Forms of the Novella

Forms of the Novella

Ten Short Novels

David H. Richter

Queens College of The City University of New York

Alfred A. Knopf, New York

To the memory of Anne Hirsch and Sarah Ehrlich

This is a Borzoi Book
Published by Alfred A. Knopf, Inc.

First Edition

98765432

Copyright © 1981 by Alfred A. Knopf, Inc.

Book design: Teresa Harmon
Cover design: Teresa Harmon

Library of Congress Cataloging in Publication Data
Main entry under title:

Forms of the novella.

   Bibliography: p.
   CONTENTS: Gogol, N. The overcoat.—Melville, H. Billy
Budd, sailor.—James, H. The Aspern papers.—[etc.]
   1. Fiction—19th century. 2. Fiction—20th century. I. Richter,
David H., 1945-
PN6120.2.F6   808.83   80-21528
ISBN 0-394-32030-1

Manufactured in the United States of America

Acknowledgments

The Overcoat from THE COLLECTED TALES AND PLAYS OF NIKOLAI GOGOL, edited by David Garnett and Leonard J. Kent and published by Alfred A. Knopf, Inc. Reprinted by permission of Leonard J. Kent.

Billy Budd, Sailor, © 1962 by The University of Chicago. All rights reserved. Reprinted by permission of The University of Chicago Press, Harrison Hayford, and Merton M. Sealts, Jr.

The Dead from DUBLINERS by James Joyce. Originally published by B. W. Huebsch, Inc., in 1916. © 1967 by the Estate of James Joyce. All rights reserved. Reprinted by permission of Viking Penguin Inc.

The Metamorphosis, reprinted by permission of Schocken Books, Inc., from THE PENAL COLONY by Franz Kafka. Copyright © 1948 by Schocken Books, Inc. Copyright renewed © 1975 by Schocken Books, Inc.

St. Mawr from ST. MAWR AND THE MAN WHO DIED by D. H. Lawrence. Copyright 1925 and renewed 1953 by Frieda Lawrence Ravagli. Reprinted by permission of Alfred A. Knopf, Inc.

Pale Horse, Pale Rider, copyright 1937, 1965, by Katherine Anne Porter. Reprinted from her volume PALE HORSE, PALE RIDER by permission of Harcourt Brace Jovanovich, Inc.

The Crying of Lot 49 by Thomas Pynchon. Copyright © 1965, 1966 by Thomas Pynchon. Reprinted by permission of Lippincott & Crowell.

Preface

Novellas are sophisticated but accessible works of fiction that, although relatively brief, often attain much of the variety and breadth of scope of full-length novels. Because they give rise to nearly as much discussion as lengthier works and can be read, even re-read, in the limited time at the student's disposal, novellas make ideal texts for courses in fiction.

Any anthology is likely to reflect the tastes and prejudices of its editor. This one is no exception, but other principles have operated here as well. I have tried to strike an appropriate balance between the unusual and the commonplace, for one thing. Included are four classic and popular novellas (*Billy Budd, Heart of Darkness, The Dead,* and *The Metamorphosis*); three others that are more rarely seen (*The Overcoat, The Aspern Papers,* and *Pale Horse, Pale Rider*); and three excellent novellas that have not, as far as I know, been previously anthologized (*The Awakening, St. Mawr,* and *The Crying of Lot 49*). The historical range runs from the mid-nineteenth century to the present; the range of forms— including melodrama and tragedy, satire and fable—is that of the genre as a whole. Two of the novellas are by women, and several others touch strongly on feminist issues. Only two of the novellas are translations—those by Gogol and Kafka; for both I have chosen the best available English rendering. And I have tried to select the best editions of the English-language texts—for example, the definitive Hayford-Sealts edition of *Billy Budd*. I have added, where necessary, brief footnotes to explain proper names, foreign phrases, and technical terms not found in college dictionaries.

The introduction, somewhat more extensive than in similar collections, is a guide to the formal analysis of fiction, particularly the novella forms included in this anthology. It is designed to serve as a dictionary of critical terms that are used to discuss fiction and discriminate among its various forms, effects, and techniques. More than this, it aspires to provide a coherent method of analyzing fiction that relates the choices of plot structure, characterization, values, language, and narrative technique to the artistic purpose they serve. It may be read sequentially or sampled in easy stages.

The headnotes that precede each novella aim to convey a sense of the author's life, career, and principal concerns. These too are somewhat fuller than in comparable textbooks. Each headnote also includes a brief and selective bibliography, intended as a guide for the student in further study or research, giving (1) the most reliable edition in which to read the rest of the author's works; (2) the best or most recent full-fledged biographies; (3) studies of the author's work as a whole; and (4) criticism of the anthologized novella.

No one carries a project of this size to completion without a great deal of assistance from institutions and individuals. My research and textual transcriptions took place at the Paul Klapper Library of Queens College, the library of the University of Cincinnati, the Regenstein Library of the University of Chicago, and the Robarts Library of the University of Toronto. Much of the manuscript was typed by the Word Processing Service of Queens College under the able direction of Pearl Sigberman, and by the ever-helpful secretaries of the English Department, Ruth Stern, Helen Gross, and Ruth Kurke. Colleagues and friends who have read parts of the manuscript at some stage of its preparation, or who have contributed helpful suggestions, include Professor Brian Corman, Erindale College, University of Toronto; Dr. Margaret Ehrhart; Professor Wayne Franklin, University of Iowa; Professor Daniel Howard, Rutgers University; Professor Donald McQuade, Queens College; Professor James H. Pickering, Michigan State University; Ms. Jonna Gormely Semeiks; and Professor Mary Doyle Springer, St. Mary's College. The contents and style of this work owe much to the generosity of these scholars; any errors and blunders are my own. This book would have been impossible, of course, without the assistance, the faith, and at times the prodding, of the editorial staff of the College Department of Alfred A. Knopf; let me single out for mention, among the many who have worked on this project, Richard Garretson, David Follmer, Christine Pellicano, and John Sturman. Finally, I have dedicated this book to the memory of my two aunts, Anne Hirsch and Sarah Ehrlich, who, while this was in progress, were taken from me to what I hope is a *lichtigen gan-eden.*

David Richter
New York, N.Y.

Contents

Forms
of the
Novella

Introduction

Most of us read fiction, at times at any rate, as a form of escape. We turn to novels to give us what our daily existence often lacks: romance, adventure, and above all a sense of coherence. Much of what any of us knows of human nature is learned through fiction—movies and television programs as well as short stories, novellas, and novels—any narrative that creates characters, people like ourselves or different, and shows them in action. Fiction exposes us to ideas we would otherwise have never encountered, to ways of life that have vanished, to places we will never visit and people we will never meet. Fiction is literally untrue, yet it teaches us as well as scientific treatises do.

Prose fiction narratives teach us especially well because there we can know the characters from within. We know Flaubert's Madame Bovary and Joyce's Stephen Dedalus better than we can know any human being, with the possible exception of ourselves, for we know their secret thoughts and desires, which even the people we know most intimately usually hide. And novels are excellent teachers because we read them rather than passively see them. To enter the author's world, we must exercise our own imaginations and build for ourselves the fictional world that exists only as black marks upon white paper. And the imagined worlds authors force us to construct for ourselves are more powerful, somehow, than those that a film director can create for us, for we have invested our own mental energies in building them.

The understanding or analysis of fiction is nothing more or less than seeing it as a created experience, moving us to appropriate emotions or convincing us of its ideas, through the means of action, character, and technique. People sometimes talk as if analyzing fiction destroys the enjoyment it gives us. But unless we have enjoyed a fiction, unless we have responded to it and been moved by its imaginative re-creation of life, we cannot begin to analyze it, for we will lack that intuitive appreciation of the artist's intention that is the basis for any critical understanding. Analysis will make us less naive about the sources of a

1

novel's power, but not less willing to put ourselves under its spell again. Analysis is our tribute to the author, to the artistic choices that shaped the work we have enjoyed, and to which we will return for pleasure or solace.

I. What Is a Novella? The Problem of Magnitude

Fiction, like breakfast cereal and detergent, is packaged in different sizes: small, medium, and large. The short story and the novel are the small and large packages; the terms "novella" and "short novel" designate the middle size. The tales in this collection run between 14,000 and 65,000 words—from twice the length of the average short story to half the length of the average novel. While one occasionally encounters precise quantitative definitions of the novella (15,000 to 50,000 words is one popular formula), numerical boundaries are by nature arbitrary and uninformative. Like middle age, the middle size in fiction is more a matter of character than of numbers.

At the same time, as Norman Friedman has shown, quantity does have an impact on qualities, and magnitude, measured in a more significant way than the counting of words, plays a large part in determining the powers and limits of literary forms. The four following levels of magnitude, moving from the smallest to the largest, are of importance in analyzing literature:

1. *Speech*   A *speech* is the continuous utterance of a single character in a closed situation (a situation is "closed" when no new characters or facts are introduced from beginning to end). Most lyric poems are of this magnitude.

2. *Scene*   The interaction of two or more characters in a closed situation is called a *scene*. Many dramatic poems are of this order of magnitude, as are many short stories—such as Edgar Allan Poe's "A Cask of Amontillado" and Ernest Hemingway's "A Clean Well-Lighted Place."

3. *Episode*   An *episode* consists of two or more scenes that lead to a culminating incident. At this level we find narrative poems, most one-act plays, and most short stories. The culminating incident, which can

be used to portray a surprising twist of fate, to convey a poignant or ironic revelation of character, or to drive home a significant idea or thesis, is responsible for the characteristic effects of the short story.

4. *Plot or Story Line* A *plot* is a system of episodes linked through probability, often involving a major change in the fortunes or the consciousness of the protagonist. Most full-length plays, epic poems, novellas, and novels are of this level of magnitude, with complex lines of probability that work to produce or impede the major change.

While these distinctions suggest that there is a genuine difference in magnitude between the short story on the one hand and the novella and the novel on the other, the two latter forms cannot be so easily distinguished. Other elements in the study and analysis of fiction, however, enable us to come closer to seeing the qualititative differences that derive from their different lengths.

II. *Mimetic vs. Didactic Fiction*

"What's the point of that story?" is a question one often hears, and it is a question that the person telling an anecdote often has no idea how to deal with. Some stories have a point, in the sense that they lead the listener toward a general truth about the real world, to inculcate—or to question—the values we live by. Other stories have no point in this sense; they are told for the sake of their own inherent interest, for the sympathy or sorrow or laughter that the story itself can generate.

Literary fictions fall into these two categories as well, and most are of the latter sort—*mimetic* fictions—which represent some human experience in language for the sake of its power to inspire the appropriate emotional effect. The artist's choices of plot, characters, and language are governed by the necessity of calling up that particular sequence of feelings in his or her audience. *Didactic* fictions, on the other hand, represent human experience for the sake of altering the audience's attitudes toward the world at large. The events, the characters, and the language are chosen to maximize the impact of the author's thesis, and our emotional involvement in the fiction is subordinate to our understanding of the author's ideas, message, or thesis. Didactic fictions are structurally different from mimetic ones, and we will discuss them later on in this introduction. What follows directly concerns itself primarily with the problems relevant to the forms of mimetic fiction.

III. Mimetic Fiction

A. The Question of the Protagonist

Most mimetic fictions have a single protagonist—the agent to whom the principal change, presented in the plot, occurs. Identifying the protagonist is crucial to any further analysis of the fiction. This is easy when the protagonist is the most "heroic" person in the story, its most sympathetic, or its narrator—but he or she may be none of these. Generally, the protagonist is that person about whom we are most made to care—though we must remember that our feelings may not be positive but negative, as in Shakespeare's *Richard III*.

B. Characterization

Protagonists and the other characters who populate narratives may be presented, in E. M. Forster's famous distinction, as either "flat" or "round." Round characters are presented with sufficient internal complexity to be able to change, in the course of the action, without shocking us by their inconsistent behavior. Flat characters may be vivid or drab, but they are all puppets. If they act "out of character" they cease to convince us.

The presence of flat characters within a work is not a sign of poor artistry. Many minor roles do not require round characters to fill them, and the attention that complex individuals in subordinate functions would draw from the central figures might easily upset the perceived shape of the story. The Shakespeare who created Hamlet created the pasteboard Rosencrantz and Guildenstern in the same play.

Characters, flat or round, may be described for us or introduced in dramatic action, leading us to deduce their character from their words and deeds. The latter seems, on the face of it, the more artistic way of proceeding, but this is not always so. It may be more economical to present a character's description, and surely it would be no boon to the reader, whenever a dull or stupid character needed to be introduced, to present him or her being foolish and boring for pages on end till the reader got the point.

Aristotle's strictures on character in the *Poetics* still hold good today. Characters should be functional within the plot; consistent—or, if they are round characters, at least fairly predictable in the sorts of change they undergo; true to life; and true to type (in the sense that a character presented as a successful executive, say, should have the aggressiveness requisite to such success). Truth to life, which implies individuality, and truth to type, which implies representativeness, grind against one another a bit: which one will be emphasized generally depends on the character's function within the plot.

C. The Problem of Unity

Unity of plot means simply that the action or experience presented is a single action, rather than several distinct actions or a fraction of one. The classic, Aristotelian notion of a unified action is one that has a beginning, a middle, and an end. The plot begins from an initially stable situation, becomes unstable, leads to further complications, and is finally resolved with the introduction of a new stability.

To take a familiar plot, that of *Hamlet*, we would have to say that the plot begins when the ghost of the late king instructs Hamlet to revenge his murder. In the "middle," the action is complicated by Hamlet's rational and irrational delays—his desire to test the ghost's veracity and Claudius's guilt; his reluctance to slay Claudius while the latter seems to be at prayer; and his mistaken killing of Polonius, which leads Claudius to arrange a counterplot against Hamlet. In the counterplot—still part of the "middle"—Hamlet escapes from the voyage to England Claudius had meant to be his last, but falls victim to Laertes's poisoned foil. As his death approaches, Hamlet stabs Claudius, completing his revenge—and the plot. With all the major agents dead, the new stability must be imposed from outside the plot by Fortinbras, the Norwegian prince who arrives to pick up the pieces.

The plot *presupposes* events that precede its beginning: the murder by Claudius of the elder Hamlet, the adultery between Gertrude and Claudius, even the birth of Prince Hamlet some thirty years before the opening of the play. But the plot does not include these events. Without the ghost's command, Hamlet might have been suspicious of his uncle, and Claudius might have been distrustful of Hamlet, but the matter would have rested there. The command, the initiating incident of the plot, is what calls Hamlet's internal and external conflicts into being. We should also note that the beginning of the plot is not at the beginning of the play; the audience watches *Hamlet* for thirty or forty minutes before the plot, properly speaking, begins. The information presented in those minutes—the disturbed state of Denmark, the uncomfortable relations between Claudius and Hamlet, Polonius's cyni-

cism about Hamlet's love for Ophelia, and so on—could be called
exposition. But what is right for *Hamlet* is not right for every play: *King
Lear* begins its plot at the very first scene, *Othello* not until the second
act. And in some plays, like *Oedipus the King*, the initiating incident of
the plot occurs *before* the play begins.

Prose fictions are like plays in this respect: the plot and the narrative
do not necessarily open together. Sometimes a plot that requires a great
deal of exposition (like that of Dickens's *Great Expectations*) will not
begin until a quarter of the novel is over. Other novels open in the
midst of the plot and present the beginning in flashbacks (as in F. Scott
Fitzgerald's *Tender Is the Night*). And novels frequently go on after the
plot ends; it was practically a convention of the Victorian novel to
conclude with a lengthy epilogue telling what happened to all the major characters after the end of the plot.

It is the individual work, its plot and its power, that determines the
relation between action and narration, plot and its representation. But
generally, the relative brevity of the novella permits less exposition
than is possible in the novel, usually only a page or two before the plot
begins. Epilogues are briefer, if they exist at all. And the flashback,
when used in the novella, more often provides exposition for a plot
already begun than it presents the first stages of the plot itself.

D. The Power of the Plot

As we have said, the purpose of mimetic fiction is to inspire an emotional effect. But what determines these emotional effects? Here are
three factors residing in the plot:

1. The moral quality of the protagonist inspires us with more or less
   definite *desires* regarding him or her. Depending on his or her character, and on the values the narrative sets forth, we wish the protagonist
   good or bad fortune, with greater or lesser ardor.
2. The events of the plot set up lines of probability that inspire us with
   more or less definite *expectations* regarding the protagonist's fate. We
   may expect him or her to have good or bad fortune, in greater or
   lesser degree, temporarily or permanently. We may also have indeterminate expectations, either because the author presents us with two
   possible fates for the protagonist or because the author keeps us in
   suspense without closely defining the alternatives at all.
3. The protagonist has a more or less definite degree of *responsibility* for
   what happens. We may be made to feel that his or her character,
   exercised through choices, largely determines his or her fate, or, on

the other hand, that the outcome is the result of the actions of other agents, or of Chance, or of Destiny. If the protagonist has a high degree of responsibility, then it matters whether he or she acted in full knowledge or as the result of a mistake of some sort.

The emotional impact of a narrative will, to a large extent, depend on the interrelationship of these three factors—all of them have to be taken into account. These factors allow us to make some broad generic distinctions between types of plots, and some surprisingly subtle ones. For example, the plots of most so-called romantic comedies (*Twelfth Night, A Midsummer Night's Dream, Tom Jones, Pride and Prejudice,* and so on) all share the feature of presenting sympathetic protagonists in actions that lead us to expect a happy ending. It is the expectation, rather than the ending itself, that leads us to read them as comedies; they have, by virtue of this expectation, a "feel" to them that is different from (say) a melodrama that chances to end happily.

For all their differences, these works are more like each other than any of them is like, for example, *Volpone* or *The Egoist,* whose plots are also called "comic." The protagonists of these two works inspire not sympathy but fascination and repugnance; we desire and expect their fall and just punishment, and a happy ending not for them but for their intended victims. The power of these works is closer to certain types of tragedy than to the romantic comedies. Tragedies like Shakespeare's *Richard III* have as protagonists fascinatingly evil villains whose desired and expected downfall transpires to the satisfaction of the audience. The main difference between the punitive plots that are called "comedies" and those called "tragedies" seems to be the degree of punishment meted out; Richard, in the "tragedy," is killed, while Volpone, in the "comedy," deserves and receives less severe returns.

E. THE FOCUS OF FATE

The factors we have just discussed—our desires, our expectations, our sense of the protagonist's degree of responsibility for what happens to him or her—all refer to the protagonist's *fate*. In many, perhaps most, plots the fate of the protagonist is primarily defined in terms of his or her fortunes or circumstances—health, social status, reputation, love relationships, and so on. In the last century or so, however, many plots have defined the fate of the protagonist in terms of a change in *consciousness*. In plots of this kind, the focus of our concern may be on the protagonist's developing capacity for making mature moral decisions (as in Dickens's *Great Expectations*) or, conversely, on his or her ethical degeneration (as in André Gide's *The Immoralist*). Alternatively, the focus may be on a crisis, in which the protagonist's already formed moral character is tested by temptations; he or she wavers between doing right and suffering the consequences or taking an easy way out at the cost of self-contempt (as in Hemingway's *The Old Man and the Sea*). In the first two cases our concern is with positive and negative moral change realized in action; in the last case, particularly if the protagonist surmounts the temptation, the moral change is only a dreaded possibility, yet still the focus of our concern.

In still other plots of consciousness, our concern may be less with changes in *character* than with changes in *thought*. Here the focus is on the protagonist's struggle to come to terms with experience, to make meaningful sense of his or her life. In some cases the struggle is successful (as in Saul Bellow's *Herzog*), while in others the opportunity to learn and to enlarge one's world is missed by the protagonist (as in James's *The Aspern Papers*). In still others, learning takes the form of disillusionment, and our feelings about it will depend on whether the protagonist's romantic illusions are portrayed as nobler than the sordid realities he finds (as in Fitzgerald's *The Great Gatsby*) or as follies he is better off without (as in Philip Roth's *Goodbye, Columbus*).

In some novels and novellas, the protagonist's fortunes, character, and thought are *all* altered, simultaneously or successively, and in cases of this sort it may or may not be easy to single out the primary change on which our desires and expectations are focused. In a novel like Hemingway's *For Whom the Bell Tolls*, for example, the protagonist, Robert Jordan, successfully surmounts a test of his ideals, but the cost will be his death in battle. In James's *The Ambassadors*, Lambert Strether refuses to betray the deepened and widened view of life he has achieved, but the cost will be loneliness and poverty. These two novels have superficially "unhappy" endings. But if these works have plots of consciousness, then we must see the price the protagonists pay as a measure of the immense value we are to place on their integrity of character or vision.

F. Simple vs. Complex Plots

Most plots are *dynamic*: they involve some change in the protagonist's situation or our understanding of it. In *simple* plots, the protagonist's situation moves from its initial to its final state along a single line of probability: he or she moves, in a series of episodes, from triumph to triumph, ending at the height of fortune, or, conversely, degenerates successively, at each turn of events, ending in death or some lesser doom. *Complex plots*, on the other hand, employ two or more lines of probability that work against one another: the protagonist's fortune is subject to reversals at one or more points in the action. Simple plots are typical of the short story, complex plots of the novel—though there are many exceptions. The novella, which is similar to the novel in magnitude, is closer to the short story in this. Tragedy, for example, where it appears in the novella, is usually of the degenerative kind, in which a sympathetic protagonist gradually succumbs to forces beyond his or her control, ending in a doom of disillusionment or death. High comedy, high tragedy, and complex melodrama, which are found frequently in the novel, are seldom seen in the novella.

IV. Didactic Fiction

A. SATIRE AND APOLOGUE

Didactic fictions represent experience in order to alter the reader's attitudes toward the world. We can distinguish two very broad general types of didactic fiction.

Satires are works organized so as to ridicule specific targets in the real world—particular people and institutions, or traits held by groups of people or by humanity at large. Satires that run to the length of a full-scale novel are rather rare—*Gulliver's Travels* is the only one that is widely known and read, and its targets are many and varied. Satires that focus on a single important target tend to run to novella length or not much longer. Kurt Vonnegut's satire on the amorality of atomic scientists (*Cat's Cradle*), Evelyn Waugh's satire on American funeral practices (*The Loved One*), and Philip Roth's satire on Richard Nixon (*Our Gang*) are interesting modern examples of the form. The action in a satire may be loose and episodic rather than tightly organized into a plot; the characters may be unrealistic or even inconsistent. We would not find these features tolerable in a mimetic work, but in a satire, where the purpose is ridicule, they are entirely in place.

Apologues are fictions organized so as to convince the reader of the truth of a particular thesis, or doctrine, or view of the world; they are fictional imitations of arguments. Apologues vary enormously in the complexity of their theses. Some, like Samuel Johnson's *Rasselas*, are organized around a doctrine as simple and straightforward as "there is no perfect, secure earthly happiness"; others, like Camus's *The Stranger*, present doctrines of such novelty and difficulty that whole treatises would be required to explicate them fully.

Many mimetic works also contain ideas, discussions of metaphysics or theology, social policy or abstract ethics—Dostoevsky's *Crime and Punishment* and Mann's *The Magic Mountain* are two examples in which intellectual matters take up a goodly proportion of the work. Nevertheless, there is a difference of kind between such "novels of ideas" and apologues. As Sheldon Sacks puts it, in mimetic fiction, "the most intellectual belief, the most extended social criticism, the most penetrating ethical comment, become integral parts of a whole work only as they move us to the appropriate response to the created characters, which, finally, makes possible the appropriate experience." In the apologue, on the other hand, the characters and the action "become integral parts of a complete work only as they move us to some realization—implicit or formulated—about the world external to the literary creation itself."

The didactic purposes of these works have some important technical consequences. Most important, perhaps, is the fact that none of these forms has a plot with the sort of unity that was defined in section III-C. Didactic fictions have action, of course, as well as sequences of events of some complexity, but the organizing principle of the story is relevance to the instructional purpose of the whole. For this reason, the action sequences of didactic works are frequently episodic rather than tightly structured; they often lack that sense of full resolution that is common in mimetic plots.

How can we tell when we are reading an apologue? This is not an easy question to answer. Some apologues label themselves with an explicit statement such as the opening sentence of *Rasselas*: "Ye who listen with credulity to the whispers of fancy, and pursue with eagerness the phantom of hope . . . attend to the history of Rasselas prince of Abyssinia." Some employ characters with type-names: Bunyan's *Pilgrim's Progress*, for example, with characters named Christian, Evangelist, Obstinate, and Pliable, could not be taken for anything but an allegory. These techniques are dated, but some modern writers have used slightly different methods to make us feel that the characters are exemplary rather than individual, with universal problems rather than ones peculiar to themselves. The opening of Camus's *The Plague*, for example, stresses the "ordinariness" of the town of Oran. In the course of a page or two, the narrator defines his town as just like every place else, but ever so much more so—and thus sets the stage for a fable in which the effects of bubonic plague upon the town are shown to be emblematic of man's confrontation with the absurdity of the universe. And frequently type-names are used with more subtlety than Bunyan's: Winston Smith, the central character of Orwell's *1984*, is a type-name for Mr. Average British Citizen. Or nameless characters, like the narrator of Ralph Ellison's *Invisible Man*, help us see them as types. Other signals of the apologue, as Mary Doyle Springer has suggested, include any or all of the following: (1) an episodic or unsatisfying plot structure; (2) use of the present tense for narrative; (3) heavy-handed authorial commentary; (4) settings where the various human types are traditionally gathered—aboard ships, in prisons, at parties; (5) relative lack of dialogue. A word of caution here, however: any, perhaps all, of the above signals may be present in a mimetic work; these are indications—hints, not definite signs—that this is a didactic form.

B. ALLEGORY AND FABLE

How do didactic fictions work to make their theses convincing? What relationship is set up between the fictional world and our real one? There are two basic patterns. One is the allegory. A one-to-one correspondence is set up between the objects and characters in the fiction and beings, persons, and ideas in the real world. We find its narrative embodiments in apologues like *Pilgrim's Progress* and in satires like *Animal Farm*. The second pattern, the *fable*, works not in terms of the interrelationships among symbolic parts, but as a symbolic whole, in representing the meaning of an abstract principle or viewpoint. The parable of the Good Samaritan, for example, is a fable that illustrates the commandment "Love thy neighbor as thyself." Each detail of plot, characterization, and language is chosen in order to make us understand the meaning of "loving one's neighbor," but the individual elements do not have a symbolic significance that can be detached from the fiction and equated on a one-for-one basis with ideas in the external world. This is the form that many modern apologues and satires take.

One relatively common subtype of the fable—and one that is particularly suited to the novella—is what Mary Springer has called the "example apologue," a narrative in which the experiences of a single individual character are used to present what is typical of the way of life of a group in the external world. In works of this sort, as Springer has put it, the general statement embodied in the fiction takes the form "It is like this to be a ———." In the case of Solzhenitsyn's *One Day in the Life of Ivan Denisovich*, the blank would be filled in with "prisoner in a Soviet labor camp"; in the case of Dostoevsky's *The Gambler*, with "roulette addict"; and so on.

V. Typical Forms of the Novella

As we have already suggested, the scale of the novella, its middle magnitude relative to the novel and the short story, predisposes it to certain forms. Didactic fictions, which, like sermons, are most effective when they are kept reasonably short, have been popular forms of the novella since its inception in the mid-eighteenth century, and continue to be so today: satires, fables, and example apologues are to be found in most collections, including this one. High comedy, classic tragedy, and complex melodrama, which require reversals and multiple lines of probability, are, on the other hand, difficult to achieve in 50,000 words or less. Among plots of character, full-scale representations of a character's development tend also to be too unwieldy for the novella. The most usual sort of mimetic plots in the novella are the pathetic or degenerative tragedy, described in section III-F, and some of the plots of consciousness, especially the plots of "testing," "learning," and "disillusionment" described in section III-E. The latter are serious plots that may be resolved favorably or unfavorably: the protagonist may pass or fail a test of character; disillusionment may be a curse or a blessing. This collection contains a number of examples of these mimetic forms.

VI. Narrative Technique

Once the author has decided to tell a certain sort of story about certain sorts of characters to achieve a certain sort of emotional or intellectual impact, he or she must then make a host of further decisions about how the story is to be told.* These decisions, which concern how information reaches the reader, in what order and with what authority,

---

*This is not to say that all authors make their choices in this precise order; analytically, though, technique is subordinate to form and purpose, and has to be considered afterwards.

come under the heading of narrative technique, about which many critical studies have been written. The best of these studies, Wayne Booth's *The Rhetoric of Fiction*, has supplied most of the distinctions used in the brief guide that follows.

A. AUTHORS AND THEIR MASKS

We must make a few distinctions between authors themselves and the various voices they employ. There is, in the first place, the man or woman who created the story. Biographers can give us some access to his or her personality and concerns, but we should not confuse the *real author* with the sense of him or her that we derive from the stories. This writing personality, termed the *implied author* or the "author's second self," is the ultimate source of the values in the work being read. And when we talk of Melville's beliefs, we are using a kind of shorthand for the "Melville" we can infer from *Billy Budd, Sailor*, say, who may or may not be identical with the "Melville" of *Moby Dick*, and who bears some unknown relationship to the real man himself. Next, there is the *narrator* of the story, who may be identical with the implied author—or radically different. We shall discuss this problem at greater length. Finally, there are the *characters* of the story: one or more of them may actually be the narrator—and in a sense *any* character whom we observe speaking and thinking becomes, for the time, the narrator.

B. THE NARRATOR'S ROLES

Narrators may either be reticent or assume a definite role in telling the story. Undramatized narrators (like the third-person voice of *The Awakening*) are indistinguishable from the implied author. The dramatized narrator, on the other hand, can take a great variety of forms.

The first-person narrator is the most obvious sort of dramatized storyteller, but this classification hides at least as much as it reveals. Some first-person narrators, like the "I" who tells *The Overcoat*, are observers who play no part whatever in the story beyond reporting it; others, like Nick in *The Great Gatsby*, affect as well as report the plot; still others, like the I-narrator of *The Aspern Papers*, are themselves the protagonists. The decision to place the narrator outside the plot, at its edge, or at its center is clearly as important as whether to make the narrator first-person or third-person.

Third-person narratives become "dramatic" in character whenever the narrative takes up the point of view of one of the story's agents, though, here again, there are many possibilities.

1. The "reflector"   In this mode of narration, the point of view rests with a single character, and the third-person voice is practically a camera recording the focal character's experiences, feelings, and thoughts. The narrative of *Pale Horse, Pale Rider*, for example, follows Miranda so closely that, when she is delirious, it is hard to separate her visions from reality. The effect of this type of third-person narration is very similar to a first-person point of view, though in some ways it is more flexible. Brief exposition that might be out of character for an I-narrator to relate, for example, or authorial commentary can be introduced into narratives without permanently disturbing the central focus.

2. Multiple reflectors   This technique presents the successive subjective views of several characters in the story. Joyce's *Ulysses*, for example, presents the perspectives of Stephen Dedalus, Leopold Bloom, and Molly Bloom.

3. Mixed techniques   Many narratives are neither purely objective—told by an apparently neutral observer who knows only what anyone present would see and hear—nor purely subjective—told from the perspective of a single character or set of characters. Joyce's *The Dead*, to take one example, begins from the point of view of the servant-girl, Lily, then backs off to a more objective stance, then briefly enters the consciousness of Gabriel's aunts, next presents a panorama of the musical party, and only gradually settles down to convey the subjective thoughts and feelings of Gabriel Conroy, the protagonist. While it would be true to say that *The Dead* is told primarily from Gabriel's point of view, it is important to note that Joyce decided to show us Gabriel from the outside before fastening us to his perspective. We can thus "size him up" before surrendering to his vision of experience.

These narrational styles did not develop, of course, in this historical order. In the eighteenth century, novelists favored the first-person narrative, with the story told either by a single narrator, in a memoir (as in Defoe's *Moll Flanders*), or by two or more separate narrators, in the form of letters between various correspondents (as in Richardson's *Clarissa*); or, alternatively, they used an omniscient point of view centered in a dramatized narrator who was licensed to present a wide variety of editorial commentary (as in Fielding's *Tom Jones*). In the early nine-teenth century, Jane Austen experimented with the use of a character as a narrative reflector, a technique that George Eliot and Henry James developed further, effacing progressively the third-person narrator's commentary, telling less and showing more. By the early twentieth century, in works like Joyce's *Portrait of the Artist* and Woolf's *Mrs. Dalloway*, we find strict uses of the single and multiple reflector approach. And in the closest approach to drama, some of Hemingway's short stories (like "The Killers") use a technique in which there is neither commentary nor reflector. We are presented with literally de-scribed scene, action, and dialogue, and the authorial presence is taken nearly to the vanishing point. Of course, the development of a new technique does not make the older ones obsolete: the first-person memoir and the editorializing narrator continue to be used today.

C. The Varieties of Distance

The narrator, the characters, and the implied author of a story are not merely technically different from one another; they may differ from one another in their moral values, intellectual capacities, and in a vari-ety of other ways that affect the impact of the tale.

1. *Implied author vs. narrator*   A narrator whose norms are different from those of the implied author is often called an "unreliable narra-tor"; this term, however, covers an extremely wide variety of situations. Narrators usually are reliable reporters of the facts of the story—though when the narrator is demonstrably mentally impaired (like Benjy in Faulkner's *The Sound and the Fury*), the reader may have trouble reconstructing the actual events. More usually, the narrator's distance from the implied author is on the moral axis: his or her judgments are warped or self-serving, and we must be on our guard against taking them at face value. And this is sometimes difficult, the more so since our close acquaintance with the narrator—first person or reflector, it makes no difference—predisposes us to find him or her sympathetic. Even a sadistic or psychopathic narrator can seduce us a long way toward adopting his or her point of view, and we can be rather easily fooled into agreeing with the judgments of a narrator who is merely egocentric and conniving. Most unreliable narrators are characters in the stories they tell, but even an editorializing "omniscient" narrator

may be unreliable at times, as in Gogol's *The Overcoat*. The "I" who tells that story is afraid of offending the sensibilities of the St. Petersburg bureaucracy, for which the "Gogol" we infer from the tale has little respect. The ironies of Gogol's novella appear not only in the tale itself but in the way it is told.

2. *Narrator vs. characters* A narrator's greater or lesser distance from the characters will tend to make them more or less sympathetic to us. The distance may be primarily moral (Marlow and Kurtz in *Heart of Darkness*), primarily intellectual (the I-narrator and Akaky Akakievich in *The Overcoat*), or even physical—as in *The Metamorphosis*, where the protagonist is an insect. An especially interesting and powerful form of distance occurs when the narrator is the protagonist speaking from the vantage point of time: in *Heart of Darkness*, for example, Marlow-the-narrator already knows what Marlow-the-character is in the process of learning for the first time.

3. *Author vs. characters* The author's distance from the characters will vary as much as the narrator's. Depending on the narrator's degree of reliability, these distances may be identical or widely different. Some authors keep all the characters more or less remote from us, maintaining an *aesthetic* distance that keep the agents on a "storybook" level and defeats our desire to "identify with" the author's creations. Others allow, even encourage, us to become almost submerged. The former is true of *The Overcoat* and *The Crying of Lot 49*, the latter of *The Awakening* and *Pale Horse, Pale Rider*.

D. Scene vs. Summary

At every moment throughout the story, the author must decide what parts of the narrative are to be dramatized as scenes, complete with action, dialogue, and description, and which are to be told through summary. In general, scene is more vivid than summary—though it is possible to write drab scenes and sparkling summaries, of course—and the choice of which parts of the plot to present as scene will affect the way the story takes shape in the mind of the reader.

One might think that summary would be reserved for those elements of a story, like an uneventful journey, that would be dull to present at full length, but the matter is not so simple. On the one hand, some novelists, in a *tour de force*, have made a character's coming down a flight of stairs into a vivid and suspenseful event. And on the other hand, novelists often collapse into summary a state of affairs that would provide many fascinating scenes. But had such scenes been present, they might have misled the reader about the focus of the work. Perhaps the hardest thing an apprentice novelist learns is how to write a thrilling scene—and the second hardest could well be how to tell when not to.

E. PRIVILEGE

A narrator's privilege refers to the ability to tell us more than could be known through the senses or through rational deduction; total privilege is usually referred to as "omniscience." The variations of privilege are enormous, from next to nothing (in an "objectively" told story like Hemingway's "The Killers") to the nearly complete omniscience of the narrators of *Tom Jones* and *St. Mawr*. Even the most completely privileged narrator, of course, does not tell all that he or she knows; the narrator presumably knows how the story ends, for example, but withholds that information until the proper time.

The most important sort of privilege is that of giving interior views of the story's characters. The narrator of *Pale Horse, Pale Rider,* is privileged to explore Miranda's conscious and unconscious mind—but is given no inside views of any other character. The narrator of *The Overcoat* can tell us about any character he wishes, but his views are superficial for the most part. The narrator of *Billy Budd* gives us deep views of Captain Vere, but he finds Claggart mysteriously opaque. In general, the more extended the inside views we are given of characters and the deeper they penetrate, the more sympathetic we are likely to find them, regardless of how much their values differ from those of the implied author.

It is important to remember that matters of narrative technique are means, not ends in themselves; they can be judged only relative to how they serve the controlling principle of the story. Flashbacks, dream sequences, stream of consciousness, unreliable narrators—these are all devices that exist solely to enhance our discovery of the emotional or intellectual core of the narrative. Most novelists make their decisions about narrative technique intuitively or instinctively. Authors are more apt to tinker with a story, revising and reshaping it till it "works" the way they had wanted it to, than to bring it to speedy birth from a pat outline. And the tinkering may be done totally in the author's mind.

Katherine Anne Porter is said to have written one of her most famous stories, "Flowering Judas," in a single night, but the story had actually been percolating in her brain for many years. On the other hand, writers like Henry James seem to have been entirely conscious of what they were doing and why they were doing it. James's notebooks are filled with elaborate technical memoranda and theoretical ideas. Yet even James, master craftsman though he was, seldom wrote his stories just as he had planned them. Quite the contrary: when one compares his notebooks with the finished tales, one finds many stories that altered drastically between conception and completion. Characters once central fade into the background, while narrators invented at first to observe the action later usurp the position of the protagonist.

F. Diction and Style

Once a plot with a particular power has been selected, and the many decisions that comprise "narrative technique" made in order to enhance that power, the novelist must make innumerable decisions involving the choice of words. Techniques of poetic analysis may help the student decide whether the appropriate decisions were in fact made.

In the formal analysis of fiction, one must be warned not to overemphasize the importance of stylistic decisions. In any lyric poem, the precise words are often all-important; that is why translations of the lyric generally fail to convey the beauty of the original—poetry, it has been said, is what gets lost in translation. But the novel generally translates quite well, and it is conversely true that style is here far less significant.

G. Irony

In the most general sense, irony is saying one thing and meaning something else. The most common form of irony we meet with in daily life is sarcasm; if a friend were to compliment me, in a strained and overemphatic tone of voice, on my handsome outfit, I would immediately look down to see if my suit were stained or my socks mismatched. Tone of voice is not easily conveyed in fiction, and the writer must use other means of letting the reader know that he does not mean what he says. An example of such *verbal irony* can be seen in this passage from Voltaire's *Candide*:

After the earthquake, which had destroyed three-quarters of Lisbon, the country's wise men had found no more efficacious means of preventing total ruin than to give the people a fine auto-da-fé; it was decided by the University of Coimbra that the spectacle of a few persons burned by a slow fire in a great ceremony is an infallible secret for keeping the earth from quaking.

Once we have inferred that Voltaire cannot believe, as the "wise men" of Lisbon do, that heresy causes earthquakes and executions prevent them, we can understand the passage as a satirical attack on the superstitious cruelty of self-styled "Christians" rather than, as the passage would literally be taken, as an endorsement of their practices.

Only vaguely analogous to verbal irony is *dramatic irony*. Dramatic irony usually involves a character who holds mistaken expectations of what will happen, or mistaken notions of what has happened. For example, Agamemnon, not knowing that his wife is about to murder him, thanks the gods for having allowed him to return home safely from Troy. This sort of irony is intensified if the audience is aware of the truth. Strictly speaking, though, the audience need not be complicit in dramatic ironies; it may share the character's delusion and be surprised and shocked at the ironic turn of events.

Dramatic irony can operate in plays, narrative poetry, and prose fiction—wherever there are characters and a plot. A third form of irony, *narrative irony*, is possible only where there is a narrator, primarily in prose fiction. Narrative irony occurs when a narrator's values, ideas, and beliefs are at odds with those of the implied author; to arrive at an accurate sense of the narrative, the reader must discount the unreliable narrator's bias and distortion, which derive from the erroneous or self-justifying values with which he or she colors the presentation of the story.

H. Symbolism

Any object, character, or action invested with meaning beyond its literal significance can be said to be "symbolic," and works of fiction often require us to understand them on both symbolic and literal levels. Sometimes this is easy and sometimes not; the difficulties come as often from overinterpretation (seeing something as a symbol that is not meant to be one) and from misinterpretation (assigning the wrong significance) as from overliteral reading.

Part of the problem derives from the existence of traditional symbols that come from Christian and pagan iconography. The ancient meanings of the cross (suffering and redemption), of the lamb (divine love), and of the serpent (evil) may predispose us to see the traditional meanings wherever we encounter these objects, whether that is appropriate or not. A serpent may usually stand for evil, but sometimes, particularly in the work of D. H. Lawrence, it may stand for the phallus, and beyond that for a satisfying and redemptive sexuality. Writers, when using traditional symbols in a completely new way, must make it clear what they are doing; an author who symbolizes vicious hatred in a lamb runs the risk that the reader will miss the point.

Symbols may also be invented for the occasion. An overcoat, for most of us, is an ordinary garment, advisable to have in the winter. In Gogol's *The Overcoat*, though, the coat seems to have vast significance: Akaky's possession of his overcoat grows to symbolize his full participation in humanity. Before the coat, Akaky is antisocial and asexual; with it, he becomes convivial and experiences sexual longings for the first time; after he loses it, he dies. Gogol must go to a good deal of trouble to invest the overcoat with such a weight of meaning. Later Russian writers, though, counting on their audience's familiarity with the story, were able to adopt Gogol's symbol at bargain rates.

Conflicts between traditional meanings of symbols and what may be their specific meaning within a given work cause problems for even highly experienced readers. One controversy focuses on the meaning of the snow that falls softly throughout Joyce's *The Dead*. The traditional meaning of the snow, from its conventional associations with coldness and hence with death, is at odds with associations throughout the work that link it with freshness, vitality, community, and life. It would be tempting to call off the whole question and claim that the snow is just literal snow. Not only, however, is Joyce himself an inveterate dealer in symbols who would not waste such an opportunity, but so is the character, Gabriel Conroy, who experiences the snow: "Gabriel . . . asked himself what is a woman standing on the stairs in the shadow, listening to distant music, a symbol of."

It is important not to miss symbols, but it is equally important not to be so concerned with them that one neglects the literal meaning of the narrative. Most symbols, like Gogol's overcoat and Conrad's journey, are tolerably obvious symbols of something, even if their meaning is not utterly transparent. And overreading can have its dangers: Oedipa Maas, the heroine of *The Crying of Lot 49*, is a cautionary example—a woman who sees symbolic significance in so many places that she wonders whether the world is a hieroglyph to be deciphered—or whether she herself is crazy. It is a thought that has occurred to more than one possessed seeker after meanings.

VII. Literary Analysis

Careful attention to the language of a text will often help one to find and understand the artistic significance of irony, symbolism, and other narrative techniques that require nonliteral reading. Something of what is involved in formal literary analysis might be indicated by a brief look at the opening paragraph of one of Joyce's short stories, "Araby":

> North Richmond Street, being blind, was a quiet street except at the hour when the Christian Brothers' School set the boys free. An uninhabited house of two storeys stood at the blind end, detached from its neighbors in a square ground. The other houses of the street, conscious of decent lives within them, gazed at one another with brown imperturbable faces.

This seems like a fairly ordinary description of a middle-class neighborhood till one reads that the houses are "conscious of decent lives within them" and "gazed at one another." This personification turns the cityscape into something new and potentially significant, in the context of the story as a whole. The personification of the houses, the creation of a living landscape, permits us to go beyond literal reading and encourages us to see North Richmond Street as a self-portrait of the first-person narrator who is the protagonist of Joyce's tale.

Thus we might conjecture that the "blind" street—literally a dead end—is meant to suggest both the blocked and frustrated quality of the twelve-year-old boy who tells the story, and his spiritual blindness or naivete as well. We might guess that he feels himself, like the uninhabited house, detached and alienated from his fellows, perhaps with some consciousness of sin or guilt that would contrast with the "decent lives" in the houses with the "imperturbable faces." The "two storeys" of the isolated house, too, might refer to some split within the boy, perhaps, given his age and his education, a division between his religious idealism and the sexual longings that are beginning to well up within him. This split is further suggested by the contrast between the noise when the boys have been "set free" and the "quiet street" when they are confined in the Christian Brothers' School.

Here, in brief summary, is the plot of "Araby": An adolescent boy, who has focused both his religious ideals and his sexual fantasies into the worship of a schoolmate's sister, goes to a Dublin bazaar—which she longs to attend but cannot—in romantic quest of a gift for her. After many frustrations, he arrives at the bazaar when it is nearly closing, finds it cheap and tawdry, commonplace instead of romantically exotic, and, painfully disillusioned with it and with himself, "I saw myself as a creature driven and derided by vanity; and my eyes burned with anguish and anger." Clearly, no one could predict such a plot on the basis of the first three sentences of the story, but it is equally clear that the language of the opening paragraph carefully prepares us for a great many of the spiritual conflicts which the story as a whole will detail. They appear as covert metaphors within the literal texture of what is apparently only a physical description of a street.

The style of novels does not always reveal covert metaphors—or any other single figure of speech—but most fiction is written so that the language subtly reinforces (or undercuts) the significance of the story line. Careful attention to language, which may be most easily paid when rereading a text, can often reveal a great deal that one tends to miss the first time through.

A. Thought and Values

In didactic narratives, a thesis, doctrine, or view of the world is the organizing principle of the work as a whole. But even in mimetic fictions, thought remains a highly significant element. In some, like *The Brothers Karamazov* and *St. Mawr*, abstract ideas are enormously important as influences on character and action, and they must be understood if the narratives themselves are to be properly experienced. In a more general sense, though, thought has its place even in the least intellectual-seeming novels: novels of manners, crime stories, or the like. Specifically, we must at the bare minimum be made to sympathize with some of the characters and to find others hateful, and we cannot be counted upon to make the precise judgments required without being given values, to which we give at least notional assent, either explicitly or implicitly within the work. (By "notional assent" I mean that we agree to judge the characters by these values temporarily and hypothetically, without permanently and actually committing ourselves to them.) One of the questions we must ask ourselves, in analyzing any work—mimetic or didactic—is what the norms of the fiction are—these values may be moral, intellectual, aesthetic, or some combination of the three—and how the various characters stand in relation to them.

How hard the author has to work to guarantee the reader's acceptance of his or her norms depends primarily upon how far they are apart to begin with. Katherine Anne Porter needs very little rhetoric to win our assent to the superior value of individuality and love over abstract patriotism. But some novelists—the Marquis de Sade is an extreme example—may be unable to gain our notional acceptance of their values, regardless of how hard they try. Yet there are more ambiguous cases. Is the feminist reader wrong to respond angrily to sexism in a novelist like Fielding, who wrote long before the emancipation of women? Is the Jewish reader wrong to take umbrage at the presentation of a Jew as criminal in Dickens's *Oliver Twist*? Too parochial an attachment to our current beliefs can close us off to much of the pleasure of literary experience, and to the broadening of our horizons that fiction offers us; if we are able to process only information consistent with what we already know, we can never grow.

B. Beyond Formal Analysis

This introduction has aimed to provide a series of general questions that may help the reader analyze the novellas in this collection, and narratives in general. The focus has been on the purposes that novelists have used as the organizing principles of fiction, and the means that authors have chosen to accomplish these purposes. But such formal problems are not the only ones works of fiction raise, nor are they necessarily the most interesting. Let us glance briefly at some of the other perspectives one might use to illuminate a literary work.

1. *Biography*   Novels, however intricate as formal structures, do not grow of themselves like crystals: they are made by people, men and women whose personal histories and public concerns predispose them to invent one sort of fictional narrative rather than another. Some works of fiction are more or less autobiographical; works like *Heart of Darkness* and *Pale Horse, Pale Rider*, fictional reconstructions of real experiences that Conrad and Porter lived through, may have been motivated by their authors' desire better to understand themselves. Other works may be motivated by conscious social or philosophical concerns of the authors: Dickens's *Oliver Twist*, for example, drew some of its

inspiration from his outrage over the Poor Law of 1834 and the misery it was causing. Many novels have complex origins; James's *The Aspern Papers* derives partly from an anecdote he heard, partly from his relations with a woman writer in Florence, and partly from a long-term philosophical concern with the problems of visiting the dead past.

But conscious motives are not the only ones people possess, as Freudian psychology has made clear. Novelists' creations, like ordinary men and women's dreams and fantasies, may embody their unconscious desires and dreads. Thus we may view the prevalence of orphans in Dickens's novels in reference to the trauma in the novelist's youth when he thought himself abandoned by his parents. These orphans, who either are adopted by wealthy and loving benefactors or die abandoned and are extravagantly mourned, may represent Dickens's private fantasies, dating from his childhood, and called up in moments of normal adult isolation. Similarly, in *The Metamorphosis*, the transformation of Gregor Samsa into an insect threatened and destroyed by his hostile father may owe a good deal to Kafka's tormented relationship to his own father. We can understand a great deal about literature through the judicious use of Freudian psychology; it requires, of course, immense tact and care, and an intensive study of the biographical record which, even in the best of cases, is unlikely to be ideally complete.

2. History   In a rather more general way, novels bear the marks of the times in which they were written. Even narratives with no social message will tend to reflect their milieu, so that works written around the same time, by different authors with different experiences and ideas, may have much in common with each other, and may differ in significant ways from novels written much earlier or later. *St. Mawr* and *Pale Horse, Pale Rider*, two novellas written between the world wars, both give us the sense of crumbling worlds, of societies with rigid rules but no firm values to rely on, of isolated individuals who find little help from institutions in making peace with themselves or finding meaning in life. And these characteristics are shared by a good many other works of the period—Hemingway's *The Sun Also Rises*, Woolf's *To the Lighthouse*, Evelyn Waugh's *Vile Bodies*, Sinclair Lewis's *Babbitt*, and poetry and drama as well. These features are characteristic of the modern sensibility; in earlier works, before the romantic movement, say, the individual is more likely to be a threat to institutions than the other way around, and the values of society and community are more solidly maintained. Comparing any of the between-the-wars narratives with novels by Fielding or Austen will quickly display these differences.

3. *Myth and Archetype* According to the psychological theories of Carl Gustav Jung, the primary source for fantasy, dream, and art is not the personal unconscious of Freud, which Jung considered a "thin" layer just below the threshold of awareness, but the collective unconscious, a vast storehouse of symbols common to the human species as a whole. In this theory, the resemblances between the myths of various primitive peoples, the folk tales and epics of the nations of the East and the West, and universal iconographical symbols like the cross and the mandala are explained as manifestations of archetypes residing within this unconscious. Effective literary works also derive from the archetypes. The heroes and villains of fiction are displaced versions of the archetypal images of God and the Devil; women derive from the archetypal Earth Mother, in one or another of her manifestations as progenitor, mistress, and destroyer; voyages come from the archetypal night journey from life through death to a new rebirth.

The archetypes are human universals, and as such have the power of relating a literary work not merely to others of its own time and place, but also to the literature of any milieu, and to myth as well. Thus Marlow's voyage in *Heart of Darkness* would be related not only to Oedipa Maas's journey through the night world of San Francisco in *The Crying of Lot 49*, but to night journeys throughout recorded time: Odysseus's descent into Hades, Dante's tour through the Inferno, the Egyptian *Book of the Dead*, the Biblical story of Joseph, and many, many more. This form of criticism allows the reader to see all of literature as a vast and permanent tradition, ordered into an eternal artifice of human dreams.

These three modes of criticism—biographical, historical, and archetypal—can be seen, Norman Friedman has shown, as three concentric circles expanding outward from the formal study of the literary work. The formal analysis of the narrative in question gives us a sense of the novel in its concrete individuality—what it is and how it is put together. Biographical criticism then relates the novel, as the product of an individual artist, to the mind that created that work along with others. Historical criticism sees the work as the product of its time, similar to others that share its milieu, and different from the works of other ages and cultures. And finally, archetypal criticism views the literary creation as one manifestation of the total myth of humankind, potentially akin to any artifact whatever. As we move outward from the center, the work appears against a widening sequence of contexts, each of which broadens and enriches what went before, leaving us with a sense of the inexhaustibility of the literary experience.

Bibliography

The reader is referred to the following works of literary theory, from which most of the ideas in the Introduction were derived.

Booth, Wayne C. *The Rhetoric of Fiction.* Chicago: University of Chicago Press, 1961.

Crane, Ronald S. "The Concept of Plot and the Plot of *Tom Jones*," in R. S. Crane, ed., *Critics and Criticism.* Chicago: University of Chicago Press, 1952.

Forster, E. M. *Aspects of the Novel.* New York: Harcourt, Brace and World, 1927.

Friedman, Norman. *Form and Meaning in Fiction.* Athens: University of Georgia Press, 1975.

Olson, Elder. "An Outline of Poetic Theory," in R. S. Crane, op. cit.

Richter, David H. *Fable's End.* Chicago: University of Chicago Press, 1974.

Sacks, Sheldon. *Fiction and the Shape of Belief.* Berkeley: University of California Press, 1964.

Springer, Mary Doyle. *Forms of the Modern Novella.* Chicago: University of Chicago Press, 1975.

The Overcoat

Nikolai Gogol

When we look at the life of Nikolai Vasilievich Gogol (1809-1852), we immediately discover a mass of strange contradictions. Born a Ukrainian, he wrote in Russian; immensely intelligent and ambitious, his performance at school was at best mediocre. He rose swiftly in the civil service through his high-placed connections, then mercilessly satirized the system that allowed him to do so. He was at thirty a fop and a dandy, and at forty a mystical ascetic. He celebrated the immensity of Russia and the glory of its future, but he spent nine of his last thirteen years away from its soil traveling in Western Europe. We can come to terms with some of these peculiar oppositions if we understand that Gogol felt deeply from his earliest youth that God had marked him out for some special destiny. To know that one is called—but not to have any idea what one has been called on to do—this accounts for the turmoil, the many false starts of Gogol's youth, and the tragedy of his last years.

As a slovenly and sickly schoolboy, Gogol had already acquired a dreamy and self-centered personality; he found more to interest him in his own imagination than in the books he was asked to study. In his young manhood he tried several careers before—and even after—he had begun to find success as a writer. His ambition to act on the stage, prompted by his friends' praise of his dramatic improvisations, collapsed at his first public audition when an attack of nerves made his performance a complete fiasco. He went into the Imperial Chancery, where he found powerful patronage that guaranteed swift advancement, but he resigned for fear of becoming trapped in petty paperwork. He taught for a time in a boarding school for nobly born young ladies, and in 1833 (when his reputation as a writer was already on the rise) managed to get himself appointed Professor of History at St. Petersburg University. Here he planned out a four-volume history of Russia and an eight-volume history of the Ukraine, neither of which was ever written; here he gave a series of lectures which (according to Turgenev, who attended some of them) were completely incoherent.

The beginning of Gogol's writing career was almost equally unpromising. His first published work, *Hans Kuechelgarten*, a Byronic verse drama written when he was eighteen and published in 1829, was viciously panned by the leading Moscow critics, and Gogol's main satisfaction was in having had the work printed anonymously. But in 1831 Gogol was introduced to Alexander Pushkin—then and to this day considered Russia's greatest poet. Pushkin was impressed by Gogol's wit and talent and he sponsored the young man in the artistic salons he frequented. This paved the way for Gogol's first literary success, his humorous and grotesque sketches of Ukrainian life entitled *Evenings on the Farm near Dikanka* (1831-1832). And after his abortive attempt to become Russia's greatest historian, Gogol returned to his first love, the stage, and wrote the most celebrated Russian comedy, a satire on provincial life called *The Inspector-General* (1836). This farce played to full houses throughout its run, but the response to the play was not entirely favorable: Gogol's ridiculous exposure of bribery and corruption in high places and of the smugness of petty civil servants cut too deep to please the Establishment he had held up to laughter. Gogol took the indignation of the infuriated few more seriously than the howls of responsive hilarity from the audience at large, and, beginning to feel like a scorned prophet, he left for an extended European tour.

On his return three years later, his friends saw a new Gogol, more serious, more dignified, and with the first signs of the religious mysticism that was later to consume him. He was already at work on his epic novel, *Dead Souls* (1842), which he hoped would develop into a Russian *Divine Comedy* that would lead the Slavic races toward their salvation. Despite problems with censorship, Gogol managed to see through the press the first part of *Dead Souls*, a subtle but biting satire on provincial folly and avarice. It was also at this time, when he was at the height of his powers, that Gogol wrote and published his greatest short novel, *The Overcoat* (1842).

On the pretext of his health, Gogol returned to Western Europe, where he spent the next six years in travel. France and Italy had earlier nurtured his talent, but this time—at the age of only thirty-three—Gogol's inspiration seems to have dried up. He tried to force himself to write and succeeded only in making himself desperately ill, spiritually and physically. His works toward the end of this European tour were allegorical or direct sermons to the Russian people, who were irritated, amused, and finally bored by them.

On his return to Russia in 1849, Gogol's religious mania was well advanced. He alternated between periods of effervescent cheerfulness—during which he worked on the second part of *Dead Souls*—and long stretches of black despair. Manipulated by a fanatical Orthodox priest, Matvey Konstantinovsky, Gogol denounced his former idol Pushkin, burned most of his unpublished work (including all but a small part of the continuation of *Dead Souls*), and turned morbidly away from life to a mystical vision beyond. Father Matvey visited Gogol on February 6, 1852—the beginning of Lent—and from that day on Gogol went into a strict and suicidal fast which ended when death came two weeks later. Like his father, Gogol had had visions which directed the principal choices of his life; like his father, he had felt himself to be haunted by the Devil. And his last delirious words (''faster . . . faster . . . get me a ladder'') bespoke his terror of the Demon within him. On February 24, the pagan, secular intellectuals of Moscow all turned out to pay their respects to the severely Orthodox writer who had taken himself from their midst.

One of the finest Russian authors of the nineteenth century, Gogol's influence has been immense. He is usually looked upon as the father of that school of Russian authors specializing in the ironic, the fantastic, and the grotesque, a school that included Dostoyevsky and Chekhov in the later nineteenth century, as well as Bely and Nabokov in the twentieth. Gogol and his sponsor Pushkin, both driven, both tragically fated, share the palm as founders of an internationally famed Russian literature.

Biography   Readable full-length biographies of Gogol include those by David Magarshack, *Nikolai Gogol* (New York: Grove Press, 1957), and Henri Troyat, *Divided Soul: The Life of Gogol* (New York: Minerva Press, 1973). Biographical sketches are also in the works by Nabokov and Setchkarev listed below.

Editions and Translations   The most convenient edition of Gogol for the English-speaking reader is Leonard J. Kent, ed., *The Collected Tales and Plays of Nikolai Gogol* (New York: Pantheon Books, 1964). This collection does not include *Dead Souls*, which is available in an edition edited and translated by Bernard Guilbert Guerney (New York: The Modern Library, 1965). Most Russian-speaking critics are contemptuous of the translations of Gogol in English; one exception to this general disdain is the praise of Vladimir Nabokov—himself a superb English stylist—for the Guerney translation of *Dead Souls*.

Criticism   Most Gogol criticism is written in Russian and is still untranslated. A few good studies of his art available in English include Vladimir Nabokov, *Nikolai Gogol* (London: Nicholson and Watson, 1947), and Vsevolod Setchkarev, *Gogol: His Life and Works* (New York: New York University Press, 1965). Robert Maguire's collection of essays about Gogol, *Gogol from the Twentieth Century* (Princeton: Princeton University Press, 1974), brings together a number of previously untranslated articles, including two, by Boris Eichenbaum and Dmitry Chizhevsky, on *The Overcoat*.

The Overcoat [1]

Translated by Leonard J. Kent

In the department of . . . but I had better not mention which department. There is nothing in the world more touchy than a department, a regiment, a government office, and, in fact, any sort of official body. Nowadays every private individual considers all society insulted in his person. I have been told that very lately a complaint was lodged by a

---

[1] It is usually agreed that the theme of this story was suggested to Gogol by a tale about an indigent clerk who loved to hunt but had no money to buy a gun. After enormous

police inspector of which town I don't remember, and that in this complaint he set forth clearly that the institutions of the State were in danger and that his sacred name was being taken in vain; and, in proof thereof, he appended to his complaint an enormously long volume of some romantic work in which a police inspector appeared on every tenth page, occasionally, indeed, in an intoxicated condition. And so, to avoid any unpleasantness, we had better call the department of which we are speaking "a certain department."

And so, in a *certain department* there was a *certain clerk*; a clerk of whom it cannot be said that he was very remarkable; he was short, somewhat pock-marked, with rather reddish hair and rather dim, bleary eyes, with a small bald patch on the top of his head, with wrinkles on both sides of his cheeks and the sort of complexion which is usually described as hemorrhoidal . . . nothing can be done about that, it is the Petersburg climate. As for his grade in the civil service (for among us a man's rank is what must be established first) he was what is called a perpetual titular councilor, a class at which, as we all know, various writers who indulge in the praiseworthy habit of attacking those who cannot defend themselves jeer and jibe to their hearts' content. This clerk's surname was Bashmachkin. From the very name it is clear that it must have been derived from a shoe (*bashmak*); but when and under what circumstances it was derived from a shoe, it is impossible to say. Both his father and his grandfather and even his brother-in-law, and all the Bashmachkins without exception wore boots, which they simply

---

privation, the tale continued, the clerk finally saved enough to buy one. On his first hunting trip, however, he dropped it into the water and it was lost forever. Grief-stricken, the moribund clerk was saved from death by the generosity of his fellow workers, who bought him a new gun. Despite very important differences there is obviously a strong thematic thread which ties this to *The Overcoat*. Professor Stilman notes three possible sources. The first, the story of the indigent clerk. The second, "facts or anecdotes recorded in the diary of Pushkin . . ." and the entry in Pushkin's diary which Professor Stilman quotes notes that strange occurrences had made the streets unsafe—such occurrences consisting mainly of furniture jumping around, thieves very active in the streets. And third, a possible source which was uncovered by F. C. Driessen, a Dutch scholar, namely, a legend of a sixteenth-century saint of the Orthodox Church, Saint Akaky, who died after being abused for nine years by his elder. The elder, the legend continues, was stricken with guilt and, obsessed with the thought that Akaky was still alive, he visited his grave, where he heard his voice saying, "I am not dead, for a man who lived in obedience may not die." We consider this last possible source highly unlikely. Rather we would suggest Akaky is "Akaky" (as was his father) because the name is so suggestive, something of which the language-conscious Gogol could not conceivably have been unaware; indeed, to a native Russian who has never read or heard of the story, the name is provocative, the resemblance to *kaka* (defecation) being quite impossible to miss, and Gogol's fondness for the word is evident from a reading of the Russian text. (Translator)

resoled two or three times a year. His name was Akaky Akakievich. Perhaps it may strike the reader as a rather strange and contrived name, but I can assure him that it was not contrived at all, that the circumstances were such that it was quite out of the question to give him any other name. Akaky Akakievich was born toward nightfall, if my memory does not deceive me, on the twenty-third of March. His mother, the wife of a government clerk, a very good woman, made arrangements in due course to christen the child. She was still lying in bed, facing the door, while on her right hand stood the godfather, an excellent man called Ivan Ivanovich Yeroshkin, one of the head clerks in the Senate, and the godmother, the wife of a police official and a woman of rare qualities, Arina Semeonovna Belobriushkova. Three names were offered to the happy mother for selection—Mokky, Sossy, or the name of the martyr Khozdazat. "No," thought the poor lady, "they are all such names!" To satisfy her, they opened the calendar at another page, and the names which turned up were: Trifily, Dula, Varakhasy. "What an infliction!" said the mother. "What names they all are! I really never heard such names. Varadat or Varukh would be bad enough, but Trifily and Varakhasy!" They turned over another page and the names were: Pavsikakhy and Yakhisy. "Well, I see," said the mother, "it is clear that it is his fate. Since that is how it is, he had better be named after his father; his father is Akaky; let the son be Akaky, too." This was how he came to be Akaky Akakievich. The baby was christened and cried and made sour faces during the ceremony, as though he foresaw that he would be a titular councilor. So that was how it all came to pass. We have reported it here so that the reader may see for himself that it happened quite inevitably and that to give him any other name was out of the question.

No one has been able to remember when and how long ago he entered the department, nor who gave him the job. Regardless of how many directors and higher officials of all sorts came and went, he was always seen in the same place, in the same position, at the very same duty, precisely the same copying clerk, so that they used to declare that he must have been born a copying clerk, uniform, bald patch, and all. No respect at all was shown him in the department. The porters, far from getting up from their seats when he came in, took no more notice of him than if a simple fly had flown across the reception room. His superiors treated him with a sort of despotic aloofness. The head clerk's assistant used to throw papers under his nose without even saying "Copy this" or "Here is an interesting, nice little case" or some agreeable remark of the sort, as is usually done in well-bred offices.

And he would take it, gazing only at the paper without looking to see who had put it there and whether he had the right to do so; he would take it and at once begin copying it. The young clerks jeered and made jokes at him to the best of their clerkly wit, and told before his face all sorts of stories of their own invention about him; they would say of his landlady, an old woman of seventy, that she beat him, would ask when the wedding was to take place, and would scatter bits of paper on his head, calling them snow. Akaky Akakievich never answered a word, however, but behaved as though there were no one there. It had no influence on his work; in the midst of all this teasing, he never made a single mistake in his copying. It was only when the jokes became too unbearable, when they jolted his arm, and prevented him from going on with his work, that he would say: "Leave me alone! Why do you insult me?" and there was something touching in the words and in the voice in which they were uttered. There was a note in it of something that aroused compassion, so that one young man, new to the office, who, following the example of the rest, had allowed himself to tease him, suddenly stopped as though cut to the heart, and from that time on, everything was, as it were, changed and appeared in a different light to him. Some unseen force seemed to repel him from the companions with whom he had become acquainted because he thought they were well-bred and decent men. And long afterward, during moments of the greatest gaiety, the figure of the humble little clerk with a bald patch on his head appeared before him with his heart-rending words: "Leave me alone! Why do you insult me?" and within those moving words he heard others: "I am your brother." And the poor young man hid his face in his hands, and many times afterward in his life he shuddered, seeing how much inhumanity there is in man, how much savage brutality lies hidden under refined, cultured politeness, and, my God! even in a man whom the world accepts as a gentleman and a man of honor. . . .

It would be hard to find a man who lived for his work as did Akaky Akakievich. To say that he was zealous in his work is not enough; no, he loved his work. In it, in that copying, he found an interesting and pleasant world of his own. There was a look of enjoyment on his face; certain letters were favorites with him, and when he came to them he was delighted; he chuckled to himself and winked and moved his lips, so that it seemed as though every letter his pen was forming could be read in his face. If rewards had been given according to the measure of zeal in the service, he might to his amazement have even found himself a civil councilor; but all he gained in the service, as the wits, his fellow clerks, expressed it, was a button in his buttonhole[2] and hemorrhoids where he sat. It cannot be said, however, that no notice had ever been taken of him. One director, being a good-natured man and anxious to reward him for his long service, sent him something a little more important than his ordinary copying; he was instructed to make some sort of report from a finished document for another office; the work consisted only of altering the headings and in places changing the first person into the third. This cost him so much effort that he was covered with perspiration: he mopped his brow and said at last, "No, I'd rather copy something."

From that time on they left him to his copying forever. It seemed as though nothing in the world existed for him except his copying. He gave no thought at all to his clothes; his uniform was—well, not green but some sort of rusty, muddy color. His collar was very low and narrow, so that, although his neck was not particularly long, yet, standing out of the collar, it looked as immensely long as those of the dozens of plaster kittens with nodding heads which foreigners carry about on their heads and peddle in Russia. And there were always things sticking to his uniform, either bits of hay or threads; moreover, he had a special knack of passing under a window at the very moment when various garbage was being flung out into the street, and so was continually carrying off bits of melon rind and similar litter on his hat. He had never once in his life noticed what was being done and what was going on in the street, all those things at which, as we all know, his colleagues, the young clerks, always stare, utilizing their keen sight so well that they notice anyone on the other side of the street with a trouser strap hanging loose—an observation which always calls forth a sly grin. Whatever Akaky Akakievich looked at, he saw nothing but his clear, evenly written lines, and it was only perhaps when a horse suddenly appeared from nowhere and placed its head on his shoulder, and with its nostrils blew a real gale upon his cheek, that he would notice that he was not in the middle of his writing, but rather in the middle of the street.

On reaching home, he would sit down at once at the table, hurriedly eat his soup and a piece of beef with an onion; he did not notice the taste at all but ate it all with the flies and anything else that Providence happened to send him. When he felt that his stomach was beginning to be full, he would get up from the table, take out a bottle of ink and

---

[2]Whereas most clerks of long service wore a medal of achievement. (TRANSLATOR.)

begin copying the papers he had brought home with him. When he had none to do, he would make a copy especially for his own pleasure, particularly if the document were remarkable not for the beauty of its style but because it was addressed to some new or distinguished person.

Even at those hours when the gray Petersburg sky is completely overcast and the whole population of clerks have dined and eaten their fill, each as best he can, according to the salary he receives and his personal tastes; when they are all resting after the scratching of pens and bustle of the office, their own necessary work and other people's, and all the tasks that an overzealous man voluntarily sets himself even beyond what is necessary; when the clerks are hastening to devote what is left of their time to pleasure; some more enterprising are flying to the theater, others to the street to spend their leisure staring at women's hats, some to spend the evening paying compliments to some attractive girl, the star of a little official circle, while some—and this is the most frequent of all—go simply to a fellow clerk's apartment on the third or fourth story, two little rooms with a hall or a kitchen, with some pretensions to style, with a lamp or some such article that has cost many sacrifices of dinners and excursions—at the time when all the clerks are scattered about the apartments of their friends, playing a stormy game of whist, sipping tea out of glasses, eating cheap biscuits, sucking in smoke from long pipes, telling, as the cards are dealt, some scandal that has floated down from higher circles, a pleasure which the Russian can never by any possibility deny himself, or, when there is nothing better to talk about, repeating the everlasting anecdote of the commanding officer who was told that the tail had been cut off the horse on the Falconet monument[3]—in short, even when everyone was eagerly seeking entertainment, Akaky Akakievich did not indulge in any amusement. No one could say that they had ever seen him at an evening party. After working to his heart's content, he would go to bed, smiling at the thought of the next day and wondering what God would send him to copy. So flowed on the peaceful life of a man who knew how to be content with his fate on a salary of four hundred rubles,[4] and so perhaps it would have flowed on to extreme old age, had it not been for the various disasters strewn along the road of life, not only of titular, but even of privy, actual court, and all other coun-

---

[3] Famous statue of Peter the First.

[4] About $5,000 in today's currency.

cilors, even those who neither give counsel to others nor accept it themselves.

There is in Petersburg a mighty foe of all who receive a salary of about four hundred rubles. That foe is none other than our northern frost, although it is said to be very good for the health. Between eight and nine in the morning, precisely at the hour when the streets are filled with clerks going to their departments, the frost begins indiscriminately giving such sharp and stinging nips at all their noses that the poor fellows don't know what to do with them. At that time, when even those in the higher grade have a pain in their brows and tears in their eyes from the frost, the poor titular councilors are sometimes almost defenseless. Their only protection lies in running as fast as they can through five or six streets in a wretched, thin little overcoat and then warming their feet thoroughly in the porter's room, till all their faculties and talents for their various duties thaw out again after having been frozen on the way. Akaky Akakievich had for some time been feeling that his back and shoulders were particularly nipped by the cold, although he did try to run the regular distance as fast as he could. He wondered at last whether there were any defects in his overcoat. After examining it thoroughly in the privacy of his home, he discovered that in two or three places, on the back and the shoulders, it had become a regular sieve; the cloth was so worn that you could see through it and the lining was coming out. I must note that Akaky Akakievich's overcoat had also served as a butt for the jokes of the clerks. It had even been deprived of the honorable name of overcoat and had been referred to as the "dressing gown."[5] It was indeed of rather a peculiar make. Its collar had been growing smaller year by year as it served to patch the other parts. The patches were not good specimens of the tailor's art, and they certainly looked clumsy and ugly. On seeing what was wrong, Akaky Akakievich decided that he would have to take the overcoat to Petrovich, a tailor who lived on the fourth floor up a back staircase, and, in spite of having only one eye and being pockmarked all over his face, was rather successful in repairing the trousers and coats of clerks and others—that is, when he was sober, be it understood, and had no other enterprise in his mind. Of this tailor I ought not, of course, say much, but since it is now the rule that the character of every person in a novel must be completely described, well, there's nothing I can do but describe Petrovich too. At

---

[5]*Kapot*, usually a woman's garment. (TRANSLATOR)

first he was called simply Grigory, and was a serf belonging to some gentleman or other. He began to be called Petrovich[6] from the time that he got his freedom and began to drink rather heavily on every holiday, at first only on the main holidays, but afterward, on all church holidays indiscriminately, wherever there was a cross in the calendar. In this he was true to the customs of his forefathers, and when he quarreled with his wife he used to call her a worldly woman and a German. Since we have now mentioned the wife, it will be necessary to say a few words about her, too, but unfortunately not much is known about her, except indeed that Petrovich had a wife and that she wore a cap and not a kerchief, but apparently she could not boast of beauty; anyway, none but soldiers of the guard peered under her cap when they met her, and they twitched their mustaches and gave vent to a rather peculiar sound.

As he climbed the stairs leading to Petrovich's—which, to do them justice, were all soaked with water and slops and saturated through and through with that smell of ammonia which makes the eyes smart, and is, as we all know, inseparable from the backstairs of Petersburg houses—Akaky Akakievich was already wondering how much Petrovich would ask for the job, and inwardly resolving not to give more than two rubles. The door was open, because Petrovich's wife was frying some fish and had so filled the kitchen with smoke that you could not even see the cockroaches. Akaky Akakievich crossed the kitchen unnoticed by the good woman, and walked at last into a room where he saw Petrovich sitting on a big, wooden, unpainted table with his legs tucked under him like a Turkish pasha. The feet, as is usual with tailors when they sit at work, were bare; and the first object that caught Akaky Akakievich's eye was the big toe, with which he was already familiar, with a misshapen nail as thick and strong as the shell of a tortoise. Around Petrovich's neck hung a skein of silk and another of thread and on his knees was a rag of some sort. He had for the last three minutes been trying to thread his needle, but could not get the thread into the eye and so was very angry with the darkness and indeed with the thread itself, muttering in an undertone: "She won't go in, the savage! You wear me out, you bitch." Akaky Akakievich was unhappy that he had come just at the minute when Petrovich was in a bad humor; he liked to give him an order when he was a little "elevated," or, as his wife expressed it, "had fortified himself with vodka,

---

[6]Customarily, serfs were addressed by first name only, while free men were addressed either by first name and patronymic or just the patronymic. (Translator)

the one-eyed devil." In such circumstances Petrovich was as a rule very ready to give way and agree, and invariably bowed and thanked him. Afterward, it is true, his wife would come wailing that her husband had been drunk and so had asked too little, but adding a single ten-kopek piece would settle that. But on this occasion Petrovich was apparently sober and consequently curt, unwilling to bargain, and the devil knows what price he would be ready to demand. Akaky Akakievich realized this, and was, as the saying is, beating a retreat, but things had gone too far, for Petrovich was screwing up his solitary eye very attentively at him and Akaky Akakievich involuntarily said: "Good day, Petrovich!"

"I wish you a good day, sir," said Petrovich, and squinted at Akaky Akakievich's hands, trying to discover what sort of goods he had brought.

"Here I have come to you, Petrovich, do you see . . . !"

It must be noticed that Akaky Akakievich for the most part explained himself by apologies, vague phrases, and meaningless parts of speech which have absolutely no significance whatever. If the subject were a very difficult one, it was his habit indeed to leave his sentences quite unfinished, so that very often after a sentence had begun with the words, "It really is, don't you know . . ." nothing at all would follow and he himself would be quite oblivious to the fact that he had not finished his thought, supposing he had said all that was necessary.

"What is it?" said Petrovich, and at the same time with his solitary eye he scrutinized his whole uniform from the collar to the sleeves, the back, the skirts, the buttonholes—with all of which he was very familiar since they were all his own work. Such scrutiny is habitual with tailors; it is the first thing they do on meeting one.

"It's like this, Petrovich . . . the overcoat, the cloth . . . you see everywhere else it is quite strong; it's a little dusty and looks as though it were old, but it is new and it is only in one place just a little . . . on the back, and just a little worn on one shoulder and on this shoulder, too, a little . . . do you see? that's all, and it's not much work . . ."

Petrovich took the "dressing gown," first spread it out over the table, examined it for a long time, shook his head, and put his hand out to the window sill for a round snuffbox with a portrait on the lid of some general—which general I can't exactly say, for a finger had been thrust through the spot where a face should have been, and the hole had been pasted over with a square piece of paper. After taking a pinch of snuff, Petrovich held the "dressing gown" up in his hands and looked at it against the light, and again he shook his head; then he turned it with the lining upward and once more shook his head; again he took off the lid with the general pasted up with paper and stuffed a pinch into his nose, shut the box, put it away, and at last said: "No, it can't be repaired; a wretched garment!" Akaky Akakievich's heart sank at those words.

"Why can't it, Petrovich?" he said, almost in the imploring voice of a child. "Why, the only thing is, it is a bit worn on the shoulders; why, you have got some little pieces . . ."

"Yes, the pieces will be found all right," said Petrovich, "but it can't be patched, the stuff is rotten; if you put a needle in it, it would give way."

"Let it give way, but you just put a patch on it."

"There is nothing to put a patch on. There is nothing for it to hold on to; there is a great strain on it; it is not worth calling cloth; it would fly away at a breath of wind."

"Well, then, strengthen it with something—I'm sure, really, this is . . . !"

"No," said Petrovich resolutely, "there is nothing that can be done, the thing is no good at all. You had far better, when the cold winter weather comes, make yourself leg wrappings out of it, for there is no warmth in stockings; the Germans invented them just to make money." (Petrovich enjoyed a dig at the Germans occasionally.) "And as for the overcoat, it is obvious that you will have to have a new one."

At the word "new" there was a mist before Akaky Akakievich's eyes, and everything in the room seemed blurred. He could see nothing clearly but the general with the piece of paper over his face on the lid of Petrovich's snuffbox.

"A new one?" he said, still feeling as though he were in a dream; "why, I haven't the money for it."

"Yes, a new one," Petrovich repeated with barbarous composure.

"Well, and if I did have a new one, how much would it . . . ?"

"You mean what will it cost?"

"Yes."

"Well, at least one hundred and fifty rubles," said Petrovich, and he compressed his lips meaningfully. He was very fond of making an effect; he was fond of suddenly disconcerting a man completely and then squinting sideways to see what sort of a face he made.

"A hundred and fifty rubles for an overcoat!" screamed poor Akaky Akakievich—it was perhaps the first time he had screamed in his life, for he was always distinguished by the softness of his voice.

"Yes," said Petrovich, "and even then it depends on the coat. If I were to put marten on the collar, and add a hood with silk linings, it would come to two hundred."

"Petrovich, please," said Akaky Akakievich in an imploring voice, not hearing and not trying to hear what Petrovich said, and missing all his effects, "repair it somehow, so that it will serve a little longer."

"No, that would be wasting work and spending money for nothing," said Petrovich, and after that Akaky Akakievich went away completely crushed, and when he had gone Petrovich remained standing for a long time with his lips pursed up meaningfully before he began his work again, feeling pleased that he had not demeaned himself or lowered the dignity of the tailor's art.

When he got into the street, Akaky Akakievich felt as though he was in a dream. "So that is how it is," he said to himself. "I really did not think it would be this way . . . " and then after a pause he added, "So that's it! So that's how it is at last! and I really could never have supposed it would be this way. And there . . . " There followed another long silence, after which he said: "So that's it! well, it really is so utterly unexpected . . . who would have thought . . . what a circumstance . . . " Saying this, instead of going home he walked off in quite the opposite direction without suspecting what he was doing. On the way a clumsy chimney sweep brushed the whole of his sooty side against him and blackened his entire shoulder; a whole hatful of plaster scattered upon him from the top of a house that was being built. He noticed nothing of this, and only after he had jostled against a policeman who had set his halberd down beside him and was shaking some snuff out of his horn into his rough fist, he came to himself a little and then only because the policeman said: "Why are you poking yourself right in one's face, haven't you enough room on the street?" This made him look around and turn homeward; only there he began to collect his thoughts, to see his position in a clear and true light, and began talking to himself no longer incoherently but reasonably and openly as with a sensible friend with whom one can discuss the most intimate and vital matters. "No," said Akaky Akakievich, "it is no use talking to Petrovich now; just now he really is . . . his wife must have been giving it to him. I had better go to him on Sunday morning; after Saturday night he will have a crossed eye and be sleepy, so he'll want a little drink and his wife won't give him a kopek. I'll slip ten kopeks into his hand and then he will be more accommodating and maybe take the overcoat . . . "

So reasoning with himself, Akaky Akakievich cheered up and waited until the next Sunday; then, seeing from a distance Petrovich's wife leaving the house, he went straight in. Petrovich certainly had a crossed eye after Saturday. He could hardly hold his head up and was very drowsy; but, despite all that, as soon as he heard what Akaky Akakievich was speaking about, it seemed as though the devil had nudged him. "I can't," he said, "you must order a new one." Akaky Akakievich at once slipped a ten-kopek piece into his hand. "I thank you, sir, I will have just a drop to your health, but don't trouble yourself about the overcoat; it is no good for anything. I'll make you a fine new coat; you can have faith in me for that."

Akaky Akakievich would have said more about repairs, but Petrovich, without listening, said: "A new one I'll make you without fail; you can rely on that; I'll do my best. It could even be like the fashion that is popular, with the collar to fasten with silver-plated hooks under a flap."

Then Akaky Akakievich saw that there was no escape from a new overcoat and he was utterly depressed. How indeed, for what, with what money could he get it? Of course he could to some extent rely on the bonus for the coming holiday, but that money had long ago been appropriated and its use determined beforehand. It was needed for new trousers and to pay the cobbler an old debt for putting some new tops on some old boots, and he had to order three shirts from a seamstress as well as two items of undergarments which it is indecent to mention in print; in short, all that money absolutely must be spent, and even if the director were to be so gracious as to give him a holiday bonus of forty-five or even fifty, instead of forty rubles, there would be still left a mere trifle, which would be but a drop in the ocean compared to the fortune needed for an overcoat. Though, of course, he knew that Petrovich had a strange craze for suddenly demanding the devil knows what enormous price, so that at times his own wife could not help crying out: "Why, you are out of your wits, you idiot! Another time he'll undertake a job for nothing, and here the devil has bewitched him to ask more than he is worth himself." Though, of course, he knew that Petrovich would undertake to make it for eighty rubles, still where would he get those eighty rubles? He might manage half of that sum; half of it could be found, perhaps even a little more; but where could he get the other half? . . . But, first of all, the reader ought to know where that first half was to be found. Akaky Akakievich had the habit every time he spent a ruble of putting aside two kopeks in a little box which he kept locked, with a slit in the lid for dropping in the money. At the end of every six months he would inspect the pile of coppers there and change them for small silver. He had done this for a long time, and in the course of many years the sum had mounted up to forty rubles and so he had half the money in his hands, but where was he to get the other half; where was he to get another forty rubles? Akaky Akakievich thought and thought and decided at last that he would have to diminish his ordinary expenses, at least for a year; give up burning candles in the evening, and if he had to do any work he must go into the landlady's room and work by her candle; that as he walked along the streets he must walk as lightly and carefully as possible, almost on tiptoe, on the cobbles and flagstones, so that his soles might last a little longer than usual; that he must send his linen to the wash less frequently, and that, to preserve it from being worn, he must take it off every day when he came home and sit in a thin cotton dressing gown, a very ancient garment which Time itself had spared. To tell the truth, he found it at first rather difficult to get used to these privations, but after a while it became a habit and went smoothly enough—he even became quite accustomed to being hungry in the evening; on the other hand, he had spiritual nourishment, for he carried ever in his thoughts the idea of his future overcoat. His whole existence had in a sense become fuller, as though he had married, as though some other person were present with him, as though he were no longer alone but an agreeable companion had consented to walk the path of life hand in hand with him, and that companion was none other than the new overcoat with its thick padding and its strong, durable lining. He became, as it were, more alive, even more strong-willed, like a man who has set before himself a definite goal. Uncertainty, indecision, in fact all the hesitating and vague characteristics, vanished from his face and his manners. At times there was a gleam in his eyes; indeed, the most bold and audacious ideas flashed through his mind. Why not really have marten on the collar? Meditation on the subject always made him absent-minded. On one occasion when he was copying a document, he very nearly made a mistake, so that he almost cried out "ough" aloud and crossed himself. At least once every month he went to Petrovich to talk about the overcoat: where it would be best to buy the cloth, and what color it should be, and what price; and, though he returned home a little anxious, he was always pleased at the thought that at last the time was at hand when everything would be bought and the overcoat would be made. Things moved even faster than he had anticipated. Contrary to all expectations, the director bestowed on Akaky Akakievich a bonus of no less than sixty rubles. Whether it was that he had an inkling that Akaky Akakievich needed a coat, or whether it happened by luck, owing to this he found he had twenty rubles extra. This circumstance hastened the course of affairs. Another two or three months of partial starvation and Akaky Akakievich had actually saved up nearly eighty rubles. His heart, as a rule very tranquil, began to throb. The very first day he set out with Petrovich for the shops. They bought some very good cloth, and no wonder, since they had been thinking of it for more than six months, and scarcely a month had passed without their going out to the shop to compare prices; now Petrovich himself declared that there was no better cloth to be had. For the lining they chose calico, but of such good quality, that in Petrovich's words it was even better than silk, and actually as strong and handsome to look at. Marten they did not buy, because it was too expensive, but instead they chose cat fur, the best to be found in the shop—cat which in the distance might almost be taken for marten. Petrovich was busy making the coat for two weeks, because there was a great deal of quilting; otherwise it would have been ready sooner. Petrovich charged twelve rubles for the work; less than that it hardly could have been; everything was sewn with silk, with fine double seams, and Petrovich went over every seam afterwards with his own teeth, imprinting various patterns with them. It was . . . it is hard to say precisely on what day, but probably on the most triumphant day in the life of Akaky Akakievich, that Petrovich at last brought the overcoat. He brought it in the morning, just before it was time to set off for the department. The overcoat could not have arrived at a more opportune time, because severe frosts were just beginning and seemed threatening to become even harsher. Petrovich brought the coat himself as a good tailor should. There was an expression of importance on his face, such as Akaky Akakievich had never seen there before. He seemed fully conscious of having completed a work of no little importance and of having shown by his own example the gulf that separates tailors who only put in linings and do repairs from those who make new coats. He took the coat out of the huge handkerchief in which he had brought it (the handkerchief had just come home from the wash); he then folded it up and put it in his pocket for future use. After taking out the overcoat, he looked at it with much pride and holding it in both hands, threw it very deftly over Akaky Akakievich's shoulders, then pulled it down and smoothed it out behind with his hands, then draped it about Akaky Akakievich somewhat jauntily. Akaky Akakievich, a practical man, wanted to try it with his arms in the sleeves. Petrovich helped him to put it on, and it looked splendid with his arms in the sleeves, too. In fact, it turned out that the overcoat was completely and entirely successful. Petrovich did not let slip the occasion for observing that it was only because he lived in a small street and had no signboard, and because he had known Akaky Akakievich so long, that he had done it so cheaply, and that on Nevsky Prospekt they would have asked him seventy-five rubles for the tailoring alone. Akaky Akakievich had no inclination to discuss this with Petrovich; besides he was frightened of the big sums that Petrovich was fond of flinging airily about in conversation. He paid him, thanked him, and went off, with his new overcoat on, to the department. Petrovich followed him out and stopped in the street, staring for a long time at the coat from a distance and then purposely turned off and, taking a short cut through a side street, came back into the street, and got another view of the coat from the other side, that is, from the front.

Meanwhile Akaky Akakievich walked along in a gay holiday mood. Every second he was conscious that he had a new overcoat on his shoulders, and several times he actually laughed from inward satisfaction. Indeed, it had two advantages: one that it was warm and the other that it was good. He did not notice how far he had walked at all and he suddenly found himself in the department; in the porter's room he took off the overcoat, looked it over, and entrusted it to the porter's special care. I cannot tell how it happened, but all at once everyone in the department learned that Akaky Akakievich had a new overcoat and that the "dressing gown" no longer existed. They all ran out at once into the cloakroom to look at Akaky Akakievich's new overcoat; they began welcoming him and congratulating him so that at first he could do nothing but smile and then felt positively embarrassed. When, coming up to him, they all began saying that he must "sprinkle" the new overcoat and that he ought at least to buy them all a supper, Akaky Akakievich lost his head completely and did not know what to do, how to get out of it, nor what to answer. A few minutes later, flushing crimson, he even began assuring them with great simplicity that it was not a new overcoat at all, that it wasn't much, that it was an old overcoat. At last one of the clerks, indeed the assistant of the head clerk of the room, probably in order to show that he wasn't too proud to mingle with those beneath him, said: "So be it, I'll give a party instead of Akaky Akakievich and invite you all to tea with me this evening; as luck would have it, it is my birthday." The clerks naturally congratulated the assistant head clerk and eagerly accepted the invitation. Akaky Akakievich was beginning to make excuses, but they all declared that it was uncivil of him, that it would be simply a shame and a disgrace and that he could not possibly refuse. So, he finally relented, and later felt pleased about it when he remembered that through this he would have the opportunity of going out in the evening, too, in his new overcoat. That whole day was for Akaky Akakievich the most triumphant and festive day in his life. He returned home in the happiest frame of mind, took off the overcoat, and hung it carefully on the wall, admiring the cloth and lining once more, and then pulled out his old "dressing gown," now completely falling apart, and put it next to his new overcoat to compare the two. He glanced at it and laughed: the difference was enormous! And long afterwards he went on laughing at dinner, as the position in which the "dressing gown" was placed recurred to his mind. He dined in excellent spirits and after dinner wrote nothing, no papers at all, but just relaxed for a little while on his bed, till it got dark; then, without putting things off, he dressed, put on his overcoat, and went out into the street. Where precisely the clerk who had invited him lived we regret to say we cannot tell; our memory is beginning to fail sadly, and everything there in Petersburg, all the streets and houses, are so blurred and muddled in our head that it is a very difficult business to put anything in orderly fashion. Regardless of that, there is no doubt that the clerk lived in the better part of the town and consequently a very long distance from Akaky Akakievich. At first Akaky Akakievich had to walk through deserted streets, scantily lighted, but as he approached his destination the streets became more lively, more full of people, and more brightly lighted; passers-by began to be more frequent, ladies began to appear, here and there beautifully dressed, and beaver collars were to be seen on the men. Cabmen with wooden, railed sledges, studded with brass-topped nails, were less frequently seen; on the other hand, jaunty drivers in raspberry-colored velvet caps, with lacquered sledges and bearskin rugs, appeared and carriages with decorated boxes dashed along the streets, their wheels crunching through the snow.

Akaky Akakievich looked at all this as a novelty; for several years he had not gone out into the streets in the evening. He stopped with curiosity before a lighted shop window to look at a picture in which a beautiful woman was represented in the act of taking off her shoe and displaying as she did so the whole of a very shapely leg, while behind her back a gentleman with whiskers and a handsome imperial on his chin was sticking his head in at the door. Akaky Akakievich shook his head and smiled and then went on his way. Why did he smile? Was it because he had come across something quite unfamiliar to him, though every man retains some instinctive feeling on the subject, or was it that he reflected, like many other clerks, as follows: "Well, those Frenchmen! It's beyond anything! If they go in for anything of the sort, it really is . . . !" Though possibly he did not even think that; there is no creeping into a man's soul and finding out all that he thinks. At last he reached the house in which the assistant head clerk lived in fine style; there was a lamp burning on the stairs, and the apartment was on the second floor. As he went into the hall Akaky Akakievich saw rows of galoshes. Among them in the middle of the room stood a hissing samovar puffing clouds of steam. On the walls hung coats and cloaks among which some actually had beaver collars or velvet panels. From the other side of the wall there came noise and talk which suddenly became clear and loud when the door opened and the footman came out with a tray full of empty glasses, a jug of cream, and a basket of biscuits. It was evident that the clerks had arrived long before and had already drunk their first glass of tea. Akaky Akakievich, after hanging up his coat with his own hands, went into the room, and at the same moment there flashed before his eyes a vision of candles, clerks, pipes and card tables, together with the confused sounds of conversation rising up on all sides and the noise of moving chairs. He stopped very awkwardly in the middle of the room, looking about and trying to think of what to do, but he was noticed and received with a shout and they all went at once into the hall and again took a look at his overcoat. Though Akaky Akakievich was somewhat embarrassed, yet being a simplehearted man, he could not help being pleased at seeing how they all admired his coat. Then of course they all abandoned him and his coat, and turned their attention as usual to the tables set for whist. All this—the noise, the talk, and the crowd of people—was strange and wonderful to Akaky Akakievich. He simply did not know how to behave, what to do with his arms and legs and his whole body; at last he sat down beside the players, looked at the cards, stared first at one and then at another of the faces, and in a little while, feeling bored, began to yawn—especially since it was long past the time at which he usually went to bed. He tried to say goodbye to his hosts, but they would not let him go, saying that he absolutely must have a glass of champagne in honor of the new coat. An hour later supper was served, consisting of salad, cold veal, pastry and pies from the bakery, and champagne. They made Akaky Akakievich drink two glasses after which he felt that things were much more cheerful, though he could not forget that it was twelve o'clock, and that he ought to have been home long ago. That his host might not take it into his head to detain him, he slipped out of the room, hunted in the hall for his coat, which he found, not without regret, lying on the floor, shook it, removed some fluff from it, put it on, and went down the stairs into the street. It was still light in the streets. Some little grocery shops, those perpetual clubs for servants and all sorts of people, were open; others which were closed showed, however, a long streak of light at every crack of the door, proving that they were not yet deserted, and probably maids and menservants were still finishing their conversation and discussion, driving their masters to utter perplexity as to their whereabouts. Akaky Akakievich walked along in a cheerful state of mind; he was even on the point of running, goodness knows why, after a lady of some sort who passed by like lightning with every part of her frame in violent motion. He checked himself at once, however, and again walked along very gently, feeling positively surprised at the inexplicable impulse that had seized him. Soon the deserted streets, which are not particularly cheerful by day and even less so in the evening, stretched before him. Now they were still more dead and deserted; the light of street lamps was scantier, the oil evidently running low; then came wooden houses and fences; not a soul anywhere; only the snow gleamed on the streets and the low-pitched slumbering hovels looked black and gloomy with their closed shutters. He approached the spot where the street was intersected by an endless square, which looked like a fearful desert with its houses scarcely visible on the far side.

In the distance, goodness knows where, there was a gleam of light from some sentry box which seemed to be at the end of the world. Akaky Akakievich's lightheartedness faded. He stepped into the square, not without uneasiness, as though his heart had a premonition of evil. He looked behind him and to both sides—it was as though the sea were all around him. "No, better not look," he thought, and walked on, shutting his eyes, and when he opened them to see whether the end of the square was near, he suddenly saw standing before him, almost under his very nose, some men with mustaches; just what they were like he could not even distinguish. There was a mist before his eyes, and a throbbing in his chest. "Why, that overcoat is mine!" said one of them in a voice like a clap of thunder, seizing him by the collar. Akaky Akakievich was on the point of shouting "Help" when another put a fist the size of a clerk's head against his lips, saying: "You just shout now." Akaky Akakievich felt only that they took the overcoat off, and gave him a kick with their knees, and he fell on his face in the snow and was conscious of nothing more. A few minutes later he recovered consciousness and got up on his feet, but there was no one there. He felt that it was cold on the ground and that he had no overcoat, and began screaming, but it seemed as though his voice would not carry to the end of the square. Overwhelmed with despair and continuing to scream, he ran across the square straight to the sentry box beside which stood a policeman leaning on his halberd and, so it seemed, looking with curiosity to see who the devil the man was who was screaming and running toward him from the distance. As Akaky Akakievich reached him, he began breathlessly shouting that he was asleep and not looking after his duty not to see that a man was being robbed. The policeman answered that he had seen nothing, that he had only seen him stopped in the middle of the square by two men, and supposed that they were his friends, and that, instead of abusing him for nothing, he had better go the next day to the police inspector, who would certainly find out who had taken the overcoat. Akaky Akakievich ran home in a terrible state: his hair, which was still comparatively abundant on his temples and the back of his head, was completely disheveled; his sides and chest and his trousers were all covered with snow. When his old landlady heard a fearful knock at the door, she jumped hurriedly out of bed and, with only one slipper on, ran to open it, modestly holding her chemise over her bosom; but when she opened it she stepped back, seeing in what a state Akaky Akakievich was. When he told her what had happened, she clasped her hands in horror and said that he must go straight to the district commissioner, because the local police inspector would deceive him, make promises and lead him a dance; that it would be best of all to go to the district commissioner, and that she knew him, because Anna, the Finnish girl who was once her cook, was now in service as a nurse at the commissioner's; and that she often saw him himself when he passed by their house, and that he used to be every Sunday at church too, saying his prayers and at the same time looking good-humoredly at everyone, and that therefore by every token he must be a kind-hearted man. After listening to this advice, Akaky Akakievich made his way very gloomily to his room, and how he spent that night I leave to the imagination of those who are in the least able to picture the position of others.

Early in the morning he set off to the police commissioner's but was told that he was asleep. He came at ten o'clock, he was told again that he was asleep; he came at eleven and was told that the commissioner was not at home; he came at dinnertime, but the clerks in the anteroom would not let him in, and insisted on knowing what was the matter and what business had brought him and exactly what had happened; so that at last Akaky Akakievich for the first time in his life tried to show the strength of his character and said curtly that he must see the commissioner himself, that they dare not refuse to admit him, that he had come from the department on government business, and that if he made complaint of them they would see. The clerks dared say nothing to this, and one of them went to summon the commissioner. The latter received his story of being robbed of his overcoat in an extremely peculiar manner. Instead of attending to the main point, he began asking Akaky Akakievich questions: why had he been coming home so late? wasn't he going, or hadn't he been, to some bawdy house? so that Akaky Akakievich was overwhelmed with confusion, and went away without knowing whether or not the proper measures would be taken regarding his overcoat. He was absent from the office all that day (the only time that it had happened in his life). Next day he appeared with a pale face, wearing his old "dressing gown" which had become a still more pitiful sight. The news of the theft of the overcoat—though there were clerks who did not let even this chance slip of jeering at Akaky Akakievich—touched many of them. They decided on the spot to get up a collection for him, but collected only a very trifling sum, because the clerks had already spent a good deal contributing to the director's portrait and on the purchase of a book, at the suggestion of the head of their department, who was a friend of the author, and so the total realized was very insignificant. One of the clerks, moved by compassion, ventured at any rate to assist Akaky Akakievich with good advice, telling him not to go to the local police inspector, because, though it might happen that the latter might succeed in finding his overcoat because he wanted to impress his superiors, it would remain in the possession of the police unless he presented legal proofs that it belonged to him; he urged that by far the best thing would be to appeal to a Person of Consequence; that the Person of Consequence, by writing and getting into communication with the proper authorities, could push the matter through more successfully. There was nothing else to do. Akaky Akakievich made up his mind to go to the Person of Consequence. What precisely was the nature of the functions of the Person of Consequence has remained a matter of uncertainty. It must be noted that this Person of Consequence had only lately become a person of consequence, and until recently had been a person of no consequence. Though, indeed, his position even now was not reckoned of consequence in comparison with others of still greater consequence. But there is always to be found a circle of persons to whom a person of little consequence in the eyes of others is a person of consequence. It is true that he did his utmost to increase the consequence of his position in various ways, for instance by insisting that his subordinates should come out onto the stairs to meet him when he arrived at his office; that no one should venture to approach him directly but all proceedings should follow the strictest chain of command; that a collegiate registrar should report the matter to the governmental secretary; and the governmental secretary to the titular councilor or whomsoever it might be, and that business should only reach him through this channel. Everyone in Holy Russia has a craze for imitation; everyone apes and mimics his superiors. I have actually been told that a titular councilor who was put in charge of a small separate office, immediately partitioned off a special room for himself, calling it the head office, and posted lackeys at the door with red collars and gold braid, who took hold of the handle of the door and opened it for everyone who went in, though the "head office" was so tiny that it was with difficulty that an ordinary writing desk could be put into it. The manners and habits of the Person of Consequence were dignified and majestic, but hardly subtle. The chief foundation of his system was strictness; "strictness, strictness, and—strictness!" he used to say, and at the last word he would look very significantly at the person he was addressing, though, indeed, he had no reason to do so, for the dozen clerks who made up the whole administrative mechanism of his office stood in appropriate awe of him; any clerk who saw him in the distance would leave his work and remain standing at attention till his superior had left the room. His conversation with his subordinates was usually marked by severity and almost confined to three phrases: "How dare you? Do you know to whom you are speaking? Do you understand who I am?" He was, however, at heart a good-natured man, pleasant and obliging with his colleagues; but his advancement to a high rank had completely turned his head. When he received it, he was perplexed, thrown off his balance, and quite at a loss as to how to behave. If he chanced to be with his equals, he was still quite a decent man, a very gentlemanly man, in fact, and in many ways even an intelligent man; but as soon as he was in company with men who were even one grade below him, there was simply no doing anything with him: he sat silent and his position excited compassion, the more so as he himself felt that he might have been spending his time to so much more advantage. At times there could be seen in his eyes an intense desire to join in some interesting conversation, but he was restrained by the doubt whether it would not be too much on his part, whether it would not be too great a familiarity and lowering of his dignity, and in consequence of these reflections he remained everlastingly in the same mute condition, only uttering from time to time monosyllabic sounds, and in this way he gained the reputation of being a terrible bore.

So this was the Person of Consequence to whom our friend Akaky Akakievich appealed, and he appealed to him at a most unpropitious moment, very unfortunate for himself, though fortunate, indeed, for the Person of Consequence. The latter happened to be in his study, talking in the very best of spirits with an old friend of his childhood who had only just arrived and whom he had not seen for several years. It was at this moment that he was informed that a man called Bashmachkin was asking to see him. He asked abruptly, "What sort of man is he?" and received the answer, "A government clerk." "Ah! he can wait. I haven't time now," said the Person of Consequence. Here I must observe that this was a complete lie on the part of the Person of Consequence; he had time; his friend and he had long ago said all they had to say to each other and their conversation had begun to be broken by very long pauses during which they merely slapped each other on the knee, saying, "So that's how things are, Ivan Abramovich!"—"So that's it, Stepan Varlamovich!" but, despite that, he told the clerk to wait in order to show his friend, who had left the civil service some years before and was living at home in the country, how long clerks had to wait for him. At last, after they had talked or rather been silent to their heart's content and had smoked a cigar in very comfortable armchairs with sloping backs, he seemed suddenly to recollect, and said to the secretary, who was standing at the door with papers for his signature: "Oh, by the way, there is a clerk waiting, isn't there? tell him he can come in." When he saw Akaky Akakievich's meek appearance and old uniform, he turned to him at once and said: "What do you want?" in a firm and abrupt voice, which he had purposely rehearsed in his own room in solitude before the mirror for a week before receiving his present post and the grade of a general. Akaky Akakievich, who was overwhelmed with appropriate awe beforehand, was somewhat confused and, as far as his tongue would allow him, explained to the best of his powers, with even more frequent "ers" than usual, that he had had a perfectly new overcoat and now he had been robbed of it in the most inhuman way, and that now he had come to beg him by his intervention either to correspond with his honor, the head police commissioner, or anybody else, and find the overcoat. This mode of proceeding struck the general for some reason as too familiar. "What next, sir?" he went on abruptly. "Don't you know the way to proceed? To whom are you addressing yourself? Don't you know how things are done? You ought first to have handed in a petition to the office; it would have gone to the head clerk of the room, and to the head clerk of the section; then it would have been handed to the secretary and the secretary would have brought it to me . . ."

"But, your Excellency," said Akaky Akakievich, trying to gather the drop of courage he possessed and feeling at the same time that he was perspiring all over, "I ventured, your Excellency, to trouble you because secretaries . . . er . . . are people you can't depend on . . ."

"What? what? what?" said the Person of Consequence, "where did you get hold of that attitude? where did you pick up such ideas? What insubordination is spreading among young men against their superiors and their chiefs!" The Person of Consequence did not apparently observe that Akaky Akakievich was well over fifty, and therefore if he could have been called a young man it would only have been in comparison with a man of seventy. "Do you know to whom you are speaking? Do you understand who I am? Do you understand that, I ask you?" At this point he stamped, and raised his voice to such a powerful note that Akaky Akakievich was not the only one to be terrified. Akaky Akakievich was positively petrified; he staggered, trembling all over, and could not stand; if the porters had not run up to support him, he would have flopped on the floor; he was led out almost unconscious. The Person of Consequence, pleased that the effect had surpassed his expectations and enchanted at the idea that his words could even deprive a man of consciousness, stole a sideway glance at his friend to see how he was taking it, and perceived not without satisfaction that his friend was feeling very uncertain and even beginning to be a little terrified himself.

How he got downstairs, how he went out into the street—of all that Akaky Akakievich remembered nothing; he had no feeling in his arms or his legs. In all his life he had never been so severely reprimanded by a general, and this was by one of another department, too. He went out into the snowstorm that was whistling through the streets, with his mouth open, and as he went he stumbled off the pavement; the wind, as its way is in Petersburg, blew upon him from all points of the compass and from every side street. In an instant it had blown a quinsy into his throat, and when he got home he was not able to utter a word; he went to bed with a swollen face and throat. That's how violent the effects of an appropriate reprimand can be!

Next day he was in a high fever. Thanks to the gracious assistance of the Petersburg climate, the disease made more rapid progress than could have been expected, and when the doctor came, after feeling his pulse he could find nothing to do but prescribe a poultice, and that simply so that the patient might not be left without the benefit of medical assistance; however, two days later he informed him that his end was at hand, after which he turned to Akaky Akakievich's landlady and said: "And you had better lose no time, my good woman, but order him now a pine coffin, for an oak one will be too expensive for him." Whether Akaky Akakievich heard these fateful words or not, whether they produced a shattering effect upon him, and whether he regretted his pitiful life, no one can tell, for he was constantly in delirium and fever. Apparitions, each stranger than the one before, were continually haunting him: first he saw Petrovich and was ordering him to make an overcoat trimmed with some sort of traps for robbers, who were, he believed, continually under the bed, and he was calling his landlady every minute to pull out a thief who had even got under the quilt; then he kept asking why his old "dressing gown" was hanging before him when he had a new overcoat; then he thought he was standing before the general listening to the appropriate reprimand and saying, "I am sorry, your Excellency"; then finally he became abusive, uttering the most awful language, so that his old landlady positively crossed herself, having never heard anything of the kind from him before, and the more horrified because these dreadful words followed immediately upon the phrase "your Excellency." Later on, his talk was merely a medley of nonsense, so that it was quite unintelligible; all that was evident was that his incoherent words and thoughts were concerned with nothing but the overcoat. At last poor Akaky Akakievich gave up the ghost. No seal was put upon his room nor upon his things, because, in the first place, he had no heirs and, in the second, the property left was very small, to wit, a bundle of quills, a quire of white government paper, three pairs of socks, two or three buttons that had come off his trousers, and the "dressing gown" with which the reader is already familiar. Who came into all this wealth God only knows; even I who tell the tale must admit that I have not bothered to inquire. And Petersburg carried on without Akaky Akakievich, as though, indeed, he had never been in the city. A creature had vanished and departed whose cause no one had championed, who was dear to no one, of interest to no one, who never attracted the attention of a naturalist, though the latter does not disdain to fix a common fly upon a pin and look at him under the microscope—a creature who bore patiently the jeers of the office and for no particular reason went to his grave, though even he at the very end of his life was visited by an exalted guest in the form of an overcoat that for one instant brought color into his poor, drab life—a creature on whom disease fell as it falls upon the heads of the mighty ones of this world . . . !

Several days after his death, a messenger from the department was sent to his lodgings with instructions that he should go at once to the office, for his chief was asking for him; but the messenger was obliged to return without him, explaining that he could not come, and to the inquiry "Why?" he added, "Well, you see, the fact is he is dead; he was buried three days ago." This was how they learned at the office of the death of Akaky Akakievich, and the next day there was sitting in his seat a new clerk who was very much taller and who wrote not in the same straight handwriting but made his letters more slanting and crooked.

But who could have imagined that this was not all there was to tell about Akaky Akakievich, that he was destined for a few days to make his presence felt in the world after his death, as though to make up for his life having been unnoticed by anyone? But so it happened, and our little story unexpectedly finishes with a fantastic ending.

Rumors were suddenly floating about Petersburg that in the neighborhood of the Kalinkin Bridge and for a little distance beyond, a corpse[7] had begun appearing at night in the form of a clerk looking for a stolen overcoat, and stripping from the shoulders of all passers-by, regardless of grade and calling, overcoats of all descriptions—trimmed with cat fur or beaver or padded, lined with raccoon, fox, and bear—made, in fact, of all sorts of skin which men have adapted for the covering of their own. One of the clerks of the department saw the corpse with his own eyes and at once recognized it as Akaky Akakievich; but it excited in him such terror that he ran away as fast as his legs could carry him and so could not get a very clear view of him, and only saw him hold up his finger threateningly in the distance.

From all sides complaints were continually coming that backs and shoulders, not of mere titular councilors, but even of upper court councilors, had been exposed to catching cold, as a result of being stripped of their overcoats. Orders were given to the police to catch the corpse regardless of trouble or expense, dead or alive, and to punish him severely, as an example to others, and, indeed, they very nearly succeeded in doing so. The policeman of one district in Kiryushkin Alley snatched a corpse by the collar on the spot of the crime in the very act of attempting to snatch a frieze overcoat from a retired musician, who used, in his day, to play the flute. Having caught him by the collar, he shouted until he had brought two other policemen whom he ordered to hold the corpse while he felt just a minute in his boot to get out a

---

[7]Mrs. Garnett excepted, this is often translated "ghost," but there is no doubt of Gogol's intention. He uses the word *mertverts* (corpse) and not *prividenye* (ghost). To confuse the two is damaging to Gogol's delight in the fantastic, and seriously alters the tone of the story. (TRANSLATOR)

snuffbox in order to revive his nose which had six times in his life been frostbitten, but the snuff was probably so strong that not even a dead man could stand it. The policeman had hardly had time to put his finger over his right nostril and draw up some snuff in the left when the corpse sneezed violently right into the eyes of all three. While they were putting their fists up to wipe their eyes, the corpse completely vanished, so that they were not even sure whether he had actually been in their hands. From that time forward, the policemen had such a horror of the dead that they were even afraid to seize the living and confined themselves to shouting from the distance: "Hey, you! Move on!" and the clerk's body began to appear even on the other side of the Kalinkin Bridge, terrorizing all timid people.

We have, however, quite neglected the Person of Consequence, who may in reality almost be said to be the cause of the fantastic ending of this perfectly true story. To begin with, my duty requires me to do justice to the Person of Consequence by recording that soon after poor Akaky Akakievich had gone away crushed to powder, he felt something not unlike regret. Sympathy was a feeling not unknown to him; his heart was open to many kindly impulses, although his exalted grade very often prevented them from being shown. As soon as his friend had gone out of his study, he even began brooding over poor Akaky Akakievich, and from that time forward, he was almost every day haunted by the image of the poor clerk who had been unable to survive the official reprimand. The thought of the man so worried him that a week later he actually decided to send a clerk to find out how he was and whether he really could help him in any way. And when they brought him word that Akaky Akakievich had died suddenly in delirium and fever, it made a great impression on him; his conscience reproached him and he was depressed all day. Anxious to distract his mind and to forget the unpleasant incident, he went to spend the evening with one of his friends, where he found respectable company, and what was best of all, almost everyone was of the same grade so that he was able to be quite uninhibited. This had a wonderful effect on his spirits. He let himself go, became affable and genial—in short, spent a very agreeable evening. At supper he drank a couple of glasses of champagne—a proceeding which we all know is not a bad recipe for cheerfulness. The champagne made him inclined to do something unusual, and he decided not to go home yet but to visit a lady of his acquaintance, a certain Karolina Ivanovna—a lady apparently of German extraction, for whom he entertained extremely friendly feelings. It must be noted that the Person of Consequence was a man no longer young. He was an excellent husband, and the respectable father of a family. He had two sons, one already serving in an office, and a nice-looking daughter of sixteen with a rather turned-up, pretty little nose, who used to come every morning to kiss his hand, saying: *"Bon jour, Papa."* His wife, who was still blooming and decidedly good-looking, indeed, used first to give him her hand to kiss and then turning his hand over would kiss it. But though the Person of Consequence was perfectly satisfied with the pleasant amenities of his domestic life, he thought it proper to have a lady friend in another quarter of the town. This lady friend was not a bit better looking nor younger than his wife, but these puzzling things exist in the world and it is not our business to criticize them. And so the Person of Consequence went downstairs, got into his sledge, and said to his coachman, "To Karolina Ivanovna." While luxuriously wrapped in his warm fur coat he remained in that agreeable frame of mind sweeter to a Russian than anything that could be invented, that is, when one thinks of nothing while thoughts come into the mind by themselves, one pleasanter than the other, without your having to bother following them or looking for them. Full of satisfaction, he recalled all the amusing moments of the evening he had spent, all the phrases that had started the intimate circle of friends laughing; many of them he repeated in an undertone and found them as amusing as before, and so, very naturally, laughed very heartily at them again. From time to time, however, he was disturbed by a gust of wind which, blowing suddenly, God knows why or where from, cut him in the face, pelting him with flakes of snow, puffing out his coat collar like a sail, or suddenly flinging it with unnatural force over his head and giving him endless trouble to extricate himself from it. All at once, the Person of Consequence felt that someone had clutched him very tightly by the collar. Turning around he saw a short man in a shabby old uniform, and not without horror recognized him as Akaky Akakievich. The clerk's face was white as snow and looked like that of a corpse, but the horror of the Person of Consequence was beyond all bounds when he saw the mouth of the corpse distorted into speech, and breathing upon him the chill of the grave, it uttered the following words: "Ah, so here you are at last! At last I've . . . er . . . caught you by the collar. It's your overcoat I want; you refused to help me and abused me into the bargain! So now give me yours!" The poor Person of Consequence very nearly dropped dead. Resolute and determined as he was in his office and before subordinates in general, and though anyone looking at his manly air and figure would have said: "Oh, what a man of character!" yet in this situation he felt, like very many persons of heroic appearance, such terror that not without reason he began to be afraid he would have some sort of fit. He actually flung his overcoat off his shoulders as far as he could and shouted to his coachman in an unnatural voice: "Drive home! Let's get out of here!" The coachman, hearing the tone which he had only heard in critical moments and then accompanied by something even more tangible, hunched his shoulders up to his ears in case of worse following, swung his whip, and flew on like an arrow. In a little over six minutes, the Person of Consequence was at the entrance of his own house. Pale, panic-stricken, and without his overcoat, he arrived home instead of at Karolina Ivanovna's, dragged himself to his own room, and spent the night in great distress, so that next morning his daughter said to him at breakfast, "You look very pale today, Papa"; but her papa remained mute and said not a word to anyone of what had happened to him, where he had been, and where he had been going. The incident made a great impression upon him. Indeed, it happened far more rarely that he said to his subordinates, "How dare you? Do you understand who I am?" and he never uttered those words at all until he had first heard all the facts of the case.

What was even more remarkable is that from that time on the apparition of the dead clerk ceased entirely; apparently the general's overcoat had fitted him perfectly; anyway nothing more was heard of overcoats being snatched from anyone. Many restless and anxious people refused, however, to be pacified, and still maintained that in remote parts of the town the dead clerk went on appearing. One policeman, in Kolomna, for instance, saw with his own eyes an apparition appear from behind a house; but, being by natural constitution somewhat frail—so much so that on one occasion an ordinary grown-up suckling pig, making a sudden dash out of some private building, knocked him off his feet to the great amusement of the cabmen standing around, whom he fined two kopeks each for snuff for such disrespect—he did not dare to stop it, and so followed it in the dark until the apparition suddenly looked around and, stopping, asked him: "What do you want?" displaying a huge fist such as you never see even among the living. The policeman said: "Nothing," and turned back on the spot. This apparition, however, was considerably taller and adorned with immense mustaches, and, directing its steps apparently toward Obukhov Bridge, vanished into the darkness of the night.

Billy Budd, Sailor

Herman Melville

Perhaps the most persistent myth about artists is that of the genius born out of his time, misunderstood by his contemporaries, creating his masterpiece in lonely isolation and unveiling it to a deafening silence, neither rediscovered nor given his true evaluation until long after his death. This sad scenario happens less often than is commonly supposed and is rarer with novelists than most other kinds of artists—possibly because, since they generally write about men and women in society, novelists tend to have a firmer grasp of their times and its principal concerns. Yet there have been many exceptions, and the myth was realized, in an almost classically tragic form, in the career of Herman Melville.

Melville was born on August 1, 1819, in New York City, the third of eight children. His mother's family, the Gansevoorts, were wealthy and solid citizens in upstate New York. The Melvilles, from whom Herman received much of his temperament, were talented, multifaceted, unstable individualists who had pursued business careers in Boston and in revolutionary France. His father, Allan Melville, was a genial and gentlemanly merchant-importer; Herman, who idolized him, must have spent a good deal of his early youth following his father around the wharves of New York harbor where much of his business was conducted. This idyll was shattered in 1830 when, as a result of imprudent investments, Allan Melville went bankrupt and was forced to move to Albany near his wife's relations. There he began business once more, but two years later he suffered another collapse—mental and physical as well as economic: he died mad in 1832. For the next seven years, the Melville family underwent a series of advances and reverses. During this time Herman for various brief spans went to school, worked in a bank, loafed on his uncle Thomas Melville's Pittsfield, Massachusetts, estate, studied surveying and engineering, and served as a schoolmaster. All this might be seen as a richly varied life, had it not been for the immense pressure to find a permanent situation that would end their hand-to-mouth existence, and for the emotional demands of Herman's mother, Maria Melville, who seems in her widowhood to have looked to her children to provide the support and security she had lost at the death of her husband. According to Newton Arvin, Melville's mother became "more and more the exacting, aggressive, overbearing, haughty and worldly woman," and her disappointment with Herman created an intense love-hate relationship which played havoc with his emotional development.

To escape all these pressures, Melville went to sea in 1839 and spent most of the next five years aboard ships—a merchant vessel, several whalers, and a man-of-war. His first voyage, on the cargo ship *St. Lawrence*, made only the routine transatlantic crossing between New York and Liverpool, but on board Melville served his apprenticeship, learned the hard, routine duties that make up the bulk of the common sailor's life at sea, and experienced the tyranny of captains and officers as well as the companionship and mutual affection of working seamen—themes that run like a common thread through all his novels of the sea. The second voyage began on board the whaler *Acushnet* and took Melville to more picturesque areas—the Azores, the whaling grounds off the coasts of South America, the perilous passage of Cape Horn, and finally the Polynesian Islands of the South Pacific. Life on a whaler in the 1840s was, if anything, harder than on merchant ships, and in addition it was embittered by the violent and arbitrary conduct of the master. Provoked beyond endurance, Melville jumped ship at Nuku Hiva in the Marquesas group and, accompanied by a friend, Toby Greene, went off to explore the interior of the island, the valley of Taipi Vai.

Here Melville and Greene became the guests—or prisoners—of a tribe of natives which Melville later called the Typees. Though the tribe had a well-deserved reputation for cannibalism, they treated their visitors well, probably adopted them into the tribe, but refused to let them leave. Eventually Greene was allowed to go to a port settlement to obtain medicines for Melville, who was suffering from a festering leg wound. He never returned (Melville later learned that he had been shanghaied aboard another ship), and Melville was left alone among the savages for several weeks. During that time Melville saw this primitive society from inside, participated in their work, their crafts, their orgiastic celebrations, and indulged the primordial side of his own complex nature. But the idyll could not last, and Melville soon burned with homesickness and longed to return to civilization. He succeeded both in having a message of his whereabouts taken to the coast and in hobbling on his lame leg to meet the boat sent to find him. It was the *Lucy Ann*, a whaler bound for Tahiti.

On Tahiti, Melville found himself in the midst of further adventure. The crew of the *Lucy Ann* mutinied and refused to continue the voyage, and Melville, after initially opposing the rebellion, joined the mutineers. On the authority of the British consul, Melville was thrown into the makeshift prison at Papeete, put in irons, and interrogated for a possible trial. But once the *Lucy Ann* had recruited a new crew and put to sea the case was dropped and Melville, together with several companions from the ship, was turned loose to lead the life of a beachcomber. Characteristically, Melville enjoyed the ease and freedom of Polynesian life for a time, but after a couple of months he found it palling on him and asked to be taken aboard the *Charles and Henry*, an American whaler that took him to Hawaii. There he signed aboard the frigate *United States*—a man-of-war that had fought in the War of 1812—and became an enlisted man in the American navy.

The year Melville spent aboard the *United States* was the one brief period in his life when he was subject to military discipline, and as such it must constitute the subjective source of much of *Billy Budd, Sailor.* It was in part the brutality of navy life that made a tremendous impression upon him; the first order Melville received after his enlistment seems to have been to witness punishment—a fellow seaman being lashed by a cat-o'-nine-tails till he bled—and Melville was forced to witness no fewer than 163 floggings during this year. There is no evidence that Melville was ever himself the victim of the "cat" (though he must have had nightmares about it). But every seaman was put through his paces by means of arbitrary physical coercion, and Melville found himself in silent but deeply felt rebellion against it. Strangely enough, Melville loved the order that was the *result* of discipline, and hated and feared the occasional moments of chaos or anarchy that occurred when orders were bungled or misunderstood. What he rebelled against was the *source* of the discipline: the paternalistic authority of the captain, ruling through fear of punishment, rather than through the spontaneous love and loyalty for him instilled within the men.

Melville's best friend aboard the *United States* was John J. Chase, the "Jack Chase" to whom *Billy Budd, Sailor* is dedicated. Chase was apparently a "Handsome Sailor" like Budd—courageous, candid, and with immense personal charm. Independent himself, and a lover of independence in others, Chase had deserted his ship in Peru to fight for the liberation of South America and had been reinstated into the navy after a mere reprimand. Chase took the younger Melville under his wing and became his "sea-tutor and sire." They were close comrades until the frigate arrived in Boston and they went their separate ways. It was the end of Melville's life as a sailor and the beginning of his career as a novelist.

That career began, ironically enough, with an immense success. Melville's first book, *Typee*, written in the first months after he had returned to his mother's house in Lansingburgh, New York, was an imaginative reconstruction of his second voyage to Nuku Hiva and his brief isolation among the cannibal tribes there. Upon its publication in 1846, Melville awoke to find himself a literary celebrity of the first order. He followed it up quickly with *Omoo* (1847), a tale based upon his beachcombing months on Tahiti, and unlike most sequels, it was received with equal enthusiasm by the public. These two novels are seldom read today and are looked upon as Melville's least characteristic works, for they lack almost entirely the tormented questioning, the depth of perception beneath the surface of physical action that marks his masterpieces. But on the strength of the popular success he had achieved, Melville courted and married in 1847 Elizabeth Shaw, a staid, well-bred young lady of Boston who remained deeply devoted to and entirely uncomprehending of Melville for the next forty-five years.

Melville continued to write at the same breathless pace with which he had started, but without the same success. *Mardi* (1849) was a dull and confused work, yet one which, for all its inadequacies of form and style, marks a deepening of Melville's moral perceptions. *Redburn*, published the same year, is a chronicle of Melville's apprentice voyage whose "inward subject," according to one critic, "is the initiation of innocence into evil." *White-Jacket* (1850) takes up Melville's last voyage on the American man-of-war. Marred, perhaps, by its didactic exposition of minute details of naval life and by a moralistic outrage at the brutishness of naval discipline, it shows in places the psychological intensity and the brooding concern over the problem of evil that allies this minor work with *Moby-Dick* and *Billy Budd, Sailor*. All these books made money for Melville and his new but growing family, but none allowed him to advance in fame or in wealth.

It was in 1850 also that Melville, moving with his family to a house near Pittsfield, met and became friends with Nathaniel Hawthorne. Hawthorne was fifteen years older than Melville, and both men were fearfully busy—Hawthorne was writing *The House of the Seven Gables* at the same time that Melville was composing *Moby-Dick*—but their acquaintance progressed to some sort of intimacy in the short time they were neighbors. Hawthorne's diary records that upon one evening, "Melville and I had a talk about time and eternity, things of this world and of the next, and books, and publishers, and all possible and impossible matters, that lasted pretty deep into the night, and if truth must be told, we smoked cigars even within the sacred precincts of the sitting room." The two men were not only intellectual companions, but partners in "domestic crime."

Moby-Dick came out in 1851. It was Melville's masterpiece, in which his comic and tragic perceptions of life reached their highest point, an epic of whaling, but also an epic of the American character, and the chronicle of an inquest into the meaning of the universe, man's place in nature, and the origins and significance of evil. Encyclopedic, allegorical, digressive by turns, the novel knits together all its strands into a grand, Faustian, romantic tragedy. If one were forced to choose the greatest work of art to have come out of America to date, many, perhaps most, literary critics would choose *Moby-Dick*. Yet on its appearance it was reviled by the reviewers as much as it was praised, and it was far from being a popular success. The style was called "maniacal—mad as a March hare—mowing, gibbering, screaming," and one critic suggested that the novel and Mr. Melville together belonged in a lunatic asylum. Had Melville been a less conscientious artist, he could have gone back to the easy, travelogue style of his first two successful books. Instead he wrote *Pierre* (1852), a study in sin, madness, and death, which was greeted with a virtual orgy of abuse, and which pretty much finished Melville's reputation as a writer. He subsequently wrote a number of short stories, a derivative novel called *Israel Potter* (1855), a collection of novellas, *The Piazza Tales* (1856), and his darkest work, *The Confidence-Man: His Masquerade* (1857). The response was, if anything, worse than the scandal caused by *Pierre*: his works were considered boring and indigestible, rather than strangely mad. Melville was only thirty-six when he finished writing *The Confidence-Man*: it was the last novel of his published during his lifetime.

Melville survived his renown by over thirty-five years, drifting from one venture to another until he was appointed an inspector of customs of the port of New York. There, for twenty years until his retirement in 1885, Melville carried out his dull duties with conspicuous probity, examining cargo ships and reporting violations to his superiors in the office in Gansevoort Street, where he would be reminded of the prominence of his mother's family. He lived to see the deaths of both his sons, Malcolm and Stanwix, the former by suicide. His literary productions in the last half of his life consisted of a few volumes of poetry, including *Clarel* (1876), which saw print only through a subsidy given by his uncle. His last work, which occupied him, off and on, through the last three years of his life, was the novella *Billy Budd, Sailor*, which he completed in April 1891, but which remained in manuscript at his death and was not published until 1924. He died quietly, and in almost complete obscurity, on September 28, 1891.

Until 1917, Melville's reputation seems to have slept—he is mentioned in the literary histories of the period before World War I as a very minor writer. But beginning with Carl Van Doren's praise of *Moby-Dick* as a great and original romance in the *Cambridge History of American Literature*, Melville was resurrected, his works reprinted, and his stature within the American tradition grew until now, sixty years after the Melville revival began, he is generally thought of as one of the finest novelists of his own or, indeed, of any time.

Biography   Jan Leyda's *The Melville Log* (New York: Harcourt Brace, 1951) presents Melville's life largely through his own words. The standard biography to date is Leon Howard, *Herman Melville: A Biography* (Berkeley: University of California Press, 1951). Newton Arvin's *Herman Melville* (New York: Viking, 1957) looks at Melville from a Freudian perspective.

Editions   Until recently, the Melville canon was represented by the sixteen-volume Standard Edition (London, 1922–1924). Now, however, the fiction and poetry are being issued in the Newberry Library edition, under the general editorship of Harrison Hayford. The text of *Billy Budd, Sailor*, prepared through the exhaustive analysis of the surviving manuscript, was edited by Harrison Hayford and Merton M. Sealts, Jr., and originally published by the University of Chicago Press in 1962.

General Criticism   The list of works on Melville is immense, but one might single out John D. Seelye, *Melville: The Ironic Diagram* (Evanston: Northwestern University Press, 1970); Edgar A. Dryden, *Melville's Thematics of Form* (Baltimore: Johns Hopkins University Press, 1968); H. Bruce Franklin, *The Wake of the Gods: Melville's Mythology* (Stanford: Stanford University Press, 1963); Warner Berthoff, *The Example of Melville* (Princeton: Princeton University Press, 1962); and Merlin Bowen, *The Long Encounter: Self and Experience in the Writings of Herman Melville* (Chicago: University of Chicago Press, 1960).

Criticism of Billy Budd, Sailor   On the problems of irony in *Billy Budd*, a persistent issue in the criticism, see E. L. Grant Watson, "Melville's Testament of Acceptance," *New England Quarterly* 6 (1933), 319–327; Phil Withim, "*Billy Budd*: Testament of Resistance," *Modern Language Quarterly* 20 (1959), 115–127; Richard Fogle, "*Billy Budd*—Acceptance or Irony," *Tulane Studies in English* 8 (1958), 107–113; and Edward H. Rosenberry, "The Problem of *Billy Budd*," *PMLA* 80 (1965), 489–498; along with Bowen and Seelye, above.

Other interesting studies of sources, analogues, and literary relations include: Charles Roberts Anderson, "The Genesis of *Billy Budd*," *American Literature* 12 (1940), 328–346; Ray Browne, "*Billy Budd*: Gospel of Democracy,"*Nineteenth-Century Fiction* 17 (1963), 321–337; Hayford and Sealts's "Introduction" to the edition of *Billy Budd* listed above; William Bysshe Stein, "*Billy Budd*: The Nightmare of History," *Criticism* 3 (1961), 237–250; C. B. Ives, "*Billy Budd* and the Articles of War," *American Literature*, 34 (1962), 31–39; and Karl E. Zink, "Herman Melville and the Forms: Irony and Social Criticism in *Billy Budd*," *Accent* 12 (1952), 131–139. Many of these essays—and others—are to be found in Howard P. Vincent, *Billy Budd: A Collection of Critical Essays* (Englewood Cliffs, N.J.: Prentice-Hall, 1971), or in William T. Stafford, *Melville's Billy Budd and the Critics* (Belmont, Calif.: Wadsworth Publishing Company, 1968).

Billy Budd, Sailor
(An Inside Narrative)

DEDICATED

TO

JACK CHASE

ENGLISHMAN

Wherever that great heart may now be
Here on Earth or harbored in Paradise
Captain of the Maintop
in the year 1843
in the U.S. Frigate
United States

I

In the time before steamships, or then more frequently than now, a stroller along the docks of any considerable seaport would occasionally have his attention arrested by a group of bronzed mariners, man-of-war's men or merchant sailors in holiday attire, ashore on liberty. In certain instances they would flank, or like a bodyguard quite surround, some superior figure of their own class, moving along with them like

Aldebaran[1] among the lesser lights of his constellation. That signal object was the "Handsome Sailor" of the less prosaic time alike of the military and merchant navies. With no perceptible trace of the vainglorious about him, rather with the offhand unaffectedness of natural regality, he seemed to accept the spontaneous homage of his shipmates.

A somewhat remarkable instance recurs to me. In Liverpool, now half a century ago, I saw under the shadow of the great dingy streetwall of Prince's Dock (an obstruction long since removed) a common sailor so intensely black that he must needs have been a native African of the unadulterate blood of Ham—a symmetric figure much above the average height. The two ends of a gay silk handkerchief thrown loose about the neck danced upon the displayed ebony of his chest, in his ears were big hoops of gold, and a Highland bonnet with a tartan band set off his shapely head. It was a hot noon in July; and his face, lustrous with perspiration, beamed with barbaric good humor. In jovial sallies right and left, his white teeth flashing into view, he rollicked along, the center of a company of his shipmates. These were made up of such an assortment of tribes and complexions as would have well fitted them to be marched up by Anacharsis Cloots[2] before the bar of the first French Assembly as Representatives of the Human Race. At each spontaneous tribute rendered by the wayfarers to this black pagod[3] of a fellow—the tribute of a pause and stare, and less frequently an exclamation—the motley retinue showed that they took that sort of pride in the evoker of it which the Assyrian priests doubtless showed for their grand sculptured Bull when the faithful prostrated themselves.

To return. If in some cases a bit of a nautical Murat[4] in setting forth his person ashore, the Handsome Sailor of the period in question evinced nothing of the dandified Billy-be-Dam, an amusing character all but extinct now, but occasionally to be encountered, and in a form yet more amusing than the original, at the tiller of the boats on the tempestuous Erie Canal or, more likely, vaporing in the groggeries along the towpath. Invariably a proficient in his perilous calling, he was also more or less of a mighty boxer or wrestler. It was strength and

---

[1]Brightest star in the constellation of Taurus.
[2]French revolutionary (1755-1794).
[3]Pagoda; also, the idol inside a pagoda.
[4]A foppish general under Napoleon, later made King of Naples (1767-1815).

beauty. Tales of his prowess were recited. Ashore he was the champion; afloat the spokesman; on every suitable occasion always foremost. Close-reefing[5] topsails in a gale, there he was, astride the weather yardarm-end, foot in the Flemish horse as stirrup, both hands tugging at the earing as at a bridle, in very much the attitude of young Alexander curbing the fiery Bucephalus.[6] A superb figure, tossed up as by the horns of Taurus against the thunderous sky, cheerily hallooing to the strenuous file along the spar.

The moral nature was seldom out of keeping with the physical make. Indeed, except as toned by the former, the comeliness and power, always attractive in masculine conjunction, hardly could have drawn the sort of honest homage the Handsome Sailor in some examples received from his less gifted associates.

Such a cynosure, at least in aspect, and something such too in nature, though with important variations made apparent as the story proceeds, was welkin-eyed[7] Billy Budd—or Baby Budd, as more familiarly, under circumstances hereafter to be given, he at last came to be called—aged twenty-one, a foretopman of the British fleet toward the close of the last decade of the eighteenth century. It was not very long prior to the time of the narration that follows that he had entered the King's service, having been impressed on the Narrow Seas[8] from a homeward-bound English merchantman into a seventy-four[9] outward bound, H.M.S. *Bellipotent;* which ship, as was not unusual in those hurried days, having been obliged to put to sea short of her proper complement of men. Plump upon Billy at first sight in the gangway the boarding officer, Lieutenant Ratcliffe, pounced, even before the merchantman's crew was formally mustered on the quarter-deck for his deliberate inspection. And him only he elected. For whether it was because the other men when ranged before him showed to ill advantage after Billy, or whether he had some scruples in view of the merchantman's being rather short-handed, however it might be, the officer contented himself

---

[5]In foul weather, sails must be "reefed," or folded over so as to expose less surface to the high wind. The sailor's job involves climbing the mast to the yard-arm from which the sail hangs, working his way out along a foot-rope (the "flemish horse"), and hauling up the bottom edge of the sail, securing it with a rope (the "earing").

[6]The wild horse of Alexander the Great (356-323 B.C.).

[7]Eyes as blue as the sky.

[8]Summarily drafted into the Royal Navy on the Irish Sea or English Channel.

[9]A seventy-four–gun man-of-war.

with his first spontaneous choice. To the surprise of the ship's company, though much to the lieutenant's satisfaction, Billy made no demur. But, indeed, any demur would have been as idle as the protest of a goldfinch popped into a cage.

Noting this uncomplaining acquiescence, all but cheerful, one might say, the shipmaster turned a surprised glance of silent reproach at the sailor. The shipmaster was one of those worthy mortals found in every vocation, even the humbler ones—the sort of person whom everybody agrees in calling "a respectable man." And—nor so strange to report as it may appear to be—though a ploughman of the troubled waters, lifelong contending with the intractable elements, there was nothing this honest soul at heart loved better than simple peace and quiet. For the rest, he was fifty or thereabouts, a little inclined to corpulence, a prepossessing face, unwhiskered, and of an agreeable color—a rather full face, humanely intelligent in expression. On a fair day with a fair wind and all going well, a certain musical chime in his voice seemed to be the veritable unobstructed outcome of the innermost man. He had much prudence, much conscientiousness, and there were occasions when these virtues were the cause of overmuch disquietude in him. On a passage, so long as his craft was in any proximity to land, no sleep for Captain Graveling. He took to heart those serious responsibilities not so heavily borne by some shipmasters.

Now while Billy Budd was down in the forecastle[10] getting his kit together, the *Bellipotent's* lieutenant, burly and bluff, nowise disconcerted by Captain Graveling's omitting to proffer the customary hospitalities on an occasion so unwelcome to him, an omission simply caused by preoccupation of thought, unceremoniously invited himself into the cabin, and also to a flask from the spirit locker, a receptacle which his experienced eye instantly discovered. In fact he was one of those sea dogs in whom all the hardship and peril of naval life in the great prolonged wars of his time never impaired the natural instinct for sensuous enjoyment. His duty he always faithfully did; but duty is sometimes a dry obligation, and he was for irrigating its aridity, whensoever possible, with a fertilizing decoction of strong waters. For the cabin's proprietor there was nothing left but to play the part of the enforced host with whatever grace and alacrity were practicable. As necessary adjuncts to the flask, he silently placed tumbler and water jug before the irrepressible guest. But excusing himself from partaking

---

[10]Area at the front of the ship where the common sailors bunked.

just then, he dismally watched the unembarrassed officer deliberately diluting his grog a little, then tossing it off in three swallows, pushing the empty tumbler away, yet not so far as to be beyond easy reach, at the same time settling himself in his seat and smacking his lips with high satisfaction, looking straight at the host.

These proceedings over, the master broke the silence; and there lurked a rueful reproach in the tone of his voice: "Lieutenant, you are going to take my best man from me, the jewel of 'em."

"Yes, I know," rejoined the other, immediately drawing back the tumbler preliminary to a replenishing. "Yes, I know. Sorry."

"Beg pardon, but you don't understand, Lieutenant. See here, now. Before I shipped that young fellow, my forecastle was a rat-pit of quarrels. It was black times, I tell you, aboard the *Rights* here. I was worried to that degree my pipe had no comfort for me. But Billy came; and it was like a Catholic priest striking peace in an Irish shindy. Not that he preached to them or said or did anything in particular; but a virtue went out of him, sugaring the sour ones. They took to him like hornets to treacle; all but the buffer[11] of the gang, the big shaggy chap with the fire-red whiskers. He indeed, out of envy, perhaps, of the newcomer, and thinking such a 'sweet and pleasant fellow,' as he mockingly designated him to the others, could hardly have the spirit of a gamecock, must needs bestir himself in trying to get up an ugly row with him. Billy forebore with him and reasoned with him in a pleasant way—he is something like myself, Lieutenant, to whom aught like a quarrel is hateful—but nothing served. So, in the second dogwatch one day, the Red Whiskers in presence of the others, under pretense of showing Billy just whence a sirloin steak was cut—for the fellow had once been a butcher—insultingly gave him a dig under the ribs. Quick as lightning Billy let fly his arm. I dare say he never meant to do quite as much as he did, but anyhow he gave the burly fool a terrible drubbing. It took about half a minute, I should think. And, lord bless you, the lubber was astonished at the celerity. And will you believe it, Lieutenant, the Red Whiskers now really loves Billy—loves him, or is the biggest hypocrite that ever I heard of. But they all love him. Some of 'em do his washing, darn his old trousers for him; the carpenter is at odd times making a pretty little chest of drawers for him. Anybody will do anything for Billy Budd; and it's the happy family here. But now, Lieutenant, if that young fellow goes—I know how it will be aboard the *Rights*. Not again very soon shall I, coming up from dinner, lean over

---

[11]Bully.

the capstan smoking a quiet pipe—no, not very soon again, I think. Ay, Lieutenant, you are going to take away the jewel of 'em; you are going to take away my peacemaker!" And with that the good soul had really some ado in checking a rising sob.

"Well," said the lieutenant, who had listened with amused interest to all this and now was waxing merry with his tipple; "well, blessed are the peacemakers, especially the fighting peacemakers. And such are the seventy-four beauties some of which you see poking their noses out of the portholes of yonder warship lying to for me," pointing through the cabin window at the *Bellipotent.* "But courage! Don't look so downhearted, man. Why, I pledge you in advance the royal approbation. Rest assured that His Majesty will be delighted to know that in a time when his hardtack is not sought for by sailors with such avidity as should be, a time also when some shipmasters privily resent the borrowing from them a tar or two for the service; His Majesty, I say, will be delighted to learn that *one* shipmaster at least cheerfully surrenders to the King the flower of his flock, a sailor who with equal loyalty makes no dissent.—But where's my beauty? Ah," looking through the cabin's open door, "here he comes; and, by Jove, lugging along his chest—Apollo with his portmanteau!—My man," stepping out to him, "you can't take that big box aboard a warship. The boxes there are mostly shot boxes. Put your duds in a bag, lad. Boot and saddle for the cavalryman, bag and hammock for the man-of-war's man."

The transfer from chest to bag was made. And, after seeing his man into the cutter and then following him down, the lieutenant pushed off from the *Rights-of-Man.* That was the merchant ship's name, though by her master and crew abbreviated in sailor fashion into the *Rights.* The hardheaded Dundee owner was a staunch admirer of Thomas Paine, whose book in rejoinder to Burke's arraignment of the French Revolution had then been published for some time and had gone everywhere.[12] In christening his vessel after the title of Paine's volume the man of Dundee was something like his contemporary shipowner, Stephen Girard of Philadelphia, whose sympathies, alike with his native land[13] and its liberal philosophers, he evinced by naming his ships after Voltaire, Diderot, and so forth.

---

[12]Edmund Burke's *Reflections on the Revolution in France* (1790) had stressed the necessity of conserving traditions in political affairs to assure the stability of government and law; Thomas Paine's *The Rights of Man* (1791) asserted abstract human rights over such stability. These ideas are central themes in *Billy Budd.*

[13]Girard (1750–1831) had been born in France and lived there till 1787.

But now, when the boat swept under the merchantman's stern, and officer and oarsmen were noting—some bitterly and others with a grin—the name emblazoned there; just then it was that the new recruit jumped up from the bow where the coxswain had directed him to sit, and waving hat to his silent shipmates sorrowfully looking over at him from the taffrail, bade the lads a genial good-bye. Then, making a salutation as to the ship herself, "And good-bye to you too, old *Rights-of-Man*."

"Down, sir!" roared the lieutenant, instantly assuming all the rigor of his rank, though with difficulty repressing a smile.

To be sure, Billy's action was a terrible breach of naval decorum. But in that decorum he had never been instructed; in consideration of which the lieutenant would hardly have been so energetic in reproof but for the concluding farewell to the ship. This he rather took as meant to convey a covert sally on the new recruit's part, a sly slur at impressment in general, and that of himself in especial. And yet, more likely, if satire it was in effect, it was hardly so by intention, for Billy, though happily endowed with the gaiety of high health, youth, and a free heart, was yet by no means of a satirical turn. The will to it and the sinister dexterity were alike wanting. To deal in double meanings and insinuations of any sort was quite foreign to his nature.

As to his enforced enlistment, that he seemed to take pretty much as he was wont to take any vicissitude of weather. Like the animals, though no philosopher, he was, without knowing, practically a fatalist. And it may be that he rather liked this adventurous turn in his affairs, which promised an opening into novel scenes and martial excitements.

Aboard the *Bellipotent* our merchant sailor was forthwith rated as an able seaman and assigned to the starboard watch of the foretop.[14] He was soon at home in the service, not at all disliked for his unpretentious good looks and a sort of genial happy-go-lucky air. No merrier man in his mess: in marked contrast to certain other individuals included like himself among the impressed portion of the ship's company; for these when not actively employed were sometimes, and more particularly in the last dogwatch when the drawing near of twilight induced revery, apt to fall into a saddish mood which in some partook of sullenness. But they were not so young as our foretopmen, and no few of them must have known a hearth of some sort, others may have

---

[14]Members of a ship's crew were divided into two groups, the port and starboard watches. Billy's duties principally involve sail handling—the topsail of the foremast—typically a job for a young and agile seaman.

had wives and children left, too probably, in uncertain circumstances, and hardly any but must have had acknowledged kith and kin, while for Billy, as will shortly be seen, his entire family was practically invested in himself.

II

Though our new-made foretopman was well received in the top and on the gun decks, hardly here was he that cynosure he had previously been among those minor ship's companies of the merchant marine, with which companies only had he hitherto consorted.

He was young; and despite his all but fully developed frame, in aspect looked even younger than he really was, owing to a lingering adolescent expression in the as yet smooth face all but feminine in purity of natural complexion but where, thanks to his seagoing, the lily was quite suppressed and the rose had some ado visibly to flush through the tan.

To one essentially such a novice in the complexities of factitious life, the abrupt transition from his former and simpler sphere to the ampler and more knowing world of a great warship; this might well have abashed him had there been any conceit or vanity in his composition. Among her miscellaneous multitude, the *Bellipotent* mustered several individuals who however inferior in grade were of no common natural stamp, sailors more signally susceptive of that air which continuous martial discipline and repeated presence in battle can in some degree impart even to the average man. As the Handsome Sailor, Billy Budd's position aboard the seventy-four was something analogous to that of a rustic beauty transplanted from the provinces and brought into competition with the highborn dames of the court. But this change of circumstances he scarce noted. As little did he observe that something about him provoked an ambiguous smile in one or two harder faces among the bluejackets. Nor less unaware was he of the peculiar favorable effect his person and demeanor had upon the more intelligent gentlemen of the quarter-deck.[15] Nor could this well have been otherwise. Cast in a mold peculiar to the finest physical examples of those Englishmen in whom the Saxon strain would seem not at all to partake of any Norman or other admixture, he showed in face that humane look of reposeful good nature which the Greek sculptor in some instances gave

---

[15]The quarter-deck was officers' country.

to his heroic strong man, Hercules. But this again was subtly modified by another and pervasive quality. The ear, small and shapely, the arch of the foot, the curve in mouth and nostril, even the indurated hand dyed to the orange-tawny of the toucan's bill, a hand telling alike of the halyards and tar bucket; but, above all, something in the mobile expression, and every chance attitude and movement, something suggestive of a mother eminently favored by Love and the Graces; all this strangely indicated a lineage in direct contradiction to his lot. The mysteriousness here became less mysterious through a matter of fact elicited when Billy at the capstan was being formally mustered into the service. Asked by the officer, a small, brisk little gentleman as it chanced, among other questions, his place of birth, he replied, "Please, sir, I don't know."

"Don't know where you were born? Who was your father?"

"God knows, sir."

Struck by the straightforward simplicity of these replies, the officer next asked, "Do you know anything about your beginning?"

"No, sir. But I have heard that I was found in a pretty silk-lined basket hanging one morning from the knocker of a good man's door in Bristol."

"*Found*, say you? Well," throwing back his head and looking up and down the new recruit; "well, it turns out to have been a pretty good find. Hope they'll find some more like you, my man; the fleet sadly needs them."

Yes, Billy Budd was a foundling, a presumable by-blow, and, evidently, no ignoble one. Noble descent was as evident in him as in a blood horse.

For the rest, with little or no sharpness of faculty or any trace of the wisdom of the serpent, nor yet quite a dove, he possessed that kind and degree of intelligence going along with the unconventional rectitude of a sound human creature, one to whom not yet has been proffered the questionable apple of knowledge. He was illiterate; he could not read, but he could sing, and like the illiterate nightingale was sometimes the composer of his own song.

Of self-consciousness he seemed to have little or none, or about as much as we may reasonably impute to a dog of Saint Bernard's breed.

Habitually living with the elements and knowing little more of the land than as a beach, or, rather, that portion of the terraqueous[16] globe

---

[16]Composed of land and water. "Doxies" are prostitutes, "tapsters" bartenders, and a "fiddler's green" the sailor's paradise where drink and women are readily furnished.

providentially set apart for dance-houses, doxies, and tapsters, in short what sailors call a "fiddler's green," his simple nature remained unsophisticated by those moral obliquities which are not in every case incompatible with that manufacturable thing known as respectability. But are sailors, frequenters of fiddlers' greens, without vices? No; but less often than with landsmen do their vices, so called, partake of crookedness of heart, seeming less to proceed from viciousness than exuberance of vitality after long constraint: frank manifestations in accordance with natural law. By his original constitution aided by the co-operating influences of his lot, Billy in many respects was little more than a sort of upright barbarian, much such perhaps as Adam presumably might have been ere the urbane Serpent wriggled himself into his company.

And here be it submitted that apparently going to corroborate the doctrine of man's Fall, a doctrine now popularly ignored, it is observable that where certain virtues pristine and unadulterate peculiarly characterize anybody in the external uniform of civilization, they will upon scrutiny seem not to be derived from custom or convention, but rather to be out of keeping with these, as if indeed exceptionally transmitted from a period prior to Cain's city and citified man. The character marked by such qualities has to an unvitiated taste an untampered-with flavor like that of berries, while the man thoroughly civilized, even in a fair specimen of the breed, has to the same moral palate a questionable smack as of a compounded wine. To any stray inheritor of these primitive qualities found, like Caspar Hauser,[17] wandering dazed in any Christian capital of our time, the good-natured poet's[18] famous invocation, near two thousand years ago, of the good rustic out of his latitude in the Rome of the Caesars, still appropriately holds:

Honest and poor, faithful in word and thought,
What hath thee, Fabian, to the city brought?

Though our Handsome Sailor had as much of masculine beauty as one can expect anywhere to see; nevertheless, like the beautiful woman in one of Hawthorne's minor tales,[19] there was just one thing amiss in him. No visible blemish indeed, as with the lady; no, but an occasional

---

[17]A wild boy found wandering the streets of Nuremberg in 1828.
[18]The "good-natured poet" is the ferocious Roman satirist Martial.
[19]Georgiana in "The Birthmark."

liability to a vocal defect. Though in the hour of elemental uproar or peril he was everything that a sailor should be, yet under sudden provocation of strong heart-feeling his voice, otherwise singularly musical, as if expressive of the harmony within, was apt to develop an organic hesitancy, in fact more or less of a stutter or even worse. In this particular Billy was a striking instance that the arch interferer, the envious marplot of Eden, still has more or less to do with every human consignment to this planet of Earth. In every case, one way or another he is sure to slip in his little card, as much as to remind us—I too have a hand here.

The avowal of such an imperfection in the Handsome Sailor should be evidence not alone that he is not presented as a conventional hero, but also that the story in which he is the main figure is no romance.

III

At the time of Billy Budd's arbitrary enlistment into the *Bellipotent* that ship was on her way to join the Mediterranean fleet. No long time elapsed before the junction was effected. As one of that fleet the seventy-four participated in its movements, though at times on account of her superior sailing qualities, in the absence of frigates, dispatched on separate duty as a scout and at times on less temporary service. But with all this the story has little concernment, restricted as it is to the inner life of one particular ship and the career of an individual sailor.

It was the summer of 1797. In the April of that year had occurred the commotion at Spithead followed in May by a second and yet more serious outbreak in the fleet at the Nore. The latter is known, and without exaggeration in the epithet, as "the Great Mutiny." It was indeed a demonstration more menacing to England than the contemporary manifestoes and conquering and proselyting armies of the French Directory. To the British Empire the Nore Mutiny was what a strike in the fire brigade would be to London threatened by general arson. In a crisis when the kingdom might well have anticipated the famous signal that some years later published along the naval line of battle what it was that upon occasion England expected of Englishmen[20]; *that* was the time when at the mastheads of the three-deckers and seventy-fours moored in her own roadstead—a fleet the right arm of a Power then all

---

[20]Admiral Nelson's signal to the fleet at Trafalgar: England expects every man to do his duty.

but the sole free conservative one of the Old World—the bluejackets, to be numbered by thousands, ran up with huzzas the British colors with the union and cross wiped out; by that cancellation transmuting the flag of founded law and freedom defined, into the enemy's red meteor of unbridled and unbounded revolt. Reasonable discontent growing out of practical grievances in the fleet[21] had been ignited into irrational combustion as by live cinders blown across the Channel from France in flames.

The event converted into irony for a time those spirited strains of Dibdin[22]—as a song-writer no mean auxiliary to the English government at that European conjuncture—strains celebrating, among other things, the patriotic devotion of the British tar: "And as for my life, 'tis the King's!"

Such an episode in the Island's grand naval story her naval historians naturally abridge, one of them (William James) candidly acknowledging that fain would he pass it over did not "impartiality forbid fastidiousness." And yet his mention is less a narration than a reference, having to do hardly at all with details. Nor are these readily to be found in the libraries. Like some other events in every age befalling states everywhere, including America, the Great Mutiny was of such character that national pride along with views of policy would fain shade it off into the historical background. Such events cannot be ignored, but there is a considerate way of historically treating them. If a well-constituted individual refrains from blazoning aught amiss or calamitous in his family, a nation in the like circumstance may without reproach be equally discreet.

Though after parleyings between government and the ringleaders, and concessions by the former as to some glaring abuses, the first uprising—that at Spithead—with difficulty was put down, or matters for the time pacified; yet at the Nore the unforeseen renewal of insurrection on a yet larger scale, and emphasized in the conferences that ensued by demands deemed by the authorities not only inadmissible but aggressively insolent, indicated—if the Red Flag did not sufficiently do so—what was the spirit animating the men. Final suppression, how-

---

[21]This wartime naval strike grew out of dissatisfaction with pay (often stolen by dishonest pursers), food (often inedible), and working conditions (no leaves were granted, sometimes for years; ships were understaffed and hence overworked). The relatively quiet mutiny at Spithead resulted in an easing of the seamen's lot; the radical mutiny at the Nore was put down harshly.

[22]Charles Dibdin (1745–1814), dramatist and song-writer.

ever, there was; but only made possible perhaps by the unswerving loyalty of the marine corps and a voluntary resumption of loyalty among influential sections of the crews.

To some extent the Nore Mutiny may be regarded as analogous to the distempering irruption of contagious fever in a frame constitutionally sound, and which anon throws it off.

At all events, of these thousands of mutineers were some of the tars who not so very long afterwards—whether wholly prompted thereto by patriotism, or pugnacious instinct, or by both—helped to win a coronet for Nelson at the Nile, and the naval crown of crowns for him at Trafalgar.[23] To the mutineers, those battles and especially Trafalgar were a plenary absolution and a grand one. For all that goes to make up scenic naval display and heroic magnificence in arms, those battles, especially Trafalgar, stand unmatched in human annals.

IV

In this matter of writing, resolve as one may to keep to the main road, some bypaths have an enticement not readily to be withstood. I am going to err into such a bypath. If the reader will keep me company I shall be glad. At the least, we can promise ourselves that pleasure which is wickedly said to be in sinning, for a literary sin the divergence will be.

Very likely it is no new remark that the inventions of our time have at last brought about a change in sea warfare in degree corresponding to the revolution in all warfare effected by the original introduction from China into Europe of gunpowder. The first European firearm, a clumsy contrivance, was, as is well known, scouted by no few of the knights as a base implement, good enough peradventure for weavers too craven to stand up crossing steel with steel in frank fight. But as ashore knightly valor, though shorn of its blazonry, did not cease with the knights, neither on the seas—though nowadays in encounters there a certain kind of displayed gallantry be fallen out of date as hardly applicable under changed circumstances—did the nobler qualities of

---

[23]For his victory in the Battle of the Nile (1798), Nelson was made a baron; Nelson was killed in 1805 at Trafalgar and became, in effect, the saint and martyr of the British Navy.

such naval magnates as Don John of Austria, Doria, Van Tromp, Jean Bart, the long line of British admirals, and the American Decaturs of 1812 become obsolete with their wooden walls.

Nevertheless, to anybody who can hold the Present at its worth without being inappreciative of the Past, it may be forgiven, if to such an one the solitary old hulk at Portsmouth, Nelson's *Victory*, seems to float there, not alone as the decaying monument of a fame incorruptible, but also as a poetic reproach, softened by its picturesqueness, to the *Monitors*[24] and yet mightier hulls of the European ironclads. And this not altogether because such craft are unsightly, unavoidably lacking the symmetry and grand lines of the old battleships, but equally for other reasons.

There are some, perhaps, who while not altogether inaccessible to that poetic reproach just alluded to, may yet on behalf of the new order be disposed to parry it; and this to the extent of iconoclasm, if need be. For example, prompted by the sight of the star inserted in the *Victory*'s quarter-deck designating the spot where the Great Sailor fell, these martial utilitarians may suggest considerations implying that Nelson's ornate publication of his person in battle[25] was not only unnecessary, but not military, nay, savored of foolhardiness and vanity. They may add, too, that at Trafalgar it was in effect nothing less than a challenge to death; and death came; and that but for his bravado the victorious admiral might possibly have survived the battle, and so, instead of having his sagacious dying injunctions overruled by his immediate successor in command, he himself when the contest was decided might have brought his shattered fleet to anchor, a proceeding which might have averted the deplorable loss of life by shipwreck in the elemental tempest that followed the martial one.

Well, should we set aside the more than disputable point whether for various reasons it was possible to anchor the fleet, then plausibly enough the Benthamites[26] of war may urge the above. But the *might-have-been* is but boggy ground to build on. And, certainly, in foresight as to the larger issue of an encounter, and anxious preparations for it—

---

[24]First American ironclad warship, used in the Civil War.
[25]Nelson wore his decorations while commanding the *Victory* at Trafalgar, making him a tempting target to French sharpshooters, who succeeded in putting a bullet through his spine.
[26]Pragmatists.

buoying the deadly way and mapping it out, as at Copenhagen[27]—few commanders have been so painstakingly circumspect as this same reckless declarer of his person in fight.

Personal prudence, even when dictated by quite other than selfish considerations, surely is no special virtue in a military man; while an excessive love of glory, impassioning a less burning impulse, the honest sense of duty, is the first. If the name *Wellington* is not so much of a trumpet to the blood as the simpler name *Nelson*, the reason for this may perhaps be inferred from the above. Alfred[28] in his funeral ode on the victor of Waterloo ventures not to call him the greatest soldier of all time, though in the same ode he invokes Nelson as "the greatest sailor since our world began."

At Trafalgar Nelson on the brink of opening the fight sat down and wrote his last brief will and testament. If under the presentiment of the most magnificent of all victories to be crowned by his own glorious death, a sort of priestly motive led him to dress his person in the jewelled vouchers of his own shining deeds; if thus to have adorned himself for the altar and the sacrifice were indeed vainglory, then affectation and fustian is each more heroic line in the great epics and dramas, since in such lines the poet but embodies in verse those exaltations of sentiment that a nature like Nelson, the opportunity being given, vitalizes into acts.

V

Yes, the outbreak at the Nore was put down. But not every grievance was redressed. If the contractors, for example, were no longer permitted to ply some practices peculiar to their tribe everywhere, such as providing shoddy cloth, rations not sound, or false in the measure; not the less impressment, for one thing, went on. By custom sanctioned for centuries, and judicially maintained by a Lord Chancellor as late as Mansfield,[29] that mode of manning the fleet, a mode now fallen into a sort of abeyance but never formally renounced, it was not practicable

---

[27]In 1801, the Danes had removed the channel buoys from the port of Copenhagen as a defensive measure. Nelson carefully sounded and re-marked the harbor before leading his fleet in for his first major victory.

[28]Lord Tennyson.

[29]William Murray, Lord Mansfield (1705-1793), Lord Chief Justice of England from 1756.

to give up in those years. Its abrogation would have crippled the indispensable fleet, one wholly under canvas, no steam power, its innumerable sails and thousands of cannon, everything in short, worked by muscle alone; a fleet the more insatiate in demand for men, because then multiplying its ships of all grades against contingencies present and to come of the convulsed Continent.[30]

Discontent foreran the Two Mutinies, and more or less it lurkingly survived them. Hence it was not unreasonable to apprehend some return of trouble sporadic or general. One instance of such apprehensions: In the same year with this story, Nelson, then Rear Admiral Sir Horatio, being with the fleet off the Spanish coast, was directed by the admiral in command to shift his pennant from the *Captain* to the *Theseus*; and for this reason: that the latter ship having newly arrived on the station from home, where it had taken part in the Great Mutiny, danger was apprehended from the temper of the men; and it was thought that an officer like Nelson was the one, not indeed to terrorize the crew into base subjection, but to win them, by force of his mere presence and heroic personality, back to an allegiance if not as enthusiastic as his own yet as true.

So it was that for a time, on more than one quarter-deck, anxiety did exist. At sea, precautionary vigilance was strained against relapse. At short notice an engagement might come on. When it did, the lieutenants assigned to batteries felt it incumbent on them, in some instances, to stand with drawn swords behind the men working the guns.

VI

But on board the seventy-four in which Billy now swung his hammock, very little in the manner of the men and nothing obvious in the demeanor of the officers would have suggested to an ordinary observer that the Great Mutiny was a recent event. In their general bearing and conduct the commissioned officers of a warship naturally take their tone from the commander, that is if he have that ascendancy of character that ought to be his.

Captain the Honorable Edward Fairfax Vere, to give his full title, was a bachelor of forty or thereabouts, a sailor of distinction even in a time

---

[30]The British naval war and blockade against first the revolutionary government of France, then the empire of Napoleon, would continue until 1814.

prolific of renowned seamen. Though allied to the higher nobility,[31] his advancement had not been altogether owing to influences connected with that circumstance. He had seen much service, been in various engagements, always acquitting himself as an officer mindful of the welfare of his men, but never tolerating an infraction of discipline; thoroughly versed in the science of his profession, and intrepid to the verge of temerity, though never injudiciously so. For his gallantry in the West Indian waters as flag lieutenant under Rodney in that admiral's crowning victory over De Grasse, he was made a post captain.

Ashore, in the garb of a civilian, scarce anyone would have taken him for a sailor, more especially that he never garnished unprofessional talk with nautical terms, and grave in his bearing, evinced little appreciation of mere humor. It was not out of keeping with these traits that on a passage when nothing demanded his paramount action, he was the most undemonstrative of men. Any landsman observing this gentleman not conspicuous by his stature and wearing no pronounced insignia, emerging from his cabin to the open deck, and noting the silent deference of the officers retiring to leeward, might have taken him for the King's guest, a civilian aboard the King's ship, some highly honorable discreet envoy on his way to an important post. But in fact this unobtrusiveness of demeanor may have proceeded from a certain unaffected modesty of manhood sometimes accompanying a resolute nature, a modesty evinced at all times not calling for pronounced action, which shown in any rank of life suggests a virtue aristocratic in kind. As with some others engaged in various departments of the world's more heroic activities, Captain Vere though practical enough upon occasion would at times betray a certain dreaminess of mood. Standing alone on the weather side of the quarter-deck, one hand holding by the rigging, he would absently gaze off at the blank sea. At the presentation to him then of some minor matter interrupting the current of his thoughts, he would show more or less irascibility; but instantly he would control it.

In the navy he was popularly known by the appellation "Starry Vere." How such a designation happened to fall upon one who whatever his sterling qualities was without any brilliant ones, was in this wise: A favorite kinsman, Lord Denton, a freehearted fellow, had been the first to meet and congratulate him upon his return to England from his West Indian cruise; and but the day previous turning over a copy of Andrew Marvell's poems had lighted, not for the first time, however,

---

[31]His title, "the Honorable," suggests that he is the younger son of an earl or viscount.

upon the lines entitled "Appleton House," the name of one of the seats of their common ancestor, a hero in the German wars of the seventeenth century, in which poem occur the lines:

> This 'tis to have been from the first
> In a domestic heaven nursed,
> Under the discipline severe
> Of Fairfax and the starry Vere.[32]

And so, upon embracing his cousin fresh from Rodney's great victory wherein he had played so gallant a part, brimming over with just family pride in the sailor of their house, he exuberantly exclaimed, "Give ye joy, Ed; give ye joy, my starry Vere!" This got currency, and the novel prefix serving in familiar parlance readily to distinguish the *Bellipotent*'s captain from another Vere his senior, a distant relative, an officer of like rank in the navy, it remained permanently attached to the surname.

VII

In view of the part that the commander of the *Bellipotent* plays in scenes shortly to follow, it may be well to fill out that sketch of him outlined in the previous chapter.

Aside from his qualities as a sea officer Captain Vere was an exceptional character. Unlike no few of England's renowned sailors, long and arduous service with signal devotion to it had not resulted in absorbing and *salting* the entire man. He had a marked leaning toward everything intellectual. He loved books, never going to sea without a newly replenished library, compact but of the best. The isolated leisure, in some cases so wearisome, falling at intervals to commanders even during a war cruise, never was tedious to Captain Vere. With nothing of that literary taste which less heeds the thing conveyed than the vehicle, his bias was toward those books to which every serious mind of superior order occupying any active post of authority in the world naturally inclines: books treating of actual men and events no matter of what era—history, biography, and unconventional writers like Montaigne,

---

[32]The subject of the poem is Mary Fairfax, whom Marvell tutored at Appleton House; "Fairfax and the starry Vere" are her father and mother, Thomas Fairfax and Anne Vere.

who, free from cant and convention, honestly and in the spirit of common sense philosophize upon realities. In this line of reading he found confirmation of his own more reserved thoughts—confirmation which he had vainly sought in social converse, so that as touching most fundamental topics, there had got to be established in him some positive convictions which he forefelt would abide in him essentially unmodified so long as his intelligent part remained unimpaired. In view of the troubled period in which his lot was cast, this was well for him. His settled convictions were as a dike against those invading waters of novel opinion social, political, and otherwise, which carried away as in a torrent no few minds in those days, minds by nature not inferior to his own. While other members of that aristocracy to which by birth he belonged were incensed at the innovators mainly because their theories were inimical to the privileged classes, Captain Vere disinterestedly opposed them not alone because they seemed to him insusceptible of embodiment in lasting institutions, but at war with the peace of the world and the true welfare of mankind.

With minds less stored than his and less earnest, some officers of his rank, with whom at times he would necessarily consort, found him lacking in the companionable quality, a dry and bookish gentleman, as they deemed. Upon any chance withdrawal from their company one would be apt to say to another something like this: "Vere is a noble fellow, Starry Vere. 'Spite the gazettes,[33] Sir Horatio" (meaning him who became Lord Nelson) "is at bottom scarce a better seaman or fighter. But between you and me now, don't you think there is a queer streak of the pedantic running through him? Yes, like the King's yarn[34] in a coil of navy rope?"

Some apparent ground there was for this sort of confidential criticism; since not only did the captain's discourse never fall into the jocosely familiar, but in illustrating of any point touching the stirring personages and events of the time he would be as apt to cite some historic character or incident of antiquity as he would be to cite from the moderns. He seemed unmindful of the circumstance that to his bluff company such remote allusions, however pertinent they might really be, were altogether alien to men whose reading was mainly confined to the journals. But considerateness in such matters is not easy to

---

[33]Despite the gazettes—newspapers of the time which publicized heroic actions at sea.
[34]A colored yarn identifying the rope as government property—so that it could not be stolen and sold.

natures constituted like Captain Vere's. Their honesty prescribes to them directness, sometimes far-reaching like that of a migratory fowl that in its flight never heeds when it crosses a frontier.

VIII

The lieutenants and other commissioned gentlemen forming Captain Vere's staff it is not necessary here to particularize, nor needs it to make any mention of any of the warrant officers. But among the petty officers was one who, having much to do with the story, may as well be forthwith introduced. His portrait I essay, but shall never hit it. This was John Claggart, the master-at-arms. But that sea title may to landsmen seem somewhat equivocal. Originally, doubtless, that petty officer's function was the instruction of the men in the use of arms, sword or cutlass. But very long ago, owing to the advance in gunnery making hand-to-hand encounters less frequent and giving to niter and sulphur the pre-eminence over steel, that function ceased; the master-at-arms of a great warship becoming a sort of chief of police charged among other matters with the duty of preserving order on the populous lower gun decks.

Claggart was a man about five-and-thirty, somewhat spare and tall, yet of no ill figure upon the whole. His hand was too small and shapely to have been accustomed to hard toil. The face was a notable one, the features all except the chin cleanly cut as those on a Greek medallion; yet the chin, beardless as Tecumseh's, had something of strange protuberant broadness in its make that recalled the prints of the Reverend Dr. Titus Oates, the historic deponent with the clerical drawl in the time of Charles II and the fraud of the alleged Popish Plot.[35] It served Claggart in his office that his eye could cast a tutoring glance. His brow was of the sort phrenologically associated with more than average intellect; silken jet curls partly clustering over it, making a foil to the pallor below, a pallor tinged with a faint shade of amber akin to the hue of time-tinted marbles of old. This complexion, singularly contrasting with the red or deeply bronzed visages of the sailors, and in

---

[35]In 1678, Titus Oates (1649–1705) fabricated the story of a plot by Catholics to assassinate Charles II and set his Catholic brother on the throne; though entirely fictitious, the "Popish Plot" created widespread hysteria, and a number of wholly innocent Catholic courtiers and lords paid with their lives for their supposed complicity in the nonexistent conspiracy.

part the result of his official seclusion from the sunlight, though it was not exactly displeasing, nevertheless seemed to hint of something defective or abnormal in the constitution and blood. But his general aspect and manner were so suggestive of an education and career incongruous with his naval function that when not actively engaged in it he looked like a man of high quality, social and moral, who for reasons of his own was keeping incog.[36] Nothing was known of his former life. It might be that he was an Englishman; and yet there lurked a bit of accent in his speech suggesting that possibly he was not such by birth, but through naturalization in early childhood. Among certain grizzled sea gossips of the gun decks and forecastle went a rumor perdue that the master-at-arms was a *chevalier*[37] who had volunteered into the King's navy by way of compounding for some mysterious swindle whereof he had been arraigned at the King's Bench. The fact that nobody could substantiate this report was, of course, nothing against its secret currency. Such a rumor once started on the gun decks in reference to almost anyone below the rank of a commissioned officer would, during the period assigned to this narrative, have seemed not altogether wanting in credibility to the tarry old wiseacres of a man-of-war crew. And indeed a man of Claggart's accomplishments, without prior nautical experience entering the navy at mature life, as he did, and necessarily allotted at the start to the lowest grade in it; a man too who never made allusion to his previous life ashore; these were circumstances which in the dearth of exact knowledge as to his true antecedents opened to the invidious a vague field for unfavorable surmise.

But the sailors' dogwatch gossip concerning him derived a vague plausibility from the fact that now for some period the British navy could so little afford to be squeamish in the matter of keeping up the muster rolls, that not only were press gangs notoriously abroad both afloat and ashore, but there was little or no secret about another matter, namely, that the London police were at liberty to capture any able-bodied suspect, any questionable fellow at large, and summarily ship him to the dockyard or fleet. Furthermore, even among voluntary enlistments there were instances where the motive thereto partook neither of patriotic impulse nor yet of a random desire to experience a bit of sea life and martial adventure. Insolvent debtors of minor grade, together with the promiscuous lame ducks of morality, found in the

---

[36]Incognito.
[37]A soldier-of-fortune, an adventurer.

navy a convenient and secure refuge, secure because, once enlisted aboard a King's ship, they were as much in sanctuary as the transgressor of the Middle Ages harboring himself under the shadow of the altar. Such sanctioned irregularities, which for obvious reasons the government would hardly think to parade at the time and which consequently, and as affecting the least influential class of mankind, have all but dropped into oblivion, lend color to something for the truth whereof I do not vouch, and hence have some scruple in stating; something I remember having seen in print though the book I cannot recall; but the same thing was personally communicated to me now more than forty years ago by an old pensioner in a cocked hat with whom I had a most interesting talk on the terrace at Greenwich, a Baltimore Negro, a Trafalgar man. It was to this effect: In the case of a warship short of hands whose speedy sailing was imperative, the deficient quota, in lack of any other way of making it good, would be eked out by drafts culled direct from the jails. For reasons previously suggested it would not perhaps be easy at the present day directly to prove or disprove the allegation. But allowed as a verity, how significant would it be of England's straits at the time confronted by those wars which like a flight of harpies rose shrieking from the din and dust of the fallen Bastille.[38] That era appears measurably clear to us who look back at it, and but read of it. But to the grandfathers of us graybeards, the more thoughtful of them, the genius of it presented an aspect like that of Camoëns' Spirit of the Cape, an eclipsing menace mysterious and prodigious.[39] Not America was exempt from apprehension. At the height of Napoleon's unexampled conquests, there were Americans who had fought at Bunker Hill who looked forward to the possibility that the Atlantic might prove no barrier against the ultimate schemes of this French portentous upstart from the revolutionary chaos who seemed in act of fulfilling judgment prefigured in the Apocalypse.

But the less credence was to be given to the gun-deck talk touching Claggart, seeing that no man holding his office in a man-of-war can ever hope to be popular with the crew. Besides, in derogatory comments upon anyone against whom they have a grudge, or for any reason or no reason mislike, sailors are much like landsmen: they are apt to exaggerate or romance it.

---

[38]Parisian prison, the storming of which signaled the start of the French Revolution, on July 14, 1789.

[39]In the Portuguese national epic, the *Lusiads*, by Luiz Vaz de Camões (1524-1580), the Spirit of the Cape, Adamastor, is a vast monster that attempts to destroy the hero.

About as much was really known to the *Bellipotent's* tars of the master-at-arms' career before entering the service as an astronomer knows about a comet's travels prior to its first observable appearance in the sky. The verdict of the sea quidnuncs[40] has been cited only by way of showing what sort of moral impression the man made upon rude uncultivated natures whose conceptions of human wickedness were necessarily of the narrowest, limited to ideas of vulgar rascality—a thief among the swinging hammocks during a night watch, or the man-brokers and land-sharks of the seaports.

It was no gossip, however, but fact that though, as before hinted, Claggart upon his entrance into the navy was, as a novice, assigned to the least honorable section of a man-of-war's crew, embracing the drudgery, he did not long remain there. The superior capacity he immediately evinced, his constitutional sobriety, an ingratiating deference to superiors, together with a peculiar ferreting genius manifested on a singular occasion; all this, capped by a certain austere patriotism, abruptly advanced him to the position of master-at-arms.

Of this maritime chief of police the ship's corporals, so called, were the immediate subordinates, and compliant ones; and this, as is to be noted in some business departments ashore, almost to a degree inconsistent with entire moral volition. His place put various converging wires of underground influence under the chief's control, capable when astutely worked through his understrappers of operating to the mysterious discomfort, if nothing worse, of any of the sea commonalty.

IX

Life in the foretop well agreed with Billy Budd. There, when not actually engaged on the yards yet higher aloft, the topmen, who as such had been picked out for youth and activity, constituted an aerial club lounging at ease against the smaller stun'sails rolled up into cushions, spinning yarns like the lazy gods, and frequently amused with what was going on in the busy world of the decks below. No wonder then that a young fellow of Billy's disposition was well content in such society. Giving no cause of offense to anybody, he was always alert at a call. So in the merchant service it had been with him. But now such a punctiliousness in duty was shown that his topmates would sometimes good-naturedly laugh at him for it. This heightened alacrity had its

---

[40]Gossips.

cause, namely, the impression made upon him by the first formal gang-way-punishment he had ever witnessed, which befell the day following his impressment. It had been incurred by a little fellow, young, a novice afterguardsman absent from his assigned post when the ship was being put about; a dereliction resulting in a rather serious hitch to that maneuver, one demanding instantaneous promptitude in letting go and making fast. When Billy saw the culprit's naked back under the scourge, gridironed with red welts and worse, when he marked the dire expression in the liberated man's face as with his woolen shirt flung over him by the executioner he rushed forward from the spot to bury himself in the crowd, Billy was horrified. He resolved that never through remissness would he make himself liable to such a visitation or do or omit aught that might merit even verbal reproof. What then was his surprise and concern when ultimately he found himself getting into petty trouble occasionally about such matters as the stowage of his bag or something amiss in his hammock, matters under the police oversight of the ship's corporals of the lower decks, and which brought down on him a vague threat from one of them.

So heedful in all things as he was, how could this be? He could not understand it, and it more than vexed him. When he spoke to his young topmates about it they were either lightly incredulous or found something comical in his unconcealed anxiety. "Is it your bag, Billy?" said one. "Well, sew yourself up in it, bully boy, and then you'll be sure to know if anybody meddles with it."

Now there was a veteran aboard who because his years began to disqualify him for more active work had been recently assigned duty as mainmastman in his watch, looking to the gear belayed at the rail roundabout that great spar near the deck. At off-times the foretopman had picked up some acquaintance with him, and now in his trouble it occurred to him that he might be the sort of person to go to for wise counsel. He was an old Dansker[41] long anglicized in the service, of few words, many wrinkles, and some honorable scars. His wizened face, time-tinted and weather-stained to the complexion of an antique parchment, was here and there peppered blue by the chance explosion of a gun cartridge in action.

He was an *Agamemnon* man, some two years prior to the time of this story having served under Nelson when still captain in that ship immortal in naval memory, which dismantled and in part broken up to

---

[41]A Dane.

her bare ribs is seen a grand skeleton in Haden's etching.[42] As one of a boarding party from the *Agamemnon* he had received a cut slantwise along one temple and cheek leaving a long pale scar like a streak of dawn's light falling athwart the dark visage. It was on account of that scar and the affair in which it was known that he had received it, as well as from his blue-peppered[43] complexion, that the Dansker went among the *Bellipotent*'s crew by the name of "Board-Her-in-the-Smoke."

Now the first time that his small weasel eyes happened to light on Billy Budd, a certain grim internal merriment set all his ancient wrinkles into antic play. Was it that his eccentric unsentimental old sapience, primitive in its kind, saw or thought it saw something which in contrast with the warship's environment looked oddly incongruous in the Handsome Sailor? But after slyly studying him at intervals, the old Merlin's equivocal merriment was modified; for now when the twain would meet, it would start in his face a quizzing sort of look, but it would be but momentary and sometimes replaced by an expression of speculative query as to what might eventually befall a nature like that, dropped into a world not without some mantraps and against whose subtleties simple courage lacking experience and address, and without any touch of defensive ugliness, is of little avail; and where such innocence as man is capable of does yet in a moral emergency not always sharpen the faculties or enlighten the will.

However it was, the Dansker in his ascetic way rather took to Billy. Nor was this only because of a certain philosophic interest in such a character. There was another cause. While the old man's eccentricities, sometimes bordering on the ursine, repelled the juniors, Billy, undeterred thereby, revering him as a salt hero, would make advances, never passing the old *Agamemnon* man without a salutation marked by that respect which is seldom lost on the aged, however crabbed at times or whatever their station in life.

There was a vein of dry humor, or what not, in the mastman; and, whether in freak of patriarchal irony touching Billy's youth and athletic frame, or for some other and more recondite reason, from the first in addressing him he always substituted *Baby* for Billy, the Dansker in fact being the originator of the name by which the foretopman eventually became known aboard ship.

Well then, in his mysterious little difficulty going in quest of the

---

[42]Sir Francis Seymour Haden's 1870 etching, "The Breaking-up of the *Agamemnon*."
[43]Burned and tattooed by black-powder.

wrinkled one, Billy found him off duty in a dogwatch ruminating by himself, seated on a shot box of the upper gun deck, now and then surveying with a somewhat cynical regard certain of the more swaggering promenaders there. Billy recounted his trouble, again wondering how it all happened. The salt seer attentively listened, accompanying the foretopman's recital with queer twitchings of his wrinkles and problematical little sparkles of his small ferret eyes. Making an end of his story, the foretopman asked, "And now, Dansker, do tell me what you think of it."

The old man, shoving up the front of his tarpaulin and deliberately rubbing the long slant scar at the point where it entered the thin hair, laconically said, "Baby Budd, *Jemmy Legs*" (meaning the master-at-arms) "is down on you."

"*Jemmy Legs!*" ejaculated Billy, his welkin eyes expanding. "What for? Why, he calls me 'the sweet and pleasant young fellow,' they tell me."

"Does he so?" grinned the grizzled one; then said, "Ay, Baby lad, a sweet voice has Jemmy Legs."

"No, not always. But to me he has. I seldom pass him but there comes a pleasant word."

"And that's because he's down upon you, Baby Budd."

Such reiteration, along with the manner of it, incomprehensible to a novice, disturbed Billy almost as much as the mystery for which he had sought explanation. Something less unpleasingly oracular he tried to extract; but the old sea Chiron, thinking perhaps that for the nonce he had sufficiently instructed his young Achilles,[44] pursed his lips, gathered all his wrinkles together, and would commit himself to nothing further.

Years, and those experiences which befall certain shrewder men subordinated lifelong to the will of superiors, all this had developed in the Dansker the pithy guarded cynicism that was his leading characteristic.

The next day an incident served to confirm Billy Budd in his incredulity as to the Dansker's strange summing up of the case submitted. The ship at noon, going large before the wind, was rolling on her course, and he below at dinner and engaged in some sportful talk with the members of his mess, chanced in a sudden lurch to spill the entire

---

[44]The centaur Chiron, according to legend, was the tutor of the heroic Achilles.

contents of his soup pan upon the new-scrubbed deck. Claggart, the master-at-arms, official rattan[45] in hand, happened to be passing along the battery in a bay of which the mess was lodged, and the greasy liquid streamed just across his path. Stepping over it, he was proceeding on his way without comment, since the matter was nothing to take notice of under the circumstances, when he happened to observe who it was that had done the spilling. His countenance changed. Pausing, he was about to ejaculate something hasty at the sailor, but checked himself, and pointing down to the streaming soup, playfully tapped him from behind with his rattan, saying in a low musical voice peculiar to him at times, "Handsomely done, my lad! And handsome is as handsome did it, too!" And with that passed on. Not noted by Billy as not coming within his view was the involuntary smile, or rather grimace, that accompanied Claggart's equivocal words. Aridly it drew down the thin corners of his shapely mouth. But everybody taking his remark as meant for humorous, and at which therefore as coming from a superior they were bound to laugh "with counterfeited glee," acted accordingly; and Billy, tickled, it may be, by the allusion to his being the Handsome Sailor, merrily joined in; then addressing his messmates exclaimed, "There now, who says that Jemmy Legs is down on me!"

"And who said he was, Beauty?" demanded one Donald with some surprise. Whereat the foretopman looked a little foolish, recalling that it was only one person, Board-Her-in-the-Smoke, who had suggested what to him was the smoky idea that this master-at-arms was in any peculiar way hostile to him. Meantime that functionary, resuming his path, must have momentarily worn some expression less guarded than that of the bitter smile, usurping the face from the heart—some distorting expression perhaps, for a drummer-boy heedlessly frolicking along from the opposite direction and chancing to come into light collision with his person was strangely disconcerted by his aspect. Nor was the impression lessened when the official, impetuously giving him a sharp cut with the rattan, vehemently exclaimed, "Look where you go!"

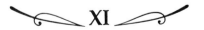

XI

What was the matter with the master-at-arms? And, be the matter what it might, how could it have direct relation to Billy Budd, with whom prior to the affair of the spilled soup he had never come into any

---

[45]Cane for inflicting mild summary punishment.

special contact official or otherwise? What indeed could the trouble have to do with one so little inclined to give offense as the merchant-ship's "peacemaker," even him who in Claggart's own phrase was "the sweet and pleasant young fellow"? Yes, why should Jemmy Legs, to borrow the Dansker's expression, be "down" on the Handsome Sailor? But, at heart and not for nothing, as the late chance encounter may indicate to the discerning, down on him, secretly down on him, he assuredly was.

Now to invent something touching the more private career of Clag-gart, something involving Billy Budd, of which something the latter should be wholly ignorant, some romantic incident implying that Clag-gart's knowledge of the young blue-jacket began at some period ante-rior to catching sight of him on board the seventy-four—all this, not so difficult to do, might avail in a way more or less interesting to account for whatever of enigma may appear to lurk in the case. But in fact there was nothing of the sort. And yet the cause necessarily to be assumed as the sole one assignable is in its very realism as much charged with that prime element of Radcliffian romance, the mysterious, as any that the ingenuity of the author of *The Mysteries of Udolpho*[46] could devise. For what can more partake of the mysterious than an antipathy spontane-ous and profound such as is evoked in certain exceptional mortals by the mere aspect of some other mortal, however harmless he may be, if not called forth by this very harmlessness itself?

Now there can exist no irritating juxtaposition of dissimilar personal-ities comparable to that which is possible aboard a great warship fully manned and at sea. There, every day among all ranks, almost every man comes into more or less of contact with almost every other man. Wholly there to avoid even the sight of an aggravating object one must needs give it Jonah's toss[47] or jump overboard himself. Imagine how all this might eventually operate on some peculiar human creature the direct reverse of a saint!

But for the adequate comprehending of Claggart by a normal nature these hints are insufficient. To pass from a normal nature to him one must cross "the deadly space between." And this is best done by in-direction.

Long ago an honest scholar, my senior, said to me in reference to one

---

[46]Gothic novel (1794-95) by Ann Radcliffe (1764-1823), noted for mysterious happenings eventually given rational explanations.
[47]Into the sea.

who like himself is now no more, a man so unimpeachably respectable that against him nothing was ever openly said though among the few something was whispered, "Yes, X——is a nut not to be cracked by the tap of a lady's fan. You are aware that I am the adherent of no organized religion, much less of any philosophy built into a system. Well, for all that, I think that to try and get into X——, enter his labyrinth and get out again, without a clue derived from some source other than what is known as 'knowledge of the world'—that were hardly possible, at least for me."

"Why," said I, "X——, however singular a study to some, is yet human, and knowledge of the world assuredly implies the knowledge of human nature, and in most of its varieties."

"Yes, but a superficial knowledge of it, serving ordinary purposes. But for anything deeper, I am not certain whether to know the world and to know human nature be not two distinct branches of knowledge, which while they may coexist in the same heart, yet either may exist with little or nothing of the other. Nay, in an average man of the world, his constant rubbing with it blunts that finer spiritual insight indispensable to the understanding of the essential in certain exceptional characters, whether evil ones or good. In a matter of some importance I have seen a girl wind an old lawyer about her little finger. Nor was it the dotage of senile love. Nothing of the sort. But he knew law better than he knew the girl's heart. Coke and Blackstone[48] hardly shed so much light into obscure spiritual places as the Hebrew prophets. And who were they? Mostly recluses."

At the time, my inexperience was such that I did not quite see the drift of all this. It may be that I see it now. And, indeed, if that lexicon which is based on Holy Writ were any longer popular, one might with less difficulty define and denominate certain phenomenal men. As it is, one must turn to some authority not liable to the charge of being tinctured with the biblical element.

In a list of definitions included in the authentic translation of Plato, a list attributed to him, occurs this: "Natural Depravity: a depravity according to nature," a definition which, though savoring of Calvinism, by no means involves Calvin's dogma as to total mankind.[49] Evidently

---

[48]Learned commentators on the laws of England of the sixteenth and eighteenth centuries, respectively.

[49]The doctrine that, except for a small group of Elect individuals, the mass of mankind is doomed, predestined for the fires of Hell.

its intent makes it applicable but to individuals. Not many are the examples of this depravity which the gallows and jail supply. At any rate, for notable instances, since these have no vulgar alloy of the brute in them, but invariably are dominated by intellectuality, one must go elsewhere. Civilization, especially if of the austerer sort, is auspicious to it. It folds itself in the mantle of respectability. It has its certain negative virtues serving as silent auxiliaries. It never allows wine to get within its guard. It is not going too far to say that it is without vices or small sins. There is a phenomenal pride in it that excludes them. It is never mercenary or avaricious. In short, the depravity here meant partakes nothing of the sordid or sensual. It is serious, but free from acerbity. Though no flatterer of mankind it never speaks ill of it.

But the thing which in eminent instances signalizes so exceptional a nature is this: Though the man's even temper and discreet bearing would seem to intimate a mind peculiarly subject to the law of reason, not the less in heart he would seem to riot in complete exemption from that law, having apparently little to do with reason further than to employ it as an ambidexter implement for effecting the irrational. That is to say: Toward the accomplishment of an aim which in wantonness of atrocity would seem to partake of the insane, he will direct a cool judgment sagacious and sound. These men are madmen, and of the most dangerous sort, for their lunacy is not continuous, but occasional, evoked by some special object; it is protectively secretive, which is as much as to say it is self-contained, so that when, moreover, most active it is to the average mind not distinguishable from sanity, and for the reason above suggested: that whatever its aims may be—and the aim is never declared—the method and the outward proceeding are always perfectly rational.

Now something such an one was Claggart, in whom was the mania of an evil nature, not engendered by vicious training or corrupting books or licentious living, but born with him and innate, in short "a depravity according to nature."

Dark sayings are these, some will say. But why? Is it because they somewhat savor of Holy Writ in its phrase "mystery of iniquity"?[50] If they do, such savor was far enough from being intended, for little will it commend these pages to many a reader of today.

The point of the present story turning on the hidden nature of the

---

[50] In 2 Thessalonians 2:7, "the mystery of inquity doth already work."

master-at-arms has necessitated this chapter. With an added hint or two in connection with the incident at the mess, the resumed narrative must be left to vindicate, as it may, its own credibility.

XII

That Claggart's figure was not amiss, and his face, save the chin, well molded, has already been said. Of these favorable points he seemed not insensible, for he was not only neat but careful in his dress. But the form of Billy Budd was heroic; and if his face was without the intellectual look of the pallid Claggart's, not the less was it lit, like his, from within, though from a different source. The bonfire in his heart made luminous the rose-tan in his cheek.

In view of the marked contrast between the persons of the twain, it is more than probable that when the master-at-arms in the scene last given applied to the sailor the proverb "Handsome is as handsome does," he there let escape an ironic inkling, not caught by the young sailors who heard it, as to what it was that had first moved him against Billy, namely, his significant personal beauty.

Now envy and antipathy, passions irreconcilable in reason, nevertheless in fact may spring conjoined like Chang and Eng[51] in one birth. Is Envy then such a monster? Well, though many an arraigned mortal has in hopes of mitigated penalty pleaded guilty to horrible actions, did ever anybody seriously confess to envy? Something there is in it universally felt to be more shameful than even felonious crime. And not only does everybody disown it, but the better sort are inclined to incredulity when it is in earnest imputed to an intelligent man. But since its lodgment is in the heart not the brain, no degree of intellect supplies a guarantee against it. But Claggart's was no vulgar form of the passion. Nor, as directed toward Billy Budd, did it partake of that streak of apprehensive jealousy that marred Saul's visage perturbedly brooding on the comely young David.[52] Claggart's envy struck deeper. If askance he eyed the good looks, cheery health, and frank enjoyment of young life in Billy Budd, it was because these went along with a nature that, as Claggart magnetically felt, had in its simplicity never willed malice or experienced the reactionary bite of that serpent. To him, the spirit

---

[51]The original "Siamese twins," who lived 1811–1874.
[52]In 1 Samuel 18, King Saul is envious of David's popularity and plots his death.

lodged within Billy, and looking out from his welkin eyes as from windows, that ineffability it was which made the dimple in his dyed cheek, suppled his joints, and dancing in his yellow curls made him pre-eminently the Handsome Sailor. One person excepted, the master-at-arms was perhaps the only man in the ship intellectually capable of adequately appreciating the moral phenomenon presented in Billy Budd. And the insight but intensified his passion, which assuming various secret forms within him, at times assumed that of cynic disdain, disdain of innocence—to be nothing more than innocent! Yet in an aesthetic way he saw the charm of it, the courageous free-and-easy temper of it, and fain would have shared it, but he despaired of it.

With no power to annul the elemental evil in him, though readily enough he could hide it; apprehending the good, but powerless to be it; a nature like Claggart's, surcharged with energy as such natures almost invariably are, what recourse is left to it but to recoil upon itself and, like the scorpion for which the Creator alone is responsible, act out to the end the part allotted it.

XIII

Passion, and passion in its profoundest, is not a thing demanding a palatial stage whereon to play its part. Down among the groundlings, among the beggars and rakers of the garbage, profound passion is enacted. And the circumstances that provoke it, however trivial or mean, are no measure of its power. In the present instance the stage is a scrubbed gun deck, and one of the external provocations a man-of-war's man's spilled soup.

Now when the master-at-arms noticed whence came that greasy fluid streaming before his feet, he must have taken it—to some extent wilfully, perhaps—not for the mere accident it assuredly was, but for the sly escape of a spontaneous feeling on Billy's part more or less answering to the antipathy on his own. In effect a foolish demonstration, he must have thought, and very harmless, like the futile kick of a heifer, which yet were the heifer a shod stallion would not be so harmless. Even so was it that into the gall of Claggart's envy he infused the vitriol of his contempt. But the incident confirmed to him certain telltale reports purveyed to his ear by "Squeak," one of his more cunning corporals, a grizzled little man, so nicknamed by the sailors on account of his squeaky voice and sharp visage ferreting about the dark corners of the lower decks after interlopers, satirically suggesting to them the idea of a rat in a cellar.

From his chief's employing him as an implicit tool in laying little traps for the worriment of the foretopman—for it was from the master-at-arms that the petty persecutions heretofore adverted to had proceeded—the corporal, having naturally enough concluded that his master could have no love for the sailor, made it his business, faithful understrapper that he was, to foment the ill blood by perverting to his chief certain innocent frolics of the good-natured foretopman, besides inventing for his mouth sundry contumelious epithets he claimed to have overheard him let fall. The master-at-arms never suspected the veracity of these reports, more especially as to the epithets, for he well knew how secretly unpopular may become a master-at-arms, at least a master-at-arms of those days, zealous in his function, and how the bluejackets shoot at him in private their raillery and wit; the nickname by which he goes among them (Jemmy Legs) implying under the form of merriment their cherished disrespect and dislike. But in view of the greediness of hate for pabulum it hardly needed a purveyor to feed Claggart's passion.

An uncommon prudence is habitual with the subtler depravity, for it has everything to hide. And in case of an injury but suspected, its secretiveness voluntarily cuts it off from enlightenment or disillusion; and, not unreluctantly, action is taken upon surmise as upon certainty. And the retaliation is apt to be in monstrous disproportion to the supposed offense; for when in anybody was revenge in its exactions aught else but an inordinate usurer? But how with Claggart's conscience? For though consciences are unlike as foreheads, every intelligence, not excluding the scriptural devils who "believe and tremble," has one. But Claggart's conscience being but the lawyer to his will, made ogres of trifles, probably arguing that the motive imputed to Billy in spilling the soup just when he did, together with the epithets alleged, these, if nothing more, made a strong case against him; nay, justified animosity into a sort of retributive righteousness. The Pharisee[53] is the Guy Fawkes prowling in the hid chambers[54] underlying some natures like Claggart's. And they can really form no conception of an unreciprocated malice. Probably the master-at-arms' clandestine persecution of

---

[53]Hypocrite.
[54]Guy Fawkes (1570–1606) plotted to place gunpowder in the underground "hid chambers" of the Houses of Parliament and blow them up.

Billy was started to try the temper of the man; but it had not developed any quality in him that enmity could make official use of or even pervert into plausible self-justification; so that the occurrence at the mess, petty if it were, was a welcome one to that peculiar conscience assigned to be the private mentor of Claggart; and, for the rest, not improbably it put him upon new experiments.

XIV

Not many days after the last incident narrated, something befell Billy Budd that more graveled him than aught that had previously occurred.

It was a warm night for the latitude; and the foretopman, whose watch at the time was properly below, was dozing on the uppermost deck whither he had ascended from his hot hammock, one of hundreds suspended so closely wedged together over a lower gun deck that there was little or no swing to them. He lay as in the shadow of a hillside, stretched under the lee of the booms, a piled ridge of spare spars amidships between foremast and mainmast among which the ship's largest boat, the launch, was stowed. Alongside of three other slumberers from below, he lay near that end of the booms which approaches the foremast; his station aloft on duty as a foretopman being just over the deck-station of the forecastlemen, entitling him according to usage to make himself more or less at home in that neighborhood.

Presently he was stirred into semiconsciousness by somebody, who must have previously sounded the sleep of the others, touching his shoulder, and then, as the foretopman raised his head, breathing into his ear in a quick whisper, "Slip into the lee forechains, Billy; there is something in the wind. Don't speak. Quick, I will meet you there," and disappearing.

Now Billy, like sundry other essentially good-natured ones, had some of the weaknesses inseparable from essential good nature; and among these was a reluctance, almost an incapacity of plumply saying *no* to an abrupt proposition not obviously absurd on the face of it, nor obviously unfriendly, nor iniquitous. And being of warm blood, he had not the phlegm[55] tacitly to negative any proposition by unresponsive inaction. Like his sense of fear, his apprehension as to aught outside of

---

[55]Coldness, torpor.

the honest and natural was seldom very quick. Besides, upon the present occasion, the drowse from his sleep still hung upon him.

However it was, he mechanically rose and, sleepily wondering what could be in the wind, betook himself to the designated place, a narrow platform, one of six, outside of the high bulwarks and screened by the great deadeyes and multiple columned lanyards of the shrouds and backstays[56]; and, in a great warship of that time, of dimensions commensurate to the hull's magnitude; a tarry balcony in short, overhanging the sea, and so secluded that one mariner of the *Bellipotent*, a Nonconformist[57] old tar of a serious turn, made it even in daytime his private oratory.

In this retired nook the stranger soon joined Billy Budd. There was no moon as yet; a haze obscured the starlight. He could not distinctly see the stranger's face. Yet from something in the outline and carriage, Billy took him, and correctly, for one of the afterguard.

"Hist! Billy," said the man, in the same quick cautionary whisper as before. "You were impressed, weren't you? Well, so was I"; and he paused, as to mark the effect. But Billy, not knowing exactly what to make of this, said nothing. Then the other: "We are not the only impressed ones, Billy. There's a gang of us.—Couldn't you—help—at a pinch?"

"What do you mean?" demanded Billy, here thoroughly shaking off his drowse.

"Hist, hist!" the hurried whisper now growing husky. "See here," and the man held up two small objects faintly twinkling in the night-light; "see, they are yours, Billy, if you'll only——"

But Billy broke in, and in his resentful eagerness to deliver himself his vocal infirmity somewhat intruded. "D—d—damme, I don't know what you are d—d—driving at, or what you mean, but you had better g—g—go where you belong!" For the moment the fellow, as confounded, did not stir; and Billy, springing to his feet, said, "If you d—don't start, I'll t—t—toss you back over the r—rail!" There was no mistaking this and the mysterious emissary decamped, disappearing in the direction of the mainmast in the shadow of the booms.

"Hallo, what's the matter?" here came growling from a forecastle-

---

[56]Deadeyes are wooden blocks to which ropes are attached; lanyards are short ropes used to fasten shrouds; shrouds and backstays are ropes which help secure the masts of a sailing ship.

[57]Protestant not belonging to the Church of England.

man awakened from his deck-doze by Billy's raised voice. And as the foretopman reappeared and was recognized by him: "Ah, Beauty, is it you? Well, something must have been the matter, for you st—st—stuttered."

"Oh," rejoined Billy, now mastering the impediment, "I found an afterguardsman in our part of the ship here, and I bid him be off where he belongs."

"And is that all you did about it, Foretopman?" gruffly demanded another, an irascible old fellow of brick-colored visage and hair who was known to his associate forecastlemen as "Red Pepper." "Such sneaks I should like to marry to the gunner's daughter!"—by that expression meaning that he would like to subject them to disciplinary castigation over a gun.

However, Billy's rendering of the matter satisfactorily accounted to these inquirers for the brief commotion, since of all the sections of a ship's company the forecastlemen, veterans for the most part and bigoted in their sea prejudices, are the most jealous in resenting territorial encroachments, especially on the part of any of the afterguard, of whom they have but a sorry opinion—chiefly landsmen, never going aloft except to reef or furl the mainsail, and in no wise competent to handle a marlinspike or turn in a deadeye, say.

XV

This incident sorely puzzled Billy Budd. It was an entirely new experience, the first time in his life that he had ever been personally approached in underhand intriguing fashion. Prior to this encounter he had known nothing of the afterguardsman, the two men being stationed wide apart, one forward and aloft during his watch, the other on deck and aft.

What could it mean? And could they really be guineas, those two glittering objects the interloper had held up to his (Billy's) eyes? Where could the fellow get guineas? Why, even spare buttons are not so plentiful at sea. The more he turned the matter over, the more he was nonplussed, and made uneasy and discomfited. In his disgustful recoil from an overture which, though he but ill comprehended, he instinctively knew must involve evil of some sort, Billy Budd was like a young horse fresh from the pasture suddenly inhaling a vile whiff from some chemical factory, and by repeated snortings trying to get it out of his nostrils and lungs. This frame of mind barred all desire of holding further parley with the fellow, even were it but for the purpose of gaining some enlightenment as to his design in approaching him. And yet he was not without natural curiosity to see how such a visitor in the dark would look in broad day.

He espied him the following afternoon in his first dogwatch below, one of the smokers on that forward part of the upper gun deck allotted to the pipe.[58] He recognized him by his general cut and build more than by his round freckled face and glassy eyes of pale blue, veiled with lashes all but white. And yet Billy was a bit uncertain whether indeed it were he—yonder chap about his own age chatting and laughing in freehearted way, leaning against a gun; a genial young fellow enough to look at, and something of a rattlebrain, to all appearance. Rather chubby too for a sailor, even an afterguardsman. In short, the last man in the world, one would think, to be overburdened with thoughts, especially those perilous thoughts that must needs belong to a conspirator in any serious project, or even to the underling of such a conspirator.

Although Billy was not aware of it, the fellow, with a sidelong watchful glance, had perceived Billy first, and then noting that Billy was looking at him, thereupon nodded a familiar sort of friendly recognition as to an old acquaintance, without interrupting the talk he was engaged in with the group of smokers. A day or two afterwards, chancing in the evening promenade on a gun deck to pass Billy, he offered a flying word of good-fellowship, as it were, which by its unexpectedness, and equivocalness under the circumstances, so embarrassed Billy that he knew not how to respond to it, and let it go unnoticed.

Billy was now left more at a loss than before. The ineffectual speculations into which he was led were so disturbingly alien to him that he did his best to smother them. It never entered his mind that here was a matter which, from its extreme questionableness, it was his duty as a loyal bluejacket to report in the proper quarter. And, probably, had such a step been suggested to him, he would have been deterred from taking it by the thought, one of novice magnanimity, that it would savor overmuch of the dirty work of a telltale. He kept the thing to himself. Yet upon one occasion he could not forbear a little disburdening himself to the old Dansker, tempted thereto perhaps by the influence of a balmy night when the ship lay becalmed; the twain, silent for

---

[58]Where smoking was permitted.

the most part, sitting together on deck, their heads propped against the bulwarks. But it was only a partial and anonymous account that Billy gave, the unfounded scruples above referred to preventing full disclosure to anybody. Upon hearing Billy's version, the sage Dansker seemed to divine more than he was told; and after a little meditation, during which his wrinkles were pursed as into a point, quite effacing for the time that quizzing expression his face sometimes wore: "Didn't I say so, Baby Budd?"

"Say what?" demanded Billy.

"Why, *Jemmy Legs* is *down* on you."

"And what," rejoined Billy in amazement, "has *Jemmy Legs* to do with that cracked afterguardsman?"

"Ho, it was an afterguardsman, then. A cat's-paw, a cat's-paw!" And with that exclamation, whether it had reference to a light puff of air[59] just then coming over the calm sea, or a subtler relation to the afterguardsman, there is no telling, the old Merlin gave a twisting wrench with his black teeth at his plug of tobacco, vouchsafing no reply to Billy's impetuous question, though now repeated, for it was his wont to relapse into grim silence when interrogated in skeptical sort as to any of his sententious oracles, not always very clear ones, rather partaking of that obscurity which invests most Delphic[60] deliverances from any quarter.

Long experience had very likely brought this old man to that bitter prudence which never interferes in aught and never gives advice.

XVI

Yes, despite the Dansker's pithy insistence as to the master-at-arms being at the bottom of these strange experiences of Billy on board the *Bellipotent*, the young sailor was ready to ascribe them to almost anybody but the man who, to use Billy's own expression, "always had a pleasant word for him." This is to be wondered at. Yet not so much to be wondered at. In certain matters, some sailors even in mature life remain unsophisticated enough. But a young seafarer of the disposition of our athletic foretopman is much of a child-man. And yet a child's

---

[59]A "cat's paw" meant a light breeze as well as someone manipulated for an underhanded purpose.

[60]The oracle of Apollo at Delphi was notorious for ambiguous prophecies.

utter innocence is but its blank ignorance, and the innocence more or less wanes as intelligence waxes. But in Billy Budd intelligence, such as it was, had advanced while yet his simple-mindedness remained for the most part unaffected. Experience is a teacher indeed; yet did Billy's years make his experience small. Besides, he had none of that intuitive knowledge of the bad which in natures not good or incompletely so foreruns experience, and therefore may pertain, as in some instances it too clearly does pertain, even to youth.

And what could Billy know of man except of man as a mere sailor? And the old-fashioned sailor, the veritable man before the mast, the sailor from boyhood up, he, though indeed of the same species as a landsman, is in some respects singularly distinct from him. The sailor is frankness, the landsman is finesse. Life is not a game with the sailor, demanding the long head—no intricate game of chess where few moves are made in straightforwardness and ends are attained by indirection, an oblique, tedious, barren game hardly worth that poor candle burnt out in playing it.

Yes, as a class, sailors are in character a juvenile race. Even their deviations are marked by juvenility, this more especially holding true with the sailors of Billy's time. Then too, certain things which apply to all sailors do more pointedly operate here and there upon the junior one. Every sailor, too, is accustomed to obey orders without debating them; his life afloat is externally ruled for him; he is not brought into that promiscuous commerce with mankind where unobstructed free agency on equal terms—equal superficially, at least—soon teaches one that unless upon occasion he exercise a distrust keen in proportion to the fairness of the appearance, some foul turn may be served him. A ruled undemonstrative distrustfulness is so habitual, not with business-men so much as with men who know their kind in less shallow relations than business, namely, certain men of the world, that they come at last to employ it all but unconsciously; and some of them would very likely feel real surprise at being charged with it as one of their general characteristics.

XVII

But after the little matter at the mess Billy Budd no more found himself in strange trouble at times about his hammock or his clothes bag or what not. As to that smile that occasionally sunned him, and the pleasant passing word, these were, if not more frequent, yet if anything more pronounced than before.

But for all that, there were certain other demonstrations now. When Claggart's unobserved glance happened to light on belted Billy rolling along the upper gun deck in the leisure of the second dogwatch, exchanging passing broadsides of fun with other young promenaders in the crowd, that glance would follow the cheerful sea Hyperion[61] with a settled meditative and melancholy expression, his eyes strangely suffused with incipient feverish tears. Then would Claggart look like the man of sorrows. Yes, and sometimes the melancholy expression would have in it a touch of soft yearning, as if Claggart could even have loved Billy but for fate and ban. But this was an evanescence, and quickly repented of, as it were, by an immitigable look, pinching and shriveling the visage into the momentary semblance of a wrinkled walnut. But sometimes catching sight in advance of the foretopman coming in his direction, he would, upon their nearing, step aside a little to let him pass, dwelling upon Billy for the moment with the glittering dental satire of a Guise.[62] But upon any abrupt unforeseen encounter a red light would flash forth from his eye like a spark from an anvil in a dusk smithy. That quick, fierce light was a strange one, darted from orbs which in repose were of a color nearest approaching a deeper violet, the softest of shades.

Though some of these caprices of the pit could not but be observed by their object, yet were they beyond the construing of such a nature. And the thews of Billy were hardly compatible with that sort of sensitive spiritual organization which in some cases instinctively conveys to ignorant innocence an admonition of the proximity of the malign. He thought the master-at-arms acted in a manner rather queer at times. That was all. But the occasional frank air and pleasant word went for what they purported to be, the young sailor never having heard as yet of the "too fair-spoken man."

Had the foretopman been conscious of having done or said anything to provoke the ill will of the official, it would have been different with him, and his sight might have been purged if not sharpened. As it was, innocence was his blinder.

---

[61]In Greek legend, a handsome youth beloved of Apollo.
[62]The dukes of Guise were known less for satire than for conspiracy against the French crown.

So was it with him in yet another matter. Two minor officers, the armorer and captain of the hold, with whom he had never exchanged a word, his position in the ship not bringing him into contact with them, these men now for the first began to cast upon Billy, when they chanced to encounter him, that peculiar glance which evidences that the man from whom it comes has been some way tampered with, and to the prejudice of him upon whom the glance lights. Never did it occur to Billy as a thing to be noted or a thing suspicious, though he well knew the fact, that the armorer and captain of the hold, with the ship's yeoman, apothecary, and others of that grade, were by naval usage messmates of the master-at-arms, men with ears convenient to his confidential tongue.

But the general popularity that came from our Handsome Sailor's manly forwardness upon occasion and irresistible good nature, indicating no mental superiority tending to excite an invidious feeling, this good will on the part of most of his shipmates made him the less to concern himself about such mute aspects toward him as those whereto allusion has just been made, aspects he could not so fathom as to infer their whole import.

As to the afterguardsman, though Billy for reasons already given necessarily saw little of him, yet when the two did happen to meet, invariably came the fellow's offhand cheerful recognition, sometimes accompanied by a passing pleasant word or two. Whatever that equivocal young person's original design may really have been, or the design of which he might have been the deputy, certain it was from his manner upon these occasions that he had wholly dropped it.

It was as if his precocity of crookedness (and every vulgar villain is precocious) had for once deceived him, and the man he had sought to entrap as a simpleton had through his very simplicity ignominiously baffled him.

But shrewd ones may opine that it was hardly possible for Billy to refrain from going up to the afterguardsman and bluntly demanding to know his purpose in the initial interview so abruptly closed in the forechains. Shrewd ones may also think it but natural in Billy to set about sounding some of the other impressed men of the ship in order to discover what basis, if any, there was for the emissary's obscure suggestions as to plotting disaffection aboard. Yes, shrewd ones may so think. But something more, or rather something else than mere shrewdness is perhaps needful for the due understanding of such a character as Billy Budd's.

As to Claggart, the monomania in the man—if that indeed it were—

as involuntarily disclosed by starts in the manifestations detailed, yet in general covered over by his self-contained and rational demeanor; this, like a subterranean fire, was eating its way deeper and deeper in him. Something decisive must come of it.

XVIII

After the mysterious interview in the forechains, the one so abruptly ended there by Billy, nothing especially germane to the story occurred until the events now about to be narrated.

Elsewhere it has been said that in the lack of frigates (of course better sailers than line-of-battle ships) in the English squadron up the Straits[63] at that period, the *Bellipotent* 74 was occasionally employed not only as an available substitute for a scout, but at times on detached service of more important kind. This was not alone because of her sailing qualities, not common in a ship of her rate, but quite as much, probably, that the character of her commander, it was thought, specially adapted him for any duty where under unforeseen difficulties a prompt initiative might have to be taken in some matter demanding knowledge and ability in addition to those qualities implied in good seamanship. It was on an expedition of the latter sort, a somewhat distant one, and when the *Bellipotent* was almost at her furthest remove from the fleet, that in the latter part of an afternoon watch she unexpectedly came in sight of a ship of the enemy. It proved to be a frigate. The latter, perceiving through the glass that the weight of men and metal would be heavily against her, invoking her light heels crowded sail to get away. After a chase urged almost against hope and lasting until about the middle of the first dogwatch, she signally succeeded in effecting her escape.

Not long after the pursuit had been given up, and ere the excitement incident thereto had altogether waned away, the master-at-arms, ascending from his cavernous sphere, made his appearance cap in hand by the mainmast respectfully waiting the notice of Captain Vere, then solitary walking the weather side of the quarter-deck, doubtless somewhat chafed at the failure of the pursuit. The spot where Claggart stood was the place allotted to men of lesser grades seeking some more particular interview either with the officer of the deck or the captain him-

---

[63]The Straits of Gibraltar; the squadron thus employed is the Mediterranean fleet.

self. But from the latter it was not often that a sailor or petty officer of those days would seek a hearing; only some exceptional cause would, according to established custom, have warranted that.

Presently, just as the commander, absorbed in his reflections, was on the point of turning aft in his promenade, he became sensible of Claggart's presence, and saw the doffed cap held in deferential expectancy. Here be it said that Captain Vere's personal knowledge of this petty officer had only begun at the time of the ship's last sailing from home, Claggart then for the first, in transfer from a ship detained for repairs, supplying on board the *Bellipotent* the place of a previous master-at-arms disabled and ashore.

No sooner did the commander observe who it was that now deferentially stood awaiting his notice than a peculiar expression came over him. It was not unlike that which uncontrollably will flit across the countenance of one at unawares encountering a person who, though known to him indeed, has hardly been long enough known for thorough knowledge, but something in whose aspect nevertheless now for the first provokes a vaguely repellent distaste. But coming to a stand and resuming much of his wonted official manner, save that a sort of impatience lurked in the intonation of the opening word, he said, "Well? What is it, Master-at-arms?"

With the air of a subordinate grieved at the necessity of being a messenger of ill tidings, and while conscientiously determined to be frank yet equally resolved upon shunning overstatement, Claggart at this invitation, or rather summons to disburden, spoke up. What he said, conveyed in the language of no uneducated man, was to the effect following, if not altogether in these words, namely, that during the chase and preparations for the possible encounter he had seen enough to convince him that at least one sailor aboard was a dangerous character in a ship mustering some who not only had taken a guilty part in the late serious troubles, but others also who, like the man in question, had entered His Majesty's service under another form than enlistment.

At this point Captain Vere with some impatience interrupted him: "Be direct, man; say *impressed men*."

Claggart made a gesture of subservience, and proceeded. Quite lately he (Claggart) had begun to suspect that on the gun decks some sort of movement prompted by the sailor in question was covertly going on, but he had not thought himself warranted in reporting the suspicion so long as it remained indistinct. But from what he had that afternoon observed in the man referred to, the suspicion of something clandestine going on had advanced to a point less removed from certainty. He deeply felt, he added, the serious responsibility assumed in making a report involving such possible consequences to the individual mainly concerned, besides tending to augment those natural anxieties which every naval commander must feel in view of extraordinary outbreaks so recent as those which, he sorrowfully said it, it needed not to name.[64]

Now at the first broaching of the matter Captain Vere, taken by surprise, could not wholly dissemble his disquietude. But as Claggart went on, the former's aspect changed into restiveness under something in the testifier's manner in giving his testimony. However, he refrained from interrupting him. And Claggart, continuing, concluded with this: "God forbid, your honor, that the *Bellipotent's* should be the experience of the——"

"Never mind that!" here peremptorily broke in the superior, his face altering with anger, instinctively divining the ship that the other was about to name, one in which the Nore Mutiny had assumed a singularly tragical character that for a time jeopardized the life of its commander. Under the circumstances he was indignant at the purposed allusion. When the commissioned officers themselves were on all occasions very heedful how they referred to the recent events in the fleet, for a petty officer unnecessarily to allude to them in the presence of his captain, this struck him as a most immodest presumption. Besides, to his quick sense of self-respect it even looked under the circumstances something like an attempt to alarm him. Nor at first was he without some surprise that one who so far as he had hitherto come under his notice had shown considerable tact in his function should in this particular evince such lack of it.

But these thoughts and kindred dubious ones flitting across his mind were suddenly replaced by an intuitional surmise which, though as yet obscure in form, served practically to affect his reception of the ill tidings. Certain it is that, long versed in everything pertaining to the complicated gun-deck life, which like every other form of life has its secret mines and dubious side, the side popularly disclaimed, Captain Vere did not permit himself to be unduly disturbed by the general tenor of his subordinate's report.

Furthermore, if in view of recent events prompt action should be taken at the first palpable sign of recurring insubordination, for all that, not judicious would it be, he thought, to keep the idea of lingering disaffection alive by undue forwardness in crediting an informer, even

---

[64]The Great Mutinies.

if his own subordinate and charged among other things with police surveillance of the crew. This feeling would not perhaps have so prevailed with him were it not that upon a prior occasion the patriotic zeal officially evinced by Claggart had somewhat irritated him as appearing rather supersensible[65] and strained. Furthermore, something even in the official's self-possessed and somewhat ostentatious manner in making his specifications strangely reminded him of a bandsman, a perjurous witness in a capital case before a court-martial ashore of which when a lieutenant he (Captain Vere) had been a member.

Now the peremptory check given to Claggart in the matter of the arrested allusion was quickly followed up by this: "You say that there is at least one dangerous man aboard. Name him."

"William Budd, a foretopman, your honor."

"William Budd!" repeated Captain Vere with unfeigned astonishment. "And mean you the man that Lieutenant Ratcliffe took from the merchantman not very long ago, the young fellow who seems to be so popular with the men—Billy, the Handsome Sailor, as they call him?"

"The same, your honor; but for all his youth and good looks, a deep one. Not for nothing does he insinuate himself into the good will of his shipmates, since at the least they will at a pinch say—all hands will—a good word for him, and at all hazards. Did Lieutenant Ratcliffe happen to tell your honor of that adroit fling of Budd's, jumping up in the cutter's bow under the merchantman's stern when he was being taken off? It is even masked by that sort of good-humored air that at heart he resents his impressment. You have but noted his fair cheek. A mantrap may be under the ruddy-tipped daisies."

Now the Handsome Sailor as a signal figure among the crew had naturally enough attracted the captain's attention from the first. Though in general not very demonstrative to his officers, he had congratulated Lieutenant Ratcliffe upon his good fortune in lighting on such a fine specimen of the *genus homo*, who in the nude might have posed for a statue of young Adam before the Fall. As to Billy's adieu to the ship *Rights-of-Man*, which the boarding lieutenant had indeed reported to him, but, in a deferential way, more as a good story than aught else, Captain Vere, though mistakenly understanding it as a satiric sally, had but thought so much the better of the impressed man for it; as a military sailor, admiring the spirit that could take an arbitrary enlistment so merrily and sensibly. The foretopman's conduct,

---

[65]Oversensitive.

too, so far as it had fallen under the captain's notice, had confirmed the first happy augury, while the new recruit's qualities as a "sailor-man" seemed to be such that he had thought of recommending him to the executive officer for promotion to a place that would more frequently bring him under his own observation, namely, the captaincy of the mizzentop, replacing there in the starboard watch a man not so young whom partly for that reason he deemed less fitted for the post. Be it parenthesized here that since the mizzentopmen have not to handle such breadths of heavy canvas as the lower sails on the mainmast and foremast, a young man if of the right stuff not only seems best adapted to duty there, but in fact is generally selected for the captaincy of that top, and the company under him are light hands and often but striplings. In sum, Captain Vere had from the beginning deemed Billy Budd to be what in the naval parlance of the time was called a "King's bargain": that is to say, for His Britannic Majesty's navy a capital investment at small outlay or none at all.

After a brief pause, during which the reminiscences above mentioned passed vividly through his mind and he weighed the import of Claggart's last suggestion conveyed in the phrase "mantrap under the daisies," and the more he weighed it the less reliance he felt in the informer's good faith, suddenly he turned upon him and in a low voice demanded: "Do you come to me, Master-at-arms, with so foggy a tale? As to Budd, cite me an act or spoken word of his confirmatory of what you in general charge against him. Stay," drawing nearer to him; "heed what you speak. Just now, and in a case like this, there is a yardarm-end for the false witness."

"Ah, your honor!" sighed Claggart, mildly shaking his shapely head as in sad deprecation of such unmerited severity of tone. Then, bridling—erecting himself as in virtuous self-assertion—he circumstantially alleged certain words and acts which collectively, if credited, led to presumptions mortally inculpating Budd. And for some of these averments, he added, substantiating proof was not far.

With gray eyes impatient and distrustful essaying to fathom to the bottom Claggart's calm violet ones, Captain Vere again heard him out; then for the moment stood ruminating. The mood he evinced, Claggart—himself for the time liberated from the other's scrutiny—steadily regarded with a look difficult to render: a look curious of the operation of his tactics, a look such as might have been that of the spokesman of the envious children of Jacob deceptively imposing upon the troubled patriarch the blood-dyed coat of young Joseph.

Though something exceptional in the moral quality of Captain Vere made him, in earnest encounter with a fellow man, a veritable touch-stone of that man's essential nature, yet now as to Claggart and what was really going on in him his feeling partook less of intuitional convic-tion than of strong suspicion clogged by strange dubieties. The per-plexity he evinced proceeded less from aught touching the man informed against—as Claggart doubtless opined—than from consider-ations how best to act in regard to the informer. At first, indeed, he was naturally for summoning that substantiation of his allegations which Claggart said was at hand. But such a proceeding would result in the matter at once getting abroad, which in the present stage of it, he thought, might undesirably affect the ship's company. If Claggart was a false witness—that closed the affair. And therefore, before trying the accusation, he would first practically test the accuser; and he thought this could be done in a quiet, undemonstrative way.

The measure he determined upon involved a shifting of the scene, a transfer to a place less exposed to observation than the broad quarter-deck. For although the few gun-room officers there at the time had, in due observance of naval etiquette, withdrawn to leeward the moment Captain Vere had begun his promenade on the deck's weather side; and though during the colloquy with Claggart they of course ventured not to diminish the distance; and though throughout the interview Captain Vere's voice was far from high, and Claggart's silvery and low; and the wind in the cordage and the wash of the sea helped the more to put them beyond earshot; nevertheless, the interview's continuance already had attracted observation from some topmen aloft and other sailors in the waist or further forward.

Having determined upon his measures, Captain Vere forthwith took action. Abruptly turning to Claggart, he asked. "Master-at-arms, is it now Budd's watch aloft?"

"No, your honor."

Whereupon, "Mr. Wilkes!" summoning the nearest midshipman. "Tell Albert to come to me." Albert was the captain's hammock-boy, a sort of sea valet in whose discretion and fidelity his master had much confidence. The lad appeared.

"You know Budd, the foretopman?"

"I do, sir."

"Go find him. It is his watch off. Manage to tell him out of earshot that he is wanted aft. Contrive it that he speaks to nobody. Keep him in talk yourself. And not till you get well aft here, not till then let him know that the place where he is wanted is my cabin. You understand.

Go.—Master-at-arms, show yourself on the decks below, and when you think it time for Albert to be coming with his man, stand by quietly to follow the sailor in."

XIX

Now when the foretopman found himself in the cabin, closeted there, as it were, with the captain and Claggart, he was surprised enough. But it was a surprise unaccompanied by apprehension or distrust. To an immature nature essentially honest and humane, forewarning intimations of subtler danger from one's kind come tardily if at all. The only thing that took shape in the young sailor's mind was this: Yes, the captain, I have always thought, looks kindly upon me. Wonder if he's going to make me his coxswain. I should like that. And may be now he is going to ask the master-at-arms about me.

"Shut the door there, sentry," said the commander; "stand without, and let nobody come in.—Now, Master-at-arms, tell this man to his face what you told of him to me," and stood prepared to scrutinize the mutually confronting visages.

With the measured step and calm collected air of an asylum physician approaching in the public hall some patient beginning to show indications of a coming paroxysm, Claggart deliberately advanced within short range of Billy and, mesmerically looking him in the eye, briefly recapitulated the accusation.

Not at first did Billy take it in. When he did, the rose-tan of his cheek looked struck as by white leprosy. He stood like one impaled and gagged. Meanwhile the accuser's eyes, removing not as yet from the blue dilated ones, underwent a phenomenal change, their wonted rich violet color blurring into a muddy purple. Those lights of human intelligence, losing human expression, were gelidly protruding like the alien eyes of certain uncatalogued creatures of the deep. The first mesmeristic glance was one of serpent fascination; the last was as the paralyzing lurch of the torpedo fish.

"Speak, man!" said Captain Vere to the transfixed one, struck by his aspect even more than by Claggart's. "Speak! Defend yourself!" Which appeal caused but a strange dumb gesturing and gurgling in Billy; amazement at such an accusation so suddenly sprung on inexperienced nonage; this, and, it may be, horror of the accuser's eyes, serving to bring out his lurking defect and in this instance for the time intensifying it into a convulsed tongue-tie; while the intent head and entire form straining in an agony of ineffectual eagerness to obey the injunction to speak and defend himself, gave an expression to the face like that of a condemned vestal priestess in the moment of being buried alive, and in the first struggle against suffocation.

Though at the time Captain Vere was quite ignorant of Billy's liability to vocal impediment, he now immediately divined it, since vividly Billy's aspect recalled to him that of a bright young schoolmate of his whom he had once seen struck by much the same startling impotence in the act of eagerly rising in the class to be foremost in response to a testing question put to it by the master. Going close up to the young sailor, and laying a soothing hand on his shoulder, he said, "There is no hurry, my boy. Take your time, take your time." Contrary to the effect intended, these words so fatherly in tone, doubtless touching Billy's heart to the quick, prompted yet more violent efforts at utterance— efforts soon ending for the time in confirming the paralysis, and bringing to his face an expression which was as a crucifixion to behold. The next instant, quick as the flame from a discharged cannon at night, his right arm shot out, and Claggart dropped to the deck. Whether intentionally or but owing to the young athlete's superior height, the blow had taken effect full upon the forehead, so shapely and intellectual-looking a feature in the master-at-arms; so that the body fell over lengthwise, like a heavy plank tilted from erectness. A gasp or two, and he lay motionless.

"Fated boy," breathed Captain Vere in tone so low as to be almost a whisper, "what have you done! But here, help me."

The twain raised the felled one from the loins up into a sitting position. The spare form flexibly acquiesced, but inertly. It was like handling a dead snake. They lowered it back. Regaining erectness, Captain Vere with one hand covering his face stood to all appearance as impassive as the object at his feet. Was he absorbed in taking in all the bearings of the event and what was best not only now at once to be done, but also in the sequel? Slowly he uncovered his face; and the effect was as if the moon emerging from eclipse should reappear with quite another aspect than that which had gone into hiding. The father in him, manifested towards Billy thus far in the scene, was replaced by the military disciplinarian. In his official tone he bade the foretopman retire to a stateroom aft (pointing it out), and there remain till thence summoned. This order Billy in silence mechanically obeyed. Then going to the cabin door where it opened on the quarter-deck, Captain Vere said to the sentry without, "Tell somebody to send Albert here."

When the lad appeared, his master so contrived it that he should not catch sight of the prone one. "Albert," he said to him, "tell the surgeon I wish to see him. You need not come back till called."

When the surgeon entered—a self-poised character of that grave sense and experience that hardly anything could take him aback— Captain Vere advanced to meet him, thus unconsciously intercepting his view of Claggart, and, interrupting the other's wonted ceremonious salutation, said, "Nay. Tell me how it is with yonder man," directing his attention to the prostrate one.

The surgeon looked, and for all his self-command somewhat started at the abrupt revelation. On Claggart's always pallid complexion, thick black blood was now oozing from nostril and ear. To the gazer's professional eye it was unmistakably no living man that he saw.

"Is it so, then?" said Captain Vere, intently watching him. "I thought it. But verify it." Whereupon the customary tests confirmed the surgeon's first glance, who now, looking up in unfeigned concern, cast a look of intense inquisitiveness upon his superior. But Captain Vere, with one hand to his brow, was standing motionless. Suddenly, catching the surgeon's arm convulsively, he exclaimed, pointing down to the body, "It is the divine judgment on Ananias![66] Look!"

Disturbed by the excited manner he had never before observed in the *Bellipotent*'s captain, and as yet wholly ignorant of the affair, the prudent surgeon nevertheless held his peace, only again looking an earnest interrogatory as to what it was that had resulted in such a tragedy.

But Captain Vere was now again motionless, standing absorbed in thought. Again starting, he vehemently exclaimed, "Struck dead by an angel of God! Yet the angel must hang!"

At these passionate interjections, mere incoherences to the listener as yet unapprised of the antecedents, the surgeon was profoundly discomposed. But now, as recollecting himself, Captain Vere in less passionate tone briefly related the circumstances leading up to the event. "But come; we must dispatch," he added. "Help me to remove him" (meaning the body) "to yonder compartment," designating one opposite that where the foretopman remained immured. Anew disturbed by a request that, as implying a desire for secrecy, seemed unaccountably strange to him, there was nothing for the subordinate to do but comply.

---

[66]Ananias is struck dead for perjury in Acts 5.

"Go now," said Captain Vere with something of his wonted manner. "Go now. I presently shall call a drumhead court.[67] Tell the lieutenants what has happened, and tell Mr. Mordant" (meaning the captain of marines), "and charge them to keep the matter to themselves."

XX

Full of disquietude and misgiving, the surgeon left the cabin. Was Captain Vere suddenly affected in his mind, or was it but a transient excitement, brought about by so strange and extraordinary a tragedy? As to the drumhead court, it struck the surgeon as impolitic, if nothing more. The thing to do, he thought, was to place Billy Budd in confinement, and in a way dictated by usage, and postpone further action in so extraordinary a case to such time as they should rejoin the squadron, and then refer it to the admiral. He recalled the unwonted agitation of Captain Vere and his excited exclamations, so at variance with his normal manner. Was he unhinged?

But assuming that he is, it is not so susceptible of proof. What then can the surgeon do? No more trying situation is conceivable than that of an officer subordinate under a captain whom he suspects to be not mad, indeed, but yet not quite unaffected in his intellects. To argue his order to him would be insolence. To resist him would be mutiny.

In obedience to Captain Vere, he communicated what had happened to the lieutenants and captain of marines, saying nothing as to the captain's state. They fully shared his own surprise and concern. Like him too, they seemed to think that such a matter should be referred to the admiral.[68]

XXI

Who in the rainbow can draw the line where the violet tint ends and the orange tint begins? Distinctly we see the difference of the colors, but where exactly does the one first blendingly enter into the other? So

---

[67]A summary court-martial.

[68]Normally, any criminal offense at sea requiring punishment more severe than one dozen lashes was tried by a court-martial called by the admiral of the fleet. Such was the naval law of the time, but it was ignored in practice by many a commander.

with sanity and insanity. In pronounced cases there is no question about them. But in some supposed cases, in various degrees supposedly less pronounced, to draw the exact line of demarcation few will undertake, though for a fee becoming considerate some professional experts will. There is nothing namable but that some men will, or undertake to, do it for pay.

Whether Captain Vere, as the surgeon professionally and privately surmised, was really the sudden victim of any degree of aberration, every one must determine for himself by such light as this narrative may afford.

That the unhappy event which has been narrated could not have happened at a worse juncture was but too true. For it was close on the heel of the suppressed insurrections, an aftertime very critical to naval authority, demanding from every English sea commander two qualities not readily interfusable—prudence and rigor. Moreover, there was something crucial in the case.

In the jugglery of circumstances preceding and attending the event on board the *Bellipotent*, and in the light of that martial code whereby it was formally to be judged, innocence and guilt personified in Claggart and Budd in effect changed places. In a legal view the apparent victim of the tragedy was he who had sought to victimize a man blameless; and the indisputable deed of the latter, navally regarded, constituted the most heinous of military crimes. Yet more. The essential right and wrong involved in the matter, the clearer that might be, so much the worse for the responsibility of a loyal sea commander, inasmuch as he was not authorized to determine the matter on that primitive basis.

Small wonder then that the *Bellipotent*'s captain, though in general a man of rapid decision, felt that circumspectness not less than promptitude was necessary. Until he could decide upon his course, and in each detail; and not only so, but until the concluding measure was upon the point of being enacted, he deemed it advisable, in view of all the circumstances, to guard as much as possible against publicity. Here he may or may not have erred. Certain it is, however, that subsequently in the confidential talk of more than one or two gun rooms and cabins he was not a little criticized by some officers, a fact imputed by his friends and vehemently by his cousin Jack Denton to professional jealousy of Starry Vere. Some imaginative ground for invidious comment there was. The maintenance of secrecy in the matter, the confining all knowledge of it for a time to the place where the homicide occurred, the quarter-deck cabin; in these particulars lurked some resemblance to the policy adopted in those tragedies of the palace which have occurred more than once in the capital[69] founded by Peter the Barbarian.

The case indeed was such that fain would the *Bellipotent*'s captain have deferred taking any action whatever respecting it further than to keep the foretopman a close prisoner till the ship rejoined the squadron and then submitting the matter to the judgment of his admiral. But a true military officer is in one particular like a true monk. Not with more of self-abnegation will the latter keep his vows of monastic obedience than the former his vows of allegiance to martial duty.

Feeling that unless quick action was taken on it, the deed of the foretopman, so soon as it should be known on the gun decks, would tend to awaken any slumbering embers of the Nore among the crew, a sense of the urgency of the case overruled in Captain Vere every other consideration. But though a conscientious disciplinarian, he was no lover of authority for mere authority's sake. Very far was he from embracing opportunities for monopolizing to himself the perils of moral responsibility, none at least that could properly be referred to an official superior or shared with him by his official equals or even subordinates. So thinking, he was glad it would not be at variance with usage[70] to turn the matter over to a summary court of his own officers, reserving to himself, as the one on whom the ultimate accountability would rest, the right of maintaining a supervision of it, or formally or informally interposing at need. Accordingly a drumhead court was summarily convened, he electing the individuals composing it: the first lieutenant, the captain of marines, and the sailing master.

In associating an officer of marines with the sea lieutenant and the sailing master in a case having to do with a sailor, the commander perhaps deviated from general custom. He was prompted thereto by the circumstance that he took that soldier to be a judicious person, thoughtful, and not altogether incapable of grappling with a difficult case unprecedented in his prior experience. Yet even as to him he was not without some latent misgiving, for withal he was an extremely good-natured man, an enjoyer of his dinner, a sound sleeper, and inclined to obesity—a man who though he would always maintain his manhood in battle might not prove altogether reliable in a moral dilemma involving aught of the tragic. As to the first lieutenant and the sailing master, Captain Vere could not but be aware that though honest

---

[69]St. Petersburg, founded by Czar Peter the Great of Russia.
[70]Actually this was, as the surgeon and the other officers think, "at variance with usage," though whether Melville knew this is uncertain.

natures, of approved gallantry upon occasion, their intelligence was mostly confined to the matter of active seamanship and the fighting demands of their profession.

The court was held in the same cabin where the unfortunate affair had taken place. This cabin, the commander's, embraced the 'entire area under the poop deck. Aft, and on either side, was a small stateroom, the one now temporarily a jail and the other a dead-house,[71] and a yet smaller compartment, leaving a space between expanding forward into a goodly oblong of length coinciding with the ship's beam. A skylight of moderate dimension was overhead, and at each end of the oblong space were two sashed porthole windows easily convertible back into embrasures for short carronades.[72]

All being quickly in readiness, Billy Budd was arraigned, Captain Vere necessarily appearing as the sole witness in the case, and as such temporarily sinking his rank, though singularly maintaining it in a matter apparently trivial, namely, that he testified from the ship's weather side, with that object having caused the court to sit on the lee side.[73] Concisely he narrated all that had led up to the catastrophe, omitting nothing in Claggart's accusation and deposing as to the manner in which the prisoner had received it. At this testimony the three officers glanced with no little surprise at Billy Budd, the last man they would have suspected either of the mutinous design alleged by Claggart or the undeniable deed he himself had done. The first lieutenant, taking judicial primacy and turning toward the prisoner, said, "Captain Vere has spoken. Is it or is it not as Captain Vere says?"

In response came syllables not so much impeded in the utterance as might have been anticipated. They were these: "Captain Vere tells the truth. It is just as Captain Vere says, but it is not as the master-at-arms said. I have eaten the King's bread and I am true to the King."

"I believe you, my man," said the witness, his voice indicating a suppressed emotion not otherwise betrayed.

"God will bless you for that, your honor!" not without stammering said Billy, and all but broke down. But immediately he was recalled to self-control by another question, to which with the same emotional difficulty of utterance he said, "No, there was no malice between us. I never bore malice against the master-at-arms. I am sorry that he is

---

[71]Morgue.

[72]Cannon.

[73]The "weather" side of a ship—the side from which the wind is blowing—sits higher than the "lee" side; Vere thus stands looking down at the court.

dead. I did not mean to kill him. Could I have used my tongue I would not have struck him. But he foully lied to my face and in presence of my captain, and I had to say something, and I could only say it with a blow, God help me!"

In the impulsive aboveboard manner of the frank one the court saw confirmed all that was implied in words that just previously had perplexed them, coming as they did from the testifier to the tragedy and promptly following Billy's impassioned disclaimer of mutinous intent—Captain Vere's words, "I believe you, my man."

Next it was asked of him whether he knew of or suspected aught savoring of incipient trouble (meaning mutiny, though the explicit term was avoided) going on in any section of the ship's company.

The reply lingered. This was naturally imputed by the court to the same vocal embarrassment which had retarded or obstructed previous answers. But in main it was otherwise here, the question immediately recalling to Billy's mind the interview with the afterguardsman in the forechains. But an innate repugnance to playing a part at all approaching that of an informer against one's own shipmates—the same erring sense of uninstructed honor which had stood in the way of his reporting the matter at the time, though as a loyal man-of-war's man it was incumbent on him, and failure so to do, if charged against him and proven, would have subjected him to the heaviest of penalties[74]; this, with the blind feeling now his that nothing really was being hatched, prevailed with him. When the answer came it was a negative.

"One question more," said the officer of marines, now first speaking and with a troubled earnestness. "You tell us that what the master-at-arms said against you was a lie. Now why should he have so lied, so maliciously lied, since you declare there was no malice between you?"

At that question, unintentionally touching on a spiritual sphere wholly obscure to Billy's thoughts, he was nonplussed, evincing a confusion indeed that some observers, such as can readily be imagined, would have construed into involuntary evidence of hidden guilt. Nevertheless, he strove some way to answer, but all at once relinquished the vain endeavor, at the same time turning an appealing glance towards Captain Vere as deeming him his best helper and friend. Captain Vere, who had been seated for a time, rose to his feet, addressing the interrogator. "The question you put to him comes naturally enough. But how can he rightly answer it?—or anybody else, unless indeed it be

---

[74]Concealing a mutinous plot was a hanging offense.

he who lies within there," designating the compartment where lay the corpse. "But the prone one there will not rise to our summons. In effect, though, as it seems to me, the point you make is hardly material. Quite aside from any conceivable motive actuating the master-at-arms, and irrespective of the provocation to the blow, a martial court must needs in the present case confine its attention to the blow's consequence, which consequence justly is to be deemed not otherwise than as the striker's deed."

This utterance, the full significance of which it was not at all likely that Billy took in, nevertheless caused him to turn a wistful interrogative look toward the speaker, a look in its dumb expressiveness not unlike that which a dog of generous breed might turn upon his master, seeking in his face some elucidation of a previous gesture ambiguous to the canine intelligence. Nor was the same utterance without marked effect upon the three officers, more especially the soldier. Couched in it seemed to them a meaning unanticipated, involving a prejudgment on the speaker's part. It served to augment a mental disturbance previously evident enough.

The soldier once more spoke, in a tone of suggestive dubiety addressing at once his associates and Captain Vere: "Nobody is present— none of the ship's company, I mean—who might shed lateral light, if any is to be had, upon what remains mysterious in this matter."

"That is thoughtfully put," said Captain Vere; "I see your drift. Ay, there is a mystery; but, to use a scriptural phrase, it is a 'mystery of iniquity,' a matter for psychologic theologians to discuss. But what has a military court to do with it? Not to add that for us any possible investigation of it is cut off by the lasting tongue-tie of—him—in yonder," again designating the mortuary stateroom. "The prisoner's deed—with that alone we have to do."

To this, and particularly the closing reiteration, the marine soldier, knowing not how aptly to reply, sadly abstained from saying aught. The first lieutenant, who at the outset had not unnaturally assumed primacy in the court, now overrulingly instructed by a glance from Captain Vere, a glance more effective than words, resumed that primacy. Turning to the prisoner, "Budd," he said, and scarce in equable tones, "Budd, if you have aught further to say for yourself, say it now."

Upon this the young sailor turned another quick glance toward Captain Vere; then, as taking a hint from that aspect, a hint confirming his own instinct that silence was now best, replied to the lieutenant, "I have said all, sir."

The marine—the same who had been the sentinel without the cabin door at the time that the foretopman, followed by the master-at-arms, entered it—he, standing by the sailor throughout these judicial proceedings, was now directed to take him back to the after compartment originally assigned to the prisoner and his custodian. As the twain disappeared from view, the three officers, as partially liberated from some inward constraint associated with Billy's mere presence, simultaneously stirred in their seats. They exchanged looks of troubled indecision, yet feeling that decide they must and without long delay. For Captain Vere, he for the time stood—unconsciously with his back toward them, apparently in one of his absent fits—gazing out from a sashed porthole to windward upon the monotonous blank of the twilight sea. But the court's silence continuing, broken only at moments by brief consultations, in low earnest tones, this served to arouse him and energize him. Turning, he to-and-fro paced the cabin athwart; in the returning ascent to windward climbing the slant deck in the ship's lee roll, without knowing it symbolizing thus in his action a mind resolute to surmount difficulties even if against primitive instincts strong as the wind and the sea. Presently he came to a stand before the three. After scanning their faces he stood less as mustering his thoughts for expression than as one inly deliberating how best to put them to well-meaning men not intellectually mature, men with whom it was necessary to demonstrate certain principles that were axioms to himself. Similar impatience as to talking is perhaps one reason that deters some minds from addressing any popular assemblies.

When speak he did, something, both in the substance of what he said and his manner of saying it, showed the influence of unshared studies modifying and tempering the practical training of an active career. This, along with his phraseology, now and then was suggestive of the grounds whereon rested that imputation of a certain pedantry socially alleged against him by certain naval men of wholly practical cast, captains who nevertheless would frankly concede that His Majesty's navy mustered no more efficient officer of their grade than Starry . Vere.

What he said was to this effect: "Hitherto I have been but the witness, little more; and I should hardly think now to take another tone, that of your coadjutor for the time, did I not perceive in you—at the crisis too—a troubled hesitancy, proceeding, I doubt not, from the clash of military duty with moral scruple—scruple vitalized by compassion. For the compassion, how can I otherwise than share it? But, mindful of paramount obligations, I strive against scruples that may tend to enervate decision. Not, gentlemen, that I hide from myself that the case is an exceptional one. Speculatively regarded, it well might be referred to a jury of casuists. But for us here, acting not as casuists or moralists, it is a case practical, and under martial law practically to be dealt with. "But your scruples: do they move as in a dusk? Challenge them. Make them advance and declare themselves. Come now; do they import something like this: If, mindless of palliating circumstances, we are bound to regard the death of the master-at-arms as the prisoner's deed, then does that deed constitute a capital crime whereof the penalty is a mortal one. But in natural justice is nothing but the prisoner's overt act to be considered? How can we adjudge to summary and shameful death a fellow creature innocent before God, and whom we feel to be so?—Does that state it aright? You sign sad assent. Well, I too feel that, the full force of that. It is Nature. But do these buttons that we wear attest that our allegiance is to Nature? No, to the King. Though the ocean, which is inviolate Nature primeval, though this be the element where we move and have our being as sailors, yet as the King's officers lies our duty in a sphere correspondingly natural? So little is that true, that in receiving our commissions we in the most important regards ceased to be natural free agents. When war is declared are we the commissioned fighters previously consulted? We fight at command. If our judgments approve the war, that is but coincidence. So in other particulars. So now. For suppose condemnation to follow these present proceedings. Would it be so much we ourselves that would condemn as it would be martial law operating through us? For that law and the rigor of it, we are not responsible. Our vowed responsibility is in this: That however pitilessly that law may operate in any instances, we nevertheless adhere to it and administer it.

"But the exceptional in the matter moves the hearts within you. Even so too is mine moved. But let not warm hearts betray heads that should be cool. Ashore in a criminal case, will an upright judge allow himself off the bench to be waylaid by some tender kinswoman of the accused seeking to touch him with her tearful plea? Well, the heart here, sometimes the feminine in man, is as that piteous woman, and hard though it be, she must here be ruled out."

He paused, earnestly studying them for a moment; then resumed.

"But something in your aspect seems to urge that it is not solely the heart that moves in you, but also the conscience, the private conscience. But tell me whether or not, occupying the position we do, private conscience should not yield to that imperial one formulated in the code[75] under which alone we officially proceed?"

---

[75]The Articles of War.

Here the three men moved in their seats, less convinced than agitated by the course of an argument troubling but the more the spontaneous conflict within.

Perceiving which, the speaker paused for a moment; then abruptly changing his tone, went on.

"To steady us a bit, let us recur to the facts.—In wartime at sea a man-of-war's man strikes his superior in grade, and the blow kills. Apart from its effect the blow itself is, according to the Articles of War, a capital crime. Furthermore——"

"Ay, sir," emotionally broke in the officer of marines, "in one sense it was. But surely Budd purposed neither mutiny nor homicide."

"Surely not, my good man. And before a court less arbitrary and more merciful than a martial one, that plea would largely extenuate. At the Last Assizes[76] it shall acquit. But how here? We proceed under the law of the Mutiny Act. In feature no child can resemble his father more than that Act resembles in spirit the thing from which it derives—War. In His Majesty's service—in this ship, indeed—there are Englishmen forced to fight for the King against their will. Against their conscience, for aught we know. Though as their fellow creatures some of us may appreciate their position, yet as navy officers what reck we of it? Still less recks the enemy. Our impressed men he would fain cut down in the same swath with our volunteers. As regards the enemy's naval conscripts, some of whom may even share our own abhorrence of the regicidal[77] French Directory, it is the same on our side. War looks but to the frontage, the appearance. And the Mutiny Act, War's child, takes after the father. Budd's intent or non-intent is nothing to the purpose.

"But while, put to it by those anxieties in you which I cannot but respect, I only repeat myself—while thus strangely we prolong proceedings that should be summary—the enemy may be sighted and an engagement result. We must do; and one of two things must we do— condemn or let go."

"Can we not convict and yet mitigate the penalty?" asked the sailing master, here speaking, and falteringly, for the first.

"Gentlemen, were that clearly lawful for us under the circumstances, consider the consequences of such clemency. The people" (meaning

---

[76]The Last Judgment of God.
[77]In 1793 the French revolutionary government had condemned and guillotined Louis XVI.

the ship's company) "have native sense; most of them are familiar with our naval usage and tradition; and how would they take it? Even could you explain to them—which our official position forbids—they, long molded by arbitrary discipline, have not that kind of intelligent responsiveness that might qualify them to comprehend and discriminate. No, to the people the foretopman's deed, however it be worded in the announcement, will be plain homicide committed in a flagrant act of mutiny. What penalty for that should follow, they know. But it does not follow. *Why?* they will ruminate. You know what sailors are. Will they not revert to the recent outbreak at the Nore? Ay. They know the well-founded alarm—the panic it struck throughout England. Your clement sentence they would account pusillanimous. They would think that we flinch, that we are afraid of them—afraid of practicing a lawful rigor singularly demanded at this juncture, lest it should provoke new troubles. What shame to us such a conjecture on their part, and how deadly to discipline. You see then, whither, prompted by duty and the law, I steadfastly drive. But I beseech you, my friends, do not take me amiss. I feel as you do for this unfortunate boy. But did he know our hearts, I take him to be of that generous nature that he would feel even for us on whom in this military necessity so heavy a compulsion is laid."

With that, crossing the deck he resumed his place by the sashed porthole, tacitly leaving the three to come to a decision. On the cabin's opposite side the troubled court sat silent. Loyal lieges, plain and practical, though at bottom they dissented from some points Captain Vere had put to them, they were without the faculty, hardly had the inclination, to gainsay one whom they felt to be an earnest man, one too not less their superior in mind than in naval rank. But it is not improbable that even such of his words as were not without influence over them, less came home to them than his closing appeal to their instinct as sea officers: in the forethought he threw out as to the practical consequences to discipline, considering the unconfirmed tone of the fleet at the time, should a man-of-war's man's violent killing at sea of a superior in grade be allowed to pass for aught else than a capital crime demanding prompt infliction of the penalty.

Not unlikely they were brought to something more or less akin to that harassed frame of mind which in the year 1842 actuated the commander of the U.S. brig-of-war *Somers* to resolve, under the so-called Articles of War, Articles modeled upon the English Mutiny Act, to resolve upon the execution at sea of a midshipman and two sailors as mutineers designing the seizure of the brig. Which resolution was carried out though in a time of peace and within not many days' sail of home. An act vindicated by a naval court of inquiry subsequently convened ashore. History, and here cited without comment. True, the circumstances on board the *Somers* were different from those on board the *Bellipotent*. But the urgency felt, well-warranted or otherwise, was much the same.[78]

Says a writer whom few know,[79] "Forty years after a battle it is easy for a noncombatant to reason about how it ought to have been fought. It is another thing personally and under fire to have to direct the fighting while involved in the obscuring smoke of it. Much so with respect to other emergencies involving considerations both practical and moral, and when it is imperative promptly to act. The greater the fog the more it imperils the steamer, and speed is put on though at the hazard of running somebody down. Little ween the snug card players in the cabin of the responsibilities of the sleepless man on the bridge."

In brief, Billy Budd was formally convicted and sentenced to be hung at the yardarm in the early morning watch, it being now night. Otherwise, as is customary in such cases, the sentence would forthwith have been carried out. In wartime on the field or in the fleet, a mortal punishment decreed by a drumhead court—on the field sometimes decreed by but a nod from the general—follows without delay on the heel of conviction, without appeal.[80]

XXII

It was Captain Vere himself who of his own motion communicated the finding of the court to the prisoner, for that purpose going to the compartment where he was in custody and bidding the marine there to withdraw for the time.

Beyond the communication of the sentence, what took place at this interview was never known. But in view of the character of the twain briefly closeted in that stateroom, each radically sharing in the rarer qualities of our nature—so rare indeed as to be all but incredible to

---

[78]Melville's cousin, Guert Gansevoort, had been a lieutenant aboard the *Somers* and a member of the summary court-martial that condemned three mutineers to death.

[79]Melville himself.

[80]According to naval law, this was true only in cases of mutiny; sentences of death for other offenses were to be confirmed by the Lords Commissioners of the Admiralty before being carried out. Again, whether Melville knew this is uncertain.

average minds however much cultivated—some conjectures may be ventured.

It would have been in consonance with the spirit of Captain Vere should he on this occasion have concealed nothing from the condemned one—should he indeed have frankly disclosed to him the part he himself had played in bringing about the decision, at the same time revealing his actuating motives. On Billy's side it is not improbable that such a confession would have been received in much the same spirit that prompted it. Not without a sort of joy, indeed, he might have appreciated the brave opinion of him implied in his captain's making such a confidant of him. Nor, as to the sentence itself, could he have been insensible that it was imparted to him as to one not afraid to die. Even more may have been. Captain Vere in end may have developed the passion sometimes latent under an exterior stoical or indifferent. He was old enough to have been Billy's father. The austere devotee of military duty, letting himself melt back into what remains primeval in our formalized humanity, may in end have caught Billy to his heart, even as Abraham may have caught young Isaac on the brink of resolutely offering him up in obedience to the exacting behest.[81] But there is no telling the sacrament, seldom if in any case revealed to the gadding world, wherever under circumstances at all akin to those here attempted to be set forth two of great Nature's nobler order embrace. There is privacy at the time, inviolable to the survivor; and holy oblivion, the sequel to each diviner magnanimity, providentially covers all at last.

The first to encounter Captain Vere in act of leaving the compartment was the senior lieutenant. The face he beheld, for the moment one expressive of the agony of the strong, was to that officer, though a man of fifty, a startling revelation. That the condemned one suffered less than he who mainly had effected the condemnation was apparently indicated by the former's exclamation in the scene soon perforce to be touched upon.

 XXIII

Of a series of incidents within a brief term rapidly following each other, the adequate narration may take up a term less brief, especially if explanation or comment here and there seem requisite to the better

---

[81]The sacrifice of Isaac, in Genesis 22.

understanding of such incidents. Between the entrance into the cabin of him who never left it alive, and him who when he did leave it left it as one condemned to die; between this and the closeted interview just given, less than an hour and a half had elapsed. It was an interval long enough, however, to awaken speculations among no few of the ship's company as to what it was that could be detaining in the cabin the master-at-arms and the sailor; for a rumor that both of them had been seen to enter it and neither of them had been seen to emerge, this rumor had got abroad upon the gun decks and in the tops, the people of a great warship being in one respect like villagers, taking microscopic note of every outward movement or non-movement going on. When therefore, in weather not at all tempestuous, all hands were called in the second dogwatch, a summons under such circumstances not usual in those hours, the crew were not wholly unprepared for some announcement extraordinary, one having connection too with the continued absence of the two men from their wonted haunts.

There was a moderate sea at the time; and the moon, newly risen and near to being at its full, silvered the white spar deck wherever not blotted by the clear-cut shadows horizontally thrown of fixtures and moving men. On either side the quarter-deck the marine guard under arms was drawn up; and Captain Vere, standing in his place surrounded by all the wardroom officers, addressed his men. In so doing, his manner showed neither more nor less than that properly pertaining to his supreme position aboard his own ship. In clear terms and concise he told them what had taken place in the cabin: that the master-at-arms was dead, that he who had killed him had been already tried by a summary court and condemned to death, and that the execution would take place in the early morning watch. The word *mutiny* was not named in what he said. He refrained too from making the occasion an opportunity for any preachment as to the maintenance of discipline, thinking perhaps that under existing circumstances in the navy the consequence of violating discipline should be made to speak for itself.

Their captain's announcement was listened to by the throng of standing sailors in a dumbness like that of a seated congregation of believers in hell listening to the clergyman's announcement of his Calvinistic text.

At the close, however, a confused murmur went up. It began to wax. All but instantly, then, at a sign, it was pierced and suppressed by shrill whistles of the boatswain and his mates. The word was given to about ship.

To be prepared for burial Claggart's body was delivered to certain petty officers of his mess. And here, not to clog the sequel with lateral matters, it may be added that at a suitable hour, the master-at-arms was committed to the sea with every funeral honor properly belonging to his naval grade.

In this proceeding as in every public one growing out of the tragedy strict adherence to usage was observed. Nor in any point could it have been at all deviated from, either with respect to Claggart or Billy Budd, without begetting undesirable speculations in the ship's company, sailors, and more particularly men-of-war's men, being of all men the greatest sticklers for usage. For similar cause, all communication between Captain Vere and the condemned one ended with the closeted interview already given, the latter being now surrendered to the ordinary routine preliminary to the end. His transfer under guard from the captain's quarters was effected without unusual precautions—at least no visible ones. If possible, not to let the men so much as surmise that their officers anticipate aught amiss from them is the tacit rule in a military ship. And the more that some sort of trouble should really be apprehended, the more do the officers keep that apprehension to themselves, though not the less unostentatious vigilance may be augmented. In the present instance, the sentry placed over the prisoner had strict orders to let no one have communication with him but the chaplain. And certain unobtrusive measures were taken absolutely to insure this point.

XXIV

In a seventy-four of the old order the deck known as the upper gun deck was the one covered over by the spar deck, which last, though not without its armament, was for the most part exposed to the weather. In general it was at all hours free from hammocks; those of the crew swinging on the lower gun deck and berth deck, the latter being not only a dormitory but also the place for the stowing of the sailors' bags, and on both sides lined with the large chests or movable pantries of the many messes of the men.

On the starboard side of the *Bellipotent*'s upper gun deck, behold Billy Budd under sentry lying prone in irons in one of the bays formed by the regular spacing of the guns comprising the batteries on either side. All these pieces were of the heavier caliber of that period. Mounted on lumbering wooden carriages, they were hampered with cumbersome harness of breeching and strong side-tackles for running them out.

Guns and carriages, together with the long rammers and shorter lin-
stocks lodged in loops overhead—all these, as customary, were painted
black; and the heavy hempen breechings, tarred to the same tint, wore
the like livery of the undertakers. In contrast with the funeral hue of
these surroundings, the prone sailor's exterior apparel, white jumper
and white duck trousers, each more or less soiled, dimly glimmered in
the obscure light of the bay like a patch of discolored snow in early
April lingering at some upland cave's black mouth. In effect he is already in his shroud, or the garments that shall serve him in lieu of one.
Over him but scarce illuminating him, two battle lanterns swing from
two massive beams of the deck above. Fed with the oil supplied by the
war contractors (whose gains, honest or otherwise, are in every land an
anticipated portion of the harvest of death), with flickering splashes of
dirty yellow light they pollute the pale moonshine all but ineffectually
struggling in obstructed flecks through the open ports from which the
tampioned cannon protrude. Other lanterns at intervals serve but to
bring out somewhat the obscurer bays which, like small confessionals
or side-chapels in a cathedral, branch from the long dim-vistaed broad
aisle between the two batteries of that covered tier.

Such was the deck where now lay the Handsome Sailor. Through the
rose-tan of his complexion no pallor could have shown. It would have
taken days of sequestration from the winds and the sun to have
brought about the effacement of that. But the skeleton in the cheek-
bone at the point of its angle was just beginning delicately to be defined under the warm-tinted skin. In fervid hearts self-contained, some
brief experiences devour our human tissue as secret fire in a ship's hold
consumes cotton in the bale.

But now lying between the two guns, as nipped in the vise of fate,
Billy's agony, mainly proceeding from a generous young heart's virgin
experience of the diabolical incarnate and effective in some men—the
tension of that agony was over now. It survived not the something
healing in the closeted interview with Captain Vere. Without movement, he lay as in a trance, that adolescent expression previously noted
as his taking on something akin to the look of a slumbering child in the
cradle when the warm hearth-glow of the still chamber at night plays
on the dimples that at whiles mysteriously form in the cheek, silently
coming and going there. For now and then in the gyved[82] one's trance

---

[82]Bound.

a serene happy light born of some wandering reminiscence or dream would diffuse itself over his face, and then wane away only anew to return.

The chaplain, coming to see him and finding him thus, and perceiving no sign that he was conscious of his presence, attentively regarded him for a space, then slipping aside, withdrew for the time, peradventure feeling that even he, the minister of Christ though receiving his stipend from Mars,[83] had no consolation to proffer which could result in a peace transcending that which he beheld. But in the small hours he came again. And the prisoner, now awake to his surroundings, noticed his approach, and civilly, all but cheerfully, welcomed him. But it was to little purpose that in the interview following, the good man sought to bring Billy Budd to some godly understanding that he must die, and at dawn. True, Billy himself freely referred to his death as a thing close at hand; but it was something in the way that children will refer to death in general, who yet among their other sports will play a funeral with hearse and mourners.

Not that like children Billy was incapable of conceiving what death really is. No, but he was wholly without irrational fear of it, a fear more prevalent in highly civilized communities than those so-called barbarous ones which in all respects stand nearer to unadulterate Nature. And, as elsewhere said, a barbarian Billy radically was—as much so, for all the costume, as his countrymen the British captives, living trophies, made to march in the Roman triumph of Germanicus.[84] Quite as much so as those later barbarians, young men probably, and picked specimens among the earlier British converts to Christianity, at least nominally such, taken to Rome (as today converts from lesser isles of the sea may be taken to London), of whom the Pope of that time,[85] admiring the strangeness of their personal beauty so unlike the Italian stamp, their clear ruddy complexion and curled flaxen locks, exclaimed, "Angles" (meaning *English*, the modern derivative), "Angles, do you call them? And is it because they look so like angels?" Had it been later in time, one would think that the Pope had in mind Fra Angelico's[86] seraphs, some of whom, plucking apples in gardens of the Hesperides,

---

[83]The Roman god of War.
[84]Roman general whose triumph in A.D. 17 included British prisoners.
[85]Gregory the Great, pope from 590 to 604.
[86]Florentine friar and painter of the early fifteenth century.

have the faint rosebud complexion of the more beautiful English girls.

If in vain the good chaplain sought to impress the young barbarian with ideas of death akin to those conveyed in the skull, dial, and crossbones on old tombstones, equally futile to all appearance were his efforts to bring home to him the thought of salvation and a Savior. Billy listened, but less out of awe or reverence, perhaps, than from a certain natural politeness, doubtless at bottom regarding all that in much the same way that most mariners of his class take any discourse abstract or out of the common tone of the workaday world. And this sailor way of taking clerical discourse is not wholly unlike the way in which the primer of Christianity, full of transcendent miracles, was received long ago on tropic isles by any superior *savage*, so called—a Tahitian, say, of Captain Cook's time or shortly after that time. Out of natural courtesy he received, but did not appropriate. It was like a gift placed in the palm of an outreached hand upon which the fingers do not close.

But the *Bellipotent's* chaplain was a discreet man possessing the good sense of a good heart. So he insisted not in his vocation here. At the instance of Captain Vere, a lieutenant had apprised him of pretty much everything as to Billy; and since he felt that innocence was even a better thing than religion wherewith to go to Judgment, he reluctantly withdrew; but in his emotion not without first performing an act strange enough in an Englishman, and under the circumstances yet more so in any regular priest. Stooping over, he kissed on the fair cheek his fellow man, a felon in martial law, one whom though on the confines of death he felt he could never convert to a dogma; nor for all that did he fear for his future.

Marvel not that having been made acquainted with the young sailor's essential innocence the worthy man lifted not a finger to avert the doom of such a martyr to martial discipline. So to do would not only have been as idle as invoking the desert, but would also have been an audacious transgression of the bounds of his function, one as exactly prescribed to him by military law as that of the boatswain or any other naval officer. Bluntly put, a chaplain is the minister of the Prince of Peace serving in the host of the God of War—Mars. As such, he is as incongruous as a musket would be on the altar at Christmas. Why, then, is he there? Because he indirectly subserves the purpose attested by the cannon; because too he lends the sanction of the religion of the meek to that which practically is the abrogation of everything but brute Force.

XXV

The night so luminous on the spar deck, but otherwise on the cavernous ones below, levels so like the tiered galleries in a coal mine—the luminous night passed away. But like the prophet in the chariot disappearing in heaven and dropping his mantle to Elisha,[87] the withdrawing night transferred its pale robe to the breaking day. A meek, shy light appeared in the East, where stretched a diaphanous fleece of white furrowed vapor. That light slowly waxed. Suddenly *eight bells* was struck aft, responded to by one louder metallic stroke from forward. It was four o'clock in the morning. Instantly the silver whistles were heard summoning all hands to witness punishment. Up through the great hatchways rimmed with racks of heavy shot the watch below came pouring, overspreading with the watch already on deck the space between the mainmast and foremast including that occupied by the capacious launch and the black booms tiered on either side of it, boat and booms making a summit of observation for the powder-boys and younger tars. A different group comprising one watch of topmen leaned over the rail of that sea balcony, no small one in a seventy-four, looking down on the crowd below. Man or boy, none spake but in whisper, and few spake at all. Captain Vere—as before, the central figure among the assembled commissioned officers—stood nigh the break of the poop deck facing forward. Just below him on the quarterdeck the marines in full equipment were drawn up much as at the scene of the promulgated sentence.

At sea in the old time, the execution by halter of a military sailor was generally from the foreyard. In the present instance, for special reasons the mainyard was assigned.[88] Under an arm of that yard the prisoner was presently brought up, the chaplain attending him. It was noted at the time, and remarked upon afterwards, that in this final scene the good man evinced little or nothing of the perfunctory. Brief speech indeed he had with the condemned one, but the genuine Gospel was less on his tongue than in his aspect and manner towards him. The

---

[87]In 2 Kings 2:11-13, the prophet Elijah, drawn up to heaven in a fiery chariot, drops his mantle to his successor in prophecy, Elisha.

[88]Perhaps because the foremast was Billy's duty-station, perhaps because the waist of the ship could be more effectively guarded in the event of protest on the part of the crew.

final preparations personal to the latter being speedily brought to an end by two boatswain's mates, the consummation impended. Billy stood facing aft. At the penultimate moment, his words, his only ones, words wholly unobstructed in the utterance, were these: "God bless Captain Vere!" Syllables so unanticipated coming from one with the ignominious hemp about his neck—a conventional felon's benediction directed aft towards the quarters of honor; syllables too delivered in the clear melody of a singing bird on the point of launching from the twig—had a phenomenal effect, not unenhanced by the rare personal beauty of the young sailor, spiritualized now through late experiences so poignantly profound.

Without volition, as it were, as if indeed the ship's populace were but the vehicles of some vocal current electric, with one voice from alow and aloft came a resonant sympathetic echo: "God bless Captain Vere!" And yet at that instant Billy alone must have been in their hearts, even as in their eyes.

At the pronounced words and spontaneous echo that voluminously rebounded them, Captain Vere, either through stoic self-control or a sort of momentary paralysis induced by emotional shock, stood erectly rigid as a musket in the ship-armorer's rack.

The hull, deliberately recovering from the periodic roll to leeward, was just regaining an even keel when the last signal, a preconcerted dumb one, was given. At the same moment it chanced that the vapory fleece hanging low in the East was shot through with a soft glory as of the fleece of the Lamb of God seen in mystical vision, and simultaneously therewith, watched by the wedged mass of upturned faces, Billy ascended; and, ascending, took the full rose of the dawn.

In the pinioned figure arrived at the yard-end, to the wonder of all no motion was apparent, none save that created by the slow roll of the hull in moderate weather, so majestic in a great ship ponderously cannoned.

XXVI

When some days afterwards, in reference to the singularity just mentioned, the purser, a rather ruddy, rotund person more accurate as an accountant than profound as a philosopher, said at mess to the surgeon, "What testimony to the force lodged in will power," the latter, saturnine, spare, and tall, one in whom a discreet causticity went along with a manner less genial than polite, replied, "Your pardon, Mr. Purser. In a hanging scientifically conducted—and under special orders

I myself directed how Budd's was to be effected—any movement following the completed suspension and originating in the body suspended, such movement indicates mechanical spasm[89] in the muscular system. Hence the absence of that is no more attributable to will power, as you call it, than to horsepower—begging your pardon."

"But this muscular spasm you speak of, is not that in a degree more or less invariable in these cases?"

"Assuredly so, Mr. Purser."

"How then, my good sir, do you account for its absence in this instance?"

"Mr. Purser, it is clear that your sense of the singularity in this matter equals not mine. You account for it by what you call will power—a term not yet included in the lexicon of science. For me, I do not, with my present knowledge, pretend to account for it at all. Even should we assume the hypothesis that at the first touch of the halyards the action of Budd's heart, intensified by extraordinary emotion at its climax, abruptly stopped—much like a watch when in carelessly winding it up you strain at the finish, thus snapping the chain—even under that hypothesis how account for the phenomenon that followed?"

"You admit, then, that the absence of spasmodic movement was phenomenal."

"It was phenomenal, Mr. Purser, in the sense that it was an appearance the cause of which is not immediately to be assigned."

"But tell me, my dear sir," pertinaciously continued the other, "was the man's death effected by the halter, or was it a species of euthanasia?"[90]

"*Euthanasia*, Mr. Purser, is something like your *will power*: I doubt its authenticity as a scientific term—begging your pardon again. It is at once imaginative and metaphysical—in short, Greek.—But," abruptly changing his tone, "there is a case in the sick bay that I do not care to leave to my assistants. Beg your pardon, but excuse me." And rising from the mess he formally withdrew.

XXVII

The silence at the moment of execution and for a moment or two continuing thereafter, a silence but emphasized by the regular wash of the sea against the hull or the flutter of a sail caused by the helmsman's

---

[89]Erection and orgasm, almost invariable in a hanged man, as the purser suggests.
[90]Here, a death without pain or suffering.

eyes being tempted astray, this emphasized silence was gradually disturbed by a sound not easily to be verbally rendered. Whoever has heard the freshet-wave of a torrent suddenly swelled by pouring showers in tropical mountains, showers not shared by the plain; whoever has heard the first muffled murmur of its sloping advance through precipitous woods may form some conception of the sound now heard. The seeming remoteness of its source was because of its murmurous indistinctness, since it came from close by, even from the men massed on the ship's open deck. Being inarticulate, it was dubious in significance further than it seemed to indicate some capricious revulsion of thought or feeling such as mobs ashore are liable to, in the present instance possibly implying a sullen revocation on the men's part of their involuntary echoing of Billy's benediction. But ere the murmur had time to wax into clamor it was met by a strategic command, the more telling that it came with abrupt unexpectedness: "Pipe down the starboard watch, Boatswain, and see that they go."

Shrill as the shriek of the sea hawk, the silver whistles of the boatswain and his mates pierced that ominous low sound, dissipating it; and yielding to the mechanism of discipline the throng was thinned by one-half. For the remainder, most of them were set to temporary employments connected with trimming the yards and so forth, business readily to be got up to serve occasion by any officer of the deck.

Now each proceeding that follows a mortal sentence pronounced at sea by a drumhead court is characterized by promptitude not perceptibly merging into hurry, though bordering that. The hammock, the one which had been Billy's bed when alive, having already been ballasted with shot and otherwise prepared to serve for his canvas coffin, the last offices of the sea undertakers, the sailmaker's mates, were now speedily completed. When everything was in readiness a second call for all hands, made necessary by the strategic movement before mentioned, was sounded, now to witness burial.

The details of this closing formality it needs not to give. But when the tilted plank let slide its freight into the sea, a second strange human murmur was heard, blended now with another inarticulate sound proceeding from certain larger seafowl who, their attention having been attracted by the peculiar commotion in the water resulting from the heavy sloped dive of the shotted hammock into the sea, flew screaming to the spot. So near the hull did they come, that the stridor or bony creak of their gaunt double-jointed pinions was audible. As the ship under light airs passed on, leaving the burial spot astern, they still kept circling it low down with the moving shadow of their outstretched wings and the croaked requiem of their cries.

Upon sailors as superstitious as those of the age preceding ours, men-of-war's men too who had just beheld the prodigy of repose in the form suspended in air, and now foundering in the deeps; to such mariners the action of the seafowl, though dictated by mere animal greed for prey, was big with no prosaic significance. An uncertain movement began among them, in which some encroachment was made. It was tolerated but for a moment. For suddenly the drum beat to quarters, which familiar sound happening at least twice every day, had upon the present occasion a signal peremptoriness in it. True martial discipline long continued superinduces in average man a sort of impulse whose operation at the official word of command much resembles in its promptitude the effect of an instinct.

The drumbeat dissolved the multitude, distributing most of them along the batteries of the two covered gun decks. There, as wonted, the guns' crews stood by their respective cannon erect and silent. In due course the first officer, sword under arm and standing in his place on the quarter-deck, formally received the successive reports of the sworded lieutenants commanding the sections of batteries below; the last of which reports being made, the summed report he delivered with the customary salute to the commander. All this occupied time, which in the present case was the object in beating to quarters at an hour prior to the customary one. That such variance from usage was authorized by an officer like Captain Vere, a martinet[91] as some deemed him, was evidence of the necessity for unusual action implied in what he deemed to be temporarily the mood of his men. "With mankind," he would say, "forms, measured forms, are everything; and that is the import couched in the story of Orpheus with his lyre spellbinding the wild denizens of the wood."[92] And this he once applied to the disruption of forms going on across the Channel and the consequence thereof.

At this unwonted muster at quarters, all proceeded as at the regular hour. The band on the quarter-deck played a sacred air, after which the chaplain went through the customary morning service. That done, the

---

[91]A stringent disciplinarian.

[92]In Greek legend, Orpheus, a hero and musician, first of the bards, was said to have charmed all nature with his music.

drum beat the retreat; and toned by music and religious rites subserving the discipline and purposes of war, the men in their wonted orderly manner dispersed to the places allotted them when not at the guns.

And now it was full day. The fleece of low-hanging vapor had vanished, licked up by the sun that late had so glorified it. And the circumambient air in the clearness of its serenity was like smooth white marble in the polished block not yet removed from the marble-dealer's yard.

XXVIII

The symmetry of form attainable in pure fiction cannot so readily be achieved in a narration essentially having less to do with fable than with fact. Truth uncompromisingly told will always have its ragged edges; hence the conclusion of such a narration is apt to be less finished than an architectural finial.

How it fared with the Handsome Sailor during the year of the Great Mutiny has been faithfully given. But though properly the story ends with his life, something in way of sequel will not be amiss. Three brief chapters will suffice.

In the general rechristening under the Directory of the craft originally forming the navy of the French monarchy, the *St. Louis* line-of-battle ship was named the *Athée* (the *Atheist*). Such a name, like some other substituted ones in the Revolutionary fleet, while proclaiming the infidel audacity of the ruling power, was yet, though not so intended to be, the aptest name, if one consider it, ever given to a warship; far more so indeed than the *Devastation*, the *Erebus* (the *Hell*), and similar names bestowed upon fighting ships.

On the return passage to the English fleet from the detached cruise during which occurred the events already recorded, the *Bellipotent* fell in with the *Athée*. An engagement ensued, during which Captain Vere, in the act of putting his ship alongside the enemy with a view of throwing his boarders across her bulwarks, was hit by a musket ball from a porthole of the enemy's main cabin. More than disabled, he dropped to the deck and was carried below to the same cockpit where some of his men already lay. The senior lieutenant took command. Under him the enemy was finally captured, and though much crippled was by rare good fortune successfully taken into Gibraltar, an English port not very distant from the scene of the fight. There, Captain Vere with the rest of the wounded was put ashore. He lingered for some days, but the end came. Unhappily he was cut off too early for the Nile and Trafalgar. The spirit that 'spite its philosophic austerity may yet have indulged in the most secret of all passions, ambition, never attained to the fulness of fame.

Not long before death, while lying under the influence of that magical drug[93] which, soothing the physical frame, mysteriously operates on the subtler element in man, he was heard to murmur words inexplicable to his attendant: "Billy Budd, Billy Budd." That these were not the accents of remorse would seem clear from what the attendant said to the *Bellipotent*'s senior officer of marines, who, as the most reluctant to condemn of the members of the drumhead court, too well knew, though here he kept the knowledge to himself, who Billy Budd was.

XXIX

Some few weeks after the execution, among other matters under the head of "News from the Mediterranean," there appeared in a naval chronicle of the time, an authorized weekly publication, an account of the affair. It was doubtless for the most part written in good faith, though the medium, partly rumor, through which the facts must have reached the writer served to deflect and in part falsify them. The account was as follows:

On the tenth of the last month a deplorable occurrence took place on board H.M.S. *Bellipotent*. John Claggart, the ship's master-at-arms, discovering that some sort of plot was incipient among an inferior section of the ship's company, and that the ringleader was one William Budd; he, Claggart, in the act of arraigning the man before the captain, was vindictively stabbed to the heart by the suddenly drawn sheath knife of Budd.

The deed and the implement employed sufficiently suggest that though mustered into the service under an English name the assassin was no Englishman, but one of those aliens adopting English cognomens whom the present extraordinary necessities of the service have caused to be admitted into it in considerable numbers.

The enormity of the crime and the extreme depravity of the criminal appear the greater in view of the character of the victim, a middle-aged man respectable and discreet, belonging to that minor official grade, the petty officers, upon whom, as none know better than the commissioned gentle-

---

[93]Opium.

men, the efficiency of His Majesty's navy so largely depends. His function was a responsible one, at once onerous and thankless; and his fidelity in it the greater because of his strong patriotic impulse. In this instance as in so many other instances in these days, the character of this unfortunate man signally refutes, if refutation were needed, the peevish saying attributed to the late Dr. Johnson, that patriotism is the last refuge of a scoundrel.

The criminal paid the penalty of his crime. The promptitude of the punishment has proved salutary. Nothing amiss is now apprehended aboard H.M.S. *Bellipotent*.

The above, appearing in a publication now long ago superannuated and forgotten, is all that hitherto has stood in human record to attest what manner of men respectively were John Claggart and Billy Budd.

XXX

Everything is for a term venerated in navies. Any tangible object associated with some striking incident of the service is converted into a monument. The spar from which the foretopman was suspended was for some few years kept trace of by the bluejackets. Their knowledges followed it from ship to dockyard and again from dockyard to ship, still pursuing it even when at last reduced to a mere dockyard boom. To them a chip of it was as a piece of the Cross. Ignorant though they were of the secret facts of the tragedy, and not thinking but that the penalty was somehow unavoidably inflicted from the naval point of view, for all that, they instinctively felt that Billy was a sort of man as incapable of mutiny as of wilful murder. They recalled the fresh young image of the Handsome Sailor, that face never deformed by a sneer or subtler vile freak of the heart within. This impression of him was doubtless deepened by the fact that he was gone, and in a measure mysteriously gone. On the gun decks of the *Bellipotent*, the general estimate of his nature and its unconscious simplicity eventually found rude utterance from another foretopman, one of his own watch, gifted, as some sailors are, with an artless *poetic* temperament. The tarry hand made some lines which, after circulating among the shipboard crews for a while, finally got rudely printed at Portsmouth as a ballad. The title given to it was the sailor's.

BILLY IN THE DARBIES[94]

Good of the chaplain to enter Lone Bay
And down on his marrowbones here and pray

---

[94]Handcuffs.

For the likes just o' me, Billy Budd.—But, look:
Through the port comes the moonshine astray!
It tips the guard's cutlass and silvers this nook;
But 'twill die in the dawning of Billy's last day.
A jewel-block they'll make of me tomorrow,
Pendant pearl from the yardarm-end
Like the eardrop I gave to Bristol Molly—
O, 'tis me, not the sentence they'll suspend.
Ay, ay, all is up; and I must up too,
Early in the morning, aloft from alow.
On an empty stomach now never it would do.
They'll give me a nibble—bit o' biscuit ere I go.
Sure, a messmate will reach me the last parting cup;
But, turning heads away from the hoist and the belay,
Heaven knows who will have the running of me up!
No pipe to those halyards.—But aren't it all sham?
A blur's in my eyes; it is dreaming that I am.
A hatchet to my hawser? All adrift to go?
The drum roll to grog, and Billy never know?
But Donald he has promised to stand by the plank;
So I'll shake a friendly hand ere I sink.
But—no! It is dead then I'll be, come to think.
I remember Taff the Welshman when he sank.
And his cheek it was like the budding pink.
But me they'll lash in hammock, drop me deep.
Fathoms down, fathoms down, how I'll dream fast asleep.
I feel it stealing now. Sentry, are you there?
Just ease these darbies at the wrist,
And roll me over fair!
I am sleepy, and the oozy weeds about me twist.

Appendix

The Cancelled "Preface" to
Billy Budd, Sailor

The following text, printed by F. B. Freeman as the preface to his 1948 edition of *Billy Budd*, was found by Hayford and Sealts (see p. 61) to have been originally designed for a place toward the middle of the narrative. Late in

Melville's revisions, the passage was actually cancelled, and it does not appear in the edition as printed here, though some scholars speculate that Melville might have restored it to the printed text had he lived. Despite their uncanonical status, the two paragraphs are referred to so often by critics for their clues to Melville's political attitudes that we have reprinted them here.

The year 1797, the year of this narrative, belongs to a period which as every thinker now feels, involved a crisis for Christendom not exceeded in its undetermined momentousness at the time by any other era whereof there is record. The opening proposition made by the Spirit of that Age involved rectification of the Old World's hereditary wrongs. In France, to some extent, this was bloodily effected. But what then? Straightway the Revolution itself became a wrong-doer, one more oppressive than the kings. Under Napoleon it enthroned upstart kings, and initiated that prolonged agony of continual war whose final throe was Waterloo. During those years not the wisest could have foreseen that the outcome of all would be what to some thinkers apparently it has since turned out to be—a political advance along nearly the whole line for Europeans.

Now, as elsewhere hinted, it was something caught from the Revolutionary Spirit that at Spithead emboldened the man-of-war's men to rise against real abuses, long-standing ones, and afterwards at the Nore to make inordinate and aggressive demands—successful resistance to which was confirmed only when the ringleaders were hung for an admonitory spectacle to the anchored fleet. Yet in a way analogous to the operation of the Revolution at large—the Great Mutiny, though by Englishmen naturally deemed monstrous at the time, doubtless gave the first latent prompting to most important reforms in the British navy.

The Aspern Papers

Henry James

Born an American, influenced by the French, a naturalized British subject, Henry James was a relentless experimenter with technique and subject matter who brought a new sophistication to the art of fiction. His father, Henry James, Sr., was one of the more remarkable men of his age, a restless intellectual and religious mystic with, as one of his contemporaries put it, ''the look of a broker, and the brains and heart of a Pascal.'' A close acquaintance of Ralph Waldo Emerson, Nathaniel Hawthorne, and many of the other New England luminaries of the pre-Civil War period, James's father wrote philosophical and theological works with a complete disdain for popularity, which his inherited income of ten thousand dollars a year permitted him to do. He also had a devoted wife and a large family, into which Henry James, Jr., was born on April 15, 1843, the second son of five children.

Afraid that his offspring would grow up in too conventional a mold, James, Sr., moved Henry and his famous elder brother, William, from one school to another in New York City, Albany, Paris, Geneva, London, Boulogne, and Bonn. Apart from the broadening effects of travel, the idea seems to have been that, though some sort of formal education was necessary for the children, no teacher or school should gain exclusive control over their minds. The instant one of the boys became attached to his masters, his father would yank him away. The other intent was to avoid the pragmatic professionalism of American education, which was as prevalent then as now. The elder James wished to instill some of his own eclecticism and amateurism into his talented children, but the result of his systematic avoidance of system was, paradoxically, that both the older boys became ardently professional in their chosen fields, William as a psychologist and philosopher, Henry as a novelist and man of letters.

The beginnings of James's literary career seem to have occurred after the family returned to America in 1860. William, who wished to try painting as a career, became a student in the studio of William Morris Hunt in Newport, Rhode Island. He was accompanied by Henry, who was passionately devoted to his brother, though the latter treated him all his life with an elder's disdain. Henry had even less artistic talent than did William, but the cosmopolitan Hunt and his friends introduced him to the work of the French writers Balzac and

Mérimée, which James read, admired, and translated. After another abortive move toward a career—a year at Harvard Law School—James returned to his family, following its moves from Newport to Cambridge and then to Boston, and attempted to write stories of his own. His first published effort, "A Tragedy of Error," appeared anonymously in 1864. "The Story of a Year," the first work to bear his name, came out in the *Atlantic Monthly* in March 1865. At around the same time, James began to write literary criticism for the prestigious *North American Review*, edited by two influential Brahmins of the Boston literary scene, James Russell Lowell and Charles Eliot Norton. James's sense of his vocation solidified under the friendship and admiration of Lowell and Norton. He was supported also by the young William Dean Howells, then an assistant editor of the *Atlantic Monthly*, who encouraged his periodical to publish James's stories and became a lifelong friend. James published a dozen stories and scores of reviews between "A Tragedy of Error" and "A Passionate Pilgrim"(1871), his first mature work. His apprentice years were industrious, and the stories works of deliberate craft, but they are hardly masterpieces. James later called them "subaqueous," implying that they shimmered brilliantly but lacked solid outlines, and he dropped the one novel of the period, *Watch and Ward* (1871), from the canon of his works. He had become a writer in America, but it was not until he moved to Europe that he was to find his true voice.

In personal terms, the years between James's return to America from his peripatetic education and his decision to make his home in Europe were not happy ones. In 1861, while helping to put out a fire, James suffered a severe injury ("a horrid even if obscure hurt," he called it) that kept him from enlisting in the Union Army during the Civil War. Just what the injury was is not certain, and James's reticence has given rise to lurid speculation that it was an injury to the groin that castrated him. His biographer, Leon Edel, however, finds that the evidence rather suggests a blow to a spinal disc or sacroiliac that gave James recurrent back pain for the rest of his life. The other permanent loss James suffered was the death from tuberculosis of his young cousin Minny Temple, whom he idolized as the quintessence of youth and womanhood, and with whom he may have been quietly in love. He wrote to his brother William after her death about their relations: "I always looked forward with a certain eagerness to the day when I should have regained my natural lead, and one friendship, on my part, at least, might become more active and masculine." How romantic was James's attachment to Minny Temple? Since James never married, nor is he known to have formed a sexual relationship with any woman or man, either before Minny's death or after it, it is tempting to see Minny Temple as the focus of a romantic tragedy and her death as the trauma which confirmed James in his bachelor celibacy. Certainly James enshrined her image, as he foresaw he would, in two of his most glorious American heroines, Isabel Archer in *The Portrait of a Lady* and Milly Theale in *The Wings of the Dove*. But sexual identity is most often determined long before one's twenty-seventh year, so that, while Minny's death cast its shadow over James's life, it is unlikely to have so profoundly influenced its course. Because of his rootless youth, James had long been drifting toward a style of living that would be filled with friends and acquaintances but empty of more intimate relationships.

Throughout the early 1870s James flirted, more and more seriously, with the idea of leaving America and making Europe his permanent home. His travels with his family and his peripatetic education had made the cities of Europe almost as familiar to him as New York, Newport, and Cambridge. And thanks to his immense talent and industry, and the literary reputation these had gained him, he could support himself by his pen. Most of all he had the sense that the literary man in America was doomed to a buried life, like Hawthorne's, if he rose above mere entertainment and tried to plumb the depths of the American character and conscience. In Europe, on the other hand, there was a richness of culture and history that America lacked, and there the artist, if he had the enveloping imagination of a Balzac, could become the lion of his society and could be looked up to as a Master of art and life. James's decision was slow in coming. He was delayed by his sense that he knew and loved the American mind as he could not know that of Europe, and by a genuine attachment to the individualistic freedom fostered by the myth and adventure of the younger continent. He tested the water with lengthy trips to Europe, writing travel pieces as well as fiction and essays, and tasted life in Florence and Paris before deciding, in 1877, to make London his principal home.

James's work, in the years leading up to and away from his move to London, is marked by growing power and complexity and by the emergence of his special interest in the "international theme": the impact of Europe upon Americans and of Americans upon Europe. While some of the fiction of this period— like *The Europeans* (1878)—pokes gentle fun at the provinciality and puritanism of the American character and at its inability to assimilate the grander culture of the Continent, James more often emphasizes the innocence and freedom of his Americans and contrasts them with the corruption and decadence of the older civilizations. His painter-hero in *Roderick Hudson* (1874) is destroyed partly through his own lack of discipline, partly through the attractions of the wayward, bohemian life he finds in Rome. Christopher Newman, the hero of *The American* (1875), is ultimately frustrated in his romance with a delicate French beauty by the designs of her haughty and conniving family, who take advantage of his idealistic nature at every turn. And in "Daisy Miller" (1878)—the James story most popular in his own lifetime, and perhaps today as well—the author's concern is less with the rebellious American girl at its center than with its narrator, an American so Europeanized that he cannot comprehend the essential innocence and purity of Daisy's character until he has, by his failure to understand, rejected and destroyed her. The culmination of James's fiction in this period is *The Portrait of a Lady* (1881). Its story of a young American girl whose inherited fortune, left her to grant freedom and scope to her individualistic nature, only leaves her prey to a coldly egocentric expatriate, is as satisfyingly melodramatic as James's earlier novels. But James's real achievement was in his portrayal of Isabel Archer's moral and emotional growth in the course of her disillusionment—a portrait of such intricacy, vividness, and depth as to make this work not only one of the high points of Victorian fiction but also one of the experiments in technique that mark the transition between the "social" novel of the nineteenth century and the psychological realism of the twentieth.

James's treatment of the "international theme," with its distrust of the too-Europeanized American, perhaps reflects the ease with which he made his way into British society and his fear that he would lose his American character there. With the aid of an introduction from Henry Adams, James joined the circle of Richard Monckton Milnes, Lord Houghton, where he met such celebrities as Heinrich Schliemann, the discoverer of Troy, Poet Laureate Alfred, Lord Tennyson, and Prime Minister William Gladstone. He was also awarded an honorary membership at the Atheneum, one of England's most exclusive gentlemen's clubs. At the same time, there were limits to James's acceptance in British society; he was appreciated for his brilliant talk and admired as an artist, but he always remained "in" British society, never "of" it. Constantly invited to dine out and to spend weekends at his friends' country houses, James never joined the most intimate circles of the aristocracy. James himself decried the amount of time his social life took from his writing and, tempting as it would be to see his compulsive sociability as pure waste, one should remember that his experiences gave him fresh material to fictionalize, prevented his stories from settling into a single mold, and gave him the semblance of a life when he was in danger of having only a career. Then too, intellectual friendships, like those with Robert Louis Stevenson and Edmund Gosse, transcended the merely social connections of these London years.

As James was in the process of finding a new homeland in England, his family circle in America was destroyed by the successive deaths of his mother and father in 1882, followed the next year by that of a younger brother. In 1884, his sister Alice, a neurasthenic invalid, came over to settle near him, and James devoted his share of the family inheritance, as well as a good deal of his time, to making her last eight years as comfortable as possible.

What James could not know, as he moved into his forties, was that he had already passed the peak of his public popularity with "Daisy Miller" and *The Portrait of a Lady* and that the glory he had sought in coming to England was henceforth largely to elude him. The three major novels of the middle and late 1880s, *The Bostonians* (1886), *The Princess Casamassima* (1886), and *The Tragic Muse* (1890) were both critical and popular failures and, while they have found appreciators today, are still not ranked with James's greatest work.

The most admired product of this transitional period in James's life and work is his novella *The Aspern Papers*, which he wrote during an eight-month stay in Florence in 1887 and published the following year. *The Aspern Papers* was based on an item of gossip James heard about one Captain Silsbee, a fanatical collector of Shelley memorabilia, who inveigled his way into the household of Claire Clairmont, who had been Byron's mistress many years before. Silsbee had hoped to get his hands on some Shelley-Byron correspondence in Clairmont's possession, but fled when he learned that the price would be marriage to her spinster niece. Recently, Leon Edel has suggested that events closer to James's own life may have played some part in the tale. The Florentine villa James inhabited was rented by the American writer Constance Fenimore Woolson, a great-niece of James Fenimore Cooper. While James was working in one wing, Woolson moved into the other, and though things remained quite proper, she seems to have developed a romantic attachment to James, one-sided to be sure. And so it may have been Woolson's portrait James drew in the character of the niece, Tina Bordereau, in *The Aspern Papers*.

With the sales of his novels in decline and his patrimony committed to the support of his invalid sister, James decided to turn dramatist in the early 1890s. He hoped for a relatively rapid financial return at worst, and at best the conquest of the London stage. It is true that James's experiments with fictional point of view were moving his art toward a more dramatic style, but his concern with subtleties and delicate nuances was unsuited to the broad strokes of successful theater. His first effort, a dramatization of *The American* (1891), ran seventy performances and made James a little money; his second, *Disengaged*, was withdrawn while still in rehearsal. The third effort was an unmitigated disaster. *Guy Domville*, written in 1893 and produced in 1895, was a complicated costume melodrama whose star was forced to speak stilted lines that drew jeers and wit from the gallery. In revenge, the matinee idol playing the lead drew the unsuspecting James out before the footlights, where he was greeted by a "crescendo of booing" that ended, then and there, his theatrical ambitions.

From 1897 on James withdrew from London to the provincial town of Rye, where he rented and later purchased the small but stately Lamb House. In place of his usual role as guest at various aristocratic establishments, he delighted in playing host to a varied group of talented new friends, which included Edith Wharton, Stephen Crane, Joseph Conrad, Hugh Walpole, and H. G. Wells. And he worked, with ever greater intensity, at the fiction that was his metier. The novels of the late 1890s, *What Maisie Knew* (1897) and *The Awkward Age* (1899), are daring experiments with technique that manage to be witty and moving works of art as well. The former traces the complex sexual entanglements of a divorced couple from the point of view of the unwanted child who oscillates between their households. The latter uses an almost purely dramatic technique—dialogue almost completely supplants narration—in its satirical but poignant exposé of the marriage market of fashionable London. There is a new assurance in these novels that points unmistakably to the last novels of James's "major phase."

In the three novels of this period, *The Wings of the Dove* (1902), *The Ambassadors* (1903), and *The Golden Bowl* (1904), James brought his art to its culmination. These works return, in a sense, to the "international theme" of his earlier years, for they all involve the conflict between American innocence and European experience. All turn upon a sexual betrayal whose discovery forms the turning point of the novel. What is new here is the use of characters of extraordinary refinement of sensibility, with imaginations responsive to the slightest nuance of word or gesture, conveyed with a style matched to the subtle and intricate texture of the subject matter. James's language is abstract and involuted or racy and metaphorical by turns; it is easy to lose one's track on the steep slopes of these novels, and many readers, even ones who admire James's earlier work, find the rewards are not worth the difficulties. But for those who can penetrate the surface of late James, there is the pleasure, over and above that of an ordinary novel, of finding oneself gradually refashioned into as subtle a creature as the exquisite characters, with their capacity for imaginative understanding. It is the effort James puts us to that makes us sensitive, and our consciousness of this unused talent is its own reward.

While the sales of *The Golden Bowl* were unusually large—due most probably to a trip James took back to America in 1904—James never regained the popularity he had enjoyed before 1881. He had hoped to make himself financially secure through the publication of the New York Edition of his works, a twenty-six-volume set for which he painstakingly revised his best stories and tales (1907–1909). But the returns were disappointing, so much so that his friend Edith Wharton made a secret arrangement with their common publisher to divert some of her own royalties to his account. He had become a writer's writer, though, if he was not the public's, and an entire generation of English and American novelists looked to him for advice and assistance, for tactful but sharp-eyed criticism of their work, and for the warm friendship that was his personal gift. To them, at least, he was the Master.

In his last years, James began writing his memoirs, and his *A Small Boy and Others* (1913) and *Notes of a Son and Brother* (1914) have given us great insights into himself and the remarkable family that produced him. The outbreak of the First World War broke the quiet of his final days. Though past seventy and in failing health, James involved himself in relief activities, visiting hospitals for refugees and giving comfort to the displaced and the wounded. As an expression of his solidarity with the British cause during America's neutrality, James applied for British citizenship, which was granted in July 1915. In recognition of both his literary and patriotic efforts, King George V put him on his next honors list, awarding James the Order of Merit. Disabled by heart trouble and pneumonia brought on by his exertions, James died on February 26, 1916.

Biography   The texture of James's life shows up in its highest relief in Leon Edel's five-volume *The Life of Henry James* (Philadelphia: Lippincott, 1953–1972). A good brief overview is *Henry James: His Life and Writings*, by F. W. Dupee (Garden City, N.Y.: Anchor, 1956).

Editions   James revised his major works for the "New York Edition" of his collected works (Scribner, 1907–1917, 26 vols.). No uniform edition of the novels as they were originally published yet exists, though many of the paperback editions of his novels follow the text of the first rather than the revised edition. A complete edition of James's short fiction in its first published form is the *Complete Tales of Henry James*, edited by Leon Edel (Philadelphia: Lippincott, 1962–1964, 12 vols.). James's *Notebooks*, invaluable for the study of the development of his art, were edited by F. O. Matthiessen and K. B. Murdoch (New York: Oxford University Press, 1947).

Bibliography   LeRoy Phillips: *A Bibliography of the Writings of Henry James* (Boston: Milford House, 1974); Beatrice Ricks: *Henry James: A Bibliography of Secondary Works* (Metuchen, N.J.: Scarecrow, 1975).

General Criticism   A few of the major works on James include Joseph Warren Beach, *The Method of Henry James* (New Haven: Yale University Press, 1918); F. O. Matthiessen, *Henry James: The Major Phase* (New York: Oxford University Press, 1944); Dorothea Krook, *The Ordeal of Consciousness in Henry James* (Cambridge: Cambridge University Press, 1948); Seymour Chatman, *The Later Style of Henry James* (New York: Barnes & Noble, 1972).

***Criticism of* The Aspern Papers**   William Bysshe Stein, "The Aspern Papers: a Comedy of Masks," *Nineteenth-Century Fiction* 14 (September, 1959), 172–178; Sam S. Baskett, "The Sense of the Present in *The Aspern Papers*," *Proceedings of the Michigan Academy of Science, Arts and Letters* 44 (1959), 381–388; Wayne C. Booth, *The Rhetoric of Fiction* (Chicago: University of Chicago Press, 1961), pp. 354-364.

A Note on the Text   The following reprinting of *The Aspern Papers* follows the text of the New York Edition (1909).

The Aspern Papers

I

I had taken Mrs. Prest into my confidence; without her in truth I should have made but little advance, for the fruitful idea in the whole business dropped from her friendly lips. It was she who found the short cut and loosed the Gordian knot. It is not supposed easy for women to rise to the large free view of anything, anything to be done; but they sometimes throw off a bold conception—such as a man would n't have risen to—with singular serenity. "Simply make them take you in on the footing of a lodger"—I don't think that unaided I should have risen to that. I was beating about the bush, trying to be ingenious, wondering by what combination of arts I might become an acquaintance, when she offered this happy suggestion that the way to become an acquaintance was first to become an intimate. Her actual knowledge of the Misses Bordereau was scarcely larger than mine, and indeed I had brought with me from England some definite facts that were new to her. Their name had been mixed up ages before with one of the greatest names of the century, and they now lived obscurely in Venice, lived on very small means, unvisited, unapproachable, in a sequestered and dilapidated old palace: this was the substance of my friend's impression of them. She herself had been established in Venice some fifteen years and had done a great deal of good there; but the circle of her benevolence had never embraced the two shy, mysterious and, as was somehow supposed, scarcely respectable Americans—they were believed to have lost in their long exile all national quality, besides being as their name implied of some remoter French affiliation[1]— who asked no favours and desired no attention. In the early years of her residence she had made an attempt to see them, but this had been successful only as regards the little one, as Mrs. Prest called the niece; though in fact I afterwards found her the bigger of the two in inches. She had heard Miss Bordereau was ill and had a suspicion she was in want, and had gone to the house to offer aid, so that if there were suffering, American suffering in particular, she should n't have it on her conscience. The "little one" had received her in the great cold tarnished Venetian *sala*, the central hall of the house, paved with marble and roofed with dim cross-beams, and had n't even asked her to sit down. This was not encouraging for me, who wished to sit so fast, and I remarked as much to Mrs. Prest. She replied however with profundity, "Ah, but there's all the difference: I went to confer a favour and you'll go to ask one. If they're proud you'll be on the right side." And she offered to show me their house to begin with—to row me thither in her gondola. I let her know I had already been to look at it half a dozen times; but I accepted her invitation, for it charmed me to hover about the place. I had made my way to it the day after my arrival in Venice— it had been described to me in advance by the friend in England to whom I owed definite information as to their possession of the papers—laying siege to it with my eyes while I considered my plan of campaign. Jeffrey Aspern had never been in it that I knew of, but some note of his voice seemed to abide there by a roundabout implication and in a "dying fall."

Mrs. Prest knew nothing about the papers, but was interested in my curiosity, as always in the joys and sorrows of her friends. As we went, however, in her gondola, gliding there under the sociable hood with the bright Venetian picture framed on either side by the movable window, I saw how my eagerness amused her and that she found my interest in my possible spoil a fine case of monomania. "One would think you expected from it the answer to the riddle of the universe,"

---

[1]"Bordereau" in French means, appropriately enough, memorandum.

she said; and I denied the impeachment only by replying that if I had to choose between that precious solution and a bundle of Jeffrey Aspern's letters I knew indeed which would appear to me the greater boon. She pretended to make light of his genius and I took no pains to defend him. One does n't defend one's god: one's god is in himself a defence. Besides, to-day, after his long comparative obscuration, he hangs high in the heaven of our literature for all the world to see; he's a part of the light by which we walk. The most I said was that he was no doubt not a woman's poet; to which she rejoined aptly enough that he had been at least Miss Bordereau's. The strange thing had been for me to discover in England that she was still alive: it was as if I had been told Mrs. Siddons was, or Queen Caroline, or the famous Lady Hamilton, for it seemed to me that she belonged to a generation as extinct. "Why she must be tremendously old—at least a hundred," I had said; but on coming to consider dates I saw it not strictly involved that she should have far exceeded the common span. None the less she was of venerable age and her relations with Jeffrey Aspern had occurred in her early womanhood. "That's her excuse," said Mrs. Prest half-sententiously and yet also somewhat as if she were ashamed of making a speech so little in the real tone of Venice. As if a woman needed an excuse for having loved the divine poet! He had been not only one of the most brilliant minds of his day—and in those years, when the century was young, there were, as every one knows, many—but one of the most genial men and one of the handsomest.

The niece, according to Mrs. Prest, was of minor antiquity, and the conjecture was risked that she was only a grand-niece. This was possible; I had nothing but my share in the very limited knowledge of my English fellow worshipper John Cumnor, who had never seen the couple. The world, as I say, had recognised Jeffrey Aspern, but Cumnor and I had recognised him most. The multitude to-day flocked to his temple, but of that temple he and I regarded ourselves as the appointed ministers. We held, justly, as I think, that we had done more for his memory than any one else, and had done it simply by opening lights into his life. He had nothing to fear from us because he had nothing to fear from the truth, which alone at such a distance of time we could be interested in establishing. His early death had been the only dark spot, as it were, on his fame, unless the papers in Miss Bordereau's hands should perversely bring out others. There had been an impression about 1825 that he had "treated her badly," just as there had been an impression that he had "served," as the London populace says, several other ladies in the same masterful way. Each of these cases Cumnor and I had been able to investigate, and we had never failed to acquit him conscientiously of any grossness. I judged him perhaps more indulgently than my friend; certainly, at any rate, it appeared to me that no man could have walked straighter in the given circumstances. These had been almost always difficult and dangerous. Half the women of his time, to speak liberally, had flung themselves at his head, and while the fury raged—the more that it was very catching—accidents, some of them very grave, had not failed to occur. He was not a woman's poet, as I had said to Mrs. Prest, in the modern phase of his reputation; but the situation had been different when the man's own voice was mingled with his song. That voice, by every testimony, was one of the most charming ever heard. "Orpheus and the Maenads!"[2] had been of course my foreseen judgement when first I turned over his correspondence. Almost all the Maenads were unreasonable and many of them unbearable; it struck me that he had been kinder and more considerate than in his place—if I could imagine myself in any such box—I should have found the trick of.

It was certainly strange beyond all strangeness, and I shall not take up space with attempting to explain it, that whereas among all these other relations and in these other directions of research we had to deal with phantoms and dust, the mere echoes of echoes, the one living source of information that had lingered on into our time had been unheeded by us. Every one of Aspern's contemporaries had, according to our belief, passed away; we had not been able to look into a single pair of eyes into which his had looked or to feel a transmitted contact in any aged hand that his had touched. Most dead of all did poor Miss Bordereau appear, and yet she alone had survived. We exhausted in the course of months our wonder that we had not found her out sooner, and the substance of our explanation was that she had kept so quiet. The poor lady on the whole had had reason for doing so. But it was a revelation to us that self-effacement on such a scale had been possible in the latter half of the nineteenth century—the age of newspapers and telegrams and photographs and interviewers. She had taken no great trouble for it either—had n't hidden herself away in an undiscoverable hole, had boldly settled down in a city of exhibition. The one apparent secret of her safety had been that Venice contained so many much greater curiosities. And then accident had somehow favoured her, as was shown for example in the fact that Mrs. Prest had never

---

[2]A legendary Greek hero with magical talent for music, Orpheus was killed by the Maenads, a group of maddened women, when he refused to sing for them.

happened to name her to me, though I had spent three weeks in Venice—under her nose, as it were—five years before. My friend indeed had not named her much to any one; she appeared almost to have forgotten the fact of her continuance. Of course Mrs. Prest had n't the nerves of an editor. It was meanwhile no explanation of the old woman's having eluded us to say that she lived abroad, for our researches had again and again taken us—not only by correspondence but by personal enquiry—to France, to Germany, to Italy, in which countries, not counting his important stay in England, so many of the too few years of Aspern's career had been spent. We were glad to think at least that in all our promulgations—some people now consider I believe that we have overdone them—we had only touched in passing and in the most discreet manner on Miss Bordereau's connexion. Oddly enough, even if we had had the material—and we had often wondered what could have become of it—this would have been the most difficult episode to handle.

The gondola stopped, the old palace was there; it was a house of the class which in Venice carries even in extreme dilapidation the dignified name. "How charming! It's grey and pink!" my companion exclaimed; and that is the most comprehensive description of it. It was not particularly old, only two or three centuries; and it had an air not so much of decay as of quiet discouragement, as if it had rather missed its career. But its wide front, with a stone balcony from end to end of the *piano nobile* or most important floor, was architectural enough, with the aid of various pilasters and arches; and the stucco with which in the intervals it had long ago been endued was rosy in the April afternoon. It overlooked a clean melancholy rather lonely canal, which had a narrow *riva* or convenient footway on either side. "I don't know why—there are no brick gables," said Mrs. Prest, "but this corner has seemed to me before more Dutch than Italian, more like Amsterdam than like Venice. It's eccentrically neat, for reasons of its own; and though you may pass on foot scarcely any one ever thinks of doing so. It's as negative—considering *where* it is—as a Protestant Sunday. Perhaps the people are afraid of the Misses Bordereau. I dare say they have the reputation of witches."

I forget what answer I made to this—I was given up to two other reflexions. The first of these was that if the old lady lived in such a big and imposing house she could n't be in any sort of misery and therefore would n't be tempted by a chance to let a couple of rooms. I expressed this fear to Mrs. Prest, who gave me a very straight answer. "If she did n't live in a big house how could it be a question of her having rooms to spare? If she were not amply lodged you'd lack ground to approach her. Besides, a big house here, and especially in this *quartier perdu*,[3] proves nothing at all: it's perfectly consistent with a state of penury. Dilapidated old palazzi, if you'll go out of the way for them, are to be had for five shillings a year. And as for the people who live in them—no, until you've explored Venice socially as much as I have, you can form no idea of their domestic desolation. They live on nothing, for they've nothing to live on." The other idea that had come into my head was connected with a high blank wall which appeared to confine an expanse of ground on one side of the house. Blank I call it, but it was figured over with the patches that please a painter, repaired breaches, crumblings of plaster, extrusions of brick that had turned pink with time; while a few thin trees, with the poles of certain rickety trellises, were visible over the top. The place was a garden and apparently attached to the house. I suddenly felt that so attached it gave me my pretext.

I sat looking out on all this with Mrs. Prest (it was covered with the golden glow of Venice) from the shade of our *felze*, and she asked me if I would go in then, while she waited for me, or come back another time. At first I couldn't decide—it was doubtless very weak of me. I wanted still to think I *might* get a footing, and was afraid to meet failure, for it would leave me, as I remarked to my companion, without another arrow for my bow. "Why not another?" she enquired as I sat there hesitating and thinking it over; and she wished to know why even now and before taking the trouble of becoming an inmate—which might be wretchedly uncomfortable after all, even if it succeeded—I hadn't the resource of simply offering them a sum of money down. In that way I might get what I wanted without bad nights.

"Dearest lady," I exclaimed, "excuse the impatience of my tone when I suggest that you must have forgotten the fact—surely I communicated it to you—which threw me on your ingenuity. The old woman won't have her relics and tokens so much as spoken of; they're personal, delicate, intimate, and she hasn't the feelings of the day, God bless her! If I should sound that note first I should certainly spoil the game. I can arrive at my spoils only by putting her off her guard, and I can put her off her guard only by ingratiating diplomatic arts. Hypocrisy, duplicity are my only chance. I'm sorry for it, but there's no baseness I wouldn't commit for Jeffrey Aspern's sake. First I must take tea

---

[3]Deserted neighborhood.

with her—then tackle the main job." And I told over what had happened to John Cumnor on his respectfully writing to her. No notice whatever had been taken of his first letter, and the second had been answered very sharply, in six lines, by the niece. "Miss Bordereau requested her to say that she could n't imagine what he meant by troubling them. They had none of Mr. Aspern's 'literary remains,' and if they *had* would n't have dreamed of showing them to any one on any account whatever. She could n't imagine what he was talking about and begged he would let her alone." I certainly did n't want to be met that way.

"Well," said Mrs. Prest after a moment and all provokingly, "perhaps they really have n't anything. If they deny it flat how are you sure?"

"John Cumnor's sure, and it would take me long to tell you how his conviction, or his very strong presumption—strong enough to stand against the old lady's not unnatural fib—has built itself up. Besides, he makes much of the internal evidence of the niece's letter."

"The internal evidence?"

"Her calling him 'Mr. Aspern.' "

"I don't see what that proves."

"It proves familiarity, and familiarity implies the possession of mementoes, of tangible objects. I can't tell you how that 'Mr.' affects me— how it bridges over the gulf of time and brings our hero near to me— nor what an edge it gives to my desire to see Juliana. You don't say 'Mr.' Shakespeare."

"Would I, any more, if I had a box full of his letters?"

"Yes, if he had been your lover and some one wanted them." And I added that John Cumnor was so convinced, and so all the more convinced by Miss Bordereau's tone, that he would have come himself to Venice on the undertaking were it not for the obstacle of his having, for any confidence, to disprove his identity with the person who had written to them, which the old ladies would be sure to suspect in spite of dissimulation and a change of name. If they were to ask him point-blank if he were not their snubbed correspondent it would be too awkward for him to lie; whereas I was fortunately not tied in that way. I was a fresh hand—I could protest without lying.

"But you'll have to take a false name," said Mrs. Prest. "Juliana lives out of the world as much as it is possible to live, but she has none the less probably heard of Mr. Aspern's editors. She perhaps possesses what you've published."

"I've thought of that," I returned; and I drew out of my pocket-book a visiting-card neatly engraved with a well-chosen *nom de guerre*.[4]

"You're very extravagant—it adds to your immorality. You might have done it in pencil or ink," said my companion.

"This looks more genuine."

"Certainly you've the courage of your curiosity. But it will be awkward about your letters; they won't come to you in that mask."

"My banker will take them in and I shall go every day to get them. It will give me a little walk."

"Shall you depend all on that?" asked Mrs. Prest. "Are n't you coming to see me?"

"Oh you'll have left Venice for the hot months long before there are any results. I'm prepared to roast all summer—as well as through the long hereafter perhaps you'll say! Meanwhile John Cumnor will bombard me with letters addressed, in my feigned name, to the care of the padrona."

"She'll recognise his hand," my companion suggested.

"On the envelope he can disguise it."

"Well, you're a precious pair! Does n't it occur to you that even if you're able to say you're not Mr. Cumnor in person they may still suspect you of being his emissary?"

"Certainly, and I see only one way to parry that."

"And what may that be?"

I hesitated a moment. "To make love to the niece."

"Ah," cried my friend, "wait till you see her!"

II

"I must work the garden—I must work the garden," I said to myself five minutes later and while I waited, upstairs, in the long dusky sala, where the bare scagliola floor gleamed vaguely in a chink of the closed shutters. The place was impressive, yet looked somehow cold and cautious. Mrs. Prest had floated away, giving me a rendezvous at the end of half an hour by some neighbouring water-steps; and I had been let into the house, after pulling the rusty bell-wire, by a small red-headed and white-faced maid-servant, who was very young and not ugly and wore clicking pattens and a shawl in the fashion of a hood. She had not

_____

4Pseudonym; in particular, a spy's false name.

contented herself with opening the door from above by the usual arrangement of a creaking pulley, though she had looked down at me first from an upper window, dropping the cautious challenge which in Italy precedes the act of admission. I was irritated as a general thing by this survival of medieval manners, though as so fond, if yet so special, an antiquarian I suppose I ought to have liked it; but, with my resolve to be genial from the threshold at any price, I took my false card out of my pocket and held it up for her, smiling as if it were a magic token. It had the effect of one indeed, for it brought her, as I say, all the way down. I begged her to hand it to her mistress, having first written on it in Italian the words: "Could you very kindly see a gentleman, a travelling American, for a moment?" The little maid wasn't hostile—even that was perhaps something gained. She coloured, she smiled and looked both frightened and pleased. I could see that my arrival was a great affair, that visits in such a house were rare and that she was a person who would have liked a bustling place. When she pushed forward the heavy door behind me I felt my foot in the citadel and promised myself ever so firmly to keep it there. She pattered across the damp stony lower hall and I followed her up the high staircase—stonier still, as it seemed—without an invitation. I think she had meant I should wait for her below, but such was not my idea, and I took up my station in the sala. She flitted, at the far end of it, into impenetrable regions, and I looked at the place with my heart beating as I had known it to do in dentists' parlours. It had a gloomy grandeur, but owed its character almost all to its noble shape and to the fine architectural doors, as high as those of grand frontages, which, leading into the various rooms, repeated themselves on either side at intervals. They were surmounted with old faded painted escutcheons, and here and there in the spaces between them hung brown pictures, which I noted as speciously bad, in battered and tarnished frames that were yet more desirable than the canvases themselves. With the exception of several straw-bottomed chairs that kept their backs to the wall the grand obscure vista contained little else to minister to effect. It was evidently never used save as a passage, and scantly even as that. I may add that by the time the door through which the maid-servant had escaped opened again my eyes had grown used to the want of light.

I hadn't meanwhile meant by my private ejaculation that I must myself cultivate the soil of the tangled enclosure which lay beneath the windows, but the lady who came toward me from the distance over the hard shining floor might have supposed as much from the way in which, as I went rapidly to meet her, I exclaimed, taking care to speak

Italian: "The garden, the garden—do me the pleasure to tell me if it's yours!"

She stopped short, looking at me with wonder; and then, "Nothing here is mine," she answered in English, coldly and sadly.

"Oh, you're English; how delightful!" I ingenuously cried. "But surely the garden belongs to the house?"

"Yes, but the house does n't belong to me." She was a long lean pale person, habited apparently in a dull-coloured dressing gown, and she spoke very simply and mildly. She did n't ask me to sit down, any more than years before—if she were the niece—she had asked Mrs. Prest, and we stood face to face in the empty pompous hall.

"Well then, would you kindly tell me to whom I must address myself? I'm afraid you'll think me horribly intrusive, but you know I *must* have a garden—upon my honour I must!"

Her face was not young, but it was candid; it was not fresh, but it was clear. She had large eyes which were not bright, and a great deal of hair which was not "dressed," and long fine hands which were—possibly—not clean. She clasped these members almost convulsively as, with a confused alarmed look, she broke out: "Oh don't take it away from us; we like it ourselves!"

"You have the use of it then?"

"Oh yes. If it was n't for that—!" And she gave a wan vague smile.

"Is n't it a luxury, precisely? That's why, intending to be in Venice some weeks, possibly all summer, and having some literary work, some reading and writing to do, so that I must be quiet and yet if possible a great deal in the open air—that's why I've felt a garden to be really indispensable. I appeal to your own experience," I went on with as sociable a smile as I could risk. "Now can't I look at yours?"

"I don't know, I don't understand," the poor woman murmured, planted there and letting her weak wonder deal—helplessly enough, as I felt—with my strangeness.

"I mean only from one of those windows—such grand ones as you have here—if you'll let me open the shutters." And I walked toward the back of the house. When I had advanced halfway I stopped and waited as in the belief she would accompany me. I had been of necessity quite abrupt, but I strove at the same time to give her the impression of extreme courtesy. "I've looked at furnished rooms all over the place, and it seems impossible to find any with a garden attached. Naturally in a place like Venice gardens are rare. It's absurd if you like, for a man, but I can't live without flowers."

"There are none to speak of down there." She came nearer, as if, though she mistrusted me, I had drawn her by an invisible thread. I went on again, and she continued as she followed me: "We've a few, but they're very common. It costs too much to cultivate them; one has to have a man."

"Why should n't I be the man?" I asked. "I'll work without wages; or rather I'll put in a gardener. You shall have the sweetest flowers in Venice."

She protested against this with a small quaver of sound that might have been at the same time a gush of rapture for my free sketch. Then she gasped: "We don't know you—we don't know you."

"You know me as much as I know you; or rather much more, because you know my name. And if you're English I'm almost a countryman."

"We're not English," said my companion, watching me in practical submission while I threw open the shutters of one of the divisions of the wide high window.

"You speak the language so beautifully: might I ask what you are?" Seen from above the garden was in truth shabby, yet I felt at a glance that it had great capabilities. She made no rejoinder, she was so lost in her blankness and gentleness, and I exclaimed: "You don't mean to say you're also by chance American?"

"I don't know. We used to be."

"Used to be? Surely you have n't changed?"

"It's so many years ago. We don't seem to be anything now."

"So many years that you've been living here?" Well, I don't wonder at that; it's a grand old house. I suppose you all use the garden," I went on, "but I assure you I should n't be in your way. I'd be very quiet and stay quite in one corner."

"We all use it?" she repeated after me vaguely, not coming close to the window but looking at my shoes. She appeared to think me capable of throwing her out.

"I mean all your family—as many as you are."

"There's only one other than me. She's very old. She never goes down."

I feel again my thrill at this close identification of Juliana; in spite of which, however, I kept my head. "Only one other in all this great house!" I feigned to be not only amazed but almost scandalised. "Dear lady, you must have space then to spare!"

"To spare?" she repeated—almost as for the rich unwonted joy to her of spoken words.

"Why you surely don't live (two quiet women—I see *you* are quiet, at any rate) in fifty rooms!" Then with a burst of hope and cheer I put the question straight. "Could n't you for a good rent *let* me two or three? That would set me up!"

I had now struck the note that translated my purpose, and I need n't reproduce the whole of the tune I played. I ended by making my entertainer believe me an undesigning person, though of course I did n't even attempt to persuade her I was not an eccentric one. I repeated that I had studies to pursue; that I wanted quiet; that I delighted in a garden and had vainly sought one up and down the city: that I would undertake that before another month was over the dear old house should be smothered in flowers. I think it was the flowers that won my suit, for I afterwards found that Miss Tina—for such the name of this high tremulous spinster proved somewhat incongruously to be—had an insatiable appetite for them. When I speak of my suit as won I mean that before I left her she had promised me she would refer the question to her aunt. I invited information as to who her aunt might be and she answered "Why Miss Bordereau!" with an air of surprise, as if I might have been expected to know. There were contradictions like this in Miss Tina which, as I observed later, contributed to make her rather pleasingly incalculable and interesting. It was the study of the two ladies to live so that the world should n't talk of them or touch them, and yet they had never altogether accepted the idea that it did n't hear of them. In Miss Tina at any rate a grateful susceptibility to human contact had not died out, and contact of a limited order there would be if I should come to live in the house.

"We've never done anything of the sort; we've never had a lodger or any kind of inmate." So much as this she made a point of saying to me. "We're very poor, we live very badly—almost on nothing. The rooms are very bare—those you might take; they've nothing at all in them. I don't know how you'd sleep, how you'd eat."

"With your permission I could easily put in a bed and a few tables and chairs. *C'est la moindre des choses*⁵ and the affair of an hour or two. I know a little man from whom I can hire for a trifle what I should so briefly want, what I should use; my gondolier can bring the things round in his boat. Of course in this great house you must have a second kitchen, and my servant, who's a wonderfully handy fellow"— this personage was an evocation of the moment—"can easily cook me a chop there. My tastes and habits are of the simplest: I live on flow-

---

⁵It's the least little thing.

ers!" And then I ventured to add that if they were very poor it was all the more reason they should let their rooms. They were bad economists—I had never heard of such a waste of material.

I saw in a moment my good lady had never before been spoken to in any such fashion—with a humorous firmness that did n't exclude sympathy, that was quite founded on it. She might easily have told me that my sympathy was impertinent, but this by good fortune did n't occur to her. I left her with the understanding that she would submit the question to her aunt and that I might come back the next day for their decision.

"The aunt will refuse; she'll think the whole proceeding very *louche!*"[6] Mrs. Prest declared shortly after this, when I had resumed my place in her gondola. She had put the idea into my head and now—so little are women to be counted on—she appeared to take a despondent view of it. Her pessimism provoked me and I pretended to have the best hopes; I went so far as to boast of a distinct prevision of success. Upon this Mrs. Prest broke out: "Oh I see what's in your head! You fancy you've made such an impression in five minutes that she's dying for you to come and can be depended on to bring the old one around. If you do get in you'll count it as a triumph."

I did count it as a triumph, but only for the commentator—in the last analysis—not for the man, who had not the tradition of personal conquest. When I went back on the morrow the little maid-servant conducted me straight through the long sala—it opened there as before in large perspective and was lighter now, which I thought a good omen—into the apartment from which the recipient of my former visit had emerged on that occasion. It was a spacious shabby parlour with a fine old painted ceiling under which a strange figure sat alone at one of the windows. They come back to me now almost with the palpitation they caused, the successive states marking my consciousness that as the door of the room closed behind me I was really face to face with the Juliana of some of Aspern's most exquisite and most renowned lyrics. I grew used to her afterwards, though never completely; but as she sat there before me my heart beat as fast as if the miracle of resurrection had taken place for my benefit. Her presence seemed somehow to contain and express his own, and I felt nearer to him at that first moment of seeing her than I ever had been before or ever have been since. Yes, I remember my emotions in their order, even including a curious

---

[6]Suspicious.

little tremor that took me when I saw the niece not to be there. With
her, the day before, I had become sufficiently familiar, but it almost
exceeded my courage—much as I had longed for the event—to be left
alone with so terrible a relic as the aunt. She was too strange, too
literally resurgent. Then came a check from the perception that we
were n't really face to face, inasmuch as she had over her eyes a horrible green shade which served for her almost as a mask. I believed for
the instant that she had put it on expressly, so that from underneath it
she might take me all in without my getting at herself. At the same
time it created a presumption of some ghastly death's-head lurking
behind it. The divine Juliana as a grinning skull—the vision hung there
until it passed. Then it came to me that she *was* tremendously old—so
old that death might take her at any moment, before I should have
time to compass my end. The next thought was a correction to that; it
lighted up the situation. She would die next week, she would die to-
morrow—then I could pounce on her possessions and ransack her
drawers. Meanwhile she sat there neither moving nor speaking. She
was very small and shrunken, bent forward with her hands in her lap.
She was dressed in black and her head was wrapped in a piece of old
black lace which showed no hair.

My emotion keeping me silent she spoke first, and the remark she
made was exactly the most unexpected.

III

"Our house is very far from the centre, but the little canal is very *comme
il faut*."[7]

"It's the sweetest corner of Venice and I can imagine nothing more
charming," I hastened to reply. The old lady's voice was very thin and
weak, but it had an agreeable, cultivated murmur and there was wonder in the thought that that individual note had been in Jeffrey
Aspern's ear.

"Please to sit down there. I hear very well," she said quietly, as if
perhaps I had been shouting; and the chair she pointed to was at a
certain distance. I took possession of it, assuring her I was perfectly
aware of my intrusion and of my not having been properly introduced,
and that I could but throw myself on her indulgence. Perhaps the other

---

[7]Suitable; proper.

lady, the one I had had the honour of seeing the day before, would have explained to her about the garden. That was literally what had given me courage to take a step so unconventional. I had fallen in love at first sight with the whole place—she herself was probably so used to it that she did n't know the impression it was capable of making on a stranger—and I had felt it really a case to risk something. Was her own kindness in receiving me a sign that I was not wholly out in my calculation? It would make me extremely happy to think so. I could give her my word of honour that I was a most respectable inoffensive person and that as a co-tenant of the palace, so to speak, they would be barely conscious of my existence. I would conform to any regulation, any restrictions, if they would only let me enjoy the garden. Moreover I should be delighted to give her references, guarantees; they would be of the very best, both in Venice and in England, as well as in America.

She listened to me in perfect stillness and I felt her look at me with great penetration, though I could see only the lower part of her bleached and shrivelled face. Independently of the refining process of old age it had a delicacy which once must have been great. She had been very fair, she had had a wonderful complexion. She was silent a little after I had ceased speaking; then she began: "If you're so fond of a garden why don't you go to *terra firma*, where there are so many far better than this?"

"Oh it's the combination!" I answered, smiling; and then with rather a flight of fancy: "It's the idea of a garden in the middle of the sea."

"This is n't the middle of the sea; you can't so much as see the water."

I stared a moment, wondering if she wished to convict me of fraud. "Can't see the water? Why, dear madam, I can come up to the very gate in my boat."

She appeared inconsequent, for she said vaguely in reply to this: "Yes, if you've got a boat. I have n't any; it's many years since I've been in one of the *gondole*." She uttered these words as if they designed a curious far-away craft known to her only by hearsay.

"Let me assure you of the pleasure with which I would put mine at your service!" I returned. I had scarcely said this however before I became aware that the speech was in questionable taste and might also do me the injury of making me appear too eager, too possessed of a hidden motive. But the old woman remained impenetrable and her attitude worried me by suggesting that she had a fuller vision of me than I had of her. She gave me no thanks for my somewhat extravagant offer, but remarked that the lady I had seen the day before was her niece; she would presently come in. She had asked her to stay away a little on purpose—had had her reasons for seeing me first alone. She relapsed into silence and I turned over the fact of these unmentioned reasons and the question of what might come yet; also that of whether I might venture on some judicious remark in praise of her companion. I went so far as to say I should be delighted to see our absent friend again: she had been so very patient with me, considering how odd she must have thought me—a declaration which drew from Miss Bordereau another of her whimsical speeches.

"She has very good manners; I bred her up myself!" I was on the point of saying that that accounted for the easy grace of the niece, but I arrested myself in time, and the next moment the old woman went on: "I don't care who you may be—I don't want to know: it signifies very little to-day." This had all the air of being a formula of dismissal, as if her next words would be that I might take myself off now that she had had the amusement of looking on the face of such a monster of indiscretion. Therefore I was all the more surprised when she added in her soft venerable quaver: "You may have as many rooms as you like—if you'll pay me a good deal of money."

I hesitated but an instant, long enough to measure what she meant in particular by this condition. First it struck me that she must really have a large sum in her mind; then I reasoned quickly that her idea of a large sum would probably not correspond to my own. My deliberation, I think, was not so visible as to diminish the promptitude with which I replied: "I will pay with pleasure and of course in advance whatever you may think it proper to ask me."

"Well then, a thousand francs a month," she said instantly, while her baffling green shade continued to cover her attitude.

The figure, as they say, was startling and my logic had been at fault. The sum she had mentioned was, by the Venetian measure of such matters, exceedingly large; there was many an old palace in an out-of-the-way corner that I might on such terms have enjoyed the whole of the year. But so far as my resources allowed I was prepared to spend money, and my decision was quickly taken. I would pay her with a smiling face what she asked; but in that case I would make it up by getting hold of my "spoils" for nothing. Moreover if she had asked five times as much I should have risen to the occasion, so odious would it have seemed to me to stand chaffering with Aspern's Juliana. It was queer enough to have a question of money with her at all. I assured her that her views perfectly met my own and that on the morrow I should have the pleasure of putting three months' rent into her hand. She received this announcement with apparent complacency and with no discoverable sense that after all it would become her to say that I ought to see the rooms first. This did n't occur to her, and indeed her serenity was mainly what I wanted. Our little agreement was just concluded when the door opened and the younger lady appeared on the threshold. As soon as Miss Bordereau saw her niece she cried out almost gaily: "He'll give three thousand—three thousand to-morrow!"

Miss Tina stood still, her patient eyes turning from one of us to the other; then she brought out, scarcely above her breath: "Do you mean francs?"

"Did you mean francs or dollars?" the old woman asked of me at this.

"I think francs were what you said," I sturdily smiled.

"That's very good," said Miss Tina, as if she had felt how overreaching her own question might have looked.

"What do *you* know? You're ignorant," Miss Bordereau remarked; not with acerbity but with a strange soft coldness.

"Yes, of money—certainly of money!" Miss Tina hastened to concede.

"I'm sure you've your own fine branches of knowledge," I took the liberty of saying genially. There was something painful to me, somehow, in the turn the conversation had taken, in the discussion of dollars and francs.

"She had a very good education when she was young. I looked into that myself," said Miss Bordereau. Then she added: "But she has learned nothing since."

"I've always been with *you*," Miss Tina rejoined very mildly, and of a certainty with no intention of an epigram.

"Yes, but for that—!" her aunt declared with more satirical force. She evidently meant that but for this her niece would have never got on at all; the point of the observation however being lost on Miss Tina, though she blushed at hearing her history revealed to a stranger. Miss Bordereau went on, addressing herself to me: "And what time will you come to-morrow with the money?"

"The sooner the better. If it suits you I'll come at noon."

"I'm always here, but I have my hours," said the old woman as if her convenience were not to be taken for granted.

"You mean the times when you receive?"

"I never receive. But I'll see you at noon, when you come with the money."

"Very good, I shall be punctual." To which I added: "May I shake hands with you on our contract?" I thought there ought to be some little form; it would make me really feel easier, for I was sure there would be no other. Besides, though Miss Bordereau could n't to-day be called personally attractive and there was something even in her wasted antiquity that bade one stand at one's distance, I felt an irresistible desire to hold in my own for a moment the hand Jeffrey Aspern had pressed.

For a minute she made no answer, and I saw that my proposal failed to meet with her approbation. She indulged in no movement of withdrawal, which I half-expected; she only said coldly: "I belong to a time when that was not the custom."

I felt rather snubbed but I exclaimed good-humouredly to Miss Tina "Oh you'll do as well!" I shook hands with her while she assented with a small flutter. "Yes, yes, to show it's all arranged!"

"Shall you bring the money in gold?" Miss Bordereau demanded as I was turning to the door.

I looked at her a moment. "Are n't you a little afraid, after all, of keeping such a sum as that in the house?" It was not that I was annoyed at her avidity, but was truly struck with the disparity between such a treasure and such scanty means of guarding it.

"Whom should I be afraid of if I'm not afraid of you?" she asked with her shrunken grimness.

"Ah well," I laughed, "I shall be in point of fact a protector and I'll bring gold if you prefer."

"Thank you," the old woman returned with dignity and with an inclination of her head which evidently signified my dismissal. I passed out of the room, thinking how hard it would be to circumvent her. As I stood in the sala again I saw that Miss Tina had followed me, and I supposed that as her aunt had neglected to suggest I should take a look at my quarters it was her purpose to repair the omission. But she made no such overture; she only stood there with a dim, though not a languid smile, and with an effect of irresponsible incompetent youth almost comically at variance with the faded facts of her person. She was not infirm, like her aunt, but she struck me as more deeply futile, because her inefficiency was inward, which was not the case with Miss Bordereau's. I waited to see if she would offer to show me the rest of the house, but I did n't precipitate the question, inasmuch as my plan was from this moment to spend as much time as possible in her society. A minute indeed elapsed before I committed myself.

"I've had better fortune than I hoped. It was very kind of her to see me. Perhaps you said a good word for me."

"It was the idea of money," said Miss Tina.

"And did you suggest that?"

"I told her you'd perhaps pay largely."

"What made you think that?"

"I told her I thought you were rich."

"And what put that into your head?"

"I don't know; the way you talked."

"Dear me, I must talk differently now," I returned. "I'm sorry to say it's not the case."

"Well," said Miss Tina, "I think that in Venice the *forestieri*[8] in general often give a great deal for something that after all is n't much." She appeared to make this remark with a comforting intention, to wish to remind me that if I had been extravagant I was n't foolishly singular. We walked together along the sala, and as I took its magnificent measure I observed that I was afraid it would n't form a part of my *quartiere*. Were my rooms by chance to be among those that opened into it? "Not if you go above—to the second floor," she answered as if she had rather taken for granted I would know my proper place.

"And I infer that that's where your aunt would like me to be."

"She said your apartments ought to be very distinct."

"That certainly would be best." And I listened with respect while she told me that above I should be free to take whatever I might like; that there was another staircase, but only from the floor on which we stood, and that to pass from it to the garden-level or to come up to my lodging I should have in effect to cross the great hall. This was an immense point gained; I foresaw that it would constitute my whole leverage in my relations with the two ladies. When I asked Miss Tina how I was to manage at present to find my way up she replied with an access of that sociable shyness which constantly marked her manner:

"Perhaps you can't. I don't see—unless I should go with you." She evidently had n't thought of this before.

We ascended to the upper floor and visited a long succession of empty rooms. The best of them looked over the garden; some of the others had above the opposite rough-tiled house-tops a view of the blue lagoon. They were all dusty and even a little disfigured with long neglect, but I saw that by spending a few hundred francs I should be able to make three or four of them habitable enough. My experiment was turning out costly, yet now that I had all but taken possession I

---

[8]Foreigners.

ceased to allow this to trouble me. I mentioned to my companion a few of the things I should put in, but she replied rather more precipitately than usual that I might do exactly what I liked: she seemed to wish to notify me that the Misses Bordereau would take none but the most veiled interest in my proceedings. I guessed that her aunt had instructed her to adopt this tone, and I may as well say now that I came afterwards to distinguish perfectly (as I believed) between the speeches she made on her own responsibility and those the old woman imposed upon her. She took no notice of the unswept condition of the rooms and indulged neither in explanations nor in apologies. I said to myself that this was a sign Juliana and her niece—disenchanting idea!—were untidy persons with a low Italian standard; but I afterwards recognised that a lodger who had forced an entrance had no *locus standi* as a critic. We looked out of a good many windows, for there was nothing within the rooms to look at, and still I wanted to linger. I asked her what several different objects in the prospect might be, but in no case did she appear to know. She was evidently not familiar with the view—it was as if she had not looked at it for years—and I presently saw that she was too preoccupied with something else to pretend to care for it. Suddenly she said—the remark was not suggested:

"I don't know whether it will make any difference to you, but the money is for me."

"The money—?"

"The money you're going to bring."

"Why you'll make me wish to stay here two or three years!" I spoke as benevolently as possible, though it had begun to act upon my nerves that these women so associated with Aspern should so constantly bring the pecuniary question back.

"That would be very good for me," she answered almost gaily.

"You put me on my honour!"

She looked as if she failed to understand this, but went on: "She wants me to have more. She thinks she's going to die."

"Ah not soon I hope!" I cried with genuine feeling. I had perfectly considered the possibility of her destroying her documents on the day she should feel her end at hand. I believed that she would cling to them till then, and I was as convinced of her reading Aspern's letters over every night or at least pressing them to her withered lips. I would have given a good deal for some view of those solemnities. I asked Miss Tina if her venerable relative were seriously ill, and she replied that she was only very tired—she had lived so extraordinarily long. That was what she said herself—she wanted to die for a change. Besides, all her friends had been dead for ages; either they ought to have remained or she ought to have gone. That was another thing her aunt often said: she was not at all resigned—resigned, that is, to life.

"But people don't die when they like, do they?" Miss Tina enquired. I took the liberty of asking why, if there was actually enough money to maintain both of them, there would not be more than enough in case of her being left alone. She considered this difficult problem a moment and then said: "Oh well, you know, she takes care of me. She thinks that when I'm alone I shall be a great fool and shan't know how to manage."

"I should have supposed rather that you took care of *her*. I'm afraid she's very proud."

"Why, have you discovered that already?" Miss Tina cried with a dimness of glad surprise.

"I was shut up with her there for a considerable time and she struck me, she interested me extremely. It did n't take me long to make my discovery. She won't have much to say to me while I'm here."

"No, I don't think she will," my companion averred.

"Do you suppose she has some suspicion of me?"

Miss Tina's honest eyes gave me no sign I had touched a mark. "I should n't think so—letting you in after all so easily."

"You call it easily? She has covered her risk," I said. "But where is it one could take an advantage of her?"

"I ought n't to tell you if I knew, ought I?" And Miss Tina added, before I had time to reply to this, smiling dolefully: "Do you think we've any weak points?"

"That's exactly what I'm asking. You'd only have to mention them for me to respect them religiously."

She looked at me hereupon with that air of timid but candid and even gratified curiosity with which she had confronted me from the first; after which she said: "There's nothing to tell. We're terribly quiet. I don't know how the days pass. We've no life."

"I wish I might think I should bring you a little."

"Oh we know what we want," she went on. "It's all right."

There were twenty things I desired to ask her: how in the world they did live; whether they had any friends or visitors, any relations in America or in other countries. But I judged such probings premature; I must leave it to a later chance. "Well, don't *you* be proud," I contented myself with saying. "Don't hide from me altogether."

"Oh I must stay with my aunt," she returned without looking at me. And at the same moment, abruptly, without any ceremony of parting, she quitted me and disappeared, leaving me to make my own way downstairs. I stayed a while longer, wandering about the bright desert—the sun was pouring in—of the old house, thinking the situation over on the spot. Not even the pattering little *serva* came to look after me, and I reflected that after all this treatment showed confidence.

IV

Perhaps it did, but all the same, six weeks later, towards the middle of June, the moment when Mrs. Prest undertook her annual migration, I had made no measurable advance. I was obliged to confess to her that I had no results to speak of. My first step had been unexpectedly rapid, but there was no appearance it would be followed by a second. I was a thousand miles from taking tea with my hostesses—that privilege of which, as I reminded my good friend, we both had a vision. She reproached me with lacking boldness and I answered that even to be bold you must have an opportunity: you may push on through a breach, but you can't batter down a dead wall. She returned that the breach I had already made was big enough to admit an army and accused me of wasting precious hours in whimpering in her salon when I ought to have been carrying on the struggle in the field. It is true that I went to see her very often—all on the theory that it would console me (I freely expressed my discouragement) for my want of success on my own premises. But I began to feel that it did n't console me to be perpetually chaffed for my scruples, especially since I was really so vigilant; and I was rather glad when my ironic friend closed her house for the summer. She had expected to draw amusement from the drama of my intercourse with the Misses Bordereau, and was disappointed that the intercourse, and consequently the drama, had not come off. "They'll lead you to your ruin," she said before she left Venice. "They'll get all your money without showing you a scrap." I think I settled down to my business with more concentration after her departure.

It was a fact that up to that time I had not, save on a single brief occasion, had even a moment's contact with my queer hostesses. The exception had occurred when I carried them according to my promise the terrible three thousand francs. Then I found Miss Tina awaiting me in the hall, and she took the money from my hand with a promptitude that prevented my seeing her aunt. The old lady had promised to receive me, yet apparently thought nothing of breaking that vow. The money was contained in a bag of chamois leather, of respectable dimensions, which my banker had given me, and Miss Tina had to make a big fist to receive it. This she did with extreme solemnity, though I tried to treat the affair as a little joke. It was in no jocular strain, yet it was with a clearness akin to a brightness that she enquired, weighing the money in her two palms: "Don't you think it's too much?" To which I replied that this would depend on the amount of pleasure I should get for it. Hereupon she turned away from me quickly, as she had done the day before, murmuring in a tone different from any she had used hitherto: "Oh pleasure, pleasure—there's no pleasure in this house!"

After that, for a long time, I never saw her, and I wondered the common chances of the day should n't have helped us to meet. It could only be evident that she was immensely on her guard against them; and in addition to this the house was so big that for each other we were lost in it. I used to look out for her hopefully as I crossed the sala in my comings and goings, but I was not rewarded with a glimpse of the tail of her dress. It was as if she never peeped out of her aunt's apartment. I used to wonder what she did there week after week and year after year. I had never met so stiff a policy of seclusion; it was more than keeping quiet—it was like hunted creatures feigning death. The two ladies appeared to have no visitors whatever and no sort of contact with the world. I judged at least that people could n't have come to the house and that Miss Tina could n't have gone out without my catching some view of it. I did what I disliked myself for doing—considering it but as once in a way: I questioned my servant about their habits and let him infer that I should be interested in any information he might glean. But he gleaned amazingly little for a knowing Venetian: it must be added that where there is a perpetual fast there are very few crumbs on the floor. His ability in other ways was sufficient, if not quite all I had attributed to him on the occasion of my first interview with Miss Tina. He had helped my gondolier to bring me round a boat-load of furniture; and when these articles had been carried to the top of the palace and distributed according to our associated wisdom he organised my household with such dignity as answered to its being composed exclusively of himself. He made me in short as comfortable as I could be with my indifferent prospects. I should have been glad if he had fallen in love with Miss Bordereau's maid or, failing this, had taken her in aversion: either event might have brought about some catastrophe, and a catastrophe might have led to some parley. It was my idea that she would have been sociable, and I myself on various occasions saw her flit to and fro on domestic errands, so that I was sure she was accessible. But I tasted of no gossip from that fountain, and I afterwards learned that Pasquale's affections were fixed upon an object that made him heedless of other women. This was a young lady with a powdered face, a yellow cotton gown and much leisure, who used often to come to see him. She practised, at her convenience, the art of a stringer of beads—these ornaments are made in Venice to profusion; she had her pocket full of them and I used to find them on the floor of my apartment—and kept an eye on the possible rival in the house. It was not for me of course to make the domestics tattle, and I never said a word to Miss Bordereau's cook.

It struck me as a proof of the old woman's resolve to have nothing to do with me that she should never have sent me a receipt for my three months' rent. For some days I looked out for it and then, when I had given it up, wasted a good deal of time in wondering what her reason had been for neglecting so indispensable and familiar a form. At first I was tempted to send her a reminder; after which I put by the idea—against my judgement as to what was right in the particular case—on the general ground of wishing to keep quiet. If Miss Bordereau suspected me of ulterior aims she would suspect me less if I should be businesslike, and yet I consented not to be. It was possible she intended her omission as an impertinence, a visible irony, to show how she could overreach people who attempted to overreach her. On that hypothesis it was well to let her see that one did n't notice her little tricks. The real reading of the matter, I afterwards gathered, was simply the poor lady's desire to emphasize the fact that I was in the enjoyment of a favour as rigidly limited as it had been liberally bestowed. She had given me part of her house, but she would n't add to that so much as a morsel of paper with her name on it. Let me say that even at first this did n't make me too miserable, for the whole situation had the charm of its oddity. I foresaw that I should have a summer after my own literary heart, and the sense of playing with my opportunity was much greater after all than any sense of being played with. There could be no Venetian business without patience, and since I adored the place I was much more in the spirit of it for having laid in a large provision. That spirit kept me perpetual company and seemed to look out at me from the revived immortal face—in which all his genius shone—of the great poet who was my prompter. I had invoked him and he had come; he hovered before me half the time; it was as if his bright ghost had returned to earth to assure me he regarded the affair as his own no less than as mine and that we should see it fraternally and fondly to a conclusion. It was as if he had said: "Poor dear, be easy with her; she has some natural prejudices; only give her time. Strange as it may appear to you she was very attractive in 1820. Meanwhile are n't we in Venice together, and what better place is there for the meeting of dear friends? See how it glows with the advancing summer; how the sky and the sea and the rosy air and the marble of the palaces all shimmer and melt together." My eccentric private errand became a part of the general romance and the general glory—I felt even a mystic companionship, a moral fraternity with all those who in the past had been in the service of art. They had worked for beauty, for a devotion; and what else was I doing? That element was in everything that Jeffrey Aspern had written, and I was only bringing it to light.

I lingered in the sala when I went to and fro; I used to watch—as long as I thought decent—the door that led to Miss Bordereau's part of the house. A person observing me might have supposed I was trying to cast a spell on it or attempting some odd experiment in hypnotism. But I was only praying it might open or thinking what treasure probably lurked behind it. I hold it singular, as I look back, that I should never have doubted for a moment that the sacred relics were there; never have failed to know the joy of being beneath the same roof with them. After all they were under my hand—they had not escaped me yet; and they made my life continuous, in a fashion, with the illustrious life they had touched at the other end. I lost myself in this satisfaction to the point of assuming—in my quiet extravagance—that poor Miss Tina also went back, and still went back, as I used to phrase it. She did indeed, the gentle spinster, but not quite so far as Jeffrey Aspern, who was simple hearsay to her quite as he was to me. Only she had lived for years with Juliana, she had seen and handled all mementoes and—even though she was stupid—some esoteric knowledge had rubbed off on her. That was what the old woman represented—esoteric knowledge; and this was the idea with which my critical heart used to thrill. It literally beat faster often, of an evening when I had been out, as I stopped with my candle in the re-echoing hall on my way up to bed. It was as if at such a moment as that, in the stillness and after the long contradiction of the day, Miss Bordereau's secrets were in the air, the wonder of her survival more vivid. These were the acute impressions. I had them in another form, with more of a certain shade of reciprocity, during the hours I sat in the garden looking up over the top of my book at the closed windows of my hostess. In these windows no sign of life ever appeared; it was as if, for fear of my catching a glimpse of them, the two ladies passed their days in the dark. But this only emphasised their having matters to conceal; which was what I had wished to prove.

Their motionless shutters became as expressive as eyes consciously closed, and I took comfort in the probability that, though invisible themselves, they kept me in view between the lashes.

I made a point of spending as much time as possible in the garden, to justify the picture I had originally given of my horticultural passion. And I not only spent time, but (hang it! as I said) spent precious money. As soon as I had got my rooms arranged and could give the question proper thought I surveyed the place with a clever expert and made terms for having it put in order. I was sorry to do this, for personally I liked it better as it was, with its weeds and its wild rich tangle, its sweet characteristic Venetian shabbiness. I had to be consistent, to keep my promise that I would smother the house in flowers. Moreover I clung to the fond fancy that by flowers I should make my way—I should succeed by big nosegays. I would batter the old women with lilies—I would bombard their citadel with roses. Their door would have to yield to the pressure when a mound of fragrance should be heaped against it. The place in truth had been brutally neglected. The Venetian capacity for dawdling is of the largest, and for a good many days unlimited litter was all my gardener had to show for his ministrations. There was a great digging of holes and carting about of earth, and after a while I grew so impatient that I had thoughts of sending for my "results" to the nearest stand. But I felt sure my friends would see through the chinks of their shutters where such tribute *could n't* have been gathered, and might so make up their minds against my veracity. I possessed my soul and finally, though the delay was long, perceived some appearances of bloom. This encouraged me and I waited serenely enough till they multiplied. Meanwhile the real summer days arrived and began to pass, and as I look back upon them they seem to me almost the happiest of my life. I took more and more care to be in the garden whenever it was not too hot. I had an arbour arranged and a low table and an armchair put into it; and I carried out books and portfolios—I had always some business of writing in hand—and worked and waited and mused and hoped, while the golden hours elapsed and the plants drank in the light and the inscrutable old palace turned pale and then, as the day waned, began to recover and flush and my papers rustled in the wandering breeze of the Adriatic.

Considering how little satisfaction I got from it at first it is wonderful I should n't have grown more tired of trying to guess what mystic rites of ennui the Misses Bordereau celebrated in their darkened rooms; whether this had always been the tenor of their life and how in previous years they had escaped elbowing their neighbours. It was supposable they had then had other habits, forms and resources; that they must once have been young or at least middle-aged. There was no end to the questions it was possible to ask about them and no end to the answers it was not possible to frame. I had known many of my countrypeople in Europe and was familiar with the strange ways they were liable to take up there; but the Misses Bordereau formed altogether a new type of the American absentee. Indeed it was clear the American name had ceased to have any application to them—I had seen this in the ten minutes I spent in the old woman's room. You could never have said whence they came from the appearance of either of them; wherever it was they had long ago shed and unlearned all native marks and notes. There was nothing in them one recognised or fitted, and, putting the question of speech aside, they might have been Norwegians or Spaniards. Miss Bordereau, after all, had been in Europe nearly three quarters of a century; it appeared by some verses addressed to her by Aspern on the occasion of his own second absence from America— verses of which Cumnor and I had after infinite conjecture established solidly enough the date—that she was even then, as a girl of twenty, on the foreign side of the sea. There was a profession in the poem—I hope not just for the phrase—that he had come back for her sake. We had no real light on her circumstances at that moment, any more than we had upon her origin, which we believed to be the sort usually spoken of as modest. Cumnor had a theory that she had been a governess in some family in which the poet visited and that, in consequence of her position, there was from the first something unavowed, or rather something quite clandestine, in their relations. I on the other hand had hatched a little romance according to which she was the daughter of an artist, a painter or a sculptor, who had left the Western world, when the century was fresh, to study in the ancient schools. It was essential to my hypothesis that this amiable man should have lost his wife, should have been poor and unsuccessful and should have had a second daughter of a disposition quite different from Juliana's. It was also indispensable that he should have been accompanied to Europe by these young ladies and should have established himself there for the remainder of a struggling saddened life. There was a further implication that Miss Bordereau had had in her youth a perverse and reckless, albeit a generous and fascinating character, and that she had braved some wondrous chances. By what passions had she been ravaged, by what adventures and sufferings had she been blanched, what store of memories had she laid away for the monotonous future?

I asked myself these things as I sat spinning theories about her in my arbour and the bees droned in the flowers. It was incontestable that, whether for right or for wrong, most readers of certain of Aspern's poems (poems not as ambiguous as the sonnets—scarcely more divine, I think—of Shakespeare) had taken for granted that Juliana had not always adhered to the steep footway of renunciation. There hovered about her name a perfume of impenitent passion, an intimation that she had not been exactly as the respectable young person in general. Was this a sign that her singer had betrayed her, had given her away, as we say nowadays, to posterity? Certain it is that it would have been difficult to put one's finger on the passage in which her fair fame suffered injury. Moreover was not any fame fair enough that was so sure of duration and was associated with works immortal through their beauty? It was a part of my idea that the young lady had had a foreign lover—and say an unedifying tragical rupture—before her meeting with Jeffrey Aspern. She had lived with her father and sister in a queer old-fashioned expatriated artistic Bohemia of the days when the aesthetic was only the academic and the painters who knew the best models for *contadina* and *pifferaro*[9] wore peaked hats and long hair. It was a society less awake than the coteries of to-day—in its ignorance of the wonderful chances, the opportunities of the early bird, with which its path was strewn—to tatters of old stuff and fragments of old crockery; so that Miss Bordereau appeared not to have picked up or have inherited many objects of importance. There was no enviable *bric-à-brac*, with its provoking legend of cheapness, in the room in which I had seen her. Such a fact as that suggested bareness, but none the less it worked happily into the sentimental interest I had always taken in the early movements of my countrymen as visitors to Europe. When Americans went abroad in 1820 there was something romantic, almost heroic in it, as compared with the perpetual ferryings of the present hour, the hour at which photography and other conveniences have annihilated surprise. Miss Bordereau had sailed with her family on a tossing brig in the days of long voyages and sharp differences; she had had her emotions on the top of yellow diligences, passed the night at inns where she dreamed of travellers' tales, and was most struck, on reaching the Eternal City, with the elegance of Roman pearls and scarfs and mosaic brooches. There was something touching to me in all that, and my imagination frequently went back to the period. If Miss Bordereau carried it there of course Jeffrey Aspern had at other times done so with

---

[9]Peasant girl and piper—traditional "picturesque" subjects in the early nineteenth century.

greater force. It was a much more important fact, if one was looking at his genius critically, that he had lived in the days before the general transfusion. It had happened to me to regret that he had known Europe at all; I should have liked to see what he would have written without that experience, by which he had incontestably been enriched. But as his fate had ruled otherwise I went with him—I tried to judge how the general old order would have struck him. It was not only there, however, I watched him; the relations he had entertained with the special new had even a livelier interest. His own country after all had had most of his life, and his muse, as they said at that time, was essentially American. That was originally what I had prized him for: that at a period when our native land was nude and crude and provincial, when the famous "atmosphere" it is supposed to lack was not even missed, when literature was lonely there and art and form almost impossible, he had found means to live and write like one of the first; to be free and general and not at all afraid; to feel, understand and express everything.

V

I was seldom at home in the evening, for when I attempted to occupy myself in my apartments the lamplight brought in a swarm of noxious insects, and it was too hot for closed windows. Accordingly I spent the late hours either on the water—the moonlights of Venice are famous—or in the splendid square which serves as a vast forecourt to the strange old church of Saint Mark. I sat in front of Florian's café eating ices, listening to music, talking with acquaintances: the traveller will remember how the immense cluster of tables and little chairs stretches like a promontory into the smooth lake of the Piazza. The whole place, of a summer's evening, under the stars and with all the lamps, all the voices and light footsteps on marble—the only sounds of the immense arcade that encloses it—is an open-air saloon dedicated to cooling drinks and to a still finer degustation, that of the splendid impressions received during the day. When I did n't prefer to keep mine to myself there was always a stray tourist, disencumbered of his Bädeker,[10] to discuss them with, or some domesticated painter rejoicing in the return of the season of strong effects. The great basilica, with its low domes and bristling embroideries, the mystery of its mosaic and sculpture,

---

[10]The standard guidebook to Europe of that day.

looked ghostly in the tempered gloom, and the sea-breeze passed between the twin columns of the Piazzetta, the lintels of a door no longer
guarded, as gently as if a rich curtain swayed there. I used sometimes
on these occasions to think of the Misses Bordereau and of the pity of
their being shut up in apartments which in the Venetian July even
Venetian vastness couldn't relieve of some stuffiness. Their life
seemed miles away from the life of the Piazza, and no doubt it was
really too late to make the austere Juliana change her habits. But poor
Miss Tina would have enjoyed one of Florian's ices, I was sure; sometimes I even had thoughts of carrying one home to her. Fortunately my
patience bore fruit and I was not obliged to do anything so ridiculous.

One evening about the middle of July I came in earlier than usual—
I forget what chance had led to this—and instead of going up to my
quarters made my way into the garden. The temperature was very
high; it was such a night as one would gladly have spent in the open
air, and I was in no hurry to go to bed. I had floated home in my
gondola, listening to the slow splash of the oar in the dark narrow
canals, and now the only thought that occupied me was that it would
be good to recline at one's length in the fragrant darkness on a garden-
bench. The odour of the canal was doubtless at the bottom of that
aspiration, and the breath of the garden, as I entered it, gave consistency to my purpose. It was delicious—just such an air as must have
trembled with Romeo's vows when he stood among the thick flowers
and raised his arms to his mistress's balcony. I looked at the windows
of the palace to see if by chance the example of Verona—Verona not
being far off—had been followed; but everything was dim, as usual,
and everything was still. Juliana might on the summer nights of her
youth have murmured down from open windows at Jeffrey Aspern, but
Miss Tina was not a poet's mistress any more than I was a poet. This
however didn't prevent my gratification from being great as I became
aware on reaching the end of the garden that my younger padrona was
seated in one of the bowers. At first I made out but an indistinct figure,
not in the least counting on such an overture from one of my hostesses;
it even occurred to me that some enamoured maid-servant had stolen
in to keep a tryst with her sweetheart. I was going to turn away, not to
frighten her, when the figure rose to its height and I recognised Miss
Bordereau's niece. I must do myself the justice that I didn't wish to
frighten her either, and much as I had longed for some such accident I
should have been capable of retreating. It was as if I had laid a trap for
her by coming home earlier than usual and by adding to that oddity
my invasion of the garden. As she rose she spoke to me, and then I

guessed that perhaps, secure in my almost inveterate absence, it was her nightly practice to take a lonely airing. There was no trap in truth, because I had had no suspicion. At first I took the words she uttered for an impatience of my arrival; but as she repeated them—I had n't caught them clearly—I had the surprise of hearing her say: "Oh dear, I'm so glad you've come!" She and her aunt had in common the property of unexpected speeches. She came out of the arbour almost as if to throw herself in my arms.

I hasten to add that I escaped this ordeal and that she did n't even then shake hands with me. It was an ease to her to see me and presently she told me why—because she was nervous when out-of-doors at night alone. The plants and shrubs looked so strange in the dark, and there were all sorts of queer sounds—she could n't tell what they were—like the noises of animals. She stood close to me, looking about her with an air of greater security but without any demonstration of interest in me as an individual. Then I felt how little nocturnal prowlings could have been her habit, and I was also reminded—I had been afflicted by the same in talking with her before I took possession—that it was impossible to allow too much for her simplicity.

"You speak as if you were lost in the backwoods," I cheeringly laughed. "How you manage to keep out of this charming place when you've only three steps to take to get into it is more than I've yet been able to discover. You hide away amazingly so long as I'm on the premises, I know; but I had a hope you peeped out a little at other times. You and your poor aunt are worse off than Carmelite nuns in their cells. Should you mind telling me how you exist without air, without exercise, without any sort of human contact? I don't see how you carry on the common business of life."

She looked at me as if I had spoken a strange tongue, and her answer was so little of one that I felt it make for irritation. "We go to bed very early—earlier than you'd believe." I was on the point of saying that this only deepened the mystery, but she gave me some relief by adding: "Before you came we were n't so private. But I've never been out at night."

"Never in these fragrant alleys, blooming here under your nose?"

"Ah," said Miss Tina, "they were never nice till now!" There was a finer sense in this and a flattering comparison, so that it seemed to me I had gained some advantage. As I might follow that further by establishing a good grievance I asked her why, since she thought my garden nice, she had never thanked me in any way for the flowers I had been sending up in such quantities for the previous three weeks. I had not been discouraged—there had been, as she would have observed, a daily armful; but I had been brought up in the common forms and a word of recognition now and then would have touched me in the right place.

"Why I did n't know they were for me!"

"They were for both of you. Why should I make a difference?"

Miss Tina reflected as if she might be thinking of a reason for that, but she failed to produce one. Instead of this she asked abruptly: "Why in the world do you want so much to know us?"

"I ought after all to make a difference," I replied. "That question's your aunt's; it is n't yours. You would n't ask if you had n't been put up to it."

"She did n't tell me to ask you," Miss Tina replied without confusion. She was indeed the oddest mixture of shyness and straightness.

"Well, she has often wondered about it herself and expressed her wonder to you. She has insisted on it, so that she has put the idea into your head that I'm insufferably pushing. Upon my word I think I've been very discreet. And how completely your aunt must have lost every tradition of sociability, to see anything out of the way in the idea that respectable intelligent people, living as we do under the same roof, should occasionally exchange a remark! What could be more natural? We're of the same country and have at least some of the same tastes, since, like you, I'm intensely fond of Venice."

My friend seemed incapable of grasping more than one clause in any proposition, and she now spoke quickly, eagerly, as if she were answering my whole speech. "I'm not in the least fond of Venice. I should like to go far away!"

"Has she always kept you back so?" I went on, to show her I could be as irrelevant as herself.

"She told me to come out to-night; she has told me very often," said Miss Tina. "It is I who would n't come. I don't like to leave her."

"Is she too weak, is she really failing?" I demanded, with more emotion, I think, than I meant to betray. I measured this by the way her eyes rested on me in the darkness. It embarrassed me a little, and to turn the matter off I continued genially: "Do let us sit down together comfortably somewhere—while you tell me all about her."

Miss Tina made no resistance to this. We found a bench less secluded, less confidential, as it were, than the one in the arbour; and we were still sitting there when I heard midnight ring out from those clear bells of Venice which vibrate with a solemnity of their own over the lagoon and hold the air so much more than the chimes of other places.

We were together for more than an hour, and our interview gave, as it struck me, a great lift to my undertaking. Miss Tina accepted the situation without a protest; she had avoided me for three months, yet now she treated me almost as if these three months had made me an old friend. If I had chosen I might have gathered from this that though she had avoided me she had given a good deal of consideration to doing so. She paid no attention to the flight of time—never worried at my keeping her so long away from her aunt. She talked freely, answering questions and asking them and not even taking advantage of certain longish pauses by which they were naturally broken to say she thought she had better go in. It was almost as if she were waiting for something— something I might say to her—and intended to give me my opportunity. I was the more struck by this as she told me how much less well her aunt had been for a good many days, and in a way that was rather new. She was markedly weaker; at moments she showed no strength at all; yer more than ever she wished to be left alone. That was why she had told her to come out—not even to remain in her own room, which was alongside; she pronounced poor Miss Tina "a worry, a bore and a source of aggravation." She sat still for hours altogether, as if for long sleep; she had always done that, musing and dozing; but at such times formerly she gave, in breaks, some small sign of life, of interest, liking her companion to be near her with her work. This sad personage confided to me that at present her aunt was so motionless as to create the fear she was dead; moreover she scarce ate or drank—one could n't see what she lived on. The great thing was that she still on most days got up; the serious job was to dress her, to wheel her out of her bedroom. She clung to as many of her old habits as possible and had always, little company as they had received for years, made a point of sitting in the great parlour.

I scarce knew what to think of this—of Miss Tina's sudden conversion to sociability and of the strange fact that the more the old woman appeared to decline to her end the less she should desire to be looked after. The story hung indifferently together, and I even asked myself if it might n't be a trap laid for me, the result of a design to make me show my hand. I could n't have told why my companions (as they could only by courtesy be called) should have this purpose—why they should try to trip up so lucrative a lodger. But at any hazard I kept on my guard, so that Miss Tina should n't have occasion again to ask me what I might really be "up to." Poor woman, before we parted for the night my mind was at rest as to what *she* might be. She was up to nothing at all.

She told me more about their affairs than I had hoped; there was no need to be prying, for it evidently drew her out simply to feel me listen and care. She ceased wondering why I *should*, and at last, while describing the brilliant life they had led years before, she almost chattered. It was Miss Tina who judged it brilliant; she said that when they first came to live in Venice, years and years back—I found her essentially vague about dates and the order in which events had occurred—there was never a week they had n't some visitor or did n't make some pleasant *passeggio*[11] in the town. They had seen all the curiosities; they had even been to the Lido[12] in a boat—she spoke as if I might think there was a way on foot; they had had a collation there, brought in three baskets and spread out on the grass. I asked her what people they had known and she said Oh very nice ones—the Cavaliere Bombicci and the Contessa Altemura, with whom they had had a great friendship! Also English people—the Churtons and the Goldies and Mrs. Stock-Stock, whom they had loved dearly; she was dead and gone, poor dear. That was the case with most of their kind circle—this expression was Miss Tina's own; though a few were left, which was a wonder considering how they had neglected them. She mentioned the names of two or three Venetian old women; of a certain doctor, very clever, who was so attentive—he came as a friend, he had really given up practice; of the *avvocato*[13] Pochintesta, who wrote beautiful poems and had addressed one to her aunt. These people came to see them without fail every year, usually at the *capo d'anno*,[14] and of old her aunt used to make them some little present—her aunt and she together: small things that she, Miss Tina, turned out with her own hand, paper lampshades, or mats for the decanters of wine at dinner, or those woollen things that in cold weather are worn on the wrists. The last few years there had n't been many presents; she could n't think what to make and her aunt had lost interest and never suggested. But the people came all the same; if the good Venetians liked you once they liked you for ever.

There was affecting matter enough in the good faith of this sketch of former social glories; the picnic at the Lido had remained vivid through the ages and poor Miss Tina evidently was of the impression that she had had a dashing youth. She had in fact had a glimpse of the Venetian

---

[11]Trip or tour.
[12]The fashionable seashore of Venice.
[13]Lawyer.
[14]New Year's Day.

world in its gossiping home-keeping parsimonious professional walks; for I noted for the first time how nearly she had acquired by contact the trick of the familiar soft-sounding almost infantile prattle of the place. I judged her to have imbibed this invertebrate dialect from the natural way the names of things and people—most purely local—rose to her lips. If she knew little of what they represented she knew still less of anything else. Her aunt had drawn in—the failure of interest in the table-mats and lamp-shades was a sign of that—and she had n't been able to mingle in society or to entertain it alone; so that her range of reminiscence struck one as an old world altogether. Her tone, had n't it been so decent, would have seemed to carry one back to the queer rococo Venice of Goldoni and Casanova.[15] I found myself mistakenly think of her too as one of Jeffrey Aspern's contemporaries; this came from her having so little in common with my own. It was possible, I indeed reasoned, that she had n't even heard of him; it might very well be that Juliana had forborne to lift for innocent eyes the veil that covered the temple of her glory. In this case she perhaps would n't know of the existence of the papers, and I welcomed that presumption—it made me feel safe with her—till I remembered we had believed the letter of disavowal received by Cumnor to be in the handwriting of the niece. If it had been dictated to her she had of course to know what it was about; though the effect of it withal was to repudiate the idea of any connexion with the poet. I held it probable at all events that Miss Tina had n't read a word of his poetry. Moreover if, with her companion, she had always escaped invasion and research, there was little occasion for her having got it into her head that people were "after" the letters. People had not been after them, for people had n't heard of them. Cumnor's fruitless feeler would have been a solitary accident.

When midnight sounded Miss Tina got up; but she stopped at the door of the house only after she had wandered two or three times with me round the garden. "When shall I see you again?" I asked before she went in; to which she replied with promptness that she should like to come out the next night. She added however that she should n't come—she was so far from doing everything she liked.

"You might do a few things *I* like," I quite sincerely sighed.

"Oh you—I don't believe you!" she murmured at this, facing me with her simple solemnity.

----

[15]Two eighteenth-century Venetian writers, neither noted for his high moral tone.

"Why don't you believe me?"

"Because I don't understand you."

"That's just the sort of occasion to have faith." I could n't say more, though I should have liked to, as I saw I only mystified her; for I had no wish to have it on my conscience that I might pass for having made love to her. Nothing less should I have seemed to do had I continued to beg a lady to "believe in me" in an Italian garden on a midsummer night. There was some merit in my scruples, for Miss Tina lingered and lingered: I made out in her the conviction that she should n't really soon come down again and the wish therefore to protract the present. She insisted too on making the talk between us personal to ourselves; and altogether her behaviour was such as would have been possible only to a perfectly artless and a considerably witless woman.

"I shall like the flowers better now that I know them also meant for me."

"How could you have doubted it? If you'll tell me the kind you like best I'll send a double lot."

"Oh I like them all best!" Then she went on familiarly: "Shall you study—shall you read and write—when you go up to your rooms?"

"I don't do that at night—at this season. The lamplight brings in the animals."

"You might have known that when you came."

"I did know it!"

"And in winter do you work at night?"

"I read a good deal, but I don't often write." She listened as if these details had a rare interest, and suddenly a temptation quite at odds with the prudence I had been teaching myself glimmered at me in her plain mild face. Ah yes, she was safe and I could make her safer! It seemed to me from one moment to another that I could n't wait longer—that I really must take a sounding. So I went on: "In general before I go to sleep (very often in bed; it's a bad habit, but I confess to it) I read some great poet. In nine cases out of ten it's a volume of Jeffrey Aspern."

I watched her well as I pronounced that name, but I saw nothing wonderful. Why should I indeed? Was n't Jeffrey Aspern the property of the human race?

"Oh *we* read him—we *have* read him," she quietly replied.

"He's my poet of poets—I know him almost by heart."

For an instant Miss Tina hesitated; then her sociability was too much for her. "Oh by heart—that's nothing;" and, though dimly, she quite lighted. "My aunt used to know him, to know him"—she paused an instant and I wondered what she was going to say—"to know him as a visitor."

"As a visitor?" I guarded my tone.

"He used to call on her and take her out."

I continued to stare. "My dear lady, he died a hundred years ago!"

"Well," she said amusingly, "my aunt's a hundred and fifty."

"Mercy on us!" I cried; "why did n't you tell me before? I should like so to ask her about him."

"She would n't care for that—she would n't tell you," Miss Tina returned.

"I don't care what she cares for! She *must* tell me—it's not a chance to be lost."

"Oh you should have come twenty years ago. Then she still talked about him."

"And what did she say?" I eagerly asked.

"I don't know—that he liked her immensely."

"And she—did n't she like *him*?"

"She said he was a god." Miss Tina gave me this information flatly, without expression; her tone might have made it a piece of trivial gossip. But it stirred me deeply as she dropped the words into the summer night; their sound might have been the light rustle of an old unfolded love-letter.

"Fancy, fancy!" I murmured. And then: "Tell me this, please—has she got a portrait of him? They're distressingly rare."

"A portrait? I don't know," said Miss Tina; and now there was a discomfiture in her face. "Well, good-night!" she added; and she turned into the house.

I accompanied her into the wide dusky stone-paved passage that corresponded on the ground floor with our great sala. It opened at one end into the garden, at the other upon the canal, and was lighted now only by the small lamp always left for me to take up as I went to bed. An extinguished candle which Miss Tina apparently had brought down with her stood on the same table with it. "Good-night, good-night!" I replied, keeping beside her as she went to get her light. "Surely you'd know, should n't you, if she had one?"

"If she had what?" the poor lady asked, looking at me queerly over the flame of her candle.

"A portrait of the god. I don't know what I would n't give to see it."

"I don't know what she has got. She keeps her things locked up." And Miss Tina went away toward the staircase with the sense evidently of having said too much.

I let her go—I wished not to frighten her—and I contented myself with remarking that Miss Bordereau would n't have locked up such a glorious possession as that: a thing a person would be proud of and hang up in a prominent place on the parlour-wall. Therefore of course she had n't any portrait. Miss Tina made no direct answer to this and, candle in hand, with her back to me, mounted two or three degrees. Then she stopped short and turned round, looking at me across the dusky space.

"Do you write—do you write?" There was a shake in her voice—she could scarcely bring it out.

"Do I write? Oh don't speak of my writing on the same day with Aspern's!"

"Do you write about *him*—do you pry into his life?"

"Ah that's your aunt's question; it can't be yours!" I said in a tone of slightly wounded sensibility.

"All the more reason then that you should answer it. Do you, please?"

I thought I had allowed for all the falsehoods I should have to tell, but I found that in fact when it came to the point I had n't. Besides, now that I had an opening there was a kind of relief in being frank. Lastly—it was perhaps fanciful, even fatuous—I guessed that Miss Tina personally would n't in the last resort be less my friend. So after a moment's hesitation I answered: "Yes, I've written about him and I'm looking for more material. In heaven's name have you got any?"

"*Santo Dio!*"[16] she exclaimed without heeding my question; and she hurried upstairs and out of sight. I might count upon her in the last resort, but for the present she was visibly alarmed. The proof of it was that she began to hide again, so that for a fortnight I kept missing her. I found my patience ebbing and after four or five days of this I told the gardener to stop the "floral tributes."

VI

One afternoon, at last, however, as I came down from my quarters to go out, I found her in the sala; it was our first encounter on that ground since I had come to the house. She put on no air of being there by accident; there was an ignorance of such arts in her honest angular

---

[16]Holy God!

diffidence. That I might be quite sure she was waiting for me she mentioned it at once, but telling me with it that Miss Bordereau wished to see me: she would take me into the room at that moment if I had time. If I had been late for a love-tryst I would have stayed for this, and I quickly signified that I should be delighted to wait on my benefactress. "She wants to talk with you—to know you," Miss Tina said, smiling as if she herself appreciated that idea; and she led me to the door of her aunt's apartment. I stopped her a moment before she had opened it, looking at her with great curiosity. I told her that this was a great satisfaction to me and a great honour; but all the same I should like to ask what had made Miss Bordereau so markedly and suddenly change. It had been only the other day that she would n't suffer me near her. Miss Tina was not embarrassed by my question; she had as many little unexpected serenities, plausibilities almost, as if she told fibs, but the odd part of them was that they had on the contrary their source in her truthfulness. "Oh my aunt varies," she answered; "it's so terribly dull—I suppose she's tired."

"But you told me she wanted more and more to be alone."

Poor Miss Tina coloured as if she found me too pushing. "Well, if you don't believe she wants to see you, I have n't invented it! I think people often are capricious when they're very old."

"That's perfectly true. I only wanted to be clear as to whether you've repeated to her what I told you the other night."

"What you told me?"

"About Jeffrey Aspern—that I'm looking for materials."

"If I had told her do you think she'd have sent for you?"

"That's exactly what I want to know. If she wants to keep him to herself she might have sent for me to tell me so."

"She won't speak of him," said Miss Tina. Then as she opened the door she added in a lower tone: "I told her nothing."

The old woman was sitting in the same place in which I had seen her last, in the same position, with the same mystifying bandage over her eyes. Her welcome was to turn her almost invisible face to me and show me that while she sat silent she saw me clearly. I made no motion to shake hands with her; I now felt too well that this was out of place for ever. It had been sufficiently enjoined on me that she was too sacred for trivial modernisms—too venerable to touch. There was something so grim in her aspect—it was partly the accident of her green shade— as I stood there to be measured, that I ceased on the spot to doubt her suspecting me, though I did n't in the least myself suspect that Miss Tina had n't just spoken the truth. She had n't betrayed me, but the old woman's brooding instinct had served her; she had turned me over and over in the long still hours and had guessed. The worst of it was that she looked terribly like an old woman who at a pinch would, even like Sardanapalus,[17] burn her treasure. Miss Tina pushed a chair forward, saying to me, "This will be a good place for you to sit." As I took possession of it I asked after Miss Bordereau's health; expressed the hope that in spite of the hot weather it was satisfactory. She answered that it was good enough—good enough; that it was a great thing to be alive.

"Oh as to that, it depends upon what you compare it with!" I returned with a laugh.

"I don't compare—I don't compare. If I did that I should have given everything up long ago."

I liked to take this for a subtle allusion to the rapture she had known in the society of Jeffrey Aspern—though it was true that such an allusion would have accorded ill with the wish I imputed to her to keep him buried in her soul. What it accorded with was my constant conviction that no human being had ever had a happier social gift than his, and what it seemed to convey was that nothing in the world was worth speaking of if one pretended to speak of that. But one did n't pretend! Miss Tina sat down beside her aunt, looking as if she had reason to believe some wonderful talk would come off between us.

"It's about the beautiful flowers," said the old lady; "you sent us so many—I ought to have thanked you for them before. But I don't write letters and I receive company but at long intervals."

She had n't thanked me while the flowers continued to come, but she departed from her custom so far as to send for me as soon as she began to fear they would n't come any more. I noted this; I remembered what an acquisitive propensity she had shown when it was a question of extracting gold from me, and I privately rejoiced at the happy thought I had had in suspending my tribute. She had missed it and was willing to make a concession to bring it back. At the first sign of this concession I could only go to meet her. "I'm afraid you have n't had many, of late, but they shall begin again immediately—to-morrow, to-night."

"Oh do send us some to-night!" Miss Tina cried as if it were a great affair.

"What else should you do with them? It is n't a manly taste to make a bower of your room," the old woman remarked.

---

[17]A legendary Assyrian nobleman, subject of a play by Byron.

"I don't make a bower of my room, but I'm exceedingly fond of growing flowers, of watching their ways. There's nothing unmanly in that; it has been the amusement of philosophers, of statesmen in retirement; even I think of great captains."

"I suppose you know you can sell them—those you don't use," Miss Bordereau went on. "I dare say they would n't give you much for them; still, you could make a bargain."

"Oh I've never in my life made a bargain, as you ought pretty well to have gathered. My gardener disposes of them and I ask no questions."

"I'd ask a few, I can promise you!" said Miss Bordereau; and it was so I first heard the strange sound of her laugh, which was as if the faint "walking" ghost of her old-time tone had suddenly cut a caper. I could n't get used to the idea that this vision of pecuniary profit was most what drew out the divine Juliana.

"Come into the garden yourself and pick them; come as often as you like; come every day. The flowers are all for you," I pursued, addressing Miss Tina and carrying off this veracious statement by treating it as an innocent joke. "I can't imagine why she does n't come down," I added for Miss Bordereau's benefit.

"You must make her come; you must come up and fetch her," the old woman said to my stupefaction. "That odd thing you've made in the corner will do very well for her to sit in."

The allusion to the most elaborate of my shady coverts, a sketchy "summer-house," was irreverent; it confirmed the impression I had already received that there was a flicker of impertinence in Miss Bordereau's talk, a vague echo of the boldness or the archness of her adventurous youth and which had somehow automatically outlived passions and faculties. None the less I asked: "Would n't it be possible for you to come down there yourself? Would n't it do you good to sit there in the shade and the sweet air?"

"Oh sir, when I move out of this it won't be to sit in the air, and I'm afraid that any that may be stirring around me won't be particularly sweet! It will be a very dark shade indeed. But that won't be just yet," Miss Bordereau continued cannily, as if to correct any hopes this free glance at the last receptacle of her mortality might lead me to entertain. "I've sat here many a day and have had enough of arbours in my time. But I'm not afraid to wait till I'm called."

Miss Tina had expected, as I felt, rare conversation, but perhaps she found it less gracious on her aunt's side—considering I had been sent for with a civil intention—than she had hoped. As to give the position a turn that would put our companion in a light more favourable she said to me: "Did n't I tell you the other night that she had sent me out? You see I can do what I like!"

"Do you pity her—do you teach her to pity herself?" Miss Bordereau demanded, before I had time to answer this appeal. "She has a much easier life than I had at her age."

"You must remember it has been quite open to me," I said, "to think you rather inhuman."

"Inhuman? That's what the poets used to call the women a hundred years ago. Don't try that; you won't do as well as they!" Juliana went on. "There's no more poetry in the world—that I know of at least. But I won't bandy words with you," she said, and I well remember the old-fashioned artificial sound she gave the speech. "You make me talk, talk, talk! It is n't good for me at all." I got up at this and told her I would take no more of her time; but she detained me to put a question. "Do you remember, the day I saw you about the rooms, that you offered us the use of your gondola?" And when I assented promptly, struck again with her disposition to make a "good thing" of my being there and wondering what she now had in her eye, she produced: "Why don't you take that girl out in it and show her the place?"

"Oh dear aunt, what do you want to do with me?" cried the "girl" with a piteous quaver. "I know all about the place!"

"Well then go with him and explain!" said Miss Bordereau, who gave an effect of cruelty to her implacable power of retort. This showed her as a sardonic profane cynical old woman. "Have n't we heard that there have been all sorts of changes in all these years? You ought to see them, and at your age—I don't mean because you're so young—you ought to take the chances that come. You're old enough, my dear, and this gentleman won't hurt you. He'll show you the famous sunsets, if they still go on—*do* they go on? The sun set for me so long ago. But that's not a reason. Besides, I shall never miss you; you think you're too important. Take her to the Piazza; it used to be very pretty," Miss Bordereau continued, addressing herself to me. "What have they done with the funny old church? I hope it has n't tumbled down. Let her look at the shops; she may take some money, she may buy what she likes."

Poor Miss Tina had got up, discountenanced and helpless, and as we stood there before her aunt it would certainly have struck a spectator of the scene that our venerable friend was making rare sport of us. Miss Tina protested in a confusion of exclamations and murmurs; but I lost no time in saying that if she would do me the honour to accept the hospitality of my boat I would engage she really should n't be bored. Or if she did n't want so much of my company the boat itself, with the gondolier, was at her service; he was a capital oar and she might have every confidence. Miss Tina, without definitely answering this speech, looked away from me and out of the window, quite as if about to weep, and I remarked that once we had Miss Bordereau's approval we could easily come to an understanding. We would take an hour, whichever she liked, one of the very next days. As I made my obeisance to the old lady I asked her if she would kindly permit me to see her again.

For a moment she kept me; then she said: "Is it very necessary to your happiness?"

"It diverts me more than I can say."

"You're wonderfully civil. Don't you know it almost kills *me?*"

"How can I believe that when I see you more animated, more brilliant than when I came in?"

"That's very true, aunt," said Miss Tina. "I think it does you good."

"Is n't it touching, the solicitude we each have that the other shall enjoy herself?" sneered Miss Bordereau. "If you think me brilliant to-day you don't know what you're talking about; you've never seen an agreeable woman. What do you people know about good society?" she cried; but before I could tell her, "Don't try to pay me a compliment; I've been spoiled," she went on. "My door's shut, but you may sometimes knock."

With this she dismissed me and I left the room. The latch closed behind me, but Miss Tina, contrary to my hope, had remained within. I passed slowly across the hall and before taking my way downstairs waited a little. My hope was answered; after a minute my conductress followed me. "That's a delightful idea about the Piazza," I said. "When will you go—to-night, to-morrow?"

She had been disconcerted, as I have mentioned, but I had already perceived, and I was to observe again, that when Miss Tina was embarrassed she did n't—as most women would have in like case—turn away, floundering and hedging, but came closer, as it were, with a deprecating, a clinging appeal to be spared, to be protected. Her attitude was a constant prayer for aid and explanation, and yet no woman in the world could have been less of a comedian. From the moment you were kind to her she depended on you absolutely; her self-consciousness dropped and she took the greatest intimacy, the innocent intimacy that was all she could conceive, for granted. She did n't know, she now declared, what possessed her aunt, who had changed so quickly, who had got some idea. I replied that she must catch the idea and let me have it: we would go and take an ice together at Florian's and she should report while we listened to the band.

"Oh it will take me a long time to be able to 'report'!" she said rather ruefully; and she could promise me this satisfaction neither for that night nor for the next. I was patient now, however, for I felt I had only to wait; and in fact at the end of the week, one lovely evening after dinner, she stepped into my gondola, to which in honour of the occasion I had attached a second oar.

We swept in the course of five minutes into the Grand Canal; whereupon she uttered a murmur of ecstasy as fresh as if she had been a tourist just arrived. She had forgotten the splendour of the great waterway on a clear summer evening, and how the sense of floating between marble palaces and reflected lights disposed the mind to freedom and ease. We floated long and far, and though my friend gave no high-pitched voice to her glee I was sure of her full surrender. She was more than pleased, she was transported; the whole thing was an immense liberation. The gondola moved with slow strokes, to give her time to enjoy it, and she listened to the plash of the oars, which grew louder and more musically liquid as we passed into narrow canals, as if it were a revelation of Venice. When I asked her how long it was since she had thus floated she answered: "Oh I don't know; a long time—not since my aunt began to be ill." This was not the only show of her extreme vagueness about the previous years and the line marking off the period of Miss Bordereau's eminence. I was not at liberty to keep her out long, but we took a considerable *giro* before going to the Piazza. I asked her no questions, holding off by design from her life at home and the things I wanted to know; I poured, rather, treasures of information about the objects before and around us into her ears, describing also Florence and Rome, discoursing on the charms and advantages of travel. She reclined, receptive, on the deep leather cushions, turned her eyes conscientiously to everything I noted and never mentioned to me till some time afterwards that she might be supposed to know Florence better than I, as she had lived there for years with her kinswoman. At last she said with the shy impatience of a child: "Are we not really going to the Piazza? That's what I want to see!" I immediately gave the order that we should go straight, after which we sat silent with the expectation of arrival. As some time still passed, however, she broke out of her own movement: "I've found out what's the matter with my aunt: she's afraid you'll go!"

I quite gasped. "What has put that into her head?"

"She has an idea you've not been happy. That's why she's different now."

"You mean she wants to make me happier?"

"Well, she wants you not to go. She wants you to stay."

"I suppose you mean on account of the rent," I remarked candidly. Miss Tina's candour but profited. "Yes, you know; so that I shall have more."

"How much does she want you to have?" I asked with all the gaiety I now felt. "She ought to fix the sum, so that I may stay until it's made up."

"Oh that would n't please me," said Miss Tina. "It would be unheard of, your taking that trouble."

"But suppose I should have my own reasons for staying in Venice?"

"Then it would be better for you to stay in some other house."

"And what would your aunt say to that?"

"She would n't like it at all. But I should think you'd do well to give up your reasons and go away altogether."

"Dear Miss Tina," I said, "it's not so easy to give up my reasons!"

She made no immediate answer to this, but after a moment broke out afresh: "I think I know what your reasons are!"

"I dare say, because the other night I almost told you how I wished you'd help me to make them good."

"I can't do that without being false to my aunt."

"What do you mean by being false to her?"

"Why she would never consent to what you want. She has been asked, she has been written to. It makes her fearfully angry."

"Then she *has* papers of value?" I precipitately cried.

"Oh she has everything!" sighed Miss Tina with a curious weariness, a sudden lapse into gloom.

These words caused all my pulses to throb, for I regarded them as precious evidence. I felt them too deeply to speak, and in the interval, the gondola approached the Piazzetta. After we had disembarked I asked my companion if she would rather walk round the square or go and sit before the great café; to which she replied that she would do whichever I liked best—I must only remember again how little time she had. I assured her there was plenty to do both, and we made the circuit of the long arcades. Her spirits revived at the sight of the bright shop-windows, and she lingered and stopped, admiring or disapproving of their contents, asking me what I thought of things, theorising about prices. My attention wandered from her; her words of a while before

"Oh she has everything!" echoed so in my consciousness. We sat down at last in the crowded circle at Florian's, finding an unoccupied table among those that were ranged in the square. It was a splendid night and all the world out-of-doors; Miss Tina could n't have wished the elements more auspicious for her return to society. I saw she felt it all even more than she told, but her impressions were well-nigh too many for her. She had forgotten the attraction of the world and was learning that she had for the best years of her life been rather mercilessly cheated of it. This did n't make her angry; but as she took in the charming scene her face had, in spite of its smile of appreciation, the flush of a wounded surprise. She did n't speak, sunk in the sense of opportunities, for ever lost, that ought to have been easy; and this gave me a chance to say to her: "Did you mean a while ago that your aunt has a plan of keeping me on by admitting me occasionally to her presence?"

"She thinks it will make a difference with you if you sometimes see her. She wants you so much to stay that she's willing to make that concession."

"And what good does she consider I think it will do me to see her?"

"I don't know; it must be interesting," said Miss Tina simply. "You told her you found it so."

"So I did; but everyone does n't think that."

"No, of course not, or more people would try."

"Well, if she's capable of making that reflexion she's capable also of making this further one," I went on: "that I must have a particular reason for not doing as others do, in spite of the interest she offers—for not leaving her alone." Miss Tina looked as if she failed to grasp this rather complicated proposition; so I continued: "If you've not told her what I said to you the other night may she not at least have guessed it?"

"I don't know—she's very suspicious."

"But she has n't been made so by indiscreet curiosity, by persecution?"

"No, no; it is n't that," said Miss Tina, turning on me a troubled face. "I don't know how to say it; it's on account of something—ages ago, before I was born—in her life."

"Something? What sort of thing?"—and I asked it as if I could have no idea.

"Oh she has never told me." And I was sure my friend spoke the truth.

Her extreme limpidity was almost provoking, and I felt for the moment that she would have been more satisfactory if she had been less ingenuous. "Do you suppose it's something to which Jeffrey Aspern's letters and papers—I mean the things in her possession—have reference?"

"I dare say it is!" my companion exclaimed as if this were a very happy suggestion. "I've never looked at any of those things."

"None of them? Then how do you know what they are?"

"I don't," said Miss Tina placidly. "I've never had them in my hands. But I've seen them when she has had them out."

"Does she have them out very often?"

"Not now, but she used to. She's very fond of them."

"In spite of their being compromising?"

"Compromising?" Miss Tina repeated as if vague as to what that meant. I felt almost as one who corrupts the innocence of youth.

"I allude to their containing painful memories."

"Oh I don't think anything's painful."

"You mean there's nothing to affect her reputation?"

An odder look even than usual came at this into the face of Miss Bordereau's niece—a confession, it seemed, of helplessness, an appeal to me to deal fairly, generously with her. I had brought her to the Piazza, placed her among charming influences, paid her an attention she appreciated, and now I appeared to show it all as a bribe—a bribe to make her turn in some way against her aunt. She was of a yielding nature and capable of doing anything to please a person markedly kind to her; but the greatest kindness of all would be not to presume too much on this. It was strange enough, as I afterwards thought, that she had not the least air of resenting my want of consideration for her aunt's character, which would have been in the worst possible taste if anything less vital—from my point of view—had been at stake. I don't think she really measured it. "Do you mean she ever did something bad?" she asked in a moment.

"Heaven forbid I should say so, and it's none of my business. Besides, if she did," I agreeably put it, "that was in other ages, in another world. But why should n't she destroy her papers?"

"Oh she loves them too much."

"Even now, when she may be near her end?"

"Perhaps when she's sure of that she will."

"Well, Miss Tina," I said, "that's just what I should like you to prevent."

"How can I prevent it?"

"Could n't you get them away from her?"

"And give them to you?"

This put the case, superficially, with sharp irony, but I was sure of her not intending that. "Oh I mean that you might let me see them and look them over. It is n't for myself, or that I should want them at any cost to anyone else. It's simply that they would be of such immense interest to the public, such immeasurable importance as a contribution to Jeffrey Aspern's history."

She listened to me in her usual way, as if I abounded in matters she had never heard of, and I felt almost as base as the reporter of a newspaper who forces his way into a house of mourning. This was marked when she presently said: "There was a gentleman who some time ago wrote to her in very much those words. He also wanted her papers."

"And did she answer him?" I asked, rather ashamed of not having my friend's rectitude.

"Only when he had written two or three times. He made her very angry."

"And what did she say?"

"She said he was a devil," Miss Tina replied categorically.

"She used that expression in her letter?"

"Oh no; she said it to me. She made me write to him."

"And what did you say?"

"I told him there were no papers at all."

"Ah, poor gentleman!" I groaned.

"I knew there were, but I wrote what she bade me."

"Of course you had to do that. But I hope I shan't pass for a devil."

"It will depend upon what you ask me to do for you," my companion smiled.

"Oh if there's a chance of *your* thinking so my affair 's in a bad way! I shan't ask you to steal for me, nor even to fib—for you *can't* fib, unless on paper. But the principal thing is this—to prevent her destroying the papers."

"Why I've no control of her," said Miss Tina. "It's she who controls me."

"But she does n't control her own arms and legs, does she? The way she would naturally destroy her letters would be to burn them. Now she can't burn them without fire, and she can't get fire unless you give it her."

"I've always done everything she has asked," my poor friend pleaded. "Besides, there's Olimpia."

I was on the point of saying that Olimpia was probably corruptible, but I thought it best not to sound that note. So I simply put it that this frail creature might perhaps be managed.

"Every one can be managed by my aunt," said Miss Tina. And then she remembered that her holiday was over; she must go home.

I laid my hand on her arm, across the table, to stay her a moment. "What I want of you is a general promise to help me."

"Oh how *can* I, how *can* I?" she asked, wondering and troubled. She was half-surprised, half-frightened at my attaching that importance to her, at my calling on her for action.

"This is the main thing: to watch our friend carefully and warn me in time, before she commits that dreadful sacrilege."

"I can't watch her when she makes me go out."

"That's very true."

"And when you do too."

"Mercy on us—do you think she'll have done anything to-night?"

"I don't know. She's very cunning."

"Are you trying to frighten me?" I asked.

I felt this question sufficiently answered when my companion murmured in a musing, almost envious way: "Oh but she loves them—she loves them!"

This reflexion, repeated with such emphasis, gave me great comfort; but to obtain more of that balm I said: "If she should n't intend to destroy the objects we speak of before her death she'll probably have made some disposition by will."

"By will?"

"Has n't she made a will for your benefit?"

"Ah she has so little to leave. That's why she likes money," said Miss Tina.

"Might I ask, since we're really talking things over, what you and she live on?"

"On some money that comes from America, from a gentleman—I think a lawyer—in New York. He sends it every quarter. It is n't much!"

"And won't she have disposed of that?"

My companion hesitated—I saw she was blushing. "I believe it's mine," she said; and the look and tone which accompanied these words betrayed so the absence of the habit of thinking of herself that I almost thought her charming. The next instant she added: "But she had in an *avvocato* here once, ever so long ago. And some people came and signed something."

"They were probably witnesses. And you were n't asked to sign? Well then," I argued, rapidly and hopefully, "it's because you're the legatee. She must have left all her documents to you!"

"If she has it's with very strict conditions," Miss Tina responded, rising quickly, while the movement gave the words a small character of decision. They seemed to imply that the bequest would be accompanied with a proviso that the articles bequeathed should remain concealed from every inquisitive eye, and that I was very much mistaken if I thought her the person to depart from an injunction so absolute.

"Oh of course you'll have to abide by the terms," I said; and she uttered nothing to mitigate the rigour of this conclusion. None the less, later on, just before we disembarked at her own door after a return which had taken place almost in silence, she said to me abruptly: "I'll do what I can to help you." I was grateful for this—it was very well so far as it went; but it did n't keep me from remembering that night in a worried waking hour that I now had her word for it to re-enforce my own impression that the old woman was full of craft.

VII

The fear of what this side of her character might have led her to do made me nervous for days afterwards. I waited for an intimation from Miss Tina; I almost read it as her duty to keep me informed, to let me know definitely whether or not Miss Bordereau had sacrificed her treasures. But as she gave no sign I lost patience and determined to put the case to the very touch of my own senses. I sent late one afternoon to ask if I might pay the ladies a visit, and my servant came back with surprising news. Miss Bordereau could be approached without the least difficulty; she had been moved out into the sala and was sitting by the window that overlooked the garden. I descended and found this picture correct; the old lady had been wheeled forth into the world and had a certain air, which came mainly perhaps from some brighter element in her dress, of being prepared again to have converse with it. It had not yet, however, begun to flock about her; she was perfectly alone and, though the door leading to her own quarters stood open, I had at first no glimpse of Miss Tina. The window at which she sat had the afternoon shade and, one of the shutters having been pushed back, she could see the pleasant garden, where the summer sun had by this time dried up too many of the plants—she could see the yellow light and the long shadows.

"Have you come to tell me you'll take the rooms for six months more?" she asked as I approached her, startling me by something coarse in her cupidity almost as much as if she had n't already given me a specimen of it. Juliana's desire to make our acquaintance lucrative had been, as I have sufficiently indicated, a false note in my image of the woman who had inspired a great poet with immortal lines; but I may say here definitely that I after all recognised large allowance to be made for her. It was I who had kindled the unholy flame; it was I who put into her head that she had the means of making money. She appeared never to have thought of that; she had been living wastefully for years, in a house five times too big for her, on a footing that I could explain only by the presumption that, excessive as it was, the space she enjoyed cost her next to nothing and that, small as were her revenues, they left her, for Venice, an appreciable margin. I had descended on her one day and taught her to calculate, and my almost extravagant comedy on the subject of the garden had presented me irresistibly in the light of a victim. Like all persons who achieve the miracle of changing their point of view late in life, she had been intensely converted: she had seized my hint with a desperate tremulous clutch.

I invited myself to go and get one of the chairs that stood, at a distance, against the wall—she had given herself no concern as to whether I should sit or stand; and while I placed it near her I began gaily: "Oh dear madam, what an imagination you have, what an intellectual sweep! I'm a poor devil of a man of letters who lives from day to day. How can I take palaces by the year? My existence is precarious. I don't know whether six months hence I shall have bread to put in my mouth. I've treated myself for once; it has been an immense luxury. But when it comes to going on—!"

"Are your rooms too dear? if they are you can have more for the same money," Juliana responded. "We can arrange, we can *combinare*, as they say here."

"Well yes, since you ask me, they're too dear, much too dear," I said. "Evidently you suppose me richer than I am."

She looked at me as from the mouth of her cave. "If you write books don't you sell them?"

"Do you mean don't people buy them? A little, a very little—not so much as I could wish. Writing books, unless one be a great genius—and even then!—is the last road to fortune. I think there's no more money to be made by good letters."

"Perhaps you don't choose nice subjects. What do you write about?" Miss Bordereau implacably pursued.

"About the books of other people. I'm a critic, a commentator, an historian, in a small way." I wondered what she was coming to.

"And what other people now?"

"Oh better ones than myself: the great writers mainly—the great philosophers and poets of the past; those who are dead and gone and can't, poor darlings, speak for themselves."

"And what do you say about them?"

"I say they sometimes attached themselves to very clever women!" I replied as for pleasantness. I had measured, as I thought, my risk, but as my words fell upon the air they were to strike me as imprudent. However, I had launched them and I was n't sorry, for perhaps after all the old woman would be willing to treat. It seemed tolerably obvious that she knew my secret: why therefore drag the process out? But she did n't take what I said as a confession; she only asked:

"Do you think it's right to rake up the past?"

"I don't feel that I know what you mean by raking it up. How can we get at it unless we dig a little? The present has such a rough way of treading it down."

"Oh I like the past, but I don't like critics," my hostess declared with her hard complacency.

"Neither do I, but I like their discoveries."

"Are n't they mostly lies?"

"The lies are what they sometimes discover," I said, smiling at the quiet impertinence of this. "They often lay bare the truth."

"The truth is God's, it is n't man's: we had better leave it alone. Who can judge of it?—who can say?"

"We're terribly in the dark, I know," I admitted; "but if we give up trying what becomes of all the fine things? What becomes of the work I just mentioned, that of the great philosophers and poets? It's all vain words if there's nothing to measure it by."

"You talk as if you were a tailor," said Miss Bordereau whimsically; and then she added quickly and in a different manner: "This house is very fine; the proportions are magnificent. To-day I wanted to look at this part again. I made them bring me out here. When your man came just now to learn if I would see you I was on the point of sending for you to ask you if you did n't mean to go on. I wanted to judge what I'm letting you have. This sala is very grand," she pursued like an auctioneer, moving a little, as I guessed, her invisible eyes. "I don't believe you often have lived in such a house, eh?"

"I can't often afford to!" I said.

"Well then how much will you give me for six months?"

I was on the point of exclaiming—and the air of excruciation on my face would have denoted a moral fact—"Don't, Juliana; for *his* sake, don't!" But I controlled myself and asked less passionately: "Why should I remain so long as that?"

"I thought you liked it," said Miss Bordereau with her shrivelled dignity.

"So I thought I should."

For a moment she said nothing more, and I left my own words to suggest to her what they might. I half-expected her to say, coldly enough, that if I had been disappointed we need n't continue the discussion, and this in spite of the fact that I believed her now to have in her mind—however it had come there—what would have told her that my disappointment was natural. But to my extreme surprise she ended by observing: "If you don't think we've treated you well enough perhaps we can discover some way of treating you better." This speech was somehow so incongruous that it made me laugh again, and I excused myself by saying that she talked as if I were a sulky boy pouting in the corner and having to be "brought round." I had n't a grain of complaint to make; and could anything have exceeded Miss Tina's graciousness in accompanying me a few nights before to the Piazza? At this the old woman went on: "Well, you brought it on yourself!" And then in a different tone: "She's a very fine girl." I assented cordially to this proposition, and she expressed the hope that I did so not merely to be obliging, but that I really liked her. Meanwhile I wondered still more what Miss Bordereau was coming to. "Except for me, to-day," she said, "she has n't a relation in the world." Did she by describing her niece as amiable and unencumbered wish to represent her as a *parti*?[18]

It was perfectly true that I could n't afford to go on with my rooms at a fancy price and that I had already devoted to my undertaking almost all the hard cash I had set apart for it. My patience and my time were by no means exhausted, but I should be able to draw upon them only on a more usual Venetian basis. I was willing to pay the precious personage with whom my pecuniary dealings were such a discord twice as much as any other *padrona di casa*[19] would have asked, but I was n't willing to pay her twenty times as much. I told her so plainly, and my plainness appeared to have some success, for she exclaimed: "Very good; you've done what I asked—you've made an offer!"

[18]A marriageable person.
[19]Landlady.

"Yes, but not for half a year. Only by the month."

"Oh I must think of that then." She seemed disappointed that I would n't tie myself to a period, and I guessed that she wished both to secure me and to discourage me; to say severely: "Do you dream that you can get off with less than six months? Do you dream that even by the end of that time you'll be appreciably nearer your victory?" What was most in my mind was that she had a fancy to play me the trick of making me engage myself when in fact she had sacrificed her treasure. There was a moment when my suspense on this point was so acute that I all but broke out with the question, and what kept it back was but an instinctive recoil—lest it should be a mistake—from the last violence of self-exposure. She was such a subtle old witch that one could never tell where one stood with her. You may imagine whether it cleared up the puzzle when, just after she had said she would think of my proposal and without any formal transition, she drew out of her pocket with an embarrassed hand a small object wrapped in crumpled white paper. She held it there a moment and then resumed: "Do you know much about curiosities?"

"About curiosities?"

"About antiquities, the old gimcracks that people pay so much for to-day. Do you know the kind of price they bring?"

I thought I saw what was coming, but I said ingenuously: "Do you want to buy something?"

"No, I want to sell. What would an amateur give me for that?" She unfolded the white paper and made a motion for me to take from her a small oval portrait. I possessed myself of it with fingers of which I could only hope that they did n't betray the intensity of their clutch, and she added: "I would part with it only for a good price."

At the first glance I recognised Jeffrey Aspern, and was well aware that I flushed with the act. As she was watching me however I had the consistency to exclaim: "What a striking face! Do tell me who he is."

"He's an old friend of mine, a very distinguished man in his day. He gave it me himself, but I'm afraid to mention his name, lest you never should have heard of him, critic and historian as you are. I know the world goes fast and one generation forgets another. He was all the fashion when I was young."

She was perhaps amazed at my assurance, but I was surprised at hers; at her having the energy, in her state of health and at her time of life, to wish to sport with me to that tune simply for her private entertainment—the humour to test me and practise on me and befool me. This at least was the interpretation that I put upon her production of the relic, for I could n't believe she really desired to sell it or cared for any information I might give her. What she wished was to dangle it before my eyes and put a prohibitive price on it. "The face comes back to me, it torments me," I said, turning the object this way and that and looking at it very critically. It was a careful but not a supreme work of art, larger than the ordinary miniature and representing a young man with a remarkably handsome face, in a high-collared green coat and a buff waistcoat. I felt in the little work a virtue of likeness and judged it to have been painted when the model was about twenty-five. There are, as all the world knows, three other portraits of the poet in existence, but none of so early a date as this elegant image. "I've never seen the original, clearly a man of a past age, but I've seen other reproductions of this face," I went on. "You expressed doubt of this generation's having heard of the gentleman, but he strikes me for all the world as a celebrity. Now who is he? I can't put my finger on him—I can't give him a label. Was n't he a writer? Surely he's a poet." I was determined that it should be she, not I, who should first pronounce Jeffrey Aspern's name.

My resolution was taken in ignorance of Miss Bordereau's extremely resolute character, and her lips never formed in my hearing the syllables that meant so much for her. She neglected to answer my question, but raised her hand to take back the picture, using a gesture which though impotent was in a high degree peremptory. "It's only a person who should know for himself that would give me my price," she said with a certain dryness.

"Oh then you have a price?" I did n't restore the charming thing; not from any vindictive purpose, but because I instinctively clung to it. We looked at each other hard while I retained it.

"I know the least I would take. What it occurred to me to ask you about is the most I shall be able to get."

She made a movement, drawing herself together as if, in a spasm of dread at having lost her prize, she had been impelled to the immense effort of rising to snatch it from me. I instantly placed it in her hand again, saying as I did so: "I should like to have it myself, but with your ideas it would be quite beyond my mark."

She turned the small oval plate over in her lap, with its face down, and I heard her catch her breath as after a strain or an escape. This however did not prevent her saying in a moment: "You'd buy a likeness of a person you don't know by an artist who has no reputation?"

"The artist may have no reputation, but that thing's wonderfully well painted," I replied, to give myself a reason.

"It's lucky you thought of saying that, because the painter was my father."

"That makes the picture indeed precious!" I returned with gaiety; and I may add that a part of my cheer came from this proof I had been right in my theory of Miss Bordereau's origin. Aspern had of course met the young lady on his going to her father's studio as a sitter. I observed to Miss Bordereau that if she would entrust me with her property for twenty-four hours I should be happy to take advice on it; but she made no other reply than to slip it in silence into her pocket. This convinced me still more that she had no sincere intention of selling it during her lifetime, though she may have desired to satisfy herself as to the sum her niece, should she leave it to her, might expect eventually to obtain for it. "Well, at any rate, I hope you won't offer it without giving me notice," I said as she remained irresponsive. "Remember me as a possible purchaser."

"I should want your money first!" she returned with unexpected rudeness; and then, as if she bethought herself that I might well complain of such a tone and wished to turn the matter off, asked abruptly what I talked about with her niece when I went out with her that way of an evening.

"You speak as if we had set up the habit," I replied. "Certainly I should be very glad if it were to become our pleasant custom. But in that case I should feel a still greater scruple at betraying a lady's confidence."

"Her confidence? Has my niece confidence?"

"Here she is—she can tell you herself," I said; for Miss Tina now appeared on the threshold of the old woman's parlour. "Have you confidence, Miss Tina? Your aunt wants very much to know."

"Not in her, not in her!" the younger lady declared, shaking her head with a dolefulness that was neither jocular nor affected. "I don't know what to do with her; she has fits of horrid imprudence. She's so easily tired—and yet she has begun to roam, to drag herself about the house." And she looked down at her yoke-fellow of long years with a vacancy of wonder, as if all their contact and custom had n't made her perversities, on occasion, any more easy to follow.

"I know what I'm about. I'm not losing my mind. I dare say you'd like to think so," said Miss Bordereau with a crudity of cynicism.

"I don't suppose you came out here yourself. Miss Tina must have had to lend you a hand," I interposed for conciliation.

"Oh she insisted we should push her; and when she insists!" said Miss Tina, in the same tone of apprehension; as if there were no knowing what service she disapproved of her aunt might force her next to render.

"I've always got most things done I wanted, thank God! The people I've lived with have humoured me," the old woman continued, speaking out of the white ashes of her vanity.

I took it pleasantly up. "I suppose you mean they've obeyed you."

"Well whatever it is—when they like one."

"It's just because I like you that I want to resist," said Miss Tina with a nervous laugh.

"Oh I suspect you'll bring Miss Bordereau upstairs next to pay me a visit," I went on; to which the old lady replied:

"Oh no; I can keep an eye on you from here!"

"You're very tired; you'll certainly be ill to-night!" cried Miss Tina.

"Nonsense, dear; I feel better at this moment than I've done for a month. To-morrow I shall come out again. I want to be where I can see this clever gentleman."

"Should n't you perhaps see me better in your sitting-room?" I asked.

"Don't you mean should n't you have a better chance at *me?*" she returned, fixing me a moment with her green shade.

"Ah I have n't that anywhere! I look at you but don't see you."

"You agitate her dreadfully—and that's not good," said Miss Tina, giving me a reproachful deterrent headshake.

"I want to watch you—I want to watch you!" Miss Bordereau went on.

"Well then let us spend as much of our time together as possible—I don't care where. That will give you every facility."

"Oh I've seen you enough for to-day. I'm satisfied. Now I'll go home," Juliana said. Miss Tina laid her hands on the back of the wheeled chair and began to push, but I begged her to let me take her place. "Oh yes, you may move me this way—you shan't in any other!" the old woman cried as she felt herself propelled firmly and easily over the smooth hard floor. Before we reached the door of her own apartment she bade me stop, and she took a long last look up and down the noble sala. "Oh it's a prodigious house!" she murmured; after which I pushed her forward. When we had entered the parlour Miss Tina let me know she should now be able to manage, and at the same moment the little red-haired *donna* came to meet her mistress. Miss Tina's idea was evidently to get her aunt immediately back to bed. I confess that in spite of this urgency I was guilty of the indiscretion of lingering; it held me there to feel myself so close to the objects I coveted—which would be probably put away somewhere in the faded unsociable room. The place had indeed a bareness that suggested no hidden values; there were neither dusky nooks nor curtained corners, neither massive cabinets nor chests with iron bands. Moreover it was possible, it was perhaps even likely, that the old lady had consigned her relics to her bedroom, to some battered box that was shoved under the bed, to the drawer of some lame dressing-table, where they would be in the range of vision by the dim night-lamp. None the less I turned an eye on every article of furniture, on every conceivable cover for a hoard, and noticed that there were half a dozen things with drawers, and in particular a tall old secretary with brass ornaments of the style of the Empire—a receptacle somewhat infirm but still capable of keeping rare secrets. I don't know why this article so engaged me, small purpose as I had of breaking into it; but I stared at it so hard that Miss Tina noticed me and changed colour. Her doing this made me think I was right and that, wherever they might have been before, the Aspern papers at that moment languished behind the peevish little lock of the secretary. It was hard to turn my attention from the dull mahogany front when I reflected that a plain panel divided me from the goal of my hopes; but I gathered up my slightly scattered prudence and with an effort took leave of my hostess. To make the effort graceful I said to her that I should certainly bring her an opinion about the little picture.

"The little picture?" Miss Tina asked in surprise.

"What do *you* know about it, my dear?" the old woman demanded. "You need n't mind. I've fixed my price."

"And what may that be?"

"A thousand pounds."

"Oh Lord!" cried poor Miss Tina irrepressibly.

"Is that what she talks to you about?" said Miss Bordereau.

"Imagine your aunt's wanting to know!" I had to separate from my younger friend with only those words, though I should have liked immensely to add: "For heaven's sake meet me to-night in the garden!"

VIII

As it turned out the precaution had not been needed, for three hours later, just as I had finished my dinner, Miss Tina appeared, unannounced, in the open doorway of the room in which my simple repasts were served. I remember well that I felt no surprise at seeing her; which is not a proof of my not believing in her timidity. It was immense, but in a case in which there was a particular reason for boldness it never would have prevented her from running up to my floor. I saw that she was now quite full of a particular reason; it threw her forward—made her seize me, as I rose to meet her, by the arm.

"My aunt's very ill; I think she's dying!"

"Never in the world," I answered bitterly. "Don't you be afraid!"

"Do go for a doctor—do, do! Olimpia's gone for the one we always have, but she does n't come back; I don't know what has happened to her. I told her that if he was n't at home she was to follow him where he had gone; but apparently she's following him all over Venice. I don't know what to do—she looks so as if she were sinking."

"May I see her, may I judge?" I asked. "Of course I shall be delighted to bring some one; but had n't we better send my man instead, so that I may stay with you?"

Miss Tina assented to this and I dispatched my servant for the best doctor in the neighborhood. I hurried downstairs with her, and on the way she told me that an hour after I quitted them in the afternoon Miss Bordereau had had an attack of "oppression," a terrible difficulty in breathing. This had subsided, but had left her so exhausted that she did n't come up; she seemed all spent and gone. I repeated that she was n't gone, that she would n't go yet; whereupon Miss Tina gave me a sharper sidelong glance than she had ever favoured me withal and said: "Really, what do you mean? I suppose you don't accuse her of making-believe!" I forget what reply I made to this, but I fear that in my heart I thought the old woman capable of any weird manoeuvre. Miss Tina wanted to know what I had done to her; her aunt had told her I had made her so angry. I declared I had done nothing whatsoever—I had been exceedingly careful; to which my companion rejoined that our friend had assured her she had had a scene with me—a scene that had upset her. I answered with some resentment that the scene had been of *her* making—that I could n't think what she was angry with me for unless for not seeing my way to give a thousand pounds for the portrait of Jeffrey Aspern. "And did she show you that? Oh gracious—oh deary me!" groaned Miss Tina, who seemed to feel the situation pass out of her control and the elements of her fate thicken round her. I answered her I'd give anything to possess it, yet that I had no thousand pounds; but I stopped when we came to the door of Miss Bordereau's room. I had an immense curiosity to pass it, but I thought it my duty to represent to Miss Tina that if I made the invalid angry she ought perhaps to be spared the sight of me. "The sight of you? Do you think she can *see?*" my companion demanded almost with indignation.

I did think so but forbore to say it, and I softly followed my conductress.

I remember that what I said to her as I stood for a moment beside the old woman's bed was: "Does she never show you her eyes then? Have you never seen them?" Miss Bordereau had been divested of her green shade, but—it was not my fortune to behold Juliana in her nightcap— the upper half of her face was covered by the fall of a piece of dingy lacelike muslin, a sort of extemporised hood which, wound round her head, descended to the end of her nose, leaving nothing visible but her white withered cheeks and puckered mouth, closed tightly and, as it were, consciously. Miss Tina gave me a glance of surprise, evidently not seeing a reason for my impatience. "You mean she always wears something? She does it to preserve them."

"Because they're so fine?"

"Oh to-day, to-day!" And Miss Tina shook her head speaking very low. "But they used to be magnificent!"

"Yes indeed,—we've Aspern's word for that." And as I looked again at the old woman's wrappings I could imagine her not having wished to allow any supposition that the great poet had overdone it. But I did n't waste my time in considering Juliana, in whom the appearance of respiration was so slight as to suggest that no human attention could ever help her more. I turned my eyes once more all over the room, rummaging with them the closets, the chests of drawers, the tables. Miss Tina at once noted their direction and read, I think, what was in them; but she did n't answer it, turning away restlessly, anxiously, so that I felt rebuked, with reason, for an appetite well-nigh indecent in the presence of our dying companion. All the same I took another view, endeavouring to pick out mentally the receptacle to try first, for a person who should wish to put his hand on Miss Bordereau's papers directly after her death. The place was a dire confusion; it looked like the dressing-room of an old actress. There were clothes hanging over chairs, odd-looking shabby bundles here and there, and various pasteboard boxes piled together, battered, bulging, and discoloured, which might have been fifty years old. Miss Tina after a moment noticed the direction of my eyes again, and, as if she guessed how I judged such appearances—forgetting I had no business to judge them at all—said, perhaps to defend herself from the imputation of complicity in the disorder:

"She likes it this way; we can't move things. There are old bandboxes she has had most of her life." Then she added, half-taking pity on my real thought: "Those things were *there*." And she pointed to a small low trunk which stood under a sofa that just allowed room for it. It struck me as a queer superannuated coffer, of painted wood, with elaborate handles and shrivelled straps and with the colour—it had last been endued with a coat of light green—much rubbed off. It evidently had travelled with Juliana in the olden time—in the days of her adventures, which it had shared. It would have made a strange figure arriving at a modern hotel.

"*Were* there—they are n't now?" I asked, startled by Miss Tina's implication.

She was going to answer, but at that moment the doctor came in—the doctor whom the little maid had been sent to fetch and whom she had at last overtaken. My servant, going on his own errand, had met her with her companion in tow, and in the sociable Venetian spirit, retracing his steps with them, had also come up to the threshold of the padrona's room, where I saw him peep over the doctor's shoulder. I motioned him away the more instantly that the sight of his prying face reminded me how little I myself had to do there—an admonition confirmed by the sharp way the little doctor eyed me, his air of taking me for a rival who had the field before him. He was a short fat brisk gentleman who wore the tall hat of his profession and seemed to look at everything but his patient. He kept me still in range, as if it struck him I too should be better for a dose, so that I bowed to him and left him with the women, going down to smoke a cigar in the garden. I was nervous; I could n't go further; I could n't leave the place. I don't know exactly what I thought might happen, but I felt it important to be there. I wandered about the alleys—the warm night had come on—smoking cigar after cigar and studying the light in Miss Bordereau's windows. They were open now, I could see; the situation was different. Sometimes the light moved, but not quickly; it did n't suggest the hurry of a crisis. Was the old woman dying or was she already dead? Had the doctor said that there was nothing to be done at her tremendous age but to let her quietly pass away? or had he simply announced with a look a little more conventional that the end of the end had come? Were the other two women just going and coming over the offices that follow in such a case? It made me uneasy not to be nearer, as if I thought the doctor himself might carry away the papers with him. I bit my cigar hard while it assailed me again that perhaps there were now no papers to carry!

I wandered about an hour and more. I looked out for Miss Tina at one of the windows, having a vague idea that she might come there to give me some sign. Would n't she see the red tip of my cigar in the dark and feel sure I was hanging on to know what the doctor had said? I'm afraid it's a proof of the grossness of my anxieties that I should have taken in some degree for granted at such an hour, in the midst of the greatest change that could fall on her, poor Miss Tina's having also a free mind for them. My servant came down and spoke to me; he knew nothing save that the doctor had gone after a visit of half an hour. If he had stayed half an hour then Miss Bordereau was still alive: it could n't have taken so long to attest her decease. I sent the man out of the house; there were moments when the sense of his curiosity annoyed me, and this was one of them. *He* had been watching my cigar-tip from an upper window, if Miss Tina had n't; he could n't know what I was after and I could n't tell him, though I suspected in him fantastic private theories about me which he thought fine and which, had I more exactly known them, I should have thought offensive.

I went upstairs at last, but I mounted no higher than the sala. The door of Miss Bordereau's apartment was open, showing from the parlour the dimness of a poor candle. I went toward it with a light tread, and at the same moment Miss Tina appeared and stood looking at me as I approached. "She's better, she's better," she said even before I asked. "The doctor has given her something; she woke up, came back to life while he was there. He says there's no immediate danger."

"No immediate danger? Surely he thinks her condition serious."

"Yes, because she had been excited. That affects her dreadfully."

"It will do so again then, because she works herself up. She did so this afternoon."

"Yes, she must n't come out any more," said Miss Tina with one of her lapses into a deeper detachment.

"What's the use of making such a remark as that," I permitted myself to ask, "if you begin to rattle her about again the first time she bids you?"

"I won't—I won't do it any more."

"You must learn to resist her," I went on.

"Oh yes I shall; I shall do so better if you tell me it's right."

"You must n't do it for me—you must do it for yourself. It all comes back to you, if you're scared and upset."

"Well, I'm not upset now," said Miss Tina placidly enough. "She's very quiet."

"Is she conscious again—does she speak?"

"No, she does n't speak, but she takes my hand. She holds it fast."

"Yes," I returned, "I can see what force she still has by the way she grabbed that picture this afternoon. But if she holds you fast how comes it that you're here?"

Miss Tina waited a little; though her face was in deep shadow—she had her back to the light in the parlour and I had put down my own candle far off, near the door of the sala—I thought I saw her smile ingenuously. "I came on purpose—I had heard your step."

"Why I came on tiptoe, as soundlessly as possible."

"Well, I had heard you," said Miss Tina.

"And is your aunt alone now?"

"Oh no—Olimpia sits there."

On my side I debated. "Shall we then pass in there?" And I nodded at the parlour; I wanted more and more to be on the spot.

"We can't talk there—she'll hear us."

I was on the point of replying that in that case we'd sit silent, but I felt too much this would n't do, there was something I desired so immensely to ask her. Thus I hinted we might walk a little in the sala, keeping more at the other end, where we should n't disturb our friend. Miss Tina assented unconditionally; the doctor was coming again, she said, and she would be there to meet him at the door. We strolled through the fine superfluous hall, where on the marble floor—particularly as at first we said nothing—our footsteps were more audible than I had expected. When we reached the other end—the wide window, inveterately closed, connecting with the balcony that overhung the canal—I submitted that we had best remain there, as she would see the doctor arrive the sooner. I opened the window and we passed out on the balcony. The air of the canal seemed even heavier, hotter than that of the sala. The place was hushed and void; the quiet neighbourhood had gone to sleep. A lamp, here and there, over the narrow black water, glimmered in double; the voice of a man going homeward singing, his jacket on his shoulder and his hat on his ear, came to us from a distance. This did n't prevent the scene from being very *comme il faut*, as Miss Bordereau had called it the first time I saw her. Presently a gondola passed along the canal with its slow rhythmical splash, and as we listened we watched it in silence. It did n't stop, it did n't carry the doctor; and after it had gone I said to Miss Tina:

"And where are they now—the things that were in the trunk?"

"In the trunk?"

"That green box you pointed out to me in her room. You said her papers had been there; you seemed to mean she had transferred them."

"Oh yes; they're not in the trunk," said Miss Tina.

"May I ask if you've looked?"

"Yes, I've looked—for you."

"How for me, dear Miss Tina? Do you mean you'd have given them to me if you had found them?"—and I fairly trembled with the question.

She delayed to reply and I waited. Suddenly she broke out: "I don't know what I'd do—what I would n't!"

"Would you look again—somewhere else?"

She had spoken with a strange unexpected emotion, and she went on in the same tone: "I can't—I can't—while she lies there. It is n't decent."

"No, it is n't decent," I replied gravely. "Let the poor lady rest in peace." And the words, on my lips, were not hypocritical, for I felt reprimanded and shamed.

Miss Tina added in a moment, as if she had guessed this and were sorry for me, but at the same time wished to explain that I did push her, or at least harp on the chord, too much: "I can't deceive her that way. I can't deceive her—perhaps on her deathbed."

"Heaven forbid I should ask you, though I've been guilty myself!"

"You've been guilty?"

"I've sailed under false colours." I felt now I must make a clean breast of it, must tell her I had given her an invented name on account of my fear her aunt would have heard of me and so refuse to take me in. I explained this as well as that I had really been a party to the letter addressed to them by John Cumnor months before.

She listened with great attention, almost in fact gaping for wonder, and when I had made my confession she said: "Then your real name—what is it?" She repeated it over twice when I told her, accompanying it with the exclamation "Gracious, gracious!" Then she added: "I like your own best."

"So do I"—and I felt my laugh rueful. "Ouf! it's a relief to get rid of the other."

"So it was a regular plot—a kind of conspiracy?"

"Oh a conspiracy—we were only two," I replied, leaving out of course Mrs. Prest.

She considered; I thought she was perhaps going to pronounce us very base. But this was not her way, and she remarked after a moment, as in candid impartial contemplation: "How much you must want them!"

"Oh, I do, passionately!" I grinned, I fear, to admit. And this chance made me go on, forgetting my compunction of a moment before. "How can she possibly have changed their place herself? How can she walk?

How can she arrive at that sort of muscular exertion? How can she lift
and carry things?"

"Oh when one wants and one has so much will!" said Miss Tina as if
she had thought over my question already herself and had simply had
no choice but that answer—the idea that in the dead of night, or at
some moment when the coast was clear, the old woman had been
capable of a miraculous effort.

"Have you questioned Olimpia? Has n't she helped her—has n't she
done it for her?" I asked; to which my friend replied promptly and
positively that their servant had had nothing to do with the matter,
though without admitting definitely that she had spoken to her. It was
as if she were a little shy, a little ashamed now, of letting me see how
much she had entered into my uneasiness and had me on her mind.
Suddenly she said to me without any immediate relevance:

"I rather feel you a new person, you know, now that you've a new
name."

"It is n't a new one; it's a very good old one, thank fortune!"

She looked at me a moment. "Well, I do like it better."

"Oh if you did n't I would almost go on with the other!"

"Would you really?"

I laughed again, but I returned for an answer: "Of course if she can
rummage about that way she can perfectly have burnt them."

"You must wait—you must wait," Miss Tina mournfully moralised;
and her tone ministered little to my patience, for it seemed after all to
accept that wretched possibility. I would teach myself to wait, I declared nevertheless; because in the first place I could n't otherwise and
in the second I had her promise, given me the other night, that she
would help me.

"Of course if the papers are gone that's no use," she said; not as if
she wished to recede, but only to be conscientious.

"Naturally. But if you could only find out!" I groaned, quivering
again.

"I thought you promised you'd wait."

"Oh you mean wait even for that?"

"For what then?"

"Ah nothing," I answered rather foolishly, being ashamed to tell her
what had been implied in my acceptance of delay—the idea that she
would perhaps do more for me than merely find out.

I know not if she guessed this; at all events she seemed to bethink
herself of some propriety of showing me more rigour. "I did n't promise to deceive, did I? I don't think I did."

"It does n't much matter whether you did or not, for you could n't!"
Nothing is more possible than that she would n't have contested this
even had n't she been diverted by our seeing the doctor's gondola
shoot into the little canal and approach the house. I noted that he came
as fast as if he believed our proprietress still in danger. We looked
down at him while he disembarked and then went back into the sala to
meet him. When he came up, however, I naturally left Miss Tina to go
off with him alone, only asking her leave to come back later for news.

I went out of the house and walked far, as far as the Piazza, where
my restlessness declined to quit me. I was unable to sit down; it was
very late now though there were people still at the little tables in front
of the cafés: I could but uneasily revolve, and I did so half a dozen
times. The only comfort, none the less, was in my having told Miss
Tina who I really was. At last I took my way home again, getting
gradually and all but inextricably lost, as I did whenever I went out in
Venice: so that it was considerably past midnight when I reached my
door. The sala, upstairs, was dark as usual and my lamp as I crossed it
found nothing satisfactory to show me. I was disappointed, for I had
notified Miss Tina that I would come back for a report, and I thought
she might have left a light there as a sign. The door of the ladies'
apartment was closed; which seemed a hint that my faltering friend
had gone to bed in impatience of waiting for me. I stood in the middle
of the place, considering, hoping she would hear me and perhaps peep
out, saying to myself too that she would never go to bed with her aunt
in a state so critical; she would sit up and watch—she would be in a
chair, in her dressing-gown. I went nearer the door; I stopped there and
listened. I heard nothing at all and at last I tapped gently. No answer
came and after another minute I turned the handle. There was no light
in the room; this ought to have prevented my entrance, but it had no
such effect. If I have frankly stated the importunities, the indelicacies,
of which my desire to possess myself of Jeffrey Aspern's papers had
made me capable I need n't shrink, it seems to me, from confessing this
last indiscretion. I regard it as the worst thing I did, yet there were
extenuating circumstances. I was deeply though doubtless not disinterestedly anxious for more news of Juliana, and Miss Tina had accepted
from me, as it were, a rendezvous which it might have been a point of
honour with me to keep. It may be objected that her leaving the place
dark was a positive sign that she released me, and to this I can only
reply that I wished not to be released.

The door of Miss Bordereau's room was open and I could see beyond
it the faintness of a taper. There was no sound—my footstep caused no

one to stir. I came further into the room; I lingered there lamp in hand. I wanted to give Miss Tina a chance to come to me if, as I could n't doubt, she were still with her aunt. I made no noise to call her; I only waited to see if she would n't notice my light. She did n't, and I explained this—I found afterwards I was right—by the idea that she had fallen asleep. If she had fallen asleep her aunt was not on her mind, and my explanation ought to have led me to go out as I had come. I must repeat again that I did n't, for I found myself at the same moment given up to something else. I had no definite purpose, no bad intention, but felt myself held to the spot by an acute, though absurd, sense of opportunity. Opportunity for what I could n't have said, inasmuch as it was n't in my mind that I might proceed to thievery. Even had this tempted me I was confronted with the evident fact that Miss Bordereau did n't leave her secretary, her cupboard and the drawers of her tables gaping. I had no keys, no tools and no ambition to smash her furniture. None the less it came to me that I was now, perhaps alone, unmolested, at the hour of freedom and safety, nearer to the source of my hopes than I had ever been. I held up my lamp, let the light play on the different objects as if it could tell me something. Still there was no movement from the other room. If Miss Tina was sleeping she was sleeping sound. Was she doing so—generous creature—on purpose to leave me the field? Did she know I was there and was she just keeping quiet to see what I would do—what I *could* do? Yet might I, when it came to that? She herself knew even better than I how little.

I stopped in front of the secretary, gaping at it vainly and no doubt grotesquely; for what had it to say to me after all? In the first place it was locked, and in the second it almost surely contained nothing in which I was interested. Ten to one the papers had been destroyed, and even if they had n't the keen old woman would n't have put them in such a place as that after removing them from the green trunk— would n't have transferred them, with the idea of their safety on her brain, from the better hiding-place to the worse. The secretary was more conspicuous, more exposed in a room in which she could no longer mount guard. It opened with a key, but there was a small brass handle, like a button, as well: I saw this as I played my lamp over it. I did something more, for the climax of my crisis; I caught a glimpse of the possibility that Miss Tina wished me really to understand. If she did n't so wish me, if she wished me to keep away, why had n't she locked the door of communication between the sitting-room and the sala? That would have been a definite sign that I was to leave them alone. If I did n't leave them alone she meant me to come for a purpose—a purpose now represented by the super-subtle inference that to oblige me she had unlocked the secretary. She had n't left the key, but the lid would probably move if I touched the button. This possibility pressed me hard and I bent very close to judge. I did n't propose to do anything, not even—not in the least—to let down the lid; I only wanted to test my theory, to see if the cover *would* move. I touched the button with my hand—a mere touch would tell me; and as I did so—it is embarrassing for me to relate it—I looked over my shoulder. It was a chance, an instinct, for I had really heard nothing. I almost let my luminary drop and certainly I stepped back, straightening myself up at what I saw. Juliana stood there in her night-dress, by the doorway of her room, watching me; her hands were raised, she had lifted the ever-lasting curtain that covered half her face, and for the first, the last, the only time I beheld her extraordinary eyes. They glared at me; they were like the sudden drench, for a caught burglar, of a flood of gas-light; they made me horribly ashamed. I never shall forget her strange little bent white tottering figure, with its lifted head, her attitude, her expression; neither shall I forget the tone in which as I turned, looking at her, she hissed out passionately, furiously:

"Ah you publishing scoundrel!"

I can't now say what I stammered to excuse myself, to explain; but I went toward her to tell her I meant no harm. She waved me off with her old hands, retreating before me in horror; and the next thing I knew she had fallen back with a quick spasm, as if death had descended on her, into Miss Tina's arms.

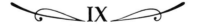

IX

I left Venice the next morning, directly on learning that my hostess had not succumbed, as I feared at the moment, to the shock I had given her—the shock I may also say she had given me. How in the world could I have supposed her capable of getting out of bed by herself? I failed to see Miss Tina before going; I only saw the *donna*, whom I entrusted with a note for her younger mistress. In this note I mentioned that I should be absent but a few days. I went to Treviso, to Bassano, to Castelfranco; I took walks and drives and looked at musty old churches with ill-lighted pictures; I spent hours seated smoking at the doors of cafés, where there were flies and yellow curtains, on the shady side of sleepy little squares. In spite of these pastimes, which were mechanical and perfunctory, I scantly enjoyed my travels: I had

had to gulp down a bitter draught and could n't get rid of the taste. It had been devilish awkward, as the young men say, to be found by Juliana in the dead of night examining the attachment of her bureau; and it had not been less so to have to believe for a good many hours after that it was highly probable I had killed her. My humiliation galled me, but I had to make the best of it, had, in writing to Miss Tina, to minimise it, as well as account for the posture in which I had been discovered. As she gave me no word of answer I could n't know what impression I made on her. It rankled for me that I had been called a publishing scoundrel, since certainly I did publish and no less certainly had n't been very delicate. There was a moment when I stood convinced that the only way to purge my dishonour was to take myself straight away on the instant; to sacrifice my hopes and relieve the two poor women for ever of the oppression of my intercourse. Then I reflected that I had better try a short absence first, for I must already have had a sense (unexpressed and dim) that in disappearing completely it would n't be merely my own hopes I should condemn to extinction. It would perhaps answer if I kept dark long enough to give the elder lady time to believe herself rid of me. That she would wish to be rid of me after this—if I was n't rid of her—was now not to be doubted: that midnight monstrosity would have cured her of the disposition to put up with my company for the sake of my dollars. I said to myself that after all I could n't abandon Miss Tina, and I continued to say this even while I noted that she quite ignored my earnest request—I had given her two or three addresses, at little towns, *poste restante*[20]—for some sign of her actual state. I would have made my servant write me news but that he was unable to manage a pen. Could n't I measure the scorn of Miss Tina's silence—little disdainful as she had ever been? Really the soreness pressed; yet if I had scruples about going back I had others about not doing so, and I wanted to put myself on a better footing. The end of it was that I did return to Venice on the twelfth day; and as my gondola gently bumped against our palace steps a fine palpitation of suspense showed me the violence my absence had done me.

I had faced about so abruptly that I had n't even telegraphed to my servant. He was therefore not at the station to meet me, but he poked out his head from an upper window when I reached the house. "They have put her into earth, *quella vecchia*,"[21] he said to me in the lower hall

---

[20]General delivery.
[21]That old woman.

while he shouldered my valise; and he grinned and almost winked as if he knew I should be pleased with his news.

"She's dead!" I cried, giving him a very different look.

"So it appears, since they've buried her."

"It's all over then? When was the funeral?"

"The other yesterday. But a funeral you could scarcely call it, signore: *roba da niente—un piccolo passeggio brutto* of two gondolas. *Poveretta!*"[22] the man continued, referring apparently to Miss Tina. His conception of funerals was that they were mainly to amuse the living.

I wanted to know about Miss Tina, how she might be and generally where; but I asked him no more questions till we had got upstairs. Now that the fact had met me I took a bad view of it, especially of the idea that poor Miss Tina had had to manage by herself after the end. What did she know about arrangements, about the steps to take in such a case? Poveretta indeed! I could only hope the doctor had given her support and that she had n't been neglected by the old friends of whom she had told me, the little band of the faithful whose fidelity consisted in coming to the house once a year. I elicited from my servant that two old ladies and an old gentleman had in fact rallied round Miss Tina and had supported her—they had come for her in a gondola of their own—during the journey to the cemetery, the little red-walled island of tombs which lies to the north of the town and on the way to Murano. It appeared from these signs that the Misses Bordereau were Catholics, a discovery I had never made, as the old woman could n't go to church and her niece, so far as I perceived, either did n't, or went to early mass in the parish before I was stirring. Certainly even the priests respected their seclusion; I had never caught the whisk of the curato's skirt. That evening, an hour later, I sent my servant down with five words on a card to ask if Miss Tina would see me a few moments. She was not in the house, where he had sought her, he told me when I came back, but in the garden walking about to refresh herself and picking the flowers quite as if they belonged to her. He had found her there and she would be happy to see me.

I went down and passed half an hour with poor Miss Tina. She always had a look of musty mourning, as if she were wearing out old robes of sorrow that would n't come to an end; and in this particular she made no different show. But she clearly had been crying, crying a great deal—simply, satisfyingly, refreshingly, with a primitive retarded sense of solitude and violence. But she had none of the airs or graces of

---

[22]Nothing at all—a mean little cortege of two gondolas. Poor little thing!

grief, and I was almost surprised to see her stand there in the first dusk with her hands full of admirable roses and smile at me with reddened eyes. Her white face, in the frame of her mantilla, looked longer, leaner than usual. I had n't doubted her being irreconcilably disgusted with me, her considering I ought to have been on the spot to advise her, to help her; and, though I believed there was no rancour in her composition and no great conviction of the importance of her affairs, I had prepared myself for a change in her manner, for some air of injury and estrangement, which should say to my conscience: "Well, you're a nice person to have professed things!" But historic truth compels me to declare that this poor lady's dull face ceased to be dull, almost ceased to be plain, as she turned it gladly to her late aunt's lodger. That touched him extremely and he thought it simplified his situation until he found it did n't. I was as kind to her that evening as I knew how to be, and I walked about the garden with her as long as seemed good. There was no explanation of any sort between us; I did n't ask her why she had n't answered my letter. Still less did I repeat what I had said to her in that communication; if she chose to let me suppose she had forgotten the position in which Miss Bordereau had surprised me and the effect of the discovery on the old woman, I was quite willing to take it that way: I was grateful to her for not treating me as if I had killed her aunt.

We strolled and strolled, though really not much passed between us save the recognition of her bereavement, conveyed in my manner and in the expression she had of depending on me now, since I let her see I still took an interest in her. Miss Tina's was no breast for the pride or the pretence of independence; she did n't in the least suggest that she knew at present what would become of her. I forbore to press on that question, however, for I certainly was not prepared to say that I would take charge of her. I was cautious; not ignobly, I think, for I felt her knowledge of life to be so small that in her unsophisticated vision there would be no reason why—since I seemed to pity her—I should n't somehow look after her. She told me how her aunt had died, very peacefully at the last, and how everything had been done afterwards by the care of her good friends—fortunately, thanks to me, she said, smiling, there was money in the house. She repeated that when once the "nice" Italians like you they are your friends for life, and when we had gone into this she asked me about my *giro*, my impressions, my adventures, the places I had seen. I told her what I could, making it up partly, I'm afraid, as in my disconcerted state I had taken little in; and after she had heard me she exclaimed, quite as if she had forgotten her aunt and her sorrow, "Dear, dear, how much I should like to do such things—to take an amusing little journey!" It came over me for the moment that I ought to propose some enterprise, say I would accompany her anywhere she liked; and I remarked at any rate that a pleasant excursion— to give her a change—might be managed; we would think of it, talk it over. I spoke never a word of the Aspern documents, asked no question as to what she had ascertained or what had otherwise happened with regard to them before Juliana's death. It was n't that I was n't on pins and needles to know, but that I thought it more decent not to show greed again so soon after the catastrophe. I hoped she herself would say something, but she never glanced that way, and I thought this natural at the time. Later on, however, that night, it occurred to me that her silence was matter for suspicion; since if she had talked of my movements, of anything so detached as the Giorgione[23] at Castelfranco, she might have alluded to what she could easily remember was in my mind. It was not to be supposed the emotion produced by her aunt's death had blotted out the recollection that I was interested in that lady's relics, and I fidgeted afterwards as it came to me that her reticence might very possibly just mean that no relics survived. We separated in the garden—it was she who said she must go in; now that she was alone on the *piano nobile* I felt that (judged at any rate by Venetian ideas) I was on rather a different footing in regard to the invasion of it. As I shook hands with her for good-night I asked if she had some general plan, had thought over what she had best do. "Oh yes, oh yes, but I have n't settled anything yet," she replied quite cheerfully. Was her cheerfulness explained by the impression that I would settle for her?

I was glad the next morning that we had neglected practical questions, as this gave me a pretext for seeing her again immediately. There was a practical enough question now to be touched on. I owed it to her to let her know formally that of course I did n't expect her to keep me on as a lodger, as also to show some interest in her own tenure, what she might have on her hands in the way of a lease. But I was not destined, as befell, to converse with her for more than an instant on either of these points. I sent her no message; I simply went down to the sala and walked to and fro there. I knew she would come out; she would promptly see me accessible. Somehow I preferred not to be shut up with her; gardens and big halls seemed better places to talk. It was a splendid morning, with something in the air that told of the waning

---

[23]A Venetian painter of the Renaissance.

of the long Venetian summer; a freshness from the sea that stirred the flowers in the garden and made a pleasant draught in the house, less shuttered and darkened now than when the old woman was alive. It was the beginning of autumn, of the end of the golden months. With this it was the end of my experiment—or would be in the course of half an hour, when I should really have learned that my dream had been reduced to ashes. After that there would be nothing left for me but to go to the station; for seriously—and as it struck me in the morning light—I could n't linger there to act as guardian to a piece of middle-aged female helplessness. If she had n't saved the papers wherein should I be indebted to her? I think I winced a little as I asked myself how much, if she *had* saved them, I should have to recognise and, as it were, reward such a courtesy. Might n't that service after all saddle me with a guardianship? If this idea did n't make me more uncomfortable as I walked up and down it was because I was convinced I had nothing to look to. If the old woman had n't destroyed everything before she pounced on me in the parlour she had done so the next day.

It took Miss Tina rather longer than I had expected to act on my calculation; but when at last she came out she looked at me without surprise. I mentioned I had been waiting for her and she asked why I had n't let her know. I was glad a few hours later on that I had checked myself before remarking that a friendly intuition might have told her: it turned to comfort for me that I had n't played even to that mild extent on her sensibility. What I did say was virtually the truth—that I was too nervous, since I expected her now to settle my fate.

"Your fate?" said Miss Tina, giving me a queer look; and as she spoke I noticed a rare change in her. Yes, she was other than she had been the evening before—less natural and less easy. She had been crying the day before and was not crying now, yet she struck me as less confident. It was as if something had happened to her during the night, or at least as if she had thought of something that troubled her—something in particular that affected her relations with me, made them more embarrassing and more complicated. Had she simply begun to feel that her aunt's not being there now altered my position?

"I mean about our papers. *Are* there any? You must know now."

"Yes, there are a great many; more than I supposed." I was struck with the way her voice trembled as she told me this.

"Do you mean you've got them in there—and that I may see them?"

"I don't think you can see them," said Miss Tina with an extraordinary expression of entreaty in her eyes, as if the dearest hope she had in the world now was that I would n't take them from her. But how could she expect me to make such a sacrifice as that after all that had passed between us? What had I come back to Venice for but to see them, to take them? My joy at learning they were still in existence was such that if the poor woman had gone down on her knees to beseech me never to mention them again I would have treated the proceeding as a bad joke. "I've got them but I can't show them," she lamentably added.

"Not even to me? Ah Miss Tina!" I broke into a tone of infinite remonstrance and reproach.

She coloured and the tears came back into her eyes; I measured the anguish it cost her to take such a stand, which a dreadful sense of duty had imposed on her. It made me quite sick to find myself confronted with that particular obstacle; all the more that it seemed to me I had been distinctly encouraged to leave it out of account. I quite held Miss Tina to have assured me that if she had no greater hindrance than that—! "You don't mean to say you made her a deathbed promise? It was precisely against your doing anything of that sort that I thought I was safe. Oh I would rather she had burnt the papers outright than have to reckon with such a treachery as that."

"No, it is n't a promise," said Miss Tina.

"Pray what is it then?"

She hung fire, but finally said: "She tried to burn them, but I prevented it. She had hid them in her bed."

"In her bed—?"

"Between the mattresses. That's where she put them when she took them out of the trunk. I can't understand how she did it, because Olimpia did n't help her. She tells me so and I believe her. My aunt only told her afterwards, so that she should n't undo the bed—anything but the sheets. So it was very badly made," added Miss Tina simply.

"I should think so! And how did she try to burn them?"

"She did n't try much; she was too weak those last days. But she told me—she charged me. Oh it was terrible! She could n't speak after that night. She could only make signs."

"And what did you do?"

"I took them away. I locked them up."

"In the secretary?"

"Yes, in the secretary," said Miss Tina, reddening again.

"Did you tell her you'd burn them?"

"No, I did n't—on purpose."

"On purpose to gratify me?"

"Yes, only for that."

"And what good will you have done me if after all you won't show them?"

"Oh none. I know that—I know that," she dismally sounded.

"And did she believe you had destroyed them?"

"I don't know what she believed at the last. I could n't tell—she was too far gone."

"Then if there was no promise and no assurance I can't see what ties you."

"Oh she hated it so—she hated it so! She was so jealous. But here's the portrait—you may have that," the poor woman announced, taking the little picture, wrapped up in the same manner in which her aunt had wrapped it, out of her pocket.

"I may have it—do you mean you give it to me?" I gasped as it passed into my hand.

"Oh yes."

"But it's worth money—a large sum."

"Well!" said Miss Tina, still with her strange look.

I did n't know what to make of it, for it could scarcely mean that she wanted to bargain like her aunt. She spoke as for making me a present. "I can't take it from you as a gift," I said, "and yet I can't afford to pay you for it according to the idea Miss Bordereau had of its value. She rated it at a thousand pounds."

"Could n't we sell it?" my friend threw off.

"God forbid! I prefer the picture to the money."

"Well then keep it."

"You're very generous."

"So are you."

"I don't know why you should think so," I returned; and this was true enough, for the good creature appeared to have in her mind some rich reference that I did n't in the least seize.

"Well, you've made a great difference for me," she said.

I looked at Jeffrey Aspern's face in the little picture, partly in order not to look at that of my companion, which had begun to trouble me, even to frighten me a little—it had taken so very odd, so strained and unnatural a cast. I made no answer to this last declaration; I but privately consulted Jeffrey Aspern's delightful eyes with my own—they were so young and brilliant and yet so wise and so deep; I asked him what on earth was the matter with Miss Tina. He seemed to smile at me with mild mockery; he might have been amused at my case. I had got into a pickle for him—as if he needed it! He was unsatisfactory for the only moment since I had known him. Nevertheless, now that I held the little picture in my hand I felt it would be a precious possession. "Is this a bribe to make me give up the papers?" I presently and all perversely asked. "Much as I value this, you know, if I were obliged to choose the papers are what I should prefer. Ah but ever so much!"

"How can you choose—how can you choose?" Miss Tina returned slowly and woefully.

"I see! Of course there's nothing to be said if you regard the interdiction that rests on you as quite insurmountable. In this case it must seem to you that to part with them would be an impiety of the worst kind, a simple sacrilege!"

She shook her head, only lost in the queerness of her case. "You'd understand if you had known her. I'm afraid," she quavered suddenly—"I'm afraid! She was terrible when she was angry."

"Yes, I saw something of that, that night. She was terrible. Then I saw her eyes. Lord, they were fine!"

"I see them—they stare at me in the dark!" said Miss Tina.

"You've grown nervous with all you've been through."

"Oh yes, very—very!"

"You must n't mind; that will pass away," I said kindly. Then I added resignedly, for it really seemed to me that I must accept the situation: "Well, so it is, and it can't be helped. I must renounce." My friend, at this, with her eyes on me, gave a low soft moan, and I went on: "I only wish to goodness she had destroyed them: then there would be nothing more to say. And I can't understand why, with her ideas, she did n't."

"Oh she lived on them!" said Miss Tina.

"You can imagine whether that makes me want less to see them," I returned not quite so desperately. "But don't let me stand here as if I had it in my soul to tempt you to anything base. Naturally, you understand, I give up my rooms. I leave Venice immediately." And I took up my hat, which I had placed on a chair. We were still rather awkwardly on our feet in the middle of the sala. She had left the door of the apartments open behind her, but had not led me that way.

A strange spasm came into her face as she saw me take my hat. "Immediately—do you mean to-day?" The tone of the words was tragic—they were a cry of desolation.

"Oh no; not so long as I can be of the least service to you."

"Well, just a day or two more—just two or three days," she panted. Then controlling herself she added in another manner: "She wanted to say something to me—the last day—something very particular. But she could n't."

"Something very particular?"

"Something more about the papers."

"And did you guess—have you any idea?"

"No, I've tried to think—but I don't know. I've thought all kinds of things."

"As for instance?"

"Well, that if you were a relation it would be different."

I wondered. "If I were a relation—?"

"If you were n't a stranger. Then it would be the same for you as for me. Anything that's mine would be yours, and you could do what you like. I should n't be able to prevent you—and you'd have no responsibility."

She brought out this droll explanation with a nervous rush and as if speaking words got by heart. They gave me the impression of a subtlety which at first I failed to follow. But after a moment her face helped me to see further, and then the queerest of lights came to me. It was embarrassing, and I bent my head over Jeffrey Aspern's portrait. What an odd expression was in his face! "Get out of it as you can, my dear fellow!" I put the picture into the pocket of my coat and said to Miss Tina: "Yes, I'll sell it for you. I shan't get a thousand pounds by any means, but I shall get something good."

She looked at me through pitiful tears, but seemed to try to smile as she returned: "We can divide the money."

"No, no, it shall all be yours." Then I went on: "I think I know what your poor aunt wanted to say. She wanted to give directions that her papers should be buried with her."

Miss Tina appeared to weigh this suggestion; after which she answered with striking decision, "Oh no, she would n't have thought that safe!"

"It seems to me that nothing could be safer."

"She had an idea that when people want to publish they're capable—!" And she paused, very red.

"Of violating a tomb? Mercy on us, what must she have thought of me!"

"She was n't just, she was n't generous!" my companion cried with sudden passion.

The light that had come into my mind a moment before spread further. "Ah don't say that, for we *are* a dreadful race." Then I pursued: "If she left a will, that may give you some idea."

"I've found nothing of the sort—she destroyed it. She was very fond of me," Miss Tina added with an effect of extreme inconsequence.

"She wanted me to be happy. And if any person should be kind to me—she wanted to speak of that."

I was almost awestricken by the astuteness with which the good lady found herself inspired, transparent astuteness as it was and stitching, as the phrase is, with white thread. "Depend upon it she did n't want to make any provision that would be agreeable to *me.*"

"No, not to you, but quite to me. She knew I should like it if you could carry out your idea. Not because she cared for you, but because she did think of me," Miss Tina went on with her unexpected persuasive volubility. "You could see the things—you could use them." She stopped, seeing I grasped the sense of her conditional—stopped long enough for me to give some sign that I did n't give. She must have been conscious, however, that though my face showed the greatest embarrassment ever painted on a human countenance it was not set as a stone, it was also full of compassion. It was a comfort to me a long time afterwards to consider that she could n't have seen in me the smallest symptom of disrespect. "I don't know what to do; I'm too tormented, I'm too ashamed!" she continued with vehemence. Then turning away from me and burying her face in her hands she burst into a flood of tears. If she did n't know what to do it may be imagined whether I knew better. I stood there dumb, watching her while her sobs resounded in the great empty hall. In a moment she was up at me again with her streaming eyes. "I'd give you everything, and she'd understand, where she is—she'd forgive me!"

"Ah Miss Tina—ah Miss Tina," I stammered for all reply. I did n't know what to do, as I say, but at a venture I made a wild vague movement in consequence of which I found myself at the door. I remember standing there and saying, "It would n't do, it would n't do!"—saying it pensively, awkwardly, grotesquely, while I looked away to the opposite end of the sala as at something very interesting. The next thing I remember is that I was downstairs and out of the house. My gondola was there and my gondolier, reclining on the cushions, sprang up as soon as he saw me. I jumped in and to his usual "*Dove commanda?*" replied, in a tone that made him stare: "Anywhere, anywhere; out into the lagoon!"

He rowed me away and I sat there prostrate, groaning softly to myself, my hat pulled over my brow. What in the name of the preposterous did she mean if she did n't mean to offer me her hand? That was the price—that was the price! And did she think I wanted it, poor deluded infatuated extravagant lady? My gondolier, behind me, must have seen my ears red as I wondered, motionless there under the fluttering *tenda*,[24] with my hidden face, noticing nothing as we passed—wondered whether her delusion, her infatuation had been my own reckless work. Did she think that I had made love to her even to get the papers? I had n't, I had n't; I repeated that over to myself for an hour, for two hours, till I was wearied if not convinced. I don't know where, on the lagoon, my gondolier took me; we floated aimlessly and with slow rare strokes. At last I became conscious that we were near the Lido, far up, on the right hand, as you turn your back to Venice, and I made him put me ashore. I wanted to walk, to move, to shed some of my bewilderment. I crossed the narrow strip and got to the sea-beach—I took my way toward Malamocco. But presently I flung myself down again on the warm sand, in the breeze, on the coarse dry grass. It took it out of me to think I had been so much at fault, that I had unwittingly but none the less deplorably trifled. But I had n't given her cause—distinctly I had n't. I had said to Mrs. Prest that I would make love to her; but it had been a joke without consequences and I had never said it to my victim. I had been as kind as possible because I really liked her; but since when had that become a crime where a woman of such an age and such an appearance was concerned? I am far from remembering clearly the succession of events and feelings during this long day of confusion, which I spent entirely in wandering about, without going home, until late at night: it only comes back to me that there were moments when I pacified my conscience and others when I lashed it into pain. I did n't laugh all day—that I do recollect; the case, however it might have struck others, seemed to me so little amusing. I should have been better employed perhaps in taking the comic side of it. At any rate, whether I had given cause or not, there was no doubt whatever that I could n't pay the price. I could n't accept the proposal. I could n't, for a bundle of tattered papers, marry a ridiculous pathetic provincial old woman. It was a proof of how little she supposed the idea would come to me that she should have decided to suggest it herself in that practical argumentative heroic way—with the timidity, however, so much more striking than the boldness, that her reasons appeared to come first and her feelings afterward.

As the day went on I grew to wish I had never heard of Aspern's relics, and I cursed the extravagant curiosity that had put John Cumnor on the scent of them. We had more than enough material without

---

[24]The awning shading the passenger of a gondola.

them, and my predicament was the just punishment of that most fatal of human follies, our not having known when to stop. It was very well to say it was no predicament, that the way out was simple, that I had only to leave Venice by the first train in the morning, after addressing Miss Tina a note which should be placed in her hand as soon as I got clear of the house; for it was strong proof of my quandary that when I tried to make up the note to my taste in advance—I would put it on paper as soon as I got home, before going to bed—I could n't think of anything but "How can I thank you for the rare confidence you've placed in me?" That would never do; it sounded exactly as if an acceptance were to follow. Of course I might get off without writing at all, but that would be brutal, and my idea was still to exclude brutal solutions. As my confusion cooled I lost myself in wonder at the importance I had attached to Juliana's crumpled scraps; the thought of them became odious to me and I was as vexed with the old witch for the superstition that had prevented her from destroying them as I was with myself for having already spent more money than I could afford in attempting to control their fate. I forget what I did, where I went after leaving the Lido and at what hour or with what recovery of composure I made my way back to my boat. I only know that in the afternoon, when the air was aglow with the sunset, I was standing before the church of Saints John and Paul and looking up at the small square-jawed face of Bartolommeo Colleoni,[25] the terrible *condottiere* who sits so sturdily astride of his huge bronze horse on the high pedestal on which Venetian gratitude maintains him. The statue is incomparable, the finest of all mounted figures, unless that of Marcus Aurelius,[26] who rides benignant before the Roman Capitol, be finer: but I was not thinking of that; I only found myself staring at the triumphant captain as if he had had an oracle on his lips. The western light shines into all his grimness at that hour and makes it wonderfully personal. But he continued to look far over my head, at the red immersion of another day—he had seen so many go down into the lagoon through the centuries—and if he were thinking of battles and stratagems they were of a different quality from any I had to tell him of. He could n't direct me what to do, gaze up at him as I might. Was it before this or after that I wandered about for an hour in the small canals, to the continued stupefaction of my gondolier,

---

[25]Once a *condottiere*—the leader of a private army of mercenaries—Colleoni became the generalissimo of the Venetian republic in the late fifteenth century.

[26]Philosopher-emperor of Rome, who reigned A.D. 161–180.

who had never seen me so restless and yet so void of a purpose and could extract from me no order but "Go anywhere—everywhere—all over the place"? He reminded me that I had not lunched and expressed therefore respectfully the hope that I would dine earlier. He had had long periods of leisure during the day, when I had left the boat and rambled, so that I was not obliged to consider him, and I told him that till the morrow, for reasons, I should touch no meat. It was an effect of poor Miss Tina's proposal, not altogether auspicious, that I had quite lost my appetite. I don't know why it happened that on this occasion I was more than ever struck with that queer air of sociability, of cousinship and family life, which makes up half the expression of Venice. Without streets and vehicles, the uproar of wheels, the brutality of horses, and with its little winding ways where people crowd together, where voices sound as in the corridors of a house, where the human step circulates as if it skirted the angles of furniture and shoes never wear out, the place has the character of an immense collective apartment, in which Piazza San Marco is the most ornamented corner and palaces and churches, for the rest, play the part of great divans of repose, tables of entertainment, expanses of decoration. And somehow the splendid common domicile, familiar domestic and resonant, also resembles a theatre with its actors clicking over bridges and, in straggling processions, tripping along fondamentas. As you sit in your gondola the footways that in certain parts edge the canals assume to the eye the importance of a stage, meeting it at the same angle, and the Venetian figures, moving to and fro against the battered scenery of their little houses of comedy, strike you as members of an endless dramatic troupe.

I went to bed that night very tired and without being able to compose an address to Miss Tina. Was this failure the reason why I became conscious the next morning as soon as I awoke of a determination to see the poor lady again the first moment she would receive me? That had something to do with it, but the oddest revulsion had taken place in my spirit. I found myself aware of this almost as soon as I opened my eyes: it made me jump out of my bed with the movement of a man who remembers that he has left the house-door ajar or a candle burning under a shelf. Was I still in time to save my goods? That question was in my heart; for what had now come to pass was that in the unconscious celebration of sleep I had swung back to a passionate appreciation of Juliana's treasure. The pieces composing it were now more precious than ever and a positive ferocity had come into my need to acquire them. The condition Miss Tina had attached to that act no longer appeared an obstacle worth thinking of, and for an hour this morning my repentant imagination brushed it aside. It was absurd I should be able to invent nothing; absurd to renounce so easily and turn away helpless from the idea that the only way to become possessed was to unite myself to her for life. I migh n't unite myself, yet I might still have what she had. I must add that by the time I went down to ask if she would see me I had invented no alternative, though in fact I drew out my dressing in the interest of my wit. This failure was humiliating, yet what could the alternative be? Miss Tina sent back word I might come; and as I descended the stairs and crossed the sala to her door— this time she received me in her aunt's forlorn parlour—I hoped she would n't think my announcement was to be "favourable." She certainly would have understood my recoil of the day before.

As soon as I came into the room I saw that she had done so, but I also saw something which had not been in my forecast. Poor Miss Tina's sense of her failure had produced a rare alteration in her, but I had been too full of stratagems and spoils to think of that. Now I took it in; I can scarcely tell how it startled me. She stood in the middle of the room with a face of mildness bent upon me, and her look of forgiveness, of absolution, made her angelic. It beautified her; she was younger; she was not a ridiculous old woman. This trick of her expression, this magic of her spirit, transfigured her, and while I still noted it I heard a whisper somewhere in the depths of my conscience: "Why not, after all—why not?" It seemed to me I *could* pay the price. Still more distinctly however than the whisper I heard Miss Tina's own voice. I was so struck with the different effect she made on me that at first I was n't clearly aware of what she was saying; then I recognised she had bade me good-bye—she said something about hoping I should be very happy.

"Good-bye—good-bye?" I repeated with an inflexion interrogative and probably foolish.

I saw she did n't feel the interrogation, she only heard the words; she had strung herself up to accepting our separation and they fell upon her ear as a proof. "Are you going to-day?" she asked. "But it does n't matter, for whenever you go I shall not see you again. I don't want to." And she smiled strangely, with an infinite gentleness. She had never doubted my having left her the day before in horror. How *could* she, since I had n't come back before night to contradict, even as a simple form, even as an act of common humanity, such an idea? And now she had the force of soul—Miss Tina with force of soul was a new conception—to smile at me in her abjection.

"What shall you do—where shall you go?" I asked.

"Oh I don't know. I've done the great thing. I've destroyed the papers."

"Destroyed them?" I wailed.

"Yes; what was I to keep them for? I burnt them last night, one by one, in the kitchen."

"One by one?" I coldly echoed it.

"It took a long time—there were so many." The room seemed to go round me as she said this and a real darkness for a moment descended on my eyes. When it passed Miss Tina was there still, but the transfiguration was over and she had changed back to a plain dingy elderly person. It was in this character she spoke as she said "I can't stay with you longer, I can't"; and it was in this character she turned her back upon me, as I had turned mine upon her twenty-four hours before, and moved to the door of her room. Here she did what I had n't done when I quitted her—she paused long enough to give me one look. I have never forgotten it and I sometimes still suffer from it, though it was not resentful. No, there was no resentment, nothing hard or vindictive in poor Miss Tina; for when, later, I sent her, as the price of the portrait of Jeffrey Aspern, a larger sum of money than I had hoped to be able to gather for her, writing to her that I had sold the picture, she kept it with thanks; she never sent it back. I wrote her that I had sold the picture, but I admitted to Mrs. Prest at the time—I met this other friend in London that autumn—that it hangs above my writing-table. When I look at it I can scarcely bear my loss—I mean of the precious papers.

The Awakening

Kate Chopin

The writer known as Kate Chopin was born Katherine O'Flaherty on February 8, 1851, in St. Louis, Missouri. She was the daughter of Thomas O'Flaherty, an immigrant from Galway who had risen to be a prosperous merchant in that booming center of river traffic. Her mother was Eliza Faris, who had become O'Flaherty's second wife at the age of fourteen; she was a society beauty of French Creole stock, people who had originally settled St. Louis by coming upriver from New Orleans. When her witty and jovial father was killed in a freak railway accident in 1855, Katherine was raised primarily by women: her mother, who in her widowhood turned more and more to the consolations of religion, and her octogenarian great-grandmother, Victoria Charleville, who aroused Kate's interest in independent women with stories of the earliest pioneer days of St. Louis.

Kate O'Flaherty was given a conventional Catholic education at the Convent of the Sacred Heart, and if she failed to turn into a conventional society belle, like most of her classmates, the reasons may lie in the losses she suffered. In 1862 both her great-grandmother and her much-admired half-brother George, a Confederate officer, died; Kate, overpowered by grief, took refuge in books. Her omnivorous reading included not only the classics of English literature, but also Goethe, Racine, Molière, and Mme. de Staël, whom she read in their original languages. When she emerged as a debutante at the age of seventeen, she was at once a woman prepared to live in society as it was and one who looked at her society with an ironic, skeptical eye. By temperament she had become an observer, reticent about herself and her own feelings—which she confided only to her diaries—but eager to draw out the gentlemen who came calling. If she was inwardly critical of the egotistical chatter she thus brought forth, her beaux never knew it; her habit of penetrating observation was to be the mainstay of her later literary career.

Though Kate was impatient of traditional women's roles, and though she admired independent women who were able to maintain themselves by their own talents, another side of her understood that it could be her pleasure, as well as her duty, to marry, so long as it were still possible in marriage to "follow her inclination" in a state of inner freedom. When she did marry, she was lucky in her choice. Her husband was Oscar Chopin, a Louisiana Creole then working in a St. Louis bank. He and Kate met at the home of mutual friends, soon fell in love, and were married the following year, in 1870. After a glamorous

European honeymoon (which was cut short by the outbreak of the Franco-Prussian War), the Chopins moved to New Orleans, where Oscar set up business as a cotton broker. Chopin's resemblance to Léonce Pontellier, Edna's husband in *The Awakening*, is strong but entirely superficial: both were Creole cotton factors, and both had homes in New Orleans and summer places on Grand Isle. But unlike Pontellier, whose wife is merely a valued possession, Oscar Chopin (according to Kate's most recent biographer) ''understood Kate and respected her individuality.'' In addition to the brilliant social life over which Kate presided, she had time and freedom for solitary rambles exploring the sophisticated and cosmopolitan city in which she had settled.

Through most of the 1870s, Oscar Chopin's business was highly successful, but a succession of poor cotton crops in 1878 and 1879 left him with outstanding loans to planters which he could not collect, so he closed out and moved near the family plantation in Natchitoches Parish in northwestern Louisiana. There he managed some farms he owned and opened a general store in Cloutierville, a small village on the Cane River. Kate kept house, raised their six children, and entered into the life of the rural community: she rode horseback, threw parties, made her home the social center of the neighborhood, and, in a more serious vein, helped the poor with advice, medicines, and food. It is probable that, had her life in Cloutierville continued in this peaceful and useful round, Kate Chopin would have remained a consumer rather than becoming a creator of literature. But in 1883 Oscar Chopin died of swamp fever, and Kate, broken as she was by her loss, gave her life new purpose for a time by taking over his management of the plantations and the business. After a year or so of this, however, when her industry had been rewarded by enough success to give her a sufficient sense of accomplishment, she yielded to her mother's entreaties, wound up her husband's affairs, and moved with her children back to St. Louis. It was only a brief reunion for Kate: in June of 1885, less than a year after her return, her mother, too, died suddenly.

Kate Chopin's response to grief at thirty-four was similar to what it had been at eleven—to withdraw to the world of books. She was helped in this by an intellectual physician, Frederick Kolbenheyer, who directed her reading to philosophy and science, particularly Darwin, Huxley, and Spencer. He also encouraged her to write fiction in the hope that she could support herself and her children by the sale of stories to magazines. She attempted to do so, and her model was the French realist Guy de Maupassant, whose untraditional simplicity and directness of thought and expression very strongly appealed to her when she began to read him in 1888. Drawing on her observation of Southern society and modeling her technique upon Maupassant, she quickly wrote and placed several short stories in the St. Louis *Post-Dispatch* and other newspapers and magazines.

In the decade that followed her entry into the world of letters, Kate Chopin published a novel, *At Fault* (1890), and nearly one hundred short stories and sketches, many of them in prestigious national magazines like *Atlantic Monthly*, *Vogue*, and the *Saturday Evening Post*. Her principal subject matter was the Creole culture of Louisiana, particularly the Cane River folk of Natchitoches Parish. She gradually gained a reputation as a "local colorist," a member of the literary movement, then twenty years old, that concerned itself with delineating the landscapes and human types of individual regions of America, exploring the diversity of the United States in the interest of harmonizing its sectionalism. The reviews of her first collection of Louisiana tales, *Bayou Folk* (1894), were enthusiastically favorable—so much so that Kate Chopin despaired of receiving any genuinely constructive criticism. Her second collection, *A Night in Acadie* (1897), was a more modest success only because it came out through a more obscure publisher. Hers was not a Horatio Alger success story, however: her first novel, rejected by the first publisher to whom she submitted it, was brought out privately under her own imprint, and she destroyed her second attempt at a novel, *Young Dr. Gosse*, when it too met with rejection. A good many of her stories, some with explicitly sexual themes, could not be placed, even when she had opened channels to a good many periodicals; these were first published from her manuscripts long after her death. In addition to her novel and short stories, Kate Chopin published translations of Maupassant, critical essays on contemporary fiction from France and the United States, and a number of poems.

During the development of Chopin's literary career she kept herself private and aloof from literary society, disdaining all forms of self-advertisement and display. She lived modestly in St. Louis with her children, entertaining her intellectual friends and distinguished visitors to the city in her parlor on her "at home" days. In an era of movements she was not a "joiner"; the one exception was the Wednesday Club of St. Louis, a social and cultural club founded by the mother of T. S. Eliot, where she attended meetings and, on one occasion, lectured on German music. Eventually, however, the lofty idealism of this group began to grate on Chopin's unpretentious and realistic nature, and she retreated to the privacy of her own salon.

Just as only a few of Kate Chopin's reviewers recognized that her talent for the portrayal of human passion went beyond the restricted world of "local color" to the more universal concerns of the masters of fiction, so only a few of Chopin's stories look forward to the themes of liberty and sensuality that run through *The Awakening*. Louise Mallard, the heroine of "The Story of an Hour," responds to the news of her husband's death first with conventional grief, then with an exultant sense of her personal freedom: "There would be no one to live for her during those coming years; she would live for herself. There would be no powerful will bending hers in that blind persistence with which men and women believe they have a right to impose a private will upon a fellow-creature. . . . And yet she had loved him—sometimes. Often she had not. What did it matter? What could love, the unsolved mystery, count for in the face of this possession of self-assertion which she suddenly recognized as the strongest impulse of her being!" And while most of Chopin's women are traditionally chaste, Mme. Farival, in "Lilacs," has affairs, and Nathalie, in "The Kiss," fails to seduce her intended lover and has to fall back for consolation on her doltish husband and his millions.

What was revolutionary about Chopin's treatment of her heroines was neither their sexual feelings nor their sins against traditional morality. To create a "fallen" woman in order to moralize over her ungoverned passion, to deliver her over to repentance, death, and the Devil, was a commonplace literary practice. To represent such an unhappy creature as the victim of social and economic forces beyond her control was to be a feature of the naturalistic novel—like *Sister Carrie* or *Maggie*—then just coming into existence. But Chopin was neither a traditional moralist nor a naturalist: her women act as free, conscious personalities, and it is Chopin's refusal to draw wholesome ethical lessons from their behavior that marks her literary imagination as decades ahead of its time.

But to be too far ahead of one's time is dangerous for an artist as sensitive as Kate Chopin. After the favorable reception of her second collection of short stories, she conceived and wrote her most remarkable work, *The Awakening*, in six short months of concentrated effort; it was accepted by the first publisher to whom she submitted it and came out in April 1899. Its portrayal of the gradual growth of sensual awareness and the passion for freedom within Edna Pontellier, a Louisiana wife and mother, is a boldly imaginative psychological study that should have been the triumph of Chopin's career. Instead, it spelled the end of that career. While one reviewer, a personal friend of Chopin, praised *The Awakening*'s "consummate art," most of the reviews were witheringly negative. The novella was blasted as morbid, unhealthy, and vulgar. More damaging, though, were the accusations that the tale belonged in the category of "gilded dirt" and "sex fiction." As a result of suggestions that *The Awakening* should be kept out of the hands of the impressionable, the novella was quietly but firmly banned, and removed from the circulating libraries that had purchased it.

There was no loud outcry against the book, no obscenity trial of the sort that had greeted the publication of Flaubert's *Madame Bovary*. Per Seyersted, Chopin's biographer, suggests that, had *The Awakening* created a public scandal, the author's individualistic and rebellious spirit would have risen to its defense, and she would have received the support of morally courageous lovers of artistic freedom across the nation. But what Chopin had to confront was not open hostility but a silent snub, which was far harder to bear. Articles about her failed to mention *The Awakening*; her customary channels of publication dried up; she was shunned by many of her former acquaintances and refused admission to the St. Louis Fine Arts Club. And although she continued to write, her much diminished output reflects the dispirited mood with which she must have reacted to this affront to her literary reputation, while the fact that she was able to publish only three stories after *The Awakening* reflects the closing doors that greeted her arrival. Kate Chopin did not long survive the decline of her artistic career. After a tiring day at the St. Louis World's Fair, she suffered a severe stroke and died two days later, on August 22, 1904.

Like Herman Melville, another novelist ahead of his time, Kate Chopin died in near-obscurity, and her rediscovery took longer even than Melville's did. One reason for this is that her reputation during her lifetime was primarily as a local colorist, and that movement, at the time of her death, was in eclipse. On the few occasions when Chopin was discussed, in literary histories and in a 1932 biography, she was treated as a regional writer; *The Awakening*, when it was not condemned, was ignored. For all practical purposes, *The Awakening* received no attention until 1946, when a French critic, Cyrille Arnavon, noted the qualities of its realism and its affinities with Flaubert and Maupassant. And it was not until the 1950s that American literary scholars began to sense the value of *The Awakening* and to reassess its pioneering significance in the history of American fiction. At the present time, however, we are in the midst of a Kate Chopin boom, spurred by a new wave of feminism that recognizes Chopin as one of its prophets and martyrs. However long it lasts—and the boom shows no sign of receding—it will leave Kate Chopin and *The Awakening* with a secure place in the pantheon of American literature.

Biography   The first biography, Daniel Rankin's *Kate Chopin and Her Creole Stories* (Philadelphia: University of Pennsylvania Press, 1932), has been superseded by Per Seyersted's *Kate Chopin: A Critical Biography* (Baton Rouge: Louisiana State University Press, 1969).

Editions   *The Complete Works of Kate Chopin* (ed. Per Seyersted, Baton Rouge: Louisiana State University Press, 1969; 2 vols.) contains not only her novels and collected short stories but also the stories and sketches available in manuscript which were not published in Chopin's lifetime.

Bibliography   See the appropriate section of Marlene Springer, *Edith Wharton and Kate Chopin: A Reference Guide* (Boston: G. K. Hall, 1976), updated by the *Kate Chopin Newsletter* or the *PMLA* Bibliography.

Criticism of The Awakening   All books entirely on Chopin have been cited above. In addition to the chapter on *The Awakening* in the Seyersted biography, see Kenneth Eble, "A Forgotten Novel: Kate Chopin's *The Awakening*," *Western Humanities Review* 10 (1956), 261–269; John R. May, "Local Color in *The Awakening*," *Southern Review* 6 (1970), 1031–1040; Donald A. Ringe, "Romantic Imagery in Kate Chopin's *The Awakening*," *American Literature* 43 (1972), 580–588; James E. Rocks, "Kate Chopin's Ironic Vision," *Louisiana Review* 1 (1972), 110–120; Otis B. Wheeler, "The Five Awakenings of Edna Pontellier," *Southern Review* 9 (1975), 118–128; and James H. Justus, "The Unawakening of Edna Pontellier," *Southern Literary Journal* 5 (1979), 107–122.

The Awakening

∽≪I≫∽

A green and yellow parrot, which hung in a cage outside the door, kept repeating over and over:

"*Allez-vous-en! Allez-vous-en! Sapristi!*[1] That's all right!"

---

[1]Go away! Go away! Dammit!

He could speak a little Spanish, and also a language which nobody understood, unless it was the mocking-bird that hung on the other side of the door, whistling his fluty notes out upon the breeze with maddening persistence.

Mr. Pontellier, unable to read his newspaper with any degree of comfort, arose with an expression and an exclamation of disgust. He walked down the gallery and across the narrow "bridges" which connected the Lebrun cottages one with the other. He had been seated before the door of the main house. The parrot and the mocking-bird were the property of Madame Lebrun, and they had the right to make all the noise they wished. Mr. Pontellier had the privilege of quitting their society when they ceased to be entertaining.

He stopped before the door of his own cottage, which was the fourth one from the main building and next to the last. Seating himself in a wicker rocker which was there, he once more applied himself to the task of reading the newspaper. The day was Sunday; the paper was a day old. The Sunday papers had not yet reached Grand Isle.[2] He was already acquainted with the market reports, and he glanced restlessly over the editorials and bits of news which he had not had time to read before quitting New Orleans the day before.

Mr. Pontellier wore eye-glasses. He was a man of forty, of medium height and rather slender build; he stooped a little. His hair was brown and straight, parted on one side. His beard was neatly and closely trimmed.

Once in a while he withdrew his glance from the newspaper and looked about him. There was more noise than ever over at the house. The main building was called "the house," to distinguish it from the cottages. The chattering and whistling birds were still at it. Two young girls, the Farival twins, were playing a duet from "Zampa" upon the piano. Madame Lebrun was bustling in and out, giving orders in a high key to a yard-boy whenever she got inside the house, and directions in an equally high voice to a dining-room servant whenever she got outside. She was a fresh, pretty woman, clad always in white with elbow sleeves. Her starched skirts crinkled as she came and went. Farther down, before one of the cottages, a lady in black was walking demurely up and down, telling her beads. A good many persons of the *pension* had gone over to the *Chênière Caminada*[3] in Beaudelet's lugger to hear mass. Some young people were out under the water-oaks playing cro-

---

[2]An island in the Gulf of Mexico, fifty miles from New Orleans.
[3]Another island nearer the Louisiana shore.

quet. Mr. Pontellier's two children were there—sturdy little fellows of four and five. A quadroon nurse followed them about with a far-away, meditative air.

Mr. Pontellier finally lit a cigar and began to smoke, letting the paper drag idly from his hand. He fixed his gaze upon a white sunshade that was advancing at snail's pace from the beach. He could see it plainly between the gaunt trunks of the water-oaks and across the stretch of yellow camomile. The Gulf looked far away, melting hazily into the blue of the horizon. The sunshade continued to approach slowly. Beneath its pink-lined shelter were his wife, Mrs. Pontellier, and young Robert Lebrun. When they reached the cottage, the two seated themselves with some appearance of fatigue upon the upper step of the porch, facing each other, each leaning against a supporting post.

"What folly! to bathe at such an hour in such heat!" exclaimed Mr. Pontellier. He himself had taken a plunge at daylight. That was why the morning seemed long to him.

"You are burnt beyond recognition," he added, looking at his wife as one looks at a valuable piece of personal property which has suffered some damage. She held up her hands, strong, shapely hands, and surveyed them critically, drawing up her lawn sleeves above the wrists. Looking at them reminded her of her rings, which she had given to her husband before leaving for the beach. She silently reached out to him, and he, understanding, took the rings from his vest pocket and dropped them into her open palm. She slipped them upon her fingers; then clasping her knees, she looked across at Robert and began to laugh. The rings sparkled upon her fingers. He sent back an answering smile.

"What is it?" asked Pontellier, looking lazily and amused from one to the other. It was some utter nonsense; some adventure out there in the water, and they both tried to relate it at once. It did not seem half so amusing when told. They realized this, and so did Mr. Pontellier. He yawned and stretched himself. Then he got up, saying he had half a mind to go over to Klein's hotel and play a game of billiards.

"Come go along, Lebrun," he proposed to Robert. But Robert admitted quite frankly that he preferred to stay where he was and talk to Mrs. Pontellier.

"Well, send him about his business when he bores you, Edna," instructed her husband as he prepared to leave.

"Here, take the umbrella," she exclaimed, holding it out to him. He accepted the sunshade, and lifting it over his head descended the steps and walked away.

"Coming back to dinner?" his wife called after him. He halted a moment and shrugged his shoulders. He felt in his vest pocket; there was a ten-dollar bill there. He did not know; perhaps he would return for the early dinner and perhaps he would not. It all depended upon the company which he found over at Klein's and the size of "the game." He did not say this, but she understood it, and laughed, nodding good-by to him.

Both children wanted to follow their father when they saw him starting out. He kissed them and promised to bring them back bonbons and peanuts.

II

Mrs. Pontellier's eyes were quick and bright; they were a yellowish brown, about the color of her hair. She had a way of turning them swiftly upon an object and holding them there as if lost in some inward maze of contemplation or thought.

Her eyebrows were a shade darker than her hair. They were thick and almost horizontal, emphasizing the depth of her eyes. She was rather handsome than beautiful. Her face was captivating by reason of a certain frankness of expression and a contradictory subtle play of features. Her manner was engaging.

Robert rolled a cigarette. He smoked cigarettes because he could not afford cigars, he said. He had a cigar in his pocket which Mr. Pontellier had presented him with, and he was saving it for his after-dinner smoke.

This seemed quite proper and natural on his part. In coloring he was not unlike his companion. A clean-shaved face made the resemblance more pronounced than it would otherwise have been. There rested no shadow of care upon his open countenance. His eyes gathered in and reflected the light and languor of the summer day.

Mrs. Pontellier reached over for a palm-leaf fan that lay on the porch and began to fan herself, while Robert sent between his lips light puffs from his cigarette. They chatted incessantly: about the things around them; their amusing adventure out in the water—it had again assumed its entertaining aspect; about the wind, the trees, the people who had gone to the *Chênière*; about the children playing croquet under the oaks, and the Farival twins, who were now performing the overture to "The Poet and the Peasant."

Robert talked a good deal about himself. He was very young, and did not know any better. Mrs. Pontellier talked a little about herself for the same reason. Each was interested in what the other said. Robert spoke of his intention to go to Mexico in the autumn, where fortune awaited him. He was always intending to go to Mexico, but some way never got there. Meanwhile he held on to his modest position in a mercantile house in New Orleans, where an equal familiarity with English, French, and Spanish gave him no small value as a clerk and correspondent.

He was spending his summer vacation, as he always did, with his mother at Grand Isle. In former times, before Robert could remember, "the house" had been a summer luxury of the Lebruns. Now, flanked by its dozen or more cottages, which were always filled with exclusive visitors from the "*Quartier Français,*"[4] it enabled Madame Lebrun to maintain the easy and comfortable existence which appeared to be her birthright.

Mrs. Pontellier talked about her father's Mississippi plantation and her girlhood home in the old Kentucky blue-grass country. She was an American woman, with a small infusion of French which seemed to have been lost in dilution. She read a letter from her sister, who was away in the East, and who had engaged herself to be married. Robert was interested and wanted to know what manner of girls the sisters were, what the father was like, and how long the mother had been dead.

When Mrs. Pontellier folded the letter it was time for her to dress for the early dinner.

"I see Léonce isn't coming back," she said, with a glance in the direction whence her husband had disappeared. Robert supposed he was not, as there were a good many New Orleans club men over at Klein's.

When Mrs. Pontellier left him to enter her room, the young man descended the steps and strolled over toward the croquet players, where, during the half-hour before dinner, he amused himself with the little Pontellier children, who were very fond of him.

III

It was eleven o'clock that night when Mr. Pontellier returned from Klein's hotel. He was in an excellent humor, in high spirits, and very talkative. His entrance awoke his wife, who was in bed and fast asleep

---

[4]The "French Quarter" of New Orleans, where most of the Creole population lived.

when he came in. He talked to her while he undressed, telling her anecdotes and bits of news and gossip that he had gathered during the day. From his trousers pockets he took a fistful of crumpled bank notes and a good deal of silver coin, which he piled on the bureau indiscriminately with keys, knife, handkerchief, and whatever else happened to be in his pockets. She was overcome with sleep, and answered him with little half utterances.

He thought it very discouraging that his wife, who was the sole object of his existence, evinced so little interest in things which concerned him, and valued so little his conversation.

Mr. Pontellier had forgotten the bonbons and peanuts for the boys. Notwithstanding he loved them very much, and went into the adjoining room where they slept to take a look at them and make sure that they were resting comfortably. The result of his investigation was far from satisfactory. He turned and shifted the youngsters about in bed. One of them began to kick and talk about a basket full of crabs.

Mr. Pontellier returned to his wife with the information that Raoul had a high fever and needed looking after. Then he lit a cigar and went and sat near the open door to smoke it.

Mrs. Pontellier was quite sure Raoul had no fever. He had gone to bed perfectly well, she said, and nothing had ailed him all day. Mr. Pontellier was too well acquainted with fever symptoms to be mistaken. He assured her the child was consuming at that moment in the next room.

He reproached his wife with her inattention, her habitual neglect of the children. If it was not a mother's place to look after children, whose on earth was it? He himself had his hands full with his brokerage business. He could not be in two places at once; making a living for his family on the street, and staying at home to see that no harm befell them. He talked in a monotonous, insistent way.

Mrs. Pontellier sprang out of bed and went into the next room. She soon came back and sat on the edge of the bed, leaning her head down on the pillow. She said nothing, and refused to answer her husband when he questioned her. When his cigar was smoked he went to bed, and in half a minute he was fast asleep.

Mrs. Pontellier was by that time thoroughly awake. She began to cry a little, and wiped her eyes on the sleeve of her *peignoir*. Blowing out the candle, which her husband had left burning, she slipped her bare feet into a pair of satin *mules* at the foot of the bed and went out on the porch, where she sat down in the wicker chair and began to rock gently to and fro.

It was then past midnight. The cottages were all dark. A single faint light gleamed out from the hallway of the house. There was no sound abroad except the hooting of an old owl in the top of a water-oak, and the everlasting voice of the sea, that was not uplifted at that soft hour. It broke like a mournful lullaby upon the night.

The tears came so fast to Mrs. Pontellier's eyes that the damp sleeve of her *peignoir* no longer served to dry them. She was holding the back of her chair with one hand; her loose sleeve had slipped almost to the shoulder of her uplifted arm. Turning, she thrust her face, steaming and wet, into the bend of her arm, and she went on crying there, not caring any longer to dry her face, her eyes, her arms. She could not have told why she was crying. Such experiences as the foregoing were not uncommon in her married life. They seemed never before to have weighed much against the abundance of her husband's kindness and a uniform devotion which had come to be tacit and self-understood.

An indescribable oppression, which seemed to generate in some unfamiliar part of her consciousness, filled her whole being with a vague anguish. It was like a shadow, like a mist passing across her soul's summer day. It was strange and unfamiliar; it was a mood. She did not sit there inwardly upbraiding her husband, lamenting at Fate, which had directed her footsteps to the path which they had taken. She was just having a good cry all to herself. The mosquitoes made merry over her, biting her firm, round arms and nipping at her bare insteps.

The little stinging, buzzing imps succeeded in dispelling a mood which might have held her there in the darkness half a night longer.

The following morning Mr. Pontellier was up in good time to take the rockaway which was to convey him to the steamer at the wharf. He was returning to the city to his business, and they would not see him again at the Island till the coming Saturday. He had regained his composure, which seemed to have been somewhat impaired the night before. He was eager to be gone, as he looked forward to a lively week in Carondelet Street.[5]

Mr. Pontellier gave his wife half of the money which he had brought away from Klein's hotel the evening before. She liked money as well as most women, and accepted it with no little satisfaction.

"It will buy a handsome wedding present for Sister Janet!" she exclaimed, smoothing out the bills as she counted them one by one.

"Oh! we'll treat Sister Janet better than that, my dear," he laughed, as he prepared to kiss her good-by.

---

[5]The New Orleans business and financial district, where cotton brokers had their offices.

The boys were tumbling about, clinging to his legs, imploring that numerous things be brought back to them. Mr. Pontellier was a great favorite, and ladies, men, children, even nurses, were always on hand to say good-by to him. His wife stood smiling and waving, the boys shouting, as he disappeared in the old rockaway down the sandy road.

A few days later a box arrived for Mrs. Pontellier from New Orleans. It was from her husband. It was filled with *friandises*,[6] with luscious and toothsome bits—the finest of fruits, *patés*, a rare bottle or two, delicious syrups, and bonbons in abundance.

Mrs. Pontellier was always very generous with the contents of such a box; she was quite used to receiving them when away from home. The *patés* and fruit were brought to the dining-room; the bonbons were passed around. And the ladies, selecting with dainty and discriminating fingers and a little greedily, all declared that Mr. Pontellier was the best husband in the world. Mrs. Pontellier was forced to admit that she knew of none better.

IV

It would have been a difficult matter for Mr. Pontellier to define to his own satisfaction or any one else's wherein his wife failed in her duty toward their children. It was something which he felt rather than perceived, and he never voiced the feeling without subsequent regret and ample atonement.

If one of the little Pontellier boys took a tumble whilst at play, he was not apt to rush crying to his mother's arms for comfort; he would more likely pick himself up, wipe the water out of his eyes and the sand out of his mouth, and go on playing. Tots as they were, they pulled together and stood their ground in childish battles with doubled fists and uplifted voices, which usually prevailed against the other mother-tots. The quadroon nurse was looked upon as a huge encumbrance, only good to button up waists and panties and to brush and part hair; since it seemed to be a law of society that hair must be parted and brushed.

In short, Mrs. Pontellier was not a mother-woman. The mother-women seemed to prevail that summer at Grand Isle. It was easy to

---

[6]Delicacies.

know them, fluttering about with extended, protective wings when any harm, real or imaginary, threatened their precious brood. They were women who idolized their children, worshiped their husbands, and esteemed it a holy privilege to efface themselves as individuals and grow wings as ministering angels.

Many of them were delicious in the rôle; one of them was the embodiment of every womanly grace and charm. If her husband did not adore her, he was a brute, deserving of death by slow torture. Her name was Adèle Ratignolle. There are no words to describe her save the old ones that have served so often to picture the bygone heroine of romance and the fair lady of our dreams. There was nothing subtle or hidden about her charms; her beauty was all there, flaming and apparent: the spun-gold hair that comb nor confining pin could restrain; the blue eyes that were like nothing but sapphires; two lips that pouted, that were so red one could only think of cherries or some other delicious crimson fruit in looking at them. She was growing a little stout, but it did not seem to detract an iota from the grace of every step, pose, gesture. One would not have wanted her white neck a mite less full or her beautiful arms more slender. Never were hands more exquisite than hers, and it was a joy to look at them when she threaded her needle or adjusted her gold thimble to her taper middle finger as she sewed away on the little night-drawers or fashioned a bodice or a bib.

Madame Ratignolle was very fond of Mrs. Pontellier, and often she took her sewing and went over to sit with her in the afternoons. She was sitting there the afternoon of the day the box arrived from New Orleans. She had possession of the rocker, and she was busily engaged in sewing upon a diminutive pair of night-drawers.

She had brought the pattern of the drawers for Mrs. Pontellier to cut out—a marvel of construction, fashioned to enclose a baby's body so effectually that only two small eyes might look out from the garment, like an Eskimo's. They were designed for winter wear, when treacherous drafts came down chimneys and insidious currents of deadly cold found their way through key-holes.

Mrs. Pontellier's mind was quite at rest concerning the present material needs of her children, and she could not see the use of anticipating and making winter night garments the subject of her summer meditations. But she did not want to appear unamiable and uninterested, so she had brought forth newspapers, which she spread upon the floor of the gallery, and under Madame Ratignolle's directions she had cut a pattern of the impervious garment.

Robert was there, seated as he had been the Sunday before, and Mrs.

Pontellier also occupied her former position on the upper step, leaning listlessly against the post. Beside her was a box of bonbons, which she held out at intervals to Madame Ratignolle.

That lady seemed at a loss to make a selection, but finally settled upon a stick of nougat, wondering if it were not too rich; whether it could possibly hurt her. Madame Ratignolle had been married seven years. About every two years she had a baby. At that time she had three babies, and was beginning to think of a fourth one. She was always talking about her "condition." Her "condition" was in no way apparent, and no one would have known a thing about it but for her persistence in making it the subject of conversation.

Robert started to reassure her, asserting that he had known a lady who had subsisted upon nougat during the entire—but seeing the color mount into Mrs. Pontellier's face he checked himself and changed the subject.

Mrs. Pontellier, though she had married a Creole, was not thoroughly at home in the society of Creoles; never before had she been thrown so intimately among them. There were only Creoles that summer at Lebrun's. They all knew each other, and felt like one large family, among whom existed the most amicable relations. A characteristic which distinguished them and which impressed Mrs. Pontellier most forcibly was their entire absence of prudery. Their freedom of expression was at first incomprehensible to her, though she had no difficulty in reconciling it with a lofty chastity which in the Creole woman seems to be inborn and unmistakable.

Never would Edna Pontellier forget the shock with which she heard Madame Ratignolle relating to old Monsieur Farival the harrowing story of one of her *accouchements*,[7] withholding no intimate detail. She was growing accustomed to like shocks, but she could not keep the mounting color back from her cheeks. Oftener than once her coming had interrupted the droll story with which Robert was entertaining some amused group of married women.

A book had gone the rounds of the *pension*. When it came her turn to read it, she did so with profound astonishment. She felt moved to read the book in secret and solitude, though none of the others had done so—to hide it from view at the sound of approaching footsteps. It was openly criticised and freely discussed at table. Mrs. Pontellier gave over being astonished, and concluded that wonders would never cease.

---

[7]Childbirths.

V

They formed a congenial group sitting there that summer afternoon—Madame Ratignolle sewing away, often stopping to relate a story or incident with much expressive gesture of her perfect hands; Robert and Mrs. Pontellier sitting idle, exchanging occasional words, glances or smiles which indicated a certain advanced stage of intimacy and *camaraderie*.

He had lived in her shadow during the past month. No one thought anything of it. Many had predicted that Robert would devote himself to Mrs. Pontellier when he arrived. Since the age of fifteen, which was eleven years before, Robert each summer at Grand Isle had constituted himself the devoted attendant of some fair dame or damsel. Sometimes it was a young girl, again a widow; but as often as not it was some interesting married woman.

For two consecutive seasons he lived in the sunlight of Mademoiselle Duvigné's presence. But she died between summers; then Robert posed as an inconsolable, prostrating himself at the feet of Madame Ratignolle for whatever crumbs of sympathy and comfort she might be pleased to vouchsafe.

Mrs. Pontellier liked to sit and gaze at her companion as she might look upon a faultless Madonna.

"Could any one fathom the cruelty beneath that fair exterior?" murmured Robert. "She knew that I adored her once, and she let me adore her. It was 'Robert, come; go; stand up; sit down; do this; do that; see if the baby sleeps; my thimble, please, that I left God knows where. Come and read Daudet to me while I sew.' "

"*Par example!*[8] I never had to ask. You were always there under my feet, like a troublesome cat."

"You mean like an adoring dog. And just as soon as Ratignolle appeared on the scene, then it *was* like a dog. '*Passez! Adieu! Allez-vous-en!*' "[9]

"Perhaps I feared to make Alphonse jealous," she interjoined, with excessive naïveté. That made them all laugh. The right hand jealous of the left! The heart jealous of the soul! But for that matter, the Creole husband is never jealous; with him the gangrene passion is one which has become dwarfed by disuse.

---

[8]Well, now!
[9]Move on! Goodbye! Go away!

Meanwhile Robert, addressing Mrs. Pontellier, continued to tell of his one time hopeless passion for Madame Ratignolle; of sleepless nights, of consuming flames till the very sea sizzled when he took his daily plunge. While the lady at the needle kept up a little running, contemptuous comment:

"*Blagueur—farceur—gros bête, va!*"[10]

He never assumed this serio-comic tone when alone with Mrs. Pontellier. She never knew precisely what to make of it; at that moment it was impossible for her to guess how much of it was jest and what proportion was earnest. It was understood that he had often spoken words of love to Madame Ratignolle, without any thought of being taken seriously. Mrs. Pontellier was glad he had not assumed a similar rôle toward herself. It would have been unacceptable and annoying.

Mrs. Pontellier had brought her sketching materials, which she sometimes dabbled with in an unprofessional way. She liked the dabbling. She felt in it satisfaction of a kind which no other employment afforded her.

She had long wished to try herself on Madame Ratignolle. Never had that lady seemed a more tempting subject than at that moment, seated there like some sensuous Madonna, with the gleam of the fading day enriching her splendid color.

Robert crossed over and seated himself on the step below Mrs. Pontellier, that he might watch her work. She handled her brushes with a certain ease and freedom which came, not from long and close acquaintance with them, but from a natural aptitude. Robert followed her work with close attention, giving forth little ejaculatory expressions of appreciation in French, which he addressed to Madame Ratignolle.

"*Mais ce n'est pas mal! Elle s'y connait, elle a de la force, oui.*"[11]

During his oblivious attention he once quietly rested his head against Mrs. Pontellier's arm. As gently she repulsed him. Once again he repeated the offense. She could not believe it to be thoughtlessness on his part; yet that was no reason she should submit to it. She did not remonstrate, except again to repulse him quietly but firmly. He offered no apology.

The picture completed bore no resemblance to Madame Ratignolle. She was greatly disappointed to find that it did not look like her. But it was a fair enough piece of work, and in many respects satisfying.

---

[10]Chatterer—joker—fool, come off it!

[11]But that's not bad! She knows what she's doing, she has some talent, yes.

Mrs. Pontellier evidently did not think so. After surveying the sketch critically she drew a broad smudge of paint across its surface, and crumpled the paper between her hands.

The youngsters came tumbling up the steps, the quadroon following at the respectful distance which they required her to observe. Mrs. Pontellier made them carry her paints and things into the house. She sought to detain them for a little talk and some pleasantry. But they were greatly in earnest. They had only come to investigate the contents of the bonbon box. They accepted without murmuring what she chose to give them, each holding out two chubby hands scoop-like, in the vain hope that they might be filled; and then away they went.

The sun was low in the west, and the breeze soft and languorous that came up from the south, charged with the seductive odor of the sea. Children, freshly befurbelowed, were gathering for their games under the oaks. Their voices were high and penetrating.

Madame Ratignolle folded her sewing, placing thimble, scissors and thread all neatly together in the roll, which she pinned securely. She complained of faintness. Mrs. Pontellier flew for the cologne water and a fan. She bathed Madame Ratignolle's face with cologne, while Robert plied the fan with unnecessary vigor.

The spell was soon over, and Mrs. Pontellier could not help wondering if there were not a little imagination responsible for its origin, for the rose tint had never faded from her friend's face.

She stood watching the fair woman walk down the long line of galleries with the grace and majesty which queens are sometimes supposed to possess. Her little ones ran to meet her. Two of them clung about her white skirts, the third she took from its nurse and with a thousand endearments bore it along in her own fond, encircling arms. Though, as everybody well knew, the doctor had forbidden her to lift so much as a pin!

"Are you going bathing?" asked Robert of Mrs. Pontellier. It was not so much a question as a reminder.

"Oh, no," she answered, with a tone of indecision. "I'm tired; I think not." Her glance wandered from his face away toward the Gulf, whose sonorous murmur reached her like a loving but imperative entreaty.

"Oh, come!" he insisted. "You mustn't miss your bath. Come on. The water must be delicious; it will not hurt you. Come."

He reached up for her big, rough straw hat that hung on a peg outside the door, and put it on her head. They descended the steps, and walked away together toward the beach. The sun was low in the west and the breeze was soft and warm.

VI

Edna Pontellier could not have told why, wishing to go to the beach with Robert, she should in the first place have declined, and in the second place have followed in obedience to one of the two contradictory impulses which impelled her.

A certain light was beginning to dawn dimly within her—the light which, showing the way, forbids it.

At that early period it served but to bewilder her. It moved her to dreams, to thoughtfulness, to the shadowy anguish which had overcome her the midnight when she had abandoned herself to tears.

In short, Mrs. Pontellier was beginning to realize her position in the universe as a human being, and to recognize her relations as an individual to the world within and about her. This may seem like a ponderous weight of wisdom to descend upon the soul of a young woman of twenty-eight—perhaps more wisdom than the Holy Ghost is usually pleased to vouchsafe to any woman.

But the beginning of things, of a world especially, is necessarily vague, tangled, chaotic, and exceedingly disturbing. How few of us ever emerge from such beginning! How many souls perish in its tumult!

The voice of the sea is seductive; never ceasing, whispering, clamoring, murmuring, inviting the soul to wander for a spell in abysses of solitude; to lose itself in mazes of inward contemplation.

The voice of the sea speaks to the soul. The touch of the sea is sensuous, enfolding the body in its soft, close embrace.

VII

Mrs. Pontellier was not a woman given to confidences, a characteristic hitherto contrary to her nature. Even as a child she had lived her own small life all within herself. At a very early period she had apprehended instinctively the dual life—that outward existence which conforms, the inward life which questions.

That summer at Grand Isle she began to loosen a little the mantle of reserve that had always enveloped her. There may have been—there must have been—influences, both subtle and apparent, working in their several ways to induce her to do this; but the most obvious was the influence of Adèle Ratignolle. The excessive physical charm of the Creole had first attracted her, for Edna had a sensuous susceptibility to beauty. Then the candor of the woman's whole existence, which every one might read, and which formed so striking a contrast to her own habitual reserve—this might have furnished a link. Who can tell what metals the gods use in forging the subtle bond which we call sympathy, which we might as well call love.

The two women went away one morning to the beach together, arm in arm, under the huge white sunshade. Edna had prevailed upon Madame Ratignolle to leave the children behind, though she could not induce her to relinquish a diminutive roll of needlework, which Adèle begged to be allowed to slip into the depths of her pocket. In some unaccountable way they had escaped from Robert.

The walk to the beach was no inconsiderable one, consisting as it did of a long, sandy path, upon which a sporadic and tangled growth that bordered it on either side made frequent and unexpected inroads. There were acres of yellow camomile reaching out on either hand. Further away still, vegetable gardens abounded, with frequent small plantations of orange or lemon trees intervening. The dark green clusters glistened from afar in the sun.

The women were both of goodly height, Madame Ratignolle possessing the more feminine and matronly figure. The charm of Edna Pontellier's physique stole insensibly upon you. The lines of her body were long, clean and symmetrical; it was a body which occasionally fell into splendid poses; there was no suggestion of the trim, stereotyped fashion-plate about it. A casual and indiscriminating observer, in passing, might not cast a second glance upon the figure. But with more feeling and discernment he would have recognized the noble beauty of its modeling, and the graceful severity of poise and movement, which made Edna Pontellier different from the crowd.

She wore a cool muslin that morning—white, with a waving vertical line of brown running through it; also a white linen collar and the big straw hat which she had taken from the peg outside the door. The hat rested any way on her yellow-brown hair, that waved a little, was heavy, and clung close to her head.

Madame Ratignolle, more careful of her complexion, had twined a gauze veil about her head. She wore dogskin gloves, with gauntlets that protected her wrists. She was dressed in pure white, with a fluffiness of ruffles that became her. The draperies and fluttering things which she wore suited her rich, luxuriant beauty as a greater severity of line could not have done.

There were a number of bath-houses along the beach, of rough but solid construction, built with small, protecting galleries facing the water. Each house consisted of two compartments, and each family at Lebrun's possessed a compartment for itself, fitted out with all the essential paraphernalia of the bath and whatever other conveniences the owners might desire. The two women had no intention of bathing; they had just strolled down to the beach for a walk and to be alone and near the water. The Pontellier and Ratignolle compartments adjoined one another under the same roof.

Mrs. Pontellier had brought down her key through force of habit. Unlocking the door of her bath-room she went inside, and soon emerged, bringing a rug, which she spread upon the floor of the gallery, and two huge hair pillows covered with crash, which she placed against the front of the building.

The two seated themselves there in the shade of the porch, side by side, with their backs against the pillows and their feet extended. Madame Ratignolle removed her veil, wiped her face with a rather delicate handkerchief, and fanned herself with the fan which she always carried suspended somewhere about her person by a long, narrow ribbon. Edna removed her collar and opened her dress at the throat. She took the fan from Madame Ratignolle and began to fan both herself and her companion. It was very warm, and for a while they did nothing but exchange remarks about the heat, the sun, the glare. But there was a breeze blowing, a choppy, stiff wind that whipped the water into froth. It fluttered the skirts of the two women and kept them for a while engaged in adjusting, readjusting, tucking in, securing hair-pins and hat-pins. A few persons were sporting some distance away in the water. The beach was very still of human sound at that hour. The lady in black was reading her morning devotions on the porch of a neighboring bath-house. Two young lovers were exchanging their hearts' yearnings beneath the children's tent, which they had found unoccupied.

Edna Pontellier, casting her eyes about, had finally kept them at rest upon the sea. The day was clear and carried the gaze out as far as the blue sky went; there were a few white clouds suspended idly over the horizon. A lateen sail was visible in the direction of Cat Island, and others to the south seemed almost motionless in the far distance.

"Of whom—of what are you thinking?" asked Adèle of her companion, whose countenance she had been watching with a little amused attention, arrested by the absorbed expression which seemed to have seized and fixed every feature into a statuesque repose.

"Nothing," replied Mrs. Pontellier, with a start, adding at once: "How stupid! But it seems to me it is the reply we make instinctively to such a question. Let me see," she went on, throwing back her head and narrowing her fine eyes till they shone like two vivid points of light. "Let me see. I was really not conscious of thinking of anything; but perhaps I can retrace my thoughts."

"Oh! never mind!" laughed Madame Ratignolle. "I am not quite so exacting. I will let you off this time. It is really too hot to think, especially to think about thinking."

"But for the fun of it," persisted Edna. "First of all, the sight of the water stretching so far away, those motionless sails against the blue sky, made a delicious picture that I just wanted to sit and look at. The hot wind beating in my face made me think—without any connection that I can trace—of a summer day in Kentucky, of a meadow that seemed as big as the ocean to the very little girl walking through the grass, which was higher than her waist. She threw out her arms as if swimming when she walked, beating the tall grass as one strikes out in the water. Oh, I see the connection now!"

"Where were you going that day in Kentucky, walking through the grass?"

"I don't remember now. I was just walking diagonally across a big field. My sun-bonnet obstructed the view. I could see only the stretch of green before me, and I felt as if I must walk on forever, without coming to the end of it. I don't remember whether I was frightened or pleased. I must have been entertained."

"Likely as not it was Sunday," she laughed; "and I was running away from prayers, from the Presbyterian service, read in a spirit of gloom by my father that chills me yet to think of."

"And have you been running away from prayers ever since, ma chère?" asked Madame Ratignolle, amused.

"No! oh, no!" Edna hastened to say. "I was a little unthinking child in those days, just following a misleading impulse without question. On the contrary, during one period of my life religion took a firm hold upon me; after I was twelve and until—until—why, I suppose until now, though I never thought much about it—just driven along by habit. But do you know," she broke off, turning her quick eyes upon Madame Ratignolle and leaning forward a little so as to bring her face quite close to that of her companion, "sometimes I feel this summer as if I were walking through the green meadow again; idly, aimlessly, unthinking and unguided."

Madame Ratignolle laid her hand over that of Mrs. Pontellier, which was near her. Seeing that the hand was not withdrawn, she clasped it firmly and warmly. She even stroked it a little, fondly, with the other hand, murmuring in an undertone, "Pauvre chérie."

The action was at first a little confusing to Edna, but she soon lent herself readily to the Creole's gentle caress. She was not accustomed to an outward and spoken expression of affection, either in herself or in others. She and her younger sister, Janet, had quarreled a good deal through force of unfortunate habit. Her older sister, Margaret, was matronly and dignified, probably from having assumed matronly and housewifely responsibilities too early in life, their mother having died when they were quite young. Margaret was not effusive; she was practical. Edna had had an occasional girl friend, but whether accidentally or not, they seemed to have been all of one type—the self-contained. She never realized that the reserve of her own character had much, perhaps everything, to do with this. Her most intimate friend at school had been one of rather exceptional intellectual gifts, who wrote fine-sounding essays, which Edna admired and strove to imitate; and with her she talked and glowed over the English classics, and sometimes held religious and political controversies.

Edna often wondered at one propensity which sometimes had inwardly disturbed her without causing any outward show or manifestation on her part. At a very early age—perhaps it was when she traversed the ocean of waving grass—she remembered that she had been passionately enamored of a dignified and sad-eyed cavalry officer who visited her father in Kentucky. She could not leave his presence when he was there, nor remove her eyes from his face, which was something like Napoleon's, with a lock of black hair falling across the forehead. But the cavalry officer melted imperceptibly out of her existence.

At another time her affections were deeply engaged by a young gentleman who visited a lady on a neighboring plantation. It was after they went to Mississippi to live. The young man was engaged to be married to the young lady, and they sometimes called upon Margaret, driving over of afternoons in a buggy. Edna was a little miss, just merging into her teens; and the realization that she herself was nothing, nothing, nothing to the engaged young man was a bitter affliction to her. But he, too, went the way of dreams.

She was a grown young woman when she was overtaken by what she supposed to be the climax of her fate. It was when the face and figure of a great tragedian began to haunt her imagination and stir her senses. The persistence of the infatuation lent it an aspect of genuineness. The hopelessness of it colored it with the lofty tones of a great passion.

The picture of the tragedian stood enframed upon her desk. Any one may possess the portrait of a tragedian without exciting suspicion or comment. (This was a sinister reflection which she cherished.) In the presence of others she expressed admiration for his exalted gifts, as she handed the photograph around and dwelt upon the fidelity of the likeness. When alone she sometimes picked it up and kissed the cold glass passionately.

Her marriage to Léonce Pontellier was purely an accident, in this respect resembling many other marriages which masquerade as the decrees of Fate. It was in the midst of her secret great passion that she met him. He fell in love, as men are in the habit of doing, and pressed his suit with an earnestness and an ardor which left nothing to be desired. He pleased her; his absolute devotion flattered her. She fancied there was a sympathy of thought and taste between them, in which fancy she was mistaken. Add to this the violent opposition of her father and her sister Margaret to her marriage with a Catholic, and we need seek no further for the motives which led her to accept Monsieur Pontellier for her husband.

The acme of bliss, which would have been a marriage with the tragedian, was not for her in this world. As the devoted wife of a man who worshiped her, she felt she would take her place with a certain dignity in the world of reality, closing the portals forever upon the realm of romance and dreams.

But it was not long before the tragedian had gone to join the cavalry officer and the engaged young man and a few others; and Edna found herself face to face with the realities. She grew fond of her husband, realizing with some unaccountable satisfaction that no trace of passion or excessive and fictitious warmth colored her affection, thereby threatening its dissolution.

She was fond of her children in an uneven, impulsive way. She would sometimes gather them passionately to her heart; she would sometimes forget them. The year before they had spent part of the summer with their grandmother Pontellier in Iberville. Feeling secure regarding their happiness and welfare, she did not miss them except with an occasional intense longing. Their absence was a sort of relief, though she did not admit this, even to herself. It seemed to free her of a responsibility which she had blindly assumed and for which Fate had not fitted her.

Edna did not reveal so much as all this to Madame Ratignolle that summer day when they sat with faces turned to the sea. But a good part of it escaped her. She had put her head down on Madame Ratignolle's shoulder. She was flushed and felt intoxicated with the sound of her own voice and the unaccustomed taste of candor. It muddled her like wine, or like a first breath of freedom.

There was the sound of approaching voices. It was Robert, surrounded by a troop of children, searching for them. The two little Pontelliers were with him, and he carried Madame Ratignolle's little girl in his arms. There were other children beside, and two nurse-maids followed, looking disagreeable and resigned.

The women at once rose and began to shake out their draperies and relax their muscles. Mrs. Pontellier threw the cushions and rug into the bath-house. The children all scampered off to the awning, and they stood there in a line, gazing upon the intruding lovers, still exchanging their vows and sighs. The lovers got up, with only a silent protest, and walked slowly away somewhere else.

The children possessed themselves of the tent, and Mrs. Pontellier went over to join them.

Madame Ratignolle begged Robert to accompany her to the house; she complained of cramp in her limbs and stiffness of the joints. She leaned draggingly upon his arm as they walked.

VIII

"Do me a favor, Robert," spoke the pretty woman at his side, almost as soon as she and Robert had started on their slow, homeward way. She looked up in his face, leaning on his arm beneath the encircling shadow of the umbrella which he had lifted.

"Granted; as many as you like," he returned, glancing down into her eyes that were full of thoughtfulness and some speculation.

"I only ask for one; let Mrs. Pontellier alone."

"*Tiens!*" he exclaimed, with a sudden, boyish laugh. "*Voilà que Madame Ratignolle est jalouse!*"[12]

"Nonsense! I'm in earnest; I mean what I say. Let Mrs. Pontellier alone."

"Why?" he asked; himself growing serious at his companion's solicitation.

"She is not one of us; she is not like us. She might make the unfortunate blunder of taking you seriously."

His face flushed with annoyance, and taking off his soft hat he began

---

[12]Well! So Madame Ratignolle is jealous!

to beat it impatiently against his leg as he walked. "Why shouldn't she take me seriously?" he demanded sharply. "Am I a comedian, a clown, a jack-in-the-box? Why shouldn't she? You Creoles! I have no patience with you! Am I always to be regarded as a feature of an amusing programme? I hope Mrs. Pontellier does take me seriously. I hope she has discernment enough to find in me something besides the *blagueur*. If I thought there was any doubt—"

"Oh, enough, Robert!" she broke into his heated outburst. "You are not thinking of what you are saying. You speak with about as little reflection as we might expect from one of those children down there playing in the sand. If your attentions to any married women here were ever offered with any intention of being convincing, you would not be the gentleman we all know you to be, and you would be unfit to associate with the wives and daughters of the people who trust you."

Madame Ratignolle had spoken what she believed to be the law and the gospel. The young man shrugged his shoulders impatiently.

"Oh! well! That isn't it," slamming his hat down vehemently upon his head. "You ought to feel that such things are not flattering to say to a fellow."

"Should our whole intercourse consist of an exchange of compliments? *Ma foi!*"[13]

"It isn't pleasant to have a woman tell you—" he went on, unheedingly, but breaking off suddenly: "Now if I were like Arobin—you remember Alcée Arobin and that story of the consul's wife at Biloxi?" And he related the story of Alcée Arobin and the consul's wife; and another about the tenor of the French Opera, who received letters which should never have been written; and still other stories, grave and gay, till Mrs. Pontellier and her possible propensity for taking young men seriously was apparently forgotten.

Madame Ratignolle, when they had regained her cottage, went in to take the hour's rest which she considered helpful. Before leaving her, Robert begged her pardon for the impatience—he called it rudeness— with which he had received her well-meant caution.

"You made one mistake, Adèle," he said, with a light smile; "there is no earthly possibility of Mrs. Pontellier ever taking me seriously. You should have warned me against taking myself seriously. Your advice might then have carried some weight and given me subject for some

---

[13]My goodness!

reflection. *Au revoir.* But you look tired," he added, solicitously. "Would you like a cup of bouillon? Shall I stir you a toddy? Let me mix you a toddy with a drop of Angostura."[14]

She acceded to the suggestion of bouillon, which was grateful and acceptable. He went himself to the kitchen, which was a building apart from the cottages and lying to the rear of the house. And he himself brought her the golden-brown bouillon, in a dainty Sèvres cup, with a flaky cracker or two on the saucer.

She thrust a bare, white arm from the curtain which shielded her open door, and received the cup from his hands. She told him he was a *bon garçon,*[15] and she meant it. Robert thanked her and turned away toward "the house."

The lovers were just entering the grounds of the *pension.* They were leaning toward each other as the water-oaks bent from the sea. There was not a particle of earth beneath their feet. Their heads might have been turned upside-down, so absolutely did they tread upon blue ether. The lady in black, creeping behind them, looked a trifle paler and more jaded than usual. There was no sign of Mrs. Pontellier and the children. Robert scanned the distance for any such apparition. They would doubtless remain away until the dinner hour. The young man ascended to his mother's room. It was situated at the top of the house, made up of odd angles and a queer, sloping ceiling. Two broad dormer windows looked out toward the Gulf, and as far across it as a man's eye might reach. The furnishings of the room were light, cool, and practical.

Madame Lebrun was busily engaged at the sewing-machine. A little black girl sat on the floor, and with her hands worked the treadle of the machine. The Creole woman does not take any chances which may be avoided of imperiling her health.

Robert went over and seated himself on the broad sill of one of the dormer windows. He took a book from his pocket and began energetically to read it, judging by the precision and frequency with which he turned the leaves. The sewing-machine made a resounding clatter in the room; it was of a ponderous, by-gone make. In the lulls, Robert and his mother exchanged bits of desultory conversation.

"Where is Mrs. Pontellier?"

---

[14]Aromatic bitters.
[15]"Nice boy" or "good waiter"—Adèle is making a play on words.

"Down at the beach with the children."

"I promised to lend her the Goncourt.[16] Don't forget to take it down when you go; it's there on the bookshelf over the small table." Clatter, clatter, clatter, bang! for the next five or eight minutes.

"Where is Victor going with the rockaway?"

"The rockaway? Victor?"

"Yes; down there in front. He seems to be getting ready to drive away somewhere."

"Call him." Clatter, clatter!

Robert uttered a shrill, piercing whistle which might have been heard back at the wharf.

"He won't look up."

Madame Lebrun flew to the window. She called, "Victor!" She waved a handkerchief and called again. The young fellow got into the vehicle and started the horse off at a gallop.

Madame Lebrun went back to the machine, crimson with annoyance. Victor was the younger son and brother— a *tête montée*,[17] with a temper which invited violence and a will which no ax could break.

"Whenever you say the word I'm ready to thrash any amount of reason into him that he's able to hold."

"If your father had only lived!" Clatter, clatter, clatter, clatter, bang! It was a fixed belief with Madame Lebrun that the conduct of the universe and all things pertaining thereto would have been manifestly of a more intelligent and higher order had not Monsieur Lebrun been removed to other spheres during the early years of their married life.

"What do you hear from Montel?" Montel was a middle-aged gentleman whose vain ambition and desire for the past twenty years had been to fill the void which Monsieur Lebrun's taking off had left in the Lebrun household. Clatter, clatter, bang, clatter!

"I have a letter somewhere," looking in the machine drawer and finding the letter in the bottom of the work-basket. "He says to tell you he will be in Vera Cruz the beginning of next month"—clatter, clatter!—"and if you still have the intention of joining him"—bang! clatter, clatter, bang!

"Why didn't you tell me so before, mother? You know I wanted—" Clatter, clatter, clatter!

---

[16]A novel, probably, by Edmond and/or Jules Goncourt, French realists of the mid-nineteenth century.

[17]An excitable fellow.

"Do you see Mrs. Pontellier starting back with the children? She will be in late to luncheon again. She never starts to get ready for luncheon till the last minute." Clatter, clatter! "Where are you going?"

"Where did you say the Goncourt was?"

IX

Every light in the hall was ablaze; every lamp turned as high as it could be without smoking the chimney or threatening explosion. The lamps were fixed at intervals against the wall, encircling the whole room. Some one had gathered orange and lemon branches, and with these fashioned graceful festoons between. The dark green of the branches stood out and glistened against the white muslin curtains which draped the windows, and which puffed, floated, and flapped at the capricious will of a stiff breeze that swept up from the Gulf.

It was a Saturday night a few weeks after the intimate conversation held between Robert and Madame Ratignolle on their way from the beach. An unusual number of husbands, fathers, and friends had come down to stay over Sunday; and they were being suitably entertained by their families, with the material help of Madame Lebrun. The dining tables had all been removed to one end of the hall, and the chairs ranged about in rows and in clusters. Each little family group had had its say and exchanged its domestic gossip earlier in the evening. There was now an apparent disposition to relax; to widen the circle of confidences and give a more general tone to the conversation.

Many of the children had been permitted to sit up beyond their usual bedtime. A small band of them were lying on their stomachs on the floor looking at the colored sheets of the comic papers which Mr. Pontellier had brought down. The little Pontellier boys were permitting them to do so, and making their authority felt.

Music, dancing, and a recitation or two were the entertainments furnished, or rather, offered. But there was nothing systematic about the programme, no appearance of prearrangement nor even premeditation.

At an early hour in the evening the Farival twins were prevailed upon to play the piano. They were girls of fourteen, always clad in the Virgin's colors, blue and white, having been dedicated to the Blessed Virgin at their baptism. They played a duet from "Zampa," and at the earnest solicitation of every one present followed it with the overture to "The Poet and the Peasant."

"*Allez-vous-en! Sapristi!*" shrieked the parrot outside the door. He was the only being present who possessed sufficient candor to admit that he was not listening to these gracious performances for the first time that summer. Old Monsieur Farival, grandfather of the twins, grew indignant over the interruption, and insisted upon having the bird removed and consigned to regions of darkness. Victor Lebrun objected; and his decrees were as immutable as those of Fate. The parrot fortunately offered no further interruption to the entertainment, the whole venom of his nature apparently having been cherished up and hurled against the twins in that one impetuous outburst.

Later a young brother and sister gave recitations, which every one present had heard many times at winter evening entertainments in the city.

A little girl performed a skirt dance in the center of the floor. The mother played her accompaniments and at the same time watched her daughter with greedy admiration and nervous apprehension. She need have had no apprehension. The child was mistress of the situation. She had been properly dressed for the occasion in black tulle and black silk tights. Her little neck and arms were bare, and her hair, artificially crimped, stood out like fluffy black plumes over her head. Her poses were full of grace, and her little black-shod toes twinkled as they shot out and upward with a rapidity and suddenness which were bewildering.

But there was no reason why every one should not dance. Madame Ratignolle could not, so it was she who gaily consented to play for the others. She played very well, keeping excellent waltz time and infusing an expression into the strains which was indeed inspiring. She was keeping up her music on account of the children, she said; because she and her husband both considered it a means of brightening the home and making it attractive.

Almost every one danced but the twins, who could not be induced to separate during the brief period when one or the other should be whirling around the room in the arms of a man. They might have danced together, but they did not think of it.

The children were sent to bed. Some went submissively; others with shrieks and protests as they were dragged away. They had been permitted to sit up till after the ice-cream, which naturally marked the limit of human indulgence.

The ice-cream was passed around with cake—gold and silver cake arranged on platters in alternate slices; it had been made and frozen during the afternoon back of the kitchen by two black women, under the supervision of Victor. It was pronounced a great success—excellent if it had only contained a little less vanilla or a little more sugar, if it had been frozen a degree harder, and if the salt might have been kept out of portions of it. Victor was proud of his achievement, and went about recommending it and urging every one to partake of it to excess.

After Mrs. Pontellier had danced twice with her husband, once with Robert, and once with Monsieur Ratignolle, who was thin and tall and swayed like a reed in the wind when he danced, she went out on the gallery and seated herself on the low window-sill, where she commanded a view of all that went on in the hall and could look out toward the Gulf. There was a soft effulgence in the east. The moon was coming up, and its mystic shimmer was casting a million lights across the distant, restless water.

"Would you like to hear Mademoiselle Reisz play?" asked Robert, coming out on the porch where she was. Of course Edna would like to hear Mademoiselle Reisz play; but she feared it would be useless to entreat her.

"I'll ask her," he said. "I'll tell her that you want to hear her. She likes you. She will come." He turned and hurried away to one of the far cottages, where Mademoiselle Reisz was shuffling away. She was dragging a chair in and out of her room, and at intervals objecting to the crying of a baby, which a nurse in the adjoining cottage was endeavoring to put to sleep. She was a disagreeable little woman, no longer young, who had quarreled with almost every one, owing to a temper which was self-assertive and a disposition to trample upon the rights of others. Robert prevailed upon her without any too great difficulty.

She entered the hall with him during a lull in the dance. She made an awkward, imperious little bow as she went in. She was a homely woman, with a small weazened face and body and eyes that glowed. She had absolutely no taste in dress, and wore a batch of rusty black lace with a bunch of artificial violets pinned to the side of her hair.

"Ask Mrs. Pontellier what she would like to hear me play," she requested of Robert. She sat perfectly still before the piano, not touching the keys, while Robert carried her message to Edna at the window. A general air of surprise and genuine satisfaction fell upon every one as they saw the pianist enter. There was a settling down, and a prevailing air of expectancy everywhere. Edna was a trifle embarrassed at being thus signaled out for the imperious little woman's favor. She would not dare to choose, and begged that Mademoiselle Reisz would please herself in her selections.

Edna was what she herself called very fond of music. Musical strains, well rendered, had a way of evoking pictures in her mind. She sometimes liked to sit in the room of mornings when Madame Ratignolle played or pacticed. One piece which that lady played Edna had entitled "Solitude." It was a short, plaintive, minor strain. The name of the piece was something else, but she called it "Solitude." When she heard it there came before her imagination the figure of a man standing beside a desolate rock on the seashore. He was naked. His attitude was one of hopeless resignation as he looked toward a distant bird winging its flight away from him.

Another piece called to her mind a dainty young woman clad in an Empire gown, taking mincing dancing steps as she came down a long avenue between tall hedges. Again, another reminded her of children at play, and still another of nothing on earth but a demure lady stroking a cat.

The very first chords which Mademoiselle Reisz struck upon the piano sent a keen tremor down Mrs. Pontellier's spinal column. It was not the first time she had heard an artist at the piano. Perhaps it was the first time she was ready, perhaps the first time her being was tempered to take an impress of the abiding truth.

She waited for the material pictures which she thought would gather and blaze before her imagination. She waited in vain. She saw no pictures of solitude, of hope, of longing, or of despair. But the very passions themselves were aroused within her soul, swaying it, lashing it, as the waves daily beat upon her splendid body. She trembled, she was choking, and the tears blinded her.

Mademoiselle was finished. She arose, and bowing her stiff, lofty bow, she went away, stopping for neither thanks nor applause. As she passed along the gallery she patted Edna upon the shoulder.

"Well, how did you like my music?" she asked. The young woman was unable to answer; she pressed the hand of the pianist convulsively. Mademoiselle Reisz perceived her agitation and even her tears. She patted her again upon the shoulder as she said:

"You are the only one worth playing for. Those others? Bah!" and she went shuffling and sidling on down the gallery toward her room.

But she was mistaken about "those others." Her playing had aroused a fever of enthusiasm. "What passion!" "What an artist!" "I have always said no one could play Chopin like Mademoiselle Reisz!" "That last prelude! *Bon Dieu*! It shakes a man!"

It was growing late, and there was a general disposition to disband. But some one, perhaps it was Robert, thought of a bath at that mystic hour and under that mystic moon.

X

At all events Robert proposed it, and there was not a dissenting voice. There was not one but was ready to follow when he led the way. He did not lead the way, however, he directed the way; and he himself loitered behind with the lovers, who had betrayed a disposition to linger and hold themselves apart. He walked between them, whether with malicious or mischievous intent was not wholly clear, even to himself.

The Pontelliers and Ratignolles walked ahead; the women leaning upon the arms of their husbands. Edna could hear Robert's voice behind them, and could sometimes hear what he said. She wondered why he did not join them. It was unlike him not to. Of late he had sometimes held away from her for an entire day, redoubling his devotion upon the next and the next, as though to make up for hours that had been lost. She missed him the days when some pretext served to take him away from her, just as one misses the sun on a cloudy day without having thought much about the sun when it was shining.

The people walked in little groups toward the beach. They talked and laughed; some of them sang. There was a band playing down at Klein's hotel, and the strains reached them faintly, tempered by the distance. There were strange, rare odors abroad—a tangle of the sea smell and of weeds and damp, new-plowed earth, mingled with the heavy perfume of a field of white blossoms somewhere near. But the night sat lightly upon the sea and the land. There was no weight of darkness; there were no shadows. The white light of the moon had fallen upon the world like the mystery and the softness of sleep.

Most of them walked into the water as though into a native element. The sea was quiet now, and swelled lazily in broad billows that melted into one another and did not break except upon the beach in little foamy crests that coiled back like slow, white serpents.

Edna had attempted all summer to learn how to swim. She had received instructions from both the men and women; in some instances from the children. Robert had pursued a system of lessons almost daily; and he was nearly at the point of discouragement in realizing the futility of his efforts. A certain ungovernable dread hung about her when in the water, unless there was a hand nearby that might reach out and reassure her.

But that night she was like the little tottering, stumbling, clutching child, who of a sudden realizes its powers, and walks for the first time alone, boldly and with over-confidence. She could have shouted for joy. She did shout for joy, as with a sweeping stroke or two she lifted her body to the surface of the water.

A feeling of exultation overtook her, as if some power of significant import had been given her to control the working of her body and her soul. She grew daring and reckless, overestimating her strength. She wanted to swim far out, where no woman had ever swum before.

Her unlooked-for achievement was the subject of wonder, applause, and admiration. Each one congratulated himself that his special teachings had accomplished this desired end.

"How easy it is!" she thought. "It is nothing," she said aloud; "why did I not discover before that it was nothing. Think of the time I have lost splashing about like a baby!" She would not join the groups in their sports and bouts, but intoxicated with her newly conquered power, she swam out alone.

She turned her face seaward to gather in an impression of space and solitude, which the vast expanse of water, meeting and melting with the moonlit sky, conveyed to her excited fancy. As she swam she seemed to be reaching out for the unlimited in which to lose herself.

Once she turned and looked out toward the shore, toward the people she had left there. She had not gone any great distance—that is, what would have been a great distance for an experienced swimmer. But to her unaccustomed vision the stretch of water behind her assumed the aspect of a barrier which her unaided strength would never be able to overcome.

A quick vision of death smote her soul, and for a second of time appalled and enfeebled her senses. But by an effort she rallied her staggering faculties and managed to regain the land.

She made no mention of her encounter with death and her flash of terror, except to say to her husband, "I thought I should have perished out there alone."

"You were not so very far, my dear; I was watching you," he told her.

Edna went at once to the bath-house, and she had put on her dry clothes and was ready to return home before the others had left the water. She started to walk away alone. They all called to her and shouted to her. She waved a dissenting hand, and went on, paying no further heed to their renewed cries which sought to detain her.

"Sometimes I am tempted to think that Mrs. Pontellier is capricious," said Madame Lebrun, who was amusing herself immensely and feared that Edna's abrupt departure might put an end to the pleasure.

"I know she is," assented Mr. Pontellier; "sometimes, not often."

Edna had not traversed a quarter of the distance on her way home before she was overtaken by Robert.

"Did you think I was afraid?" she asked him, without a shade of annoyance.

"No; I knew you weren't afraid."

"Then why did you come? Why didn't you stay out there with the others?"

"I never thought of it."

"Thought of what?"

"Of anything. What difference does it make?"

"I'm very tired," she uttered, complainingly.

"I know you are."

"You don't know anything about it. Why should you know? I never was so exhausted in my life. But it isn't unpleasant. A thousand emotions have swept through me to-night. I don't comprehend half of them. Don't mind what I'm saying; I am just thinking aloud. I wonder if I shall ever be stirred again as Mademoiselle Reisz's playing moved me to-night. I wonder if any night on earth will ever again be like this one. It is like a night in a dream. The people about me are like some uncanny, half-human beings. There must be spirits abroad to-night."

"There are," whispered Robert. "Didn't you know this was the twenty-eighth of August?"

"The twenty-eighth of August?"

"Yes. On the twenty-eighth of August, at the hour of midnight, and if the moon is shining—the moon must be shining—a spirit that has haunted these shores for ages rises up from the Gulf. With its own penetrating vision this spirit seeks some one mortal worthy to hold him company, worthy of being exalted for a few hours into realms of the semi-celestials. His search has always hitherto been fruitless, and he has sunk back, disheartened, into the sea. But to-night he found Mrs. Pontellier. Perhaps he will never wholly release her from the spell. Perhaps she will never again suffer a poor, unworthy earthling to walk in the shadow of her divine presence."

"Don't banter me," she said, wounded at what appeared to be his flippancy. He did not mind the entreaty, but the tone with its delicate note of pathos was like a reproach. He could not explain; he could not tell her that he had penetrated her soul and understood. He said nothing except to offer her his arm, for, by her own admission, she was exhausted. She had been walking alone with her arms hanging limp, letting her white skirts trail along the dewy path. She took his arm, but she did not lean upon it. She let her hand lie listlessly, as though her thoughts were elsewhere—somewhere in advance of her body, and she was striving to overtake them.

Robert assisted her into the hammock which swung from the post before her door out to the trunk of a tree.

"Will you stay here and wait for Mr. Pontellier?" he asked.

"I'll stay out here. Good-night."

"Shall I get you a pillow?"

"There's one here," she said, feeling about, for they were in the shadow.

"It must be soiled; the children have been tumbling it about."

"No matter." And having discovered the pillow, she adjusted it beneath her head. She extended herself in the hammock with a deep breath of relief. She was not a supercilious or an over-dainty woman. She was not much given to reclining in the hammock, and when she did so it was with no cat-like suggestion of voluptuous ease, but with a beneficent repose which seemed to invade her whole body.

"Shall I stay with you until Mr. Pontellier comes?" asked Robert, seating himself on the outer edge of one of the steps and taking hold of the hammock rope which was fastened to the post.

"If you wish. Don't swing the hammock. Will you get my white shawl which I left on the window-sill over at the house?"

"Are you chilly?"

"No; but I shall be presently."

"Presently?" he laughed. "Do you know what time it is? How long are you going to stay out here?"

"I don't know. Will you get the shawl?"

"Of course I will," he said, rising. He went over to the house, walking along the grass. She watched his figure pass in and out of the strips of moonlight. It was past midnight. It was very quiet.

When he returned with the shawl she took it and kept it in her hand. She did not put it around her.

"Did you say I should stay till Mr. Pontellier came back?"

"I said you might if you wished to."

He seated himself again and rolled a cigarette, which he smoked in silence. Neither did Mrs. Pontellier speak. No multitude of words could have been more significant than those moments of silence, or more pregnant with the first-felt throbbings of desire.

When the voices of the bathers were heard approaching, Robert said good-night. She did not answer him. He thought she was asleep. Again she watched his figure pass in and out of the strips of moonlight as he walked away.

XI

"What are you doing out here, Edna? I thought I should find you in bed," said her husband, when he discovered her lying there. He had walked up with Madame Lebrun and left her at the house. His wife did not reply.

"Are you asleep?" he asked, bending down close to look at her.

"No." Her eyes burned bright and intense, with no sleepy shadows, as they looked into his.

"Do you know it is past one o'clock? Come on," and he mounted the steps and went into their room.

"Edna!" called Mr. Pontellier from within, after a few moments had gone by.

"Don't wait for me," she answered. He thrust his head through the door.

"You will take cold out there," he said, irritably. "What folly is this? Why don't you come in?"

"It isn't cold; I have my shawl."

"The mosquitoes will devour you."

"There are no mosquitoes."

She heard him moving about the room, every sound indicating impatience and irritation. Another time she would have gone in at his request. She would, through habit, have yielded to his desire; not with any sense of submission or obedience to his compelling wishes, but unthinkingly, as we walk, move, sit, stand, go through the daily treadmill of the life which has been portioned out to us.

"Edna, dear, are you not coming in soon?" he asked again, this time fondly, with a note of entreaty.

"No; I am going to stay out here."

"This is more than folly," he blurted out. "I can't permit you to stay out there all night. You must come in the house instantly."

With a writhing motion she settled herself more securely in the hammock. She perceived that her will had blazed up, stubborn and resistant. She could not at that moment have done other than denied and resisted. She wondered if her husband had ever spoken to her like that before, and if she had submitted to his command. Of course she had; she remembered that she had. But she could not realize why or how she should have yielded, feeling as she then did.

"Léonce, go to bed," she said. "I mean to stay out here. I don't wish to go in, and I don't intend to. Don't speak to me like that again; I shall not answer you."

Mr. Pontellier had prepared for bed, but he slipped on an extra garment. He opened a bottle of wine, of which he kept a small and select supply in a buffet of his own. He drank a glass of the wine and went out on the gallery and offered a glass to his wife. She did not wish any. He drew up the rocker, hoisted his slippered feet on the rail, and proceeded to smoke a cigar. He smoked two cigars; then he went inside and drank another glass of wine. Mrs. Pontellier again declined to accept a glass when it was offered to her. Mr. Pontellier once more seated himself with elevated feet, and after a reasonable interval of time smoked some more cigars.

Edna began to feel like one who awakens gradually out of a dream, a delicious, grotesque, impossible dream, to feel again the realities pressing into her soul. The physical need for sleep began to overtake her; the exuberance which had sustained and exalted her spirit left her helpless and yielding to the conditions which crowded her in.

The stillest hour of the night had come, the hour before dawn, when the world seems to hold its breath. The moon hung low, and had turned from silver to copper in the sleeping sky. The old owl no longer hooted, and the water-oaks had ceased to moan as they bent their heads.

Edna arose, cramped from lying so long and still in the hammock. She tottered up the steps, clutching feebly at the post before passing into the house.

"Are you coming in, Léonce?" she asked, turning her face toward her husband.

"Yes, dear," he answered, with a glance following a misty puff of smoke. "Just as soon as I have finished my cigar."

XII

She slept but a few hours. They were troubled and feverish hours, disturbed with dreams that were intangible, that eluded her, leaving only an impression upon her half-awakened senses of something unattainable. She was up and dressed in the cool of the early morning. The air was invigorating and steadied somewhat her faculties. However, she was not seeking refreshment or help from any other source, either external or from within. She was blindly following whatever impulse moved her, as if she had placed herself in alien hands for direction, and freed her soul of responsibility.

Most of the people at that early hour were still in bed and asleep. A few, who intended to go over to the *Chênière* for mass, were moving about. The lovers, who had laid their plans the night before, were already strolling toward the wharf. The lady in black, with her Sunday prayer-book, velvet and gold-clasped, and her Sunday silver beads, was following them at no great distance. Old Monsieur Farival was up, and was more than half inclined to do anything that suggested itself. He put on his big straw hat, and taking his umbrella from the stand in the hall, followed the lady in black, never overtaking her.

The little negro girl who worked Madame Lebrun's sewing-machine was sweeping up the galleries with long, absent-minded strokes of the broom. Edna sent her up into the house to awaken Robert.

"Tell him I am going to the *Chênière*. The boat is ready; tell him to hurry."

He had soon joined her. She had never sent for him before. She had never asked for him. She had never seemed to want him before. She did not appear conscious that she had done anything unusual in commanding his presence. He was apparently equally unconscious of anything extraordinary in the situation. But his face was suffused with a quiet glow when he met her.

They went together back to the kitchen to drink coffee. There was no time for any nicety of service. They stood outside the window and the cook passed them their coffee and a roll, which they drank and ate from the window-sill. Edna said it tasted good. She had not thought of coffee nor of anything. He told her he had often noticed that she lacked forethought.

"Wasn't it enough to think of going to the *Chênière* and waking you up?" she laughed. "Do I have to think of everything?—as Léonce says when he's in a bad humor. I don't blame him; he'd never be in a bad humor if it weren't for me."

They took a short cut across the sands. At a distance they could see the curious procession moving across the wharf—the lovers, shoulder to shoulder, creeping; the lady in black, gaining steadily upon them; old Monsieur Farival, losing ground inch by inch; and a young bare-footed Spanish girl, with a red kerchief on her head and a basket on her arm, bringing up the rear.

Robert knew the girl, and he talked to her a little in the boat. No one present understood what they said. Her name was Mariequita. She had a round, sly, piquant face and pretty black eyes. Her hands were small, and she kept them folded over the handle of her basket. Her feet were broad and coarse. She did not strive to hide them. Edna looked at her feet, and noticed the sand and slime between her brown toes.

Beaudelet grumbled because Mariequita was there, taking up so much room. In reality he was annoyed at having old Monsieur Farival, who considered himself the better sailor of the two. But he would not quarrel with so old a man as Monsieur Farival, so he quarreled with Mariequita. The girl was deprecatory at one moment, appealing to Robert. She was saucy the next, moving her head up and down, making "eyes" at Robert and making "mouths" at Beaudelet.

The lovers were all alone. They saw nothing, they heard nothing. The lady in black was counting her beads for the third time. Old Monsieur Farival talked incessantly of what he knew about handling a boat, and of what Beaudelet did not know on the same subject.

Edna liked it all. She looked Mariequita up and down, from her ugly brown toes to her pretty black eyes, and back again.

"Why does she look at me like that?" inquired the girl of Robert.

"Maybe she thinks you are pretty. Shall I ask her?"

"No. Is she your sweetheart?"

"She's a married lady, and has two children."

"Oh! well! Francisco ran away with Sylvano's wife, who had four children. They took all his money and one of the children and stole his boat."

"Shut up!"

"Does she understand?"

"Oh, hush!"

"Are those two married over there—leaning on each other?"

"Of course not," laughed Robert.

"Of course not," echoed Mariequita, with a serious, confirmatory bob of the head.

The sun was high up and beginning to bite. The swift breeze seemed to Edna to bury the sting of it into the pores of her face and hands. Robert held his umbrella over her.

As they went cutting sidewise through the water, the sails bellied taut, with the wind filling and overflowing them. Old Monsieur Farival laughed sardonically at something as he looked at the sails, and Beaudelet swore at the old man under his breath.

Sailing across the bay to the *Chênière Caminada*, Edna felt as if she were being borne away from some anchorage which had held her fast, whose chains had been loosening—had snapped the night before when the mystic spirit was abroad, leaving her free to drift whithersoever she chose to set her sails. Robert spoke to her incessantly; he no longer noticed Mariequita. The girl had shrimps in her bamboo basket. They were covered with Spanish moss. She beat the moss down impatiently, and muttered to herself sullenly.

"Let us go to Grande Terre[18] to-morrow?" said Robert in a low voice.

"What shall we do there?"

"Climb up the hill to the old fort and look at the little wriggling gold snakes, and watch the lizards sun themselves."

She gazed away toward Grande Terre and thought she would like to be alone there with Robert, in the sun, listening to the ocean's roar and watching the slimy lizards writhe in and out among the ruins of the old fort.

"And the next day or the next we can sail to the Bayou Brulow," he went on.

"What shall we do there?"

"Anything—cast bait for fish."

"No; we'll go back to Grande Terre. Let the fish alone."

"We'll go wherever you like," he said. "I'll have Tonie come over and help me patch and trim my boat. We shall not need Beaudelet nor any one. Are you afraid of the pirogue?"[19]

"Oh, no."

"Then I'll take you some night in the pirogue when the moon shines. Maybe your Gulf spirit will whisper to you in which of these islands the treasures are hidden—direct you to the very spot, perhaps."

"And in a day we should be rich!" she laughed. "I'd give it all to you, the pirate gold and every bit of treasure we could dig up. I think you would know how to spend it. Pirate gold isn't a thing to be hoarded or utilized. It is something to squander and throw to the four winds, for the fun of seeing the golden specks fly."

"We'd share it, and scatter it together," he said. His face flushed.

They all went together up to the quaint little Gothic church of Our Lady of Lourdes, gleaming all brown and yellow with paint in the sun's glare.

---

[18]An island adjacent to Grand Isle.

[19]A flat-bottomed sailboat.

Only Beaudelet remained behind, tinkering at his boat, and Mariequita walked away with her basket of shrimps, casting a look of childish ill-humor and reproach at Robert from the corner of her eye.

XIII

A feeling of oppression and drowsiness overcame Edna during the service. Her head began to ache, and the lights on the altar swayed before
her eyes. Another time she might have made an effort to regain her
composure; but her one thought was to quit the stifling atmosphere of
the church and reach the open air. She arose, climbing over Robert's
feet with a muttered apology. Old Monsieur Farival, flurried, curious,
stood up, but upon seeing that Robert had followed Mrs. Pontellier, he
sank back into his seat. He whispered an anxious inquiry of the lady in
black, who did not notice him or reply, but kept her eyes fastened
upon the pages of her velvet prayer-book.

"I felt giddy and almost overcome," Edna said, lifting her hands
instinctively to her head and pushing her straw hat up from her forehead. "I couldn't have stayed through the service." They were outside
in the shadow of the church. Robert was full of solicitude.

"It was folly to have thought of going in the first place, let alone
staying. Come over to Madame Antoine's; you can rest there." He took
her arm and led her away, looking anxiously and continuously down
into her face.

How still it was, with only the voice of the sea whispering through
the reed that grew in the salt-water pools! The long line of little gray,
weather-beaten houses nestled peacefully among the orange trees. It
must always have been God's day on that low, drowsy island, Edna
thought. They stopped, leaning over a jagged fence made of sea-drift,
to ask for water. A youth, a mild-faced Acadian,[20] was drawing water
from the cistern, which was nothing more than a rusty buoy, with an
opening on one side, sunk in the ground. The water which the youth
handed to them in a tin pail was not cold to taste, but it was cool to her
heated face, and it greatly revived and refreshed her.

Madame Antoine's cot was at the far end of the village. She wel-

---

[20]Also spelled "Cajun"; a descendant of French-Canadians expelled from Nova Scotia
who settled in Louisiana.

comed them with all the native hospitality, as she would have opened
her door to let the sunlight in. She was fat, and walked heavily and
clumsily across the floor. She could speak no English, but when Robert
made her understand that the lady who accompanied him was ill and
desired to rest, she was all eagerness to make Edna feel at home and to
dispose of her comfortably.

The whole place was immaculately clean, and the big, four-posted
bed, snow-white, invited one to repose. It stood in a small side room
which looked out across a narrow grass plot toward the shed, where
there was a disabled boat lying keel upward.

Madame Antoine had not gone to mass. Her son Tonie had, but she
supposed he would soon be back, and she invited Robert to be seated
and wait for him. But he went and sat outside the door and smoked.
Madame Antoine busied herself in the large front room preparing dinner. She was boiling mullet over a few red coals in the huge fireplace.

Edna, left alone in the little side room, loosened her clothes, removing the greater part of them. She bathed her face, her neck and arms in
the basin that stood between the windows. She took off her shoes and
stockings and stretched herself in the very center of the high, white
bed. How luxurious it felt to rest thus in a strange, quaint bed, with its
sweet country odor of laurel lingering about the sheets and mattress!
She stretched her strong limbs that ached a little. She ran her fingers
through her loosened hair for a while. She looked at her round arms as
she held them straight up and rubbed them one after the other, observing closely, as if it were something she saw for the first time, the fine,
firm quality and texture of her flesh. She clasped her hands easily
above her head, and it was thus she fell asleep.

She slept lightly at first, half awake and drowsily attentive to the
things about her. She could hear Madame Antoine's heavy, scraping
tread as she walked back and forth on the sanded floor. Some chickens
were clucking outside the window, scratching for bits of gravel in the
grass. Later she heard the voices of Robert and Tonie talking under the
shed. She did not stir. Even her eyelids rested numb and heavily over
her sleepy eyes. The voices went on—Tonie's slow, Acadian drawl,
Robert's quick, soft, smooth French. She understood French imperfectly unless directly addressed, and the voices were only part of the
other drowsy, muffled sounds lulling her senses.

When Edna awoke it was with the conviction that she had slept long
and soundly. The voices were hushed under the shed. Madame Antoine's step was no longer to be heard in the adjoining room. Even the

chickens had gone elsewhere to scratch and cluck. The mosquito bar was drawn over her; the old woman had come in while she slept and let down the bar. Edna arose quietly from the bed, and looking between the curtains of the window, she saw by the slanting rays of the sun that the afternoon was far advanced. Robert was out there under the shed, reclining in the shade against the sloping keel of the overturned boat. He was reading from a book. Tonie was no longer with him. She wondered what had become of the rest of the party. She peeped out at him two or three times as she stood washing herself in the little basin between the windows.

Madame Antoine had laid some coarse, clean towels upon a chair, and had placed a box of *poudre de riz*[21] within easy reach. Edna dabbed the powder upon her nose and cheeks as she looked at herself closely in the little distorted mirror which hung on the wall above the basin. Her eyes were bright and wide awake and her face glowed.

When she had completed her toilet she walked into the adjoining room. She was very hungry. No one was there. But there was a cloth spread upon the table that stood against the wall, and a cover was laid for one, with a crusty brown loaf and a bottle of wine beside the plate. Edna bit a piece from a brown loaf, tearing it with her strong, white teeth. She poured some of the wine into the glass and drank it down. Then she went softly out of doors, and plucking an orange from the low-hanging bough of a tree, threw it at Robert, who did not know she was awake and up.

An illumination broke over his whole face when he saw her and joined her under the orange tree.

"How many years have I slept?" she inquired. "The whole island seems changed. A new race of beings must have sprung up, leaving only you and me as past relics. How many ages ago did Madame Antoine and Tonie die? and when did our people from Grand Isle disappear from the earth?"

He familiarly adjusted a ruffle upon her shoulder.

"You have slept precisely one hundred years. I was left here to guard your slumbers; and for one hundred years I have been out under the shed reading a book. The only evil I couldn't prevent was to keep a broiled fowl from drying up."

"If it has turned to stone, still will I eat it," said Edna, moving with

---

[21]Rice flour, used as a cosmetic.

him into the house. "But really, what has become of Monsieur Farival and the others?"

"Gone hours ago. When they found that you were sleeping they thought it best not to awake you. Any way, I wouldn't have let them. What was I here for?"

"I wonder if Léonce will be uneasy!" she speculated, as she seated herself at table.

"Of course not; he knows you are with me," Robert replied, as he busied himself among sundry pans and covered dishes which had been left standing on the hearth.

"Where are Madame Antoine and her son?" asked Edna.

"Gone to Vespers, and to visit some friends, I believe. I am to take you back in Tonie's boat whenever you are ready to go."

He stirred the smoldering ashes till the broiled fowl began to sizzle afresh. He served her with no mean repast, dripping the coffee anew and sharing it with her. Madame Antoine had cooked little else than the mullets, but while Edna slept Robert had foraged the island. He was childishly gratified to discover her appetite, and to see the relish with which she ate the food which he had procured for her.

"Shall we go right away?" she asked, after draining her glass and brushing together the crumbs of the crusty loaf.

"The sun isn't as low as it will be in two hours," he answered.

"The sun will be gone in two hours."

"Well, let it go; who cares!"

They waited a good while under the orange trees, till Madame Antoine came back, panting, waddling, with a thousand apologies to explain her absence. Tonie did not dare to return. He was shy, and would not willingly face any woman except his mother.

It was very pleasant to stay there under the orange trees, while the sun dipped lower and lower, turning the western sky to flaming copper and gold. The shadows lengthened and crept out like stealthy, grotesque monsters across the grass.

Edna and Robert both sat upon the ground—that is, he lay upon the ground beside her, occasionally picking at the hem of her muslin gown.

Madame Antoine seated her fat body, broad and squat, upon a bench beside the door. She had been talking all the afternoon, and had wound herself up to the story-telling pitch.

And what stories she told them! But twice in her life she had left the *Chênière Caminada*, and then for the briefest span. All her years she had squatted and waddled there upon the island, gathering legends of the

Baratarians[22] and the sea. The night came on, with the moon to lighten it. Edna could hear the whispering voices of dead men and the click of muffled gold.

When she and Robert stepped into Tonie's boat, with the red lateen sail, misty spirit forms were prowling in the shadows and among the reeds, and upon the water were phantom ships, speeding to cover.

XIV

The youngest boy, Etienne, had been very naughty, Madame Ratignolle said, as she delivered him into the hands of his mother. He had been unwilling to go to bed and had made a scene; whereupon she had taken charge of him and pacified him as well as she could. Raoul had been in bed and asleep for two hours.

The youngster was in his long white nightgown, that kept tripping him up as Madame Ratignolle led him along by the hand. With the other chubby fist he rubbed his eyes, which were heavy with sleep and ill-humor. Edna took him in her arms, and seating herself in the rocker, began to coddle and caress him, calling him all manner of tender names, soothing him to sleep.

It was not more than nine o'clock. No one had yet gone to bed but the children.

Léonce had been very uneasy at first, Madame Ratignolle said, and had wanted to start at once for the *Chênière*. But Monsieur Farival had assured him that his wife was only overcome with sleep and fatigue, that Tonie would bring her back later in the day; and he had thus been dissuaded from crossing the bay. He had gone over to Klein's, looking up some cotton broker whom he wished to see in regard to securities, exchanges, stocks, bonds, or something of the sort, Madame Ratignolle did not remember what. He said he would not remain away late. She herself was suffering from heat and oppression, she said. She carried a bottle of salts and a large fan. She would not consent to remain with Edna, for Monsieur Ratignolle was alone, and he detested above all things to be left alone.

When Etienne had fallen asleep Edna bore him into the back room, and Robert went and lifted the mosquito bar that she might lay the

---

[22]Pirates—especially the band led by Jean Lafitte, who had used Grand Isle as a head-quarters in the early nineteenth century.

child comfortably in his bed. The quadroon had vanished. When they emerged from the cottage Robert bade Edna good-night.

"Do you know we have been together the whole livelong day, Robert—since early this morning?" she said at parting.

"All but the hundred years when you were sleeping. Good-night."

He pressed her hand and went away in the direction of the beach. He did not join any of the others, but walked alone toward the Gulf.

Edna stayed outside, awaiting her husband's return. She had no desire to sleep or to retire; nor did she feel like going over to sit with the Ratignolles, or to join Madame Lebrun and a group whose animated voices reached her as they sat in conversation before the house. She let her mind wander back over her stay at Grand Isle; and she tried to discover wherein this summer had been different from any and every other summer of her life. She could only realize that she herself—her present self—was in some way different from the other self. That she was seeing with different eyes and making the acquaintance of new conditions in herself that colored and changed her environment, she did not yet suspect.

She wondered why Robert had gone away and left her. It did not occur to her to think he might have grown tired of being with her the livelong day. She was not tired, and she felt that he was not. She regretted that he had gone. It was so much more natural to have him stay when he was not absolutely required to leave her.

As Edna waited for her husband she sang low a little song that Robert had sung as they crossed the bay. It began with "Ah! *Si tu savais,*"and every verse ended with "*si tu savais.*"[23]

Robert's voice was not pretentious. It was musical and true. The voice, the notes, the whole refrain haunted her memory.

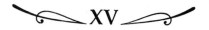

XV

When Edna entered the dining-room one evening a little late, as was her habit, an unusually animated conversation seemed to be going on. Several persons were talking at once, and Victor's voice was predominating, even over that of his mother. Edna had returned late from her bath, had dressed in some haste, and her face was flushed. Her head,

---

[23]The song is a French translation of Michael Balfe's Irish melody, "Couldst Thou But Know."

set off by her dainty white gown, suggested a rich, rare blossom. She took her seat at table between old Monsieur Farival and Madame Ratignolle.

As she seated herself and was about to begin to eat her soup, which had been served when she entered the room, several persons informed her simultaneously that Robert was going to Mexico. She laid her spoon down and looked about her bewildered. He had been with her, reading to her all the morning, and had never even mentioned such a place as Mexico. She had not seen him during the afternoon; she had heard some one say he was at the house, upstairs with his mother. This she had thought nothing of, though she was surprised when he did not join her later in the afternoon, when she went down to the beach.

She looked across at him, where he sat beside Madame Lebrun, who presided. Edna's face was a blank picture of bewilderment, which she never thought of disguising. He lifted his eyebrows with the pretext of a smile as he returned her glance. He looked embarrassed and uneasy.

"When is he going?" she asked of everybody in general, as if Robert were not there to answer for himself.

"To-night!" "This very evening!" "Did you ever!" "What possesses him?" were some of the replies she gathered, uttered simultaneously in French and English.

"Impossible!" she exclaimed. "How can a person start off from Grand Isle to Mexico at a moment's notice, as if he were going over to Klein's or to the wharf or down to the beach?"

"I said all along I was going to Mexico; I've been saying so for years!" cried Robert, in an excited and irritable tone, with the air of a man defending himself against a swarm of stinging insects.

Madame Lebrun knocked on the table with her knife handle.

"Please let Robert explain why he is going, and why he is going tonight," she called out. "Really, this table is getting to be more and more like Bedlam every day, with everybody talking at once. Sometimes—I hope God will forgive me—but positively, sometimes I wish Victor would lose the power of speech."

Victor laughed sardonically as he thanked his mother for her holy wish, of which he failed to see the benefit to anybody, except that it might afford her a more ample opportunity and license to talk herself.

Monsieur Farival thought that Victor should have been taken out in mid-ocean in his earliest youth and drowned. Victor thought there would be more logic in thus disposing of old people with an established claim for making themselves universally obnoxious. Madame Lebrun grew a trifle hysterical; Robert called his brother some sharp, hard names.

"There's nothing much to explain, mother," he said; though he explained, nevertheless—looking chiefly at Edna—that he could only meet the gentleman whom he intended to join at Vera Cruz by taking such and such a steamer, which left New Orleans on such a day; that Beaudelet was going out with his lugger-load of vegetables that night, which gave him an opportunity of reaching the city and making his vessel in time.

"But when did you make up your mind to all this?" demanded Monsieur Farival.

"This afternoon," returned Robert, with a shade of annoyance.

"At what time this afternoon?" persisted the old gentleman, with nagging determination, as if he were cross-questioning a criminal in a court of justice.

"At four o'clock this afternoon, Monsieur Farival," Robert replied, in a high voice and with a lofty air, which reminded Edna of some gentleman on the stage.

She had forced herself to eat most of her soup, and now she was picking the flaky bits of a *court bouillon*[24] with her fork.

The lovers were profiting by the general conversation on Mexico to speak in whispers of matters which they rightly considered were interesting to no one but themselves. The lady in black had once received a pair of prayer-beads of curious workmanship from Mexico, with very special indulgence attached to them, but she had never been able to ascertain whether the indulgence extended outside the Mexican border. Father Fochel of the Cathedral had attempted to explain it; but he had not done so to her satisfaction. And she begged that Robert would interest himself, and discover, if possible, whether she was entitled to the indulgence accompanying the remarkably curious Mexican prayer-beads.

Madame Ratignolle hoped that Robert would exercise extreme caution in dealing with the Mexicans, who, she considered, were a treacherous people, unscrupulous and revengeful. She trusted she did them no injustice in thus condemning them as a race. She had known personally but one Mexican, who made and sold excellent tamales, and whom she would have trusted implicitly, so soft-spoken was he. One

---

[24]Fish soup.

day he was arrested for stabbing his wife. She never knew whether he had been hanged or not.

Victor had grown hilarious, and was attempting to tell an anecdote about a Mexican girl who served chocolate one winter in a restaurant in Dauphine Street. No one would listen to him but old Monsieur Farival, who went into convulsions over the droll story.

Edna wondered if they had all gone mad, to be talking and clamoring at that rate. She herself could think of nothing to say about Mexico or the Mexicans.

"At what time do you leave?" she asked Robert.

"At ten," he told her. "Beaudelet wants to wait for the moon."

"Are you all ready to go?"

"Quite ready. I shall only take a hand-bag, and shall pack my trunk in the city."

He turned to answer some question put to him by his mother, and Edna, having finished her black coffee, left the table.

She went directly to her room. The little cottage was close and stuffy after leaving the outer air. But she did not mind; there appeared to be a hundred different things demanding her attention indoors. She began to set the toilet-stand to rights, grumbling at the negligence of the quadroon, who was in the adjoining room putting the children to bed. She gathered together stray garments that were hanging on the backs of chairs, and put each where it belonged in closet or bureau drawer. She changed her gown for a more comfortable and commodious wrapper. She rearranged her hair, combing and brushing it with unusual energy. Then she went in and assisted the quadroon in getting the boys to bed.

They were very playful and inclined to talk—to do anything but lie quiet and go to sleep. Edna sent the quadroon away to her supper and told her she need not return. Then she sat and told the children a story. Instead of soothing it excited them, and added to her wakefulness. She left them in heated argument, speculating about the conclusion of the tale which their mother promised to finish the following night.

The little black girl came in to say that Madame Lebrun would like to have Mrs. Pontellier go and sit with them over at the house till Mr. Robert went away. Edna returned answer that she had already undressed, that she did not feel quite well, but perhaps she would go over to the house later. She started to dress again, and got as far advanced as to remove her *peignoir*. But changing her mind once more she resumed the *peignoir*, and went outside and sat down before her door. She was overheated and irritable, and fanned herself energetically for a while. Madame Ratignolle came down to discover what was the matter.

"All that noise and confusion at the table must have upset me," replied Edna, "and moreover, I hate shocks and surprises. The idea of Robert starting off in such a ridiculously sudden and dramatic way! As if it were a matter of life and death! Never saying a word about it all morning when he was with me."

"Yes," agreed Madame Ratignolle. "I think it was showing us all— you especially—very little consideration. It wouldn't have surprised me in any of the others; those Lebruns are all given to heroics. But I must say I should never have expected such a thing from Robert. Are you not coming down? Come on, dear; it doesn't look friendly."

"No," said Edna, a little sullenly. "I can't go to the trouble of dressing again; I don't feel like it."

"You needn't dress; you look all right; fasten a belt around your waist. Just look at me!"

"No," persisted Edna; "but you go on. Madame Lebrun might be offended if we both stayed away."

Madame Ratignolle kissed Edna good-night, and went away, being in truth rather desirous of joining in the general and animated conversation which was still in progress concerning Mexico and the Mexicans.

Somewhat later Robert came up, carrying his hand-bag.

"Aren't you feeling well?" he asked.

"Oh, well enough. Are you going right away?"

He lit a match and looked at his watch. "In twenty minutes," he said. The sudden and brief glare of the match emphasized the darkness for a while. He sat down upon a stool which the children had left out on the porch.

"Get a chair," said Edna.

"This will do," he replied. He put on his soft hat and nervously took it off again, and wiping his face with his handkerchief, complained of the heat.

"Take the fan," said Edna, offering it to him.

"Oh, no! Thank you. It does you no good; you have to stop fanning some time, and feel all the more uncomfortable afterward."

"That's one of the ridiculous things which men always say. I have never known one to speak otherwise of fanning. How long will you be gone?"

"Forever, perhaps. I don't know. It depends upon a good many things."

"Well, in case it shouldn't be forever, how long will it be?"

"I don't know."

"This seems to me perfectly preposterous and uncalled for. I don't like it. I don't understand your motive for silence and mystery, never saying a word to me about it this morning." He remained silent, not offering to defend himself. He only said, after a moment:

"Don't part from me in an ill-humor. I never knew you to be out of patience with me before."

"I don't want to part in any ill-humor," she said. "But can't you understand? I've grown used to seeing you, to having you with me all the time, and your action seems unfriendly, even unkind. You don't even offer an excuse for it. Why, I was planning to be together, thinking of how pleasant it would be to see you in the city next winter."

"So was I," he blurted. "Perhaps that's the—" He stood up suddenly and held out his hand. "Good-by, my dear Mrs. Pontellier; good-by. You won't—I hope you won't completely forget me." She clung to his hand, striving to detain him.

"Write to me when you get there, won't you, Robert?" she entreated.

"I will, thank you. Good-by."

How unlike Robert! The merest acquaintance would have said something more emphatic than "I will, thank you; good-by," to such a request.

He had evidently already taken leave of the people over at the house, for he descended the steps and went to join Beaudelet, who was out there with an oar across his shoulder waiting for Robert. They walked away in the darkness. She could only hear Beaudelet's voice; Robert had apparently not even spoken a word of greeting to his companion.

Edna bit her handkerchief convulsively, striving to hold back and to hide, even from herself as she would have hidden from another, the emotion which was troubling—tearing—her. Her eyes were brimming with tears.

For the first time she recognized anew the symptoms of infatuation which she had felt incipiently as a child, as a girl in her earliest teens, and later as a young woman. The recognition did not lessen the reality, the poignancy of the revelation by any suggestion or promise of insta-bility. The past was nothing to her; offered no lesson which she was willing to heed. The future was a mystery which she never attempted to penetrate. The present alone was significant; was hers, to torture her as it was doing then with the biting conviction that she had lost that which she had held, that she had been denied that which her impas-sioned, newly awakened being demanded.

XVI

"Do you miss your friend greatly?" asked Mademoiselle Reisz one morning as she came creeping up behind Edna, who had just left her cottage on her way to the beach. She spent much of her time in the water since she had acquired finally the art of swimming. As their stay at Grand Isle drew near its close, she felt that she could not give too much time to a diversion which afforded her the only real pleasurable moments that she knew. When Mademoiselle Reisz came and touched her upon the shoulder and spoke to her, the woman seemed to echo the thought which was ever in Edna's mind; or, better, the feeling which constantly possessed her.

Robert's going had some way taken the brightness, the color, the meaning out of everything. The conditions of her life were in no way changed, but her whole existence was dulled, like a faded garment which seems to be no longer worth wearing. She sought him everywhere—in others whom she induced to talk about him. She went up in the mornings to Madame Lebrun's room, braving the clatter of the old sewing-machine. She sat there and chatted at intervals as Robert had done. She gazed around the room at the pictures and photographs hanging upon the wall, and discovered in some corner an old family album, which she examined with the keenest interest, appealing to Madame Lebrun for enlightenment concerning the many figures and faces which she discovered between its pages.

There was a picture of Madame Lebrun with Robert as a baby, seated in her lap, a round-faced infant with a fist in his mouth. The eyes alone in the baby suggested the man. And that was he also in kilts, at the age of five, wearing long curls and holding a whip in his hand. It made Edna laugh, and she laughed, too, at the portrait in his first long trousers; while another interested her, taken when he left for college, looking thin, long-faced, with eyes full of fire, ambition and great intentions. But there was no recent picture, none which suggested the Robert who had gone away five days ago, leaving a void and wilderness behind him.

"Oh, Robert stopped having his pictures taken when he had to pay for them himself! He found wiser use for his money, he says," explained Madame Lebrun. She had a letter from him, written before he left New Orleans. Edna wished to see the letter, and Madame Lebrun told her to look for it either on the table or the dresser, or perhaps it was on the mantelpiece.

The letter was on the bookshelf. It possessed the greatest interest and attraction for Edna; the envelope, its size and shape, the post-mark, the handwriting. She examined every detail of the outside before opening it. There were only a few lines, setting forth that he would leave the city that afternoon, that he had packed his trunk in good shape, that he was well, and sent her his love and begged to be affectionately remembered to all. There was no special message to Edna except a postscript saying that if Mrs. Pontellier desired to finish the book which he had been reading to her, his mother would find it in his room, among other books there on the table. Edna experienced a pang of jealousy because he had written to his mother rather than to her.

Every one seemed to take for granted that she missed him. Even her husband, when he came down the Saturday following Robert's departure, expressed regret that he had gone.

"How do you get on without him, Edna?" he asked.

"It's very dull without him," she admitted. Mr. Pontellier had seen Robert in the city, and Edna asked him a dozen questions or more. Where had they met? On Carondelet Street, in the morning. They had gone "in" and had a drink and a cigar together. What had they talked about? Chiefly about his prospects in Mexico, which Mr. Pontellier thought were promising. How did he look? How did he seem—grave, or gay, or how? Quite cheerful, and wholly taken up with the idea of his trip, which Mr. Pontellier found altogether natural in a young fellow about to seek fortune and adventure in a strange, queer country.

Edna tapped her foot impatiently, and wondered why the children persisted in playing in the sun when they might be under the trees. She went down and led them out of the sun, scolding the quadroon for not being more attentive.

It did not strike her as in the least grotesque that she should be making of Robert the object of conversation and leading her husband to speak of him. The sentiment which she entertained for Robert in no way resembled that which she felt for her husband, or had ever felt, or ever expected to feel. She had all her life long been accustomed to harbor thoughts and emotions which never voiced themselves. They had never taken the form of struggles. They belonged to her and were her own, and she entertained the conviction that she had a right to them and that they concerned no one but herself. Edna had once told Madame Ratignolle that she would never sacrifice herself for her children, or for any one. Then had followed a rather heated argument; the two women did not appear to understand each other or to be talking the same language. Edna tried to appease her friend, to explain.

"I would give up the unessential; I would give my money, I would give my life for my children; but I wouldn't give myself. I can't make it more clear; it's only something which I am beginning to comprehend, which is revealing itself to me."

"I don't know what you would call the essential, or what you mean by the unessential," said Madame Ratignolle, cheerfully; "but a woman who would give her life for her children could do no more than that— your Bible tells you so. I'm sure I couldn't do more than that."

"Oh, yes you could!" laughed Edna.

She was not surprised at Mademoiselle Reisz's question the morning that lady, following her to the beach, tapped her on the shoulder and asked if she did not greatly miss her young friend.

"Oh, good morning, Mademoiselle; is it you? Why, of course I miss Robert. Are you going down to bathe?"

"Why should I go down to bathe at the very end of the season when I haven't been in the surf all summer," replied the woman, disagreeably.

"I beg your pardon," offered Edna, in some embarrassment, for she should have remembered that Mademoiselle Reisz's avoidance of the water had furnished a scene for much pleasantry. Some among them thought it was on account of her false hair, or the dread of getting the violets wet, while others attributed it to the natural aversion for water sometimes believed to accompany the artistic temperament. Mademoiselle offered Edna some chocolates in a paper bag, which she took from her pocket, by way of showing that she bore no ill feeling. She habitually ate chocolates for their sustaining quality; they contained much nutriment in small compass, she said. They saved her from starvation, as Madame Lebrun's table was utterly impossible; and no one save so impertinent a woman as Madame Lebrun could think of offering such food to people and requiring them to pay for it.

"She must feel very lonely without her son," said Edna, desiring to change the subject. "Her favorite son, too. It must have been quite hard to let him go."

Mademoiselle laughed maliciously.

"Her favorite son! Oh, dear! Who could have been imposing such a tale upon you? Aline Lebrun lives for Victor, and for Victor alone. She has spoiled him into the worthless creature he is. She worships him and the ground he walks on. Robert is very well in a way, to give up all the money he can earn to the family, and keep the barest pittance for himself. Favorite son, indeed! I miss the poor fellow myself, my dear. I liked to see him and to hear him about the place—the only Lebrun who is worth a pinch of salt. He comes to see me often in the city. I like to play to him. That Victor! hanging would be too good for him. It's a wonder Robert hasn't beaten him to death long ago."

"I thought he had great patience with his brother," offered Edna, glad to be talking about Robert, no matter what was said.

"Oh! he thrashed him well enough a year or two ago," said Mademoiselle. "It was about a Spanish girl, whom Victor considered that he had some sort of claim upon. He met Robert one day talking to the girl, or walking with her, or bathing with her, or carrying her basket— I don't remember what—and he became so insulting and abusive that Robert gave him a thrashing on the spot that has kept him comparatively in order for a good while. It's about time he was getting another."

"Was her name Mariequita?" asked Edna.

"Mariequita—yes, that was it; Mariequita. I had forgotten. Oh, she's a sly one, and a bad one, that Mariequita!"

Edna looked down at Mademoiselle Reisz and wondered how she could have listened to her venom so long. For some reason she felt depressed, almost unhappy. She had not intended to go into the water; but she donned her bathing suit, and left Mademoiselle alone, seated under the shade of the children's tent. The water was growing cooler as the season advanced. Edna plunged and swam about with an abandon that thrilled and invigorated her. She remained a long time in the water, half hoping that Mademoiselle Reisz would not wait for her.

But Mademoiselle waited. She was very amiable during the walk back, and raved much over Edna's appearance in her bathing suit. She talked about music. She hoped that Edna would go to see her in the city, and wrote her address with the stub of a pencil on a piece of card which she found in her pocket.

"When do you leave?" asked Edna.

"Next Monday; and you?"

"The following week," answered Edna, adding, "It has been a pleasant summer, hasn't it, Mademoiselle?"

"Well," agreed Mademoiselle Reisz, with a shrug, "rather pleasant, if it hadn't been for the mosquitoes and the Farival twins."

XVII

The Pontelliers possessed a very charming home on Esplanade Street[25] in New Orleans. It was a large, double cottage, with a broad front

---

[25]The most fashionable neighborhood in New Orleans.

veranda, whose round, fluted columns supported the sloping roof. The house was painted a dazzling white; the outside shutters, or jalousies, were green. In the yard, which was kept scrupulously neat, were flowers and plants of every description which flourishes in South Louisiana. Within doors the appointments were perfect after the conventional type. The softest carpets and rugs covered the floors; rich and tasteful draperies hung at doors and windows. There were paintings, selected with judgment and discrimination, upon the walls. The cut glass, the silver, the heavy damask which daily appeared upon the table were the envy of many women whose husbands were less generous than Mr. Pontellier.

Mr. Pontellier was very fond of walking about his house examining its various appointments and details, to see that nothing was amiss. He greatly valued his possessions, chiefly because they were his, and derived genuine pleasure from contemplating a painting, a statuette, a rare lace curtain—no matter what—after he had bought it and placed it among his household gods.

On Tuesday afternoons—Tuesday being Mrs. Pontellier's reception day[26]—there was a constant stream of callers—women who came in carriages or in the street cars, or walked when the air was soft and distance permitted. A light-colored mulatto boy, in dress coat and bearing a diminutive silver tray for the reception of cards, admitted them. A maid, in white fluted cap, offered the callers liqueur, coffee, or chocolate, as they might desire. Mrs. Pontellier, attired in a handsome reception gown, remained in the drawing-room the entire afternoon receiving her visitors. Men sometimes called in the evening with their wives.

This had been the programme which Mrs. Pontellier had religiously followed since her marriage, six years before. Certain evenings during the week she and her husband attended the opera or sometimes the play.

Mr. Pontellier left his home in the mornings between nine and ten o'clock, and rarely returned before half-past six or seven in the evening—dinner being served at half-past seven.

He and his wife seated themselves at table one Tuesday evening, a few weeks after their return from Grand Isle. They were alone together. The boys were being put to bed; the patter of their bare, escaping feet could be heard occasionally, as well as the pursuing voice of the quadroon, lifted in mild protest and entreaty. Mrs. Pontellier did

---

[26]Ladies in society chose one day in the week to stay at home and receive callers.

not wear her usual Tuesday reception gown; she was in ordinary house dress. Mr. Pontellier, who was observant about such things, noticed it, as he served the soup and handed it to the boy in waiting.

"Tired out, Edna? Whom did you have? Many callers?" he asked. He tasted his soup and began to season it with pepper, salt, vinegar, mustard—everything within reach.

"There were a good many," replied Edna, who was eating her soup with evident satisfaction. "I found their cards when I got home; I was out."[27]

"Out!" exclaimed her husband, with something like genuine consternation in his voice as he laid down the vinegar cruet and looked at her through his glasses. "Why, what could have taken you out on Tuesday? What did you have to do?"

"Nothing. I simply felt like going out, and I went out."

"Well, I hope you left some suitable excuse," said her husband, somewhat appeased, as he added a dash of cayenne pepper to the soup.

"No, I left no excuse. I told Joe to say I was out, that was all."

"Why, my dear, I should think you'd understand by this time that people don't do such things; we've got to observe *les convenances*[28] if we ever expect to get on and keep up with the procession. If you felt you had to leave home this afternoon, you should have left some suitable explanation for your absence.

"This soup is really impossible; it's strange that woman hasn't learned yet to make a decent soup. Any free-lunch stand in town serves a better one. Was Mrs. Belthrop here?"

"Bring the tray with the cards, Joe. I don't remember who was here."

The boy retired and returned after a moment, bringing the tiny silver tray, which was covered with ladies' visiting cards. He handed it to Mrs. Pontellier.

"Give it to Mr. Pontellier," she said.

Joe offered the tray to Mr. Pontellier, and removed the soup.

Mr. Pontellier scanned the names of his wife's callers, reading some of them aloud, with comments as he read.

" 'The Misses Delasidas.' I worked a big deal in futures for their father this morning; nice girls; it's time they were getting married. 'Mrs. Belthrop.' I tell you what it is, Edna; you can't afford to snub Mrs. Belthrop. Why, Belthrop could buy and sell us ten times over. His

---

[27]To be "out" on one's "at-home" day was a major social gaffe.
[28]The proprieties.

business is worth a good, round sum to me. You'd better write her a note. 'Mrs. James Highcamp.' Hugh! the less you have to do with Mrs. Highcamp, the better. 'Madame Laforcé.' Came all the way from Carrolton, too, poor old soul. 'Miss Wiggs,' 'Mrs. Eleanor Boltons.' " He pushed the cards aside.

"Mercy!" exclaimed Edna, who had been fuming. "Why are you taking the thing so seriously and making such a fuss over it?"

"I'm not making any fuss over it. But it's just such seeming trifles that we've got to take seriously; such things count."

The fish was scorched. Mr. Pontellier would not touch it. Edna said she did not mind a little scorched taste. The roast was in some way not to his fancy, and he did not like the manner in which the vegetables were served.

"It seems to me," he said, "we spend enough money in this house to procure at least one meal a day which a man could eat and retain his self-respect."

"You used to think the cook was a treasure," returned Edna, indifferently.

"Perhaps she was when she first came; but cooks are only human. They need looking after, like any other class of persons that you employ. Suppose I didn't look after the clerks in my office, just let them run things their own way; they'd soon make a nice mess of me and my business."

"Where are you going?" asked Edna, seeing that her husband arose from table without having eaten a morsel except a taste of the highly-seasoned soup.

"I'm going to get my dinner at the club. Good night." He went into the hall, took his hat and stick from the stand, and left the house.

She was somewhat familiar with such scenes. They had often made her very unhappy. On a few previous occasions she had been completely deprived of any desire to finish her dinner. Sometimes she had gone into the kitchen to administer a tardy rebuke to the cook. Once she went to her room and studied the cookbook during an entire evening, finally writing out a menu for the week, which left her harassed with a feeling that, after all, she had accomplished no good that was worth the name.

But that evening Edna finished her dinner alone, with forced deliberation. Her face was flushed and her eyes flamed with some inward fire that lighted them. After finishing her dinner she went to her room, having instructed the boy to tell any other callers that she was indisposed.

It was a large, beautiful room, rich and picturesque in the soft, dim light which the maid had turned low. She went and stood at an open window and looked out upon the deep tangle of the garden below. All the mystery and witchery of the night seemed to have gathered there amid the perfumes and the dusky and tortuous outlines of flowers and foliage. She was seeking herself and finding herself in just such sweet, half-darkness which met her moods. But the voices were not soothing that came to her from the darkness and the sky above and the stars. They jeered and sounded mournful notes without promise, devoid even of hope. She turned back into the room and began to walk to and fro down its whole length, without stopping, without resting. She carried in her hands a thin handkerchief, which she tore into ribbons, rolled into a ball, and flung from her. Once she stopped, and taking off her wedding ring, flung it upon the carpet. When she saw it lying there, she stamped her heel upon it, striving to crush it. But her small boot heel did not make an indenture, not a mark upon the little glittering circlet.

In a sweeping passion she seized a glass from the table and flung it upon the tiles of the hearth. She wanted to destroy something. The crash and clatter were what she wanted to hear.

A maid, alarmed at the din of breaking glass, entered the room to discover what was the matter.

"A vase fell upon the hearth," said Edna. "Never mind; leave it till morning."

"Oh! you might get some of the glass in your feet, ma'am," insisted the young woman, picking up bits of the broken vase that were scattered upon the carpet. "And here's your ring, ma'am, under the chair."

Edna held out her hand, and taking the ring, slipped it upon her finger.

XVIII

The following morning Mr. Pontellier, upon leaving for his office, asked Edna if she would not meet him in town in order to look at some new fixtures for the library.

"I hardly think we need new fixtures, Léonce. Don't let us get anything new; you are too extravagant. I don't believe you ever think of saving or putting by."

"The way to become rich is to make money, my dear Edna, not to save it," he said. He regretted that she did not feel inclined to go with him and select new fixtures. He kissed her good-by, and told her she was not looking well and must take care of herself. She was unusually pale and very quiet.

She stood on the front veranda as he quitted the house, and absently picked a few sprays of jessamine that grew upon a trellis near by. She inhaled the odor of the blossoms and thrust them into the bosom of her white morning gown. The boys were dragging along the banquette[29] a small "express wagon," which they had filled with blocks and sticks. The quadroon was following them with little quick steps, having assumed a fictitious animation and alacrity for the occasion. A fruit vender was crying his wares in the street.

Edna looked straight before her with a self-absorbed expression upon her face. She felt no interest in anything about her. The street, the children, the fruit vender, the flowers growing there under her eyes, were all part and parcel of an alien world which had suddenly become antagonistic.

She went back into the house. She had thought of speaking to the cook concerning her blunders of the previous night; but Mr. Pontellier had saved her that disagreeable mission, for which she was so poorly fitted. Mr. Pontellier's arguments were usually convincing with those whom he employed. He left home feeling quite sure that he and Edna would sit down that evening, and possibly a few subsequent evenings, to a dinner deserving of the name.

Edna spent an hour or two in looking over some of her old sketches. She could see their shortcomings and defects, which were glaring in her eyes. She tried to work a little, but found she was not in the humor. Finally she gathered together a few of the sketches—those which she considered the least discreditable; and she carried them with her when, a little later, she dressed and left the house. She looked handsome and distinguished in her street gown. The tan of the seashore had left her face, and her forehead was smooth, white, and polished beneath her heavy, yellow-brown hair. There were a few freckles on her face, and a small, dark mole near the under lip and one on the temple, half-hidden in her hair.

As Edna walked along the street she was thinking of Robert. She was still under the spell of her infatuation. She had tried to forget him, realizing the inutility of remembering. But the thought of him was like an obsession, ever pressing itself upon her. It was not that she dwelt

---

[29]Sidewalk.

upon details of their acquaintance, or recalled in any special or peculiar way his personality; it was his being, his existence, which dominated her thought, fading sometimes as if it would melt into the mist of the forgotten, reviving again with an intensity which filled her with an incomprehensible longing.

Edna was on her way again to Madame Ratignolle's. Their intimacy, begun at Grand Isle, had not declined, and they had seen each other with some frequency since their return to the city. The Ratignolles lived at no great distance from Edna's home, on the corner of a side street, where Monsieur Ratignolle owned and conducted a drug store which enjoyed a steady and prosperous trade. His father had been in the business before him, and Monsieur Ratignolle stood well in the community and bore an enviable reputation for integrity and clear-headedness. His family lived in commodious apartments over the store, having an entrance on the side within the *porte cochère*.[30] There was something which Edna thought very French, very foreign, about their whole manner of living. In the large and pleasant salon which extended across the width of the house, the Ratignolles entertained their friends once a fortnight with a *soirée musicale*,[31] sometimes diversified by card-playing. There was a friend who played upon the 'cello. One brought his flute and another his violin, while there were some who sang and a number who performed upon the piano with various degrees of taste and agility. The Ratignolles' *soirées musicales* were widely known, and it was considered a privilege to be invited to them.

Edna found her friend engaged in assorting the clothes which had returned that morning from the laundry. She at once abandoned her occupation upon seeing Edna, who had been ushered without ceremony into her presence.

" 'Cité can do it as well as I; it is really her business," she explained to Edna, who apologized for interrupting her. And she summoned a young black woman, whom she instructed, in French, to be very careful in checking off the list which she handed her. She told her to notice particularly if a fine linen handkerchief of Monsieur Ratignolle's, which was missing last week, had been returned; and to be sure to set to one side such pieces as required mending and darning.

Then placing an arm around Edna's waist, she led her to the front of the house, to the salon, where it was cool and sweet with the odor of great roses that stood upon the hearth in jars.

---

[30]Porch protecting carriage passengers from inclement weather.
[31]Musical party.

Madame Ratignolle looked more beautiful than ever there at home, in a negligé which left her arms almost wholly bare and exposed the rich, melting curves of her white throat.

"Perhaps I shall be able to paint your picture one day," said Edna with a smile when they were seated. She produced the roll of sketches and started to unfold them. "I believe I ought to work again. I feel as if I wanted to be doing something. What do you think of them? Do you think it worth while to take it up again and study some more? I might study for a while with Laidpore."

She knew that Madame Ratignolle's opinion in such a matter would be next to valueless, that she herself had not alone decided, but determined; but she sought the words of praise and encouragement that would help her to put heart into her venture.

"Your talent is immense, dear!"

"Nonsense!" protested Edna, well pleased.

"Immense, I tell you," persisted Madame Ratignolle, surveying the sketches one by one, at close range, then holding them at arm's length, narrowing her eyes, and dropping her head on one side. "Surely, this Bavarian peasant is worthy of framing; and this basket of apples! never have I seen anything more lifelike. One might almost be tempted to reach out a hand and take one."

Edna could not control a feeling which bordered upon complacency at her friend's praise, ever realizing, as she did, its true worth. She retained a few of the sketches, and gave all the rest to Madame Ratignolle, who appreciated the gift far beyond its value and proudly exhibited the pictures to her husband when he came up from the store a little later for his midday dinner.

Mr. Ratignolle was one of those men who are called the salt of the earth. His cheerfulness was unbounded, and it was matched by his goodness of heart, his broad charity, and common sense. He and his wife spoke English with an accent which was only discernible through its un-English emphasis and a certain carefulness and deliberation. Edna's husband spoke English with no accent whatever. The Ratignolles understood each other perfectly. If ever the fusion of two human beings into one has been accomplished on this sphere it was surely in their union.

As Edna seated herself at table with them she thought, "Better a dinner of herbs,"[32] though it did not take her long to discover that it

---

[32]Edna is quoting Proverbs 15:17.

was no dinner of herbs, but a delicious repast, simple, choice, and in every way satisfying.

Monsieur Ratignolle was delighted to see her, though he found her looking not so well as at Grand Isle, and he advised a tonic. He talked a good deal on various topics, a little politics, some city news and neighborhood gossip. He spoke with an animation and earnestness that gave an exaggerated importance to every syllable he uttered. His wife was keenly interested in everything he said, laying down her fork the better to listen, chiming in, taking the words out of his mouth.

Edna felt depressed rather than soothed after leaving them. The little glimpse of domestic harmony which had been offered her, gave her no regret, no longing. It was not a condition of life which fitted her, and she could see in it but an appalling and hopeless ennui. She was moved by a kind of commiseration for Madame Ratignolle,—a pity for that colorless existence which never uplifted its possessor beyond the region of blind contentment, in which no moment of anguish ever visited her soul, in which she would never have the taste of life's delirium. Edna vaguely wondered what she meant by "life's delirium." It had crossed her thought like some unsought, extraneous impression.

XIX

Edna could not help but think that it was very foolish, very childish, to have stamped upon her wedding ring and smashed the crystal vase upon the tiles. She was visited by no more such outbursts, moving her to such futile expedients. She began to do as she liked and to feel as she liked. She completely abandoned her Tuesdays at home, and did not return the visits of those who had called upon her. She made no ineffectual efforts to conduct her household *en bonne ménagère*,[33] going and coming as it suited her fancy, and, so far as she was able, lending herself to any passing caprice.

Mr. Pontellier had been a rather courteous husband so long as he met a certain tacit submissiveness in his wife. But her new and unexpected line of conduct completely bewildered him. It shocked him. Then her absolute disregard for her duties as a wife angered him. When Mr. Pontellier became rude, Edna grew insolent. She had resolved never to take another step backward.

---

[33]Like a good housekeeper.

"It seems to me the utmost folly for a woman at the head of a household, and the mother of children, to spend in an atelier days which would be better employed contriving for the comfort of her family."

"I feel like painting," answered Edna. "Perhaps I shan't always feel like it."

"Then in God's name paint! but don't let the family go to the devil. There's Madame Ratignolle; because she keeps up her music, she doesn't let everything else go to chaos. And she's more of a musician than you are a painter."

"She isn't a musician, and I'm not a painter. It isn't on account of painting that I let things go."

"On account of what, then?"

"Oh! I don't know. Let me alone; you bother me."

It sometimes entered Mr. Pontellier's mind to wonder if his wife were not growing a little unbalanced mentally. He could see plainly that she was not herself. That is, he could not see that she was becoming herself and daily casting aside that fictitious self which we assume like a garment with which to appear before the world.

Her husband let her alone as she requested, and went away to his office. Edna went up to her atelier[34]—a bright room in the top of the house. She was working with great energy and interest, without accomplishing anything, however, which satisfied her even in the smallest degree. For a time she had the whole household enrolled in the service of art. The boys posed for her. They thought it amusing at first, but the occupation soon lost its attractiveness when they discovered that it was not a game arranged especially for their entertainment. The quadroon sat for hours before Edna's palette, patient as a savage, while the house-maid took charge of the children, and the drawing-room went undusted. But the house-maid, too, served her term as model when Edna perceived that the young woman's back and shoulders were molded on classic lines, and that her hair, loosened from its confining cap, became an inspiration. While Edna worked she sometimes sang low the little air, "*Ah! si tu savais!*"

It moved her with recollections. She could hear again the ripple of the water, the flapping sail. She could see the glint of the moon upon the bay, and could feel the soft, gusty beating of the hot south wind. A subtle current of desire passed through her body, weakening her hold upon the brushes and making her eyes burn.

---

[34]Studio.

There were days when she was very happy without knowing why. She was happy to be alive and breathing, when her whole being seemed to be one with the sunlight, the color, the odors, the luxuriant warmth of some perfect Southern day. She liked then to wander alone into strange and unfamiliar places. She discovered many a sunny, sleepy corner, fashioned to dream in. And she found it good to dream and to be alone and unmolested.

There were days when she was unhappy, she did not know why,— when it did not seem worth while to be glad or sorry, to be alive or dead; when life appeared to her like a grotesque pandemonium and humanity like worms struggling blindly toward inevitable annihilation. She could not work on such a day, nor weave fancies to stir her pulses and warm her blood.

XX

It was during such a mood that Edna hunted up Mademoiselle Reisz. She had not forgotten the rather disagreeable impression left upon her by their last interview; but she nevertheless felt a desire to see her— above all, to listen while she played the piano. Quite early in the afternoon she started upon her quest for the pianist. Unfortunately she had mislaid or lost Mademoiselle Reisz's card, and looking up her address in the city directory, she found that the woman lived on Bienville Street,[35] some distance away. The directory which fell into her hands was a year or more old, however, and upon reaching the number indicated, Edna discovered that the house was occupied by a respectable family of mulattoes who had *chambres garnies*[36] to let. They had been living there for six months, and knew absolutely nothing of a Mademoiselle Reisz. In fact, they knew nothing of any of their neighbors; their lodgers were all people of the highest distinction, they assured Edna. She did not linger to discuss class distinctions with Madame Pouponne, but hastened to a neighboring grocery store, feeling sure that Mademoiselle would have left her address with the proprietor.

He knew Mademoiselle Reisz a good deal better than he wanted to know her, he informed his questioner. In truth, he did not want to

---

[35]An unfashionable neighborhood near the waterfront.
[36]Furnished flats.

know her at all, or anything concerning her—the most disagreeable
and unpopular woman who ever lived in Bienville Street. He thanked
heaven she had left the neighborhood, and was equally thankful that
he did not know where she had gone.

Edna's desire to see Mademoiselle Reisz had increased tenfold since
these unlooked-for obstacles had arisen to thwart it. She was wondering who could give her the information she sought, when it suddenly
occurred to her that Madame Lebrun would be the one most likely to
do so. She knew it was useless to ask Madame Ratignolle, who was on
the most distant terms with the musician, and preferred to know nothing concerning her. She had once been almost as emphatic in expressing herself upon the subject as the corner grocer.

Edna knew that Madame Lebrun had returned to the city, for it was
the middle of November. And she also knew where the Lebruns lived,
on Chartres Street.

Their home from the outside looked like a prison, with iron bars
before the door and lower windows. The iron bars were a relic of the
old *régime*, and no one had ever thought of dislodging them. At the side
was a high fence enclosing the garden. A gate or door opening upon
the street was locked. Edna rang the bell at this side garden gate, and
stood upon the banquette, waiting to be admitted.

It was Victor who opened the gate for her. A black woman, wiping
her hands upon her apron, was close at his heels. Before she saw them
Edna could hear them in altercation, the woman—plainly an anom-
aly—claiming the right to be allowed to perform her duties, one of
which was to answer the bell.

Victor was surprised and delighted to see Mrs. Pontellier, and he
made no attempt to conceal either his astonishment or his delight. He
was a dark-browed, good-looking youngster of nineteen, greatly resembling his mother, but with ten times her impetuosity. He instructed
the black woman to go at once and inform Madame Lebrun that Mrs.
Pontellier desired to see her. The woman grumbled a refusal to do part
of her duty when she had not been permitted to do it all, and started
back to her interrupted task of weeding the garden. Whereupon Victor
administered a rebuke in the form of a volley of abuse, which, owing to
its rapidity and incoherence, was all but incomprehensible to Edna.
Whatever it was, the rebuke was convincing, for the woman dropped
her hoe and went mumbling into the house.

Edna did not wish to enter. It was very pleasant there on the side
porch, where there were chairs, a wicker lounge, and a small table. She

seated herself, for she was tired from her long tramp; and she began to rock gently and smooth out the folds of her silk parasol. Victor drew up his chair beside her. He at once explained that the black woman's offensive conduct was all due to imperfect training, as he was not there to take her in hand. He had only come up from the island the morning before, and expected to return next day. He stayed all winter at the island; he lived there, and kept the place in order and got things ready for the summer visitors.

But a man needed occasional relaxation, he informed Mrs. Pontellier, and every now and again he drummed up a pretext to bring him to the city. My! but he had had a time of it the evening before! He wouldn't want his mother to know, and he began to talk in a whisper. He was scintillant with recollections. Of course, he couldn't think of telling Mrs. Pontellier all about it, she being a woman and not comprehending such things. But it all began with a girl peeping and smiling at him through the shutters as he passed by. Oh! but she was a beauty! Certainly he smiled back, and went up and talked to her. Mrs. Pontellier did not know him if she supposed he was one to let an opportunity like that escape him. Despite herself, the youngster amused her. She must have betrayed in her look some degree of interest or entertainment. The boy grew more daring, and Mrs. Pontellier might have found herself, in a little while, listening to a highly colored story but for the timely appearance of Madame Lebrun.

That lady was still clad in white, according to her custom of the summer. Her eyes beamed an effusive welcome. Would not Mrs. Pontellier go inside? Would she partake of some refreshment? Why had she not been there before? How was that dear Mr. Pontellier and how were those sweet children? Had Mrs. Pontellier ever known such a warm November?

Victor went and reclined on the wicker lounge behind his mother's chair, where he commanded a view of Edna's face. He had taken her parasol from her hands while he spoke to her, and he now lifted it and twirled it above him as he lay on his back. When Madame Lebrun complained that it was *so* dull coming back to the city; that she saw *so* few people now; that even Victor, when he came up from the island for a day or two, had *so* much to occupy him and engage his time; then it was that the youth went into contortions on the lounge and winked mischievously at Edna. She somehow felt like a confederate in crime, and tried to look severe and disapproving.

There had been but two letters from Robert, with little in them, they told her. Victor said it was not really worth while to go inside for the letters, when his mother entreated him to go in search of them. He remembered the contents, which in truth he rattled off very glibly when put to the test.

One letter was written from Vera Cruz and the other from the City of Mexico. He had met Montel, who was doing everything toward his advancement. So far, the financial situation was no improvement over the one he had left in New Orleans, but of course the prospects were vastly better. He wrote of the City of Mexico, the buildings, the people and their habits, the conditions of life which he found there. He sent his love to the family. He inclosed a check to his mother, and hoped she would affectionately remember him to all his friends. That was about the substance of the two letters. Edna felt that if there had been a message for her, she would have received it. The despondent frame of mind in which she had left home began again to overtake her, and she remembered that she wished to find Mademoiselle Reisz.

Madame Lebrun knew where Mademoiselle Reisz lived. She gave Edna the address, regretting that she would not consent to stay and spend the remainder of the afternoon, and pay a visit to Mademoiselle Reisz some other day. The afternoon was already well advanced.

Victor escorted her out upon the banquette, lifted her parasol, and held it over her while he walked to the car with her. He entreated her to bear in mind that the disclosures of the afternoon were strictly confidential. She laughed and bantered him a little, remembering too late that she should have been dignified and reserved.

"How handsome Mrs. Pontellier looked!" said Madame Lebrun to her son.

"Ravishing!" he admitted. "The city atmosphere has improved her. Some way she doesn't seem like the same woman."

XXI

Some people contended that the reason Mademoiselle Reisz always chose apartments up under the roof was to discourage the approach of beggars, peddlars and callers. There were plenty of windows in her little front room. They were for the most part dingy, but as they were nearly always open it did not make so much difference. They often admitted into the room a good deal of smoke and soot; but at the same time all the light and air that there was came through them. From her windows could be seen the crescent of the river, the masts of ships and the big chimneys of the Mississippi steamers. A magnificent piano crowded the apartment. In the next room she slept, and in the third and last she harbored a gasoline stove on which she cooked her meals when disinclined to descend to the neighboring restaurant. It was there also that she ate, keeping her belongings in a rare old buffet, dingy and battered from a hundred years of use.

When Edna knocked at Mademoiselle Reisz's front room door and entered, she discovered that person standing beside the window, engaged in mending or patching an old prunella gaiter.[37] The little musician laughed all over when she saw Edna. Her laugh consisted of a contortion of the face and all the muscles of the body. She seemed strikingly homely, standing there in the afternoon light. She still wore the shabby lace and the artificial bunch of violets on the side of her head.

"So you remembered me at last," said Mademoiselle. "I had said to myself, 'Ah, bah! she will never come.' "

"Did you want me to come?" asked Edna with a smile.

"I had not thought much about it," answered Mademoiselle. The two had seated themselves on a little bumpy sofa which stood against the wall. "I am glad, however, that you came. I have the water boiling back there, and was just about to make some coffee. You will drink a cup with me. And how is *la belle dame?*[38] Always handsome! always healthy! always contented!" She took Edna's hand between her strong wiry fingers, holding it loosely without warmth, and executing a sort of double theme upon the back and palm.

"Yes," she went on; "I sometimes thought: 'She will never come. She promised as those women in society always do, without meaning it. She will not come.' For I really don't believe you like me, Mrs. Pontellier."

"I don't know whether I like you or not," replied Edna, gazing down at the little woman with a quizzical look.

The candor of Mrs. Pontellier's admission greatly pleased Mademoiselle Reisz. She expressed her gratification by repairing forthwith to the region of the gasoline stove and rewarding her guest with the promised cup of coffee. The coffee and the biscuit accompanying it proved very

---

[37]An old-fashioned high-buttoned shoe.
[38]The lovely lady.

acceptable to Edna, who had declined refreshment at Madame Lebrun's and was now beginning to feel hungry. Mademoiselle set the tray which she brought in upon a small table near at hand, and seated herself once again on the lumpy sofa.

"I have had a letter from your friend," she remarked, as she poured a little cream into Edna's cup and handed it to her.

"My friend?"

"Yes, your friend Robert. He wrote to me from the City of Mexico."

"Wrote to *you?*" repeated Edna in amazement, stirring her coffee absently.

"Yes, to me. Why not? Don't stir all the warmth out of your coffee; drink it. Though the letter might as well have been sent to you; it was nothing but Mrs. Pontellier from beginning to end."

"Let me see it," requested the young woman, entreatingly.

"No; a letter concerns no one but the person who writes it and the one to whom it is written."

"Haven't you just said it concerned me from beginning to end?"

"It was written about you, not to you. 'Have you seen Mrs. Pontellier? How is she looking?' he asks. 'As Mrs. Pontellier says,' or 'as Mrs. Pontellier once said.' 'If Mrs. Pontellier should call upon you, play for her that Impromptu of Chopin's, my favorite. I heard it here a day or two ago, but not as you play it. I should like to know how it affects her,' and so on, as if he supposed we were constantly in each other's society."

"Let me see the letter."

"Oh, no."

"Have you answered it?"

"No."

"Let me see the letter."

"No, and again, no."

"Then play the Impromptu for me."

"It is growing late; what time do you have to be home?"

"Time doesn't concern me. Your question seems a little rude. Play the Impromptu."

"But you have told me nothing of yourself. What are you doing?"

"Painting!" laughed Edna. "I am becoming an artist. Think of it!"

"Ah! an artist! You have pretensions, Madame."

"Why pretensions? Do you think I could not become an artist?"

"I do not know you well enough to say. I do not know your talent or your temperament. To be an artist includes much; one must possess many gifts—absolute gifts—which have not been acquired by one's own effort. And, moreover, to succeed, the artist must possess the courageous soul."

"What do you mean by the courageous soul?"

"Courageous, *ma foi!* The brave soul. The soul that dares and defies."

"Show me the letter and play for me the Impromptu. You see that I have persistence. Does that quality count for anything in art?"

"It counts with a foolish old woman whom you have captivated," replied Mademoiselle, with her wriggling laugh.

The letter was right there at hand in the drawer of the little table upon which Edna had just placed her coffee cup. Mademoiselle opened the drawer and drew forth the letter, the topmost one. She placed it in Edna's hands, and without further comment arose and went to the piano.

Mademoiselle played a soft interlude. It was an improvisation. She sat low at the instrument, and the lines of her body settled into ungraceful curves and angles that gave it an appearance of deformity. Gradually and imperceptibly the interlude melted into the soft opening minor chords of the Chopin Impromptu.

Edna did not know when the Impromptu began or ended. She sat in the sofa corner reading Robert's letter by the fading light. Mademoiselle had glided from the Chopin into the quivering love-notes of Isolde's song,[39] and back again to the Impromptu with its soulful and poignant longing.

The shadows deepened in the little room. The music grew strange and fantastic—turbulent, insistent, plaintive and soft with entreaty. The shadows grew deeper. The music filled the room. It floated out upon the night, over the housetops, the crescent of the river, losing itself in the silence of the upper air.

Edna was sobbing, just as she had wept one midnight at Grand Isle when strange, new voices awoke in her. She arose in some agitation to take her departure. "May I come again, Mademoiselle?" she asked at the threshold.

"Come whenever you feel like it. Be careful; the stairs and landings are dark; don't stumble."

Mademoiselle reëntered and lit a candle. Robert's letter was on the floor. She stooped and picked it up. It was crumpled and damp with

---

[39]Probably the "Liebestod" ("Love-death"), Isolde's aria just before she commits suicide, from Richard Wagner's opera *Tristan und Isolde.*

tears. Mademoiselle smoothed the letter out, restored it to the envelope, and replaced it in the table drawer.

XXII

One morning on his way to town, Mr. Pontellier stopped at the house of his old friend and family physician, Doctor Mandelet. The Doctor was a semi-retired physician, resting, as the saying is, upon his laurels. He bore a reputation for wisdom rather than skill—leaving the active practice of medicine to his assistants and younger contemporaries—and was much sought for in matters of consultation. A few families, united to him by bonds of friendship, he still attended when they required the services of a physician. The Pontelliers were among those.

Mr. Pontellier found the Doctor reading at the open window of his study. His house stood rather far back from the street, in the center of a delightful garden, so that it was quiet and peaceful at the old gentleman's study window. He was a great reader. He stared up disapprovingly over his eye-glasses as Mr. Pontellier entered, wondering who had the temerity to disturb him at that hour of the morning.

"Ah, Pontellier! Not sick, I hope. Come and have a seat. What news do you bring this morning?" He was quite portly, with a profusion of gray hair, and small blue eyes which age had robbed of much of their brightness but none of their penetration.

"Oh! I'm never sick, Doctor. You know that I come of tough fiber—of that old Creole race of Pontelliers that dry up and finally blow away. I came to consult—no, not precisely to consult—to talk to you about Edna. I don't know what ails her."

"Madame Pontellier not well?" marveled the Doctor. "Why, I saw her—I think it was a week ago—walking along Canal Street, the picture of health, it seemed to me."

"Yes, yes; she seems quite well," said Mr. Pontellier, leaning forward and whirling his stick between his two hands; "but she doesn't act well. She's odd, she's not like herself. I can't make her out, and I thought perhaps you'd help me."

"How does she act?" inquired the Doctor.

"Well, it isn't easy to explain," said Mr. Pontellier, throwing himself back in his chair. "She lets the housekeeping go to the dickens."

"Well, well; women are not all alike, my dear Pontellier. We've got to consider—"

"I know that; I told you I couldn't explain. Her whole attitude—

toward me and everybody and everything—has changed. You know I have a quick temper, but I don't want to quarrel or be rude to a woman, especially my wife; yet I'm driven to it, and feel like ten thousand devils after I've made a fool of myself. She's making it devilishly uncomfortable for me," he went on nervously. "She's got some sort of notion in her head concerning the eternal rights of women; and—you understand—we meet in the morning at the breakfast table."

The old gentleman lifted his shaggy eyebrows, protruded his thick nether lip, and tapped the arms of his chair with his cushioned fingertips.

"What have you been doing to her, Pontellier?"

"Doing! *Parbleu!*"

"Has she," asked the Doctor, with a smile, "has she been associating of late with a circle of pseudo-intellectual women—super-spiritual superior beings? My wife has been telling me about them."

"That's the trouble," broke in Mr. Pontellier, "she hasn't been associating with any one. She has abandoned her Tuesdays at home, has thrown over all her acquaintances, and goes tramping about by herself, moping in the street-cars, getting in after dark. I tell you she's peculiar. I don't like it; I feel a little worried over it."

This was a new aspect for the Doctor. "Nothing hereditary?" he asked seriously. "Nothing peculiar about her family antecedents, is there?"

"Oh, no, indeed! She comes of sound old Presbyterian Kentucky stock. The old gentleman, her father, I have heard, used to atone for his weekday sins with his Sunday devotions. I know for a fact that his race horses literally ran away with the prettiest bit of Kentucky farming land I ever laid eyes upon. Margaret—you know Margaret—she has all the Presbyterianism undiluted. And the youngest is something of a vixen. By the way, she gets married in a couple of weeks from now."

"Send your wife up to the wedding," exclaimed the Doctor, foreseeing a happy solution. "Let her stay among her own people for a while; it will do her good."

"That's what I want her to do. She won't go to the marriage. She says a wedding is one of the most lamentable spectacles on earth. Nice thing for a woman to say to her husband!" exclaimed Mr. Pontellier, fuming anew at the recollection.

"Pontellier," said the Doctor, after a moment's reflection, "let your wife alone for a while. Don't bother her, and don't let her bother you. Woman, my dear friend, is a very peculiar and delicate organism—a sensitive and highly organized woman, such as I know Mrs. Pontellier to be, is especially peculiar. It would require an inspired psychologist to deal successfully with them. And when ordinary fellows like you and me attempt to cope with their idiosyncracies the result is bungling. Most women are moody and whimsical. This is some passing whim of your wife, due to some cause or causes which you and I needn't try to fathom. But it will pass happily over, especially if you leave her alone. Send her around to see me."

"Oh! I couldn't do that; there'd be no reason for it," objected Mr. Pontellier.

"Then I'll go around and see her," said the Doctor. "I'll drop in to dinner some evening *en bon ami.*"[40]

"Do! by all means," urged Mr. Pontellier. "What evening will you come? Say Thursday. Will you come Thursday?" he asked, rising to take his leave.

"Very well; Thursday. My wife may possibly have some engagement for me Thursday. In case she has, I shall let you know. Otherwise, you may expect me."

Mr. Pontellier turned before leaving to say:

"I am going to New York on business very soon. I have a big scheme on hand, and want to be on the field proper to pull the ropes and handle the ribbons. We'll let you in on the inside if you say so, Doctor," he laughed.

"No, I thank you, my dear sir," returned the Doctor. "I leave such ventures to you younger men with the fever of life still in your blood."

"What I wanted to say," continued Mr. Pontellier, with his hand on the knob; "I may have to be absent for a good while. Would you advise me to take Edna along?"

"By all means, if she wishes to go. If not, leave her here. Don't contradict her. The mood will pass, I assure you. It may take a month, two, three months—possibly longer, but it will pass; have patience."

"Well, good-by, *à jeudi,*"[41] said Mr. Pontellier, as he let himself out.

The Doctor would have liked during the course of conversation to ask, "Is there any man in the case?" but he knew his Creole too well to make such a blunder as that.

He did not resume his book immediately, but sat for a while meditatively looking out into the garden.

---

[40]As a friend (as opposed to a professional visit).
[41]Till Thursday.

XXIII

Edna's father was in the city, and had been with them several days. She was not very warmly or deeply attached to him, but they had certain tastes in common, and when together they were companionable. His coming was in the nature of a welcome disturbance; it seemed to furnish a new direction for her emotions.

He had come to purchase a wedding gift for his daughter, Janet, and an outfit for himself in which he might make a creditable appearance at her marriage. Mr. Pontellier had selected the bridal gift, as every one immediately connected with him always deferred to his taste in such matters. And his suggestions on the question of dress—which too often assumes the nature of a problem—were of inestimable value to his father-in-law. But for the past few days the old gentleman had been upon Edna's hands, and in his society she was becoming acquainted with a new set of sensations. He had been a colonel in the Confederate army, and still maintained, with the title, the military bearing which had always accompanied it. His hair and mustache were white and silky, emphasizing the rugged bronze of his face. He was tall and thin, and wore his coats padded, which gave a fictitious breadth and depth to his shoulders and chest. Edna and her father looked very distinguished together, and excited a good deal of notice during their perambulations. Upon his arrival she began by introducing him to her atelier and making a sketch of him. He took the whole matter very seriously. If her talent had been ten-fold greater than it was, it would not have surprised him, convinced as he was that he had bequeathed to all of his daughters the germs of a masterful capability, which only depended upon their own efforts to be directed toward successful achievement.

Before her pencil he sat rigid and unflinching, as he had faced the cannon's mouth in days gone by. He resented the intrusion of the children, who gaped with wondering eyes at him, sitting so stiff up there in their mother's bright atelier. When they drew near he motioned them away with an expressive action of the foot, loath to disturb the fixed lines of his countenance, his arms, or his rigid shoulders.

Edna, anxious to entertain him, invited Mademoiselle Reisz to meet him, having promised him a treat in her piano playing; but Mademoiselle declined the invitation. So together they attended a *soirée musicale* at the Ratignolles'. Monsieur and Madame Ratignolle made much of the Colonel, installing him as the guest of honor and engaging him at once to dine with them the following Sunday, or any day which he might select. Madame coquetted with him in the most captivating and naïve manner, with eyes, gestures, and a profusion of compliments, till the Colonel's old head felt thirty years younger on his padded shoulders. Edna marveled, not comprehending. She herself was almost devoid of coquetry.

There were one or two men whom she observed at the *soirée musicale;* but she would never have felt moved to any kittenish display to attract their notice—to any feline or feminine wiles to express herself toward them. Their personality attracted her in an agreeable way. Her fancy selected them, and she was glad when a lull in the music gave them an opportunity to meet her and talk with her. Often on the street the glance of strange eyes had lingered in her memory, and sometimes had disturbed her.

Mr. Pontellier did not attend these *soirées musicales.* He considered them *bourgeois,* and found more diversion at the club. To Madame Ratignolle he said the music dispensed at her *soirées* was too "heavy," too far beyond his untrained comprehension. His excuse flattered her. But she disapproved of Mr. Pontellier's club, and she was frank enough to tell Edna so.

"It's a pity Mr. Pontellier doesn't stay home more in the evenings. I think you would be more—well, if you don't mind my saying it—more united, if he did."

"Oh! dear no!" said Edna, with a blank look in her eyes. "What should I do if he stayed home? We wouldn't have anything to say to each other."

She had not much of anything to say to her father, for that matter; but he did not antagonize her. She discovered that he interested her, though she realized that he might not interest her long; and for the first time in her life she felt as if she were thoroughly acquainted with him. He kept her busy serving him and ministering to his wants. It amused her to do so. She would not permit a servant or one of the children to do anything for him which she might do herself. Her husband noticed, and thought it was the expression of a deep filial attachment which he had never suspected.

The Colonel drank numerous "toddies" during the course of the day, which left him, however, imperturbed. He was an expert at concocting strong drinks. He had even invented some, to which he had given fantastic names, and for whose manufacture he required diverse ingredients that it devolved upon Edna to procure for him.

When Doctor Mandelet dined with the Pontelliers on Thursday he could discern in Mrs. Pontellier no trace of that morbid condition which her husband had reported to him. She was excited and in a manner radiant. She and her father had been to the race course, and their thoughts when they seated themselves at table were still occupied with the events of the afternoon, and their talk was still of the track. The Doctor had not kept pace with turf affairs. He had certain recollections of racing in what he called "the good old times" when the Lecompte stables flourished, and he drew upon this fund of memories so that he might not be left out and seem wholly devoid of the modern spirit. But he failed to impose upon the Colonel, and was even far from impressing him with this trumped-up knowledge of bygone days. Edna had staked her father on his last venture, with the most gratifying results to both of them. Besides, they had met some very charming people, according to the Colonel's impressions. Mrs. Mortimer Merriman and Mrs. James Highcamp, who were there with Alcée Arobin, had joined them and had enlivened the hours in a fashion that warmed him to think of.

Mr. Pontellier himself had no particular leaning toward horse-racing, and was even rather inclined to discourage it as a pastime, especially when he considered the fate of that blue-grass farm in Kentucky. He endeavored, in a general way, to express a particular disapproval, and only succeeded in arousing the ire and opposition of his father-in-law. A pretty dispute followed, in which Edna warmly espoused her father's cause and the Doctor remained neutral.

He observed his hostess attentively from under his shaggy brows, and noted a subtle change which had transformed her from the listless woman he had known into a being who, for the moment, seemed palpitant with the forces of life. Her speech was warm and energetic. There was no repression in her glance or gesture. She reminded him of some beautiful sleek animal waking up in the sun.

The dinner was excellent. The claret was warm and the champagne was cold, and under their beneficent influence the threatened unpleasantness melted and vanished with the fumes of the wine.

Mr. Pontellier warmed up and grew reminiscent. He told some amusing plantation experiences, recollections of old Iberville and his youth, when he hunted 'possum in company with some friendly darky; thrashed the pecan trees, shot the grosbec, and roamed the woods and fields in mischievous idleness.

The Colonel, with little sense of humor and of the fitness of things, related a somber episode of those dark and bitter days, in which he had acted a conspicuous part and always formed a central figure. Nor was the Doctor happier in his selection, when he told the old, ever new and curious story of the waning of a woman's love, seeking strange, new channels, only to return to its legitimate source after days of fierce unrest. It was one of the many little human documents which had been unfolded to him during his long career as a physician. The story did not seem especially to impress Edna. She had one of her own to tell, of a woman who paddled away one night with her lover in a pirogue and never came back. They were lost amid the Baratarian Islands, and no one ever heard of them or found trace of them from that day to this. It was a pure invention. She said that Madame Antoine had related it to her. That, also, was an invention. Perhaps it was a dream she had had. But every glowing word seemed real to those who listened. They could feel the hot breath of the Southern night; they could hear the long sweep of the pirogue through the glistening moonlit water, the beating of birds' wings, rising startled from among the reeds in the salt-water pools; they could see the faces of the lovers, pale, close together, rapt in oblivious forgetfulness, drifting into the unknown.

The champagne was cold, and its subtle fumes played fantastic tricks with Edna's memory that night.

Outside, away from the glow of the fire and the soft lamplight, the night was chill and murky. The Doctor doubled his old-fashioned cloak across his breast as he strode home through the darkness. He knew his fellow-creatures better than most men; knew that inner life which so seldom unfolds itself to unanointed eyes. He was sorry he had accepted Pontellier's invitation. He was growing old, and beginning to need rest and an imperturbed spirit. He did not want the secrets of other lives thrust upon him.

"I hope it isn't Arobin," he muttered to himself as he walked. "I hope to heaven it isn't Alcée Arobin."

XXIV

Edna and her father had a warm, and almost violent dispute upon the subject of her refusal to attend her sister's wedding. Mr. Pontellier declined to interfere, to interpose either his influence or his authority. He was following Doctor Mandelet's advice, and letting her do as she liked. The Colonel reproached his daughter for her lack of filial kindness and respect, her want of sisterly affection and womanly consideration. His arguments were labored and unconvincing. He doubted if Janet would accept any excuse—forgetting that Edna had offered none. He doubted if Janet would ever speak to her again, and he was sure Margaret would not.

Edna was glad to be rid of her father when he finally took off with his wedding garments and his bridal gifts, with his padded shoulders, his Bible reading, his "toddies" and ponderous oaths.

Mr. Pontellier followed him closely. He meant to stop at the wedding on his way to New York and endeavor by every means which money and love could devise to atone somewhat for Edna's incomprehensible action.

"You are too lenient, too lenient by far, Léonce," asserted the Colonel. "Authority, coercion are what is needed. Put your foot down good and hard; the only way to manage a wife. Take my word for it."

The Colonel was perhaps unaware that he had coerced his own wife into the grave. Mr. Pontellier had a vague suspicion of it which he thought it needless to mention at that late day.

Edna was not so consciously gratified at her husband's leaving home as she had been over the departure of her father. As the day approached when he was to leave her for a comparatively long stay, she grew melting and affectionate, remembering his many acts of consideration and his repeated expressions of an ardent attachment. She was solicitous about his health and his welfare. She bustled around, looking after his clothing, thinking about heavy underwear, quite as Madame Ratignolle would have done under similar circumstances. She cried when he went away, calling him her dear, good friend, and she was quite certain she would grow lonely before long and go to join him in New York.

But after all, a radiant peace settled upon her when she at last found herself alone. Even the children were gone. Old Madame Pontellier had come herself and carried them off to Iberville with their quadroon. The old madame did not venture to say she was afraid they would be neglected during Léonce's absence; she hardly ventured to think so. She was hungry for them—even a little fierce in her attachment. She did not want them to be wholly "children of the pavement," she always said when begging to have them for a space. She wished them to know the country, with its streams, its fields, its woods, its freedom, so delicious to the young. She wished them to taste something of the life their father had lived and known and loved when he, too, was a little child.

When Edna was at last alone, she breathed a big, genuine sigh of relief. A feeling that was unfamiliar but very delicious came over her. She walked all through the house, from one room to another, as if inspecting it for the first time. She tried the various chairs and lounges, as if she had never sat and reclined upon them before. And she perambulated around the outside of the house, investigating, looking to see if windows and shutters were secure and in order. The flowers were like new acquaintances; she approached them in a familiar spirit, and made herself at home among them. The garden walls were damp, and Edna called to the maid to bring out her rubber sandals. And there she stayed, and stooped, digging around the plants, trimming, picking dead, dry leaves. The children's little dog came out, interfering, getting in her way. She scolded him, laughed at him, played with him. The garden smelled so good and looked so pretty in the afternoon sunlight. Edna plucked all the bright flowers she could find, and went into the house with them, she and the little dog.

Even the kitchen assumed a sudden interesting character which she had never before perceived. She went in to give directions to the cook, to say that the butcher would have to bring much less meat, that they would require only half their usual quantity of bread, of milk and groceries. She told the cook that she herself would be greatly occupied during Mr. Pontellier's absence, and she begged her to take all thought and responsibility of the larder upon her own shoulders.

That night Edna dined alone. The candelabra, with a few candles in the center of the table, gave all the light she needed. Outside the circle of light in which she sat, the large dining-room looked solemn and shadowy. The cook, placed upon her mettle, served a delicious repast—a luscious tenderloin broiled *à point*.[42] The wine tasted good; the *marron glacé*[43] seemed to be just what she wanted. It was so pleasant, too, to dine in a comfortable *peignoir*.

She thought a little sentimentally about Léonce and the children, and wondered what they were doing. As she gave a dainty scrap or two to the doggie, she talked intimately to him about Etienne and Raoul. He was beside himself with astonishment and delight over these companionable advances. and showed his appreciation by his little quick, snappy barks and a lively agitation.

Then Edna sat in the library after dinner and read Emerson[44] until she grew sleepy. She realized that she had neglected her reading, and determined to start anew upon a course of improving studies, now that her time was completely her own to do with as she liked.

After a refreshing bath, Edna went to bed. And as she snuggled

---

[42]Medium rare.

[43]Candied chestnuts.

[44]American essayist of the Transcendentalist school; it would be appropriate if Edna were reading his famous essay "Self-Reliance."

comfortably beneath the eiderdown a sense of restfulness invaded her, such as she had not known before.

XXV

When the weather was dark and cloudy Edna could not work. She needed the sun to mellow and temper her mood to the sticking point. She had reached a stage when she seemed to be no longer feeling her way, working, when in the humor, with sureness and ease. And being devoid of ambition, and striving not toward accomplishment, she drew satisfaction from the work in itself.

On rainy or melancholy days Edna went out and sought the society of the friends she had made at Grand Isle. Or else she stayed indoors and nursed a mood with which she was becoming too familiar for her own comfort and peace of mind. It was not despair; but it seemed to her as if life were passing by, leaving its promise broken and unfulfilled. Yet there were other days when she listened, was led on and deceived by fresh promises which her youth held out to her.

She went again to the races, and again. Alcée Arobin and Mrs. Highcamp called for her one bright afternoon in Arobin's drag.[45] Mrs. Highcamp was a worldly but unaffected, intelligent, slim, tall blonde woman in the forties, with an indifferent manner and blue eyes that stared. She had a daughter who served her as a pretext for cultivating the society of young men of fashion. Alcée Arobin was one of them. He was a familiar figure at the race course, the opera, the fashionable clubs. There was a perpetual smile in his eyes, which seldom failed to awaken a corresponding cheerfulness in any one who looked into them and listened to his good-humored voice. His manner was quiet, and at times a little insolent. He possessed a good figure, a pleasing face, not overburdened with depth of thought or feeling; and his dress was that of the conventional man of fashion.

He admired Edna extravagantly, after meeting her at the races with her father. He had met her before on other occasions, but she had seemed to him unapproachable until that day. It was at his instigation that Mrs. Highcamp called to ask her to go with them to the Jockey Club to witness the turf event of the season.

There were possibly a few track men out there who knew the race

---

[45]Coach.

horse as well as Edna, but there was certainly none who knew it better. She sat between her two companions as one having authority to speak. She laughed at Arobin's pretensions, and deplored Mrs. Highcamp's ignorance. The race horse was a friend and intimate associate of her childhood. The atmosphere of the stables and the breath of the blue-grass paddock revived in her memory and lingered in her nostrils. She did not perceive that she was talking like her father as the sleek geld-ings ambled in review before them. She played for very high stakes, and fortune favored her. The fever of the game flamed in her cheeks and eyes, and it got into her blood and into her brain like an intoxicant. People turned their heads to look at her, and more than one lent an attentive ear to her utterances, hoping thereby to secure the elusive but ever-desired "tip." Arobin caught the contagion of excitement which drew him to Edna like a magnet. Mrs. Highcamp remained, as usual, unmoved, with her indifferent stare and uplifted eyebrows.

Edna stayed and dined with Mrs. Highcamp upon being urged to do so. Arobin also remained and sent away his drag.

The dinner was quiet and uninteresting, save for the cheerful efforts of Arobin to enliven things. Mrs. Highcamp deplored the absence of her daughter from the race, and tried to convey to her what she had missed by going to the "Dante reading" instead of joining them. The girl held a geranium leaf up to her nose and said nothing, but looked knowing and noncommittal. Mr. Highcamp was a plain, bald-headed man, who only talked under compulsion. He was unresponsive. Mrs. Highcamp was full of delicate courtesy and consideration toward her husband. She addressed most of her conversation to him at table. They sat in the library after dinner and read the evening papers together under the droplight; while the younger people went into the drawing-room near by and talked. Miss Highcamp played some selections from Grieg upon the piano. She seemed to have apprehended all of the composer's coldness and none of his poetry. While Edna listened she could not help wondering if she had lost her taste for music.

When the time came to go home, Mr. Highcamp grunted a lame offer to escort her, looking down at his slippered feet with tactless concern. It was Arobin who took her home. The car ride was long, and it was late when they reached Esplanade Street. Arobin asked permis-sion to enter for a second to light his cigarette—his match safe was empty. He filled his match safe, but did not light his cigarette until he left her, after she had expressed her willingness to go to the races with him again.

Edna was neither tired nor sleepy. She was hungry again, for the

Highcamp dinner, though of excellent quality, had lacked abundance. She rummaged in the larder and brought forth a slice of Gruyère and some crackers. She opened a bottle of beer which she found in the icebox. Edna felt extremely restless and excited. She vacantly hummed a fantastic tune as she poked at the wood embers on the hearth and munched a cracker.

She wanted something to happen—something, anything; she did not know what. She regretted that she had not made Arobin stay a half hour to talk over the horses with her. She counted the money she had won. But there was nothing else to do, so she went to bed, and tossed there for hours in a sort of monotonous agitation.

In the middle of the night she remembered that she had forgotten to write her regular letter to her husband; and she decided to do so next day and tell him about her afternoon at the Jockey Club. She lay wide awake composing a letter which was nothing like the one which she wrote next day. When the maid awoke her in the morning Edna was dreaming of Mr. Highcamp playing the piano at the entrance of a music store on Canal Street, while his wife was saying to Alcée Arobin, as they boarded an Esplanade Street car:

"What a pity that so much talent has been neglected! but I must go."

When, a few days later, Alcée Arobin called for Edna in his drag, Mrs. Highcamp was not with him. He said they would pick her up. But as that lady had not been apprised of his intention of picking her up, she was not at home. The daughter was just leaving the house to attend the meeting of a branch Folk Lore Society, and regretted that she could not accompany them. Arobin appeared nonplused, and asked Edna if there were any one else she cared to ask.

She did not deem it worth while to go in search of any of the fashionable acquaintances from whom she had withdrawn herself. She thought of Madame Ratignolle, but knew that her fair friend did not leave the house, except to take a languid walk around the block with her husband after nightfall. Mademoiselle Reisz would have laughed at such a request from Edna. Madame Lebrun might have enjoyed the outing, but for some reason Edna did not want her. So they went alone, she and Arobin.

The afternoon was intensely interesting to her. The excitement came back upon her like a remittent fever. Her talk grew familiar and confidential. It was no labor to become intimate with Arobin. His manner invited easy confidence. The preliminary stage of becoming acquainted was one which he always endeavored to ignore when a pretty and engaging woman was concerned.

He stayed and dined with Edna. He stayed and sat beside the wood fire. They laughed and talked; and before it was time to go he was telling her how different life might have been if he had known her years before. With ingenuous frankness he spoke of what a wicked, ill-disciplined boy he had been, and impulsively drew up his cuff to exhibit upon his wrist the scar from a saber cut which he had received in a duel outside of Paris when he was nineteen. She touched his hand as she scanned the red cicatrice on the inside of his white wrist. A quick impulse that was somewhat spasmodic impelled her fingers to close in a sort of clutch upon his hand. He felt the pressure of her pointed nails in the flesh of his palm.

She arose hastily and walked toward the mantel.

"The sight of a wound or scar always agitates and sickens me," she said. "I shouldn't have looked at it."

"I beg your pardon," he entreated, following her; "it never occurred to me that it might be repulsive."

He stood close to her, and the effrontery in his eyes repelled the old, vanishing self in her, yet drew all her awakening sensuousness. He saw enough in her face to impel him to take her hand and hold while he said his lingering good night.

"Will you go to the races again?" he asked.

"No," she said. "I've had enough of the races. I don't want to lose all the money I've won, and I've got to work when the weather is bright, instead of—"

"Yes; work; to be sure. You promised to show me your work. What morning may I come up to your atelier? To-morrow?"

"No!"

"Day after?"

"No, no."

"Oh, please don't refuse me! I know something of such things. I might help you with a stray suggestion or two."

"No. Good night. Why don't you go after you have said good night? I don't like you," she went on in a high, excited pitch, attempting to draw away her hand. She felt that her words lacked dignity and sincerity, and she knew that he felt it.

"I'm sorry you don't like me. I'm sorry I offended you. How have I offended you? What have I done? Can't you forgive me?" And he bent and pressed his lips upon her hand as if he wished never more to withdraw them.

"Mr. Arobin," she complained, "I'm greatly upset by the excitement of the afternoon; I'm not myself. My manner must have misled you in some way. I wish you to go, please." She spoke in a monotonous, dull tone. He took his hat from the table, and stood with eyes turned from her, looking into the dying fire. For a moment or two he kept an impressive silence.

"Your manner has not misled me, Mrs. Pontellier," he said finally. "My own emotions have done that. I couldn't help it. When I'm near you, how could I help it? Don't think anything of it, don't bother, please. You see, I go when you command me. If you wish me to stay away, I shall do so. If you let me come back, I—oh! you will let me come back?"

He cast one appealing glance at her, to which she made no response. Alcée Arobin's manner was so genuine that it often deceived even himself.

Edna did not care or think whether it were genuine or not. When she was alone she looked mechanically at the back of her hand which he had kissed so warmly. Then she leaned her head down on the mantel-piece. She felt somewhat like a woman who in a moment of passion is betrayed into an act of infidelity, and realizes the significance of the act without being wholly awakened from its glamour. The thought was passing vaguely through her mind, "What would he think?"

She did not mean her husband; she was thinking of Robert Lebrun. Her husband seemed to her now like a person whom she had married without love as an excuse.

She lit a candle and went up to her room. Alcée Arobin was absolutely nothing to her. Yet his presence, his manners, the warmth of his glances, and above all the touch of his lips upon her hand had acted like a narcotic upon her.

She slept a languorous sleep, interwoven with vanishing dreams.

XXVI

Alcée Arobin wrote Edna an elaborate note of apology, palpitant with sincerity. It embarrassed her; for in a cooler, quieter moment it appeared to her absurd that she should have taken his action so seriously, so dramatically. She felt sure that the significance of the whole occurrence had lain in her own self-consciousness. If she ignored his note it would give undue importance to a trivial affair. If she replied to it in a serious spirit it would still leave in his mind the impression that she had in a susceptible moment yielded to his influence. After all, it was no great matter to have one's hand kissed. She was provoked at his having written the apology. She answered in as light and bantering a spirit as she fancied it deserved, and said she would be glad to have him look in upon her at work whenever he felt the inclination and his business gave him the opportunity.

He responded at once by presenting himself at her home with all his disarming naïveté. And then there was scarcely a day which followed that she did not see him or was not reminded of him. He was prolific in pretexts. His attitude became one of good-natured subservience and tacit adoration. He was ready at all times to submit to her moods, which were as often kind as they were cold. She grew accustomed to him. They became intimate and friendly by imperceptible degrees, and then by leaps. He sometimes talked in a way that astonished her at first and brought the crimson into her face; in a way that pleased her at last, appealing to the animalism that stirred impatiently within her.

There was nothing which so quieted the turmoil of Edna's senses as a visit to Mademoiselle Reisz. It was then, in the presence of that personality which was offensive to her, that the woman, by her divine art, seemed to reach Edna's spirit and set it free.

It was misty, with heavy, lowering atmosphere, one afternoon, when Edna climbed the stairs to the pianist's apartments under the roof. Her clothes were dripping with moisture. She felt chilled and pinched as she entered the room. Mademoiselle was poking at a rusty stove that smoked a little and warmed the room indifferently. She was endeavoring to heat a pot of chocolate on the stove. The room looked cheerless and dingy to Edna as she entered. A bust of Beethoven, covered with a hood of dust, scowled at her from the mantelpiece.

"Ah! here comes the sunlight!" exclaimed Mademoiselle, rising from her knees before the stove. "Now it will be warm and bright enough; I can let the fire alone."

She closed the stove door with a bang, and approaching, assisted in removing Edna's dripping mackintosh.

"You are cold; you look miserable. The chocolate will soon be hot. But would you rather have a taste of brandy? I have scarcely touched the bottle which you brought me for my cold." A piece of red flannel was wrapped around Mademoiselle's throat; a stiff neck compelled her to hold her head on one side.

"I will take some brandy," said Edna, shivering as she removed her gloves and overshoes. She drank the liquor from the glass as a man would have done. Then flinging herself upon the uncomfortable sofa she said, "Mademoiselle, I am going to move away from my house on Esplanade Street."

"Ah!" ejaculated the musician, neither surprised nor especially interested. Nothing ever seemed to astonish her very much. She was endeavoring to adjust the bunch of violets which had become loose from its fastening in her hair. Edna drew her down upon the sofa, and taking a pin from her own hair, secured the shabby artificial flowers in their accustomed place.

"Aren't you astonished?"

"Passably. Where are you going? to New York? to Iberville? to your father in Mississippi? where?"

"Just two steps away," laughed Edna, "in a little four-room house around the corner. It looks so cozy, so inviting and restful, whenever I pass by; and it's for rent. I'm tired looking after that big house. It never seemed like mine, anyway—like home. It's too much trouble. I have to keep too many servants. I am tired bothering with them."

"That is not your true reason, *ma belle*. There is no use in telling me lies. I don't know your reason, but you have not told me the truth."

Edna did not protest or endeavor to justify herself.

"The house, the money that provides for it, are not mine. Isn't that enough reason?"

"They are your husband's," returned Mademoiselle, with a shrug and a malicious elevation of the eyebrows.

"Oh! I see there is no deceiving you. Then let me tell you: It is a caprice. I have a little money of my own from my mother's estate, which my father sends me by driblets. I won a large sum this winter on the races, and I am beginning to sell my sketches. Laidpore is more and more pleased with my work; he says it grows in force and individuality. I cannot judge of that myself, but I feel that I have gained in ease and confidence. However, as I said, I have sold a good many through Laidpore. I can live in the tiny house for little or nothing, with one servant. Old Celestine, who works occasionally for me, says she will come stay with me and do my work. I know I shall like it, like the feeling of freedom and independence."

"What does your husband say?"

"I have not told him yet. I only thought of it this morning. He will think I am demented, no doubt. Perhaps you think so."

Mademoiselle shook her head slowly. "Your reason is not yet clear to me," she said.

Neither was it quite clear to Edna herself; but it unfolded itself as she sat for a while in silence. Instinct had prompted her to put away her husband's bounty in casting off her allegiance. She did not know how it would be when he returned. There would have to be an understanding, an explanation. Conditions would in some way adjust themselves, she felt; but whatever came, she had resolved never again to belong to another than herself.

"I shall give a grand dinner before I leave the old house!" Edna exclaimed. "You will have to come to it, Mademoiselle. I will give you everything that you like to eat and drink. We shall sing and laugh and be merry for once." And she uttered a sigh that came from the very depths of her being.

If Mademoiselle happened to have received a letter from Robert during the interval of Edna's visits, she would give her the letter unsolicited. And she would seat herself at the piano and play as her humor prompted her while the young woman read the letter.

The little stove was roaring; it was red-hot, and the chocolate in the tin sizzled and sputtered. Edna went forward and opened the stove door, and Mademoiselle rising, took a letter from under the bust of Beethoven and handed it to Edna.

"Another! so soon!" she exclaimed, her eyes filled with delight. "Tell me, Mademoiselle, does he know that I see his letters?"

"Never in the world! He would be angry and would never write to me again if he thought so. Does he write to you? Never a line. Does he send you a message? Never a word. It is because he loves you, poor fool, and is trying to forget you, since you are not free to listen to him or to belong to him."

"Why do you show me his letters, then?"

"Haven't you begged for them? Can I refuse you anything? Oh! you cannot deceive me," and Mademoiselle approached her beloved instrument and began to play. Edna did not at once read the letter. She sat holding it in her hand, while the music penetrated her whole being like an effulgence, warming and brightening the dark places of her soul. It prepared her for joy and exultation.

"Oh!" she exclaimed, letting the letter fall to the floor. "Why did you not tell me?" She went and grasped Mademoiselle's hands up from the keys. "Oh! unkind! malicious! Why did you not tell me?"

"That he was coming back? No great news, *ma foi*. I wonder he did not come long ago."

"But when, when?" cried Edna, impatiently. "He does not say when."

"He says 'very soon.' You know as much about it as I do; it is all in the letter."

"But why? Why is he coming? Oh, if I thought—" and she snatched the letter from the floor and turned the pages this way and that way, looking for the reason, which was left untold.

"If I were young and in love with a man," said Mademoiselle, turning on the stool and pressing her wiry hands between her knees as she looked down at Edna, who sat on the floor holding the letter, "it seems to me he would have to be some *grand esprit*[46]; a man with the lofty aims and ability to reach them; one who stood high enough to attract the notice of his fellow-men. It seems to me if I were young and in love I should never deem a man of ordinary caliber worthy of my devotion."

"Now it is you who are telling lies and seeking to deceive me, Mademoiselle; or else you have never been in love, and know nothing about it. Why," went on Edna, clasping her knees and looking up into Mademoiselle's twisted face, "do you suppose a woman knows why she loves? Does she select? Does she say to herself: 'Go to! Here is a distinguished statesman with presidential possibilities; I shall proceed to fall in love with him.' Or, 'I shall set my heart upon this musician, whose fame is on every tongue?' Or, 'This financier, who controls the world's money markets?' "

"You are purposely misunderstanding me, *ma reine*.[47] Are you in love with Robert?"

"Yes," said Edna. It was the first time she had admitted it, and a glow overspread her face, blotching it with red spots.

"Why?" asked her companion. "Why do you love him when you ought not to?"

Edna, with a motion or two, dragged herself on her knees before Mademoiselle Reisz, who took the glowing face between her two hands.

"Why? Because his hair is brown and grows away from his temples; because he opens and shuts his eyes, and his nose is a little out of drawing; because he has two lips and a square chin, and a little finger which he can't straighten from having played baseball too energetically in his youth. Because—"

"Because you do, in short," laughed Mademoiselle. "What will you do when he comes back?" she asked.

"Do? Nothing, except feel glad and happy to be alive."

She was already glad and happy to be alive at the mere thought of

---

[46]Great intellect.
[47]My queen.

his return. The murky, lowering sky, which had depressed her a few hours before, seemed bracing and invigorating as she splashed through the streets on her way home.

She stopped at a confectioner's and ordered a huge box of bonbons for the children in Iberville. She slipped a card in the box, on which she scribbled a tender message and sent an abundance of kisses.

Before dinner in the evening Edna wrote a charming letter to her husband, telling him of her intention to move for a while into the little house around the block, and to give a farewell dinner before leaving, regretting that he was not there to share it, to help her out with the menu and assist her in entertaining the guests. Her letter was brilliant and brimming with cheerfulness.

XXVII

"What is the matter with you?" asked Arobin that evening. "I never found you in such a happy mood." Edna was tired by that time, and was reclining on the lounge before the fire.

"Don't you know the weather prophet has told us we shall see the sun pretty soon?"

"Well, that ought to be reason enough," he acquiesced. "You wouldn't give me another if I sat here all night imploring you." He sat close to her on a low tabouret, and as he spoke his fingers lightly touched the hair that fell a little over her forehead. She liked the touch of his fingers through her hair, and closed her eyes sensitively.

"One of these days," she said, "I'm going to pull myself together for a while and think—try to determine what character of a woman I am; for, candidly, I don't know. By all the codes which I am acquainted with, I am a devilishly wicked specimen of the sex. But some way I can't convince myself that I am. I must think about it."

"Don't. What's the use? Why should you bother thinking about it when I can tell you what manner of woman you are." His fingers strayed occasionally down to her warm, smooth cheeks and firm chin, which was growing a little full and double.

"Oh, yes! You will tell me that I am adorable; everything that is captivating. Spare yourself the effort."

"No; I shan't tell you anything of the sort, though I shouldn't be lying if I did."

"Do you know Mademoiselle Reisz?" she asked irrelevantly.

"The pianist? I know her by sight. I've heard her play."

"She says queer things sometimes in a bantering way that you don't notice at the time and you find yourself thinking about afterward."

"For instance?"

"Well, for instance, when I left her to-day, she put her arms around me and felt my shoulder blades, to see if my wings were strong, she said. 'The bird that would soar above the level plain of tradition and prejudice must have strong wings. It is a sad spectacle to see the weaklings bruised, exhausted, fluttering back to earth.'"

"Whither would you soar?"

"I'm not thinking of any extraordinary flights. I only half comprehend her."

"I've heard she's partially demented," said Arobin.

"She seems to me wonderfully sane," Edna replied.

"I'm told she's extremely disagreeable and unpleasant. Why have you introduced her at a moment when I desired to talk of you?"

"Oh! talk of me if you like," cried Edna, clasping her hands beneath her head; "but let me think of something else while you do."

"I'm jealous of your thoughts to-night. They're making you a little kinder than usual; but some way I feel as if they were wandering, as if they were not here with me." She only looked at him and smiled. His eyes were very near. He leaned upon the lounge with an arm extended across her, while the other hand still rested upon her hair. They continued silently to look into each other's eyes. When he leaned forward and kissed her, she clasped his head, holding his lips to hers.

It was the first kiss of her life to which her nature had really responded. It was a flaming torch that kindled desire.

XXVIII

Edna cried a little that night after Arobin left her. It was only one phase of the multitudinous emotions which had assailed her. There was with her an overwhelming feeling of irresponsibility. There was the shock of the unexpected and the unaccustomed. There was her husband's reproach looking at her from the external things around her which he had provided for her external existence. There was Robert's reproach making itself felt by a quicker, fiercer, more overpowering love, which had awakened within her toward him. Above all, there was understanding. She felt as if a mist had been lifted from her eyes, enabling her to look upon and comprehend the significance of life, that monster made up of beauty and brutality. But among the conflicting sensations which assailed her, there was neither shame nor remorse. There was a dull pang of regret because it was not the kiss of love which had inflamed her, because it was not love which had held this cup of life to her lips.

XXIX

Without even waiting for an answer from her husband regarding his opinion or wishes in the matter, Edna hastened her preparations for quitting her home on Esplanade Street and moving into the little house around the block. A feverish anxiety attended her every action in that direction. There was no moment of deliberation, no interval of repose between the thought and its fulfillment. Early upon the morning following those hours passed in Arobin's society, Edna set about securing her new abode and hurrying her arrangements for occupying it. Within the precincts of her home she felt like one who has entered and lingered within the portals of some forbidden temple in which a thousand muffled voices bade her begone.

Whatever was her own in the house, everything which she had acquired aside from her husband's bounty, she caused to be transported to the other house, supplying simple and meager deficiencies from her own resources.

Arobin found her with rolled sleeves, working in company with the house-maid when he looked in during the afternoon. She was splendid and robust, and had never appeared handsomer than in the old blue gown, with a red silk handkerchief knotted at random around her head to protect her hair from the dust. She was mounted upon a high stepladder, unhooking a picture from the wall when he entered. He had found the front door open, and had followed his ring by walking in unceremoniously.

"Come down!" he said. "Do you want to kill yourself?" She greeted him with affected carelessness, and appeared absorbed in her occupation.

If he had expected to find her languishing, reproachful, or indulging in sentimental tears, he must have been greatly surprised.

He was no doubt prepared for any emergency, ready for any one of the foregoing attitudes, just as he bent himself easily and naturally to the situation which confronted him.

"Please come down," he insisted, holding the ladder and looking up at her.

"No," she answered; "Ellen is afraid to mount the ladder. Joe is working over at the 'pigeon house'—that's the name Ellen gives it, because it's so small and looks like a pigeon house—and some one has to do this."

Arobin pulled off his coat, and expressed himself ready and willing to tempt fate in her place. Ellen brought him one of her dust-caps, and went into contortions of mirth, which she found it impossible to control, when she saw him put it on before the mirror as grotesquely as he could. Edna herself could not refrain from smiling when she fastened it at his request. So it was he who in turn mounted the ladder, unhooking pictures and curtains, and dislodging ornaments as Edna directed. When he had finished he took off his dust-cap and went out to wash his hands.

Edna was sitting on the tabouret, idly brushing the tips of a feather duster along the carpet when he came in again.

"Is there anything more you will let me do?" he asked.

"That is all," she answered. "Ellen can manage the rest." She kept the young woman occupied in the drawing-room, unwilling to be left alone with Arobin.

"What about the dinner?" he asked; "the grand event, the *coup d'état?*"[48]

"It will be the day after to-morrow. Why do you call it the '*coup d'état?*' Oh! it will be very fine; all my best of everything—crystal, silver and gold, Sèvres, flowers, music, and champagne to swim in. I'll let Léonce pay the bills. I wonder what he'll say when he sees the bills."

"And you ask me why I call it a *coup d'état?*" Arobin had put on his coat, and he stood before her and asked her if his cravat was plumb. She told him it was, looking no higher than the tip of his collar.

"When do you go to the 'pigeon house'—with all due acknowledgment to Ellen."

"Day after to-morrow, after the dinner. I shall sleep there."

"Ellen, will you very kindly get me a glass of water?" asked Arobin. "The dust in the curtains, if you will pardon me for hinting such a thing, has parched my throat to a crisp."

"While Ellen gets the water," said Edna, rising, "I will say good-by and let you go. I must get rid of this grime, and I have a million things to do and think of."

"When shall I see you?" asked Arobin, seeking to detain her, the maid having left the room.

---

[48]Sudden, violent change of government.

"At the dinner, of course. You are invited."

"Not before?—not to-night or to-morrow morning or to-morrow noon or night? or the day after morning or noon? Can't you see yourself, without my telling you, what an eternity it is?"

He had followed her into the hall and to the foot of the stairway, looking up at her as she mounted with her face half turned to him.

"Not an instant sooner," she said. But she laughed and looked at him with eyes that at once gave him courage to wait and made it torture to wait.

XXX

Though Edna had spoken of the dinner as a very grand affair, it was in truth a very small affair and very select, in so much as the guests invited were few and were selected with discrimination. She had counted upon an even dozen seating themselves at her round mahogany board, forgetting for the moment that Madame Ratignolle was to the last degree *souffrante*[49] and unpresentable, and not foreseeing that Madame Lebrun would send a thousand regrets at the last moment. So there were only ten, after all, which made a cozy, comfortable number.

There were Mr. and Mrs. Merriman, a pretty, vivacious little woman in the thirties; her husband, a jovial fellow, something of a shallowpate, who laughed a good deal at other people's witticisms, and had thereby made himself extremely popular. Mrs. Highcamp had accompanied them. Of course, there was Alcée Arobin; and Mademoiselle Reisz had consented to come. Edna had sent her a fresh bunch of violets with black lace trimmings for her hair. Monsieur Ratignolle brought himself and his wife's excuses. Victor Lebrun, who happened to be in the city, bent upon relaxation, had accepted with alacrity. There was a Miss Mayblunt, no longer in her teens, who looked at the world through lorgnettes and with the keenest interest. It was thought and said that she was intellectual; it was suspected of her that she wrote under a *nom de guerre*.[50] She had come with a gentleman by the name of Gouvernail, connected with one of the daily papers, of whom nothing special could be said, except that he was observant and seemed quiet and inoffensive. Edna herself made the tenth, and at half-past

---

[49]Ill.

[50]Pseudonym.

eight they seated themselves at table, Arobin and Monsieur Ratignolle on either side of their hostess.

Mrs. Highcamp sat between Arobin and Victor Lebrun. Then came Mrs. Merriman, Mr. Gouvernail, Miss Mayblunt, Mr. Merriman, and Mademoiselle Reisz next to Monsieur Ratignolle.

There was something extremely gorgeous about the appearance of the table, an effect of splendor conveyed by a cover of pale yellow satin under strips of lace-work. There were wax candles in massive brass candelabra, burning softly under yellow silk shades; full, fragrant roses, yellow and red, abounded. There were silver and gold, as she had said there would be, and crystal which glittered like the gems which the women wore.

The ordinary stiff dining chairs had been discarded for the occasion and replaced by the most commodious and luxurious which could be collected throughout the house. Mademoiselle Reisz, being exceedingly diminutive, was elevated upon cushions, as small children are sometimes hoisted at table upon bulky volumes.

"Something new, Edna?" exclaimed Miss Mayblunt, with lorgnette directed toward a magnificent cluster of diamonds that sparkled, that almost sputtered, in Edna's hair, just over the center of her forehead.

"Quite new; 'brand' new, in fact; a present from my husband. It arrived this morning from New York. I may as well admit that this is my birthday, and that I am twenty-nine. In good time I expect you to drink my health. Meanwhile, I shall ask you to begin with this cocktail, composed—would you say 'composed?' " with an appeal to Miss Mayblunt—"composed by my father in honor of Sister Janet's wedding."

Before each guest stood a tiny glass that looked and sparkled like a garnet gem.

"Then, all things considered," spoke Arobin, "it might not be amiss to start out by drinking the Colonel's health in the cocktail which he composed, on the birthday of the most charming of women—the daughter whom he invented."

Mr. Merriman's laugh at this sally was such a genuine outburst and so contagious that it started the dinner with an agreeable swing that never slackened.

Miss Mayblunt begged to be allowed to keep her cocktail untouched before her, just to look at. The color was marvelous! She could compare it to nothing she had ever seen, and the garnet lights which it emitted were unspeakably rare. She pronounced the Colonel an artist, and stuck to it.

Monsieur Ratignolle was prepared to take things seriously: the *mets,* the *entre-mets,*[51] the service, the decorations, even the people. He looked up from his pompano and inquired of Arobin if he were related to the gentleman of that name who formed one of the firm of Laitner and Arobin, lawyers. The young man admitted that Laitner was a warm personal friend, who permitted Arobin's name to decorate the firm's letterheads and to appear upon a shingle that graced Perdido Street.

"There are so many inquisitive people and institutions abounding," said Arobin, "that one is really forced as a matter of convenience these days to assume the virtue of an occupation if he has it not."

Monsieur Ratignolle stared a little, and turned to ask Mademoiselle Reisz if she considered the symphony concerts up to the standard which had been set the previous winter. Mademoiselle Reisz answered Monsieur Ratignolle in French, which Edna thought a little rude under the circumstances, but characteristic. Mademoiselle had only disagreeable things to say of the symphony concerts, and insulting remarks to make of all the musicians of New Orleans, singly and collectively. All her interest seemed to be centered upon the delicacies placed before her.

Mr. Merriman said that Mr. Arobin's remark about inquisitive people reminded him of a man from Waco the other day at the St. Charles Hotel—but as Mr. Merriman's stories were always lame and lacking point, his wife seldom permitted him to complete them. She interrupted him to ask if he remembered the name of the author whose book she had bought the week before to send to a friend in Geneva. She was talking "books" with Mr. Gouvernail and trying to draw from him his opinion upon current literary topics. Her husband told the story of the Waco man privately to Miss Mayblunt, who pretended to be greatly amused and to think it extremely clever.

Mrs. Highcamp hung with languid but unaffected interest upon the warm and impetuous volubility of her left-hand neighbor, Victor Lebrun. Her attention was never for a moment withdrawn after seating herself at table; and when he turned to Mrs. Merriman, who was prettier and more vivacious than Mrs. Highcamp, she waited with easy indifference for an opportunity to reclaim his attention. There was the occasional sound of music, of mandolins, sufficiently removed to be an agreeable accompaniment rather than an interruption to the conversation. Outside the soft, monotonous splash of a fountain could be heard;

---

[51]Principal and subordinate courses.

the sound penetrated into the room with the heavy odor of jessamine that came through the open windows.

The golden shimmer of Edna's satin gown spread in rich folds on either side of her. There was a soft fall of lace encircling her shoulders. It was the color of her skin, without the glow, the myriad living tints that one may sometimes discover in vibrant flesh. There was something in her attitude, in her whole appearance when she leaned her head against the high-backed chair and spread her arms, which suggested the regal woman, the one who rules, who looks on, who stands alone.

But as she sat there among her guests, she felt the old ennui overtaking her; the hopelessness which so often assailed her, which came upon her like an obsession, like something extraneous, independent of volition. It was something which announced itself; a chill breath that seemed to issue from some vast cavern wherein discords wailed. There came over her the acute longing which always summoned into her spiritual vision the presence of the beloved one, overpowering her at once with a sense of the unattainable.

The moments glided on, while a feeling of good fellowship passed around the circle like a mystic cord, holding and binding these people together with jest and laughter. Monsieur Ratignolle was the first to break the pleasant charm. At ten o'clock he excused himself. Madame Ratignolle was waiting for him at home. She was *bien souffrante*, and she was filled with vague dread, which only her husband's presence could allay.

Mademoiselle Reisz arose with Monsieur Ratignolle, who offered to escort her to the car. She had eaten well; she had tasted the good, rich wines, and they must have turned her head, for she bowed pleasantly to all as she withdrew from table. She kissed Edna upon the shoulder, and whispered: "*Bonne nuit, ma reine; soyez sage.*"[52] She had been a little bewildered upon rising, or rather, descending from her cushions, and Monsieur Ratignolle gallantly took her arm and led her away.

Mrs. Highcamp was weaving a garland of roses, yellow and red. When she had finished the garland, she laid it lightly upon Victor's black curls. He was reclining far back in the luxurious chair, holding a glass of champagne to the light.

As if a magician's wand had touched him, the garland of roses transformed him into a vision of Oriental beauty. His cheeks were the color

---

[52]Good night, my queen; be careful.

of crushed grapes, and his dusky eyes glowed with a languishing fire.

"*Sapristi!*" exclaimed Arobin.

But Mrs. Highcamp had one more touch to add to the picture. She took from the back of her chair a white silken scarf, with which she had covered her shoulders in the early part of the evening. She draped it across the boy in graceful folds, and in a way to conceal his black, conventional evening dress. He did not seem to mind what she did to him, only smiled, showing a faint gleam of white teeth, while he continued to gaze with narrowing eyes at the light through his glass of champagne.

"Oh! to be able to paint in color rather than with words!" exclaimed Miss Mayblunt, losing herself in a rhapsodic dream as she looked at him.

" 'There was a graven image of Desire
Painted with red blood on a ground of gold.' "[53]

murmured Gouvernail, under his breath.

The effect of the wine upon Victor was to change his accustomed volubility into silence. He seemed to have abandoned himself to a reverie, and to be seeing pleasing visions in the amber bead.

"Sing," entreated Mrs. Highcamp. "Won't you sing to us?"

"Let him alone," said Arobin.

"He's posing," offered Mr. Merriman; "let him have it out."

"I believe he's paralyzed," laughed Mrs. Merriman. And leaning over the youth's chair, she took the glass from his hand and held it to his lips. He sipped the wine slowly, and when he had drained the glass she laid it upon the table and wiped his lips with her little filmy handkerchief.

"Yes, I'll sing for you," he said, turning in his chair toward Mrs. Highcamp. He clasped his hands behind his head, and looking up at the ceiling began to hum a little, trying his voice like a musician tuning an instrument. Then, looking at Edna, he began to sing:

"Ah! si tu savais!"

"Stop!" she cried, "don't sing that. I don't want you to sing it," and she laid her glass so impetuously and blindly upon the table as to

---

[53]Opening lines of "A Cameo," a sonnet by Algernon Charles Swinburne.

shatter it against a carafe. The wine spilled over Arobin's legs and some of it trickled down upon Mrs. Highcamp's black gauze gown. Victor had lost all idea of courtesy, or else he thought his hostess was not in earnest, for he laughed and went on:

"Ah! si tu savais
Ce que tes yeux me disent"—[54]

"Oh! you mustn't! you mustn't," exclaimed Edna, and pushing back her chair she got up, and going behind him placed her hand over his mouth. He kissed the soft palm that pressed upon his lips.

"No, no, I won't, Mrs. Pontellier. I didn't know you meant it," looking up at her with caressing eyes. The touch of his lips was like a pleasing sting to her hand. She lifted the garland of roses from his head and flung it across the room.

"Come, Victor; you've posed long enough. Give Mrs. Highcamp her scarf."

Mrs. Highcamp undraped the scarf from about him with her own hands. Miss Mayblunt and Mr. Gouvernail suddenly conceived the notion that it was time to say good night. And Mr. and Mrs. Merriman wondered how it could be so late.

Before parting from Victor, Mrs. Highcamp invited him to call upon her daughter, who she knew would be charmed to meet him and talk French and sing French songs with him. Victor expressed his desire and intention to call upon Miss Highcamp at the first opportunity which presented itself. He asked if Arobin were going his way. Arobin was not.

The mandolin players had long since stolen away. A profound stillness had fallen upon the broad, beautiful street. The voices of Edna's disbanding guests jarred like a discordant note upon the quiet harmony of the night.

XXXI

"Well?" questioned Arobin, who had remained with Edna after the others had departed.

---

[54]If only you knew/ What your eyes are telling me.

"Well," she reiterated, and stood up, stretching her arms, and feeling the need to relax her muscles after having been so long seated.

"What next?" he asked.

"The servants are all gone. They left when the musicians did. I have dismissed them. The house has to be closed and locked, and I shall trot around to the pigeon house, and shall send Celestine over in the morning to straighten things up."

He looked around, and began to turn out some of the lights.

"What about upstairs?" he inquired.

"I think it is all right; but there may be a window or two unlatched. We had better look; you might take a candle and see. And bring me my wrap and hat on the foot of the bed in the middle room."

He went up with the light, and Edna began closing doors and windows. She hated to shut in the smoke and the fumes of the wine. Arobin found her cape and hat, which he brought down and helped her to put on.

When everything was secured and the lights put out, they left through the front door, Arobin locking it and taking the key, which he carried for Edna. He helped her down the steps.

"Will you have a spray of jessamine?" he asked, breaking off a few blossoms as he passed.

"No; I don't want anything."

She seemed disheartened, and had nothing to say. She took his arm, which he offered her, holding up the weight of her satin train with the other hand. She looked down, noticing the black line of his leg moving in and out so close to her against the yellow shimmer of her gown. There was the whistle of a railway train somewhere in the distance, and the midnight bells were ringing. They met no one in their short walk.

The "pigeon-house" stood behind a locked gate, and a shallow *parterre*[55] that had been somewhat neglected. There was a small porch, upon which a long window and the front door opened. The door opened directly into the parlor; there was no side entry. Back in the yard was a room for servants, in which old Celestine had been ensconced.

Edna had left a lamp burning low upon the table. She had succeeded in making the room look habitable and homelike. There were some

---

[55]Lawn.

books on the table and a lounge near at hand. On the floor was a fresh matting, covered with a rug or two; and on the walls hung a few tasteful pictures. But the room was filled with flowers. These were a surprise to her. Arobin had sent them, and had had Celestine distribute them during Edna's absence. Her bedroom was adjoining, and across a small passage were the dining-room and kitchen.

Edna seated herself with every appearance of discomfort.

"Are you tired?" he asked.

"Yes, and chilled, and miserable. I feel as if I had been wound up to a certain pitch—too tight—and something inside of me had snapped." She rested her head against the table upon her bare arm.

"You want to rest," he said, "and to be quiet. I'll go; I'll leave you and let you rest."

"Yes," she replied.

He stood up beside her and smoothed her hair with his soft, magnetic hand. His touch conveyed to her a certain physical comfort. She could have fallen quietly asleep there if he had continued to pass his hand over her hair. He brushed the hair upward from the nape of her neck.

"I hope you will feel happier and better in the morning," he said. "You have tried to do too much in the past few days. The dinner was the last straw; you might have dispensed with it."

"Yes," she admitted; "it was stupid."

"No, it was delightful; but it has worn you out." His hand had strayed to her beautiful shoulders, and he could feel the response of her flesh to his touch. He seated himself beside her and kissed her lightly upon the shoulder.

"I thought you were going away," she said, in an uneven voice.

"I am, after I have said good night."

"Good night," she murmured.

He did not answer, except to continue to caress her. He did not say good night until she had become supple to his gentle, seductive entreaties.

XXXII

When Mr. Pontellier learned of his wife's intention to abandon her home and take up her residence elsewhere, he immediately wrote her a letter of unqualified disapproval and remonstrance. She had given reasons which he was unwilling to acknowledge as adequate. He hoped she had not acted upon her rash impulse; and he begged her to consider first, foremost, and above all else, what people would say. He was not dreaming of scandal when he uttered this warning; that was a thing which would never have entered into his mind to consider in connection with his wife's name or his own. He was simply thinking of his financial integrity. It might get noised about that the Pontelliers had met with reverses, and were forced to conduct their *ménage*[56] on a humbler scale than heretofore. It might do incalculable mischief to his business prospects.

But remembering Edna's whimsical turn of late, and foreseeing that she had immediately acted upon her impetuous determination, he grasped the situation with his usual promptness and handled it with his well-known business tact and cleverness.

The same mail which brought to Edna his letter of disapproval carried instructions—the most minute instructions—to a well-known architect concerning the remodeling of his home, changes which he had long contemplated, and which he desired carried forward during his temporary absence.

Expert and reliable packers and movers were engaged to convey the furniture, carpets, pictures—everything movable, in short—to places of security. And in an incredibly short time the Pontellier house was turned over to the artisans. There was to be an addition—a small snuggery; there was to be frescoing, and hardwood flooring was to be put into such rooms as had not yet been subjected to this improvement.

Furthermore, in one of the daily papers appeared a brief notice to the effect that Mr. and Mrs. Pontellier were contemplating a summer sojourn abroad, and that their handsome residence on Esplanade Street was undergoing sumptuous alterations, and would not be ready for occupancy until their return. Mr. Pontellier had saved appearances!

Edna admired the skill of his maneuver, and avoided any occasion to balk his intentions. When the situation as set forth by Mr. Pontellier was accepted and taken for granted, she was apparently satisfied that it should be so.

The pigeon-house pleased her. It at once assumed the intimate character of a home, while she herself invested it with a charm which it reflected like a warm glow. There was with her a feeling of having descended in the social scale, with a corresponding sense of having risen in the spiritual. Every step which she took toward relieving her-

[56]Household.

self from obligations added to her strength and expansion as an individual. She began to look with her own eyes; to see and to apprehend the deeper undercurrents of life. No longer was she content to "feed upon opinion" when her own soul had invited her.

After a little while, a few days, in fact, Edna went up and spent a week with her children in Iberville. They were delicious February days, with all the summer's promise hovering in the air.

How glad she was to see the children! She wept for very pleasure when she felt their little arms clasping her; their hard, ruddy cheeks pressed against her own glowing cheeks. She looked into their faces with hungry eyes that could not be satisfied with looking. And what stories they had to tell their mother! About the pigs, the cows, the mules! About riding to the mill behind Gluglu; fishing back in the lake with their Uncle Jasper; picking pecans with Lidie's little black brood, and hauling chips in their express wagon. It was a thousand times more fun to haul real chips for old lame Susie's real fire than to drag painted blocks along the banquette on Esplanade Street!

She went with them herself to see the pigs and the cows, to look at the darkies laying the cane, to thrash the pecan trees, and catch fish in the back lake. She lived with them a whole week long, giving them all of herself, and gathering and filling herself with their young existence. They listened, breathless, when she told them the house in Esplanade Street was crowded with workmen, hammering, nailing, sawing, and filling the place with clatter. They wanted to know where their bed was; what had been done with their rocking-horse; and where did Joe sleep, and where had Ellen gone, and the cook? But, above all, they were fired with a desire to see the little house around the block. Was there any place to play? Were there any boys next door? Raoul, with pessimistic foreboding, was convinced that there were only girls next door. Where would they sleep, and where would papa sleep? She told them the fairies would fix it all right.

The old Madame was charmed with Edna's visit, and showered all manner of delicate attentions upon her. She was delighted to know that the Esplanade Street house was in a dismantled condition. It gave her the promise and pretext to keep the children indefinitely.

It was with a wrench and a pang that Edna left her children. She carried away with her the sound of their voices and the touch of their cheeks. All along the journey homeward their presence lingered with her like the memory of a delicious song. But by the time she had regained the city the song no longer echoed in her soul. She was again alone.

⤳ XXXIII ⤙

It happened sometimes when Edna went to see Mademoiselle Reisz that the little musician was absent, giving a lesson or making some small necessary household purchase. The key was always left in a secret hiding-place in the entry, which Edna knew. If Mademoiselle happened to be away, Edna would usually enter and wait for her return.

When she knocked at Mademoiselle Reisz's door one afternoon there was no response; so unlocking the door, as usual, she entered and found the apartment deserted, as she had expected. Her day had been quite filled up, and it was for a rest, a refuge, and to talk about Robert, that she sought out her friend.

She had worked at her canvas—a young Italian character study—all the morning, completing the work without the model; but there had been many interruptions, some incident to her modest housekeeping, and others of a social nature.

Madame Ratignolle had dragged herself over, avoiding the too public thoroughfares, she said. She complained that Edna had neglected her much of late. Besides, she was consumed with curiosity to see the little house and the manner in which it was conducted. She wanted to hear all about the dinner party; Monsieur Ratignolle had left *so* early. What had happened after he left? The champagne and grapes which Edna sent over were *too* delicious. She had so little appetite; they had refreshed and toned her stomach. Where on earth was she going to put Mr. Pontellier in that little house, and the boys? And then she made Edna promise to go to her when her hour of trial overtook her.

"At any time—any time of the day or night, dear," Edna assured her.

Before leaving Madame Ratignolle said:

"In some way you seem to me like a child, Edna. You seem to act without a certain amount of reflection which is necessary in this life. That is the reason I want to say you mustn't mind if I advise you to be a little careful while you are living here alone. Why don't you have some one come and stay with you? Wouldn't Mademoiselle Reisz come?"

"No; she wouldn't wish to come, and I shouldn't want her always with me."

"Well, the reason—you know how evil-minded the world is—some one was talking of Alcée Arobin visiting you. Of course, it wouldn't matter if Mr. Arobin had not such a dreadful reputation. Monsieur Ratignolle was telling me that his attentions alone are considered enough to ruin a woman's name."

"Does he boast of his successes?" asked Edna indifferently, squinting at her picture.

"No, I think not. I believe he is a decent fellow as far as that goes. But his character is so well known among the men. I shan't be able to come back and see you; it was very, very imprudent to-day."

"Mind the step!" cried Edna.

"Don't neglect me," entreated Madame Ratignolle; "and don't mind what I said about Arobin, or having some one to stay with you."

"Of course not," Edna laughed. "You may say anything you like to me." They kissed each other good-by. Madame Ratignolle had not far to go, and Edna stood on the porch a while watching her walk down the street.

Then in the afternoon Mrs. Merriman and Mrs. Highcamp had made their "party call." Edna felt that they might have dispensed with the formality. They had also come to invite her to play *vingt-et-un*[57] one evening at Mrs. Merriman's. She was asked to go early, to dinner, and Mr. Merriman or Mr. Arobin would take her home. Edna accepted in a half-hearted way. She sometimes felt very tired of Mrs. Highcamp and Mrs. Merriman.

Late in the afternoon she sought refuge with Mademoiselle Reisz, and stayed there alone, waiting for her, feeling a kind of repose invade her with the very atmosphere of the shabby, unpretentious little room.

Edna sat at the window, which looked out over the house-tops and across the river. The window frame was filled with pots of flowers, and she sat and picked the dry leaves from a rose geranium. The day was warm, and the breeze which blew from the river was very pleasant. She removed her hat and laid it on the piano. She went on picking the leaves and digging around the plants with her hat pin. Once she thought she heard Mademoiselle Reisz approaching. But it was a young black girl, who came in, bringing a small bundle of laundry, which she deposited in the adjoining room, and went away.

Edna seated herself at the piano, and softly picked out with one hand the bars of a piece of music which lay open before her. A half-hour went by. There was the occasional sound of people going and coming in the lower hall. She was growing interested in her occupation of picking out the aria, when there was a second rap at the door. She vaguely wondered what these people did when they found Mademoiselle's door locked.

---

[57]Twenty-one, a card game like blackjack.

"Come in," she called, turning her face toward the door. And this time it was Robert Lebrun who presented himself. She attempted to rise; she could not have done so without betraying the agitation which mastered her at sight of him, so she fell back upon the stool, only exclaiming, "Why, Robert!"

He came and clasped her hand, seemingly without knowing what he was saying or doing.

"Mrs. Pontellier! How do you happen—oh! how well you look! Is Mademoiselle Reisz not here? I never expected to see you."

"When did you come back?" asked Edna in an unsteady voice, wiping her face with her handkerchief. She seemed ill at ease on the piano stool, and he begged her to take the chair by the window. She did so, mechanically, while he seated himself on the stool.

"I returned day before yesterday," he answered, while he leaned his arm on the keys, bringing forth a crash of discordant sound.

"Day before yesterday!" she repeated aloud; and went on thinking to herself, "day before yesterday," in a sort of uncomprehending way. She had pictured him seeking her at the very first hour, and he had lived under the same sky since day before yesterday, while only by accident had he stumbled upon her. Mademoiselle must have lied when she said, "Poor fool, he loves you."

"Day before yesterday," she repeated, breaking off a spray of Mademoiselle's geranium; "then if you had not met me here to-day you wouldn't—when—that is, didn't you mean to come and see me?"

"Of course, I should have gone to see you. There have been so many things—" he turned the leaves of Mademoiselle's music nervously. "I started in at once yesterday with the old firm. After all there is as much chance for me here as there was there—that is, I might find it profitable some day. The Mexicans were not very congenial."

So he had come back because the Mexicans were not congenial; because business was as profitable here as there; because of any reason, and not because he cared to be near her. She remembered the day she sat on the floor, turning the pages of his letter, seeking the reason which was left untold.

She had not noticed how he looked—only feeling his presence; but she turned deliberately and observed him. After all, he had been absent but a few months, and was not changed. His hair—the color of hers—waved back from his temples in the same way as before. His skin was not more burned than it had been at Grand Isle. She found in his eyes, when he looked at her for one silent moment, the same tender caress, with an added warmth and entreaty which had not been there before—the same glance which had penetrated to the sleeping places of her soul and awakened them.

A hundred times Edna had pictured Robert's return, and imagined their first meeting. It was usually at her home, whither he had sought her out at once. She always fancied him expressing or betraying in some way his love for her. And here, the reality was that they sat ten feet apart, she at the window, crushing geranium leaves in her hand and smelling them, he twirling about on the piano stool, saying:

"I was very much surprised to hear of Mr. Pontellier's absence; it's a wonder Mademoiselle Reisz did not tell me; and your moving—mother told me yesterday. I should think you would have gone to New York with him, or to Iberville with the children, rather than be bothered here with housekeeping. And you are going abroad, too, I hear. We shan't have you at Grand Isle next summer; it won't seem—do you see much of Mademoiselle Reisz? She often spoke of you in the few letters she wrote."

"Do you remember that you promised to write to me when you went away?" A flush overspread his whole face.

"I couldn't believe that my letters would be of any interest to you."

"That is an excuse; it isn't the truth." Edna reached for her hat on the piano. She adjusted it, sticking the hat pin through the heavy coil of hair with some deliberation.

"Are you not going to wait for Mademoiselle Reisz?" asked Robert.

"No; I have found when she is absent this long, she is liable not to come back till late." She drew on her gloves, and Robert picked up his hat.

"Won't you wait for her?" asked Edna.

"Not if you think she will not be back till late," adding, as if suddenly aware of some discourtesy in his speech, "and I should miss the pleasure of walking home with you." Edna locked the door and put the key back in its hiding-place.

They went together, picking their way across muddy streets and sidewalks encumbered with the cheap display of small tradesmen. Part of the distance they rode in the car, and after disembarking, passed the Pontellier mansion, which looked broken and half torn asunder. Robert had never known the house, and looked at it with interest.

"I never knew you in your home," he remarked.

"I am glad you did not."

"Why?" She did not answer. They went on around the corner, and it seemed as if her dreams were coming true after all, when he followed her into the little house.

"You must stay and dine with me, Robert. You see, I am all alone, and it is so long since I have seen you. There is so much I want to ask you."

She took off her hat and gloves. He stood irresolute, making some excuse about his mother who expected him; he even muttered something about an engagement. She struck a match and lit a lamp on the table; it was growing dusk. When he saw her face in the lamp-light, looking pained, with all the soft lines gone out of it, he threw his hat aside and seated himself.

"Oh! you know I want to stay if you will let me!" he exclaimed. All the softness came back. She laughed, and went and put her hand on his shoulder.

"This is the first moment you have seemed like the old Robert. I'll go tell Celestine." She hurried away to tell Celestine to set an extra place. She even sent her off in search of some added delicacy which she had not thought of for herself. And she recommended great care in dripping the coffee and having the omelet done to a proper turn.

When she reëntered, Robert was turning over magazines, sketches, and things that lay upon the table in great disorder. He picked up a photograph, and exclaimed:

"Alcée Arobin! What on earth is his picture doing here?"

"I tried to make a sketch of his head one day," answered Edna, "and he thought the photograph might help me. It was at the other house. I thought it had been left there. I must have packed it up with my drawing materials."

"I should think you would give it back to him if you have finished with it."

"Oh! I have a great many photographs. I never think of returning them. They don't amount to anything." Robert kept on looking at the picture.

"It seems to me—do you think his head is worth drawing? Is he a friend of Mr. Pontellier's? You never said you knew him."

"He isn't a friend of Mr. Pontellier's; he's a friend of mine. I always knew him—that is, it is only of late that I know him pretty well. But I'd rather talk about you, and know what you have been seeing and doing and feeling out there in Mexico." Robert threw aside the picture.

"I've been seeing the waves and the white beach of Grand Isle; the quiet, grassy street of the *Chênière;* the old fort at Grande Terre. I've been working like a machine, and feeling like a lost soul. There was nothing interesting."

She leaned her head upon her hand to shade her eyes from the light.

"And what have you been doing and feeling all these days?" he asked.

"I've been seeing the waves and the white beach at Grand Isle; the quiet, grassy street of the *Chênière Caminada;* the old sunny fort at Grande Terre. I've been working with little more comprehension than a machine, and still feeling like a lost soul. There was nothing interesting."

"Mrs. Pontellier, you are cruel," he said, with feeling, closing his eyes and resting his head back on the chair. They remained in silence till old Celestine announced dinner.

 XXXIV

The dining-room was very small. Edna's round mahogany would have almost filled it. As it was there was but a step or two from the little table to the kitchen, to the mantel, the small buffet, and the side door that opened out onto the narrow brick-paved yard.

A certain degree of ceremony settled upon them with the announcement of dinner. There was no return to personalities. Robert related incidents of his sojourn in Mexico, and Edna talked of events likely to interest him, which had occurred during his absence. The dinner was of ordinary quality, except for the few delicacies which she had sent out to purchase. Old Celestine, with a bandana *tignon*[58] twisted about her head, hobbled in and out, taking a personal interest in everything; and she lingered occasionally to talk patois[59] with Robert, whom she had known as a boy.

He went out to a neighboring cigar stand to purchase cigarette papers, and when he came back he found that Celestine had served the black coffee in the parlor.

"Perhaps I shouldn't have come back," he said. "When you are tired of me, tell me to go."

"You never tire me. You must have forgotten the hours and hours at Grand Isle in which we grew accustomed to each other and used to being together."

"I have forgotten nothing at Grand Isle," he said, not looking at her, but rolling a cigarette. His tobacco pouch, which he laid upon the table,

---

[58]Scarf.
[59]Louisiana French dialect.

was a fantastic embroidered silk affair, evidently the handiwork of a woman.

"You used to carry your tobacco in a rubber pouch," said Edna, picking up the pouch and examining the needlework.

"Yes; it was lost."

"Where did you buy this one? In Mexico?"

"It was given to me by a Vera Cruz girl; they are very generous," he replied, striking a match and lighting his cigarette.

"They are very handsome, I suppose, those Mexican women; very picturesque, with their black eyes and their lace scarfs."

"Some are; others are hideous. Just as you find women everywhere."

"What was she like—the one who gave you the pouch? You must have known her very well."

"She was very ordinary. She wasn't of the slightest importance. I knew her well enough."

"Did you visit at her house? Was it interesting? I should like to know and hear about the people you met, and the impressions they made on you."

"There are some people who leave impressions not so lasting as the imprint of an oar upon water."

"Was she such a one?"

"It would be ungenerous for me to admit that she was of that order and kind." He thrust the pouch back in his pocket, as if to put away the subject with the trifle which had brought it up.

Arobin dropped in with a message from Mrs. Merriman, to say that the card party was postponed on account of the illness of one of her children.

"How do you do, Arobin?" said Robert, rising from the obscurity.

"Oh! Lebrun. To be sure! I heard yesterday you were back. How did they treat you down in Mexique?"

"Fairly well."

"But not well enough to keep you there. Stunning girls, though, in Mexico. I thought I should never get away from Vera Cruz when I was down there a couple of years ago."

"Did they embroider slippers and tobacco pouches and hat-bands and things for you?" asked Edna.

"Oh! my! no! I didn't get so deep in their regard. I fear they made more impression on me than I made on them."

"You were less fortunate than Robert, then."

"I am always less fortunate than Robert. Has he been imparting tender confidences?"

"I've been imposing myself long enough," said Robert, rising, and shaking hands with Edna. "Please convey my regards to Mr. Pontellier when you write."

He shook hands with Arobin and went away.

"Fine fellow, that Lebrun," said Arobin when Robert had gone. "I never heard you speak of him."

"I knew him last summer at Grand Isle," she replied. "Here is that photograph of yours. Don't you want it?"

"What do I want with it? Throw it away." She threw it back on the table.

"I'm not going to Mrs. Merriman's," she said. "If you see her, tell her so. But perhaps I had better write. I think I shall write now, and say that I am sorry her child is sick, and tell her not to count on me."

"It would be a good scheme," acquiesced Arobin. "I don't blame you; stupid lot!"

Edna opened the blotter, and having procured paper and pen, began to write the note. Arobin lit a cigar and read the evening paper, which he had in his pocket.

"What is the date?" she asked. He told her.

"Will you mail this for me when you go out?"

"Certainly." He read to her little bits out of the newspaper, while she straightened things on the table.

"What do you want to do?" he asked, throwing aside the paper. "Do you want to go out for a walk or a drive or anything? It would be a fine night to drive."

"No; I don't want to do anything but just be quiet. You go away and amuse yourself. Don't stay."

"I'll go away if I must; but I shan't amuse myself. You know that I only live when I am near you."

He stood up to bid her good night.

"Is that one of the things you always say to women?"

"I have said it before, but I don't think I ever came so near meaning it," he answered with a smile. There were no warm lights in her eyes; only a dreamy, absent look.

"Good night. I adore you. Sleep well," he said, and kissed her hand and went away.

She stayed alone in a kind of reverie—a sort of stupor. Step by step she lived over every instant of time she had been with Robert after he had entered Mademoiselle Reisz's door. She recalled his words, his looks. How few and meager they had been for her hungry heart! A vision—a transcendently seductive vision of a Mexican girl arose before her. She writhed with a jealous pang. She wondered when he would come back. He had not said he would come back. She had been with him, had heard his voice and touched his hand. But some way he had seemed nearer to her off there in Mexico.

XXXV

The morning was full of sunlight and hope. Edna could see before her no denial—only the promise of excessive joy. She lay in bed awake, with bright eyes full of speculation. "He loves you, poor fool." If she could but get that conviction firmly fixed in her mind, what mattered about the rest? She felt she had been childish and unwise the night before in giving herself over to despondency. She recapitulated the motives which no doubt explained Robert's reserve. They were not insurmountable; they would not hold if he really loved her; they could not hold against her own passion, which he must come to realize in time. She pictured him going to his business that morning. She even saw how he was dressed; how he walked down one street, and turned the corner of another; saw him bending over his desk, talking to people who entered the office, going to his lunch, and perhaps watching for her on the street. He would come to her in the afternoon or evening, sit and roll his cigarette, talk a little, and go away as he had done the night before. But how delicious it would be to have him there with her! She would have no regrets, nor seek to penetrate his reserve if he still chose to wear it.

Edna ate her breakfast only half dressed. The maid brought her a delicious printed scrawl from Raoul, expressing his love, asking her to send him some bonbons, and telling her they had found this morning ten tiny white pigs all lying in a row beside Lidie's big white pig.

A letter also came from her husband, saying he hoped to be back early in March, and then they would get ready for that journey abroad which he had promised her so long, which he now felt fully able to afford; he felt able to travel as people should, without any thought of small economies—thanks to his recent speculations in Wall Street.

Much to her surprise she received a note from Arobin, written at midnight from the club. It was to say good morning to her, to hope she had slept well, to assure her of his devotion, which he trusted she in some faintest manner returned.

All these letters were pleasing to her. She answered the children in a cheerful frame of mind, promising them bonbons, and congratulating them upon their happy find of the little pigs.

She answered her husband with friendly evasiveness,—not with any fixed design to mislead him, only because all sense of reality had gone out of her life; she had abandoned herself to Fate, and awaited the consequences with indifference.

To Arobin's note she made no reply. She put it under Celestine's stove-lid.

Edna worked several hours with much spirit. She saw no one but a picture dealer, who asked her if it were true that she was going abroad to study in Paris.

She said possibly she might, and he negotiated with her for some Parisian studies to reach him in time for the holiday trade in December.

Robert did not come that day. She was keenly disappointed. He did not come the following day, nor the next. Each morning she awoke with hope, and each night she was a prey to despondency. She was tempted to seek him out. But far from yielding to the impulse, she avoided any occasion which might throw her in his way. She did not go to Mademoiselle Reisz's nor pass by Madame Lebrun's, as she might have done if he had still been in Mexico.

When Arobin, one night, urged her to drive with him, she went out—out to the lake, on the Shell Road. His horses were full of mettle, and even a little unmanageable. She liked the rapid gait at which they spun along, and the quick, sharp sound of the horses' hoofs on the hard road. They did not stop anywhere to eat or drink. Arobin was not needlessly imprudent. But they ate and drank when they regained Edna's little dining-room—which was comparatively early in the evening.

It was late when he left her. It was getting to be more than a passing whim with Arobin to see her and be with her. He had detected the latent sensuality, which unfolded under his delicate sense of her nature's requirements like a torpid, torrid, sensitive blossom.

There was no despondency when she fell asleep that night; nor was there hope when she awoke in the morning.

XXXVI

There was a garden out in the suburbs; a small, leafy corner, with a few green tables under the orange trees. An old cat slept all day on the stone step in the sun, and an old *mulatresse*[60] slept her idle hours away

---

[60]Mulatto woman.

in her chair at the open window, till some one happened to knock on one of the green tables. She had milk and cream cheese to sell, and bread and butter. There was no one who could make such excellent coffee or fry a chicken so golden brown as she.

The place was too modest to attract the attention of people of fashion, and so quiet as to have escaped the notice of those in search of pleasure and dissipation. Edna had discovered it accidentally one day when the high-board gate stood ajar. She caught sight of a little green table, blotched with the checkered sunlight that filtered through the quivering leaves overhead. Within she had found the slumbering *mulatresse*, the drowsy cat, and a glass of milk which reminded her of the milk she had tasted in Iberville.

She often stopped there during her perambulations; sometimes taking a book with her, and sitting an hour or two under the trees when she found the place deserted. Once or twice she took a quiet dinner there alone, having instructed Celestine beforehand to prepare no dinner at home. It was the last place in the city she would have expected to meet any one she knew.

Still she was not astonished when, as she was partaking of a modest dinner late in the afternoon, looking into an open book, stroking the cat, which had made friends with her—she was not greatly astonished to see Robert come in at the tall garden gate.

"I am destined to see you only by accident," she said, shoving the cat off the chair beside her. He was surprised, ill at ease, almost embarrassed at meeting her thus so unexpectedly.

"Do you come here often?" he asked.

"I almost live here," she said.

"I used to drop in very often for a cup of Catiche's good coffee. This is the first time since I came back."

"She'll bring you a plate, and you will share my dinner. There's always enough for two—even three." Edna had intended to be indifferent and as reserved as he when she met him; she had reached the determination by a laborious train of reasoning, incident to one of her despondent moods. But her resolve melted when she saw him before her, seated there beside her in the little garden, as if a designing Providence had led him into her path.

"Why have you kept away from me, Robert?" she asked, closing the book that lay open upon the table.

"Why are you so personal, Mrs. Pontellier? Why do you force me to idiotic subterfuges?" he exclaimed with sudden warmth. "I suppose there's no use telling you I've been very busy, or that I've been sick, or that I've been to see you and not found you at home. Please let me off with any one of these excuses."

"You are the embodiment of selfishness," she said. "You save yourself something—I don't know what—but there is some selfish motive, and in sparing yourself you never consider for a moment what I think, or how I feel your neglect and indifference. I suppose this is what you would call unwomanly; but I have got into a habit of expressing myself. It doesn't matter to me, and you may think me unwomanly if you like."

"No; I only think you cruel, as I said the other day. Maybe not intentionally cruel; but you seem to be forcing me into disclosures which can result in nothing; as if you would have me bare a wound for the pleasure of looking at it, without the intention or power of healing it."

"I'm spoiling your dinner, Robert; never mind what I say. You haven't eaten a morsel."

"I only came in for a cup of coffee." His sensitive face was all disfigured with excitement.

"Isn't this a delightful place?" she remarked. "I am so glad it has never actually been discovered. It is so quiet, so sweet, here. Do you notice there is scarcely a sound to be heard? It's so out of the way; and a good walk from the car. However, I don't mind walking. I always feel so sorry for women who don't like to walk; they miss so much—so many rare little glimpses of life; and we women learn so little of life on the whole.

"Catiche's coffee is always hot. I don't know how she manages it, here in the open air. Celestine's coffee gets cold bringing it from the kitchen to the dining-room. Three lumps! How can you drink it so sweet? Take some of the cress with your chop; it's so biting and crisp. Then there's the advantage of being able to smoke with your coffee out here. Now, in the city—aren't you going to smoke?"

"After a while," he said, laying a cigar on the table.

"Who gave it to you?" she laughed.

"I bought it. I suppose I'm getting reckless; I bought a whole box." She was determined not to be personal again and make him uncomfortable.

The cat made friends with him, and climbed into his lap when he smoked his cigar. He stroked her silky fur, and talked a little about her. He looked at Edna's book, which he had read; and he told her the end, to save her the trouble of wading through it, he said.

Again he accompanied her back to her home; and it was after dusk when they reached the little "pigeon-house." She did not ask him to remain, which he was grateful for, as it permitted him to stay without the discomfort of blundering through an excuse which he had no intention of considering. He helped her to light the lamp; then she went into her room to take off her hat and to bathe her face and hands.

When she came back Robert was not examining the pictures and magazines as before; he sat off in the shadow, leaning his head back on the chair as if in a reverie. Edna lingered a moment beside the table, arranging the books there. Then she went across the room to where he sat. She bent over the arm of his chair and called his name.

"Robert," she said, "are you asleep?"

"No," he answered, looking up at her.

She leaned over and kissed him—a soft, cool, delicate kiss, whose voluptuous sting penetrated his whole being—then she moved away from him. He followed, and took her in his arms, just holding her close to him. She put her hand up to his face and pressed his cheek against her own. The action was full of love and tenderness. He sought her lips again. Then he drew her down upon the sofa beside him and held her hand in both of his.

"Now you know," he said, "now you know what I have been fighting against since last summer at Grand Isle; what drove me away and drove me back again."

"Why have you been fighting against it?" she asked. Her face glowed with soft lights.

"Why? Because you were not free; you were Léonce Pontellier's wife. I couldn't help loving you if you were ten times his wife; but so long as I went away from you and kept away I could help telling you so." She put her free hand up to his shoulder, and then against his cheek, rubbing it softly. He kissed her again. His face was warm and flushed.

"There in Mexico I was thinking of you all the time, and longing for you."

"But not writing to me," she interrupted.

"Something put into my head that you cared for me; and I lost my senses. I forgot everything but a wild dream of your some way becoming my wife."

"Your wife!"

"Religion, loyalty, everything would give way if only you cared."

"Then you must have forgotten that I was Léonce Pontellier's wife."

"Oh! I was demented, dreaming of wild, impossible things, recalling men who had set their wives free, we have heard of such things."

"Yes, we have heard of such things."

"I came back full of vague, mad intentions. And when I got here—"

"When you got here you never came near me!" She was still caressing his cheek.

"I realized what a cur I was to dream of such a thing, even if you had been willing."

She took his face between her hands and looked into it as if she would never withdraw her eyes more. She kissed him on the forehead, the eyes, the cheeks, and the lips.

"You have been a very, very foolish boy, wasting your time dreaming of impossible things when you speak of Mr. Pontellier setting me free! I am no longer one of Mr. Pontellier's possessions to dispose of or not. I give myself where I choose. If he were to say, 'Here, Robert, take her and be happy; she is yours,' I should laugh at you both."

His face grew a little white. "What do you mean?" he asked.

There was a knock at the door. Old Celestine came in to say that Madame Ratignolle's servant had come around the back way with a message that Madame had been taken sick and begged Mrs. Pontellier to go to her immediately.

"Yes, yes," said Edna, rising; "I promised. Tell her yes—to wait for me. I'll go back with her."

"Let me walk over with you," offered Robert.

"No," she said; "I will go with the servant." She went into her room to put on her hat, and when she came in again she sat once more upon the sofa beside him. He had not stirred. She put her arms about his neck.

"Good-by, my sweet Robert. Tell me good-by." He kissed her with a degree of passion which had not before entered into his caress, and strained her to him.

"I love you," she whispered, "only you; no one but you. It was you who awoke me last summer out of a life-long, stupid dream. Oh! you have made me so unhappy with your indifference. Oh! I have suffered, suffered! Now you are here we shall love each other, my Robert. We shall be everything to each other. Nothing else in the world is of any consequence. I must go to my friend; but you will wait for me? No matter how late; you will wait for me, Robert?"

"Don't go; don't go! Oh! Edna, stay with me," he pleaded. "Why should you go? Stay with me, stay with me."

"I shall come back as soon as I can; I shall find you here." She buried her face in his neck, and said good-by again. Her seductive voice, together with his great love for her, had enthralled his senses, had deprived him of every impulse but the longing to hold her and keep her.

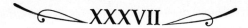

XXXVII

Edna looked in at the drug store. Monsieur Ratignolle was putting up a mixture himself, very carefully, dropping a red liquid into a tiny glass.[61] He was grateful to Edna for having come; her presence would be a comfort to his wife. Madame Ratignolle's sister, who had always been with her at such trying times, had not been able to come up from the plantation, and Adèle had been inconsolable until Mrs. Pontellier so kindly promised to come to her. The nurse had been with them at night for the past week, as she lived a great distance away. And Dr. Mandelet had been coming and going all the afternoon. They were then looking for him any moment.

Edna hastened upstairs by a private stairway that led from the rear of the store to the apartments above. The children were all sleeping in a back room. Madame Ratignolle was in the salon, whither she had strayed in her suffering impatience. She sat on the sofa, clad in an ample white *peignoir*, holding a handkerchief tight in her hand with a nervous clutch. Her face was drawn and pinched, her sweet blue eyes haggard and unnatural. All her beautiful hair had been drawn back and plaited. It lay in a long braid on the sofa pillow, coiled like a golden serpent. The nurse, a comfortable looking *Griffe*[62] woman in white apron and cap, was urging her to return to her bedroom.

"There is no use, there is no use," she said at once to Edna. "We must get rid of Mandelet; he is getting too old and careless. He said he would be here at half-past seven; now it must be eight. See what time it is, Joséphine."

The woman was possessed of a cheerful nature, and refused to take any situation too seriously, especially a situation with which she was so familiar. She urged Madame to have courage and patience. But Madame only set her teeth hard into her under lip, and Edna saw the sweat gather in beads on her white forehead. After a moment or two she uttered a profound sigh and wiped her face with the handkerchief rolled in a ball. She appeared exhausted. The nurse gave her a fresh handkerchief, sprinkled with cologne water.

"This is too much!" she cried. "Mandelet ought to be killed! Where is Alphonse? Is it possible I am to be abandoned like this—neglected by every one?"

---

[61]Probably laudanum, a narcotic elixir.
[62]Race of mixed Indian and Negro blood.

"Neglected, indeed!" exclaimed the nurse. Wasn't she there? And here was Mrs. Pontellier leaving, no doubt, a pleasant evening at home to devote to her? And wasn't Monsieur Ratignolle coming that very instant through the hall? And Joséphine was quite sure she had heard Doctor Mandelet's coupé. Yes, there it was, down at the door.

Adèle consented to go back to her room. She sat on the edge of a little low couch next to her bed.

Doctor Mandelet paid no attention to Madame Ratignolle's upbraidings. He was accustomed to them at such times, and was too well convinced of her loyalty to doubt it.

He was glad to see Edna, and wanted her to go with him into the salon and entertain him. But Madame Ratignolle would not consent that Edna should leave her for an instant. Between agonizing moments, she chatted a little, and said it took her mind off her sufferings.

Edna began to feel uneasy. She was seized with a vague dread. Her own like experiences seemed far away, unreal, and only half remembered. She recalled faintly an ecstasy of pain, the heavy odor of chloroform, a stupor which had deadened sensation, and an awakening to find a little new life to which she had given being, added to the great unnumbered multitude of souls that come and go.

She began to wish she had not come; her presence was not necessary. She might have invented a pretext for staying away; she might even invent a pretext now for going. But Edna did not go. With an inward agony, with a flaming, outspoken revolt against the ways of Nature, she witnessed the scene of torture.

She was still stunned and speechless with emotion when later she leaned over her friend to kiss her and softly say good-by. Adèle, pressing her cheek, whispered in an exhausted voice: "Think of the children, Edna. Oh think of the children! Remember them!"

XXXVIII

Edna still felt dazed when she got outside in the open air. The Doctor's coupé had returned for him and stood before the *porte cochère*. She did not wish to enter the coupé, and told Doctor Mandelet she would walk; she was not afraid, and would go alone. He directed his carriage to meet him at Mrs. Pontellier's, and he started to walk home with her.

Up—away up, over the narrow street between the tall houses, the stars were blazing. The air was mild and caressing, but cool with the breath of spring and the night. They walked slowly, the Doctor with a heavy, measured tread and his hands behind him; Edna, in an absent-minded way, as she had walked one night at Grand Isle, as if her thoughts had gone ahead of her and she was striving to overtake them.

"You shouldn't have been there, Mrs. Pontellier," he said. "That was no place for you. Adèle is full of whims at such times. There were a dozen women she might have had with her, unimpressionable women. I felt that it was cruel, cruel. You shouldn't have gone."

"Oh, well!" she answered, indifferently. "I don't know that it matters after all. One has to think of the children some time or other; the sooner the better."

"When is Léonce coming back?"

"Quite soon. Some time in March."

"And you are going abroad?"

"Perhaps—no, I am not going. I'm not going to be forced into doing things. I don't want to go abroad. I want to be let alone. Nobody has any right—except children, perhaps—and even then, it seems to me—or it did seem—" She felt that her speech was voicing the incoherency of her thoughts, and stopped abruptly.

"The trouble is," sighed the Doctor, grasping her meaning intuitively, "that youth is given up to illusions. It seems to be a provision of Nature; a decoy to secure mothers for the race. And Nature takes no account of moral consequences, of arbitrary conditions which we create, and which we feel obliged to maintain at any cost."

"Yes," she said. "The years that are gone seem like dreams—if one might go on sleeping and dreaming—but to wake up and find—oh! well! perhaps it is better to wake up after all, even to suffer, rather than to remain a dupe to illusions all one's life."

"It seems to me, my dear child," said the Doctor at parting, holding her hand, "you seem to me to be in trouble. I am not going to ask for your confidence. I will only say that if ever you feel moved to give it to me, perhaps I might help you. I know I would understand, and I tell you there are not many who would—not many, my dear."

"Some way I don't feel moved to speak of things that trouble me. Don't think I am ungrateful or that I don't appreciate your sympathy. There are periods of despondency and suffering which take possession of me. But I don't want anything but my own way. That is wanting a good deal, of course, when you have to trample upon the lives, the hearts, the prejudices of others—but no matter—still, I shouldn't want to trample upon the little lives. Oh! I don't know what I'm saying, Doctor. Good night. Don't blame me for anything."

"Yes, I will blame you if you don't come and see me soon. We will talk of things you never have dreamt of talking about before. It will do us both good. I don't want you to blame yourself, whatever comes. Good night, my child."

She let herself in at the gate, but instead of entering she sat upon the step of the porch. The night was quiet and soothing. All the tearing emotion of the last few hours seemed to fall away from her like a somber, uncomfortable garment, which she had but to loosen to be rid of. She went back to that hour before Adèle had sent for her; and her senses kindled afresh in thinking of Robert's words, the pressure of his arms, and the feeling of his lips upon her own. She could picture at that moment no greater bliss on earth than possession of the beloved one. His expression of love had already given him to her in part. When she thought that he was there at hand, waiting for her, she grew numb with the intoxication of expectancy. It was so late; he would be asleep perhaps. She would awaken him with a kiss. She hoped that he would be asleep that she might arouse him with her caresses.

Still, she remembered Adèle's voice whispering, "Think of the children; think of them." She meant to think of them; that determination had driven into her soul like a death wound—but not to-night. To-morrow would be time to think of everything.

Robert was not waiting for her in the little parlor. He was nowhere at hand. The house was empty. But he had scrawled on a piece of paper that lay in lamplight:

"I love you. Good-by—because I love you."

Edna grew faint when she read the words. She went and sat on the sofa. Then she stretched herself out there, never uttering a sound. She did not sleep. She did not go to bed. The lamp sputtered and went out. She was still awake in the morning, when Celestine unlocked the kitchen door and came in to light the fire.

XXXIX

Victor, with hammer and nails and scraps of scantling, was patching a corner of one of the galleries. Mariequita sat near by, dangling her legs, watching him work, and handing him nails from the tool-box. The sun was beating down upon them. The girl had covered her head with her apron folded into a square pad. They had been talking for an hour or more. She never tired of hearing Victor describe the dinner at Mrs. Pontellier's. He exaggerated every detail, making it appear a veritable

Lucullan[63] feast. The flowers were in tubs, he said. The champagne was quaffed from huge golden goblets. Venus rising from the foam could have presented no more entrancing a spectacle than Mrs. Pontellier, blazing with beauty and diamonds at the head of the board, while the other women were all of them youthful houris,[64] possessed of incomparable charms.

She got it into her head that Victor was in love with Mrs. Pontellier, and he gave her evasive answers, framed so as to confirm her belief. She grew sullen and cried a little, threatening to go off and leave him to his fine ladies. There were a dozen men crazy about her at the *Chênière;* and since it was the fashion to be in love with married people, why, she could run away any time she liked to New Orleans with Célina's husband.

Célina's husband was a fool, a coward, and a pig, and to prove it to her, Victor intended to hammer his head into a jelly the next time he encountered him. This assurance was very consoling to Mariequita. She dried her eyes, and grew cheerful at the prospect.

They were still talking of the dinner and the allurements of city life when Mrs. Pontellier herself slipped around the corner of the house. The two youngsters stayed dumb with amazement before what they considered to be an apparition. But it was really she in flesh and blood, looking tired and a little travel-stained.

"I walked up from the wharf," she said, "and heard the hammering. I supposed it was you, mending the porch. It's a good thing. I was always tripping over the loose planks last summer. How dreary and deserted everything looks!"

It took Victor some time to comprehend that she had come in Beaudelet's lugger, that she had come alone, and for no purpose but to rest.

"There's nothing fixed up yet, you see. I'll give you my room; it's the only place."

"Any corner will do," she assured him.

"And if you can stand Philomel's cooking," he went on, "though I might try to get her mother while you are here. Do you think she would come?" turning to Mariequita.

Mariequita thought that perhaps Philomel's mother might come for a few days, and money enough.

---

[63]From Lucius Licinius Lucullus, a Roman politician (110–56 B. C.), known for his luxurious life.

[64]Angels of the Islamic heaven.

Beholding Mrs. Pontellier make her appearance, the girl had at once suspected a lovers' rendezvous. But Victor's astonishment was so genuine, and Mrs. Pontellier's indifference so apparent, that the disturbing notion did not lodge long in her brain. She contemplated with the greatest interest this woman who gave the most sumptuous dinners in America, and who had all the men in New Orleans at her feet.

"What time will you have dinner?" asked Edna. "I'm very hungry; but don't get anything extra."

"I'll have it ready in little or no time," he said, bustling and packing away his tools. "You may go to my room to brush up and rest yourself. Mariequita will show you."

"Thank you," said Edna. "But, do you know, I have a notion to go down to the beach and take a good wash and even a little swim, before dinner?"

"The water is too cold!" they both exclaimed. "Don't think of it."

"Well, I might go down and try—dip my toes in. Why, it seems to me the sun is hot enough to have warmed the very depths of the ocean. Could you get me a couple of towels? I'd better go right away, so as to be back in time. It would be a little too chilly if I waited till this afternoon."

Mariequita ran over to Victor's room, and returned with some towels, which she gave to Edna.

"I hope you have fish for dinner," said Edna, as she started to walk away; "but don't do anything extra if you haven't."

"Run and find Philomel's mother," Victor instructed the girl. "I'll go to the kitchen and see what I can do. By Gimminy! Women have no consideration! She might have sent me word."

Edna walked on down to the beach rather mechanically, not noticing anything special except that the sun was hot. She was not dwelling upon any particular train of thought. She had done all the thinking which was necessary after Robert went away, when she lay awake upon the sofa till morning.

She had said over and over to herself: "To-day it is Arobin; to-morrow it will be some one else. It makes no difference to me, it doesn't matter about Léonce Pontellier— but Raoul and Etienne!" She understood now clearly what she had meant long ago when she said to Adèle Ratignolle that she would give up the unessential, but she would never sacrifice herself for her children.

Despondency had come upon her there in the wakeful night, and had never lifted. There was no one thing in the world that she desired. There was no human being whom she wanted near her except Robert;

and she even realized that the day would come when he, too, and the thought of him would melt out of her existence, leaving her alone. The children appeared before her like antagonists who had overcome her; who had overpowered her and sought to drag her into the soul's slavery for the rest of her days. But she knew a way to elude them. She was not thinking of these things when she walked down to the beach.

The water of the Gulf stretched out before her, gleaming with the million lights of the sun. The voice of the sea is seductive, never ceasing, whispering, clamoring, murmuring, inviting the soul to wander in abysses of solitude. All along the white beach, up and down, there was no living thing in sight. A bird with a broken wing was beating the air above, reeling, fluttering, circling disabled down, down to the water.

Edna had found her old bathing suit still hanging, faded, upon its accustomed peg.

She put it on, leaving her clothing in the bath-house. But when she was there beside the sea, absolutely alone, she cast the unpleasant, pricking garments from her, and for the first time in her life she stood naked in the open air, at the mercy of the sun, the breeze that beat upon her, and the waves that invited her.

How strange and awful it seemed to stand naked under the sky! how delicious! She felt like some new-born creature, opening its eyes in a familiar world that it had never known.

The foamy wavelets curled up to her white feet, and coiled like serpents about her ankles. She walked out. The water was chill, but she walked on. The water was deep, but she lifted her white body and reached out with a long, sweeping stroke. The touch of the sea is sensuous, enfolding the body in its soft, close embrace.

She went on and on. She remembered the night she swam far out, and recalled the terror that seized her at the fear of being unable to regain the shore. She did not look back now, but went on and on, thinking of the blue-grass meadow that she had traversed when a little child, believing that it had no beginning and no end.

Her arms and legs were growing tired.

She thought of Léonce and the children. They were a part of her life. But they need not have thought that they could possess her, body and soul. How Mademoiselle Reisz would have laughed, perhaps sneered, if she knew! "And you call yourself an artist! What pretensions, Madame! The artist must possess the courageous soul that dares and defies."

Exhaustion was pressing upon and overpowering her.

"Good-by—because I love you." He did not know—he did not understand. He would never understand. Perhaps Doctor Mandelet would have understood if she had seen him—but it was too late; the shore was far behind her, and her strength was gone.

She looked into the distance, and the old terror flamed up for an instant, then sank again. Edna heard her father's voice and her sister Margaret's. She heard the barking of an old dog that was chained to the sycamore tree. The spurs of the cavalry officer clanged as he walked across the porch. There was the hum of bees, and the musky odor of pinks filled the air.

Heart of
Darkness

Joseph Conrad

While a great many novelists have been willing or unwilling exiles from the land of their birth, only a handful have ever managed to write and achieve fame in a language other than their native tongue. Until the late Vladimir Nabokov dropped his native Russian for American English the most astounding example of literary transplantation was that of Joseph Conrad.*

He was born Jozef Teodor Konrad Nalecz Korzeniowski on December 3, 1857, at Derebczynka Manor near Berdichev in the Ukraine, the only son of a restlessly romantic Polish aristocrat with literary pretensions, whose patriotic agitation for Polish independence in 1862 resulted in his exile to the Russian hinterland. Within seven years Conrad's mother and father were both dead—victims of the Russian climate and the rigors of exile—so the eleven-year-old orphan was brought up by his uncle, Thaddeus Bobrowski, who vainly tried to instill proper middle-class values into a boy whose imagination burned for adventure. Conrad's youthful reading, the seafaring novels of Captain Marryat and the explorers' journals of Bruce and Livingstone, had made an intense impression upon him, and for two years he nagged and badgered his uncle to let him go to sea until, in 1874, when Conrad was seventeen, he was granted his wish.

For the next twenty years Conrad indulged his wanderlust to the full. First in the French, then in the British merchant marine, he sailed every sea and touched at every major port of call from Martinique to Singapore, from Amsterdam to Adelaide. Beginning as an apprentice on a rickety French hulk, he worked his way up through the ranks of seaman, mate, and master to the command of a British barque. He ran guns for Spanish revolutionaries, had a tragic love affair in Marseilles (which ended in his nearly successful attempt at suicide), and fought the gales, fires, and intolerable boredom that constitute the major hazards of the sailor's life. He did not know that he was gathering material for his second career.

---

*Nabokov's case amazes me more than Conrad's, not because he is a greater novelist, but because he had already become an established Russian author before he took up writing in English. Conrad became an Englishman before his literary career began.

In 1887 Conrad was on a voyage through the islands that are now Indonesia when he heard about and finally met a Dutch trader named William Charles Olmeijer, physically deteriorated but possessed by grandiose romantic ambitions. The man was a "character," in short, and though Conrad had encountered a good many such people in his travels, the meeting was a historic one because Conrad soon began drafting a story based on him. He wrote when in port and during the slack periods of his voyages, and the tale ultimately became his first novel, *Almayer's Folly*, published in 1895. As Conrad stated in his autobiography, "If I had not got to know Almayer pretty well it is almost certain there would never have been a line of mine in print." Why Olmeijer's pathetic story of broken dreams inspired him more than his personal experiences is not fully known, but one may speculate that Conrad as a man of thirty, whose own dreams of adventure had begun to sink to a disappointingly prosaic career as a merchant officer, was touched by the spectacle of the man whose visions had long outlived his power to make them come true.

In 1889 Conrad realized one of his youthful ambitions by taking a post as riverboat captain for the Belgian Upper-Congo Trading Company. He had been an avid reader of the journals of the great African explorers and had once put his finger on the blank space at the center of a map of Africa and boasted to his boyhood friends that when he grew up he would go there. Twenty years after Stanley had explored the Congo the Belgians were exploiting it, and Conrad got his chance to see Central Africa. The Congo journey of 1889–1890 was the basis for *Heart of Darkness*, which Conrad described as "experience pushed a little (and only very little) beyond the actual facts of the case." But the Congo did more to make Conrad a novelist than provide him with the background for his most famous novella: his four months in the jungle permanently broke his health. Plagued by recurrent fevers, a rheumatic condition of his legs, and debilitating depression, Conrad tried to return to the sea—he heroically endured two more voyages—but finally had to give up his merchant captain's career in 1894.

From 1895, when *Almayer's Folly* first appeared, until his death in 1924, Conrad's life was largely that of the professional writer. Despite his continuing ill health, aggravated by frequent nervous collapses, few years passed that did not see the appearance of a novel or a collection of short stories. *Almayer's Folly* was rapidly followed by *An Outcast of the Islands* (1896), *The Nigger of the "Narcissus"* (1897), *Tales of Unrest* (1898), and *Lord Jim* (1900). These works of the first phase of Conrad's career, together with the novellas *Youth, Typhoon, The End of the Tether,* and *Heart of Darkness* (all 1902), are all psychological tales of adventure, set either on shipboard or on the exotic coasts of the Orient. Their origins are to be found in Conrad's own experience and his imaginative reconstruction of the lives of men he actually knew. They are an enormously varied group of tales, united in their concern for the moral struggle of the isolated individual to find a source of value outside the bounds of civilized society. Confronted by dangers from the elements, from brutal or savage men, from within the tortured, dark, secret self, his protagonists triumph—or are overwhelmed—as they succeed or fail at discovering the elementary virtues of courage, restraint, and self-sacrifice.

The great, grimly fatalistic novels of Conrad's middle period include *Nostromo* (1904), *The Secret Agent* (1907), *Under Western Eyes* (1911), and *Victory* (1915). Unlike the earlier works and some of the other fiction he wrote during this decade, these novels leave the area of seafaring adventure for the broader realm of politics. *Nostromo*, the novel in which Conrad worked on the largest canvas, with the greatest sustained success, portrays the inexorable forces that lead to the creation and then the dissolution of a South American republic. *The Secret Agent* and *Under Western Eyes* confront the problems of anarchism, rebellion, and political terrorism, and how the souls of well-intentioned men are inevitably warped by their political ends. *Victory* takes up politics from the outside: it is the tragedy of a good man who has tried to preserve his purity by living apart from society, and who finds that he has lost the faith in humanity he needs to struggle successfully against evil. It is upon these pessimistic novels, together with *Lord Jim* and *Heart of Darkness*, that Conrad's reputation rests.

For most of his first two decades as a novelist, the period of his greatest achievement, Conrad had a growing reputation in literary circles. The Polish sea captain who spoke with a thick accent all his life (and preferred speaking French to English) was adopted as a comrade by all the major literary figures of his time. His friends and admirers ranged from the philistine H. G. Wells and the bourgeois John Galsworthy to the refined and aesthetically adventurous Henry James and Ford Madox Ford. But while connoisseurs of fiction ranked Conrad among the most important writers of the day, popular success eluded him. He had married in 1896 and fathered two sons, and the expense of his small and far from lavish household was not met by the sales of his books. Even a government grant of £500 awarded to Conrad in 1905 and a small annual pension of £100 in 1910 could not prevent him from running up large debts to his publishers.

The turning point for Conrad's public reputation came late in his career. In 1914, with the appearance of *Chance*—a novel which, ironically, is almost unread today—Conrad became a best-seller. But with the exception of *Victory*, the works of Conrad's last decade are generally considered inferior to those of his early and middle years. *Within the Tides* (1915), *The Shadow-Line* (1917), *The Arrow of Gold* (1919), *The Rescue* (1920), and *The Rover* (1923) return to the adventurous themes of his early work, but with a slackening of imaginative power and of verbal self-discipline. For Conrad as for many writers—Faulkner is the outstanding American example—public recognition came during his lifetime but not until his creative talents had begun to fade.

The financial reward of his belated success made it possible for Conrad and his family to travel. The world-renowned son of the patriotic nobleman made a triumphant return to Poland which suddenly turned into a nightmare when the First World War broke out and the Conrads, British citizens by naturalization or birth, were nearly interned by the Austrians, with whom England was now at war. But the aid of the American ambassador in Vienna enabled the novelist and his family to cross the lines to Italy and return home. His unaccustomed wealth also helped ease the burden of his declining physical condition, for in his last years both Conrad and his wife were near-invalids. He died after a series of heart attacks on August 3, 1924, and was buried in the Catholic cemetery in Canterbury, where his epitaph is the couplet from Spenser which he had chosen as the epigraph to *The Rover* :

Sleep after toyle, port after stormie seas,
Ease after warre, death after life, does greatly please.

Biography   Conrad wrote several volumes of autobiographical reminiscences, especially *A Personal Record* (1912) and *Notes on Life and Letters* (1921). Gerard Jean-Aubry, Conrad's authorized biographer, put out a short, lively book called *The Sea Dreamer* in its English translation (New York: Archon Books, 1967). More accurate and trustworthy recent lives of Conrad are Jocelyn Baines, *Joseph Conrad: A Critical Biography* (New York: McGraw-Hill, 1959); Frederick R. Karl, *Joseph Conrad: The Three Lives* (New York: Farrar, Straus and Giroux, 1979); and the first part of a projected multivolume biography, Ian Watt, *Conrad in the Nineteenth Century* (Berkeley: University of California Press, 1979). And see also Bernard Mayer, *Joseph Conrad: A Psychoanalytical Biography* (Princeton: Princeton University Press, 1970).

Editions   In general, the most reliable edition of Conrad is the Doubleday-Dent *Collected Works* of 1923-1928 (New York and London; 22 vols.); most volumes of this edition were thoroughly revised and corrected by the author. But it has recently been shown that the *Youth* volume, containing *Heart of Darkness*, was printed unrevised from plates of a 1920 edition which Conrad never saw and which is riddled with printer's errors. The best text for *Heart of Darkness*, and the one on which the present reprint is based, is the limited William Heinemann edition (20 vols., 1921-1927).

Bibliography   Theodore G. Ehrsam, *A Bibliography of Joseph Conrad* (Metuchen, N.J.: Scarecrow Press, 1969), and Maurice Beebe, "Criticism of Joseph Conrad: A Selected Checklist," *Modern Fiction Studies* X (Spring 1964), 81-106.

General Criticism   The single most valuable recent study of Conrad is Albert Guerard's *Conrad the Novelist* (Cambridge, Mass.: Harvard University Press, 1958). Guerard's central thesis and sound, sensible approach to the novels make his book indispensable. Other important works include the chapters on Conrad in David Daiches's *The Novel and the Modern World* (Chicago: University of Chicago Press, 1939); Paul Wiley's *Conrad's Measure of Man* (Madison: University of Wisconsin Press, 1954); Thomas Moser's *Joseph Conrad: Achievement and Decline* (Cambridge, Mass.: Harvard University Press, 1957); J. I. M. Stewart's *Joseph Conrad* (New York: Dodd, Mead, 1968); David Thorburn's *Conrad's Romanticism* (New Haven: Yale University Press, 1971); and Peter Glassman's *Language and Being: Joseph Conrad and the Literature of Personality* (New York: Columbia University Press, 1976).

Criticism of Heart of Darkness   In addition to the sections on *Heart of Darkness* in the general studies of Conrad listed above, see Lillian Feder,

"Marlow's Descent into Hell," *Nineteenth-Century Fiction* 9 (March 1955), 280-292; Leonard F. Dean, "The Tragic Pattern in Conrad's *Heart of Darkness*," *College English* 6 (1944), 100-104; Frederick C. Crews, "The Power of Darkness," *Partisan Review* 34 (Fall 1967), 507-525; James Guetti, "*Heart of Darkness* and the Failure of the Imagination," *Sewanee Review* 73 (1965), 488-504; William Bysshe Stein, "The Lotus Posture and *Heart of Darkness*," *Modern Fiction Studies* 2 (1956-1957), 167-170; Kenneth Bruffee, "The Lesser Nightmare," *Modern Language Quarterly* 25 (1964), 322-329; Florence Ridley, "The Ultimate Meaning of *Heart of Darkness*," *Nineteenth-Century Fiction* 18 (1963), 43-53; William York Tindall, "Apology for Marlow," in Robert C. Rathbun and Martin Steinmann, eds., *From Jane Austen to Joseph Conrad* (Minneapolis: University of Minnesota Press, 1958), pp. 274-285; Frederick R. Karl, "Introduction to the Danse Macabre: Conrad's *Heart of Darkness*," *Modern Fiction Studies* 14 (1968), 143-156; and Garrett Stewart, "Lying as Dying in *Heart of Darkness*," *PMLA* 95 (1980), 319-331.

Heart of Darkness

I

The *Nellie*, a cruising yawl, swung to her anchor without a flutter of the sails, and was at rest. The flood had made, the wind was nearly calm, and being bound down the river, the only thing for it was to come to and wait for the turn of the tide.

The sea-reach of the Thames stretched before us like the beginning of an interminable waterway. In the offing the sea and the sky were welded together without a joint, and in the luminous space the tanned sails of the barges drifting up with the tide seemed to stand still in red clusters of canvas sharply peaked, with gleams of varnished sprits. A haze rested on the low shores that ran out to sea in vanishing flatness. The air was dark above Gravesend, and farther back still seemed condensed into a mournful gloom, brooding motionless over the biggest, and the greatest, town on earth.

The Director of Companies was our captain and our host. We four affectionately watched his back as he stood in the bows looking to seaward. On the whole river there was nothing that looked half so nautical. He resembled a pilot, which to a seaman is trustworthiness personified. It was difficult to realise his work was not out there in the luminous estuary, but behind him, within the brooding gloom.

Between us there was, as I have already said somewhere, the bond of the sea. Besides holding our hearts together through long periods of separation, it had the effect of making us tolerant of each other's yarns—and even convictions. The Lawyer—the best of old fellows— had, because of his many years and many virtues, the only cushion on deck, and was lying on the only rug. The Accountant had brought out already a box of dominoes, and was toying architecturally with the bones. Marlow sat cross-legged right aft, leaning against the mizzen-mast. He had sunken cheeks, a yellow complexion, a straight back, an ascetic aspect, and, with his arms dropped, the palms of hands outwards, resembled an idol. The Director, satisfied the anchor had good hold, made his way aft and sat down amongst us. We exchanged a few words lazily. Afterwards there was silence on board the yacht. For some reason or other we did not begin that game of dominoes. We felt meditative, and fit for nothing but placid staring. The day was ending in a serenity of still and exquisite brilliance. The water shone pacifically; the sky, without a speck, was a benign immensity of unstained light; the very mist on the Essex marshes was like a gauzy and radiant fabric, hung from the wooded rises inland, and draping the low shores in diaphanous folds. Only the gloom to the west, brooding over the upper reaches, became more sombre every minute, as if angered by the approach of the sun.

And at last, in its curved and imperceptible fall, the sun sank low, and from glowing white changed to a dull red without rays and without heat, as if about to go out suddenly, stricken to death by the touch of that gloom brooding over a crowd of men.

Forthwith a change came over the waters, and the serenity became less brilliant but more profound. The old river in its broad reach rested unruffled at the decline of day, after ages of good service done to the race that peopled its banks, spread out in the tranquil dignity of a waterway leading to the uttermost ends of the earth. We looked at the venerable stream not in the vivid flush of a short day that comes and departs for ever, but in the august light of abiding memories. And indeed nothing is easier for a man who has, as the phrase goes, "fol-lowed the sea" with reverence and affection, than to evoke the great spirit of the past upon the lower reaches of the Thames. The tidal current runs to and fro in its unceasing service, crowded with memories of men and ships it has borne to the rest of home or to the battles of the sea. It had known and served all the men of whom the nation is proud, from Sir Francis Drake to Sir John Franklin,[1] knights all, titled and untitled—the great knights-errant of the sea. It had borne all the ships whose names are like jewels flashing in the night of time, from the *Golden Hind* returning with her round flanks full of treasure, to be visited by the Queen's Highness and thus pass out of the gigantic tale, to the *Erebus* and *Terror*, bound on other conquests—and that never returned. It had known the ships and the men. They had sailed from Deptford, from Greenwich, from Erith—the adventurers and the settlers; kings' ships and the ships of men on 'Change[2]; captains, admirals, the dark "interlopers" of the Eastern trade, and the commissioned "generals" of East India fleets. Hunters for gold or pursuers of fame, they all had gone out on that stream, bearing the sword, and often the torch, messengers of the might within the land, bearers of a spark from the sacred fire. What greatness had not floated on the ebb of that river into the mystery of an unknown earth! . . . The dreams of men, the seed of commonwealths, the germs of empires.

The sun set; the dusk fell on the stream, and lights began to appear along the shore. The Chapman lighthouse, a three-legged thing erect on a mud-flat, shone strongly. Lights of ships moved in the fairway—a great stir of lights going up and going down. And farther west on the upper reaches the place of the monstrous town[3] was still marked ominously on the sky, a brooding gloom in sunshine, a lurid glare under the stars.

"And this also," said Marlow suddenly, "has been one of the dark places of the earth."

He was the only man of us who still "followed the sea." The worst that could be said of him was that he did not represent his class. He was a seaman, but he was a wanderer too, while most seamen lead, if one may so express it, a sedentary life. Their minds are of the stay-at-home order, and their home is always with them—the ship; and so is their country—the sea. One ship is very much like another, and the sea is always the same. In the immutability of their surroundings the foreign shores, the foreign faces, the changing immensity of life, glide

---

[1]Sailing in the *Golden Hind*, Sir Francis Drake had circumnavigated the globe in the 1580s in search of Spanish treasure; Sir John Franklin was a Victorian explorer who commanded the *Erebus* and the *Terror* in his unsuccessful quest for the Northwest Passage—an Arctic route from Europe over North America into the Pacific. Franklin died in 1847 and the rest of his party by the end of the following year.

[2]The London Stock Exchange.

[3]London.

past, veiled not by a sense of mystery but by a slightly disdainful ignorance; for there is nothing mysterious to a seaman unless it be the sea itself, which is the mistress of his existence and as inscrutable as Destiny. For the rest, after his hours of work, a casual stroll or a casual spree on shore suffices to unfold for him the secret of a whole continent, and generally he finds the secret not worth knowing. The yarns of seamen have a direct simplicity, the whole meaning of which lies within the shell of a cracked nut. But Marlow was not typical (if his propensity to spin yarns be excepted), and to him the meaning of an episode was not inside like a kernel but outside, enveloping the tale which brought it out only as a glow brings out a haze, in the likeness of one of these misty halos that sometimes are made visible by the spectral illumination of moonshine.

His remark did not seem at all surprising. It was just like Marlow. It was accepted in silence. No one took the trouble to grunt even; and presently he said, very slow:

"I was thinking of very old times, when the Romans first came here, nineteen hundred years ago—the other day. . . . Light came out of this river since—you say Knights? Yes; but it is like a running blaze on a plain, like a flash of lightning in the clouds. We live in the flicker—may it last as long as the old earth keeps rolling! But darkness was here yesterday. Imagine the feelings of a commander of a fine—what d'ye call 'em?—trireme[4] in the Mediterranean, ordered suddenly to the north; run overland across the Gauls in a hurry; put in charge of one of these craft the legionaries—a wonderful lot of handy men they must have been too—used to build, apparently by the hundred, in a month or two, if we may believe what we read. Imagine him here—the very end of the world, a sea the colour of lead, a sky the colour of smoke, a kind of ship about as rigid as a concertina—and going up this river with stores, or orders, or what you like. Sandbanks, marshes, forests, savages—precious little to eat fit for a civilised man, nothing but Thames water to drink. No Falernian wine here, no going ashore. Here and there a military camp lost in a wilderness, like a needle in a bundle of hay—cold, fog, tempests, disease, exile, and death—death skulking in the air, in the water, in the bush. They must have been dying like flies here. Oh yes—he did it. Did it very well, too, no doubt, and without thinking much about it either, except afterwards to brag of what he had gone through in his time, perhaps. They were men

---

[4]A war galley with three banks of oars.

enough to face the darkness. And perhaps he was cheered by keeping his eye on a chance of promotion to the fleet at Ravenna by and by, if he had good friends in Rome and survived the awful climate. Or think of a decent young citizen in a toga—perhaps too much dice, you know—coming out here in the train of some prefect, or tax-gatherer, or trader, even, to mend his fortunes. Land in a swamp, march through the woods, and in some inland post feel the savagery, the utter savagery, had closed round him—all that mysterious life of the wilderness that stirs in the forest, in the jungles, in the hearts of wild men. There's no initiation either into such mysteries. He has to live in the midst of the incomprehensible, which is also detestable. And it has a fascination, too, that goes to work upon him. The fascination of the abomination—you know. Imagine the growing regrets, the longing to escape, the powerless disgust, the surrender, the hate."

He paused.

"Mind," he began again, lifting one arm from the elbow, the palm of the hand outwards, so that, with his legs folded before him, he had the pose of a Buddha preaching in European clothes and without a lotus-flower—"Mind, none of us would feel exactly like this. What saves us is efficiency—the devotion to efficiency. But these chaps were not much account, really. They were no colonists; their administration was merely a squeeze, and nothing more, I suspect. They were conquerors, and for that you want only brute force—nothing to boast of, when you have it, since your strength is just an accident arising from the weakness of others. They grabbed what they could get for the sake of what was to be got. It was just robbery with violence, aggravated murder on a great scale, and men going at it blind—as is very proper for those who tackle a darkness. The conquest of the earth, which mostly means the taking it away from those who have a different complexion or slightly flatter noses than ourselves, is not a pretty thing when you look into it too much. What redeems it is the idea only. An idea at the back of it; not a sentimental pretence but an idea; and an unselfish belief in the idea—something you can set up, and bow down before, and offer a sacrifice to. . . ."

He broke off. Flames glided in the river, small green flames, red flames, white flames, pursuing, overtaking, joining, crossing each other—then separating slowly or hastily. The traffic of the great city went on in the deepening night upon the sleepless river. We looked on, waiting patiently—there was nothing else to do till the end of the flood; but it was only after a long silence, when he said, in a hesitating voice, "I suppose you fellows remember I did once turn fresh-water sailor for a bit," that we knew we were fated, before the ebb began to run, to hear about one of Marlow's inconclusive experiences.

"I don't want to bother you much with what happened to me personally," he began, showing in this remark the weakness of many tellers of tales who seem so often unaware of what their audience would best like to hear; "yet to understand the effect of it on me you ought to know how I got out there, what I saw, how I went up that river to the place where I first met the poor chap. It was the farthest point of navigation and the culminating point of my experience. It seemed somehow to throw a kind of light on everything about me—and into my thoughts. It was sombre enough too—and pitiful—not extraordinary in any way—not very clear either. No, not very clear. And yet it seemed to throw a kind of light.

"I had then, as you remember, just returned to London after a lot of Indian Ocean, Pacific, China Seas—a regular dose of the East—six years or so, and I was loafing about, hindering you fellows in your work and invading your homes, just as though I had got a heavenly mission to civilise you. It was very fine for a time, but after a bit I did get tired of resting. Then I began to look for a ship—I should think the hardest work on earth. But the ships wouldn't even look at me. And I got tired of that game too.

"Now when I was a little chap I had a passion for maps. I would look for hours at South America, or Africa, or Australia, and lose myself in all the glories of exploration. At that time there were many blank spaces on the earth, and when I saw one that looked particularly inviting on a map (but they all look that) I would put my finger on it and say, When I grow up I will go there. The North Pole was one of these places, I remember. Well, I haven't been there yet, and shall not try now. The glamour's off. Other places were scattered about the Equator, and in every sort of latitude all over the two hemispheres. I have been in some of them, and . . . well, we won't talk about that. But there was one yet—the biggest, the most blank, so to speak—that I had a hankering after.

"True, by this time it was not a blank space any more. It had got filled since my boyhood with rivers and lakes and names. It had ceased to be a blank space of delightful mystery—a white patch for a boy to dream gloriously over. It had become a place of darkness. But there was in it one river especially, a mighty big river, that you could see on the map, resembling an immense snake uncoiled, with its head in the sea, its body at rest curving afar over a vast country, and its tail lost in the depths of the land.[5] And as I looked at the map of it in a shop-window, it fascinated me as a snake would a bird—a silly little bird. Then I remembered there was a big concern, a Company for trade on that river. Dash it all! I thought to myself, they can't trade without using some kind of craft on that lot of fresh water—steamboats! Why shouldn't I try to get charge of one? I went on along Fleet Street, but could not shake off the idea. The snake had charmed me.

"You understand it was a Continental concern, that Trading Society; but I have a lot of relations living on the Continent, because it's cheap and not so nasty as it looks, they say.

"I am sorry to own I began to worry them. This was already a fresh departure for me. I was not used to get things that way, you know. I always went my own road and on my own legs where I had a mind to go. I wouldn't have believed it of myself; but, then—you see—I felt somehow I must get there by hook or by crook. So I worried them. The men said, 'My dear fellow,' and did nothing. Then—would you believe it?—I tried the women. I, Charlie Marlow, set the women to work—to get a job. Heavens! Well, you see, the notion drove me. I had an aunt, a dear enthusiastic soul. She wrote: 'It will be delightful. I am ready to do anything, anything for you. It is a glorious idea. I know the wife of a very high personage in the Administration, and also a man who has lots of influence with,' etc. etc. She was determined to make no end of fuss to get me appointed skipper of a river steamboat, if such was my fancy.

"I got my appointment—of course; and I got it very quick. It appears the Company had received news that one of their captains had been killed in a scuffle with the natives. This was my chance, and it made me the more anxious to go. It was only months and months afterwards, when I made the attempt to recover what was left of the body, that I heard the original quarrel arose from a misunderstanding about some hens. Yes, two black hens. Fresleven—that was the fellow's name, a Dane—thought himself wronged somehow in the bargain, so he went ashore and started to hammer the chief of the village with a stick. Oh, it didn't surprise me in the least to hear this, and at the same time to be told that Fresleven was the gentlest, quietest creature that ever walked on two legs. No doubt he was; but he had been a couple of years already out there engaged in the noble cause, you know, and he prob-

---

[5]The Congo.

ably felt the need at last of asserting his self-respect in some way. Therefore he whacked the old nigger mercilessly, while a big crowd of his people watched him, thunderstruck, till some man—I was told the chief's son—in desperation at hearing the old chap yell, made a tentative jab with a spear at the white man—and of course it went quite easy between the shoulder-blades. Then the whole population cleared into the forest, expecting all kinds of calamities to happen, while, on the other hand, the steamer Fresleven commanded left also in a bad panic, in charge of the engineer, I believe. Afterwards nobody seemed to trouble much about Fresleven's remains, till I got out and stepped into his shoes. I couldn't let it rest, though; but when an opportunity offered at last to meet my predecessor, the grass growing through his ribs was tall enough to hide his bones. They were all there. The supernatural being had not been touched after he fell. And the village was deserted, the huts gaped black, rotting, all askew within the fallen enclosures. A calamity had come to it, sure enough. The people had vanished. Mad terror had scattered them, men, women, and children, through the bush, and they had never returned. What became of the hens I don't know either. I should think the cause of progress got them, anyhow. However, through this glorious affair I got my appointment, before I had fairly begun to hope for it.

"I flew around like mad to get ready, and before forty-eight hours I was crossing the Channel to show myself to my employers, and sign the contract. In a very few hours I arrived in a city that always makes me think of a whited sepulchre.[6] Prejudice no doubt. I had no difficulty in finding the Company's offices. It was the biggest thing in the town, and everybody I met was full of it. They were going to run an oversea empire, and make no end of coin by trade.

"A narrow and deserted street in deep shadow, high houses, innumerable windows with venetian blinds, a dead silence, grass sprouting between the stones, imposing carriage archways right and left, immense double doors standing ponderously ajar. I slipped through one of these cracks, went up a swept and ungarnished staircase, as arid as a desert, and opened the first door I came to. Two women, one fat and the other slim, sat on straw-bottomed chairs, knitting black wool. The slim one got up and walked straight at me—still knitting with downcast eyes—and only just as I began to think of getting out of her way, as you would for a somnambulist, stood still, and looked up. Her dress was as plain as an umbrella-cover, and she turned round without a

---

[6]Brussels.

word and preceded me into a waiting-room. I gave my name, and looked about. Deal table in the middle, plain chairs all round the walls, on one end a large shining map, marked with all the colours of a rainbow. There was a vast amount of red[7]—good to see at any time, because one knows that some real work is done in there, a deuce of a lot of blue, a little green, smears of orange, and, on the East Coast, a purple patch, to show where the jolly pioneers of progress drink the jolly lager-beer. However, I wasn't going into any of these. I was going into the yellow. Dead in the centre. And the river was there—fascinating—deadly—like a snake. Ough! A door opened, a white-haired secretarial head, but wearing a compassionate expression, appeared, and a skinny forefinger beckoned me into the sanctuary. Its light was dim, and a heavy writing-desk squatted in the middle. From behind that structure came out an impression of pale plumpness in a frock-coat. The great man himself. He was five feet six, I should judge, and had his grip on the handle-end of ever so many millions. He shook hands, I fancy, murmured vaguely, was satisfied with my French. *Bon voyage.*

"In about forty-five seconds I found myself again in the waiting-room with the compassionate secretary, who, full of desolation and sympathy, made me sign some document. I believe I undertook amongst other things not to disclose any trade secrets. Well, I am not going to.

"I began to feel slightly uneasy. You know I am not used to such ceremonies, and there was something ominous in the atmosphere. It was just as though I had been let into some conspiracy—I don't know—something not quite right; and I was glad to get out. In the outer room the two women knitted black wool feverishly. People were arriving, and the younger one was walking back and forth introducing them. The old one sat on her chair. Her flat cloth slippers were propped up on a foot-warmer, and a cat reposed on her lap. She wore a starched white affair on her head, had a wart on one cheek, and silver-rimmed spectacles hung on the tip of her nose. She glanced at me above the glasses. The swift and indifferent placidity of that look troubled me. Two youths with foolish and cheery countenances were being piloted over, and she threw at them the same quick glance of unconcerned wisdom. She seemed to know all about them and about me too. An eerie feeling came over me. She seemed uncanny and fateful. Often far away there I thought of these two, guarding the door of Darkness,

---

[7] Traditional color of British colonies; the blue probably represents the French, the green and orange the Italian and Portuguese, and the purple the German colony of Tanganyika.

knitting black wool as for a warm pall, one introducing, introducing continuously to the unknown, the other scrutinising the cheery and foolish faces with unconcerned old eyes. *Ave!* Old knitter of black wool. *Morituri te salutant.*[8] Not many of those she looked at ever saw her again—not half, by a long way.

"There was yet a visit to the doctor. 'A simple formality,' assured me the secretary, with an air of taking an immense part in all my sorrows. Accordingly a young chap wearing his hat over the left eyebrow, some clerk I suppose—there must have been clerks in the business, though the house was as still as a house in a city of the dead—came from somewhere upstairs, and led me forth. He was shabby and careless, with ink-stains on the sleeves of his jacket, and his cravat was large and billowy, under a chin shaped like the toe of an old boot. It was a little too early for the doctor, so I proposed a drink, and thereupon he developed a vein of joviality. As we sat over our vermuths he glorified the Company's business, and by and by I expressed casually my surprise at him not going out there. He became very cool and collected all at once. 'I am not such a fool as I look, quoth Plato to his disciples,' he said sententiously, emptied his glass with great resolution, and we rose.

"The old doctor felt my pulse, evidently thinking of something else the while. 'Good, good for there,' he mumbled, and then with a certain eagerness asked me whether I would let him measure my head. Rather surprised, I said Yes, when he produced a thing like callipers and got the dimensions back and front and every way, taking notes carefully. He was an unshaven little man in a threadbare coat like a gaberdine, with his feet in slippers, and I thought him a harmless fool. 'I always ask leave, in the interests of science, to measure the crania of those going out there,' he said. 'And when they come back too?' I asked. 'Oh, I never see them,' he remarked; 'and, moreover, the changes take place inside, you know.' He smiled, as if at some quiet joke. 'So you are going out there. Famous. Interesting too.' He gave me a searching glance, and made another note. 'Ever any madness in your family?' he asked, in a matter-of-fact tone. I felt very annoyed. 'Is that question in the interests of science too?' 'It would be,' he said, without taking notice of my irritation, 'interesting for science to watch the mental changes of individuals on the spot, but . . .' 'Are you an alienist?'[9] I

---

[8]Hail! They who are about to die salute thee. (A slight variant of the gladiators' traditional greeting to the top-ranking spectators in the arena.)

[9]Psychiatrist.

interrupted. 'Every doctor should be—a little,' answered that original imperturbably. 'I have a little theory which you Messieurs who go out there must help me to prove. This is my share in the advantages my country shall reap from the possession of such a magnificent dependency. The mere wealth I leave to others. Pardon my questions, but you are the first Englishman coming under my observation . . .' I hastened to assure him I was not in the least typical. 'If I were,' said I, 'I wouldn't be talking like this with you.' 'What you say is rather profound, and probably erroneous,' he said, with a laugh. 'Avoid irritation more than exposure to the sun. Adieu. How do you English say, eh? Good-bye. Ah! Good-bye. Adieu. In the tropics one must before everything keep calm.' . . . He lifted a warning forefinger. . . . '*Du calme, du calme. Adieu.*'

"One thing more remained to do—say good-bye to my excellent aunt. I found her triumphant. I had a cup of tea—the last decent cup of tea for many days—and in a room that most soothingly looked just as you would expect a lady's drawing-room to look, we had a long quiet chat by the fireside. In the course of these confidences it became quite plain to me I had been represented to the wife of the high dignitary, and goodness knows to how many more people besides, as an exceptional and gifted creature—a piece of good fortune for the Company— a man you don't get hold of every day. Good Heavens! and I was going to take charge of a two-penny-halfpenny river-steamboat with a penny whistle attached! It appeared, however, I was also one of the Workers, with a capital—you know. Something like an emissary of light, something like a lower sort of apostle. There had been a lot of such rot let loose in print and talk just about that time, and the excellent woman, living right in the rush of all that humbug, got carried off her feet. She talked about 'weaning those ignorant millions from their horrid ways,' till, upon my word, she made me quite uncomfortable. I ventured to hint that the Company was run for profit.

" 'You forget, dear Charlie, that the labourer is worthy of his hire,' she said brightly. It's queer how out of touch with truth women are. They live in a world of their own, and there had never been anything like it, and never can be. It is too beautiful altogether, and if they were to set it up it would go to pieces before the first sunset. Some confounded fact we men have been living contentedly with ever since the day of creation would start up and knock the whole thing over.

"After this I got embraced, told to wear flannel, be sure to write often, and so on—and I left. In the street—I don't know why—a queer

feeling came to me that I was an impostor. Odd thing that I, who used
to clear out for any part of the world at twenty-four hours' notice, with
less thought than most men give to the crossing of a street, had a
moment—I won't say of hesitation, but of startled pause, before this
commonplace affair. The best way I can explain it to you is by saying
that, for a second or two, I felt as though, instead of going to the centre
of a continent, I were about to set off for the centre of the earth.

"I left in a French steamer, and she called in every blamed port they
have out there, for, as far as I could see, the sole purpose of landing
soldiers and custom-house officers. I watched the coast. Watching a
coast as it slips by the ship is like thinking about an enigma. There it is
before you—smiling, frowning, inviting, grand, mean, insipid, or savage, and always mute with an air of whispering, Come and find out.
This one was almost featureless, as if still in the making, with an aspect
of monotonous grimness. The edge of a colossal jungle, so dark green
as to be almost black, fringed with white surf, ran straight, like a ruled
line, far, far away along a blue sea whose glitter was blurred by a
creeping mist. The sun was fierce, the land seemed to glisten and drip
with steam. Here and there greyish-whitish specks showed up clus-
tered inside the white surf, with a flag flying above them perhaps—
settlements some centuries old, and still no bigger than pin-heads on
the untouched expanse of their background. We pounded along,
stopped, landed soldiers; went on, landed custom-house clerks to levy
toll in what looked like a God-forsaken wilderness, with a tin shed and
a flag-pole lost in it; landed more soldiers—to take care of the custom-
house clerks presumably. Some, I heard, got drowned in the surf; but
whether they did or not, nobody seemed particularly to care. They
were just flung out there, and on we went. Every day the coast looked
the same, as though we had not moved; but we passed various places—
trading places—with names like Gran' Bassam, Little Popo; names that
seemed to belong to some sordid farce acted in front of a sinister back-
cloth. The idleness of a passenger, my isolation amongst all these men
with whom I had no point of contact, the oily and languid sea, the
uniform sombreness of the coast, seemed to keep me away from the
truth of things, within the toil of a mournful and senseless delusion.
The voice of the surf heard now and then was a positive pleasure, like
the speech of a brother. It was something natural, that had its reason,
that had a meaning. Now and then a boat from the shore gave one a
momentary contact with reality. It was paddled by black fellows. You
could see from afar the white of their eyeballs glistening. They

shouted, sang; their bodies streamed with perspiration; they had faces like grotesque masks—these chaps; but they had bone, muscle, a wild vitality, an intense energy of movement, that was as natural and true as the surf along their coast. They wanted no excuse for being there. They were a great comfort to look at. For a time I would feel I belonged still to a world of straightforward facts; but the feeling would not last long. Something would turn up to scare it away. Once, I remember, we came upon a man-of-war anchored off the coast. There wasn't even a shed there, and she was shelling the bush. It appears the French had one of their wars going on thereabouts. Her ensign dropped limp like a rag; the muzzles of the long six-inch guns stuck out all over the low hull; the greasy, slimy swell swung her up lazily and let her down, swaying her thin masts. In the empty immensity of earth, sky, and water, there she was, incomprehensible, firing into a continent. Pop, would go one of the six-inch guns; a small flame would dart and vanish, a little white smoke would disappear, a tiny projectile would give a feeble screech— and nothing happened. Nothing could happen. There was a touch of insanity in the proceeding, a sense of lugubrious drollery in the sight; and it was not dissipated by somebody on board assuring me earnestly there was a camp of natives—he called them enemies!—hidden out of sight somewhere.

"We gave her her letters (I heard the men in that lonely ship were dying of fever at the rate of three a day) and went on. We called at some more places with farcical names, where the merry dance of death and trade goes on in a still and earthy atmosphere as of an overheated catacomb; all along the formless coast bordered by dangerous surf, as if Nature herself had tried to ward off intruders; in and out of rivers, streams of death in life, whose banks were rotting into mud, whose waters, thickened into slime, invaded the contorted mangroves, that seemed to writhe at us in the extremity of an impotent despair. No-where did we stop long enough to get a particularised impression, but the general sense of vague and oppressive wonder grew upon me. It was like a weary pilgrimage amongst hints for nightmares.

"It was upward of thirty days before I saw the mouth of the big river. We anchored off the seat of the government. But my work would not begin till some two hundred miles farther on. So as soon as I could I made a start for a place thirty miles higher up.

"I had my passage on a little sea-going steamer. Her captain was a Swede, and knowing me for a seaman, invited me on the bridge. He was a young man, lean, fair, and morose, with lanky hair and a shuffling gait. As we left the miserable little wharf, he tossed his head contemptuously at the shore. 'Been living there?' he asked. I said, 'Yes.' 'Fine lot these government chaps—are they not?' he went on, speaking English with great precision and considerable bitterness. 'It is funny what some people will do for a few francs a month. I wonder what becomes of that kind when it goes up country?' I said to him I expected to see that soon. 'So-o-o!' he exclaimed. He shuffled athwart, keeping one eye ahead vigilantly. 'Don't be too sure,' he continued. 'The other day I took up a man who hanged himself on the road. He was a Swede, too.' 'Hanged himself! Why, in God's name?' I cried. He kept on looking out watchfully. 'Who knows? The sun too much for him, or the country perhaps.'

"At last we opened a reach. A rocky cliff appeared, mounds of turned-up earth by the shore, houses on a hill, others with iron roofs, amongst a waste of excavations, or hanging to the declivity. A continuous noise of the rapids above hovered over this scene of inhabited devastation. A lot of people, mostly black and naked, moved about like ants. A jetty projected into the river. A blinding sunlight drowned all this at times in a sudden recrudescence of glare. 'There's your Company's station,' said the Swede, pointing to three wooden barrack-like structures on the rocky slope. 'I will send your things up. Four boxes did you say? So. Farewell.'

"I came upon a boiler wallowing in the grass, then found a path leading up the hill. It turned aside for the boulders, and also for an undersized railway truck lying there on its back with its wheels in the air. One was off. The thing looked as dead as the carcass of some animal. I came upon more pieces of decaying machinery, a stack of rusty rails. To the left a clump of trees made a shady spot, where dark things seemed to stir feebly. I blinked, the path was steep. A horn tooted to the right, and I saw the black people run. A heavy and dull detonation shook the ground, a puff of smoke came out of the cliff, and that was all. No change appeared on the face of the rock. They were building a railway. The cliff was not in the way or anything; but this objectless blasting was all the work going on.

"A slight clinking behind me made me turn my head. Six black men advanced in a file, toiling up the path. They walked erect and slow, balancing small baskets full of earth on their heads, and the clink kept time with their footsteps. Black rags were wound round their loins, and the short ends behind waggled to and fro like tails. I could see every rib, the joints of their limbs were like knots in a rope; each had an iron collar on his neck, and all were connected together with a chain whose bights swung between them, rhythmically clinking. Another report from the cliff made me think suddenly of that ship of war I had seen firing into a continent. It was the same kind of ominous voice; but these men could by no stretch of imagination be called enemies. They were called criminals, and the outraged law, like the bursting shells, had come to them, an insoluble mystery from the sea. All their meagre breasts panted together, the violently dilated nostrils quivered, the eyes stared stonily uphill. They passed me within six inches, without a glance, with that complete, deathlike indifference of unhappy savages. Behind this raw matter one of the reclaimed, the product of the new forces at work, strolled despondently, carrying a rifle by its middle. He had a uniform jacket with one button off, and seeing a white man on the path, hoisted his weapon to his shoulder with alacrity. This was simple prudence, white men being so much alike at a distance that he could not tell who I might be. He was speedily reassured, and with a large, white, rascally grin, and a glance at his charge, seemed to take me into partnership in his exalted trust. After all, I also was a part of the great cause of these high and just proceedings.

"Instead of going up, I turned and descended to the left. My idea was to let that chain-gang get out of sight before I climbed the hill. You know I am not particularly tender; I've had to strike and to fend off. I've had to resist and to attack sometimes—that's only one way of resisting—without counting the exact cost, according to the demands of such sort of life as I had blundered into. I've seen the devil of violence, and the devil of greed, and the devil of hot desire; but, by all the stars! these were strong, lusty, red-eyed devils, that swayed and drove men— men, I tell you. But as I stood on this hillside, I foresaw that in the blinding sunshine of that land I would become acquainted with a flabby, pretending, weak-eyed devil of a rapacious and pitiless folly. How insidious he could be, too, I was only to find out several months later and a thousand miles farther. For a moment I stood appalled, as though by a warning. Finally I descended the hill, obliquely, towards the trees I had seen.

"I avoided a vast artificial hole somebody had been digging on the slope, the purpose of which I found it impossible to divine. It wasn't a quarry or a sandpit, anyhow. It was just a hole. It might have been connected with the philanthropic desire of giving the criminals something to do. I don't know. Then I nearly fell into a very narrow ravine, almost no more than a scar in the hillside. I discovered that a lot of imported drainage-pipes for the settlement had been tumbled in there. There wasn't one that was not broken. It was a wanton smash-up. At last I got under the trees. My purpose was to stroll into the shade for a moment; but no sooner within than it seemed to me I had stepped into the gloomy circle of some Inferno. The rapids were near, and an uninterrupted, uniform, headlong, rushing noise filled the mournful stillness of the grove, where not a breath stirred, not a leaf moved, with a mysterious sound—as though the tearing pace of the launched earth had suddenly become audible.

"Black shapes crouched, lay, sat between the trees, leaning against the trunks, clinging to the earth, half coming out, half effaced within the dim light, in all the attitudes of pain, abandonment, and despair. Another mine on the cliff went off, followed by a slight shudder of the soil under my feet. The work was going on. The work! And this was the place where some of the helpers had withdrawn to die.

"They were dying slowly—it was very clear. They were not enemies, they were not criminals, they were nothing earthly now—nothing but black shadows of disease and starvation, lying confusedly in the greenish gloom. Brought from all the recesses of the coast in all the legality of time contracts, lost in uncongenial surroundings, fed on unfamiliar food, they sickened, became inefficient and were then allowed to crawl away and rest. These moribund shapes were free as air—and nearly as thin. I began to distinguish the gleam of the eyes under the trees. Then, glancing down, I saw a face near my hand. The black bones reclined at full length with one shoulder against the tree, and slowly the eyelids rose and the sunken eyes looked up at me, enormous and vacant, a kind of blind, white flicker in the depths of the orbs, which died out slowly. The man seemed young—almost a boy—but you know with them it's hard to tell. I found nothing else to do but to offer him one of my good Swede's ship's biscuits I had in my pocket. The fingers closed slowly on it and held—there was no other movement and no other glance. He had tied a bit of white worsted round his neck—Why? Where did he get it? Was it a badge—an ornament—a charm—a propitiatory act? Was there any idea at all connected with it? It looked startling round his black neck, this bit of white thread from beyond the seas.

"Near the same tree two more bundles of acute angles sat with their legs drawn up. One, with his chin propped on his knees, stared at nothing, in an intolerable and appalling manner: his brother phantom rested its forehead, as if overcome with a great weariness; and all about others were scattered in every pose of contorted collapse, as in some picture of a massacre or a pestilence. While I stood horror-struck, one of these creatures rose to his hands and knees, and went off on all-fours towards the river to drink. He lapped out of his hand, then sat up in the sunlight, crossing his shins in front of him, and after a time let his woolly head fall on his breastbone.

"I didn't want any more loitering in the shade, and I made haste towards the station. When near the buildings I met a white man, in such an unexpected elegance of get-up that in the first moment I took him for a sort of vision. I saw a high starched collar, white cuffs, a light alpaca jacket, snowy trousers, a clean necktie, and varnished boots. No hat. Hair parted, brushed, oiled, under a green-lined parasol held in a big white hand. He was amazing, and had a pen-holder behind his ear.

"I shook hands with this miracle, and I learned he was the Company's chief accountant, and that all the book-keeping was done at this station. He had come out for a moment, he said, 'to get a breath of fresh air.' The expression sounded wonderfully odd, with its suggestion of sedentary desk-life. I wouldn't have mentioned the fellow to you at all, only it was from his lips that I first heard the name of the man who is so indissolubly connected with the memories of that time. Moreover, I respected the fellow. Yes; I respected his collars, his vast cuffs, his brushed hair. His appearance was certainly that of a hairdresser's dummy; but in the great demoralisation of the land he kept up his appearance. That's backbone. His starched collars and got-up shirt-fronts were achievements of character. He had been out nearly three years; and, later, I could not help asking him how he managed to sport such linen. He had just the faintest blush, and said modestly, 'I've been teaching one of the native women about the station. It was difficult. She had a distaste for the work.' Thus this man had verily accomplished something. And he was devoted to his books, which were in apple-pie order.

"Everything else in the station was in a muddle,—heads, things, buildings. Strings of dusty niggers with splay feet arrived and departed; a stream of manufactured goods, rubbishy cottons, beads, and brass-wire sent into the depths of darkness, and in return came a precious trickle of ivory.

"I had to wait in the station for ten days—an eternity. I lived in a hut in the yard, but to be out of the chaos I would sometimes get into the accountant's office. It was built of horizontal planks, and so badly put together that, as he bent over his high desk, he was barred from neck to heels with narrow strips of sunlight. There was no need to open the big shutter to see. It was hot there too; big flies buzzed fiendishly, and did not sting, but stabbed. I sat generally on the floor, while, of faultless appearance (and even slightly scented), perching on a high stool, he wrote, he wrote. Sometimes he stood up for exercise. When a truckle-bed with a sick man (some invalided agent from up-country) was put in there, he exhibited a gentle annoyance. 'The groans of this sick person,' he said, 'distract my attention. And without that it is extremely difficult to guard against clerical errors in this climate.'

"One day he remarked, without lifting his head, 'In the interior you will no doubt meet Mr. Kurtz.' On my asking who Mr. Kurtz was, he said he was a first-class agent; and seeing my disappointment at this information, he added slowly, laying down his pen, 'He is a very re-markable person.' Further questions elicited from him that Mr. Kurtz was at present in charge of a trading-post, a very important one, in the true ivory-country, at 'the very bottom of there. Sends in as much ivory as all the others put together . . .' He began to write again. The sick man was too ill to groan. The flies buzzed in a great peace.

"Suddenly there was a growing murmur of voices and a great tramp-ing of feet. A caravan had come in. A violent babble of uncouth sounds burst out on the other side of the planks. All the carriers were speaking together, and in the midst of the uproar the lamentable voice of the chief agent was heard 'giving it up' tearfully for the twentieth time that day. . . . He rose slowly. 'What a frightful row,' he said. He crossed the room gently to look at the sick man, and returning, said to me, 'He does not hear.' 'What! Dead?' I asked, startled. 'No, not yet,' he an-swered, with great composure. Then, alluding with a toss of the head to the tumult in the station-yard, 'When one has got to make correct entries, one comes to hate those savages—hate them to the death.' He remained thoughtful for a moment. 'When you see Mr. Kurtz,' he went on, 'tell him from me that everything here'—he glanced at the desk—'is very satisfactory. I don't like to write to him—with those messengers of ours you never know who may get hold of your letter—at that Central Station.' He stared at me for a moment with his mild, bulging eyes. 'Oh, he will go far, very far,' he began again. 'He will be a some-body in the Administration before long. They, above—the Council in Europe, you know—mean him to be.'

"He turned to his work. The noise outside had ceased, and presently in going out I stopped at the door. In the steady buzz of flies the homeward-bound agent was lying flushed and insensible; the other, bent over his books, was making correct entries of perfectly correct transactions; and fifty feet below the doorstep I could see the still tree-tops of the grove of death.

"Next day I left that station at last, with a caravan of sixty men, for a two-hundred-mile tramp.

"No use telling you much about that. Paths, paths, everywhere; a stamped-in network of paths spreading over the empty land, through long grass, through burnt grass, through thickets, down and up chilly ravines, up and down stony hills ablaze with heat; and a solitude, a solitude, nobody, not a hut. The population had cleared out a long time ago. Well, if a lot of mysterious niggers armed with all kinds of fearful weapons suddenly took to travelling on the road between Deal and Gravesend, catching the yokels right and left to carry heavy loads for them, I fancy every farm and cottage thereabouts would get empty very soon. Only here the dwellings were gone too. Still, I passed through several abandoned villages. There's something pathetically childish in the ruins of grass walls. Day after day, with the stamp and shuffle of sixty pair of bare feet behind me, each pair under a 60-lb. load. Camp, cook, sleep; strike camp, march. Now and then a carrier dead in harness, at rest in the long grass near the path, with an empty water-gourd and his long staff lying by his side. A great silence around and above. Perhaps on some quiet night the tremor of far-off drums, sinking, swelling, a tremor vast, faint; a sound weird, appealing, suggestive, and wild—and perhaps with as profound a meaning as the sound of bells in a Christian country. Once a white man in an unbuttoned uniform, camping on the path with an armed escort of lank Zanzibaris, very hospitable and festive—not to say drunk. Was looking after the up-keep of the road, he declared. Can't say I saw any road or any upkeep, unless the body of a middle-aged negro, with a bullet-hole in the fore-head, upon which I absolutely stumbled three miles farther on, may be considered as a permanent improvement. I had a white companion too, not a bad chap, but rather too fleshy and with the exasperating habit of fainting on the hot hillsides, miles away from the least bit of shade and water. Annoying, you know, to hold your own coat like a parasol over a man's head while he is coming to. I couldn't help asking him once what he meant by coming there at all. 'To make money, of course. What do you think?' he said scornfully. Then he got fever, and had to be carried in a hammock slung under a pole. As he weighed sixteen stone[10] I had no end of rows with the carriers. They jibbed, ran away, sneaked off with their loads in the night—quite a mutiny. So, one evening, I made a speech in English with gestures, not one of which was lost to the sixty pairs of eyes before me, and the next morning I started the hammock off in front all right. An hour afterwards I came

---

[10] 224 pounds.

upon the whole concern wrecked in a bush—man, hammock, groans, blankets, horrors. The heavy pole had skinned his poor nose. He was very anxious for me to kill somebody, but there wasn't the shadow of a carrier near. I remembered the old doctor—'It would be interesting for science to watch the mental changes of individuals, on the spot.' I felt I was becoming scientifically interesting. However, all that is to no purpose. On the fifteenth day I came in sight of the big river again, and hobbled into the Central Station. It was on a back water surrounded by scrub and forest, with a pretty border of smelly mud on one side, and on the three others enclosed by a crazy fence of rushes. A neglected gap was all the gate it had, and the first glance at the place was enough to let you see the flabby devil was running that show. White men with long staves in their hands appeared languidly from amongst the buildings, strolling up to take a look at me, and then retired out of sight somewhere. One of them, a stout, excitable chap with black moustaches, informed me with great volubility and many digressions, as soon as I told him who I was, that my steamer was at the bottom of the river. I was thunderstruck. What, how, why? Oh, it was 'all right.' The 'manager himself' was there. All quite correct. 'Everybody had behaved splendidly! splendidly!'—'You must,' he said in agitation, 'go and see the general manager at once. He is waiting.'

"I did not see the real significance of that wreck at once. I fancy I see it now, but I am not sure—not at all. Certainly the affair was too stupid—when I think of it—to be altogether natural. Still . . . But at the moment it presented itself simply as a confounded nuisance. The steamer was sunk. They had started two days before in a sudden hurry up the river with the manager on board, in charge of some volunteer skipper, and before they had been out three hours they tore the bottom out of her on stones, and she sank near the south bank. I asked myself what I was to do there, now my boat was lost. As a matter of fact, I had plenty to do in fishing my command out of the river. I had to set about it the very next day. That, and the repairs when I brought the pieces to the station, took some months.

"My first interview with the manager was curious. He did not ask me to sit down after my twenty-mile walk that morning. He was commonplace in complexion, in feature, in manners, and in voice. He was of middle size and of ordinary build. His eyes, of the usual blue, were perhaps remarkably cold, and he certainly could make his glance fall on one as trenchant and heavy as an axe. But even at these times the rest of his person seemed to disclaim the intention. Otherwise there was only an indefinable, faint expression of his lips, something stealthy—a smile—not a smile—I remember it, but I can't explain. It was unconscious, this smile was, though just after he had said something it got intensified for an instant. It came at the end of his speeches like a seal applied on the words to make the meaning of the commonest phrase appear absolutely inscrutable. He was a common trader, from his youth up employed in these parts—nothing more. He was obeyed, yet he inspired neither love nor fear, nor even respect. He inspired uneasiness. That was it! Uneasiness. Not a definite mistrust—just uneasiness—nothing more. You have no idea how effective such a . . . a . . . faculty can be. He had no genius for organising, for initiative, or for order even. That was evident in such things as the deplorable state of the station. He had no learning, and no intelligence. His position had come to him—why? Perhaps because he was never ill . . . He had served three terms of three years out there . . . Because triumphant health in the general rout of constitutions is a kind of power in itself. When he went home on leave he rioted on a large scale—pompously. Jack[11] ashore—with a difference—in externals only. This one could gather from his casual talk. He originated nothing, he could keep the routine going—that's all. But he was great. He was great by this little thing that it was impossible to tell what could control such a man. He never gave that secret away. Perhaps there was nothing within him. Such a suspicion made one pause—for out there there were no external checks. Once when various tropical diseases had laid low almost every 'agent' in the station, he was heard to say, 'Men who come out here should have no entrails.' He sealed the utterance with that smile of his, as though it had been a door opening into a darkness he had in his keeping. You fancied you had seen things—but the seal was on. When annoyed at meal-times by the constant quarrels of the white men about precedence, he ordered an immense round table to be made, for which a special house had to be built. This was the station's mess-room. Where he sat was the first place—the rest were nowhere. One felt this to be his unalterable conviction. He was neither civil nor uncivil. He was quiet. He allowed his 'boy'—an overfed young negro from the coast—to treat the white men, under his very eyes, with provoking insolence.

"He began to speak as soon as he saw me. I had been very long on the road. He could not wait. Had to start without me. The up-river stations had to be relieved. There had been so many delays already that

---

[11]Slang for a common seaman.

he did not know who was dead and who was alive, and how they got on—and so on, and so on. He paid no attention to my explanations, and, playing with a stick of sealing-wax, repeated several times that the situation was 'very grave, very grave.' There were rumours that a very important station was in jeopardy, and its chief, Mr. Kurtz, was ill. Hoped it was not true. Mr. Kurtz was . . . I felt weary and irritable. Hang Kurtz, I thought. I interrupted him by saying I had heard of Mr. Kurtz on the coast. 'Ah! So they talk of him down there,' he murmured to himself. Then he began again, assuring me Mr. Kurtz was the best agent he had, an exceptional man, of the greatest importance to the Company; therefore I could understand his anxiety. He was, he said, 'very, very uneasy.' Certainly he fidgeted on his chair a good deal, exclaimed, 'Ah, Mr. Kurtz!' broke the stick of sealing-wax and seemed dumbfounded by the accident. Next thing he wanted to know 'how long it would take to' . . . I interrupted him again. Being hungry, you know, and kept on my feet too, I was getting savage. 'How can I tell?' I said. 'I haven't even seen the wreck yet—some months, no doubt.' All this talk seemed to me so futile. 'Some months,' he said. 'Well, let us say three months before we can make a start. Yes. That ought to do the affair.' I flung out of his hut (he lived all alone in a clay hut with a sort of verandah) muttering to myself my opinion of him. He was a chattering idiot. Afterwards I took it back when it was borne in upon me startlingly with what extreme nicety he had estimated the time requisite for the 'affair.'

"I went to work the next day, turning, so to speak, my back on that station. In that way only it seemed to me I could keep my hold on the redeeming facts of life. Still, one must look about sometimes; and then I saw this station, these men strolling aimlessly about in the sunshine of the yard. I asked myself sometimes what it all meant. They wandered here and there with their absurd long staves in their hands, like a lot of faithless pilgrims bewitched inside a rotten fence. The word 'ivory' rang in the air, was whispered, was sighed. You would think they were praying to it. A taint of imbecile rapacity blew through it all, like a whiff from some corpse. By Jove! I've never seen anything so unreal in my life. And outside, the silent wilderness surrounding this cleared speck on the earth struck me as something great and invincible, like evil or truth, waiting patiently for the passing away of this fantastic invasion.

"Oh, those months! Well, never mind. Various things happened. One evening a grass shed full of calico, cotton prints, beads, and I don't know what else, burst into a blaze so suddenly that you would have thought the earth had opened to let an avenging fire consume all that trash. I was smoking my pipe quietly by my dismantled steamer, and saw them all cutting capers in the light, with their arms lifted high, when the stout man with moustaches came tearing down to the river, a tin pail in his hand, assured me that everybody was 'behaving splendidly, splendidly,' dipped about a quart of water and tore back again. I noticed there was a hole in the bottom of his pail.

"I strolled up. There was no hurry. You see the thing had gone off like a box of matches. It had been hopeless from the very first. The flame had leaped high, driven everybody back, lighted up everything—and collapsed. The shed was already a heap of embers glowing fiercely. A nigger was being beaten near by. They said he had caused the fire in some way; be that as it may, he was screeching most horribly. I saw him, later, for several days, sitting in a bit of shade looking very sick and trying to recover himself: afterwards he arose and went out—and the wilderness without a sound took him into its bosom again. As I approached the glow from the dark I found myself at the back of two men, talking. I heard the name of Kurtz pronounced, then the words, 'take advantage of this unfortunate accident.' One of the men was the manager. I wished him a good evening. 'Did you ever see anything like it—eh? it is incredible,' he said, and walked off. The other man remained. He was a first-class agent, young, gentlemanly, a bit reserved, with a forked little beard and a hooked nose. He was stand-offish with the other agents, and they on their side said he was the manager's spy upon them. As to me, I had hardly ever spoken to him before. We got into talk, and by and by we strolled away from the hissing ruins. Then he asked me to his room, which was in the main building of the station. He struck a match, and I perceived that this young aristocrat had not only a silver-mounted dressing-case but also a whole candle all to himself. Just at that time the manager was the only man supposed to have any right to candles. Native mats covered the clay walls; a collection of spears, assegais,[12] shields, knives, was hung up in trophies. The business entrusted to this fellow was the making of bricks—so I had been informed; but there wasn't a fragment of a brick anywhere in the station, and he had been there more than a year—waiting. It seems he could not make bricks without something, I don't know what—straw maybe. Anyway, it could not be found there, and as it was not likely to be sent from Europe, it did not appear clear to me what he was waiting

---

[12]Throwing spears.

for. An act of special creation perhaps. However, they were all waiting—all the sixteen or twenty pilgrims of them—for something; and
upon my word it did not seem an uncongenial occupation, from the
way they took it, though the only thing that ever came to them was
disease—as far as I could see. They beguiled the time by backbiting
and intriguing against each other in a foolish kind of way. There was
an air of plotting about that station, but nothing came of it, of course.
It was as unreal as everything else—as the philanthropic pretence of
the whole concern, as their talk, as their government, as their show of
work. The only real feeling was a desire to get appointed to a trading-
post where ivory was to be had, so that they could earn percentages.
They intrigued and slandered and hated each other only on that account—but as to effectually lifting a little finger—oh no. By Heavens!
there is something after all in the world allowing one man to steal a
horse while another must not look at a halter. Steal a horse straight
out. Very well. He has done it. Perhaps he can ride. But there is a way
of looking at a halter that would provoke the most charitable of saints
into a kick.

"I had no idea why he wanted to be sociable, but as we chatted in
there it suddenly occurred to me the fellow was trying to get at something—in fact, pumping me. He alluded constantly to Europe, to the
people I was supposed to know there—putting leading questions as to
my acquaintances in the sepulchral city, and so on. His little eyes glittered like mica discs—with curiosity—though he tried to keep up a bit
of superciliousness. At first I was astonished, but very soon I became
awfully curious to see what he could find out from me. I couldn't
possibly imagine what I had in me to make it worth his while. It was
very pretty to see how he baffled himself, for in truth my body was full
only of chills, and my head had nothing in it but that wretched steamboat business. It was evident he took me for a perfectly shameless
prevaricator. At last he got angry, and, to conceal a movement of furious annoyance, he yawned. I rose. Then I noticed a small sketch in oils,
on a panel, representing a woman, draped and blindfolded, carrying a
lighted torch. The background was sombre—almost black. The movement of the woman was stately, and the effect of the torchlight on the
face was sinister.

"It arrested me, and he stood by civilly, holding an empty half-pint
champagne bottle (medical comforts) with the candle stuck in it. To my
question he said Mr. Kurtz had painted this—in this very station more
than a year ago—while waiting for means to go to his trading-post.
'Tell me, pray,' said I, 'who is this Mr. Kurtz?'

" 'The chief of the Inner Station,' he answered in a short tone, looking away. 'Much obliged,' I said, laughing. 'And you are the brickmaker of the Central Station. Every one knows that.' He was silent for a while. 'He is a prodigy,' he said at last. 'He is an emissary of pity, and science, and progress, and devil knows what else. We want,' he began to declaim suddenly, 'for the guidance of the cause entrusted to us by Europe, so to speak, higher intelligence, wide sympathies, a singleness of purpose.' 'Who says that?' I asked. 'Lots of them,' he replied. 'Some even write that; and so *he* comes here, a special being, as you ought to know.' 'Why ought I to know?' I interrupted, really surprised. He paid no attention. 'Yes. To-day he is chief of the best station, next year he will be assistant-manager, two years more and . . . but I daresay you know what he will be in two years' time. You are of the new gang—the gang of virtue. The same people who sent him specially also recommended you. Oh, don't say no. I've my own eyes to trust.' Light dawned upon me. My dear aunt's influential acquaintances were producing an unexpected effect upon that young man. I nearly burst into a laugh. 'Do you read the Company's confidential correspondence?' I asked. He hadn't a word to say. It was great fun. 'When Mr. Kurtz,' I continued severely, 'is General Manager, you won't have the opportunity.'

"He blew the candle out suddenly, and we went outside. The moon had risen. Black figures strolled about listlessly, pouring water on the glow, whence proceeded a sound of hissing; steam ascended in the moonlight; the beaten nigger groaned somewhere. 'What a row the brute makes!' said the indefatigable man with the moustaches, appearing near us. 'Serve him right. Transgression—punishment—bang! Pitiless, pitiless. That's the only way. This will prevent all conflagrations for the future. I was just telling the manager . . .' He noticed my companion, and became crestfallen all at once. 'Not in bed yet,' he said, with a kind of servile heartiness; 'it's so natural. Ha! Danger—agitation.' He vanished. I went on to the river-side, and the other followed me. I heard a scathing murmur at my ear. 'Heaps of muffs—go to.' The pilgrims could be seen in knots gesticulating, discussing. Several had still their staves in their hands. I verily believe they took these sticks to bed with them. Beyond the fence the forest stood up spectrally in the moonlight, and through the dim stir, through the faint sounds of that lamentable courtyard, the silence of the land went home to one's very heart—its mystery, its greatness, the amazing reality of its concealed life. The hurt nigger moaned feebly somewhere near by, and then fetched a deep sigh that made me mend my pace away from there. I felt a hand introducing itself under my arm. 'My dear sir,' said the fellow, 'I don't want to be misunderstood, and especially by you, who will see Mr. Kurtz long before I can have that pleasure. I wouldn't like him to get a false idea of my disposition. . . .'

"I let him run on, this papier-mâché Mephistopheles, and it seemed to me that if I tried I could poke my forefinger through him, and would find nothing inside but a little loose dirt, maybe. He, don't you see, had been planning to be assistant-manager by and by under the present man, and I could see that the coming of that Kurtz had upset them both not a little. He talked precipitately, and I did not try to stop him. I had my shoulders against the wreck of my steamer, hauled up on the slope like a carcass of some big river animal. The smell of mud, of primeval mud, by Jove! was in my nostrils, the high stillness of primeval forest was before my eyes; there were shiny patches on the black creek. The moon had spread over everything a thin layer of silver—over the rank grass, over the mud, upon the wall of matted vegetation standing higher than the wall of a temple, over the great river I could see through a sombre gap glittering, glittering, as it flowed broadly by without a murmur. All this was great, expectant, mute, while the man jabbered about himself. I wondered whether the stillness on the face of the immensity looking at us two were meant as an appeal or as a menace. What were we who had strayed in here? Could we handle that dumb thing, or would it handle us? I felt how big, how confoundedly big, was that thing that couldn't talk and perhaps was deaf as well. What was in there? I could see a little ivory coming out from there, and I had heard Mr. Kurtz was in there. I had heard enough about it too—God knows! Yet somehow it didn't bring any image with it—no more than if I had been told an angel or a fiend was in there. I believed it in the same way one of you might believe there are inhabitants in the planet Mars. I knew once a Scotch sailmaker who was certain, dead sure, there were people in Mars. If you asked him for some idea how they looked and behaved, he would get shy and mutter something about 'walking on all-fours.' If you as much as smiled, he would—though a man of sixty—offer to fight you. I would not have gone so far as to fight for Kurtz, but I went for him near enough to a lie. You know I hate, detest, and can't bear a lie, not because I am straighter than the rest of us, but simply because it appals me. There is a taint of death, a flavour of mortality in lies—which is exactly what I hate and detest in the world—what I want to forget. It makes me miserable and sick, like biting something rotten would do. Temperament, I suppose. Well, I went near enough to it by letting the young fool there believe anything he liked to imagine as to my influence in Europe. I became in an instant as much of a pretence as the rest of the bewitched pilgrims. This simply because I had a notion it somehow would be of help to that Kurtz whom at the time I did not see—you understand. He was just a word for me. I did not see the man in the name any more than you do. Do you see him? Do you see the story? Do you see anything? It seems to me I am trying to tell you a dream—making a vain attempt, because no relation of a dream can convey the dream-sensation, that commingling of absurdity, surprise, and bewilderment in a tremor of struggling revolt, that notion of being captured by the incredible which is of the very essence of dreams. . . ."

He was silent for a while.

". . . No, it is impossible; it is impossible to convey the life-sensation of any given epoch of one's existence—that which makes its truth, its meaning—its subtle and penetrating essence. It is impossible. We live, as we dream—alone. . . ."

He paused again as if reflecting, then added:

"Of course in this you fellows see more than I could then. You see me, whom you know. . . ."

It had become so pitch dark that we listeners could hardly see one another. For a long time already he, sitting apart, had been no more to us than a voice. There was not a word from anybody. The others might have been asleep, but I was awake. I listened, I listened on the watch for the sentence, for the word, that would give me the clue to the faint uneasiness inspired by this narrative that seemed to shape itself without human lips in the heavy night-air of the river.

". . . Yes—I let him run on," Marlow began again, "and think what he pleased about the powers that were behind me. I did! And there was nothing behind me! There was nothing but that wretched, old, mangled steamboat I was leaning against, while he talked fluently about 'the necessity for every man to get on.' 'And when one comes out here, you conceive, it is not to gaze at the moon.' Mr. Kurtz was a 'universal genius,' but even a genius would find it easier to work with 'adequate tools—intelligent men.' He did not make bricks—why, there was a physical impossibility in the way—as I was well aware; and if he did secretarial work for the manager, it was because 'no sensible man rejects wantonly the confidence of his superiors.' Did I see it? I saw it. What more did I want? What I really wanted was rivets, by Heaven! Rivets. To get on with the work—to stop the hole. Rivets I wanted. There were cases of them down at the coast—cases—piled up—burst—split! You kicked a loose rivet at every second step in that station yard on the hillside. Rivets had rolled into the grove of death. You could fill your pockets with rivets for the trouble of stooping down—and there wasn't one rivet to be found where it was wanted. We had plates that would do, but nothing to fasten them with. And every week the messenger, a lone negro, letter-bag on shoulder and staff in hand, left our station for the coast. And several times a week a coast caravan came in with trade goods—ghastly glazed calico that made you shudder only to look at it, glass beads value about a penny a quart, confounded spotted cotton handkerchiefs. And no rivets. Three carriers could have brought all that was wanted to set that steamboat afloat.

"He was becoming confidential now, but I fancy my unresponsive attitude must have exasperated him at last, for he judged it necessary to inform me he feared neither God nor devil, let alone any mere man. I said I could see that very well, but what I wanted was a certain quantity of rivets—and rivets were what really Mr. Kurtz wanted, if he had only known it. Now letters went to the coast every week. . . . 'My dear sir,' he cried, 'I write from dictation.' I demanded rivets. There was a way— for an intelligent man. He changed his manner; became very cold, and suddenly began to talk about a hippopotamus; wondered whether sleeping on board the steamer (I stuck to my salvage night and day) I wasn't disturbed. There was an old hippo that had the bad habit of getting out on the bank and roaming at night over the station grounds. The pilgrims used to turn out in a body and empty every rifle they could lay hands on at him. Some even had sat up o' nights for him. All this energy was wasted, though. 'That animal has a charmed life,' he said; 'but you can say this only of brutes in this country. No man—you apprehend me?—no man here bears a charmed life.' He stood there for a moment in the moonlight with his delicate hooked nose set a little askew, and his mica eyes glittering without a wink, then, with a curt Good-night, he strode off. I could see he was disturbed and considerably puzzled, which made me feel more hopeful than I had been for days. It was a great comfort to turn from that chap to my influential friend, the battered, twisted, ruined, tin-pot steamboat. I clambered on board. She rang under my feet like an empty Huntley & Palmer biscuit-tin kicked along a gutter; she was nothing so solid in make, and rather less pretty in shape, but I had expended enough hard work on her to make me love her. No influential friend would have served me better. She had given me a chance to come out a bit—to find out what I could do. No, I don't like work. I had rather laze about and think of all the fine things that can be done. I don't like work—no man does—but I like what is in the work—the chance to find yourself. Your own reality—for yourself, not for others—what no other man can ever know. They can only see the mere show, and never can tell what it really means.

"I was not surprised to see somebody sitting aft, on the deck, with his legs dangling over the mud. You see I rather chummed with the few mechanics there were in that station, whom the other pilgrims naturally despised—on account of their imperfect manners, I suppose. This was the foreman—a boiler-maker by trade—a good worker. He was a lank, bony, yellow-faced man, with big intense eyes. His aspect was worried, and his head was as bald as the palm of my hand; but his hair in falling seemed to have stuck to his chin, and had prospered in the new locality, for his beard hung down to his waist. He was a widower with six young children (he had left them in charge of a sister of his to come out there), and the passion of his life was pigeon-flying. He was an enthusiast and a connoisseur. He would rave about pigeons. After work hours he used sometimes to come over from his hut for a talk about his children and his pigeons; at work, when he had to crawl in the mud under the bottom of the steamboat, he would tie up that beard of his in a kind of white serviette[13] he brought for the purpose. It had loops to go over his ears. In the evening he could be seen squatted on the bank rinsing that wrapper in the creek with great care, then spreading it solemnly on a bush to dry.

"I slapped him on the back and shouted 'We shall have rivets!' He scrambled to his feet exclaiming 'No! Rivets!' as though he couldn't believe his ears. Then in a low voice, 'You . . . eh?' I don't know why we behaved like lunatics. I put my finger to the side of my nose and nodded mysteriously. 'Good for you!' he cried, snapped his fingers above his head, lifting one foot. I tried a jig. We capered on the iron deck. A frightful clatter came out of that hulk, and the virgin forest on the other bank of the creek sent it back in a thundering roll upon the sleeping station. It must have made some of the pilgrims sit up in their hovels. A dark figure obscured the lighted doorway of the manager's hut, vanished, then, a second or so after, the doorway itself vanished too. We stopped, and the silence driven away by the stamping of our feet flowed back again from the recesses of the land. The great wall of vegetation, an exuberant and entangled mass of trunks, branches, leaves, boughs, festoons, motionless in the moonlight, was like a rioting invasion of soundless life, a rolling wave of plants, piled up, crested,

---

[13]Napkin.

ready to topple over the creek, to sweep every little man of us out of his little existence. And it moved not. A deadened burst of mighty splashes and snorts reached us from afar, as though an ichthyosaurus had been taking a bath of glitter in the great river. 'After all,' said the boiler-maker in a reasonable tone, 'why shouldn't we get the rivets?' Why not, indeed! I did not know of any reason why we shouldn't. 'They'll come in three weeks,' I said confidently.

"But they didn't. Instead of rivets there came an invasion, an infliction, a visitation. It came in sections during the next three weeks, each section headed by a donkey carrying a white man in new clothes and tan shoes, bowing from that elevation right and left to the impressed pilgrims. A quarrelsome band of footsore sulky niggers trod on the heels of the donkey; a lot of tents, camp-stools, tin boxes, white cases, brown bales would be shot down in the courtyard, and the air of mystery would deepen a little over the muddle of the station. Five such instalments came, with their absurd air of disorderly flight with the loot of innumerable outfit shops and provision stores, that, one would think, they were lugging, after a raid, into the wilderness for equitable division. It was an inextricable mess of things decent in themselves but that human folly made look like the spoils of thieving.

"This devoted band called itself the Eldorado Exploring Expedition, and I believe they were sworn to secrecy. Their talk, however, was the talk of sordid buccaneers: it was reckless without hardihood, greedy without audacity, and cruel without courage; there was not an atom of foresight or of serious intention in the whole batch of them, and they did not seem aware these things are wanted for the work of the world. To tear treasure out of the bowels of the land was their desire, with no more moral purpose at the back of it than there is in burglars breaking into a safe. Who paid the expenses of the noble enterprise I don't know; but the uncle of our manager was leader of that lot.

"In exterior he resembled a butcher in a poor neighbourhood, and his eyes had a look of sleepy cunning. He carried his fat paunch with ostentation on his short legs, and during the time his gang infested the station spoke to no one but his nephew. You could see these two roaming about all day long with their heads close together in an everlasting confab.

"I had given up worrying myself about the rivets. One's capacity for that kind of folly is more limited than you would suppose. I said Hang!—and let things slide. I had plenty of time for meditation, and now and then I would give some thought to Kurtz. I wasn't very interested in him. No. Still, I was curious to see whether this man, who had come out equipped with moral ideas of some sort, would climb to the top after all, and how he would set about his work when there."

II

"One evening as I was lying flat on the deck of my steamboat, I heard voices approaching—and there were the nephew and the uncle strolling along the bank. I laid my head on my arm again, and had nearly lost myself in a doze, when somebody said in my ear, as it were: 'I am as harmless as a little child, but I don't like to be dictated to. Am I the manager—or am I not? I was ordered to send him there. It's incredible.' . . . I became aware that the two were standing on the shore alongside the forepart of the steamboat, just below my head. I did not move; it did not occur to me to move: I was sleepy. 'It *is* unpleasant,' grunted the uncle. 'He has asked the Administration to be sent there,' said the other, 'with the idea of showing what he could do; and I was instructed accordingly. Look at the influence that man must have. Is it not frightful?' They both agreed it was frightful, then made several bizarre remarks: 'Make rain and fine weather—one man—the Council—by the nose'—bits of absurd sentences that got the better of my drowsiness, so that I had pretty near the whole of my wits about me when the uncle said, 'The climate may do away with this difficulty for you. Is he alone there?' 'Yes,' answered the manager; 'he sent his assistant down the river with a note to me in these terms: "Clear this poor devil out of the country, and don't bother sending more of that sort. I had rather be alone than have the kind of men you can dispose of with me." It was more than a year ago. Can you imagine such impudence?' 'Anything since then?' asked the other hoarsely. 'Ivory,' jerked the nephew; 'lots of it—prime sort—lots—most annoying, from him.' 'And with that?' questioned the heavy rumble. 'Invoice,' was the reply fired out, so to speak. Then silence. They had been talking about Kurtz.

"I was broad awake by this time, but, lying perfectly at ease, remained still, having no inducement to change my position. 'How did that ivory come all this way?' growled the elder man, who seemed very vexed. The other explained that it had come with a fleet of canoes in charge of an English half-caste clerk Kurtz had with him; that Kurtz had apparently intended to return himself, the station being by that time bare of goods and stores, but after coming three hundred miles, had suddenly decided to go back, which he started to do alone in a small dugout with four paddlers, leaving the half-caste to continue down the river with the ivory. The two fellows there seemed astounded at anybody attempting such a thing. They were at a loss for an adequate motive. As for me, I seemed to see Kurtz for the first time. It was a distinct glimpse: the dugout, four paddling savages, and the lone white man turning his back suddenly on the headquarters, on relief, on thoughts of home—perhaps; setting his face towards the depths of the wilderness, towards his empty and desolate station. I did not know the motive. Perhaps he was just simply a fine fellow who stuck to his work for its own sake. His name, you understand, had not been pronounced once. He was 'that man.' The half-caste, who, as far as I could see, had conducted a difficult trip with great prudence and pluck, was invariably alluded to as 'that scoundrel.' The 'scoundrel' had reported that the 'man' had been very ill—had recovered imperfectly. . . . The two below me moved away then a few paces, and strolled back and forth at some little distance. I heard: 'Military post—doctor—two hundred miles— quite alone now—unavoidable delays—nine months—no news— strange rumours.' They approached again, just as the manager was saying, 'No one, as far as I know, unless a species of wandering trader—a pestilential fellow, snapping ivory from the natives.' Who was it they were talking about now? I gathered in snatches that this was some man supposed to be in Kurtz's district, and of whom the manager did not approve. 'We will not be free from unfair competition till one of these fellows is hanged for an example,' he said. 'Certainly,' grunted the other; 'get him hanged! Why not? Anything—anything can be done in this country. That's what I say; nobody here, you understand, *here,* can endanger your position. And why? You stand the climate—you outlast them all. The danger is in Europe; but there before I left I took care to—' They moved off and whispered, then their voices rose again. 'The extraordinary series of delays is not my fault. I did my possible.' The fat man sighed, 'Very sad.' 'And the pestiferous absurdity of his talk,' continued the other; 'he bothered me enough when he was here. "Each station should be like a beacon on the road towards better things, a centre for trade of course, but also for humanising, improving, instructing." Conceive you—that ass! And he wants to be manager! No, it's——' Here he got choked by excessive indignation, and I lifted my head the least bit. I was surprised to see how near they were—right under me. I could have spat upon their hats. They were looking on the ground, absorbed in thought. The manager was switching his leg with a slender twig: his sagacious relative lifted his head. 'You have been well since you came out this time?' he asked. The other gave a start. 'Who? I? Oh! Like a charm—like a charm. But the rest—oh, my goodness! All sick. They die so quick, too, that I haven't the time to send them out of the country—it's incredible!' 'H'm. Just so,' grunted the uncle. 'Ah! my boy, trust to this—I say, trust to this.' I saw him extend his short flipper of an arm for a gesture that took in the forest, the creek, the mud, the river—seemed to beckon with a dishonouring flourish before the sunlit face of the land a treacherous appeal to the lurking death, to the hidden evil, to the profound darkness of its heart. It was so startling that I leaped to my feet and looked back at the edge of the forest, as though I had expected an answer of some sort to that black display of confidence. You know the foolish notions that come to one sometimes. The high stillness confronted these two figures with its ominous patience, waiting for the passing away of a fantastic invasion.

"They swore aloud together—out of sheer fright, I believe—then, pretending not to know anything of my existence, turned back to the station. The sun was low; and leaning forward side by side, they seemed to be tugging painfully uphill their two ridiculous shadows of unequal length, that trailed behind them slowly over the tall grass without bending a single blade.

"In a few days the Eldorado Expedition went into the patient wilderness, that closed upon it as the sea closes over a diver. Long afterwards the news came that all the donkeys were dead. I know nothing as to the fate of the less valuable animals. They, no doubt, like the rest of us, found what they deserved. I did not inquire. I was then rather excited at the prospect of meeting Kurtz very soon. When I say very soon I mean it comparatively. It was just two months from the day we left the creek when we came to the bank below Kurtz's station.

"Going up that river was like travelling back to the earliest beginnings of the world, when vegetation rioted on the earth and the big trees were kings. An empty stream, a great silence, an impenetrable forest. The air was warm, thick, heavy, sluggish. There was no joy in the brilliance of sunshine. The long stretches of the waterway ran on, deserted, into the gloom of overshadowed distances. On silvery sandbanks hippos and alligators sunned themselves side by side. The broadening waters flowed through a mob of wooded islands; you lost your way on that river as you would in a desert, and butted all day long against shoals, trying to find the channel, till you thought yourself bewitched and cut off for ever from everything you had known once—somewhere—far away—in another existence perhaps. There were moments when one's past came back to one, as it will sometimes when you have not a moment to spare to yourself; but it came in the shape of an unrestful and noisy dream, remembered with wonder amongst the overwhelming realities of this strange world of plants, and water, and silence. And this stillness of life did not in the least resemble a peace. It was the stillness of an implacable force brooding over an inscrutable intention. It looked at you with a vengeful aspect. I got used to it afterwards; I did not see it any more; I had no time. I had to keep guessing at the channel; I had to discern, mostly by inspiration, the signs of hidden banks; I watched for sunken stones; I was learning to clap my teeth smartly before my heart flew out, when I shaved by a fluke some infernal sly old snag that would have ripped the life out of the tin-pot steamboat and drowned all the pilgrims; I had to keep a look-out for the signs of dead wood we could cut up in the night for next day's steaming. When you have to attend to things of that sort, to the mere incidents of the surface, the reality—the reality, I tell you— fades. The inner truth is hidden—luckily, luckily. But I felt it all the same; I felt often its mysterious stillness watching me at my monkey tricks, just as it watches you fellows performing on your respective tight-ropes for—what is it? half a crown a tumble——"

"Try to be civil, Marlow," growled a voice, and I knew there was at least one listener awake besides myself.

"I beg your pardon. I forgot the heartache which makes up the rest of the price. And indeed what does the price matter, if the trick be well done? You do your tricks very well. And I didn't do badly either, since I managed not to sink that steamboat on my first trip. It's a wonder to me yet. Imagine a blindfolded man set to drive a van over a bad road. I sweated and shivered over that business considerably, I can tell you. After all, for a seaman, to scrape the bottom of the thing that's sup- posed to float all the time under his care is the unpardonable sin. No one may know of it, but you never forget the thump—eh? A blow on the very heart. You remember it, you dream of it, you wake up at night and think of it—years after—and go hot and cold all over. I don't pretend to say that steamboat floated all the time. More than once she had to wade for a bit, with twenty cannibals splashing around and pushing. We had enlisted some of these chaps on the way for a crew. Fine fellows—cannibals—in their place. They were men one could work with, and I am grateful to them. And, after all, they did not eat each other before my face: they had brought along a provision of hippo-meat which went rotten, and made the mystery of the wilder- ness stink in my nostrils. Phoo! I can sniff it now. I had the manager on board and three or four pilgrims with their staves—all complete. Some- times we came upon a station close by the bank, clinging to the skirts of the unknown, and the white men rushing out of a tumble-down hovel, with great gestures of joy and surprise and welcome, seemed very strange—had the appearance of being held there captive by a spell. The word 'ivory' would ring in the air for a while—and on we went again into the silence, along empty reaches, round the still bends, between the high walls of our winding way, reverberating in hollow claps the ponderous beat of the stern-wheel. Trees, trees, millions of trees, massive, immense, running up high; and at their foot, hugging the bank against the stream, crept the little begrimed steamboat, like a sluggish beetle crawling on the floor of a lofty portico. It made you feel very small, very lost, and yet it was not altogether depressing, that feeling. After all, if you were small, the grimy beetle crawled on—which was just what you wanted it to do. Where the pilgrims imagined it crawled to I don't know. To some place where they expected to get something, I bet! For me it crawled towards Kurtz—exclusively; but when the steam-pipes started leaking we crawled very slow. The reaches opened before us and closed behind, as if the forest had stepped leisurely across the water to bar the way for our return. We penetrated deeper and deeper into the heart of darkness. It was very quiet there. At night sometimes the roll of drums behind the curtain of trees would run up the river and remain sustained faintly, as if hovering in the air high over our heads, till the first break of day. Whether it meant war, peace, or prayer we could not tell. The dawns were heralded by the descent of a chill stillness; the woodcutters slept, their fires burned low; the snapping of a twig would make you start. We were wanderers on a prehistoric earth, on an earth that wore the aspect of an unknown planet. We could have fancied ourselves the first of men taking possession of an accursed inheritance, to be subdued at the cost of profound anguish and of excessive toil. But suddenly, as we struggled round a bend, there would be a glimpse of rush walls, of peaked grass-roofs, a burst of yells, a whirl of black limbs, a mass of hands clapping, of feet stamping, of bodies swaying, of eyes rolling, under the droop of heavy and motionless foliage. The steamer toiled along slowly on the edge of a black and incomprehensible frenzy. The prehistoric man was cursing us, praying to us, welcoming us—who could tell? We were cut off from the comprehension of our surroundings; we glided past like phantoms, wondering and secretly appalled, as sane men would be before an enthusiastic outbreak in a madhouse. We could not understand because we were too far and could not remember, because we were travelling in the night of first ages, of those ages that are gone, leaving hardly a sign—and no memories.

"The earth seemed unearthly. We are accustomed to look upon the shackled form of a conquered monster, but there—there you could look at a thing monstrous and free. It was unearthly, and the men were—— No, they were not inhuman. Well, you know, that was the worst of it—this suspicion of their not being inhuman. It would come slowly to one. They howled and leaped, and spun, and made horrid faces; but what thrilled you was just the thought of their humanity—like yours—the thought of your remote kinship with this wild and passionate uproar. Ugly. Yes, it was ugly enough; but if you were man enough you would admit to yourself that there was in you just the faintest trace of a response to the terrible frankness of that noise, a dim suspicion of there being a meaning in it which you—you so remote from the night of first ages—could comprehend. And why not? The mind of man is capable of anything—because everything is in it, all the past as well as all the future. What was there after all? Joy, fear, sorrow, devotion, valour, rage—who can tell?—but truth—truth stripped of its cloak of time. Let the fool gape and shudder—the man knows, and can look on without a wink. But he must at least be as much of a man as these on the shore. He must meet that truth with his own true stuff—with his own inborn strength. Principles? Principles won't do. Acquisitions, clothes, pretty rags—rags that would fly off at the first good shake. No; you want a deliberate belief. An appeal to me in this fiendish row—is there? Very well; I hear; I admit, but I have a voice too, and for good or evil mine is the speech that cannot be silenced. Of course, a fool, what with sheer fright and fine sentiments, is always safe. Who's that grunting? You wonder I didn't go ashore for a howl and a dance? Well, no—I didn't. Fine sentiments, you say? Fine sentiments be hanged! I had no time. I had to mess about with white-lead and strips of woollen blanket helping to put bandages on those leaky steam-pipes—I tell you. I had to watch the steering, and circumvent those snags, and get the tin-pot along by hook or by crook. There was surface-truth enough in these things to save a wiser man. And between whiles I had to look after the savage who was fireman. He was an improved specimen; he could fire up a vertical boiler. He was there below me, and, upon my word, to look at him was as edifying as seeing a dog in a parody of breeches and a feather hat, walking on his hind legs. A few months of training had done for that really fine chap. He squinted at the steam-gauge and at the water-gauge with an evident effort of intrepidity—and he had filed teeth too, the poor devil, and the wool of his pate shaved into queer patterns, and three ornamental scars on each of his cheeks. He ought to have been clapping his hands and stamping his feet on the bank, instead of which he was hard at work, a thrall to strange witchcraft, full of improving knowledge. He was useful because he had been instructed; and what he knew was this—that should the water in that transparent thing disappear, the evil spirit inside the boiler would get angry through the greatness of his thirst, and take a terrible vengeance. So he sweated and fired up and watched the glass fearfully (with an impromptu charm, made of rags, tied to his arm, and a piece of polished bone, as big as a watch, stuck flatways through his lower lip), while the wooded banks slipped past us slowly, the short noise was left behind, the interminable miles of silence—and we crept on, towards Kurtz. But the snags were thick, the water was treacherous and shallow, the boiler seemed indeed to have a sulky devil in it, and thus neither that fireman nor I had any time to peer into our creepy thoughts.

"Some fifty miles below the Inner Station we came upon a hut of reeds, an inclined and melancholy pole, with the unrecognisable tatters of what had been a flag of some sort flying from it, and a neatly stacked wood-pile. This was unexpected. We came to the bank, and on the stack of firewood found a flat piece of board with some faded pencil-writing on it. When deciphered it said: 'Wood for you. Hurry up. Approach cautiously.' There was a signature, but it was illegible—not Kurtz—a much longer word. 'Hurry up.' Where? Up the river? 'Approach cautiously.' We had not done so. But the warning could not have been meant for the place where it could be only found after approach. Something was wrong above. But what—and how much? That was the question. We commented adversely upon the imbecility of that telegraphic style. The bush around said nothing, and would not let us look very far, either. A torn curtain of red twill hung in the doorway of the hut, and flapped sadly in our faces. The dwelling was dismantled; but we could see a white man had lived there not very long ago. There remained a rude table—a plank on two posts; a heap of rubbish reposed in a dark corner, and by the door I picked up a book. It had lost its covers, and the pages had been thumbed into a state of extremely dirty softness; but the back had been lovingly stitched afresh with white cotton thread, which looked clean yet. It was an extraordinary find. Its title was, *An Inquiry into some Points of Seamanship*, by a man Towser, Towson—some such name—Master in His Majesty's Navy. The matter looked dreary reading enough, with illustrative diagrams and repulsive tables of figures, and the copy was sixty years old. I handled this amazing antiquity with the greatest possible tenderness, lest it should dissolve in my hands. Within, Towson or Towser was inquiring earnestly into the breaking strain of ships' chains and tackle, and other such matters. Not a very enthralling book; but at the first glance you could see there a singleness of intention, an honest concern for the right way of going to work, which made these humble pages, thought out so many years ago, luminous with another than a professional light. The simple old sailor, with his talk of chains and purchases, made me forget the jungle and the pilgrims in a delicious sensation of having come upon something unmistakably real. Such a book being there was wonderful enough; but still more astounding were the notes pencilled in the margin, and plainly referring to the text. I couldn't believe my eyes! They were in cipher! Yes, it looked like cipher. Fancy a man lugging with him a book of that description into this nowhere and studying it—and making notes—in cipher at that! It was an extravagant mystery.

"I had been dimly aware for some time of a worrying noise, and when I lifted my eyes I saw the wood-pile was gone, and the manager, aided by all the pilgrims, was shouting at me from the river-side. I slipped the book into my pocket. I assure you to leave off reading was like tearing myself away from the shelter of an old and solid friendship.

"I started the lame engine ahead. 'It must be this miserable trader—this intruder,' exclaimed the manager, looking back malevolently at the place we had left. 'He must be English,' I said. 'It will not save him from getting into trouble if he is not careful,' muttered the manager darkly. I observed with assumed innocence that no man was safe from trouble in this world.

"The current was more rapid now, the steamer seemed at her last gasp, the stern-wheel flopped languidly, and I caught myself listening on tiptoe for the next beat of the float, for in sober truth I expected the wretched thing to give up every moment. It was like watching the last flickers of a life. But still we crawled. Sometimes I would pick out a tree a little way ahead to measure our progress towards Kurtz by, but I lost it invariably before we got abreast. To keep the eyes so long on one thing was too much for human patience. The manager displayed a beautiful resignation. I fretted and fumed and took to arguing with myself whether or no I would talk openly with Kurtz; but before I could come to any conclusion it occurred to me that my speech or my silence, indeed any action of mine, would be a mere futility. What did it matter what any one knew or ignored? What did it matter who was manager? One gets sometimes such a flash of insight. The essentials of this affair lay deep under the surface, beyond my reach, and beyond my power of meddling.

"Towards the evening of the second day we judged ourselves about eight miles from Kurtz's station. I wanted to push on; but the manager looked grave, and told me the navigation up there was so dangerous that it would be advisable, the sun being very low already, to wait where we were till next morning. Moreover, he pointed out that if the warning to approach cautiously were to be followed, we must approach in daylight—not at dusk, or in the dark. This was sensible enough. Eight miles meant nearly three hours' steaming for us, and I could also see suspicious ripples at the upper end of the reach. Nevertheless, I was annoyed beyond expression at the delay, and most unreasonably too, since one night more could not matter much after so many months. As we had plenty of wood, and caution was the word, I brought up in the middle of the stream. The reach was narrow, straight, with high sides like a railway cutting. The dusk came gliding into it long before the sun had set. The current ran smooth and swift, but a dumb immobility sat on the banks. The living trees, lashed together by the creepers and every living bush of the undergrowth, might have been changed into stone, even to the slenderest twig, to the lightest leaf. It was not sleep—it seemed unnatural, like a state of trance. Not the faintest sound of any kind could be heard. You looked on amazed, and began to suspect yourself of being deaf—then the night came suddenly, and struck you blind as well. About three in the morning some large fish leaped, and the loud splash made me jump as though a gun had been fired. When the sun rose there was a white fog, very warm and clammy, and more blinding than the night. It did not shift or drive; it was just there, standing all round you like something solid. At eight or nine, perhaps, it lifted as a shutter lifts. We had a glimpse of the towering multitude of trees, of the immense matted jungle, with the blazing little ball of sun hanging over it—all perfectly still—and then the white shutter came down again, smoothly, as if sliding in greased grooves. I ordered the chain, which we had begun to heave in, to be paid out again. Before it stopped running with a muffled rattle, a cry, a very loud cry, as of infinite desolation, soared slowly in the opaque air. It ceased. A complaining clamour, modulated in savage discords, filled our ears. The sheer unexpectedness of it made my hair stir under my cap. I don't know how it struck the others: to me it seemed as though the mist itself had screamed, so suddenly, and apparently from all sides at once, did this tumultuous and mournful uproar arise. It culminated in a hurried outbreak of almost intolerably excessive shrieking, which stopped short, leaving us stiffened in a variety of silly attitudes, and obstinately listening to the nearly as appalling and excessive silence. 'Good God!

What is the meaning——?' stammered at my elbow one of the pilgrims—a little fat man, with sandy hair and red whiskers, who wore side-spring boots, and pink pyjamas tucked into his socks. Two others remained open-mouthed a whole minute, then dashed into the little cabin, to rush out incontinently and stand darting scared glances, with Winchesters at 'ready' in their hands. What we could see was just the steamer we were on, her outlines blurred as though she had been on the point of dissolving, and a misty strip of water, perhaps two feet broad, around her—and that was all. The rest of the world was nowhere, as far as our eyes and ears were concerned. Just nowhere. Gone, disappeared; swept off without leaving a whisper or a shadow behind.

"I went forward, and ordered the chain to be hauled in short, so as to be ready to trip the anchor and move the steamboat at once if necessary. 'Will they attack?' whispered an awed voice. 'We will all be butchered in this fog,' murmured another. The faces twitched with the strain, the hands trembled slightly, the eyes forgot to wink. It was very curious to see the contrast of expressions of the white men and of the black fellows of our crew, who were as much strangers to that part of the river as we, though their homes were only eight hundred miles away. The whites, of course greatly discomposed, had besides a curious look of being painfully shocked by such an outrageous row. The others had an alert, naturally interested expression; but their faces were essentially quiet, even those of the one or two who grinned as they hauled at the chain. Several exchanged short, grunting phrases, which seemed to settle the matter to their satisfaction. Their head-man, a young, broad-chested black, severely draped in dark-blue fringed cloths, with fierce nostrils and his hair all done up artfully in oily ringlets, stood near me. 'Aha!' I said, just for good fellowship's sake. 'Catch 'im,' he snapped, with a bloodshot widening of his eyes and a flash of sharp teeth—'catch 'im. Give 'im to us.' 'To you, eh?' I asked; 'what would you do with them?' 'Eat 'im!' he said curtly, and, leaning his elbow on the rail, looked out into the fog in a dignified and profoundly pensive attitude. I would no doubt have been properly horrified, had it not occurred to me that he and his chaps must be very hungry: that they must have been growing increasingly hungry for at least this month past. They had been engaged for six months (I don't think a single one of them had any clear idea of time, as we at the end of countless ages have. They still belonged to the beginnings of time— had no inherited experience to teach them, as it were), and of course, as long as there was a piece of paper written over in accordance with some farcical law or other made down the river, it didn't enter anybody's head to trouble how they would live. Certainly they had brought with them some rotten hippo-meat, which couldn't have lasted very long, anyway, even if the pilgrims hadn't, in the midst of a shocking hullaba-loo, thrown a considerable quantity of it overboard. It looked like a high-handed proceeding; but it was really a case of legitimate self-defence. You can't breathe dead hippo waking, sleeping, and eating, and at the same time keep your precarious grip on existence. Besides that, they had given them every week three pieces of brass wire, each about nine inches long; and the theory was they were to buy their provisions with that currency in river-side villages. You can see how *that* worked. There were either no villages, or the people were hostile, or the director, who like the rest of us fed out of tins, with an occa-sional old he-goat thrown in, didn't want to stop the steamer for some more or less recondite reason. So, unless they swallowed the wire itself, or made loops of it to snare the fishes with, I don't see what good their extravagant salary could be to them. I must say it was paid with a regularity worthy of a large and honourable trading company. For the rest, the only thing to eat—though it didn't look eatable in the least—I saw in their possession was a few lumps of some stuff like half-cooked dough, of a dirty lavender colour, they kept wrapped in leaves, and now and then swallowed a piece of, but so small that it seemed done more for the look of the thing than for any serious purpose of sustenance. Why in the name of all the gnawing devils of hunger they didn't go for us—they were thirty to five—and have a good tuck-in for once, amazes me now when I think of it. They were big powerful men, with not much capacity to weigh the consequences, with courage, with strength, even yet, though their skins were no longer glossy and their muscles no longer hard. And I saw that something restraining, one of those human secrets that baffle probability, had come into play there. I looked at them with a swift quickening of interest—not because it occurred to me I might be eaten by them before very long, though I own to you that just then I perceived—in a new light, as it were—how unwholesome the pilgrims looked, and I hoped, yes, I positively hoped, that my aspect was not so—what shall I say?—so—unappetising: a touch of fantastic vanity which fitted well with the dream-sensation that pervaded all my days at that time. Perhaps I had a little fever too. One can't live with one's finger everlastingly on one's pulse. I had often 'a little fever,' or a little touch of other things—the playful paw-strokes of the wilderness, the preliminary trifling before the more serious on-slaught which came in due course. Yes; I looked at them as you would on any human being, with a curiosity of their impulses, motives, capacities, weaknesses, when brought to the test of an inexorable physical necessity. Restraint! What possible restraint? Was it superstition, disgust, patience, fear—or some kind of primitive honour? No fear can stand up to hunger, no patience can wear it out, disgust simply does not exist where hunger is; and as to superstition, beliefs, and what you may call principles, they are less than chaff in a breeze. Don't you know the devilry of lingering starvation, its exasperating torment, its black thoughts, its sombre and brooding ferocity? Well, I do. It takes a man all his inborn strength to fight hunger properly. It's really easier to face bereavement, dishonour, and the perdition of one's soul—than this kind of prolonged hunger. Sad, but true. And these chaps too had no earthly reason for any kind of scruple. Restraint! I would just as soon have expected restraint from a hyena prowling amongst the corpses of a battlefield. But there was the fact facing me—the fact dazzling, to be seen, like the foam on the depths of the sea, like a ripple on an unfathomable enigma, a mystery greater—when I thought of it— than the curious, inexplicable note of desperate grief in this savage clamour that had swept by us on the river-bank, behind the blind whiteness of the fog.

"Two pilgrims were quarrelling in hurried whispers as to which bank. 'Left.' 'No, no; how can you? Right, right, of course.' 'It is very serious,' said the manager's voice behind me; 'I would be desolated if anything should happen to Mr. Kurtz before we came up.' I looked at him, and had not the slightest doubt he was sincere. He was just the kind of man who would wish to preserve appearances. That was his restraint. But when he muttered something about going on at once, I did not even take the trouble to answer him. I knew, and he knew, that it was impossible. Were we to let go our hold of the bottom, we would be absolutely in the air—in space. We wouldn't be able to tell where we were going to—whether up or down stream, or across—till we fetched against one bank or the other—and then we wouldn't know at first which it was. Of course I made no move. I had no mind for a smash-up. You couldn't imagine a more deadly place for a shipwreck. Whether drowned at once or not, we were sure to perish speedily in one way or another. 'I authorise you to take all the risks,' he said, after a short silence. 'I refuse to take any,' I said shortly; which was just the answer he expected, though its tone might have surprised him. 'Well, I must defer to your judgment. You are captain,' he said, with marked civility. I turned my shoulder to him in sign of my appreciation, and looked into the fog. How long would it last? It was the most hopeless look-out. The approach to this Kurtz grubbing for ivory in the wretched bush was beset by as many dangers as though he had been an enchanted princess sleeping in a fabulous castle. 'Will they attack, do you think?' asked the manager, in a confidential tone.

"I did not think they would attack, for several obvious reasons. The thick fog was one. If they left the bank in their canoes they would get lost in it, as we would be if we attempted to move. Still, I had also judged the jungle of both banks quite impenetrable—and yet eyes were in it, eyes that had seen us. The river-side bushes were certainly very thick; but the undergrowth behind was evidently penetrable. However, during the short lift I had seen no canoes anywhere in the reach—certainly not abreast of the steamer. But what made the idea of attack inconceivable to me was the nature of the noise—of the cries we had heard. They had not the fierce character boding of immediate hostile intention. Unexpected, wild, and violent as they had been, they had given me an irresistible impression of sorrow. The glimpse of the steamboat had for some reason filled those savages with unrestrained grief. The danger, if any, I expounded, was from our proximity to a great human passion let loose. Even extreme grief may ultimately vent itself in violence—but more generally takes the form of apathy. . . .

"You should have seen the pilgrims stare! They had no heart to grin, or even to revile me; but I believe they thought me gone mad—with fright, maybe. I delivered a regular lecture. My dear boys, it was no good bothering. Keep a look-out? Well, you may guess I watched the fog for the signs of lifting as a cat watches a mouse; but for anything else our eyes were of no more use to us than if we had been buried miles deep in a heap of cotton-wool. It felt like it too—choking, warm, stifling. Besides, all I said, though it sounded extravagant, was absolutely true to fact. What we afterwards alluded to as an attack was really an attempt at repulse. The action was very far from being aggressive—it was not even defensive, in the usual sense: it was undertaken under the stress of desperation, and in its essence was purely protective.

"It developed itself, I should say, two hours after the fog lifted, and its commencement was at a spot, roughly speaking, about a mile and a half below Kurtz's station. We had just floundered and flopped round a bend, when I saw an islet, a mere grassy hummock of bright green, in the middle of the stream. It was the only thing of the kind; but as we opened the reach more, I perceived it was the head of a long sandbank, or rather of a chain of shallow patches stretching down the middle of the river. They were discoloured, just awash, and the whole lot was seen just under the water, exactly as a man's backbone is seen running down the middle of his back under the skin. Now, as far as I did see, I could go to the right or to the left of this. I didn't know either channel, of course. The banks looked pretty well alike, the depth appeared the same; but as I had been informed the station was on the west side, I naturally headed for the western passage.

"No sooner had we fairly entered it than I became aware it was much narrower than I had supposed. To the left of us there was the long uninterrupted shoal, and to the right a high steep bank heavily over-grown with bushes. Above the bush the trees stood in serried ranks. The twigs overhung the current thickly, and from distance to distance a large limb of some tree projected rigidly over the stream. It was then well on in the afternoon, the face of the forest was gloomy, and a broad strip of shadow had already fallen on the water. In this shadow we steamed up—very slowly, as you may imagine. I sheered her well in-shore—the water being deepest near the bank, as the sounding-pole informed me.

"One of my hungry and forbearing friends was sounding in the bows just below me. This steamboat was exactly like a decked scow. On the deck there were two little teak-wood houses, with doors and windows. The boiler was in the fore-end, and the machinery right astern. Over the whole there was a light roof, supported on stanchions. The funnel projected through that roof, and in front of the funnel a small cabin built of light planks served for a pilot-house. It contained a couch, two camp-stools, a loaded Martini-Henry[14] leaning in one cor-ner, a tiny table, and the steering-wheel. It had a wide door in front and a broad shutter at each side. All these were always thrown open, of course. I spent my days perched up there on the extreme fore-end of that roof, before the door. At night I slept, or tried to, on the couch. An athletic black belonging to some coast tribe, and educated by my poor predecessor, was the helmsman. He sported a pair of brass earrings, wore a blue cloth wrapper from the waist to the ankles, and thought all the world of himself. He was the most unstable kind of fool I had ever seen. He steered with no end of a swagger while you were by; but if he lost sight of you, he became instantly the prey of an abject funk, and would let that cripple of a steamboat get the upper hand of him in a minute.

"I was looking down at the sounding-pole, and feeling much an-noyed to see at each try a little more of it stick out of that river, when

---

[14]A powerful rifle.

I saw my poleman give up the business suddenly, and stretch himself flat on the deck, without even taking the trouble to haul his pole in. He kept hold on it though, and it trailed in the water. At the same time the fireman, whom I could also see below me, sat down abruptly before his furnace and ducked his head. I was amazed. Then I had to look at the river mighty quick, because there was a snag in the fairway. Sticks, little sticks, were flying about—thick: they were whizzing before my nose, dropping below me, striking behind me against my pilot-house. All this time the river, the shore, the woods, were very quiet—perfectly quiet. I could only hear the heavy splashing thump of the stern-wheel and the patter of these things. We cleared the snag clumsily. Arrows, by Jove! We were being shot at! I stepped in quickly to close the shutter on the land-side. That fool-helmsman, his hands on the spokes, was lifting his knees high, stamping his feet, champing his mouth, like a reined-in horse. Confound him! And we were staggering within ten feet of the bank. I had to lean right out to swing the heavy shutter, and I saw a face amongst the leaves on the level with my own, looking at me very fierce and steady; and then suddenly, as though a veil had been removed from my eyes, I made out, deep in the tangled gloom, naked breasts, arms, legs, glaring eyes—the bush was swarming with human limbs in movement, glistening, of bronze colour. The twigs shook, swayed, and rustled, the arrows flew out of them, and then the shutter came to. 'Steer her straight,' I said to the helmsman. He held his head rigid, face forward; but his eyes rolled, he kept on lifting and setting down his feet gently, his mouth foamed a little. 'Keep quiet!' I said in a fury. I might just as well have ordered a tree not to sway in the wind. I darted out. Below me there was a great scuffle of feet on the iron deck; confused exclamations; a voice screamed, 'Can you turn back?' I caught sight of a V-shaped ripple on the water ahead. What? Another snag! A fusillade burst out under my feet. The pilgrims had opened with their Winchesters, and were simply squirting lead into that bush. A deuce of a lot of smoke came up and drove slowly forward. I swore at it. Now I couldn't see the ripple or the snag either. I stood in the doorway, peering, and the arrows came in swarms. They might have been poisoned, but they looked as though they wouldn't kill a cat. The bush began to howl. Our wood-cutters raised a warlike whoop; the report of a rifle just at my back deafened me. I glanced over my shoulder, and the pilot-house was yet full of noise and smoke when I made a dash at the wheel. The fool-nigger had dropped everything, to throw the shutter open and let off that Martini-Henry. He stood before the wide opening, glaring, and I yelled at him to come back, while I straightened the sudden twist out of that steamboat. There was no room to turn even if I had wanted to, the snag was somewhere very near ahead in that confounded smoke, there was no time to lose, so I just crowded her into the bank—right into the bank, where I knew the water was deep.

"We tore slowly along the overhanging bushes in a whirl of broken twigs and flying leaves. The fusillade below stopped short, as I had foreseen it would when the squirts got empty. I threw my head back to a glinting whiz that traversed the pilot-house, in at one shutter-hole and out at the other. Looking past that mad helmsman, who was shaking the empty rifle and yelling at the shore, I saw vague forms of men running bent double, leaping, gliding, distinct, incomplete, evanescent. Something big appeared in the air before the shutter, the rifle went overboard, and the man stepped back swiftly, looked at me over his shoulder in an extraordinary, profound, familiar manner, and fell upon my feet. The side of his head hit the wheel twice, and the end of what appeared a long cane clattered round and knocked over a little camp-stool. It looked as though after wrenching that thing from somebody ashore he had lost his balance in the effort. The thin smoke had blown away, we were clear of the snag, and looking ahead I could see that in another hundred yards or so I would be free to sheer off, away from the bank; but my feet felt so very warm and wet that I had to look down. The man had rolled on his back and stared straight up at me; both his hands clutched that cane. It was the shaft of a spear that, either thrown or lunged through the opening, had caught him in the side just below the ribs; the blade had gone in out of sight, after making a frightful gash; my shoes were full; a pool of blood lay very still, gleaming dark-red under the wheel; his eyes shone with an amazing lustre. The fusillade burst out again. He looked at me anxiously, gripping the spear like something precious, with an air of being afraid I would try to take it away from him. I had to make an effort to free my eyes from his gaze and attend to the steering. With one hand I felt above my head for the line of the steam-whistle, and jerked out screech after screech hurriedly. The tumult of angry and warlike yells was checked instantly, and then from the depths of the woods went out such a tremulous and prolonged wail of mournful fear and utter despair as may be imagined to follow the flight of the last hope from the earth. There was a great commotion in the bush; the shower of arrows stopped, a few dropping shots rang out sharply—then silence, in which the languid beat of the stern-wheel came plainly to my ears. I put the helm hard a-starboard at the moment when the pilgrim in pink pyjamas, very hot and agitated, appeared in the doorway. 'The manager sends me——' he began in an official tone, and stopped short. 'Good God!' he said, glaring at the wounded man.

"We two whites stood over him, and his lustrous and inquiring glance enveloped us both. I declare it looked as though he would presently put to us some question in an understandable language; but he died without uttering a sound, without moving a limb, without twitching a muscle. Only in the very last moment, as though in response to some sign we could not see, to some whisper we could not hear, he frowned heavily, and that frown gave to his black death-mask an inconceivably sombre, brooding, and menacing expression. The lustre of inquiring glance faded swiftly into vacant glassiness. 'Can you steer?' I asked the agent eagerly. He looked very dubious; but I made a grab at his arm, and he understood at once I meant him to steer whether or no. To tell you the truth, I was morbidly anxious to change my shoes and socks. 'He is dead,' murmured the fellow, immensely impressed. 'No doubt about it,' said I, tugging like mad at the shoe-laces. 'And by the way, I suppose Mr. Kurtz is dead as well by this time.'

"For the moment that was the dominant thought. There was a sense of extreme disappointment, as though I had found out I had been striving after something altogether without a substance. I couldn't have been more disgusted if I had travelled all this way for the sole purpose of talking with Mr. Kurtz. Talking with . . . I flung one shoe overboard, and became aware that that was exactly what I had been looking forward to—a talk with Kurtz. I made the strange discovery that I had never imagined him as doing, you know, but as discoursing. I didn't say to myself, 'Now I will never see him,' or 'Now I will never shake him by the hand,' but, 'Now I will never hear him.' The man presented himself as a voice. Not of course that I did not connect him with some sort of action. Hadn't I been told in all the tones of jealousy and admiration that he had collected, bartered, swindled, or stolen more ivory than all the other agents together? That was not the point. The point was in his being a gifted creature, and that of all his gifts the one that stood out pre-eminently, that carried with it a sense of real presence, was his ability to talk, his words—the gift of expression, the bewildering, the illuminating, the most exalted and the most contemptible, the pulsating stream of light, or the deceitful flow from the heart of an impenetrable darkness.

"The other shoe went flying unto the devil-god of that river. I thought, By Jove! it's all over. We are too late; he has vanished—the gift has vanished, by means of some spear, arrow, or club. I will never

hear that chap speak after all—and my sorrow had a startling extravagance of emotion, even such as I had noticed in the howling sorrow of
these savages in the bush. I couldn't have felt more of lonely desolation
somehow, had I been robbed of a belief or had missed my destiny in
life. . . . Why do you sigh in this beastly way, somebody? Absurd?
Well, absurd. Good Lord! mustn't a man ever—— Here, give me some
tobacco." . . .

There was a pause of profound stillness, then a match flared, and
Marlow's lean face appeared, worn, hollow, with downward folds and
dropped eyelids, with an aspect of concentrated attention; and as he
took vigorous draws at his pipe, it seemed to retreat and advance out of
the night in the regular flicker of the tiny flame. The match went out.

"Absurd!" he cried. "This is the worst of trying to tell . . . Here you
all are, each moored with two good addresses, like a hulk with two
anchors, a butcher round one corner, a policeman round another, excellent appetites, and temperature normal—you hear—normal from
year's end to year's end. And you say, Absurd! Absurd be—exploded!
Absurd! My dear boys, what can you expect from a man who out of
sheer nervousness had just flung overboard a pair of new shoes? Now
I think of it, it is amazing I did not shed tears. I am, upon the whole,
proud of my fortitude. I was cut to the quick at the idea of having lost
the inestimable privilege of listening to the gifted Kurtz. Of course I
was wrong. The privilege was waiting for me. Oh yes, I heard more
than enough. And I was right, too. A voice. He was very little more
than a voice. And I heard—him—it—this voice—other voices—all of
them were so little more than voices—and the memory of that time
itself lingers around me, impalpable, like a dying vibration of one immense jabber, silly, atrocious, sordid, savage, or simply mean, without
any kind of sense. Voices, voices—even the girl herself—now——"

He was silent for a long time.

"I laid the ghost of his gifts at last with a lie," he began suddenly.
"Girl! What? Did I mention a girl? Oh, she is out of it—completely.
They—the women I mean—are out of it—should be out of it. We must
help them to stay in that beautiful world of their own, lest ours gets
worse. Oh, she had to be out of it. You should have heard the disin-
terred body of Mr. Kurtz saying, 'My Intended.' You would have perceived directly then how completely she was out of it. And the lofty
frontal bone of Mr. Kurtz! They say the hair goes on growing sometimes, but this—ah—specimen was impressively bald. The wilderness
had patted him on the head, and, behold, it was like a ball—an ivory
ball; it had caressed him, and—lo !—he had withered; it had taken him,

loved him, embraced him, got into his veins, consumed his flesh, and sealed his soul to its own by the inconceivable ceremonies of some devilish initiation. He was its spoiled and pampered favourite. Ivory? I should think so. Heaps of it, stacks of it. The old mud shanty was bursting with it. You would think there was not a single tusk left either above or below the ground in the whole country. 'Mostly fossil,' the manager had remarked disparagingly. It was no more fossil than I am; but they call it fossil when it is dug up. It appears these niggers do bury the tusks sometimes—but evidently they couldn't bury this parcel deep enough to save the gifted Mr. Kurtz from his fate. We filled the steamboat with it, and had to pile a lot on the deck. Thus he could see and enjoy as long as he could see, because the appreciation of this favour had remained with him to the last. You should have heard him say, 'My ivory.' Oh yes, I heard him. 'My Intended, my ivory, my station, my river, my——' everything belonged to him. It made me hold my breath in expectation of hearing the wilderness burst into a prodigious peal of laughter that would shake the fixed stars in their places. Everything belonged to him—but that was a trifle. The thing was to know what he belonged to, how many powers of darkness claimed him for their own. That was the reflection that made you creepy all over. It was impossible—it was not good for one either—trying to imagine. He had taken a high seat amongst the devils of the land—I mean literally. You can't understand. How could you?—with solid pavement under your feet, surrounded by kind neighbours ready to cheer you or to fall on you, stepping delicately between the butcher and the policeman, in the holy terror of scandal and gallows and lunatic asylums—how can you imagine what particular region of the first ages a man's untrammelled feet may take him into by the way of solitude—utter solitude without a policeman—by the way of silence—utter silence, where no warning voice of a kind neighbour can be heard whispering of public opinion? These little things make all the great difference. When they are gone you must fall back upon your own innate strength, upon your own capacity for faithfulness. Of course you may be too much of a fool to go wrong—too dull even to know you are being assaulted by the powers of darkness. I take it, no fool ever made a bargain for his soul with the devil: the fool is too much of a fool, or the devil too much of a devil—I don't know which. Or you may be such a thunderingly exalted creature as to be altogether deaf and blind to anything but heavenly sights and sounds. Then the earth for you is only a standing place—and whether to be like this is your loss or your gain I won't pretend to say. But most of us are neither one nor the other. The earth for us is a place to live in, where we must put up with sights, with sounds, with smells, too, by Jove!—breathe dead hippo, so to speak, and not be contaminated. And there, don't you see? your strength comes in, the faith in your ability for the digging of unostentatious holes to bury the stuff in—your power of devotion, not to yourself, but to an obscure, back-breaking business. And that's difficult enough. Mind, I am not trying to excuse or even explain—I am trying to account to myself for—for—Mr. Kurtz—for the shade of Mr. Kurtz. This initiated wraith from the back of Nowhere honoured me with its amazing confidence before it vanished altogether. This was because it could speak English to me. The original Kurtz had been educated partly in England, and— as he was good enough to say himself—his sympathies were in the right place. His mother was half-English, his father was half-French. All Europe contributed to the making of Kurtz; and by and by I learned that, most appropriately, the International Society for the Suppression of Savage Customs had entrusted him with the making of a report, for its future guidance. And he had written it too. I've seen it. I've read it. It was eloquent, vibrating with eloquence, but too high-strung, I think. Seventeen pages of close writing he had found time for! But this must have been before his—let us say—nerves went wrong, and caused him to preside at certain midnight dances ending with unspeakable rites, which—as far as I reluctantly gathered from what I heard at various times—were offered up to him—do you understand?—to Mr. Kurtz himself. But it was a beautiful piece of writing. The opening paragraph, however, in the light of later information, strikes me now as ominous. He began with the argument that we whites, from the point of development we had arrived at, 'must necessarily appear to them [savages] in the nature of supernatural beings—we approach them with the might as of a deity,' and so on, and so on. 'By the simple exercise of our will we can exert a power for good practically unbounded,' etc. etc. From that point he soared and took me with him. The peroration was magnificent, though difficult to remember, you know. It gave me the notion of an exotic Immensity ruled by an august Benevolence. It made me tingle with enthusiasm. This was the unbounded power of eloquence— of words—of burning noble words. There were no practical hints to interrupt the magic current of phrases, unless a kind of note at the foot of the last page, scrawled evidently much later, in an unsteady hand, may be regarded as the exposition of a method. It was very simple, and at the end of that moving appeal to every altruistic sentiment it blazed at you, luminous and terrifying, like a flash of lightning in a serene sky: 'Exterminate all the brutes!' The curious part was that he had apparently forgotten all about that valuable postscriptum, because, later on, when he in a sense came to himself, he repeatedly entreated me to take good care of 'my pamphlet' (he called it), as it was sure to have in the future a good influence upon his career. I had full information about all these things, and, besides, as it turned out, I was to have the care of his memory. I've done enough for it to give me the indisputable right to lay it, if I choose, for an everlasting rest in the dust-bin of progress, amongst all the sweepings and, figuratively speaking, all the dead cats of civilisation. But then, you see, I can't choose. He won't be forgotten. Whatever he was, he was not common. He had the power to charm or frighten rudimentary souls into an aggravated witch-dance in his honour; he could also fill the small souls of the pilgrims with bitter misgivings: he had one devoted friend at least, and he had conquered one soul in the world that was neither rudimentary nor tainted with self-seeking. No; I can't forget him, though I am not prepared to affirm the fellow was exactly worth the life we lost in getting to him. I missed my late helmsman awfully—I missed him even while his body was still lying in the pilot-house. Perhaps you will think it passing strange this regret for a savage who was no more account than a grain of sand in a black Sahara. Well, don't you see, he had done something, he had steered; for months I had him at my back—a help—an instrument. It was a kind of partnership. He steered for me—I had to look after him, I worried about his deficiencies, and thus a subtle bond had been created, of which I only became aware when it was suddenly broken. And the intimate profundity of that look he gave me when he received his hurt remains to this day in my memory—like a claim of distant kinship affirmed in a supreme moment.

"Poor fool! If he had only left that shutter alone. He had no restraint, no restraint—just like Kurtz—a tree swayed by the wind. As soon as I had put on a dry pair of slippers, I dragged him out, after first jerking the spear out of his side, which operation I confess I performed with my eyes shut tight. His heels leaped together over the little door-step; his shoulders were pressed to my breast; I hugged him from behind desperately. Oh! he was heavy, heavy; heavier than any man on earth, I should imagine. Then without more ado I tipped him overboard. The current snatched him as though he had been a wisp of grass, and I saw the body roll over twice before I lost sight of it for ever. All the pilgrims and the manager were then congregated on the awning-deck about the pilot-house, chattering at each other like a flock of excited magpies, and there was a scandalised murmur at my heartless promptitude. What they wanted to keep that body hanging about for I can't guess.

Embalm it, maybe. But I had also heard another, and a very ominous, murmur on the deck below. My friends the wood-cutters were likewise scandalised, and with a better show of reason—though I admit that the reason itself was quite inadmissible. Oh, quite! I had made up my mind that if my late helmsman was to be eaten, the fishes alone should have him. He had been a very second-rate helmsman while alive, but now he was dead he might have become a first-class temptation, and possibly cause some startling trouble. Besides, I was anxious to take the wheel, the man in pink pyjamas showing himself a hopeless duffer at the business.

"This I did directly the simple funeral was over. We were going half-speed, keeping right in the middle of the stream, and I listened to the talk about me. They had given up Kurtz, they had given up the station; Kurtz was dead, and the station had been burnt—and so on, and so on. The red-haired pilgrim was beside himself with the thought that at least this poor Kurtz had been properly revenged. 'Say! We must have made a glorious slaughter of them in the bush. Eh? What do you think? Say?' He positively danced, the bloodthirsty little gingery[15] beggar. And he had nearly fainted when he saw the wounded man! I could not help saying, 'You made a glorious lot of smoke, anyhow.' I had seen, from the way the tops of the bushes rustled and flew, that almost all the shots had gone too high. You can't hit anything unless you take aim and fire from the shoulder; but these chaps fired from the hip with their eyes shut. The retreat, I maintained—and I was right—was caused by the screeching of the steam-whistle. Upon this they forgot Kurtz, and began to howl at me with indignant protests.

"The manager stood by the wheel murmuring confidentially about the necessity of getting well away down the river before dark at all events, when I saw in the distance a clearing on the river-side and the outlines of some sort of building. 'What's this?' I asked. He clapped his hands in wonder. 'The station!' he cried. I edged in at once, still going half-speed.

"Through my glasses I saw the slope of a hill interspersed with rare trees and perfectly free from undergrowth. A long decaying building on the summit was half buried in the high grass; the large hole in the peaked roof gaped black from afar; the jungle and the woods made a background. There was no enclosure or fence of any kind; but there had been one apparently, for near the house half a dozen slim posts

---

[15]Red-haired or, perhaps, feisty.

remained in a row, roughly trimmed, and with their upper ends ornamented with round carved balls. The rails, or whatever there had been
between, had disappeared. Of course the forest surrounded all that.
The river-bank was clear, and on the water side I saw a white man
under a hat like a cart-wheel beckoning persistently with his whole
arm. Examining the edge of the forest above and below, I was almost
certain I could see movements—human forms gliding here and there. I
steamed past prudently, then stopped the engines and let her drift
down. The man on the shore began to shout, urging us to land. 'We
have been attacked,' screamed the manager. 'I know—I know. It's all
right,' yelled back the other, as cheerful as you please. 'Come along. It's
all right. I am glad.'

"His aspect reminded me of something I had seen—something funny
I had seen somewhere. As I manoeuvred to get alongside, I was asking
myself, 'What does this fellow look like?' Suddenly I got it. He looked
like a harlequin. His clothes had been made of some stuff that was
brown holland probably, but it was covered with patches all over, with
bright patches, blue, red, and yellow—patches on the back, patches on
the front, patches on elbows, on knees; coloured binding round his
jacket, scarlet edging at the bottom of his trousers; and the sunshine
made him look extremely gay and wonderfully neat withal, because
you could see how beautifully all this patching had been done. A
beardless, boyish face, very fair, no features to speak of, nose peeling,
little blue eyes, smiles and frowns chasing each other over that open
countenance like sunshine and shadow on a wind-swept plain. 'Look
out, captain!' he cried; 'there's a snag lodged in here last night.' What!
Another snag? I confess I swore shamefully. I had nearly holed my
cripple, to finish off that charming trip. The harlequin on the bank
turned his little pug-nose up to me. 'You English?' he asked, all smiles.
'Are you?' I shouted from the wheel. The smiles vanished, and he
shook his head as if sorry for my disappointment. Then he brightened
up. 'Never mind!' he cried encouragingly. 'Are we in time?' I asked. 'He
is up there,' he replied, with a toss of the head up the hill, and becoming gloomy all of a sudden. His face was like the autumn sky, overcast
one moment and bright the next.

"When the manager, escorted by the pilgrims, all of them armed to
the teeth, had gone to the house, this chap came on board. 'I say, I
don't like this. These natives are in the bush,' I said. He assured me
earnestly it was all right. 'They are simple people,' he added; 'well, I am
glad you came. It took me all my time to keep them off.' 'But you said
it was all right,' I cried. 'Oh, they meant no harm,' he said; and as I

stared he corrected himself, 'Not exactly.' Then vivaciously, 'My faith, your pilot-house wants a clean-up!' In the next breath he advised me to keep enough steam on the boiler to blow the whistle in case of any trouble. 'One good screech will do more for you than all your rifles. They are simple people,' he repeated. He rattled away at such a rate he quite overwhelmed me. He seemed to be trying to make up for lots of silence, and actually hinted, laughing, that such was the case. 'Don't you talk with Mr. Kurtz?' I said. 'You don't talk with that man—you listen to him,' he exclaimed with severe exaltation. 'But now——' He waved his arm, and in the twinkling of an eye was in the uttermost depths of despondency. In a moment he came up again with a jump, possessed himself of both my hands, shook them continuously, while he gabbled: 'Brother sailor . . . honour . . . pleasure . . . delight . . . introduce myself . . . Russian . . . son of an arch-priest . . . Government of Tambov . . . What? Tobacco! English tobacco; the excellent English tobacco! Now, that's brotherly. Smoke? Where's a sailor that does not smoke?'

"The pipe soothed him, and gradually I made out he had run away from school, had gone to sea in a Russian ship; ran away again; served some time in English ships; was now reconciled with the arch-priest. He made a point of that. 'But when one is young one must see things, gather experience, ideas; enlarge the mind.' 'Here!' I interrupted. 'You can never tell! Here I met Mr. Kurtz,' he said, youthfully solemn and reproachful. I held my tongue after that. It appears he had persuaded a Dutch trading-house on the coast to fit him out with stores and goods, and had started for the interior with a light heart, and no more idea of what would happen to him than a baby. He had been wandering about that river for nearly two years alone, cut off from everybody and every-thing. 'I am not so young as I look. I am twenty-five,' he said. 'At first old Van Shuyten would tell me to go to the devil,' he narrated with keen enjoyment; 'but I stuck to him, and talked and talked, till at last he got afraid I would talk the hind-leg off his favourite dog, so he gave me some cheap things and a few guns, and told me he hoped he would never see my face again. Good old Dutchman, Van Shuyten. I sent him one small lot of ivory a year ago, so that he can't call me a little thief when I get back. I hope he got it. And for the rest, I don't care. I had some wood stacked for you. That was my old house. Did you see?'

"I gave him Towson's book. He made as though he would kiss me, but restrained himself. 'The only book I had left, and I thought I had lost it,' he said, looking at it ecstatically. 'So many accidents happen to a man going about alone, you know. Canoes get upset sometimes—and sometimes you've got to clear out so quick when the people get angry.' He thumbed the pages. 'You made notes in Russian?' I asked. He nodded. 'I thought they were written in cipher,' I said. He laughed, then became serious. 'I had lots of trouble to keep these people off,' he said. 'Did they want to kill you?' I asked. 'Oh no!' he cried, and checked himself. 'Why did they attack us?' I pursued. He hesitated, then said shame-facedly, 'They don't want him to go.' 'Don't they?' I said curiously. He nodded a nod full of mystery and wisdom. 'I tell you,' he cried, 'this man has enlarged my mind.' He opened his arms wide, staring at me with his little blue eyes that were perfectly round."

III

"I looked at him, lost in astonishment. There he was before me, in motley, as though he had absconded from a troupe of mimes, enthusiastic, fabulous. His very existence was improbable, inexplicable, and altogether bewildering. He was an insoluble problem. It was inconceivable how he had existed, how he had succeeded in getting so far, how he had managed to remain—why he did not instantly disappear. 'I went a little farther,' he said, 'then still a little farther—till I had gone so far that I don't know how I'll ever get back. Never mind. Plenty time. I can manage. You take Kurtz away quick—quick—I tell you.' The glamour of youth enveloped his parti-coloured rags, his destitution, his loneliness, the essential desolation of his futile wanderings. For months—for years—his life hadn't been worth a day's purchase; and there he was gallantly, thoughtlessly alive, to all appearance indestructible solely by the virtue of his few years and of his unreflecting audacity. I was seduced into something like admiration—like envy. Glamour urged him on, glamour kept him unscathed. He surely wanted nothing from the wilderness but space to breathe in and to push on through. His need was to exist, and to move onwards at the greatest possible risk, and with a maximum of privation. If the absolutely pure, uncalculating, unpractical spirit of adventure had ever ruled a human being, it ruled this be-patched youth. I almost envied him the possession of this modest and clear flame. It seemed to have consumed all thought of self so completely, that, even while he was talking to you, you forgot that it was he—the man before your eyes—who had gone through these things. I did not envy him his devotion to Kurtz, though. He had not meditated over it. It came to him, and he accepted it with a sort of eager fatalism. I must say that to me it appeared about the most dangerous thing in every way he had come upon so far.

"They had come together unavoidably, like two ships becalmed near each other, and lay rubbing sides at last. I suppose Kurtz wanted an audience, because on a certain occasion, when encamped in the forest, they had talked all night, or more probably Kurtz had talked. 'We talked of everything,' he said, quite transported at the recollection. 'I forgot there was such a thing as sleep. The night did not seem to last an hour. Everything! Everything! . . . Of love too.' 'Ah, he talked to you of love!' I said, much amused. 'It isn't what you think,' he cried, almost passionately. 'It was in general. He made me see things—things.'

"He threw his arms up. We were on deck at the time, and the head-man of my wood-cutters, lounging near by, turned upon him his heavy and glittering eyes. I looked round, and I don't know why, but I assure you that never, never before, did this land, this river, this jungle, the very arch of this blazing sky, appear to me so hopeless and so dark, so impenetrable to human thought, so pitiless to human weakness. 'And, ever since, you have been with him, of course?' I said.

"On the contrary. It appears their intercourse had been very much broken by various causes. He had, as he informed me proudly, man-aged to nurse Kurtz through two illnesses (he alluded to it as you would to some risky feat), but as a rule Kurtz wandered alone, far in the depths of the forest. 'Very often coming to this station, I had to wait days and days before he would turn up,' he said. 'Ah, it was worth waiting for!—sometimes.' 'What was he doing? exploring or what?' I asked. 'Oh yes, of course'; he had discovered lots of villages, a lake too—he did not know exactly in what direction; it was dangerous to inquire too much—but mostly his expeditions had been for ivory. 'But he had no goods to trade with by that time,' I objected. 'There's a good lot of cartridges left even yet,' he answered, looking away. 'To speak plainly, he raided the country,' I said. He nodded. 'Not alone, surely!' He muttered something about the villages round that lake. 'Kurtz got the tribe to follow him, did he?' I suggested. He fidgeted a little. 'They adored him,' he said. The tone of these words was so extraordinary that I looked at him searchingly. It was curious to see his mingled eagerness and reluctance to speak of Kurtz. The man filled his life, occupied his thoughts, swayed his emotions. 'What can you expect?' he burst out; 'he came to them with thunder and lightning, you know—and they had never seen anything like it—and very terrible. He could be very terri-ble. You can't judge Mr. Kurtz as you would an ordinary man. No, no, no! Now—just to give you an idea—I don't mind telling you, he wanted to shoot me too one day—but I don't judge him.' 'Shoot you!' I cried. 'What for?' 'Well, I had a small lot of ivory the chief of that village near my house gave me. You see I used to shoot game for them. Well, he wanted it, and wouldn't hear reason. He declared he would shoot me unless I gave him the ivory and then cleared out of the country, because he could do so, and had a fancy for it, and there was nothing on earth to prevent him killing whom he jolly well pleased. And it was true too. I gave him the ivory. What did I care! But I didn't clear out. No, no. I couldn't leave him. I had to be careful, of course, till we got friendly again for a time. He had his second illness then. Afterwards I had to keep out of the way; but I didn't mind. He was living for the most part in those villages on the lake. When he came down to the river, sometimes he would take to me, and sometimes it was better for me to be careful. This man suffered too much. He hated all this, and somehow he couldn't get away. When I had a chance I begged him to try and leave while there was time; I offered to go back with him. And he would say yes, and then he would remain; go off on another ivory hunt; disappear for weeks; forget himself amongst these people—forget himself—you know.' 'Why! he's mad,' I said. He protested indignantly. Mr. Kurtz couldn't be mad. If I had heard him talk, only two days ago, I wouldn't dare hint at such a thing. . . . I had taken up my binoculars while we talked, and was looking at the shore, sweeping the limit of the forest at each side and at the back of the house. The consciousness of there being people in that bush, so silent, so quiet—as silent and quiet as the ruined house on the hill—made me uneasy. There was no sign on the face of nature of this amazing tale that was not so much told as suggested to me in desolate exclamations, completed by shrugs, in interrupted phrases, in hints ending in deep sighs. The woods were unmoved, like a mask—heavy, like the closed door of a prison—they looked with their air of hidden knowledge, of patient expectation, of unapproachable silence. The Russian was explaining to me that it was only lately that Mr. Kurtz had come down to the river, bringing along with him all the fighting men of that lake tribe. He had been absent for several months—getting himself adored, I suppose—and had come down unexpectedly, with the intention to all appearance of making a raid either across the river or down stream. Evidently the appetite for more ivory had got the better of the—what shall I say?—less material aspirations. However, he had got much worse suddenly. 'I heard he was lying helpless, and so I came up—took my chance,' said the Russian. 'Oh, he is bad, very bad.' I directed my glass to the house. There were no signs of life, but there were the ruined roof, the long mud wall peeping above the grass, with three little square window-holes, no two of the same size; all this brought within reach of my hand, as it were. And then I made a brusque movement, and one of the remaining posts of that vanished fence leaped up in the field of my glass. You remember I told you I had been struck at the distance by certain attempts at ornamentation, rather remarkable in the ruinous aspect of the place. Now I had suddenly a nearer view, and its first result was to make me throw my head back as if before a blow. Then I went carefully from post to post with my glass, and I saw my mistake. These round knobs were not ornamental but symbolic; they were expressive and puzzling, striking and disturbing—food for thought and also for vultures if there had been any looking down from the sky; but at all events for such ants as were industrious enough to ascend the pole. They would have been even more impressive, those heads on the stakes, if their faces had not been turned to the house. Only one, the first I had made out, was facing my way. I was not so shocked as you may think. The start back I had given was really nothing but a movement of surprise. I had expected to see a knob of wood there, you know. I returned deliberately to the first I had seen—and there it was, black, dried, sunken, with closed eyelids—a head that seemed to sleep at the top of that pole, and, with the shrunken dry lips showing a narrow white line of the teeth, was smiling too, smiling continuously at some endless and jocose dream of that eternal slumber.

"I am not disclosing any trade secrets. In fact the manager said afterwards that Mr. Kurtz's methods had ruined the district. I have no opinion on that point, but I want you clearly to understand that there was nothing exactly profitable in these heads being there. They only showed that Mr. Kurtz lacked restraint in the gratification of his various lusts, that there was something wanting in him—some small matter which, when the pressing need arose, could not be found under his magnificent eloquence. Whether he knew of this deficiency himself I can't say. I think the knowledge came to him at last—only at the very last. But the wilderness had found him out early, and had taken on him a terrible vengeance for the fantastic invasion. I think it had whispered to him things about himself which he did not know, things of which he had no conception till he took counsel with this great solitude—and the whisper had proved irresistibly fascinating. It echoed loudly within him because he was hollow at the core. . . . I put down the glass, and the head that had appeared near enough to be spoken to seemed at once to have leaped away from me into inaccessible distance.

"The admirer of Mr. Kurtz was a bit crestfallen. In a hurried, indistinct voice he began to assure me he had not dared to take these—say, symbols—down. He was not afraid of the natives; they would not stir till Mr. Kurtz gave the word. His ascendancy was extraordinary. The camps of these people surrounded the place, and the chiefs came every day to see him. They would crawl . . . 'I don't want to know anything of the ceremonies used when approaching Mr. Kurtz,' I shouted. Curious, this feeling that came over me that such details would be more intolerable than those heads drying on the stakes under Mr. Kurtz's windows. After all, that was only a savage sight, while I seemed at one bound to have been transported into some lightless region of subtle horrors, where pure, uncomplicated savagery was a positive relief, being something that had a right to exist—obviously—in the sunshine. The young man looked at me with surprise. I suppose it did not occur to him that Mr. Kurtz was no idol of mine. He forgot I hadn't heard any of these splendid monologues on, what was it? on love, justice, conduct of life—or what not. If it had come to crawling before Mr. Kurtz, he crawled as much as the veriest savage of them all. I had no idea of the conditions, he said: these heads were the heads of rebels. I shocked him excessively by laughing. Rebels! What would be the next definition I was to hear? There had been enemies, criminals, workers—and these were rebels. Those rebellious heads looked very subdued to me on their sticks. 'You don't know how such a life tries a man like Kurtz,' cried Kurtz's last disciple. 'Well, and you?' I said. 'I! I! I am a simple man. I have no great thoughts. I want nothing from anybody. How can you compare me to . . . ?' His feelings were too much for speech, and suddenly he broke down. 'I don't understand,' he groaned. 'I've been doing my best to keep him alive, and that's enough. I had no hand in all this. I have no abilities. There hasn't been a drop of medicine or a mouthful of invalid food for months here. He was shamefully abandoned. A man like this, with such ideas. Shamefully! Shamefully! I— I—haven't slept for the last ten nights. . . .'

"His voice lost itself in the calm of the evening. The long shadows of the forests had slipped downhill while we talked, had gone far beyond the ruined hovel, beyond the symbolic row of stakes. All this was in the gloom, while we down there were yet in the sunshine, and the stretch of the river abreast of the clearing glittered in a still and dazzling splendour, with a murky and overshadowed bend above and below. Not a living soul was seen on the shore. The bushes did not rustle.

"Suddenly round the corner of the house a group of men appeared, as though they had come up from the ground. They waded waist-deep in the grass, in a compact body, bearing an improvised stretcher in their midst. Instantly, in the emptiness of the landscape, a cry arose whose shrillness pierced the still air like a sharp arrow flying straight to the very heart of the land; and, as if by enchantment, streams of human beings—of naked human beings—with spears in their hands, with bows, with shields, with wild glances and savage movements, were poured into the clearing by the dark-faced and pensive forest. The bushes shook, the grass swayed for a time, and then everything stood still in attentive immobility.

" 'Now, if he does not say the right thing to them we are all done for,' said the Russian at my elbow. The knot of men with the stretcher had stopped too, half-way to the steamer, as if petrified. I saw the man on the stretcher sit up, lank and with an uplifted arm, above the shoulders of the bearers. 'Let us hope that the man who can talk so well of love in general will find some particular reason to spare us this time,' I said. I resented bitterly the absurd danger of our situation, as if to be at the mercy of that atrocious phantom had been a dishonouring necessity. I could not hear a sound, but through my glasses I saw the thin arm extended commandingly, the lower jaw moving, the eyes of that apparition shining darkly far in its bony head that nodded with grotesque jerks. Kurtz—Kurtz—that means 'short' in German—don't it? Well, the name was as true as everything else in his life—and death. He looked at least seven feet long. His covering had fallen off, and his body emerged from it pitiful and appalling as from a winding-sheet. I could see the cage of his ribs all astir, the bones of his arm waving. It was as though an animated image of death carved out of old ivory had been shaking its hand with menaces at a motionless crowd of men made of dark and glittering bronze. I saw him open his mouth wide— it gave him a weirdly voracious aspect, as though he had wanted to swallow all the air, all the earth, all the men before him. A deep voice reached me faintly. He must have been shouting. He fell back suddenly. The stretcher shook as the bearers staggered forward again, and almost at the same time I noticed that the crowd of savages was vanishing without any perceptible movement of retreat, as if the forest that had ejected these beings so suddenly had drawn them in again as the breath is drawn in a long aspiration.

"Some of the pilgrims behind the stretcher carried his arms—two shot-guns, a heavy rifle, and a light revolver-carbine—the thunderbolts of that pitiful Jupiter.[16] The manager bent over him murmuring as he

---

[16]Jupiter, chief god of the Romans, was pictured wielding thunderbolts as weapons.

walked beside his head. They laid him down in one of the little cabins—just a room for a bed-place and a camp-stool or two, you know. We had brought his belated correspondence, and a lot of torn envelopes and open letters littered his bed. His hand roamed feebly amongst these papers. I was struck by the fire of his eyes and the composed languor of his expression. It was not so much the exhaustion of disease. He did not seem in pain. This shadow looked satiated and calm, as though for the moment it had had its fill of all the emotions.

"He rustled one of the letters, and looking straight in my face said, 'I am glad.' Somebody had been writing to him about me. These special recommendations were turning up again. The volume of tone he emitted without effort, almost without the trouble of moving his lips, amazed me. A voice! a voice! It was grave, profound, vibrating, while the man did not seem capable of a whisper. However, he had enough strength in him—factitious no doubt—to very nearly make an end of us, as you shall hear directly.

"The manager appeared silently in the doorway; I stepped out at once and he drew the curtain after me. The Russian, eyed curiously by the pilgrims, was staring at the shore. I followed the direction of his glance.

"Dark human shapes could be made out in the distance, flitting indistinctly against the gloomy border of the forest, and near the river two bronze figures, leaning on tall spears, stood in the sunlight under fantastic head-dresses of spotted skins, warlike and still in statuesque repose. And from right to left along the lighted shore moved a wild and gorgeous apparition of a woman.

"She walked with measured steps, draped in striped and fringed cloths, treading the earth proudly, with a slight jingle and flash of barbarous ornaments. She carried her head high; her hair was done in the shape of a helmet; she had brass leggings to the knee, brass wire gauntlets to the elbow, a crimson spot on her tawny cheek, innumerable necklaces of glass beads on her neck; bizarre things, charms, gifts of witch-men, that hung about her, glittered and trembled at every step. She must have had the value of several elephant tusks upon her. She was savage and superb, wild-eyed and magnificent; there was something ominous and stately in her deliberate progress. And in the hush that had fallen suddenly upon the whole sorrowful land, the immense wilderness, the colossal body of the fecund and mysterious life seemed to look at her, pensive, as though it had been looking at the image of its own tenebrous and passionate soul.

"She came abreast of the steamer, stood still, and faced us. Her long shadow fell to the water's edge. Her face had a tragic and fierce aspect of wild sorrow and of dumb pain mingled with the fear of some struggling, half-shaped resolve. She stood looking at us without a stir, and like the wilderness itself, with an air of brooding over an inscrutable purpose. A whole minute passed, and then she made a step forward. There was a low jingle, a glint of yellow metal, a sway of fringed draperies, and she stopped as if her heart failed her. The young fellow by my side growled. The pilgrims murmured at my back. She looked at us all as if her life had depended upon the unswerving steadiness of her glance. Suddenly she opened her bared arms and threw them up rigid above her head, as though in an uncontrollable desire to touch the sky, and at the same time the swift shadows darted out on the earth, swept around on the river, gathering the steamer in a shadowy embrace. A formidable silence hung over the scene.

"She turned away slowly, walked on, following the bank, and passed into the bushes to the left. Once only her eyes gleamed back at us in the dusk of the thickets before she disappeared.

" 'If she had offered to come aboard I really think I would have tried to shoot her,' said the man of patches nervously. 'I had been risking my life every day for the last fortnight to keep her out of the house. She got in one day and kicked up a row about those miserable rags I picked up in the storeroom to mend my clothes with. I wasn't decent. At least it must have been that, for she talked like a fury to Kurtz for an hour, pointing at me now and then. I don't understand the dialect of this tribe. Luckily for me, I fancy Kurtz felt too ill that day to care, or there would have been mischief. I don't understand. . . . No—it's too much for me. Ah, well, it's all over now.'

"At this moment I heard Kurtz's deep voice behind the curtain: 'Save me!—save the ivory, you mean. Don't tell me. Save *me*! Why, I've had to save you. You are interrupting my plans now. Sick! Sick! Not so sick as you would like to believe. Never mind. I'll carry my ideas out yet—I will return. I'll show you what can be done. You with your little peddling notions—you are interfering with me. I will return. I . . .'

"The manager came out. He did me the honour to take me under the arm and lead me aside. 'He is very low, very low,' he said. He considered it necessary to sigh, but neglected to be consistently sorrowful. 'We have done all we could for him—haven't we? But there is no disguising the fact, Mr. Kurtz has done more harm than good to the Company. He did not see the time was not ripe for vigorous action. Cautiously, cautiously—that's my principle. We must be cautious yet. The district is closed to us for a time. Deplorable! Upon the whole, the trade will suffer. I don't deny there is a remarkable quantity of ivory—mostly fossil. We must save it, at all events—but look how precarious the position is—and why? Because the method is unsound.' 'Do you,' said I, looking at the shore, 'call it "unsound method"?' 'Without doubt,' he exclaimed hotly. 'Don't you?' . . . 'No method at all,' I murmured after a while. 'Exactly,' he exulted. 'I anticipated this. Shows a complete want of judgment. It is my duty to point it out in the proper quarter.' 'Oh,' said I, 'that fellow—what's his name?—the brickmaker, will make a readable report for you.' He appeared confounded for a moment. It seemed to me I had never breathed an atmosphere so vile, and I turned mentally to Kurtz for relief—positively for relief. 'Nevertheless, I think Mr. Kurtz is a remarkable man,' I said with emphasis. He started, dropped on me a cold heavy glance, said very quietly, 'He *was*,' and turned his back on me. My hour of favour was over; I found myself lumped along with Kurtz as a partisan of methods for which the time was not ripe; I was unsound! Ah! but it was something to have at least a choice of nightmares.

"I had turned to the wilderness really, not to Mr. Kurtz, who, I was ready to admit, was as good as buried. And for a moment it seemed to me as if I also were buried in a vast grave full of unspeakable secrets. I felt an intolerable weight oppressing my breast, the smell of the damp earth, the unseen presence of victorious corruption, the darkness of an impenetrable night. . . . The Russian tapped me on the shoulder. I heard him mumbling and stammering something about 'brother seaman—couldn't conceal—knowledge of matters that would affect Mr. Kurtz's reputation.' I waited. For him evidently Mr. Kurtz was not in his grave; I suspect that for him Mr. Kurtz was one of the immortals. 'Well!' said I at last, 'speak out. As it happens, I am Mr. Kurtz's friend—in a way.'

"He stated with a good deal of formality that had we not been 'of the same profession,' he would have kept the matter to himself without regard to consequences. He suspected 'there was an active ill-will towards him on the part of these white men that——' 'You are right,' I said, remembering a certain conversation I had overheard. 'The manager thinks you ought to be hanged.' He showed a concern at this intelligence which amused me at first. 'I had better get out of the way quietly,' he said earnestly. 'I can do no more for Kurtz now, and they would soon find some excuse. What's to stop them? There's a military post three hundred miles from here.' 'Well, upon my word,' said I, 'perhaps you had better go if you have any friends amongst the savages near by.' 'Plenty,' he said. 'They are simple people—and I want nothing, you know.' He stood biting his lip, then: 'I don't want any harm to happen to these whites here, but of course I was thinking of Mr. Kurtz's reputation—but you are a brother seaman and——' 'All right,' said I, after a time. 'Mr. Kurtz's reputation is safe with me.' I did not know how truly I spoke.

"He informed me, lowering his voice, that it was Kurtz who had ordered the attack to be made on the steamer. 'He hated sometimes the idea of being taken away—and then again . . . But I don't understand these matters. I am a simple man. He thought it would scare you away—that you would give it up, thinking him dead. I could not stop him. Oh, I had an awful time of it this last month.' 'Very well,' I said. 'He is all right now.' 'Ye-e-es,' he muttered, not very convinced apparently. 'Thanks,' said I; 'I shall keep my eyes open.' 'But quiet—eh?' he urged anxiously. 'It would be awful for his reputation if anybody here——' I promised a complete discretion with great gravity. 'I have a canoe and three black fellows waiting not very far. I am off. Could you give me a few Martini-Henry cartridges?' I could, and did, with proper secrecy. He helped himself, with a wink at me, to a handful of my tobacco. 'Between sailors—you know—good English tobacco.' At the door of the pilot-house he turned round— 'I say, haven't you a pair of shoes you could spare?' He raised one leg. 'Look.' The soles were tied with knotted strings sandal-wise under his bare feet. I rooted out an old pair, at which he looked with admiration before tucking it under his left arm. One of his pockets (bright red) was bulging with cartridges, from the other (dark blue) peeped 'Towson's Inquiry,' etc. etc. He seemed to think himself excellently well equipped for a renewed encounter with the wilderness. 'Ah! I'll never, never meet such a man again. You ought to have heard him recite poetry—his own too it was, he told me. Poetry!' He rolled his eyes at the recollection of these delights. 'Oh, he enlarged my mind!' 'Good-bye,' said I. He shook hands and vanished in the night. Sometimes I ask myself whether I had ever really seen him—whether it was possible to meet such a phenomenon! . . .

"When I woke up shortly after midnight his warning came to my mind with its hint of danger that seemed, in the starred darkness, real enough to make me get up for the purpose of having a look round. On the hill a big fire burned, illuminating fitfully a crooked corner of the station-house. One of the agents with a picket of a few of our blacks, armed for the purpose, was keeping guard over the ivory; but deep within the forest, red gleams that wavered, that seemed to sink and rise from the ground amongst confused columnar shapes of intense blackness, showed the exact position of the camp where Mr. Kurtz's adorers were keeping their uneasy vigil. The monotonous beating of a big drum filled the air with muffled shocks and a lingering vibration. A steady droning sound of many men chanting each to himself some weird incantation came out from the black, flat wall of the woods as the humming of bees comes out of a hive, and had a strange narcotic effect upon my half-awake senses. I believe I dozed off leaning over the rail, till an abrupt burst of yells, an overwhelming outbreak of a pent-up and mysterious frenzy, woke me up in a bewildered wonder. It was cut short all at once, and the low droning went on with an effect of audible and soothing silence. I glanced casually into the little cabin. A light was burning within, but Mr. Kurtz was not there.

"I think I would have raised an outcry if I had believed my eyes. But I didn't believe them at first—the thing seemed so impossible. The fact is, I was completely unnerved by a sheer blank fright, pure abstract terror, unconnected with any distinct shape of physical danger. What made this emotion so overpowering was—how shall I define it?—the moral shock I received, as if something altogether monstrous, intolerable to thought and odious to the soul, had been thrust upon me unexpectedly. This lasted of course the merest fraction of a second, and then the usual sense of commonplace, deadly danger, the possibility of a sudden onslaught and massacre, or something of the kind, which I saw impending, was positively welcome and composing. It pacified me, in fact, so much, that I did not raise an alarm.

"There was an agent buttoned up inside an ulster[17] and sleeping on a chair on deck within three feet of me. The yells had not awakened him; he snored very slightly; I left him to his slumbers and leaped ashore. I did not betray Mr. Kurtz—it was ordered I should never betray him—it was written I should be loyal to the nightmare of my choice. I was anxious to deal with this shadow by myself alone—and to this day I don't know why I was so jealous of sharing with any one the peculiar blackness of that experience.

"As soon as I got on the bank I saw a trail—a broad trail through the grass. I remember the exultation with which I said to myself, 'He can't walk—he is crawling on all-fours—I've got him.' The grass was wet with dew. I strode rapidly with clenched fists. I fancy I had some vague notion of falling upon him and giving him a drubbing. I don't know. I had some imbecile thoughts. The knitting old woman with the cat

---

[17]Overcoat.

obtruded herself upon my memory as a most improper person to be sitting at the other end of such an affair. I saw a row of pilgrims squirting lead in the air out of Winchesters held to the hip. I thought I would never get back to the steamer, and imagined myself living alone and unarmed in the woods to an advanced age. Such silly things—you know. And I remember I confounded the beat of the drum with the beating of my heart, and was pleased at its calm regularity.

"I kept to the track though—then stopped to listen. The night was very clear; a dark blue space, sparkling with dew and starlight, in which black things stood very still. I thought I could see a kind a motion ahead of me. I was strangely cocksure of everything that night. I actually left the track and ran in a wide semicircle (I verily believe chuckling to myself) so as to get in front of that stir, of that motion I had seen—if indeed I had seen anything. I was circumventing Kurtz as though it had been a boyish game.

"I came upon him, and, if he had not heard me coming, I would have fallen over him too, but he got up in time. He rose, unsteady, long, pale, indistinct, like a vapour exhaled by the earth, and swayed slightly, misty and silent before me; while at my back the fires loomed between the trees, and the murmur of many voices issued from the forest. I had cut him off cleverly; but when actually confronting him I seemed to come to my senses, I saw the danger in its right proportion. It was by no means over yet. Suppose he began to shout? Though he could hardly stand, there was still plenty of vigour in his voice. 'Go away— hide yourself,' he said, in that profound tone. It was very awful. I glanced back. We were within thirty yards from the nearest fire. A black figure stood up, strode on long black legs, waving long black arms, across the glow. It had horns—antelope horns, I think—on its head. Some sorcerer, some witch-man, no doubt: it looked fiend-like enough. 'Do you know what you are doing?' I whispered. 'Perfectly,' he answered, raising his voice for that single word: it sounded to me far off and yet loud, like a hail through a speaking-trumpet. If he makes a row we are lost, I thought to myself. This clearly was not a case for fisti- cuffs, even apart from the very natural aversion I had to beat that Shadow—this wandering and tormented thing. 'You will be lost,' I said—'utterly lost.' One gets sometimes such a flash of inspiration, you know. I did say the right thing, though indeed he could not have been more irretrievably lost than he was at this very moment, when the foundations of our intimacy were being laid—to endure—to endure— even to the end—even beyond.

" 'I had immense plans,' he muttered irresolutely. 'Yes,' said I; 'but if you try to shout I'll smash your head with——' There was not a stick or a stone near. 'I will throttle you for good,' I corrected myself. 'I was on the threshold of great things,' he pleaded, in a voice of longing, with a wistfulness of tone that made my blood run cold. 'And now for this stupid scoundrel——' 'Your success in Europe is assured in any case,' I affirmed steadily. I did not want to have the throttling of him, you understand—and indeed it would have been very little use for any practical purpose. I tried to break the spell—the heavy, mute spell of the wilderness—that seemed to draw him to its pitiless breast by the awakening of forgotten and brutal instincts, by the memory of gratified and monstrous passions. This alone, I was convinced, had driven him out to the edge of the forest, to the bush, towards the gleam of fires, the throb of drums, the drone of weird incantations; this alone had beguiled his unlawful soul beyond the bounds of permitted aspirations. And, don't you see, the terror of the position was not in being knocked on the head—though I had a very lively sense of that danger too—but in this, that I had to deal with a being to whom I could not appeal in the name of anything high or low. I had, even like the niggers, to invoke him—himself—his own exalted and incredible degradation. There was nothing either above or below him, and I knew it. He had kicked himself loose of the earth. Confound the man! he had kicked the very earth to pieces. He was alone, and I before him did not know whether I stood on the ground or floated in the air. I've been telling you what we said—repeating the phrases we pronounced—but what's the good? They were common everyday words—the familiar, vague sounds exchanged on every waking day of life. But what of that? They had behind them, to my mind, the terrific suggestiveness of words heard in dreams, of phrases spoken in nightmares. Soul! If anybody had ever struggled with a soul, I am the man. And I wasn't arguing with a lunatic either. Believe me or not, his intelligence was perfectly clear—concentrated, it is true, upon himself with horrible intensity, yet clear; and therein was my only chance—barring, of course, the killing him there and then, which wasn't so good, on account of unavoidable noise. But his soul was mad. Being alone in the wilderness, it had looked within itself, and, by Heavens! I tell you, it had gone mad. I had—for my sins, I suppose, to go through the ordeal of looking into it myself. No eloquence could have been so withering to one's belief in mankind as his final burst of sincerity. He struggled with himself too. I saw it—I heard it. I saw the inconceivable mystery of a soul that knew no restraint, no faith, and no fear, yet struggling blindly with itself. I kept my head pretty well; but when I had him at last stretched on the couch, I wiped my forehead, while my legs shook under me as though I had carried half a ton on my back down that hill. And yet I had only supported him, his bony arm clasped round my neck—and he was not much heavier than a child.

"When next day we left at noon, the crowd, of whose presence behind the curtain of trees I had been acutely conscious all the time, flowed out of the woods again, filled the clearing, covered the slope with a mass of naked, breathing, quivering, bronze bodies. I steamed up a bit, then swung down-stream, and two thousand eyes followed the evolutions of the splashing, thumping, fierce river-demon beating the water with its terrible tail and breathing black smoke into the air. In front of the first rank, along the river, three men, plastered with bright red earth from head to foot, strutted to and fro restlessly. When we came abreast again, they faced the river, stamped their feet, nodded their horned heads, swayed their scarlet bodies; they shook towards the fierce river-demon a bunch of black feathers, a mangy skin with a pendent tail—something that looked like a dried gourd; they shouted periodically together strings of amazing words that resembled no sounds of human language; and the deep murmurs of the crowd, interrupted suddenly, were like the responses of some satanic litany.

"We had carried Kurtz into the pilot-house: there was more air there. Lying on the couch, he stared through the open shutter. There was an eddy in the mass of human bodies, and the woman with helmeted head and tawny cheeks rushed out to the very brink of the stream. She put out her hands, shouted something, and all that wild mob took up the shout in a roaring chorus of articulated, rapid, breathless utterance.

" 'Do you understand this?' I asked.

"He kept on looking out past me with fiery, longing eyes, with a mingled expression of wistfulness and hate. He made no answer, but I saw a smile, a smile of indefinable meaning, appear on his colourless lips that a moment after twitched convulsively. 'Do I not?' he said slowly, gasping, as if the words had been torn out of him by a supernatural power.

"I pulled the string of the whistle, and I did this because I saw the pilgrims on deck getting out their rifles with an air of anticipating a jolly lark. At the sudden screech there was a movement of abject terror through that wedged mass of bodies. 'Don't! don't you frighten them away,' cried some one on deck disconsolately. I pulled the string time after time. They broke and ran, they leaped, they crouched, they swerved, they dodged the flying terror of the sound. The three red chaps had fallen flat, face down on the shore, as though they had been shot dead. Only the barbarous and superb woman did not so much as flinch, and stretched tragically her bare arms after us over the sombre and glittering river.

"And then that imbecile crowd down on the deck started their little fun, and I could see nothing more for smoke.

"The brown current ran swiftly out of the heart of darkness, bearing us down towards the sea with twice the speed of our upward progress; and Kurtz's life was running swiftly too, ebbing, ebbing out of his heart into the sea of inexorable time. The manager was very placid, he had no vital anxieties now, he took us both in with a comprehensive and satisfied glance: the 'affair' had come off as well as could be wished. I saw the time approaching when I would be left alone of the party of 'unsound method.' The pilgrims looked upon me with disfavour. I was, so to speak, numbered with the dead. It is strange how I accepted this unforeseen partnership, this choice of nightmares forced upon me in the tenebrous land invaded by these mean and greedy phantoms.

"Kurtz discoursed. A voice! a voice! It rang deep to the very last. It survived his strength to hide in the magnificent folds of eloquence the barren darkness of his heart. Oh, he struggled! he struggled! The wastes of his weary brain were haunted by shadowy images now— images of wealth and fame revolving obsequiously round his unextinguishable gift of noble and lofty expression. My Intended, my station, my career, my ideas—these were the subjects for the occasional utterances of elevated sentiments. The shade of the original Kurtz frequented the bedside of the hollow sham, whose fate it was to be buried presently in the mould of primeval earth. But both the diabolic love and the unearthly hate of the mysteries it had penetrated fought for the possession of that soul satiated with primitive emotions, avid of lying fame, of sham distinction, of all the appearances of success and power.

"Sometimes he was contemptibly childish. He desired to have kings meet him at railway stations on his return from some ghastly Nowhere, where he intended to accomplish great things. 'You show them you have in you something that is really profitable, and then there will be no limits to the recognition of your ability,' he would say. 'Of course you must take care of the motives—right motives—always.' The long reaches that were like one and the same reach, monotonous bends that were exactly alike, slipped past the steamer with their multitude of secular[18] trees looking patiently after this grimy fragment of another world, the forerunner of change, of conquest, of trade, of massacres, of blessings. I looked ahead—piloting. 'Close the shutter,' said Kurtz suddenly one day; 'I can't bear to look at this.' I did so. There was a silence. 'Oh, but I will wring your heart yet!' he cried at the invisible wilderness.

"We broke down—as I had expected—and had to lie up for repairs at the head of an island. This delay was the first thing that shook Kurtz's confidence. One morning he gave me a packet of papers and a photograph—the lot tied together with a shoe-string. 'Keep this for me,' he said. 'This noxious fool' (meaning the manager) 'is capable of prying into my boxes when I am not looking.' In the afternoon I saw him. He was lying on his back with closed eyes, and I withdrew quietly, but I heard him mutter, 'Live rightly, die, die . . .' I listened. There was nothing more. Was he rehearsing some speech in his sleep, or was it a fragment of a phrase from some newspaper article? He had been writing for the papers and meant to do so again, 'for the furthering of my ideas. It's a duty.'

"His was an impenetrable darkness. I looked at him as you peer down at a man who is lying at the bottom of a precipice where the sun never shines. But I had not much time to give him, because I was helping the engine-driver to take to pieces the leaky cylinders, to straighten a bent connecting-rod, and in other such matters. I lived in an infernal mess of rust, filings, nuts, bolts, spanners,[19] hammers, ratchet-drills—things I abominate, because I don't get on with them. I tended the little forge we fortunately had aboard; I toiled wearily in a wretched scrap-heap—unless I had the shakes too bad to stand.

"One evening coming in with a candle I was startled to hear him say a little tremulously, 'I am lying here in the dark waiting for death.' The light was within a foot of his eyes. I forced myself to murmur, 'Oh, nonsense!' and stood over him as if transfixed.

"Anything approaching the change that came over his features I have never seen before, and hope never to see again. Oh, I wasn't touched. I was fascinated. It was as though a veil had been rent. I saw on that ivory face the expression of sombre pride, of ruthless power, of craven terror—of an intense and hopeless despair. Did he live his life

---

[18]Ancient.
[19]Wrenches.

again in every detail of desire, temptation, and surrender during that supreme moment of complete knowledge? He cried in a whisper at some image, at some vision—he cried out twice, a cry that was no more than a breath:

" 'The horror! The horror!'

"I blew the candle out and left the cabin. The pilgrims were dining in the mess-room, and I took my place opposite the manager, who lifted his eyes to give me a questioning glance, which I successfully ignored. He leaned back, serene, with that peculiar smile of his sealing the unexpressed depths of his meanness. A continuous shower of small flies streamed upon the lamp, upon the cloth, upon our hands and faces. Suddenly the manager's boy put his insolent black head in the doorway, and said in a tone of scathing contempt:

" 'Mistah Kurtz—he dead.'

"All the pilgrims rushed out to see. I remained, and went on with my dinner. I believe I was considered brutally callous. However, I did not eat much. There was a lamp in there—light, don't you know—and outside it was so beastly, beastly dark. I went no more near the remarkable man who had pronounced a judgment upon the adventures of his soul on this earth. The voice was gone. What else had been there? But I am of course aware that next day the pilgrims buried something in a muddy hole.

"And then they very nearly buried me.

"However, as you see, I did not go to join Kurtz there and then. I did not. I remained to dream the nightmare out to the end, and to show my loyalty to Kurtz once more. Destiny. My destiny! Droll thing life is—that mysterious arrangement of merciless logic for a futile purpose. The most you can hope from it is some knowledge of yourself—that comes too late—a crop of unextinguishable regrets. I have wrestled with death. It is the most unexciting contest you can imagine. It takes place in an impalpable greyness, with nothing underfoot, with nothing around, without spectators, without clamour, without glory, without the great desire of victory, without the great fear of defeat, in a sickly atmosphere of tepid scepticism, without much belief in your own right, and still less in that of your adversary. If such is the form of ultimate wisdom, then life is a greater riddle than some of us think it to be. I was within a hair's-breadth of the last opportunity for pronouncement, and I found with humiliation that probably I would have nothing to say. This is the reason why I affirm that Kurtz was a remarkable man. He had something to say. He said it. Since I had peeped over the edge myself, I understand better the meaning of his stare, that could not see the flame of the candle, but was wide enough to embrace the whole universe, piercing enough to penetrate all the hearts that beat in the darkness. He had summed up—he had judged. 'The horror!' He was a remarkable man. After all, this was the expression of some sort of belief; it had candour, it had conviction, it had a vibrating note of revolt in its whisper, it had the appalling face of a glimpsed truth—the strange commingling of desire and hate. And it is not my own extremity I remember best—a vision of greyness without form filled with physical pain, and a careless contempt for the evanescence of all things—even of this pain itself. No! It is his extremity that I seem to have lived through. True, he had made that last stride, he had stepped over the edge, while I had been permitted to draw back my hesitating foot. And perhaps in this is the whole difference; perhaps all the wisdom, and all truth, and all sincerity, are just compressed into that inappreciable moment of time in which we step over the threshold of the invisible. Perhaps! I like to think my summing-up would not have been a word of careless contempt. Better his cry—much better. It was an affirmation, a moral victory paid for by innumerable defeats, by abominable terrors, by abominable satisfactions. But it was a victory! That is why I have remained loyal to Kurtz to the last, and even beyond, when a long time after I heard once more, not his own voice, but the echo of his magnificent eloquence thrown to me from a soul as translucently pure as a cliff of crystal.

"No, they did not bury me, though there is a period of time which I remember mistily, with a shuddering wonder, like a passage through some inconceivable world that had no hope in it and no desire. I found myself back in the sepulchral city resenting the sight of people hurrying through the streets to filch a little money from each other, to devour their infamous cookery, to gulp their unwholesome beer, to dream their insignificant and silly dreams. They trespassed upon my thoughts. They were intruders whose knowledge of life was to me an irritating pretence, because I felt so sure they could not possibly know the things I knew. Their bearing, which was simply the bearing of commonplace individuals going about their business in the assurance of perfect safety, was offensive to me like the outrageous flauntings of folly in the face of a danger it is unable to comprehend. I had no particular desire to enlighten them, but I had some difficulty in restraining myself from laughing in their faces, so full of stupid importance. I daresay I was not very well at that time. I tottered about the streets—there were various affairs to settle—grinning bitterly at perfectly respectable persons. I admit my behaviour was inexcusable, but then my temperature was seldom normal in these days. My dear aunt's endeavours to 'nurse up my strength' seemed altogether beside the mark. It was not my strength that wanted nursing, it was my imagination that wanted soothing. I kept the bundle of papers given me by Kurtz, not knowing exactly what to do with it. His mother had died lately, watched over, as I was told, by his Intended. A clean-shaved man, with an official manner and wearing gold-rimmed spectacles, called on me one day and made inquiries, at first circuitous, afterwards suavely pressing, about what he was pleased to denominate certain 'documents.' I was not surprised, because I had had two rows with the manager on the subject out there. I had refused to give up the smallest scrap out of that package, and I took the same attitude with the spectacled man. He became darkly menacing at last, and with much heat argued that the Company had the right to every bit of information about its 'territories.' And, said he, 'Mr. Kurtz's knowledge of unexplored regions must have been necessarily extensive and peculiar—owing to his great abilities and to the deplorable circumstances in which he had been placed: therefore——' I assured him Mr. Kurtz's knowledge, however extensive, did not bear upon the problems of commerce or administration. He invoked then the name of science. 'It would be an incalculable loss if,' etc. etc. I offered him the report on the 'Suppression of Savage Customs,' with the post-scriptum torn off. He took it up eagerly, but ended by sniffing at it with an air of contempt. 'This is not what we had a right to expect,' he remarked. 'Expect nothing else,' I said. 'There are only private letters.' He withdrew upon some threat of legal proceedings, and I saw him no more; but another fellow, calling himself Kurtz's cousin, appeared two days later, and was anxious to hear all the details about his dear relative's last moments. Incidentally he gave me to understand that Kurtz had been essentially a great musician. 'There was the making of an immense success,' said the man, who was an organist, I believe, with lank grey hair flowing over a greasy coat-collar. I had no reason to doubt his statement; and to this day I am unable to say what was Kurtz's profession, whether he ever had any—which was the greatest of his talents. I had taken him for a painter who wrote for the papers, or else for a journalist who could paint—but even the cousin (who took snuff during the interview) could not tell me what he had been—exactly. He was a universal genius—on that point I agreed with the old chap, who thereupon blew his nose noisily into a large cotton handkerchief and withdrew in senile agitation, bearing off some family letters and memoranda without importance. Ultimately a journalist anxious to know something of the fate of his 'dear colleague' turned up. This visitor informed me Kurtz's proper sphere ought to have been politics 'on the popular side.' He had furry straight eyebrows, bristly hair cropped short, an eyeglass on a broad ribbon, and, becoming expansive, confessed his opinion that Kurtz really couldn't write a bit—'but Heavens! how that man could talk! He electrified large meetings. He had faith—don't you see?—he had the faith. He could get himself to believe anything—anything. He would have been a splendid leader of an extreme party.' 'What party?' I asked. 'Any party,' answered the other. 'He was an—an—extremist.' Did I not think so? I assented. Did I know, he asked, with a sudden flash of curiosity, 'what it was that had induced him to go out there?' 'Yes,' said I, and forthwith handed him the famous Report for publication, if he thought fit. He glanced through it hurriedly, mumbling all the time, judged 'it would do,' and took himself off with this plunder.

"Thus I was left at last with a slim packet of letters and the girl's portrait. She struck me as beautiful—I mean she had a beautiful expression. I know that the sunlight can be made to lie too, yet one felt that no manipulation of light and pose could have conveyed the delicate shade of truthfulness upon those features. She seemed ready to listen without mental reservation, without suspicion, without a thought for herself. I concluded I would go and give her back her portrait and those letters myself. Curiosity? Yes; and also some other feeling perhaps. All that had been Kurtz's had passed out of my hands: his soul, his body, his station, his plans, his ivory, his career. There remained only his memory and his Intended—and I wanted to give that up too to the past, in a way—to surrender personally all that remained of him with me to that oblivion which is the last word of our common fate. I don't defend myself. I had no clear perception of what it was I really wanted. Perhaps it was an impulse of unconscious loyalty, or the fulfilment of one of those ironic necessities that lurk in the facts of human existence. I don't know. I can't tell. But I went.

"I thought his memory was like the other memories of the dead that accumulate in every man's life—a vague impress on the brain of shadows that had fallen on it in their swift and final passage; but before the high and ponderous door, between the tall houses of a street as still and decorous as a well-kept alley in a cemetery, I had a vision of him on the stretcher, opening his mouth voraciously, as if to devour all the earth with all its mankind. He lived then before me; he lived as much as he had ever lived—a shadow insatiable of splendid appearances, of frightful realities; a shadow darker than the shadow of the night, and draped nobly in the folds of a gorgeous eloquence. The vision seemed to enter the house with me—the stretcher, the phantom-bearers, the wild crowd of obedient worshippers, the gloom of the forests, the glitter of the reach between the murky bends, the beat of the drum, regular and muffled like the beating of a heart—the heart of a conquering darkness. It was a moment of triumph for the wilderness, an invading and vengeful rush which, it seemed to me, I would have to keep back alone for the salvation of another soul. And the memory of what I had heard him say afar there, with the horned shapes stirring at my back, in the glow of fires, within the patient woods, those broken phrases came back to me, were heard again in their ominous and terrifying simplicity. I remembered his abject pleading, his abject threats, the colossal scale of his vile desires, the meanness, the torment, the tempestuous anguish of his soul. And later on I seemed to see his collected languid manner, when he said one day, 'This lot of ivory now is really mine. The Company did not pay for it. I collected it myself at a very great personal risk. I am afraid they will try to claim it as theirs though. H'm. It is a difficult case. What do you think I ought to do—resist? Eh? I want no more than justice.' . . . He wanted no more than justice—no more than justice. I rang the bell before a mahogany door on the first floor, and while I waited he seemed to stare at me out of the glassy panel—stare with that wide and immense stare embracing, condemning, loathing all the universe. I seemed to hear the whispered cry, 'The horror! The horror!'

"The dusk was falling. I had to wait in a lofty drawing-room with three long windows from floor to ceiling that were like three luminous and bedraped columns. The bent gilt legs and backs of the furniture shone in indistinct curves. The tall marble fireplace had a cold and monumental whiteness. A grand piano stood massively in a corner; with dark gleams on the flat surfaces like a sombre and polished sarcophagus. A high door opened—closed. I rose.

"She came forward, all in black, with a pale head, floating toward me in the dusk. She was in mourning. It was more than a year since his death, more than a year since the news came; she seemed as though she would remember and mourn for ever. She took both my hands in hers and murmured, 'I had heard you were coming.' I noticed she was not very young—I mean not girlish. She had a mature capacity for fidelity, for belief, for suffering. The room seemed to have grown darker, as if all the sad light of the cloudy evening had taken refuge on her forehead. This fair hair, this pale visage, this pure brow, seemed surrounded by an ashy halo from which the dark eyes looked out at me. Their glance was guileless, profound, confident, and trustful. She carried her sorrowful head as though she were proud of that sorrow, as though she would say, I—I alone know how to mourn for him as he deserves. But while we were still shaking hands, such a look of awful desolation came upon her face that I perceived she was one of those creatures that are not the playthings of Time. For her he had died only yesterday. And, by Jove! the impression was so powerful that for me too he seemed to have died only yesterday—nay, this very minute. I saw her and him in the same instant of time—his death and her sorrow—I saw her sorrow in the very moment of his death. Do you understand? I saw them together—I heard them together. She had said, with a deep catch of the breath, 'I have survived'; while my strained ears seemed to hear distinctly, mingled with her tone of despairing regret, the summing-up whisper of his eternal condemnation. I asked myself what I was doing there, with a sensation of panic in my heart as though I had blundered into a place of cruel and absurd mysteries not fit for a human being to behold. She motioned me to a chair. We sat down. I laid the packet gently on the little table, and she put her hand over it. . . . 'You knew him well,' she murmured, after a moment of mourning silence.

" 'Intimacy grows quickly out there,' I said. 'I knew him as well as it is possible for one man to know another.'

" 'And you admired him,' she said. 'It was impossible to know him and not to admire him. Was it?'

" 'He was a remarkable man,' I said unsteadily. Then before the appealing fixity of her gaze, that seemed to watch for more words on my lips, I went on, 'It was impossible not to——'

" 'Love him,' she finished eagerly, silencing me into an appalled dumbness. 'How true! how true! But when you think that no one knew him so well as I! I had all his noble confidence. I knew him best.'

" 'You knew him best,' I repeated. And perhaps she did. But with every word spoken the room was growing darker, and only her forehead, smooth and white, remained illumined by the unextinguishable light of belief and love.

" 'You were his friend,' she went on. 'His friend,' she repeated, a little louder. 'You must have been, if he had given you this, and sent you to me. I feel I can speak to you—and oh! I must speak. I want you—you who have heard his last words—to know I have been worthy of him. . . . It is not pride. . . . Yes! I am proud to know I understood him better than any one on earth—he told me so himself. And since his mother died I have had no one—no one—to—to——'

"I listened. The darkness deepened. I was not even sure whether he had given me the right bundle. I rather suspect he wanted me to take care of another batch of his papers which, after his death, I saw the manager examining under the lamp. And the girl talked, easing her pain in the certitude of my sympathy; she talked as thirsty men drink. I had heard that her engagement with Kurtz had been disapproved by her people. He wasn't rich enough or something. And indeed I don't know whether he had not been a pauper all his life. He had given me some reason to infer that it was his impatience of comparative poverty that drove him out there.

" '. . . Who was not his friend who had heard him speak once?' she was saying. 'He drew men towards him by what was best in them.' She looked at me with intensity. 'It is the gift of the great,' she went on, and the sound of her low voice seemed to have the accompaniment of all the other sounds, full of mystery, desolation, and sorrow, I had ever heard—the ripple of the river, the soughing of the trees swayed by the wind, the murmurs of the crowds, the faint ring of incomprehensible words cried from afar, the whisper of a voice speaking from beyond the threshold of an eternal darkness. 'But you have heard him! You know!' she cried.

" 'Yes, I know,' I said with something like despair in my heart, but bowing my head before the faith that was in her, before that great and saving illusion that shone with an unearthly glow in the darkness, in the triumphant darkness from which I could not have defended her— from which I could not even defend myself.

" 'What a loss to me—to us!'—she corrected herself with beautiful generosity; then added in a murmur, 'To the world.' By the last gleams of twilight I could see the glitter of her eyes, full of tears—of tears that would not fall.

" 'I have been very happy—very fortunate—very proud,' she went on. 'Too fortunate. Too happy for a little while. And now I am unhappy for—for life.'

"She stood up; her fair hair seemed to catch all the remaining light in a glimmer of gold. I rose too.

" 'And of all this,' she went on mournfully, 'of all his promise, and of all his greatness, of his generous mind, of his noble heart, nothing remains—nothing but a memory. You and I——'

" 'We shall always remember him,' I said hastily.

" 'No!' she cried. 'It is impossible that all this should be lost—that such a life should be sacrificed to leave nothing—but sorrow. You know what vast plans he had. I knew of them too—I could not perhaps understand—but others knew of them. Something must remain. His words, at least, have not died.'

" 'His words will remain,' I said.

" 'And his example,' she whispered to herself. 'Men looked up to him—his goodness shone in every act. His example——'

" 'True,' I said; 'his example too. Yes, his example. I forgot that.'

" 'But I do not. I cannot—I cannot believe—not yet. I cannot believe that I shall never see him again, that nobody will see him again, never, never, never.'

"She put out her arms as if after a retreating figure, stretching them back and with clasped pale hands across the fading and narrow sheen of the window. Never see him! I saw him clearly enough then. I shall see this eloquent phantom as long as I live, and I shall see her too, a tragic and familiar Shade, resembling in this gesture another one, tragic also, and bedecked with powerless charms, stretching bare brown arms over the glitter of the infernal stream, the stream of darkness. She said suddenly very low, 'He died as he lived.'

" 'His end,' said I, with dull anger stirring in me, 'was in every way worthy of his life.'

" 'And I was not with him,' she murmured. My anger subsided before a feeling of infinite pity.

" 'Everything that could be done——' I mumbled.

" 'Ah, but I believed in him more than any one on earth—more than his own mother, more than—himself. He needed me! Me! I would have treasured every sigh, every word, every sign, every glance.'

"I felt like a chill grip on my chest. 'Don't,' I said, in a muffled voice.

" 'Forgive me. I—I—have mourned so long in silence—in silence. . . . You were with him—to the last? I think of his loneliness. Nobody near to understand him as I would have understood. Perhaps no one to hear . . .'

" 'To the very end,' I said shakily. 'I heard his very last words. . . .' I stopped in a fright.

" 'Repeat them,' she murmured in a heartbroken tone. 'I want—I want—something—something—to—to live with.'

"I was on the point of crying at her, 'Don't you hear them?' The dusk was repeating them in a persistent whisper all around us, in a whisper that seemed to swell menacingly like the first whisper of a rising wind. 'The horror! The horror!'

" 'His last word—to live with,' she insisted. 'Don't you understand I loved him—I loved him—I loved him!'

"I pulled myself together and spoke slowly.

" 'The last word he pronounced was—your name.'

"I heard a light sigh and then my heart stood still, stopped dead short by an exulting and terrible cry, by the cry of inconceivable triumph and of unspeakable pain. 'I knew it—I was sure!' . . . She knew. She was sure. I heard her weeping; she had hidden her face in her hands. It seemed to me that the house would collapse before I could escape, that the heavens would fall upon my head. But nothing happened. The heavens do not fall for such a trifle. Would they have fallen, I wonder, if I had rendered Kurtz that justice which was his due? Hadn't he said he wanted only justice? But I couldn't. I could not tell her. It would have been too dark—too dark altogether. . . ."

Marlow ceased, and sat apart, indistinct and silent, in the pose of a meditating Buddha. Nobody moved for a time. "We have lost the first of the ebb," said the Director suddenly. I raised my head. The offing was barred by a black bank of clouds, and the tranquil waterway leading to the uttermost ends of the earth flowed sombre under an overcast sky—seemed to lead into the heart of an immense darkness.

The Dead

James Joyce

The early years of James Joyce are better known than those of most other modern novelists because they form the substance, little disguised, of his first novel, *A Portrait of the Artist as a Young Man* (1916). He was born in Dublin on February 2, 1882, the eldest of the ten surviving children of May Murray and John Stanislaus Joyce. Joyce's family, at the time of his birth, was relatively well-to-do. His father, a grandiloquent man-about-town with a fine tenor voice, in politics an avid Parnellite, had been awarded as a political favor a post in the Dublin Rates Office that paid well and demanded little real work. Ambitious for his firstborn, he sent Joyce at the early age of six to the finest preparatory school in Ireland, the Jesuit-run Clongowes Wood College. *Portrait* recounts Joyce's homesick misery at Clongowes; this was undoubtedly a transient stage in his life at that school, for he soon came to stand at the head of his class in both his academic and religious studies.

In 1891 Joyce wrote his first recorded poem, a topical piece occasioned by the death of Parnell that satirized that leader's betrayers. In the same year, as the result of a civic reorganization, John Joyce's job was eliminated. He was, after much delay, awarded a pension of one-third of his salary, and for a time he was able to keep up most of his expensive habits by selling some family property near Cork. But he was unable to find another easy, lucrative position, and preferred to be idle than to take the jobs he could get. The Joyce family began its long, slow descent into a not terribly genteel poverty. One of the first luxuries to be sacrificed was James Joyce's tuition at Clongowes Wood; he was removed from that school and sent, for two years, to a mediocre Christian Brothers' school in Dublin.

Joyce was spared some of the consequences of his father's imprudence by a combination of his own brilliance and a fortunate accident. In a chance meeting with Father John Conmee, the former rector of Clongowes, Joyce's father mentioned his son's withdrawal from school. Conmee, who remembered Joyce very well, used his influence to get the boy admitted without fees to Belvedere College in Dublin, where Conmee was prefect of studies. At Belvedere Joyce continued his distinguished performance, winning three "exhibitions"—national examinations with substantial money prizes—and treating his parents to unaccustomed little luxuries with some of the proceeds.

It was during the Belvedere years, though, while he kept up the façade of the successful schoolboy, that Joyce laid the foundations of his rebellion and exile.

A brief encounter with a prostitute after an evening at the theater began Joyce's sexual initiation, and the precocious fourteen-year-old followed the experience with surreptitious visits to Nighttown—Dublin's red-light district—financed out of his exhibition prizes. The conflict between the unholy mysteries of sex and the sacred mysteries of his training at Belvedere was intense. Joyce had been chosen prefect of the Sodality of the Blessed Virgin Mary, and he would preside over the adoration of the Virgin while his lips still recalled a whore's "lewd kiss." The crisis came on a retreat when, after a ferocious hellfire sermon, Joyce experienced a violent revulsion to his adolescent sexuality and underwent a highly spiritual phase of purgation, fasting, and prayer. But this too had its reaction: after some months of piety, during which Joyce seriously contemplated entering the priesthood, he began to understand that his conversion had been extorted from him. While he remained a nominal Catholic all his life, the forms had become empty for him, and Joyce knew that his vocation lay elsewhere, in the priesthood of the imagination.

In 1898 Joyce graduated from Belvedere and entered University College, Dublin, the Catholic university founded by Cardinal Newman to compete with the more prestigious Protestant institution, Trinity College. By this time, Joyce's aesthetic sensibility, developed at Belvedere, had come to the fore, while his sense of himself as an active rebel against the conventional pieties of his time had replaced his former satisfaction with academic success and recognition. His literary idol was Henrik Ibsen—himself an exile and a rebel against his society—whose work was thought scandalous by turn-of-the-century Dublin, but whom Joyce defended in literary papers and in public debates. Not yet in his twenties, Joyce attacked the narrowness and provincialism of the Irish intellectuals and nationalists and looked toward Europe as a scene of greater vision and freedom. By 1902, when he took his degree, Joyce was ready to break with home, religion, and country—the shackles he felt were binding him—and to search for his own vision and freedom abroad.

His creative work from this period has not survived except by accident—Joyce destroyed most of it himself. There was a full-length play, imitative of Ibsen, and a good deal of poetry, self-indulgent and with echoes of Byron, Yeats, and the symbolists. What is most interesting, for the course of his later career, is a group of short prose pieces which Joyce called "epiphanies." Literally a "showing forth," an epiphany, to Joyce, was a dramatic or lyrical moment of spiritual revelation. Some of these epiphanies are radiantly beautiful, while others are revelations of vulgarity, dullness, or stupidity. What is important is that they make manifest the special quality, the "whatness" of a given moment and manifest it so clearly that no commentary on the part of the writer could be necessary. About forty of Joyce's epiphanies have survived; this one, after a few changes, was reprinted as part of the conclusion of *Portrait*:

> The spell of arms and voices—the white arms of roads, their promise of close embraces, and the black arms of tall ships that stand against the moon, their tale of distant nations. They are held out to say: We are alone,—come. And the voices

say with them, We are your people. And the air is thick with their company as they call to me their kinsman, making ready to go, shaking the wings of their exultant and terrible youth.

None of the surviving epiphanies was used in the *Dubliners* stories, but many contain similar moments of revelation, like Gabriel's vision at the end of *The Dead.*

Despite the seriousness with which Joyce took literature and despite his sense of the necessity of exile, his early twenties were a series of false starts. In 1902 he traveled to Paris to begin studying medicine but quickly dropped out for want of money to pay his fees. He lingered in Paris for a while, writing reviews for the Dublin *Daily Express* and teaching English to private pupils, till a telegram, MOTHER DYING COME HOME FATHER, summoned him back to Dublin. After his mother's death, Joyce considered the possibility of an operatic career. Like his father, Joyce had an excellent tenor voice, and when he entered a competition against well-known contestants (including the great John McCormick) he would have been judged the winner but for his refusal to sight-sing a set piece. Yet his voice, though sweet and true, was not sufficiently strong to support a career, so in 1904 Joyce took a teaching post at a school in a Dublin suburb.

In June 1904, Joyce met and fell in love with a young woman with the somewhat comic name of Nora Barnacle. Tall, pretty, with a jaunty way about her, but nearly uneducated and with no interest in literature, she was not the girl one would have expected to become the consort of a great master of modern letters, but her understanding and uncritical acceptance of him was perhaps just what Joyce needed. When Joyce's father heard the name of his son's sweetheart, he is said to have remarked: "Barnacle? She'll never leave him then." He was right; she stuck to him all her life. The date of their first evening out together, June 16, is the day on which Joyce set his novel *Ulysses.* Nora was the model for many of the women in Joyce's fiction, notably Gretta Conroy in *The Dead.* Like Gretta, Nora was a country-bred girl from Galway, in the west of Ireland, and Joyce even gave Gretta an episode from Nora's past— a former lover named Michael who died young.

In addition to her love and acceptance, Nora gave Joyce the courage to make the final break with Ireland. In September she agreed to live with him and, since they could not do so in Dublin, Joyce hastily borrowed a small sum to pay their fare to Paris. With little planning or forethought about how and where they might live, the couple embarked for the Continent. Except for two brief trips, one to found Dublin's first cinema in 1909 (it collapsed the next year), the other to try to arrange the publication of *Dubliners* in 1912 (he failed), Joyce never returned to Ireland. After brief stays in Pola, a port on the Adriatic Sea, and in Rome, Joyce took up teaching languages at the Berlitz school in Trieste, where he and Nora lived until 1915 and where their two children, Giorgio and Lucia, were born. Not until 1931 were Joyce and Nora legally married.

At the time Joyce left Ireland he was working on three projects. The least problematic was a collection of poetry entitled *Chamber Music*, which was published in London in 1907. The second was an autobiographical novel whose seed was a brief sketch called "A Portrait of the Artist," written in 1904; Joyce was engaged in expanding this sketch into a full-length novel to be called *Stephen Hero*. The most frustrating of his projects was a collection of short stories, of which Joyce wrote: "I call the series *Dubliners* to betray the soul of that hemiplegia or paralysis which many consider a city." The original manuscript contained twelve stories, three each in the four "phases" of childhood, adolescence, maturity, and public life; they were written at white heat in late 1904 through 1905 and quickly accepted by Grant Richards, a Dublin publisher. But Richards's printer feared prosecution for obscenity or libel, and Joyce had to fight fiercely to get his collection published as he had written it. By 1907 the *Dubliners* manuscript was completed by the addition of two more stories and *The Dead*, the novella that acts as the capstone and conclusion of the whole series. But it was not until 1914 that Richards was finally persuaded to offer *Dubliners* to the public.

The year 1914 is a watershed of Joyce's career, for it marks not only the publication of *Dubliners*, but Joyce's discovery by poet Ezra Pound and editor Harriet Shaw Weaver, both potent forces in European literary circles. Joyce had begun refining *Stephen Hero*—which had wound up a wordy and unwieldy novel of over sixty chapters—into the evocative and dramatic *A Portrait of the Artist as a Young Man*. He showed the first chapter to Pound, who was enthusiastic about it and arranged for its serial publication in Weaver's literary magazine, *The Egoist*, where it appeared during 1914-1915 before its book publication in 1916. While the experimentalism of *Portrait* is overshadowed by that of Joyce's later novels, it remains a remarkable technical achievement, nearly perfect in the economy of its form and the objectivity of its treatment of the most personal of subjects. Using symbolism and a series of distinct styles, Joyce conveyed the inner life of his protagonist in his progress from early childhood to the assumption of his mature destiny: "to forge in the smithy of my soul the uncreated conscience of my race." In *Portrait*, Joyce convincingly and movingly delineated the formation of his own poetic temperament.

The year 1914 also marks the outset of Joyce's work on his greatest achievement, *Ulysses*, which he worked on in Trieste, in Zurich—to which the Joyce family moved during the First World War—and in Paris, where they settled in 1920. There, Joyce was delighted to find himself no longer ignored, but the head of a literary movement. His fame derived not only from the publication of *Dubliners* and *Portrait*, but also from the chapters of *Ulysses* that had been appearing, thanks to Pound, in the New York-based *Little Review* from 1918 to 1920, when the U.S. Post Office halted further publication on grounds of obscenity. By this point, Joyce was no longer teaching at Berlitz academies. He and his family were able to live, in a bohemian fashion, partly from the advances and royalties of his publications, but mainly from the generosity of wealthy friends and admirers who wished to set him free from financial cares and enable him to write full-time in complete independence. Joyce spent his first two years in Paris completing and revising *Ulysses*, which was published there by the Shakespeare Press in 1922. Despite its obvious seriousness, the uncompromising language and vision of *Ulysses* made it impossible to publish in Britain and America, and readers had to smuggle copies back from Paris until Justice Woolsey's 1933 decision cleared the way for its American publication.

Ulysses is an impossible book to describe adequately in brief. It covers one day (June 16, 1904) in the life of three Dubliners, a day in which nothing very much happens, which ends as inconclusively as it began—and yet it is a novel of amazing breadth and scope, an encyclopedic portrait of modern life. On one level, it conveys the flickering, fugitive thoughts of its characters, the hideous and tawdry domestic details of their lives, dissecting them with a surgical precision hitherto unknown in fiction; on another level it presents Leopold and Molly Bloom and Stephen Dedalus as the modern symbolic equivalents of Odysseus, Penelope, and Telemachus in Homer's epic, while a complex network of parallels constantly relates and contrasts the characters to their Homeric counterparts. On still another level, Joyce stylistically plays with the forms of rhetoric and the types of narrative technique. One chapter is related as a catechism of questions and answers; another is told in a sequence of parodies of English literature from Anglo-Saxon to the present day—and beyond. Yet, as Walton Litz has suggested, the ultimate triumph of *Ulysses* goes beyond its psychological naturalism, its mythic and symbolic structure, its stylistic experimentation, to the elemental drama of Bloom's search for a son and Stephen's search for a father, and the spiritual profundity that underlies all of Joyce's artistry. It is his masterpiece, and one with which we are still struggling to come to terms.

Joyce spent the next seventeen years, from 1922 to 1939, writing his last novel, *Finnegans Wake*. They were years of growing fame and easing circumstances, but they were also years of personal pain and sorrow. The deterioration of his eyesight, despite treatments and surgery, progressed until he became nearly blind, while his daughter Lucia, always unstable, had a nervous breakdown and was ultimately to be institutionalized in Switzerland. Meanwhile he devoted himself to completing his "monster," a book that cannot be read, only studied.

In *Ulysses* Joyce tried to universalize his three Dubliners through their symbolic relation with Greek epic characters. He attempted something even larger, a universal history, in *Finnegans Wake*. The title refers to an Irish tavern song about the hod-carrier, Tim Finnegan, who breaks his skull in a drunken fall and is miraculously "resurrected" at his own wake, revitalized by a noggin of spilled whisky. The theme of death and resurrection and the broader theme of the cyclical character of human history, in which civilizations evolve, collapse, and are reborn, govern the structure of the novel, which is itself cyclical, beginning in mid-sentence and ending in the middle of the same sentence—as though the novel, like life itself, were continuous with no beginning and no end. The language is English, but with misspellings that call up puns in a dozen other tongues, making covert reference to historical figures from Gilgamesh to the Marx Brothers. Yet behind all the erudite play is the primordial arena of the family, the Father struggling with his Sons, the conflict of Brother with Brother, the relation of Man to life-giving or -devouring Woman. It is a book in which Joyce strove to give voice to the eternal dream of humanity, taking place on a single never-ending night of dreams. Within its own terms, *Finnegans Wake* is a triumph, but its terms are so uncompromising and its immediate rewards to the reader are so slender that it has never been and will probably never be a popular book. As Joyce himself knew, his last novel, the most difficult ever written, would be fully understood only by the handful of specialists willing to devote their lives to mastering its complexities.

Finnegans Wake came out on the eve of the Second World War, and the Joyce family was forced to flee Paris as it fell before the advancing German armies. They found a refuge in Zurich, where they had spent the first war, but Joyce was no longer young and energetic. Rather, he was prematurely aged and suffering from an ulcer aggravated by his addiction to drink. The ulcer perforated, and despite surgery and transfusions, the loss of blood could not be controlled. Joyce died on January 13, 1941, in his fifty-ninth year. By the time of his death, James Joyce had become a legend and an icon, as much known for what he had sacrificed in the service of his art—friends, country, family, and faith—as for his contributions to that art themselves. He remains today the archetypal modern writer, against whom all others are measured, because, as Richard Ellmann put it in the opening of his fine biography, "We are all still learning to be Joyce's contemporaries, to understand our interpreter."

Biography   The irreplaceable modern biography is Richard Ellmann's *James Joyce* (New York: Oxford University Press, 1959). Specialized biographies include Kevin Sullivan's *Joyce Among the Jesuits* (on Joyce's school days) (New York: Columbia University Press, 1958) and Frank Budgen's *James Joyce and the Making of 'Ulysses'* by a friend of Joyce who knew him best during the period 1918–1921 (Bloomington: Indiana University Press, 1960).

Editions   Critical editions of Joyce's fiction, based upon the first printings and on available manuscripts, are only recently beginning to appear. For *Dubliners*, the edition of choice, and the one from which the text of *The Dead* was prepared, is the Viking Critical Library edition, edited by Robert Scholes and A. Walton Litz (1969). For *Portrait of the Artist*, again the Viking Critical Library edition, edited by Chester Anderson. For *Ulysses*, there is only the old Random House edition, revised 1959, but in need of further revision. For *Finnegans Wake*, the best text is the Viking Compass Book.

Bibliography   Joyce's own works are comprehensively examined in John J. Slocum and Herbert Cahoon's *A Bibliography of James Joyce* (New Haven: Yale University Press, 1953). Joyce criticism bibliographies include Maurice Beebe and A. Walton Litz, "Criticism of James Joyce: A Selected Checklist" in *Modern Fiction Studies* 4 (1958), 71–99; and Robert Deming, *A Bibliography of James Joyce Studies* (Lawrence: University of Kansas Press, 1964).

General Criticism   A small library could be filled with works about Joyce alone. Some of the most significant, though, would have to include: Hugh Kenner, *Dublin's Joyce* (Bloomington: Indiana University Press, 1956); William

York Tindall, *A Reader's Guide to James Joyce* (New York: Farrar, Straus & Giroux, 1959); Harry Levin, *James Joyce: A Critical Introduction* (New York: New Directions, 1960); and S. L. Goldberg, *James Joyce* (New York: Evergreen Books, 1962).

Criticism of **The** **Dead**   See "The Backgrounds of *The Dead*," pp. 252–263 of the Ellmann biography; Bernard Benstock's "The Dead" in Clive Hart, ed., *James Joyce's Dubliners* (New York: Viking Press, 1969), pp. 153–169; Warren Beck, *Joyce's Dubliners: Substance, Vision and Art* (Durham, N.C.: Duke University Press, 1969); C. C. Loomis, Jr., "Structure and Sympathy in *The Dead*," *PMLA* 75 (March 1960), 149–151; Homer Brown, *James Joyce's Early Fiction* (Cleveland: Case Western Reserve University Press, 1972); Florence L. Walzl, "Gabriel and Michael: The Conclusion of 'The Dead,' " in *James Joyce Quarterly* 4 (1966), 17–31; Brendan P. O Hehir, "Structural Symbol in Joyce's *The Dead*," *Twentieth Century Literature* 3 (April 1957), 3–13; Robert Bierman, "Structural Elements in *The Dead*," *James Joyce Quarterly* 4 (Fall 1966), 42–45; Andrew Lytle, "A Reading of James Joyce's *The Dead*," *Sewanee Review* 77 (Spring 1969), 193–216; John D. and Ruth A. Boyd, "The Love Triangle in Joyce's *The Dead*," *University of Toronto Quarterly* 42 (Spring 1973), 202–217; and John W. Foster, "Passage Through *The Dead*," *Criticism* 15 (Spring 1973), 91–108.

The Dead

Lily, the caretaker's daughter, was literally run off her feet. Hardly had she brought one gentleman into the little pantry behind the office on the ground floor and helped him off with his overcoat than the wheezy hall-door bell clanged again and she had to scamper along the bare hallway to let in another guest. It was well for her she had not to attend to the ladies also. But Miss Kate and Miss Julia had thought of that and had converted the bathroom upstairs into a ladies' dressing-room. Miss Kate and Miss Julia were there, gossiping and laughing and fussing, walking after each other to the head of the stairs, peering down over the banisters and calling down to Lily to ask her who had come.

It was always a great affair, the Misses Morkan's annual dance. Everybody who knew them came to it, members of the family, old friends of the family, the members of Julia's choir, any of Kate's pupils that were grown up enough and even some of Mary Jane's pupils too. Never once had it fallen flat. For years and years it had gone off in splendid style as long as anyone could remember; ever since Kate and Julia, after the death of their brother Pat, had left the house in Stoney Batter and

p.o.v. begins objective,
→ *tucked with Aunts diction*

taken Mary Jane, their only niece, to live with them in the dark gaunt house on Usher's Island, the upper part of which they had rented from Mr Fulham, the cornfactor on the ground floor. That was a good thirty years ago if it was a day. Mary Jane, who was then a little girl in short clothes, was now the main prop of the household for she had[1] the organ in Haddington Road. She had been through the Academy and gave a pupils' concert every year in the upper room of the Antient Concert Rooms. Many of her pupils belonged to better-class families on the Kingstown and Dalkey line. Old as they were, her aunts also did their share. Julia, though she was quite grey, was still the leading soprano in Adam and Eve's,[2] and Kate, being too feeble to go about much, gave music lessons to beginners on the old square piano in the back room. Lily, the caretaker's daughter, did housemaid's work for them. Though their life was modest they believed in eating well; the best of everything: diamond-bone sirloins, three-shilling tea and the best bottled stout. But Lily seldom made a mistake in the orders so that she got on well with her three mistresses. They were fussy, that was all. But the only thing they would not stand was back answers.

Of course they had a good reason to be fussy on such a night. And then it was long after ten o'clock and yet there was no sign of Gabriel and his wife. Besides they were dreadfully afraid that Freddy Malins might turn up screwed.[3] They would not wish for worlds that any of Mary Jane's pupils should see him under the influence; and when he was like that it was sometimes very hard to manage him. Freddy Malins always came late but they wondered what could be keeping Gabriel: and that was what brought them every two minutes to the banisters to ask Lily had Gabriel or Freddy come.

——O, Mr Conroy, said Lily to Gabriel when she opened the door for him, Miss Kate and Miss Julia thought you were never coming. Good-night, Mrs Conroy.

——I'll engage they did, said Gabriel, but they forget that my wife here takes three mortal hours to dress herself.

He stood on the mat, scraping the snow from his goloshes, while Lily led his wife to the foot of the stairs and called out:

——Miss Kate, here's Mrs Conroy.

Kate and Julia came toddling down the dark stairs at once. Both of

first mention of G

↑ expo

scene ↓

---

[1] Played.
[2] A church.
[3] Drunk.

them kissed Gabriel's wife, said she must be perished alive and asked was Gabriel with her.

——Here I am right as the mail, Aunt Kate! Go on up. I'll follow, called out Gabriel from the dark.

He continued scraping his feet vigorously while the three women went upstairs, laughing, to the ladies' dressing-room. A light fringe of snow lay like a cape on the shoulders of his overcoat and like toecaps on the toes of his goloshes; and, as the buttons of his overcoat slipped with a squeaking noise through the snow-stiffened frieze, a cold fragrant air from out-of-doors escaped from crevices and folds.

——Is it snowing again, Mr Conroy? asked Lily.

She had preceded him into the pantry to help him off with his overcoat. Gabriel smiled at the three syllables she had given his surname and glanced at her. She was a slim, growing girl, pale in complexion and with hay-coloured hair. The gas in the pantry made her look still paler. Gabriel had known her when she was a child and used to sit on the lowest step nursing a rag doll.

——Yes, Lily, he answered, and I think we're in for a night of it.

He looked up at the pantry ceiling, which was shaking with the stamping and shuffling of feet on the floor above, listened for a moment to the piano and then glanced at the girl, who was folding his overcoat carefully at the end of a shelf.

——Tell me, Lily, he said in a friendly tone, do you still go to school?

——O no, sir, she answered. I'm done schooling this year and more.

——O, then, said Gabriel gaily, I suppose we'll be going to your wedding one of these fine days with your young man, eh?

The girl glanced back at him over her shoulder and said with great bitterness:

——The men that is now is only all palaver and what they can get out of you.

Gabriel coloured as if he felt he had made a mistake and, without looking at her, kicked off his goloshes and flicked actively with his muffler at his patent-leather shoes.

He was a stout tallish young man. The high colour of his cheeks pushed upwards even to his forehead where it scattered itself in a few formless patches of pale red; and on his hairless face there scintillated restlessly the polished lenses and the bright gilt rims of the glasses which screened his delicate and restless eyes. His glossy black hair was parted in the middle and brushed in a long curve behind his ears where it curled slightly beneath the groove left by his hat.

When he had flicked lustre into his shoes he stood up and pulled his

waistcoat down more tightly on his plump body. Then he took a coin
rapidly from his pocket.

——O Lily, he said, thrusting it into her hand, it's Christmas-time,
isn't it? Just . . . here's a little. . . .

He walked rapidly towards the door.

——O no, sir! cried the girl, following him. Really, sir, I wouldn't
take it.

——Christmas-time! Christmas-time! said Gabriel, almost trotting to
the stairs and waving his hand to her in deprecation.

The girl, seeing that he had gained the stairs, called out after him:

——Well, thank you, sir.

He waited outside the drawing-room door until the waltz should
finish, listening to the skirts that swept against it and to the shuffling of
feet. He was still discomposed by the girl's bitter and sudden retort. It
had cast a gloom over him which he tried to dispel by arranging his
cuffs and the bows of his tie. Then he took from his waistcoat pocket a
little paper and glanced at the headings he had made for his speech. He
was undecided about the lines from Robert Browning for he feared
they would be above the heads of his hearers. Some quotation that
they could recognise from Shakespeare or from the Melodies[4] would be
better. The indelicate clacking of the men's heels and the shuffling of
their soles reminded him that their grade of culture differed from his.
He would only make himself ridiculous by quoting poetry to them
which they could not understand. They would think that he was airing
his superior education. He would fail with them just as he had failed
with the girl in the pantry. He had taken up a wrong tone. His whole
speech was a mistake from first to last, an utter failure.

Just then his aunts and his wife came out of the ladies' dressing-
room. His aunts were two small plainly dressed old women. Aunt Julia
was an inch or so the taller. Her hair, drawn low over the tips of her
ears, was grey; and grey also, with darker shadows, was her large flac-
cid face. Though she was stout in build and stood erect her slow eyes
and parted lips gave her the appearance of a woman who did not know
where she was or where she was going. Aunt Kate was more vivacious.
Her face, healthier than her sister's, was all puckers and creases, like a
shrivelled red apple, and her hair, braided in the same old-fashioned
way, had not lost its ripe nut colour.

They both kissed Gabriel frankly. He was their favourite nephew,

---

[4]Thomas Moore's nineteenth-century collection of Irish songs.

the son of their dead elder sister, Ellen, who had married T. J. Conroy of the Port and Docks.

——Gretta tells me you're not going to take a cab back to Monkstown to-night, Gabriel, said Aunt Kate.

——No, said Gabriel, turning to his wife, we had quite enough of that last year, hadn't we? Don't you remember, Aunt Kate, what a cold Gretta got out of it? Cab windows rattling all the way, and the east wind blowing in after we passed Merrion. Very jolly it was. Gretta caught a dreadful cold.

Aunt Kate frowned severely and nodded her head at every word.

——Quite right, Gabriel, quite right, she said. You can't be too careful.

——But as for Gretta there, said Gabriel, she'd walk home in the snow if she were let.

Mrs Conroy laughed.

——Don't mind him, Aunt Kate, she said. He's really an awful bother, what with green shades for Tom's eyes at night and making him do the dumb-bells, and forcing Eva to eat the stirabout.[5] The poor child! And she simply hates the sight of it! . . . O, but you'll never guess what he makes me wear now!

She broke out into a peal of laughter and glanced at her husband, whose admiring and happy eyes had been wandering from her dress to her face and hair. The two aunts laughed heartily, too, for Gabriel's solicitude was a standing joke with them.

——Goloshes! said Mrs Conroy. That's the latest. Whenever it's wet underfoot I must put on my goloshes. To-night even he wanted me to put them on, but I wouldn't. The next thing he'll buy me will be a diving suit.

Gabriel laughed nervously and patted his tie reassuringly while Aunt Kate nearly doubled herself, so heartily did she enjoy the joke. The smile soon faded from Aunt Julia's face and her mirthless eyes were directed towards her nephew's face. After a pause she asked:

——And what are goloshes, Gabriel?

——Goloshes, Julia! exclaimed her sister. Goodness me, don't you know what goloshes are? You wear them over your . . . over your boots, Gretta, isn't it?

——Yes, said Mrs Conroy. Guttapercha[6] things. We both have a pair now. Gabriel says everyone wears them on the continent.

---

[5]Porridge.
[6]India rubber.

——O, on the continent, murmured Aunt Julia, nodding her head slowly.

Gabriel knitted his brows and said, as if he were slightly angered:

——It's nothing very wonderful but Gretta thinks it very funny because she says the word reminds her of Christy Minstrels.

——But tell me, Gabriel, said Aunt Kate, with brisk tact. Of course, you've seen about the room. Gretta was saying . . .

——O, the room is all right, replied Gabriel. I've taken one in the Gresham.

——To be sure, said Aunt Kate, by far the best thing to do. And the children, Gretta, you're not anxious about them?

——O, for one night, said Mrs Conroy. Besides, Bessie will look after them.

——To be sure, said Aunt Kate again. What a comfort it is to have a girl like that, one you can depend on! There's that Lily, I'm sure I don't know what has come over her lately. She's not the girl she was at all.

Gabriel was about to ask his aunt some questions on this point but she broke off suddenly to gaze after her sister who had wandered down the stairs and was craning her neck over the banisters.

——Now, I ask you, she said, almost testily, where is Julia going? Julia! Julia! Where are you going?

Julia, who had gone halfway down one flight, came back and announced blandly:

——Here's Freddy.

At the same moment a clapping of hands and a final flourish of the pianist told that the waltz had ended. The drawing-room door was opened from within and some couples came out. Aunt Kate drew Gabriel aside hurriedly and whispered into his ear:

——Slip down, Gabriel, like a good fellow and see if he's all right, and don't let him up if he's screwed. I'm sure he's screwed. I'm sure he is.

Gabriel went to the stairs and listened over the banisters. He could hear two persons talking in the pantry. Then he recognised Freddy Malins' laugh. He went down the stairs noisily.

——It's such a relief, said Aunt Kate to Mrs Conroy, that Gabriel is here. I always feel easier in my mind when he's here. . . . Julia, there's Miss Daly and Miss Power will take some refreshment. Thanks for your beautiful waltz, Miss Daly. It made lovely time.

A tall wizen-faced man, with a stiff grizzled moustache and swarthy skin, who was passing out with his partner said:

——And may we have some refreshment too, Miss Morkan?

———Julia, said Aunt Kate summarily, and here's Mr Browne and Miss Furlong. Take them in, Julia, with Miss Daly and Miss Power.

———I'm the man for the ladies, said Mr Browne, pursing his lips until his moustache bristled and smiling in all his wrinkles. You know, Miss Morkan, the reason they are so fond of me is—

He did not finish his sentence, but, seeing that Aunt Kate was out of earshot, at once led the three young ladies into the back room. The middle of the room was occupied by two square tables placed end to end, and on these Aunt Julia and the caretaker were straightening and smoothing a large cloth. On the sideboard were arranged dishes and plates, and glasses and bundles of knives and forks and spoons. The top of the closed square piano served also as a sideboard for viands and sweets. At a smaller sideboard in one corner two young men were standing, drinking hop-bitters.

Mr Browne led his charges thither and invited them all, in jest, to some ladies' punch, hot, strong, and sweet. As they said they never took anything strong he opened three bottles of lemonade for them. Then he asked one of the young men to move aside, and, taking hold of the decanter, filled out for himself a goodly measure of whisky. The young men eyed him respectfully while he took a trial sip.

———God help me, he said, smiling, it's the doctor's orders.

His wizened face broke into a broader smile, and the three young ladies laughed in musical echo to his pleasantry, swaying their bodies to and fro, with nervous jerks of their shoulders. The boldest said:

———O, now, Mr Browne, I'm sure the doctor never ordered anything of the kind.

Mr Browne took another sip of his whisky and said, with sidling mimicry:

———Well, you see, I'm like the famous Mrs Cassidy, who is reported to have said: *Now, Mary Grimes, if I don't take it, make me take it, for I feel I want it.*

His hot face had leaned forward a little too confidentially and he had assumed a very low Dublin accent so that the young ladies, with one instinct, received his speech in silence. Miss Furlong, who was one of Mary Jane's pupils, asked Miss Daly what was the name of the pretty waltz she had played; and Mr Browne, seeing that he was ignored, turned promptly to the two young men who were more appreciative.

A red-faced young woman, dressed in pansy, came into the room, excitedly clapping her hands and crying:

———Quadrilles! Quadrilles!

Close on her heels came Aunt Kate, crying:

——Two gentlemen and three ladies, Mary Jane!

——O, here's Mr Bergin and Mr Kerrigan, said Mary Jane. Mr Kerrigan, will you take Miss Power? Miss Furlong, may I get you a partner, Mr Bergin. O, that'll just do now.

——Three ladies, Mary Jane, said Aunt Kate.

The two young gentlemen asked the ladies if they might have the pleasure, and Mary Jane turned to Miss Daly.

——O, Miss Daly, you're really awfully good, after playing for the last two dances, but really we're so short of ladies to-night.

——I don't mind in the least, Miss Morkan.

——But I've a nice partner for you, Mr Bartell D'Arcy, the tenor. I'll get him to sing later on. All Dublin is raving about him. *[margin: D'Arcy]*

——Lovely voice, lovely voice! said Aunt Kate.

As the piano had twice begun the prelude to the first figure Mary Jane led her recruits quickly from the room. They had hardly gone when Aunt Julia wandered slowly into the room, looking behind her at something.

——What is the matter, Julia? asked Aunt Kate anxiously. Who is it?

Julia, who was carrying in a column of table-napkins, turned to her sister and said, simply, as if the question had surprised her:

——It's only Freddy, Kate, and Gabriel with him.

In fact right behind her Gabriel could be seen piloting Freddy Malins *[margin: descr. of Freddy Malins]* across the landing. The latter, a young man of about forty, was of Gabriel's size and build, with very round shoulders. His face was fleshy and pallid, touched with colour only at the thick hanging lobes of his ears and at the wide wings of his nose. He had coarse features, a blunt nose, a convex and receding brow, tumid and protruded lips. His heavy-lidded eyes and the disorder of his scanty hair made him look sleepy. He was laughing heartily in a high key at a story which he had been telling Gabriel on the stairs and at the same time rubbing the knuckles of his left fist backwards and forwards into his left eye.

——Good-evening, Freddy, said Aunt Julia.

Freddy Malins bade the Misses Morkan good-evening in what seemed an offhand fashion by reason of the habitual catch in his voice and then, seeing that Mr Browne was grinning at him from the sideboard, crossed the room on rather shaky legs and began to repeat in an undertone the story he had just told Gabriel.

——He's not so bad, is he? said Aunt Kate to Gabriel.

Gabriel's brows were dark but he raised them quickly and answered:

——O no, hardly noticeable.   understatement

——Now, isn't he a terrible fellow! she said. And his poor mother made him take the pledge on New Year's Eve. But come on, Gabriel, into the drawing-room.

Before leaving the room with Gabriel she signalled to Mr Browne by frowning and shaking her forefinger in warning to and fro. Mr Browne nodded in answer and, when she had gone, said to Freddy Malins:

——Now, then, Teddy, I'm going to fill you out a good glass of lemonade just to buck you up.

Freddy Malins, who was nearing the climax of his story, waved the offer aside impatiently but Mr. Browne, having first called Freddy Malins' attention to a disarray in his dress, filled out and handed him a full glass of lemonade. Freddy Malins' left hand accepted the glass mechanically, his right hand being engaged in the mechanical readjustment of his dress. Mr Browne, whose face was once more wrinkling with mirth, poured out for himself a glass of whisky while Freddy Malins exploded, before he had well reached the climax of his story, in a kink of high-pitched bronchitic laughter and, setting down his untasted and overflowing glass, began to rub the knuckles of his left fist backwards and forwards into his left eye, repeating words of his last phrase as well as his fit of laughter would allow him.

Gabriel could not listen while Mary Jane was playing her Academy piece, full of runs and difficult passages, to the hushed drawing-room. He liked music but the piece she was playing had no melody for him and he doubted whether it had any melody for the other listeners, though they had begged Mary Jane to play something. Four young men, who had come from the refreshment-room to stand in the doorway at the sound of the piano, had gone away quietly in couples after a few minutes. The only persons who seemed to follow the music were Mary Jane herself, her hands racing along the key-board or lifted from it at the pauses like those of a priestess in momentary imprecation, and Aunt Kate standing at her elbow to turn the page.

Gabriel's eyes, irritated by the floor, which glittered with beeswax under the heavy chandelier, wandered to the wall above the piano. A picture of the balcony scene in *Romeo and Juliet* hung there and beside it was a picture of the two murdered princes in the Tower[7] which Aunt Julia had worked in red, blue and brown wools when she was a girl. Probably in the school they had gone to as girls that kind of work had

Mary Jane's awful piano piece

---

[7]An illustration of a scene from *Richard III*.

been taught, for one year his mother had worked for him as a birthday present a waistcoat of purple tabinet, with little foxes' heads upon it, lined with brown satin and having round mulberry buttons. It was strange that his mother had had no musical talent though Aunt Kate used to call her the brains carrier of the Morkan family. Both she and Julia had always seemed a little proud of their serious and matronly sister. Her photograph stood before the pierglass. She held an open book on her knees and was pointing out something in it to Constantine who, dressed in a man-o'-war suit, lay at her feet. It was she who had chosen the names for her sons for she was very sensible of the dignity of family life. Thanks to her, Constantine was now senior curate in Balbriggan and, thanks to her, Gabriel himself had taken his degree in the Royal University. A shadow passed over his face as he remembered her sullen opposition to his marriage. Some slighting phrases she had used still rankled in his memory; she had once spoken of Gretta as being country cute and that was not true of Gretta at all. It was Gretta who had nursed her during all her last long illness in their house at Monkstown.

He knew that Mary Jane must be near the end of her piece for she was playing again the opening melody with runs of scales after every bar and while he waited for the end the resentment died down in his heart. The piece ended with a trill of octaves in the treble and a final deep octave in the bass. Great applause greeted Mary Jane as, blushing and rolling up her music nervously, she escaped from the room. The most vigorous clapping came from the four young men in the doorway who had gone away to the refreshment-room at the beginning of the piece but had come back when the piano had stopped.

Lancers were arranged. Gabriel found himself partnered with Miss Ivors. She was a frank-mannered talkative young lady, with a freckled face and prominent brown eyes. She did not wear a low-cut bodice and the large brooch which was fixed in the front of her collar bore on it an Irish device.

When they had taken their places she said abruptly:

——I have a crow to pluck with you.

——With me? said Gabriel.

She nodded her head gravely.

——What is it? asked Gabriel, smiling at her solemn manner.

——Who is G. C.? answered Miss Ivors, turning her eyes upon him.

Gabriel coloured and was about to knit his brows, as if he did not understand, when she said bluntly:

————O, innocent Amy! I have found out that you write for *The Daily Express*.[8] Now, aren't you ashamed of yourself?

————Why should I be ashamed of myself? asked Gabriel, blinking his eyes and trying to smile.

————Well, I'm ashamed of you, said Miss Ivors frankly. To say you'd write for a rag like that. I didn't think you were a West Briton.[9]

A look of perplexity appeared on Gabriel's face. It was true that he wrote a literary column every Wednesday in *The Daily Express*, for which he was paid fifteen shillings. But that did not make him a West Briton surely. The books he received for review were almost more welcome than the paltry cheque. He loved to feel the covers and turn over the pages of newly printed books. Nearly every day when his teaching in the college was ended he used to wander down the quays to the second-hand booksellers, to Hickey's on Bachelor's Walk, to Webb's or Massey's on Aston's Quay, or to O'Clohissey's in the by-street. He did not know how to meet her charge. He wanted to say that literature was above politics. But they were friends of many years' standing and their careers had been parallel, first at the University and then as teachers: he could not risk a grandiose phrase with her. He continued blinking his eyes and trying to smile and murmured lamely that he saw nothing political in writing reviews of books.

When their turn to cross had come he was still perplexed and in-attentive. Miss Ivors promptly took his hand in a warm grasp and said in a soft friendly tone:

————Of course, I was only joking. Come, we cross now.

When they were together again she spoke of the University question and Gabriel felt more at ease. A friend of hers had shown her his review of Browning's poems. That was how she had found out the secret: but she liked the review immensely. Then she said suddenly:

————O, Mr Conroy, will you come for an excursion to the Aran Isles[10] this summer? We're going to stay there a whole month. It will be splendid out in the Atlantic. You ought to come. Mr Clancy is coming, and Mr Kilkelly and Kathleen Kearney. It would be splendid for Gretta too if she'd come. She's from Connacht,[11] isn't she?

————Her people are, said Gabriel shortly.

---

8 A daily newspaper that opposed Irish nationalism.

9 An Irishman with British sympathies.

10 Primitive, Irish-speaking islands off the western coast of Ireland.

11 A beautiful but primitive district on the western coast of Ireland.

——But you will come, won't you? said Miss Ivors, laying her warm hand eagerly on his arm.

——The fact is, said Gabriel, I have already arranged to go—

——Go where? asked Miss Ivors.

——Well, you know, every year I go for a cycling tour with some fellows and so—

——But where? asked Miss Ivors.

——Well, we usually go to France or Belgium or perhaps Germany, said Gabriel awkwardly.

——And why do you go to France and Belgium, said Miss Ivors, instead of visiting your own land?

——Well, said Gabriel, it's partly to keep in touch with the languages and partly for a change.

——And haven't you your own language to keep in touch with— Irish? asked Miss Ivors.

——Well, said Gabriel, if it comes to that, you know, Irish is not my language.

Their neighbors had turned to listen to the cross-examination. Gabriel glanced right and left nervously and tried to keep his good humour under the ordeal which was making a blush invade his forehead.

——And haven't you your own land to visit, continued Miss Ivors, that you know nothing of, your own people, and your own country?

——O, to tell you the truth, retorted Gabriel suddenly, I'm sick of my own country, sick of it!

——Why? asked Miss Ivors.

Gabriel did not answer for his retort had heated him.

——Why? repeated Miss Ivors.

They had to go visiting together and, as he had not answered her, Miss Ivors said warmly:

——Of course, you've no answer.

Gabriel tried to cover his agitation by taking part in the dance with great energy. He avoided her eyes for he had seen a sour expression on her face. But when they met in the long chain he was surprised to feel his hand firmly pressed. She looked at him from under her brows for a moment quizzically until he smiled. Then, just as the chain was about to start again, she stood on tiptoe and whispered into his ear:

——West Briton!

When the lancers were over Gabriel went away to a remote corner of the room where Freddy Malins' mother was sitting. She was a stout feeble old woman with white hair. Her voice had a catch in it like her son's and she stuttered slightly. She had been told that Freddy had

old mrs. molin

come and that he was nearly all right. Gabriel asked her whether she had had a good crossing. She lived with her married daughter in Glasgow, and came to Dublin on a visit once a year. She answered placidly that she had had a beautiful crossing and that the captain had been most attentive to her. She spoke also of the beautiful house her daughter kept in Glasgow, and of all the nice friends they had there. While her tongue rambled on Gabriel tried to banish from his mind all memory of the unpleasant incident with Miss Ivors. Of course the girl or woman, or whatever she was, was an enthusiast but there was a time for all things. Perhaps he ought not to have answered her like that. But she had no right to call him a West Briton before people, even in joke. She had tried to make him ridiculous before people, heckling him and staring at him with her rabbit's eyes.

He saw his wife making her way towards him through the waltzing couples. When she reached him she said into his ear:

——Gabriel, Aunt Kate wants to know won't you carve the goose as usual. Miss Daly will carve the ham and I'll do the pudding.

——All right, said Gabriel.

——She's sending in the younger ones first as soon as this waltz is over so that we'll have the table to ourselves.

——Were you dancing? asked Gabriel.

——Of course I was. Didn't you see me? What words had you with Molly Ivors?

——No words. Why? Did she say so?

——Something like that. I'm trying to get that Mr D'Arcy to sing. He's full of conceit, I think.

——There were no words, said Gabriel moodily, only she wanted me to go for a trip to the west of Ireland and I said I wouldn't.

His wife clasped her hands excitedly and gave a little jump.

——O, do go, Gabriel, she cried. I'd love to see Galway again.

——You can go if you like, said Gabriel coldly.

She looked at him for a moment, then turned to Mrs Malins and said:

——There's a nice husband for you, Mrs Malins.

While she was threading her way back across the room Mrs Malins, without adverting to the interruption, went on to tell Gabriel what beautiful places there were in Scotland and beautiful scenery. Her son-in-law brought them every year to the lakes and they used to go fishing. Her son-in-law was a splendid fisher. One day he caught a fish, a beautiful big big fish, and the man in the hotel boiled it for their dinner.

Gabriel hardly heard what she said. Now that supper was coming near he began to think again about his speech and about the quotation. When he saw Freddy Malins coming across the room to visit his mother Gabriel left the chair free for him and retired into the embrasure of the window. The room had already cleared and from the back room came the clatter of plates and knives. Those who still remained in the drawing-room seemed tired of dancing and were conversing quietly in little groups. Gabriel's warm trembling fingers tapped the cold pane of the window. How cool it must be outside! How pleasant it would be to walk out alone, first along by the river and then through the park! The snow would be lying on the branches of trees and forming a bright cap on the top of the Wellington Monument. How much more pleasant it would be there than at the supper-table!

He ran over the headings of his speech: Irish hospitality, sad memories, the Three Graces, Paris, the quotation from Browning. He repeated to himself a phrase he had written in his review: *One feels that one is listening to a thought-tormented music.* Miss Ivors had praised the review. Was she sincere? Had she really any life of her own behind all her propagandism? There had never been any ill-feeling between them until that night. It unnerved him to think that she would be at the supper-table, looking up at him while he spoke with her critical quizzing eyes. Perhaps she would not be sorry to see him fail in his speech. An idea came into his mind and gave him courage. He would say, alluding to Aunt Kate and Aunt Julia: *Ladies and Gentlemen, the generation which is now on the wane among us may have had its faults but for my part I think it had certain qualities of hospitality, of humour, of humanity, which the new and very serious and hypereducated generation that is growing up around us seems to me to lack.* Very good: that was one for Miss Ivors. What did he care that his aunts were only two ignorant old women?

A murmur in the room attracted his attention. Mr Browne was advancing from the door, gallantly escorting Aunt Julia, who leaned upon his arm, smiling and hanging her head. An irregular musketry of applause escorted her also as far as the piano and then, as Mary Jane seated herself on the stool, and Aunt Julia, no longer smiling, half turned so as to pitch her voice fairly into the room, gradually ceased. Gabriel recognised the prelude. It was that of an old song of Aunt Julia's—*Arrayed for the Bridal.* Her voice, strong and clear in tone, attacked with great spirit the runs which embellish the air and though she sang very rapidly she did not miss even the smallest of the grace notes. To follow the voice, without looking at the singer's face, was to feel and share the excitement of swift and secure flight. Gabriel applauded loudly with all the others at the close of the song and loud applause was borne in from the invisible supper-table. It sounded so genuine that a little colour struggled into Aunt Julia's face as she bent to replace in the music-stand the old leather-bound song-book that had her initials on the cover. Freddy Malins, who had listened with his head perched sideways to hear her better, was still applauding when everyone else had ceased and talking animatedly to his mother who nodded her head gravely and slowly in acquiescence. At last, when he could clap no more, he stood up suddenly and hurried across the room to Aunt Julia whose hand he seized and held in both his hands, shaking it when words failed him or the catch in his voice proved too much for him.

——I was just telling my mother, he said, I never heard you sing so well, never. No, I never heard your voice so good as it is to-night. Now! Would you believe that now? That's the truth. Upon my word and honour that's the truth. I never heard your voice sound so fresh and so . . . so clear and fresh, never.

Aunt Julia smiled broadly and murmured something about compliments as she released her hand from his grasp. Mr Browne extended his open hand towards her and said to those who were near him in the manner of a showman introducing a prodigy to an audience:

——Miss Julia Morkan, my latest discovery!

He was laughing very heartily at himself when Freddy Malins turned to him and said:

——Well, Browne, if you're serious you might make a worse discovery. All I can say is I never heard her sing half so well as long as I am coming here. And that's the honest truth.

——Neither did I, said Mr Browne. I think her voice has greatly improved.

Aunt Julia shrugged her shoulders and said with meek pride:

——Thirty years ago I hadn't a bad voice as voices go.

——I often told Julia, said Aunt Kate emphatically, that she was simply thrown away in that choir. But she never would be said by me.

She turned as if to appeal to the good sense of the others against a refractory child while Aunt Julia gazed in front of her, a vague smile of reminiscence playing on her face.

——No, continued Aunt Kate, she wouldn't be said or led by anyone, slaving there in that choir night and day, night and day. Six o'clock on Christmas morning! And all for what?

——Well, isn't it for the honour of God, Aunt Kate? asked Mary Jane, twisting round on the piano-stool and smiling.

Mary Jane: diplomat

Aunt Kate turned fiercely on her niece and said:

——I know all about the honour of God, Mary Jane, but I think it's not at all honourable for the pope to turn out the women out of the choirs that have slaved there all their lives and put little whipper-snappers of boys over their heads.[12] I suppose it is for the good of the Church if the pope does it. But it's not just, Mary Jane, and it's not right.

She had worked herself into a passion and would have continued in defence of her sister for it was a sore subject with her but Mary Jane, seeing that all the dancers had come back, intervened pacifically:

——Now, Aunt Kate, you're giving scandal to Mr Browne who is of the other persuasion. Protestant

Aunt Kate turned to Mr Browne, who was grinning at this allusion to his religion, and said hastily:

——O, I don't question the pope's being right. I'm only a stupid old woman and I wouldn't presume to do such a thing. But there's such a thing as common everyday politeness and gratitude. And if I were in Julia's place I'd tell that Father Healy straight up to his face . . .

——And besides, Aunt Kate, said Mary Jane, we really are all hungry and when we are all hungry we are all very quarrelsome.

——And when we are thirsty we are also quarrelsome, added Mr Browne.

——So that we had better go to supper, said Mary Jane, and finish the discussion afterwards.

On the landing outside the drawing-room Gabriel found his wife and Mary Jane trying to persuade Miss Ivors to stay for supper. But Miss Ivors, who had put on her hat and was buttoning her cloak, would not stay. She did not feel in the least hungry and she had already overstayed her time.

Miss Ivors leaves

——But only for ten minutes, Molly, said Mrs Conroy. That won't delay you.

——To take a pick itself, said Mary Jane, after all your dancing.

——I really couldn't, said Miss Ivors.

——I am afraid you didn't enjoy yourself at all, said Mary Jane hopelessly.

——Ever so much, I assure you, said Miss Ivors, but you really must let me run off now.

---

[12]In 1903, an encyclical of Pope Pius X had ordered the replacement of women in choirs by boy sopranos.

————But how can you get home? asked Mrs Conroy.

————O, it's only two steps up the quay.

Gabriel hesitated a moment and said:

————If you will allow me, Miss Ivors, I'll see you home if you really are obliged to go.

But Miss Ivors broke away from them.

————I won't hear of it, she cried. For goodness sake go in to your suppers and don't mind me. I'm quite well able to take care of myself.

————Well, you're the comical girl, Molly, said Mrs Conroy frankly.

————*Beannacht libh*,[13] cried Miss Ivors, with a laugh, as she ran down the staircase.

Mary Jane gazed after her, a moody puzzled expression on her face, while Mrs Conroy leaned over the banisters to listen for the hall-door. Gabriel asked himself was he the cause of her abrupt departure. But she did not seem to be in an ill humour: she had gone away laughing. He stared blankly down the staircase.

At that moment Aunt Kate came toddling out of the supper-room, almost wringing her hands in despair.

————Where is Gabriel? she cried. Where on earth is Gabriel? There's everyone waiting in there, stage to let, and nobody to carve the goose!

————Here I am, Aunt Kate! cried Gabriel, with sudden animation, ready to carve a flock of geese, if necessary.

A fat brown goose lay at one end of the table and at the other end, on a bed of creased paper strewn with sprigs of parsley, lay a great ham, stripped of its outer skin and peppered over with crust crumbs, a neat paper frill round its shin and beside this was a round of spiced beef. Between these rival ends ran parallel lines of side-dishes: two little minsters of jelly, red and yellow; a shallow dish full of blocks of blancmange and red jam, a large green leaf-shaped dish with a stalk-shaped handle, on which lay bunches of purple raisins and peeled almonds, a companion dish on which lay a solid rectangle of Smyrna figs, a dish of custard topped with grated nutmeg, a small bowl full of chocolates and sweets wrapped in gold and silver papers and a glass vase in which stood some tall celery stalks. In the centre of the table there stood, as sentries to a fruit-stand which upheld a pyramid of oranges and American apples, two squat old-fashioned decanters of cut glass, one containing port and the other dark sherry. On the closed square piano a pudding in a huge yellow dish lay in waiting and behind

---

[13]Good-night.

it were three squads of bottles of stout and ale and minerals,[14] drawn up according to the colours of their uniforms, the first two black, with brown and red labels, the third and smallest squad white, with transverse green sashes.

Gabriel took his seat boldly at the head of the table and, having looked to the edge of the carver, plunged his fork firmly into the goose. He felt quite at ease now for he was an expert carver and liked nothing better than to find himself at the head of a well-laden table.

——Miss Furlong, what shall I send you? he asked. A wing or a slice of the breast?

——Just a small slice of the breast.

——Miss Higgins, what for you?

——O, anything at all, Mr Conroy.

While Gabriel and Miss Daly exchanged plates of goose and plates of ham and spiced beef Lily went from guest to guest with a dish of hot floury potatoes wrapped in a white napkin. This was Mary Jane's idea and she had also suggested apple sauce for the goose but Aunt Kate had said that plain roast goose without apple sauce had always been good enough for her and she hoped she might never eat worse. Mary Jane waited on her pupils and saw that they got the best slices and Aunt Kate and Aunt Julia opened and carried across from the piano bottles of stout and ale for the gentlemen and bottles of minerals for the ladies. There was a great deal of confusion and laughter and noise, the noise of orders and counter-orders, of knives and forks, of corks and glass-stoppers. Gabriel began to carve second helpings as soon as he had finished the first round without serving himself. Everyone protested loudly so that he compromised by taking a long draught of stout for he had found the carving hot work. Mary Jane settled down quietly to her supper but Aunt Kate and Aunt Julia were still toddling round the table, walking on each other's heels, getting in each other's way and giving each other unheeded orders. Mr Browne begged of them to sit down and eat their suppers and so did Gabriel but they said there was time enough so that, at last, Freddy Malins stood up and, capturing Aunt Kate, plumped her down on her chair amid general laughter.

When everyone had been well served Gabriel said, smiling:

——Now, if anyone wants a little more of what vulgar people call stuffing let him or her speak.

A chorus of voices invited him to begin his own supper and Lily

---

[14]Carbonated beverages.

came forward with three potatoes which she had reserved for him.

——Very well, said Gabriel amiably, as he took another preparatory draught, kindly forget my existence, ladies and gentlemen, for a few minutes.

He set to his supper and took no part in the conversation with which the table covered Lily's removal of the plates. The subject of talk was the opera company which was then at the Theatre Royal. Mr Bartell D'Arcy, the tenor, a dark-complexioned young man with a smart moustache, praised very highly the leading contralto of the company but Miss Furlong thought she had a rather vulgar style of production. Freddy Malins said there was a negro chieftain singing in the second part of the Gaiety pantomime who had one of the finest tenor voices he had ever heard.

——Have you heard him? he asked Mr Bartell D'Arcy across the table.

——No, answered Mr Bartell D'Arcy carelessly.

——Because, Freddy Malins explained, now I'd be curious to hear your opinion of him. I think he has a grand voice.

——It takes Teddy to find out the really good things, said Mr Browne familiarly to the table.

——And why couldn't he have a voice too? asked Freddy Malins sharply. Is it because he's only a black?

Nobody answered this question and Mary Jane led the table back to the legitimate opera. One of her pupils had given her a pass for *Mignon*. Of course it was very fine, she said, but it made her think of poor Georgina Burns. Mr Browne could go back farther still, to the old Italian companies that used to come to Dublin—Tietjens, Ilma de Murzka, Campanini, the great Trebelli, Giuglini, Ravelli, Aramburo.[15] Those were the days, he said, when there was something like singing to be heard in Dublin. He told too of how the top gallery of the old Royal used to be packed night after night, of how one night an Italian tenor had sung five encores to *Let Me Like a Soldier Fall*, introducing a high C every time, and of how the gallery boys would sometimes in their enthusiasm unyoke the horses from the carriage of some great *prima donna* and pull her themselves through the streets to her hotel. Why did they never play the grand old operas now, he asked, *Dinorah, Lucrezia Borgia*? Because they could not get the voices to sing them: that was why.

---

[15]Great singers of the 1870s and 1880s.

D'Arcy: present

——O, well, said Mr Bartell D'Arcy, I presume there are as good singers to-day as there were then.

——Where are they? asked Mr Browne defiantly.

——In London, Paris, Milan, said Mr Bartell D'Arcy warmly. I suppose Caruso, for example, is quite as good, if not better than any of the men you have mentioned.

——Maybe so, said Mr Browne. But I may tell you I doubt it strongly.

——O, I'd give anything to hear Caruso sing, said Mary Jane.

——For me, said Aunt Kate, who had been picking a bone, there was only one tenor. To please me, I mean. But I suppose none of you ever heard of him.

——Who was he, Miss Morkan? asked Mr Bartell D'Arcy politely.

——His name, said Aunt Kate, was Parkinson. I heard him when he was in his prime and I think he had then the purest tenor voice that was ever put into a man's throat.

——Strange, said Mr Bartell D'Arcy. I never even heard of him.

——Yes, yes, Miss Morkan is right, said Mr Browne. I remember hearing of old Parkinson but he's too far back for me.

——A beautiful pure sweet mellow English tenor, said Aunt Kate with enthusiasm.

Gabriel having finished, the huge pudding was transferred to the table. The clatter of forks and spoons began again. Gabriel's wife served out spoonfuls of the pudding and passed the plates down the table. Midway down they were held up by Mary Jane, who replenished them with raspberry or orange jelly or with blancmange and jam. The pudding was of Aunt Julia's making and she received praises for it from all quarters. She herself said that it was not quite brown enough.

——Well, I hope, Miss Morkan, said Mr Browne, that I'm brown enough for you because, you know, I'm all brown.

All the gentlemen, except Gabriel, ate some of the pudding out of compliment to Aunt Julia. As Gabriel never ate sweets the celery had been left for him. Freddy Malins also took a stalk of celery and ate it with his pudding. He had been told that celery was a capital thing for the blood and he was just then under doctor's care. Mrs Malins, who had been silent all through the supper, said that her son was going down to Mount Melleray in a week or so. The table then spoke of Mount Melleray, how bracing the air was down there, how hospitable the monks were and how they never asked for a penny-piece from their guests.

——And do you mean to say, asked Mr Browne incredulously, that

*supper talk: dead opera singers,
monks who sleep in coffins*

a chap can go down there and put up there as if it were a hotel and live on the fat end of the land and then come away without paying a farthing?

——O, most people give some donation to the monastery when they leave, said Mary Jane.

——I wish we had an institution like that in our Church, said Mr Browne candidly.

He was astonished to hear that the monks never spoke, got up at two in the morning and slept in their coffins. He asked what they did it for.

——That's the rule of the order, said Aunt Kate firmly.

——Yes, but why? asked Mr Browne.

Aunt Kate repeated that it was the rule, that was all. Mr Browne still seemed not to understand. Freddy Malins explained to him, as best he could, that the monks were trying to make up for the sins committed by all the sinners in the outside world. The explanation was not very clear for Mr Browne grinned and said:

——I like that idea very much but wouldn't a comfortable spring bed do them as well as a coffin?

——The coffin, said Mary Jane, is to remind them of their last end.

As the subject had grown lugubrious it was buried in a silence of the table during which Mrs Malins could be heard saying to her neighbour in an indistinct undertone:

——They are very good men, the monks, very pious men.

The raisins and almonds and figs and apples and oranges and chocolates and sweets were now passed about the table and Aunt Julia invited all the guests to have either port or sherry. At first Mr Bartell D'Arcy refused to take either but one of his neighbours nudged him and whispered something to him upon which he allowed his glass to be filled. Gradually as the last glasses were being filled the conversation ceased. A pause followed, broken only by the noise of the wine and by unsettlings of chairs. The Misses Morkan, all three, looked down at the tablecloth. Someone coughed once or twice and then a few gentlemen patted the table gently as a signal for silence. The silence came and Gabriel pushed back his chair and stood up.

The patting at once grew louder in encouragement and then ceased altogether. Gabriel leaned his ten trembling fingers on the tablecloth and smiled nervously at the company. Meeting a row of upturned faces he raised his eyes to the chandelier. The piano was playing a waltz tune and he could hear the skirts sweeping against the drawing-room door. People, perhaps, were standing in the snow on the quay outside, gazing up at the lighted windows and listening to the waltz music. The air was

*monks,
coffins*

snow

G.'s speech

G's speech

pure there. In the distance lay the park where the trees were weighted with snow. The Wellington Monument wore a gleaming cap of snow that flashed westward over the white field of Fifteen Acres.

He began:

——Ladies and Gentlemen.

——It has fallen to my lot this evening, as in years past, to perform a very pleasing task but a task for which I am afraid my poor powers as a speaker are all too inadequate.

——No, no! said Mr Browne.

——But, however that may be, I can only ask you to-night to take the will for the deed and to lend me your attention for a few moments while I endeavour to express to you in words what my feelings are on this occasion.

——Ladies and Gentlemen. It is not the first time that we have gathered together under this hospitable roof, around this hospitable board. It is not the first time that we have been the recipients—or perhaps, I had better say, the victims—of the hospitality of certain good ladies.

He made a circle in the air with his arm and paused. Everyone laughed or smiled at Aunt Kate and Aunt Julia and Mary Jane who all turned crimson with pleasure. Gabriel went on more boldly:

——I feel more strongly with every recurring year that our country has no tradition which does it so much honour and which it should guard so jealously as that of its hospitality. It is a tradition that is unique as far as my experience goes (and I have visited not a few places abroad) among the modern nations. Some would say, perhaps, that with us it is rather a failing than anything to be boasted of. But granted even that, it is, to my mind, a princely failing, and one that I trust will long be cultivated among us. Of one thing, at least, I am sure. As long as this one roof shelters the good ladies aforesaid—and I wish from my heart it may do so for many and many a long year to come—the tradition of genuine warm-hearted courteous Irish hospitality, which our forefathers have handed down to us and which we in turn must hand down to our descendants, is still alive among us.

A hearty murmur of assent ran round the table. It shot through Gabriel's mind that Miss Ivors was not there and that she had gone away discourteously: and he said with confidence in himself:

——Ladies and Gentlemen.

——A new generation is growing up in our midst, a generation actuated by new ideas and new principles. It is serious and enthusiastic for these new ideas and its enthusiasm, even when it is misdirected, is, I believe, in the main sincere. But we are living in a sceptical and, if I may use the phrase, a thought-tormented age: and sometimes I fear that this new generation, educated or hypereducated as it is, will lack those qualities of humanity, of hospitality, of kindly humour which belonged to an older day. Listening to-night to the names of all those great singers of the past it seemed to me, I must confess, that we were living in a less spacious age. Those days might, without exaggeration, be called spacious days: and if they are gone beyond recall let us hope, at least, that in gatherings such as this we shall still speak of them with pride and affection, still cherish in our hearts the memory of those dead and gone great ones whose fame the world will not willingly let die.

——Hear, hear! said Mr Browne loudly.

——But yet, continued Gabriel, his voice falling into a softer inflection, there are always in gatherings such as this sadder thoughts that will recur to our minds: thoughts of the past, of youth, of changes, of absent faces that we miss here to-night. Our path through life is strewn with many such sad memories: and were we to brood upon them always we could not find the heart to go on bravely with our work among the living. We have all of us living duties and living affections which claim, and rightly claim, our strenuous endeavors.

——Therefore, I will not linger on the past. I will not let any gloomy moralising intrude upon us here to-night. Here we are gathered together for a brief moment from the bustle and rush of our everyday routine. We are met here as friends, in the spirit of good fellowship, as colleagues, also to a certain extent, in the true spirit of *camaraderie*, and as the guests of—what shall I call them?—the Three Graces[16] of the Dublin musical world. *Kate, Julia, Mary Jane.*

The table burst into applause and laughter at this sally. Aunt Julia vainly asked each of her neighbours in turn to tell her what Gabriel had said.

——He says we are the Three Graces, Aunt Julia, said Mary Jane.

Aunt Julia did not understand but she looked up, smiling, at Gabriel, who continued in the same vein:

——Ladies and Gentlemen.

——I will not attempt to play to-night the part that Paris played on another occasion.[17] I will not attempt to choose between them. The task would be an invidious one and one beyond my poor powers. For when I view them in turn, whether it be our chief hostess herself, whose good

---

[16]In Greek mythology, the companions of the Muses.
[17]Paris judged a beauty contest between Hera, Athena, and Aphrodite.

heart, whose too good heart, has become a byword with all who know her, or her sister, who seems to be gifted with perennial youth and whose singing must have been a surprise and a revelation to us all to-night, or, last but not least, when I consider our youngest hostess, talented, cheerful, hard-working and the best of nieces, I confess, Ladies and Gentlemen, that I do not know to which of them I should award the prize.

Gabriel glanced down at his aunts and, seeing the large smile on Aunt Julia's face and the tears which had risen to Aunt Kate's eyes, hastened to his close. He raised his glass of port gallantly, while every member of the company fingered a glass expectantly, and said loudly:

——Let us toast them all three together. Let us drink to their health, wealth, long life, happiness, and prosperity and may they long continue to hold the proud and self-won position which they hold in their profession and the position of honour and affection which they hold in our hearts.

All the guests stood up, glass in hand, and, turning towards the three seated ladies, sang in unison, with Mr Browne as leader:

> For they are jolly gay fellows,
> For they are jolly gay fellows,
> For they are jolly gay fellows,
> Which nobody can deny.

Aunt Kate was making frank use of her handkerchief and even Aunt Julia seemed moved. Freddy Malins beat time with his pudding-fork and the singers turned towards one another, as if in melodious conference, while they sang, with emphasis:

> Unless he tells a lie,
> Unless he tells a lie.

Then, turning once more towards their hostesses, they sang:

> For they are jolly gay fellows,
> For they are jolly gay fellows,
> For they are jolly gay fellows,
> Which nobody can deny.

The acclamation which followed was taken up beyond the door of the supper-room by many of the other guests and renewed time after time, Freddy Malins acting as officer with his fork on high.

guests'
departure

leaving

The piercing morning air came into the hall where they were stand-ing so that Aunt Kate said:

——Close the door, somebody. Mrs Malins will get her death of cold.

——Browne is out there, Aunt Kate, said Mary Jane.

——Browne is everywhere, said Aunt Kate, lowering her voice.

Mary Jane laughed at her tone.

——Really, she said archly, he is very attentive.

——He has been laid on[18] here like the gas, said Aunt Kate in the same tone, all during the Christmas.

She laughed herself this time good-humouredly and then added quickly:

——But tell him to come in, Mary Jane, and close the door. I hope to goodness he didn't hear me.

At that moment the hall-door was opened and Mr Browne came in from the doorstep, laughing as if his heart would break. He was dressed in a long green overcoat with mock astrakhan cuffs and collar and wore on his head an oval fur cap. He pointed down the snow-covered quay from where the sound of shrill prolonged whistling was borne in.

——Teddy will have all the cabs in Dublin out, he said.

Gabriel advanced from the little pantry behind the office, struggling into his overcoat and, looking round the hall, said:

——Gretta not down yet?

——She's getting on her things, Gabriel, said Aunt Kate.

——Who's playing up there? asked Gabriel.

——Nobody. They're all gone.

——O no, Aunt Kate, said Mary Jane. Bartell D'Arcy and Miss O'Callaghan aren't gone yet.

——Someone is strumming at the piano, anyhow, said Gabriel.

Mary Jane glanced at Gabriel and Mr Browne and said with a shiver:

——It makes me feel cold to look at you two gentlemen muffled up like that. I wouldn't like to face your journey home at this hour.

——I'd like nothing better this minute, said Mr Browne stoutly, than a rattling fine walk in the country or a fast drive with a good spanking goer between the shafts.

——We used to have a very good horse and trap at home, said Aunt Julia sadly.

---

[18]Supplied.

——The never-to-be-forgotten Johnny, said Mary Jane, laughing.
Aunt Kate and Gabriel laughed too.

——Why, what was wonderful about Johnny? asked Mr Browne.

——The late lamented Patrick Morkan, our grandfather, that is, explained Gabriel, commonly known in his later years as the old gentleman, was a glue-boiler.

——O, now, Gabriel, said Aunt Kate, laughing, he had a starch mill.

——Well, glue or starch, said Gabriel, the old gentleman had a horse by the name of Johnny. And Johnny used to work in the old gentleman's mill, walking round and round in order to drive the mill. That was all very well; but now comes the tragic part about Johnny. One fine day the old gentleman thought he'd like to drive out with the quality to a military review in the park.

——The Lord have mercy on his soul, said Aunt Kate compassionately.

——Amen, said Gabriel. So the old gentleman, as I said, harnessed Johnny and put on his best tall hat and his very best stock collar and drove out in grand style from his ancestral mansion somewhere near Back Lane, I think.

Everyone laughed, even Mrs Malins, at Gabriel's manner and Aunt Kate said:

——O now, Gabriel, he didn't live in Back Lane, really. Only the mill was there.

——Out from the mansion of his forefathers, continued Gabriel, he drove with Johnny. And everything went on beautifully until Johnny came in sight of King Billy's statue[19]: and whether he fell in love with the horse King Billy sits on or whether he thought he was back again in the mill, anyhow he began to walk around the statue.

Gabriel paced in a circle round the hall in his goloshes amid the laughter of the others.

——Round and round he went, said Gabriel, and the old gentleman, who was a very pompous gentleman, was highly indignant. *Go on, sir! What do you mean, sir? Johnny! Johnny! Most extraordinary conduct! Can't understand the horse!*

The peals of laughter which followed Gabriel's imitation of the event were interrupted by a resounding knock at the hall-door. Mary Jane ran to open it and let in Freddy Malins. Freddy Malins, with his hat

---

[19]Statue of William III, who decisively defeated James II and an army of Irish nationalists at the Battle of the Boyne (1690).

well back on his head and his shoulders humped with cold, was puffing and steaming after his exertions.

——I could only get one cab, he said.

——O, we'll find another along the quay, said Gabriel.

——Yes, said Aunt Kate. Better not keep Mrs Malins standing in the draught.

Mrs Malins was helped down the front steps by her son and Mr Browne and, after many manœuvres, hoisted into the cab. Freddy Malins clambered in after her and spent a long time settling her on the seat, Mr Browne helping him with advice. At last she was settled comfortably and Freddy Malins invited Mr Browne into the cab. There was a good deal of confused talk, and then Mr Browne got into the cab. The cabman settled his rug over his knees, and bent down for the address. The confusion grew greater and the cabman was directed differently by Freddy Malins and Mr Browne, each of whom had his head out a window of the cab. The difficulty was to know where to drop Mr Browne along the route and Aunt Kate, Aunt Julia and Mary Jane helped the discussion from the doorstep with cross-directions and contradictions and abundance of laughter. As for Freddy Malins, he was speechless with laughter. He popped his head in and out of the window every moment, to the great danger of his hat, and told his mother how the discussion was progressing till at last Mr Browne shouted out to the bewildered cabman above the din of everybody's laughter:

——Do you know Trinity College?

——Yes, sir, said the cabman.

——Well, drive bang up against Trinity College gates, said Mr Browne, and then we'll tell you where to go. You understand now?

——Yes, sir, said the cabman.

——Make like a bird for Trinity College.

——Right, sir, cried the cabman.

The horse was whipped up and the cab rattled off along the quay amid a chorus of laughter and adieus.

Gabriel had not gone to the door with the others. He was in a dark part of the hall gazing up the staircase. A woman was standing near the top of the first flight, in the shadow also. He could not see her face but he could see the terracotta and salmonpink panels of her skirt which the shadow made appear black and white. It was his wife. She was leaning on the banisters, listening to something. Gabriel was surprised at her stillness and strained his ear to listen also. But he could hear little save the noise of laughter and dispute on the front steps, a few chords struck on the piano and a few notes of a man's voice singing.

He stood still in the gloom of the hall, trying to catch the air that the voice was singing and gazing up at his wife. There was grace and mystery in her attitude as if she were a symbol of something. He asked himself what is a woman standing on the stairs in the shadow, listening to distant music, a symbol of. If he were a painter he would paint her in that attitude. Her blue felt hat would show off the bronze of her hair against the darkness and the dark panels of her skirt would show off the light ones. *Distant Music* he would call the picture if he were a painter.

The hall-door was closed; and Aunt Kate, Aunt Julia and Mary Jane came down the hall, still laughing.

——Well, isn't Freddy terrible? said Mary Jane. He's really terrible.

Gabriel said nothing but pointed up the stairs towards where his wife was standing. Now that the hall-door was closed the voice and the piano could be heard more clearly. Gabriel held up his hand for them to be silent. The song seemed to be in the old Irish tonality and the singer seemed uncertain both of his words and of his voice. The voice, made plaintive by distance and by the singer's hoarseness, faintly illuminated the cadence of the air with words expressing grief:

> O, the rain falls on my heavy locks
> And the dew wets my skin,
> My babe lies cold . . .

——O, exclaimed Mary Jane. It's Bartell D'Arcy singing and he wouldn't sing all the night. O, I'll get him to sing a song before he goes.

——O do, Mary Jane, said Aunt Kate.

Mary Jane brushed past the others and ran to the staircase but before she reached it the singing stopped and the piano was closed abruptly.

——O, what a pity! she cried. Is he coming down, Gretta?

Gabriel heard his wife answer yes and saw her come down towards them. A few steps behind her were Mr Bartell D'Arcy and Miss O'Callaghan.

——O, Mr D'Arcy, cried Mary Jane, it's downright mean of you to break off like that when we were all in raptures listening to you.

——I have been at him all the evening, said Miss O'Callaghan, and Mrs Conroy too and he told us he had a dreadful cold and couldn't sing.

——O, Mr D'Arcy, said Aunt Kate, now that was a great fib to tell.

——Can't you see that I'm as hoarse as a crow? said Mr D'Arcy roughly.

He went into the pantry hastily and put on his overcoat. The others, taken aback by his rude speech, could find nothing to say. Aunt Kate wrinkled her brows and made signs to the others to drop the subject. Mr D'Arcy stood swathing his neck carefully and frowning.

——It's the weather, said Aunt Julia, after a pause.

——Yes, everybody has colds, said Aunt Kate readily, everybody.

——They say, said Mary Jane, we haven't had snow like it for thirty years; and I read this morning in the newspapers that the snow is general all over Ireland.

——I love the look of snow, said Aunt Julia sadly.

——So do I, said Miss O'Callaghan. I think Christmas is never really Christmas unless we have the snow on the ground.

——But poor Mr D'Arcy doesn't like the snow, said Aunt Kate, smiling.

Mr D'Arcy came from the pantry, fully swathed and buttoned, and in a repentant tone told them the history of his cold. Everyone gave him advice and said it was a great pity and urged him to be very careful of his throat in the night air. Gabriel watched his wife who did not join in the conversation. She was standing right under the dusty fanlight and the flame of the gas lit up the rich bronze of her hair which he had seen her drying at the fire a few days before. She was in the same attitude and seemed unaware of the talk about her. At last she turned towards them and Gabriel saw that there was colour on her cheeks and that her eyes were shining. A sudden tide of joy went leaping out of his heart.

——Mr D'Arcy, she said, what is the name of that song you were singing?

——It's called *The Lass of Aughrim*, said Mr D'Arcy, but I couldn't remember it properly. Why? Do you know it?

——*The Lass of Aughrim*, she repeated. I couldn't think of the name.

——It's a very nice air, said Mary Jane. I'm sorry you were not in voice to-night.

——Now, Mary Jane, said Aunt Kate, don't annoy Mr D'Arcy. I won't have him annoyed.

Seeing that all were ready to start she shepherded them to the door where good-night was said:

——Well, good-night, Aunt Kate, and thanks for the pleasant evening.

——Good-night, Gabriel. Good-night, Gretta!

——Good-night, Aunt Kate, and thanks ever so much. Good-night, Aunt Julia.

——O, good-night, Gretta, I didn't see you.
——Good-night, Mr D'Arcy. Good-night, Miss O'Callaghan.
——Good-night, Miss Morkan.
——Good-night, again.
——Good-night, all. Safe home.
——Good-night. Good-night.

The morning was still dark. A dull yellow light brooded over the houses and the river; and the sky seemed to be descending. It was slushy underfoot; and only streaks and patches of snow lay on the roofs, on the parapets of the quay and on the area railings. The lamps were still burning redly in the murky air and, across the river, the palace of the Four Courts stood out menacingly against the heavy sky.

She was walking on before him with Mr Bartell D'Arcy, her shoes in a brown parcel tucked under one arm and her hands holding her skirt up from the slush. She had no longer any grace of attitude but Gabriel's eyes were still bright with happiness. The blood went bounding along his veins; and the thoughts went rioting through his brain, proud, joyful, tender, valorous.

She was walking on before him so lightly and so erect that he longed to run after her noiselessly, catch her by the shoulders and say something foolish and affectionate into her ear. She seemed to him so frail that he longed to defend her against something and then to be alone with her. Moments of their secret life together burst like stars upon his memory. A heliotrope envelope was lying beside his breakfast-cup and he was caressing it with his hand. Birds were twittering in the ivy and the sunny web of the curtain was shimmering along the floor: he could not eat for happiness. They were standing on the crowded platform and he was placing a ticket inside the warm palm of her glove. He was standing with her in the cold, looking in through a grated window at a man making bottles in a roaring furnace. It was very cold. Her face, fragrant in the cold air, was quite close to his; and suddenly she called out to the man at the furnace:

——Is the fire hot, sir?

But the man could not hear her with the noise of the furnace. It was just as well. He might have answered rudely.

A wave of yet more tender joy escaped from his heart and went coursing in warm flood along his arteries. Like the tender fires of stars moments of their life together, that no one knew of or would ever know of, broke upon and illuminated his memory. He longed to recall to her those moments, to make her forget the years of their dull existence together and remember only their moments of ecstasy. For the years, he felt, had not quenched his soul or hers. Their children, his writing, her household cares had not quenched all their souls' tender fire. In one letter that he had written to her then he had said: *Why is it that words like these seem so dull and cold? Is it because there is no word tender enough to be your name?*

Like distant music these words that he had written years before were borne towards him from the past. He longed to be alone with her. When the others had gone away, when he and she were in their room in the hotel, then they would be alone together. He would call her softly:

——Gretta!

Perhaps she would not hear at once: she would be undressing. Then something in his voice would strike her. She would turn and look at him. . . .

At the corner of Winetavern Street they met a cab. He was glad of its rattling noise as it saved him from conversation. She was looking out of the window and seemed tired. The others spoke only a few words, pointing out some building or street. The horse galloped along wearily under the murky morning sky, dragging his old rattling box after his heels, and Gabriel was again in a cab with her, galloping to catch the boat, galloping to their honeymoon.

As the cab drove across O'Connell Bridge Miss O'Callaghan said:

——They say you never cross O'Connell Bridge without seeing a white horse.

——I see a white man this time, said Gabriel.

——Where? asked Mr Bartell D'Arcy.

 Gabriel pointed to the statue,[20] on which lay patches of snow. Then he nodded familiarly to it and waved his hand.

——Good-night, Dan, he said gaily.

When the cab drew up before the hotel Gabriel jumped out and, in spite of Mr Bartell D'Arcy's protest, paid the driver. He gave the man a shilling over his fare. The man saluted and said:

——A prosperous New Year to you, sir.

——The same to you, said Gabriel cordially.

She leaned for a moment on his arm in getting out of the cab and while standing at the curbstone, bidding the others good-night. She leaned lightly on his arm, as lightly as when she had danced with him

---

[20]Of Daniel O'Connell, who fought for Irish independence in the early nineteenth century.

hotel room

a few hours before. He had felt proud and happy then, happy that she was his, proud of her grace and wifely carriage. But now, after the kindling again of so many memories, the first touch of her body, musical and strange and perfumed, sent through him a keen pang of lust. Under cover of her silence he pressed her arm closely to his side; and, as they stood at the hotel door, he felt that they had escaped from their lives and duties, escaped from home and friends and run away together with wild and radiant hearts to a new adventure.

An old man was dozing in a great hooded chair in the hall. He lit a candle in the office and went before them to the stairs. They followed him in silence, their feet falling in soft thuds on the thickly carpeted stairs. She mounted the stairs behind the porter, her head bowed in the ascent, her frail shoulders curved as with a burden, her skirt girt tightly about her. He could have flung his arms about her hips and held her still for his arms were trembling with desire to seize her and only the stress of his nails against the palms of his hands held the wild impulse of his body in check. The porter halted on the stairs to settle his guttering candle. They halted too on the steps below him. In the silence Gabriel could hear the falling of the molten wax into the tray and the thumping of his own heart against his ribs.

The porter led them along a corridor and opened a door. Then he set his unstable candle down on a toilet-table and asked at what hour they were to be called in the morning.

——Eight, said Gabriel.

The porter pointed to the tap of the electric-light and began a muttered apology but Gabriel cut him short.

——We don't want any light. We have light enough from the street. And I say, he added, pointing to the candle, you might remove that handsome article, like a good man.

The porter took up his candle again, but slowly for he was surprised by such a novel idea. Then he mumbled good-night and went out. Gabriel shot the lock to.

A ghostly light from the street lamp lay in a long shaft from one window to the door. Gabriel threw his overcoat and hat on a couch and crossed the room towards the window. He looked down into the street in order that his emotion might calm a little. Then he turned and leaned against a chest of drawers with his back to the light. She had taken off her hat and cloak and was standing before a large swinging mirror, unhooking her waist. Gabriel paused for a few moments, watching her, and then said:

——Gretta!

She turned away from the mirror slowly and walked along the shaft of light towards him. Her face looked so serious and weary that the words would not pass Gabriel's lips. No, it was not the moment yet.

——You looked tired, he said.

——I am a little, she answered.

——You don't feel ill or weak?

——No, tired: that's all.

She went on to the window and stood there, looking out. Gabriel waited again and then, fearing that indifference was about to conquer him, he said abruptly:

——By the way, Gretta!

——What is it?

——You know that poor fellow Malins? he said quickly.

——Yes. What about him?

——Well, poor fellow, he's a decent sort of chap after all, continued Gabriel in a false voice. He gave me back that sovereign I lent him and I didn't expect it really. It's a pity he wouldn't keep away from that Browne, because he's not a bad fellow at heart.

He was trembling now with annoyance. Why did she seem so abstracted? He did not know how he could begin. Was she annoyed, too, about something? If she would only turn to him or come to him of her own accord! To take her as she was would be brutal. No, he must see some ardour in her eyes first. He longed to be master of her strange mood.

——When did you lend him the pound? she asked, after a pause.

Gabriel strove to restrain himself from breaking out into brutal language about the sottish Malins and his pound. He longed to cry to her from his soul, to crush her body against his, to overmaster her. But he said:

——O, at Christmas, when he opened that little Christmas-card shop in Henry Street.

He was in such a fever of rage and desire that he did not hear her come from the window. She stood before him for an instant, looking at him strangely. Then, suddenly raising herself on tiptoe and resting her hands lightly on his shoulders, she kissed him.

——You are a very generous person, Gabriel, she said.

Gabriel, trembling with delight at her sudden kiss and at the quaintness of her phrase, put his hands on her hair and began smoothing it back, scarcely touching it with his fingers. The washing had made it fine and brilliant. His heart was brimming over with happiness. Just when he was wishing for it she had come to him of her own accord.

Perhaps her thoughts had been running with his. Perhaps she had felt the impetuous desire that was in him and then the yielding mood had come upon her. Now that she had fallen to him so easily he wondered why he had been so diffident.

He stood, holding her head between his hands. Then, slipping one arm swiftly about her body and drawing her towards him, he said softly:

——Gretta dear, what are you thinking about?

She did not answer nor yield wholly to his arm. He said again, softly:

——Tell me what it is, Gretta. I think I know what is the matter. Do I know?

She did not answer at once. Then she said in an outburst of tears:

——O, I am thinking about that song, *The Lass of Aughrim*.

She broke loose from him and ran to the bed and, throwing her arms across the bed-rail, hid her face. Gabriel stood stock-still for a moment in astonishment and then followed her. As he passed in the way of the cheval-glass he caught sight of himself in full length, his broad, well-filled shirt-front, the face whose expression always puzzled him when he saw it in a mirror and his glimmering gilt-rimmed eyeglasses. He halted a few paces from her and said:

——What about the song? Why does that make you cry?

She raised her head from her arms and dried her eyes with the back of her hand like a child. A kinder note than he had intended went into his voice.

——Why, Gretta? he asked.

——I am thinking about a person long ago who used to sing that song.

——And who was the person long ago? asked Gabriel, smiling.

——It was a person I used to know in Galway when I was living there with my grandmother, she said.

The smile passed away from Gabriel's face. A dull anger began to gather again at the back of his mind and the dull fires of his lust began to glow angrily in his veins.

——Someone you were in love with? he asked ironically.

——It was a young boy I used to know, she answered, named Michael Furey. He used to sing that song, *The Lass of Aughrim*. He was very delicate.

Gabriel was silent. He did not wish her to think that he was interested in this delicate boy.

——I can see him so plainly, she said after a moment. Such eyes as he had: big dark eyes! And such an expression in them—an expression!

——O then, you were in love with him? said Gabriel.

——I used to go out walking with him, she said, when I was in Galway.

A thought flew across Gabriel's mind.

Perhaps that was why you wanted to go to Galway with that Ivors girl? he said coldly.

She looked at him and asked in surprise:

——What for?

Her eyes made Gabriel feel awkward. He shrugged his shoulders and said:

——How do I know? To see him perhaps.

She looked away from him along the shaft of light towards the window in silence.

——He is dead, she said at length. He died when he was only seventeen. Isn't it a terrible thing to die so young as that?

——What was he? asked Gabriel, still ironically.

——He was in the gasworks, she said.

Gabriel felt humiliated by the failure of his irony and by the evocation of this figure from the dead, a boy in the gasworks. While he had been full of memories of their secret life together, full of tenderness and joy and desire, she had been comparing him in her mind with another. A shameful consciousness of his own person assailed him. He saw himself as a ludicrous figure, acting as a pennyboy for his aunts, a nervous well-meaning sentimentalist, orating to vulgarians and idealising his own clownish lusts, the pitiable fatuous fellow he had caught a glimpse of in the mirror. Instinctively he turned his back more to the light lest she might see the shame that burned upon his forehead.

epiphany

He tried to keep up his tone of cold interrogation but his voice when he spoke was humble and indifferent.

——I suppose you were in love with this Michael Furey, Gretta, he said.

——I was great with him at that time, she said.

Her voice was veiled and sad. Gabriel, feeling now how vain it would be to try to lead her whither he had purposed, caressed one of her hands and said, also sadly:

——And what did he die of so young, Gretta? Consumption, was it?

——I think he died for me, she answered.

A vague terror seized Gabriel at this answer as if, at that hour when he had hoped to triumph, some impalpable and vindictive being was coming against him, gathering forces against him in its vague world. But he shook himself free of it with an effort of reason and continued to caress her hand. He did not question her again for he felt that she would tell him of herself. Her hand was warm and moist: it did not respond to his touch but he continued to caress it just as he had caressed her first letter to him that spring morning.

——It was in the winter, she said, about the beginning of the winter when I was going to leave my grandmother's and come up here to the convent. And he was ill at the time in his lodgings in Galway and wouldn't be let out and his people in Oughterard were written to. He was in decline, they said, or something like that. I never knew rightly.

She paused for a moment and sighed.

——Poor fellow, she said. He was very fond of me and he was such a gentle boy. We used to go out together, walking, you know, Gabriel, like the way they do in the country. He was going to study singing only for his health. He had a very good voice, poor Michael Furey.

——Well; and then? asked Gabriel.

——And then when it came to the time for me to leave Galway and come up to the convent he was much worse and I wouldn't be let see him so I wrote a letter saying I was going up to Dublin and would be back in the summer and hoping he would be better then.

She paused for a moment to get her voice under control and then went on:

——Then the night before I left I was in my grandmother's house in Nuns' Island, packing up, and I heard gravel thrown up against the window. The window was so wet I couldn't see so I ran downstairs as I was and slipped out the back into the garden and there was the poor fellow at the end of the garden, shivering.

——And did you not tell him to go back? asked Gabriel.

——I implored of him to go home at once and told him he would get his death in the rain. But he said he did not want to live. I can see his eyes as well as well! He was standing at the end of the wall where there was a tree.

——And did he go home? asked Gabriel.

——Yes, he went home. And when I was only a week in the convent he died and he was buried in Oughterard where his people came from. O, the day I heard that, that he was dead!

She stopped, choking with sobs, and, overcome by emotion, flung herself face downward on the bed, sobbing in the quilt. Gabriel held her hand for a moment longer, irresolutely, and then, shy of intruding on her grief, let it fall gently and walked quietly to the window.

She was fast asleep.

Gabriel, leaning on his elbow, looked for a few moments unresentfully on her tangled hair and half-open mouth, listening to her deep-drawn breath. So she had had that romance in her life: a man had died for her sake. It hardly pained him now to think how poor a part he, her husband, had played in her life. He watched her while she slept as though he and she had never lived together as man and wife. His curious eyes rested long upon her face and on her hair: and, as he thought of what she must have been then, in that time of her first girlish beauty, a strange friendly pity for her entered his soul. He did not like to say even to himself that her face was no longer beautiful but he knew it was no longer the face for which Michael Furey had braved death.

Perhaps she had not told him all the story. His eyes moved to the chair over which she had thrown some of her clothes. A petticoat string dangled to the floor. One boot stood upright, its limp upper fallen down: the fellow of it lay upon its side. He wondered at his riot of emotions of an hour before. From what had it proceeded? From his aunt's supper, from his own foolish speech, from the wine and dancing, the merry-making when saying good-night in the hall, the pleasure of the walk along the river in the snow. Poor Aunt Julia! She, too, would soon be a shade with the shade of Patrick Morkan and his horse. He had caught that haggard look upon her face for a moment when she was singing *Arrayed for the Bridal*. Soon, perhaps, he would be sitting in that same drawing-room, dressed in black, his silk hat on his knees. The blinds would be drawn down and Aunt Kate would be sitting beside him, crying and blowing her nose and telling him how Julia had died. He would cast about in his mind for some words that might console her, and would find only lame and useless ones. Yes, yes: that would happen very soon.

The air of the room chilled his shoulders. He stretched himself cautiously along the sheets and lay down beside his wife. One by one they were all becoming shades. Better pass boldly into that other world, in the full glory of some passion, than fade and wither dismally with age. He thought of how she who lay beside him had locked in her heart for so many years that image of her lover's eyes when he had told her that he did not wish to live.

Generous tears filled Gabriel's eyes. He had never felt like that himself towards any woman but he knew that such a feeling must be love. The tears gathered more thickly in his eyes and in the partial darkness he imagined he saw the form of a young man standing under a dripping tree. Other forms were near. His soul had approached that region where dwell the vast hosts of the dead. He was conscious of, but could not apprehend, their wayward and flickering existence. His own identity was fading out into a grey impalpable world: the solid world itself which these dead had one time reared and lived in was dissolving and dwindling.

A few light taps upon the pane made him turn to the window. It had begun to snow again. He watched sleepily the flakes, silver and dark, falling obliquely against the lamplight. The time had come for him to set out on his journey westward. Yes, the newspapers were right: snow was general all over Ireland. It was falling on every part of the dark central plain, on the treeless hills, falling softly upon the Bog of Allen[21] and, farther westward, softly falling into the dark mutinous Shannon waves.[22] It was falling, too, upon every part of the lonely churchyard on the hill where Michael Furey lay buried. It lay thickly drifted on the crooked crosses and headstones, on the spears of the little gate, on the barren thorns. His soul swooned slowly as he heard the snow falling faintly through the universe and faintly falling, like the descent of their last end, upon all the living and the dead.

---

[21]Several miles west of Dublin.
[22]River on the western coast of Ireland.

The Metamorphosis

Franz Kafka

The brief, tormented life of Franz Kafka began in Prague on July 3, 1883. His father, Hermann Kafka, the son of a butcher, had worked his way up from a peddler's pack to become the owner of a wholesale women's wear firm. A living example of how a powerful and aggressive man could succeed in life despite his initial poverty and his despised Jewish nationality, Kafka's father respected only those qualities that had contributed to his prosperity. But his first child and only son was as unlike him as it was possible to be. Where his father was physically robust, a man of strength and appetite, Franz was thin and frail, sickly both as a child and an adult. Where his father was a man of the world, Franz was an intellectual and a dreamer. Hermann Kafka's unsuccessful attempt to force his son into his mold, his tyrannical domination, his contempt for his son's qualities, and his disapproval of all his son's plans and ambitions marked the younger Kafka for life. He grew up embittered and alienated, feeling himself not merely a failure but one who had been rejected by what he called the "court of last appeal." Franz Kafka never forgave his father for this. In 1919, at the age of thirty-six, he composed a 15,000-word letter to his then aging father, an astonishing document, accusatory and calmly explanatory by turns, in which he tried to resolve the question of "why am I afraid of you." The letter, which Kafka sent through his mother, was never delivered: Julie Kafka knew that Hermann would not understand.

The Prague in which Kafka grew up, and which we see through his fiction as a shadowy, unreal, impersonal city, may have been another source of alienation. It was then the capital of the Kingdom of Bohemia within the Austro-Hungarian Empire, populated primarily by Czechs but managed and ruled by a German-speaking minority. In the twenty years that preceded the break-up of the empire in 1918, nationalistic feeling ran high, and Kafka, a German-speaking Jew, would have been the target of two distinct sorts of ethnic hatred. Kafka remained loyal, however, to the Jewish origins of both sides of his family (his mother's forebears, the Löwys, included several rabbis); he studied Judaism and Hebrew, wrote a lecture on Yiddish, and identified strongly with the plight of Eastern European Jews living outside the relatively tolerant empire. And though, as a speaker of German, Kafka might have been expected to sympathize with the ruling classes of Prague, he instead learned Czech and interested himself in the national aspirations of the oppressed majority. In both these things Kafka may have been reacting against the example of his father, whose secular and assimilated style of Jewishness left his son with a need for deeper roots, and whose contempt for his Czech workers and for their language ("the language of servants," he had called it) disturbed Kafka's liberalism and love of justice.

Kafka's schooling was entirely conventional, designed to fit him for success in the business world. He went first to a local elementary school, then to the German Gymnasium (a secondary academy), and finally to Karl-Ferdinand University in Prague, from which he received his doctorate in jurisprudence in 1906. Kafka disliked the study of law and practiced it only for the single year required for entry into the Austrian civil service. In 1908, after taking a brief commercial course in insurance, Kafka entered as a probationer into the bureaucracy of the Workers' Accident Insurance Company, a government agency in Prague. He was a diligent and successful civil servant, noted for his kindness and humanity as well as for his intellectual gifts, and in the fourteen years until his health completely broke, Kafka rose through the ranks to the post of senior secretary, the highest position for which his training had fitted him. It was, in many ways, a humdrum vocation, yet it can be said to have contributed to Kafka's writing career in two quite different ways: it provided the office scenes for *The Trial*, and the brief working day (eight in the morning till two) left Kafka free to write for much of the afternoon and evening. And the calm routine of his office work must have been a refuge from the intensity and self-torture with which Kafka approached his two main personal preoccupations, women and literature.

Kafka's relations with women have come under a great deal of psychoanalytical scrutiny, partly because his dealings with them were so complex and ambivalent, and partly because he left behind him in his diaries and his voluminous correspondence with them such a rich mass of material to analyze. Though what lies behind is not easy to understand, the facts themselves can be stated quite simply. From 1912 to 1917 Kafka was deeply involved with Felice Bauer, a charming and intelligent but in many respects commonplace young woman from Berlin whom he had met at the home of Max Brod, his best friend. The relationship began through letters of ever-increasing intimacy—at one time Kafka was writing three letters a day to Felice—but their visits were infrequent, at least in part because Kafka's fears about meeting her were stronger than his longings. In the spring of 1914 they were engaged, but two months later Kafka dissolved the engagement. The relationship then went into a second cycle similar to the first: early in 1915, Kafka and Felice were reunited, engaged again in July 1917, but in December the engagement was broken once more and their relations came to an end. The pattern was repeated yet once more between 1918 and 1920 with another woman, Julie Wohryzek.

Both Felice and Julie were domestically oriented Jewish girls, unintellectual and in many ways uncomprehending of Kafka's art and thought. Kafka's next love was quite different: Milena Ješenská was a Gentile Czech married to a Jewish scholar and critic, a frequent visitor to Prague literary circles, and a journalist and translator in her own right. It was via the correspondence arising out of the Czech translation of part of his *Amerika* that Milena became involved with Kafka and she was, as most commentators agree, the only woman in Kafka's life who fully understood his genius. Their stormy correspondence was followed by a brief and passionate love affair (an engagement was this time out of the question, of course) and then, inevitably, by Kafka's rejection of her. Perhaps the happiest of Kafka's relationships took place in the last year of his life, after his advancing case of tuberculosis had forced his retirement from business. While at a sanatorium on the Baltic, Kafka met Dora Dymant, an Eastern European girl of Hasidic background. Though she was not even twenty, less than half Kafka's age, she fell deeply in love with him, and he responded, perhaps for the first time in his life, without his usual agonies of self-torture. While his health permitted it, they lived together in a little apartment in a suburb of Berlin and, in his last days, when he had to be under constant medical care, she continued to nurse him. To the end, despite the disapproval of both his parents and hers and despite the refusal of her rabbi to perform the ceremony, he nourished the hope of marrying Dora and of going to live with her in Palestine. There was no time, though: less than a year after their relationship began, on July 3, 1924, he was dead.

The simplest and easiest explanation of Kafka's agonies over the women in his life is the one Kafka himself gave in his diaries and his letters to Felice: the conflict between domestic life and his literary work. In his diaries for 1913, Kafka listed seven reasons "for and against my marriage," and except for his "inability to bear living alone," all the arguments are against marriage, including "the fear of being tied to anyone," the sense that he "must be alone a great deal," since all he had "accomplished was only the result of being alone," the fear that domestic happiness would come only "at the expense of my writing. Not that, not that!" And in a letter of the same year, Kafka asked Felice how she would like living with a husband who "returns from the office at 2:30 or 3, lies down, sleeps until 7 or 8, hurriedly has supper, takes an hour's walk, and then starts writing, and writes till 1 or 2? Could you really stand that?" Psychoanalytic writers, on the other hand, have suggested—some of them dogmatically—that Kafka was really a homosexual whose fear of marriage betokened a deeply rooted disgust with women's bodies and with the sexual act itself. In this view, his avowed longing for conveniently absent women would be a clever way of denying his homosexuality; his elaborate explanations of why he delayed meeting with Felice and Milena would be rationalizations for his genuine aversion. It is not wholly convincing, however, in that it leaves unexplained his relatively unclouded affair with Dora, and it is also puzzling that Kafka, who so endlessly analyzed himself in his diaries and letters, should have given no hint that he suspected this of himself. Still another explanation—and it is the one I find most satisfying—derives from the self-hatred that Kafka's father instilled into him from his childhood. Kafka's idealistic desires to marry and found a family were always sincere, I think, but his powerful feelings of worthlessness prevented him from ever pursuing his ideal. In his undelivered letter to his father, Kafka suggested this himself. From the moment he makes up his mind to marry, he says, he becomes so worried that he can scarcely sleep: "It is the general pressure of anxiety, of weakness, of self-contempt." In his last year, when he knew that death was imminent and that he would be in no danger of marrying and having to act as a father, the pressure was off Kafka. He could be easy and cheerful with Dora because she posed no threat to the dying man.

At the time of his death, Kafka had published two short novels, *The Metamorphosis* (1915) and *In the Penal Colony* (1919), and a collection of short stories, *The Country Doctor* (1919). He put his second short-story collection, *The Hunger Artist*, into final form while on his deathbed, and the book appeared posthumously (1924). His last testament, written at a time of deep despondency in 1922, appointed Max Brod his literary executor and directed him to destroy all his unpublished work. If Brod had followed Kafka's expressed intention, Kafka would, as one commentator has stated, "scarcely be remembered, or if he were, he would probably be ranked as a writer of promise who composed some startling short stories." His rank in twentieth-century letters would have been minor or nonexistent. But Brod was, as Kafka probably knew, the last person in the world to heed his orders. He idolized Kafka and had written glowing accounts of his friend's work. He disregarded Kafka's will and devoted much of the rest of his life to preparing the unpublished manuscripts for the press and to publicizing Kafka's genius. Brod issued *The Trial* in 1925, *The Castle* in 1926, and *Amerika* in 1927. All three had to be assembled from disarranged manuscript fragments, all have missing chapters, and all but *The Trial* lack their endings. Despite their unfinished state, it is on these novels, and mainly on *The Trial* and *The Castle*, that Kafka's reputation primarily rests.

The Trial, begun as early as 1914, is the story of Joseph K., who is arrested without warning on the morning of his thirtieth birthday, charged with a crime whose nature he is never told, and brutally executed precisely one year later. His struggles to prove his innocence, or to come to terms with the Law—which comes to seem more and more metaphysical as the novel progresses—make up the plot of the novel. *The Castle*, written in 1922, is about another intense, but equally vague and amorphous, quest. The hero, known only as K., either is or is pretending to be the official Land-Surveyor appointed by the Count at whose Castle he arrives. K.'s attempts to gain the recognition of the Castle's hierarchy of officials (who seem determined to exclude him as an intruder) take the form of a siege waged aggressively on both sides. Both these novels are written surrealistically, with a strange mixture of vivid, realistic description and weird events and imagery, all conveyed in a precise, luminous style whose very clarity heightens the uncanny effect of the stories.

Since Kafka's novels defy literal interpretation, his critics have attempted to read them as allegories of one sort or another. From a psychoanalytical perspective, they have been read as attempts, on Kafka's part, to dramatize his tragic conflict with his disapproving and distant father. The silent but condemnatory Law and the inaccessible Castle would in this reading be symbolic representations of Hermann Kafka; the anxious and guilt-ridden but audacious heroes, versions of the author himself. From a political perspective, *The Trial* has been seen as a prophecy of the totalitarian state holding human beings and their freedom in its arbitrary power. Similarly, *The Castle* has been described as an allegory of the Jews in Europe, ambivalently tolerated or persecuted intruders besieging its institutions. Most influential, however, has been the religious and philosophical interpretation, which was relentlessly voiced by Max Brod, Kafka's earliest appreciator. In one version of this view, at least, *The Trial* represents humanity's always unfulfilled quest for the absolute values once associated with Divine Law in an absurd world darkened by the death of belief. *The Castle,* attacking the same problem from a slightly altered perspective, represents the search for Grace, for a Promised Land, from a God who arbitrarily declines to guarantee His reward to either faith or good works. No one of these views has ever entirely displaced the others, and the significance of Kafka's novels is likely to be debated as long as he continues to be read— that is, as long as people suffer from guilt and anxiety threatened by the world's incomprehensible order.

Biography   Max Brod's life of his friend is available in English as *Franz Kafka: A Biography* (New York: Schocken, 1963). An excellent alternative is to read Kafka's autobiographical writings themselves—the diaries and the letters to Felice Bauer, Milena Ješenská, and his father—through which the flavor of his personality comes directly. A shorter option is *I Am a Memory Come Alive,* a set of selections from these materials skillfully arranged by editor Nahum Glatzer into a well-structured autobiography (New York: Schocken, 1974).

Editions   Kafka's works, many found in fragmentary form at his death, have been admirably edited by Max Brod and his successors. They are available, in excellent translations, in a fourteen-volume Schocken edition (New York: 1946–1974). Most of the volumes are available in a uniform paperback edition, which includes Kafka's diaries and letters as well as his fiction.

Bibliography   See Maurice Beebe and Naomi Christensen, ''Criticism of Franz Kafka: A Selected Checklist,'' in *Modern Fiction Studies* 8 (1962), 80–100; most complete is Angel Flores, *A Kafka Bibliography: 1908–1976* (New York: Gordian Press, 1976).

General Criticism   Paul Eisner, *Kafka and Prague* (New York: Arts, Inc., 1950); Heinz Politzer, *Franz Kafka: Parable and Paradox* (Ithaca, N.Y.: Cornell University Press, 1962); Ronald Gray, ed., *Kafka: A Collection of Critical Essays* (Englewood Cliffs, N.J.: Prentice-Hall, 1962); Angel Flores, ed., *The Kafka Problem* (New York: New Directions, 1963); Michael Kowal, *Franz Kafka: Problems in Interpretation* (New Haven: Yale University dissertation, 1962); Charles Neider, *The Frozen Sea: A Study of Franz Kafka* (New York: Oxford University Press, 1948); Martin Greenberg, *The Terror of Art: Kafka and Modern Literature* (New York: Oxford University Press, 1968); James Rolleston,

Kafka's Narrative Theater (University Park, Pa.: State University Press, 1974); Meno Spann, *Franz Kafka* (Boston: Twayne, 1977); and Henry Sussman, *Franz Kafka: Geometrician of Metaphor* (Madison, Wisc.: Coda Press, 1979).

Criticism of The Metamorphosis   In addition to sections or chapters on *The Metamorphosis* in the books above, see: Walter Sokel, "Kafka's *Metamorphosis:* Rebellion and Punishment," *Monatshefte* 48 (1956), 203-214; Norman Holland, "Realism and Unrealism: Kafka's *Metamorphosis*," *Modern Fiction Studies* 4 (1958), 143-150; F. D. Luke, "*The Metamorphosis*," in Angel Flores, ed., *Franz Kafka Today* (Madison: University of Wisconsin Press, 1958); Mark Spilka, "Kafka's Sources for *The Metamorphosis*," *Comparative Literature* 11 (1959), 289-307; Norman Friedman, "Kafka's *Metamorphosis*: A Literal Reading," *Approach* 49 (1963), 26-34; Stanley Corngold, "Kafka's *Die Verwandlung*: Metamorphosis of the Metaphor," *Mosaic* 3, iv (1970), 91-106; Sander L. Gilman, "A View of Kafka's Treatment of Actuality in *Die Verwandlung*," *Germanic Notes* 2, iv (1971), 26-30; Suzanne Wolkerfeld, "Christian Symbolism in Kafka's *The Metamorphosis*," *Studies in Short Fiction* 10 (1973), 205-207; and Carol Helmstetter Cantrell, "*The Metamorphosis*: Kafka's Study of a Family," *Modern Fiction Studies* 23 (1977-1978), 578-586. See also Stanley Corngold's book, *The Commentators' Despair: The Interpretation of Kafka's* Metamorphosis (Port Washington, N.Y.: Kennikat Press, 1973), which analyzes more than one hundred critical interpretations of *The Metamorphosis*.

The Metamorphosis

Translated by Willa and Edwin Muir

I

As Gregor Samsa awoke one morning from uneasy dreams he found himself transformed in his bed into a gigantic insect. He was lying on his hard, as it were armor-plated, back and when he lifted his head a little he could see his domelike brown belly divided into stiff arched segments on top of which the bed quilt could hardly keep in position and was about to slide off completely. His numerous legs, which were pitifully thin compared to the rest of his bulk, waved helplessly before his eyes.

What has happened to me? he thought. It was no dream. His room, a regular human bedroom, only rather too small, lay quiet between the four familiar walls. Above the table on which a collection of cloth samples was unpacked and spread out—Samsa was a commercial traveler—hung the picture which he had recently cut out of an illustrated magazine and put into a pretty gilt frame. It showed a lady, with a fur cap on and a fur stole, sitting upright and holding out to the spectator a huge fur muff into which the whole of her forearm had vanished!

Gregor's eyes turned next to the window, and the overcast sky—one could hear raindrops beating on the window gutter—made him quite melancholy. What about sleeping a little longer and forgetting all this nonsense, he thought, but it could not be done, for he was accustomed to sleep on his right side and in his present condition he could not turn himself over. However violently he forced himself toward his right side he always rolled onto his back again. He tried it at least a hundred times, shutting his eyes to keep from seeing his struggling legs, and only desisted when he began to feel in his side a faint dull ache he had never experienced before.

Oh God, he thought, what an exhausting job I've picked on! Traveling about day in, day out. It's much more irritating work than doing the actual business in the office, and on top of that there's the trouble of constant traveling, of worrying about train connections, the bed and irregular meals, casual acquaintances that are always new and never become intimate friends. The devil take it all! He felt a slight itching up on his belly; slowly pushed himself on his back nearer to the top of the bed so that he could lift his head more easily; identified the itching place which was surrounded by many small white spots the nature of which he could not understand and made to touch it with a leg, but drew the leg back immediately, for the contact made a cold shiver run through him.

He slid again into his former position. This getting up early, he thought, makes one quite stupid. A man needs his sleep. Other commercials live like harem women. For instance, when I come back to the hotel of a morning to write up the orders I've got, these others are only sitting down to breakfast. Let me just try that with my chief; I'd be sacked on the spot. Anyhow, that might be quite a good thing for me, who can tell? If I didn't have to hold my hand because of my parents I'd have given notice long ago, I'd have gone to the chief and told him exactly what I think of him. That would knock him endways from his desk! It's a queer way of doing, too, this sitting on high at a desk and talking down to employees, especially when they have to come quite near because the chief is hard of hearing. Well, there's still hope; once I've saved enough money to pay back my parents' debts to him—that should take another five or six years—I'll do it without fail. I'll cut myself completely loose then. For the moment, though, I'd better get up, since my train goes at five.

He looked at the alarm clock ticking on the chest. Heavenly Father! he thought. It was half-past six o'clock and the hands were quietly moving on, it was even past the half-hour, it was getting on toward a quarter to seven. Had the alarm clock not gone off? From the bed one could see that it had been properly set for four o'clock; of course it must have gone off. Yes, but was it possible to sleep quietly through that ear-splitting noise? Well, he had not slept quietly, yet apparently all the more soundly for that. But what was he to do now? The next train went at seven o'clock; to catch that he would need to hurry like mad and his samples weren't even packed up, and he himself wasn't feeling particularly fresh and active. And even if he did catch the train he wouldn't avoid a row with the chief, since the firm's porter would have been waiting for the five o'clock train and would have long since reported his failure to turn up. The porter was a creature of the chief's, spineless and stupid. Well, supposing he were to say he was sick? But that would be most unpleasant and would look suspicious, since during his five years' employment he had not been ill once. The chief himself would be sure to come with the sick-insurance doctor, would reproach his parents with their son's laziness, and would cut all excuses short by referring to the insurance doctor, who of course regarded all mankind as perfectly healthy malingerers. And would he be so far wrong on this occasion? Gregor really felt quite well, apart from a drowsiness that was utterly superfluous after such a long sleep, and he was even unusually hungry.

As all this was running through his mind at top speed without his being able to decide to leave his bed—the alarm clock had just struck a quarter to seven—there came a cautious tap at the door behind the head of his bed. "Gregor," said a voice—it was his mother's—"it's a quarter to seven. Hadn't you a train to catch?" That gentle voice! Gregor had a shock as he heard his own voice answering hers, unmistakably his own voice, it was true, but with a persistent horrible twittering squeak behind it like an undertone, which left the words in their clear shape only for the first moment and then rose up reverberating around them to destroy their sense, so that one could not be sure one had heard them rightly. Gregor wanted to answer at length and explain everything, but in the circumstances he confined himself to saying: "Yes, yes, thank you, Mother, I'm getting up now." The wooden door between them must have kept the change in his voice from being noticeable outside, for his mother contented herself with this statement and shuffled away. Yet this brief exchange of words had made the other members of the family aware that Gregor was still in the house, as they had not expected, and at one of the side doors his father was already knocking, gently, yet with his fist. "Gregor, Gregor," he called, "What's the matter with you?" And after a little while he called again in a deeper voice: "Gregor! Gregor!" At the other side door his sister was saying in a low, plaintive tone: "Gregor? Aren't you well? Are you needing anything?" He answered them both at once: "I'm just ready," and did his best to make his voice sound as normal as possible by enunciating the words very clearly and leaving long pauses between them. So his father went back to his breakfast, but his sister whispered: "Gregor, open the door, do." However, he was not thinking of opening the door, and felt thankful for the prudent habit he had acquired in traveling of locking all doors during the night, even at home.

His immediate intention was to get up quietly without being disturbed, to put on his clothes and above all eat his breakfast, and only then consider what else was to be done, since in bed, he was well aware, his meditations would come to no sensible conclusion. He remembered that often enough in bed he had felt small aches and pains, probably caused by awkward postures, which had proved purely imaginary once he got up, and he looked forward eagerly to seeing this morning's delusions gradually fall away. That the change in his voice was nothing but the precursor of a severe chill, a standing ailment of commercial travelers, he had not the least possible doubt.

To get rid of the quilt was quite easy; he had only to inflate himself a little and it fell off by itself. But the next move was difficult, especially because he was so uncommonly broad. He would have needed arms and hands to hoist himself up; instead he had only the numerous little legs which never stopped waving in all directions and which he could not control in the least. When he tried to bend one of them it was the first to stretch itself straight; and did he succeed at last in making it do what he wanted, all the other legs meanwhile waved the more wildly in a high degree of unpleasant agitation. "But what's the use of lying idle in bed," said Gregor to himself.

He thought that he might get out of bed with the lower part of his body first, but this lower part, which he had not yet seen and of which he could form no clear conception, proved too difficult to move; it shifted so slowly; and when finally, almost wild with annoyance, he gathered his forces together and thrust out recklessly, he had miscalculated the direction and bumped heavily against the lower end of the bed, and the stinging pain he felt informed him that precisely this lower part of his body was at the moment most sensitive.

So he tried to get the top part of himself out first, and cautiously moved his head toward the edge of the bed. That proved easy enough, and despite its breadth and mass the bulk of his body at last slowly followed the movement of his head. Still, when he finally got his head free over the edge of the bed he felt too scared to go on advancing, for after all if he let himself fall in this way it would take a miracle to keep his head from being injured. And at all costs he must not lose consciousness now, precisely now; he would rather stay in bed.

But when after a repetition of the same efforts he lay in his former position again, sighing, and watched his little legs struggling against each other more wildly than ever, if that were possible, and saw no way of bringing any order into this arbitrary confusion, he told himself again that it was impossible to stay in bed and that the most sensible course was to risk everything for the smallest hope of getting away from it. At the same time he did not forget to remind himself occasionally that cool reflection, the coolest possible, was much better than desperate resolves. In such moments he focused his eyes as sharply as possible on the window, but, unfortunately, the prospect of the morning fog, which muffled even the other side of the narrow street, brought him little encouragement and comfort. "Seven o'clock already," he said to himself when the alarm clock chimed again, "seven o'clock already and still such a thick fog." And for a little while he lay quiet, breathing lightly, as if perhaps expecting such complete repose to restore all things to their real and normal condition.

But then he said to himself: "Before it strikes a quarter past seven I must be quite out of this bed, without fail. Anyhow, by that time someone will have come from the office to ask for me, since it opens before seven." And he set himself to rocking his whole body at once in a regular rhythm, with the idea of swinging it out of the bed. If he tipped himself out in that way he could keep his head from injury by lifting it at an acute angle when he fell. His back seemed to be hard and was not likely to suffer from a fall on the carpet. His biggest worry was the loud crash he would not be able to help making, which would probably cause anxiety, if not terror, behind all the doors. Still, he must take the risk.

When he was already half out of the bed—the new method was more a game than an effort, for he needed only to hitch himself across by rocking to and fro—it struck him how simple it would be if he could get help. Two strong people—he thought of his father and the servant girl—would be amply sufficient; they would only have to thrust their arms under his convex back, lever him out of the bed, bend down with their burden, and then be patient enough to let him turn himself right over onto the floor, where it was to be hoped his legs would then find their proper function. Well, ignoring the fact that the doors were all locked, ought he really to call for help? In spite of his misery he could not suppress a smile at the very idea of it.

He had got so far that he could barely keep his equilibrium when he rocked himself strongly, and he would have to nerve himself very soon for the final decision since in five minutes' time it would be quarter past seven—when the front doorbell rang. "That's someone from the office," he said to himself, and grew almost rigid, while his little legs only jigged about all the faster. For a moment everything stayed quiet. "They're not going to open the door," said Gregor to himself, catching at some kind of irrational hope. But then of course the servant girl went as usual to the door with her heavy tread and opened it. Gregor needed only to hear the first good morning of the visitor to know immediately who it was—the chief clerk himself. What a fate, to be condemned to work for a firm where the smallest omission at once gave rise to the gravest suspicion! Were all employees in a body nothing but scoundrels, was there not among them one single loyal devoted man who, had he wasted only an hour or so of the firm's time in a morning, was so tormented by conscience as to be driven out of his mind and actually incapable of leaving his bed? Wouldn't it really have been sufficient to send an apprentice to inquire—if any inquiry were necessary at all—did the chief clerk himself have to come and thus indicate to the entire family, an innocent family, that this suspicious circumstance could be investigated by no one less versed in affairs than himself? And more through the agitation caused by these reflections than through any strength of will Gregor swung himself out of bed with all his strength. His fall was broken to some extent by the carpet, his back, too, was less stiff than he thought, and so there was merely a dull thud, not so very startling. Only he had not lifted his head carefully enough and had hit it; he turned it and rubbed it on the carpet in pain and irritation.

"That was something falling down in there," said the chief clerk in the next room to the left. Gregor tried to suppose to himself that something like what had happened to him today might someday happen to the chief clerk; one really could not deny that it was possible. But as if in brusque reply to this supposition the chief clerk took a couple of firm steps in the next-door room and his patent leather boots creaked.

From the right-hand room his sister was whispering to inform him of the situation: "Gregor, the chief clerk's here." "I know," muttered Gregor to himself; but he didn't dare to make his voice loud enough for his sister to hear it.

"Gregor," said his father now from the left-hand room, "the chief clerk has come and wants to know why you didn't catch the early train. We don't know what to say to him. Besides, he wants to talk to you in person. So open the door, please. He will be good enough to excuse the untidiness of your room." "Good morning, Mr. Samsa," the chief clerk was calling amiably meanwhile. "He's not well," said his mother to the visitor, while his father was still speaking through the door, "he's not well, sir, believe me. What else would make him miss a train! The boy thinks about nothing but his work. It makes me almost cross the way he never goes out in the evenings; he's been here the last eight days and has stayed at home every single evening. He just sits there quietly at the table reading a newspaper or looking through railway timetables. The only amusement he gets is doing fretwork. For instance, he spent two or three evenings cutting out a little picture frame; you would be surprised to see how pretty it is; it's hanging in his room; you'll see it in a minute when Gregor opens the door. I must say I'm glad you've come, sir; we should never have got him to unlock the door by ourselves; he's so obstinate; and I'm sure he's unwell, though he wouldn't have it be so this morning." "I'm just coming," said Gregor slowly and carefully, not moving an inch for fear of losing one word of the conversation. "I can't think of any other explanation, madame," said the chief clerk, "I hope it's nothing serious. Although on the other hand I must say that we men of business—fortunately or unfortunately—very often simply have to ignore any slight indisposition, since business must be attended to." "Well, can the chief clerk come in now?" asked Gregor's father impatiently, again knocking on the door. "No," said Gregor. In the left-hand room a painful silence followed this refusal, in the right-hand room his sister began to sob.

Why didn't his sister join the others? She was probably newly out of bed and hadn't even begun to put on her clothes yet. Well, why was she crying? Because he wouldn't get up and let the chief clerk in, because he was in danger of losing his job, and because the chief would begin dunning his parents again for the old debts? Surely these were things one didn't need to worry about for the present. Gregor was still at home and not in the least thinking of deserting the family. At the moment, true, he was lying on the carpet and no one who knew the condition he was in could seriously expect him to admit the chief clerk.

But for such a small discourtesy, which could be plausibly explained away somehow later on, Gregor could hardly be dismissed on the spot. And it seemed to Gregor that it would be much more sensible to leave him in peace for the present than to trouble him with tears and entreaties. Still, of course, their uncertainty bewildered them all and excused their behavior.

"Mr. Samsa," the chief clerk called now in a louder voice, "what's the matter with you? Here you are, barricading yourself in your room, giving only 'yes' and 'no' for answers, causing your parents a lot of unnecessary trouble and neglecting—I mention this only in passing—neglecting your business duties in an incredible fashion. I am speaking here in the name of your parents and of your chief, and I beg you quite seriously to give me an immediate and precise explanation. You amaze me, you amaze me. I thought you were a quiet, dependable person, and now all at once you seem bent on making a disgraceful exhibition of yourself. The chief did hint to me early this morning a possible explanation for your disappearance—with reference to the cash payments that were entrusted to you recently—but I almost pledged my solemn word of honor that this could not be so. But now that I see how incredibly obstinate you are, I no longer have the slightest desire to take your part at all. And your position in the firm is not so unassailable. I came with the intention of telling you all this in private, but since you are wasting my time so needlessly I don't see why your parents shouldn't hear it too. For some time past your work has been most unsatisfactory; this is not the season of the year for a business boom, of course, we admit that, but a season of the year for doing no business at all, that does not exist, Mr. Samsa, must not exist."

"But, sir," cried Gregor, beside himself and in his agitation forgetting everything else, "I'm just going to open the door this very minute. A slight illness, an attack of giddiness, has kept me from getting up. I'm still lying in bed. But I feel all right again. I'm getting out of bed now. Just give me a moment or two longer! I'm not quite so well as I thought. But I'm all right, really. How a thing like that can suddenly strike one down! Only last night I was quite well, my parents can tell you, or rather I did have a slight presentiment. I must have showed some sign of it. Why didn't I report it at the office! But one always thinks that an indisposition can be got over without staying in the house. Oh sir, do spare my parents! All that you're reproaching me with now has no foundation; no one has ever said a word to me about it. Perhaps you haven't looked at the last orders I sent in. Anyhow, I can still catch the eight o'clock train, I'm much the better for my few hours' rest. Don't let me detain you here, sir; I'll be attending to business very soon, and do be good enough to tell the chief so and to make my excuses to him!"

And while all this was tumbling out pell-mell and Gregor hardly knew what he was saying, he had reached the chest quite easily, perhaps because of the practice he had had in bed, and was now trying to lever himself upright by means of it. He meant actually to open the door, actually to show himself and speak to the chief clerk; he was eager to find out what the others, after all their insistence, would say at the sight of him. If they were horrified then the responsibility was no longer his and he could stay quiet. But if they took it calmly, then he had no reason either to be upset, and could really get to the station for the eight o'clock train if he hurried. At first he slipped down a few times from the polished surface of the chest, but at length with a last heave he stood upright; he paid no more attention to the pains in the lower part of his body, however they smarted. Then he let himself fall against the back of a nearby chair, and clung with his little legs to the edges of it. That brought him into control of himself again and he stopped speaking, for now he could listen to what the chief clerk was saying.

"Did you understand a word of it?" the chief clerk was asking; "surely he can't be trying to make fools of us?" "Oh dear," cried his mother in tears, "perhaps he's terribly ill and we're tormenting him. Grete! Grete!" she called out then. "Yes Mother?" called his sister from the other side. They were calling to each other across Gregor's room. "You must go this minute for the doctor. Gregor is ill. Go for the doctor, quick. Did you hear how he was speaking?" "That was no human voice," said the chief clerk in a voice noticeably low beside the shrillness of the mother's. "Anna! Anna!" his father was calling through the hall to the kitchen, clapping his hands, "get a locksmith at once!" And the two girls were already running through the hall with a swish of skirts—how could his sister have got dressed so quickly?—and were tearing the front door open. There was no sound of its closing again; they had evidently left it open, as one does in houses where some great misfortune has happened.

But Gregor was now much calmer. The words he uttered were no longer understandable, apparently, although they seemed clear enough to him, even clearer than before, perhaps because his ear had grown accustomed to the sound of them. Yet at any rate people now believed that something was wrong with him, and were ready to help him. The positive certainty with which these first measures had been taken comforted him. He felt himself drawn once more into the human circle and hoped for great and remarkable results from both the doctor and the locksmith, without really distinguishing precisely between them. To make his voice as clear as possible for the decisive conversation that was now imminent he coughed a little, as quietly as he could, of course, since this noise might not sound like a human cough for all he was able to judge. In the next room meanwhile there was complete silence. Perhaps his parents were sitting at the table with the chief clerk, whispering, perhaps they were all leaning against the door and listening.

Slowly Gregor pushed the chair toward the door, then let go of it, caught hold of the door for support—the soles at the end of his little legs were somewhat sticky—and rested against it for a moment after his efforts. Then he set himself to turning the key in the lock with his mouth. It seemed, unhappily, that he hadn't really any teeth—what could he grip the key with?—but on the other hand his jaws were certainly very strong; with their help he did manage to set the key in motion, heedless of the fact that he was undoubtedly damaging them somewhere, since a brown fluid issued from his mouth, flowed over the key, and dripped on the floor. "Just listen to that," said the chief clerk next door; "he's turning the key." That was a great encouragement to Gregor; but they should all have shouted encouragement to him, his father and mother too: "Go on, Gregor," they should have called out, "keep going, hold on to that key!" And in the belief that they were all following his efforts intently, he clenched his jaws recklessly on the key with all the force at his command. As the turning of the key progressed, he circled around the lock, holding on now only with his mouth, pushing on the key, as required, or pulling it down again with all the weight of his body. The louder click of the finally yielding lock literally quickened Gregor. With a deep breath of relief he said to himself: "So I didn't need the locksmith," and laid his head on the handle to open the door wide.

Since he had to pull the door toward him, he was still invisible when it was really wide open. He had to edge himself slowly around the near half of the double door, and to do it very carefully if he was not to fall plump upon his back just on the threshold. He was still carrying out this difficult maneuver, with no time to observe anything else, when he heard the chief clerk utter a loud "Oh!"—it sounded like a gust of wind—and now he could see the man, standing as he was nearest to the door, clapping one hand before his open mouth and slowly backing away as if driven by some invisible steady pressure. His mother—in spite of the chief clerk's being there her hair was still undone and sticking up in all directions—first clasped her hands and looked at his father, then took two steps toward Gregor and fell on the floor among her outspread skirts, her face quite hidden on her breast. His father knotted his fist with a fierce expression on his face as if he meant to knock Gregor back into his room, then looked uncertainly around the living room, covered his eyes with his hands, and wept till his great chest heaved.

Gregor did not go now into the living room, but leaned against the inside of the firmly shut wing of the door, so that only half his body was visible and his head above it bending sideways to look at the others. The light had meanwhile strengthened; on the other side of the street one could see clearly a section of the endlessly long, dark gray building opposite—it was a hospital—abruptly punctuated by its row of regular windows; the rain was still falling, but only in large singly discernible and literally singly splashing drops. The breakfast dishes were set out on the table lavishly, for breakfast was the most important meal of the day to Gregor's father, who lingered it out for hours over various newspapers. Right opposite Gregor on the wall hung a photograph of himself in military service, as a lieutenant, hand on sword, a carefree smile on his face, inviting one to respect his uniform and military bearing. The door leading to the hall was open, and one could see that the front door stood open too, showing the landing beyond and the beginning of the stairs going down.

"Well," said Gregor, knowing perfectly that he was the only one who had retained any composure, "I'll put my clothes on at once, pack up my samples, and start off. Will you only let me go? You see, sir, I'm not obstinate, and I'm willing to work; traveling is a hard life, but I couldn't live without it. Where are you going, sir? To the office? Yes? Will you give a true account of all this? One can be temporarily incapacitated, but that's just the moment for remembering former services and bearing in mind that later on, when the incapacity has been got over, one will certainly work with all the more industry and concentration. I'm loyally bound to serve the chief, you know that very well. Besides, I have to provide for my parents and my sister. I'm in great difficulties, but I'll get out of them again. Don't make things any worse for me than they are. Stand up for me in the firm. Travelers are not popular there, I know. People think they earn sacks of money and just have a good time. A prejudice there's no particular reason for revising. But you, sir, have a more comprehensive view of affairs than the rest of the staff, yes, let me tell you in confidence, a more comprehensive view than the chief himself, who, being the owner, lets his judgment easily be swayed against one of his employees. And you know very well that the traveler, who is never seen in the office almost the whole year around, can so easily fall a victim to gossip and ill luck and unfounded complaints, which he mostly knows nothing about, except when he comes back exhausted from his rounds, and only then suffers in person from their evil consequences, which he can no longer trace back to the original causes. Sir, sir, don't go away without a word to me to show that you think me in the right at least to some extent!"

But at Gregor's very first words the chief clerk had already backed away and only stared at him with parted lips over one twitching shoulder. And while Gregor was speaking he did not stand still one moment but stole away toward the door, without taking his eyes off Gregor, yet only an inch at a time, as if obeying some secret injunction to leave the room. He was already at the hall, and the suddenness with which he took his last step out of the living room would have made one believe he had burned the sole of his foot. Once in the hall he stretched his right arm before him toward the staircase, as if some supernatural power were waiting there to deliver him.

Gregor perceived that the chief clerk must on no account be allowed to go away in this frame of mind if his position in the firm were not to be endangered to the utmost. His parents did not understand this so well; they had convinced themselves in the course of years that Gregor was settled for life in this firm, and besides they were so preoccupied with their immediate troubles that all foresight had forsaken them. Yet Gregor had this foresight. The chief clerk must be detained, soothed, persuaded, and finally won over; the whole future of Gregor and his family depended on it! If only his sister had been there! She was intelligent; she had begun to cry while Gregor was still lying quietly on his back. And no doubt the chief clerk, so partial to ladies, would have been guided by her; she would have shut the door of the flat and in the hall talked him out of his horror. But she was not there, and Gregor would have to handle the situation himself. And without remembering that he was still unaware what powers of movement he possessed, without even remembering that his words in all possibility, indeed in all likelihood, would again be unintelligible, he let go the wing of the door, pushed himself through the opening, started to walk toward the chief clerk, who was already ridiculously clinging with both hands to the railing on the landing; but immediately, as he was feeling for a support, he fell down with a little cry upon all his numerous legs. Hardly was he down when he experienced for the first time this morning a sense of physical comfort; his legs had firm ground under them; they were completely obedient, as he noted with joy; they even strove to carry him forward in whatever direction he chose; and he was inclined to believe that a final relief from all his sufferings was at hand. But in the same moment as he found himself on the floor, rocking with suppressed eagerness to move, not far from his mother, indeed just in front of her, she, who had seemed so completely crushed, sprang all at once to her feet, her arms and fingers outspread, cried: "Help, for God's sake, help!" bent her head down as if to see Gregor better, yet on the contrary kept backing senselessly away; had quite forgotten that the laden table stood behind her; sat upon it hastily, as if in absence of mind, when she bumped into it; and seemed altogether unaware that the big coffeepot beside her was upset and pouring coffee in a flood over the carpet.

"Mother, Mother," said Gregor in a low voice and looked up at her. The chief clerk, for the moment, had quite slipped from his mind; instead, he could not resist snapping his jaws together at the sight of the streaming coffee. That made his mother scream again, she fled from the table and fell into the arms of his father, who hastened to catch her. But Gregor now had no time to spare for his parents; the chief clerk was already on the stairs; with his chin on the banisters he was taking one last backward look. Gregor made a spring, to be as sure as possible of overtaking him; the chief clerk must have divined his intention, for he leaped down several steps and vanished; he was still yelling "Ugh!" and it echoed through the whole staircase.

Unfortunately, the flight of the chief clerk seemed completely to upset Gregor's father, who had remained relatively calm until now, for instead of running after the man himself, or at least not hindering Gregor in his pursuit, he seized in his right hand the walking stick that the chief clerk had left behind on a chair, together with a hat and greatcoat, snatched in his left hand a large newspaper from the table, and began stamping his feet and flourishing the stick and the newspaper to drive Gregor back into his room. No entreaty of Gregor's availed, indeed no entreaty was even understood, however humbly he bent his head his father only stamped on the floor the more loudly. Behind his father his mother had torn open a window, despite the cold weather, and was leaning far out of it with her face in her hands. A strong draught set in from the street to the staircase, the window curtains blew in, the newspapers on the table fluttered, stray pages whisked over the floor. Pitilessly Gregor's father drove him back, hissing and crying "Shoo!" like a savage. But Gregor was quite unpracticed in walking backwards, it really was a slow business. If he only had a chance to turn around he could get back to his room at once, but he was afraid of exasperating his father by the slowness of such a rotation and at any moment the stick in his father's hand might hit him a fatal blow on the back or on the head. In the end, however, nothing else was left for him to do since to his horror he observed that in moving backwards he could not even control the direction he took; and so, keeping an anxious eye on his father all the time over his shoulder, he began to turn around as quickly as he could, which was in reality very slowly. Perhaps his father noted his good intentions, for he did not interfere except every now and then to help him in the maneuver from a distance with the point of the stick. If only he would have stopped making that unbearable hissing noise! It made Gregor quite lose his head. He had turned around almost completely when the hissing noise so distracted him that he even turned a little the wrong way again. But when at last his head was fortunately right in front of the doorway, it appeared that his body was too broad simply to get through the opening. His father, of course, in his present mood was far from thinking of such a thing as opening the other half of the door, to let Gregor have enough space. He had merely the fixed idea of driving Gregor back into his room as quickly as possible. He would never have suffered Gregor to make the circumstantial preparations for standing up on end and perhaps slipping his way through the door. Maybe he was now making more noise than ever to urge Gregor forward, as if no obstacle impeded him; to Gregor, anyhow, the noise in his rear sounded no longer like the voice of one single father; this was really no joke, and Gregor thrust himself—come what might—into the doorway. One side of his body rose up, he was tilted at an angle in the doorway, his flank was quite bruised, horrid blotches stained the white door, soon he was stuck fast and, left to himself, could not have moved at all, his legs on one side fluttered trembling in the air, those on the other were crushed painfully to the floor—when from behind his father gave him a strong push which was literally a deliverance and he flew far into the room, bleeding freely. The door was slammed behind him with the stick, and then at last there was silence.

II

Not until it was twilight did Gregor awake out of a deep sleep, more like a swoon than a sleep. He would certainly have waked up of his own accord not much later, for he felt himself sufficiently rested and well slept, but it seemed to him as if a fleeting step and a cautious shutting of the door leading into the hall had aroused him. The electric lights in the street cast a pale sheen here and there on the ceiling and the upper surfaces of the furniture, but down below, where he lay, it was dark. Slowly, awkwardly trying out his feelers, which he now first learned to appreciate, he pushed his way to the door to see what had been happening there. His left side felt like one single long, unpleasantly tense scar, and he had actually to limp on his two rows of legs. One little leg, moreover, had been severely damaged in the course of that morning's events—it was almost a miracle that only one had been damaged—and trailed uselessly behind him.

He had reached the door before he discovered what had really drawn him to it: the smell of food. For there stood a basin filled with fresh milk in which floated little sops of white bread. He could almost have laughed with joy, since he was now still hungrier than in the morning, and he dipped his head almost over the eyes straight into the milk. But soon in disappointment he withdrew it again; not only did he find it difficult to feed because of his tender left side—and he could only feed with the palpitating collaboration of his whole body—he did not like the milk either, although milk had been his favorite drink and that was certainly why his sister had set it there for him, indeed it was almost with repulsion that he turned away from the basin and crawled back to the middle of the room.

He could see through the crack of the door that the gas was turned on in the living room, but while usually at this time his father made a habit of reading the afternoon newspaper in a loud voice to his mother and occasionally to his sister as well, not a sound was now to be heard. Well, perhaps his father had recently given up this habit of reading aloud, which his sister had mentioned so often in conversation and in her letters. But there was the same silence all around, although the flat was certainly not empty of occupants. "What a quiet life our family has been leading," said Gregor to himself, and as he sat there motionless staring into the darkness he felt great pride in the fact that he had been able to provide such a life for his parents and sister in such a fine flat. But what if all the quiet, the comfort, the contentment were now to end in horror? To keep himself from being lost in such thoughts Gregor took refuge in movement and crawled up and down the room.

Once during the long evening one of the side doors was opened a little and quickly shut again, later the other side door too; someone had apparently wanted to come in and then thought better of it. Gregor now stationed himself immediately before the living-room door, determined to persuade any hesitating visitor to come in or at least to discover who it might be; but the door was not opened again and he waited in vain. In the early morning, when the doors were locked, they had all wanted to come in, now that he had opened one door and the other had apparently been opened during the day, no one came in and even the keys were on the other side of the doors.

It was late at night before the gas went out in the living room, and Gregor could easily tell that his parents and his sister had all stayed awake until then, for he could clearly hear the three of them stealing away on tiptoe. No one was likely to visit him, not until the morning, that was certain; so he had plenty of time to meditate at his leisure on how he was to arrange his life afresh. But the lofty, empty room in which he had to lie flat on the floor filled him with an apprehension he could not account for, since it had been his very own room for the past five years—and with a half-unconscious action, not without a slight feeling of shame, he scuttled under the sofa, where he felt comfortable at once, although his back was a little cramped and he could not lift his head up, and his only regret was that his body was too broad to get the whole of it under the sofa.

He stayed there all night, spending the time partly in a light slumber, from which his hunger kept waking him up with a start, and partly in worrying and sketching vague hopes, which all led to the same conclusion, that he must lie low for the present and, by exercising patience and the utmost consideration, help the family to bear the inconvenience he was bound to cause them in his present condition.

Very early in the morning, it was still almost night, Gregor had the chance to test the strength of his new resolutions, for his sister, nearly fully dressed, opened the door from the hall and peered in. She did not see him at once, yet when she caught sight of him under the sofa—well, he had to be somewhere, he couldn't have flown away, could he?—she was so startled that without being able to help it she slammed the door shut again. But as if regretting her behavior she opened the door again immediately and came in on tiptoe, as if she were visiting an invalid or even a stranger. Gregor had pushed his head forward to the very edge of the sofa and watched her. Would she notice that he had left the milk standing, and not for lack of hunger, and would she bring in some other kind of food more to his taste? If she did not do it of her own accord, he would rather starve than draw her attention to the fact, although he felt a wild impulse to dart out from under the sofa, throw himself at her feet, and beg her for something to eat. But his sister at once noticed, with surprise, that the basin was still full, except for a little milk that had been spilled all around it, she lifted it immediately, not with her bare hands, true, but with a cloth and carried it away. Gregor was wildly curious to know what she would bring instead, and made various speculations about it. Yet what she actually did next, in the goodness of her heart, he could never have guessed at. To find out what he liked she brought him a whole selection of food, all set out on an old newspaper. There were old, half-decayed vegetables, bones from last night's supper covered with a white sauce that had thickened; some raisins and almonds; a piece of cheese that Gregor would have called uneatable two days ago; a dry roll of bread, a buttered roll, and a roll both buttered and salted. Besides all that, she set down again the same basin, into which she had poured some water, and which was apparently to be reserved for his exclusive use. And with fine tact, knowing that Gregor would not eat in her presence, she withdrew quickly and even turned the key, to let him understand that he could take his ease as much as he liked. Gregor's legs all whizzed toward the food. His wounds must have healed completely, moreover, for he felt no disability, which amazed him and made him reflect how more than a month ago he had cut one finger a little with a knife and had still suffered pain from the wound only the day before yesterday. Am I less sensitive now? he thought, and sucked greedily at the cheese, which above all the other edibles attracted him at once and strongly. One after another and with tears of satisfaction in his eyes he quickly devoured the cheese, the vegetables, and the sauce; the fresh food, on the other hand, had no charms for him, he could not even stand the smell of it and actually dragged away to some little distance the things he could eat. He had long finished his meal and was only lying lazily on the same spot when his sister turned the key slowly as a sign for him to retreat. That roused him at once, although he was nearly asleep, and he hurried under the sofa again. But it took considerable self-control for him to stay under the sofa, even for the short time his sister was in the room, since the large meal had swollen his body somewhat and he was so cramped he could hardly breathe. Slight attacks of breathlessness affected him and his eyes were starting a little out of his head as he watched his unsuspecting sister sweeping together with a broom not only the remains of what he had eaten but even the things he had not touched, as if these were now of no use to anyone, and hastily shoveling it all into a bucket, which she covered with a wooden lid and carried away. Hardly had she turned her back when Gregor came from under the sofa and stretched and puffed himself out.

In this manner Gregor was fed, once in the early morning while his parents and the servant girl were still asleep, and a second time after they had all had their midday dinner, for then his parents took a short nap and the servant girl could be sent out on some errand or other by his sister. Not that they would have wanted him to starve, of course, but perhaps they could not have borne to know more about his feeding than from hearsay, perhaps too his sister wanted to spare them such little anxieties wherever possible, since they had quite enough to bear as it was.

Under what pretext the doctor and the locksmith had been got rid of on that first morning Gregor could not discover, for since what he said was not understood by the others it never struck any of them, not even his sister, that he could understand what they said, and so whenever his sister came into his room he had to content himself with hearing her utter only a sigh now and then and an occasional appeal to the saints. Later on, when she had got a little used to the situation—of course she could never get completely used to it—she sometimes threw out a remark which was kindly meant or could be so interpreted. "Well, he liked his dinner today," she would say when Gregor had made a good clearance of his food; and when he had not eaten, which gradually happened more and more often, she would say almost sadly: "Everything's been left standing again."

But although Gregor could get no news directly, he overheard a lot from the neighboring rooms, and as soon as voices were audible, he would run to the door of the room concerned and press his whole body against it. In the first few days especially there was no conversation that did not refer to him somehow, even if only indirectly. For two whole days there were family consultations at every mealtime about what should be done; but also between meals the same subject was discussed, for there were always at least two members of the family at home, since no one wanted to be alone in the flat and to leave it quite empty was unthinkable. And on the very first of these days the household cook—it was not quite clear what and how much she knew of the situation—went down on her knees to his mother and begged leave to go, and when she departed, a quarter of an hour later, gave thanks for her dismissal with tears in her eyes as if for the greatest benefit that could have been conferred on her, and without any prompting swore a solemn oath that she would never say a single word to anyone about what had happened.

Now Gregor's sister had to cook too, helping her mother; true, the cooking did not amount to much, for they ate scarcely anything. Gregor was always hearing one of the family vainly urging another to eat and getting no answer but: "Thanks, I've had all I want," or something similar. Perhaps they drank nothing either. Time and again his sister kept asking his father if he wouldn't like some beer and offered kindly to go and fetch it herself, and when he made no answer suggested that she could ask the concierge to fetch it, so that he need feel no sense of obligation, but then a round "No" came from his father and no more was said about it.

In the course of that very first day Gregor's father explained the family's financial position and prospects to both his mother and his sister. Now and then he rose from the table to get some voucher or memorandum out of the small safe he had rescued from the collapse of his business five years earlier. One could hear him opening the compli-cated lock and rustling papers out and shutting it again. This statement made by his father was the first cheerful information Gregor had heard since his imprisonment. He had been of the opinion that nothing at all was left over from his father's business; at least his father had never said anything to the contrary, and of course he had never asked him directly. At that time Gregor's sole desire was to do his utmost to help the family to forget as soon as possible the catastrophe that had over-whelmed the business and thrown them all into a state of complete despair. And so he had set to work with unusual ardor and almost overnight had become a commercial traveler instead of a little clerk, with of course much greater chances of earning money, and his success was immediately translated into good round coin which he could lay on the table for his amazed and happy family. These had been fine times, and they had never recurred, at least not with the same sense of glory, although later on Gregor had earned so much money that he was able to meet the expenses of the whole household and did so. They had simply got used to it, both the family and Gregor; the money was gratefully accepted and gladly given, but there was no special uprush of warm feeling. With his sister alone had he remained intimate, and it was a secret plan of his that she, who loved music, unlike himself, and could play movingly on the violin, should be sent next year to study at the Conservatorium, despite the great expense that would entail, which must be made up in some other way. During his brief visits home the Conservatorium was often mentioned in the talks he had with his sis-ter, but always as merely a beautiful dream which could never come true, and his parents discouraged even these innocent references to it; yet Gregor had made up his mind firmly about it and meant to an-nounce the fact with due solemnity on Christmas Day.

Such were the thoughts, completely futile in his present condition, that went through his head as he stood clinging upright to the door and listening. Sometimes out of sheer weariness he had to give up listening and let his head fall negligently against the door, but he always had to pull himself together again at once, for even the slight sound his head made was audible next door and brought all conversation to a stop. "What can he be doing now?" his father would say after a while, obviously turning toward the door, and only then would the interrupted conversation gradually be set going again.

Gregor was now informed as amply as he could wish—for his father tended to repeat himself in his explanations, partly because it was a long time since he had handled such matters and partly because his mother could not always grasp things at once—that a certain amount of investments, a very small amount it was true, had survived the wreck of their fortunes and had even increased a little because the dividends had not been touched meanwhile. And besides that, the money Gregor brought home every month—he had kept only a few dollars for himself—had never quite been used up and now amounted to a small capital sum. Behind the door Gregor nodded his head eagerly, rejoiced at this evidence of unexpected thrift and foresight. True, he could really have paid off some more of his father's debts to the chief with this extra money, and so brought much nearer the day on which he could quit his job, but doubtless it was better the way his father had arranged it.

Yet this capital was by no means sufficient to let the family live on the interest of it; for one year, perhaps, or at the most two, they could live on the principal, that was all. It was simply a sum that was not to be touched and should be kept for a rainy day; money for living expenses would have to be earned. Now his father was still hale enough but an old man, and he had done no work for the past five years and could not be expected to do much; during these five years, the first years of leisure in his laborious though unsuccessful life, he had grown rather fat and become sluggish. And Gregor's old mother, how was she to earn a living with her asthma, which troubled her even when she walked through the flat and kept her lying on a sofa every other day panting for breath beside an open window? And was his sister to earn her bread, she who was still a child of seventeen and whose life hitherto had been so pleasant, consisting as it did in dressing herself nicely, sleeping long, helping in the housekeeping, going out to a few modest entertainments, and above all playing the violin? At first whenever the need for earning money was mentioned Gregor let go his hold on the door and threw himself down on the cool leather sofa beside it, he felt so hot with shame and grief.

Often he just lay there the long nights through without sleeping at all, scrabbling for hours on the leather. Or he nerved himself to the great effort of pushing an armchair to the window, then crawled up over the window sill and, braced against the chair, leaned against the windowpanes, obviously in some recollection of the sense of freedom that looking out of a window always used to give him. For in reality day by day things that were even a little way off were growing dimmer to his sight; the hospital across the street, which he used to execrate for being all too often before his eyes, was now quite beyond his range of vision, and if he had not known that he lived in Charlotte Street, a quiet street but still a city street, he might have believed that his window gave on a desert waste where gray sky and gray land blended indistinguishably into each other. His quick-witted sister only needed to observe twice that the armchair stood by the window; after that whenever she had tidied the room she always pushed the chair back to the same place at the window and even left the inner casements open.

If he could have spoken to her and thanked her for all she had to do for him, he could have borne her ministrations better; as it was, they oppressed him. She certainly tried to make as light as possible of whatever was disagreeable in her task, and as time went on she succeeded, of course, more and more, but time brought more enlightenment to Gregor too. The very way she came in distressed him. Hardly was she in the room when she rushed to the window, without even taking time to shut the door, careful as she was usually to shield the sight of Gregor's room from the others, and as if she were almost suffocating tore the casements open with hasty fingers, standing then in the open draught for a while even in the bitterest cold and drawing deep breaths. This noisy scurry of hers upset Gregor twice a day; he would crouch trembling under the sofa all the time, knowing quite well that she would certainly have spared him such a disturbance had she found it at all possible to stay in his presence without opening the window.

On one occasion, about a month after Gregor's metamorphosis, when there was surely no reason for her to be still startled at his appearance, she came a little earlier than usual and found him gazing out of the window, quite motionless, and thus well placed to look like a bogey. Gregor would not have been surprised had she not come in at all, for she could not immediately open the window while he was there, but not only did she retreat, she jumped back as if in alarm and banged the door shut; a stranger might well have thought that he had been lying in wait for her there meaning to bite her. Of course he hid himself under the sofa at once, but he had to wait until midday before she came again, and she seemed more ill at ease than usual. This made him realize how repulsive the sight of him still was to her, and that it was bound to go on being repulsive, and what an effort it must cost her not to run away even from the sight of the small portion of his body that stuck out from under the sofa. In order to spare her that, therefore, one day he carried a sheet on his back to the sofa—it cost him four hours' labor—and arranged it there in such a way as to hide him completely, so that even if she were to bend down she could not see him. Had she considered the sheet unnecessary, she would certainly have stripped it off the sofa again, for it was clear enough that this curtaining and confining of himself was not likely to conduce to Gregor's comfort, but she left it where it was, and Gregor even fancied that he caught a thankful glance from her eye when he lifted the sheet a very little with his head to see how she was taking the new arrangement.

For the first fortnight his parents could not bring themselves to the point of entering his room, and he often heard them expressing their appreciation of his sister's activities, whereas formerly they had frequently scolded her for being as they thought a somewhat useless daughter. But now, both of them often waited outside the door, his father and his mother, while his sister tidied his room, and as soon as she came out she had to tell them exactly how things were in the room, what Gregor had eaten, how he had conducted himself this time, and whether there was not perhaps some slight improvement in his condition. His mother, moreover, began relatively soon to want to visit him, but his father and sister dissuaded her at first with arguments which Gregor listened to very attentively and altogether approved. Later, however, she had to be held back by main force, and when she cried out: "Do let me in to Gregor, he is my unfortunate son! Can't you understand that I must go to him?" Gregor thought that it might be well to have her come in, not every day, of course, but perhaps once a week; she understood things, after all, much better than his sister, who was only a child despite the efforts she was making and had perhaps taken on so difficult a task merely out of childish thoughtlessness.

Gregor's desire to see his mother was soon fulfilled. During the daytime he did not want to show himself at the window, out of consideration for his parents, but he could not crawl very far around the few square yards of floor space he had, nor could he bear lying quietly at rest all during the night, while he was fast losing any interest he had ever taken in food, so that for mere recreation he had formed the habit of crawling crisscross over the walls and ceiling. He especially enjoyed hanging suspended from the ceiling; it was much better than lying on the floor; one could breathe more freely; one's body swung and rocked lightly; and in the almost blissful absorption induced by this suspension it could happen to his own surprise that he let go and fell plump on the floor. Yet he now had his body much better under control than formerly, and even such a big fall did him no harm. His sister at once remarked the new distraction Gregor had found for himself—he left traces behind him of the sticky stuff on his soles wherever he crawled—and she got the idea in her head of giving him as wide a field as possible to crawl in and of removing the pieces of furniture that hindered him, above all the chest of drawers and the writing desk. But that was more than she could manage all by herself; she did not dare ask her father to help her; and as for the servant girl, a young creature of sixteen who had the courage to stay on after the cook's departure, she could not be asked to help, for she had begged as a special favor that she might keep the kitchen door locked and open it only on a definite summons; so there was nothing left but to apply to her mother at an hour when her father was out. And the old lady did come, with exclamations of joyful eagerness, which, however, died away at the door of Gregor's room. Gregor's sister, of course, went in first, to see that everything was in order before letting his mother enter. In great haste Gregor pulled the sheet lower and rucked it more in folds so that it really looked as if it had been thrown accidentally over the sofa. And this time he did not peer out from under it; he renounced the pleasure of seeing his mother on this occasion and was only glad that she had come at all. "Come in, he's out of sight," said his sister, obviously leading her mother in by the hand. Gregor could now hear the two women struggling to shift the heavy old chest from its place, and his sister claiming the greater part of the labor for herself, without listening to the admonitions of her mother, who feared she might overstrain herself. It took a long time. After at least a quarter of an hour's tugging his mother objected that the chest had better be left where it was, for in the first place it was too heavy and could never be got out before his father came home, and standing in the middle of the room like that it would only hamper Gregor's movements, while in the second place it was not at all certain that removing the furniture would be doing a service to Gregor. She was inclined to think to the contrary; the sight of the naked walls made her own heart heavy, and why shouldn't Gregor have the same feeling, considering that he had been used to his furniture for so long and might feel forlorn without it. "And doesn't it look," she concluded in a low voice—in fact she had been almost whispering all the time as if to avoid letting Gregor, whose exact whereabouts she did not know, hear even the tones of her voice, for she was convinced that he could not understand her words—"doesn't it look as if we were showing him, by taking away his furniture, that we have given up hope of his ever getting better and are just leaving him coldly to himself? I think it would be best to keep his room exactly as it has always been, so that when he comes back to us he will find everything unchanged and be able all the more easily to forget what has happened in between."

On hearing these words from his mother Gregor realized that the lack of all direct human speech for the past two months together with the monotony of family life must have confused his mind, otherwise he could not account for the fact that he had quite earnestly looked forward to having his room emptied of furnishing. Did he really want his warm room, so comfortably fitted with old family furniture, to be turned into a naked den in which he would certainly be able to crawl unhampered in all directions but at the price of shedding simultaneously all recollection of his human background? He had indeed been so near the brink of forgetfulness that only the voice of his mother, which he had not heard for so long, had drawn him back from it. Nothing should be taken out of his room; everything must stay as it was; he could not dispense with the good influence of the furniture on his state of mind; and even if the furniture did hamper him in his senseless crawling around and around, that was no drawback but a great advantage.

Unfortunately his sister was of the contrary opinion; she had grown accustomed, and not without reason, to consider herself an expert in Gregor's affairs as against her parents, and so her mother's advice was now enough to make her determined on the removal not only of the chest and the writing desk, which had been her first intention, but of all the furniture except the indispensable sofa. This determination was not, of course, merely the outcome of childish recalcitrance and of the self-confidence she had recently developed so unexpectedly and at such cost; she had in fact perceived that Gregor needed a lot of space to crawl about in, while on the other hand he never used the furniture at all, so far as could be seen. Another factor might also have been the enthusiastic temperament of an adolescent girl, which seeks to indulge itself on every opportunity and which now tempted Grete to exaggerate the horror of her brother's circumstances in order that she might do all the more for him. In a room where Gregor lorded it all alone over empty walls no one save herself was likely ever to set foot.

And so she was not to be moved from her resolve by her mother, who seemed moreover to be ill at ease in Gregor's room and therefore unsure of herself, was soon reduced to silence, and helped her daughter as best she could to push the chest outside. Now, Gregor could do without the chest, if need be, but the writing desk he must retain. As soon as the two women had got the chest out of his room, groaning as they pushed it, Gregor stuck his head out from under the sofa to see how he might intervene as kindly and cautiously as possible. But as bad luck would have it, his mother was the first to return, leaving Grete clasping the chest in the room next door where she was trying to shift it all by herself, without of course moving it from the spot. His mother however was not accustomed to the sight of him, it might sicken her and so in alarm Gregor backed quickly to the other end of the sofa, yet could not prevent the sheet from swaying a little in front. That was enough to put her on the alert. She paused, stood still for a moment, and then went back to Grete.

Although Gregor kept reassuring himself that nothing out of the way was happening, but only a few bits of furniture were being changed around, he soon had to admit that all this trotting to and fro of the two women, their little ejaculations, and the scraping of furniture along the floor affected him like a vast disturbance coming from all sides at once, and however much he tucked in his head and legs and cowered to the very floor he was bound to confess that he would not be able to stand it for long. They were clearing his room out; taking away everything he loved; the chest in which he kept his fret saw and other tools was already dragged off; they were now loosening the writing desk which had almost sunk into the floor, the desk at which he had done all his homework when he was at the commercial academy, at the grammar school before that, and, yes, even at the primary school—he had no more time to waste in weighing the good intentions of the two women, whose existence he had by now almost forgotten, for they were so exhausted that they were laboring in silence and nothing could be heard but the heavy scuffling of their feet.

And so he rushed out—the women were just leaning against the writing desk in the next room to give themselves a breather—and four times changed his direction, since he really did not know what to rescue first, then on the wall opposite, which was already otherwise cleared, he was struck by the picture of the lady muffled in so much fur and quickly crawled up to it and pressed himself to the glass, which was a good surface to hold on to and comforted his hot belly. This picture at least, which was entirely hidden behind him, was going to be removed by nobody. He turned his head toward the door of the living room so as to observe the women when they came back.

They had not allowed themselves much of a rest and were already coming; Grete had twined her arm around her mother and was almost supporting her. "Well, what shall we take now?" said Grete, looking around. Her eyes met Gregor's from the wall. She kept her composure, presumably because of her mother, bent her head down to her mother, to keep her from looking up, and said, although in a fluttering, unpremeditated voice: "Come, hadn't we better go back to the living room for a moment?" Her intentions were clear enough to Gregor, she wanted to bestow her mother in safety and then chase him down from the wall. Well, just let her try it! He clung to his picture and would not give it up. He would rather fly in Grete's face.

But Grete's words had succeeded in disquieting her mother, who took a step to one side, caught sight of the huge brown mass on the flowered wallpaper, and before she was really conscious that what she saw was Gregor, screamed in a loud, hoarse voice: "Oh God, oh God!" fell with outspread arms over the sofa as if giving up, and did not move. "Gregor!" cried his sister, shaking her fist and glaring at him. This was the first time she had directly addressed him since his metamorphosis. She ran into the next room for some aromatic essence with which to rouse her mother from her fainting fit. Gregor wanted to help too—there was still time to rescue the picture—but he was stuck fast to the glass and had to tear himself loose; he then ran after his sister into the next room as if he could advise her, as he used to do; but then had to stand helplessly behind her; she meanwhile searched among various small bottles and when she turned around started in alarm at the sight of him; one bottle fell on the floor and broke; a splinter of glass cut Gregor's face and some kind of corrosive medicine splashed him; without pausing a moment longer Grete gathered up all the bottles she could carry and ran to her mother with them; she banged the door shut with her foot. Gregor was now cut off from his mother, who was perhaps nearly dying because of him; he dared not open the door for fear of frightening away his sister, who had to stay with her mother; there was nothing he could do but wait; and harassed by self-reproach and worry he began now to crawl to and fro, over everything, walls, furniture, and ceiling, and finally in his despair, when the whole room seemed to be reeling around him, fell down onto the middle of the big table.

A little while elapsed, Gregor was still lying there feebly and all around was quiet, perhaps that was a good omen. Then the doorbell rang. The servant girl was of course locked in her kitchen, and Grete would have to open the door. It was his father. "What's been happening?" were his first words; Grete's face must have told him everything. Grete answered in a muffled voice, apparently hiding her head on his breast: "Mother has been fainting, but she's better now. Gregor's broken loose." "Just what I expected," said his father, "just what I've been telling you, but you women would never listen." It was clear to Gregor that his father had taken the worst interpretation of Grete's all too brief statement and was assuming that Gregor had been guilty of some violent act. Therefore Gregor must now try to propitiate his father, since he had neither time nor means for an explanation. And so he fled to the door of his own room and crouched against it, to let his father see as soon as he came in from the hall that his son had the good intention of getting back into his room immediately and that it was not necessary to drive him there, but that if only the door were opened he would disappear at once.

Yet his father was not in the mood to perceive such fine distinctions. "Ah!" he cried as soon as he appeared, in a tone that sounded at once angry and exultant. Gregor drew his head back from the door and lifted it to look at his father. Truly, this was not the father he had imagined to himself; admittedly he had been too absorbed of late in his new recreation of crawling over the ceiling to take the same interest as before in what was happening elsewhere in the flat, and he ought really to be prepared for some changes. And yet, and yet, could that be his father? The man who used to lie wearily sunk in bed whenever Gregor set out on a business journey; who welcomed him back of an evening lying in a long chair in a dressing gown; who could not really rise to his feet but only lifted his arms in greeting, and on the rare occasions when he did go out with his family, on one or two Sundays a year and on highest holidays, walked between Gregor and his mother, who were slow walkers anyhow, even more slowly than they did, muffled in his old greatcoat, shuffling laboriously forward with the help of his crook-handled stick which he set down most cautiously at every step and, whenever he wanted to say anything, nearly always came to a full stop and gathered his escort around him? Now he was standing there in fine shape; dressed in a smart blue uniform with gold buttons, such as bank messengers wear; his strong double chin bulged over the stiff collar of his jacket; from under his bushy eyebrows his black eyes darted fresh and penetrating glances; his onetime tangled white hair had been combed flat on either side of a shining and carefully exact parting. He pitched his cap, which bore a gold monogram, probably the badge of some bank, in a wide sweep across the whole room onto a sofa and with the tail-ends of his jacket thrown back, his hands in his trouser pockets, advanced with a grim visage toward Gregor. Likely enough he did not himself know what he meant to do; at any rate he lifted his feet uncommonly high, and Gregor was dumbfounded at the enormous size of his shoe soles. But Gregor could not risk standing up to him, aware as he had been from the very first day of his new life that his father believed only the severest measures suitable for dealing with him. And so he ran before his father, stopping only when he stopped and scuttling forward again when his father made any kind of move. In this way they circled the room several times without anything decisive happening, indeed the whole operation did not even look like a pursuit because it was carried out so slowly. And so Gregor did not leave the floor, for he feared that his father might take as a piece of peculiar wickedness any excursion of his over the walls of the ceiling. All the same, he could not stay this course much longer, for while his father took one step he had to carry out a whole series of movements. He was already beginning to feel breathless, just as in his former life his lungs had not been very dependable. As he was staggering along, trying to concentrate his energy on running, hardly keeping his eyes open; in his dazed state never even thinking of any other escape than simply going forward; and having almost forgotten that the walls were free to him, which in this room were well provided with finely carved pieces of furniture full of knobs and crevices—suddenly something lightly flung landed close behind him and rolled before him. It was an apple; a second apple followed immediately; Gregor came to a stop in alarm; there was no point in running on, for his father was determined to bombard him. He had filled his pockets with fruit from the dish on the sideboard and was now shying apple after apple, without taking particularly good aim for the moment. The small red apples rolled about the floor as if magnetized and cannoned into each other. An apple thrown without much force grazed Gregor's back and glanced off harmlessly. But another following immediately landed right on his back and sank in; Gregor wanted to drag himself forward, as if this startling, incredible pain could be left behind him; but he felt as if nailed to the spot and flattened himself out in a complete derangement of all his senses. With his last conscious look he saw the door of his room being torn open and his mother rushing out ahead of his screaming sister, in her underbodice, for her daughter had loosened her clothing to let her breathe more freely and recover from her swoon, he saw his mother rushing toward his father, leaving one after another behind her on the floor her loosened petticoats, stumbling over her petticoats straight to his father and embracing him, in complete union with him—but here Gregor's sight began to fail—with her hands clasped around his father's neck as she begged for her son's life.

The serious injury done to Gregor, which disabled him for more than a month—the apple went on sticking in his body as a visible reminder, since no one ventured to remove it—seemed to have made even his father recollect that Gregor was a member of the family, despite his present condition and repulsive shape, and ought not to be treated as an enemy, that, on the contrary, family duty required the suppression of disgust and the exercise of patience, nothing but patience.

And although his injury had impaired, probably forever, his powers of movement, and for the time being it took him long, long minutes to creep across his room like an old invalid—there was no question now of crawling up the wall—yet in his own opinion he was sufficiently compensated for this worsening of his condition by the fact that toward evening the living-room door, which he used to watch intently for an hour or two beforehand, was always thrown open, so that lying in the darkness of his room, invisible to the family, he could see them all at the lamp-lit table and listen to their talk, by general consent as it were, very different from his earlier eavesdropping.

True, their intercourse lacked the lively character of former times, which he had always called to mind with a certain wistfulness in the small hotel bedrooms where he had been wont to throw himself down, tired out, on damp bedding. They were now mostly very silent. Soon after supper his father would fall asleep in his armchair; his mother and sister would admonish each other to be silent; his mother, bending low over the lamp, stitched at fine sewing for an underwear firm; his sister, who had taken a job as a salesgirl, was learning shorthand and French in the evenings on the chance of bettering herself. Sometimes his father woke up, and as if quite unaware that he had been sleeping said to his mother: "What a lot of sewing you're doing today!" and at once fell asleep again, while the two women exchanged a tired smile.

With a kind of mulishness his father persisted in keeping his uniform on even in the house; his dressing gown hung uselessly on its peg and he slept fully dressed where he sat, as if he were ready for service at any moment and even here only at the beck and call of his superior. As a result, his uniform, which was not brand-new to start with, began to look dirty, despite all the loving care of the mother and sister to keep it clean, and Gregor often spent whole evenings gazing at the many greasy spots on the garment, gleaming with gold buttons always in a high state of polish, in which the old man sat sleeping in extreme discomfort and yet quite peacefully.

As soon as the clock struck ten his mother tried to rouse his father with gentle words and to persuade him after that to get into bed, for sitting there he could not have a proper sleep and that was what he needed most, since he had to go on duty at six. But with the mulishness that had obsessed him since he became a bank messenger he always insisted on staying longer at the table, although he regularly fell asleep again and in the end only with the greatest trouble could be got out of his armchair and into his bed. However insistently Gregor's mother and sister kept urging him with gentle reminders, he would go on slowly shaking his head for a quarter of an hour, keeping his eyes shut, and refuse to get to his feet. The mother plucked at his sleeve, whispering endearments in his ear, the sister left her lessons to come to her mother's help, but Gregor's father was not to be caught. He would only sink down deeper in his chair. Not until the two women hoisted him up by the armpits did he open his eyes and look at them both, one after the other, usually with the remark: "This is a life. This is the peace and quiet of my old age." And leaning on the two of them he would heave himself up, with difficulty, as if he were a great burden to himself, suffer them to lead him as far as the door and then wave them off and go on alone, while the mother abandoned her needlework and the sister her pen in order to run after him and help him farther.

Who could find time, in this overworked and tired-out family, to bother about Gregor more than was absolutely needful? The household was reduced more and more; the servant girl was turned off; a gigantic bony charwoman with white hair flying around her head came in morning and evening to do the rough work; everything else was done by Gregor's mother, as well as great piles of sewing. Even various family ornaments, which his mother and sister used to wear with pride at parties and celebrations, had to be sold, as Gregor discovered of an evening from hearing them all discuss the prices obtained. But what they lamented most was the fact that they could not leave the flat which was much too big for their present circumstances, because they could not think of any way to shift Gregor. Yet Gregor saw well enough that consideration for him was not the main difficulty preventing the removal, for they could have easily shifted him in some suitable box with a few air holes in it; what really kept them from moving into another flat was rather their own complete hopelessness and the belief that they had been singled out for a misfortune such as had never happened to any of their relations or acquaintances. They fulfilled to the uttermost all that the world demands of poor people, the father fetched breakfast for the small clerks in the bank, the mother devoted her energy to making underwear for strangers, the sister trotted to and fro behind the counter at the behest of customers, but more than this they had not the strength to do. And the wound in Gregor's back began to nag at him afresh when his mother and sister, after getting his father into bed, came back again, left their work lying, drew close to each other, and sat cheek by cheek; when his mother, pointing towards his room, said: "Shut that door now, Grete," and he was left again in darkness, while next door the women mingled their tears or perhaps sat dry-eyed staring at the table.

Gregor hardly slept at all by night or by day. He was often haunted by the idea that next time the door opened he would take the family's affairs in hand again just as he used to do; once more, after this long interval, there appeared in his thoughts the figures of the chief and the chief clerk, the commercial travelers and the apprentices, the porter who was so dull-witted, two or three friends in other firms, a chamber-maid in one of the rural hotels, a sweet and fleeting memory, a cashier in a milliner's shop, whom he had wooed earnestly but too slowly— they all appeared, together with strangers or people he had quite forgotten, but instead of helping him and his family they were one and all unapproachable and he was glad when they vanished. At other times he would not be in the mood to bother about his family, he was only filled with rage at the way they were neglecting him, and although he had no clear idea of what he might care to eat he would make plans for getting into the larder to take the food that was after all his due, even if he were not hungry. His sister no longer took thought to bring him what might especially please him, but in the morning and at noon before she went to business hurriedly pushed into his room with her foot any food that was available, and in the evening cleared it out again with one sweep of the broom, heedless of whether it had been merely tasted, or—as most frequently happened—left untouched. The cleaning of his room, which she now did always in the evenings, could not have been more hastily done. Streaks of dirt stretched along the walls, here and there lay balls of dust and filth. At first Gregor used to station himself in some particularly filthy corner when his sister arrived, in order to reproach her with it, so to speak. But he could have sat there for weeks without getting her to make any improvement; she could see the dirt as well as he did, but she had simply made up her mind to leave it alone. And yet, with a touchiness that was new to her, which seemed anyhow to have infected the whole family, she jealously guarded her claim to be the sole caretaker of Gregor's room. His mother once subjected his room to a thorough cleaning, which was achieved only by means of several buckets of water—all this dampness of course upset Gregor too and he lay widespread, sulky, and motionless on the sofa—but she was well punished for it. Hardly had his sister noticed the changed aspect of his room that evening than she rushed in high dudgeon into the living room and, despite the imploringly raised hands of her mother, burst into a storm of weeping, while her parents—her father had of course been startled out of his chair—looked on at first in helpless amazement; then they too began to go into action; the father reproached the mother on his right for not having left the cleaning of Gregor's room to his sister; shrieked at the sister on his left that never again was she to be allowed to clean Gregor's room; while the mother tried to pull the father into his bedroom, since he was beyond himself with agitation; the sister, shaken with sobs, then beat upon the table with her small fists; and Gregor hissed loudly with rage because not one of them thought of shutting the door to spare him such a spectacle and so much noise.

Still, even if the sister, exhausted by her daily work, had grown tired of looking after Gregor as she did formerly, there was no need for his mother's intervention or for Gregor's being neglected at all. The charwoman was there. This old widow, whose strong bony frame had enabled her to survive the worst a long life could offer, by no means recoiled from Gregor. Without being in the least curious she had once by chance opened the door of his room and at the sight of Gregor, who, taken by surprise, began to rush to and fro although no one was chasing him, merely stood there with her arms folded. From that time she never failed to open his door a little for a moment, morning and evening, to have a look at him. At first she even used to call him to her, with words which apparently she took to be friendly, such as: "Come along, then, you old dung beetle!" or "Look at the old dung beetle, then!" To such allocutions Gregor made no answer, but stayed motionless where he was, as if the door had never been opened. Instead of being allowed to disturb him so senselessly whenever the whim took her, she should rather have been ordered to clean out his room daily, that charwoman! Once, early in the morning—heavy rain was lashing on the windowpanes, perhaps a sign that spring was on the way—Gregor was so exasperated when she began addressing him again that he ran at her, as if to attack her, although slowly and feebly enough. But the charwoman, instead of showing fright merely lifted high a chair that happened to be beside the door, and as she stood there with her mouth wide open it was clear that she meant to shut it only when she brought the chair down on Gregor's back. "So you're not coming any nearer?" she asked, as Gregor turned away again, and quietly put the chair back into the corner.

Gregor was now hardly eating anything. Only when he happened to pass the food laid out for him did he take a bit of something in his mouth as a pastime, kept it there for an hour at a time, and usually spat it out again. At first he thought it was chagrin over the state of his room that prevented him from eating, yet he soon got used to the various changes in his room. It had become a habit in the family to push into his room things there was no room for elsewhere, and there were plenty of these now, since one of the rooms had been let to three lodgers. These serious gentlemen—all three of them with full beards, as Gregor once observed through a crack in the door—had a passion for order, not only in their own room but, since they were now members of the household, in all its arrangements, especially in the kitchen. Superfluous, not to say dirty, objects they could not bear. Besides, they had brought with them most of the furnishings they needed. For this reason many things could be dispensed with that it was no use trying to sell but that should not be thrown away either. All of them found their way into Gregor's room. The ash can likewise and the kitchen garbage can. Anything that was not needed for the moment was simply flung into Gregor's room by the charwoman, who did everything in a hurry; fortunately Gregor usually saw only the object, whatever it was, and the hand that held it. Perhaps she intended to take the things away again as time and opportunity offered, or to collect them until she could throw them all out in a heap, but in fact they just lay wherever she happened to throw them, except when Gregor pushed his way through the junk heap and shifted it somewhat, at first out of necessity, because he had not room enough to crawl, but later with increasing enjoyment, although after such excursions, being sad and weary to death, he would lie motionless for hours. And since the lodgers often ate their supper at home in the common living room, the living-room door stayed shut many an evening, yet Gregor reconciled himself quite easily to the shutting of the door, for often enough on evenings when it was opened he had disregarded it entirely and lain in the darkest corner of his room, quite unnoticed by the family. But on one occasion the charwoman left the door open a little and it stayed ajar even when the lodgers came in for supper and the lamp was lit. They set themselves at the top end of the table where formerly Gregor and his father and mother had eaten their meals, unfolded their napkins, and took knife and fork in hand. At once his mother appeared in the other doorway with a dish of meat and close behind her his sister with a dish of potatoes piled high. The food steamed with a thick vapor. The lodgers bent over the food set before them as if to scrutinize it before eating, in fact the man in the middle, who seemed to pass for an authority with the other two, cut a piece of meat as it lay on the dish, obviously to discover if it were tender or should be sent back to the kitchen. He showed satisfaction, and Gregor's mother and sister, who had been watching anxiously, breathed freely and began to smile.

The family itself took its meals in the kitchen. Nonetheless, Gregor's father came into the living room before going into the kitchen and with one prolonged bow, cap in hand, made a round of the table. The lodgers all stood up and murmured something in their beards. When they were alone again they ate their food in almost complete silence. It seemed remarkable to Gregor that among the various noises coming from the table he could always distinguish the sound of their masticating teeth, as if this were a sign to Gregor that one needed teeth in order to eat, and that with toothless jaws even of the finest make one could do nothing. "I'm hungry enough," said Gregor sadly to himself, "but not for that kind of food. How these lodgers are stuffing themselves, and here I am dying of starvation!"

On that very evening—during the whole of his time there Gregor could not remember ever having heard the violin—the sound of violin-playing came from the kitchen. The lodgers had already finished their supper, the one in the middle had brought out a newspaper and given the other two a page apiece, and now they were leaning back at ease reading and smoking. When the violin began to play they pricked up their ears, got to their feet, and went on tiptoe to the hall door where they stood huddled together. Their movements must have been heard in the kitchen, for Gregor's father called out: "Is the violin-playing disturbing you, gentlemen? It can be stopped at once." "On the contrary," said the middle lodger, "could not Fräulein Samsa come and play in this room, beside us, where it is much more convenient and comfortable?" "Oh certainly," cried Gregor's father, as if he were the violin-player. The lodgers came back into the living room and waited. Presently Gregor's father arrived with the music stand, his mother carrying the music and his sister with the violin. His sister quietly made everything ready to start playing; his parents, who had never let rooms before and so had an exaggerated idea of the courtesy due to lodgers, did not venture to sit down on their own chairs; his father leaned against the door, the right hand thrust between two buttons of his livery coat, which was formally buttoned up; but his mother was offered a chair by one of the lodgers and, since she left the chair just where he had happened to put it, sat down in a corner to one side.

Gregor's sister began to play; the father and mother, from either side, intently watched the movements of her hands. Gregor, attracted by the playing, ventured to move forward a little until his head was actually inside the living room. He felt hardly any surprise at his growing lack of consideration for the others; there had been a time when he prided himself on being considerate. And yet just on this occasion he had more reason than ever to hide himself, since, owing to the amount of dust that lay thick in his room and rose into the air at the slightest movement, he too was covered with dust; fluff and hair and remnants of food trailed with him, caught on his back and along his sides; his indifference to everything was much too great for him to turn on his back and scrape himself clean on the carpet, as once he had done several times a day. And in spite of his condition, no shame deterred him from advancing a little over the spotless floor of the living room.

To be sure, no one was aware of him. The family was entirely absorbed in the violin-playing; the lodgers, however, who first of all had stationed themselves, hands in pockets, much too close behind the music stand so that they could all have read the music, which must have bothered his sister, had soon retreated to the window, half whispering with downbent heads, and stayed there while his father turned an anxious eye on them. Indeed, they were making it more than obvious that they had been disappointed in their expectation of hearing good or enjoyable violin-playing, that they had had more than enough of the performance and only out of courtesy suffered a continued disturbance of their peace. From the way they all kept blowing the smoke of their cigars high in the air through nose and mouth one could divine their irritation. And yet Gregor's sister was playing so beautifully. Her face leaned sideways, intently, and sadly her eyes followed the notes of music. Gregor crawled a little farther forward and lowered his head to the ground so that it might be possible for his eyes to meet hers. Was he an animal, that music had such an effect upon him? He felt as if the way were opening before him to the unknown nourishment he craved. He was determined to push forward till he reached his sister, to pull at her skirt and so let her know that she was to come into his room with her violin, for no one here appreciated her playing as he would appreciate it. He would never let her out of his room, at least, not so long as he lived; his frightful appearance would become, for the first time, useful to him; he would watch all the doors of his room at once and spit at intruders; but his sister should need no constraint, she should stay with him of her own free will; she should sit beside him on the sofa, bend down her ear to him, and hear him confide that he had had the firm intention of sending her to the Conservatorium, and that, but for his mishap, last Christmas—surely Christmas was long past?—he would have announced it to everybody without allowing a single objection. After this confession his sister would be so touched that she would burst into tears, and Gregor would then raise himself to her shoulder, and kiss her on the neck, which, now that she went to business, she kept free of any ribbon or collar.

"Mr. Samsa!" cried the middle lodger to Gregor's father, and pointed, without wasting any more words, at Gregor, now working himself slowly forward. The violin fell silent, the middle lodger first smiled to his friends with a shake of the head and then looked at Gregor again. Instead of driving Gregor out, his father seemed to think it more needful to begin by soothing down the lodgers, although they were not at all agitated and apparently found Gregor more entertaining than the violin-playing. He hurried toward them and, spreading out his arms, tried to urge them back into their own room and at the same time to block their view of Gregor. They now began to be really a little angry, one could not tell whether because of the old man's behavior or because it had just dawned on them that all unwittingly they had such a neighbor as Gregor next door. They demanded explanations of his father, they waved their arms like him, tugged uneasily at their beards, and only with reluctance backed toward their room. Meanwhile Gregor's sister, who stood there as if lost when her playing was so abruptly broken off, came to life again, pulled herself together all at once after standing for a while holding violin and bow in nervelessly hanging hands and staring at her music, pushed her violin into the lap of her mother, who was still sitting in her chair fighting asthmatically for breath, and ran into the lodgers' room to which they were now being shepherded by her father rather more quickly than before. One could see pillows and blankets on the beds flying under her accustomed fingers and being laid in order. Before the lodgers had actually reached their room she had finished making the beds and slipped out.

The old man seemed once more to be so possessed by his mulish self-assertiveness that he was forgetting all the respect he should show to his lodgers. He kept driving them on and driving them on until in the very door of the bedroom the middle lodger stamped his foot loudly on the floor and so brought him to a halt. "I beg to announce," said the lodger, lifting one hand and looking also at Gregor's mother and sister, "that because of the disgusting conditions prevailing in this household and family"—here he spat on the floor with emphatic brevity—"I give you notice on the spot. Naturally I won't pay you a penny for the days I have lived here, on the contrary I shall consider bringing an action for damages against you, based on claims—believe me—that will be easily susceptible of proof." He ceased and stared straight in front of him, as if he expected something. In fact his two friends at once rushed into the breach with these words: "And we too give you notice on the spot." On that he seized the door handle and shut the door with a slam.

Gregor's father, groping with his hands, staggered forward and fell into his chair; it looked as if he were stretching himself there for his ordinary evening nap, but the marked jerkings of his head, which were as if uncontrollable, showed that he was far from asleep. Gregor had simply stayed quietly all the time on the spot where the lodgers had espied him. Disappointment at the failure of his plan, perhaps also the weakness arising from extreme hunger, made it impossible for him to move. He feared, with a fair degree of certainty, that at any moment the general tension would discharge itself in a combined attack upon him, and he lay waiting. He did not react even to the noise made by the violin as it fell off his mother's lap from under her trembling fingers and gave out a resonant note.

"My dear parents," said his sister, slapping her hand on the table by way of introduction, "things can't go on like this. Perhaps you don't realize that, but I do. I won't utter my brother's name in the presence of this creature, and so all I say is: we must try to get rid of it. We've tried to look after it and to put up with it as far as humanly possible, and I don't think anyone could reproach us in the slightest."

"She is more than right," said Gregor's father to himself. His mother, who was still choking for lack of breath, began to cough hollowly into her hand with a wild look in her eyes.

His sister rushed over to her and held her forehead. His father's thoughts seemed to have lost their vagueness at Grete's words, he sat more upright, fingering his service cap that lay among the plates still lying on the table from the lodgers' supper, and from time to time looked at the still form of Gregor.

"We must try to get rid of it," his sister now said explicitly to her father, since her mother was coughing too much to hear a word, "it will be the death of both of you, I can see that coming. When one has to work as hard as we do, all of us, one can't stand this continual torment at home on top of it. At least I can't stand it any longer." And she burst into such a passion of sobbing that her tears dropped on her mother's face, where she wiped them off mechanically.

"My dear," said the old man sympathetically, and with evident understanding, "but what can we do?"

Gregor's sister merely shrugged her shoulders to indicate the feeling of helplessness that had now overmastered her during her weeping fit, in contrast to her former confidence.

"If he could understand us," said her father, half questioningly; Grete, still sobbing, vehemently waved a hand to show how unthinkable that was.

"If he could understand us," repeated the old man, shutting his eyes to consider his daughter's conviction that understanding was impossible, "then perhaps we might come to some agreement with him. But as it is—"

"He must go," cried Gregor's sister, "that's the only solution, Father. You must try to get rid of the idea that this is Gregor. The fact that we've believed it for so long is the root of all our trouble. But how can it be Gregor? If this were Gregor, he would have realized long ago that human beings can't live with such a creature, and he'd have gone away on his own accord. Then we wouldn't have any brother, but we'd be able to go on living and keep his memory in honor. As it is, this creature persecutes us, drives away our lodgers, obviously wants the whole apartment to himself, and would have us all sleep in the gutter. Just look, Father," she shrieked all at once, "he's at it again!" And in an access of panic that was quite incomprehensible to Gregor she even quitted her mother, literally thrusting the chair from her as if she would rather sacrifice her mother than stay so near to Gregor, and rushed behind her father, who also rose up, being simply upset by her agitation, and half spread his arms out as if to protect her.

Yet Gregor had not the slightest intention of frightening anyone, far less his sister. He had only begun to turn around in order to crawl back to his room, but it was certainly a startling operation to watch, since because of his disabled condition he could not execute the difficult turning movements except by lifting his head and then bracing it against the floor over and over again. He paused and looked around. His good intention seemed to have been recognized; the alarm had only been momentary. Now they were all watching him in melancholy silence. His mother lay in her chair, her legs outstretched and pressed together, her eyes almost closing for sheer weariness; his father and his sister were sitting beside each other, his sister's arm around the old man's neck.

Perhaps I can go on turning around now, thought Gregor, and began his labors again. He could not stop himself from panting with the effort, and had to pause now and then to take breath. Nor did anyone harass him, he was left entirely to himself. When he had completed the turn-around he began at once to crawl straight back. He was amazed at the distance separating him from his room and could not understand how in his weak state he had managed to accomplish the same journey so recently, almost without remarking it. Intent on crawling as fast as possible, he barely noticed that not a single word, not an ejaculation from his family, interfered with his progress. Only when he was already in the doorway did he turn his head around, not completely, for his neck muscles were getting stiff, but enough to see that nothing had changed behind him except that his sister had risen to her feet. His last glance fell on his mother, who was not quite overcome by sleep.

Hardly was he well inside his room when the door was hastily pushed shut, locked, and bolted. The sudden noise in his rear startled him so much that his little legs gave beneath him. It was his sister who had shown such haste. She had been standing ready waiting and had made a light spring forward, Gregor had not even heard her coming, and she cried "At last!" to her parents as she turned the key in the lock.

"And what now?" said Gregor to himself, looking around in the darkness. Soon he made a discovery that he was now unable to stir a limb. This did not surprise him, rather it seemed unnatural that he should ever actually have been able to move on these feeble little legs. Otherwise he felt relatively comfortable. True, his whole body was aching, but it seemed that the pain was gradually growing less and would finally pass away. The rotting apple in his back and the inflamed area around it, all covered with soft dust, already hardly troubled him. He thought of his family with tenderness and love. The decision that he must disappear was one that he held to even more strongly than his sister, if that were possible. In this state of vacant and peaceful meditation he remained until the tower clock struck three in the morning. The first broadening of light in the world outside the window entered his consciousness once more. Then his head sank to the floor of its own accord and from his nostrils came the last faint flicker of his breath.

When the charwoman arrived early in the morning—what between her strength and her impatience she slammed all the doors so loudly, never mind how often she had been begged not to do so, that no one in the whole apartment could enjoy any quiet sleep after her arrival—she noticed nothing unusual as she took her customary peep into Gregor's room. She thought he was lying motionless on purpose, pretending to be in the sulks; she credited him with every kind of intelligence. Since she happened to have the long-handled broom in her hand she tried to tickle him up with it from the doorway. When that too produced no action she felt provoked and poked at him a little harder, and only when she had pushed him along the floor without meeting any resistance was her attention aroused. It did not take her long to establish the truth of the matter, and her eyes widened, she let out a whistle, yet did not waste much time over it but tore open the door of the Samsas' bedroom and yelled into the darkness at the top of her voice: "Just look at this, it's dead; it's lying here dead and done for!"

Mr. and Mrs. Samsa started up in their double bed and before they realized the nature of the charwoman's announcement had some difficulty in overcoming the shock of it. But then they got out of bed quickly, one on either side, Mr. Samsa throwing a blanket over his shoulders, Mrs. Samsa in nothing but her nightgown; in this array they entered Gregor's room. Meanwhile the door of the living room opened, too, where Grete had been sleeping since the advent of the lodgers; she was completely dressed as if she had not been to bed, which seemed to be confirmed also by the paleness of her face. "Dead?" said Mrs. Samsa, looking questioningly at the charwoman, although she would have investigated for herself, and the fact was obvious enough without investigation. "I should say so," said the charwoman, proving her words by pushing Gregor's corpse a long way to one side with her broomstick. Mrs. Samsa made a movement as if to stop her, but checked it. "Well," said Mr. Samsa, "now thanks be to God." He crossed himself, and the three women followed his example. Grete, whose eyes never left the corpse, said: "Just see how thin he was. It's such a long time since he's eaten anything. The food came out again just as it went in." Indeed, Gregor's body was completely flat and dry, as could only now be seen when it was no longer supported by the legs and nothing prevented one from looking closely at it.

"Come in beside us, Grete, for a little while," said Mrs. Samsa with a tremulous smile, and Grete, not without looking back at the corpse, followed her parents into their bedroom. The charwoman shut the door and opened the window wide. Although it was so early in the morning a certain softness was perceptible in the fresh air. After all, it was already the end of March.

The three lodgers emerged from their room and were surprised to see no breakfast; they had been forgotten. "Where's our breakfast?" said the middle lodger peevishly to the charwoman. But she put her finger to her lips and hastily, without a word, indicated by gestures that they should go into Gregor's room. They did so and stood, their hands in the pockets of their somewhat shabby coats, around Gregor's corpse in the room where it was now fully light.

At that the door of the Samsas' bedroom opened and Mr. Samsa appeared in his uniform, his wife on one arm, his daughter on the other. They all looked a little as if they had been crying; from time to time Grete hid her face on her father's arm.

"Leave my house at once!" said Mr. Samsa, and pointed to the door without disengaging himself from the women. "What do you mean by that?" said the middle lodger, taken somewhat aback, with a feeble smile. The two others put their hands behind them and kept rubbing them together, as if in gleeful expectation of a fine set-to in which they were bound to come off the winners. "I mean just what I say," answered Mr. Samsa, and advanced in a straight line with his two companions toward the lodger. He stood his ground at first quietly, looking at the floor as if his thoughts were taking a new pattern in his head. "Then let us go, by all means," he said, and looked up at Mr. Samsa as if in a sudden access of humility he were expecting some renewed sanction for this decision. Mr. Samsa merely nodded briefly once or twice with meaning eyes. Upon that the lodger really did go with long strides into the hall, his two friends had been listening and had quite stopped rubbing their hands for some moments and now went scuttling after him as if afraid that Mr. Samsa might get into the hall before them and cut them off from their leader. In the hall they all three took their hats from the rack, their sticks from the umbrella stand, bowed in silence, and quitted the apartment. With a suspiciousness that proved quite unfounded Mr. Samsa and the two women followed them out to the landing; leaning over the banister they watched the three figures slowly but surely going down the long stairs, vanishing from sight at a certain turn of the staircase on every floor and coming into view again after a moment or so; the more they dwindled, the more the Samsa family's interest in them dwindled, and when a butcher's boy met and passed them on the stairs coming up proudly with a tray on his head, Mr. Samsa and the two women soon left the landing and as if a burden had been lifted from them went back into their apartment.

They decided to spend this day in resting and going for a stroll; they had not only deserved such a respite from work, but absolutely needed it. And so they sat down at the table and wrote three notes of excuse,

Mr. Samsa to his board of management, Mrs. Samsa to her employer, and Grete to the head of her firm. While they were writing, the charwoman came in to say that she was going now, since her morning's work was finished. At first they only nodded without looking up, but as she kept hovering there they eyed her irritably. "Well?" said Mr. Samsa. The charwoman stood grinning in the doorway as if she had good news to impart to the family but meant not to say a word unless properly questioned. The small ostrich feather standing upright on her hat, which had annoyed Mr. Samsa ever since she was engaged, was waving gaily in all directions. "Well, what is it then?" asked Mrs. Samsa, who obtained more respect from the charwoman than the others. "Oh," said the charwoman, giggling so amiably that she could not at once continue, "just this, you don't need to bother how to get rid of the thing next door. It's been seen to already." Mrs. Samsa and Grete bent over their letters again, as if preoccupied; Mr. Samsa, who perceived that she was eager to begin describing it all in detail, stopped her with a decisive hand. But since she was not allowed to tell her story, she remembered the great hurry she was in, obviously deeply huffed: "Bye, everybody," she said, whirling off violently, and departed with a frightful slamming of doors.

"She'll be given notice tonight," said Mr. Samsa, but neither from his wife nor his daughter did he get any answer, for the charwoman seemed to have shattered again the composure they had barely achieved. They rose, went to the window and stayed there, clasping each other tight. Mr. Samsa turned in his chair to look at them and quietly observed them for a little. Then he called out: "Come along, now, do. Let bygones be bygones. And you might have some consideration for me." The two of them complied at once, hastened to him, caressed him, and quickly finished their letters.

Then they all three left the apartment together, which was more than they had done for months, and went by tram into the open country outside the town. The tram, in which they were the only passengers, was filled with warm sunshine. Leaning comfortably back in their seats they canvassed their prospects for the future, and it appeared on closer inspection that these were not at all bad, for the jobs they had got, which so far they had never really discussed with each other, were all three admirable and likely to lead to better things later on. The greatest immediate improvement in their condition would of course arise from moving to another house; they wanted to take a smaller and cheaper but also better situated and more easily run apartment than the one they had, which Gregor had selected. While they were thus conversing, it struck both Mr. and Mrs. Samsa, almost at the same moment, as they became aware of their daughter's increasing vivacity, that in spite of all the sorrow of recent times, which had made her cheeks pale, she had bloomed into a pretty girl with a good figure. They grew quieter and half unconsciously exchanged glances of complete agreement, having come to the conclusion that it would soon be time to find a good husband for her. And it was like a confirmation of their new dreams and excellent intentions that at the end of the journey their daughter sprang to her feet first and stretched her young body.

St. Mawr

D. H. Lawrence

David Herbert Lawrence was born on September 11, 1885, in Eastwood, England, a coal town in the industrial Midlands near the city of Nottingham. His father was a miner, his mother a former schoolteacher from a once-wealthy family, and Lawrence's childhood, as he portrayed it in somewhat distorted form in *Sons and Lovers*, was largely shaped by their conflicting styles and intentions. Arthur Lawrence, as there depicted, was a man addicted to drink who used his hands on his family as brutally as he used them down in the pit, yet he was possessed of a masculine vigor and tenacity that kept him from being totally contemptible. Lydia Beardsall Lawrence was a more subtle tyrant than her husband, and one whose influence on the writer was far harder to throw off, since she ruled by love rather than fear. Her willing sacrifices procured young Lawrence his education at Nottingham High School and Ilkeston teachers college, and she kept her delicate son from a strenuous stint in the mines, which he could not have long survived. But her close intimacy with her son produced a powerful oedipal bond that warped his post-adolescent development and delayed his emergence into full personal and artistic freedom.

Sons and Lovers principally chronicles the war for Lawrence's soul between his mother and Jessie Chambers, Lawrence's first love and the discoverer of his literary talents. It was on visits to Jessie at her parents' farm that Lawrence began to read philosophy and to free himself from his mother's fundamentalist Christianity, and it was there he began to read and to write symbolist poetry. Jessie Chambers launched Lawrence's literary career by sending a group of his poems to Ford Madox Ford, who published them in his *English Review* in 1909. But the battle for Lawrence's soul was one Jessie was destined to lose. Though the writer was to have several love affairs, Platonic and otherwise, during his early manhood, he was spiritually incapable of giving himself wholly to another woman until well after his mother's death.

The first phase of Lawrence's literary career, 1909–1912, corresponds roughly to the years he spent as a secondary-school teacher at Croydon, south of London. He wrote during that time a volume of highly charged love poetry and three novels: *The White Peacock* (1911), which was well received by the reviewers; *The Trespasser* (1912), which was justly neglected; and *Sons and Lovers* (1913), the autobiographical treatment of his adolescence that was Lawrence's emancipation proclamation. *Sons and Lovers* demonstrated Lawrence's mastery of the conventional form of the novel and of one of its most traditional subjects, the coming to maturity of a young man. It was also the last of Lawrence's novels to be conventional in either sense. On the acceptance of this novel Lawrence also left the teaching profession, at which he was talented but to which he was not really committed. From 1912 on he lived on the often meager proceeds of his writing. And it was in 1912, too, that Lawrence met the woman who was finally to lay to rest the ghostly influence of his mother.

Frieda von Richthofen Weekley was the wife of one of Lawrence's Nottingham professors and the daughter of a noble Prussian family (Manfred von Richthofen, the Red Baron of the German Air Force in World War I, was her first cousin). During a few springtime meetings she and Lawrence fell deeply in love, and she agreed to leave her much-older husband and their children to go away with him. Their life together was passionate and stormy before and after their marriage in 1914, but they wandered through the world together, never staying very long in any one place, nearly inseparable till the writer's death. It was upon Frieda that Lawrence based many of the women in his novels who awaken to the dark violence of their own natures and to a new fulfillment in and beyond sex.

The second phase of Lawrence's writing is dominated by a single fiction that bore the working title of *The Sisters* and that was eventually split into *The Rainbow* (1915) and *Women in Love* (1920). The lengthy and intense pair of novels, considered by most Lawrence scholars the high-water mark of his creative work, begins as a family saga, modulates into a tragic love story, and continues with an analytical examination of two couples' quests for emotional fulfillment. The form this complex story takes is original, almost outrageous, with a daringly free use of myth and symbolism, and an open expression of sexual feelings and acts that resulted in *The Rainbow* being suppressed and *Women in Love* nearly sharing its fate. More dangerous and shocking than the sex in these novels, though, is their political and prophetic strain. In these works Lawrence, the miner's son, tried to come to terms with industrialism, its destructive impact on the English landscape, and its insidious, dehumanizing effect upon the souls of the English people, from the proletariat to the captains of the coal mines. Both novels combine depth psychology influenced by Freud with trenchant sociopolitical speculation. *Women in Love*, however, is the deeper and the bitterer of the two books because it was a product of World War I, an event that strengthened Lawrence's nightmare vision of humanity on the brink of collective suicide.

The war years were difficult ones for Lawrence, not least because Frieda's Prussian ancestry made them politically suspect. The Lawrences' cottage in Cornwall was searched by the police, and they were expelled from the Cornish coast for fear they might signal to German submarines. Nor were they allowed to leave the country—their passport applications were denied. The prospect of totalitarianism and of mass self-destruction, which Lawrence prophetically foresaw, summoned up in the writer the visionary scheme of founding a utopian community on some island that could survive the universal wreckage. Lawrence spent a decade dreaming of Rananim—as he called his utopia—

and inviting various friends to help him establish it. But Lawrence's friends always disappointed him, sooner or later, or fell foul of his increasingly bitter rages, and the dream never got any farther than the planning stage. Among the friends Lawrence made, and subsequently lost, during this period of progressive alienation were writers Katherine Mansfield and John Middleton Murry (who, with the Lawrence themselves, were the two couples anatomized in *Women in Love*); Lady Ottoline Morrell and the other wits and intellectuals of the Bloomsbury Group who gathered at Garsington, her country house; Lord Bertrand Russell, whom Lawrence satirized; and Aldous Huxley, who idolized Lawrence and became his most famous disciple.

Late in 1919, the Lawrences left England for Italy and continued their eastward journey to Sicily, Ceylon, Australia, Tahiti, Mexico, and the western United States, always in search of a community of kindred souls. His output during this period, 1920–1925, is immense and includes not only poetry and fiction, but travel literature, history, criticism, and psychology. Lawrence's analysis of the destructive tendencies of Western civilization had led him to the conclusion that the fault lay in the overemphasis of the intellect and the corresponding neglect of that instinctual, darker knowledge that proceeds from the body. Accordingly, he studied primitive cultures, hoping to find in them the mystical knowledge that might provide the key to successful living. His fiction in this period includes the so-called leadership novels: *Aaron's Rod* (1922), *Kangaroo* (1923), and *The Plumed Serpent* (1926). Imaginatively inferior to his earlier novels and marred by preachiness, by excessive explanation rather than dramatic representation, these fictions center on Lawrence's quest for an ideal charismatic leader whose dark power and spiritual force could counter the dehumanizing tendencies of European society. It is on the basis of these works that Lawrence has been accused of fascism, and while there are major differences—Lawrence was horrified by the regimentation of human life and by the mechanical progress that fascism worshipped—it is only fair to admit that Lawrence's ideas and those of Hitler and Mussolini sprang from similar motives. They shared, at the very least, a search for the sort of leadership that would bring back community to an increasingly fragmented world, a respect for the more primitive values of physical strength and spiritual courage, and a contempt for the collectivist anthill into which European society was turning.

Lawrence's quest for the primitive ended at the Kiowa Ranch in the mountains of New Mexico, which he celebrated in his greatest novella, *St. Mawr* (1925). There, amid the desperate beauty of the Sangre de Cristo Mountains, Lawrence came to see that primitivism, too, had its characteristic defect, for, balancing the sordidness of machine civilization with its ash heaps and tin cans was the sordidness of savagery, "the vast and unrelenting will of the swarming lower life, working for ever against man's attempt at a higher life, a further created being." Nobility in man was in the *struggle* for the higher life, but that higher life, once attained, allowed for no further transcendence. It was a bitter conclusion for a prophet to reach—and one that forced him to renounce his quest for leadership and community and to search for value in retreat, in the unity that a man and a woman could privately share.

So Lawrence retreated himself, first to England—briefly, for he was soon disgusted with his homeland—then to Italy, where he wrote the two most important works of his last phase, *Lady Chatterley's Lover* (1928) and *The Man Who Died* (1929). The latter is a brilliantly blasphemous reworking of the Resurrection, in which Lawrence's crucified prophet finds greater meaning in the delights of the body than in his former spiritual powers over his flock. The former, Lawrence's most scandalous work, contains such explicit descriptions of the sexual awakening of its heroine that it could not be printed in England and America for more than thirty years. More permissive times have lessened the shock of its erotic realism but not its indictment of the "tragic age" that divorces man from his land, his fellow man, his love, his own body. As an introduction to the ideas of the mature Lawrence its power is unsurpassed.

D. H. Lawrence had begun life as a delicate child with weak lungs, and his years of constant travel had undermined his fragile health. Though he long refused to admit the fact, he had contracted tuberculosis while living in primitive conditions in Mexico, and the last five years of his life were a protracted losing battle against the debility of that disease. Death finally claimed him at Vence, on the French Riviera, on March 1, 1930. His ashes were eventually taken to his ranch above Taos, New Mexico, where they form the center of a Lawrence "shrine" that his devoted readers can still visit today.

Biography Harry T. Moore's *The Life and Works of D. H. Lawrence* (London: Allen and Unwin, 1951) analyzes nearly all of Lawrence's literary output in the context of his biography. Edward H. Niehls in *D. H. Lawrence: A Composite Biography* (Madison: University of Wisconsin Press, 1957–1959; 3 vols.) has put together bits and pieces of Lawrence's letters and memorial fragments about Lawrence to create a life in its participants' own words. Lawrence's life in America is remembered by Mabel Dodge Luhan in *Lorenzo in Taos* (New York: Alfred A. Knopf, 1932) and by his artist friend Knud Merrild in *A Poet and Two Painters: A Memoir of D. H. Lawrence* (New York: Viking Press, 1939). The most up-to-date treatments of Lawrence's life are Paul Delany, *D. H. Lawrence's Nightmare: The Writer and His Circle in the Years of the Great War* (New York: Basic Books, 1978) and Keith M. Sagar, *The Life of D. H. Lawrence* (New York: Pantheon, 1980).

Editions The major uniform edition of Lawrence's works, the Phoenix edition published by William Heinemann, Ltd. (London, 1954–1957), abounds in misprints; more reliable are the paperback editions published in the United States by Vintage and by Viking-Penguin. A critical edition of Lawrence seems to be needed.

Bibliography See Warren Roberts, *A Bibliography of D. H. Lawrence* (London: Hart-Davis, 1963), and the extensive bibliography appended to Keith Sagar, *The Art of D. H. Lawrence* (Cambridge: Cambridge University Press, 1976), updated by the annual checklists in the *D. H. Lawrence Review*.

General Criticism   In addition to Moore and Sagar, above, the most important studies of Lawrence would have to include F. R. Leavis's *D. H. Lawrence: Novelist* (New York: Alfred A. Knopf, 1956); Graham Hough's *The Dark Sun: A Study of D. H. Lawrence* (New York: Macmillan, 1957); Eliseo Vivas's *D. H. Lawrence: The Failure and Triumph of Art* (Evanston: Northwestern University Press, 1960); Eugene Goodheart's *The Utopian Vision of D. H. Lawrence* (Chicago: University of Chicago Press, 1963); and Julian Moynahan's *The Deed of Life: The Novels and Tales of D. H. Lawrence* (Princeton: Princeton University Press, 1963); John Worthen, *D. H. Lawrence and the Idea of the Novel* (Totowa, N.J.: Rowman & Littlefield, 1979); and Donald Gutierrez, *Lapsing Out: Embodiments of Death and Rebirth in the Last Writings of D. H. Lawrence* (Cranbury, N.J.: Fairleigh Dickinson University Press, 1980).

Criticism of St. Mawr   All the above works on Lawrence contain chapters or parts of chapters on *St. Mawr*. In addition to these, see Alan Wilde, ''The Illusion of *St. Mawr:* Technique and Vision in D. H. Lawrence's Novel,'' *PMLA* 79 (1964), 164-170; Bob L. Smith, ''D. H. Lawrence's *St.Mawr:* Transposition of Myth,'' *Arizona Quarterly* 24 (1968), 197-208; James C. Cowan, *D. H. Lawrence's American Journey* (Cleveland: Case Western Reserve University Press, 1970), pp. 81-98; Jerry Wasserman, ''*St. Mawr* and the Search for Community,'' *Mosaic* 5, ii (1972), 113-123; and Michael Ragussis, ''The False Myth of *St. Mawr:* Lawrence and the Subterfuge of Art,'' *Papers on Literature and Language* 11 (1975), 186-196.

St. Mawr

Lou Witt had had her own way so long that by the age of twenty-five she didn't know where she was. Having one's own way landed one completely at sea.

To be sure, for a while she had failed in her grand love affair with Rico. And then she had had something really to despair about. But even that had worked out as she wanted. Rico had come back to her, and was dutifully married to her. And now, when she was twenty-five and he was three months older, they were a charming married couple. He flirted with other women still, to be sure. He wouldn't be the handsome Rico if he didn't. But she had "got" him. Oh, yes! You had only to see the uneasy backward glance at her, from his big blue eyes: just like a horse that is edging away from its master: to know how completely he was mastered.

She, with her odd little *museau*,[1] not exactly pretty, but very attractive; and her quaint air of playing at being well-bred, in a sort of charade game; and her queer familiarity with foreign cities and foreign languages; and the lurking sense of being an outsider everywhere, like a sort of gipsy, who is at home anywhere and nowhere; all this made up her charm and her failure. She didn't quite belong.

Of course she was American: Louisiana family, moved down to Texas. And she was moderately rich, with no close relation except her mother. But she had been sent to school in France when she was twelve, and since she had finished school, she had drifted from Paris to Palermo, Biarritz to Vienna and back via Munich to London, then down again to Rome. Only fleeting trips to her America.

So what sort of American was she, after all?

And what sort of European was she either? She didn't "belong" anywhere. Perhaps most of all in Rome, among the artists and the Embassy people.

It was in Rome she had met Rico. He was an Australian, son of a government official in Melbourne, who had been made a baronet.[2] So one day Rico would be Sir Henry, as he was the only son. Meanwhile he floated around Europe on a very small allowance—his father wasn't rich in capital—and was being an artist.

They met in Rome when they were twenty-two, and had a love affair in Capri. Rico was handsome, elegant, but mostly he had spots of paint on his trousers and he ruined a necktie pulling it off. He behaved in a most floridly elegant fashion, fascinating to the Italians. But at the same time he was canny and shrewd and sensible as any young poser could be, and, on principle, good-hearted, anxious. He was anxious for his future, and anxious for his place in the world, he was poor, and suddenly wasteful in spite of all his tension of economy, and suddenly spiteful in spite of all his ingratiating efforts, and suddenly ungrateful in spite of all his burden of gratitude, and suddenly rude in spite of all his good manners, and suddenly detestable in spite of all his suave, courtier-like amiability.

He was fascinated by Lou's quaint aplomb, her experiences, her "knowledge," her *gamine*[3] knowingness, her aloneness, her pretty clothes that were sometimes an utter failure, and her southern "drawl"

---

[1]Face, in French slang.
[2]The holder of a hereditary knighthood.
[3]Tomboy.

that was sometimes so irritating. That sing-song which was so American. Yet she used no Americanisms at all, except when she lapsed into her odd spasms of acid irony, when she was very American indeed!

And she was fascinated by Rico. They played to each other like two butterflies at one flower. They pretended to be very poor in Rome—he *was* poor: and very rich in Naples. Everybody stared their eyes out at them. And they had that love affair in Capri.

But they reacted badly on each other's nerves. She became ill. Her mother appeared. He couldn't stand Mrs. Witt, and Mrs. Witt couldn't stand him. There was a terrible fortnight. Then Lou was popped into a convent nursing-home in Umbria, and Rico dashed off to Paris. Nothing would stop him. He must go back to Australia.

He went to Melbourne, and while there his father died, leaving him a baronet's title and an income still very moderate. Lou visited America once more, as the strangest of strange lands to her. She came away disheartened, panting for Europe, and, of course, doomed to meet Rico again.

They couldn't get away from one another, even though in the course of their rather restrained correspondence he informed her that he was "probably" marrying a very dear girl, friend of his childhood, only daughter of one of the oldest families in Victoria. Not saying much.

He didn't commit the probability, but reappeared in Paris, wanting to paint his head off, terribly inspired by Cezanne and by old Renoir.[4] He dined at the Rotonde with Lou and Mrs. Witt, who, with her queer democratic New Orleans sort of conceit, looked round the drinking-hall with savage contempt, and at Rico as part of the show. "Certainly," she said, "when these people here have got any money, they fall in love on a full stomach. And when they've got no money, they fall in love with a full pocket. I never was in a more disgusting place. They take their love like some people take after-dinner pills."

She would watch with her arching, full, strong grey eyes, sitting there erect and silent in her well-bought American clothes. And then she would deliver some such charge of grape-shot. Rico always writhed.

Mrs. Witt hated Paris: "this sordid, unlucky city," she called it. "Something unlucky is bound to happen to me in this sinister, unclean

---

[4]Paul Cézanne (1839–1906) and August Renoir (1841–1919) were two French Impressionist painters of completely different styles and character; the Rotonde was a fashionable café in the artistic bohemia of Montparnasse.

town," she said. "I feel *contagion* in the air of this place. For heaven's sake, Louise, let us go to Morocco or somewhere."

"No, mother dear, I can't now. Rico has proposed to me, and I have accepted him. Let us think about a wedding, shall we?"

"There!" said Mrs. Witt. "I said it was an unlucky city!"

And the peculiar look of extreme New Orleans annoyance came round her sharp nose. But Lou and Rico were both twenty-four years old, and beyond management. And anyhow, Lou would be Lady Carrington. But Mrs. Witt was exasperated beyond exasperation. She would almost rather have preferred Lou to elope with one of the great, evil porters at Les Halles.[5] Mrs. Witt was at the age when the malevolent male in man, the old Adam, begins to loom above all the social tailoring. And yet—and yet—it was better to have Lady Carrington for a daughter, seeing Lou was that sort.

There was a marriage, after which Mrs. Witt departed to America. Lou and Rico leased a little old house in Westminster, and began to settle into a certain layer of English society. Rico was becoming an almost fashionable portrait-painter. At least, *he* was almost fashionable, whether his portraits were or not. And Lou too was almost fashionable: almost a hit. There was some flaw somewhere. In spite of their appearances, both Rico and she would never quite go down in any society. They were the drifting artist sort. Yet neither of them was content to be of the drifting artist sort. They wanted to fit in, to make good.

Hence the little house in Westminster, the portraits, the dinners, the friends, and the visits. Mrs. Witt came and sardonically established herself in a suite in a quiet but good-class hotel not far off. Being on the spot. And her terrible grey eyes with the touch of a leer looked on at the hollow mockery of things. As if *she* knew of anything better!

Lou and Rico had a curious exhausting effect on one another: neither knew why. They were fond of one another. Some inscrutable bond held them together. But it was strange vibration of the nerves, rather than of the blood. A nervous attachment, rather than a sexual love. A curious tension of will, rather than a spontaneous passion. Each was curiously under the domination of the other. They were a pair—they had to be together. Yet quite soon they shrank from one another. This attachment of the will and the nerves was destructive. As soon as one felt strong, the other felt ill. As soon as the ill one recovered strength, down went the one who had been well.

---

[5]Until recently, the central market for meat and vegetables in Paris.

And soon, tacitly, the marriage became more like a friendship, Platonic. It was a marriage, but without sex. Sex was shattering and exhausting, they shrank from it, and became like brother and sister. But still they were husband and wife. And the lack of physical relation was a secret source of uneasiness and chagrin to both of them. They would neither of them accept it. Rico looked with contemplative, anxious eyes at other women.

Mrs. Witt kept track of everything, watching, as it were, from outside the fence, like a potent well-dressed demon, full of uncanny energy and a shattering sort of sense. She said little: but her small, occasionally biting remarks revealed her attitude of contempt for the *ménage.*[6]

Rico entertained clever and well-known people. Mrs. Witt would appear, in her New York gowns and few good jewels. She was handsome, with her vigorous grey hair. But her heavy-lidded grey eyes were the despair of any hostess. They looked too many shattering things. And it was but too obvious that these clever, well-known English people got on her nerves terribly, with their finickiness and their fine-drawn discriminations. She wanted to put her foot through all these fine-drawn distinctions. She thought continually of the house of her girlhood, the plantation, the Negroes, the planters: the sardonic grimness that underlay all the big, shiftless life. And she wanted to cleave with some of this grimness of the big, dangerous America, into the safe, finicky drawing-rooms of London. So naturally she was not popular.

But being a woman of energy, she had to do *something.* During the latter part of the war she had worked with the American Red Cross in France, nursing. She loved men—real men. But, on close contact, it was difficult to define what she meant by "real" men. She never met any.

Out of the debacle of the war she had emerged with an odd piece of debris, in the shape of Geronimo Trujillo. He was an American, son of a Mexican father and a Navajo Indian mother, from Arizona. When you knew him well, you recognized the real half-breed, though at a glance he might pass as a sunburnt citizen of any nation, particularly of France. He looked like a certain sort of Frenchman, with his curiously set dark eyes, his straight black hair, his thin black moustache, his rather long cheeks, and his almost slouching, diffident, sardonic bear-

---

[6]Household.

ing. Only when you knew him, and looked right into his eyes, you saw that unforgettable glint of the Indian.

He had been badly shell-shocked, and was for a time a wreck. Mrs. Witt, having nursed him into convalescence, asked him where he was going next. He didn't know. His father and mother were dead, and he had nothing to take him back to Phoenix, Arizona. Having had an education in one of the Indian high schools, the unhappy fellow had now no place in life at all. Another of the many misfits.

There was something of the Paris *Apache*[7] in his appearance: but he was all the time withheld, and nervously shut inside himself. Mrs. Witt was intrigued by him.

"Very well, Phoenix," she said, refusing to adopt his Spanish name, "I'll see what I can do."

What she did was to get him a place on a sort of manor farm, with some acquaintances of hers. He was very good with horses, and had a curious success with turkeys and geese and fowls.

Some time after Lou's marriage, Mrs. Witt reappeared in London, from the country, with Phoenix in tow, and a couple of horses. She decided that she would ride in the Park in the morning, and see the world that way. Phoenix was to be her groom.

So, to the great misgiving of Rico, behold Mrs. Witt in splendidly tailored habit and perfect boots, a smart black hat on her smart grey hair, riding a grey gelding as smart as she was, and looking down her conceited, inquisitive, scornful, aristocratic-democratic Louisiana nose at the people in Piccadilly, as she crossed to the Row, followed by the taciturn shadow of Phoenix, who sat on a chestnut with three white feet as if he had grown there.

Mrs. Witt, like many other people, always expected to find the real *beau monde* and the real *grand monde*[8] somewhere or other. She didn't quite give in to what she saw in the Bois de Boulogne, or in Monte Carlo, or on the Pincio; all a bit shoddy, and not very *beau* and not at all *grand*. There she was, with her grey eagle eye, her splendid complexion and her weapon-like health of a woman of fifty, dropping her eyelids a little, very slightly nervous, but completely prepared to despise the *monde* she was entering in Rotten Row.

---

[7]In French, not an Indian but a hooligan or petty criminal.

[8]The "beautiful world" and the "great world": respectively, fashionable society and the aristocracy. Rotten Row is the elite bridle path in London's Hyde Park.

In she sailed, and up and down that regatta-canal of horsemen and horsewomen under the trees of the Park. And yes, there were lovely girls with fair hair down their backs, on happy ponies. And awfully well-groomed papas, and tight mammas who looked as if they were going to pour tea between the ears of their horses, and converse with banal skill, one eye on the teapot, one on the visitor with whom she was talking, and all the rest of her hostess' argus-eyes[9] upon everybody in sight. That alert argus capability of the English matron was startling and a bit horrifying. Mrs. Witt would at once think of the old Negro mammies, away in Louisiana. And her eyes became dagger-like as she watched the clipped, shorn, mincing young Englishmen. She refused to look at the prosperous Jews.

It was still the days before motor-cars were allowed in the Park, but Rico and Lou, sliding round Hyde Park Corner and up Park Lane in their car, would watch the steely horsewoman and the saturnine groom with a sort of dismay. Mrs. Witt seemed to be pointing a pistol at the bosom of every other horseman or horsewoman, and announcing: *Your virility or your life! Your femininity or your life!* She didn't know herself what she really wanted them to be: but it was something as democratic as Abraham Lincoln, and as aristocratic as a Russian Czar, as highbrow as Arthur Balfour,[10] and as taciturn and unideal as Phoenix. Everything at once.

There was nothing for it: Lou had to buy herself a horse and ride at her mother's side, for very decency's sake. Mrs. Witt was *so* like a smooth, levelled, gun-metal pistol, Lou had to be a sort of sheath. And she really looked pretty, with her clusters of dark, curly, New Orleans hair, like grapes, and her quaint brown eyes that didn't quite match, and that looked a bit sleepy and vague, and at the same time quick as a squirrel's. She was slight and elegant, and a tiny bit rakish, and somebody suggested she might be in the movies.

Nevertheless, they were in the society columns next morning—*two new and striking figures in the Row this morning were Lady Henry Carrington and her mother Mrs. Witt,* etc. And Mrs. Witt liked it, let her say what she might. So did Lou. Lou liked it immensely. She simply luxuriated in the sun of publicity.

"Rico dear, you must get a horse."

---

[9]In Greek mythology, Argus was a monster with a hundred eyes.
[10]Conservative Prime Minister and Foreign Secretary of the British Government (1848–1930).

The tone was soft and southern and drawling, but the overtone had a decisive finality. In vain Rico squirmed—he had a way of writhing and squirming which perhaps he had caught at Oxford. In vain he protested that he couldn't ride, and that he didn't care for riding. He got quite angry, and his handsome arched nose tilted and his upper lip lifted from his teeth, like a dog that is going to bite. Yet daren't quite bite.

And that was Rico. He daren't quite bite. Not that he was really afraid of the others. He was afraid of himself, once he let himself go. He might rip up in an eruption of lifelong anger all this pretty-pretty picture of a charming young wife and a delightful little home and a fascinating success as a painter of fashionable and, at the same time, "great" portraits: with colour, wonderful colour, and, at the same time, form, marvellous form. He had composed this little *tableau vivant*[11] with great effort. He didn't want to erupt like some suddenly wicked horse—Rico was really more like a horse than a dog, a horse that might go nasty any moment. For the time, he was good, very good, dangerously good.

"Why, Rico dear, I thought you used to ride so much, in Australia, when you were young? Didn't you tell me all about it, hm?"—and as she ended on that slow, singing *hm?* which acted on him like an irritant and a drug, he knew he was beaten.

Lou kept the sorrel mare in a mews just behind the house in Westminster, and she was always slipping round to the stables. She had a funny little nostalgia for the place: something that really surprised her. She had never had the faintest notion that she cared for horses and stables and grooms. But she did. She was fascinated. Perhaps it was her childhood's Texas associations come back. Whatever it was, her life with Rico in the elegant little house, and all her social engagements, seemed like a dream, the substantial reality of which was those mews in Westminster, her sorrel mare, the owner of the mews, Mr. Saintsbury, and the grooms he employed. Mr. Saintsbury was a horsy elderly man like an old maid, and he loved the sound of titles.

"Lady Carrington!—well, I never! You've come to us for a bit of company again, I see. I don't know whatever we shall do if you go away, we shall be that lonely!" and he flashed his old-maid's smile at her. "No matter how grey the morning, your Ladyship would make a beam of sunshine. Poppy is all right, I think . . ."

---

[11]A staged sustained pose; literally, a "living picture."

Poppy was the sorrel mare with the no white feet and the startled eye, and she was all right. And Mr. Saintsbury was smiling with the old-maid's mouth, and showing all his teeth.

"Come across with me, Lady Carrington, and look at a new horse just up from the country? I think he's worth a look, and I believe you have a moment to spare, your Ladyship."

Her Ladyship had too many moments to spare. She followed the sprightly, elderly, clean-shaven man across the yard to a loose box, and waited while he opened the door.

In the inner dark she saw a handsome bay horse with his clean ears pricked like daggers from his naked head as he swung handsomely round to stare at the open doorway. He had big, black, brilliant eyes, with a sharp questioning glint, and that air of tense, alert quietness which betrays an animal that can be dangerous.

"Is he quiet?" Lou asked.

"Why—yes—my Lady! He's quiet, with those that know how to handle him. Cup! my boy! Cup my beauty! Cup then! St. Mawr!"

Loquacious even with the animals, he went softly forward and laid his hand on the horse's shoulder, soft and quiet as a fly settling. Lou saw the brilliant skin of the horse crinkle a little in apprehensive anticipation, like the shadow of the descending hand on a bright red-gold liquid. But then the animal relaxed again.

"Quiet with those that know how to handle him, and a bit of a ruffian with those that don't. Isn't that the ticket, eh, St. Mawr?"

"What is his name?" Lou asked.

The man repeated it, with a slight Welsh twist.[12] "He's from the Welsh borders, belonging to a Welsh gentleman, Mr. Griffith Edwards. But they're wanting to sell him."

"How old is he?" asked Lou.

"About seven years—seven years and five months," said Mr. Saintsbury, dropping his voice as if it were a secret.

"Could one ride him in the Park?"

"Well—yes! I should say a gentleman who knew how to handle him could ride him very well and make a very handsome figure in the Park."

Lou at once decided that this handsome figure should be Rico's. For she was already half in love with St. Mawr. He was of such a lovely

---

[12]"Mawr" in Welsh means big, great, or high; no St. Mawr, so spelled, is recognized in the Catholic church.

red-gold colour, and a dark, invisible fire seemed to come out of him. But in his big black eyes there was a lurking afterthought. Something told her that the horse was not quite happy: that somewhere deep in his animal consciousness lived a dangerous, half-revealed resentment, a diffused sense of hostility. She realized that he was sensitive, in spite of his flaming, healthy strength, and nervous with a touchy uneasiness that might make him vindictive.

"Has he got any tricks?" she asked.

"Not that I know of, my Lady: not tricks exactly. But he's one of these temperamental creatures, as they say. Though *I* say, every horse is temperamental, when you come down to it. But this one, it is as if he was a trifle raw somewhere. Touch this raw spot, and there's no answering for him."

"Where is he raw?" asked Lou, somewhat mystified. She thought he might really have some physical sore.

"Why, that's hard to say, my Lady. If he was a human being, you'd say something had gone wrong in his life. But with a horse, it's not that, exactly. A high-bred animal like St. Mawr needs understanding, and I don't know as anybody has quite got the hang of him. I confess I haven't myself. But I do realize that he is a special animal and needs a special sort of touch, and I'm willing he should have it, did I but know exactly what it is."

She looked at the glowing bay horse that stood there with his ears back, his face averted, but attending as if he were some lightning-conductor. He was a stallion. When she realized this, she became more afraid of him.

"Why does Mr. Griffith Edwards want to sell him?" she asked.

"Well—my Lady—they raised him for stud purposes—but he didn't answer. There are horses like that: don't seem to fancy the mares, for some reason. Well, anyway, they couldn't keep him for the stud. And as you see, he's a powerful, beautiful hackney,[13] clean as a whistle, and eaten up with his own power. But there's no putting him between the shafts. He won't stand it. He's a fine saddle-horse, beautiful action, and lovely to ride. But he's got to be handled, and there you are."

Lou felt there was something behind the man's reticence.

"Has he ever made a break?" she asked, apprehensive.

"Made a break?" replied the man. "Well, if I must admit it, he's had two accidents. Mr. Griffith Edwards' son rode him a bit wild, away

---

[13] A heavily muscled breed of horse, once used for carriages.

there in the forest of Deane, and the young fellow had his skull smashed in, against a low oak-bough. Last autumn, that was. And some time back, he crushed a groom against the side of the stall— injured him fatally. But they were both accidents, my Lady. Things will happen."

The man spoke in a melancholy, fatalistic way. The horse, with his ears laid back, seemed to be listening tensely, his face averted. He looked like something finely bred and passionate, that has been judged and condemned.

"May I say *how do you do?*" she said to the horse, drawing a little nearer in her white, summery dress, and lifting her hand that glittered with emeralds and diamonds.

He drifted away from her, as if some wind blew him. Then he ducked his head, and looked sideways at her, from his black, full eye.

"I think I'm all right," she said, edging nearer, while he watched her.

She laid her hand on his side, and gently stroked him. Then she stroked his shoulder, and then the hard, tense arch of his neck. And she was startled to feel the vivid heat of his life come through to her, through the lacquer of red-gold gloss. So slippery with vivid, hot life!

She paused, as if thinking, while her hand rested on the horse's sun-arched neck. Dimly, in her weary young-woman's soul, an ancient understanding seemed to flood in.

She wanted to buy St. Mawr.

"I think," she said to Saintsbury, "if I can, I will buy him."

The man looked at her long and shrewdly.

"Well, my Lady," he said at last, "there shall be nothing kept from you. But what would your Ladyship do with him, if I may make so bold?"

"I don't know," she replied, vaguely. "I might take him to America."

The man paused once more, then said:

"They say it's been the making of some horses, to take them over the water, to Australia or such places. It might repay you—you never know."

She wanted to buy St. Mawr. She wanted him to belong to her. For some reason the sight of him, his power, his alive, alert intensity, his unyieldingness, made her want to cry.

She never did cry: except sometimes with vexation, or to get her own way. As far as weeping went, her heart felt as dry as a Christmas walnut. What was the good of tears, anyhow? You had to keep on holding on, in this life, never give way, and never give in. Tears only left one weakened and ragged.

But now, as if that mysterious fire of the horse's body had split some rock in her, she went home and hid herself in her room, and just cried. The wild, brilliant, alert head of St. Mawr seemed to look at her out of another world. It was as if she had had a vision, as if the walls of her own world had suddenly melted away, leaving her in a great darkness, in the midst of which the large, brilliant eyes of that horse looked at her with demonish question, while his naked ears stood up like daggers from the naked lines of his inhuman head, and his great body glowed red with power.

What was it? Almost like a god looking at her terribly out of the everlasting dark, she had felt the eyes of that horse; great, glowing, fearsome eyes, arched with a question, and containing a white blade of light like a threat. What was his non-human question, and his uncanny threat? She didn't know. He was some splendid demon, and she must worship him.

She hid herself away from Rico. She could not bear the triviality and superficiality of her human relationships. Looming like some god out of the darkness was the head of that horse, with the wide, terrible, questioning eyes. And she felt that it forbade her to be her ordinary, commonplace self. It forbade her to be just Rico's wife, young Lady Carrington, and all that.

It haunted her, the horse. It had looked at her as she had never been looked at before: terrible, gleaming, questioning eyes arching out of the darkness, and backed by all the fire of that great ruddy body. What did it mean, and what ban did it put upon her? She felt it put a ban on her heart: wielded some uncanny authority over her, that she dared not, could not understand.

No matter where she was, what she was doing, at the back of her consciousness loomed a great, over-aweing figure out of a dark background: St. Mawr, looking at her without really seeing her, yet gleaming a question at her, from his wide terrible eyes, and gleaming a sort of menace, doom. Master of doom, he seemed to be!

"You are thinking about something, Lou dear!" Rico said to her that evening.

He was so quick and sensitive to detect her moods—so exciting in this respect. And his big, slightly prominent blue eyes, with the whites a little bloodshot, glanced at her quickly, with searching, and anxiety, and a touch of fear, as if his conscience were always uneasy. He, too, was rather like a horse—but for ever quivering with a sort of cold, dangerous mistrust, which he covered with anxious love.

At the middle of his eyes was a central powerlessness, that left him anxious. It used to touch her to pity, that central look of powerlessness in him. But now, since she had seen the full, dark, passionate blaze of power and of different life in the eyes of the thwarted horse, the anxious powerlessness of the man drove her mad. Rico was so handsome, and he was so self-controlled, he had a gallant sort of kindness and a real worldly shrewdness. One had to admire him: at least *she* had to. But after all, and after all, it was a bluff, an attitude. He kept it all working in himself, deliberately. It was an attitude. She read psychologists who said that everything was an attitude. Even the best of everything. But now she realized that, with men and women, everything is an attitude only when something else is lacking. Something is lacking and they are thrown back on their own devices. That black fiery flow in the eyes of the horse was not "attitude." It was something much more terrifying, and real, the only thing that was real. Gushing from the darkness in menace and question, and blazing out in the splendid body of the horse.

"Was I thinking about something?" she replied, in her slow, amused, casual fashion. As if everything was so casual and easy to her. And so it was, from the hard, polished side of herself. But that wasn't the whole story.

"I think you were, Loulina, May we offer the penny?"

"Don't trouble," she said. "I was thinking, if I was thinking of anything, about a bay horse called St. Mawr."—Her secret *almost* crept into her eyes.

"The name is awfully attractive," he said with a laugh.

"Not so attractive as the creature himself. I'm going to buy him."

"Not really!" he said. "But why?"

"He *is* so attractive. I'm going to buy him for you."

"For *me!* Darling! how you do take me for granted! He may not be in the least attractive to me. As you know, I have hardly any feeling for horses at all.—Besides, how much does he cost?"

"That I don't know, Rico dear. But I'm sure you'll love him, for my sake."—She felt, now, she was merely playing for her own ends.

"Lou dearest, *don't* spend a fortune on a horse for me, which I *don't* want. Honestly, I prefer a car."

"Won't you ride with me in the Park, Rico?"

"Honestly, dear Lou, I don't want to."

"Why not, dear boy? You'd look so beautiful. I wish you would.— And anyhow, come with me to look at St. Mawr."

Rico was divided. He had a certain uneasy feeling about horses. At the same time, he *would* like to cut a handsome figure in the Park.

They went across to the mews. A little Welsh groom was watering the brilliant horse.

"Yes, dear, he certainly *is* beautiful: such a marvellous colour! Almost orange! But rather large, I should say, to ride in the Park."

"No, for you he's perfect. You are so tall."

"He'd be marvellous in a composition. That colour!"

And all Rico could do was to gaze with the artist's eye at the horse, with a glance at the groom.

"Don't you think the man is rather fascinating too?" he said, nursing his chin artistically and penetratingly.

The groom, Lewis, was a little, quick, rather bow-legged, loosely built fellow of indeterminate age, with a mop of black hair and little black beard. He was grooming the brilliant St. Mawr, out in the open. The horse was really glorious: like a marigold, with a pure golden sheen, a shimmer of green-gold lacquer, upon a burning red-orange. There on the shoulder you saw the yellow lacquer glisten. Lewis, a little scrub of a fellow, worked absorbedly, unheedingly, at the horse, with an absorption that was almost ritualistic. He seemed the attendant shadow of the ruddy animal.

"He goes with the horse," said Lou. "If we buy St. Mawr, we get the man thrown in."

"They'd be *so* amusing to paint: such an extraordinary contrast! But, darling, I *hope* you won't insist on buying the horse. It's so frightfully expensive."

"Mother will help me.—You'd look so well on him, Rico."

"If ever I dared take the liberty of getting on his back——!"

"Why not?" She went quickly across the cobbled yard.

"Good morning, Lewis. How is St. Mawr?"

Lewis straightened himself and looked at her under the falling mop of his black hair.

"All right," he said.

He peered straight at her from under his overhanging black hair. He had pale-grey eyes, that looked phosphorescent, and suggested the eyes of a wildcat peering intent from under the darkness of some bush where it lies unseen. Lou, with her brown, unmatched, oddly perplexed eyes, felt herself found out.—"He's a common little fellow," she thought to herself. "But he knows a woman and a horse, at sight."— Aloud she said, in her southern drawl:

"How do you think he'd be with Sir Henry?"

Lewis turned his remote, coldly watchful eyes on the young baronet. Rico was tall and handsome and balanced on his hips. His face was long and well-defined, and with the hair taken straight back from the brow. It seemed as well-made as his clothing, and as perpetually presentable. You could not imagine his face dirty, or scrubby and unshaven, or bearded, or even moustached. It was perfectly prepared for social purposes. If his head had been cut off, like John the Baptist's, it would have been a thing complete in itself, would not have missed the body in the least. The body was perfectly tailored. The head was one of the famous "talking heads" of modern youth, with eyebrows a trifle Mephistophelian, large blue eyes a trifle bold, and curved mouth thrilling to death to kiss.

Lewis, the groom, staring from between his bush of hair and his beard, watched like an animal from the underbrush. And Rico was still sufficiently a colonial to be uneasily aware of the underbrush, uneasy under the watchfulness of the pale-grey eyes, and uneasy in that man-to-man exposure which is characteristic of the democratic colonies and of America. He knew he must ultimately be judged on his merits as a man, alone without a background: an ungarnished colonial.

This lack of background, this defenceless man-to-man business which left him at the mercy of every servant, was bad for his nerves. For he was *also* an artist. He bore up against it in a kind of desperation, and was easily moved to rancorous resentment. At the same time he was free of the Englishman's water tight *suffisance*.[14] He really was aware that he would have to hold his own all alone, thrown alone on his own defences in the universe. The extreme democracy of the Colonies had taught him this.

And this the little aboriginal Lewis recognized in him. He recognized also Rico's curious hollow misgiving, fear of some deficiency in himself, beneath all his handsome, young-hero appearance.

"He'd be all right with anybody as would meet him half-way," said Lewis, in the quick Welsh manner of speech, impersonal.

"You hear, Rico!" said Lou in her sing-song, turning to her husband.

"Perfectly, darling!"

"Would you be willing to meet St. Mawr half-way, hmm?"

"All the way, darling! Mahomet would go *all* the way to that mountain. Who would dare do otherwise?"

He spoke with a laughing, yet piqued sarcasm.

"Why, I think St. Mawr would understand perfectly," she said in the soft voice of a woman haunted by love. And she went and laid her

---

[14]Conceit, self-possession.

hand on the slippery, life-smooth shoulder of the horse. He, with his strange equine head lowered, its exquisite fine lines reaching a little snake-like forward, and his ears a little back, was watching her sideways, from the corner of his eye. He was in a state of absolute mistrust, like a cat crouching to spring.

"St. Mawr!" she said. "St. Mawr! What is the matter? Surely you and I are all right!"

And she spoke softly, dreamily stroked the animal's neck. She could feel a response gradually coming from him. But he would not lift up his head. And when Rico suddenly moved nearer, he sprang with a sudden jerk backwards, as if lightning exploded in his four hoofs.

The groom spoke a few low words in Welsh. Lou, frightened, stood with lifted hand arrested. She had been going to stroke him.

"Why did he do that?" she said.

"They gave him a beating once or twice," said the groom in a neutral voice, "and he doesn't forget."

She could hear a neutral sort of judgment in Lewis' voice. And she thought of the "raw spot."

Not any raw spot at all. A battle between two worlds. She realized that St. Mawr drew his hot breaths in another world from Rico's, from our world. Perhaps the old Greek horses had lived in St. Mawr's world. And the old Greek heroes, even Hippolytus,[15] had known it.

With their strangely naked equine heads, and something of a snake in their way of looking round, and lifting their sensitive, dangerous muzzles, they moved in a prehistoric twilight where all things loomed phantasmagoric, all on one plane, sudden presences suddenly jutting out of the matrix. It was another world, an older, heavily potent world. And in this world the horse was swift and fierce and supreme, undominated and unsurpassed.—"Meet him half-way," Lewis said. But halfway across from our human world to that terrific equine twilight was not a small step. It was a step, she knew, that Rico could never take.

St. Mawr was bought, and Lewis was hired along with him. At first, Lewis rode him behind Lou, in the Row, to get him going. He behaved perfectly.

Phoenix, the half-Indian, was very jealous when he saw the black-bearded Welsh groom on St. Mawr.

---

[15]In Euripides's tragedy of the same name, Hippolytus, cursed by his father, is killed when Poseidon sends a sea monster who frightens the horses he is driving so that they bolt out of control and drag him to death.

"What horse you got there?" he asked, looking at the other man with the curious unseeing stare in his hard, Navajo eyes, in which the Indian glint moved like a spark upon a dark chaos. In Phoenix's high-boned face there was all the race-misery of the dispossessed Indian, with an added blankness left by shell-shock. But at the same time, there was that unyielding, save to death, which is characteristic of his tribe: his mother's tribe. Difficult to say what subtle thread bound him to the Navajo, and made his destiny a Red Man's destiny still.

They were a curious pair of grooms, following the correct, and yet extraordinary, pair of American mistresses. Mrs. Witt and Phoenix both rode with long stirrups and straight leg, sitting close to the saddle, without posting. Phoenix looked as if he and the horse were all one piece, he never seemed to rise in the saddle at all, neither trotting nor galloping, but sat like a man riding bareback. And all the time he stared around, at the riders in the Row, at the people grouped outside the rail, chatting, at the children walking with their nurses, as if he were looking at a mirage, in whose actuality he never believed for a moment. London was all a sort of dark mirage to him. His wide, nervous-looking brown eyes, with a smallish brown pupil that showed the white all round, seemed to be focused on the far distance, as if he could not see things too near. He was watching the pale deserts of Arizona shimmer with moving light, the long mirage of a shallow lake ripple, the great pallid concave of earth and sky expanding with interchanged light. And a horse-shape loom large and portentous in the mirage, like some prehistoric beast.

That was real to him: the phantasm of Arizona. But this London was something his eye passed over, as a false mirage.

He looked too smart in his well-tailored groom's clothes, so smart, he might have been one of the satirized new-rich. Perhaps it was a sort of half-breed physical assertion that came through his clothing, the savage's physical assertion of himself. Anyhow, he looked "common," rather horsy and loud.

Except his face. In the golden suavity of his high-boned Indian face, that was hairless, with hardly any eyebrows, there was a blank, lost look that was almost touching. The same startled blank look was in his eyes. But in the smallish dark pupils the dagger-point of light still gleamed unbroken.

He was a good groom, watchful, quick, and on the spot in an instant if anything went wrong. He had a curious, quiet power over the horses, unemotional, unsympathetic, but silently potent. In the same way, watching the traffic of Piccadilly with his blank, glinting eye, he would calculate everything instinctively, as if it were an enemy, and pilot Mrs. Witt by the strength of his silent will. He threw around her the tense watchfulness of her own America, and made her feel at home.

"Phoenix," she said, turning abruptly in her saddle as they walked the horses past the sheltering policeman at Hyde Park Corner, "I can't tell you how glad I am to have something a hundred per cent American at the back of me, when I go through these gates."

She looked at him from dangerous grey eyes as if she meant it indeed, in vindictive earnest. A ghost of a smile went up to his high cheek-bones, but he did not answer.

"Why, mother?" said Lou, sing-song. "It feels to me so friendly——!"

"Yes, Louise, it does. *So* friendly! That's why I mistrust it so entirely——"

And she set off at a canter up the Row, under the green trees, her face like the face of Medusa[16] at fifty, a weapon in itself. She stared at everything and everybody, with that stare of cold dynamite waiting to explode them all. Lou posted trotting at her side, graceful and elegant, and faintly amused. Behind came Phoenix, like a shadow, with his yellowish, high-boned face still looking sick. And at his side, on the big brilliant bay horse, the smallish, black-bearded Welshman.

Between Phoenix and Lewis there was a latent but unspoken and wary sympathy. Phoenix was terribly impressed by St. Mawr, he could not leave off staring at him. And Lewis rode the brilliant, handsome-moving stallion so very quietly, like an insinuation.

Of the two men, Lewis looked the darker, with his black beard coming up to his thick black eyebrows. He was swarthy, with a rather short nose, and the uncanny pale-grey eyes that watched everything and cared about nothing. He cared about nothing in the world, except, at the present, St. Mawr. People did not matter to him. He rode his horse and watched the world from the vantage-ground of St. Mawr, with a final indifference.

"You have been with that horse long?" asked Phoenix.

"Since he was born."

Phoenix watched the action of St. Mawr as they went. The bay moved proud and springy, but with perfect good sense, among the stream of riders. It was a beautiful June morning, the leaves overhead were thick and green; there came the first whiff of lime-tree scent. To

---

[16]In Greek legend, a monster who turned to stone anyone who looked into her face.

Phoenix, however, the city was a sort of nightmare mirage, and to Lewis it was a sort of prison. The presence of people he felt as a prison around him.

Mrs. Witt and Lou were turning, at the end of the Row, bowing to some acquaintances. The grooms pulled aside. Mrs. Witt looked at Lewis with a cold eye.

"It seems an extraordinary thing to me, Louise," she said, "to see a groom with a beard."

"It isn't usual, mother," said Lou. "Do you mind?"

"Not at all. At least, I think I don't. I get very tired of modern bare-faced young men, *very!* The clean, pure boy, don't you know! Doesn't it make you tired?—No, I think a groom with a beard is quite attractive."

She gazed into the crowd defiantly, perching her finely shod toe with warlike firmness on the stirrup-iron. Then suddenly she reined in, and turned her horse towards the grooms.

"Lewis!" she said. "I want to ask you a question. Supposing, now, that Lady Carrington wanted you to shave off that beard, what should you say?"

Lewis instinctively put up his hand to the said beard.

"They've wanted me to shave it off, Mam," he said. "But I've never done it."

"But why? Tell me why."

"It's part of me, Mam."

Mrs. Witt pulled on again.

"Isn't that extraordinary, Louise?" she said. "Don't you like the way he says *Mam?* It sounds so impossible to me. Could any woman think of herself as Mam? Never, since Queen Victoria! But—do you know?— it hadn't occurred to me that a man's beard was really part of him. It always seemed to me that men wore their beards, like they wear their neckties, for show. I shall always remember Lewis for saying his beard was part of him. Isn't it curious, the way he rides? He seems to sink himself in the horse. When I speak to him, I'm not sure whether I'm speaking to a man or to a horse."

A few days later, Rico himself appeared on St. Mawr, for the morning ride. He rode self-consciously, as he did everything, and he was just a little nervous. But his mother-in-law was benevolent. She made him ride between her and Lou, like three ships slowly sailing abreast.

And that very day, who should come driving in an open carriage through the Park but the Queen Mother! Dear old Queen Alexandra, there was a flutter everywhere. And she bowed expressly to Rico, mistaking him, no doubt, for somebody else.

"Do you know," said Rico as they sat at lunch, he and Lou and Mrs. Witt, in Mrs. Witt's sitting-room in the dark, quiet hotel in Mayfair, "I really like riding St. Mawr *so* much. He really is a noble animal.—If ever I am made a Lord—which heaven forbid!—I shall be Lord St. Mawr."

"You mean," said Mrs. Witt, "his real lordship would be the horse?"

"Very possible, I admit," said Rico, with a curl of his long upper lip.

"Don't you think, mother," said Lou, "there *is* something quite noble about St. Mawr? He strikes me as the first noble thing I have ever seen."

"Certainly I've not seen any *man* that could compare with him. Because these English noblemen—well! I'd rather look at a Negro Pullman-boy, if I was looking for what *I* call nobility."

Poor Rico was getting crosser and crosser. There was a devil in Mrs. Witt. She had a hard, bright devil inside her, that she seemed to be able to let loose at will.

She let it loose the next day, when Rico and Lou joined her in the Row. She was silent but deadly with the horses, balking them in every way. She suddenly crowded over against the rail, in front of St. Mawr, so that the stallion had to rear to pull himself up. Then, having a clear track, she suddenly set off at a gallop, like an explosion, and the stallion, all on edge, set off after her.

It seemed as if the whole Park, that morning, were in a state of nervous tension. Perhaps there was thunder in the air. But St. Mawr kept on dancing and pulling at the bit, and wheeling sideways up against the railing, to the terror of the children and the onlookers, who squealed and jumped back suddenly, sending the nerves of the stallion into a rush like rockets. He reared and fought as Rico pulled him round.

Then he went on: dancing, pulling, springily progressing sideways, possessed with all the demons of perversity. Poor Rico's face grew longer and angrier. A fury rose in him, which he could hardly control. He hated his horse, and viciously tried to force him to a quiet, straight trot. Up went St. Mawr on his hind legs, to the terror of the Row. He got the bit in his teeth, and began to fight.

But Phoenix, cleverly, was in front of him.

"You get off, Rico!" called Mrs. Witt's voice, with all the calm of her wicked exultance.

And almost before he knew what he was doing, Rico had sprung lightly to the ground, and was hanging on to the bridle of the rearing stallion.

Phoenix also lightly jumped down, and ran to St. Mawr, handing his bridle to Rico. Then began a dancing and a splashing, a rearing and a plunging. St. Mawr was being wicked. But Phoenix, the indifference of conflict in his face, sat tight and immovable, without any emotion, only the heaviness of his impersonal will settling down like a weight, all the time, on the horse. There was, perhaps, a curious barbaric exultance in bare, dark will devoid of emotion or personal feeling.

So they had a little display in the Row for almost five minutes, the brilliant horse rearing and fighting. Rico, with a stiff long face, scrambled on to Phoenix's horse, and withdrew to a safe distance. Policemen came, and an officious mounted police rode up to save the situation. But it was obvious that Phoenix, detached and apparently unconcerned, but barbarically potent in his will, would bring the horse to order.

Which he did, and rode the creature home. Rico was requested not to ride St. Mawr in the Row any more, as the stallion was dangerous to public safety. The authorities knew all about him.

Where ended the first fiasco of St. Mawr.

"We didn't get on very well with his lordship this morning," said Mrs. Witt triumphantly.

"No, he didn't like his company *at all!*" Rico snarled back.

He wanted Lou to sell the horse again.

"I doubt if anyone would buy him, dear," she said. "He's a known character."

"Then make a gift of him—to your mother," said Rico with venom.

"Why to mother?" asked Lou innocently.

"She might be able to cope with him—or he with her!" The last phrase was deadly. Having delivered it, Rico departed.

Lou remained at a loss. She felt almost always a little bit dazed, as if she could not see clear nor feel clear. A curious deadness upon her, like the first touch of death. And through this cloud of numbness, or deadness, came all her muted experiences.

Why was it? She did not know. But she felt that in some way it came from a battle of wills. Her mother, Rico, herself, it was always an unspoken, unconscious battle of wills, which was gradually numbing and paralysing her. She knew Rico meant nothing but kindness by her. She knew her mother only wanted to watch over her. Yet always there was this tension of will, that was so numbing. As if at the depths of him, Rico were always angry, though he seemed so "happy" on the top. And Mrs. Witt was organically angry. So they were like a couple of bombs, timed to explode some day, but ticking on like two ordinary timepieces in the meanwhile.

She had come definitely to realize this: that Rico's anger was wound up tight at the bottom of him, like a steel spring that kept his works going, while he himself was "charming," like a bomb-clock with Sèvres paintings or Dresden figures on the outside. But his very charm was a sort of anger, and his love was a destruction in itself. He just couldn't help it.

And she? Perhaps she was a good deal the same herself. Wound up tight inside, and enjoying herself being "lovely." But wound up tight on some tension that, she realized now with wonder, was really a sort of anger. This, the mainspring that drove her on the round of "joys."

She used really to enjoy the tension, and the *élan* it gave her. While she knew nothing about it. So long as she felt it really was life and happiness, this *élan*, this tension and excitement of "enjoying oneself."

Now suddenly she doubted the whole show. She attributed to it the curious numbness that was overcoming her, as if she couldn't feel any more.

She wanted to come unwound. She wanted to escape this battle of wills.

Only St. Mawr gave her some hint of the possibility. He was so powerful, and so dangerous. But in his dark eye, that looked, with its cloudy brown pupil, a cloud within a dark fire, like a world beyond our world, there was a dark vitality glowing, and within the fire, another sort of wisdom. She felt sure of it: even when he put his ears back, and bared his teeth, and his great eyes came bolting out of his naked horse's head, and she saw demons upon demons in the chaos of his horrid eyes.

Why did he seem to her like some living background, into which she wanted to retreat? When he reared his head and neighed from his deep chest, like deep wind-bells resounding, she seemed to hear the echoes of another darker, more spacious, more dangerous, more splendid world than ours, that was beyond her. And there she wanted to go.

She kept it utterly a secret, to herself. Because Rico would just have lifted his long upper lip, in his bare face, in a condescending sort of "understanding." And her mother would, as usual, have suspected her of sidestepping. People, all the people she knew, seemed so entirely contained within their cardboard let's-be-happy world. Their wills were fixed like machines on happiness, or fun, or the-best-ever. This ghastly cheery-o! touch, that made all her blood go numb.

Since she had really seen St. Mawr looming fiery and terrible in an outer darkness, she could not believe the world she lived in. She could not believe it was actually happening, when she was dancing in the afternoon at Claridge's, or in the evening at the Carlton,[17] sliding about with some suave young man who wasn't like a man at all to her. Or down in Sussex for the week-end with the Enderleys: the talk, the eating and drinking, the flirtation, the endless dancing: it all seemed far more bodiless and, in a strange way, wraithlike, than any fairy-story. She seemed to be eating Barmecide[18] food, that had been conjured up out of thin air, by the power of words. She seemed to be talking to handsome young bare-faced unrealities, not men at all: as she slid about with them, in the perpetual dance, they too seemed to have been conjured up out of air, merely for this soaring, slithering dance-business. And she could not believe that, when the lights went out, they wouldn't melt back into thin air again, and complete nonentity. The strange nonentity of it all! Everything just conjured up, and nothing real. *"Isn't this the best ever!"* they would beamingly assert, like the wraiths of enjoyment, without any genuine substance. And she would beam back: *"Lots of fun!"*

She was thankful the season was over and everybody was leaving London. She and Rico were due to go to Scotland, but not till August.[19] In the meantime they would go to her mother.

Mrs. Witt had taken a cottage in Shropshire, on the Welsh border, and had moved down there with Phoenix and her horses. The open, heather-and-bilberry-covered hills were splendid for riding.

Rico consented to spend the month in Shropshire, because for near neighbours Mrs. Witt had the Manbys, at Corrabach Hall. The Manbys were rich Australians returned to the old country and set up as Squires, all in full blow. Rico had known them in Victoria: they were of good family: and the girls made a great fuss of him.

So down went Lou and Rico, Lewis, Poppy and St. Mawr, to Shrewsbury, then out into the country. Mrs. Witt's "cottage" was a tall red-

---

[17]Fashionable London hotels.

[18]In the *Arabian Nights*, one of the Barmecides (the rulers of Baghdad) holds a banquet at which all the festal dishes are empty.

[19]Fashionable people left London when the courts and Parliament rose in June, went to the country or to the coast for yacht-racing in midsummer, and converged in Scotland in August for the start of the hunting season.

brick Georgian house looking straight on to the churchyard, and the dark, looming big church.

"I never knew what a comfort it would be," said Mrs. Witt, "to have gravestones under my drawing-room windows, and funerals for lunch."

She really did take a strange pleasure in sitting in her panelled room, that was painted grey, and watching the Dean or one of the curates officiating at the graveside, among a group of black country mourners with black-bordered handkerchiefs luxuriantly in use.

"Mother!" said Lou. "I think it's gruesome!"

She had a room at the back, looking over the walled garden and the stables. Nevertheless there was the *boom! boom!* of the passing-bell, and the chiming and pealing on Sundays. The shadow of the church, indeed! A very audible shadow, making itself heard insistently.

The Dean was a big, burly, fat man with a pleasant manner. He was a gentleman, and a man of learning in his own line. But he let Mrs. Witt know that he looked down on her just a trifle—as a parvenu[20] American, a Yankee—though she never was a Yankee: and at the same time he had a sincere respect for her, as a rich woman. Yes, a sincere respect for her, as a rich woman.

Lou knew that every Englishman, especially of the upper classes, has a wholesome respect for riches. But then, who hasn't?

The Dean was more *impressed* by Mrs. Witt than by little Lou. But to Lady Carrington he was charming: she was *almost* "one of us," you know. And he was very gracious to Rico: "your father's splendid colonial service."

Mrs. Witt had now a new pantomime to amuse her: the Georgian house, her own pew in church—it went with the old house: a village of thatched cottages—some of them with corrugated iron over the thatch: the cottage people, farm labourers and their families, with a few, a very few, outsiders: the wicked little group of cottages down at Mile End, famous for ill living. The Mile-Enders were all Allisons and Jephsons, and inbred, the Dean said: result of working through the centuries at the quarry, and living isolated there at Mile End.

Isolated! Imagine it! A mile and a half from the railway station, ten miles from Shrewsbury. Mrs. Witt thought of Texas, and said:

_____

[20]Newly rich.

"Yes, they are *very* isolated, away down there!"

And the Dean never for a moment suspected sarcasm.

But there she had the whole thing staged complete for her: English village life. Even miners breaking in to shatter the rather stuffy, unwholesome harmony.—All the men touched their caps to her, all the women did a bit of a reverence, the children stood aside for her, if she appeared in the street.

They were all poor again: the labourers could no longer afford even a glass of beer in the evenings, since the Glorious War.[21]

"Now I think that *is* terrible," said Mrs. Witt. "Not to be able to get away from those stuffy, squalid, picturesque cottages for an hour in the evening, to drink a glass of beer."

"It's a pity, I do agree with you, Mrs. Witt. But Mr. Watson has organized a men's reading-room, where the men can smoke and play dominoes, and read if they wish."

"But that," said Mrs. Witt, "is not the same as that cosy parlour in the 'Moon and Stars.' "

"I quite agree," said the Dean. "It isn't."

Mrs. Witt marched to the landlord of the "Moon and Stars," and asked for a glass of cider.

"I want," she said, in her American accent, "these poor labourers to have their glass of beer in the evenings."

"They want it themselves," said Harvey.

"Then they must have it——"

The upshot was, she decided to supply one large barrel of beer per week and the landlord was to sell it to the labourers at a penny a glass.

"My own country has gone dry," she asserted. "But not because we can't *afford* it."

By the time Lou and Rico appeared, she was deep in. She actually interfered very little: the barrel of beer was her one public act. But she *did* know everybody by sight, already, and she *did* know everybody's circumstances. And she had attended one prayer-meeting, one mother's meeting, one sewing-bee, one "social," one Sunday School meeting, one Band of Hope meeting, and one Sunday School treat. She ignored the poky little Wesleyan and Baptist chapels, and was true-blue Episcopalian.

"How strange these picturesque old villages are, Louise!" she said,

---

[21]World War I left in its wake a major recession with severe unemployment and reduced wages.

with a duskiness around her sharp, well-bred nose. "How *easy* it all seems, all on a definite pattern. And how false! And underneath, *how corrupt!*"

She gave that queer, triumphant leer from her grey eyes, and queer demonish wrinkles seemed to twitter on her face.

Lou shrank away. She was beginning to be afraid of her mother's insatiable curiosity, that always looked for the snake under the flowers. Or rather, for the maggots.

Always this same morbid interest in other people and their doings, their privacies, their dirty linen. Always this air of alertness for personal happenings, personalities, personalities, personalities. Always this subtle criticism and appraisal of other people, this analysis of other people's motives. If anatomy presupposes a corpse, then psychology presupposes a world of corpses. Personalities, which means personal criticism and analysis, presupposes a whole world-laboratory of human psyches waiting to be vivisected. If you cut a thing up, of course it will smell. Hence, nothing raises such an infernal stink, at last, as human psychology.

Mrs. Witt was a pure psychologist, a fiendish psychologist. And Rico, in his way, was a psychologist too. But he had a formula. "Let's *know* the worst, dear! But let's look on the bright side, and believe the best."

"Isn't the Dean a priceless old darling!" said Rico at breakfast.

And it had begun. Work had started in the psychic vivisection laboratory.

"Isn't he wonderful!" said Lou vaguely.

"So delightfully worldly!—*Some of us are not born to make money, dear boy. Luckily for us, we can marry it.*"—Rico made a priceless face.

"Is Mrs. Vyner so rich?" asked Lou.

"She is, quite a wealthy woman—in coal," replied Mrs. Witt. "But the Dean is surely worth his weight, even in gold. And he's a massive figure. I can imagine there would be great satisfaction in having him for a husband."

"Why, mother?" asked Lou.

"Oh, such a presence! One of these old Englishmen, that nobody can put in their pocket. You can't imagine his wife asking him to thread her needle. Something, after all, so *robust!* So different from *young* Englishmen, who all seem to me like ladies, perfect ladies."

"*Somebody* has to keep up the tradition of the perfect lady," said Rico.

"I know it," said Mrs. Witt. "And if the women won't do it, the young gentlemen take on the burden. They bear it very well."

It was in full swing, the cut and thrust. And poor Lou, who had reached the point of stupefaction in the game, felt she did not know what to do with herself.

Rico and Mrs. Witt were deadly enemies, yet neither could keep clear of the other. It might have been they who were married to one another, their duel and their duet were so relentless.

But Rico immediately started the social round: first the Manbys: then motor twenty miles to luncheon at Lady Tewkesbury's: then young Mr. Burns came flying down in his aeroplane from Chester: then they must motor to the sea, to Sir Edward Edwards' place, where there was a moonlight bathing-party. Everything intensely thrilling, and so innerly wearisome, Lou felt.

But back of it all was St. Mawr, looming like a bonfire in the dark. He really was a tiresome horse to own. He worried the mares, if they were in the same paddock with him, always driving them round. And with any other horse he just fought with definite intent to kill. So he had to stay alone.

"That St. Mawr, he's a bad horse," said Phoenix.

"Maybe!" said Lewis.

"You don't like quiet horses?" said Phoenix.

"Most horses *is* quiet," said Lewis. "St. Mawr, he's different."

"Why don't he never get any foals?"

"Doesn't want to, I should think. Same as me."

"What good is a horse like that? Better shoot him, before he kill somebody."

"What good'll they get, shooting St. Mawr?" said Lewis.

"If he kills somebody!" said Phoenix.

But there was no answer.

The two grooms both lived over the stables, and Lou, from her window, saw a good deal of them. They were two quiet men, yet she was very much aware of their presence, aware of Phoenix's rather high square shoulders and his fine, straight, vigorous black hair that tended to stand up assertively on his head, as he went quietly drifting about his various jobs. He was not lazy, but he did everything with a sort of diffidence, as if from a distance, and handled his horses carefully, cautiously, and cleverly, but without sympathy. He seemed to be holding something back, all the time, unconsciously, as if in his very being there was some secret. But it was a secret of *will*. His quiet, reluctant movements, as if he never really wanted to do anything; his long flat-stepping stride; the permanent challenge in his high cheek-bones, the

Indian glint in his eyes, and his peculiar stare, watchful and yet unseeing, made him unpopular with the women servants.

Nevertheless, women had a certain fascination for him: he would stare at the pretty young maids with an intent blank stare, when they were not looking. Yet he was rather overbearing, domineering with them, and they resented him. It was evident to Lou that he looked upon himself as belonging to the Master, not to the servant class. When he flirted with the maids, as he very often did, for he had a certain crude ostentatiousness, he seemed to let them feel that he despised them as inferiors, servants, while he admired their pretty charms, as fresh country maids.

"I'm fair nervous of that Phoenix," said Fanny, the fair-haired maid. "He makes you feel what he'd do to you if he could."

"He'd better not try with me," said Mabel. "I'd scratch his cheeky eyes out. Cheek!—for it's nothing else! He's nobody—common as they're made!"

"He makes you feel you was there for him to trample on," said Fanny.

"Mercy, you *are* soft! If anybody's that, it's him. Oh, my, Fanny, you've no right to let a fellow make you feel like *that!* Make *them* feel that *they're* dirt, for *you* to trample on: which they are!"

Fanny, however, being a shy little blond thing, wasn't good at assuming the trampling rôle. She was definitely nervous of Phoenix. And he enjoyed it. An invisible smile seemed to creep up his cheek-bones, and the glint moved in his eyes as he teased her. He tormented her by his very presence, as he knew.

He would come silently up when she was busy, and stand behind her perfectly still, so that she was unaware of his presence. Then, silently, he would *make* her aware. Till she glanced nervously round and, with a scream, saw him.

One day Lou watched this little play. Fanny had been picking over a bowl of black currants, sitting on the bench under the maple-tree in a corner of the yard. She didn't look round till she had picked up her bowl to go to the kitchen. Then there was a scream and a crash.

When Lou came out, Phoenix was crouching down silently gathering up the currants, which the little maid, scarlet and trembling, was collecting into another bowl. Phoenix seemed to be smiling down his back.

"Phoenix!" said Lou. "I wish you wouldn't startle Fanny!"

He looked up, and she saw the glint of ridicule in his eyes.

"Who, me?" he said.

"Yes, you. You go up behind Fanny, to startle her. You're not to do it."

He slowly stood erect, and lapsed into his peculiar invisible silence. Only for a second his eyes glanced at Lou's, and then she saw the cold anger, the gleam of malevolence and contempt. He could not bear being commanded, or reprimanded, by a woman.

Yet it was even worse with a man.

"What's that, Lou?" said Rico, appearing all handsome and in the picture, in white flannels with an apricot silk shirt.

"I'm telling Phoenix he's not to torment Fanny!"

"Oh!" and Rico's voice immediately became his father's, the important government official's. "Certainly *not!* Most certainly *not!*" He looked at the scattered currants and the broken bowl. Fanny melted into tears. "This, I suppose, is some of the results! Now look here, Phoenix, you're to leave the maids strictly alone. I shall ask them to report to me whenever, or *if* ever, you interfere with them. But I hope you *won't* interfere with them—in any way. You understand?"

As Rico became more and more Sir Henry and the government official, Lou's bones melted more and more into discomfort. Phoenix stood in his peculiar silence, the invisible smile on his cheek-bones.

"You understand what I'm saying to you?" Rico demanded, in intensified acid tones.

But Phoenix only stood there, as it were behind a cover of his own will, and looked back at Rico with a faint smile on his face and the glint moving in his eyes.

"Do you intend to answer?" Rico's upper lip lifted nastily.

"Mrs. Witt is my boss," came from Phoenix.

The scarlet flew up Rico's throat and flushed his face, his eyes went glaucous. Then quickly his face turned yellow.

Lou looked at the two men: her husband, whose rages, over-controlled, were organically terrible; the half-breed, whose dark-coloured lips were widened in a faint smile of derision, but in whose eyes caution and hate were playing against one another. She realized that Phoenix would accept *her* reprimand, or her mother's, because he could despise the two of them as mere women. But Rico's bossiness aroused murder pure and simple.

She took her husband's arm.

"Come, dear!" she said, in her half plaintive way. "I'm sure Phoenix understands. We all understand. Go to the kitchen, Fanny, never mind the currants. There are plenty more in the garden."

Rico was always thankful to be drawn quickly, submissively away from his own rage. He was afraid of it. He was afraid lest he should fly at the groom in some horrible fashion. The very thought horrified him. But in actuality he came very near to it.

He walked stiffly, feeling paralysed by his own fury. And those words, *Mrs. Witt is my boss*, were like hot acid in his brain. An insult!

"By the way, Belle-Mère!"[22] he said when they joined Mrs. Witt—she hated being called Belle-Mère, and once said: "If I'm the bell-mare, are you one of the colts?"—she also hated his voice of smothered fury—"I had to speak to Phoenix about persecuting the maids. He took the liberty of informing me that you were his boss, so perhaps you had better speak to him."

"I certainly will. I believe they're my maids, and nobody else's, so it's my duty to look after them. Who was he persecuting?"

"I'm the responsible one, mother," said Lou——

Rico disappeared in a moment. He must get out: get away from the house. How? Something was wrong with the car. Yet he must get away, away. He would go over to Corrabach. He would ride St. Mawr. He had been talking about the horse, and Flora Manby was dying to see him. She had said: "Oh, I can't *wait* to see that marvellous horse of yours."

He would ride him over. It was only seven miles. He found Lou's maid Elena, and sent her to tell Lewis. Meanwhile, to soothe himself, he dressed himself most carefully in white riding-breeches and a shirt of purple silk crêpe, with a flowing black tie spotted red like a ladybird, and black riding-boots. Then he took a *chic* little white hat with a black band.

St. Mawr was saddled and waiting, and Lewis had saddled a second horse.

"Thanks, Lewis, I'm going alone!" said Rico.

This was the first time he had ridden St. Mawr in the country, and he was nervous. But he was also in the hell of a smothered fury. All his careful dressing had not really soothed him. So his fury consumed his nervousness.

He mounted with a swing, blind and rough. St. Mawr reared.

"Stop that!" snarled Rico, and put him to the gate.

Once out in the village street, the horse went dancing sideways. He insisted on dancing at the sidewalk, to the exaggerated terror of the children. Rico, exasperated, pulled him across. But no, he wouldn't go down the centre of the village street. He began dancing and edging on

---

[22]Mother-in-law.

to the other sidewalk, so the foot-passengers fled into the shops in terror.

The devil was in him. He would turn down every turning where he was not meant to go. He reared with panic at a furniture van. He *insisted* on going down the wrong side of the road. Rico was riding him with a martingale, and he could see the rolling, bloodshot eye.

"Damn you, *go!*" said Rico, giving him a dig with the spurs.

And away they went, down the high road, in a thunderbolt. It was a hot day, with thunder threatening, so Rico was soon in a flame of heat. He held on tight, with fixed eyes, trying all the time to rein in the horse. What he really was afraid of was that the brute would shy suddenly, as he galloped. Watching for this, he didn't care when they sailed past the turning to Corrabach.

St. Mawr flew on, in a sort of *élan*. Marvellous, the power and life in the creature! There was really a great joy in the motion. If only he wouldn't take the corners at a gallop, nearly swerving Rico off! Luckily the road was clear. To ride, to ride at this terrific gallop, on into eternity!

After several miles, the horse slowed down, and Rico managed to pull him into a lane that might lead to Corrabach. When all was said and done, it was a wonderful ride. St. Mawr could go like the wind, but with that luxurious heavy ripple of life which is like nothing else on earth. It seemed to carry one at once into another world, away from the life of the nerves.

So Rico arrived after all something of a conqueror at Corrabach. To be sure, he was perspiring, and so was his horse. But he was a hero from another, heroic world.

"Oh, such a hot ride!" he said, as he walked on to the lawn at Corrabach Hall. "Between the sun and the horse, really!—between two fires!"

"Don't you trouble, you're looking dandy, a bit hot and flushed like," said Flora Manby. "Let's go and see your horse."

And her exclamation was: "Oh, he's *lovely!* He's *fine!* I'd love to try him once——"

Rico decided to accept the invitation to stay overnight at Corrabach. Usually he was very careful, and refused to stay, unless Lou was with him. But they telephoned to the post office at Chomesbury, would Mr. Jones please send a message to Lady Carrington that Sir Henry was staying the night at Corrabach Hall, but would be home next day? Mr. Jones received the request with unction, and said he would go over himself to give the message to Lady Carrington.

Lady Carrington was in the walled garden. The peculiarity of Mrs. Witt's house was that, for grounds proper, it had the churchyard.

"I never thought, Louise, that one day I should have an old English churchyard for my lawns and shrubbery and park, and funeral mourners for my herds of deer. It's curious. For the first time in my life a funeral has become a real thing to me. I feel I could write a book on them."

But Louise only felt intimidated.

At the back of the house was a flagged court-yard, with stables and a maple-tree in a corner, and big doors opening on to the village street. But at the side was a walled garden, with fruit-trees and currant-bushes and a great bed of rhubarb, and some tufts of flowers, peonies, pink roses, sweet-williams. Phoenix, who had a certain taste for gardening, would be out there thinning the carrots or tying up the lettuce. He was not lazy. Only he would not take work seriously, as a job. He would be quite amused tying up lettuces, and would tie up head after head, quite prettily. Then, becoming bored, he would abandon his task, light a cigarette, and go and stand on the threshold of the big doors, in full view of the street, watching, and yet completely indifferent.

After Rico's departure on St. Mawr, Lou went into the garden. And there she saw Phoenix working in the onion-bed. He was bending over, in his own silence, busy with nimble, amused fingers among the grassy young onions. She thought he had not seen her, so she went down another path to where a swing bed hung under the apple-trees. There she sat with a book and a bundle of magazines. But she did not read.

She was musing vaguely. Vaguely, she was glad that Rico was away for a while. Vaguely, she felt a sense of bitterness, of complete futility: the complete futility of her living. This left her drifting in a sea of utter chagrin. And Rico seemed to her the symbol of the futility. Vaguely, she was aware that something else existed, but she didn't know where it was or what it was.

In the distance she could see Phoenix's dark, rather tall-built head, with its black, fine, intensely living hair tending to stand on end, like a brush with long, very fine black bristles. His hair, she thought, betrayed him as an animal of a different species. He was growing a little bored by weeding onions: that also she could tell. Soon he would want some other amusement.

Presently Lewis appeared. He was small, energetic, a little bit bow-legged, and he walked with a slight strut. He wore khaki riding-breeches, leather gaiters, and a blue shirt. And, like Phoenix, he rarely had any cap or hat on his head. His thick black hair was parted at the

side and brushed over heavily sideways, dropping on his forehead at
the right. It was very long, a real mop, under which his eyebrows were
dark and steady.

"Seen Lady Carrington?" he asked of Phoenix.

"Yes, she's sitting on that swing over there—she's been there quite
awhile."

The wretch—he had seen her from the very first!

Lewis came striding over, looking towards her with his pale-grey
eyes, from under his mop of hair.

"Mr. Jones from the post office wants to see you, my Lady, with a
message from Sir Henry."

Instantly alarm took possession of Lou's soul.

"Oh!—Does he want to see me personally?—What message? Is anything wrong?"—And her voice trailed out over the last word, with a
sort of anxious nonchalance.

"I don't think it's anything amiss," said Lewis reassuringly.

"Oh! You don't"—the relief came into her voice. Then she looked at
Lewis with a slight, winning smile in her unmatched eyes. "I'm so
afraid of St. Mawr, you know." Her voice was soft and cajoling. Phoenix was listening in the distance.

"St. Mawr's all right, if you don't do nothing to him," Lewis replied.

"I'm sure he is!—But how is one to know when one is doing something to him?—Tell Mr. Jones to come here, please," she concluded, on
a changed tone.

Mr. Jones, a man of forty-five, thickset, with a fresh complexion and
rather foolish brown eyes, and a big brown moustache, came prancing
down the path, smiling rather fatuously, and doffing his straw hat with
a gorgeous bow the moment he saw Lou sitting in her slim white frock
on the coloured swing bed under the trees with their hard green apples.

"Good morning, Mr. Jones!"

"Good morning, Lady Carrington.—If I may say so, what a picture
you make—a beautiful picture——"

He beamed under his big brown moustache like the greatest lady-
killer.

"Do I!—Did Sir Henry say he was all right?"

"He didn't *say* exactly, but I should expect he is all right——" and
Mr. Jones delivered his message, in the mayonnaise of his own unction.

"Thank you so much, Mr. Jones. It's awfully good of you to come
and tell me. Now I shan't worry about Sir Henry *at all*."

"It's a great pleasure to come and deliver a satisfactory message to
Lady Carrington. But it won't be kind to Sir Henry if you don't worry

about him *at all* in his absence. We all enjoy being worried about by those we love—so long as there is nothing to worry about of course!"

"Quite!" said Lou. "Now won't you take a glass of port and a biscuit, or a whisky and soda? And thank you ever so much."

"Thank *you*, my Lady. I might drink a whisky and soda, since you are so good."

And he beamed fatuously.

"Let Mr. Jones mix himself a whisky and soda, Lewis," said Lou.

"Heavens!" she thought, as the postmaster retreated a little uncomfortably down the garden path, his bald spot passing in and out of the sun, under the trees. "How ridiculous everything is, how ridiculous, ridiculous!" Yet she didn't really dislike Mr. Jones and his interlude.

Phoenix was melting away out of the garden. He had to follow the fun.

"Phoenix!" Lou called. "Bring me a glass of water, will you? Or send somebody with it."

He stood in the path looking round at her.

"All right!" he said.

And he turned away again.

She did not like being alone in the garden. She liked to have the men working somewhere near. Curious how pleasant it was to sit there in the garden when Phoenix was about, or Lewis. It made her feel she could never be lonely or jumpy. But when Rico was there, she was all aching nerve.

Phoenix came back with a glass of water, lemon juice, sugar, and a small bottle of brandy. He knew Lou liked a spoonful of brandy in her iced lemonade.

"How thoughtful of you, Phoenix!" she said. "Did Mr. Jones get his whisky?"

"He was just getting it."

"That's right.—By the way, Phoenix, I wish you wouldn't get mad if Sir Henry speaks to you. He is *really* so kind."

She looked up at the man. He stood there watching her in silence, the invisible smile on his face, and the inscrutable Indian glint moving in his eyes. What was he thinking? There was something passive and almost submissive about him, but, underneath this, an unyielding resistance and cruelty: yes, even cruelty. She felt that, on top, he was submissive and attentive, bringing her her lemonade as she liked it, without being told: thinking for her quite subtly. But underneath there was an unchanging hatred. He submitted circumstantially, he worked for a wage. And, even circumstantially, he *liked* his mistress—*la patrona*—and her daughter. But much deeper than any circumstance, or any circumstantial liking, was the categorical hatred upon which he was founded, and with which he was powerless. His liking for Lou and for Mrs. Witt, his serving them and working for a wage, was all sidetracking his own nature, which was grounded on hatred of their very existence. But what was he to do? He had to live. Therefore he had to serve, to work for a wage, and even to be faithful.

And yet *their* existence made his own existence negative. If he was to exist, positively, they would have to cease to exist. At the same time, a fatal sort of tolerance made him serve these women, and go on serving.

"Sir Henry is *so* kind to everybody," Lou insisted.

The half-breed met her eyes, and smiled uncomfortably.

"Yes, he's a kind man," he replied, as if sincerely.

"Then why do you mind if he speaks to you?"

"I don't mind," said Phoenix glibly.

"But you do. Or else you wouldn't make him so angry."

"Was he angry?—I don't know," said Phoenix.

"He was very angry. And you *do* know."

"No, I don't know if he's angry. I don't know," the fellow persisted. And there was a glib sort of satisfaction in his tone.

"That's awfully unkind of you, Phoenix," she said, growing offended in her turn.

"No, I don't know if he's angry. I don't want to make him angry. I don't know——"

He had taken on a tone of naïve ignorance, which at once gratified her pride as a woman, and deceived her.

"Well, you believe me when I tell you you *did* make him angry, don't you?"

"Yes, I believe when you tell me."

"And you promise me, won't you, not to do it again? It's *so* bad for him—so bad for his nerves, and for his eyes. It makes them inflamed, and injures his eyesight. And you know, as an artist, it's terrible if anything happens to his eyesight——"

Phoenix was watching her closely, to take it in. He still was not good at understanding continuous, logical statement. Logical connexion in speech seemed to stupefy him, make him stupid. He understood in disconnected assertions of fact. But he had gathered what she said. "He gets mad at you. When he gets mad, it hurts his eyes. His eyes hurt him. He can't see, because his eyes hurt him. He wants to paint a picture, he can't. He can't paint a picture, he can't see clear——"

Yes, he had understood. She saw he had understood. The bright glint of satisfaction moved in his eyes.

"So now promise me, won't you, you won't make him mad again: you won't make him angry?"

"No, I won't make him angry. I don't do anything to make him angry," Phoenix answered, rather glibly.

"And you do understand, don't you? You do know how kind he is: how he'd do a good turn to anybody?"

"Yes, he's a kind man," said Phoenix.

"I'm so glad you realize.—There, that's luncheon! How nice it is to sit here in the garden, when everybody is nice to you! No, I can carry the tray, don't you bother."

But he took the tray from her hand, and followed her to the house. And as he walked behind her, he watched the slim white nape of her neck, beneath the clustering of her bobbed hair, something as a stoat watches a rabbit he is following.

In the afternoon Lou retreated once more to her place in the garden. There she lay, sitting with a bunch of pillows behind her, neither reading nor working, just musing. She learned the new joy: to do absolutely nothing, but to lie and let the sunshine filter through the leaves, to see the bunch of red-hot-poker flowers pierce scarlet into the afternoon, beside the comparative neutrality of some foxgloves. The mere colour of hard red, like the big oriental poppies that had fallen, and these poker flowers, lingered in her consciousness like a communication.

Into this peaceful indolence, when even the big, dark-grey tower of the church beyond the wall and the yew-trees was keeping its bells in silence, advanced Mrs. Witt, in a broad panama hat and a white dress.

"Don't you want to ride, or do something, Louise?" she asked ominously.

"Don't you want to be peaceful, mother?" retorted Louise.

"Yes—an *active* peace.—I can't *believe* that my daughter can be content to lie on a hammock and do *nothing*, not even read or improve her mind, the greater part of the day."

"Well, your daughter *is* content to do that. It's her greatest pleasure."

"I know it. I can see it. And it surprises me *very* much. When I was your age, I was never still. I had so much *go*——"

" 'Those maids, thank God,
Are 'neath the sod,
And all their generation.'

"No, but mother, I only take life differently. Perhaps you used up that sort of *go*. I'm the harem type, mother: only I never want the men inside the lattice."

"Are you really my daughter?—Well! A woman never knows what will happen to her.—I'm an *American* woman, and I suppose I've got to remain one, no matter where I am.—What did you want, Lewis?"

The groom had approached down the path.

"If I am to saddle Poppy?" said Lewis.

"No, apparently *not!*" replied Mrs. Witt. "Your mistress prefers the hammock to the saddle."

"Thank you, Lewis. What mother says is true this afternoon, at least." And she gave him a peculiar little cross-eyed smile.

"Who," said Mrs. Witt to the man, "has been cutting at your hair?"

There was a moment of silent resentment.

"I did it myself, Mam! Sir Henry said it was too long."

"He certainly spoke the truth.—But I believe there's a barber in the village on Saturdays—or you could ride over to Shrewsbury.—Just turn round, and let me look at the back. Is it the money?"

"No, Mam. I don't like these fellows touching my head."

He spoke coldly, with a certain hostile reserve that at once piqued Mrs. Witt.

"Don't you really!" she said. "But it's quite *impossible* for you to go about as you are. It gives you a half-witted appearance. Go now into the yard, and get a chair and a dust-sheet. I'll cut your hair."

The man hesitated, hostile.

"Don't be afraid, I know how it's done. I've cut the hair of many a poor wounded boy in hospital: and shaved them too. *You've got such a touch, nurse!* Poor fellow, he was dying, though none of us knew it.— Those are compliments I value, Louise.—Get that chair now, and a dust-sheet. I'll borrow your hair-scissors from Elena, Louise."

Mrs. Witt, happily on the war-path, was herself again. She didn't care for work, actual work. But she loved trimming. She loved arranging unnatural and pretty salads, devising new and piquant-looking ice-creams, having a turkey stuffed exactly as she knew a stuffed turkey in Louisiana, with chestnuts and butter and stuff, or showing a servant how to turn waffles on a waffle-iron, or to bake a ham with brown sugar and cloves and a moistening of rum. She liked pruning rose-trees, or beginning to cut a yew-hedge into shape. She liked ordering her own and Louise's shoes, with an exactitude and a knowledge of shoemaking that sent the salesmen crazy. She was a demon in shoes. Reappearing from America, she would pounce on her daughter. "Louise, throw those shoes away. Give them to one of the maids."—"But, mother, they are some of the best French shoes. I like them."—"Throw them away. A shoe has only two excuses for existing: perfect comfort or perfect appearance. Those have neither. I have brought you some shoes."—Yes, she had brought ten pairs of shoes from New York. She knew her daughter's foot as she knew her own.

So now she was in her element, looming behind Lewis as he sat in the middle of the yard swathed in a dust-sheet. She had on an overall and a pair of wash-leather gloves, and she poised a pair of long scissors like one of the fates. In her big hat she looked curiously young, but with the youth of a bygone generation. Her heavy-lidded, laconic grey eyes were alert, studying the groom's black mop of hair. Her eyebrows made thin, uptilting black arches on her brow. Her fresh skin was slightly powdered, and she was really handsome, in a bold, bygone, eighteenth-century style. Some of the curious, adventurous stoicism of the eighteenth century: and then a certain blatant American efficiency.

Lou, who had strayed into the yard to see, looked so much younger and so many thousands of years older than her mother, as she stood in her wisp-like diffidence, the clusters of grape-like bobbed hair hanging beside her face, with its fresh colouring and its ancient weariness, her slightly squinting eyes, that were so disillusioned they were becoming faun-like.

"Not too short, mother, not too short!" she remonstrated, as Mrs. Witt, with a terrific flourish of efficiency, darted at the man's black hair, and the thick flakes fell like black snow.

"Now, Louise, I'm right in this job, please don't interfere.—Two things I hate to see: a man with his wool in his neck and ears: and a bare-faced young man who looks as if he'd bought his face as well as his hair from a men's beauty-specialist."

And efficiently she bent down, clip—clip—clipping! while Lewis sat utterly immobile, with sunken head, in a sort of despair.

Phoenix stood against the stable door, with his restless, eternal cigarette. And in the kitchen doorway the maids appeared and fled, appeared and fled in delight. The old gardener, a fixture who went with the house, creaked in and stood with his legs apart, silent in intense condemnation.

"First time I ever see such a thing!" he muttered to himself, as he creaked on into the garden. He was a bad-tempered old soul, who thoroughly disapproved of the household, and would have given notice, but that he knew which side his bread was buttered: and there was butter unstinted on his bread, in Mrs. Witt's kitchen.

Mrs. Witt stood back to survey her handiwork, holding those terrifying shears with their beak erect. Lewis lifted his head and looked stealthily round, like a creature in a trap.

"Keep still!" she said. "I haven't finished."

And she went for his front hair, with vigour, lifting up long layers and snipping off the ends artistically: till at last he sat with a black aureole upon the floor, and his ears standing out with curious new alertness from the sides of his clean-clipped head.

"Stand up," she said, "and let me look."

He stood up, looking absurdly young, with the hair all cut away from his neck and ears, left thick only on top. She surveyed her work with satisfaction.

"You look so much younger," she said, "you would be surprised. Sit down again."

She clipped the back of his neck with the shears, and then, with a very slight hesitation, she said:

"Now about the beard!"

But the man rose suddenly from the chair, pulling the dust-cloth from his neck with desperation.

"No, I'll do that myself," he said, looking her in the eyes with a cold light in his pale-grey, uncanny eyes.

She hesitated in a kind of wonder at his queer male rebellion.

"Now, listen, I shall do it much better than you—and besides," she added hurriedly, snatching at the dust-cloth he was flinging on the chair, "I haven't quite finished round the ears."

"I think I shall do," he said, again looking her in the eyes, with a cold, white gleam of finality. "Thank you for what you've done."

And he walked away to the stable.

"You'd better sweep up here," Mrs. Witt called.

"Yes, Mam," he replied, looking round at her again with an odd resentment, but continuing to walk away.

"However!" said Mrs. Witt. "I suppose he'll do."

And she divested herself of gloves and overall, and walked indoors to wash and to change. Lou went indoors too.

"It is extraordinary what hair that man has!" said Mrs. Witt. "Did I tell you when I was in Paris I saw a woman's face in the hotel that I thought I knew? I couldn't place her, till she was coming towards me. *Aren't you Rachel Fannière?* she said. *Aren't you Janette Leroy?* We hadn't seen each other since we were girls of twelve and thirteen, at school in New Orleans. Oh! she said to me. *Is every illusion doomed to perish? You had such wonderful golden curls! All my life I've said: Oh, if only I had such lovely hair as Rachel Fannière! I've seen those beautiful golden curls of yours all my life. And now I meet you, you're grey!* Wasn't that terrible, Louise? Well, that man's hair made me think of it—so thick and curious. It's strange what a difference there is in hair, I suppose it's because he's just an animal—no mind! There's nothing I admire in a man like a good *mind*. Your father was a very clever man, and all the men I've admired have been clever. But isn't it curious now, I've never cared much to touch their hair. How strange life is! If it gives one thing, it takes away another.—And even those poor boys in hospital: I have shaved them, or cut their hair, like a mother, never thinking anything of it. Lovely, intelligent, clean boys most of them were. Yet it never did anything to me. I never knew before that something could happen to one from a person's *hair*! Like to Janette Leroy from my curls when I was a child. And now I'm grey, as she says.—I wonder how old a man Lewis is, Louise! Didn't he look absurdly young, with his ears pricking up?"

"I think Rico said he was forty or forty-one."

"And never been married?"

"No—not as far as I know."

"Isn't that curious now!—just an animal! no mind! A man with no mind! I've always thought that the *most* despicable thing. Yet such wonderful hair to touch. Your Henry has quite a good mind, yet I would simply shrink from touching his hair.—I suppose one likes stroking a cat's fur, just the same. Just the animal in man. Curious that I never seem to have met it, Louise. Now I come to think of it, he has the eyes of a human cat: a human tomcat. Would you call him stupid? Yes, he's very stupid."

"No, mother, he's not stupid. He only doesn't care about our sort of things."

"Like an animal! But what a strange look he has in his eyes! a strange sort of intelligence! and a confidence in himself. Isn't that curious, Louise, in a man with as little mind as he has? Do you know, I should say he could see through a woman pretty well."

"Why, mother!" said Lou impatiently. "I think one gets so tired of your men with mind, as you call it. There are so many of that sort of clever men. And there are lots of men who aren't very clever, but are rather nice: and lots are stupid. It seems to me there's something else besides mind and cleverness, or niceness or cleanness. Perhaps it is the animal. Just think of St. Mawr! I've thought so much about him. We call him an animal, but we never know what it means. He seems a far greater mystery to me than a clever man. He's a horse. Why can't one say in the same way, of a man: *He's a man?* There seems no mystery in being a man. But there's a terrible mystery in St. Mawr."

Mrs. Witt watched her daughter quizzically.

"Louise," she said, "you won't tell me that the mere animal is all that counts in a man. I will never believe it. Man is wonderful because he is able to *think*."

"But is he?" cried Lou, with sudden exasperation. "Their thinking seems to me all so childish: like stringing the same beads over and over again. Ah, men! They and their thinking are all so *paltry*. How can you be impressed?"

Mrs. Witt raised her eyebrows sardonically.

"Perhaps I'm not—any more," she said with a grim smile.

"But," she added, "I still can't see that I am to be impressed by the mere animal in man. The animals are the same as we are. It seems to me they have the same feelings and wants as we do, in a commonplace way. The only difference is that they have no minds: no human minds, at least. And no matter what you say, Louise, lack of mind makes the commonplace."

Lou knitted her brows nervously.

"I suppose it does, mother.—But men's minds *are* so commonplace: look at Dean Vyner and his mind! Or look at Arthur Balfour, as a shining example. Isn't *that* commonplace, that cleverness? I would hate St. Mawr to be spoilt by such a mind."

"Yes, Louise, so would I. Because the men you mention are really old women, knitting the same pattern over and over again. Nevertheless, I shall never alter my belief that real mind is all that matters in a man, and it's *that* that we women love."

"Yes, mother!—But what *is* real mind? The old woman who knits the most complicated pattern? Oh, I can hear all their needles clicking, the clever men! As a matter of fact, mother, I believe Lewis has far more real mind than Dean Vyner or any of the clever ones. He has a good intuitive mind, he knows things without thinking them."

"That may be, Louise! But he is a servant. He is *under*. A real man should never be under. And then you could never be intimate with a man like Lewis."

"I don't want intimacy, mother. I'm too tired of it all. I love St. Mawr because he isn't intimate. He stands where one can't get at him. And he burns with life. And where does his life come from, to him? That's the mystery. That great burning life in him, which never is dead. Most men have a deadness in them that frightens me so, because of my own deadness. Why can't men get their life straight, like St. Mawr, and then think? Why can't they think quick, mother: quick as a woman: only farther than we do? Why isn't men's thinking quick like fire, mother? Why is it so slow, so dead, so deadly dull?"

"I can't tell you, Louise. My own opinion of the men of to-day has grown very small. But I can live in spite of it."

"No, mother. We seem to be living off old fuel, like the camel when he lives off his hump. Life doesn't rush into us, as it does even into St. Mawr, and he's a dependent animal. I can't live, mother. I just can't."

"I don't see why not. I'm full of life."

"I know you are, mother. But I'm not, and I'm your daughter.—And don't misunderstand me, mother. I don't want to be an animal like a horse or a cat or a lioness, though they all fascinate me, the way they get their life *straight*, not from a lot of old tanks, as we do. I don't admire the cave-man, and that sort of thing. But think, mother, if we could get our lives straight from the source, as the animals do, and still be ourselves. You don't like men yourself. But you've no idea how men just tire me out: even the very thought of them. You say they are too animal. But they're not, mother. It's the animal in them has gone perverse, or cringing, or humble, or domesticated, like dogs. I don't know one single man who is a proud living animal. I know they've left off really thinking. But then men always do leave off really thinking, when the last bit of wild animal dies in them."

"Because we have minds——"

"We have no minds once we are tame, mother. Men are all women, knitting and crocheting words together."

"I can't altogether agree, you know, Louise."

"I know you don't.—You like clever men. But clever men are mostly such unpleasant *animals*. As animals, so very unpleasant. And in men like Rico, the animal has gone queer and wrong. And in those nice clean boys you liked so much in the war, there is no wild animal left in them. They're all tame dogs, even when they're brave and well-bred. They're all tame dogs, mother, with human masters. There's no mystery in them."

"What do you want, Louise? You *do* want the caveman who'll knock you on the head with a club."

"Don't be silly, mother. That's much more your subconscious line, you admirer of Mind.—I don't consider the cave-man is real human animal at all. He's a brute, a degenerate. A pure animal man would be as lovely as a deer or a leopard, burning like a flame fed straight from underneath. And he'd be part of the unseen, like a mouse is, even. And he'd never cease to wonder, he'd breathe silence and unseen wonder, as the partridges do, running in the stubble. He'd be all the animals in turn, instead of one fixed, automatic thing, which he is now, grinding on the nerves.—Ah, no, mother, I want the wonder back again, or I shall die. I don't want to be like you, just criticizing and annihilating these dreary people, and enjoying it."

"My dear daughter, whatever else the human animal might be, he'd be a dangerous commodity."

"I wish he would, mother. I'm dying of these empty, dangerless men, who are only sentimental and spiteful."

"Nonsense, you're not dying."

"I am, mother. And I should be dead if there weren't St. Mawr and Phoenix and Lewis in the world."

"St. Mawr and Phoenix and Lewis! I thought you said they were servants!"

"That's the worst of it. If only they were masters! If only there were some men with as much natural life as they have, and their brave, quick minds that commanded instead of serving!"

"There are no such men," said Mrs. Witt, with a certain grim satisfaction.

"I know it. But I'm young, and I've got to live. And the thing that is offered me as life just starves me, starves me to death, mother. What am I to do? You enjoy shattering people like Dean Vyner. But I am young, I can't live that way."

"That may be."

It had long ago struck Lou how much more her mother realized and understood than ever Rico did. Rico was afraid, always afraid of realizing. Rico, with his good manners and his habitual kindness, and that peculiar imprisoned sneer of his.

He arrived home next morning on St. Mawr, rather flushed and gaudy, and over-kind, with an *empressé* [23] anxiety about Lou's welfare which spoke too many volumes. Especially as he was accompanied by Flora Manby, and by Flora's sister Elsie, and Elsie's husband, Frederick Edwards. They all came on horseback.

"Such awful ages since I saw you!" said Flora to Lou. "Sorry if we burst in on you. We're only just saying *How do you do?* and going on to the inn. They've got rooms all ready for us there. We thought we'd stay

---

[23]Gushing.

just one night over here, and ride to-morrow to the Devil's Chair. Won't you come? Lots of fun! Isn't Mrs. Witt at home?"

Mrs. Witt was out for the moment. When she returned she had on her curious stiff face, yet she greeted the newcomers with a certain cordiality: she felt it would be diplomatic, no doubt.

"There *are* two rooms here," she said, "and if you care to poke into them, why, we shall be *delighted* to have you. But I'll show them to you first, because they are poor, inconvenient rooms, with no running water and *miles* from the baths."

Flora and Elsie declared that they were "perfectly darling sweet rooms—not overcrowded."

"Well," said Mrs. Witt, "the conveniences certainly don't fill up much space. But if you like to take them for what they are——"

"Why, we feel absolutely overwhelmed, don't we, Elsie!—But we've no clothes——"

Suddenly the silence had turned into a house-party. The Manby girls appeared to lunch in fine muslin dresses, bought in Paris, fresh as daisies. Women's clothing takes up so little space, especially in summer! Fred Edwards was one of those blond Englishmen with a little brush moustache and those strong blue eyes which were always attempting the sentimental, but which Lou, in her prejudice, considered cruel: upon what grounds, she never analysed. However, he took a gallant tone with her at once, and she had to seem to simper. Rico, watching her, was so relieved when he saw the simper coming.

It had begun again, the whole clockwork of "lots of fun!"

"Isn't Fred flirting perfectly outrageously with Lady Carrington!—She looks so *sweet!*" cried Flora, over her coffee-cup. "Don't you mind, Harry!"

They called Rico "Harry"! His boy-name.

"Only a very little," said Harry. "*L'uomo é cacciatore.*"

"Oh, now, what does that mean?" cried Flora, who always thrilled to Rico's bits of affectation.

"It means," said Mrs. Witt, leaning forward and speaking in her most suave voice, "that man is a hunter."

Even Flora shrank under the smooth acid of the irony.

"Oh, well now!" she cried. "If he is, then what is woman?"

"The hunted," said Mrs. Witt, in a still smoother acid.

"At least," said Rico, "she is always *game!*"

"Ah, is she though!" came Fred's manly, well-bred tones. "I'm not so sure."

Mrs. Witt looked from one man to the other, as if she were dropping them down the bottomless pit.

Lou escaped to look at St. Mawr. He was still moist where the saddle had been. And he seemed a little bit extinguished, as if virtue had gone out of him.

But when he lifted his lovely naked head, like a bunch of flames, to see who it was had entered, she saw he was still himself. For ever sensitive and alert, his head lifted like the summit of a fountain. And within him the clean bones striking to the earth, his hoofs intervening between him and the ground like lesser jewels.

He knew her and did not resent her. But he took no notice of her. He would never "respond." At first she had resented it. Now she was glad. He would never be intimate, thank heaven.

She hid herself away till tea-time, but she could not hide from the sound of voices. Dinner was early, at seven. Dean Vyner came—Mrs. Vyner was an invalid—and also an artist who had a studio in the village and did etchings. He was a man of about thirty-eight, and poor, just beginning to accept himself as a failure, as far as making money goes. But he worked at his etchings and studied esoteric matters like astrology and alchemy. Rico patronized him, and was a little afraid of him. Lou could not quite make him out. After knocking about Paris and London and Munich, he was trying to become staid, and to persuade himself that English village life, with squire and dean in the background, humble artist in the middle, and labourer in the common foreground, was a genuine life. His self-persuasion was only moderately successful. This was betrayed by the curious arrest in his body: he seemed to have to force himself into movement: and by the curious duplicity in his yellow-grey, twinkling eyes, that twinkled and expanded like a goat's; with mockery, irony, and frustration.

"Your face is curiously like Pan's,"[24] said Lou to him at dinner.

It was true, in a commonplace sense. He had the tilted eyebrows, the twinkling goaty look, and the pointed ears of a goat-Pan.

"People have said so," he replied. "But I'm afraid it's not the face of the Great God Pan. Isn't it rather the Great Goat Pan!"

"I say, that's good!" cried Rico. "The Great Goat Pan!"

"I have always found it difficult," said the Dean, "to see the Great God Pan in that goat-legged old father of satyrs. He may have a good deal of influence—the world will always be full of goaty old satyrs. But

---

[24]The Greek god of nature and fertility, portrayed as a youth with goat's horns and feet; the Greek word *pan* means "all."

we find them somewhat vulgar. Even our late King Edward.[25] The goaty old satyrs are too comprehensible to me to be venerable, and I fail to see a Great God in the father of them all."

"Your ears should be getting red," said Lou to Cartwright. She, too, had an odd squinting smile that suggested nymphs, so irresponsible and unbelieving.

"Oh, no, nothing personal!" cried the Dean.

"I am not sure," said Cartwright, with a small smile. "But don't you imagine Pan once *was* a Great God, before the anthropomorphic Greeks turned him into half a man?"

"Ah!—maybe. That is very possible. But—I have noticed the limitation in myself—my mind has no grasp whatsoever of Europe before the Greeks arose. Mr. Wells' Outline[26] does not help me there, either," the Dean added with a smile.

"But what was Pan before he was a man with goat legs?" asked Lou.

"Before he looked like me?" said Cartwright, with a faint grin. "I should say he was the God that is hidden in everything. In those days you saw the thing, you never saw the God in it: I mean in the tree or the fountain or the animal. If you ever saw the God instead of the thing, you died. If you saw it with the naked eye, that is. But in the night you might see the God. And you knew it was there."

"The modern pantheist not only sees the God in everything, he takes photographs of it," said the Dean.

"Oh, and the divine pictures he paints!" cried Rico.

"Quite!" said Cartwright.

"But if they never *saw* the God in the thing, the old ones, how did they know he was there? How did they have any Pan at all?" said Lou.

"Pan was the hidden mystery—the hidden cause. That's how it was a Great God. Pan wasn't *he* at all: not even a Great God. He was Pan. All: what you see when you see in full. In the daytime you see the thing. But if your third eye is open, which sees only the things that can't be seen, you may see Pan within the thing, hidden: you may see with your third eye, which is darkness."

"Do you think I might see Pan in a horse, for example?"

"Easily. In St. Mawr!"—Cartwright gave her a knowing look.

"But," said Mrs. Witt, "it would be difficult, I should say, to open the third eye and see Pan in a man."

---

[25] Edward VII, who reigned 1901–1910, was well known to have kept a succession of mistresses while he was Prince of Wales, a scandalous matter in the reign of his mother, Queen Victoria.

[26] H. G. Wells (1866–1946) published his highly rationalistic *Outline of History* in 1920.

"Probably," said Cartwright, smiling. "In man he is overvisible: the old satyr: the fallen Pan."

"Exactly!" said Mrs. Witt. And she fell into a muse. "The fallen Pan!" she re-echoed. "Wouldn't a man be wonderful in whom Pan hadn't fallen!"

Over the coffee in the grey drawing-room she suddenly asked: "Supposing, Mr. Cartwright, one *did* open the third eye and see Pan in an actual man—I wonder what it would be like."

She half lowered her eyelids and tilted her face in a strange way, as if she were tasting something, and not quite sure.

"I wonder!" he said, smiling his enigmatic smile. But she could see he did not understand.

"Louise!" said Mrs. Witt at bedtime. "Come into my room for a moment, I want to ask you something."

"What is it, mother?"

"You, you *get* something from what Mr. Cartwright said, about seeing Pan with the third eye? Seeing Pan in something?"

Mrs. Witt came rather close, and tilted her face with strange insinuating question at her daughter.

"I think I do, mother."

"In what?"—The question came as a pistol-shot.

"I think, mother," said Lou reluctantly, "in St. Mawr."

"In a horse!"—Mrs. Witt contracted her eyes slightly. "Yes, I can see that. I know what you mean. It *is* in St. Mawr. It *is*! But in St. Mawr it makes me *afraid*——" she dragged out the word. Then she came a step closer. "But, Louise, did you ever see it in a man?"

"What, mother?"

"Pan. Did you ever see Pan in a man, as you see Pan in St. Mawr?"

Louise hesitated.

"No, mother, I don't think I did. When I look at men with my third eye, as you call it—I think I see—mostly—a sort of—pancake." She uttered the last word with a despairing grin, not knowing quite what to say.

"Oh, Louise, isn't that it! Doesn't one always see a pancake!—Now listen, Louise. Have you ever been in love?"

"Yes, as far as I understand it."

"Listen now. Did you ever see Pan in the man you loved? Tell me if you did."

"As I see Pan in St. Mawr?—no, mother." And suddenly her lips began to tremble and the tears came to her eyes.

"Listen, Louise.—I've been in love innumerable times—and *really* in love twice. Twice!—yet for fifteen years I've left off wanting to have anything to do with a man, really. For fifteen years! And why?—Do you know?—Because I couldn't see that peculiar hidden Pan in any of them. And I became that I needed to. I needed it. But it wasn't there. Not in any man. Even when I was in love with a man, it was for other things: because I *understood* him so well, or he understood me, or we had such sympathy. Never the hidden Pan.—Do you understand what I mean? Unfallen Pan!"

"More or less, mother."

"But now my third eye is coming open, I believe. I am tired of all these men like breakfast cakes, with a teaspoonful of mind or a teaspoonful of spirit in them, for baking-powder. Isn't it extraordinary that young man Cartwright talks about Pan, but he knows nothing of it at all? He knows nothing of the unfallen Pan: only the fallen Pan with goat legs and a leer—and that sort of power, don't you know——"

"But what do you know of the unfallen Pan, mother?"

"Don't ask me, Louise! I feel all of a tremble, as if I was just on the verge."

She flashed a little look of incipient triumph, and said good night.

An excursion on horseback had been arranged for the next day, to two old groups of rocks, called the Angel's Chair and the Devil's Chair, which crowned the moor-like hills looking into Wales, ten miles away. Everybody was going—they were to start early in the morning, and Lewis would be the guide, since no one exactly knew the way.

Lou got up soon after sunrise. There was a summer scent in the trees of early morning, and monkshood flowers stood up dark and tall, with shadows. She dressed in the green linen riding-skirt her maid had put ready for her, with a close bluish smock.

"Are you going out already, dear?" called Rico from his room.

"Just to smell the roses before we start, Rico."

He appeared in the doorway in his yellow silk pyjamas. His large blue eyes had that rolling irritable look and the slightly bloodshot whites which made her want to escape.

"Booted and spurred!—the *energy!*" he cried.

"It's a lovely day to ride," she said.

"A lovely day to do anything *except* ride!" he said. "Why spoil the day riding!"—A curious bitter-acid escaped into his tone. It was evident he hated the excursion.

"Why, we needn't go if you don't want to, Rico."

"Oh, I'm sure I shall love it, once I get started. It's all this business of *starting*, with horses and paraphernalia——"

Lou went into the yard. The horses were drinking at the trough under the pump, their colours strong and rich in the shadow of the tree.

"You're not coming with us, Phoenix?" she said.

"Lewis, he's riding my horse."

She could tell Phoenix did not like being left behind.

By half past seven everybody was ready. The sun was in the yard, the horses were saddled. They came swishing their tails. Lewis brought out St. Mawr from his separate box, speaking to him very quietly in Welsh: a murmuring, soothing little speech. Lou, alert, could see that he was uneasy.

"How is St. Mawr this morning?" she asked.

"He's all right. He doesn't like so many people. He'll be all right once he's started."

The strangers were in the saddle: they moved out to the deep shade of the village road outside. Rico came to his horse to mount. St. Mawr jumped away as if he had seen the devil.

"Steady, fool!" cried Rico.

The bay stood with his four feet spread, his neck arched, his big dark eye glancing sideways with that watchful, frightening look.

"You shouldn't be irritable with him, Rico!" said Lou. "Steady then, St. Mawr! Be steady."

But a certain anger rose also in her. The creature was so big, so brilliant, and so stupid, standing there with his hind legs spread, ready to jump aside or to rear terrifically, and his great eye glancing with a sort of suspicious frenzy. What was there to be suspicious of, after all?—Rico would do him no harm.

"No one will harm you, St. Mawr," she reasoned, a bit exasperated.

The groom was talking quietly, murmuringly, in Welsh. Rico was slowly advancing again, to put his foot in the stirrup. The stallion was watching from the corner of his eye, a strange glare of suspicious frenzy burning stupidly. Any moment his immense physical force might be let loose in a frenzy of panic—or malice. He was really very irritating.

"Probably he doesn't like that apricot shirt," said Mrs. Witt, "although it tones into him wonderfully well."

She pronounced it *ap*-ricot,[27] and it irritated Rico terribly.

---

[27]The common American pronunciation; the British, including Oxford-educated Rico, would say "*ape*-ricot."

"Ought we to have *asked* him before we put it on?" he flashed, his upper lip lifting venomously.

"I should say you should," replied Mrs. Witt coolly.

Rico turned with a sudden rush to the horse. Back went the great animal, with a sudden splashing crash of hoofs on the cobble-stones, and Lewis hanging on like a shadow. Up went the forefeet, showing the belly.

"The thing is accursed," said Rico, who had dropped the reins in sudden shock, and stood marooned. His rage overwhelmed him like a black flood.

"Nothing in the world is so irritating as a horse that is acting up," thought Lou.

"Say, Harry!" called Flora from the road. "Come out here into the road to mount him."

Lewis looked at Rico and nodded. Then, soothing the big, quivering animal, he led him springily out to the road under the trees, where the three friends were waiting. Lou and her mother got quickly into the saddle to follow. And in another moment Rico was mounted and bouncing down the road in the wrong direction, Lewis following on the chestnut. It was some time before Rico could get St. Mawr round. Watching him from behind, those waiting could judge how the young Baronet hated it.

But at last they set off—Rico ahead, unevenly but quietly, with the two Manby girls, Lou following with the fair young man who had been in a cavalry regiment and who kept looking round for Mrs. Witt.

"Don't look round for me," she called. "I'm riding behind, out of the dust."

Just behind Mrs. Witt came Lewis. It was a whole cavalcade trotting in the morning sun past the cottages and the cottage gardens, round the field that was the recreation ground, into the deep hedges of the lane.

"Why is St. Mawr so bad at starting? Can't you get him into better shape?" she asked over her shoulder.

"Beg your pardon, Mam!"

Lewis trotted a little nearer. She glanced over her shoulder at him, at his dark, unmoved face, his cool little figure.

"I think *Mam!* is so ugly. Why not leave it out!" she said. Then she repeated her question.

"St. Mawr doesn't trust anybody," Lewis replied.

"Not you?"

"Yes, he trusts me—mostly."

"Then why not other people?"

"They're different."

"All of them?"

"About all of them."

"How are they different?"

He looked at her with his remote, uncanny grey eyes.

They rode on slowly, up the steep rise of the wood, then down into a glade where ran a little railway built for hauling some mysterious mineral out of the hill, in wartime, and now already abandoned. Even on this countryside the dead hand of the war lay like a corpse decomposing.

They rode up again, past the foxgloves under the trees. Ahead the brilliant St. Mawr and the sorrel and grey horses were swimming like butterflies through the sea of bracken, glittering from sun to shade, shade to sun. Then once more they were on a crest, and through the thinning trees could see the slopes of the moors beyond the next dip.

Soon they were in the open, rolling hills, golden in the morning and empty save for a couple of distant bilberry-pickers, whitish figures pick—pick—picking with curious, rather disgusting assiduity. The horses were on an old trail which climbed through the pinky tips of heather and ling, across patches of green bilberry. Here and there were tufts of harebells blue as bubbles.

They were out, high on the hills. And there to west lay Wales, folded in crumpled folds, goldish in the morning light, with its moor-like slopes and patches of corn uncannily distinct. Between was a hollow, wide valley of summer haze, showing white farms among trees, and grey slate roofs.

"Ride beside me," she said to Lewis. "Nothing makes me want to go back to America like the old look of these little villages.—You have never been to America?"

"No, Mam."

"Don't you ever want to go?"

"I wouldn't mind going."

"But you're not just crazy to go?"

"No, Mam."

"Quite content as you are?"

He looked at her, and his pale, remote eyes met hers.

"I don't fret myself," he replied.

"Not about anything at all—ever?"

His eyes glanced ahead, at the other riders.

"No, Mam!" he replied, without looking at her.

She rode a few moments in silence.

"What is that over there?" she asked, pointing across the valley. "What is it called?"

"Yon's Montgomery."

"Montgomery! and is that *Wales*——?" She trailed the ending curiously.

"Yes, Mam."

"Where you come from?"

"No, Mam! I come from Merioneth."

"Not from Wales? I thought you were Welsh?"

"Yes, Mam. Merioneth *is* Wales."

"And you are Welsh?"

"Yes, Mam."

"I had a Welsh grandmother. But I come from Louisiana, and when I go back home, the Negroes still call me Miss Rachel. *Oh, my, it's little Miss Rachel come back home. Why, ain't I mighty glad to see you—u, Miss Rachel!* That gives me such a strange feeling, you know."

The man glanced at her curiously, especially when she imitated the Negroes.

"Do you feel strange when you go home?" she asked.

"I was brought up by an aunt and uncle," he said. "I never go to see them."

"And you don't have any home?"

"No, Mam."

"No wife nor anything?"

"No, Mam."

"But what do you do with your life?"

"I keep to myself."

"And care about nothing?"

"I mind St. Mawr."

"But you've not always had St. Mawr—and you won't always have him.—Were you in the war?"

"Yes, Mam."

"At the front?"

"Yes, Mam—but I was a groom."

"And you came out all right?"

"I lost my little finger from a bullet."

He held up his small, dark left hand, from which the little finger was missing.

"And did you like the war—or didn't you?"

"I didn't like it."

Again his pale-grey eyes met hers, and they looked so non-human and uncommunicative, so without connexion, and inaccessible, she was troubled.

"Tell me," she said. "Did you never want a wife and a home and children, like other men?"

"No, Mam. I never wanted a home of my own."

"Nor a wife of your own?"

"No, Mam."

"Nor children of your own?"

"No, Mam."

She reined in her horse.

"Now wait a minute," she said. "Now tell me why."

His horse came to standstill, and the two riders faced one another.

"Tell me why—I must know why you never wanted a wife and children and a home. I must know why you're not like other men."

"I never felt like it," he said. "I made my life with horses."

"Did you hate people very much? Did you have a very unhappy time as a child?"

"My aunt and uncle didn't like me, and I didn't like them."

"So you've never liked anybody?"

"Maybe not," he said. "Not to get as far as marrying them."

She touched her horse and moved on.

"Isn't that curious!" she said. "I've loved people, at various times. But I don't believe I've ever liked anybody, except a few of our Negroes. I don't like Louise, though she's my daughter and I love her. But I don't really *like* her.—I think you're the first person I've ever liked since I was on our plantation, and we had some *very fine* Negroes.—And I think that's very curious.—Now I want to know if you like *me*."

She looked at him searchingly, but he did not answer.

"Tell me," she said. "I don't mind if you say no. But tell me if you like me. I feel I must know."

The flicker of a smile went over his face—a very rare thing with him.

"Maybe I do," he said. He was thinking that she put him on a level with a Negro slave on a plantation: in his idea, Negroes were still slaves. But he did not care where she put him.

"Well, I'm glad—I'm glad if you like me. Because you *don't* like most people. I know that."

They had passed the hollow where the old Aldecar Chapel hid in damp isolation, beside the ruined mill, over the stream that came down from the moors. Climbing the sharp slope, they saw the folded hills like great shut fingers, with steep, deep clefts between. On the near sky-line was a bunch of rocks; and away to the right another bunch.

"Yon's the Angel's Chair," said Lewis, pointing to the nearer rocks.

"And yon's the Devil's Chair, where we're going."

"Oh!" said Mrs. Witt. "And aren't we going to the Angel's Chair?"

"No, Mam."

"Why not?"

"There's nothing to see there. The other's higher, and bigger, and that's where folks mostly go."

"Is that so!—They give the Devil the higher seat in this country, do they? I think they're right."—And as she got no answer, she added: "You believe in the Devil, don't you?"

"I never met him," he answered, evasively.

Ahead, they could see the other horses twinkling in a cavalcade up the slope, the black, the bay, the two greys and the sorrel, sometimes bunching, sometimes straggling. At a gate all waited for Mrs. Witt. The fair young man fell in beside her, and talked hunting at her. He had hunted the fox over these hills, and was vigorously excited locating the spot where the hounds gave the first cry, etc.

"Really!" said Mrs. Witt. "*Really!* Is that so!"

If irony could have been condensed to prussic acid,[28] the fair young man would have ended his life's history with his reminiscences.

They came at last, trotting in file along a narrow track between heather, along the saddle of a hill, to where the knot of pale granite suddenly cropped out. It was one of those places where the spirit of aboriginal England still lingers, the old savage England, whose last blood flows still in a few Englishmen, Welshmen, Cornishmen. The rocks, whitish with weather of all the ages, jutted against the blue August sky, heavy with age-moulded roundnesses.

Lewis stayed below with the horses, the party scrambled rather awkwardly, in their riding-boots, up the foot-worn boulders. At length they stood in the place called the Chair, looking west, west towards Wales, that rolled in golden folds upwards. It was neither impressive nor a very picturesque landscape: the hollow valley with farms, and then the rather bare upheaval of hills, slopes with corn and moor and pasture, rising like a barricade, seemingly high, slantingly. Yet it had a strange effect on the imagination.

"Oh, mother," said Lou, "doesn't it make you feel old, old, older than anything ever was?"

---

[28]Cyanide.

"It certainly does seem aged," said Mrs. Witt.

"It makes me want to die," said Lou. "I feel we've lasted almost too long."

"Don't say that, Lady Carrington. Why, you're a spring chicken yet: or shall I say an unopened rosebud?" remarked the fair young man.

"No," said Lou. "All these millions of ancestors have used all the life up. We're not really alive, in the sense that they were alive."

"But who?" said Rico. "Who are *they?*"

"The people who lived on these hills, in the days gone by."

"But the same people still live on the hills, darling. It's just the same stock."

"No, Rico. That old fighting stock that worshipped devils among these stones—I'm sure they did——"

"But look here, do you mean they were any better than we are?" asked the fair young man.

Lou looked at him quizzically.

"We don't exist," she said, squinting at him oddly.

"I jolly well know I do," said the fair young man.

"I consider these days are the best ever, especially for girls," said Flora Manby. "And anyhow they're our own days, so I don't jolly well see the use of crying them down."

They were all silent, with the last echoes of emphatic *joie de vivre*[29] trumpeting on the air, across the hills of Wales.

"Spoken like a brick, Flora," said Rico. "Say it again, we may not have the Devil's Chair for a pulpit next time."

"I do," reiterated Flora. "I think this is the best age there ever was for a girl to have a good time in. I read all through H. G. Wells' history, and I shut it up and thanked my stars I live in nineteen-twenty odd, not in some other beastly date when a woman had to cringe before mouldy domineering men."

After this they turned to scramble to another part of the rocks, to the famous Needle's Eye.

"Thank you so much, I am really better without help," said Mrs. Witt to the fair young man, as she slid downwards till a piece of grey silk stocking showed above her tall boot. But she got her toe in a safe place, and in a moment stood beside him, while he caught her arm protectingly. He might as well have caught the paw of a mountain lion protectingly.

---

[29]Carefree enjoyment of living.

"I should like *so* much to know," she said suavely, looking into his eyes with a demonish straight look, "what makes you so certain that you exist."

He looked back at her, and his jaunty blue eyes went baffled. Then a slow, hot, salmon-coloured flush stole over his face, and he turned abruptly round.

The Needle's Eye was a hole in the ancient grey rock, like a window, looking to England: England at the moment in shadow. A stream wound and glinted in the flat shadow, and beyond that the flat, insignificant hills heaped in mounds of shade. Cloud was coming—the English side was in shadow. Wales was still in the sun, but the shadow was spreading. The day was going to disappoint them. Lou was a tiny bit chilled already.

Luncheon was still several miles away. The party hastened down to the horses. Lou picked a few sprigs of ling, and some harebells, and some straggling yellow flowers: not because she wanted them, but to distract herself. The atmosphere of "enjoying ourselves" was becoming cruel to her: it sapped all the life out of her. "Oh, if only I needn't enjoy myself," she moaned inwardly. But the Manby girls were enjoying themselves so much. "I think it's frantically lovely up here," said the other one—not Flora—Elsie.

"It *is* beautiful, isn't it! I'm *so* glad you like it," replied Rico. And he was really relieved and gratified, because the other one said she was enjoying it so frightfully. He dared not say to Lou, as he wanted to: "I'm afraid, Lou darling, you don't love it as much as we do."—He was afraid of her answer: "No, dear, I don't love it at all! I want to be away from these people."

Slightly piqued, he rode on with the Manby group, and Lou came behind with her mother. Cloud was covering the sky with grey. There was a cold wind. Everybody was anxious to get to the farm for luncheon, and be safely home before rain came.

They were riding along one of the narrow little foot-tracks, mere groves of grass between heather and bright green bilberry. The blond young man was ahead, then his wife, then Flora, then Rico. Lou, from a little distance, watched the glossy, powerful haunches of St. Mawr swaying with life, always too much life, like a menace. The fair young man was whistling a new dance tune.

"That's an awfully attractive tune," Rico called. "Do whistle it again, Fred, I should like to memorize it."

Fred began to whistle it again.

At that moment St. Mawr exploded again, shied sideways as if a bomb had gone off, and kept backing through the heather.

"Fool!" cried Rico, thoroughly unnerved: he had been terribly sideways in the saddle, Lou had feared he was going to fall. But he got his seat, and pulled the reins viciously, to bring the horse to order, and put him on the track again. St. Mawr began to rear: his favourite trick. Rico got him forward a few yards, when up he went again.

"Fool!" yelled Rico, hanging in the air.

He pulled the horse over backwards on top of him.

Lou gave a loud, unnatural, horrible scream: she heard it herself, at the same time as she heard the crash of the falling horse. Then she saw a pale gold belly, and hoofs that worked and flashed in the air, and St. Mawr writhing, straining his head terrifically upwards, his great eyes starting from the naked lines of his nose. With a great neck arching cruelly from the ground, he was pulling frantically at the reins, which Rico still held tight.—Yes, Rico, lying strangely sideways, his eyes also starting from his yellow-white face, among the heather, still clutched the reins.

Young Edwards was rushing forward, and circling round the writhing, immense horse, whose pale-gold, inverted bulk seemed to fill the universe.

"Let him get up, Carrington! Let him get up!" he was yelling, darting warily near, to get the reins.—Another spasmodic convulsion of the horse.

Horror! The young man reeled backwards with his face in his hands. He had got a kick in the face. Red blood running down his chin!

Lewis was there, on the ground, getting the reins out of Rico's hands. St. Mawr gave a great curve like a fish, spread his forefeet on the earth and reared his head, looking round in a ghastly fashion. His eyes were arched, his nostrils wide, his face ghastly in a sort of panic. He rested thus, seated with his forefeet planted and his face in panic, almost like some terrible lizard, for several moments. Then he heaved sickeningly to his feet, and stood convulsed, trembling.

There lay Rico, crumpled and rather sideways, staring at the heavens from a yellow, dead-looking face. Lewis, glancing round in a sort of horror, looked in dread at St. Mawr again. Flora had been hovering.— She now rushed screeching to the prostrate Rico:

"Harry! Harry! you're not dead! Oh, Harry! Harry! Harry!"

Lou had dismounted.—She didn't know when. She stood a little way off, as if spellbound, while Flora cried *Harry! Harry! Harry!*

Suddenly Rico sat up.

"Where is the horse?" he said.

At the same time an added whiteness came on his face, and he bit his lip with pain, and he fell prostrate again in a faint. Flora rushed to put her arm round him.

Where was the horse? He had backed slowly away, in an agony of suspicion, while Lewis murmured to him in vain. His head was raised again, the eyes still starting from their sockets, and a terrible guilty, ghostlike look on his face. When Lewis drew a little nearer, he twitched and shrank like a shaken steel spring, away—not to be touched. He seemed to be seeing legions of ghosts, down the dark avenues of all the centuries that have lapsed since the horse became subject to man.

And the other young man? He was still standing, at a little distance, with his face in his hands, motionless, the blood falling on his white shirt, and his wife at his side, pleading, distracted.

Mrs. Witt too was there, as if cast in steel, watching. She made no sound and did not move, only, from a fixed, impassive face, watched each thing.

"Do tell me what you think is the matter?" Lou pleaded, distracted, to Flora, who was supporting Rico and weeping torrents of unknown tears.

Then Mrs. Witt came forward and began in a very practical manner to unclose the shirt-neck and feel the young man's heart. Rico opened his eyes again, said *"Really!"* and closed his eyes once more.

"It's fainting!" said Mrs. Witt. "We have no brandy."

Lou, too weary to be able to feel anything, said:

"I'll go and get some."

She went to her alarmed horse, who stood among the others with her head down, in suspense. Almost unconsciously Lou mounted, set her face ahead, and was riding away.

Then Poppy shied too, with a sudden start, and Lou pulled up. "Why?" she said to her horse. "Why did you do that?"

She looked around, and saw in the heather a glimpse of yellow and black.

"A snake!" she said wonderingly.

And she looked closer.

It was a dead adder that had been drinking at a reedy pool in a little depression just off the road, and had been killed with stones. There it lay, also crumpled, its head crushed, its gold-and-yellow back still glittering dully, and a bit of pale-blue belly showing, killed that morning.

Lou rode on, her face set towards the farm. An unspeakable weariness had overcome her. She could not even suffer. Weariness of spirit left her in a sort of apathy.

And she had a vision, a vision of evil. Or not strictly a vision. She became aware of evil, evil, evil, rolling in great waves over the earth. Always she had thought there was no such thing—only a mere negation of good. Now, like an ocean to whose surface she had risen, she saw the dark-grey waves of evil rearing in a great tide.

And it had swept mankind away without mankind's knowing. It had caught up the nations as the rising ocean might lift the fishes, and was sweeping them on in a great tide of evil. They did not know. The people did not know. They did not even wish it. They wanted to be good and to have everything joyful and enjoyable. Everything joyful and enjoyable: for everybody. This was what they wanted, if you asked them.

But at the same time, they had fallen under the spell of evil. It was a soft, subtle thing, soft as water, and its motion was soft and imperceptible, as the running of a tide is invisible to one who is out on the ocean. And they were all out on the ocean, being borne along in the current of the mysterious evil, creatures of the evil principle, as fishes are creatures of the sea.

There was no relief. The whole world was enveloped in one great flood. All the nations, the white, the brown, the black, the yellow, all were immersed in the strange tide of evil that was subtly, irresistibly rising. No one, perhaps, deliberately wished it. Nearly every individual wanted peace and a good time all round: everybody to have a good time.

But some strange thing had happened, and the vast, mysterious force of positive evil was let loose. She felt that from the core of Asia the evil welled up, as from some strange pole, and slowly was drowning earth.

It was something horrifying, something you could not escape from. It had come to her as in a vision, when she saw the pale-gold belly of the stallion upturned, the hoofs working wildly, the wicked curved hams of the horse, and then the evil straining of that arched, fish-like neck, with the dilated eyes of the head. Thrown backwards, and working its hoofs in the air. Reversed, and purely evil.

She saw the same in people. They were thrown backwards, and writhing with evil. And the rider, crushed, was still reining them down.

What did it mean? Evil, evil, and a rapid return to the sordid chaos. Which was wrong, the horse or the rider? Or both?

She thought with horror of St. Mawr, and of the look on his face. But she thought with horror, a colder horror, of Rico's face as he snarled *Fool!* His fear, his impotence as a master, as a rider, his presumption. And she thought with horror of those other people, so glib, so glibly evil.

What did they want to do, those Manby girls? Undermine, undermine, undermine. They wanted to undermine Rico, just as that fair young man would have liked to undermine her. Believe in nothing, care about nothing: but keep the surface easy, and have a good time. *Let us undermine one another. There is nothing to believe in, so let us undermine everything. But look out! No scenes, no spoiling the game. Stick to the rules of the game. Be sporting, and don't do anything that would make a commotion. Keep the game going smooth and jolly, and bear your bit like a sport. Never, by any chance, injure your fellow man openly. But always injure him secretly. Make a fool of him, and undermine his nature. Break him up by undermining him, if you can. It's good sport.*

The evil! The mysterious potency of evil. She could see it all the time, in individuals, in society, in the press. There it was in socialism and bolshevism: the same evil. But bolshevism made a mess of the outside of life, so turn it down. Try fascism. Fascism would keep the surface of life intact, and carry on the undermining business all the better. All the better sport. Never draw blood. Keep the haemorrhage internal, invisible.

And as soon as fascism makes a break—which it is bound to, because all evil works up to a break—then turn it down. With gusto, turn it down.

Mankind, like a horse, ridden by a stranger, smooth-faced, evil rider. Evil himself, smooth-faced and pseudo-handsome, riding mankind past the dead snake, to the last break.

Mankind no longer its own master. Ridden by this pseudo-handsome ghoul of outward loyalty, inward treachery, in a game of betrayal, betrayal, betrayal. The last of the gods of our era, Judas supreme!

People performing outward acts of loyalty, piety, self-sacrifice. But inwardly bent on undermining, betraying. Directing all their subtle evil will against any positive living thing. Masquerading as the ideal, in order to poison the real.

Creation destroys as it goes, throws down one tree for the rise of another. But ideal mankind would abolish death, multiply itself million upon million, rear up city upon city, save every parasite alive, until the accumulation of mere existence is swollen to a horror. But go on saving life, the ghastly salvation army of ideal mankind. At the same time secretly, viciously, potently undermine the natural creation, betray it with kiss after kiss, destroy it from the inside, till you have the swollen rottenness of our teeming existence.—But keep the game going. Nobody's going to make another bad break, such as Germany and Russia made.[30]

Two bad breaks the secret evil has made: in Germany and in Russia. Watch it! Let evil keep a policeman's eye on evil! The surface of life must remain unruptured. Production must be heaped upon production. And the natural creation must be betrayed by many more kisses, yet. Judas is the last God, and, by heaven, the most potent.

But even Judas made a break: hanged himself, and his bowels gushed out. Not long after his triumph.

Man must destroy as he goes, as trees fall for trees to rise. The accumulation of life and things means rottenness. Life must destroy life, in the unfolding of creation. We save up life at the expense of the unfolding, till all is full of rottenness. Then at last, we make a break.

What's to be done? Generally speaking, nothing. The dead will have to bury their dead, while the earth stinks of corpses. The individual can but depart from the mass, and try to cleanse himself. Try to hold fast to the living thing, which destroys as it goes, but remains sweet. And in his soul fight, fight, fight to preserve that which is life in him from the ghastly kisses and poison-bites of the myriad evil ones. Retreat to the desert, and fight. But in his soul adhere to that which is life itself, creatively destroying as it goes: destroying the stiff old thing to let the new bud come through. The one passionate principle of creative being, which recognizes the natural good, and has a sword for the swarms of evil. Fights, fights, fights to protect itself. But with itself, is strong and at peace.

Lou came to the farm, and got brandy, and asked the men to come out to carry in the injured.

It turned out that the kick in the face had knocked a couple of young Edward's teeth out, and would disfigure him a little.

"To go through the war, and then get this!" he mumbled, with a vindictive glance at St. Mawr.

And it turned out that Rico had two broken ribs and a crushed ankle. Poor Rico, he would limp for life.

---

[30]A reference, probably, to Germany's aggression in World War I and to the chaos of the Russian Revolution.

"I want St. Mawr *shot!*" was almost his first word, when he was in bed at the farm and Lou was sitting beside him.

"What good would that do, dear?" she said.

"The brute is evil. I want him *shot!*"

Rico could make the last word sound like the spitting of a bullet.

"Do you want to shoot him yourself?"

"No. But I want to have him shot. I shall never be easy till I know he has a bullet through him. He's got a wicked character. I don't feel you are safe, with him down there. I shall get one of the Manbys' game-keepers to shoot him. You might tell Flora—or I'll tell her myself, when she comes."

"Don't talk about it now, dear. You've got a temperature."

Was it true, St. Mawr was evil? She would never forget him writhing and lunging on the ground, nor his awful face when he reared up. But then that noble look of his: surely he was not mean? Whereas all evil had an inner meanness, mean! Was he mean? Was he meanly treacherous? Did he know he could kill, and meanly wait his opportunity?

She was afraid. And if this were true, then he *should* be shot. Perhaps he ought to be shot.

This thought haunted her. Was there something mean and treacherous in St. Mawr's spirit, the vulgar evil? If so, then have him shot. At moments, an anger would rise in her, as she thought of his frenzied rearing, and his mad, hideous writhing on the ground, and in the heat of her anger she would want to hurry down to her mother's house and have the creature shot at once. It would be a satisfaction, and a vindication of human rights. Because, after all, Rico was considerate of the brutal horse. But not a spark of consideration did the stallion have for Rico. No, it was the slavish malevolence of a domesticated creature that kept cropping up in St. Mawr. The slave, taking his slavish vengeance, then dropping back into subservience.

All the slaves of this world, accumulating their preparations for slavish vengeance, and then, when they have taken it, ready to drop back into servility. Freedom! Most slaves can't be freed, no matter how you let them loose. Like domestic animals, they are, in the long run, more afraid of freedom than of masters: and freed by some generous master, they will at last crawl back to some mean boss, who will have no scruples about kicking them. Because, for them, far better kicks and servility than the hard, lonely responsibility of real freedom.

The wild animal is at every moment intensely self-disciplined, poised in the tension of self-defence, self-preservation, and self-assertion. The moments of relaxation are rare and most carefully chosen. Even sleep is watchful, guarded, unrelaxing, the wild courage pitched one degree higher than the wild fear. Courage, the wild thing's courage to maintain itself alone and living in the midst of a diverse universe.

Did St. Mawr have this courage?

And did Rico?

Ah, Rico! He was one of mankind's myriad conspirators, who conspire to live in absolute physical safety, whilst willing the minor disintegration of all positive living.

But St. Mawr? Was it the natural wild thing in him which caused these disasters? Or was it the slave, asserting himself for vengeance?

If the latter, let him be shot. It would be a great satisfaction to see him dead.

But if the former——

When she could leave Rico with the nurse, she motored down to her mother for a couple of days. Rico lay in bed at the farm.

Everything seemed curiously changed. There was a new silence about the place, a new coolness. Summer had passed with several thunderstorms, and the blue, cool touch of autumn was about the house. Dahlias and perennial yellow sunflowers were out, the yellow of ending summer, the red coals of early autumn. First mauve tips of Michaelmas daisies were showing. Something suddenly carried her away to the great bare spaces of Texas, the blue sky, the flat, burnt earth, the miles of sunflowers. Another sky, another silence, towards the setting sun.

And suddenly, she craved again for the more absolute silence of America. English stillness was so soft, like an inaudible murmur of voices, of presences. But the silence in the empty spaces of America was still unutterable, almost cruel.

St. Mawr was in a small field by himself: she could not bear that he should be always in stable. Slowly she went through the gate towards him. And he stood there looking at her, the bright bay creature.

She could tell he was feeling somewhat subdued, after his late escapade. He was aware of the general human condemnation: the human damning. But something obstinate and uncanny in him made him not relent.

"Hello! St. Mawr!" she said, as she drew near, and he stood watching her, his ears pricked, his big eyes glancing sideways at her.

But he moved away when she wanted to touch him.

"Don't trouble," she said. "I don't want to catch you or do anything to you."

He stood still, listening to the sound of her voice, and giving quick, small glances at her. His underlip trembled. But he did not blink. His eyes remained wide and unrelenting. There was a curious malicious obstinacy in him which aroused her anger.

"I don't want to touch you," she said. "I only want to look at you, and even you can't prevent that."

She stood gazing hard at him, wanting to know, to settle the question of his meanness or his spirit. A thing with a brave spirit is not mean.

He was uneasy as she watched him. He pretended to hear something, the mares two fields away, and he lifted his head and neighed. She knew the powerful, splendid sound so well: like bells made of living membrane. And he looked so noble again, with his head tilted up, listening, and his male eyes looking proudly over the distance, eagerly.

But it was all a bluff.

He knew, and became silent again. And as he stood there a few yards away from her, his head lifted and wary, his body full of power and tension, his face slightly averted from her, she felt a great animal sadness come from him. A strange animal atmosphere of sadness, that was vague and disseminated through the air, and made her feel as though she breathed grief. She breathed it into her breast, as if it were a great sigh down the ages, that passed into her breast. And she felt a great woe: the woe of human unworthiness. The race of men judged in the consciousness of the animals they have subdued, and there found unworthy, ignoble.

Ignoble men, unworthy of the animals they have subjugated, bred the woe in the spirit of their creatures. St. Mawr, that bright horse, one of the kings of creation in the order below man, it had been a fulfilment for him to serve the brave, reckless, perhaps cruel men of the past, who had a flickering, rising flame of nobility in them. To serve that flame of mysterious further nobility. Nothing matters but that strange flame, of inborn nobility that obliges men to be brave, and onward plunging. And the horse will bear him on.

But now where is the flame of dangerous, forward-pressing nobility in men? Dead, dead, guttering out in a stink of self-sacrifice whose feeble light is a light of exhaustion and *laissez-faire*.

And the horse, is he to go on carrying man forward into this?—this gutter?

No! Man wisely invents motor-cars and other machines, automobile and locomotive. The horse is superannuated, for man.

But alas, man is even more superannuated, for the horse.

Dimly in a woman's muse, Lou realized this, as she breathed the horse's sadness, his accumulated vague woe from the generations of latter-day ignobility. And a grief and a sympathy flooded her, for the horse. She realized now how his sadness recoiled into these frenzies of obstinacy and malevolence. Underneath it all was grief, an unconscious, vague, pervading animal grief, which perhaps only Lewis understood, because he felt the same. The grief of the generous creature which sees all ends turning to the morass of ignoble living.

She did not want to say any more to the horse: she did not want to look at him any more. The grief flooded her soul, that made her want to be alone. She knew now what it all amounted to. She knew that the horse, born to serve nobly, had waited in vain for someone noble to serve. His spirit knew that nobility had gone out of men. And this left him high and dry, in a sort of despair.

As she walked away from him, towards the gate, slowly he began to walk after her.

Phoenix came striding through the gate towards her. "You not afraid of that horse?" he asked sardonically, in his quiet, subtle voice.

"Not at the present moment," she replied, even more quietly, looking direct at him. She was not in any mood to be jeered at.

And instantly the sardonic grimace left his face, followed by the sudden blankness, and the look of race-misery in the keen eyes.

"Do you want me to be afraid?" she said, continuing to the gate.

"No, I don't want it," he replied, dejected.

"Are you afraid of him yourself?" she said, glancing round. St. Mawr had stopped, seeing Phoenix, and had turned away again.

"I'm not afraid of no horses," said Phoenix.

Lou went on quietly. At the gate, she asked him:

"Don't you like St. Mawr, Phoenix?"

"I like him. He's a very good horse."

"Even after what he's done to Sir Henry?"

"That don't make no difference to him being a good horse."

"But suppose he'd done it to you?"

"I don't care. I say it my own fault."

"Don't you think he is wicked?"

"I don't think so. He don't kick anybody. He don't bite anybody. He don't pitch, he don't buck, he don't do nothing."

"He rears," said Lou.

"Well, what is rearing!" said the man, with a slow, contemptuous smile.

"A good deal, when a horse falls back on you."

"That horse don't want to fall back on you, if you don't make him. If you know how to ride him.—That horse want his own way sometime. If you don't let him, you got to fight him. Then look out!"

"Look out he doesn't kill you, you mean!"

"Look out you don't let him," said Phoenix, with his slow, grim, sardonic smile.

Lou watched the smooth, golden face with its thin line of moustache and its sad eyes with the glint in them. Cruel—there was something cruel in him, right down in the abyss of him. But at the same time, there was an aloneness, and a grim little satisfaction in a fight, and the peculiar courage of an inherited despair. People who inherit despair may at last turn it into greater heroism. It was almost so with Phoenix. Three quarters of his blood was probably Indian and the remaining quarter, that came through the Mexican father, had the Spanish-American despair to add to the Indian. It was almost complete enough to leave him free to be heroic.

"What are we going to do with him, though?" she asked.

"Why don't you and Mrs. Witt go back to America—you never been West. You go West."

"Where, to California?"

"No. To Arizona or New Mexico or Colorado or Wyoming, anywhere. Not to California."

Phoenix looked at her keenly, and she saw the desire dark in him. He wanted to go back. But he was afraid to go back alone, empty-handed, as it were. He had suffered too much, and in that country his sufferings would overcome him, unless he had some other background. He had been too much in contact with the white world, and his own world was too dejected, in a sense, too hopeless for his own hopelessness. He needed an alien contact to give him relief.

But he wanted to go back. His necessity to go back was becoming too strong for him.

"What is it like in Arizona?" she asked. "Isn't it all pale-coloured sand and alkali, and a few cactuses, and terribly hot and deathly?"

"No!" he cried. "I don't take you there. I take you to the mountains—trees—" he lifted up his hand and looked at the sky—"big trees—pine! *Pino—real* and *pinovetes*, smell good. And then you come down, *piñon*, not very tall, and *cedro*, cedar, smell good in the fire. And then you see the desert, away below, go miles and miles, and where the canyon go, the crack where it look red! I know, I been there, working a cattle ranch."

He looked at her with a haunted glow in his dark eyes. The poor fellow was suffering from nostalgia. And as he glowed at her in that queer mystical way, she too seemed to see that country, with its dark, heavy mountains holding in their lap the great stretches of pale, creased, silent desert that still is virgin of idea, its word unspoken.

Phoenix was watching her closely and subtly. He wanted something of her. He wanted it intensely, heavily, and he watched her as if he could force her to give it him. He wanted her to take him back to America, because, rudderless, he was afraid to go back alone. He wanted her to take him back: avidly he wanted it. She was to be the means to his end.

Why shouldn't he go back by himself? Why should he crave for her to go too? Why should he want her there?

There was no answer, except that he did.

"Why, Phoenix," she said, "I might possibly go back to America. But you know, Sir Henry would never go there. He doesn't like America, though he's never been. But I'm sure he'd never go there to live."

"Let him stay here," said Phoenix abruptly, the sardonic look on his face as he watched her face. "You come, and let him stay here."

"Ah, that's a whole story!" she said, and moved away.

As she went, he looked after her, standing silent and arrested and watching as an Indian watches.—It was not love. Personal love counts so little when the greater griefs, the greater hopes, the great despairs and the great resolutions come upon us.

She found Mrs. Witt rather more silent, more firmly closed within herself, than usual. Her mouth was shut tight, her brows were arched rather more imperiously than ever, she was revolving some inward problem about which Lou was far too wise to enquire.

In the afternoon Dean Vyner and Mrs. Vyner came to call on Lady Carrington.

"What bad luck this is, Lady Carrington!" said the Dean. "Knocks Scotland on the head for you this year, I'm afraid. How did you leave your husband?"

"He seems to be doing as well as he could do!" said Lou.

"But how *very* unfortunate!" murmured the invalid Mrs. Vyner. "Such a handsome young man, in the bloom of youth! Does he suffer much pain?"

"Chiefly his foot," said Lou.

"Oh, I *do* so hope they'll be able to restore the ankle. Oh, how dreadful to be lamed at his age!"

"The doctor doesn't know. There *may* be a limp," said Lou.

"That horse has certainly left his mark on two good-looking young fellows," said the Dean. "If you don't mind my saying so, Lady Carrington, I think he's a bad egg."

"Who, St. Mawr?" said Lou, in her American sing-song.

"Yes, Lady Carrington," murmured Mrs. Vyner, in her invalid's low tone. "Don't you think he ought to be put away? He seems to me the incarnation of cruelty. His neigh. It goes through me like knives. Cruel! Cruel! Oh, I think he should be put away."

"How put away?" mumured Lou, taking on an invalid's low tone herself.

"Shot, I suppose," said the Dean.

"It is quite painless. He'll know nothing," murmured Mrs. Vyner hastily. "And think of the harm he has done already! Horrible! Horrible!" she shuddered. "Poor Sir Henry lame for life, and Eddy Edwards disfigured. Besides all that has gone before. Ah, no, such a creature ought not to live!"

"To live, and have a groom to look after him and feed him," said the Dean. "It's a bit thick, while he's smashing up the very people that give him bread—or oats, since he's a horse. But I suppose you'll be wanting to get rid of him?"

"Rico does," murmured Lou.

"Very naturally. So should I. A vicious horse is worse than a vicious man—except that you are free to put him six feet underground, and end his vice finally, by your own act."

"Do you think St. Mawr is vicious?" said Lou.

"Well, of course—if we're driven to definitions!—I *know* he's dangerous."

"And do you think we ought to shoot everything that is dangerous?" asked Lou, her colour rising.

"But, Lady Carrington, have you consulted your husband? Surely his wish should be law, in a matter of this sort! And on such an occasion! For *you*, who are a woman, it is enough that the horse is cruel, cruel, evil! I felt it long before anything happened. That evil male cruelty! Ah!" and Mrs. Vyner clasped her hands convulsively.

"I suppose," said Lou slowly, "that St. Mawr is really Rico's horse: I gave him to him, I suppose. But I don't believe I could let him shoot him, for all that."

"Ah, Lady Carrington," said the Dean breezily, "you can shift the responsibility. The horse is a public menace, put it at that. We can get an order to have him done away with, at the public expense. And among ourselves we can find some suitable compensation for you, as a mark of sympathy. Which, believe me, is very sincere! One hates to have to destroy a fine-looking animal. But I would sacrifice a dozen rather than have our Rico limping."

"Yes, indeed," murmured Mrs. Vyner.

"Will you excuse me one moment, while I see about tea?" said Lou, rising and leaving the room. Her colour was high, and there was a glint in her eye. These people almost roused her to hatred. Oh, these awful, house-bred, house-inbred human beings, how repulsive they were!

She hurried to her mother's dressing-room. Mrs. Witt was very carefully putting a touch of red on her lips.

"Mother, they want to shoot St. Mawr," she said.

"I know," said Mrs. Witt, as calmly as if Lou had said tea was ready.

"Well—" stammered Lou, rather put out, "don't you think it cheek?"

"It depends, I suppose, on the point of view," said Mrs. Witt dispassionately, looking closely at her lips. "I don't think the English climate agrees with me. I need something to stand up against, no matter whether it's great heat or great cold. This climate, like the food and the people, is most always lukewarm or tepid, one or the other. And the tepid and the lukewarm are not really my line." She spoke with a slow drawl.

"But they're in the drawing-room, mother, trying to force me to have St. Mawr killed."

"What about tea?" said Mrs. Witt.

"I don't care," said Lou.

Mrs. Witt worked the bell-handle.

"I suppose, Louise," she said, in her most beaming eighteenth-century manner, "that these are your guests, so you will preside over the ceremony of pouring out."

"No, mother, you do it. I can't smile to-day."

"I can," said Mrs. Witt.

And she bowed her head slowly, with a faint, ceremoniously effusive smile, as if handing a cup of tea.

Lou's face flickered to a smile.

"Then you pour out for them. You can stand them better than I can."

"Yes," said Mrs. Witt. "I saw Mrs. Vyner's hat coming across the churchyard. It looks so like a crumpled cup and saucer, that I have been saying to myself ever since: *Dear Mrs. Vyner, can't I fill your cup?*— and then pouring tea into that hat. And I hear the Dean responding: *My head is covered with cream, my cup runneth over.*—That is the way they make *me* feel."

They marched downstairs, and Mrs. Witt poured tea with that devastating correctness which made Mrs. Vyner, who was utterly impervious to sarcasm, pronounce her "indecipherably vulgar."

But the Dean was the old bulldog, and he had set his teeth in a subject.

"I was talking to Lady Carrington about that stallion, Mrs. Witt."

"Did you say stallion?" asked Mrs. Witt, with perfect neutrality.

"Why, yes, I presume that's what he is."

"I presume so," said Mrs. Witt colourlessly.

"I'm afraid Lady Carrington is a little sensitive on the wrong score," said the Dean.

"I beg your pardon," said Mrs. Witt, leaning forward in her most colourless polite manner. "You mean stallion's score?"

"Yes," said the Dean testily. "The horse St. Mawr."

"The stallion St. Mawr," echoed Mrs. Witt, with utmost mild vagueness. She completely ignored Mrs. Vyner, who felt plunged like a specimen into methylated spirit. There was a moment's full stop.

"Yes?" said Mrs. Witt naïvely.

"You agree that we can't have any more of these accidents to your young men?" said the Dean rather hastily.

"I certainly do!" Mrs. Witt spoke very slowly, and the Dean's lady began to look up. She might find a loophole through which to wriggle into the contest. "You know, Dean, that my son-in-law calls me, for preference, *belle-mère!* It sounds so awfully English when he says it; I always see myself as an old grey mare with a bell round her neck, leading a bunch of horses." She smiled a prim little smile, *very* conversationally. "Well!" and she pulled herself up from the aside. "Now, as the bell-mare of the bunch of horses, I shall see to it that my son-in-law doesn't go too near that stallion again. That stallion won't stand mischief."

She spoke so earnestly that the Dean looked at her with round wide eyes, completely taken aback.

"We all know, Mrs. Witt, that the author of the mischief is St. Mawr himself," he said, in a loud tone.

"Really! you think *that?*" Her voice went up in American surprise. "Why, how *strange*——!" and she lingered over the last word.

"Strange, eh?—After what's just happened?" said the Dean, with a deadly little smile.

"Why, yes! Most strange! I saw with my own eyes my son-in-law pull that stallion over backwards, and hold him down with the reins as tight as he could hold them; pull St. Mawr's head backwards on to the ground, till the groom had to crawl up and force the reins out of my son-in-law's hands. Don't you think that was mischievous on Sir Henry's part?"

The Dean was growing purple. He made an apoplectic movement with his hand. Mrs. Vyner was turned to a seated pillar of salt, strangely dressed up.

"Mrs. Witt, you are playing on words."

"No, Dean Vyner, I am not. My son-in-law pulled that horse over backwards and pinned him down with the reins."

"I am sorry for the horse," said the Dean, with heavy sarcasm.

"I am *very*," said Mrs. Witt, "sorry for that stallion: *very!*"

Here Mrs. Vyner rose as if a chair-spring had suddenly propelled her to her feet. She was streaky pink in the face.

"Mrs. Witt," she panted, "you misdirect your sympathies. That poor young man—in the beauty of youth!"

"Isn't he *beautiful*——" murmured Mrs. Witt, extravagantly in sympathy. "He is my daughter's husband!" And she looked at the petrified Lou.

"Certainly!" panted the Dean's wife. "And you can defend that—that——"

"That stallion," said Mrs. Witt. "But you see, Mrs. Vyner," she added, leaning forward female and confidential, "if the old grey mare doesn't defend the stallion, who will? All the blooming young ladies will defend my beautiful son-in-law. You feel so *warmly* for him yourself! I'm an American woman, and I always have to stand up for the accused. And I stand up for that stallion. I say it is not right. He was pulled over backwards and then pinned down by my son-in-law—who may have meant to do it, or may not. And now people abuse him.— Just tell everybody, Mrs. Vyner and Dean Vyner"—she looked round at the Dean—"that the *belle-mère's* sympathies are with the stallion."

She looked from one to the other with a faint and gracious little bow, her black eyebrows arching in her eighteenth-century face like black rainbows, and her full, bold grey eyes absolutely incomprehensible.

"Well, it's a peculiar message to have to hand round, Mrs. Witt," the Dean began to boom, when she interrupted him by laying her hand on his arm and leaning forward, looking up into his face like a clinging, pleading female.

"Oh, but *do* hand it, Dean, *do* hand it," she pleaded, gazing intently into his face.

He backed uncomfortably from that gaze.

"Since you wish it," he said, in a chest voice.

"I most certainly *do*——" she said, as if she were wishing the sweetest wish on earth. Then, turning to Mrs. Vyner:

"Good-bye, Mrs. Vyner. We *do* appreciate your coming, my daughter and I."

"I came out of kindness——" said Mrs. Vyner.

"Oh, I know it, I know it," said Mrs. Witt. "Thank you *so* much. Good-bye! Good-bye, Dean! Who is taking the morning service on Sunday? I hope it is you, because I want to come."

"It *is* me," said the Dean. "Good-bye! Well, good-bye, Lady Carrington. I shall be going over to see our young man to-morrow, and will gladly take you or anything you have to send."

"Perhaps mother would like to go," said Lou, softly, plaintively.

"Well, we shall see," said the Dean. "Good-bye for the present!"

Mother and daughter stood at the window watching the two cross the churchyard. Dean and wife knew it, but daren't look round, and daren't admit the fact to one another.

Lou was grinning with a complete grin that gave her an odd, dryad or faun look, intensified.

"It was almost as good as pouring tea into her hat," said Mrs. Witt serenely. "People like that tire me out. I shall take a glass of sherry."

"So will I, mother.—It was even better than pouring tea in her hat.— You meant, didn't you, if you poured tea in her hat, to put cream and sugar in first?"[31]

"I did," said Mrs. Witt.

But after the excitement of the encounter had passed away, Lou felt as if her life had passed away too. She went to bed, feeling she could stand no more.

In the morning she found her mother sitting at a window watching a funeral. It was raining heavily, so that some of the mourners even wore mackintosh coats. The funeral was in the poorer corner of the churchyard, where another new grave was covered with wreaths of sodden, shrivelling flowers.—The yellowish coffin stood on the wet earth, in the rain: the curate held his hat, in a sort of permanent salute, above his head, like a little umbrella as he hastened on with the service. The people seemed too wet to weep more wet.

---

[31]Putting milk and sugar in the cup before pouring tea was *not done*. People who did so were called "miffers," an acronym for Milk In First.

It was a long coffin.

"Mother, do you really *like* watching?" asked Lou irritably, as Mrs. Witt sat in complete absorption.

"I do, Louise, I really enjoy it."

"Enjoy, mother!"—Lou was almost disgusted.

"I'll tell you why. I imagine I'm the one in the coffin—this is a girl of eighteen, who died of consumption—and those are my relatives, and I'm watching them put me away. And you know, Louise, I've come to the conclusion that hardly anybody in the world really lives, and so hardly anybody really dies. They may well say: *O Death, where is thy sting-a-ling-a-ling?* Even Death can't sting those that have never really lived.—I always used to want that—to die without death stinging me.— And I'm sure the girl in the coffin is saying to herself: *Fancy Aunt Emma putting on a drab slicker, and wearing it while they bury me. Doesn't show much respect. But then my mother's family always were common!* I feel there should be a solemn burial of a roll of newspapers containing the account of the death and funeral, next week. It would be just as serious: the grave of all the world's remarks——"

"I don't want to think about it, mother. One ought to be able to laugh at it. I want to laugh at it."

"Well, Louise, I think it's just as great a mistake to laugh at everything as to cry at everything. Laughter's not the one panacea, either. I should *really* like, before I do come to be buried in a box, to know where I am. That young girl in that coffin never was anywhere—any more than the newspaper remarks on her death and burial. And I begin to wonder if I've ever been anywhere. I seem to have been a daily sequence of newspaper remarks, myself. I'm sure I never really conceived you and gave you birth. It all happened in newspaper notices. It's a newspaper fact that you are my child, and that's about all there is to it."

Lou smiled as she listened.

"I always knew you were philosophic, mother. But I never dreamed it would come to elegies in a country churchyard, written to your motherhood."

"*Exactly*, Louise! Here I sit and sing the elegy to my own motherhood. I never had any motherhood, except in newspaper fact. I never was a wife, except in newspaper notices. I never was a young girl, except in newspaper remarks. Bury everything I ever said or that was said about me, and you've buried *me*. But since Kind Words Can Never Die, I can't be buried, and death has no sting-a-ling-a-ling for *me*!—Now listen to me, Louise: I want death to be real to me—not as it was to that young girl. I *want* it to hurt me, Louise. If it hurts me enough, I shall know I was alive."

She set her face and gazed under half-dropped lids at the funeral, stoic, fate-like, and yet, for the first time, with a certain pure wistfulness of a young, virgin girl. This frightened Lou very much. She was so used to the matchless Amazon in her mother, that when she saw her sit there still, wistful, virginal, tender as a girl who has never taken armour, wistful at the window that only looked on graves, a serious terror took hold of the young woman. The terror of *too late!*

Lou felt years, centuries older than her mother, at that moment, with the tiresome responsibility of youth to protect and guide their elders.

"What can we do about it, mother?" she asked protectively.

"Do nothing, Louise. I'm not going to have anybody wisely steering my canoe, now I feel the rapids are near. I shall go with the river. Don't you pretend to do anything for me. I've done enough mischief myself, that way. I'm going down the stream, at last."

There was a pause.

"But in actuality, what?" asked Lou, a little ironically.

"I don't quite know. Wait awhile."

"Go back to America?"

"That is possible."

"I may come too."

"I've always waited for you to go back of your own will."

Lou went away, wandering round the house. She was so unutterably tired of everything—weary of the house, the graveyard, weary of the thought of Rico. She would have to go back to him to-morrow, to nurse him. Poor old Rico, going on like an amiable machine from day to day. It wasn't his fault. But his life was a rattling nullity, and her life rattled in null correspondence. She had hardly strength enough to stop rattling and be still. Perhaps she had not strength enough.

She did not know. She felt so weak that unless something carried her away, she would go on rattling her bit in the great machine of human life till she collapsed, and her rattle rattled itself out, and there was a sort of barren silence where the sound of her had been.

She wandered out in the rain, to the coach-house where Lewis and Phoenix were sitting facing one another, one on a bin, the other on the inner door-step.

"Well," she said, smiling oddly. "What's to be done?"

The two men stood up. Outside, the rain fell steadily on the flag-stones of the yard, past the leaves of trees. Lou sat down on the little iron step of the dogcart.

"That's cold," said Phoenix. "You sit here." And he threw a yellow horse-blanket on the box where he had been sitting.

"I don't want to take your seat," she said.

"All right, you take it."

He moved across and sat gingerly on the shaft of the dogcart.[32]—Lou seated herself, and loosened her soft tartan shawl. Her face was pink and fresh, and her dark hair curled almost merrily in the damp. But under her eyes were the finger-prints of deadly weariness.

She looked up at the two men, again smiling in her odd fashion. "What are we going to do?" she asked.

They looked at her closely, seeking her meaning.

"What about?" said Phoenix, a faint smile reflecting on his face, merely because she smiled.

"Oh, everything," she said, hugging her shawl again. "You know what they want? They want to shoot St. Mawr."

The two men exchanged glances.

"Who want it?" said Phoenix.

"Why—all our *friends!*" She made a little *moue.*[33] "Dean Vyner does."

Again the men exchanged glances. There was a pause. Then Phoenix said, looking aside:

"The boss is selling him."

"Who?"

"Sir Henry."—The half-breed always spoke the title with difficulty, and with a sort of sneer. "He sell him to Miss Manby."

"How do you know?"

"The man from Corrabach told me last night. Flora, she say it."

Lou's eyes met the sardonic, empty-seeing eyes of Phoenix direct. There was too much sarcastic understanding. She looked aside.

"What else did he say?" she asked.

"I don't know," said Phoenix, evasively. "He say they cut him—else shoot him. Think they cut him—and if he die, he die."

Lou understood. He meant they would geld St. Mawr—at his age. She looked at Lewis. He sat with his head down, so she could not see his face.

"Do you think it is true?" she asked. "Lewis? Do you think they would try to geld St. Mawr—to make him a gelding?"

---

[32]A light carriage.

[33]Grimace.

Lewis looked up at her. There was a faint deadly glimmer of contempt on his face.

"Very likely, Mam," he said.

She was afraid of his cold, uncanny pale eyes, with their uneasy grey dawn of contempt. These two men, with their silent, deadly inner purpose, were not like other men. They seemed like two silent enemies of all the other men she knew. Enemies in the great white camp, disguised as servants, waiting the incalculable opportunity. What the opportunity might be, none knew.

"Sir Henry hasn't mentioned anything to me about selling St. Mawr to Miss Manby," she said.

The derisive flicker of a smile came on Phoenix's face.

"He sell him first, and tell you then," he said, with his deadly impassive manner.

"But do you really think so?" she asked.

It was extraordinary how much corrosive contempt Phoenix could convey, saying nothing. She felt it almost as an insult. Yet it was a relief to her.

"You know, I can't believe it. I can't believe Sir Henry would want to have St. Mawr mutilated. I believe he'd rather shoot him."

"You think so?" said Phoenix, with a faint grin.

Lou turned to Lewis.

"Lewis, will you tell me what you truly think?"

Lewis looked at her with a hard, straight, fearless British stare.

"That man Philips was in the 'Moon and Stars' last night. He said Miss Manby told him she was buying St. Mawr, and she asked him if he thought it would be safe to cut him, and make a horse of him. He said it would be better, take some of the nonsense out of him. He's no good for a sire, anyhow——"

Lewis dropped his head again, and tapped a tattoo with the toe of his rather small foot.

"And what do you think?" said Lou.—It occurred to her how sensible and practicable Miss Manby was, so much more so than the Dean.

Lewis looked up at her with his pale eyes.

"It won't have anything to do with me," he said. "I shan't go to Corrabach Hall."

"What will you do, then?"

Lewis did not answer. He looked at Phoenix.

"Maybe him and me go to America," said Phoenix, looking at the void.

"Can he get in?" said Lou.

"Yes, he can. I know how," said Phoenix.

"And the money?" she said.

"We got money."

There was a silence, after which she asked of Lewis:

"You'd leave St. Mawr to his fate?"

"I can't help his fate," said Lewis. "There's too many people in the world for me to help anything."

"Poor St. Mawr!"

She went indoors again, and up to her room: then higher, to the top rooms of the tall Georgian house. From one window she could see the fields in the rain. She could see St. Mawr himself, alone as usual, standing with his head up, looking across the fences. He was streaked dark with rain. Beautiful, with his poised head and massive neck, and his supple hindquarters. He was neighing to Poppy. Clear on the wet wind came the sound of his bell-like, stallion's calling, that Mrs. Vyner called cruel. It was a strange noise, with a splendour that belonged to another world-age. The mean cruelty of Mrs. Vyner's humanitarianism, the barren cruelty of Flora Manby, the eunuch cruelty of Rico. Our whole eunuch civilization, nasty-minded as eunuchs are, with their kind of sneaking, sterilizing cruelty.

Yet even she herself, seeing St. Mawr's conceited march along the fence, could not help addressing him:

"Yes, my boy! If you knew what Miss Flora Manby was preparing for you! She'll sharpen a knife that will settle you."

And Lou called her mother.

The two American women stood high at the window, overlooking the wet, close, hedged-and-fenced English landscape. Everything enclosed, enclosed, to stifling. The very apples on the trees looked so shut in, it was impossible to imagine any speck of "Knowledge" lurking inside them. Good to eat, good to cook, good even for show. But the wild sap of untamable and inexhaustible knowledge—no! Bred out of them. Geldings, even the apples.

Mrs. Witt listened to Lou's half-humorous statements.

"You must admit, mother, Flora is a sensible girl," she said.

"I admit it, Louise."

"She goes straight to the root of the matter."

"And eradicates the root. Wise girl! And what is your answer?"

"I don't know, mother. What would you say?"

"I know what I should say."

"Tell me."

"I should say: *Miss Manby, you may have my husband, but not my horse. My husband won't need emasculating, and my horse I won't have you meddle with. I'll preserve one last male thing in the museum of this world, if I can.*" Lou listened, smiling faintly.

"That's what I will say," she replied at length. "The funny thing is, mother, they think all their men with their bare faces or their little quotation-marks moustaches *are* so tremendously male. That fox-hunting one!"

"I know it. Like little male motor-cars. Give him a little gas, and start him on the low gear, and away he goes: all his male gear rattling, like a cheap motor-car."

"I'm afraid I dislike men altogether, mother."

"You may, Louise. Think of Flora Manby, and how you love the fair sex."

"After all, St. Mawr is better. And I'm glad if he gives them a kick in the face."

"Ah, Louise!" Mrs. Witt suddenly clasped her hands with wicked passion. "*Ay, qué gozo!* [34] as our Juan used to say, on your father's ranch in Texas." She gazed in a sort of wicked ecstasy out of the window.

They heard Lou's maid softly calling Lady Carrington from below. Lou went to the stairs.

"What is it?"

"Lewis wants to speak to you, my Lady."

"Send him into the sitting-room."

The two women went down.

"What is it, Lewis?" asked Lou.

"Am I to bring in St. Mawr, in case they send for him from Corrabach?"

"No," said Lou swiftly.

"Wait a minute," put in Mrs. Witt. "What makes you think they will send for St. Mawr from Corrabach, Lewis?" she asked, suave as a grey leopard cat.

"Miss Manby went up to Flints Farm with Dean Vyner this morning, and they've just come back. They stopped the car, and Miss Manby got out at the field gate, to look at St. Mawr. I'm thinking if she made the

_____

[34] Ah, what a joy!

bargain with Sir Henry, she'll be sending a man over this afternoon, and if I'd better brush St. Mawr down a bit, in case."

The man stood strangely still, and the words came like shadows of his real meaning. It was a challenge.

"I see," said Mrs. Witt slowly.

Lou's face darkened. She too saw.

"So that is her game," she said. "That is why they got me down here."

"Never mind, Louise," said Mrs. Witt. Then to Lewis: "Yes, please bring in St. Mawr. You wish it, don't you, Louise?"

"Yes," hesitated Lou. She saw by Mrs. Witt's closed face that a counter-move was prepared.

"And, Lewis," said Mrs. Witt, "my daughter may wish you to ride St. Mawr this afternoon—not to Corrabach Hall."

"Very good, Madam."

Mrs. Witt sat silent for some time, after Lewis had gone, gathering inspiration from the wet, grisly gravestones.

"Don't you think it's time we made a move, daughter?" she asked.

"Any move," said Lou desperately.

"Very well then.—My dearest friends, and my *only* friends, in this country, are in Oxfordshire. I will set off to *ride* to Merriton this afternoon, and Lewis will ride with me on St. Mawr."

"But you can't ride to Merriton in an afternoon," said Lou.

"I know it. I shall ride across country. I shall *enjoy* it, Louise.—Yes.— I shall consider I am on my way back to America. I am most deadly tired of this country. From Merriton I shall make my arrangements to go to America, and take Lewis and Phoenix and St. Mawr along with me. I think they want to go.—You will decide for yourself."

"Yes, I'll come too," said Lou casually.

"Very well. I'll start immediately after lunch, for I can't *breathe* in this place any longer. Where are Henry's automobile maps?"

Afternoon saw Mrs. Witt, in a large waterproof cape, mounted on her horse, Lewis, in another cape, mounted on St. Mawr, trotting through the rain, splashing in the puddles, moving slowly southwards. They took the open country, and would pass quite near to Flints Farm. But Mrs. Witt did not care. With great difficulty she had managed to fasten a small waterproof roll behind her, containing her night things. She seemed to breathe the first breath of freedom.

And sure enough, an hour or so after Mrs. Witt's departure, arrived Flora Manby in a splashed-up motor-car, accompanied by her sister, and bringing a groom and a saddle.

"Do you know, Harry sold me St. Mawr," she said. "I'm just wild to get that horse in hand."

"How?" said Lou.

"Oh, I don't know. There are ways. Do you mind if Philips rides him over now, to Corrabach?—Oh, I forgot, Harry sent you a note."

Dearest Loulina: Have you been gone from here two days or two years? It seems the latter. You are terribly missed. Flora wanted so much to buy St. Mawr, to save us further trouble, that I have sold him to her. She is giving me what we paid: rather, what you paid; so of course the money is yours. I am thankful we are rid of the animal, and that he falls into competent hands—I asked her please to remove him from your charge to-day. And I can't tell how much easier I am in my mind, to think of him gone. You are coming back to me to-morrow, aren't you? I shall think of nothing else but you, till I see you. *A rivederti*,[35] darling dear! R.

"I'm so sorry," said Lou. "Mother went on horseback to see some friends, and Lewis went with her on St. Mawr. He knows the road."

"She'll be back this evening?" said Flora.

"I don't know. Mother is so uncertain. She may be away a day or two."

"Well, here's the cheque for St. Mawr."

"No, I won't take it now—no, thank you—not till mother comes back with the goods."

Flora was chagrined. The two women knew they hated one another. The visit was a brief one.

Mrs. Witt rode on in the rain, which abated as the afternoon wore down, and the evening came without rain, and with a suffusion of pale yellow light. All the time she had trotted in silence, with Lewis just behind her. And she scarcely saw the heather-covered hills with the deep clefts between them, nor the oak-woods, nor the lingering fox-gloves, nor the earth at all. Inside herself she felt a profound repugnance for the English country: she preferred even the crudeness of Central Park in New York.

And she felt an almost savage desire to get away from Europe, from everything European. Now she was really *en route*, she cared not a straw for St. Mawr or for Lewis or anything. Something just writhed inside her, all the time, against Europe. That closeness, that sense of cohesion,

---

[35]In Italian, "until I see thee."

that sense of being fused into a lump with all the rest—no matter how much distance you kept—this drove her mad. In America the cohesion was a matter of choice and will. But in Europe it was organic, like the helpless particles of one sprawling body. And the great body in a state of incipient decay.

She was a woman of fifty-one: and she seemed hardly to have lived a day. She looked behind her—the thin trees and swamps of Louisiana, the sultry, sub-tropical excitement of decaying New Orleans, the vast bare dryness of Texas, with mobs of cattle in an illumined dust! The half-European thrills of New York! The false stability of Boston! A clever husband, who was a brilliant lawyer, but who was far more thrilled by his cattle ranch than by his law: and who drank heavily and died. The years of first widowhood in Boston, consoled by a self-satisfied sort of intellectual courtship from clever men.—For curiously enough, while she wanted it, she had always been able to compel men to pay court to her. All kinds of men.—Then a rather dashing time in New York—when she was in her early forties. Then the long *visual* philandering in Europe. She left off "loving," save through the eye, when she came to Europe. And when she made her trips to America, she found it was finished there also, her "loving."

What was the matter? Examining herself, she had long ago decided that her nature was a destructive force. But then, she justified herself, she had only destroyed that which was destructible. If she could have found something indestructible, especially in men, though she would have fought against it, she would have been glad at last to be defeated by it.

That was the point. She really wanted to be defeated, in her own eyes. And nobody had ever defeated her. Men were never really her match. A woman of terrible strong health, she felt even that in her strong limbs there was far more electric power than in the limbs of any man she had met. That curious fluid electric force, that could make any man kiss her hand, if she so willed it. A queen, as far as she wished. And not having been very clever at school, she always had the greatest respect for the mental powers. Her own were not mental powers. Rather electric, as of some strange physical dynamo within her. So she had been ready to bow before Mind.

But alas! After a brief time, she had found Mind, at least the man who was supposed to have the mind, bowing before her. Her own peculiar dynamic force was stronger than the force of Mind. She could make Mind kiss her hand.

And not by any sensual tricks. She did not really care about sensualities, especially as a younger woman. Sex was a mere adjunct. She cared about the mysterious, intense, dynamic sympathy that could flow between her and some "live" man—a man who was highly conscious, a real live wire. That she cared about.

But she had never rested until she had made the man she admired: and admiration was the root of her attraction to any man: made him kiss her hand. In both senses, actual and metaphorical. Physical and metaphysical. Conquered his country.

She had always succeeded. And she believed that, if she cared, she always *would* succeed. In the world of living men. Because of the power that was in her, in her arms, in her strong, shapely, but terrible hands, in all the great dynamo of her body.

For this reason she had been so terribly contemptuous of Rico, and of Lou's infatuation. Ye Gods! What was Rico in the scale of men!

Perhaps she despised the younger generation too easily. Because she did not see its sources of power, she concluded it was powerless. Whereas perhaps the power of accommodating oneself to any circumstance and committing oneself to no circumstance is the last triumph of mankind.

Her generation had had its day. She had had her day. The world of her men had sunk into a sort of insignificance. And with a great contempt she despised the world that had come into place instead: the world of Rico and Flora Manby, the world represented, to her, by the Prince of Wales.[36]

In such a world there was nothing even to conquer. It gave everything and gave nothing to everybody and anybody all the time. *Dio benedetto!* as Rico would say. A great complicated tangle of nonentities ravelled in nothingness. So it seemed to her.

Great God! This was the generation she had helped to bring into the world.

She had had her day. And, as far as the mysterious battle of life went, she had won all the way. Just as Cleopatra, in the mysterious business of a woman's life, won all the way.

Though that bald tough Caesar had drawn his iron from the fire without losing much of its temper. And he had gone his way. And Antony surely was splendid to die with.

In her life there had been no tough Caesar to go his way in cold

---

[36]At the time of *St. Mawr*, Edward, Prince of Wales, was the darling of café society; later, in 1936, he ascended the throne as Edward VIII, abdicated to marry an American divorcée the same year, and became the Duke of Windsor.

blood, away from her. Her men had gone from her like dogs on three legs, into the crowd. And certainly there was no gorgeous Antony to die for and with.

Almost she was tempted in her heart to cry: "Conquer me, O God, before I die!"—But then she had a terrible contempt for the God that was supposed to rule this universe. She felt she could make *Him* kiss her hand. Here she was, a woman of fifty-one, past the change of life. And her great dread was to die an empty, barren death. Oh, if only Death might open dark wings of mystery and consolation! To die an easy, barren death. To pass out as she had passed in, without mystery or the rustling of darkness! That was her last, final, ashy dread.

"Old!" she said to herself. "I am not *old!* I have lived many years, that is all. But I am as timeless as an hour-glass that turns morning and night, and spills the hours of sleep one way, the hours of consciousness the other way, without itself being affected. Nothing in all my life has ever truly affected me.—I believe Cleopatra only tried the asp, as she tried her pearls in wine, to see if it would really, really have any effect on her. Nothing had ever really had any effect on her, neither Caesar nor Antony nor any of them. Never once had she really been lost, lost to herself. Then try death, see if that trick would work. If she would lose herself to herself that way.—Ah, death——!"

But Mrs. Witt mistrusted death too. She felt she might pass out as a bed of asters passes out in autumn, to mere nothingness.—And something in her longed to die, at least, *positively*: to be folded then at last into throbbing wings of mystery, like a hawk that goes to sleep. Not like a thing made into a parcel and put into the last rubbish-heap.

So she rode trotting across the hills, mile after mile, in silence. Avoiding the roads, avoiding everything, avoiding everybody, just trotting forwards, towards night.

And by nightfall they had travelled twenty-five miles. She had motored around this country, and knew the little towns and the inns. She knew where she would sleep.

The morning came beautiful and sunny. A woman so strong in health, why should she ride with the fact of death before her eyes? But she did.

Yet in sunny morning she must do something about it.

"Lewis!" she said. "Come here and tell me something, please! Tell me," she said, "do you believe in God?"

"In God!" he said, wondering. "I never think about it."

"But do you say your prayers?"

"No, Mam!"

"Why don't you?"

He thought about it for some minutes.

"I don't like religion. My aunt and uncle were religious."

"You don't like religion," she repeated. "And you don't believe in God.—Well, then——"

"Nay!" he hesitated. "I never said I didn't believe in God.—Only I'm sure I'm not a Methodist. And I feel a fool in a proper church. And I feel a fool saying my prayers.—And I feel a fool when ministers and parsons come getting at me.—I never think about God, if folks don't try to make me." He had a small, sly smile, almost gay.

"And you don't like feeling a fool?" She smiled rather patronizingly.

"No, Mam."

"Do I make you feel a fool?" she asked, dryly.

He looked at her without answering.

"Why don't you answer?" she said, pressing.

"I think you'd like to make a fool of me sometimes," he said.

"Now?" she pressed.

He looked at her with that slow, distant look.

"Maybe!" he said, rather unconcernedly.

Curiously, she couldn't touch him. He always seemed to be watching her from a distance, as if from another country. Even if she made a fool of him, something in him would all the time be far away from her, not implicated.

She caught herself up in the personal game, and returned to her own isolated question. A vicious habit made her start the personal tricks. She didn't want to, really.

There was something about this little man—sometimes, to herself, she called him *Little Jack Horner, Sat in a corner*—that irritated her and made her want to taunt him. His peculiar little inaccessibility, that was so tight and easy.

Then again, there was something, his way of looking at her as if he looked from out of another country, a country of which he was an inhabitant, and where she had never been: this touched her strangely. Perhaps behind this little man was the mystery. In spite of the fact that in actual life, in her world, he was only a groom, almost *chétif*[37] with his legs a little bit horsy and bowed; and of no education, saying *Yes, Mam!* and *No, Mam!* and accomplishing nothing, simply nothing at all on the face of the earth. Strictly a nonentity.

---

[37]Worthless or mean.

And yet, what made him perhaps the only real entity to her, his seeming to inhabit another world than hers. A world dark and still, where language never ruffled the growing leaves, and seared their edges like a bad wind.

Was it an illusion, however? Sometimes she thought it was. Just bunkum, which she had faked up, in order to have something to mystify about.

But then, when she saw Phoenix and Lewis silently together, she knew there *was* another communion, silent, excluding her. And sometimes when Lewis was alone with St. Mawr: and once, when she saw him pick up a bird that had stunned itself against a wire: she had realized another world, silent, where each creature is alone in its own aura of silence, the mystery of power: as Lewis had power with St. Mawr, and even with Phoenix.

The visible world, and the invisible. Or rather, the audible and the inaudible. She had lived so long, and so completely, in the visible, audible world. She would not easily admit that other, inaudible. She always wanted to jeer, as she approached the brink of it.

Even now, she wanted to jeer at the little fellow, because of his holding himself inaccessible within the inaudible, silent world. And she knew he knew it.

"Did you never want to be rich, and be a gentleman, like Sir Henry?" she asked.

"I would many times have liked to be rich. But I never exactly wanted to be a gentleman," he said.

"Why not?"

"I can't exactly say. I should be uncomfortable if I was like they are."

"And are you comfortable now?"

"When I'm let alone."

"And do they let you alone? Does the world let you alone?"

"No, they don't."

"Well, then——"

"I keep to myself all I can."

"And are you comfortable, as you call it, when you keep to yourself?"

"Yes, I am."

"But when you keep to yourself, what do you keep to? What precious treasure have you to keep to?"

He looked, and saw she was jeering.

"None," he said. "I've got nothing of that sort."

She rode impatiently on ahead.

And the moment she had done so, she regretted it. She might put the little fellow, with contempt, out of her reckoning. But no, she would not do it.

She had put so much out of her reckoning: soon she would be left in an empty circle, with her empty self at the centre.

She reined in again.

"Lewis!" she said. "I don't want you to take offence at anything I say."

"No, Mam."

"I don't want you to say just *No, Mam!* all the time!" she cried impulsively. "Promise me."

"Yes, Mam!"

"But really! Promise me you won't be offended at whatever I say."

"Yes, Mam!"

She looked at him searchingly. To her surprise, she was almost in tears. A woman of her years! And with a servant!

But his face was blank and stony, with a stony, distant look of pride that made him inaccessible to her emotions. He met her eyes again: with that cold, distant look, looking straight into her hot, confused, pained self. So cold and as if merely refuting her. He didn't believe her, nor trust her, nor like her even. She was an attacking enemy to him. Only he stayed really far away from her, looking down at her from a sort of distant hill where her weapons could not reach: not quite.

And at the same time, it hurt him in a dumb, living way, that she made these attacks on him. She could see the cloud of hurt in his eyes, no matter how distantly he looked at her.

They bought food in a village shop, and sat under a tree near a field where men were already cutting oats, in a warm valley. Lewis had stabled the horses for a couple of hours, to feed and rest. But he came to join her under the tree, to eat.—He sat at a little distance from her, with the bread and cheese in his small brown hands, eating silently, and watching the harvesters. She was cross with him, and therefore she was stingy, would give him nothing to eat but dry bread and cheese. Herself, she was not hungry.—So all the time he kept his face a little averted from her. As a matter of fact, he kept his whole being averted from her, away from her. He did not want to touch her, nor to be touched by her. He kept his spirit there, alert, on its guard, but out of contact. It was as if he had unconsciously accepted the battle, the old battle. He was her target, the old object of her deadly weapons. But he refused to shoot back. It was as if he caught all her missiles in full flight, before they touched him, and silently threw them on the ground behind him. And in some essential part of himself he ignored her, staying in another world.

That other world! Mere male armour of artificial imperviousness! It angered her.

Yet she knew, by the way he watched the harvesters, and the grasshoppers popping into notice, that it was another world. And when a girl went by, carrying food to the field, it was at him she glanced. And he gave that quick, animal little smile that came from him unawares. Another world!

Yet also, there was a sort of meanness about him: a *suffisance!* A keep-yourself-for-yourself, and don't give yourself away.

Well!—she rose impatiently.

It was hot in the afternoon, and she was rather tired. She went to the inn and slept, and did not start again till tea-time.

Then they had to ride rather late. The sun sank, among a smell of cornfields, clear and yellow-red behind motionless dark trees. Pale smoke rose from cottage chimneys. Not a cloud was in the sky, which held the upward-floating light like a bowl inverted on purpose. A new moon sparkled and was gone. It was beginning of night.

Away in the distance, they saw a curious pinkish glare of fire, probably furnaces. And Mrs. Witt thought she could detect the scent of furnace smoke, or factory smoke. But then she always said that of the English air: it was never quite free of the smell of smoke, coal-smoke.

They were riding slowly on a path through fields, down a long slope. Away below was a puther of lights. All the darkness seemed full of half-spent crossing lights, a curious uneasiness. High in the sky a star seemed to be walking. It was an aeroplane with a light. Its buzz rattled above. Not a space, not a speck of this country that wasn't humanized, occupied by the human claim. Not even the sky.

They descended slowly through a dark wood, which they had entered through a gate. Lewis was all the time dismounting and opening gates, letting her pass, shutting the gate and mounting again.

So, in a while she came to the edge of the wood's darkness, and saw the open pale concave of the world beyond. The darkness was never dark. It shook with the concussion of many invisible lights, lights of towns, villages, mines, factories, furnaces, squatting in the valleys and behind all the hills.

Yet, as Rachel Witt drew rein at the gate emerging from the wood, a very big, soft star fell in heaven, cleaving the hubbub of this human night with a gleam from the greater world.

"See! a star falling!" said Lewis, as he opened the gate.

"I saw it," said Mrs. Witt, walking her horse past him.

There was a curious excitement of wonder, or magic, in the little man's voice. Even in this night something strange had stirred awake in him.

"You ask me about God," he said to her, walking his horse alongside in the shadow of the wood's edge, the darkness of the old Pan, that kept our artificially lit world at bay. "I don't know about God. But when I see a star fall like that out of long-distance places in the sky: and the moon sinking saying Good-bye! Good-bye! Good-bye! and nobody listening: I think I hear something, though I wouldn't call it God."

"What then?" said Rachel Witt.

"And you smell the smell of oak-leaves now," he said, "now the air is cold. They smell to me more alive than people. The trees hold their bodies hard and still, but they watch and listen with their leaves. And I think they say to me: *Is that you passing there, Morgan Lewis? All right, you pass quickly, we shan't do anything to you. You are like a holly-bush.*"

"Yes," said Rachel Witt, dryly. "*Why?*"

"All the time, the trees grow, and listen. And if you cut a tree down without asking pardon, trees will hurt you some time in your life, into the night-time."

"I suppose," said Rachel Witt, "that's an old superstition."

"They say that ash-trees don't like people. When the other people were most in the country—I mean like what they call fairies, that have all gone now—they liked ash-trees best. And you know the little green things with little small nuts in them, that come flying down from ash-trees—*pigeons*, we call them—they're the seeds—the other people used to catch them and eat them before they fell to the ground. And that made the people so they could hear trees living and feeling things.— But when all these people that there are now came to England, they liked the oak-trees best, because their pigs ate the acorns. So now you can tell the ash-trees are mad, they want to kill all these people. But the oak-trees are many more than the ash-trees."

"And do you eat the ash-tree seeds?" she asked.

"I always ate them when I was little. Then I wasn't frightened of ash-trees, like most of the others. And I wasn't frightened of the moon. If you didn't go near the fire all day, and if you didn't eat any cooked food nor anything that had been in the sun, but only things like turnips or radishes or pig-nuts, and then went without any clothes on, in the full moon, then you could see the people in the moon, and go with them. They never have fire, and they never speak, and their bodies are clear almost like jelly. They die in a minute if there's a bit of fire near them. But they know more than we. Because unless fire touches them, they never die. They see people live and they see people perish, and they say people are only like twigs on a tree, you break them off the tree, and kindle with them. You make a fire of them, and they are gone, the fire is gone, everything is gone. But the people of the moon don't die, and fire is nothing to them. They look at it from the distance of the sky, and see it burning things up, people all appearing and disappearing like twigs that come in spring and you cut them in autumn and make a fire of them and they are gone. And they say: what do people matter? If you want to matter, you must become a moon-boy. Then, all your life, fire can't blind you and people can't hurt you. Because at full moon you can join the moon people, and go through the air and pass any cool places, pass through rocks and through the trunks of trees, and when you come to people lying warm in bed, you punish them."

"How?"

"You sit on the pillow where they breathe, and you put a web across their mouth, so they can't breathe the fresh air that comes from the moon. So they go on breathing the same air again and again, and that makes them more and more stupefied. The sun gives out heat, but the moon gives out fresh air. That's what the moon people do: they wash the air clean with moonlight."

He was talking with a strange eager naïveté that amused Rachel Witt, and made her a little uncomfortable in her skin. Was he after all no more than a sort of imbecile?

"Who told you all this stuff?" she asked abruptly.

And, as abruptly, he pulled himself up.

"We used to say it, when we were children."

"But you don't believe it? It *is* only childishness, after all."

He paused a moment or two.

"No," he said, in his ironical little day-voice. "I know I shan't make anything but a fool of myself, with that talk. But all sorts of things go through our heads, and some seem to linger, and some don't. But you asking me about God put it into my mind, I suppose. I don't know what sort of things I believe in: only I know it's not what the chapel-folks believe in. We, none of us believe in them when it comes to earning a living, or, with you people, when it comes to spending your fortune. Then we know that bread costs money, and even your sleep you have to pay for.—That's work. Or, with you people, it's just owning property and seeing you get your value for your money.—But a man's mind is always full of things. And some people's minds, like my aunt and uncle, are full of religion and hell for everybody except themselves. And some people's minds are all money, money, money, and how to get hold of something they haven't got hold of yet. And some people, like you, are always curious about what everybody else in the world is after. And some people are all for enjoying themselves and being thought much of, and some, like Lady Carrington, don't know what to do with themselves. Myself, I don't want to have in my mind the things other people have in their minds. I'm one that likes my own things best. And if, when I see a bright star fall, like to-night, I think to myself: *There's movement in the sky. The world is going to change again. They're throwing something to us from the distance, and we've got to have it, whether we want it or not. To-morrow there will be a difference for everybody, thrown out of the sky upon us, whether we want it or not:* then that's how I want to think, so let me please myself."

"You know what a shooting star actually is, I suppose?—and that there are always many in August, because we pass through a region of them?"

"Yes, Mam, I've been told. But stones don't come at us from the sky for nothing. Either it's like when a man tosses an apple to you out of his orchard, as you go by, or it's like when somebody shies a stone at you, to cut your head open. You'll never make me believe the sky is like an empty house with a slate falling from the roof. The world has its own life, the sky has a life of its own, and never is it like stones rolling down a rubbish-heap and falling into a pond. Many things twitch and twitter within the sky, and many things happen beyond us. My own way of thinking is my own way."

"I never knew you talk so much."

"No, Mam. It's your asking me that about God. Or else it's the night-time. I don't believe in God and being good and going to heaven. Neither do I worship idols, so I'm not a heathen, as my aunt called me. Never from a boy did I want to believe the things they kept grinding in their guts at home, and at Sunday School, and at school. A man's mind has to be full of something, so I keep to what we used to think as lads. It's childish nonsense, I know it. But it suits me. Better than other people's stuff. Your man Phoenix is about the same, when he lets on.— Anyhow, it's my own stuff, that we believed as lads, and I like it better than other people's stuff.—You asking about God made me let on. But I would never belong to any club, or trades-union, and God's the same to my mind."

With this he gave a little kick to his horse, and St. Mawr went dancing excitedly along the highway they now entered, leaving Mrs. Witt to trot after as rapidly as she could.

When she came to the hotel, to which she had telegraphed for rooms, Lewis disappeared, and she was left thinking hard.

It was not till they were twenty miles from Merriton, riding through a slow morning mist, and she had a rather far-away, wistful look on her face, unusual for her, that she turned to him in the saddle and said: "Now don't be surprised, Lewis, at what I am going to say. I am going to ask you, now, supposing I wanted to marry you, what should you say?"

He looked at her quickly, and was at once on his guard.

"That you didn't mean it," he replied hastily.

"Yes,"—she hesitated, and her face looked wistful and tired.—"Supposing I *did* mean it. Supposing I did *really*, from my heart, want to marry you and be a wife to you—"she looked away across the fields—"then what should you say?"

Her voice sounded sad, a little broken.

"Why, Mam!" he replied, knitting his brow and shaking his head a little. "I should say you didn't mean it, you know. Something would have come over you."

"But supposing I *wanted* something to come over me?"

He shook his head.

"It would never do, Mam! Some people's flesh and blood is kneaded like bread: and that's me. And some are rolled like fine pastry, like Lady Carrington. And some are mixed with gunpowder. They're like a cartridge you put in a gun, Mam."

She listened impatiently.

"Don't talk," she said, "about bread and cakes and pastry, it all means nothing. You used to answer short enough, *Yes, Mam! No, Mam!* That will do now. Do you mean *Yes!* or *No?*"

His eyes met hers. She was again hectoring.

"No, Mam!" he said, quite neutral.

"Why?"

As she waited for his answer, she saw the foundations of his loquacity dry up, his face go distant and mute again, as it always used to be, till these last two days, when it had had a funny touch of inconsequential merriness.

He looked steadily into her eyes, and his look was neutral, sombre, and hurt. He looked at her as if infinite seas, infinite spaces divided him and her. And his eyes seemed to put her away beyond some sort of fence. An anger congealed cold like lava, set impassive against her and all her sort.

"No, Mam. I couldn't give my body to any woman who didn't respect it."

"But I do respect it, I do!"—she flushed hot like a girl.

"No, Mam. Not as *I* mean it," he replied.

There was a touch of anger against her in his voice, and a distance of distaste.

"And how do *you* mean it?" she replied, the full sarcasm coming back into her tones. She could see that as a woman to touch and fondle he saw her as repellent: only repellent.

"I have to be a servant to women now," he said, "even to earn my wage. I could never touch with my body a woman whose servant I was."

"You're not my servant: my daughter pays your wages.—And all that is beside the point, between a man and a woman."

"No woman who I touched with my body should ever speak to me as you speak to me, or think of me as you think of me," he said.

"But—" she stammered, "I think of you—with love. And can you be so unkind as to notice the way I speak? You know it's only my way."

"You, as a woman," he said, "you have no respect for a man."

"Respect! Respect!" she cried. "I'm likely to lose what respect I have left. I know I can *love* a man. But whether a man can love a woman——"

"No," said Lewis. "I never could, and I think I never shall. Because I don't want to. The thought of it makes me feel shame."

"What do you mean?" she cried.

"Nothing in the world," he said, "would make me feel such shame as to have a woman shouting at me, or mocking at me, as I see women mocking and despising the men they marry. No woman shall touch my body, and mock me or despise me. No woman."

"But men must be mocked, or despised even, sometimes."

"No. Not this man. Not by the woman I touch with my body."

"Are you perfect?"

"I don't know. But if I touch a woman with my body it must put a lock on her, to respect what I will never have despised: never!"

"What will you never have despised?"

"My body! And my touch upon the woman."

"Why insist so on your body?"—And she looked at him with a touch of contemptuous mockery, raillery.

He looked her in the eyes, steadily, and coldly, putting her away from him, and himself far away from her.

"Do you expect that any woman will stay your humble slave to-day?" she asked cuttingly.

But he only watched her, coldly, distant, refusing any connexion.

"Between men and women, it's a question of give and take. A man can't expect *always* to be humbly adored."

He watched her still, cold, rather pale, putting her far from him. Then he turned his horse and set off rapidly along the road, leaving her to follow.

She walked her horse and let him go, thinking to herself:

"There's a little bantam cock. And a groom! Imagine it! Thinking he can dictate to a woman!"

She was in love with him. And he, in an odd way, was in love with her. She had known it by the odd, uncanny merriment in him, and his unexpected loquacity. But he would not have her come physically near him. Unapproachable there as a cactus, guarding his "body" from her contact. As if contact with her would be mortal insult and fatal injury to his marvellous "body."

What a little cock-sparrow!

Let him ride ahead. He would have to wait for her somewhere.

She found him at the entrance to the next village. His face was pallid and set. She could tell he felt he had been insulted, so he had congealed into stiff insentience.

"At the bottom of all men is the same," she said to herself: "An empty, male conceit of themselves."

She too rode up with a face like a mask, and straight on to the hotel.

"Can you serve dinner to myself and my servant?" she asked at the inn: which, fortunately for her, accommodated motorists, otherwise they would have said *No!*

"I think," said Lewis as they came in sight of Merriton, "I'd better give Lady Carrington a week's notice."

A complete little stranger! And an impudent one.

"Exactly as you please," she said.

She found several letters from her daughter at Marshall Place.

"Dear Mother: No sooner had you gone off than Flora appeared, not at all in the bud, but rather in full blow. She demanded her victim: Shylock demanding the pound of flesh: and wanted to hand over the shekels.

"Joyfully I refused them. She said 'Harry' was much better, and invited him and me to stay at Corrabach Hall till he was quite well: it would be less strain on your household while he was still in bed and helpless. So the plan is that he shall be brought down on Friday, if he is really fit for the journey, and we drive straight to Corrabach. I am packing his bags and mine, clearing up our traces: his trunks to go to Corrabach, mine to stay here and make up their minds.—I am going to Flints Farm again to-morrow, dutifully, though I am no flower for the bedside.—I do so want to know if Rico has already called her Fiorita: or perhaps Florecita. It reminds me of old William's joke: *Now yuh tell me, little Missy: which is the best posy that grow?* And the hushed whisper in which he said the answer: *The Collyposy!*[38] Oh, dear, I am so tired of feeling spiteful, but how else is one to feel?

"You looked most prosaically romantic, setting off in a rubber cape, followed by Lewis. Hope the roads were not very slippery, and that you had a good time, *à la Mademoiselle de Maupin.*[39] Do remember, dear, not to devour little Lewis before you have got half-way——"

"Dear Mother: I half expected word from you before I left, but nothing came. Forrester drove me up here just before lunch. Rico seems much better, almost himself, and a little more than that. He broached our staying at Corrabach very tactfully. I told him Flora had asked me, and it seemed a good plan. Then I told him about St. Mawr. He was a little piqued, and there was a pause of very disapproving silence. Then he said: *Very well, darling. If you wish to keep the animal, do so by all means. I make a present of him again.* Me: *That's so good of you, Rico. Because I know revenge is sweet.* Rico: *Revenge, Loulina! I don't think I was selling him for vengeance! Merely to get rid of him to Flora, who can keep better hold over him.* Me: *But you know, dear, she was going to geld him!* Rico: *I don't think anybody knew it. We only wondered if it were possible, to make him more amenable. Did she tell you?* Me: *No—Phoenix did. He had it from a groom.* Rico: *Dear me! A concatenation of grooms! So your mother rode off with Lewis, and carried St. Mawr out of danger! I understand! Let us hope worse won't befall.* Me: *Whom?* Rico: *Never mind, dear! It's so lovely to see you. You are looking rested. I thought those Countess of Witton roses the most marvellous things in the world, till you came, now they're quite in the background.* He had some very lovely red roses, in a crystal bowl: the room smelled of roses. Me: *Where did they*

---

[38]Rico plays on Flora's name by translating its meaning—"flower"—into affectionate diminutives in Italian and Spanish. Old William's joke also involves a play on words: "posy" means "flower"; the answer is therefore "cauliflower."

[39]Title character of an 1835 novel by Théophile Gautier known for its "pagan eroticism."

come from? Rico: *Oh, Flora brought them!* Me: *Bowl and all?* Rico: *Bowl and all! Wasn't it dear of her?* Me: *Why, yes! But then she's the goddess of flowers, isn't she?* Poor darling, he was offended that I should twit him while he is ill, so I relented. He has had a couple of marvellous invalid's bed-jackets sent from London: one a pinkish yellow, with rose-arabesque facings: this one in fine cloth. But unfortunately he has already dropped soup on it. The other is a lovely silvery and blue and green soft brocade. He had that one on to receive me, and I at once complimented him on it. He has got a new ring too: sent by Aspasia Wein-gartner, a rather lovely intaglio of Priapus[40] under an apple bough, at least so he says it is. He made a naughty face, and said: *The Priapus stage is rather advanced for poor me.* I asked what the Priapus stage was, but he said: *Oh, nothing!* Then nurse said: *There's a big classical dictionary that Miss Manby brought up, if you wish to see it.* So I have been studying the Classical Gods. The world always was a queer place. It's a very queer one when Rico is the god Priapus. He would go round the orchard painting lifelike apples on the trees, and inviting nymphs to come and eat them. And the nymphs would pretend they were real: *Why, Sir Prippy, what stunningly naughty apples!* There's nothing so artificial as sinning nowadays. I suppose it once was real.

"I'm bored here: wish I had my horse."

"Dear Mother: I'm so glad you are enjoying your ride. I'm sure it is like riding into history, like the Yankee at the Court of King Arthur, in those old by-lanes and Roman roads. They still fascinate me: at least, more before I get there than when I am actually there. I begin to feel real American and to resent the past. Why doesn't the past decently bury itself, instead of sitting waiting to be admired by the present?

"Phoenix brought Poppy. I am so fond of her: rode for five hours yesterday. I was glad to get away from this farm. The doctor came, and said Rico would be able to go down to Corrabach to-morrow. Flora came to hear the bulletin, and sailed back full of zest. Apparently Rico is going to do a portrait of her, sitting up in bed. What a mercy the bed-clothes won't be mine when Priapus wields his palette from the pillow.

"Phoenix thinks you intend to go to America with St. Mawr, and that I am coming too, leaving Rico this side.—I wonder. I feel so unreal, nowadays, as if I too were nothing more than a painting by Rico on a

---

[40]The phallic god of the Romans.

mill-board. I feel almost too unreal even to make up my mind to anything. It is terrible when the life-flow dies out of one, and everything is like cardboard, and oneself is like cardboard. I'm sure it is worse than being dead. I realized it yesterday when Phoenix and I had a picnic lunch by a stream. You see I must imitate you in all things. He found me some water-cresses, and they tasted so damp and *alive*, I knew how deadened I was. Phoenix wants us to go and have a ranch in Arizona, and raise horses, with St. Mawr, if willing, for Father Abraham. I wonder if it matters what one does: if it isn't all the same thing over again. Only Phoenix, his funny blank face, makes my heart melt and go sad. But I believe he'd be cruel too. I saw it in his face when he didn't know I was looking. Anything though, rather than this deadness and this paint-Priapus business. *Au revoir*, mother dear! Keep on having a good time——"

"Dear Mother: I had your letter from Merriton: am so glad you arrived safe and sound in body and temper. There was such a funny letter from Lewis, too: I enclose it. What makes him take this extraordinary line? But I'm writing to tell him to take St. Mawr to London, and wait for me there. I have telegraphed Mrs. Squire to get the house ready for me: I shall go straight there.

"Things developed here as they were bound to. I just couldn't bear it. No sooner was Rico put in the automobile than a self-conscious importance came over him, like when the wounded hero is carried into the middle of the stage. *Why so solemn, Rico dear?* I asked him, trying to laugh him out of it. *Not solemn, dear, only feeling a little transient.* I don't think he knew himself what he meant. Flora was on the steps as the car drew up, dressed in severe white. She only needed an apron, to become a nurse: or a veil, to become a bride. Between the two, she had an unbearable air of a woman in seduced circumstances, as the *Times* said. She ordered two menservants about in subdued, you would have said hushed, but competent tones. And then I saw there was a touch of the priestess about her as well: Cassandra preparing for her violation: Iphigenia, with Rico for Orestes, on a stretcher: he looking like Adonis,[41]

---

[41]A melange of classical references. Cassandra, daughter of Priam, King of Troy, was violated by Aias, a Greek chieftain, on the night Troy fell. Iphigenia was the daughter of the Greek leader, Agamemnon, supposedly sacrificed to allow the fleet to sail to Troy, but transported by a miracle to barbarian Tauris, where she met her brother Orestes and saved him from death. Adonis, a handsome Greek shepherd, was unsuccessfully pursued by Aphrodite, goddess of love; he was slain by a boar.

fully prepared to be an unconscionable time in dying. They had given him a lovely room, downstairs, with doors opening on to a little garden all of its own. I believe it was Flora's boudoir. I left nurse and the men to put him to bed. Flora was hovering anxiously in the passage outside. *Oh, what a marvellous room! Oh, how colourful, how beautiful!* came Rico's tones, the hero behind the scenes. I must say, it was like a harvest festival, with roses and gaillardias in the shadow, and cornflowers in the light, and a bowl of grapes, and nectarines among leaves. *I'm so anxious that he should be happy,* Flora said to me in the passage. *You know him best. Is there anything else I could do for him?* Me: *Why, if you went to the piano and sang, I'm sure he'd love it. Couldn't you sing: Oh, my love is like a rred, rred rrose!*—You know how Rico imitates Scotch!

"Thank goodness I have a bedroom upstairs: nurse sleeps in a little antechamber to Rico's room. The Edwards are still here, the blond young man with some very futuristic plaster on his face. *Awfully good of you to come!* he said to me, looking at me out of one eye, and holding my hand fervently. How's that for cheek? *It's awfully good of Miss Manby to let me come,* said I. He: *Ah, but Flora is always a sport, a topping good sport!*

"I don't know what's the matter, but it just all put me into a fiendish temper. I felt I couldn't sit there at luncheon with that bright, youthful company, and hear about their tennis and their polo and their hunting and have their flirtatiousness making me sick. So I asked for a tray in my room. Do as I might, I couldn't help being horrid.

"Oh, and Rico! He really is too awful. Lying there in bed with every ear open, like Adonis waiting to be persuaded not to die. Seizing a hushed moment to take Flora's hand and press it to his lips, murmuring: *How awfully good you are to me, dear Flora!* And Flora: *I'd be better if I knew how, Harry!* So cheerful with it all! No, it's too much. My sense of humour is leaving me: which means, I'm getting into too bad a temper to be able to ridicule it all. I suppose I feel in the minority. It's an awful thought, to think that most all the young people in the world are brimming with *libido*. How awful!

"I said to Rico: *You're very comfortable here, aren't you?* He: *Comfortable! It's comparative heaven.* Me: *Would you mind if I went away?* A deadly pause. He is deadly afraid of being left alone with Flora. He feels safe so long as I am about, and he can take refuge in his marriage ties. He: *Where do you want to go, dear?* Me: *To mother. To London. Mother is planning to go to America, and she wants me to go.* Rico: *But you don't want to go t-h-e-e-e!* You know, mother, how Rico can put a venomous emphasis on a word, till it suggests pure poison. It nettled me. *I'm not sure,* I said. Rico: *Oh, but you can't stand that awful America.* Me: *I want to try again.* Rico: *But, Lou*

*dear, it will be winter before you get there. And this is absolutely the wrong
moment for me to go over there. I am only just making headway over here. When
I am absolutely sure of a position in England, then we nip across the Atlantic and
scoop in a few dollars, if you like. Just now, even when I am well, would be fatal.
I've only just sketched in the outline of my success in London, and one ought to
arrive in New York ready-made as a famous and important Artist.* Me: *But
mother and I didn't think of going to New York. We thought we'd sail straight to
New Orleans—if we could: or to Havana. And then go West to Arizona.* The
poor boy looked at me in such distress. *But, Loulina darling, do you mean
you want to leave me in the lurch for the winter season? You can't mean it. We're
just getting on so splendidly, really!*—I was surprised at the depth of feeling
in his voice: how tremendously his career as an artist—a popular artist—matters to him. I can never believe it.—You know, mother, you
and I feel alike about daubing paint on canvas: every possible daub
that can be daubed has already been done, so people ought to leave off.
Rico is so shrewd. I always think he's got his tongue in his cheek, and
I'm always staggered once more to find that he takes it absolutely
seriously. His career! The Modern British Society of Painters: perhaps
even the Royal Academy! Those people we see in London, and those
portraits Rico does! He may even be a second Laslow, or a thirteenth
Orpen,[42] and die happy! Oh! mother! How can it really matter to *anybody!*

"But I was really rather upset, when I realized how his heart was
fixed on his career, and that I might be spoiling everything for him. So
I went away to think about it. And then I realized how unpopular you
are, and how unpopular I shall be myself, in a little while. A sort of
hatred for people has come over me. I hate their ways and their bunk,
and I feel like kicking them in the face, as St. Mawr did that young
man. Not that I should ever do it. And I don't think I should ever have
made my final announcement to Rico, if he hadn't been such a beautiful pig in clover, here at Corrabach Hall. He has known the Manbys all
his life; they and he are sections of one engine. He would be far happier with Flora: or I won't say happier, because there is something in
him which rebels: but he would on the whole fit much better. I myself
am at the end of my limit, and beyond it. I can't 'mix' any more, and I
refuse to. I feel like a bit of eggshell in the mayonnaise: the only thing

---

[42]Sir William Orpen (1878-1931) was an academic painter of the period; Philip de László
(1869-1937) was a Hungarian-born portrait painter. Both were fashionable and very
successful financially, but they were never taken seriously as artists.

is to take it out, you can't beat it in. I *know* I shall cause a fiasco, even in Rico's career, if I stay. I shall go on being rude and hateful to people as I am at Corrabach, and Rico will lose all his nerve.

"So I have told him. I said this evening, when no one was about: *Rico dear, listen to me seriously. I can't stand these people. If you ask me to endure another week of them, I shall either become ill or insult them, as mother does. And I don't want to do either.* Rico: *But, darling, isn't everybody perfect to you!* Me: *I tell you, I shall just make a break, like St. Mawr, if I don't get out. I simply can't stand people.*—The poor darling, his face goes blank and anxious. He knows what I mean, because, except that they tickle his vanity all the time, he hates them as much as I do. But his vanity is the chief thing to him. He: *Lou darling, can't you wait till I get up, and we can go away to the Tyrol or somewhere for a spell?* Me: *Won't you come with me to America, to the South-west? I believe it's marvellous country.*—I saw his face switch into hostility; quite vicious. He: *Are you so keen on spoiling everything for me? Is that what I married you for? Do you do it deliberately?* Me: *Everything is already spoilt for me. I tell you I can't stand people, your Floras and your Aspasias, and your forthcoming young Englishmen. After all, I am an American, like mother, and I've got to go back.* He: *Really! And am I to come along as part of the luggage, labelled cabin!* Me: *You do as you wish, Rico.* He: *I wish to God you did as you wished, Lou dear. I'm afraid you do as Mrs. Witt wishes. I've always heard that the holiest thing in the world was a mother.* Me: *No, dear, it's just that I can't stand people.* He (with a snarl): *And I suppose I'm lumped in as* PEOPLE! And when he'd said it, it was true. We neither of us said anything for a time. Then he said, calculating: *Very well, dear! You take a trip to the land of stars and stripes, and I'll stay here and go on with my work. And when you've seen enough of their stars and tasted enough of their stripes, you can come back and take your place again with me.*—We left it at that.

"You and I are supposed to have important business connected with our estates in Texas—it sounds so well—so we are making a hurried trip to the States, as they call them. I shall leave for London early next week——"

Mrs. Witt read this long letter with satisfaction. She herself had one strange craving: to get back to America. It was not that she idealized her native country: she was a tartar of restlessness there, quite as much as in Europe. It was not that she expected to arrive at any blessed abiding-place. No, in America she would go on fuming and chafing the same. But at least she would be in America, in her own country. And that was what she wanted.

She picked up the sheet of poor paper, that had been folded in Lou's letter. It was the letter from Lewis, quite nicely written. "Lady Carrington, I write to tell you and Sir Henry that I think I had better quit your service, as it would be more comfortable all round. If you will write and tell me what you want me to do with St. Mawr, I will do whatever you tell me. With kind regards to Lady Carrington and Sir Henry, I remain, Your obedient servant, Morgan Lewis."

Mrs. Witt put the letter aside, and sat looking out of the window. She felt, strangely, as if already her soul had gone away from her actual surroundings. She was there, in Oxfordshire, in the body, but her spirit had departed elsewhere. A listlessness was upon her. It was with an effort she roused herself, to write to her lawyer in London, to get her release from her English obligations. Then she wrote to the London hotel.

For the first time in her life she wished she had a maid, to do little things for her. All her life, she had had too much energy to endure anyone hanging round her, personally. Now she gave up. Her wrists seemed numb, as if the power in her were switched off.

When she went down, they said Lewis had asked to speak to her. She had hardly seen him since they had arrived at Merriton.

"I've had a letter from Lady Carrington, Mam. She says will I take St. Mawr to London and wait for her there. But she says I am to come to you, Mam, for definite orders."

"Very well, Lewis. I shall be going to London in a few days' time. You arrange for St. Mawr to go up one day this week, and you will take him to the Mews. Come to me for anything you want. And don't talk of leaving my daughter. We want you to go with St. Mawr to America, with us and Phoenix."

"And your horse, Mam?"

"I shall leave him here at Merriton. I shall give him to Miss Atherton."

"Very good, Mam!"

"Dear Daughter: I shall be in my old quarters in Mayfair next Saturday, calling the same day at your house to see if everything is ready for you. Lewis has fixed up with the railway: he goes to town to-morrow. The reason of his letter was that I had asked him if he would care to marry me, and he turned me down with emphasis. But I will tell you about it. You and I are the scribe and the Pharisee; I never could write a letter, and you could never leave off——"

"Dearest Mother: I smelt something rash, but I know it's no use saying: How *could* you? I only wonder, though, that you should think of marriage. You know, dear, I ache in every fibre to be left alone, from all that sort of thing. I feel all bruises, like one who has been assassinated. I do so understand why Jesus said: *Noli me tangere.* Touch me not, I am not yet ascended unto the Father. Everything had hurt him so much, wearied him so beyond endurance, he felt he could not bear one little human touch on his body. I am like that. I can hardly bear even Elena to hand me a dress. As for a man—and marriage—ah, no! *Noli me tangere, homo!* I am not yet ascended unto the Father. Oh, leave me alone, leave me alone! That is all my cry to all the world.

"Curiously, I feel that Phoenix understands what I feel. He leaves me so understandingly alone, he almost gives me my sheath of aloneness: or at least, he protects me in my sheath. I am grateful for him.

"Whereas Rico feels my aloneness as a sort of shame to himself. He wants at least a blinding *pretence* of intimacy. Ah, intimacy! The thought of it fills me with aches, and the pretence of it exhausts me beyond myself.

"Yes, I long to go away to the West, to be away from the world like one dead and in another life, in a valley that life has not yet entered.

"Rico asked me: What are you doing with St. Mawr? When I said we were taking him with us, he said: *Oh, the corpus delicti!*[43] Whether that means anything I don't know. But he has grown sarcastic beyond my depth.

"I shall see you to-morrow——"

Lou arrived in town, at the dead end of August, with her maid and Phoenix. How wonderful it seemed to have London empty of all her set: her own little house to herself, with just the housekeeper and her own maid. The fact of being alone in those surroundings was so wonderful. It made the surroundings themselves seem all the more ghostly. Everything that had been actual to her was turning ghostly: even her little drawing-room was the ghost of a room, belonging to the dead people who had known it, or to all the dead generations that had brought such a room into being, evolved it out of their quaint domestic desires. And now, in herself, those desires were suddenly spent: gone out like a lamp that suddenly dies. And then she saw her pale, delicate

---

[43]The evidence of a crime committed.

room with its little green agate bowl and its two little porcelain birds and its soft, roundish chairs, turned into something ghostly, like a room set out in a museum. She felt like fastening little labels on the furniture: *Lady Louise Carrington Lounge Chair, Last used August, 1923.* Not for the benefit of posterity: but to remove her own self into another world, another realm of existence.

"My house, my house, my house, how can I ever have taken so much pains about it!" she kept saying to herself. It was like one of her old hats, suddenly discovered neatly put away in an old hatbox. And what a horror: an old "fashionable" hat!

Lewis came to see her, and he sat there in one of her delicate mauve chairs, with his feet on a delicate old carpet from Turkestan, and she just wondered. He wore his leather gaiters and khaki breeches as usual, and a faded blue shirt. But his beard and hair were trimmed, he was tidy. There was a certain fineness of contour about him, a certain subtle gleam, which made him seem, apart from his rough boots, not at all gross, or coarse, in that setting of rather silky, oriental furnishings. Rather he made the Asiatic, sensuous exquisiteness of her old rugs and her old white Chinese figures seem a weariness. Beauty! What was beauty, she asked herself? The oriental exquisiteness seemed to her all like dead flowers whose hour had come, to be thrown away.

Lou could understand her mother's wanting, for a moment, to marry him. His detachedness and his acceptance of something in destiny which people cannot accept. Right in the middle of him he accepted something from destiny, that gave him a quality of eternity. He did not care about persons, people, even events. In his own odd way, he was an aristocrat, unaccessible in his aristocracy. But it was the aristocracy of the invisible powers, the greater influences, nothing to do with human society.

"You don't really want to leave St. Mawr, do you?" Lou asked him. "You don't really want to quit, as you said?"

He looked at her steadily, from his pale-grey eyes, without answering, not knowing what to say.

"Mother told me what she said to you.—But she doesn't mind, she says you are entirely within your rights. She has a real regard for you. But we mustn't let our regards run us into actions which are beyond our scope, must we? That makes everything unreal. But you will come with us to America with St. Mawr, won't you? We depend on you."

"I don't want to be uncomfortable," he said.

"Don't be," she smiled. "I myself hate unreal situations—I feel I can't stand them any more. And most marriages are unreal situations. But apart from anything exaggerated, you like being with mother and me, don't you?"

"Yes, I do. I like Mrs. Witt as well. But not——"

"I know. There won't be any more of that——"

"You see, Lady Carrington," he said, with a little heat, "I'm not by nature a marrying man. And I should feel I was selling myself."

"Quite!—Why do you think you are not a marrying man, though?"

"Me! I don't feel myself after I've been with women." He spoke in a low tone, looking down at his hands. "I feel messed up. I'm better to keep to myself.—Because—" and here he looked up with a flare in his eyes—"women—they only want to make you give in to them, so that they feel almighty, and you feel small."

"Don't you like feeling small?" Lou smiled. "And don't you want to make them give in to you?"

"Not me," he said. "I don't want nothing. Nothing, I want."

"Poor mother!" said Lou. "She thinks if she feels moved by a man, it must result in marriage—or that kind of thing. Surely she makes a mistake. I think you and Phoenix and mother and I might live somewhere in a far-away wild place, and make a good life: so long as we didn't begin to mix up marriage, or love or that sort of thing, into it. It seems to me men and women have really hurt one another so much, nowadays, that they had better stay apart till they have learned to be gentle with one another again. Not all this forced passion and destructive philandering. Men and women should stay apart, till their hearts grow gentle towards one another again. Now, it's only each one fighting for his own—or her own—underneath the cover of tenderness."

"*Dear!—darling!—Yes, my love!*" mocked Lewis, with a faint smile of amused contempt.

"Exactly. People always say *dearest!* when they hate each other most."

Lewis nodded, looking at her with a sudden sombre gloom in his eyes. A queer bitterness showed on his mouth. But even then, he was so still and remote.

The housekeeper came and announced The Honourable[44] Laura Ridley. This was like a blow in the face of Lou. She rose hurriedly—and Lewis rose, moving to the door.

"Don't go, please, Lewis," said Lou—and then Laura Ridley appeared

---

[44] A title used by the sons and daughters of barons and viscounts.

in the doorway. She was a woman a few years older than Lou, but she looked younger. She might have been a shy girl of twenty-two, with her fresh complexion, her hesitant manner, her round, startled brown eyes, her bobbed hair.

"Hello!" said the new-comer. "Imagine your being back! I saw you in Paddington."

Those sharp eyes would see everything.

"I thought everyone was out of town," said Lou. "This is Mr. Lewis."

Laura gave him a little nod, then sat on the edge of her chair.

"No," she said. "I did go to Ireland to my people, but I came back. I prefer London when I can be more or less alone in it. I thought I'd just run in for a moment, before you're gone again.—Scotland, isn't it?"

"No, mother and I are going to America."

"America! Oh, I thought it was Scotland."

"It was. But we have suddenly to go to America."

"I see!—And what about Rico?"

"He is staying on in Shropshire. Didn't you hear of his accident?"

Lou told about it briefly.

"But how awful!" said Laura. "But there! I knew it! I had a premonition when I saw that horse. We had a horse that killed a man. Then my father got rid of it. But ours was a mare, that one. Yours is a boy."

"A full-grown man, I'm afraid."

"Yes, of course, I remember.—But how awful! I suppose you won't ride in the Row. The awful people that ride there nowadays, anyhow! Oh, aren't they awful! Aren't people monstrous, really! My word, when I see the horses crossing Hyde Park corner, on a wet day, and coming down smash on those slippery stones, giving their riders a fractured skull!—No joke!"

She enquired details of Rico.

"Oh, I suppose I shall see him when he gets back," she said. "But I'm sorry you are going. I shall miss you, I'm afraid. Though you won't be staying long in America. No one stays there longer than they can help."

"I think the winter through, at least," said Lou.

"Oh, all the winter! So long? I'm sorry to hear *that*. You're one of the few, very few people one can talk *really* simply with. Extraordinary, isn't it, how few really simple people there are! And they get fewer and fewer. I stayed a fortnight with my people, and a week of that I was in bed. It was really horrible. They really try to take the life out of one, *really*! Just because one won't be as they are, and play their game. I simply refused, and came away."

"But you can't cut yourself off altogether," said Lou.

"No, I suppose not. One has to see somebody. Luckily one has a few artists for friends. They're the only real people, anyhow——" She glanced round inquisitively at Lewis, and said, with a slight, impertinent elvish smile on her virgin face:

"Are you an artist?"

"No, Mam!" he said. "I'm a groom."

"Oh, I see!" She looked him up and down.

"Lewis is St. Mawr's master," said Lou.

"Oh, the horse! the terrible horse!" She paused a moment. Then again she turned to Lewis with that faint smile, slightly condescending, slightly impertinent, slightly flirtatious.

"Aren't you afraid of him?" she asked.

"No, Mam."

"Aren't you *really!*—And can you always master him?"

"Mostly. He knows me."

"Yes! I suppose that's it."—She looked him up and down again, then turned away to Lou.

"What have you been painting lately?" said Lou. Laura was not a bad painter.

"Oh, hardly anything. I haven't been able to get on at all. This is one of my bad intervals."

Here Lewis rose, and looked at Lou.

"All right," she said. "Come in after lunch, and we'll finish those arrangements."

Laura gazed after the man, as he dived out of the room, as if her eyes were gimlets that could bore into his secret.

In the course of the conversation she said:

"What a curious little man that was!"

"Which?"

"The groom who was here just now. *Very* curious! Such peculiar eyes. I shouldn't wonder if he had psychic powers."

"What sort of psychic powers?" said Lou.

"Could *see* things.—And hypnotic too. He might have hypnotic powers."

"What makes you think so?"

"He gives me that sort of feeling. Very curious! Probably he hypnotizes the horse.—Are you leaving the horse here, by the way, in stable?"

"No, taking him to America."

"Taking him to America! How extraordinary!"

"It's mother's idea. She thinks he might be valuable as a stock horse on a ranch. You know we still have interest in a ranch in Texas."

"Oh, I see! Yes, probably he'd be very valuable, to improve the breed of the horses over there.—My father has some very lovely hunters. Isn't it disgraceful, he would never let me ride!"

"Why?"

"Because we girls weren't important, in his opinion.—So you're taking the horse to America! With the little man?"

"Yes, St. Mawr will hardly behave without him."

"I see!—I see—ee—ee! Just you and Mrs. Witt and the little man. I'm sure you'll find he has psychic powers."

"I'm afraid I'm not so good at finding things out," said Lou.

"Aren't you? No, I suppose not. I am. I have a flair. I sort of *smell* things.—Then the horse is already here, is he? When do you think you'll sail?"

"Mother is finding a merchant boat that will go to Galveston, Texas, and take us along with the horse. She knows people who will find the right thing. But it takes time."

"What a much nicer way to travel than on one of those great liners! Oh, how awful they are! So vulgar! Floating palaces they call them! My word, the people inside the palaces!—Yes, I should say that would be a much pleasanter way of travelling: on a cargo boat."

Laura wanted to go down to the Mews to see St. Mawr. The two women went together.

St. Mawr stood in his box, bright and tense as usual.

"Yes!" said Laura Ridley, with a slight hiss. "Yes! Isn't he beautiful! Such very perfect legs!"—She eyed him round with those gimlet, sharp eyes of hers. "Almost a pity to let him go out of England. We need some of his perfect *bone*, I feel.—But his eye! Hasn't he got a look in it, my word!"

"I can never see that he looks wicked," said Lou.

"Can't you!"—Laura had a slight hiss in her speech, a sort of aristo-cratic decision in her enunciation, that got on Lou's nerves.—"He looks wicked to me!"

"He's not *mean*," said Lou. "He'd never do anything mean to you."

"Oh, mean! I dare say not. No! I'll grant him that, he gives fair warning. His eye says Beware!—But isn't he a beauty, *isn't* he!" Lou could feel the peculiar reverence for St. Mawr's breeding, his show qualities. Herself, all she cared about was the horse himself, his real nature. "Isn't it extraordinary," Laura continued, "that you never get a *really*, perfectly satisfactory animal! There's always something wrong.

And in men too. Isn't it curious? there's always something—something wrong—or something missing. Why is it?"

"I don't know," said Lou. She felt unable to cope with any more. And she was glad when Laura left her.

The days passed slowly, quietly, London almost empty of Lou's acquaintances. Mrs. Witt was busy getting all sorts of papers and permits: such a fuss! The battle light was still in her eye. But about her nose was a dusky, pinched look that made Lou wonder.

Both women wanted to be gone: they felt they had already flown in spirit, and it was weary having the body left behind.

At last all was ready: they only awaited the telegram to say when their cargo-boat would sail. Trunks stood there packed, like great stones locked for ever. The Westminster house seemed already a shell. Rico wrote and telegraphed, tenderly, but there was a sense of relentless effort in it all, rather than of any real tenderness. He had taken his position.

Then the telegram came, the boat was ready to sail.

"There now!" said Mrs. Witt, as if it had been a sentence of death.

"Why do you look like that, mother?"

"I feel I haven't an ounce of energy left in my body."

"But how queer, for you, mother. Do you think you are ill?"

"No, Louise. I just feel that way: as if I hadn't an ounce of energy left in my body."

"You'll feel yourself again, once you are away."

"Maybe I shall."

After all, it was only a matter of telephoning. The hotel and railway porters and taxi-men would do the rest.

It was a grey, cloudy day, cold even. Mother and daughter sat in a cold first-class carriage and watched the little Hampshire country-side go past: little, old, unreal it seemed to them both, and passing away like a dream whose edges only are in consciousness. Autumn! Was this autumn? Were these trees, fields, villages? It seemed but the dim, dissolving edges of a dream, without inward substance.

At Southampton it was raining: and just a chaos, till they stepped on to a clean boat, and were received by a clean young captain, quite sympathetic, and quite a gentleman. Mrs. Witt, however, hardly looked at him, but went down to her cabin and lay down in her bunk.

There, lying concealed, she felt the engines start, she knew the voyage had begun. But she lay still. She saw the clouds and the rain, and refused to be disturbed.

Lou had lunch with the young captain, and she felt she ought to be flirty. The young man was so polite and attentive. And she wished so much she were alone.

Afterwards, she sat on deck and saw the Isle of Wight pass shadowly, in a misty rain. She didn't know it was the Isle of Wight. To her, it was just the lowest bit of the British Isles. She saw it fading away: and with it, her life, going like a clot of shadow in a mist of nothingness. She had no feelings about it, none: neither about Rico, nor her London house, nor anything. All passing in a grey curtain of rainy drizzle, like a death, and she with not a feeling left.

They entered the Channel, and felt the slow heave of the sea. And soon the clouds broke in a little wind. The sky began to clear. By mid-afternoon it was blue summer, on the blue, running waters of the Channel. And soon, the ship steering for Santander, there was the coast of France, the rock twinkling like some magic world.

The magic world! And back of it, that post-war Paris which Lou knew only too well, and which depressed her so thoroughly. Or that post-war Monte Carlo, the Riviera still more depressing even than Paris. No, one must not land, even on magic coasts. Else you found yourself in a railway station and a "centre of civilization" in five minutes.

Mrs. Witt hated the sea, and stayed, as a rule, practically the whole time of the crossing, in her bunk. There she was now, silent, shut up like a steel trap, as in her tomb. She did not even read. Just lay and stared at the passing sky. And the only thing to do was to leave her alone.

Lewis and Phoenix hung on the rail, and watched everything. Or they went down to see St. Mawr. Or they stood talking in the doorway of the wireless operator's cabin. Lou begged the captain to give them jobs to do.

The queer, transitory, unreal feeling, as the ship crossed the great, heavy Atlantic. It was rather bad weather. And Lou felt, as she had felt before, that this grey, wolf-like, cold-blooded Ocean hated men and their ships and their smoky passage. Heavy grey waves, a low-sagging sky: rain: yellow, weird evening with snatches of sun: so it went on. Till they got way South, into the westward-running stream. Then they began to get blue weather and blue water.

To go South! Always to go South, away from the arctic horror as far as possible! That was Lou's instinct. To go out of the clutch of greyness and low skies, of sweeping rain, and of slow, blanketing snow. Never again to see the mud and rain and snow of a northern winter, nor to feel the idealistic, Christianized tension of the now irreligious North.

As they neared Havana, and the water sparkled at night with phosphorus, and the flying-fishes came like drops of bright water, sailing out of the massive-slippery waves, Mrs. Witt emerged once more. She still had that shut-up, deadly look on her face. But she prowled round the deck, and manifested at least a little interest in affairs not her own. Here at sea, she hardly remembered the existence of St. Mawr or Lewis or Phoenix. She was not very deeply aware even of Lou's existence.— But, of course, it would all come back, once they were on land.

They sailed in hot sunshine out of a blue, blue sea, past the castle into the harbour at Havana. There was a lot of shipping: and this was already America. Mrs. Witt had herself and Lou put ashore immediately. They took a motor-car and drove at once to the great boulevard that is the centre of Havana. Here they saw a long rank of motor-cars, all drawn up ready to take a couple of hundred American tourists for one more tour. There were the tourists, all with badges in their coats, lest they should get lost.

"They get so drunk by night," said the driver in Spanish, "that the policemen find them lying in the road—turn them over, see the badge—and, hup!—carry them to their hotel." He grinned sardonically.

Lou and her mother lunched at the Hotel d'Angleterre, and Mrs. Witt watched transfixed while a couple of her countrymen, a stout successful man and his wife, lunched abroad. They had cocktails—then lobster—and a bottle of hock—then a bottle of champagne—then a half-bottle of port.—And Mrs. Witt rose in haste as the liqueurs came. For that successful man and his wife had gone on imbibing with a sort of fixed and deliberate will, apparently tasting nothing, but saying to themselves: Now we're drinking Rhine wine! Now we're drinking 1912 champagne. Yah, Prohibition! Thou canst not put it over me.—Their complexions became more and more lurid. Mrs. Witt fled, fearing a Havana debacle. But she said nothing.

In the afternoon, they motored into the country, to see the great brewery gardens, the new villa suburb, and through the lanes past the old, decaying plantations with palm-trees. In one lane they met the fifty motor-cars with the two hundred tourists all with badges on their chests and self-satisfaction on their faces. Mrs. Witt watched in grim silence.

"*Plus ça change, plus c'est la même chose,*" said Lou, with a wicked little smile. "*On n'est pas mieux ici,*[45] mother."

---

[45]The more things change, the more they remain the same. We are not better off here.

"I know it," said Mrs. Witt.

The hotels by the sea were all shut up: it was not yet the "season." Not till November. And then!—Why, then Havana would be an American city, in full leaf of green dollar bills. The green leaf of American prosperity shedding itself recklessly, from every roaming sprig of a tourist, over this city of sunshine and alcohol. Green leaves unfolded in Pittsburgh and Chicago, showering in winter downfall in Havana.

Mother and daughter drank tea in a corner of the Hotel d'Angleterre once more, and returned to the ferry.

The Gulf of Mexico was blue and rippling, with the phantom of islands on the south. Great porpoises rolled and leaped, running in front of the ship in the clear water, diving, travelling in perfect motion, straight, with the tip of the ship touching the tip of their tails, then rolling over, corkscrewing, and showing their bellies as they went. Marvellous! The marvellous beauty and fascination of natural wild things! The horror of man's unnatural life, his heaped-up civilization!

The flying-fishes burst out of the sea in clouds of silvery, transparent motion. Blue above and below, the Gulf seemed a silent, empty, timeless place where man did not really reach. And Lou was again fascinated by the glamour of the universe.

But bump! She and her mother were in a first-class hotel again, calling down the telephone for the bell-boy and ice-water. And soon they were in a Pullman, off towards San Antonio.

It was America, it was Texas. They were at their ranch, on the great level of yellow autumn, with the vast sky above. And after all, from the hot wide sky, and the hot, wide, red earth, there *did* come something new, something not used up. Lou *did* feel exhilarated.

The Texans were there, tall blond people, ingenuously cheerful, ingenuously, childishly intimate, as if the fact that you had never seen them before was as nothing compared to the fact that you'd all been living in one room together all your lives, so that nothing was hidden from either of you. The one room being the mere shanty of the world in which we all live. Strange, uninspired cheerfulness, filling, as it were, the blank of complete incomprehension.

And off they set in their motor-cars, chiefly high-legged Fords, rattling away down the red trails between yellow sunflowers or sere grass or dry cotton, away, away into great distances, cheerfully raising the dust of haste. It left Lou in a sort of blank amazement. But it left her amused, not depressed. The old screws of emotion and intimacy that had been screwed down so tightly upon her fell out of their holes, here. The Texan intimacy weighed no more on her than a postage stamp, even if, for the moment, it stuck as close. And there was a certain underneath recklessness, even a stoicism, in all the apparently childish people, which left one free. They might appear childish: but they stoically depended on themselves alone, in reality. Not as in England, where every man waited to pour the burden of himself upon you. St. Mawr arrived safely, a bit bewildered. The Texans eyed him closely, struck silent, as ever, by anything pure-bred and beautiful. He was somehow too beautiful, too perfected, in this great open country. The long-legged Texan horses, with their elaborate saddles, seemed somehow more natural.

Even St. Mawr felt himself strange, as it were naked and singled out, in this rough place. Like a jewel among stones, a pearl before swine, maybe. But the swine were no fools. They knew a pearl from a grain of maize, and a grain of maize from a pearl. And they knew what they wanted. When it was pearls, it was pearls; though chiefly it was maize. Which shows good sense. They could see St. Mawr's points. Only he needn't draw the point too fine, or it would just not pierce the tough skin of this country.

The ranch-man mounted him—just threw a soft skin over his back, jumped on, and away down the red trail, raising the dust among the tall wild yellow of sunflowers, in the hot wild sun. Then back again in a fume, and the man slipped off.

"He's got the stuff in him, he sure has," said the man.

And the horse seemed pleased with this rough handling. Lewis looked on in wonder, and a little envy.

Lou and her mother stayed a fortnight on the ranch. It was all so queer: so crude, so rough, so easy, so artificially civilized, and so meaningless. Lou could not get over the feeling that it all meant nothing. There were no roots of reality at all. No consciousness below the surface, no meaning in anything save the obvious, the blatantly obvious. It was like life enacted in a mirror. Visually, it was wildly vital. But there was nothing behind it. Or like a cinematograph: flat shapes, exactly like men, but without any substance of reality, rapidly rattling away with talk, emotions, activity, all in the flat, nothing behind it. No deeper consciousness at all.—So it seemed to her.

One moved from dream to dream, from phantasm to phantasm.

But at least this Texan life, if it had no bowels, no vitals, at least it could not prey on one's own vitals. It was this much better than Europe.

Lewis was silent, and rather piqued. St. Mawr had already made advances to the boss' long-legged, arched-necked, glossy-maned Texan mare. And the boss was pleased.

What a world!

Mrs. Witt eyed it all shrewdly. But she failed to participate. Lou was a bit scared at the emptiness of it all, and the queer, phantasmal self-consciousness. Cowboys just as self-conscious as Rico, far more sentimental, inwardly vague and unreal. Cowboys that went after their cows in black Ford motor-cars: and who self-consciously saw Lady Carrington falling to them, as elegant young ladies from the East fall to the noble cowboy of the films, or in Zane Grey. It was all film-psychology.

And at the same time, these boys led a hard, hard life, often dangerous and gruesome. Nevertheless, inwardly they were self-conscious film-heroes. The boss himself, a man over forty, long and lean and with a great deal of stringy energy, showed off before her in a strong silent manner, existing for the time being purely in his imagination of the sort of picture he made to her, the sort of impression he made on her.

So they all were, coloured up like a Zane Grey book-jacket, all of them living in the mirror. The kind of picture they made to somebody else.

And at the same time, with energy, courage, and a stoical grit getting their work done, and putting through what they had to put through.

It left Lou blank with wonder. And in the face of this strange cheerful living in the mirror—a rather cheap mirror at that—England began to seem real to her again.

Then she had to remember herself back in England. And no, O God, England was not real either, except poisonously.

What was real? What under heaven was real?

Her mother had gone dumb and, as it were, out of range. Phoenix was a bit assured and bouncy, back more or less in his own conditions. Lewis was a bit impressed by the emptiness of everything, the *lack* of concentration. And St. Mawr followed at the heels of the boss' long-legged black Texan mare, almost slavishly.

What, in heaven's name, was one to make of it all?

Soon, she could not stand this sort of living in a film-setting, with the mechanical energy of "making good," that is, making money, to keep the show going. The mystic duty to "make good," meaning to make the ranch pay a laudable interest on the "owners' " investment. Lou herself being one of the owners. And the interest that came to her, from her father's will, being the money she spent to buy St. Mawr and to fit up that house in Westminster. Then also the mystic duty to "feel good." Everybody had to *feel good, fine!* "How are you this morning, Mr. Latham?"—"*Fine!* Eh! Don't you feel good out here, eh, Lady Carrington?"—"*Fine!*"—Lou pronounced it with the same ringing conviction. It was Coué all the time![46]

"Shall we stay here long, mother?" she asked.

"Not a day longer than you want to, Louise. I stay entirely for your sake."

"Then let us go, mother."

They left St. Mawr and Lewis. But Phoenix wanted to come along. So they motored to San Antonio, got into the Pullman, and travelled as far as El Paso. Then they changed to go North. Santa Fe would be at least "easy." And Mrs. Witt had acquaintances there.

They found the fiesta over in Santa Fe: Indians, Mexicans, artists had finished their great effort to amuse and attract the tourists. *Welcome, Mr. Tourist,* said a great board on one side of the high road. And on the other side, a little nearer to town: *Thank You, Mr. Tourist.*

"*Plus ça change——*" Lou began.

"*Ça ne change jamais*—except for the worse!" said Mrs. Witt, like a pistol going off. And Lou held her peace, after she had sighed to herself, and said in her own mind: "*Welcome Also Mrs. and Miss Tourist!*"

There was no getting a word out of Mrs. Witt, these days. Whereas Phoenix was becoming almost loquacious.

They stayed awhile in Santa Fe, in the clean, comfortable, "homely" hotel, where "every room had its bath": a spotless white bath, with very hot water night and day. The tourists and commercial travellers sat in the big hall down below, every body living in the mirror! And, of course, they knew Lady Carrington down to her shoe-soles. And they all expected her to know them down to their shoe-soles. For the only object of the mirror is to reflect images.

For two days mother and daughter ate in the salad-bowl intimacy of the dining-room. Then Mrs. Witt struck, and telephoned down, every meal-time, for her meal in her room. She got to staying in bed later and later, as on the ship. Lou became uneasy. This was worse than Europe.

Phoenix was still there, as a sort of half-friend, half-servant retainer. He was perfectly happy, roving round among the Mexicans and Indi-

---

[46]Émile Coué (1857–1926) was a French psychotherapist who developed a technique of healing through autosuggestion: the patient would repeat, "Every day and in every way, I am becoming better and better."

ans, talking Spanish all day, and telling about England and his two
mistresses, rolling the ball of his own importance.

"I'm afraid we've got Phoenix for life," said Lou.

"Not unless we wish," said Mrs. Witt indifferently. And she picked
up a novel which she didn't want to read, but which she was going to
read.

"What shall we do next, mother?" Lou asked.

"As far as I am concerned, there is no next," said Mrs. Witt.

"Come, mother! Let's go back to Italy or somewhere, if it's as bad as
that."

"Never again, Louise, shall I cross that water. I have come home to
die."

"I don't see much home about it—the Gonzales Hotel in Santa Fe."

"Indeed not! But as good as anywhere else, to die in."

"Oh, mother, don't be silly! Shall we look for somewhere where we
can be by ourselves?"

"I leave it to you, Louise. I have made my last decision."

"What is that, mother."

"Never, never to make another decision."

"Not even to decide to die?"

"No, not even that."

"Or *not* to die?"

"Not that either."

Mrs. Witt shut up like a trap. She refused to rise from her bed that
day.

Lou went to consult Phoenix. The result was, the two set out to look
at a little ranch that was for sale.

It was autumn, and the loveliest time in the South-west, where there
is no spring, snow blowing into the hot lap of summer; and no real
summer, hail falling in thick ice, from the thunderstorms: and even no
very definite winter, hot sun melting the snow and giving an impression of spring at any time. But autumn there is, when the winds of the
desert are almost still, and the mountains fume no clouds. But morning
comes cold and delicate, upon the wild sunflowers and the puffing,
yellow-flowered greasewood. For the desert blooms in autumn. In
spring it is grey ash all the time, and only the strong breath of the
summer sun, and the heavy splashing of thunder rain, succeed at last,
by September, in blowing it into soft, puffy yellow fire.

It was such a delicate morning when Lou drove out with Phoenix
towards the mountains, to look at this ranch that a Mexican wanted to
sell. For the brief moment the high mountains had lost their snow: it

would be back again in a fortnight: and stood dim and delicate with autumn haze. The desert stretched away pale, as pale as the sky, but silvery and sere, with hummock-mounds of shadow, and long wings of shadow, like the reflection of some great bird. The same eagle-shadows came like rude paintings of the outstretched bird, upon the mountains, where the aspens were turning yellow. For the moment, the brief moment, the great desert-and-mountain landscape had lost its certain cruelty, and looked tender, dreamy. And many, many birds were flickering around.

Lou and Phoenix bumped and hesitated over a long trail: then wound down into a deep canyon: and then the car began to climb, climb, climb, in steep rushes, and in long heart-breaking, uneven pulls. The road was bad, and driving was no joke. But it was the sort of road Phoenix was used to. He sat impassive and watchful, and kept on, till his engine boiled. He was *himself* in this country: impassive, detached, self-satisfied, and silently assertive. Guarding himself at every moment, but on his guard, sure of himself. Seeing no difference at all between Lou or Mrs. Witt and himself, except that they had money and he had none, while he had a native importance which they lacked. He depended on them for money, they on him for the power to live out here in the West. Intimately, he was as good as they. Money was their only advantage.

As Lou sat beside him in the front seat of the car, where it bumped less than behind, she felt this. She felt a peculiar tough-necked arrogance in him, as if he were asserting himself to put something over her. He wanted her to allow him to make advances to her, to allow him to suggest that he should be her lover. And then, finally, she would marry him, and he would be on the same footing as she and her mother.

In return, he would look after her, and give her his support and countenance, as a man, and stand between her and the world. In this sense, he would be faithful to her, and loyal. But as far as other women went, Mexican women or Indian women: why, that was none of her business. His marrying her would be a pact between two aliens, on behalf of one another, and he would keep his part of it all right. But himself, as a private man and a predative alien-blooded male, this had nothing to do with her. It didn't enter into her scope and count. She was one of these nervous white women with lots of money. She was very nice too. But as a *squaw*—as a real woman in a shawl whom a man went after for the pleasure of the night—why, she hardly counted. One of these white women who talk clever and know things like a man. She could hardly expect a half-savage male to acknowledge her as his female counterpart.—No! She had the bucks! And she had all the paraphernalia of the white man's civilization, which a savage can play with and so escape his own hollow boredom. But his own real female counterpart?—Phoenix would just have shrugged his shoulders, and thought the question not worth answering. How could there be any answer in *her* to the phallic male in him? Couldn't! Yet it would flatter his vanity and his self-esteem immensely, to possess her. That would be possessing the very clue to the white man's overwhelming world. And if she would let him possess her, he would be absolutely loyal to her, as far as affairs and appearances went. Only, the aboriginal phallic male in him simply couldn't recognize her as a woman at all. In this respect, she didn't exist. It needed the shawled Indian or Mexican women, with their squeaky, plaintive voices, their shuffling, watery humility, and the dark glances of their big, knowing eyes. When an Indian woman looked at him from under her black fringe, with dark, half-secretive suggestion in her big eyes: and when she stood before him hugged in her shawl, in such apparently complete quiescent humility: and when she spoke to him in her mousy squeak of a high, plaintive voice, as if it were difficult for her female bashfulness even to emit so much sound: and when she shuffled away with her legs wide apart, because of her wide-topped, white, high buckskin boots with tiny white feet, and her dark-knotted hair so full of hard, yet subtle lure: and when he remembered the almost watery softness of the Indian woman's dark, warm flesh: then he was a male, an old, secretive, rat-like male. But before Lou's straightforwardness and utter sexual incompetence, he just stood in contempt. And to him, even a French *cocotte*[47] was utterly devoid of the right sort of sex. She couldn't really move him. She couldn't satisfy the furtiveness in him. He needed this plaintive, squeaky, dark-fringed Indian quality. Something furtive and soft and rat-like, really to rouse him.

Nevertheless he was ready to trade his sex, which, in his opinion, every white woman was secretly pining for, for the white woman's money and social privileges. In the daytime, all the thrill and excitement of the white man's motor-cars and moving pictures and ice-cream sodas and so forth. In the night, the soft, watery-soft warmth of an Indian or half-Indian woman. This was Phoenix's idea of life for himself.

Meanwhile, if a white woman gave him the privileges of the white

---

[47]Courtesan.

man's world, he would do his duty by her as far as all that went.

Lou, sitting very, very still beside him as he drove the car: he was not a very good driver, not quick and marvellous as some white men are, particularly some French chauffeurs she had known, but usually a little behindhand in his movements: she knew more or less all that he felt. More or less she divined as a woman does. Even from a certain rather assured stupidity of his shoulders, and a certain rather stupid assertiveness of his knees, she knew him.

But she did not judge him too harshly. Somewhere deep, deep in herself she knew she too was at fault. And this made her sometimes inclined to humble herself, as a woman, before the furtive assertiveness of this underground, "knowing" savage. He was so different from Rico.

Yet, after all, *was* he? In his rootlessness, his drifting, his real meaninglessness, was he different from Rico? And his childish, spellbound absorption in the motor-car, or in the moving pictures, or in an ice-cream soda—was it very different from Rico? Anyhow, was it really any better? Pleasanter, perhaps, to a woman, because of the childishness of it.

The same with his opinion of himself as a sexual male! So childish, really, it was almost thrilling to a woman. But then, so stupid also, with that furtive lurking in holes and imagining it could not be detected. He imagined he kept himself dark, in his sexual rat-holes. He imagined he was not detected!

No, no, Lou was not such a fool as she looked, in his eyes anyhow. She knew what she wanted. She wanted relief from the nervous tension and irritation of her life, she wanted to escape from the friction which is the whole stimulus in modern social life. She wanted to be still: only that, to be very, very still, and recover her own soul.

When Phoenix presumed she was looking for some secretly sexual male such as himself, he was ridiculously mistaken. Even the illusion of the beautiful St. Mawr was gone. And Phoenix, roaming round like a sexual rat in promiscuous back yards!—*Merci, mon cher!* For that was all he was: a sexual rat in the great barn-yard of man's habitat, looking for female rats!

Merci, mon cher! You are had.

Nevertheless, in his very mistakenness, he was a relief to her. His mistake was amusing rather than impressive. And the fact that one-half of his intelligence was a complete dark blank, that too was a relief.

Strictly, and perhaps in the best sense, he was a servant. His very unconsciousness and his very limitation served as a shelter, as one

shelters within the limitations of four walls. The very decided limits to
his intelligence were a shelter to her. They made her feel safe.

But that feeling of safety did not deceive her. It was the feeling one
derived from having a *true* servant attached to one, a man whose psychic limitations left him incapable of anything but service, and whose
strong flow of natural life, at the same time, made him need to serve.

And Lou, sitting there so very still and frail, yet self-contained, had
not lived for nothing. She no longer wanted to fool herself. She had no
desire at all to fool herself into thinking that a Phoenix might be a
husband and a mate. No desire that way at all. His obtuseness was a
servant's obtuseness. She was grateful to him for serving, and she paid
him a wage. Moreover, she provided him with something to do, to
occupy his life. In a sense, she gave him his life, and rescued him from
his own boredom. It was a balance.

He did not know what she was thinking. There was a certain physical sympathy between them. His obtuseness made him think it was
also a sexual sympathy.

"It's a nice trip, you and me," he said suddenly, turning and looking
her in the eyes with an excited look, and ending on a foolish little
laugh.

She realized that she should have sat in the back seat.

"But it's a bad road," she said. "Hadn't you better stop and put the
sides of the hood up? your engine is boiling."

He looked away with a quick switch of interest to the red thermometer in front of his machine.

"She's boiling," he said, stopping, and getting out with a quick alacrity to go to look at the engine.

Lou got out also, and went to the back seat, shutting the door decisively.

"I think I'll ride at the back," she said; "it gets so frightfully hot in
front, when the engine heats up.—Do you think she needs some water?
Have you got some in the canteen?"

"She's full," he said, peering into the steaming valve.

"You can run a bit out, if you think there's any need. I wonder if it's
much further!"

"*Quien sabe!*"[48] said he, slightly impertinent.

She relapsed into her own stillness. She realized how careful, how
very careful she must be of relaxing into sympathy, and reposing, as it

---

[48]Who knows?

were, on Phoenix. He would read it as a sexual appeal. Perhaps he couldn't help it. She had only herself to blame. He was obtuse, as a man and a savage. He had only one interpretation, sex, for any woman's approach to him.

And she knew, with the last clear knowledge of weary disillusion, that she did not want to be mixed up in Phoenix's sexual promiscuities. The very thought was an insult to her. The crude, clumsy servant-male: no, no, not that. He was a good fellow, a very good fellow, as far as he went. But he fell far short of physical intimacy.

"No, no," she said to herself, "I was wrong to ride in the front seat with him. I must sit alone, just alone. Because sex, mere sex, is repellent to me. I will never prostitute myself again. Unless something touches my very spirit, the very quick of me, I will stay alone, just alone. Alone, and give myself only to the unseen presences, serve only the other, unseen presences."

She understood now the meaning of the Vestal Virgins, the Virgins of the holy fire in the old temples. They were symbolic of herself, of woman weary of the embrace of incompetent men, weary, weary, weary of all that, turning to the unseen gods, the unseen spirits, the hidden fire, and devoting herself to that, and that alone. Receiving thence her pacification and her fulfilment.

Not these little, incompetent, childish, self-opinionated men! Not these to touch her. She watched Phoenix's rather stupid shoulders, as he drove the car on between the piñon-trees and the cedars of the narrow mesa ridge, to the mountain foot. He was a good fellow. But let him run among women of his own sort. Something was beyond him. And this something must remain beyond him, never allow itself to come within his reach. Otherwise he would paw it and mess it up, and be as miserable as a child that has broken its father's watch.

No, no! She had loved an American, and lived with him for a fortnight. She had had a long, intimate friendship with an Italian. Perhaps it was love on his part. And she had yielded to him. Then her love and marriage to Rico.

And what of it all? Nothing. It was almost nothing. It was as if only the outside of herself, her top layers, were human. This inveigled her into intimacies. As soon as the intimacy penetrated, or attempted to penetrate, inside her, it was a disaster. Just a humiliation and a breaking down.

Within these outer layers of herself lay the successive inner sanctuaries of herself. And these were inviolable. She accepted it.

"I am not a marrying woman," she said to herself. "I am not a lover nor a mistress nor a wife. It is no good. Love can't really come into me from the outside, and I can never, never mate with any man, since the mystic new man will never come to me. No, no, let me know myself and my rôle. I am one of the eternal Virgins, serving the eternal fire. My dealings with men have only broken my stillness and messed up my doorways. It has been my own fault. I ought to stay virgin, and still, very, very still, and serve the most perfect service. I want my temple and my loneliness and my Apollo mystery of the inner fire. And with men, only the delicate, subtler, more remote relations. No coming near. A coming near only breaks the delicate veils, and broken veils, like broken flowers, only lead to rottenness."

She felt a great peace inside herself as she made this realization. And a thankfulness. Because, after all, it seemed to her that the hidden fire was alive and burning in this sky, over the desert, in the mountains. She felt a certain latent holiness in the very atmosphere, a young spring-fire of latent holiness, such as she had never felt in Europe, or in the East. "For me," she said, as she looked away at the mountains in shadow and the pale-warm desert beneath, with wings of shadow upon it: "For me, this place is sacred. It is blessed."

But as she watched Phoenix: as she remembered the motor-cars and tourists, and the rather dreary Mexicans of Santa Fe, and the lurking, invidious Indians, with something of a rat-like secretiveness and defeatedness in their bearing, she realized that the latent fire of the vast landscape struggled under a great weight of dirt-like inertia. She had to mind the dirt, most carefully and vividly avoid it and keep it away from her, here in this place that at last seemed sacred to her.

The motor-car climbed up, past the tall pine-trees, to the foot of the mountains, and came at last to a wire gate, where nothing was to be expected. Phoenix opened the gate, and they drove on, through more trees, into a clearing where dried-up bean-plants were yellow.

"This man got no water for his beans," said Phoenix. "Not got much beans this year."

They climbed slowly up the incline, through more pine-trees, and out into another clearing, where a couple of horses were grazing. And there they saw the ranch itself, little low cabins with patched roofs, under a few pine-trees, and facing the long twelve-acre clearing, or field, where the Michaelmas daisies were purple mist, and spangled with clumps of yellow flowers.

"Not got no alfalfa here neither!" said Phoenix, as the car waded past the flowers. "Must be a dry place up here. Got no water, sure they haven't."

Yet it was the place Lou wanted. In an instant, her heart sprang to it. The instant the car stopped, and she saw the two cabins inside the rickety fence, the rather broken corral beyond, and, behind all, tall, blue balsam pines, the round hills, the solid uprise of the mountain flank: and, getting down, she looked across the purple and gold of the clearing, downwards at the ring of pine-trees standing so still, so crude and untamable, the motionless desert beyond the bristles of the pine crests, a thousand feet below: and, beyond the desert, blue mountains, and far, far-off blue mountains in Arizona: "*This is the place*," she said to herself.

This little tumble-down ranch, only a homestead of a hundred and sixty acres, was, as it were, man's last effort towards the wild heart of the Rockies, at this point. Sixty years before, a restless schoolmaster had wandered out from the East, looking for gold among the mountains. He found a very little, then no more. But the mountains had got hold of him, he could not go back.

There was a little trickling spring of pure water, a thread of treasure perhaps better than gold. So the schoolmaster took up a homestead on the lot where this little spring arose. He struggled, and got himself his log cabin erected, his fence put up, sloping at the mountain-side through the pine-trees and dropping into the hollows where the ghost-white mariposa lilies stood leafless and naked in flower, in spring, on tall invisible stems. He made the long clearing for alfalfa.

And fell so into debt, that he had to trade his homestead away, to clear his debt. Then he made a tiny living teaching the children of the few American prospectors who had squatted in the valleys, beside the Mexicans.

The trader who got the ranch tackled it with a will. He built another log cabin, and a big corral, and brought water from the canyon two miles and more across the mountain slope, in a little runnel ditch, and more water, piped a mile or more down the little canyon immediately above the cabins. He got a flow of water for his houses: for, being a true American, he felt he could not *really* say he had conquered his environment till he had got running water, taps, and wash-hand basins inside his house.

Taps, running water and wash-hand basins he accomplished. And, undaunted through the years, he prepared the basin for a fountain in the little fenced-in enclosure, and he built a little bath-house. After a number of years, he sent up the enamelled bath-tub to be put in the little log bath-house on the little wild ranch hung right against the savage Rockies, above the desert.

But here the mountains finished him. He was a trader down below, in the Mexican village. This little ranch was, as it were, his hobby, his ideal. He and his New England wife spent their summers there: and turned on the taps in the cabins and turned them off again, and felt really that civilization had conquered.

All this plumbing from the savage ravines of the canyons—one of them nameless to this day—cost, however, money. In fact, the ranch cost a great deal of money. But it was all to be got back. The big clearing was to be irrigated for alfalfa, the little clearing for beans, and the third clearing, under the corral, for potatoes. All these things the trader could trade to the Mexicans, very advantageously.

And, moreover, since somebody had started a praise of the famous goat's cheese made by Mexican peasants in New Mexico, goats there should be.

Goats there were: five hundred of them, eventually. And they fed chiefly in the wild mountain hollows, the no-man's-land. The Mexicans call them fire-mouths, because everything they nibble dies. Not because of their flaming mouths, really, but because they nibble a live plant down, down to the quick, till it can put forth no more.

So, the energetic trader, in the course of five or six years, had got the ranch ready. The long three-roomed cabin was for him and his New England wife. In the two-roomed cabin lived the Mexican family who really had charge of the ranch. For the trader was mostly fixed to his store, seventeen miles away, down in the Mexican village.

The ranch lay over eight thousand feet up, the snows of winter came deep and the white goats, looking dirty yellow, swam in snow with their poor curved horns poking out like dead sticks. But the corral had a long, cosy, shut-in goat-shed all down one side, and into this crowded the five hundred, their acrid goat-smell rising like hot acid over the snow. And the thin, pock-marked Mexican threw them alfalfa out of the log barn. Until the hot sun sank the snow again, and froze the surface, when patter-patter went the two thousand little goat-hoofs, over the silver-frozen snow, up at the mountain. Nibble, nibble, nibble, the fire-mouths, at every tender twig. And the goat-bell climbed, and the baa-ing came from among the dense and shaggy pine-trees. And sometimes, in a soft drift under the trees, a goat, or several goats, went through, into the white depths, and some were lost thus, to reappear dead and frozen at the thaw.

By evening, they were driven down again, like a dirty yellowish-white stream carrying dark sticks on its yeasty surface, tripping and bleating over the frozen snow, past the bustling dark-green pine-trees, down to the trampled mess of the corral. And everywhere, everywhere over the snow, yellow stains and dark pills of goat-droppings melting into the surface crystal. On still, glittering nights, when the frost was hard, the smell of goats came up like some uncanny acid fire, and great stars sitting on the mountain's edge seemed to be watching like the eyes of a mountain lion, brought by the scent. Then the coyotes in the near canyon howled and sobbed, and ran like shadows over the snow. But the goat corral had been built tight.

In the course of years the goat-herd had grown from fifty to five hundred, and surely that was increase. The goat-milk cheeses sat drying on their little racks. In spring, there was a great flowing and skipping of kids. In summer and early autumn, there was a pest of flies, rising from all that goat-smell and that cast-out whey of goats'-milk, after the cheese-making. The rats came, and the pack-rats, swarming.

And, after all, it was difficult to sell or trade the cheeses, and little profit to be made. And, in dry summers, no water came down in the narrow ditch-channel, that straddled in wooden runnels over the deep clefts in the mountain-side. No water meant no alfalfa. In winter the goats scarcely drank at all. In summer they could be watered at the little spring. But the thirsty land was not so easy to accommodate.

Five hundred fine white Angora goats, with their massive handsome padres! They were beautiful enough. And the trader made all he could of them. Come summer, they were run down into the narrow tank filled with the fiery dipping fluid. Then their lovely white wool was clipped. It was beautiful, and valuable, but comparatively little of it.

And it all cost, cost, cost. And a man was always let down. At one time no water. At another a poison-weed. Then a sickness. Always, some mysterious malevolence fighting, fighting against the will of man. A strange invisible influence coming out of the livid rock-fastnesses in the bowels of those uncreated Rocky Mountains, preying upon the will of man, and slowly wearing down his resistance, his onward-pushing spirit. The curious, subtle thing, like a mountain fever, got into the blood, so that the men at the ranch, and the animals with them, had bursts of queer, violent, half-frenzied energy, in which, however, they were wont to lose their wariness. And then, damage of some sort. The horses ripped and cut themselves, or they were struck by lightning, the men had great hurts, or sickness. A curious disintegration working all the time, a sort of malevolent breath, like a stupefying, irritant gas, coming out of the unfathomed mountains.

The pack-rats with their bushy tails and big ears came down out of the hills, and were jumping and bouncing about: symbols of the curious debasing malevolence that was in the spirit of the place. The Mexicans in charge, good honest men, worked all they could. But they were like most of the Mexicans in the South-west, as if they had been pithed, to use one of Kipling's words. As if the invidious malevolence of the country itself had slowly taken all the pith of manhood from them, leaving a hopeless sort of corpus of a man.

And the same happened to the white men, exposed to the open country. Slowly, they were pithed. The energy went out of them. And, more than that, the interest. An inertia of indifference invading the soul, leaving the body healthy and active, but wasting the soul, the living interest, quite away.

It was the New England wife of the trader who put most energy into the ranch. She looked on it as her home. She had a little white fence put all round the two cabins: the bright brass water-taps she kept shining in the two kitchens: outside the kitchen door she had a little kitchen garden and nasturtiums, after a great fight with invading animals, that nibbled everything away. And she got so far as the preparation of the round concrete basin which was to be a little pool, under the few enclosed pine-trees between the two cabins, a pool with a tiny fountain jet.

But this, with the bath-tub, was her limit, as the five hundred goats were her man's limit. Out of the mountains came two breaths of influence: the breath of the curious, frenzied energy, that took away one's intelligence as alcohol or any other stimulus does: and then the most strange invidiousness that ate away the soul. The woman loved her ranch, almost with passion. It was she who felt the stimulus, more than the men. It seemed to enter her like a sort of sex passion, intensifying her ego, making her full of violence and of blind female energy. The energy, and the blindness of it! A strange blind frenzy, like an intoxication while it lasted. And the sense of beauty that thrilled her New England woman's soul.

Her cabin faced the slow down-slope of the clearing, the alfalfa field: her long, low cabin, crouching under the great pine-tree that threw up its trunk sheer in front of the house, in the yard. That pine-tree was the guardian of the place. But a bristling, almost demonish guardian, from the far-off crude ages of the world. Its great pillar of pale, flaky-ribbed copper rose there in strange callous indifference, and the grim permanence, which is in pine-trees. A passionless, non-phallic column, rising in the shadows of the pre-sexual world, before the hot-blooded ithyphallic column ever erected itself. A cold, blossomless, resinous sap surging and oozing gum, from that pallid brownish bark. And the wind hissing in the needles, like a vast nest of serpents. And the pine cones falling plumb as the hail hit them. Then lying all over the yard, open in the sun like wooden roses, but hard, sexless, rigid with a blind will.

Past the column of that pine-tree, the alfalfa field sloped gently down, to the circling guard of pine-trees, from which silent, living barrier isolated pines rose to ragged heights at intervals, in blind assertiveness. Strange, those pine-trees! In some lights all their needles glistened like polished steel, all subtly glittering with a whitish glitter among darkness, like real needles. Then again, at evening, the trunks would flare up orange-red, and the tufts would be dark, alert tufts like a wolf's tail touching the air. Again, in the morning sunlight they would be soft and still, hardly noticeable. But all the same, present, and watchful. Never sympathetic, always watchfully on their guard, and resistant, they hedged one in with the aroma and the power and the slight horror of the pre-sexual primeval world. The world where each creature was crudely limited to its own ego, crude and bristling and cold, and then crowding in packs like pine-trees and wolves.

But beyond the pine-trees, ah, there beyond, there was beauty for the spirit to soar in. The circle of pines, with the loose trees rising high and ragged at intervals, this was the barrier, the fence to the foreground. Beyond was only distance, the desert a thousand feet below, and beyond.

The desert swept its great fawn-coloured circle around, away beyond and below like a beach, with a long mountain-side of pure blue shadow closing in the near corner, and strange bluish hummocks of mountains rising like wet rock from a vast strand, away in the middle distance, and beyond, in the farthest distance, pale blue crests of mountains looking over the horizon, from the west, as if peering in from another world altogether.

Ah, that was beauty!—perhaps the most beautiful thing in the world. It was pure beauty, *absolute* beauty! There! That was it. To the little woman from New England, with her tense, fierce soul and her egoistic passion of service, this beauty was absolute, a *ne plus ultra*.[49] From her doorway, from her porch, she could watch the vast, eagle-like wheeling of the daylight, that turned as the eagles which lived in the near rocks turned overhead in the blue, turning their luminous, dark-edged-patterned bellies and under-wings upon the pure air, like winged orbs. So the daylight made the vast turn upon the desert, brushing the far-

---

[49]Something ultimate.

thest outwatching mountains. And sometimes the vast strand of the desert would float with curious undulations and exhalations amid the blue fragility of mountains, whose upper edges were harder than the floating bases. And sometimes she would see the little brown adobe houses of the village Mexicans, twenty miles away, like little cube crystals of insect-houses dotting upon the desert, very distinct, with a cottonwood-tree or two rising near. And sometimes she would see the far-off rocks, thirty miles away, where the canyon made a gateway between the mountains. Quite clear, like an open gateway out of a vast yard, she would see the cut-out bit of the canyon-passage. And on the desert itself, curious puckered folds of mesa-sides. And a blackish crack which in places revealed the otherwise invisible canyon of the Rio Grande. And beyond everything, the mountains like icebergs showing up from an outer sea. Then later, the sun would go down blazing above the shallow cauldron of simmering darkness, and the round mountain of Colorado would lump up into uncanny significance, northwards. That was always rather frightening. But morning came again, with the sun peeping over the mountain slopes and lighting the desert away in the distance long, long before it lighted on her yard. And then she would see another valley, like magic and very lovely, with green fields and long tufts of cottonwood-trees, and a few long-cubical adobe houses, lying floating in shallow light below, like a vision.

Ah! it was beauty, beauty absolute, at any hour of the day: whether the perfect clarity of morning, or the mountains beyond the simmering desert at noon, or the purple lumping of northern mounds under a red sun at night. Or whether the dust whirled in tall columns, travelling across the desert far away, like pillars of cloud by day, tall, leaning pillars of dust hastening with ghostly haste: or whether, in the early part of the year, suddenly in the morning a whole sea of solid white would rise rolling below, a solid mist from melted snow, ghost-white under the mountain sun, the world below blotted out: or whether the black rain and cloud streaked down, far across the desert, and lightning stung down with sharp white stings on the horizon: or the cloud travelled and burst overhead, with rivers of fluid blue fire running out of heaven and exploding on earth, and hail coming down like a world of ice shattered above: or the hot sun rode in again: or snow fell in heavy silence: or the world was blinding white under a blue sky, and one must hurry under the pine-trees for shelter against that vast, white, back-beating light which rushed up at one and made one almost unconscious, amid the snow.

It was always beauty, *always!* It was always great, and splendid, and, for some reason, natural. It was never grandiose or theatrical. Always, for some reason, perfect. And quite simple, in spite of it all. So it was, when you watched the vast and living landscape. The landscape lived, and lived as the world of the gods, unsullied and unconcerned. The great circling landscape lived its own life, sumptuous and uncaring. Man did not exist for it.

And if it had been a question simply of living through the eyes, into the *distance*, then this would have been Paradise, and the little New England woman on her ranch would have found what she was always looking for, the earthly paradise of the spirit.

But even a woman cannot live only into the distance, the beyond. Willy-nilly she finds herself juxtaposed to the near things, the thing in itself. And willy-nilly she is caught up into the fight with the immediate object.

The New England woman had fought to make the nearness as perfect as the distance: for the distance was absolute beauty. She had been confident of success. She had felt quite assured, when the water came running out of her bright brass taps, the wild water of the hills caught, tricked into the narrow iron pipes, and led tamely to her kitchen, to jump out over her sink, into her wash-basin, at her service. *There!* she said. I have tamed the waters of the mountain to my service.

So she had, for the moment.

At the same time, the invisible attack was being made upon her. While she revelled in the beauty of the luminous world that wheeled around and below her, the grey, rat-like spirit of the inner mountains was attacking her from behind. She could not keep her attention. And, curiously, she could not keep even her speech. When she was saying something, suddenly the next word would be gone out of her, as if a pack-rat had carried it off. And she sat blank, stuttering, staring in the empty cupboard of her mind, like Mother Hubbard, and seeing the cupboard bare. And this irritated her husband intensely.

Her chickens, of which she was so proud, were carried away. Or they strayed. Or they fell sick. At first she could cope with their circumstances. But after a while, she couldn't. She couldn't care. A drug-like numbness possessed her spirit, and at the very middle of her, she couldn't care what happened to her chickens.

The same when a couple of horses were struck by lightning. It frightened her. The rivers of fluid fire that suddenly fell out of the sky and exploded on the earth near by, as if the whole earth had burst like a bomb, frightened her from the very core of her, and made her know, secretly and with cynical certainty, *that there was no merciful God in the heavens.* A very tall, elegant pine-tree just above her cabin took the lightning, and stood tall and elegant as before, but with a white seam spiralling from its crest, all down its tall trunk, to earth. The perfect scar, white and long as lightning itself. And every time she looked at it, she said to herself, in spite of herself: *There is no Almighty loving God. The God there is shaggy as the pine-trees, and horrible as the lightning.* Outwardly, she never confessed this. Openly, she thought of her dear New England Church as usual. But in the violent undercurrent of her woman's soul, after the storms, she would look at that living seamed tree, and the voice would say in her, almost savagely: *What nonsense about Jesus and a God of Love, in a place like this! This is more awful and more splendid. I like it better.* The very chipmunks, in their jerky helter-skelter, the blue jays wrangling in the pine-tree in the dawn, the grey squirrel undulating to the tree-trunk, then pausing to chatter at her and scold her, with a shrewd fearlessness, as if she were the alien, the outsider, the creature that should not be permitted among the trees, all destroyed the illusion she cherished, of love, universal love. There was no love on this ranch. There was life, intense, bristling life, full of energy, but also with an undertone of savage sordidness.

The black ants in her cupboard, the pack-rats bouncing on her ceiling like hippopotamuses in the night, the two sick goats: there was a peculiar undercurrent of squalor, flowing under the curious *tussle* of wild life. That was it. The wild life, even the life of the trees and flowers, seemed one bristling, hair-raising tussle. The very flowers came up bristly, and many of them were fang-mouthed, like the dead-nettle: and none had any real scent. But they were very fascinating, too, in their very fierceness. In May, the curious columbines of the stream-beds, columbines scarlet outside and yellow in, like the red and yellow of a herald's uniform: farther from the dove nothing could be: then the beautiful rosy-blue of the great tufts of the flower they called bluebell, but which was really a flower of the snapdragon family: these grew in powerful beauty in the little clearing of the pine-trees, followed by the flower the settlers had mysteriously called herb honeysuckle: a tangle of long drops of pure fire-red, hanging from slim invisible stalks of smoke-colour. The purest, most perfect vermilion scarlet, cleanest fire-colour, hanging in long drops like a shower of fire-rain that is just going to strike the earth. A little later, more in the open, there came another sheer fire-red flower, sparking, fierce red stars running up a bristly grey ladder, as if the earth's fire-centre had blown out some red sparks, white-speckled and deadly inside, puffing for a moment in the day air.

So it was! the alfalfa field was one raging, seething conflict of plants trying to get hold. One dry year, and the bristly wild things had got hold: the spiky, blue-leaved thistle-poppy with its moon-white flowers, the low clumps of blue nettle-flower, the later rush, after the sereness of June and July, the rush of red sparks and Michaelmas daisies, and the tough wild sunflowers, strangling and choking the dark, tender green of the clover-like alfalfa! A battle, a battle, with banners of bright scarlet and yellow.

When a really defenceless flower did issue, like the moth-still, ghost-centred mariposa lily, with its inner moth-dust of yellow, it came invisible. There was nothing to be seen but a hair of greyish grass near the oak-scrub. Behold, this invisible long stalk was balancing a white, ghostly, three-petalled flower, naked out of nothingness. A mariposa lily!

Only the pink wild roses smelled sweet, like the old world. They were sweet brier-roses. And the dark-blue harebells among the oak-scrub, like the ice-dark bubbles of the mountain flowers in the Alps, the Alpenglocken.

The roses of the desert are the cactus flowers, crystal of translucent yellow or of rose-colour. But set among spines the devil himself must have conceived in a moment of sheer ecstasy.

Nay, it was a world before and after the God of Love. Even the very humming-birds hanging about the flowering squawberry-bushes, when the snow had gone, in May, they were before and after the God of Love. And the blue jays were crested dark with challenge, and the yellow-and-dark woodpecker was fearless like a warrior in war-paint, as he struck the wood. While on the fence the hawks sat motionless, like dark fists clenched under heaven, ignoring man and his ways.

Summer, it was true, unfolded the tender cottonwood leaves, and the tender aspen. But what a tangle and a ghostly aloofness in the aspen thickets high up on the mountains, the coldness that is in the eyes and the long cornelian talons of the bear.

Summer brought the little wild strawberries, with their savage aroma, and the late summer brought the rose-jewel raspberries in the valley cleft. But how lonely, how harsh-lonely and menacing it was, to be alone in that shadowy, steep cleft of a canyon just above the cabins, picking raspberries, while the thunder gathered thick and blue-purple at the mountain tops. The many wild raspberries hanging rose-red in the thickets. But the stream bed below all silent, waterless. And the trees all bristling in silence, and waiting like warriors at an outpost. And the berries waiting for the sharp-eyed, cold, long-snouted bear to come rambling and shaking his heavy sharp fur. The berries grew for the bears, and the little New England woman, with her uncanny sensitiveness to underlying influences, felt all the time she was stealing. Stealing the wild raspberries in the secret little canyon behind her home. And when she had made them into jam, she could almost taste the theft in her preserves.

She confessed nothing of this. She tried even to confess nothing of her dread. But she was afraid. Especially she was conscious of the prowling, intense aerial electricity all the summer, after June. The air was thick with wandering currents of fierce electric fluid, waiting to discharge themselves. And almost every day there was the rage and battle of thunder. But the air was never cleared. There was no relief. However the thunder raged, and spent itself, yet, afterwards, among the sunshine was the strange lurking and wandering of the electric currents, moving invisible, with strange menace, between the atoms of the air. She knew. Oh, she knew!

And her love for her ranch turned sometimes into a certain repulsion. The underlying rat-dirt, the everlasting bristling tussle of the wild life, with the tangle and the bones strewing. Bones of horses struck by lightning, bones of dead cattle, skulls of goats with little horns: bleached, unburied bones. Then the cruel electricity of the mountains. And then, most mysterious but worst of all, the animosity of the spirit of place: the crude, half-created spirit of place, like some serpent-bird for ever attacking man, in a hatred of man's onward-struggle towards further creation.

The seething cauldron of lower life, seething on the very tissue of the higher life, seething the soul away, seething at the marrow. The vast and unrelenting will of the swarming lower life, working for ever against man's attempt at a higher life, a further created being.

At last, after many years, the little woman admitted to herself that she was glad to go down from the ranch when November came with snows. She was glad to come to a more human home, her house in the village. And as winter passed by, and spring came again, she knew she did not want to go up to the ranch again. It had broken something in her. It had hurt her terribly. It had maimed her for ever in her hope, her belief in paradise on earth. Now, she hid from herself her own corpse, the corpse of her New England belief in a world ultimately all for love. The belief, and herself with it, was a corpse. The gods of those inner mountains were grim and invidious and relentless, huger than man, and lower than man. Yet man could never master them.

The little woman in her flower-garden away below, by the stream-irrigated village, hid away from the thought of it all. She would not go to the ranch any more.

The Mexicans stayed in charge, looking after the goats. But the place didn't pay. It didn't pay, not quite. It had paid. It might pay. But the effort, the effort! And as the marrow is eaten out of a man's bones and the soul out of his belly, contending with the strange rapacity of savage life, the lower stage of creation, he cannot make the effort any more.

Then also, the war came, making many men give up their enterprises at civilization.

Every new stroke of civilization has cost the lives of countless brave men, who have fallen defeated by the "dragon," in their efforts to win the apples of the Hesperides, or the fleece of gold.[50] Fallen in their efforts to overcome the old, half-sordid savagery of the lower stages of creation, and win to the next stage.

For all savagery is half sordid. And man is only himself when he is fighting on and on, to overcome the sordidness.

And every civilization, when it loses its inward vision and its cleaner energy, falls into a new sort of sordidness, more vast and more stupendous than the old savage sort. An Augean stable[51] of metallic filth.

And all the time, man has to rouse himself afresh, to cleanse the new accumulations of refuse. To win from the crude wild nature the victory and the power to make another start, and to cleanse behind him the century-deep deposits of layer upon layer of refuse: even of tin cans.

The ranch dwindled. The flock of goats declined. The water ceased to flow. And at length the trader gave it up.

He rented the place to a Mexican, who lived on the handful of beans he raised, and who was being slowly driven out by the vermin.

And now arrived Lou, new blood to the attack. She went back to Santa Fe, saw the trader and a lawyer, and bought the ranch for twelve hundred dollars. She was so pleased with herself.

She went upstairs to tell her mother.

"Mother, I've bought a ranch."

---

[50]Legendary feats: Hercules succeeded in plucking the golden apples of the Hesperides, and Jason in stealing the Golden Fleece.

[51]Another of the labors of Hercules was cleaning the stables of Augeus.

"It is just as well, for I can't stand the noise of automobiles outside here another week."

"It is quiet on my ranch, mother: the stillness simply speaks."

"I had rather it held its tongue. I am simply drugged with all the bad novels I have read. I feel as if the sky was a big cracked bell and a million clappers were hammering human speech out of it."

"Aren't you interested in my ranch, mother?"

"I hope I may be, by and by."

Mrs. Witt actually got up the next morning, and accompanied her daughter in the hired motor-car, driven by Phoenix, to the ranch: which was called Las Chivas.[52] She sat like a pillar of salt, her face looking what the Indians call a False Face, meaning a mask. She seemed to have crystallized into neutrality. She watched the desert with its tufts of yellow greasewood go lurching past: she saw the fallen apples on the ground in the orchards near the adobe cottages: she looked down into the deep arroyo, and at the stream they forded in the car, and at the mountains blocking up the sky ahead, all with indifference. High on the mountains was snow: lower, blue-grey livid rock: and below the livid rock the aspens were expiring their daffodil-yellow, this year, and the oak-scrub was dark and reddish, like gore. She saw it all with a sort of stony indifference.

"Don't you think it's lovely?" said Lou.

"I can *see* it is lovely," replied her mother.

The Michaelmas daisies in the clearing as they drove up to the ranch were sharp-rayed with purple, like a coming night.

Mrs. Witt eyed the two log cabins, one of which was dilapidated and practically abandoned. She looked at the rather rickety corral, whose long planks had silvered and warped in the fierce sun. On one of the roof-planks a pack-rat was sitting erect like an old Indian keeping watch on a pueblo roof. He showed his white belly, and folded his hands and lifted his big ears, for all the world like an old immobile Indian.

"Isn't it for all the world as if *he* were the real boss of the place, Louise?" she said cynically.

And, turning to the Mexican, who was a rag of a man but a pleasant, courteous fellow, she asked him why he didn't shoot the rat.

"Not worth a shell!" said the Mexican, with a faint hopeless smile.

---

[52]The She-Goats.

Mrs. Witt paced round and saw everything: it did not take long. She gazed in silence at the water of the spring, trickling out of an iron pipe into a barrel, under the cottonwood-tree in an arroyo.

"Well, Louise," she said, "I am glad you feel competent to cope with so much hopelessness and so many rats."

"But, mother, you must admit it is beautiful."

"Yes, I suppose it is. But, to use one of your Henry's phrases, beauty is a cold egg, as far as I am concerned."

"Rico never would have said that beauty was a cold egg to him."

"No, he wouldn't. He sits on it like a broody old hen on a china imitation.—Are you going to bring him here?"

"*Bring* him!—No. But he can come if he likes," stammered Lou.

"*Oh—h!* won't it be beau—ti—ful!" cried Mrs. Witt, rolling her head and lifting her shoulders in savage imitation of her son-in-law.

"Perhaps he won't come, mother," said Lou, hurt.

"He will most certainly come, Louise, to see what's doing: unless you tell him you don't want him."

"Anyhow, I needn't think about it till spring," said Lou, anxiously pushing the matter aside.

Mrs. Witt climbed the steep slope above the cabins, to the mouth of the little canyon. There she sat on a fallen tree, and surveyed the world beyond: a world not of men.

She could not fail to be roused.

"What is your idea in coming here, daughter?" she asked.

"I love it here, mother."

"But what do you expect to achieve by it?"

"I was rather hoping, mother, to escape achievement. I'll tell you—and you mustn't get cross if it sounds silly. As far as people go, my heart is quite broken. As far as people go, I don't want any more. I can't stand any more. What heart I ever had for it—for life with people—is quite broken. I want to be alone, mother: with you here, and Phoenix perhaps to look after horses and drive a car. But I want to be by myself, really."

"With Phoenix in the background! Are you sure he won't be coming into the foreground before long?"

"No, mother, no more of that. If I've got to say it, Phoenix is a servant: he's really placed, as far as I can see. Always the same, playing about in the old back yard. I can't take those men seriously. I can't fool round with them, or fool myself about them. I can't and I won't fool myself any more, mother, especially about men. They don't count. So why should you want them to pay me out?"

For the moment, this silenced Mrs. Witt. Then she said:

"Why, I don't want it. Why should I? But after all you've got to live. You've never *lived* yet: not in my opinion."

"Neither, mother, in my opinion, have you," said Lou dryly.

And this silenced Mrs. Witt altogether. She had to be silent, or angrily on the defensive. And the latter she wouldn't be. She couldn't, really, in honesty.

"What do you call life?" Lou continued. "Wriggling half naked at a public show, and going off in a taxi to sleep with some half-drunken fool who thinks he's a man because—oh, mother, I don't even want to think of it. I know you have a lurking idea that *that is life*. Let it be so then. But leave me out. Men in that aspect simply nauseate me: so grovelling and ratty. Life in that aspect simply drains all my life away. I tell you, for all that sort of thing, I'm broken, absolutely broken: if I wasn't broken to start with."

"Well, Louise," said Mrs. Witt after a pause, "I'm convinced that ever since men and women were men and women, people who took things seriously, and had time for it, got their hearts broken. Haven't I had mine broken? It's as sure as having your virginity broken: and it amounts to about as much. It's a beginning rather than an end."

"So it is, mother. It's the beginning of something else, and the end of something that's done with. I *know*, and there's no altering it, that I've got to live differently. It sounds silly, but I don't know how else to put it. I've got to live for something that matters, way, way down in me. And I think sex would matter, to my very soul, if it was really sacred. But cheap sex kills me."

"You have had a fancy for rather cheap men, perhaps."

"Perhaps I have. Perhaps I should always be a fool, where people are concerned. Now I want to leave off that kind of foolery. There's something else, mother, that I want to give myself to. I know it. I know it absolutely. Why should I let myself be shouted down any more?"

Mrs. Witt sat staring at the distance, her face a cynical mask.

"What is the something bigger? And *pray*, what is it bigger than?" she asked, in that tone of honeyed suavity which was her deadliest poison. "I want to learn. I am out to know. I'm terribly intrigued by it. Something bigger! Girls in my generation occasionally entered convents, for *something bigger*. I always wondered if they found it. They seemed to me inclined in the imbecile direction, but perhaps that was because I was *something less*——"

There was a definite pause between the mother and daughter, a silence that was a pure breach. Then Lou said:

"You know quite well I'm not conventy, mother, whatever else I am—even a bit of an imbecile. But that kind of religion seems to me the other half of men. Instead of running after them, you run away from them, and get the thrill that way. I don't hate men *because* they're men, as nuns do. I dislike them because they're not men enough: babies, and playboys, and poor things showing off all the time, even to themselves. I don't say I'm any better. I only wish, with all my soul, that some men *were* bigger and stronger and *deeper* than I am . . ."

"How do you know they're not?" asked Mrs. Witt.

"How *do* I know?——" said Lou mockingly.

And the pause that was a breach resumed itself. Mrs. Witt was teasing with a little stick the bewildered black ants among the fir-needles.

"And no doubt you are right about men," she said at length. "But at your age, the only sensible thing is to try and keep up the illusion. After all, as you say, you may be no better."

"I may be no better. But keeping up the illusion means fooling myself. And I won't do it. When I see a man who is even a bit attractive to me—even as much as Phoenix—I say to myself: *Would you care for him afterwards? Does he really mean anything to you, except just a sensation?*—And I know he doesn't. No, mother, of this I am convinced: either my taking a man shall have a meaning and a mystery that penetrates my very soul, or I will keep to myself.—And what I know is that the time has come for me to keep to myself. No more messing about."

"Very well, daughter. You will probably spend your life keeping to yourself."

"Do you think I mind! There's something else for me, mother. There's something else even that loves me and wants me. I can't tell you what it is. It's a spirit. And it's here, on this ranch. It's here, in this landscape. It's something more real to me than men are, and it soothes me, and it holds me up. I don't know what it is, definitely. It's something wild, that will hurt me sometimes and will wear me down sometimes. I know it. But it's something big, bigger than men, bigger than people, bigger than religion. It's something to do with wild America. And it's something to do with me. It's a mission, if you like. I am imbecile enough for that!—But it's my mission to keep myself for the spirit that is wild, and has waited so long here: even waited for such as me. Now I've come! Now I'm here. Now I am where I want to be: with the spirit that wants me.—And that's how it is. And neither Rico nor Phoenix nor anybody else really matters to me. They are in the world's back yard. And I am here, right deep in America, where there's a wild spirit wants me, a wild spirit more than men. And it doesn't want to save me either. It needs me. It craves for me. And to it, my sex is deep and sacred, deeper than I am, with a deep nature aware deep down of my sex. It saves me from cheapness, mother. And even you could never do that for me."

Mrs. Witt rose to her feet, and stood looking far, far away, at the turquoise ridge of mountains half sunk under the horizon.

"How much did you say you paid for Las Chivas?" she asked.

"Twelve hundred dollars," said Lou, surprised.

"Then I call it cheap, considering all there is to it: even the name."

Pale Horse, Pale Rider

Katherine Anne Porter

Considering how long she was a part of the American literary scene, Katherine Anne Porter is somewhat of a mystery. While her writing career spanned more than fifty years, less is known about her than about authors of comparable fame, and many details of her life are matters for speculation. The mystery is in part of Porter's own making, for she was evasive about some segments of her biography and downright misleading about others. Until her journals and diaries are published—if they ever are—a comprehensive life of this major American author will remain an impossible dream. What follows is an unavoidable mixture of established facts, guesswork, and unfilled gaps.

Katherine Anne Porter was born on May 15, 1890, in Indian Creek, Texas. She has described her birthplace on a tributary of the Colorado River as "soft blackland farming country, full of fruits and flowers and birds, with good hunting and good fishing." Her parents, Harrison Porter and Mary Alice Jones, were relatively recent settlers in central Texas, but their ancestors had played a major role in the founding of America. Her paternal family included a friend of Washington and Lafayette, and her mother's great-grandfather was a brother of Daniel Boone. Porter was the third of five children. In 1892, when she was two years old, her mother died, and the family moved to nearby Kyle, Texas, where Harrison Porter's widowed mother lived.

This grandmother, named Catherine Anne Porter, was a dominant force in the development of the writer. She was a representative of the "old order" of Southern aristocracy, a woman of wealth and good family whose fortunes were overturned by the Civil War, and in her old age an aggressive, eccentric spokesman for the civilization that was no more. In her short story "The Source," Porter described her grandmother's big secretaries filled with "shabby old sets of Dickens, Scott, Thackeray, Dr. Johnson's dictionary, the volumes of Pope and Milton and Dante and Shakespeare" that formed her taste in literature. But Catherine Porter was more than an intellectual influence on her granddaughter. In her autobiographical fiction Sophia Jane Rhea (as she is called there) emerges as an almost mythic force:

> . . . the Grandmother developed a character truly portentous under the discipline
> of trying to change the characters of others. Her husband . . . feared her deadly

willfulness, her certainty that her ways were not only right but beyond criticism, that her feelings were important, even in the lightest matter. . . . She was gay and sweet and decorous, full of vanity and incredibly exalted daydreams which threatened now and again to cast her over the edge of some mysteriously forbidden frenzy.

Her independence, her originality, her perfectionism were values that became incorporated into the author's life and art.

When Catherine Porter died in 1901, the family group broke up, and Katherine Anne was placed in a Catholic convent school, or perhaps a succession of such schools. The Porters were Methodists, not Catholics, though, and it has been suggested that the convent schools were chosen because they were cheaper than other boarding schools. (One of the persistent ambiguities about Porter is when she was converted to Catholicism. It may have been during her convent education, or it may have been after her near-fatal illness in 1919.) According to her friend Glenway Wescott, she was ''an uneven student: A in history and composition and other subjects having to do with literature, but, she admits, 'D in everything else, including deportment, which sometimes went down to E and stopped there.' '' At the age of sixteen, Porter escaped from the convent in order to marry; the name of her first husband, from whom she was divorced three years later, is not known.

For most of the next ten years, Katherine Anne Porter supported herself as a journalist, working for newspapers in Chicago, San Antonio, Denver, and perhaps other cities as well. It was not glamorous reporting but hack interviews and theater criticism, and if it was in one sense a step toward a literary career, it was not one she recommended in later years to budding writers: she suggested that one would do better as a waitress than a journalist because the latter job occupied too much of one's mind. At points between her jobs as a gypsy newspaperwoman, she was a movie extra and a music hall entertainer. While Porter was blessed with a strong constitution, she had occasional spells of ill health. At one time a case of bronchitis was misdiagnosed as a rare form of tuberculosis; she spent months in a sanatorium with her eyes covered by a green baize cloth because her doctor had observed that, even with every other form of stimulation taken from her, her restless staring at the ceiling would send her into a fever.

While working for the *Rocky Mountain News* in Denver toward the end of World War I, she was victim of the Spanish influenza epidemic that devastated the United States at that time. Porter recovered, eventually, but her soldier lover, who had contracted the disease from her, died ot it. This incident is the seed of *Pale Horse, Pale Rider.*

After her recovery, Porter moved to New York, where for a brief time she worked as a ghostwriter from an apartment in Greenwich Village. In that artists' colony, she made the acquaintance of a number of Mexican painters, who told her about the renaissance in Mexican art that was just beginning, that was ''where the exciting things are going to happen.'' She got more excitement than she bargained for, for she arrived in Mexico in the middle of the Obregón revolution of 1920-1921. ''When I got on the Mexican train,'' she later said to an interviewer, ''the whole roof was covered with soldiers and rifles. . . . So I said to this man who spoke to me, 'What's going on, what's happening?' And he said, 'Well, we're having a little revolution down here.' I thought this was interesting, kind of exhilarating, you know.'' Through her study of art, Porter became involved with a group of revolutionaries who had taken over the National Museum, and she ultimately became engaged in political activities there, carrying ''messages to people living in dark alleys.'' When the revolution succeeded, she became a sort of unofficial cultural ambassador for the Obregón government, which was trying to achieve recognition by the United States. Porter became involved in trying to place an extensive exhibition of Mexican art in American museums and galleries. After a great deal of diplomatic frustration, she finally succeeded in placing the entire exhibit, tens of thousands of art works from a variety of periods, with a Los Angeles dealer, and it was from this show, according to Porter, that American interest in Mexican art stemmed.

Her own literary career has its beginnings in this period as well. Porter's first published stories, ''María Concepción,'' ''Virgin Violeta,'' and ''The Martyr,'' are all products of her first visit to Mexico in 1920-1922; they came out between 1922 and 1924 in the *Century Magazine* under the prestigious editorship of Carl Van Doren. During the 1920s, Porter continued to write stories, supporting herself by book reviewing in New York and by acting in the Little Theatre of Fort Worth, Texas. Her first collection of short stories, *Flowering Judas*, was published in 1930.

On the basis of *Flowering Judas*, Porter won a Guggenheim Fellowship in 1931, which she spent in Mexico. The time there was less productive than her first visit, according to Porter, on account of the disruptive influence of the demonically self-destructive poet Hart Crane, who was, like her, on a Guggenheim. Their initial friendship and subsequent furious quarrel turned, it seems, on Crane's alcoholic and homosexual excesses, which outraged her. The incident suggests that, despite her gypsy life and bohemian tastes, Katherine Anne Porter was still (as one critic has put it) ''her grandmother's child, with a fixed moral code and definite ideas on right and wrong sexual and moral behavior.'' After her breach with Crane, Porter took her first trip to Europe on an ocean liner between Vera Cruz and Bremerhaven, Germany, that ultimately became the basis for her only novel, *Ship of Fools.*

While in Europe in 1933, Porter met and married Eugene Pressley of the American foreign service. The marriage ended in divorce four years later, and Porter returned to America, to New Orleans. In 1938 she married Albert Erskine, a professor at Louisiana State University, and she lived with him in Baton Rouge until that marriage, too, ended in divorce in 1942. While most of the experiences upon which she based her fiction took place in her youth in Texas, or during her bohemian days in New York, it was the relatively quiet period from the mid-1930s to the mid-1940s that was her most productive time. In those years she published her three novellas, *Old Mortality, Noon Wine,* and *Pale Horse, Pale Rider.* This last novella, which Porter considers her finest work, gave its name to the collection, published in 1939, that won her the Gold Medal for Literature and resulted in her election to the National Institute of Arts and Letters. And it was in those years that she also published her second collection of short stories, *The Leaning Tower* (1944), and wrote many of the essays that appear in her anthology of prose, *The Days Before* (1952).

As a result of the critical success of her short stories and novellas, Katherine Anne Porter was able to stop the hack journalism with which she had once supported herself, and was able to live and work partly on the royalties from her fiction, partly on a secondary career as a visiting lecturer at various American universities. She would work privately, sometimes at writers' colonies like Yaddo. Then, when her funds were running low, she would accept an academic appointment to Stanford, the University of Chicago, or another college that could succeed in luring her. Her life as an itinerant academic ended around 1960, when a Ford Foundation grant gave Porter the leisure and perhaps the impetus to complete the novel that she had been promising the world since 1940, and of which she had released bits and pieces over many years through a number of small literary magazines. *Ship of Fools* was finally finished and published in 1962. Aided by Porter's growing reputation—as well as by an unprecedented $50,000 advertising campaign—it became a runaway bestseller.

If *Ship of Fools* is not Porter's greatest work, it is certainly her longest and her most controversial. The title is taken from a medieval satire by the German Sebastian Brant, an allegorical poem from which she also took the "simple almost universal image of the ship of this world on its voyage to eternity." In Porter's novel, the voyage of the *Vera* (from the Latin word "veritas," meaning "truth") from Mexico to Germany just before Hitler's rise to power is a study in human folly and depravity of every conceivable variety. As a portrait of the modern world, it is bleak beyond redemption, for the few morally upright characters are weak and ineffectual; the majority, violent, bigoted, perverted repositories of one or more of the seven deadly sins, hold sway over them. The initial critical reception of *Ship of Fools* was laudatory almost without exception, which fueled the novel's sales as much, perhaps, as did its selection by the Book-of-the-Month Club. But before long a critical backlash set in. For those whose expectations were raised by Porter's deep and intensely revealing psychological stories, *Ship of Fools* was dismayingly dark and far too much on the surface of her characters. Her lack of sympathy with her "fools" convinced more than one critic that "the soul of humanity is lacking." In particular, her loathsome portrayal of sexuality in the novel struck some readers as either puritanically moralistic or morbidly prurient. While it is impossible to argue against her critics' distaste for Porter's ethical views, the technical "defects" of the novel may be seen to derive not from any failure on the author's part but from an inadequate critical vocabulary. Like Brant's poem, *Ship of Fools* is an apologue, a fictional work organized not around plot and character but instead by a moral thesis. Its organization requires it to be broad rather than deep, and those who admired Porter for her concentrated stories and novellas came to *Ship of Fools* expecting something that the work, by its very nature, could not give them.

After *Ship of Fools*, Katherine Anne Porter published very little. Her *Collected Stories* (1965), which won the National Book Award and the Pulitzer Prize for Fiction, reprinted her three previous collections, together with a few early stories that had never appeared before in book form. Her *Collected Essays* (1970) reprinted and updated her former anthology of prose writing. In 1977 Porter published her first entirely new work in fifteen years, a memoir of her participation in the protest over the Sacco-Vanzetti case called *The Never-Ending Wrong*. From the early 1960s until her death on September 18, 1980, Katherine Anne Porter lived at College Park, Maryland, site of the state university to which she willed her manuscripts.

For a life-span of ninety years and a writing career of well over half a century, Katherine Anne Porter's reputation rests on an astonishingly small body of work. Her entire output of fiction fits into two volumes of moderate size totalling perhaps a thousand pages. But artistry is a matter of quality, not quantity: the legion of authors who can turn out a volume every year or two cannot match her high standards of craftsmanship or the perfection of her style. She was without any lengthy formal education, and she was no one's disciple. She joined no literary clique for mutual admiration, support, and publicity. Her work was guided by no models, only by her innate sense of language, feeling, and form. And it must be said that her stubborn independence, originality, and perfectionism served her well, for she is widely regarded as one of the finest American writers of this century.

Biography   No full-length biography of Katherine Anne Porter has yet appeared. For further information see Robert Penn Warren's "Introduction" to *Katherine Anne Porter: A Collection of Critical Essays* (Englewood Cliffs, N.J.: Prentice-Hall, 1979) and George Hendrick's *Katherine Anne Porter* (New York: Twayne, 1965); in the latter work, biographical detail is interwoven with perceptive criticism of Porter's work.

Editions   For the stories and short novels, the best edition is *The Collected Stories of Katherine Anne Porter* (New York: Harcourt, Brace, and World, 1965); for the essays, see *Collected Essays* (New York: Harcourt Brace Jovanovich, 1970); her one novel is *Ship of Fools* (Boston: Little, Brown, 1962).

Bibliography   Most complete is Louise Waldrip and Shirley Ann Bauer, *A Bibliography of the Works . . . and . . . the Criticism of the Works of Katherine Anne Porter* (Metuchen, N.J.: Scarecrow Press, 1969), updated with Robert F. Kiernan's *Katherine Anne Porter and Carson McCullers: A Reference Guide* (Boston: G. K. Hall, 1976).

General Criticism   In addition to Warren and Hendrick, above, see Harry Mooney, Jr., *The Fiction and Criticism of Katherine Anne Porter* (Pittsburgh: University of Pittsburgh Press, 1957); Ray B. West, Jr., *Katherine Anne Porter*

(Minneapolis: University of Minnesota Press, 1963); and William L. Nance, *Katherine Anne Porter and the Art of Rejection* (Chapel Hill: University of North Carolina Press, 1963).

Criticism of Pale Horse, Pale Rider In addition to sections on *Pale Horse, Pale Rider* in the books cited above, see S. H. Poss, "Variations on a Theme in Four Short Stories of Katherine Anne Porter," *Twentieth Century Literature* 4 (1958), 21–29; Sarah Youngblood, "Structure and Imagery in Katherine Anne Porter's *Pale Horse, Pale Rider*," *Modern Fiction Studies* 5 (1959), 344–352; Charles A. Allen, "The Nouvelles of Katherine Anne Porter," *University of Kansas City Review* 29 (1962), 87–93; Jean Alexander, "Katherine Anne Porter's Ship in the Jungle," *Twentieth Century Literature* 11 (1966), 179–188; and Philip R. Yanella, "Problems of Dislocation in *Pale Horse, Pale Rider*," *Studies in Short Fiction* 6 (1969), 637–642.

Pale Horse, Pale Rider

In sleep she knew she was in her bed, but not the bed she had lain down in a few hours since, and the room was not same but it was a room she had known somewhere. Her heart was a stone lying upon her breast outside of her; her pulses lagged and paused, and she knew that something strange was going to happen, even as the early morning winds were cool through the lattice, the streaks of light were dark blue and the whole house was snoring in its sleep.

Now I must get up and go while they are all quiet. Where are my things? Things have a will of their own in this place and hide where they like. Daylight will strike a sudden blow on the roof startling them all up to their feet; faces will beam asking, Where are you going, What are you doing, What are you thinking, How do you feel, Why do you say such things, What do you mean? No more sleep. Where are my boots and what horse shall I ride? Fiddler or Graylie or Miss Lucy with the long nose and the wicked eye? How I have loved this house in the morning before we are all awake and tangled together like badly cast fishing lines. Too many people have been born here, and have wept too much here, and have laughed too much, and have been too angry and outrageous with each other here. Too many have died in this bed already, there are far too many ancestral bones propped up on the mantelpieces, there have been too damned many antimacassars in this house, she said loudly, and oh, what accumulation of storied dust never allowed to settle in peace for one moment.

And the stranger? Where is that lank greenish stranger I remember hanging about the place, welcomed by my grandfather, my great-aunt, my five times removed cousin, my decrepit hound and my silver kitten? Why did they take to him, I wonder? And where are they now? Yet I saw him pass the window in the evening. What else besides them did I have in the world? Nothing. Nothing is mine, I have only nothing but it is enough, it is beautiful and it is all mine. Do I even walk about in my own skin or is it something I have borrowed to spare my modesty? Now what horse shall I borrow for this journey I do not mean to take, Graylie or Miss Lucy or Fiddler who can jump ditches in the dark and knows how to get the bit between his teeth? Early morning is best for me because trees are trees in one stroke, stones are stones set in shades known to be grass, there are no false shapes or surmises, the road is still asleep with the crust of dew unbroken. I'll take Graylie because he is not afraid of bridges.

Come now, Graylie, she said, taking his bridle, we must outrun Death and the Devil.[1] You are no good for it, she told the other horses standing saddled before the stable gate, among them the horse of the stranger, gray also, with tarnished nose and ears. The stranger swung into his saddle beside her, leaned far towards her and regarded her without meaning, the blank still stare of mindless malice that makes no threats and can bide its time. She drew Graylie around sharply, urged him to run. He leaped the low rose hedge and the narrow ditch beyond, and the dust of the lane flew heavily under his beating hoofs. The stranger rode beside her, easily, lightly, his reins loose in his half-closed hand, straight and elegant in dark shabby garments that flapped upon his bones; his pale face smiled in an evil trance, he did not glance at her. Ah, I have seen this fellow before, I know this man if I could place him. He is no stranger to me.

She pulled Graylie up, rose in her stirrups and shouted, I'm not going with you this time—ride on! Without pausing or turning his head the stranger rode on. Graylie's ribs heaved under her, her own ribs rose and fell, Oh, why am I so tired, I must wake up. "But let me get a fine yawn first," she said, opening her eyes and stretching, "a slap

---

[1]The imagery of this dream recalls that of Revelation 6:7.

of cold water in my face, for I've been talking in my sleep again, I heard myself but what was I saying?"

Slowly, unwillingly, Miranda drew herself up inch by inch out of the pit of sleep, waited in a daze for life to begin again. A single word struck in her mind, a gong of warning, reminding her for the day long what she forgot happily in sleep, and only in sleep. The war, said the gong, and she shook her head. Dangling her feet idly with their slippers hanging, she was reminded of the way all sorts of persons sat upon her desk at the newspaper office. Every day she found someone there, sitting upon her desk instead of the chair provided, dangling his legs, eyes roving, full of his important affairs, waiting to pounce about something or other. "*Why* won't they sit in the chair? Should I put a sign on it, saying, 'For God's sake, sit here'?"

Far from putting up a sign, she did not even frown at her visitors. Usually she did not notice them at all until their determination to be seen was greater than her determination not to see them. Saturday, she thought, lying comfortable in her tub of hot water, will be pay day, as always. Or I hope always. Her thoughts roved hazily in a continual effort to bring together and unite firmly the disturbing oppositions in her day-to-day existence, where survival, she could see clearly, had become a series of feats of sleight of hand. I owe—let me see, I wish I had pencil and paper—well, suppose I *did* pay five dollars now on a Liberty Bond, I couldn't possibly keep it up. Or maybe. Eighteen dollars a week. So much for rent, so much for food, and I mean to have a few things besides. About five dollars' worth. Will leave me twenty-seven cents. I suppose I can make it. I suppose I should be worried. I am worried. Very well, now I am worried and what next? Twenty-seven cents. That's not so bad. Pure profit, really. Imagine if they should suddenly raise me to twenty I should then have two dollars and twenty-seven cents left over. But they aren't going to raise me to twenty. They are in fact going to throw me out if I don't buy a Liberty Bond. I hardly believe that. I'll ask Bill. (Bill was the city editor.) I wonder if a threat like that isn't a kind of blackmail. I don't believe even a Lusk Committeeman[2] can get away with that.

Yesterday there had been two pairs of legs dangling, on either side of her typewriter, both pairs stuffed thickly into funnels of dark expen-

---

[2]Named after Clayton Lusk, a New York State Senator who was in charge of investigating sedition during and after World War I, Lusk committees were local groups, usually self-appointed, enforcing patriotic activities.

sive-looking material. She noticed at a distance that one of them was oldish and one was youngish, and they both of them had a stale air of borrowed importance which apparently they had got from the same source. They were both much too well nourished and the younger one wore a square little mustache. Being what they were, no matter what their business was it would be something unpleasant. Miranda had nodded at them, pulled out her chair and without removing her cap or gloves had reached into a pile of letters and sheets from the copy desk as if she had not a moment to spare. They did not move, or take off their hats. At last she had said "Good morning" to them, and asked if they were, perhaps, waiting for her?

The two men slid off the desk, leaving some of her papers rumpled, and the oldish man had inquired why she had not bought a Liberty Bond. Miranda had looked at him then, and got a poor impression. He was a pursy-faced man, gross-mouthed, with little lightless eyes, and Miranda wondered why nearly all of those selected to do the war work at home were of his sort. He might be anything at all, she thought; advance agent for a road show, promoter of a wildcat oil company, a former saloon keeper announcing the opening of a new cabaret, an automobile salesman—any follower of any one of the crafty, haphazard callings. But he was now all Patriot, working for the government. "Look here," he asked her, "do you know there's a war, or don't you?"

Did he expect an answer to that? Be quiet, Miranda told herself, this was bound to happen. Sooner or later it happens. Keep your head. The man wagged his finger at her, "Do you?" he persisted, as if he were prompting an obstinate child.

"Oh, the war," Miranda had echoed on a rising note and she almost smiled at him. It was habitual, automatic, to give that solemn, mystically uplifted grin when you spoke the words or heard them spoken. *"C'est la guerre,"* whether you could pronounce it or not, was even better, and always, always, you shrugged.

"Yeah," said the younger man in a nasty way, "the war." Miranda, startled by the tone, met his eye; his stare was really stony, really viciously cold, the kind of thing you might expect to meet behind a pistol on a deserted corner. This expression gave temporary meaning to a set of features otherwise nondescript, the face of those men who have no business of their own. "We're having a war, and some people are buying Liberty Bonds and others just don't seem to get around to it," he said. "That's what we mean."

Miranda frowned with nervousness, the sharp beginnings of fear.

"Are you selling them?" she asked, taking the cover off her typewriter and putting it back again.

"No, we're not selling them," said the older man. "We're just asking you why you haven't bought one." The voice was persuasive and ominous.

Miranda began to explain that she had no money, and did not know where to find any, when the older man interrupted: "That's no excuse, no excuse at all, and you know it, with the Huns overrunning martyred Belgium."

"With our American boys fighting and dying in Belleau Wood," said the younger man, "anybody can raise fifty dollars to help beat the Boche."

Miranda said hastily, "I have eighteen dollars a week and not another cent in the world. I simply cannot buy anything."

"You can pay for it five dollars a week," said the older man (they had stood there cawing back and forth over her head), "like a lot of other people in this office, and a lot of other offices besides are doing."

Miranda, desperately silent, had thought, "Suppose I were not a coward, but said what I really thought? Suppose I said to hell with this filthy war? Suppose I asked that little thug, What's the matter with you, why aren't you rotting in Belleau Wood? I wish you were . . ."

She began to arrange her letters and notes, her fingers refusing to pick up things properly. The older man went on making his little set speech. It was hard, of course. Everybody was suffering, naturally. Everybody had to do his share. But as to that, a Liberty Bond was the safest investment you could make. It was just like having the money in the bank. Of course. The government was back of it and where better could you invest?

"I agree with you about that," said Miranda, "but I haven't any money to invest."

And of course, the man had gone on, it wasn't so much her fifty dollars that was going to make any difference. It was just a pledge of good faith on her part. A pledge of good faith that she was a loyal American doing her duty. And the thing was safe as a church. Why, if he had a million dollars he'd be glad to put every last cent of it in these Bonds. . . . "You can't lose by it," he said, almost benevolently, "and you can lose a lot if you don't. Think it over. You're the only one in this whole newspaper office that hasn't come in. And every firm in this city has come in one hundred percent. Over at the *Daily Clarion* nobody had to be asked twice."

"They pay better over there," said Miranda. "But next week, if I can. Not now, next week."

"See that you do," said the younger man. "This ain't any laughing matter."

They lolled away, past the Society Editor's desk, past Bill the City Editor's desk, past the long copy desk where old man Gibbons sat all night shouting at intervals, "Jarge! Jarge!" and the copy boy would come flying. "Never say *people* when you mean *persons*," old man Gibbons had instructed Miranda, "and never say *practically*, say *virtually*, and don't for God's sake ever so long as I am at this desk use the barbarism *inasmuch* under any circumstances whatsoever. Now you're educated, you may go." At the head of the stairs her inquisitors had stopped in their fussy pride and vainglory, lighting cigars and wedging their hats more firmly over their eyes.

Miranda turned over in the soothing water, and wished she might fall asleep there, to wake up only when it was time to sleep again. She had a burning slow headache, and noticed it now, remembering she had waked up with it and it had in fact begun the evening before. While she dressed she tried to trace the insidious career of her headache, and it seemed reasonable to suppose it had started with the war. "It's been a headache, all right, but not quite like this." After the Committeemen had left, yesterday, she had gone to the cloakroom and had found Mary Townsend, the Society Editor, quietly hysterical about something. She was perched on the edge of the shabby wicker couch with ridges down the center, knitting on something rose-colored. Now and then she would put down her knitting, seize her head with both hands and rock, saying, "My *God*," in a surprised, inquiring voice. Her column was called Ye Towne Gossyp, so of course everybody called her Towney. Miranda and Towney had a great deal in common, and liked each other. They had both been real reporters once, and had been sent together to "cover" a scandalous elopement, in which no marriage had taken place, after all, and the recaptured girl, her face swollen, had sat with her mother, who was moaning steadily under a mound of blankets. They had both wept painfully and implored the young reporters to suppress the worst of the story. They had suppressed it, and the rival newspaper printed it all the next day. Miranda and Towney had then taken their punishment together, and had been degraded publicly to routine female jobs, one to the theaters, the other to society. They had this in common, that neither of them could see what else they could possibly have done, and they knew they were considered fools by the rest of the staff—nice girls, but fools. At sight of Miranda, Towney had broken out in a rage. "I can't do it, I'll never be able to raise the money, I told them, I can't, I can't, but they wouldn't listen."

Miranda said, "I knew I wasn't the only person in this office who couldn't raise five dollars. I told them I couldn't, too, and I can't."

"My *God*," said Towney, in the same voice, "they told me I'd lose my job—"

"I'm going to ask Bill," Miranda said; "I don't believe Bill would do that."

"It's not up to Bill," said Towney. "He'd have to if they got after him. Do you suppose they could put us in jail?"

"I don't know," said Miranda. "If they do, we won't be lonesome." She sat down beside Towney and held her own head. "What kind of soldier are you knitting that for? It's a sprightly color, it ought to cheer him up."

"Like hell," said Towney, her needles going again. "I'm making this for myself. That's that."

"Well," said Miranda, "we won't be lonesome and we'll catch up on our sleep." She washed her face and put on fresh make-up. Taking clean gray gloves out of her pocket she went out to join a group of young women fresh from the country club dances, the morning bridge, the charity bazaar, the Red Cross workrooms, who were wallowing in good works. They gave tea dances and raised money, and with the money they bought quantities of sweets, fruit, cigarettes, and magazines for the men in the cantonment hospitals. With this loot they were now setting out, a gay procession of high-powered cars and brightly tinted faces to cheer the brave boys who already, you might very well say, had fallen in defense of their country. It must be frightfully hard on them, the dears, to be floored like this when they're all crazy to get overseas and into the trenches as quickly as possible. Yes, and some of them are the cutest things you ever saw, I didn't know there were so many good-looking men in this country, good heavens, I said, where do they come from? Well, my dear, you may ask yourself that question, who knows where they did come from? You're quite right, the way I feel about it is this, we must do everything we can to make them contented, but I draw the line at talking to them. I told the chaperons at those dances for enlisted men, I'll dance with them, every dumbbell who asks me, but I will NOT talk to them, I said, even if there is a war. So I danced hundreds of miles without opening my mouth except to say, Please keep your knees to yourself. I'm glad we gave those dances up. Yes, and the men stopped coming, anyway. But listen, I've heard that a great many of the enlisted men come from very good families; I'm not good at catching names, and those I did catch I'd never heard before, so I don't know . . . but it seems to me if they were from good families, you'd know it, wouldn't you? I mean, if a man is well bred he doesn't step on your feet, does he? At least not that. I used to have a pair of sandals ruined at every one of those dances. Well, I think any kind of social life is in very poor taste just now, I think we should all put on our Red Cross head dresses and wear them for the duration of the war—

Miranda, carrying her basket and her flowers, moved in among the young women, who scattered out and rushed upon the ward uttering girlish laughter meant to be refreshingly gay, but there was a grim determined clang in it calculated to freeze the blood. Miserably embarrassed at the idiocy of her errand, she walked rapidly between the long rows of high beds, set foot to foot with a narrow aisle between. The men, a selected presentable lot, sheets drawn up to their chins, not seriously ill, were bored and restless, most of them willing to be amused at anything. They were for the most part picturesquely bandaged as to arm or head, and those who were not visibly wounded invariably replied "Rheumatism" if some tactless girl, who had been solemnly warned never to ask this question, still forgot and asked a man what his illness was. The good-natured, eager ones, laughing and calling out from their hard narrow beds, were soon surrounded. Miranda, with her wilting bouquet and her basket of sweets and cigarettes, looking about, caught the unfriendly bitter eye of a young fellow lying on his back, his right leg in a cast and pulley. She stopped at the foot of his bed and continued to look at him, and he looked back with an unchanged, hostile face. Not having any, thank you and be damned to the whole business, his eyes said plainly to her, and will you be so good as to take your trash off my bed? For Miranda had set it down, leaning over to place it where he might be able to reach it if he would. Having set it down, she was incapable of taking it up again, but hurried away, her face burning, down the long aisle and out into the cool October sunshine, where the dreary raw barracks swarmed and worked with an aimless life of scurrying, dun-colored insects; and going around to a window near where he lay, she looked in, spying upon her soldier. He was lying with his eyes closed, his eyebrows in a sad bitter frown. She could not place him at all, she could not imagine where he came from nor what sort of being he might have been "in life," she said to herself. His face was young and the features sharp and plain, the hands were not laborer's hands but not well-cared-for hands either. They were

good useful properly shaped hands, lying there on the coverlet. It occurred to her that it would be her luck to find him, instead of a jolly
hungry puppy glad of a bite to eat and a little chatter. It is like turning
a corner absorbed in your painful thoughts and meeting your state of
mind embodied, face to face, she said. "My own feelings about this
whole thing, made flesh. Never again will I come here, this is no sort of
thing to be doing. This is disgusting," she told herself plainly. "Of
course I would pick him out," she thought, getting into the back seat of
the car she came in, "serves me right, I know better."

Another girl came out looking· very tired and climbed in beside her.
After a short silence, the girl said in a puzzled way, "I don't know what
good it does, really. Some of them wouldn't take anything at all. I don't
like this, do you?"

"I hate it," said Miranda.

"I suppose it's all right, though," said the girl, cautiously.

"Perhaps," said Miranda, turning cautious also.

That was for yesterday. At this point Miranda decided there was no
good in thinking of yesterday, except for the hour after midnight she
had spent dancing with Adam. He was in her mind so much, she hardly
knew when she was thinking about him directly. His image was simply
always present in more or less degree, he was sometimes nearer the
surface of her thoughts, the pleasantest, the only really pleasant
thought she had. She examined her face in the mirror between the
windows and decided that her uneasiness was not all imagination. For
three days at least she had felt odd and her expression was unfamiliar.
She would have to raise that fifty dollars somehow, she supposed, or
who knows what can happen? She was hardened to stories of personal
disaster, of outrageous accusations and extraordinarily bitter penalties
that had grown monstrously out of incidents very little more important
than her failure—her refusal—to buy a Bond. No, she did not find
herself a pleasing sight, flushing and shiny, and even her hair felt as if
it had decided to grow in the other direction. I must do something
about this, I can't let Adam see me like this, she told herself, knowing
that even now at that moment he was listening for the turn of her door
knob, and he would be in the hallway, or on the porch when she came
out, as if by sheerest coincidence. The noon sunlight cast cold slanting
shadows in the room where, she said, I suppose I live, and this day is
beginning badly, but they all do now, for one reason or another. In a
drowse, she sprayed perfume on her hair, put on her moleskin cap and
jacket, now in their second winter, but still good, still nice to wear,
again being glad she had paid a frightening price for them. She had

enjoyed them all this time, and in no case would she have had the money now. Maybe she could manage for that Bond. She could not find the lock without leaning to search for it, then stood undecided a moment possessed by the notion that she had forgotten something she would miss seriously later on.

Adam was in the hallway, a step outside his own door; he swung about as if quite startled to see her, and said, "Hello. I don't have to go back to camp today after all—isn't that luck?"

Miranda smiled at him gaily because she was always delighted at the sight of him. He was wearing his new uniform, and he was all olive and tan and tawny, hay colored and sand colored from hair to boots. She half noticed again that he always began by smiling at her; that his smile faded gradually; that his eyes became fixed and thoughtful as if he were reading in a poor light.

They walked out together into the fine fall day, scuffling bright ragged leaves under their feet, turning their faces up to a generous sky really blue and spotless. At the first corner they waited for a funeral to pass, the mourners seated straight and firm as if proud in their sorrow.

"I imagine I'm late," said Miranda, "as usual. What time is it?"

"Nearly half past one," he said, slipping back his sleeve with an exaggerated thrust of his arm upward. The young soldiers were still self-conscious about their wrist watches. Such of them as Miranda knew were boys from southern and southwestern towns, far off the Atlantic seaboard, and they had always believed that only sissies wore wrist watches. "I'll slap you on the wrist watch," one vaudeville comedian would simper to another, and it was always a good joke, never stale.

"I think it's a most sensible way to carry a watch," said Miranda. "You needn't blush."

"I'm nearly used to it," said Adam, who was from Texas. "We've been told time and again how all the he-manly regular army men wear them. It's the horrors of war," he said; "are we downhearted? I'll say we are."

It was the kind of patter going the rounds. "You look it," said Miranda.

He was tall and heavily muscled in the shoulders, narrow in the waist and flanks, and he was infinitely buttoned, strapped, harnessed into a uniform as tough and unyielding in cut as a strait jacket, though the cloth was fine and supple. He had his uniforms made by the best tailor he could find, he confided to Miranda one day when she told him how squish he was looking in his new soldier suit. "Hard enough to make anything of the outfit, anyhow," he told her. "It's the least I can do for my beloved country, not to go around looking like a tramp." He was twenty-four years old and a Second Lieutenant in an Engineers Corps, on leave because his outfit expected to be sent over shortly. "Came in to make my will," he told Miranda, "and get a supply of toothbrushes and razor blades. By what gorgeous luck do you suppose," he asked her, "I happened to pick on your rooming house? How did I know you were there?"

Strolling, keeping step, his stout polished well-made boots setting themselves down firmly beside her thin-soled black suède, they put off as long as they could the end of their moment together, and kept up as well as they could their small talk that flew back and forth over little grooves worn in the thin upper surface of the brain, things you could say and hear clink reassuringly at once without disturbing the radiance which played and darted about the simple and lovely miracle of being two persons named Adam and Miranda, twenty-four years old each, alive and on the earth at the same moment: "Are you in the mood for dancing, Miranda?" and "I'm always in the mood for dancing, Adam!" but there were things in the way, the day that ended with dancing was a long way to go.

He really did look, Miranda thought, like a fine healthy apple this morning. One time or another in their talking, he had boasted that he had never had a pain in his life that he could remember. Instead of being horrified at this monster, she approved his monstrous uniqueness. As for herself, she had had too many pains to mention, so she did not mention them. After working for three years on a morning newspaper she had an illusion of maturity and experience; but it was fatigue merely, she decided, from keeping what she had been brought up to believe were unnatural hours, eating casually at dirty little restaurants, drinking bad coffee all night, and smoking too much. When she said something of her way of living to Adam, he studied her face a few seconds as if he had never seen it before, and said in a forthright way, "Why, it hasn't hurt you a bit, I think you're beautiful," and left her dangling there, wondering if he had thought she wished to be praised. She did wish to be praised, but not at that moment. Adam kept unwholesome hours too, or had in the ten days they had known each other, staying awake until one o'clock to take her out for supper; he smoked also continually, though if she did not stop him he was apt to explain to her exactly what smoking did to the lungs. "But," he said, "does it matter so much if you're going to war, anyway?"

"No," said Miranda, "and it matters even less if you're staying at home knitting socks. Give me a cigarette, will you?" They paused at another corner, under a half-foliaged maple, and hardly glanced at a funeral procession approaching. His eyes were pale tan with orange flecks in them, and his hair was the color of a haystack when you turn the weathered top back to the clear straw beneath. He fished out his cigarette case and snapped his silver lighter at her, snapped it several times in his own face, and they moved on, smoking.

"I can see you knitting socks," he said. "That would be just your speed. You know perfectly well you can't knit."

"I do worse," she said, soberly; "I write pieces advising other young women to knit and roll bandages and do without sugar and help win the war."

"Oh, well," said Adam, with the easy masculine morals in such questions, "that's merely your job, that doesn't count."

"I wonder," said Miranda. "How did you manage to get an extension of leave?"

"They just gave it," said Adam, "for no reason. The men are dying like flies out there, anyway. This funny new disease. Simply knocks you into a cocked hat."

"It seems to be a plague," said Miranda, "something out of the Middle Ages. Did you ever see so many funerals, ever?"

"Never did. Well, let's be strong minded and not have any of it. I've got four days more straight from the blue and not a blade of grass must grow under our feet. What about tonight?"

"Same thing," she told him, "but make it about half past one. I've got a special job beside my usual run of the mill."

"What a job you've got," said Adam, "nothing to do but run from one dizzy amusement to another and then write a piece about it."

"Yes, it's too dizzy for words," said Miranda. They stood while a funeral passed, and this time they watched it in silence. Miranda pulled her cap to an angle and winked in the sunlight, her head swimming slowly "like goldfish," she told Adam, "my head swims. I'm only half awake, I must have some coffee."

They lounged on their elbows over the counter of a drug store. "No more cream for the stay-at-homes," she said, "and only one lump of sugar. I'll have two or none; that's the kind of martyr I'm being. I mean to live on boiled cabbage and wear shoddy from now on and get in good shape for the next round. No war is going to sneak up on me again."

"Oh, there won't be any more wars, don't you read the newspapers?" asked Adam. "We're going to mop 'em up this time, and they're going to stay mopped, and this is going to be all."

"So they told me," said Miranda, tasting her bitter lukewarm brew and making a rueful face. Their smiles approved of each other, they felt they had got the right tone, they were taking the war properly. Above all, thought Miranda, no tooth-gnashing, no hair-tearing, it's noisy and unbecoming and it doesn't get you anywhere.

"Swill," said Adam rudely, pushing back his cup. "Is that all you're having for breakfast?"

"It's more than I want," said Miranda.

"I had buckwheat cakes, with sausage and maple syrup, and two bananas, and two cups of coffee, at eight o'clock, and right now, again, I feel like a famished orphan left in the ashcan. I'm all set," said Adam, "for broiled steak and fried potatoes and—"

"Don't go on with it," said Miranda, "it sounds delirious to me. Do all that after I'm gone." She slipped from the high seat, leaned against it slightly, glanced at her face in her round mirror, rubbed rouge on her lips and decided that she was past praying for.

"There's something terribly wrong," she told Adam. "I feel too rotten. It can't just be the weather, and the war."

"The weather is perfect," said Adam, "and the war is simply too good to be true. But since when? You were all right yesterday."

"I don't know," she said slowly, her voice sounding small and thin. They stopped as always at the open door before the flight of littered steps leading up to the newspaper loft. Miranda listened for a moment to the rattle of typewriters above, the steady rumble of presses below. "I wish we were going to spend the whole afternoon on a park bench," she said, "or drive to the mountains."

"I do too," he said; "let's do that tomorrow."

"Yes, tomorrow, unless something else happens. I'd like to run away," she told him; "let's both."

"Me?" said Adam. "Where I'm going there's no running to speak of. You mostly crawl about on your stomach here and there among the debris. You know, barbed wire and such stuff. It's going to be the kind of thing that happens once in a lifetime." He reflected a moment, and went on, "I don't know a darned thing about it, really, but they make it sound awfully messy. I've heard so much about it I feel as if I had been there and back. It's going to be an anticlimax," he said, "like seeing the pictures of a place so often you can't see it at all when you actually get there. Seems to me I've been in the army all my life."

Six months, he meant. Eternity. He looked so clear and fresh, and he had never had a pain in his life. She had seen them when they had been there and back and they never looked like this again. "Already the returned hero," she said, "and don't I wish you were."

"When I learned the use of the bayonet in my first training camp," said Adam, "I gouged the vitals out of more sandbags and sacks of hay than I could keep track of. They kept bawling at us, 'Get him, get that Boche, stick him before he sticks you'—and we'd go for those sandbags like wildfire, and honestly, sometimes I felt a perfect fool for getting so worked up when I saw the sand trickling out. I used to wake up in the night sometimes feeling silly about it."

"I can imagine," said Miranda. "It's perfect nonsense." They lingered, unwilling to say good-by. After a little pause, Adam, as if keeping up the conversation, asked, "Do you know what the average life expectation of a sapping party[3] is after it hits the job?"

"Something speedy, I suppose."

"Just nine minutes," said Adam; "I read that in your own newspaper not a week ago."

"Make it ten and I'll come along," said Miranda.

"Not another second," said Adam, "exactly nine minutes, take it or leave it."

"Stop bragging," said Miranda. "Who figured that out?"

"A noncombatant," said Adam, "a fellow with rickets."

This seemed very comic, they laughed and leaned towards each other and Miranda heard herself being a little shrill. She wiped the tears from her eyes. "My, it's a funny war," she said; "isn't it? I laugh every time I think about it."

Adam took her hand in both of his and pulled a little at the tips of her gloves and sniffed them. "What nice perfume you have," he said, "and such a lot of it, too. I like a lot of perfume on gloves and hair," he said, sniffing again.

"I've got probably too much," she said. "I can't smell or see or hear today. I must have a fearful cold."

"Don't catch cold," said Adam; "my leave is nearly up and it will be the last, the very last." She moved her fingers in her gloves as he pulled at the fingers and turned her hands as if they were something new and curious and of great value, and she turned shy and quiet. She liked him, she liked him, and there was more than this but it was no good

---

[3]An engineering platoon engaged in undermining an enemy trench.

even imagining, because he was not for her nor for any woman, being beyond experience already, committed without any knowledge or act of his own to death. She took back her hands. "Good-by," she said finally, "until tonight."

She ran upstairs and looked back from the top. He was still watching her, and raised his hand without smiling. Miranda hardly ever saw anyone look back after he had said good-by. She could not help turning sometimes for one glimpse more of the person she had been talking with, as if that would save too rude and too sudden a snapping of even the lightest bond. But people hurried away, their faces already changed, fixed, in their straining towards their next stopping place, already absorbed in planning their next act or encounter. Adam was waiting as if he expected her to turn, and under his brows fixed in a strained frown, his eyes were very black.

At her desk she sat without taking off jacket or cap, slitting envelopes and pretending to read the letters. Only Chuck Rouncivale, the sports reporter, and Ye Towne Gossyp were sitting on her desk today, and them she liked having there. She sat on theirs when she pleased. Towney and Chuck were talking and they went on with it.

"They say," said Towney, "that it is really caused by germs brought by a German ship to Boston, a camouflaged ship, naturally, it didn't come in under its own colors. Isn't that ridiculous?"

"Maybe it was a submarine," said Chuck, "sneaking in from the bottom of the sea in the dead of night. Now that sounds better."

"Yes, it does," said Towney; "they always slip up somewhere in these details . . . and they think the germs were sprayed over the city— it started in Boston, you know—and somebody reported seeing a strange, thick, greasy-looking cloud float up out of Boston Harbor and spread slowly all over that end of town. I think it was an old woman who saw it."

"Should have been," said Chuck.

"I read it in a New York newspaper," said Towney; "so it's bound to be true."

Chuck and Miranda laughed so loudly at this that Bill stood up and glared at them. "Towney still reads the newspapers," explained Chuck.

"Well, what's funny about that?" asked Bill, sitting down again and frowning into the clutter before him.

"It was a noncombatant saw that cloud," said Miranda.

"Naturally," said Towney.

"Member of the Lusk Committee, maybe," said Miranda.

"The Angel of Mons," said Chuck, "or a dollar-a-year man."[4]

Miranda wished to stop hearing, and talking, she wished to think for just five minutes of her own about Adam, really to think about him, but there was no time. She had seen him first ten days ago, and since then they had been crossing streets together, darting between trucks and limousines and pushcarts and farm wagons; he had waited for her in doorways and in little restaurants that smelled of stale frying fat; they had eaten and danced to the urgent whine and bray of jazz orchestras, they had sat in dull theaters because Miranda was there to write a piece about the play. Once they had gone to the mountains and, leaving the car, had climbed a stony trail, and had come out on a ledge upon a flat stone, where they sat and watched the lights change on a valley landscape that was, no doubt, Miranda said, quite apocryphal— "We need not believe it, but it is fine poetry," she told him; they had leaned their shoulders together there, and had sat quite still, watching. On two Sundays they had gone to the geological museum, and had pored in shared fascination over bits of meteors, rock formations, fossilized tusks and trees, Indian arrows, grottoes from the silver and gold lodes. "Think of those old miners washing out their fortunes in little pans beside the streams," said Adam, "and inside the earth there was this—" and he had told her he liked better those things that took long to make; he loved airplanes too, all sorts of machinery, things carved out of wood or stone. He knew nothing much about them, but he recognized them when he saw them. He had confessed that he simply could not get through a book, any kind of book except textbooks on engineering; reading bored him to crumbs; he regretted now he hadn't brought his roadster, but he hadn't thought he would need a car; he loved driving, he wouldn't expect her to believe how many hundreds of miles he could get over in a day . . . he had showed her snapshots of himself at the wheel of his roadster; of himself sailing a boat, looking very free and windblown, all angles, hauling on the ropes; he would have joined the air force, but his mother had hysterics every time he mentioned it. She didn't seem to realize that dog fighting in the air was a good deal safer than sapping parties on the ground at night. But he

---

[4]The "Angel of Mons" was a patriotic myth referring to the supposed divine protection of a British retreat in the opening campaign of World War I. Dollar-a-year men were wealthy people who took government jobs in war operations and propaganda at that salary.

hadn't argued, because of course she did not realize about sapping parties. And here he was, stuck, on a plateau a mile high with no water for a boat and his car at home, otherwise they could really have had a good time. Miranda knew he was trying to tell her what kind of person he was when he had his machinery with him. She felt she knew pretty well what kind of person he was, and would have liked to tell him that if he thought he had left himself at home in a boat or an automobile, he was much mistaken. The telephones were ringing, Bill was shouting at somebody who kept saying, "Well, but listen, well, but listen—" but nobody was going to listen, of course, nobody. Old man Gibbons bellowed in despair, "Jarge, Jarge—"

"Just the same," Towney was saying in her most complacent patriotic voice. "Hut Service is a fine idea, and we should all volunteer even if they don't want us." Towney does well at this, thought Miranda, look at her; remembering the rose-colored sweater and the tight rebellious face in the cloakroom. Towney was now all open-faced glory and goodness, willing to sacrifice herself for her country. "After all," said Towney, "I *can* sing and dance well enough for the Little Theater, and I could write their letters for them, and at a pinch I might drive an ambulance. I have driven a Ford for years."

Miranda joined in: "Well, I can sing and dance too, but who's going to do the bed-making and the scrubbing up? Those huts are hard to keep, and it would be a dirty job and we'd be perfectly miserable; and as I've got a hard dirty job and am perfectly miserable, I'm going to stay at home."

"I think the women should keep out of it," said Chuck Rouncivale. "They just add skirts to the horrors of war." Chuck had bad lungs and fretted a good deal about missing the show. "I could have been there and back with a leg off by now; it would have served the old man right. Then he'd either have to buy his own hooch or sober up."

Miranda had seen Chuck on pay day giving the old man money for hooch. He was a good-humored ingratiating old scoundrel, too, that was the worst of him. He slapped his son on the back and beamed upon him with the bleared eye of paternal affection while he took his last nickel.

"It was Florence Nightingale ruined wars," Chuck went on. "What's the idea of petting soldiers and binding up their wounds and soothing their fevered brows? That's not war. Let 'em perish where they fall. That's what they're there for."

"You can talk," said Towney, with a slantwise glint at him.

"What's the idea?" asked Chuck, flushing and hunching his shoulders. "You know I've got this lung, or maybe half of it anyway by now."

"You're much too sensitive," said Towney. "I didn't mean a thing."

Bill had been raging about, chewing his half-smoked cigar, his hair standing up in a brush, his eyes soft and lambent but wild, like a stag's. He would never, thought Miranda, be more than fourteen years old if he lived for a century, which he would not, at the rate he was going. He behaved exactly like city editors in the moving pictures, even to the chewed cigar. Had he formed his style on the films, or had scenario writers seized once for all on the type Bill in its inarguable purity? Bill was shouting to Chuck: "*And if he comes back here take him up the alley and saw his head off by hand!*"

Chuck said, "He'll be back, don't worry." Bill said mildly, already off on another track, "Well, saw him off." Towney went to her own desk, but Chuck sat waiting amiably to be taken to the new vaudeville show. Miranda, with two tickets, always invited one of the reporters to go with her on Monday. Chuck was lavishly hardboiled and professional in his sports writing, but he had told Miranda that he didn't give a damn about sports, really; the job kept him out in the open, and paid him enough to buy the old man's hooch. He preferred shows and didn't see why women always had the job.

"Who does Bill want sawed today?" asked Miranda.

"That hoofer you panned in this morning's," said Chuck. "He was up here bright and early asking for the guy that writes up show business. He said he was going to take the goof who wrote that piece up the alley and bop him the nose. He said . . ."

"I hope he's gone," said Miranda; "I do hope he had to catch a train."

Chuck stood up and arranged his maroon-colored turtle-necked sweater, glanced down at the peasoup tweed plus fours and the hobnailed tan boots which he hoped would help to disguise the fact that he had a bad lung and didn't care for sports, and said, "He's long gone by now, don't worry. Let's get going; you're late as usual."

Miranda, facing about, almost stepped on the toes of a little drab man in a derby hat. He might have been a pretty fellow once, but now his mouth drooped where he had lost his side teeth, and his sad red-rimmed eyes had given up coquetry. A thin brown wave of hair was combed out with brilliantine and curled against the rim of the derby. He didn't move his feet, but stood planted with a kind of inert resistance, and asked Miranda: "Are you the so-called dramatic critic on this hick newspaper?"

"I'm afraid I am," said Miranda.

"Well," said the little man, "I'm just asking for one minute of your valuable time." His underlip shot out, he began with shaking hands to fish about in his waistcoat pocket. "I just hate to let you get away with it, that's all." He riffled through a collection of shabby newspaper clippings. "Just give these the once-over, will you? And then let me ask you if you think I'm gonna stand for being knocked by a tanktown critic," he said, in a toneless voice; "look here, here's Buffalo, Chicago, Saint Looey, Philadelphia, Frisco, besides New York. Here's the best publications in the business, *Variety*, the *Billboard*, they all broke down and admitted that Danny Dickerson knows his stuff. So you don't think so, hey? That's all I wanta ask you."

"No, I don't," said Miranda, as bluntly as she could, "and I can't stop to talk about it."

The little man leaned nearer, his voice shook as if he had been nervous for a long time. "Look here, what was there you didn't like about me? Tell me that."

Miranda said, "You shouldn't pay any attention at all. What does it matter what I think?"

"I don't care what you think, it ain't that," said the little man, "but these things get round and booking agencies back East don't know how it is out here. We get panned in the sticks and they think it's the same as getting panned in Chicago, see? They don't know the difference. They don't know that the more high class an act is the more the hick critics pan it. But I've been called the best in the business by the best in the business and I wanta know what you think is wrong with me."

Chuck said, "Come on, Miranda, curtain's going up." Miranda handed the little man his clippings, they were mostly ten years old, and tried to edge past him. He stepped before her again and said without much conviction, "If you was a man I'd knock your block off." Chuck got up at that and lounged over, taking his hands out of his pockets, and said, "Now you've done your song and dance you'd better get out. Get the hell out now before I throw you downstairs."

The little man pulled at the top of his tie, a small blue tie with red polka dots, slightly frayed at the knot. He pulled it straight and repeated as if he had rehearsed it, "Come out in the alley." The tears filled his thickened red lids. Chuck said, "Ah, shut up," and followed Miranda, who was running towards the stairs. He overtook her on the sidewalk. "I left him sniveling and shuffling his publicity trying to find the joker," said Chuck, "the poor old heel."

Miranda said, "There's too much of everything in this world just now. I'd like to sit down here on the curb, Chuck, and die, and never again see—I wish I could lose my memory and forget my own name . . . I wish—"

Chuck said, "Toughen up, Miranda. This is no time to cave in. Forget that fellow. For every hundred people in show business, there are ninety-nine like him. But you don't manage right, anyway. You bring it on yourself. All you have to do is play up the headliners, and you needn't even mention the also-rans. Try to keep in mind that Rypinsky has got show business cornered in this town; please Rypinsky and you'll please the advertising department, please them and you'll get a raise. Hand-in-glove, my poor dumb child, will you never learn?"

"I seem to keep learning all the wrong things," said Miranda, hopelessly.

"You do for a fact," Chuck told her cheerfully. "You are as good at it as I ever saw. Now do you feel better?"

"This is a rotten show you've invited me to," said Chuck. "Now what are you going to do about it? If I were writing it up, I'd—"

"Do write it up," said Miranda. "You write it up this time. I'm getting ready to leave, anyway, but don't tell anybody yet."

"You mean it? All my life," said Chuck, "I've yearned to be a so-called dramatic critic on a hick newspaper, and this is positively my first chance."

"Better take it," Miranda told him. "It may be your last." She thought, This is the beginning of the end of something. Something terrible is going to happen to me. I shan't need bread and butter where I'm going. I'll will it to Chuck, he has a venerable father to buy hooch for. I hope they let him have it. Oh, Adam, I hope I see you once more before I go under with whatever is the matter with me. "I wish the war were over," she said to Chuck, as if they had been talking about that. "I wish it were over and I wish it had never begun."

Chuck had got out his pad and pencil and was already writing his review. What she had said seemed safe enough but how would he take it? "I don't care how it started or when it ends," said Chuck, scribbling away, "I'm not going to be there."

All the rejected men talked like that, thought Miranda. War was the one thing they wanted, now they couldn't have it. Maybe they had wanted badly to go, some of them. All of them had a sidelong eye for the women they talked with about it, a guarded resentment which said, "Don't pin a white feather on me, you bloodthirsty female. I've offered my meat to the crows and they won't have it." The worst thing about war for the stay-at-homes is there isn't anyone to talk to any more. The Lusk Committee will get you if you don't watch out. Bread will win the war. Work will win, sugar will win, peach pits will win the war. Nonsense. *Not* nonsense, I tell you, there's some kind of valuable high explosive to be got out of peach pits. So all the happy housewives hurry during the canning season to lay their baskets of peach pits on the altar of their country. It keeps them busy and makes them feel useful, and all these women running wild with the men away are dangerous, if they aren't given something to keep their little minds out of mischief. So rows of young girls, the intact cradles of the future, with their pure serious faces framed becomingly in Red Cross wimples, roll cockeyed bandages that will never reach a base hospital, and knit sweaters that will never warm a manly chest, their minds dwelling lovingly on all the blood and mud and the next dance at the Acanthus Club for the officers of the flying corps. Keeping still and quiet will win the war.

"I'm simply not going to be there," said Chuck, absorbed in his review. No, Adam will be there, thought Miranda. She slipped down in the chair and leaned her head against the dusty plush, closed her eyes and faced for one instant that was a lifetime the certain, the overwhelming and awful knowledge that there was nothing at all ahead for Adam and for her. Nothing. She opened her eyes and held her hands together palms up, gazing at them and trying to understand oblivion.

"Now look at this," said Chuck, for the lights had come on and the audience was rustling and talking again. "I've got it all done, even before the headliner comes on. It's old Stella Mayhew, and she's always good, she's been good for forty years, and she's going to sing 'O the blues ain't nothin' but the easy-going heart disease.' That's all you need to know about her. Now just glance over this. Would you be willing to sign it?"

Miranda took the pages and stared at them conscientiously, turning them over, she hoped, at the right moment, and gave them back. "Yes, Chuck, yes, I'd sign that. But I won't. We must tell Bill you wrote it, because it's your start, maybe."

"You don't half appreciate it," said Chuck. "You read it too fast. Here, listen to this—" and he began to mutter excitedly. While he was reading she watched his face. It was a pleasant face with some kind of spark of life in it, and a good severity in the modeling of the brow above the nose. For the first time since she had known him she wondered what Chuck was thinking about. He looked preoccupied and unhappy, he wasn't so frivolous as he sounded. The people were crowding into the aisle, bringing out their cigarette cases ready to strike a match the instant they reached the lobby; women with waved hair clutched at their wraps, men stretched their chins to ease them of their stiff collars, and Chuck said, "We might as well go now." Miranda, buttoning her jacket, stepped into the moving crowd, thinking, What did I ever know about them? There must be a great many of them here who think as I do, and we dare not say a word to each other of our desperation, we are speechless animals letting ourselves be destroyed, and why? Does anybody here believe the things we say to each other?

Stretched in unease on the ridge of the wicker couch in the cloakroom, Miranda waited for time to pass and leave Adam with her. Time seemed to proceed with more than usual eccentricity, leaving twilight gaps in her mind for thirty minutes which seemed like a second, and then hard flashes of light that shone clearly on her watch proving that three minutes is an intolerable stretch of waiting, as if she were hanging by her thumbs. At last it was reasonable to imagine Adam stepping out of the house in the early darkness into blue mist that might soon be rain, he would be on the way, and there was nothing to think about him, after all. There was only the wish to see him and the fear, the present threat, of not seeing him again; for every step they took towards each other seemed perilous, drawing them apart instead of together, as a swimmer in spite of his most determined strokes is yet drawn slowly backward by the tide. "I don't want to love," she would think in spite of herself, "not Adam, there is no time and we are not ready for it and yet this is all we have—"

And there he was on the sidewalk, with his foot on the first step, and Miranda almost ran down to meet him. Adam, holding her hands, asked, "Do you feel well now? Are you hungry? Are you tired? Will you feel like dancing after the show?"

"Yes to everything," said Miranda, "yes, yes. . . ." Her head was like a feather, and she steadied herself on his arm. The mist was still mist that might be rain later, and though the air was sharp and clean in her mouth, it did not, she decided, make breathing any easier. "I hope the show is good, or at least funny," she told him, "but I promise nothing."

It was a long, dreary play, but Adam and Miranda sat very quietly together waiting patiently for it to be over. Adam carefully and seriously pulled off her glove and held her hand as if he were accustomed to holding her hand in theaters. Once they turned and their eyes met, but only once, and the two pairs of eyes were equally steady and noncommittal. A deep tremor set up in Miranda, and she set about resisting herself methodically as if she were closing windows and doors and fastening down curtains against a rising storm. Adam sat watching the monotonous play with a strange shining excitement, his face quite fixed and still.

When the curtain rose for the third act, the third act did not take place at once. There was instead disclosed a backdrop almost covered with an American flag improperly and disrespectfully exposed, nailed at each upper corner, gathered in the middle and nailed again, sagging dustily. Before it posed a local dollar-a-year man, now doing his bit as a Liberty Bond salesman. He was an ordinary man past middle life, with a neat little melon buttoned into his trousers and waistcoat, an opinionated tight mouth, a face and figure in which nothing could be read save the inept sensual record of fifty years. But for once in his life he was an important fellow in an impressive situation, and he reveled, rolling his words in an actorish tone.

"Looks like a penguin," said Adam. They moved, smiled at each other, Miranda reclaimed her hand, Adam folded his together and they prepared to wear their way again through the same old moldy speech with the same old dusty backdrop. Miranda tried not to listen, but she heard. These vile Huns—glorious Belleau Wood—our keyword is Sacrifice—Martyred Belgium—give till it hurts—our noble boys Over There—Big Berthas—the death of civilization—the Boche—

"My head aches," whispered Miranda. "Oh, why won't he hush?"

"He won't," whispered Adam. "I'll get you some aspirin."

"In Flanders Field the poppies grow, Between the crosses row on row"—"He's getting into the home stretch," whispered Adam—atrocities, innocent babes hoisted on Boche bayonets—your child and my child—if our children are spared these things, then let us say with all reverence that these dead have not died in vain—the war, the *war*, the WAR to end WAR, war for Democracy, for humanity, safe world forever and ever—and to prove our faith in Democracy to each other, and to the world, let everybody get together and buy Liberty Bonds and do without sugar and wool socks—was that it? Miranda asked herself, Say that over, I didn't catch the last line. Did you mention Adam? If you didn't I'm not interested. What about Adam, you little pig? And what are we going to sing this time, "Tipperary" or "There's a Long, Long Trail"? Oh, please do let the show go on and get over with. I must write a piece about it before I can go dancing with Adam and we have no time. Coal, oil, iron, gold, international finance, why don't you tell us about them, you little liar?

The audience rose and sang, "There's a Long, Long Trail A-winding," their opened mouths black and faces pallid in the reflected footlights; some of the faces grimaced and wept and had shining streaks like snail's tracks on them. Adam and Miranda joined in at the tops of their voices, grinning shamefacedly at each other once or twice.

In the street, they lit their cigarettes and walked slowly as always. "Just another nasty old man who would like to see the young ones killed," said Miranda in a low voice; "the tom-cats try to eat the little tom-kittens, you know. They don't fool you really, do they, Adam?" The young people were talking like that about the business by then. They felt they were seeing pretty clearly through that game. She went on, "I hate these potbellied baldheads, too fat, too old, too cowardly, to go to war themselves, they know they're safe; it's you they are sending instead—"

Adam turned eyes of genuine surprise upon her. "Oh, *that* one," he said. "Now what could the poor sap do if they did take him? It's not his fault," he explained, "he can't do anything but talk." His pride in his youth, his forbearance and tolerance and contempt for that unlucky being breathed out of his very pores as he strolled, straight and relaxed in his strength. "What *could* you expect of him, Miranda?"

She spoke his name often, and he spoke hers rarely. The little shock of pleasure the sound of her name in his mouth gave her stopped her answer. For a moment she hesitated, and began at another point of attack. "Adam," she said, "the worst of war is the fear and suspicion and the awful expression in all the eyes you meet . . . as if they had pulled down the shutters over their minds and their hearts and were peering out at you, ready to leap if you make one gesture or say one word they do not understand instantly. It frightens me; I live in fear too, and no one should have to live in fear. It's the skulking about, and the lying. It's what war does to the mind and the heart, Adam, and you can't separate these two—what it does to them is worse than what it can do to the body."

Adam said soberly, after a moment, "Oh, yes, but suppose one comes back whole? The mind and the heart sometimes get another chance, but if anything happens to the poor old human frame, why, it's just out of luck, that's all."

"Oh, yes," mimicked Miranda. "It's just out of luck, that's all."

"If I didn't go," said Adam, in a matter-of-fact voice, "I couldn't look myself in the face."

So that's all settled. With her fingers flattened on his arm, Miranda was silent, thinking about Adam. No, there was no resentment or re-volt in him. Pure, she thought, all the way through, flawless, complete, as the sacrificial lamb must be. The sacrificial lamb strode along casually, accommodating his long pace to hers, keeping her on the inside of the walk in the good American style, helping her across street corners as if she were a cripple—"I hope we don't come to a mud puddle, he'll carry me over it"—giving off whiffs of tobacco smoke, a manly smell of scentless soap, freshly cleaned leather and freshly washed skin, breathing through his nose and carrying his chest easily. He threw back his head and smiled into the sky which still misted, promising rain. "Oh, boy," he said, "what a night. Can't you hurry that review of yours so we can get started?"

He waited for her before a cup of coffee in the restaurant next to the pressroom, nicknamed The Greasy Spoon. When she came down at last, freshly washed and combed and powdered, she saw Adam first, sitting near the dingy big window, face turned to the street, but looking down. It was an extraordinary face, smooth and fine and golden in the shabby light, but now set in a blind melancholy, a look of pained suspense and disillusion. For just one split second she got a glimpse of Adam when he would have been older, the face of the man he would not live to be. He saw her then, rose, and the bright glow was there.

Adam pulled their chairs together at their table; they drank hot tea and listened to the orchestra jazzing "Pack Up Your Troubles."

"In an old kit bag, and smoil, smoil, smoil," shouted half a dozen boys under the draft age, gathered around a table near the orchestra. They yelled incoherently, laughed in great hysterical bursts of something that appeared to be merriment, and passed around under the tablecloth flat bottles containing a clear liquid—for in this western city founded and built by roaring drunken miners, no one was allowed to take his alcohol openly—splashed it into their tumblers of ginger ale, and went on singing, "It's a Long Way to Tipperary." When the tune changed to "Madelon," Adam said, "Let's dance." It was a tawdry little place, crowded and hot and full of smoke, but there was nothing better. The music was gay; and life is completely crazy anyway, thought Miranda, so what does it matter? This is what we have, Adam and I, this is all we're going to get, this is the way it is with us. She wanted to say, "Adam, come out of your dream and listen to me. I have pains in my chest and my head and my heart and they're real. I am in pain all over, and you are in such danger as I can't bear to think about, and why can we not save each other?" When her hand tightened on his shoulder his arm tightened about her waist instantly, and stayed there, holding firmly. They said nothing but smiled continually at each other, odd changing smiles as though they had found a new language. Miranda, her face near Adam's shoulder, noticed a dark young pair sitting at a corner table, each with an arm around the waist of the other, their heads together, their eyes staring at the same thing, whatever it was, that hovered in space before them. Her right hand lay on the table, his hand over it, and her face was a blur with weeping. Now and then he raised her hand and kissed it, and set it down and held it, and her eyes would fill again. They were not shameless, they had merely forgotten where they were, or they had no other place to go, perhaps. They said not a word, and the small pantomime repeated itself, like a melancholy short film running monotonously over and over again. Miranda envied them. She envied that girl. At least she can weep if that helps, and he does not even have to ask, What is the matter? Tell me. They had cups of coffee before them, and after a long while—Miranda and Adam had danced and sat down again twice—when the coffee was quite cold, they drank it suddenly, then embraced as before, without a word and scarcely a glance at each other. Something was done and settled between them, at least; it was enviable, enviable, that they could sit quietly together and have the same expression on their faces while they looked into the hell they shared, no matter what kind of hell, it was theirs, they were together.

At the table nearest Adam and Miranda a young woman was leaning on her elbow, telling her young man a story. "And I don't like him because he's too fresh. He kept on asking me to take a drink and I kept telling him, I don't drink and he said, Now look here, I want a drink the worst way and I think it's mean of you not to drink with me, I can't sit up here and drink by myself, he said. I told him, You're not by yourself in the first place; I like that, I said, and if you want a drink go ahead and have it, I told him, why drag *me* in? So he called the waiter and ordered ginger ale and two glasses and drank straight ginger ale like I always do but he poured a shot of hooch in his. He was awfully proud of that hooch, said he made it himself out of potatoes. Nice homemade likker, warm from the pipe, he told me, three drops of this and your ginger ale will taste like Mumm's Extry. But I said, No, and I mean no, can't you get that through your bean? He took another drink and said, Ah, come on, honey, don't be so stubborn, this'll make your shimmy shake. So I just got tired of the argument, and I said, I don't need to drink, to shake my shimmy, I can strut my stuff on tea, I said. Well, why don't you then, he wanted to know, and I just told him—"

She knew she had been asleep for a long time when all at once without even a warning footstep or creak of the door hinge, Adam was in the room turning on the light, and she knew it was he, though at first she was blinded and turned her head away. He came over at once and sat on the side of the bed and began to talk as if he were going on with something they had been talking about before. He crumpled a square of paper and tossed it in the fireplace.

"You didn't get my note," he said. "I left it under the door. I was called back suddenly to camp for a lot of inoculations. They kept me longer than expected, I was late. I called the office and they told me you were not coming in today. I called Miss Hobbe here and she said you were in bed and couldn't come to the telephone. Did she give you my message?"

"No," said Miranda drowsily, "but I think I have been asleep all day. Oh, I do remember. There was a doctor here. Bill sent him. I was at the telephone once, for Bill told me he would send an ambulance and have me taken to the hospital. The doctor tapped my chest and left a prescription and said he would be back, but he hasn't come."

"Where is it, the prescription?" asked Adam.

"I don't know. He left it, though, I saw him."

Adam moved about searching the tables and the mantelpiece. "Here it is," he said. "I'll be back in a few minutes. I must look for an all-night drug store. It's after one o'clock. Good-by."

Good-by, good-by. Miranda watched the door where he had disappeared for quite a while, then closed her eyes, and thought, When I am not here I cannot remember anything about this room where I have lived for nearly a year, except that the curtains are too thin and there was never any way of shutting out the morning light. Miss Hobbe had promised heavier curtains, but they had never appeared. When Miranda in her dressing gown had been at the telephone that morning, Miss Hobbe had passed through, carrying a tray. She was a little red-haired nervously friendly creature, and her manner said all too plainly that the place was not paying and she was on the ragged edge.

"My dear *child*," she said sharply, with a glance at Miranda's attire, "what is the matter?"

Miranda, with the receiver to her ear, said, "Influenza, I think."

"*Horrors*," said Miss Hobbe, in a whisper, and the tray wavered in her hands. "Go back to bed at once . . . go at *once!*"

"I must talk to Bill first," Miranda had told her, and Miss Hobbe had hurried on and had not returned. Bill had shouted directions at her, promising everything, doctor, nurse, ambulance, hospital, her check every week as usual, everything, but she was to get back to bed and stay there. She dropped into bed, thinking that Bill was the only person she had ever seen who actually tore his own hair when he was excited enough . . . I suppose I should ask to be sent home, she thought, it's a respectable old custom to inflict your death on the family if you can manage it. No, I'll stay here, this is my business, but not in this room, I hope . . . I wish I were in the cold mountains in the snow, that's what I should like best; and all about her rose the measured ranges of the Rockies wearing their perpetual snow, their majestic blue laurels of cloud, chilling her to the bone with their sharp breath. Oh, no, I must have warmth—and her memory turned and roved after another place she had known first and loved best, that now she could see only in drifting fragments of palm and cedar, dark shadows and a sky that warmed without dazzling, as this strange sky had dazzled without warming her; there was the long slow wavering of gray moss in the drowsy oak shade, the spacious hovering of buzzards overhead, the smell of crushed water herbs along a bank, and without warning a broad tranquil river into which flowed all the rivers she had known. The walls shelved away in one deliberate silent movement on either side, and a tall sailing ship was moored near by, with a gangplank weathered to blackness touching the foot of her bed. Back of the ship was jungle and even as it appeared before her, she knew it was all she had ever read or had been told or felt or thought about jungles; a writhing terribly alive and secret place of death, creeping with tangles of spotted serpents, rainbow-colored birds with malign eyes, leopards with humanly wise faces and extravagantly crested lions; screaming long-armed monkeys tumbling among broad fleshy leaves that glowed with sulphur-colored light and exuded the ichor of death, and rotting trunks of unfamiliar trees sprawled in crawling slime. Without surprise, watching from her pillow, she saw herself run swiftly down this gangplank to the slanting deck, and standing there, she leaned on the rail and waved gaily to herself in bed, and the slender ship spread its wings and sailed away into the jungle. The air trembled with the shattering scream and the hoarse bellow of voices all crying together, rolling and colliding above her like ragged storm-clouds, and the words became two words only rising and falling and clamoring about her head. Danger, danger, danger, the voices said, and War, war, war. There was her door half open, Adam standing with his hand on the knob, and Miss Hobbe with her face all out of shape with terror was crying shrilly, "I tell you, they must come for her *now*, or I'll put her on the sidewalk . . . I tell you, this is a plague, a plague, my God, and I've got a houseful of people to think about!"

Adam said, "I know that. They'll come for her tomorrow morning."

"Tomorrow morning, my God, they'd better come now!"

"They can't get an ambulance," said Adam, "and there aren't any beds. And we can't find a doctor or a nurse. They're all busy. That's all there is to it. You stay out of the room, and I'll look after her."

"Yes, you'll look after her, I can see that," said Miss Hobbe, in a particularly unpleasant tone.

"Yes, that's what I said," answered Adam, drily, "and you keep out."

He closed the door carefully. He was carrying an assortment of misshapen packages, and his face was astonishingly impassive.

"Did you hear that?" he asked, leaning over and speaking very quietly.

"Most of it," said Miranda, "It's a nice prospect, isn't it?"

"I've got your medicine," said Adam, "and you're to begin with it this minute. She can't put you out."

"So it's really as bad as that," said Miranda.

"It's as bad as anything can be," said Adam, "all the theaters and nearly all the shops and restaurants are closed, and the streets have been full of funerals all day and ambulances all night—"

"But not one for me," said Miranda, feeling hilarious and lightheaded. She sat up and beat her pillow into shape and reached for her robe. "I'm glad you're here, I've been having a nightmare. Give me a cigarette, will you, and light one for yourself and open all the windows and sit near one of them. You're running a risk," she told him, "don't you know that? Why do you do it?"

"Never mind," said Adam, "take your medicine," and offered her two large cherry-colored pills. She swallowed them promptly and instantly vomited them up. *"Do* excuse me," she said, beginning to laugh. "I'm so sorry." Adam without a word and with a very concerned expression washed her face with a wet towel, gave her some cracked ice from one of the packages, and firmly offered her two more pills. "That's what they always did at home," she explained to him, "and it worked." Crushed with humiliation, she put her hands over her face and laughed again, painfully.

"There are two more kinds yet," said Adam, pulling her hands from her face and lifting her chin. "You've hardly begun. And I've got other things, like orange juice and ice cream—they told me to feed you ice cream—and coffee in a thermos bottle, and a thermometer. You have to work through the whole lot so you'd better take it easy."

"This time last night we were dancing," said Miranda, and drank something from a spoon. Her eyes followed him about the room, as he did things for her with an absent-minded face, like a man alone; now and again he would come back, and slipping his hand under her head, would hold a cup or a tumbler to her mouth, and she drank, and followed him with her eyes again, without a clear notion of what was happening.

"Adam," she said, "I've just thought of something. Maybe they forgot St. Luke's Hospital. Call the sisters there and ask them not to be so selfish with their silly old rooms. Tell them I only want a very small dark ugly one for three days, or less. Do try them, Adam."

He believed, apparently, that she was still more or less in her right mind, for she heard him at the telephone explaining in his deliberate voice. He was back again almost at once, saying, "This seems to be my day for getting mixed up with peevish old maids. The sister said that even if they had a room you couldn't have it without doctor's orders. But they didn't have one, anyway. She was pretty sour about it."

"Well," said Miranda in a thick voice, "I think that's abominably rude and mean, don't you?" She sat up with a wild gesture of both arms, and began to retch again, violently.

"Hold it, as you were," called Adam, fetching the basin. He held her head, washed her face and hands with ice water, put her head straight on the pillow, and went over and looked out of the window. "Well," he said at last, sitting beside her again, "they haven't got a room. They haven't got a bed. They haven't even got a baby crib, the way she talked. So I think that's straight enough, and we may as well dig in."

"Isn't the ambulance coming?"

"Tomorrow, maybe."

He took off his tunic and hung it on the back of a chair. Kneeling before the fireplace, he began carefully to set kindling sticks in the shape of an Indian tepee, with a little paper in the center for them to lean upon. He lighted this and placed other sticks upon them, and larger bits of wood. When they were going nicely he added still heavier wood, and coal a few lumps at a time, until there was a good blaze, and a fire that would not need rekindling. He rose and dusted his hands together, the fire illuminated him from the back and his hair shone.

"Adam," said Miranda, "I think you're very beautiful." He laughed out at this, and shook his head at her. "What a hell of a word," he said, "for me." "It was the first that occurred to me," she said, drawing up on her elbow to catch the warmth of the blaze. "That's a good job, that fire."

He sat on the bed again, dragging up a chair and putting his feet on the rungs. They smiled at each other for the first time since he had come in that night. "How do you feel now?" he asked.

"Better, much better," she told him. "Let's talk. Let's tell each other what we meant to do."

"You tell me first," said Adam. "I want to know about you."

"You'd get the notion I had a very sad life," she said, "and perhaps it was, but I'd be glad enough to have it now. If I could have it back, it would be easy to be happy about almost anything at all. That's not true, but that's the way I feel now." After a pause, she said, "There's nothing to tell, after all, if it ends now, for all this time I was getting ready for something that was going to happen later, when the time came. So now it's nothing much."

"But it must have been worth having until now, wasn't it?" he asked seriously as if it were something important to know.

"Not if this is all," she repeated obstinately.

"Weren't you ever—happy?" asked Adam, and he was plainly afraid of the word; he was shy of it as he was of the word *love*, he seemed never to have spoken it before, and was uncertain of its sound or meaning.

"I don't know," she said, "I just lived and never thought about it. I remember things I liked, though, and things I hoped for."

"I was going to be an electrical engineer," said Adam. He stopped short. "And I shall finish up when I get back," he added, after a moment.

"Don't you love being alive?" asked Miranda. "Don't you love weather and the colors at different times of the day, and all the sounds and noises like children screaming in the next lot, and automobile horns and little bands playing in the street and the smell of food cooking?"

"I love to swim, too," said Adam.

"So do I," said Miranda; "we never did swim together."

"Do you remember any prayers?" she asked him suddenly. "Did you ever learn anything at Sunday School?"

"Not much," confessed Adam without contrition. "Well, the Lord's Prayer."

"Yes, and there's Hail Mary," she said, "and the really useful one beginning, I confess to Almighty God and to blessed Mary ever virgin and to the holy Apostles Peter and Paul—"

"Catholic," he commented.

"Prayers just the same, you big Methodist. I'll bet you *are* a Methodist."

"No, Presbyterian."

"Well, what others do you remember?"

"Now I lay me down to sleep—" said Adam.

"Yes, that one, and Blessed Jesus meek and mild—you see that my religious education wasn't neglected either. I even know a prayer beginning O Apollo.[5] Want to hear it?"

"No," said Adam, "you're making fun."

"I'm not," said Miranda, "I'm trying to keep from going to sleep. I'm afraid to go to sleep, I may not wake up. Don't let me go to sleep, Adam. Do you know Matthew, Mark, Luke and John? Bless the bed I lie upon?"

"If I should die before I wake, I pray the Lord my soul to take. Is that it?" asked Adam. "It doesn't sound right, somehow."

"Light me a cigarette, please, and move over and sit near the window. We keep forgetting about fresh air. You must have it." He lighted the cigarette and held it to her lips. She took it between her fingers and dropped it under the edge of her pillow. He found it and crushed it out in the saucer under the water tumbler. Her head swam in darkness for an instant, cleared, and she sat up in panic, throwing off the covers and breaking into a sweat. Adam leaped up with an alarmed face, and almost at once was holding a cup of hot coffee to her mouth.

"You must have some too," she told him, quiet again, and they sat huddled together on the edge of the bed, drinking coffee in silence.

Adam said, "You must lie down again. You're awake now."

"Let's sing," said Miranda. "I know an old spiritual, I can remember some of the words." She spoke in a natural voice. "I'm fine now." She began in a hoarse whisper, " 'Pale horse, pale rider, done taken my lover away . . .' Do you know that song?"

"Yes," said Adam, "I heard Negroes in Texas sing it, in an oil field."

"I heard them sing it in a cotton field," she said; "it's a good song."

They sang that line together. "But I can't remember what comes next," said Adam.

" 'Pale horse, pale rider,' " said Miranda, "(We really need a good banjo) 'done taken my lover away—' " Her voice cleared and she said, "But we ought to get on with it. What's the next line?"

"There's a lot more to it than that," said Adam, "about forty verses, the rider done taken away mammy, pappy, brother, sister, the whole family besides the lover—"

"But not the singer, not yet," said Miranda. "Death always leaves

---

[5]Apollo, the Greek god of healing, sent and ended plagues.

one singer to mourn. 'Death,' " she sang, " 'oh, leave one singer to mourn—' "

" 'Pale horse, pale rider,' " chanted Adam, coming in on the beat, " 'done taken my lover away!' (I think we're good, I think we ought to get up an act—)"

"Go in Hut Service," said Miranda, "entertain the poor defenseless heroes Over There."

"We'll play banjos," said Adam; "I always wanted to play the banjo."

Miranda sighed, and lay back on the pillow and thought, I must give up, I can't hold out any longer. There was only that pain, only that room, and only Adam. There were no longer any multiple planes of living, no tough filaments of memory and hope pulling taut backwards and forwards holding her upright between them. There was only this one moment and it was a dream of time, and Adam's face, very near hers, eyes still and intent, was a shadow, and there was to be nothing more. . . .

"Adam," she said out of the heavy soft darkness that drew her down, down, "I love you, and I was hoping you would say that to me, too."

He lay down beside her with his arm under her shoulder, and pressed his smooth face against hers, his mouth moved towards her mouth and stopped. "Can you hear what I am saying? . . . What do you think I have been trying to tell you all this time?"

She turned towards him, the cloud cleared and she saw his face for an instant. He pulled the covers about her and held her, and said, "Go to sleep, darling, darling, if you will go to sleep now for one hour I will wake you up and bring you hot coffee and tomorrow we will find somebody to help. I love you, go to sleep—"

Almost with no warning at all, she floated into the darkness, holding his hand, in sleep that was not sleep but clear evening light in a small green wood, an angry dangerous wood full of inhuman concealed voices singing sharply like the whine of arrows and she saw Adam transfixed by a flight of these singing arrows that struck him in the heart and passed shrilly cutting their path through the leaves. Adam fell straight back before her eyes, and rose again unwounded and alive; another flight of arrows loosed from the invisible bow struck him again and he fell, and yet he was there before her untouched in a perpetual death and resurrection. She threw herself before him, angrily and self-ishly she interposed between him and the track of the arrow, crying, No, no, like a child cheated in a game, It's my turn now, why must you always be the one to die? and the arrows struck her cleanly through the heart and through his body and he lay dead, and she still lived, and the wood whistled and sang and shouted, every branch and leaf and blade of grass had its own terrible accusing voice. She ran then, and Adam caught her in the middle of the room, running, and said, "Darling, I must have been asleep too. What happened, you screamed terribly?"

After he had helped her to settle again, she sat with her knees drawn up under her chin, resting her head on her folded arms and began carefully searching for her words because it was important to explain clearly. "It was a very odd sort of dream, I don't know why it could have frightened me. There was something about an old-fashioned valentine. There were two hearts carved on a tree, pierced by the same arrow—you know, Adam—"

"Yes, I know, honey," he said in the gentlest sort of way, and sat kissing her on the cheek and forehead with a kind of accustomedness, as if he had been kissing her for years, "one of those lace paper things."

"Yes, and yet they were alive, and were us, you understand—this doesn't seem to be quite the way it was, but it was something like that. It was in a wood—"

"Yes," said Adam. He got up and put on his tunic and gathered up the thermos bottle. "I'm going back to that little stand and get us some ice cream and hot coffee," he told her, "and I'll be back in five minutes, and you keep quiet. Good-by for five minutes," he said, holding her chin in the palm of his hand and trying to catch her eye, "and you be very quiet."

"Good-by," she said. "I'm awake again." But she was not, and the two alert young internes from the County hospital who had arrived, after frantic urgings from the noisy city editor of the Blue Mountain *News*, to carry her away in a police ambulance, decided that they had better go down and get the stretcher. Their voices roused her, she sat up, got out of bed at once and stood glancing about brightly. "Why, you're all right," said the darker and stouter of the two young men, both extremely fit and competent-looking in their white clothes, each with a flower in his buttonhole. "I'll just carry you." He unfolded a white blanket and wrapped it around her. She gathered up the folds and asked, "But where is Adam?" taking hold of the doctor's arm. He laid a hand on her drenched forehead, shook his head, and gave her a shrewd look. "Adam?"

"Yes," Miranda told him, lowering her voice confidentially, "he was here and now he is gone."

"Oh, he'll be back," the interne told her easily, "he's just gone round the block to get cigarettes. Don't worry about Adam. He's the least of your troubles."

"Will he know where to find me?" she asked, still holding back.

"We'll leave him a note," said the interne. "Come now, it's time we got out of here."

He lifted and swung her up to his shoulder. "I feel very badly," she told him; "I don't know why."

"I'll bet you do," said he, stepping out carefully, the other doctor going before them, and feeling for the first step of the stairs. "Put your arms around my neck," he instructed her. "It won't do you any harm and it's a great help to me."

"What's your name?" Miranda asked as the other doctor opened the front door and they stepped out into the frosty sweet air.

"Hildesheim," he said, in the tone of one humoring a child.

"Well, Dr. Hildesheim, aren't we in a pretty mess?"

"We certainly are," said Dr. Hildesheim.

The second young interne, still quite fresh and dapper in his white coat, though his carnation was withering at the edges, was leaning over listening to her breathing through a stethoscope, whistling thinly, "There's a Long, Long Trail—" From time to time he tapped her ribs smartly with two fingers, whistling. Miranda observed him for a few moments until she fixed his bright busy hazel eye not four inches from hers. "I'm not unconscious," she explained, "I know what I want to say." Then to her horror she heard herself babbling nonsense, knowing it was nonsense though she could not hear what she was saying. The flicker of attention in the eye near her vanished, the second interne went on tapping and listening, hissing softly under his breath.

"I wish you'd stop whistling," she said clearly. The sound stopped. "It's a beastly tune," she added. Anything, anything at all to keep her small hold on the life of human beings, a clear line of communication, no matter what, between her and the receding world. "Please let me see Dr. Hildesheim," she said, "I have something important to say to him. I must say it now." The second interne vanished. He did not walk away, he fled into the air without a sound, and Dr. Hildesheim's face appeared in his stead.

"Dr. Hildesheim, I want to ask you about Adam."

"That young man? He's been here, and left you a note, and has gone again," said Dr. Hildesheim, "and he'll be back tomorrow and the day after." His tone was altogether too merry and flippant.

"I don't believe you," said Miranda, bitterly, closing her lips and eyes and hoping she might not weep.

"Miss Tanner," called the doctor, "have you got that note?"

Miss Tanner appeared beside her, handed her an unsealed envelope, took it back, unfolded the note and gave it to her.

"I can't see it," said Miranda, after a pained search of the page full of hasty scratches in black ink.

"Here, I'll read it," said Miss Tanner. "It says, 'They came and took you while I was away and now they will not let me see you. Maybe tomorrow they will, with my love, Adam,' " read Miss Tanner in a firm dry voice, pronouncing the words distinctly. "Now, do you see?" she asked soothingly.

Miranda, hearing the words one by one, forgot them one by one. "Oh, read it again, what does it say?" she called out over the silence that pressed upon her, reaching towards the dancing words that just escaped as she almost touched them. "That will do," said Dr. Hildesheim, calmly authoritarian. "Where is that bed?"

"There is no bed yet," said Miss Tanner, as if she said, We are short of oranges. Dr. Hildesheim said, "Well, we'll manage something," and Miss Tanner drew the narrow trestle with bright crossed metal supports and small rubbery wheels into a deep jut of the corridor, out of the way of the swift white figures darting about, whirling and skimming like water flies all in silence. The white walls rose sheer as cliffs, a dozen frosted moons followed each other in perfect self-possession down a white lane and dropped mutely one by one into a snowy abyss.

What is this whiteness and silence but the absence of pain? Miranda lay lifting the nap of her white blanket softly between eased fingers, watching a dance of tall deliberate shadows moving behind a wide screen of sheets spread upon a frame. It was there, near her, on her side of the wall where she could see it clearly and enjoy it, and it was so beautiful she had no curiosity as to its meaning. Two dark figures nodded, bent, curtsied to each other, retreated and bowed again, lifted long arms and spread great hands against the shadow of the screen; then with a single round movement, the sheets were folded back, disclosing two speechless men in white, standing, and another speechless man in white, lying on the bare springs of a white iron bed. The man on the springs was swathed smoothly from head to foot in white, with folded bands across the face, and a large stiff bow like merry rabbit ears dangled at the crown of his head.

The two living men lifted a mattress standing hunched against the wall, spread it tenderly and exactly over the dead man. Wordless and white they vanished down the corridor, pushing the wheeled bed before them. It had been an entrancing and leisurely spectacle, but now it was over. A pallid white fog rose in their wake insinuatingly and floated before Miranda's eyes, a fog in which was concealed all terror and all weariness, all the wrung faces and twisted backs and broken feet of abused, outraged living things, all the shapes of their confused pain and their estranged hearts; the fog might part at any moment and loose the horde of human torments. She put up her hand and said, Not yet, not yet, but it was too late. The fog parted and two executioners, white clad, moved towards her pushing between them with marvelously deft and practiced hands the misshapen figure of an old man in filthy rags whose scanty beard waggled under his opened mouth as he bowed his back and braced his feet to resist and delay the fate they had prepared for him. In a high weeping voice he was trying to explain to them that the crime of which he was accused did not merit the punishment he was about to receive; and except for this whining cry there was silence as they advanced. The soiled cracked bowls of the old man's hands were held before him beseechingly as a beggar's as he said, "Before God I am not guilty," but they held his arms and drew him onward, passed, and were gone.

The road to death is a long march beset with all evils, and the heart fails little by little at each new terror, the bones rebel at each step, the mind sets up its own bitter resistance and to what end? The barriers sink one by one, and no covering of the eyes shuts out the landscape of disaster, nor the sight of crimes committed there. Across the field came Dr. Hildesheim, his face a skull beneath his German helmet, carrying a naked infant writhing on the point of his bayonet, and a huge stone pot marked Poison in Gothic letters. He stopped before the well that Miranda remembered in a pasture on her father's farm, a well once dry but now bubbling with living water, and into its pure depths he threw the child and the poison, and the violated water sank back soundlessly into the earth. Miranda, screaming, ran with her arms above her head; her voice echoed and came back to her like a wolf's howl, Hildesheim is a Boche, a spy, a Hun, kill him, kill him before he kills you. . . . She woke howling, she heard the foul words accusing Dr. Hildesheim tumbling from her mouth; opened her eyes and knew she was in a bed in a small white room, with Dr. Hildesheim sitting beside her, two firm fingers on her pulse. His hair was brushed sleekly and his buttonhole flower was fresh. Stars gleamed through the window, and Dr. Hildesheim seemed to be gazing at them with no particular expression, his stethoscope dangling around his neck. Miss Tanner stood at the foot of the bed writing something on a chart.

"Hello," said Dr. Hildesheim, "at least you take it out in shouting. You don't try to get out of bed and go running around." Miranda held her eyes open with a terrible effort, saw his rather heavy, patient face clearly even as her mind tottered and slithered again, broke from its foundation and spun like a cast wheel in a ditch. "I didn't mean it, I never believed it, Dr. Hildesheim, you mustn't remember it—" and was gone again, not being able to wait for an answer.

The wrong she had done followed her and haunted her dream: this wrong took vague shapes of horror she could not recognize or name, though her heart cringed at sight of them. Her mind, split in two, acknowledged and denied what she saw in the one instant, for across an abyss of complaining darkness her reasoning coherent self watched the strange frenzy of the other coldly, reluctant to admit the truth of its visions, its tenacious remorses and despairs.

"I know those are your hands," she told Miss Tanner, "I know it, but to me they are white tarantulas, don't touch me."

"Shut your eyes," said Miss Tanner.

"Oh, no," said Miranda, "for then I see worse things," but her eyes closed in spite of her will, and the midnight of her internal torment closed about her.

Oblivion, thought Miranda, her mind feeling among her memories of words she had been taught to describe the unseen, the unknowable, is a whirlpool of gray water turning upon itself for all eternity . . . eternity is perhaps more than the distance to the farthest star. She lay on a narrow ledge over a pit that she knew to be bottomless, though she could not comprehend it; the ledge was her childhood dream of danger, and she strained back against a reassuring wall of granite at her shoulders, staring into the pit, thinking, There it is, there it is at last, it is very simple; and soft carefully shaped words like oblivion and eternity are curtains hung before nothing at all. I shall not know when it happens, I shall not feel or remember, why can't I consent now, I am lost, there is no hope for me. Look, she told herself, there it is, that is death and there is nothing to fear. But she could not consent, still shrinking stiffly against the granite wall that was her childhood dream of safety, breathing slowly for fear of squandering breath, saying desperately, Look, don't be afraid, it is nothing, it is only eternity.

Granite walls, whirlpools, stars are things. None of them is death, nor the image of it. Death is death, said Miranda, and for the dead it has no attributes. Silenced she sank easily through deeps under deeps of darkness until she lay like a stone at the farthest bottom of life, knowing herself to be blind, deaf, speechless, no longer aware of the members of her own body, entirely withdrawn from all human concerns, yet alive with a peculiar lucidity and coherence; all notions of the mind, the reasonable inquiries of doubt, all ties of blood and the desires of the heart, dissolved and fell away from her, and there remained of her only a minute fiercely burning particle of being that knew itself alone, that relied upon nothing beyond itself for its strength; not susceptible to any appeal or inducement, being itself composed entirely of one single motive, the stubborn will to live. This fiery motionless particle set itself unaided to resist destruction, to survive and to be in its own madness of being, motiveless and planless beyond that one essential end. Trust me, the hard unwinking angry point of light said. Trust me. I stay.

At once it grew, flattened, thinned to a fine radiance, spread like a great fan and curved out into a rainbow through which Miranda, enchanted, altogether believing, looked upon a deep clear landscape of sea and sand, of soft meadow and sky, freshly washed and glistening with transparencies of blue. Why, of course, of course, said Miranda, without surprise but with serene rapture as if some promise made to her had been kept long after she had ceased to hope for it. She rose from her narrow ledge and ran lightly through the tall portals of the great bow that arched in its splendor over the burning blue of the sea and the cool green of the meadow on either hand.

The small waves rolled in and over unhurriedly, lapped upon the sand in silence and retreated; the grasses flurried before a breeze that made no sound. Moving towards her leisurely as clouds through the shimmering air came a great company of human beings, and Miranda saw in an amazement of joy that they were all the living she had known. Their faces were transfigured, each in its own beauty, beyond what she remembered of them, their eyes were clear and untroubled as good weather, and they cast no shadows. They were pure identities and she knew them every one without calling their names or remembering what relation she bore to them. They surrounded her smoothly on silent feet, then turned their entranced faces again towards the sea, and she moved among them easily as a wave among waves. The drifting circle widened, separated, and each figure was alone but not solitary; Miranda, alone too, questioning nothing, desiring nothing, in the quietude of her ecstasy, stayed where she was, eyes fixed on the overwhelming deep sky where it was always morning.

Lying at ease, arms under her head, in the prodigal warmth which flowed evenly from sea and sky and meadow, within touch but not touching the serenely smiling familiar beings about her, Miranda felt without warning a vague tremor of apprehension, some small flick of distrust in her joy; a thin frost touched the edges of this confident tranquillity; something, somebody, was missing, she had lost something, she had left something valuable in another country, oh, what could it be? There are no trees, no trees here, she said in fright, I have left something unfinished. A thought struggled at the back of her mind, came clearly as a voice in her ear. Where are the dead? We have forgotten the dead, oh, the dead, where are they? At once as if a curtain had fallen, the bright landscape faded, she was alone in a strange stony place of bitter cold, picking her way along a steep path of slippery snow, calling out, Oh, I must go back! But in what direction? Pain returned, a terrible compelling pain running through her veins like heavy fire, the stench of corruption filled her nostrils, the sweetish sickening smell of rotting flesh and pus; she opened her eyes and saw pale light through a coarse white cloth over her face, knew that the smell of death was in her own body, and struggled to lift her hand. The cloth was drawn away; she saw Miss Tanner filling a hypodermic needle in her methodical expert way, and heard Dr. Hildesheim saying, "I think that will do the trick. Try another." Miss Tanner plucked firmly at Miranda's arm near the shoulder, and the unbelievable current of agony ran burning through her veins again. She struggled to cry out, saying, Let me go, let me go; but heard only incoherent sounds of animal suffering. She saw doctor and nurse glance at each other with the glance of initiates at a mystery, nodding in silence, their eyes alive with knowledgeable pride. They looked briefly at their handiwork and hurried away.

Bells screamed all off key, wrangling together as they collided in mid air, horns and whistles mingled shrilly with cries of human distress; sulphur colored light exploded through the black window pane and flashed away in darkness. Miranda waking from a dreamless sleep asked without expecting an answer, "What is happening?" for there was a bustle of voices and footsteps in the corridor, and a sharpness in the air; the far clamor went on, a furious exasperated shrieking like a mob in revolt.

The light came on, and Miss Tanner said in a furry voice, "Hear that? They're celebrating. It's the Armistice. The war is over, my dear." Her hands trembled. She rattled a spoon in a cup, stopped to listen, held the cup out to Miranda. From the ward for old bedridden women down the hall floated a ragged chorus of cracked voices singing, "My country, 'tis of thee . . ."

Sweet land . . . oh, terrible land of this bitter world where the sound of rejoicing was a clamor of pain, where ragged tuneless old women, sitting up waiting for their evening bowl of cocoa, were singing, "Sweet land of Liberty—"

"Oh, say can you see?" their hopeless voices were asking next, the hammer strokes of metal tongues drowning them out. "The war is over," said Miss Tanner, her underlip held firmly, her eyes blurred. Miranda said, "Please open the window, please, I smell death in here."

Now if real daylight such as I remember having seen in this world would only come again, but it is always twilight or just before morning, a promise of day that is never kept. What has become of the sun? That was the longest and loneliest night and yet it will not end and let the day come. Shall I ever see light again?

Sitting in a long chair, near a window, it was in itself a melancholy wonder to see the colorless sunlight slanting on the snow, under a sky drained of its blue. "Can this be my face?" Miranda asked her mirror. "Are these my own hands?" she asked Miss Tanner, holding them up to show the yellow tint like melted wax glimmering between the closed fingers. The body is a curious monster, no place to live in, how could anyone feel at home there? Is it possible I can ever accustom myself to this place? she asked herself. The human faces around her seemed dulled and tired, with no radiance of skin and eyes as Miranda remembered radiance; the once white walls of her room were now a soiled gray. Breathing slowly, falling asleep and waking again, feeling the splash of water on her flesh, taking food, talking in bare phrases with Dr. Hildesheim and Miss Tanner, Miranda looked about her with the covertly hostile eyes of an alien who does not like the country in which he finds himself, does not understand the language nor wish to learn it, does not mean to live there and yet is helpless, unable to leave it at his will.

"It is morning," Miss Tanner would say, with a sigh, for she had grown old and weary once for all in the past month, "morning again, my dear," showing Miranda the same monotonous landscape of dulled evergreens and leaden snow. She would rustle about in her starched skirts, her face bravely powdered, her spirit unbreakable as good steel, saying, "Look, my dear, what a heavenly morning, like a crystal," for she had an affection for the salvaged creature before her, the silent ungrateful human being whom she, Cornelia Tanner, a nurse who knew her business, had snatched back from death with her own hands. "Nursing is nine-tenths, just the same," Miss Tanner would tell the other nurses; "keep that in mind." Even the sunshine was Miss Tanner's own prescription for the further recovery of Miranda, this patient the doctors had given up for lost, and who yet sat here, visible proof of Miss Tanner's theory. She said, "Look at the sunshine, now," as she might be saying, "I ordered this for you, my dear, do sit up and take it."

"It's beautiful," Miranda would answer, even turning her head to look, thanking Miss Tanner for her goodness, most of all her goodness about the weather, "beautiful, I always loved it." And I might love it again if I saw it, she thought, but truth was, she could not see it. There was no light, there might never be light again, compared as it must always be with the light she had seen beside the blue sea that lay so tranquilly along the shore of her paradise. That was a child's dream of the heavenly meadow, the vision of repose that comes to a tired body in sleep, she thought, but I have seen it when I did not know it was a dream. Closing her eyes she would rest for a moment remembering that bliss which had repaid all the pain of the journey to reach it; opening them again she saw with a new anguish the dull world to which she was condemned, where the light seemed filmed over with cobwebs, all the bright surfaces corroded, the sharp planes melted and formless, all objects and beings meaningless, ah, dead and withered things that believed themselves alive!

At night, after the long effort of lying in her chair, in her extremity of grief for what she had so briefly won, she folded her painful body together and wept silently, shamelessly, in pity of herself and her lost rapture. There was no escape. Dr. Hildesheim, Miss Tanner, the nurses in the diet kitchen, the chemist, the surgeon, the precise machine of the hospital, the whole humane conviction and custom of society, conspired to pull her inseparable rack of bones and wasted flesh to its feet, to put in order her disordered mind, and to set her once more safely in the road that would lead her again to death.

Chuck Rouncivale and Mary Townsend came to see her, bringing her a bundle of letters they had guarded for her. They brought a basket of delicate small hothouse flowers, lilies of the valley with sweet peas and feathery fern, and above these blooms their faces were merry and haggard.

Mary said, "You *have* had a tussle, haven't you?" and Chuck said, "Well, you made it back, didn't you?" Then after an uneasy pause, they told her that everybody was waiting to see her again at her desk. "They've put me back on sports already, Miranda," said Chuck. For ten minutes Miranda smiled and told them how gay and what a pleasant surprise it was to find herself alive. For it will not do to betray the conspiracy and tamper with the courage of the living; there is nothing better than to be alive, everyone has agreed on that; it is past argument, and who attempts to deny it is justly outlawed. "I'll be back in no time at all," she said; "this is almost over."

Her letters lay in a heap in her lap and beside her chair. Now and then she turned one over to read the inscription, recognized this handwriting or that, examined the blotted stamps and the postmarks, and let them drop again. For two or three days they lay upon the table beside her, and she continued to shrink from them. "They will all be telling me again how good it is to be alive, they will say again they love me, they are glad I am living too, and what can I answer to that?" and her hardened, indifferent heart shuddered in despair at itself, because before it had been tender and capable of love.

Dr. Hildesheim said, "What, all these letters not opened yet?" and Miss Tanner said, "Read your letters, my dear, I'll open them for you." Standing beside the bed, she slit them cleanly with a paper knife. Miranda, cornered, picked and chose until she found a thin one in an unfamiliar handwriting. "Oh, no, now," said Miss Tanner, "take them as they come. Here, I'll hand them to you." She sat down, prepared to be helpful to the end.

What a victory, what triumph, what happiness to be alive, sang the letters in a chorus. The names were signed with flourishes like the circles in air of bugle notes, and they were the names of those she had loved best; some of those she had known well and pleasantly; and a few who meant nothing to her, then or now. The thin letter in the unfamiliar handwriting was from a strange man at the camp where Adam had been, telling her that Adam had died of influenza in the camp hospital. Adam had asked him, in case anything happened, to be sure to let her know.

If anything happened. To be sure to let her know. If anything happened. "Your friend, Adam Barclay," wrote the strange man. It had happened—she looked at the date—more than a month ago.

"I've been here a long time, haven't I?" she asked Miss Tanner, who was folding letters and putting them back in their proper envelopes.

"Oh, quite a while," said Miss Tanner, "but you'll be ready to go soon now. But you must be careful of yourself and not overdo, and you should come back now and then and let us look at you, because sometimes the aftereffects are very—"

Miranda, sitting up before the mirror, wrote carefully: "One lipstick, medium, one ounce flask Bois d'Hiver perfume, one pair of gray suède gauntlets without straps, two pairs gray sheer stockings without clocks—"

Towney, reading after her, said, "Everything without something so that it will be almost impossible to get?"

"Try it, though," said Miranda, "they're nicer without. One walking stick of silvery wood with a silver knob."

"That's going to be expensive," warned Towney. "Walking is hardly worth it."

"You're right," said Miranda, and wrote in the margin, "a nice one to match my other things. Ask Chuck to look for this, Mary. Good looking and not too heavy." Lazarus, come forth. Not unless you bring me my top hat and stick. Stay where you are then, you snob. Not at all. I'm coming forth. "A jar of cold cream," wrote Miranda, "a box of apricot powder—and, Mary, I don't need eye shadow, do I?" She glanced at her face in the mirror and away again. "Still, no one need pity this corpse if we look properly to the art of the thing."

Mary Townsend said, "You won't recognize yourself in a week."

"Do you suppose, Mary," asked Miranda, "I could have my old room back again?"

"That should be easy," said Mary. "We stored away all your things there with Miss Hobbe." Miranda wondered again at the time and trouble the living took to be helpful to the dead. But not quite dead now, she reassured herself, one foot in either world now; soon I shall cross back and be at home again. The light will seem real and I shall be glad when I hear that someone I know has escaped from death. I shall visit the escaped ones and help them dress and tell them how lucky they are, and how lucky I am still to have them. Mary will be back soon with my gloves and my walking stick, I must go now, I must begin saying good-by to Miss Tanner and Dr. Hildesheim. Adam, she said, now you need not die again, but still I wish you were here; I wish you had come back, what do you think I came back for, Adam, to be deceived like this?

At once he was there beside her, invisible but urgently present, a ghost but more alive than she was, the last intolerable cheat of her heart; for knowing it was false she still clung to the lie, the unpardonable lie of her bitter desire. She said, "I love you," and stood up trembling, trying by the mere act of her will to bring him to sight before her. If I could call you up from the grave I would, she said, if I could see your ghost I would say, I believe . . . "I believe," she said aloud. "Oh, let me see you once more." The room was silent, empty, the shade was gone from it, struck away by the sudden violence of her rising and speaking aloud. She came to herself as if out of sleep. Oh, no, that is not the way, I must never do that, she warned herself. Miss Tanner said, "Your taxicab is waiting, my dear," and there was Mary. Ready to go.

No more war, no more plague, only the dazed silence that follows the ceasing of the heavy guns; noiseless houses with the shades drawn, empty streets, the dead cold light of tomorrow. Now there would be time for everything.

The Crying of Lot 49

Thomas Pynchon

In an age of shameless personal revelation, when such literary figures as Norman Mailer are better known through talk-show appearances and other self-advertisements than through their works, Thomas Pynchon is an outstanding exception. An intensely private and reclusive man, Pynchon has successfully avoided being interviewed, photographed, or otherwise exposed to the world's gaze. So deep is Pynchon's seclusion that it seems, perversely, a pose more intriguing than that of his publicity-seeking fellow authors, and the result has been a great deal of frustrated curiosity and very few attested facts. Pynchon's friends and relations, for the most part, have cooperated with his wish to remain personally anonymous to his audience, to be known entirely in his fiction, so that whatever personal detail has appeared in periodicals has been impossible to verify. As a result, this section will not contain a full-blown biographical essay on Thomas Pynchon, because one cannot yet be written. What is possible is only a brief chronology of Pynchon's official life insofar as that has been acceptably confirmed.

Thomas Ruggles Pynchon was born in Glen Cove, New York, on May 8, 1937, the son of Thomas Pynchon, Sr., an industrial surveyor. The Pynchon family name goes back to prerevolutionary times, and the writer's consciousness of his Puritan heritage may account for his interest in history and for the apocalyptic shape of his narratives. He was educated in local public schools on Long Island, graduating second in his class from Oyster Bay High School. The yearbook photograph, showing Pynchon at sixteen, is the only one generally known. Upon graduation, he entered Cornell University in the division of engineering physics.

In 1955 Pynchon left Cornell to enlist in the United States Navy, where he served—like Benny Profane, one of the antiheroes of his first novel—in the Signal Corps. The year 1955 was a time of profound peace for America, and it is speculated that personal rather than patriotic reasons influenced the enlistment: a broken romance perhaps, or a short-lived teenage marriage. Records of that marriage, if there was one, have not surfaced, but the frequency in Pynchon's fiction of wives who lose touch with or leave their husbands (like

Oedipa Maas in *The Crying of Lot 49*, among others) has given some weight to the guess.

In 1957 Pynchon was honorably discharged from the Navy and returned to Cornell, where he transferred from engineering to the arts and sciences division. He began to take courses in creative writing and in literature—including one from Vladimir Nabokov, then teaching at Cornell. It was during his last years at college that Pynchon began to write short stories and to publish them in small literary magazines. Pynchon graduated from Cornell in 1959 with a bachelor's degree in English. Upon graduation he was offered a Woodrow Wilson Fellowship to do doctoral work in English and a position teaching creative writing at Cornell; he declined both offers. Instead, he moved to Manhattan to work on a first novel.

Before very long, however, Pynchon moved to the West Coast to take a job with the Boeing Corporation in Seattle. From 1960 to 1962 he worked as a scientific writer for Boeing—engineering aide was the official job title. Pynchon's years at Boeing—a corporation at the heart of the "military-industrial complex"—gave him an inside look at the technological imperatives shaping twentieth-century society, at mechanical weapons created to destroy humanity, and at cybernetic devices built to make people obsolete. As a former engineering student, he could appreciate not only the scientific principles upon which this technology was based but also the pleasure taken by the electronic and mechanical engineers in the clever construction of intricate mechanisms to supersede fallible humanity. As a humanist, however, he could concurrently understand that the triumph of technology spelled either the destruction of the human spirit or the devastation through nuclear holocaust of all human works. Pynchon's informed view of technology, a complicated blend of enlightened enthusiasm for the scientific intellect and moralistic abhorrence of the energies with which the quest for doom is conducted, runs through all three of Pynchon's major fictions.

V., Pynchon's first novel, was published in 1963 and won the William Faulkner Foundation Award as the best first novel of the year. Panned as often as it was praised, *V.* established Pynchon as one of the developing talents of his generation. *V.* is a long and difficult novel, with dozens of major characters and a plot that is nearly impossible to summarize. What it attempts is nothing less than an explanation of the course of Western civilization in the twentieth century and a prophecy of its fate. The novel suggests that some time in the latter half of the nineteenth century, the Western world contracted a disease from which it has been suffering ever since; that this disease is manifested in spiritual decadence of many forms, all connected with the replacement of vital human elements of culture by the Inanimate; that the disease is chronic, progressive, and fatal; and that the end of the world, either with a bang or a whimper, is around the next corner. All of Pynchon's novels center on an absurd quest. In *V.* the quest is that of Herbert Stencil for a mysterious woman who may be his mother. V. is a femme fatale in more ways than one, for in uncovering her history from 1901 to her death in 1942, Stencil exposes the progress of the Inanimate in European society. The lady V., always found amid political chaos, riot, war, and genocide, symbolizes the encroachment of the mechanical into human life—in her devotion to mechanism, in fact, she gradually replaces the parts of her body with jeweled clockwork till she becomes more thing than woman.

The background against which Stencil's quest is set is the America of 1956, and in chapters alternating with the history of V., Pynchon sketches an America that, far from being immune to the mortal disease V. represents, has taken things notably further. The arts, the sciences, politics, religion are all equally cold, mechanical, commercialized, dead. It is not gloomy stuff—Pynchon portrays the contemporary world in a series of brilliant comic pastiches—but the jokes and parodies, it eventually appears, point the same way as the history of the Lady V.—toward apocalypse. There is, of course, an antidote to the spreading Inanimate—human love. But in the world Pynchon has created, it is not an easy answer. Love degenerates too often into the mechanical frenzy of sexual passion or into chilly egoistic indifference. To "keep cool, but care" is the hip formula of Pynchon's most vital and creative character, and he knows how hard this balance is to strike. But it is the one wholly positive note in Pynchon's pessimistic vision.

Critics of V. who were dissatisfied with the fragmented quality of the narrative lines were better pleased by his second major work, The Crying of Lot 49, which continued the author's forte of comic parody and intellectual gamesmanship, but focused the action onto a single sympathetic heroine, Oedipa Maas. Published in 1966, three years after V., it was suspected that Pynchon's second work was written earlier than his first because of its greater simplicity and coherence. Actually, many of the same elements of V. are present in Lot 49, including an absurd quest through history for an entity (here called the Tristero) symbolic and subversive in nature, mysterious and violent in its manifestations. But the Tristero is a more ambivalent symbol than the Lady V., for it signifies not mechanism and inner death—the qualities toward which modern humanity seems to be aspiring—but rather a hidden counterforce to those tendencies, one that might restore life to a universe that appears to be inexorably running down. We never find out whether that counterforce is angelic or demonic—nor whether it is real or simply the imaginary focus of a mad quest—but in the Tristero Pynchon invokes the prospect of genuine human communication, the possibility of pure Christian love, in an underground group rejected by a self-destructive America. Like the apocalypse of V., the Pentecost of Lot 49 is ambiguous: we are not told whether the message is one of terror or bliss. Yet the sense of human possibility makes Lot 49 a far more affirmative work than its predecessor.

By common consent, Pynchon's masterpiece thus far is Gravity's Rainbow. Published in 1973, it shared the National Book Award for fiction that year. True to form, Pynchon declined to attend the presentation ceremonies, and so his publishers, Viking Press, sent stand-up comic "Professor" Irwin Corey to accept the award for him. Gravity's Rainbow was also selected by the judging panel for the Pulitzer Prize, but the Pulitzer advisory board overruled the committee of judges, citing the book's "obscurity and obscenity," so that no prize was awarded that year. Obscurity and obscenity were what Joyce's *Ulysses* had been accused of fifty years earlier, and *Gravity's Rainbow* seems equally monumental, equally revolutionary, and, if critic Richard Poirier is correct, equally important.

Perhaps *Finnegans Wake* is a more apt comparison than *Ulysses*, though, because *Gravity's Rainbow* is not merely a narrative of encyclopedic breadth of reference, but a work that, like Joyce's final experiment in form, demands a new mode of reading. As in Pynchon's two earlier novels, there is a central quest, this time for an experimental V-2 rocket powered by an antigravity plastic; the work, set in the months just before and after the end of World War II in Europe, has overtones of science fiction. But the complexity of the action surrounding the central quest is here several orders of magnitude greater than in *V.* or *Lot 49*. Several *hundred* characters, each with his, her, and even *its* motives and behavior patterns, swirl subplots within and about the central motif, so that no linear understanding of the novel is possible. The linking factors between the central quest, the four main plots, the two dozen major characters, and the innumerable side shows take the form of metaphorical resemblances, sometimes guided by verbal puns, but more often by "visual" cues, in the style of cinematic montage, with its juxtaposition of images. A traditional reading of *Gravity's Rainbow* would reveal only an incomprehensible chaos. As the novel teaches us its peculiar language, however, we gradually come to see that everything is intricately interconnected in an elaborate, imaginative network whose plotting is a paranoid's delight. Criticism is currently mining *Gravity's Rainbow* in an attempt to trace out its lines of construction, though whether any consensus about its form and meaning will emerge is anybody's guess. It is a relatively accessible novel, though—more so than *Finnegans Wake*, certainly—and one may savor the comedy and the desperation of its parts even if one never makes final sense of the whole. Younger readers, those who have cut their teeth on movies and television rather than the printed word, may find themselves more in tune with *Gravity's Rainbow* than their elders would, perhaps because of the cinematic style, perhaps simply because they have less to unlearn.

The Invisible Man of the contemporary literary scene, Thomas Pynchon is also the man to watch. While none of his works has met with universal praise—he is too original, too quirky, too elusive for that—it has become clear that his imaginative grasp is unique among today's novelists. This is a time of increasing fragmentation, in which we struggle more or less hopelessly to comprehend the scientific and technological principles that have come to dominate our lives. In such an age, Pynchon's vision is significant because it cuts to the root of our alienation, comprehends the fear of dehumanization that underlies the pervasive pessimism of our time, yet speaks to the hope of human connection—friendship, affection, brotherhood—that might give us something worth living for.

Editions   Pynchon's first two novels, *V.* and *The Crying of Lot 49*, were published by the J. B. Lippincott Co.; *Gravity's Rainbow* by the Viking Press. Pynchon's short stories have not yet been collected, but must be read in back issues of the magazines in which they first appeared. See:

"The Small Rain," *Cornell Writer* (March 1959).

"Mortality and Mercy in Vienna," *Epoch* 9 (Spring 1959), 195-213.

"Low-lands," *New World Writing* 16 (1960), 85-108.

"Entropy," *Kenyon Review* 22, ii (Spring 1960), 277-292.

"Under the Rose," *Noble Savage* 3 (May 1961), 113-151.

"The Secret Integration," *Saturday Evening Post* 237 (December 19, 1964), 36-51.

"The World (This One), the Flesh (Mrs. Oedipa Maas), and the Testament of Pierce Inverarity," *Esquire* 64 (December 1965), 170-173, 296-303.

"The Shrink Flips," *Cavalier* 16 (March 1966), 32-33, 88-92.

"A Journey Into the Mind of Watts," *New York Times Magazine*, June 12, 1966, 34-35, 78-84.

General Criticism   The following books on Thomas Pynchon have been published to date: Joseph W. Slade, *Thomas Pynchon* (New York: Warner Paperback Library, 1974); George Levine and David Leverenz, eds., *Mindful Pleasures: Essays on Thoman Pynchon* (Boston: Little, Brown, 1976); and Edward Mendelson, ed., *Pynchon: A Collection of Critical Essays* (Englewood Cliffs, N.J.: Prentice-Hall, 1978); William M. Plater, *Reconstructing Thomas Pynchon* (Bloomington: Indiana University Press, 1978); Mark R. Siegel, *Pynchon: Creative Paranoia in* Gravity's Rainbow (Port Washington, N.Y.: Kennikat Press, 1978); Douglas Fowler, *A Guide to Pynchon's* Gravity's Rainbow (Ann Arbor, Mich.: Ardis Press, 1979), Douglas A. Mackey, *The Rainbow Quest of Thomas Pynchon* (San Bernardino, Calif.: Borgo Press, 1980); and John O. Stark, *Thomas Pynchon and the Literature of Information* (Columbus: Ohio State University Press, 1980). In addition, collections of essays on Pynchon's fiction have been published in special Pynchon issues of *Critique: Studies in Modern Fiction* 16, ii (1974), and of *Twentieth Century Literature* 21, ii (1975).

Criticism of The Crying of Lot 49   Recommended essays include: Edward Mendelson, "The Sacred, the Profane, and *The Crying of Lot 49*," in the Mendelson collection above or in Kenneth H. Baldwin and David Kirby, eds., *Individual and Community: Variations on a Theme in American Fiction* (Durham, N.C.: Duke University Press, 1975), 182-222; Anne Mangel, "Maxwell's Demon, Entropy, Information: *The Crying of Lot 49*," *TriQuarterly* 20 (1971), 194-208; Manfred Puetz, "Thomas Pynchon's *The Crying of Lot 49*: The World is a Trystero System," *Mosaic* 7 (1974), 125-136; and John P. Leland, "Pynchon's Linguistic Demon: *The Crying of Lot 49*," *Critique* 16, ii (1974), 45-53.

The Crying of Lot 49

I

One summer afternoon Mrs Oedipa Maas came home from a Tupper-
ware party whose hostess had put perhaps too much kirsch in the
fondue to find that she, Oedipa, had been named executor, or she
supposed executrix, of the estate of one Pierce Inverarity, a California
real estate mogul who had once lost two million dollars in his spare
time but still had assets numerous and tangled enough to make the job
of sorting it all out more than honorary. Oedipa stood in the living
room, stared at by the greenish dead eye of the TV tube, spoke the
name of God, tried to feel as drunk as possible. But this did not work.
She thought of a hotel room in Mazatlán whose door had just been
slammed, it seemed forever, waking up two hundred birds down in the
lobby; a sunrise over the library slope at Cornell University that nobody out on it had seen because the slope faces west; a dry, disconso-
late tune from the fourth movement of the Bartók Concerto for
Orchestra; a whitewashed bust of Jay Gould[1] that Pierce kept over the
bed on a shelf so narrow for it she'd always had the hovering fear it
would someday topple on them. Was that how he'd died, she wondered, among dreams, crushed by the only ikon in the house? That
only made her laugh, out loud and helpless: You're so sick, Oedipa, she
told herself, or the room, which knew.

The letter was from the law firm of Warpe, Wistfull, Kubitschek and
McMingus, of Los Angeles, and signed by somebody named Metzger.
It said Pierce had died back in the spring, and they'd only just now
found the will. Metzger was to act as co-executor and special counsel in
the event of any involved litigation. Oedipa had been named also to
execute the will in a codicil dated a year ago. She tried to think back to
whether anything unusual had happened around then. Through the
rest of the afternoon, through her trip to the market in downtown
Kinneret-Among-The-Pines to buy ricotta and listen to the Muzak (to-

---

[1]U.S. financier and speculator (1836–1892), known for his 1869 attempt to corner the gold
market, which caused a nationwide panic.

day she came through the bead-curtained entrance around bar 4 of the Fort Wayne Settecento Ensemble's variorum recording of the Vivaldi Kazoo Concerto, Boyd Beaver, soloist); then through the sunned gathering of her marjoram and sweet basil from the herb garden, reading of book reviews in the latest *Scientific American*, into the layering of a lasagna, garlicking of a bread, tearing up of romaine leaves, eventually, oven on, into the mixing of the twilight's whiskey sours against the arrival of her husband, Wendell ("Mucho") Maas[2] from work, she wondered, wondered, shuffling back through a fat deckful of days which seemed (wouldn't she be first to admit it?) more or less identical, or all pointing the same way subtly like a conjurer's deck, any odd one readily clear to a trained eye. It took her till the middle of Huntley and Brinkley[3] to remember that last year at three or so one morning there had come this long-distance call from where she would never know (unless now he'd left a diary) by a voice beginning in heavy Slavic tones as second secretary at the Transylvanian Consulate, looking for an escaped bat; modulated to comic-Negro, then on into hostile Pachuco dialect, full of chingas and maricones[4]; then a Gestapo officer asking her in shrieks did she have relatives in Germany and finally his Lamont Cranston[5] voice, the one he'd talked in all the way to Mazatlán.

"Pierce, please," she managed to get in, "I thought we had——"

"But Margo," earnestly, "I've just come from Commissioner Weston, and that old man in the fun house was murdered by the same blowgun that killed Professor Quackenbush," or something.

"For God's sake," she said. Mucho had rolled over and was looking at her.

"Why don't you hang up on him," Mucho suggested, sensibly.

"I heard that," Pierce said. "I think it's time Wendell Maas had a little visit from The Shadow." Silence, positive and thorough, fell. So it was the last of his voices she ever heard. Lamont Cranston. That phone line could have pointed any direction, been any length. Its quiet ambiguity shifted over, in the months after the call, to what had been revived: memories of his face, body, things he'd given her, things she had now and then pretended not to've heard him say. It took him over, and

---

[2]In Spanish, "mucho mas" means "much more."

[3]The NBC News anchormen in the late 1960s.

[4]Spanish obscenities.

[5]On the "classic" radio melodrama, Lamont Cranston was the "real" name of "The Shadow"; Margo was his girlfriend. Professor Quackenbush, however, is a name out of a Marx Brothers movie.

to the verge of being forgotten. The shadow waited a year before visiting. But now there was Metzger's letter. Had Pierce called last year then to tell her about this codicil? Or had he decided on it later, somehow because of her annoyance and Mucho's indifference? She felt exposed, finessed, put down. She had never executed a will in her life, didn't know where to begin, didn't know how to tell the law firm in L.A. that she didn't know where to begin.

"Mucho, baby," she cried, in an access of helplessness.

Mucho Maas, home, bounded through the screen door. "Today was another defeat," he began.

"Let me tell you," she also began. But let Mucho go first.

He was a disk jockey who worked further along the Peninsula and suffered regular crises of conscience about his profession. "I don't believe any of it, Oed," he could usually get out. "I try, I truly can't," way down there, further down perhaps than she could reach, so that such times often brought her near panic. It might have been the sight of her so about to lose control that seemed to bring him back up.

"You're too sensitive." Yeah, there was so much else she ought to be saying also, but this was what came out. It was true, anyway. For a couple years he'd been a used car salesman and so hyperaware of what *that* profession had come to mean that working hours were exquisite torture to him. Mucho shaved his upper lip every morning three times with, three times against the grain to remove any remotest breath of a moustache, new blades he drew blood invariably but kept at it; bought all natural-shoulder suits, then went to a tailor to have the lapels made yet more abnormally narrow, on his hair used only water, combing it like Jack Lemmon to throw them further off. The sight of sawdust, even pencil shavings, made him wince, his own kind being known to use it for hushing sick transmissions, and though he dieted he could still not as Oedipa did use honey to sweeten his coffee for like all things viscous it distressed him, recalling too poignantly what is often mixed with motor oil to ooze dishonest into gaps between piston and cylinder wall. He walked out of a party one night because somebody used the word "creampuff," it seemed maliciously, in his hearing. The man was a refugee Hungarian pastry cook talking shop, but there was your Mucho: thin-skinned.

Yet at least he had believed in the cars. Maybe to excess: how could he not, seeing people poorer than him come in, Negro, Mexican, cracker, a parade seven days a week, bringing the most godawful of trade-ins: motorized, metal extensions of themselves, of their families and what their whole lives must be like, out there so naked for anybody, a stranger like himself, to look at, frame cockeyed, rusty underneath, fender repainted in a shade just off enough to depress the value, if not Mucho himself, inside smelling hopelessly of children, supermarket booze, two, sometimes three generations of cigarette smokers, or only of dust—and when the cars were swept out you had to look at the actual residue of these lives, and there was no way of telling what things had been truly refused (when so little he supposed came by that out of fear most of it had to be taken and kept) and what had simply (perhaps tragically) been lost: clipped coupons promising savings of 5 or 10¢, trading stamps, pink flyers advertising specials at the markets, butts, tooth-shy combs, help-wanted ads, Yellow Pages torn from the phone book, rags of old underwear or dresses that already were period costumes, for wiping your own breath off the inside of a windshield with so you could see whatever it was, a movie, a woman or car you coveted, a cop who might pull you over just for drill, all the bits and pieces coated uniformly, like a salad of despair, in a gray dressing of ash, condensed exhaust, dust, body wastes—it made him sick to look, but he had to look. If it had been an outright junkyard, probably he could have stuck things out, made a career: the violence that had caused each wreck being infrequent enough, far enough away from him, to be miraculous, as each death, up till the moment of our own, is miraculous. But the endless rituals of trade-in, week after week, never got as far as violence or blood, and so were too plausible for the impressionable Mucho to take for long. Even if enough exposure to the unvarying gray sickness had somehow managed to immunize him, he could still never accept the way each owner, each shadow, filed in only to exchange a dented, malfunctioning version of himself for another, just as futureless, automotive projection of somebody else's life. As if it were the most natural thing. To Mucho it was horrible. Endless, convoluted incest.

Oedipa couldn't understand how he could still get so upset even now. By the time he married her he'd already been two years at the station, KCUF, and the lot on the pallid, roaring arterial was far behind him, like the Second World or Korean Wars were for older husbands. Maybe, God help her, he should have been in a war, Japs in trees, Krauts in Tiger tanks, gooks with trumpets in the night he might have forgotten sooner than whatever it was about the lot that had stayed so alarmingly with him for going on five years. Five years. You comfort them when they wake pouring sweat or crying out in the language of bad dreams, yes, you hold them, they calm down, one day they lose it: she knew that. But when was Mucho going to forget? She suspected the disk jockey spot (which he'd got through his good buddy the KCUF advertising manager, who'd visited the lot once a week, the lot being a sponsor) was a way of letting the Top 200, and even the news copy that came jabbering out of the machine—all the fraudulent dream of teenage appetites—be a buffer between him and that lot.

He had believed too much in the lot, he believed not at all in the station. Yet to look at him now, in the twilit living room, gliding like a large bird in an updraft toward the sweating shakerful of booze, smiling out of his fat vortex ring's centre, you'd think all was flat calm, gold, serene.

Until he opened his mouth. "Today Funch," he told her, pouring, "had me in, wanted to talk about my image, which he doesn't like." Funch being the program director, and Mucho's great foe. "I'm too horny, now. What I should be is a young father, a big brother. These little chicks call in with requests, naked lust, to Funch's ear, throbs in every word I say. So now I'm supposed to tape all the phone talk. Funch personally will edit out anything he considers offensive, meaning all of my end of the conversation. Censorship, I told him, 'fink,' I muttered, and fled." He and Funch went through some such routine maybe once a week.

She showed him the letter from Metzger. Mucho knew all about her and Pierce: it had ended a year before Mucho married her. He read the letter and withdrew along a shy string of eyeblinks.

"What am I going to do?" she said.

"Oh, no," said Mucho, "you got the wrong fella. Not me. I can't even make out our income tax right. Execute a will, there's nothing I can tell you, see Roseman." Their lawyer.

"Mucho. Wendell. It was *over*. *Before* he put my name on it."

"Yeah, yeah. I meant only that, Oed. I'm not capable."

So next morning that's what she did, went and saw Roseman. After a half hour in front of her vanity mirror drawing and having to redraw dark lines along her eyelids that each time went ragged or wavered violently before she could take the brush away. She'd been up most of the night, after another three-in-the-morning phone call, its announcing bell clear cardiac terror, so out of nothing did it come, the instrument one second inert, the next screaming. It brought both of them instantly awake and they lay, joints unlocking, not even wanting to look at each other for the first few rings. She finally, having nothing she knew of to lose, had taken it. It was Dr Hilarius, her shrink or psychotherapist. But he sounded like Pierce doing a Gestapo officer.

"I didn't wake you up, did I," he began, dry. "You sound so frightened. How are the pills, not working?"

"I'm not taking them," she said.

"You feel threatened by them?"

"I don't know what's inside them."

"You don't believe that they're only tranquilizers."

"Do I trust you?" She didn't, and what he said next explained why not.

"We still need a hundred-and-fourth for the bridge." Chuckled aridly. The bridge, die Brücke, being his pet name for the experiment he was helping the community hospital run on effects of LSD-25, mescaline, psilocybin, and related drugs on a large sample of suburban housewives. The bridge inward. "When can you let us fit you into our schedule."

"No," she said, "you have half a million others to choose from. It's three in the morning."

"We want you." Hanging in the air over her bed she now beheld the well-known portrait of Uncle that appears in front of all our post offices, his eyes gleaming unhealthily, his sunken yellow cheeks most violently rouged, his finger pointing between her eyes. I want you. She had never asked Dr Hilarius why, being afraid of all he might answer.

"I am having a hallucination now, I don't need drugs for that."

"Don't describe it," he said quickly. "Well. Was there anything else you wanted to talk about."

"Did I call you?"

"I thought so," he said, "I had this feeling. Not telepathy. But rapport with a patient is a curious thing sometimes."

"Not this time." She hung up. And then couldn't get to sleep. But would be damned if she'd take the capsules he'd given her. Literally damned. She didn't want to get hooked in any way, she'd told him that.

"So," he shrugged, "on me you are not hooked? Leave then. You're cured."

She didn't leave. Not that the shrink held any dark power over her. But it was easier to stay. Who'd know the day she was cured? Not him, he'd admitted that himself. "Pills are different," she pleaded. Hilarius only made a face at her, one he'd made before. He was full of these delightful lapses from orthodoxy. His theory being that a face is symmetrical like a Rorschach blot, tells a story like a TAT[6] picture, excites a response like a suggested word, so why not. He claimed to have once cured a case of hysterical blindness with his number 37, the "Fu-Manchu" (many of the faces having like German symphonies both a

---

[6]Thematic Apperception Test—a psychological examination in which the subject is shown an ambiguous picture and asked to make up a story about it.

number and nickname), which involved slanting the eyes up with the index fingers, enlarging the nostrils with the middle fingers, pulling the mouth wide with the pinkies and protruding the tongue. On Hilarius it was truly alarming. And in fact, as Oedipa's Uncle Sam hallucination faded, it was this Fu-Manchu face that came dissolving in to replace it and stay with her for what was left of the hours before dawn. It put her in hardly any shape to see Roseman.

But Roseman had also spent a sleepless night, brooding over the Perry Mason television program the evening before, which his wife was fond of but toward which Roseman cherished a fierce ambivalence, wanting at once to be a successful trial lawyer like Perry Mason and, since this was impossible, to destroy Perry Mason by undermining him. Oedipa walked in more or less by surprise to catch her trusted family lawyer stuffing with guilty haste a wad of different-sized and colored papers into a desk drawer. She knew it was the rough draft of *The Profession v. Perry Mason, A Not-so-hypothetical Indictment*, and had been in progress for as long as the TV show had been on the air.

"You didn't use to look guilty, as I remember," Oedipa said. They often went to the same group therapy sessions, in a car pool with a photographer from Palo Alto who thought he was a volleyball. "That's a good sign, isn't it?"

"You might have been one of Perry Mason's spies," said Roseman. After thinking a moment he added, "Ha, ha."

"Ha, ha," said Oedipa. They looked at each other. "I have to execute a will," she said.

"Oh, go ahead then," said Roseman, "don't let me keep you."

"No," said Oedipa, and told him all.

"Why would he do a thing like that," Roseman puzzled, after reading the letter.

"You mean die?"

"No," said Roseman, "name you to help execute it."

"He was unpredictable." They went to lunch. Roseman tried to play footsie with her under the table. She was wearing boots, and couldn't feel much of anything. So, insulated, she decided not to make any fuss.

"Run away with me," said Roseman when the coffee came.

"Where?" she asked. That shut him up.

Back in the office, he outlined what she was in for: learn intimately the books and the business, go through probate, collect all debts, inventory the assets, get an appraisal of the estate, decide what to liquidate and what to hold on to, pay off claims, square away taxes, distribute legacies . . .

"Hey," said Oedipa, "can't I get somebody to do it for me?"

"Me," said Roseman, "some of it, sure. But aren't you even interested?"

"In what?"

"In what you might find out."

As things developed, she was to have all manner of revelations. Hardly about Pierce Inverarity, or herself; but about what remained yet had somehow, before this, stayed away. There had hung the sense of buffering, insulation, she had noticed the absence of an intensity, as if watching a movie, just perceptibly out of focus, that the projectionist refused to fix. And had also gently conned herself into the curious, Rapunzel-like role of a pensive girl somehow, magically, prisoner among the pines and salt fogs of Kinneret, looking for somebody to say hey, let down your hair. When it turned out to be Pierce she'd happily pulled out the pins and curlers and down it tumbled in its whispering, dainty avalanche, only when Pierce had got maybe halfway up, her lovely hair turned, through some sinister sorcery, into a great unanchored wig, and down he fell, on his ass. But dauntless, perhaps using one of his many credit cards for a shim, he'd slipped the lock on her tower door and come up the conchlike stairs, which, had true guile come more naturally to him, he'd have done to begin with. But all that had then gone on between them had never really escaped the confinement of that tower. In Mexico City they somehow wandered into an exhibition of paintings by the beautiful Spanish exile Remedios Varo: in the central painting of a triptych, titled "Bordando el Manto Terrestre,"[7] were a number of frail girls with heart-shaped faces, huge eyes, spun-gold hair, prisoners in the top room of a circular tower, embroidering a kind of tapestry which spilled out the slit windows and into a void, seeking hopelessly to fill the void: for all the other buildings and creatures, all the waves, ships and forests of the earth were contained in this tapestry, and this tapestry was the world. Oedipa, perverse, had stood in front of the painting and cried. No one had noticed; she wore dark green bubble shades. For a moment she'd wondered if the seal around her sockets were tight enough to allow the tears simply to go on and fill up the entire lens space and never dry. She could carry the sadness of the moment with her that way forever, see the world refracted through those tears, those specific tears, as if indices as yet unfound varied in important ways from cry to cry. She had looked down at her feet and known, then, because of a painting, that what she

---

[7] Weaving the garment of the earth.

stood on had only been woven together a couple thousand miles away in her own tower, was only by accident known as Mexico, and so Pierce had taken her away from nothing, there'd been no escape. What did she so desire escape from? Such a captive maiden, having plenty of time to think, soon realizes that her tower, its height and architecture, are like her ego only incidental: that what really keeps her where she is is magic, anonymous and malignant, visited on her from outside and for no reason at all. Having no apparatus except gut fear and female cunning to examine this formless magic, to understand how it works, how to measure its field strength, count its lines of force, she may fall back on superstition, or take up a useful hobby like embroidery, or go mad, or marry a disk jockey. If the tower is everywhere and the knight of deliverance no proof against its magic, what else?

She left Kinneret, then, with no idea she was moving toward anything new. Mucho Maas, enigmatic, whistling "I Want to Kiss Your Feet," a new recording by Sick Dick and the Volkswagens (an English group he was fond of at that time but did not believe in), stood with hands in pockets while she explained about going down to San Narciso for a while to look into Pierce's books and records and confer with Metzger, the co-executor. Mucho was sad to see her go, but not desperate, so after telling him to hang up if Dr Hilarius called and look after the oregano in the garden, which had contracted a strange mold, she went.

San Narciso lay further south, near L.A. Like many named places in California it was less an identifiable city than a grouping of concepts— census tracts, special purpose bond-issue districts, shopping nuclei, all overlaid with access roads to its own freeway. But it had been Pierce's domicile, and headquarters: the place he'd begun his land speculating in ten years ago, and so put down the plinth course of capital on which everything afterward had been built, however rickety or grotesque, toward the sky; and that, she supposed, would set the spot apart, give it an aura. But if there was any vital difference between it and the rest of Southern California, it was invisible on first glance. She drove into San Narciso on a Sunday, in a rented Impala. Nothing was happening. She looked down a slope, needing to squint for the sunlight, onto a vast sprawl of houses which had grown up all together, like a well-tended crop, from the dull brown earth; and she thought of the time she'd opened a transistor radio to replace a battery and seen her first printed circuit. The ordered swirl of houses and streets, from this high angle, sprang at her now with the same unexpected, astonishing clarity as the circuit card had. Though she knew even less about radios than about Southern Californians, there were to both outward patterns a hieroglyphic sense of concealed meaning, of an intent to communicate. There'd seemed no limit to what the printed circuit could have told her (if she had tried to find out); so in her first minute of San Narciso, a revelation also trembled just past the threshold of her understanding. Smog hung all round the horizon, the sun on the bright beige country-side was painful; she and the Chevy seemed parked at the centre of an odd, religious instant. As if, on some other frequency, or out of the eye of some whirlwind rotating too slow for her heated skin even to feel the centrifugal coolness of, words were being spoken. She suspected that much. She thought of Mucho, her husband, trying to believe in his job. Was it something like this he felt, looking through the soundproof glass at one of his colleagues with a headset clamped on and cueing the next record with movements stylized as the handling of chrism, censer, chalice might be for a holy man, yet really tuned in to the voice, voices, the music, its message, surrounded by it, digging it, as were all the faithful it went out to; did Mucho stand outside Studio A looking in, knowing that even if he could hear it he couldn't believe in it?

She gave it up presently, as if a cloud had approached the sun or the smog thickened, and so broken the "religious instant," whatever it might've been; started up and proceeded at maybe 70 mph along the singing blacktop, onto a highway she thought went toward Los Angeles, into a neighborhood that was little more than the road's skinny right-of-way, lined by auto lots, escrow services, drive-ins, small office buildings and factories whose address numbers were in the 70 and then 80,000's. She had never known numbers to run so high. It seemed unnatural. To her left appeared a prolonged scatter of wide, pink buildings, surrounded by miles of fence topped with barbed wire and inter-rupted now and then by guard towers: soon an entrance whizzed by, two sixty-foot missiles on either side and the name YOYODYNE lettered conservatively on each nose cone. This was San Narciso's big source of employment, the Galactronics Division of Yoyodyne, Inc., one of the giants of the aerospace industry. Pierce, she happened to know, had owned a large block of shares, had been somehow involved in negoti-ating an understanding with the county tax assessor to lure Yoyodyne here in the first place. It was part, he explained, of being a founding father.

Barbed wire again gave way to the familiar parade of more beige, prefab, cinderblock office machine distributors, sealant makers, bottled gas works, fastener factories, warehouses, and whatever. Sunday had sent them all into silence and paralysis, all but an occasional real estate office or truck stop. Oedipa had resolved to pull in at the next motel she saw, however ugly, stillness and four walls having at some point become preferable to this illusion of speed, freedom, wind in your hair, unreeling landscape—it wasn't. What the road really was, she fancied, was this hypodermic needle, inserted somewhere ahead into the vein of a freeway, a vein nourishing the mainliner L.A., keeping it happy, coherent, protected from pain, or whatever passes, with a city, for pain. But were Oedipa some single melted crystal of urban horse, L.A., really, would be no less turned on for her absence.

Still, when she got a look at the next motel, she hesitated a second. A representation in painted sheet metal of a nymph holding a white blossom towered thirty feet into the air; the sign, lit up despite the sun, said "Echo Courts." The face of the nymph was much like Oedipa's, which didn't startle her so much as a concealed blower system that kept the nymph's gauze chiton in constant agitation, revealing enormous vermilion-tipped breasts and long pink thighs at each flap. She was smiling a lipsticked and public smile, not quite a hooker's but nowhere near that of any nymph pining away with love either. Oedipa pulled into the lot, got out and stood for a moment in the hot sun and the dead-still air, watching the artificial windstorm overhead toss gauze in five-foot excursions. Remembering her idea about a slow whirlwind, words she couldn't hear.

The room would be good enough for the time she had to stay. Its door opened on a long courtyard with a swimming pool, whose surface that day was flat, brilliant with sunlight. At the far end stood a fountain, with another nymph. Nothing moved. If people lived behind the other doors or watched through the windows gagged each with its roaring air-conditioner, she couldn't see them. The manager, a dropout named Miles, maybe 16 with a Beatle haircut and a lapelless, cuffless, one-button mohair suit, carried her bags and sang to himself, possibly to her:

MILES'S SONG

Too fat to Frug,
That's what you tell me all the time,
When you really try'n' to put me down,
But I'm hip,
So close your big fat lip,

Yeah, baby,
I may be too fat to Frug,
But at least I ain't too slim to Swim.

"It's lovely," said Oedipa, "but why do you sing with an English accent when you don't talk that way?"

"It's this group I'm in," Miles explained, "the Paranoids. We're new yet. Our manager says we should sing like that. We watch English movies a lot, for the accent."

"My husband's a disk jockey," Oedipa trying to be helpful, "it's only a thousand-watt station, but if you had anything like a tape I could give it to him to plug."

Miles closed the door behind them and started in with the shifty eye. "In return for what?" Moving in on her. "Do you want what I think you want? This is the Payola Kid here, you know." Oedipa picked up the nearest weapon, which happened to be the rabbit-ear antenna off the TV in the corner. "Oh," said Miles, stopping. "You hate me too." Eyes bright through his bangs.

"You *are* a paranoid," Oedipa said.

"I have a smooth young body," said Miles, "I thought you older chicks went for that." He left after shaking her down for four bits for carrying the bags.

That night the lawyer Metzger showed up. He turned out to be so good-looking that Oedipa thought at first They, somebody up there, were putting her on. It had to be an actor. He stood at her door, behind him the oblong pool shimmering silent in a mild diffusion of light from the nighttime sky, saying, "Mrs Maas," like a reproach. His enormous eyes, lambent, extravagantly lashed, smiled out at her wickedly; she looked around him for reflectors, microphones, camera cabling, but there was only himself and a debonair bottle of French Beaujolais, which he claimed to've smuggled last year into California, this rollicking lawbreaker, past the frontier guards.

"So hey," he murmured, "after scouring motels all day to find you, I can come in there, can't I?"

Oedipa had planned on nothing more involved that evening than watching *Bonanza* on the tube. She'd shifted into stretch denim slacks and a shaggy black sweater, and had her hair all the way down. She knew she looked pretty good. "Come in," she said, "but I only have one glass."

"I," the gallant Metzger let her know, "can drink out of the bottle." He came in and sat on the floor, in his suit. Opened the bottle, poured her a drink, began to talk. It presently came out that Oedipa hadn't been so far off, thinking it was an actor. Some twenty-odd years ago, Metzger had been one of those child movie stars, performing under the name of Baby Igor. "My mother," he announced bitterly, "was really out to kasher[8] me, boy, like a piece of beef on the sink, she wanted me drained and white. Times I wonder," smoothing down the hair on the back of his head, "if she succeeded. It scares me. You know what mothers like that turn their children into."

"You certainly don't look," Oedipa began, then had second thoughts.

Metzger flashed her a big wry couple rows of teeth. "Looks don't mean a thing any more," he said. "I live inside my looks, and I'm never sure. The possibility haunts me."

"And how often," Oedipa inquired, now aware it was all words, "has that line of approach worked for you, Baby Igor?"

"Do you know," Metzger said, "Inverarity only mentioned you to me once."

"Were you close?"

"No. I drew up his will. Don't you want to know what he said?"

"No," said Oedipa, and snapped on the television set. Onto the screen bloomed the image of a child of indeterminate sex, its bare legs pressed awkward together, its shoulder-length curls mingling with the shorter hair of a St Bernard, whose long tongue, as Oedipa watched, began to swipe at the child's rosy cheeks, making the child wrinkle up its nose appealingly and say, "Aw, Murray, come on, now, you're getting me all wet."

"That's me, that's me," cried Metzger, staring, "good God."

"Which one?" asked Oedipa.

"That movie was called," Metzger snapped his fingers, "*Cashiered*."

"About you and your mother."

"About this kid and his father, who's drummed out of the British Army for cowardice, only he's covering up for a friend, see, and to redeem himself he and the kid follow the old regiment to Gallipoli, where the father somehow builds a midget submarine, and every week they slip through the Dardanelles into the Sea of Marmara and torpedo the Turkish merchantmen, the father, son, and St Bernard. The dog sits on periscope watch, and barks if he sees anything."

Oedipa was pouring wine. "You're kidding."

---

[8]To salt meat so as to extract its blood.

"Listen, listen, here's where I sing." And sure enough, the child, and dog, and a merry old Greek fisherman who had appeared from nowhere with a zither, now all stood in front of phony-Dodecanese process footage of a seashore at sunset, and the kid sang.

BABY IGOR'S SONG

'Gainst the Hun and the Turk, never once do we shirk,
My daddy, my doggie and me.
Through the perilous years, like the Three Musketeers,
We will stick just as close as can be.
Soon our sub's periscope'll aim for Constantinople,
As again we set hopeful to sea;
Once more unto the breach, for those boys on the beach,
Just my daddy, my doggie and me.

Then there was a musical bridge, featuring the fisherman and his instrument, then the young Metzger took it from the top while his aging double, over Oedipa's protests, sang harmony.

Either he made up the whole thing, Oedipa thought suddenly, or he bribed the engineer over at the local station to run this, it's all part of a plot, an elaborate, seduction, *plot.* O Metzger.

"You didn't sing along," he observed.

"I didn't *know,*" Oedipa smiled. On came a loud commercial for Fangoso Lagoons, a new housing development west of here.

"One of Inverarity's interests," Metzger noted. It was to be laced by canals with private landings for power boats, a floating social hall in the middle of an artificial lake, at the bottom of which lay restored galleons, imported from the Bahamas; Atlantean fragments of columns and friezes from the Canaries; real human skeletons from Italy; giant clamshells from Indonesia—all for the entertainment of Scuba enthusiasts. A map of the place flashed onto the screen, Oedipa drew a sharp breath, Metzger on the chance it might be for him looked over. But she'd only been reminded of her look downhill this noontime. Some immediacy was there again, some promise of hierophany[9]: printed circuit, gently curving streets, private access to the water, Book of the Dead. . . .

Before she was ready for it, back came *Cashiered.* The little subma-

---

[9]A religious manifestation.

rine, named the "Justine"[10] after the dead mother, was at the quai, singling up all lines. A small crowd was seeing it off, among them the old fisherman, and his daughter, a leggy, ringletted nymphet who, should there be a happy ending, would end up with Metzger; an English missionary nurse with a nice build on her, who would end up with Metzger's father; and even a female sheepdog with eyes on Murray the St Bernard.

"Oh, yeah," Metzger said, "this is where we have trouble in the Narrows. It's a bitch because of the Kephez minefields, but Jerry has also recently hung this net, this gigantic net, woven out of cable 2½ inches thick."

Oedipa refilled her wine glass. They lay now, staring at the screen, flanks just lightly touching. There came from the TV set a terrific explosion. "Mines!" cried Metzger, covering his head and rolling away from her. "Daddy," blubbered the Metzger in the tube, "I'm scared." The inside of the midget sub was chaotic, the dog galloping to and fro scattering saliva that mingled with the spray from a leak in the bulkhead, which the father was now plugging with his shirt. "One thing we can do," announced the father, "go to the bottom, try to get *under* the net."

"Ridiculous," said Metzger. "They'd built a gate in it, so German U-boats could get through to attack the British fleet. All our E class subs simply used that gate."

"How do you know that?"

"Wasn't I there?"

"But," began Oedipa, then saw how they were suddenly out of wine.

"Aha," said Metzger, from an inside coat pocket producing a bottle of tequila.

"No lemons?" she asked, with movie-gaiety. "No salt?"

"A tourist thing. Did Inverarity use lemons when you were there?"

"How did you know we were there?" She watched him fill her glass, growing more anti-Metzger as the level rose.

"He wrote it off that year as a business expense. I did his tax stuff."

"A cash nexus," brooded Oedipa, "you and Perry Mason, two of a kind, it's all you know about, you shysters."

"But our beauty lies," explained Metzger, "in this extended capacity for convolution. A lawyer in a courtroom, in front of any jury, becomes

---

[10]Also the name of a novel by the Marquis de Sade (1791).

an actor, right? Raymond Burr is an actor, impersonating a lawyer, who in front of a jury becomes an actor. Me, I'm a former actor who became a lawyer. They've done the pilot film of a TV series, in fact, based loosely on my career, starring my friend Manny Di Presso, a one-time lawyer who quit his firm to become an actor. Who in this pilot plays me, an actor become a lawyer reverting periodically to being an actor. The film is in an air-conditioned vault at one of the Hollywood studios, light can't fatigue it, it can be repeated endlessly."

"You're in trouble," Oedipa told him, staring at the tube, conscious of his thigh, warm through his suit and her slacks. Presently:

"The Turks are up there with searchlights," he said, pouring more tequila, watching the little submarine fill up, "patrol boats, and machine guns. You want to bet on what'll happen?"

"Of course not," said Oedipa, "the movie's made." He only smiled back. "One of your endless repetitions."

"But you still don't know," Metzger said. "You haven't seen it." Into the commercial break now roared a deafening ad for Beaconsfield Cigarettes, whose attractiveness lay in their filter's use of bone charcoal, the very best kind.

"Bones of what?" wondered Oedipa.

"Inverarity knew. He owned 51% of the filter process."

"Tell me."

"Someday. Right now it's your last chance to place your bet. Are they going to get out of it, or not?"

She felt drunk. It occurred to her, for no reason, that the plucky trio might not get out after all. She had no way to tell how long the movie had to run. She looked at her watch, but it had stopped. "This is absurd," she said, "of course they'll get out."

"How do you know?"

"All those movies had happy endings."

"All?"

"Most."

"That cuts down the probability," he told her, smug.

She squinted at him through her glass. "Then give me odds."

"Odds would give it away."

"So," she yelled, maybe a bit rattled, "I bet a bottle of something. Tequila, all right? That you didn't make it." Feeling the words had been conned out of her.

"That I didn't make it." He pondered. "Another bottle tonight would put you to sleep," he decided. "No."

"What do you want to bet, then?" She knew. Stubborn, they watched each other's eyes for what seemed five minutes. She heard commercials chasing one another into and out of the speaker of the TV. She grew more and more angry, perhaps juiced, perhaps only impatient for the movie to come back on.

"Fine then," she gave in at last, trying for a brittle voice, "it's a bet. Whatever you'd like. That you don't make it. That you will turn to carrion for the fish at the bottom of the Dardanelles, your daddy, your doggie, and you."

"Fair enough," drawled Metzger, taking her hand as if to shake on the bet and kissing its palm instead, sending the dry end of his tongue to graze briefly among her fate's furrows, the changeless salt hatchings of her identity. She wondered then if this were really happening in the same way as, say, her first time in bed with Pierce, the dead man. But then the movie came back.

The father was huddled in a shellhole on the steep cliffs of the Anzac[11] beachhead, Turkish shrapnel flying all over the place. Neither Baby Igor nor Murray the dog were in evidence. "Now what the hell," said Oedipa.

"Golly," Metzger said, "they must have got the reels screwed up."

"Is this before or after?" she asked, reaching for the tequila bottle, a move that put her left breast in the region of Metzger's nose. The irrepressibly comic Metzger made crosseyes before replying.

"That would be telling."

"Come on." She nudged his nose with the padded tip of her bra cup and poured booze. "Or the bet's off."

"Nope," Metzger said.

"At least tell me if that's his old regiment, there."

"Go ahead," said Metzger, "ask questions. But for each answer, you'll have to take something off. We'll call it Strip Botticelli."[12]

Oedipa had a marvellous idea: "Fine," she told him, "but first I'll slip into the bathroom for a second. Close your eyes, turn around, don't peek." On the screen the "River Clyde," a collier carrying 2000 men, beached at Sedd-el-Bahr in an unearthly silence. "This is it, men," a phony British accent was heard to whisper. Suddenly a host of Turkish rifles on shore opened up all together, and the massacre began.

---

[11]Australia-New Zealand Army Corps.
[12]Botticelli is a more sophisticated version of Twenty Questions.

"I know this part," Metzger told her, his eyes squeezed shut, head away from the set. "For fifty yards out the sea was red with blood. They don't show that." Oedipa skipped into the bathroom, which happened also to have a walk-in closet, quickly undressed and began putting on as much as she could of the clothing she'd brought with her: six pairs of panties in assorted colors, girdle, three pairs of nylons, three brassieres, two pairs stretch slacks, four half-slips, one black sheath, two summer dresses, half dozen A-line skirts, three sweaters, two blouses, quilted wrapper, baby blue peignoir and old Orlon muu-muu. Bracelets then, scatterpins, earrings, a pendant. It all seemed to take hours to put on and she could hardly walk when she was finished. She made the mistake of looking at herself in the full-length mirror, saw a beach ball with feet, and laughed so violently she fell over, taking a can of hair spray on the sink with her. The can hit the floor, something broke, and with a great outsurge of pressure the stuff commenced atomizing, propelling the can swiftly about the bathroom. Metzger rushed in to find Oedipa rolling around, trying to get back on her feet, amid a great sticky miasma of fragrant lacquer. "Oh, for Pete's sake," he said in his Baby Igor voice. The can, hissing malignantly, bounced off the toilet and whizzed by Metzger's right ear, missing by maybe a quarter of an inch. Metzger hit the deck and cowered with Oedipa as the can continued its high-speed caroming; from the other room came a slow, deep crescendo of naval bombardment, machine-gun, howitzer and small-arms fire, screams and chopped-off prayers of dying infantry. She looked up past his eyelids, into the staring ceiling light, her field of vision cut across by wild, flashing overflights of the can, whose pressure seemed inexhaustible. She was scared but nowhere near sober. The can knew where it was going, she sensed, or something fast enough, God or a digital machine, might have computed in advance the complex web of its travel; but she wasn't fast enough, and knew only that it might hit them at any moment, at whatever clip it was doing, a hundred miles an hour. "Metzger," she moaned, and sank her teeth into his upper arm, through the sharkskin. Everything smelled like hair spray. The can collided with a mirror and bounced away, leaving a silvery, reticulated bloom of glass to hang a second before it all fell jingling into the sink; zoomed over to the enclosed shower, where it crashed into and totally destroyed a panel of frosted glass; thence around the three tile walls, up to the ceiling, past the light, over the two prostrate bodies, amid its own whoosh and the buzzing, distorted uproar from the TV set. She could imagine no end to it; yet presently the can did give up in midflight and fall to the floor, about a foot from Oedipa's nose. She lay watching it.

"Blimey," somebody remarked. "Coo." Oedipa took her teeth out of Metzger, looked around and saw in the doorway Miles, the kid with the bangs and mohair suit, now multiplied by four. It seemed to be the group he'd mentioned, the Paranoids. She couldn't tell them apart, three of them were carrying electric guitars, they all had their mouths open. There also appeared a number of girls' faces, gazing through armpits and around angles of knees. "That's kinky," said one of the girls.

"Are you from London?" another wanted to know: "Is that a London thing you're doing?" Hair spray hung like fog, glass twinkled all over the floor.

"Lord love a duck," summarized a boy holding a passkey, and Oedipa decided this was Miles. Deferent, he began to narrate for their entertainment a surfer orgy he had been to the week before, involving a five-gallon can of kidney suet, a small automobile with a sun roof, and a trained seal.

"I'm sure this pales by comparison," said Oedipa, who'd succeeded in rolling over, "so why don't you all just, you know, go outside. And sing. None of this works without mood music. Serenade us."

"Maybe later," invited one of the other Paranoids shyly, "you could join us in the pool."

"Depends how hot it gets in here, gang," winked jolly Oedipa. The kids filed out, after plugging extension cords into all available outlets in the other room and leading them in a bundle out a window.

Metzger helped her stagger to her feet. "Anyone for Strip Botticelli?" In the other room the TV was blaring a commercial for a Turkish bath in downtown San Narciso, wherever downtown was, called Hogan's Seraglio. "Inverarity owned that too," Metzger said. "Did you know that?"

"Sadist," Oedipa yelled, "say it once more, I'll wrap the TV tube around your head."

"You're really mad," he smiled.

She wasn't, really. She said, "What the hell didn't he own?"

Metzger cocked an eyebrow at her. "You tell me."

If she was going to she got no chance, for outside, all in a shuddering deluge of thick guitar chords, the Paranoids had broken into song. Their drummer had set up precariously on the diving board, the others were invisible. Metzger came up behind her with some idea of cupping his hands around her breasts, but couldn't immediately find them because of all the clothes. They stood at the window and heard the Paranoids singing.

SERENADE

As I lie and watch the moon
On the lonely sea,
Watch it tug the lonely tide
Like a comforter over me,
The still and faceless moon
Fills the beach tonight
With only a ghost of day,
All shadow gray, and moonbeam white.
And you lie alone tonight,
As alone as I;
Lonely girl in your lonely flat, well, that's where it's at,
So hush your lonely cry.
How can I come to you, put out the moon, send back the tide?
The night has gone so gray, I'd lose the way, and it's dark inside.
No, I must lie alone,
Till it comes for me;
Till it takes the sky, the sand, the moon, and the lonely sea.
And the lonely sea . . . etc.   [FADE OUT.]

"Now then," Oedipa shivered brightly.

"First question," Metzger reminded her. From the TV set the St Bernard was barking. Oedipa looked and saw Baby Igor, disguised as a Turkish beggar lad, skulking with the dog around a set she took to be Constantinople.

"Another early reel," she said hopefully.

"I can't allow that question," Metzger said. On the doorsill the Paranoids, as we leave milk to propitiate the leprechaun, had set a fifth of Jack Daniels.

"Oboy," said Oedipa. She poured a drink. "Did Baby Igor get to Constantinople in the good submarine 'Justine'?"

"No," said Metzger. Oedipa took off an earring.

"Did he get there in, what did you call them, in an E Class submarine."

"No," said Metzger. Oedipa took off another earring.

"Did he get there overland, maybe through Asia Minor?"

"Maybe," said Metzger. Oedipa took off another earring.

"Another earring?" said Metzger.

"If I answer that, will you take something off?"

"I'll do it without an answer," roared Metzger, shucking out of his coat. Oedipa refilled her glass, Metzger had another snort from the bottle. Oedipa then sat five minutes watching the tube, forgetting she was supposed to ask questions. Metzger took his trousers off, earnestly. The father seemed to be up before a court-martial, now.

"So," she said, "an early reel. This is where he gets cashiered; ha, ha."

"Maybe it's a flashback," Metzger said. "Or maybe he gets it twice." Oedipa removed a bracelet. So it went: the succession of film fragments on the tube, the progressive removal of clothing that seemed to bring her no nearer nudity, the boozing, the tireless shivaree of voices and guitars from out by the pool. Now and then a commercial would come in, each time Metzger would say, "Inverarity's," or "Big block of shares," and later settled for nodding and smiling. Oedipa would scowl back, growing more and more certain, while a headache began to flower behind her eyes, that they among all possible combinations of new lovers had found a way to make time itself slow down. Things grew less and less clear. At some point she went into the bathroom, tried to find her image in the mirror and couldn't. She had a moment of nearly pure terror. Then remembered that the mirror had broken and fallen in the sink. "Seven years' bad luck," she said aloud. "I'll be 35." She shut the door behind her and took the occasion to blunder, almost absently, into another slip and skirt, as well as a long-leg girdle and a couple pairs of knee socks. It struck her that if the sun ever came up Metzger would disappear. She wasn't sure if she wanted him to. She came back in to find Metzger wearing only a pair of boxer shorts and fast asleep with a hardon and his head under the couch. She noticed also a fat stomach the suit had hidden. On the screen New Zealanders and Turks were impaling one another on bayonets. With a cry Oedipa rushed to him, fell on him, began kissing him to wake him up. His radiant eyes flew open, pierced her, as if she could feel the sharpness somewhere vague between her breasts. She sank with an enormous sigh that carried all rigidity like a mythical fluid from her, down next to him; so weak she couldn't help him undress her; it took him 20 minutes, rolling, arranging her this way and that, as if she thought, he were some scaled-up, short-haired, poker-faced little girl with a Barbie doll. She may have fallen asleep once or twice. She awoke at last to find herself getting laid; she'd come in on a sexual crescendo in progress, like a cut to a scene where the camera's already moving. Outside a fugue of guitars had begun, and she counted each electronic voice as it came in, till she reached six or so and recalled only three of the Paranoids played guitars; so others must be plugging in.

Which indeed they were. Her climax and Metzger's, when it came, coincided with every light in the place, including the TV tube, suddenly going out, dead, black. It was a curious experience. The Paranoids had blown a fuse. When the lights came on again, and she and Metzger lay twined amid a wall-to-wall scatter of clothing and spilled bourbon, the TV tube revealed the father, dog and Baby Igor trapped inside the darkening "Justine," as the water level inexorably rose. The dog was first to drown, in a great crowd of bubbles. The camera came in for a close-up of Baby Igor crying, one hand on the control board. Something short-circuited then and the grounded Baby Igor was electrocuted, thrashing back and forth and screaming horribly. Through one of those Hollywood distortions in probability, the father was spared electrocution so he could make a farewell speech, apologizing to Baby Igor and the dog for getting them into this and regretting that they wouldn't be meeting in heaven: "Your little eyes have seen your daddy for the last time. You are for salvation; I am for the Pit." At the end his suffering eyes filled the screen, the sound of incoming water grew deafening, up swelled that strange '30's movie music with the massive sax section, in faded the legend THE END.

Oedipa had leaped to her feet and run across to the other wall to turn and glare at Metzger. "They didn't make it!" she yelled. "You bastard, I won."

"You won me," Metzger smiled.

"What did Inverarity tell you about me," she asked finally.

"That you wouldn't be easy."

She began to cry.

"Come back," said Metzger. "Come on."

After awhile she said, "I will." And she did.

III

Things then did not delay in turning curious. If one object behind her discovery of what she was to label the Tristero System or often only The Tristero (as if it might be something's secret title) were to bring to an end her encapsulation in her tower, then that night's infidelity with

Metzger would logically be the starting point for it; logically. That's what would come to haunt her most, perhaps: the way it fitted, logically, together. As if (as she'd guessed that first minute in San Narciso) there were revelation in progress all around her.

Much of the revelation was to come through the stamp collection Pierce had left, his substitute often for her—thousands of little colored windows into deep vistas of space and time: savannahs teeming with elands and gazelles, galleons sailing west into the void, Hitler heads, sunsets, cedars of Lebanon, allegorical faces that never were, he could spend hours peering into each one, ignoring her. She had never seen the fascination. The thought that now it would all have to be inventoried and appraised was only another headache. No suspicion at all that it might have something to tell her. Yet if she hadn't been set up or sensitized, first by her peculiar seduction, then by the other, almost offhand things, what after all could the mute stamps have told her, remaining then as they would've only ex-rivals, cheated as she by death, about to be broken up into lots, on route to any number of new masters?

It got seriously under way, this sensitizing, either with the letter from Mucho or the evening she and Metzger drifted into a strange bar known as The Scope. Looking back she forgot which had come first. The letter itself had nothing much to say, had come in response to one of her dutiful, more or less rambling, twice-a-week notes to him, in which she was not confessing to her scene with Metzger because Mucho, she felt, somehow, would know. Would then proceed at a KCUF record hop to look out again across the gleaming gym floor and there in one of the giant keyholes inscribed for basketball see, groping her vertical backstroke a little awkward opposite any boy heels might make her an inch taller than, a Sharon, Linda or Michele, seventeen and what is known as a hip one, whose velveted eyes ultimately, statistically would meet Mucho's and respond, and the thing would develop then groovy as it could when you found you couldn't get statutory rape really out of the back of your law-abiding head. She knew the pattern because it had happened a few times already, though Oedipa had been most scrupulously fair about it, mentioning the practice only once, in fact, another three in the morning and out of a dark dawn sky, asking if he wasn't worried about the penal code. "Of course," said Mucho after awhile, that was all; but in his tone of voice she thought she heard more, something between annoyance and agony. She wondered then if worrying affected his performance. Having once been seventeen and ready to laugh at almost anything, she found herself then overcome by, call it a tenderness she'd never go quite to the back of lest she get bogged. It kept her from asking him any more questions. Like all their inabilities to communicate, this too had a virtuous motive.

It may have been an intuition that the letter would be newsless inside that made Oedipa look more closely at its outside, when it arrived. At first she didn't see. It was an ordinary Muchoesque envelope, swiped from the station, ordinary airmail stamp, to the left of the cancellation a blurb put on by the government, REPORT ALL OBSCENE MAIL TO YOUR POTSMASTER. Idly, she began to skim back through Mucho's letter after reading it to see if there were any dirty words. "Metzger," it occurred to her, "what is a potsmaster?"

"Guy in the scullery," replied Metzger authoritatively from the bathroom, "in charge of all the heavy stuff, canner kettles, gunboats, Dutch ovens . . ."

She threw a brassiere in at him and said, "I'm supposed to report all obscene mail to my potsmaster."

"So they make misprints," Metzger said, "let them. As long as they're careful about not pressing the wrong button, you know?"

It may have been that same evening that they happened across The Scope, a bar out on the way to L.A., near the Yoyodyne plant. Every now and again, like this evening, Echo Courts became impossible, either because of the stillness of the pool and the blank windows that faced on it, or a prevalence of teenage voyeurs, who'd all had copies of Miles's passkey made so they could check in at whim on any bizarre sexual action. This would grow so bad Oedipa and Metzger got in the habit of dragging a mattress into the walk-in closet, where Metzger would then move the chest of drawers up against the door, remove the bottom drawer and put it on top, insert his legs in the empty space, this being the only way he could lie full length in this closet, by which point he'd usually lose interest in the whole thing.

The Scope proved to be a haunt for electronics assembly people from Yoyodyne. The green neon sign outside ingeniously depicted the face of an oscilloscope tube, over which flowed an ever-changing dance of Lissajous figures.[13] Today seemed to be payday, and everyone inside to be drunk already. Glared at all the way, Oedipa and Metzger found a table in back. A wizened bartender wearing shades materialized and Metzger ordered bourbon. Oedipa, checking the bar, grew nervous.

---

[13]Hyperboloid and paraboloid curves, named for French physicist Jules-Antoine Lissajous (1822–1880).

There was this je ne sais quoi[14] about the Scope crowd: they all wore glasses and stared at you, silent. Except for a couple-three nearer the door, who were engaged in a nose-picking contest, seeing how far they could flick it across the room.

A sudden chorus of whoops and yibbles burst from a kind of juke box at the far end of the room. Everybody quit talking. The bartender tiptoed back, with the drinks.

"What's happening?" Oedipa whispered.

"That's by Stockhausen," the hip graybeard informed her, "the early crowd tends to dig your Radio Cologne sound. Later on we really swing. We're the only bar in the area, you know, has a strictly electronic music policy. Come on around Saturdays, starting midnight we have your Sinewave Session, that's a live get-together, fellas come in just to jam from all over the state, San Jose, Santa Barbara, San Diego——"

"Live?" Metzger said, "electronic music, live?"

"They put it on the tape, here, live, fella. We got a whole back room full of your audio oscillators, gunshot machines, contact mikes, everything man. That's for if you didn't bring your ax, see, but you got the feeling and you want to swing with the rest of the cats, there's always something available."

"No offense," said Metzger, with a winning Baby Igor smile.

A frail young man in a drip-dry suit slid into the seat across from them, introduced himself as Mike Fallopian, and began proselytizing for an organization known as the Peter Pinguid Society.

"You one of these right-wing nut outfits?" inquired the diplomatic Metzger.

Fallopian twinkled. "They accuse *us* of being paranoids."

"They?" inquired Metzger, twinkling also.

"Us?" asked Oedipa.

The Peter Pinguid Society was named for the commanding officer of the Confederate man-of-war "Disgruntled," who early in 1863 had set sail with the daring plan of bringing a task force around Cape Horn to attack San Francisco and thus open a second front in the War For Southern Independence. Storms and scurvy managed to destroy or discourage every vessel in this armada except the game little "Disgruntled," which showed up off the coast of California about a year later. Unknown, however, to Commodore Pinguid, Czar Nicholas II of Russia had dispatched his Far East Fleet, four corvettes and two clippers, all

---

[14] A certain something.

under the command of one Rear Admiral Popov, to San Francisco Bay, as part of a ploy to keep Britain and France from (among other things) intervening on the side of the Confederacy. Pinguid could not have chosen a worse time for an assault on San Francisco. Rumors were abroad that winter that the Reb cruisers "Alabama" and "Sumter" were indeed on the point of attacking the city, and the Russian admiral had, on his own responsibility, issued his Pacific squadron standing orders to put on steam and clear for action should any such attempt develop. The cruisers, however, seemed to prefer cruising and nothing more. This did not keep Popov from periodic reconnoitring. What happened on the 9th March, 1864, a day now held sacred by all Peter Pinguid Society members, is not too clear. Popov did send out a ship, either the corvette "Bogatir" or the clipper "Gaidamak," to see what it could see. Off the coast of either what is now Carmel-by-the-Sea, or what is now Pismo Beach, around noon or possibly toward dusk, the two ships sighted each other. One of them may have fired; if it did then the other responded; but both were out of range so neither showed a scar afterward to prove anything. Night fell. In the morning the Russian ship was gone. But motion is relative. If you believe an excerpt from the "Bogatir" or "Gaidamak" 's log, forwarded in April to the General-Adjutant in St Petersburg and now somewhere in the Krasnyi Arkhiv, it was the "Disgruntled" that had vanished during the night.

"Who cares?" Fallopian shrugged. "We don't try to make scripture out of it. Naturally that's cost us a lot of support in the Bible Belt, where we might've been expected to go over real good. The old Confederacy.

"But that was the very first military confrontation between Russia and America. Attack, retaliation, both projectiles deep-sixed forever and the Pacific rolls on. But the ripples from those two splashes spread, and grew, and today engulf us all.

"Peter Pinguid was really our first casualty. Not the fanatic our more left-leaning friends over in the Birch Society chose to martyrize."

"Was the Commodore killed, then?" asked Oedipa.

Much worse, to Fallopian's mind. After the confrontation, appalled at what had to be some military alliance between abolitionist Russia (Nicholas having freed the serfs in 1861) and a Union that paid lip-service to abolition while it kept its own industrial laborers in a kind of wage-slavery, Peter Pinguid stayed in his cabin for weeks, brooding.

"But that sounds," objected Metzger, "like he was against industrial capitalism. Wouldn't that disqualify him as any kind of anti-Communist figure?"

"You think like a Bircher," Fallopian said. "Good guys and bad guys. You never get to any of the underlying truth. Sure he was against industrial capitalism. So are we. Didn't it lead, inevitably, to Marxism? Underneath, both are part of the same creeping horror."

"Industrial *anything*," hazarded Metzger.

"There you go," nodded Fallopian.

"What happened to Peter Pinguid?" Oedipa wanted to know.

"He finally resigned his commission. Violated his upbringing and code of honor. Lincoln and the Czar had forced him to. That's what I meant when I said casualty. He and most of the crew settled near L.A.; and for the rest of his life he did little more than acquire wealth."

"How poignant," Oedipa said. "What doing?"

"Speculating in California real estate," said Fallopian. Oedipa, half-way into swallowing part of her drink, sprayed it out again in a glittering cone for ten feet easy, and collapsed in giggles.

"Wha," said Fallopian. "During the drought that year you could've bought lots in the heart of downtown L.A. for 63¢ apiece."

A great shout went up near the doorway, bodies flowed toward a fattish pale young man who'd appeared carrying a leather mailsack over his shoulder.

"Mail call," people were yelling. Sure enough, it was, just like in the army. The fat kid, looking harassed, climbed up on the bar and started calling names and throwing envelopes into the crowd. Fallopian excused himself and joined the others.

Metzger had taken out a pair of glasses and was squinting through them at the kid on the bar. "He's wearing a Yoyodyne badge. What do you make of that?"

"Some inter-office mail run," Oedipa said.

"This time of night?"

"Maybe a late shift?" But Metzger only frowned. "Be back," Oedipa shrugged, heading for the ladies' room.

On the latrine wall, among lipsticked obscenities, she noticed the following message, neatly indited in engineering lettering:

"Interested in sophisticated fun? You, hubby, girl friends. The more the merrier. Get in touch with Kirby, through WASTE only, Box 7391, L.A."

WASTE? Oedipa wondered. Beneath the notice, faintly in pencil, was a symbol she'd never seen before, a loop, triangle and trapezoid, thus:

It might be something sexual, but she somehow doubted it. She found a pen in her purse and copied the address and symbol in her memo book, thinking: God, hieroglyphics. When she came out Fallopian was back, and had this funny look on his face.

"You weren't supposed to see that," he told them. He had an envelope. Oedipa could see, instead of a postage stamp, the handstruck initials PPS.

"Of course," said Metzger. "Delivering the mail is a government monopoly. You would be opposed to that."

Fallopian gave them a wry smile. "It's not as rebellious as it looks. We use Yoyodyne's inter-office delivery. On the sly. But it's hard to find carriers, we have a big turnover. They're run on a tight schedule, and they get nervous. Security people over at the plant know something's up. They keep a sharp eye out. De Witt," pointing at the fat mailman, who was being hauled, twitching, down off the bar and offered drinks he did not want, "he's the most nervous one we've had all year."

"How extensive is this?" asked Metzger.

"Only inside our San Narciso chapter. They've set up pilot projects similar to this in the Washington and I think Dallas chapters. But we're the only one in California so far. A few of your more affluent type members do wrap their letters around bricks, and then the whole thing in brown paper, and send them Railway Express, but I don't know . . ."

"A little like copping out," Metzger sympathized.

"It's the principle," Fallopian agreed, sounding defensive. "To keep it up to some kind of a reasonable volume, each member has to send at least one letter a week through the Yoyodyne system. If you don't, you get fined." He opened his letter and showed Oedipa and Metzger.

Dear Mike, it said, how are you? Just thought I'd drop you a note. How's your book coming? Guess that's all for now. See you at The Scope.

"That's how it is," Fallopian confessed bitterly, "most of the time."

"What book did they mean?" asked Oedipa.

Turned out Fallopian was doing a history of private mail delivery in the U.S., attempting to link the Civil War to the postal reform movement that had begun around 1845. He found it beyond simple coincidence that in of all years 1861 the federal government should have set out on a vigorous suppression of those independent mail routes still surviving the various Acts of '45, '47, '51 and '55. Acts all designed to drive any private competition into financial ruin. He saw it all as a parable of power, its feeding, growth and systematic abuse, though he didn't go into it that far with her, that particular night. All Oedipa would remember about him at first, in fact, were his slender build and neat Armenian nose, and a certain affinity of his eyes for green neon. So began, for Oedipa, the languid, sinister blooming of The Tristero. Or rather, her attendance at some unique performance, prolonged as if it were the last of the night, something a little extra for whoever'd stayed this late. As if the breakaway gowns, net bras, jeweled garters and G-strings of historical figuration that would fall away were layered dense as Oedipa's own street-clothes in that game with Metzger in front of the Baby Igor movie; as if a plunge toward dawn indefinite black hours long would indeed be necessary before The Tristero could be revealed in its terrible nakedness. Would its smile, then, be coy, and would it flirt away harmlessly backstage, say good night with a Bourbon Street bow and leave her in peace? Or would it instead, the dance ended, come back down the runway, its luminous stare locked to Oedipa's, smile gone malign and pitiless; bend to her alone among the desolate rows of seats and begin to speak words she never wanted to hear?

The beginning of that performance was clear enough. It was while she and Metzger were waiting for ancillary letters to be granted representatives in Arizona, Texas, New York, and Florida, where Inverarity had developed real estate, and in Delaware, where he'd been incorporated. The two of them, followed by a convertibleful of the Paranoids Miles, Dean, Serge and Leonard and their chicks, had decided to spend the day out at Fangoso Lagoons, one of Inverarity's last big projects. The trip out was uneventful except for two or three collisions the Paranoids almost had owing to Serge, the driver, not being able to see through his hair. He was persuaded to hand over the wheel to one of the girls. Somewhere beyond the battening, urged sweep of three-bedroom houses rushing by their thousands across all the dark beige hills, somehow implicit in an arrogance or bite to the smog the more inland somnolence of San Narciso did lack, lurked the sea, the unimaginable Pacific, the one to which all surfers, beach pads, sewage disposal schemes, tourist incursions, sunned homosexuality, chartered fishing are irrelevant, the hole left by the moon's tearing-free and monument to her exile; you could not hear or even smell this but it was there, something tidal began to reach feelers in past eyes and eardrums, perhaps to arouse fractions of brain current your most gossamer microelectrode is yet too gross for finding. Oedipa had believed, long before leaving Kinneret, in some principle of the sea as redemption for Southern California (not, of course, for her own section of the state, which seemed to need none), some unvoiced idea that no matter what you did to its edges the true Pacific stayed inviolate and integrated or assumed the ugliness at any edge into some more general truth. Perhaps it was only that notion, its arid hope, she sensed as this forenoon they made their seaward thrust, which would stop short of any sea.

They came in among earth-moving machines, a total absence of trees, the usual hieratic geometry, and eventually, shimmying for the sand roads, down in a helix to a sculptured body of water named Lake Inverarity. Out in it, on a round island of fill among blue wavelets, squatted the social hall, a chunky, ogived and verdigrised, Art Nouveau reconstruction of some European pleasure-casino. Oedipa fell in love with it. The Paranoid element piled out of their car, carrying musical instruments and looking around as if for outlets under the trucked-in white sand to plug into. Oedipa from the Impala's trunk took a basket filled with cold eggplant parmigian' sandwiches from an Italian drive-in, and Metzger came up with an enormous Thermos of tequila sours. They wandered all in a loose pattern down the beach toward a small marina for what boat owners didn't have lots directly on the water.

"Hey, blokes," yelled Dean or perhaps Serge, "let's pinch a boat."

"Hear, hear," cried the girls. Metzger closed his eyes and tripped over an old anchor. "Why are you walking around," inquired Oedipa, "with your eyes closed, Metzger?"

"Larceny," Metzger said, "maybe they'll need a lawyer." A snarl rose along with some smoke from among pleasure boats strung like piglets along the pier, indicating the Paranoids had indeed started someone's outboard. "Come on, then," they called. Suddenly, a dozen boats away, a form, covered with a blue polyethylene tarp, rose up and said, "Baby Igor, I need help."

"I know that voice," said Metzger.

"Quick," said the blue tarp, "let me hitch a ride with you guys."

"Hurry, hurry," cried the Paranoids.

"Manny Di Presso," said Metzger, seeming less than delighted.

"Your actor/lawyer friend," Oedipa recalled.

"Not so loud, hey," said Di Presso, skulking as best a polyethylene cone can along the landing towards them. "They're watching. With binoculars." Metzger handed Oedipa aboard the about-to-be-hijacked vessel, a 17-foot aluminum trimaran known as the "Godzilla II," and gave Di Presso what he intended to be a hand also, but he had grabbed, it seemed, only empty plastic, and when he pulled, the entire covering came away and there stood Di Presso, in a skin-diving suit and wrap-around shades.

"I can explain," he said.

"Hey," yelled a couple voices, faintly, almost in unison, from up the beach a ways. A squat man with a crew cut, intensely tanned and also with shades, came out in the open running, one arm doubled like a wing with the hand at chest level, inside the jacket.

"Are we on camera?" asked Metzger dryly.

"This is real," chattered Di Presso, "come on." The Paranoids cast off, backed the "Godzilla II" out from the pier, turned and with a concerted whoop took off like a bat out of hell, nearly sending Di Presso over the fantail. Oedipa, looking back, could see their pursuer had been joined by another man about the same build. Both wore gray suits. She couldn't see if they were holding anything like guns.

"I left my car on the other side of the lake," Di Presso said, "but I know he has somebody watching."

"Who does," Metzger asked.

"Anthony Giunghierrace," replied ominous Di Presso, "alias Tony Jaguar."

"Who?"

"Eh, sfacim',"[15] shrugged Di Presso, and spat into their wake. The Paranoids were singing, to the tune of "Adeste Fideles":

> Hey, solid citizen, we just pinched your bo-oat,
> Hey, solid citizen, we just pinched your boat . . .

grabassing around, trying to push each other over the side. Oedipa cringed out of the way and watched Di Presso. If he had really played the part of Metzger in a TV pilot film as Metzger claimed, the casting had been typically Hollywood: they didn't look or act a bit alike.

"So," said Di Presso, "who's Tony Jaguar. Very big in Cosa Nostra, is who."

"You're an actor," said Metzger. "How are you in with them?"

"I'm a lawyer again," Di Presso said. "That pilot will never be bought, Metz, not unless you go out and do something really Darrow-like,[16] spectacular. Arouse public interest, maybe with a sensational defense."

---

[15]An Italian obscenity.

[16]Clarence Darrow (1857–1938), exceptionally eloquent defense attorney.

"Like what."

"Like win the litigation I'm bringing against the estate of Pierce Inverarity." Metzger, as much as cool Metzger could, goggled. Di Presso laughed and punched Metzger in the shoulder. "That's right, good buddy."

"Who wants that? You better talk to the other executor too." He introduced Oedipa, Di Presso tipping his shades politely. The air suddenly went cold, the sun was blotted out. The three looked up in alarm to see looming over them and about to collide the pale green social hall, its towering pointed windows, wrought-iron floral embellishments, solid silence, air somehow of waiting for them. Dean, the Paranoid at the helm, brought the boat around neatly to a small wooden dock, everybody got out, Di Presso heading nervously for an outside staircase. "I want to check on my car," he said. Oedipa and Metzger, carrying picnic stuff, followed up the stairs, along a balcony, out of the building's shadow, up a metal ladder finally to the roof. It was like walking on the head of a drum: they could hear their reverberations inside the hollow building beneath, and the delighted yelling of the Paranoids. Di Presso, Scuba suit glistening, scrambled up the side of a cupola. Oedipa spread a blanket and poured booze into cups made of white, crushed, plastic foam. "It's still there," said Di Presso, descending. "I ought to make a run for it."

"Who's your client?" asked Metzger, holding out a tequila sour.

"Fellow who's chasing me," allowed Di Presso, holding the cup between his teeth so it covered his nose and looking at them, arch.

"You run from clients?" Oedipa asked. "You *flee* ambulances?"

"He's been trying to borrow money," Di Presso said, "since I told him I couldn't get an advance against any settlement in this suit."

"You're all ready to lose, then," she said.

"My heart isn't in it," Di Presso admitted, "and if I can't even keep up payments on that XKE I bought while temporarily insane, how can I lend money?"

"Over 30 years," Metzger snorted, "that's temporary."

"I'm not so crazy I don't know trouble," Di Presso said, "and Tony J. is in it, friends. Gambling mostly, also talk he's been up to show cause to the local Table why he shouldn't be in for some discipline there. That kind of grief I do not need."

Oedipa glared. "You're a selfish schmuck."

"All the time Cosa Nostra is watching," soothed Metzger, "watching. It does not do to be seen helping those the organization does not want helped."

"I have relatives in Sicily," said Di Presso, in comic broken English. Paranoids and their chicks appeared against the bright sky, from behind turrets, gables, ventilating ducts, and moved in on the eggplant sandwiches in the basket. Metzger sat on the jug of booze so they couldn't get any. The wind had risen.

"Tell me about the lawsuit," said Metzger, trying with both hands to keep his hair in place.

"You've been into Inverarity's books," Di Presso said. "You know the Beaconsfield filter thing." Metzger made a noncommittal moue.

"Bone charcoal," Oedipa remembered.

"Yeah, well Tony Jaguar, my client, supplied some bones," said Di Presso, "he alleges. Inverarity never paid him. That's what it's about."

"Offhand," Metzger said, "it doesn't sound like Inverarity. He was scrupulous about payments like that. Unless it was a bribe. I only did his legal tax deductions, so I wouldn't have seen it if it was. What construction firm did your client work for?"

"Construction firm," squinted Di Presso.

Metzger looked around. The Paranoids and their chicks may have been out of earshot. "Human bones, right?" Di Presso nodded yes. "All right, that's how he got them. Different highway outfits in the area, ones Inverarity had bought into, they got the contracts. All drawn up in most kosher fashion, Manfred. If there was payola in there, I doubt it got written down."

"How," inquired Oedipa, "are road builders in any position to sell bones, pray?"

"Old cemeteries have to be ripped up," Metzger explained. "Like in the path of the East San Narciso Freeway, it had no right to be there, so we just barrelled on through, no sweat."

"No bribes, no freeways," Di Presso shaking his head. "These bones came from Italy. A straight sale. Some of them," waving out at the lake, "are down there, to decorate the bottom for the Scuba nuts. That's what I've been doing today, examining the goods in dispute. Till Tony started chasing, anyway. The rest of the bones were used in the R&D phase of the filter program, back around the early '50's, way before cancer. Tony Jaguar says he harvested them all from the bottom of Lago di Pietà."[17]

"My God," Metzger said, soon as this name registered. "GI's?"

"About a company," said Manny Di Presso. Lago di Pietà was near

---

[17] Lake of Piety (or Pity).

the Tyrrhenian coast, somewhere between Naples and Rome, and had been the scene of a now ignored (in 1943 tragic) battle of attrition in a minor pocket developed during the advance on Rome. For weeks, a handful of American troops, cut off and without communications, huddled on the narrow shore of the clear and tranquil lake while from the cliffs that tilted vertiginously over the beach Germans hit them day and night with plunging, enfilading fire. The water of the lake was too cold to swim: you died of exposure before you could reach any safe shore. There were no trees to build rafts with. No planes came over except an occasional Stuka with strafing in mind. It was remarkable that so few men held out so long. They dug in as far as the rocky beach would let them; they sent small raids up the cliffs that mostly never came back, but did succeed in taking out a machine-gun, once. Patrols looked for routes out, but those few that returned had found nothing. They did what they could to break out; failing, they clung to life as long as they could. But they died, every one, humbly, without a trace or a word. One day the Germans came down from the cliffs, and their enlisted men put all the bodies that were on the beach into the lake, along with what weapons and other materiel were no longer of use to either side. Presently the bodies sank; and stayed where they were till the early '50's, when Tony Jaguar, who'd been a corporal in an Italian outfit attached to the German force at Lago di Pietà and knew what was at the bottom, decided along with some colleagues to see what he could salvage. All they managed to come up with was bones. Out of some murky train of reasoning, which may have included the observed fact that American tourists, beginning then to be plentiful, would pay good dollars for almost anything; and stories about Forest Lawn and the American cult of the dead; possibly some dim hope that Senator McCarthy, and others of his persuasion, in those days having achieved a certain ascendancy over the rich cretini from across the sea, would somehow refocus attention on the fallen of WW II, especially ones whose corpses had never been found; out of some such labyrinth of assumed motives, Tony Jaguar decided he could surely unload his harvest of bones on some American someplace, through his contacts in the "family," known these days as Cosa Nostra. He was right. An import-export firm bought the bones, sold them to a fertilizer enterprise, which may have used one or two femurs for laboratory tests but eventually decided to phase entirely into menhaden[18] instead and trans-

---

[18]Small shad-like fish used primarily as fertilizer.

ferred the remaining several tons to a holding company, which stored them in a warehouse outside of Fort Wayne, Indiana, for maybe a year before Beaconsfield got interested.

"Aha," Metzger leaped. "So it was Beaconsfield bought them. Not Inverarity. The only shares he held were in Osteolysis, Inc., the company he set up to develop the filter. Never in Beaconsfield itself."

"You know, blokes," remarked one of the girls, a long-waisted, brown-haired lovely in a black knit leotard and pointed sneakers, "this all has a most bizarre resemblance to that ill, ill Jacobean revenge play[19] we went to last week."

"*The Courier's Tragedy*," said Miles, "she's right. The same kind of kinky thing, you know. Bones of lost battalion in lake, fished up, turned into charcoal——"

"They've been listening," screamed Di Presso, "those kids. All the time, somebody listens in, snoops; they bug your apartment, they tap your phone——"

"But we don't repeat what we hear," said another girl. "None of us smoke Beaconsfields anyway. We're all on pot." Laughter. But no joke: for Leonard the drummer now reached into the pocket of his beach robe and produced a fistful of marijuana cigarettes and distributed them among his chums. Metzger closed his eyes, turned his head, muttering, "Possession."

"Help," said Di Presso, looking back with a wild eye and open mouth across the lake. Another runabout had appeared and was headed toward them. Two figures in gray suits crouched behind its windshield. "Metz, I'm running for it. If he stops here don't bully him, he's my client." And he disappeared down the ladder. Oedipa with a sigh collapsed on her back and stared through the wind at the empty blue sky. Soon she heard the "Godzilla II" starting up.

"Metzger," it occurred to her, "he's taking the boat? We're marooned."

So they were, until well after the sun had set and Miles, Dean, Serge and Leonard and their chicks, by holding up the glowing roaches of their cigarettes like a flipcard section at a football game to spell out

---

[19]In the "Jacobean" period—the reign of King James I (1603-1625)—a popular dramatic form was the "revenge-tragedy," which often involved frequent, bloody, and unusual deaths knotted into a complicated and melodramatic plot. *The Courier's Tragedy*, whose plot summary follows directly, is a parody that exaggerates, though not by much, the characteristics of such plays as Webster's *The Duchess of Malfi* and Tourneur's *Revenger's Tragedy*.

alternate S's and O's, attracted the attention of the Fangoso Lagoons Security Force, a garrison against the night made up of onetime cowboy actors and L.A. motorcycle cops. The time in between had been whiled away with songs by the Paranoids, and juicing, and feeding pieces of eggplant sandwich to a flock of not too bright seagulls who'd mistaken Fangoso Lagoons for the Pacific, and hearing the plot of *The Courier's Tragedy*, by Richard Wharfinger, related near to unintelligible by eight memories unlooping progressively into regions as strange to map as their rising coils and clouds of pot smoke. It got so confusing that next day Oedipa decided to go see the play itself, and even conned Metzger into taking her.

The Courier's Tragedy was being put on by a San Narciso group known as the Tank Players, the Tank being a small area theatre located out between a traffic analysis firm and a wildcat transistor outfit that hadn't been there last year and wouldn't be this coming but meanwhile was underselling even the Japanese and hauling in loot by the steamshovelful. Oedipa and a reluctant Metzger came in on only a partly-filled house. Attendance did not swell by the time the play started. But the costumes were gorgeous and the lighting imaginative, and though the words were all spoken in Transplanted Middle Western Stage British, Oedipa found herself after five minutes sucked utterly into the landscape of evil Richard Wharfinger had fashioned for his 17th-century audiences, so preapocalyptic, death-wishful, sensually fatigued, unprepared, a little poignantly, for that abyss of civil war that had been waiting, cold and deep, only a few years ahead of them.

Angelo, then, evil Duke of Squamuglia, has perhaps ten years before the play's opening murdered the good Duke of adjoining Faggio, by poisoning the feet on an image of Saint Narcissus, Bishop of Jerusalem, in the court chapel, which feet the Duke was in the habit of kissing every Sunday at Mass. This enables the evil illegitimate son, Pasquale, to take over as regent for his half-brother Niccolò, the rightful heir and good guy of the play, till he comes of age. Pasquale of course has no intention of letting him live so long. Being in thick with the Duke of Squamuglia, Pasquale plots to do away with young Niccolò by suggesting a game of hide-and-seek and then finessing him into crawling inside of an enormous cannon, which a henchman is then to set off, hopefully blowing the child, as Pasquale recalls ruefully, later on in the third act,

Out in a bloody rain to feed our fields
Amid the Maenad roar of nitre's song
And sulfur's cantus firmus.

Ruefully, because the henchman, a likeable schemer named Ercole, is secretly involved with dissident elements in the court of Faggio who want to keep Niccolò alive, and so he contrives to stuff a young goat into the cannon instead, meanwhile smuggling Niccolò out of the ducal palace disguised as an elderly procuress.

This comes out in the first scene, as Niccolò confides his history to a friend, Domenico. Niccolò is at this point grown up, hanging around the court of his father's murderer, Duke Angelo, and masquerading as a special courier of the Thurn and Taxis family, who at the time held a postal monopoly throughout most of the Holy Roman Empire. What he is trying to do, ostensibly, is develop a new market, since the evil Duke of Squamuglia has steadfastly refused, even with the lower rates and faster service of the Thurn and Taxis system, to employ any but his own messengers in communicating with his stooge Pasquale over in neighboring Faggio. The real reason Niccolò is waiting around is of course to get a crack at the Duke.

Evil Duke Angelo, meanwhile, is scheming to amalgamate the duchies of Squamuglia and Faggio, by marrying off the only royal female available, his sister Francesca, to Pasquale the Faggian usurper. The only obstacle in the way of this union is that Francesca is Pasquale's mother—her illicit liaison with the good ex-Duke of Faggio being one reason Angelo had him poisoned to begin with. There is an amusing scene where Francesca delicately seeks to remind her brother of the social taboos against incest. They seem to have slipped her mind, replies Angelo, during the ten years he and Francesca have been having *their* affair. Incest or no, the marriage must be; it is vital to his long-range political plans. The Church will never sanction it, says Francesca. So, says Duke Angelo, I will bribe a cardinal. He has begun feeling his sister up and nibbling at her neck; the dialogue modulates into the fevered figures of intemperate desire, and the scene ends with the couple collapsing onto a divan.

The act itself closes with Domenico, to whom the naïve Niccolò started it off by spilling his secret, trying to get in to see Duke Angelo and betray his dear friend. The Duke, of course, is in his apartment busy knocking off a piece, and the best Domenico can do is an administrative assistant who turns out to be the same Ercole who once saved the life of young Niccolò and aided his escape from Faggio. This he presently confesses to Domenico, though only after having enticed that informer into foolishly bending over and putting his head into a curious black box, on the pretext of showing him a pornographic diorama. A steel vise promptly clamps onto the faithless Domenico's head and the box muffles his cries for help. Ercole binds his hands and feet with scarlet silk cords, lets him know who it is he's run afoul of, reaches into the box with a pair of pincers, tears out Domenico's tongue, stabs him a couple times, pours into the box a beaker of aqua regia, enumerates a list of other goodies, including castration, that Domenico will undergo before he's allowed to die, all amid screams, tongueless attempts to pray, agonized struggles from the victim. With the tongue impaled on his rapier Ercole runs to a burning torch set in the wall, sets the tongue aflame and waving it around like a madman concludes the act by screaming,

> Thy pitiless unmanning is most meet,
> Thinks Ercole the zany Paraclete.
> Descended this malign, Unholy Ghost,
> Let us begin thy frightful Pentecost.[20]

The lights went out, and in the quiet somebody across the arena from Oedipa distinctly said, "Ick." Metzger said, "You want to go?" "I want to see about the bones," said Oedipa.

She had to wait till the fourth act. The second was largely spent in the protracted torture and eventual murder of a prince of the church who prefers martyrdom to sanctioning Francesca's marriage to her son. The only interruptions come when Ercole, spying on the cardinal's agony, dispatches couriers to the good-guy element back in Faggio who have it in for Pasquale, telling them to spread the word that Pasquale's planning to marry his mother, calculating this ought to rile up public opinion some; and another scene in which Niccolò, passing the time of day with one of Duke Angelo's couriers, hears the tale of the Lost Guard, a body of some fifty hand-picked knights, the flower of Faggian youth, who once rode as protection for the good Duke. One day, out on manoeuvres near the frontiers of Squamuglia, they all vanished without a trace, and shortly afterward the good Duke got poisoned. Honest Niccolò, who always has difficulty hiding his feelings, observes that if the two events turn out to be at all connected, and can be traced to Duke Angelo, boy, the Duke better watch out, is all. The other courier, one Vittorio, takes offense, vowing in an aside to report this treasonable talk to Angelo at the first opportunity. Meanwhile, back in the torture room, the cardinal is now being forced to bleed into a chalice and consecrate his own blood, not to God, but to Satan. They

---

[20]The "Paraclete," the Holy Ghost seen as advocate or comforter, descended upon the Twelve Apostles on Pentecost, the fiftieth day after the Resurrection. See Acts 2:1-13.

also cut off his big toe, and he is made to hold it up like a Host and say, "This is my body," the keen-witted Angelo observing that it's the first time he's told anything like the truth in fifty years of systematic lying. Altogether, a most anti-clerical scene, perhaps intended as a sop to the Puritans of the time (a useless gesture since none of them ever went to plays, regarding them for some reason as immoral).

The third act takes place in the court of Faggio, and is spent murdering Pasquale, as the culmination of a coup stirred up by Ercole's agents. While a battle rages in the streets outside the palace, Pasquale is locked up in his patrician hothouse, holding an orgy. Present at the merrymaking is a fierce black performing ape, brought back from a recent voyage to the Indies. Of course it is somebody in an ape suit, who at a signal leaps on Pasquale from a chandelier, at the same time as half a dozen female impersonators who have up to now been lounging around in the guise of dancing girls also move in on the usurper from all parts of the stage. For about ten minutes the vengeful crew proceed to maim, strangle, poison, burn, stomp, blind and otherwise have at Pasquale, while he describes intimately his varied sensations for our enjoyment. He dies finally in extreme agony, and in marches one Gennaro, a complete nonentity, to proclaim himself interim head of state till the rightful Duke, Niccolò, can be located.

There was an intermission. Metzger lurched into the undersized lobby to smoke, Oedipa headed for the ladies' room. She looked idly around for the symbol she'd seen the other night in The Scope, but all the walls, surprisingly, were blank. She could not say why, exactly, but felt threatened by this absence of even the marginal try at communication latrines are known for.

Act IV of *The Courier's Tragedy* discloses evil Duke Angelo in a state of nervous frenzy. He has learned about the coup in Faggio, the possibility that Niccolò may be alive somewhere after all. Word has reached him that Gennaro is levying a force to invade Squamuglia, also a rumor that the Pope is about to intervene because of the cardinal's murder. Surrounded by treachery on all sides, the Duke has Ercole, whose true role he still does not suspect, finally summon the Thurn and Taxis courier, figuring he can no longer trust his own men. Ercole brings in Niccolò to await the Duke's pleasure. Angelo takes out a quill, parchment and ink, explaining to the audience but not to the good guys, who are still ignorant of recent developments, that to forestall an invasion from Faggio, he must assure Gennaro with all haste of his good intentions. As he scribbles he lets drop a few disordered and cryptic remarks about the ink he's using, implying it's a very special fluid indeed. Like:

This pitchy brew in France is "encre" hight;
In this might dire Squamuglia ape the Gaul,
For "anchor" it has ris'n, from deeps untold.

And:

The swan has yielded but one hollow quill,
The hapless mutton, but his tegument;
Yet what, transmuted swart and silken flows
Between, was neither plucked nor harshly flayed,
But gathered up, from wildly different beasts.

All of which causes him high amusement. The message to Gennaro
completed and sealed, Niccolò tucks it in his doublet and takes off for
Faggio, still unaware, as is Ercole, of the coup and his own impending
restoration as Duke of Faggio. Scene switches to Gennaro, at the head
of a small army, on route to invade Squamuglia. There is a lot of talk to
the effect that if Angelo wants peace he'd better send a messenger to
let them know before they reach the frontier, otherwise with great
reluctance they will hand his ass to him. Back to Squamuglia, where
Vittorio, the Duke's courier, reports how Niccolò has been talking treason. Somebody else runs in with news that the body of Domenico,
Niccolò's faithless friend, has been found mutilated; but tucked in his
shoe was a message, somehow scrawled in blood, revealing Niccolò's
true identity. Angelo flies into an apoplectic rage, and orders Niccolò's
pursuit and destruction. But not by his own men.

It is at about this point in the play, in fact, that things really get
peculiar, and a gentle chill, an ambiguity, begins to creep in among the
words. Heretofore the naming of names has gone on either literally or
as metaphor. But now, as the Duke gives his fatal command, a new
mode of expression takes over. It can only be called a kind of ritual
reluctance. Certain things, it is made clear, will not be spoken aloud;
certain events will not be shown onstage; though it is difficult to imagine, given the excesses of the preceding acts, what these things could
possibly be. The Duke does not, perhaps may not, enlighten us.
Screaming at Vittorio he is explicit enough about who shall *not* pursue
Niccolò: his own bodyguard he describes to their faces as vermin, za-
nies, poltroons. But who then will the pursuers be? Vittorio knows:
every flunky in the court, idling around in their Squamuglia livery and
exchanging Significant Looks, knows. It is all a big in-joke. The audiences of the time knew. Angelo knows, but does not say. As close as he
comes does not illuminate:

Let him that vizard keep unto his grave,
That vain usurping of an honour'd name;
We'll dance his masque as if it were the truth,
Enlist the poniards swift of Those who, sworn
To punctual vendetta never sleep,
Lest at the palest whisper of the name
Sweet Niccolò hath stol'n, one trice be lost
In bringing down a fell and soulless doom
Unutterable. . . .

Back to Gennaro and his army. A spy arrives from Squamuglia to tell them Niccolò's on the way. Great rejoicing, in the midst of which Gennaro, who seldom converses, only orates, begs everybody remember that Niccolò is still riding under the Thurn and Taxis colors. The cheering stops. Again, as in Angelo's court, the curious chill creeps in. Everyone onstage (having clearly been directed to do so) becomes aware of a possibility. Gennaro, even less enlightening than Angelo was, invokes the protection of God and Saint Narcissus for Niccolò, and they all ride on. Gennaro asks a lieutenant where they are; turns out it's only a league or so from the lake where Faggio's Lost Guard were last seen before their mysterious disappearance.

Meanwhile, at Angelo's palace, wily Ercole's string has run out at last. Accosted by Vittorio and half a dozen others, he's charged with the murder of Domenico. Witnesses parade in, there is the travesty of a trial, and Ercole meets his end in a refreshingly simple mass stabbing.

We also see Niccolò, in the scene following, for the last time. He has stopped to rest by the shore of a lake where, he remembers being told, the Faggian Guard disappeared. He sits under a tree, opens Angelo's letter, and learns at last of the coup and death of Pasquale. He realizes that he's riding toward restoration, the love of an entire dukedom, the coming true of all his most virtuous hopes. Leaning against the tree, he reads parts of the letter aloud, commenting, sarcastic, on what is blatantly a pack of lies devised to soothe Gennaro until Angelo can muster his own army of Squamuglians to invade Faggio. Offstage there is a sound of footpads. Niccolò leaps to his feet, staring up one of the radial aisles, hand frozen on the hilt of his sword. He trembles and cannot speak, only stutter, in what may be the shortest line ever written in blank verse: "T-t-t-t-t . . ." As if breaking out of some dream's paralysis, he begins, each step an effort, to retreat. Suddenly, in lithe and terrible silence, with dancer's grace, three figures, long-limbed, effeminate, dressed in black tights, leotards and gloves, black silk hose pulled over their faces, come capering on stage and stop, gazing at him. Their faces behind the stockings are shadowy and deformed. They wait. The lights all go out.

Back in Squamuglia Angelo is trying to muster an army, without success. Desperate, he assembles those flunkies and pretty girls who are left, ritually locks all his exits, has wine brought in, and begins an orgy.

The act ends with Gennaro's forces drawn up by the shores of the lake. An enlisted man comes on to report that a body, identified as Niccolò by the usual amulet placed around his neck as a child, has been found in a condition too awful to talk about. Again there is silence and everybody looks at everybody else. The soldier hands Gennaro a roll of parchment, stained with blood, which was found on the body. From its seal we can see it's the letter from Angelo that Niccolò was carrying. Gennaro glances at it, does a double-take, reads it aloud. It is no longer the lying document Niccolò read us excerpts from at all, but now miraculously a long confession by Angelo of all his crimes, closing with the revelation of what really happened to the Lost Guard of Faggio. They were—surprise—every one massacred by Angelo and thrown in the lake. Later on their bones were fished up again and made into charcoal, and the charcoal into ink, which Angelo, having a dark sense of humor, used in all his subsequent communications with Faggio, the present document included.

> But now the bones of these Immaculate
> Have mingled with the blood of Niccolò,
> And innocence with innocence is join'd,
> A wedlock whose sole child is miracle:
> A life's base lie, rewritten into truth.
> That truth it is, we all bear testament,
> This Guard of Faggio, Faggio's noble dead.

In the presence of the miracle all fall to their knees, bless the name of God, mourn Niccolò, vow to lay Squamuglia waste. But Gennaro ends on a note most desperate, probably for its original audience a real shock, because it names at last the name Angelo did not and Niccolò tried to:

> He that we last as Thurn and Taxis knew
> Now recks no lord but the stiletto's Thorn,
> And Tacit lies the gold once-knotted horn.
> No hallowed skein of stars can ward, I trow,
> Who's once been set his tryst with Trystero.

Trystero. The word hung in the air as the act ended and all lights were for a moment cut; hung in the dark to puzzle Oedipa Maas, but not yet to exert the power over her it was to.

The fifth act, entirely an anticlimax, is taken up by the bloodbath Gennaro visits on the court of Squamuglia. Every mode of violent death available to Renaissance man, including a lye pit, land mines, a trained falcon with envenom'd talons, is employed. It plays, as Metzger remarked later, like a Road Runner cartoon in blank verse. At the end of it about the only character left alive in a stage dense with corpses is the colorless administrator, Gennaro.

According to the program, *The Courier's Tragedy* had been directed by one Randolph Driblette. He had also played the part of Gennaro the winner. "Look, Metzger," Oedipa said, "come on backstage with me."

"You know one of them?" said Metzger, anxious to leave.

"I want to find out something. I want to talk to Driblette."

"Oh, about the bones." He had a brooding look. Oedipa said,

"I don't know. It just has me uneasy. The two things, so close."

"Fine," Metzger said, "and what next, picket the V.A.? March on Washington? God protect me," he addressed the ceiling of the little theatre, causing a few heads among those leaving to swivel, "from these lib, overeducated broads with the soft heads and bleeding hearts. I am 35 years old, and I should know better."

"Metzger," Oedipa whispered, embarrassed, "I'm a Young Republican."

"Hap Harrigan comics," Metzger now even louder, "which she is hardly old enough to read, John Wayne on Saturday afternoon slaughtering ten thousand Japs with his teeth, this is Oedipa Maas's World War II, man. Some people today can drive VW's, carry a Sony radio in their shirt pocket. Not this one, folks, she wants to right wrongs, 20 years after it's all over. Raise ghosts. All from a drunken hassle with Manny Di Presso. Forgetting her first loyalty, legal and moral, is to the estate she represents. Not to our boys in uniform, however gallant, whenever they died."

"It isn't that," she protested. "I don't care what Beaconsfield uses in its filter. I don't care what Pierce bought from the Cosa Nostra. I don't want to think about them. Or about what happened at Lago di Pietà, or cancer . . ." She looked around for words, feeling helpless.

"What then?" Metzger challenged, getting to his feet, looming. "What?"

"I don't know," she said, a little desperate. "Metzger, don't harass me. Be on my side."

"Against whom?" inquired Metzger, putting on shades.

"I want to see if there's a connection. I'm curious."

"Yes, you're curious," Metzger said. "I'll wait in the car, OK?"
Oedipa watched him out of sight, then went looking for dressing
rooms; circled the annular corridor outside twice before settling on a
door in the shadowy interval between two overhead lights. She walked
in on soft, elegant chaos, an impression of emanations, mutually interfering, from the stub-antennas of everybody's exposed nerve endings.

A girl removing fake blood from her face motioned Oedipa on into a
region of brightly-lit mirrors. She pushed in, gliding off sweating biceps
and momentary curtains of long, swung hair, till at last she stood before Driblette, still wearing his gray Gennaro outfit.

"It was great," said Oedipa.

"Feel," said Driblette, extending his arm. She felt. Gennaro's costume was gray flannel. "You sweat like hell, but nothing else would
really be him, right?"

Oedipa nodded. She couldn't stop watching his eyes. They were
bright black, surrounded by an incredible network of lines, like a laboratory maze for studying intelligence in tears. They seemed to know
what she wanted, even if she didn't.

"You came to talk about the play," he said. "Let me discourage you.
It was written to entertain people. Like horror movies. It isn't literature,
it doesn't mean anything. Wharfinger was no Shakespeare."

"Who was he?" she said.

"Who was Shakespeare. It was a long time ago."

"Could I see a script?" She didn't know what she was looking for,
exactly. Driblette motioned her over to a file cabinet next to the one
shower.

"I'd better grab a shower," he said, "before the Drop-the-Soap
crowd get here. Scripts're in the top drawer."

But they were all purple, Dittoed—worn, torn, stained with coffee.
Nothing else in the drawer. "Hey," she yelled into the shower.
"Where's the original? What did you make these copies from?"

"A paperback," Driblette yelled back. "Don't ask me the publisher.
I found it at Zapf's Used Books over by the freeway. It's an anthology,
Jacobean Revenge Plays. There was a skull on the cover."

"Could I borrow it?"

"Somebody took it. Opening night parties. I lose at least half a dozen
every time." He stuck his head out of the shower. The rest of his body
was wreathed in steam, giving his head an eerie, balloon-like buoy-

ancy. Careful, staring at her with deep amusement, he said, "There was another copy there. Zapf might still have it. Can you find the place?" Something came to her viscera, danced briefly, and went. "Are you putting me on?" For awhile the furrowed eyes only gazed back.

"Why," Driblette said at last, "is everybody so interested in texts?"

"Who else?" Too quickly. Maybe he had only been talking in general.

Driblette's head wagged back and forth. "Don't drag me into your scholarly disputes," adding "whoever you all are," with a familiar smile. Oedipa realized then, cold corpse-fingers of grue on her skin, that it was exactly the same look he'd coached his cast to give each other whenever the subject of the Trystero assassins came up. The knowing look you get in your dreams from a certain unpleasant figure. She decided to ask about this look.

"Was it written in as a stage direction? All those people, so obviously in on something. Or was that one of your touches?"

"That was my own," Driblette told her, "that, and actually bringing the three assassins onstage in the fourth act. Wharfinger didn't show them at all, you know."

"Why did you? Had you heard about them somewhere else?"

"You don't understand," getting mad. "You guys, you're like Puritans are about the Bible. So hung up with words, words. You know where that play exists, not in that file cabinet, not in any paperback you're looking for, but—" a hand emerged from the veil of shower-steam to indicate his suspended head—"in here. That's what I'm for. To give the spirit flesh. The words, who cares? They're rote noises to hold line bashes with, to get past the bone barriers around an actor's memory, right? But the reality is in *this* head. Mine. I'm the projector at the planetarium, all the closed little universe visible in the circle of that stage is coming out of my mouth, eyes, sometimes other orifices also."

But she couldn't let it quite go. "What made you feel differently than Wharfinger did about this, this Trystero." At the word, Driblette's face abruptly vanished, back into the steam. As if switched off. Oedipa hadn't wanted to say the word. He had managed to create around it the same aura of ritual reluctance here, offstage, as he had on.

"If I were to dissolve here," speculated the voice out of the drifting steam, "be washed down the drain into the Pacific, what you saw tonight would vanish too. You, that part of you so concerned, God knows how, with that little world, would also vanish. The only residue in fact would be things Wharfinger didn't lie about. Perhaps Squamuglia and

Faggio, if they ever existed. Perhaps the Thurn and Taxis mail system. Stamp collectors tell me it did exist.[21] Perhaps the other, also. The Adversary. But they would be traces, fossils. Dead, mineral, without value or potential.

"You could fall in love with me, you can talk to my shrink, you can hide a tape recorder in my bedroom, see what I talk about from wherever I am when I sleep. You want to do that? You can put together clues, develop a thesis, or several, about why characters reacted to the Trystero possibility the way they did, why the assassins came on, why the black costumes. You could waste your life that way and never touch the truth. Wharfinger supplied words and a yarn. I gave them life. That's it." He fell silent. The shower splashed.

"Driblette?" Oedipa called, after a while.

His face appeared briefly. "We could do that." He wasn't smiling. His eyes waited, at the centres of their webs.

"I'll call," said Oedipa. She left, and was all the way outside before thinking, I went in there to ask about bones and instead we talked about the Trystero thing. She stood in a nearby deserted parking lot, watching the headlights of Metzger's car come at her, and wondered how accidental it had been.

Metzger had been listening to the car radio. She got in and rode with him for two miles before realizing that the whimsies of nighttime reception were bringing them KCUF down from Kinneret, and that the disk jockey talking was her husband, Mucho.

IV

Though she saw Mike Fallopian again, and did trace the text of *The Courier's Tragedy* a certain distance, these follow-ups were no more disquieting than other revelations which now seemed to come crowding in exponentially, as if the more she collected the more would come to her, until everything she saw, smelled, dreamed, remembered, would somehow come to be woven into The Tristero.

For one thing, she read over the will more closely. If it was really Pierce's attempt to leave an organized something behind after his own

---

[21]It did exist, and Pynchon's descriptions of it throughout the novella are surprisingly accurate.

annihilation, then it was part of her duty, wasn't it, to bestow life on what had persisted, to try to be what Driblette was, the dark machine in the centre of the planetarium, to bring the estate into pulsing stelliferous Meaning, all in a soaring dome around her? If only so much didn't stand in her way: her deep ignorance of law, of investment, of real estate, ultimately of the dead man himself. The bond the probate court had had her post was perhaps their evaluation in dollars of how much did stand in her way. Under the symbol she'd copied off the latrine wall of The Scope into her memo book, she wrote *Shall I project a world?* If not project then at least flash some arrow on the dome to skitter among constellations and trace out your Dragon, Whale, Southern Cross. Anything might help.

It was some such feeling that got her up early one morning to go to a Yoyodyne stockholders' meeting. There was nothing she could do at it, yet she felt it might redeem her a little from inertia. They gave her a round white visitor's badge at one of the gates, and she parked in an enormous lot next to a quonset building painted pink and about a hundred yards long. This was the Yoyodyne Cafeteria, and scene of her meeting. For two hours Oedipa sat on a long bench between old men who might have been twins and whose hands, alternately (as if their owners were asleep and the moled, freckled hands out roaming dreamlandscapes) kept falling onto her thighs. Around them all, Negroes carried gunboats of mashed potatoes, spinach, shrimp, zucchini, pot roast, to the long, glittering steam tables, preparing to feed an invasion of Yoyodyne workers. The routine business took an hour; for another hour the shareholders and proxies and company officers held a Yoyodyne songfest. To the tune of Cornell's alma mater, they sang:

Hymn

High above the L.A. freeways,
And the traffic's whine,
Stands the well-known Galactronics
Branch of Yoyodyne.
To the end, we swear undying
Loyalty to you,
Pink pavilions bravely shining,
Palm trees tall and true.

Being led in this by the president of the company, Mr Clayton ("Bloody") Chiclitz himself; and to the tune of "Aura Lee":

GLEE

Bendix guides the warheads in,
Avco builds them nice.
Douglas, North American,
Grumman get their slice.
Martin launches off a pad,
Lockheed from a sub;
We can't get the R&D[22]
On a Piper Cub.

Convair boosts the satellite
Into orbits round;
Boeing builds the Minuteman,
We stay on the ground.
Yoyodyne, Yoyodyne,
Contracts flee thee yet.
DOD[23] has shafted thee,
Out of spite, I'll bet.

And dozens of other old favorites whose lyrics she couldn't remember. The singers were then formed into platoon-sized groups for a quick tour of the plant.

Somehow Oedipa got lost. One minute she was gazing at a mockup of a space capsule, safely surrounded by old, somnolent men; the next, alone in a great, fluorescent murmur of office activity. As far as she could see in any direction it was white or pastel: men's shirts, papers, drawing boards. All she could think of was to put on her shades for all this light, and wait for somebody to rescue her. But nobody noticed. She began to wander aisles among light blue desks, turning a corner now and then. Heads came up at the sound of her heels, engineers stared until she'd passed, but nobody spoke to her. Five or ten minutes went by this way, panic growing inside her head: there seemed no way out of the area. Then, by accident (Dr Hilarius, if asked, would accuse her of using subliminal cues in the environment to guide her to a particular person) or howsoever, she came on one Stanley Koteks, who wore wire-rim bifocals, sandals, argyle socks, and at first glance seemed too young to be working here. As it turned out he wasn't working, only doodling with a fat felt pencil this sign:

---

[22]Research and Development (contract, that is).
[23]Department of Defense.

"Hello there," Oedipa said, arrested by this coincidence. On a whim, she added, "Kirby sent me," this having been the name on the latrine wall. It was supposed to sound conspiratorial, but came out silly.

"Hi," said Stanley Koteks, deftly sliding the big envelope he'd been doodling on into an open drawer he then closed. Catching sight of her badge, "You're lost, huh?"

She knew blunt questions like, what does that symbol mean? would get her nowhere. She said, "I'm a tourist, actually. A stockholder."

"Stockholder." He gave her the once-over, hooked with his foot a swivel chair from the next desk and rolled it over for her. "Sit down. Can you really influence policy, or make suggestions they won't just file in the garbage?"

"Yes," lied Oedipa, to see where it would take them.

"See," Koteks said, "if you can get them to drop their clause on patents. That, lady, is my ax to grind."

"Patents," Oedipa said. Koteks explained how every engineer, in signing the Yoyodyne contract, also signed away the patent rights to any inventions he might come up with.

"This stifles your really creative engineer," Koteks said, adding bitterly, "wherever he may be."

"I didn't think people invented any more," said Oedipa, sensing this would goad him. "I mean, who's there been, really, since Thomas Edison? Isn't it all teamwork now?" Bloody Chiclitz, in his welcoming speech this morning, had stressed teamwork.

"Teamwork," Koteks snarled, "is one word for it, yeah. What it really is is a way to avoid responsibility. It's a symptom of the gutlessness of the whole society."

"Goodness," said Oedipa, "are you allowed to talk like that?"

Koteks looked to both sides, then rolled his chair closer. "You know the Nefastis Machine?" Oedipa only widened her eyes. "Well this was invented by John Nefastis,[24] who's up at Berkeley now. John's somebody who still invents things. Here. I have a copy of the patent." From a drawer he produced a Xeroxed wad of papers, showing a box with a sketch of a bearded Victorian on its outside, and coming out of the top two pistons attached to a crankshaft and flywheel.

"Who's that with the beard?" asked Oedipa. James Clerk Maxwell,[25]

---

[24]In Latin, "nefastis" means "forbidden" or "taboo."

[25]British physicist whose speculations on theory of heat are given factual treatment here; he was also known as "a sincere and unostentatious Christian."

explained Koteks, a famous Scotch scientist who had once postulated a tiny intelligence, known as Maxwell's Demon. The Demon could sit in a box among air molecules that were moving at all different random speeds, and sort out the fast molecules from the slow ones. Fast molecules have more energy than slow ones. Concentrate enough of them in one place and you have a region of high temperature. You can then use the difference in temperature between this hot region of the box and any cooler region, to drive a heat engine. Since the Demon only sat and sorted, you wouldn't have put any real work into the system. So you would be violating the Second Law of Thermodynamics, getting something for nothing, causing perpetual motion.

"Sorting isn't work?" Oedipa said. "Tell them down at the post office, you'll find yourself in a mailbag headed for Fairbanks, Alaska, without even a FRAGILE sticker going for you."

"It's mental work," Koteks said, "but not work in the thermodynamic sense." He went on to tell how the Nefastis Machine contained an honest-to-God Maxwell's Demon. All you had to do was stare at the photo of Clerk Maxwell, and concentrate on which cylinder, right or left, you wanted the Demon to raise the temperature in. The air would expand and push a piston. The familiar Society for the Propagation of Christian Knowledge photo, showing Maxwell in right profile, seemed to work best.

Oedipa, behind her shades, looked around carefully, trying to move her head. Nobody paid any attention to them: the air-conditioning hummed on, IBM typewriters chiggered away, swivel chairs squeaked, fat reference manuals were slammed shut, rattling blueprints folded and refolded, while high overhead the long silent fluorescent bulbs glared merrily; all with Yoyodyne was normal. Except right here, where Oedipa Maas, with a thousand other people to choose from, had had to walk uncoerced into the presence of madness.

"Not everybody can work it, of course," Koteks, having warmed to his subject, was telling her. "Only people with the gift. 'Sensitives,' John calls them."

Oedipa rested her shades on her nose and batted her eyelashes, figuring to coquette her way off this conversational hook: "Would I make a good sensitive, do you think?"

"You really want to try it? You could write to him. He only knows a few sensitives. He'd let you try."

Oedipa took out her little memo book and opened to the symbol she'd copied and the words *Shall I project a world?* "Box 573," said Koteks.

"In Berkeley."

"No," his voice gone funny, so that she looked up, too sharply, by which time, carried by a certain momentum of thought, he'd also said, "In San Francisco; there's none—" and by then knew he'd made a mistake. "He's living somewhere along Telegraph," he muttered. "I gave you the wrong address."

She took a chance: "Then the WASTE address isn't good any more." But she'd pronounced it like a word, waste. His face congealed, a mask of distrust. "It's W.A.S.T.E., lady," he told her, "an acronym, not 'waste,' and we had best not go into it any further."

"I saw it in a ladies' john," she confessed. But Stanley Koteks was no longer about to be sweet-talked.

"Forget it," he advised; opened a book and proceeded to ignore her.

She in her turn, clearly, was not about to forget it. The envelope she'd seen Koteks doodling what she'd begun to think of as the "WASTE symbol" on had come, she bet, from John Nefastis. Or somebody like him. Her suspicions got embellished by, of all people, Mike Fallopian of the Peter Pinguid Society.

"Sure this Koteks is part of some underground," he told her a few days later, "an underground of the unbalanced, possibly, but then how can you blame them for being maybe a little bitter? Look what's happening to them. In school they got brainwashed, like all of us, into believing the Myth of the American Inventor—Morse and his telegraph, Bell and his telephone, Edison and his light bulb, Tom Swift and his this or that. Only one man per invention. Then when they grew up they found they had to sign over all their rights to a monster like Yoyodyne; got stuck on some 'project' or 'task force' or 'team' and started being ground into anonymity. Nobody wanted them to invent—only perform their little role in a design ritual, already set down for them in some procedures handbook. What's it like, Oedipa, being all alone in a nightmare like that? Of course they stick together, they keep in touch. They can always tell when they come on another of their kind. Maybe it only happens once every five years, but still, immediately, they know."

Metzger, who'd come along to The Scope that evening, wanted to argue. "You're so right-wing you're left-wing," he protested. "How can you be against a corporation that wants a worker to waive his patent rights. That sounds like the surplus value theory to me, fella, and you sound like a Marxist." As they got drunker this typical Southern California dialogue degenerated further. Oedipa sat alone and gloomy. She'd decided to come tonight to The Scope not only because of the encounter with Stanley Koteks, but also because of other revelations; because it seemed that a pattern was beginning to emerge, having to do with the mail and how it was delivered.

There had been the bronze historical marker on the other side of the lake at Fangoso Lagoons. *On this site,* it read, *in 1853, a dozen Wells, Fargo men battled gallantly with a band of masked marauders in mysterious black uniforms. We owe this description to a post rider, the only witness to the massacre, who died shortly after. The only other clue was a cross, traced by one of the victims in the dust. To this day the identities of the slayers remain shrouded in mystery.* A cross? Or the initial T? The same stuttered by Niccolò in *The Courier's Tragedy.* Oedipa pondered this. She called Randolph Driblette from a pay booth to see if he'd known about this Wells, Fargo incident; if that was why he'd chosen to dress his bravos all in black. The phone buzzed on and on, into hollowness. She hung up and headed for Zapf's Used Books. Zapf himself came forward out of a wan cone of 15-watt illumination to help her find the paperback Driblette had mentioned, *Jacobean Revenge Plays.*

"It's been very much in demand," Zapf told her. The skull on the cover watched them, through the dim light.

Did he only mean Driblette? She opened her mouth to ask, but didn't. It was to be the first of many demurs.

Back at Echo Courts, Metzger in L.A. for the day on other business, she turned immediately to the single mention of the word Trystero. Opposite the line she read, in pencil, *Cf. variant, 1687 ed.* Put there maybe by some student. In a way, it cheered her. Another reading of that line might help light further the dark face of the word. According to a short preface, the text had been taken from a folio edition, undated. Oddly, the preface was unsigned. She checked the copyright page and found that the original hardcover had been a textbook, *Plays of Ford, Webster, Tourneur and Wharfinger,* published by The Lectern Press, Berkeley, California, back in 1957. She poured herself half a tumbler of Jack Daniels (the Paranoids having left them a fresh bottle the evening before) and called the L.A. library. They checked, but didn't have the hardcover. They could look it up on inter-library loan for her. "Wait," she said, having just got an idea, "the publisher's up in Berkeley. Maybe I'll try them directly." Thinking also that she could visit John Nefastis.

She had caught sight of the historical marker only because she'd gone back, deliberately, to Lake Inverarity one day, owing to this, what you might have to call, growing obsession, with "bringing something of herself"—even if that something was just her presence—to the scatter of business interests that had survived Inverarity. She would give them order, she would create constellations; next day she drove out to Vesperhaven House, a home for senior citizens that Inverarity had put up around the time Yoyodyne came to San Narciso. In its front recreation room she found sunlight coming in it seemed through every window; an old man nodding in front of a dim Leon Schlesinger cartoon show on the tube; and a black fly browsing along the pink, dandruffy arroyo of the neat part in the old man's hair. A fat nurse ran in with a can of bug spray and yelled at the fly to take off so she could kill it. The cagy fly stayed where it was. "You're bothering Mr Thoth,"[26] she yelled at the little fellow. Mr Thoth jerked awake, jarring loose the fly, which made a desperate scramble for the door. The nurse pursued, spraying poison.

"Hello," said Oedipa.

"I was dreaming," Mr Thoth told her, "about my grandfather. A very old man, at least as old as I am now, 91. I thought, when I was a boy, that he had been 91 all his life. Now I feel," laughing, "as if *I* have been 91 all my life. Oh, the stories that old man would tell. He rode for the Pony Express, back in the gold rush days. His horse was named Adolf, I remember that."

Oedipa, sensitized, thinking of the bronze marker, smiled at him as granddaughterly as she knew how and asked, "Did he ever have to fight off desperados?"

"That cruel old man," said Mr Thoth, "was an Indian killer. God, the saliva would come out in a string from his mouth whenever he talked about killing the Indians. He must have loved that part of it."

"What were you dreaming about him?"

"Oh, that," perhaps embarrassed. "It was all mixed in with a Porky Pig cartoon." He waved at the tube. "It comes into your dreams, you know. Filthy machine. Did you ever see the one about Porky Pig and the anarchist?"

She had, as a matter of fact, but she said no.

"The anarchist is dressed all in black. In the dark you can only see his eyes. It dates from the 1930's. Porky Pig is a little boy. The children told me that he has a nephew now, Cicero. Do you remember, during

---

[26]Thoth was, in Egyptian mythology, the god of learning and wisdom, and the inventor of writing.

the war, when Porky worked in a defense plant? He and Bugs Bunny. That was a good one too."

"Dressed all in black," Oedipa prompted him.

"It was mixed in so with the Indians," he tried to remember, "the dream. The Indians who wore black feathers, the Indians who weren't Indians. My grandfather told me. The feathers were white, but those false Indians were supposed to burn bones and stir the boneblack with their feathers to get them black. It made them invisible in the night, because they came at night. That was how the old man, bless him, knew they weren't Indians. No Indian ever attacked at night. If he got killed his soul would wander in the dark forever. Heathen."

"If they weren't Indians," Oedipa asked, "what were they?"

"A Spanish name," Mr Thoth said, frowning, "a Mexican name. Oh, I can't remember. Did they write it on the ring?" He reached down to a knitting bag by his chair and came up with blue yarn, needles, patterns, finally a dull gold signet ring. "My grandfather cut this from the finger of one of them he killed. Can you imagine a 91-year-old man so brutal?" Oedipa stared. The device on the ring was once again the WASTE symbol.

She looked around, spooked at the sunlight pouring in all the windows, as if she had been trapped at the centre of some intricate crystal, and said, "My God."

"And I feel him, certain days, days of a certain temperature," said Mr Thoth, "and barometric pressure. Did you know that? I feel him close to me."

"Your grandfather?"

"No, my God."

So she went to find Fallopian, who ought to know a lot about the Pony Express and Wells, Fargo if he was writing a book about them. He did, but not about their dark adversaries.

"I've had hints," he told her, "sure. I wrote to Sacramento about that historical marker, and they've been kicking it around their bureaucratic morass for months. Someday they'll come back with a source book for me to read. It will say, 'Old-timers remember the yarn about,' whatever happened. Old-timers. Real good documentation, this Californiana crap. Odds are the author will be dead. There's no way to trace it, unless you want to follow up an accidental correlation, like you got from the old man."

"You think it's really a correlation?" She thought of how tenuous it was, like a long white hair, over a century long. Two very old men. All these fatigued brain cells between herself and the truth.

"Marauders, nameless, faceless, dressed in black. Probably hired by the Federal government. Those suppressions were brutal."

"Couldn't it have been a rival carrier?"

Fallopian shrugged. Oedipa showed him the WASTE symbol, and he shrugged again.

"It was in the ladies' room, right here in The Scope, Mike."

"Women," he only said. "Who can tell what goes on with them?"

If she'd thought to check a couple lines back in the Wharfinger play, Oedipa might have made the next connection by herself. As it was she got an assist from one Genghis Cohen, who is the most eminent philatelist in the L.A. area. Metzger, acting on instructions in the will, had retained this amiable, slightly adenoidal expert, for a percent of his valuation, to inventory and appraise Inverarity's stamp collection.

One rainy morning, with mist rising off the pool, Metzger again away, the Paranoids off somewhere to a recording session, Oedipa got rung up by this Genghis Cohen, who even over the phone she could tell was disturbed.

"There are some irregularities, Miz Maas," he said. "Could you come over?"

She was somehow sure, driving in on the slick freeway, that the "irregularities" would tie in with the word Trystero. Metzger had taken the stamp albums to Cohen from safe-deposit storage a week ago in Oedipa's Impala, and then she hadn't even been interested enough to look inside them. But now it came to her, as if the rain whispered it, that what Fallopian had not known about private carriers, Cohen might.

When he opened the door of his apartment/office she saw him framed in a long succession or train of doorways, room after room receding in the general direction of Santa Monica, all soaked in rainlight. Genghis Cohen had a touch of summer flu, his fly was half open and he was wearing a Barry Goldwater sweatshirt also. Oedipa felt at once motherly. In a room perhaps a third of the way along the suite he sat her in a rocking chair and brought real homemade dandelion wine in small neat glasses.

"I picked the dandelions in a cemetery, two years ago. Now the cemetery is gone. They took it out for the East San Narciso Freeway."

She could, at this stage of things, recognize signals like that, as the epileptic is said to—an odor, color, pure piercing grace note announcing his seizure. Afterward it is only this signal, really dross, this secular announcement, and never what is revealed during the attack, that he remembers. Oedipa wondered whether, at the end of this (if it were supposed to end), she too might be left with only compiled memories of clues, announcements, intimations, but never the central truth itself, which must somehow each time be too bright for her memory to hold; which must always blaze out, destroying its own message irreversibly, leaving an overexposed blank when the ordinary world came back. In the space of a sip of dandelion wine it came to her that she would never know how many times such a seizure may already have visited, or how to grasp it should it visit again. Perhaps even in this last second—but there was no way to tell. She glanced down the corridor of Cohen's rooms in the rain and saw, for the very first time, how far it might be possible to get lost in this.

"I have taken the liberty," Genghis Cohen was saying, "of getting in touch with an Expert Committee. I haven't yet forwarded them the stamps in question, pending your own authorization and of course Mr Metzger's. However, all fees, I am sure, can be charged to the estate."

"I'm not sure I understand," Oedipa said.

"Allow me." He rolled over to her a small table, and from a plastic folder lifted with tweezers, delicately, a U.S. commemorative stamp, the Pony Express issue of 1940, 3¢ henna brown. Cancelled. "Look," he said, switching on a small, intense lamp, handing her an oblong magnifying glass.

"It's the wrong side," she said, as he swabbed the stamp gently with benzine and placed it on a black tray.

"The watermark."

Oedipa peered. There it was again, her WASTE symbol, showing up black, a little right of center.

"What is this?" she asked, wondering how much time had gone by.

"I'm not sure," Cohen said. "That's why I've referred it, and the others, to the Committee. Some friends have been around to see them too, but they're all being cautious. But see what you think of this." From the same plastic folder he now tweezed what looked like an old German stamp, with the figures ¼ in the centre, the word *Freimarke* at the top, and along the right-hand margin the legend *Thurn und Taxis*.

"They were," she remembered from the Wharfinger play, "some kind of private couriers, right?"

"From about 1300, until Bismarck bought them out in 1867, Miz Maas, they were *the* European mail service. This is one of their very few adhesive stamps. But look in the corners." Decorating each corner of the stamp, Oedipa saw a horn with a single loop in it. Almost like the WASTE symbol. "A post horn," Cohen said, "the Thurn and Taxis symbol. It was their coat of arms."

And Tacit lies the gold once-knotted horn, Oedipa remembered. Sure.

"Then the watermark you found," she said, "is nearly the same thing, except for the extra little doojigger sort of coming out of the bell."

"It sounds ridiculous," Cohen said, "but my guess is it's a mute."

She nodded. The black costumes, the silence, the secrecy. Whoever they were their aim was to mute the Thurn and Taxis post horn.

"Normally this issue, and the others, are unwatermarked," Cohen said, "and in view of other details—the hatching, number of perforations, way the paper has aged—it's obviously a counterfeit. Not just an error."

"Then it isn't worth anything."

Cohen smiled, blew his nose. "You'd be amazed how much you can sell an honest forgery for. Some collectors specialize in them. The question is, who did these? They're atrocious." He flipped the stamp over and with the tip of the tweezers showed her. The picture had a Pony Express rider galloping out of a western fort. From shrubbery over on the right-hand side and possibly in the direction the rider would be heading, protruded a single, painstakingly engraved, black feather. "Why put in a deliberate mistake?" he asked, ignoring—if he saw it—the look on her face. "I've come up so far with eight in all. Each one has an error like this, laboriously worked into the design, like a taunt. There's even a transposition— U.S. *Potsage*, of all things."

"How recent?" blurted Oedipa, louder than she needed to be.

"Is anything wrong, Miz Maas?"

She told him first about the letter from Mucho with a cancellation telling her report all obscene mail to her potsmaster.

"Odd," Cohen agreed. "The transposition," consulting a notebook, "is only on the Lincoln 4¢. Regular issue, 1954. The other forgeries run back to 1893."

"That's 70 years," she said. "He'd have to be pretty old."

"If it's the same one," said Cohen. "And what if it were as old as Thurn and Taxis? Omedio Tassis, banished from Milan, organized his first couriers in the Bergamo region around 1290."

They sat in silence, listening to rain gnaw languidly at the windows and skylights, confronted all at once by the marvellous possibility.

"Has that ever happened before?" she had to ask.

"An 800-year tradition of postal fraud. Not to my knowledge." Oedipa told him then all about old Mr Thoth's signet ring, and the symbol she'd caught Stanley Koteks doodling, and the muted horn drawn in the ladies' room at The Scope.

"Whatever it is," he hardly needed to say, "they're apparently still quite active."

"Do we tell the government, or what?"

"I'm sure they know more than we do." He sounded nervous, or suddenly in retreat. "No, I wouldn't. It isn't our business, is it?"

She asked him then about the initials W.A.S.T.E., but it was somehow too late. She'd lost him. He said no, but so abruptly out of phase now with her own thoughts he could even have been lying. He poured her more dandelion wine.

"It's clearer now," he said, rather formal. "A few months ago it got quite cloudy. You see, in spring, when the dandelions begin to bloom again, the wine goes through a fermentation. As if they remembered."

No, thought Oedipa, sad. As if their home cemetery still did exist, in a land where you could somehow walk, and not need the East San Narciso Freeway, and bones still could rest in peace, nourishing ghosts of dandelions, no one to plow them up. As if the dead really do persist, even in a bottle of wine.

Though her next move should have been to contact Randolph Driblette again, she decided instead to drive up to Berkeley. She wanted to find out where Richard Wharfinger had got his information about Trystero. Possibly also take a look at how the inventor John Nefastis picked up his mail.

As with Mucho when she'd left Kinneret, Metzger did not seem desperate at her going. She debated, driving north, whether to stop off home on the way to Berkeley or coming back. As it turned out she missed the exit for Kinneret and that solved it. She purred along up the east side of the bay, presently climbed into the Berkeley hills and arrived close to midnight at a sprawling, many-leveled, German-baroque hotel, carpeted in deep green, going in for curved corridors and ornamental chandeliers. A sign in the lobby said WELCOME CALIFORNIA CHAPTER AMERICAN DEAF-MUTE ASSEMBLY. Every light in the place burned, alarmingly bright; a truly ponderable silence occupied the building. A clerk popped up from the desk where he'd been sleeping and began making sign language at her. Oedipa considered giving him the finger to see what would happen. But she'd driven straight through, and all at once the fatigue of it had caught up with her. The clerk took her to a room with a reproduction of a Remedios Varo in it, through corridors gently curving as the streets of San Narciso, utterly silent. She fell asleep almost at once, but kept waking from a night-

mare about something in the mirror, across from ber bed. Nothing specific, only a possibility, nothing she could see. When she finally did settle into sleep, she dreamed that Mucho, her husband, was making love to her on a soft white beach that was not part of any California she knew. When she woke in the morning, she was sitting bolt upright, staring into the mirror at her own exhausted face.

She found the Lectern Press in a small office building on Shattuck Avenue. They didn't have *Plays of Ford, Webster, Tourneur and Wharfinger* on the premises, but did take her check for $12.50, gave her the address of their warehouse in Oakland and a receipt to show the people there. By the time she'd collected the book, it was afternoon. She skimmed through to find the line that had brought her all the way up here. And in the leaf-fractured sunlight, froze.

No hallowed skein of stars can ward, I trow, ran the couplet, *Who once has crossed the lusts of Angelo.*

"No," she protested aloud. "Who's once been set his tryst with Trystero." The pencilled note in the paperback had mentioned a variant. But the paperback was supposed to be a straight reprint of the book she now held. Puzzled, she saw that this edition also had a footnote:

According only to the Quarto edition (1687). The earlier Folio has a lead inserted where the closing line should have been. D'Amico has suggested that Wharfinger may have made a libellous comparison involving someone at court, and that the later 'restoration' was actually the work of the printer, Inigo Barfstable. The doubtful 'Whitechapel' version (c. 1670) has 'This tryst or odious awry, O Niccolò,' which besides bringing in a quite graceless Alexandrine, is difficult to make sense of syntactically, unless we accept the rather unorthodox though persuasive argument of J.-K. Sale that the line is really a pun on 'This trystero *dies irae*. . . .'[27] This, however, it must be pointed out, leaves the line nearly as corrupt as before, owing to no clear meaning for the word *trystero*, unless it be a pseudo-Italianate variant on *triste* (= wretched, depraved). But the 'Whitechapel' edition, besides being a fragment, abounds in such corrupt and probably spurious lines, as we have mentioned elsewhere, and is hardly to be trusted.

Then where, Oedipa wondered, does the paperback I bought at Zapf's get off with *its* "Trystero" line? Was there yet another edition, besides the Quarto, Folio, and "Whitechapel" fragment? The editor's

[27]The *dies irae* (Latin: day of wrath) is a hymn about the day of judgment sung in the requiem mass.

preface, signed this time, by one Emory Bortz, professor of English at Cal, mentioned none. She spent nearly an hour more, searching through all the footnotes, finding nothing.

"Dammit," she yelled, started the car and headed for the Berkeley campus, to find Professor Bortz.

She should have remembered the date on the book—1957. Another world. The girl in the English office informed Oedipa that Professor Bortz was no longer with the faculty. He was teaching at San Narciso College, San Narciso, California.

Of course, Oedipa thought, wry, where else? She copied the address and walked away trying to remember who'd put out the paperback. She couldn't.

It was summer, a weekday, and midafternoon; no time for any campus Oedipa knew of to be jumping, yet this one was. She came downslope from Wheeler Hall, through Sather Gate into a plaza teeming with corduroy, denim, bare legs, blonde hair, hornrims, bicycle spokes in the sun, bookbags, swaying card tables, long paper petitions dangling to earth, posters for undecipherable FSM's, YAF's, VDC's,[28] suds in the fountain, students in nose-to-nose dialogue. She moved through it carrying her fat book, attracted, unsure, a stranger, wanting to feel relevant but knowing how much of a search among alternate universes it would take. For she had undergone her own educating at a time of nerves, blandness and retreat among not only her fellow students but also most of the visible structure around and ahead of them, this having been a national reflex to certain pathologies in high places only death had had the power to cure, and this Berkeley was like no somnolent Siwash[29] out of her own past at all, but more akin to those Far Eastern or Latin American universities you read about, those autonomous culture media where the most beloved of folklores may be brought into doubt, cataclysmic of dissents voiced, suicidal of commitments chosen—the sort that bring governments down. But it was English she was hearing as she crossed Bancroft Way among the blonde children and the muttering Hondas and Suzukis; American English.

---

[28]FSM is the Free Speech Movement, a radical group involved in the student demonstrations at the Berkeley campus of the University of California around 1964; YAF stands for Young Americans for Freedom, a right-wing student group still extant. VDC has been identified as Vietnam Day Committee.

[29]A conventional name for the college in a campus musical.

Where were Secretaries James and Foster and Senator Joseph,[30] those dear daft numina who'd mothered over Oedipa's so temperate youth? In another world. Along another pattern of track, another string of decisions taken, switches closed, the faceless pointsmen who'd thrown them now all transferred, deserted, in stir, fleeing the skip-tracers, out of their skull, on horse, alcoholic, fanatic, under aliases, dead, impossible to find ever again. Among them they had managed to turn the young Oedipa into a rare creature indeed, unfit perhaps for marches and sit-ins, but just a whiz at pursuing strange words in Jacobean texts.

She pulled the Impala into a gas station somewhere along a gray stretch of Telegraph Avenue and found in a phone book the address of John Nefastis. She then drove to a pseudo-Mexican apartment house, looked for his name among the U.S. mailboxes, ascended outside steps and walked down a row of draped windows till she found his door. He had a crewcut and the same underage look as Koteks, but wore a shirt on various Polynesian themes and dating from the Truman administration.

Introducing herself, she invoked the name of Stanley Koteks. "He said you could tell me whether or not I'm a 'sensitive'."

Nefastis had been watching on his TV set a bunch of kids dancing some kind of a Watusi. "I like to watch young stuff," he explained. "There's something about a little chick that age."

"So does my husband," she said. "I understand."

John Nefastis beamed back at her, simpatico, and brought out his Machine from a workroom in back. It looked about the way his patent described it. "You know how this works?"

"Stanley gave me a kind of rundown."

He began then, bewilderingly, to talk about something called entropy. The word bothered him as much as "Trystero" bothered Oedipa. But it was too technical for her. She did gather that there were two distinct kinds of this entropy. One having to do with heat-engines, the

---

[30]Secretary Foster is probably John Foster Dulles, Secretary of State under Eisenhower from 1953 until his death in 1959. Senator Joseph is probably Joseph P. McCarthy, whose witch-hunting investigations seeking Communists in high places absorbed the United States from 1950 to 1954. Secretary James may be any of a number of people: in the Eisenhower administration there were James P. Mitchell, Secretary of Labor, 1953–1961, and James Hagerty, Eisenhower's press secretary; in the Truman administration were James F. Byrnes, Secretary of State, 1945–1947, and James Forrestal, Secretary of the Navy, 1945–1947, and Secretary of Defense, 1947–1949. The last is perhaps the most likely choice.

other to do with communication. The equation for one, back in the '30's, had looked very like the equation for the other. It was a coincidence. The two fields were entirely unconnected, except at one point: Maxwell's Demon. As the Demon sat and sorted his molecules into hot and cold, the system was said to lose entropy. But somehow the loss was offset by the information the Demon gained about what molecules were where.

"Communication is the key," cried Nefastis. "The Demon passes his data on to the sensitive, and the sensitive must reply in kind. There are untold billions of molecules in that box. The Demon collects data on each and every one. At some deep psychic level he must get through. The sensitive must receive that staggering set of energies, and feed back something like the same quantity of information. To keep it all cycling. On the secular level all we can see is one piston, hopefully moving. One little movement, against all that massive complex of information, destroyed over and over with each power stroke."

"Help," said Oedipa, "you're not reaching me."

"Entropy is a figure of speech, then," sighed Nefastis, "a metaphor. It connects the world of thermodynamics to the world of information flow. The Machine uses both. The Demon makes one metaphor not only verbally graceful, but also objectively true."

"But what," she felt like some kind of a heretic, "if the Demon exists only because the two equations look alike? Because of the metaphor?"

Nefastis smiled; impenetrable, calm, a believer. "He existed for Clerk Maxwell long before the days of the metaphor."

But had Clerk Maxwell been such a fanatic about his Demon's reality? She looked at the picture on the outside of the box. Clerk Maxwell was in profile and would not meet her eyes. The forehead was round and smooth, and there was a curious bump at the back of his head, covered by curling hair. His visible eye seemed mild and noncommittal, but Oedipa wondered what hangups, crises, spookings in the middle of the night might be developed from the shadowed subtleties of his mouth, hidden under a full beard.

"Watch the picture," said Nefastis, "and concentrate on a cylinder. Don't worry. If you're a sensitive you'll know which one. Leave your mind open, receptive to the Demon's message. I'll be back." He returned to his TV set, which was now showing cartoons. Oedipa sat through two Yogi Bears, one Magilla Gorilla and a Peter Potamus, staring at Clerk Maxwell's enigmatic profile, waiting for the Demon to communicate.

Are you there, little fellow, Oedipa asked the Demon, or is Nefastis putting me on. Unless a piston moved, she'd never know. Clerk Maxwell's hands were cropped out of the photograph. He might have been holding a book. He gazed away, into some vista of Victorian England whose light had been lost forever. Oedipa's anxiety grew. It seemed, behind the beard, he'd begun, ever so faintly, to smile. Something in his eyes, certainly, had changed . . .

And there. At the top edge of what she could see: hadn't the right-hand piston moved, a fraction? She couldn't look directly, the instructions were to keep her eyes on Clerk Maxwell. Minutes passed, pistons remained frozen in place. High-pitched, comic voices issued from the TV set. She had seen only a retinal twitch, a misfired nerve cell. Did the true sensitive see more? In her colon now she was afraid, growing more so, that nothing would happen. Why worry, she worried; Nefastis is a nut, forget it, a sincere nut. The true sensitive is the one that can share in the man's hallucinations, that's all.

How wonderful they might be to share. For fifteen minutes more she tried; repeating, if you are there, whatever you are, show yourself to me, I need you, show yourself. But nothing happened.

"I'm sorry," she called in, surprisingly about to cry with frustration, her voice breaking. "It's no use." Nefastis came to her and put an arm around her shoulders.

"It's OK," he said. "Please don't cry. Come on in on the couch. The news will be on any minute. We can do it there."

"It?" said Oedipa. "Do it? What?"

"Have sexual intercourse," replied Nefastis. "Maybe there'll be something about China tonight. I like to do it while they talk about Viet Nam, but China is best of all. You think about all those Chinese. Teeming. That profusion of life. It makes it sexier, right?"

"Gah," Oedipa screamed, and fled, Nefastis snapping his fingers through the dark rooms behind her in a hippy-dippy, oh-go-ahead-then-chick fashion he had doubtless learned from watching the TV also.

"Say hello to old Stanley," he called as she pattered down the steps into the street, flung a babushka over her license plate and screeched away down Telegraph. She drove more or less automatically until a swift boy in a Mustang, perhaps unable to contain the new sense of virility his auto gave him, nearly killed her and she realized that she was on the freeway, heading irreversibly for the Bay Bridge. It was the middle of rush hour. Oedipa was appalled at the spectacle, having thought such traffic only possible in Los Angeles, places like that. Looking down at San Francisco a few minutes later from the high point of the bridge's arc, she saw smog. Haze, she corrected herself, is what it is, haze. How can they have smog in San Francisco? Smog, according to the folklore, did not begin till farther south. It had to be the angle of the sun.

Amid the exhaust, sweat, glare and ill-humor of a summer evening on an American freeway, Oedipa Maas pondered her Trystero problem. All the silence of San Narciso—the calm surface of the motel pool, the contemplative contours of residential streets like rakings in the sand of a Japanese garden—had not allowed her to think as leisurely as this freeway madness.

For John Nefastis (to take a recent example) two kinds of entropy, thermodynamic and informational, happened, say by coincidence, to look alike, when you wrote them down as equations. Yet he had made his mere coincidence respectable, with the help of Maxwell's Demon.

Now here was Oedipa, faced with a metaphor of God knew how many parts; more than two, anyway. With coincidences blossoming these days wherever she looked, she had nothing but a sound, a word, Trystero, to hold them together.

She knew a few things about it: it had opposed the Thurn and Taxis postal system in Europe; its symbol was a muted post horn; sometime before 1853 it had appeared in America and fought the Pony Express and Wells, Fargo, either as outlaws in black, or disguised as Indians; and it survived today, in California, serving as a channel of communication for those of unorthodox sexual persuasion, inventors who believed in the reality of Maxwell's Demon, possibly her own husband, Mucho Maas (but she'd thrown Mucho's letter long away, there was no way for Genghis Cohen to check the stamp, so if she wanted to find out for sure she'd have to ask Mucho himself).

Either Trystero did exist, in its own right, or it was being presumed, perhaps fantasized by Oedipa, so hung up on and interpenetrated with the dead man's estate. Here in San Francisco, away from all tangible assets of that estate, there might still be a chance of getting the whole thing to go away and disintegrate quietly. She had only to drift tonight, at random, and watch nothing happen, to be convinced it was purely nervous, a little something for her shrink to fix. She got off the freeway at North Beach, drove around, parked finally in a steep side-street among warehouses. Then walked along Broadway, into the first crowds of evening.

But it took her no more than an hour to catch sight of a muted post horn. She was moseying along a street full of aging boys in Roos Atkins suits when she collided with a gang of guided tourists come rowdy-dowing out of a Volkswagen bus, on route to take in a few San Francisco nite spots. "Let me lay this on you," a voice spoke into her ear, "because I just left," and she found being deftly pinned outboard of one breast this big cerise ID badge, reading HI! MY NAME IS Arnold Snarb! AND I'M LOOKIN' FOR A GOOD TIME! Oedipa glanced around and saw a cherubic face vanishing with a wink in among natural shoulders and striped shirts, and away went Arnold Snarb, looking for a better time.

Somebody blew on an athletic whistle and Oedipa found herself being herded, along with other badged citizens, toward a bar called The Greek Way. Oh, no, Oedipa thought, not a fag joint, no; and for a minute tried to fight out of the human surge, before recalling how she had decided to drift tonight.

"Now in here," their guide, sweating dark tentacles into his tab collar, briefed them, "you are going to see the members of the third sex, the lavender crowd this city by the Bay is so justly famous for. To some of you the experience may seem a little queer, but remember, try not to act like a bunch of tourists. If you get propositioned it'll all be in fun, just part of the gay night life to be found here in famous North Beach. Two drinks and when you hear the whistle it means out, on the double, regroup right here. If you're well behaved we'll hit Finocchio's next." He blew the whistle twice and the tourists, breaking into a yell, swept Oedipa inside, in a frenzied assault on the bar. When things had calmed she was near the door with an unidentifiable drink in her fist, jammed against somebody tall in a suede sport coat. In the lapel of which she spied, wrought exquisitely in some pale, glimmering alloy, not another cerise badge, but a pin in the shape of the Trystero post horn. Mute and everything.

All right, she told herself. You lose. A game try, all one hour's worth. She should have left then and gone back to Berkeley, to the hotel. But couldn't.

"What if I told you," she addressed the owner of the pin, "that I was an agent of Thurn and Taxis?"

"What," he answered, "some theatrical agency?"

He had large ears, hair cropped nearly to his scalp, acne on his face, and curiously empty eyes, which now swiveled briefly to Oedipa's breasts. "How'd you get a name like Arnold Snarb?"

"If you tell me where you got your lapel pin," said Oedipa.

"Sorry."

She sought to bug him: "If it's a homosexual sign or something, that doesn't bother me."

Eyes showing nothing: "I don't swing that way," he said. "Yours either." Turned his back on her and ordered a drink. Oedipa took off her badge, put it in an ashtray and said quietly, trying not to suggest hysteria,

"Look, you have to help me. Because I really think I am going out of my head."

"You have the wrong outfit, Arnold. Talk to your clergyman."

"I use the U.S. Mail because I was never taught any different," she pleaded. "But I'm not your enemy. I don't want to be."

"What about my friend?" He came spinning around on the stool to face her again. "You want to be that, Arnold?"

"I don't know," she thought she'd better say.

He looked at her, blank: "What *do* you know?"

She told him everything. Why not? Held nothing back. At the end of it the tourists had been whistled away and he'd bought two rounds to Oedipa's three.

"I'd heard about 'Kirby,' " he said, "it's a code name, nobody real. But none of the rest, your Sinophile across the bay, or that sick play. I never thought there was a history to it."

"I think of nothing but," she said, and a little plaintive.

"And," scratching the stubble on his head, "you have nobody else to tell this to. Only somebody in a bar whose name you don't know?"

She wouldn't look at him. "I guess not."

"No husband, no shrink?"

"Both," Oedipa said, "but they don't know."

"You can't tell them?"

She met his eyes' void for a second after all, and shrugged.

"I'll tell you what I know, then," he decided. "The pin I'm wearing means I'm a member of the IA. That's Inamorati Anonymous. An inamorato is somebody in love. That's the worst addiction of all."

"Somebody is about to fall in love," Oedipa said, "you go sit with them, or something?"

"Right. The whole idea is to get to where you don't need it. I was lucky. I kicked it young. But there are sixty-year-old men, believe it or not, and women even older, who wake up in the night screaming."

"You hold meetings then, like the AA?"

"No, of course not. You get a phone number, an answering service you can call. Nobody knows anybody else's name; just the number in case it gets so bad you can't handle it alone. We're isolates, Arnold. Meetings would destroy the whole point of it."

"What about the person who comes to sit with you? Suppose you fall in love with them?"

"They go away," he said. "You never see them twice. The answering service dispatches them, and they're careful not to have any repeats." How did the post horn come in? That went back to the founding. In the early '60's a Yoyodyne executive living near L.A. and located someplace in the corporate root-system above supervisor but below vice-president, found himself, at age 39, automated out of a job. Having been since age 7 rigidly instructed in an eschatology that pointed nowhere but to a presidency and death, trained to do absolutely nothing but sign his name to specialized memoranda he could not begin to understand and to take blame for the running-amok of specialized programs that failed for specialized reasons he had to have explained to him, the executive's first thoughts were naturally of suicide. But previous training got the better of him: he could not make the decision without first hearing the ideas of a committee. He placed an ad in the personal column of the L.A. *Times,* asking whether anyone who'd been in the same fix had ever found any good reasons for not committing suicide. His shrewd assumption being that no suicides would reply, leaving him automatically with only valid inputs. The assumption was false. After a week of anxiously watching the mailbox through little Japanese binoculars his wife had given him for a going-away present (she'd left him the day after he was pink-slipped) and getting nothing but sucker-list stuff through the regular deliveries that came each noon, he was jolted out of a boozy, black-and-white dream of jumping off The Stack into rush-hour traffic, by an insistent banging at the door. It was late on a Sunday afternoon. He opened his door and found an aged bum with a knitted watch cap on his head and a hook on his hand, who presented him with a bundle of letters and loped away without a word. Most of the letters were from suicides who had failed, either through clumsiness or last-minute cowardice. None of them, however, could offer any compelling reasons for staying alive. Still the executive dithered: spent another week with pieces of paper on which he would list, in columns headed "pro" and "con," reasons for and against taking his Brody. He found it impossible, in the absence of some trigger, to come to any clear decision. Finally one day he noticed a front page story in the *Times,* complete with AP wirephoto, about a Buddhist monk in Viet Nam who had set himself on fire to protest government policies. "Groovy!" cried the executive. He went to the garage, siphoned all the gasoline from his Buick's tank, put on his green Zachary All suit with the vest, stuffed all his letters from unsuccessful suicides into a coat pocket, went in the kitchen, sat on the floor, proceeded to douse himself good with the gasoline. He was about to make the farewell flick of the wheel on his faithful Zippo, which had seen him through the Normandy hedgerows, the Ardennes, Germany, and postwar America, when he heard a key in the front door, and voices. It was his wife and some man, whom he soon recognized as the very efficiency expert at Yoyodyne who had caused him to be replaced by an IBM 7094. Intrigued by the irony of it, he sat in the kitchen and listened, leaving his necktie dipped in the gasoline as a sort of wick. From what he could gather, the efficiency expert wished to have sexual intercourse with the wife on the Moroccan rug in the living room. The wife was not unwilling. The executive heard lewd laughter, zippers, the thump of shoes, heavy breathing, moans. He took his tie out of the gasoline and started to snigger. He closed the top on his Zippo. "I hear laughing," his wife said presently. "I smell gasoline," said the efficiency expert. Hand in hand, naked, the two proceeded to the kitchen. "I was about to do the Buddhist monk thing," explained the executive. "Nearly three weeks it takes him," marvelled the efficiency expert, "to decide. You know how long it would've taken the IBM 7094? Twelve microseconds. No wonder you were replaced." The executive threw back his head and laughed for a solid ten minutes, along toward the middle of which his wife and her friend, alarmed, retired, got dressed and went out looking for the police. The executive undressed, showered and hung his suit out on the line to dry. Then he noticed a curious thing. The stamps on some of the letters in his suit pocket had turned almost white. He realized that the gasoline must have dissolved the printing ink. Idly, he peeled off a stamp and saw suddenly the image of the muted post horn, the skin of his hand showing clearly through the watermark. "A sign," he whispered, "is what it is." If he'd been a religious man he would have fallen to his knees. As it was, he only declared, with great solemnity: "My big mistake was love. From this day I swear to stay off of love: hetero, homo, bi, dog or cat, car, every kind there is. I will found a society of isolates, dedicated to this purpose, and this sign, revealed by the same gasoline that almost destroyed me, will be its emblem." And he did.

Oedipa, by now rather drunk, said, "Where is he now?"

"He's anonymous," said the anonymous inamorato. "Why not write to him through your WASTE system? Say 'Founder, IA.' "

"But I don't know how to use it," she said.

"Think of it," he went on, also drunk. "A whole underworld of suicides who failed. All keeping in touch through that secret delivery system. What do they tell each other?" He shook his head, smiling, stumbled off his stool and headed off to take a leak, disappearing into the dense crowd. He didn't come back.

Oedipa sat, feeling as alone as she ever had, now the only woman, she saw, in a room full of drunken male homosexuals. Story of my life, she thought, Mucho won't talk to me, Hilarius won't listen, Clerk Maxwell didn't even look at me, and this group, God knows. Despair came over her, as it will when nobody around has any sexual relevance to you. She gauged the spectrum of feeling out there as running from really violent hate (an Indian-looking kid hardly out of his teens, with frosted shoulder-length hair tucked behind his ears and pointed cowboy boots) to dry speculation (a hornrimmed SS type who stared at her legs trying to figure out if she was in drag), none of which could do her any good. So she got up after awhile and left The Greek Way, and entered the city again, the infected city.

And spent the rest of the night finding the image of the Trystero post horn. In Chinatown, in the dark window of a herbalist, she thought she saw it on a sign among ideographs. But the streetlight was dim. Later, on a sidewalk, she saw two of them in chalk, 20 feet apart. Between them a complicated array of boxes, some with letters, some with numbers. A kids' game? Places on a map, dates from a secret history? She copied the diagram in her memo book. When she looked up, a man, perhaps a man, in a black suit, was standing in a doorway half a block away, watching her. She thought she saw a turned-around collar but took no chances; headed back the way she'd come, pulse thundering. A bus stopped at the next corner, and she ran to catch it.

She stayed with buses after that, getting off only now and then to walk so she'd keep awake. What fragments of dreams came had to do with the post horn. Later, possibly, she would have trouble sorting the night into real and dreamed.

At some indefinite passage in night's sonorous score, it also came to her that she would be safe, that something, perhaps only her linearly fading drunkenness, would protect her. The city was hers, as, made up and sleeked so with the customary words and images (cosmopolitan, culture, cable cars) it had not been before: she had safe-passage tonight to its far blood's branchings, be they capillaries too small for more than peering into, or vessels mashed together in shameless municipal hickeys, out on the skin for all but tourists to see. Nothing of the night's could touch her; nothing did. The repetition of symbols was to be enough, without trauma as well perhaps to attenuate it or even jar it altogether loose from her memory. *She was meant to remember.* She faced that possibility as she might the toy street from a high balcony, roller-coaster ride, feeding-time among the beasts in a zoo—any death-wish that can be consummated by some minimum gesture. She touched the edge of its voluptuous field, knowing it would be lovely beyond dreams simply to submit to it; that not gravity's pull, laws of ballistics, feral ravening, promised more delight. She tested it, shivering: I am meant to remember. Each clue that comes is *supposed* to have its own clarity, its fine chances for permanence. But then she wondered if the gemlike "clues" were only some kind of compensation. To make up for her having lost the direct, epileptic Word, the cry that might abolish the night.

In Golden Gate Park she came on a circle of children in their night-clothes, who told her they were dreaming the gathering. But that the dream was really no different from being awake, because in the mornings when they got up they felt tired, as if they'd been up most of the night. When their mothers thought they were out playing they were really curled in cupboards of neighbors' houses, in platforms up in trees, in secretly-hollowed nests inside hedges, sleeping, making up for these hours. The night was empty of all terror for them, they had inside their circle an imaginary fire, and needed nothing but their own unpenetrated sense of community. They knew about the post horn, but nothing of the chalked game Oedipa had seen on the sidewalk. You used only one image and it was a jump-rope game, a little girl explained: you stepped alternately in the loop, the bell, and the mute, while your girlfriend sang:

> Tristoe, Tristoe, one, two, three,
> Turning taxi from across the sea . . .

"Thurn and Taxis, you mean?"

They'd never heard it that way. Went on warming their hands at an invisible fire. Oedipa, to retaliate, stopped believing in them.

In an all-night Mexican greasy spoon off 24th, she found a piece of her past, in the form of one Jesús Arrabal, who was sitting in a corner under the TV set, idly stirring his bowl of opaque soup with the foot of a chicken. "Hey," he greeted Oedipa, "you were the lady in Mazatlán." He beckoned her to sit.

"You remember everything," Oedipa said, "Jesús; even tourists. How is your CIA?" Standing not for the agency you think, but for a clandes-tine Mexican outfit known as the Conjuración de los Insurgentes Anarquistas,[31] traceable back to the time of the Flores Magón brothers and later briefly allied with Zapata.

"You see. In exile," waving his arms around at the place. He was part-owner here with a yucateco who still believed in the Revolution. *Their* Revolution. "And you. Are you still with that gringo who spent too much money on you? The oligarchist, the miracle?"

"He died."

"Ah, pobrecito." They had met Jesús Arrabal on the beach, where he had previously announced an anti-government rally. Nobody had showed up. So he fell to talking to Inverarity, the enemy he must, to be true to his faith, learn. Pierce, because of his neutral manners when in the presence of ill-will, had nothing to tell Arrabal; he played the rich, obnoxious gringo so perfectly that Oedipa had seen gooseflesh come up along the anarchist's forearms, due to no Pacific sea-breeze. Soon as Pierce went off to sport in the surf, Arrabal asked her if he was real, or a spy, or making fun of him. Oedipa didn't understand.

"You know what a miracle is. Not what Bakunin said. But another world's intrusion into this one. Most of the time we coexist peacefully, but when we do touch there's cataclysm. Like the church we hate, anarchists also believe in another world. Where revolutions break out spontaneous and leaderless, and the soul's talent for consensus allows the masses to work together without effort, automatic as the body itself. And yet, señá, if any of it should ever really happen that perfectly, I would also have to cry miracle. An anarchist miracle. Like your friend. He is too exactly and without flaw the thing we fight. In Mexico the privilegiado is always, to a finite percentage, redeemed—one of the people. Unmiraculous. But your friend, unless he's joking, is as terrifying to me as a Virgin appearing to an Indian."

In the years intervening Oedipa had remembered Jesús because he'd seen that about Pierce and she hadn't. As if he were, in some unsexual way, competition. Now, drinking thick lukewarm coffee from a clay pot on the back burner of the yucateco's stove and listening to Jesús talk conspiracy, she wondered if, without the miracle of Pierce to reassure him, Jesús might not have quit his CIA eventually and gone over like everybody else to the majority priistas, and so never had to go into exile.

The dead man, like Maxwell's Demon, was the linking feature in a

---

[31]Confederation of Anarchist Revolutionaries. Zapata and the Flores Magón brothers were Mexican revolutionists around 1910–1920.

coincidence. Without him neither she nor Jesús would be exactly here, exactly now. It was enough, a coded warning. What, tonight, was chance? So her eyes did fall presently onto an ancient rolled copy of the anarcho-syndicalist paper *Regeneración*. The date was 1904 and there was no stamp next to the cancellation, only the handstruck image of the post horn.

"They arrive," said Arrabal. "Have they been in the mails that long? Has my name been substituted for that of a member who's died? Has it really taken sixty years? Is it a reprint? Idle questions, I am a footsoldier. The higher levels have their reasons." She carried this thought back out into the night with her.

Down at the city beach, long after the pizza stands and rides had closed, she walked unmolested through a drifting, dreamy cloud of delinquents in summer-weight gang jackets with the post horn stitched on in thread that looked pure silver in what moonlight there was. They had all been smoking, snuffing or injecting something, and perhaps did not see her at all.

Riding among an exhausted busful of Negroes going on to graveyard shifts all over the city, she saw scratched on the back of a seat, shining for her in the brilliant smoky interior, the post horn with the legend DEATH. But unlike WASTE, somebody had troubled to write in, in pencil: DON'T EVER ANTAGONIZE THE HORN.

Somewhere near Fillmore she found the symbol tacked to the bulletin board of a laundromat, among other scraps of paper offering cheap ironing and baby sitters. *If you know what this means,* the note said, *you know where to find out more.* Around her the odor of chlorine bleach rose heavenward, like an incense. Machines chugged and sloshed fiercely. Except for Oedipa the place was deserted, and the fluorescent bulbs seemed to shriek whiteness, to which everything their light touched was dedicated. It was a Negro neighborhood. Was The Horn so dedicated? Would it Antagonize The Horn to ask? Who could she ask?

In the buses all night she listened to transistor radios playing songs in the lower stretches of the Top 200, that would never become popular, whose melodies and lyrics would perish as if they had never been sung. A Mexican girl, trying to hear one of these through snarling static from the bus's motor, hummed along as if she would remember it always, tracing post horns and hearts with a fingernail, in the haze of her breath on the window.

Out at the airport Oedipa, feeling invisible, eavesdropped on a poker game whose steady loser entered each loss neat and conscientious in a little balance-book decorated inside with scrawled post horns. "I'm averaging a 99.375 percent return, fellas," she heard him say. The others, strangers, looked at him, some blank, some annoyed. "That's averaging it out, over 23 years," he went on, trying a smile. "Always just that little percent on the wrong side of breaking even. Twenty-three years. I'll never get ahead of it. Why don't I quit?" Nobody answering.

In one of the latrines was an advertisement by AC-DC, standing for Alameda County Death Cult, along with a box number and post horn. Once a month they were to choose some victim from among the innocent, the virtuous, the socially integrated and well-adjusted, using him sexually, then sacrificing him. Oedipa did not copy the number.

Catching a TWA flight to Miami was an uncoordinated boy who planned to slip at night into aquariums and open negotiations with the dolphins, who would succeed man. He was kissing his mother passionately goodbye, using his tongue. "I'll write, ma," he kept saying. "Write by WASTE," she said, "remember. The government will open it if you use the other. The dolphins will be mad." "I love you, ma," he said. "Love the dolphins," she advised him. "Write by WASTE."

So it went. Oedipa played the voyeur and listener. Among her other encounters were a facially deformed welder, who cherished his ugliness; a child roaming the night who missed the death before birth as certain outcasts do the dear lulling blankness of the community; a Negro woman with an intricately marbled scar along the baby-fat of one cheek who kept going through rituals of miscarriage each for a different reason, deliberately as others might the ritual of birth, dedicated not to continuity but to some kind of interregnum; an aging night-watchman, nibbling at a bar of Ivory Soap, who had trained his virtuoso stomach to accept also lotions, air-fresheners, fabrics, tobaccoes and waxes in a hopeless attempt to assimilate it all, all the promise, productivity, betrayal, ulcers, before it was too late; and even another voyeur, who hung outside one of the city's still-lighted windows, searching for who knew what specific image. Decorating each alienation, each species of withdrawal, as cufflink, decal, aimless doodling, there was somehow always the post horn. She grew so to expect it that perhaps she did not see it quite as often as she later was to remember seeing it. A couple-three times would really have been enough. Or too much.

She busrode and walked on into the lightening morning, giving herself up to a fatalism rare for her. Where was the Oedipa who'd driven so bravely up here from San Narciso? That optimistic baby had come on so like the private eye in any long-ago radio drama, believing all you needed was grit, resourcefulness, exemption from hidebound cops' rules, to solve any great mystery.

But the private eye sooner or later has to get beat up on. This night's profusion of post horns, this malignant, deliberate replication, was their way of beating up. They knew her pressure points, and the ganglia of her optimism, and one by one, pinch by precision pinch, they were immobilizing her.

Last night, she might have wondered what undergrounds apart from the couple she knew of communicated by the WASTE system. By sunrise she could legitimately ask what undergrounds didn't. If miracles were, as Jesús Arrabal had postulated years ago on the beach at Mazatlán, intrusions into this world from another, a kiss of cosmic pool balls, then so must be each of the night's post horns. For here were God knew how many citizens, deliberately choosing not to communicate by U.S. Mail. It was not an act of treason, nor possibly even of defiance. But it was a calculated withdrawal, from the life of the Republic, from its machinery. Whatever else was being denied them out of hate, indifference to the power of their vote, loopholes, simple ignorance, this withdrawal was their own, unpublicized, private. Since they could not have withdrawn into a vacuum (could they?), there had to exist the separate, silent, unsuspected world.

Just before the morning rush hour, she got out of a jitney whose ancient driver ended each day in the red, downtown on Howard Street, began to walk toward the Embarcadero. She knew she looked terrible—knuckles black with eye-liner and mascara from where she'd rubbed, mouth tasting of old booze and coffee. Through an open doorway, on the stair leading up into the disinfectant-smelling twilight of a rooming house she saw an old man huddled, shaking with grief she couldn't hear. Both hands, smoke-white, covered his face. On the back of the left hand she made out the post horn, tattooed in old ink now beginning to blur and spread. Fascinated, she came into the shadows and ascended creaking steps, hesitating on each one. When she was three steps from him the hands flew apart and his wrecked face, and the terror of eyes gloried in burst veins, stopped her.

"Can I help?" She was shaking, tired.

"My wife's in Fresno," he said. He wore an old double-breasted suit, frayed gray shirt, wide tie, no hat. "I left her. So long ago, I don't remember. Now this is for her." He gave Oedipa a letter that looked like he'd been carrying it around for years. "Drop it in the," and he held up the tattoo and stared into her eyes, "you know. I can't go out there. It's too far now, I had a bad night."

"I know," she said. "But I'm new in town. I don't know where it is."

"Under the freeway." He waved her on in the direction she'd been going. "Always one. You'll see it." The eyes closed. Cammed each night out of that safe furrow the bulk of this city's waking each sunrise again set virtuously to plowing, what rich soils had he turned, what concentric planets uncovered? What voices overheard, flinders of luminescent gods glimpsed among the wallpaper's stained foliage, candle-stubs lit to rotate in the air over him, prefiguring the cigarette he or a friend must fall asleep someday smoking, thus to end among the flaming, secret salts held all those years by the insatiable stuffing of a mattress that could keep vestiges of every nightmare sweat, helpless overflowing bladder, viciously, tearfully consummated wet dream, like the memory bank to a computer of the lost? She was overcome all at once by a need to touch him, as if she could not believe in him, or would not remember him, without it. Exhausted, hardly knowing what she was doing, she came the last three steps and sat, took the man in her arms, actually held him, gazing out of her smudged eyes down the stairs, back into the morning. She felt wetness against her breast and saw that he was crying again. He hardly breathed but tears came as if being pumped. "I can't help," she whispered, rocking him, "I can't help." It was already too many miles to Fresno.

"Is that him?" a voice asked behind her, up the stairs. "The sailor?"

"He has a tattoo on his hand."

"Can you bring him up OK? That's him." She turned and saw an even older man, shorter, wearing a tall Homburg hat and smiling at them. "I'd help you but I got a little arthritis."

"Does he have to come up?" she said. "Up there?"

"Where else, lady?"

She didn't know. She let go of him for a moment, reluctant as if he were her own child, and he looked up at her. "Come on," she said. He reached out the tattooed hand and she took that, and that was how they went the rest of the way up that flight, and then the two more: hand in hand, very slowly for the man with arthritis.

"He disappeared last night," he told her. "Said he was going looking for his old lady. It's a thing he does, off and on." They entered a warren of rooms and corridors, lit by 10-watt bulbs, separated by beaverboard partitions. The old man followed them stiffly. At last he said, "Here."

In the little room were another suit, a couple of religious tracts, a rug, a chair. A picture of a saint, changing well-water to oil for Jerusalem's Easter lamps. Another bulb, dead. The bed. The mattress, waiting. She ran through then a scene she might play. She might find the landlord of this place, and bring them to court, and buy the sailor a new suit at Roos Atkins, and shirt, and shoes, and give him the bus fare to Fresno after all. But with a sigh he had released her hand, while she was so lost in the fantasy that she hadn't felt it go away, as if he'd known the best moment to let go.

"Just mail the letter," he said, "the stamp is on it." She looked and saw the familiar carmine 8¢ airmail, with a jet flying by the Capitol dome. But at the top of the dome stood a tiny figure in deep black, with its arms outstretched. Oedipa wasn't sure what exactly was supposed to be on top of the Capitol, but knew it wasn't anything like that.

"Please," the sailor said. "Go on now. You don't want to stay here." She looked in her purse, found a ten and a single, gave him the ten. "I'll spend it on booze," he said.

"Remember your friends," said the arthritic, watching the ten.

"Bitch," said the sailor. "Why didn't you wait till he was gone?" Oedipa watched him make adjustments so he'd fit easier against the mattress. That stuffed memory. Register A . . .

"Give me a cigarette, Ramírez," the sailor said. "I know you got one."

Would it be today? "Ramírez," she cried. The arthritic looked around on his rusty neck. "He's going to die," she said.

"Who isn't?" said Ramírez.

She remembered John Nefastis, talking about his Machine, and massive destructions of information. So when this mattress flared up around the sailor, in his Viking's funeral: the stored, coded years of uselessness, early death, self-harrowing, the sure decay of hope, the set of all men who had slept on it, whatever their lives had been, would truly cease to be, forever, when the mattress burned. She stared at it in wonder. It was as if she had just discovered the irreversible process. It astonished her to think that so much could be lost, even the quantity of hallucination belonging just to the sailor that the world would bear no further trace of. She knew, because she had held him, that he suffered DT's. Behind the initials was a metaphor, a delirium tremens, a trembling unfurrowing[32] of the mind's plowshare. The saint whose water can light lamps, the clairvoyant whose lapse in recall is the breath of

---

[32]*Delirium*, from the Latin, literally meant "going out of the furrow."

God, the true paranoid for whom all is organized in spheres joyful or threatening about the central pulse of himself, the dreamer whose puns probe ancient fetid shafts and tunnels of truth all act in the same special relevance to the word, or whatever it is the word is there, buffering, to protect us from. The act of metaphor then was a thrust at truth and a lie, depending where you were: inside, safe, or outside, lost. Oedipa did not know where she was. Trembling, unfurrowed, she slipped sidewise, screeching back across grooves of years, to hear again the earnest, high voice of her second or third collegiate love Ray Glozing bitching among "uhs" and the syncopated tonguing of a cavity, about his freshman calculus; "dt," God help this old tattooed man, meant also a time differential, a vanishingly small instant in which change had to be confronted at last for what it was, where it could no longer disguise itself as something innocuous like an average rate; where velocity dwelled in the projectile though the projectile be frozen in midflight, where death dwelled in the cell though the cell be looked in on at its most quick. She knew that the sailor had seen worlds no other man had seen if only because there was that high magic to low puns, because DT's must give access to dt's of spectra beyond the known sun, music made purely of Antarctic loneliness and fright. But nothing she knew of would preserve them, or him. She gave him goodbye, walked downstairs and then on, in the direction he'd told her. For an hour she prowled along the sunless, concrete underpinnings of the freeway, finding drunks, bums, pedestrians, pederasts, hookers, walking psychotic, no secret mailbox. But at last in the shadows she did come on a can with a swinging trapezoidal top, the kind you throw trash in: old and green, nearly four feet high. On the swinging part were hand-painted the initials W.A.S.T.E. She had to look closely to see the periods between the letters.

Oedipa settled back in the shadow of a column. She may have dozed off. She woke to see a kid dropping a bundle of letters into the can. She went over and dropped in the sailor's letter to Fresno; then hid again and waited. Toward midday a rangy young wino showed up with a sack; unlocked a panel at the side of the box and took out all the letters. Oedipa gave him half a block's start, then began to tail him. Congratulating herself on having thought to wear flats, at least. The carrier led her across Market then over toward City Hall. In a street close enough to the drab, stone openness of the Civic Center to be infected by its gray, he rendezvoused with another carrier, and they exchanged sacks. Oedipa decided to stick with the one she'd been following. She tailed him all the way back down the littered, shifty, loud length of Market and over on First Street to the trans-bay bus terminal, where he bought a ticket for Oakland. So did Oedipa.

They rode over the bridge and into the great, empty glare of the Oakland afternoon. The landscape lost all variety. The carrier got off in a neighborhood Oedipa couldn't identify. She followed him for hours along streets whose names she never knew, across arterials that even with the afternoon's lull nearly murdered her, into slums and out, up long hillsides jammed solid with two- or three-bedroom houses, all their windows giving blankly back only the sun. One by one his sack of letters emptied. At length he climbed on a Berkeley bus. Oedipa followed. Halfway up Telegraph the carrier got off and led her down the street to a pseudo-Mexican apartment house. Not once had he looked behind him. John Nefastis lived here. She was back where she'd started, and could not believe 24 hours had passed. Should it have been more or less?

Back in the hotel she found the lobby full of deaf-mute delegates in party hats, copied in crepe paper after the fur Chinese communist jobs made popular during the Korean conflict. They were every one of them drunk, and a few of the men grabbed her, thinking to bring her along to a party in the grand ballroom. She tried to struggle out of the silent, gesturing swarm, but was too weak. Her legs ached, her mouth tasted horrible. They swept her on into the ballroom, where she was seized about the waist by a handsome young man in a Harris tweed coat and waltzed round and round, through the rustling, shuffling hush, under a great unlit chandelier. Each couple on the floor danced whatever was in the fellow's head: tango, two-step, bossa nova, slop. But how long, Oedipa thought, could it go on before collisions became a serious hindrance? There would have to be collisions. The only alternative was some unthinkable order of music, many rhythms, all keys at once, a choreography in which each couple meshed easy, predestined. Something they all heard with an extra sense atrophied in herself. She followed her partner's lead, limp in the young mute's clasp, waiting for the collisions to begin. But none came. She was danced for half an hour before, by mysterious consensus, everybody took a break, without having felt any touch but the touch of her partner. Jesús Arrabal would have called it an anarchist miracle. Oedipa, with no name for it, was only demoralized. She curtsied and fled.

Next day, after twelve hours of sleep and no dreams to speak of, Oedipa checked out of the hotel and drove down the peninsula to Kinneret. She had decided on route, with time to think about the day preceding, to go see Dr Hilarius her shrink, and tell him all. She might well be in the cold and sweatless meathooks of a psychosis. With her own eyes she had verified a WASTE system: seen two WASTE postmen, a WASTE mailbox, WASTE stamps, WASTE cancellations. And the image of the muted post horn all but saturating the Bay Area. Yet she wanted it all to be fantasy—some clear result of her several wounds, needs, dark doubles. She wanted Hilarius to tell her she was some kind of a nut and needed a rest, and that there was no Trystero. She also wanted to know why the chance of its being real should menace her so.

She pulled into the drive at Hilarius's clinic a little after sunset. The light in his office didn't seem to be on. Eucalyptus branches blew in a great stream of air that flowed downhill, sucked to the evening sea. Halfway along the flagstone path, she was startled by an insect whirring loudly past her ear, followed at once by the sound of a gunshot. That was no insect, thought Oedipa, at which point, hearing another shot, she made the connection. In the fading light she was a clear target; the only way to go was toward the clinic. She dashed up to the glass doors, found them locked, the lobby inside dark. Oedipa picked up a rock next to a flower bed and heaved it at one of the doors. It bounced off. She was looking around for another rock when a white shape appeared inside, fluttering up to the door and unlocking it for her. It was Helga Blamm, Hilarius's sometime assistant.

"Hurry," she chattered, as Oedipa slipped inside. The woman was close to hysterical.

"What's happening?" Oedipa said.

"He's gone crazy. I tried to call the police, but he took a chair and smashed the switchboard with it."

"Dr Hilarius?"

"He thinks someone's after him." Tear streaks had meandered down over the nurse's cheekbones. "He's locked himself in the office with that rifle." A Gewehr 43, from the war, Oedipa recalled, that he kept as a souvenir.

"He shot at me. Do you think anybody will report it?"

"Well, he's shot at half a dozen people," replied Nurse Blamm, leading Oedipa down a corridor to her office. "Somebody better report it." Oedipa noticed that the window opened on a safe line of retreat.

"You could've run," she said.

Blamm, running hot water from a washbasin tap into cups and stirring in instant coffee, looked up, quizzical. "He might need somebody."

"Who's supposed to be after him?"

"Three men with submachine guns," he said. Terrorists, fanatics, that was all I got. He started breaking up the PBX." She gave Oedipa a hostile look. "Too many nutty broads, that's what did it. Kinneret is full of nothing but. He couldn't cope."

"I've been away for a while," Oedipa said. "Maybe I could find out what it is. Maybe I'd be less of a threat for him."

Blamm burned her mouth on the coffee. "Start telling him your troubles and he'll probably shoot you."

In front of his door, which she could never remember having seen closed, Oedipa stood hipshot awhile, questioning her own sanity. Why hadn't she split out through Blamm's window and read about the rest of it in the paper?

"Who is it?" Hilarius screamed, having picked up her breathing, or something.

"Mrs Maas."

"May Speer[33] and his ministry of cretins rot eternally in hell. Do you realize that half these rounds are duds?"

"May I come in? Could we talk?"

"I'm sure you'd all like that," Hilarius said.

"I'm unarmed. You can frisk me."

"While you karate-chop me in the spine, no thank you."

"Why are you resisting every suggestion I make?"

"Listen," Hilarius said after awhile, "have I seemed to you a good enough Freudian? Have I ever deviated seriously?"

"You made faces now and then," said Oedipa, "but that's minor."

His response was a long, bitter laugh. Oedipa waited. "I tried," the shrink behind the door said, "to submit myself to that man, to the ghost of that cantankerous Jew. Tried to cultivate a faith in the literal truth of everything he wrote, even the idiocies and contradictions. It was the least I could have done, nicht wahr? A kind of penance.

"And part of me must have really wanted to believe—like a child hearing, in perfect safety, a tale of horror—that the unconscious would be like any other room, once the light was let in. That the dark shapes would resolve only into toy horses and Biedermeyer furniture. That therapy could tame it after all, bring it into society with no fear of its someday reverting. I wanted to believe, despite everything my life had been. Can you imagine?"

She could not, having no idea what Hilarius had done before show-

---

[33]Albert Speer, close associate of Hitler, was second to Goering in authority over the Third Reich's war economy; he was sentenced to twenty years in prison at the Nuremberg trials.

ing up in Kinneret. Far away she now heard sirens, the electronic kind
the local cops used, that sounded like a slide-whistle being played over
a P.A. system. With linear obstinacy they grew louder.

"Yes, I hear them," Hilarius said. "Do you think anyone can protect
me from these fanatics? They walk through walls. They replicate: you
flee them, turn a corner, and there they are, coming for you again."

"Do me a favor?" Oedipa said. "Don't shoot at the cops, they're on
your side."

"Your Israeli has access to every uniform known," Hilarius said. "I
can't guarantee the safety of the 'police.' You couldn't guarantee where
they'd take me if I surrendered, could you."

She heard him pacing around his office. Unearthly siren-sounds converged on them from all over the night. "There is a face," Hilarius said,
"that I can make. One you haven't seen; no one in this country has. I
have only made it once in my life, and perhaps today in central Europe
there still lives, in whatever vegetable ruin, the young man who saw it.
He would be, now, about your age. Hopelessly insane. His name was
Zvi. Will you tell the 'police,' or whatever they are calling themselves
tonight, that I can make that face again? That it has an effective radius
of a hundred yards and drives anyone unlucky enough to see it down
forever into the darkened oubliette, among the terrible shapes, and
secures the hatch irrevocably above them? Thank you."

The sirens had reached the front door of the clinic. She heard car
doors slamming, cops yelling, suddenly a great smash as they broke in.
The office door opened then. Hilarius grabbed her by the wrist, pulled
her inside, locked the door again.

"So now I'm a hostage," Oedipa said.

"Oh," said Hilarius, "it's you."

"Well who did you think you'd been——"

"Discussing my case with? Another. There is me, there are the others. You know, with the LSD, we're finding, the distinction begins to
vanish. Egos lose their sharp edges. But I never took the drug. I chose to
remain in relative paranoia, where at least I know who I am and who
the others are. Perhaps that is why you also refused to participate, Mrs
Maas?" He held the rifle at sling arms and beamed at her. "Well, then.
You were supposed to deliver a message to me, I assume. From them.
What were you supposed to say?"

Oedipa shrugged. "Face up to your social responsibilities," she suggested. "Accept the reality principle. You're outnumbered and they
have superior firepower."

"Ah, outnumbered. We were outnumbered there too." He watched
her with a coy look.

"Where?"

"Where I made that face. Where I did my internship."

She knew then approximately what he was talking about, but to narrow it said, "Where," again.

"Buchenwald," replied Hilarius. Cops began hammering on the office door.

"He has a gun," Oedipa called, "and I'm in here."

"Who are you, lady?" She told him. "How do you spell that first name?" He also took down her address, age, phone number, next of kin, husband's occupation, for the news media. Hilarius all the while was rummaging in his desk for more ammo. "Can you talk him out of it?" the cop wanted to know. "TV folks would like to get some footage through the window. Could you keep him occupied?"

"Hang tough," Oedipa advised, "we'll see."

"Nice act you all have there," nodded Hilarius.

"You think," said Oedipa, "then, that they're trying to bring you back to Israel, to stand trial, like they did Eichmann?"[34] The shrink kept nodding. "Why? What did you do at Buchenwald?"

"I worked," Hilarius told her, "on experimentally-induced insanity. A catatonic Jew was as good as a dead one. Liberal SS circles felt it would be more humane." So they had gone at their subjects with metronomes, serpents, Brechtian[35] vignettes at midnight, surgical removal of certain glands, magic-lantern hallucinations, new drugs, threats recited over hidden loudspeakers, hypnotism, clocks that ran backward, and faces. Hilarius had been put in charge of faces. "The Allied liberators," he reminisced, "arrived, unfortunately, before we could gather enough data. Apart from the spectacular successes, like Zvi, there wasn't much we could point to in a statistical way." He smiled at the expression on her face. "Yes, you hate me. But didn't I try to atone? If I'd been a real Nazi I'd have chosen Jung, nicht wahr? But I chose Freud instead, the Jew. Freud's vision of the world had no Buchenwalds in it. Buchenwald, according to Freud, once the light was let in, would become a soccer field, fat children would learn flower-arranging and solfeggio in the strangling rooms. At Auschwitz the ovens would be

---

[34]Adolf Eichmann (1906-1962), bureaucrat who carried out Hitler's plan to exterminate "undesirable" elements such as Jews, gypsies, homosexuals, and socialists. He escaped to Argentina after the war, but was kidnapped by Israelis in 1960, tried for crimes against humanity, and executed in 1962.

[35]Bertolt Brecht (1898-1956) was a German dramatist whose plays are often expressionistic in style.

converted over to petit fours and wedding cakes, and the V-2 missiles to public housing for the elves. I tried to believe it all. I slept three hours a night trying not to dream, and spent the other 21 at the forcible acquisition of faith. And yet my penance hasn't been enough. They've come like angels of death to get me, despite all I tried to do."

"How's it going?" the cop inquired.

"Just marv," said Oedipa. "I'll let you know if it's hopeless." Then she saw that Hilarius had left the Gewehr on his desk and was across the room ostensibly trying to open a file cabinet. She picked the rifle up, pointed it at him, and said, "I ought to kill you." She knew he had wanted her to get the weapon.

"Isn't that what you've been sent to do?" He crossed and uncrossed his eyes at her; stuck out his tongue tentatively.

"I came," she said, "hoping you could talk me out of a fantasy."

"Cherish it!" cried Hilarius fiercely. "What else do any of you have? Hold it tightly by its little tentacle, don't let the Freudians coax it away or the pharmacists poison it out of you. Whatever it is, hold it dear, for when you lose it you go over by that much to the others. You begin to cease to be."

"Come on in," Oedipa yelled.

Tears sprang to Hilarius's eyes. "You aren't going to shoot?"

The cop tried the door. "It's locked, hey," he said.

"Bust it down," roared Oedipa, "and Hitler Hilarius here will foot the bill."

Outside, as a number of nervous patrolmen approached Hilarius, holding up strait jackets and billy clubs they would not need, and as three rival ambulances backed snarling up onto the lawn, jockeying for position, causing Helga Blamm between sobs to call the drivers filthy names, Oedipa spotted among searchlights and staring crowds a KCUF mobile unit, with her husband Mucho inside it, spieling into a microphone. She moseyed over past snapping flashbulbs and stuck her head in the window. "Hi."

Mucho pressed his cough button for a moment, but only smiled. It seemed odd. How could they hear a smile? Oedipa got in, trying not to make noise. Mucho thrust the mike in front of her, mumbling, "You're on, just be yourself." Then in his earnest broadcasting voice, "How do you feel about this terrible thing?"

"Terrible," said Oedipa.

"Wonderful," said Mucho. He had let her go on to give listeners a summary of what'd happened in the office. "Thank you, Mrs Edna Mosh," he wrapped up, "for your eyewitness account of this dramatic siege at the Hilarius Psychiatric Clinic. This is KCUF Mobile Two, sending it back now to 'Rabbit' Warren, at the studio." He cut his power. Something was not quite right.

"Edna Mosh?" Oedipa said.

"It'll come out the right way," Mucho said. "I was allowing for the distortion on these rigs, and then when they put it on tape."

"Where are they taking him?"

"Community hospital, I guess," Mucho said, "for observation. I wonder what they can observe."

"Israelis," Oedipa said, "coming in the windows. If there aren't any, he's crazy." Cops came over and they chatted awhile. They told her to stay around Kinneret in case there was legal action. At length she returned to her rented car and followed Mucho back to the studio. Tonight he had the one-to-six shift on the air.

In the hallway outside the loud ratcheting teletype room, Mucho upstairs in the office typing out his story, Oedipa encountered the program director, Caesar Funch. "Sure glad you're back," he greeted her, clearly at a loss for her first name.

"Oh?" said Oedipa, "and why is that."

"Frankly," confided Funch, "since you left, Wendell hasn't been himself."

"And who," said Oedipa, working herself into a rage because Funch was right, "pray, has he been, Ringo Starr?" Funch cowered. "Chubby Checker?" she pursued him toward the lobby, "the Righteous Brothers? And why tell me?"

"All of the above," said Funch, seeking to hide his head, "Mrs Maas."

"Oh, call me Edna. What do you mean?"

"Behind his back," Funch was whining, "they're calling him the Brothers N. He's losing his identity, Edna, how else can I put it? Day by day, Wendell is less himself and more generic. He enters a staff meeting and the room is suddenly full of people, you know? He's a walking assembly of man."

"It's your imagination," Oedipa said. "You've been smoking those cigarettes without the printing on them again."

"You'll see. Don't mock me. We have to stick together. Who else worries about him?"

She sat alone then on a bench outside Studio A, listening to Mucho's colleague Rabbit Warren spin records. Mucho came downstairs carrying his copy, a serenity about him she'd never seen. He used to hunch

his shoulders and have a rapid eyeblink rate, and both now were gone.
"Wait," he smiled, and dwindled down the hall. She scrutinized him
from behind, trying to see iridescences, auras.

They had some time before he was on. They drove downtown to a
pizzeria and bar, and faced each other through the fluted gold lens of a
beer pitcher.

"How are you getting on with Metzger?" he said.

"There's nothing," she said.

"Not any more, at least," said Mucho. "I could tell that when you
were talking into the mike."

"That's pretty good," Oedipa said. She couldn't figure the expression
on his face.

"It's extraordinary," said Mucho, "everything's been—wait. Listen."
She heard nothing unusual. "There are seventeen violins on that cut,"
Mucho said, "and one of them—I can't tell where he was because it's
monaural here, damn." It dawned on her that he was talking about the
Muzak. It has been seeping in, in its subliminal, unidentifiable way
since they'd entered the place, all strings, reeds, muted brass.

"What is it," she said, feeling anxious.

"His E string," Mucho said, "it's a few cycles sharp. He can't be a
studio musician. Do you think somebody could do the dinosaur bone
bit with that one string, Oed? With just his set of notes on that cut.
Figure out what his ear is like, and then the musculature of his hands
and arms, and eventually the entire man. God, wouldn't that be wonderful."

"Why should you want to?"

"He was real. That wasn't synthetic. They could dispense with live
musicians if they wanted. Put together all the right overtones at the
right power levels so it'd come out like a violin. Like I . . ." he hesitated
before breaking into a radiant smile, "you'll think I'm crazy, Oed. But
I can do the same thing in reverse. Listen to anything and take it apart
again. Spectrum analysis in my head. I can break down chords, and
timbres, and words too into all the basic frequencies and harmonics,
with all their different loudnesses, and listen to them, each pure tone,
but all at once."

"How can you do that?"

"It's like I have a separate channel for each one," Mucho said, excited, "and if I need more I just expand. Add on what I need. I don't
know how it works, but lately I can do it with people talking too. Say
'rich, chocolaty goodness.' "

"Rich, chocolaty goodness," said Oedipa.

"Yes," said Mucho, and fell silent.

"Well, *what?*" Oedipa asked after a couple minutes, with an edge to her voice.

"I noticed it the other night hearing Rabbit do a commercial. No matter who's talking, the different power spectra are the same, give or take a small percentage. So you and Rabbit have something in common now. More than that. Everybody who says the same words is the same person if the spectra are the same only they happen differently in time, you dig? But the time is arbitrary. You pick your zero point anywhere you want, that way you can shuffle each person's time line sideways till they all coincide. Then you'd have this big, God, maybe a couple hundred million chorus saying 'rich, chocolaty goodness' together, and it would all be the same voice."

"Mucho," she said, impatient but also flirting with a wild suspicion. "Is this what Funch means when he says you're coming on like a whole roomful of people?"

"That's what I am," said Mucho, "right. Everybody is." He gazed at her, having perhaps had his vision of consensus as others do orgasms, face now smooth, amiable, at peace. She didn't know him. Panic started to climb out of a dark region in her head. "Whenever I put the headset on now," he'd continued, "I really do understand what I find there. When those kids sing about 'She loves you,' yeah well, you know, she does, she's any number of people, all over the world, back through time, different colors, sizes, ages, shapes, distances from death, but she loves. And the 'you' is everybody. And herself. Oedipa, the human voice, you know, it's a flipping miracle." His eyes brimming, reflecting the color of beer.

"Baby," she said, helpless, knowing of nothing she could do for this, and afraid for him.

He put a little clear plastic bottle on the table between them. She stared at the pills in it, and then understood. "That's LSD?" she said. Mucho smiled back. "Where'd you get it?" Knowing.

"Hilarius. He broadened his program to include husbands."

"Look then," Oedipa said, trying to be businesslike, "how long has it been, that you've been on this?"

He honestly couldn't remember.

"But there may be a chance you're not addicted yet."

"Oed," looking at her puzzled, "you don't get addicted. It's not like you're some hophead. You take it because it's good. Because you hear and see things, even smell them, taste like you never could. Because the world is so abundant. No end to it, baby. You're an antenna, sending your pattern out across a million lives a night, and they're your lives too." He had this patient, motherly look now. Oedipa wanted to hit him in the mouth. "The songs, it's not just that they say something, they *are* something, in the pure sound. Something new. And my dreams have changed."

"Oh, goodo." Flipping her hair a couple times, furious, "No nightmares any more? Fine. So your latest little friend, whoever she is, she really made out. At that age, you know, they need all the sleep they can get."

"There's no girl, Oed. Let me tell you. The bad dream that I used to have all the time, about the car lot, remember that? I could never even tell you about it. But I can now. It doesn't bother me any more. It was only that sign in the lot, that's what scared me. In the dream I'd be going about a normal day's business and suddenly, with no warning, there'd be the sign. We were a member of the National Automobile Dealers' Association. N.A.D.A. Just this creaking metal sign that said nada, nada,[36] against the blue sky. I used to wake up hollering."

She remembered. Now he would never be spooked again, not as long as he had the pills. She could not quite get it into her head that the day she'd left him for San Narciso was the day she'd seen Mucho for the last time. So much of him already had dissipated.

"Oh, listen," he was saying, "Oed, dig." But she couldn't even tell what the tune was.

When it was time for him to go back to the station, he nodded toward the pills. "You could have those."

She shook her head no.

"You're going back to San Narciso?"

"Tonight, yes."

"But the cops."

"I'll be a fugitive." Later she couldn't remember if they'd said anything else. At the station they kissed goodbye, all of them. As Mucho walked away he was whistling something complicated, twelve-tone. Oedipa sat with her forehead resting on the steering wheel and remembered that she hadn't asked him about the Trystero cancellation on his letter. But by then it was too late to make any difference.

---

[36] Spanish for "nothing": the void.

VI

When she got back to Echo Courts, she found Miles, Dean, Serge and Leonard arranged around and on the diving board at the end of the swimming pool with all their instruments, so composed and motionless that some photographer, hidden from Oedipa, might have been shooting them for an album illustration.

"What's happening?" said Oedipa.

"Your young man," replied Miles, "Metzger, really put it to Serge, our counter-tenor. The lad is crackers with grief."

"He's right, missus," said Serge. "I even wrote a song about it, whose arrangement features none other than me, and it goes like this."

SERGE'S SONG

What chance has a lonely surfer boy
For the love of a surfer chick,
With all these Humbert Humbert[37] cats
Coming on so big and sick?
For me, my baby was a woman,
For him she's just another nymphet;
Why did they run around, why did she put me down,
And get me so upset?
Well, as long as she's gone away-yay,
I've had to find somebody new,
And the older generation
Has taught me what to do—
I had a date last night with an eight-year-old,
And she's a swinger just like me,
So you can find us any night up on the football field,
In back of P.S. 33 (oh, yeah),
And it's as groovy as it can be.

"You're trying to tell me something," said Oedipa.

They gave it to her then in prose. Metzger and Serge's chick had run off to Nevada, to get married. Serge, on close questioning, admitted the bit about the eight-year-old was so far only imaginary, but that he was hanging diligently around playgrounds and should have some news for

---

[37]Narrator-protagonist of Vladimir Nabokov's novel *Lolita* (1955); he is sexually attracted only to preadolescent girls, whom he calls "nymphets."

them any day. On top of the TV set in her room Metzger had left a note telling her not to worry about the estate, that he'd turned over his executorship to somebody at Warpe, Wistfull, Kubitschek and McMingus, and they should be in touch with her, and it was all squared with the probate court also. No word to recall that Oedipa and Metzger had ever been more than co-executors.

Which must mean, thought Oedipa, that that's all we were. She should have felt more classically scorned, but had other things on her mind. First thing after unpacking she was on the horn to Randolph Driblette, the director. After about ten rings an elderly lady answered. "I'm sorry, we've nothing to say."

"Well who's this," Oedipa said.

Sigh. "This is his mother. There'll be a statement at noon tomorrow. Our lawyer will read it." She hung up. Now what the hell, Oedipa wondered: what had happened to Driblette? She decided to call later. She found Professor Emory Bortz's number in the book and had better luck. A wife named Grace answered, backed by a group of children. "He's pouring a patio," she told Oedipa. "It's a highly organized joke that's been going on since about April. He sits in the sun, drinks beer with students, lobs beer bottles at seagulls. You'd better talk to him before it gets that far. Maxine, why don't you throw that at your brother, he's more mobile than I am. Did you know Emory's done a new edition of Wharfinger? It'll be out——" but the date was obliterated by a great crash, maniacal childish laughter, high-pitched squeals. "Oh, God. Have you ever met an infanticide? Come on over, it may be your only chance."

Oedipa showered, put on a sweater, skirt and sneakers, wrapped her hair in a studentlike twist, went easy on the makeup. Recognizing with a vague sense of dread that it was not a matter of Bortz's response, or Grace's, but of The Trystero's.

Driving over she passed by Zapf's Used Books, and was alarmed to find only a pile of charred rubble where the bookstore only a week ago had stood. There was still the smell of burnt leather. She stopped and went into the government surplus outlet next door. The owner informed her that Zapf, the damn fool, has set fire to his own store for the insurance. "Any kind of a wind," snarled this worthy, "it would have taken me with it. They only put up this complex here to last five years anyway. But could Zapf wait? Books." You had the feeling that it was only his good upbringing kept him from spitting. "You want to sell something used," he advised Oedipa, "find out what there's a demand for. This season now it's your rifles. Fella was in just this forenoon, bought two hundred for his drill team. I could've sold him two hundred of the swastika armbands too, only I was short, dammit."

"Government surplus swastikas?" Oedipa said.

"Hell no." He gave her an insider's wink. "Got this little factory down outside of San Diego," he told her, "got a dozen of your niggers, say, they can sure turn them old armbands out. You'd be amazed how that little number's selling. I took some space in a couple of the girlie magazines, and I had to hire two extra niggers last week just to take care of the mail."

"What's your name?" Oedipa said.

"Winthrop Tremaine," replied the spirited entrepreneur, "Winner, for short. Listen, now we're getting up an arrangement with one of the big ready-to-wear outfits in L.A. to see how SS uniforms go for the fall. We're working it in with the back-to-school campaign, lot of 37 longs, you know, teenage kid sizes. Next season we may go all the way and get out a modified version for the ladies. How would that strike you?"

"I'll let you know," Oedipa said. "I'll keep you in mind." She left, wondering if she should've called him something, or tried to hit him with any of a dozen surplus, heavy, blunt objects in easy reach. There had been no witnesses. Why hadn't she?

You're chicken, she told herself, snapping her seat belt. This is America, you live in it, you let it happen. Let it unfurl. She drove savagely along the freeway, hunting for Volkswagens. By the time she'd pulled into Bortz's subdivision, a riparian[38] settlement in the style of Fangoso Lagoons, she was only shaking and a little nauseous in the stomach.

She was greeted by a small fat girl with some blue substance smeared all over her face. "Hi," said Oedipa, "you must be Maxine."

"Maxine's in bed. She threw one of Daddy's beer bottles at Charles and it went through the window and Mama spanked her good. If she was mine I'd drown her."

"Never thought of doing it that way," said Grace Bortz, materializing from the dim living room. "Come on in." With a wet washcloth she started to clean off her child's face. "How did you manage to get away from yours today?"

"I don't have any," said Oedipa, following her into the kitchen.

---

[38]On the seashore.

Grace looked surprised. "There's a certain harassed style," she said, "you get to recognize. I thought only kids caused it. I guess not."

Emory Bortz lay half in a hammock, surrounded by three graduate students, two male, one female, all sodden with drink, and an astounding accumulation of empty beer bottles. Oedipa located a full one and seated herself on the grass. "I would like to find out," she presently plunged, "something about the historical Wharfinger. Not so much the verbal one."

"The historical Shakespeare," growled one of the grad students through a full beard, uncapping another bottle. "The historical Marx. The historical Jesus."

"He's right," shrugged Bortz, "they're dead. What's left?"

"Words."

"Pick some words," said Bortz. "Them, we can talk about."

" 'No hallowed skein of stars can ward, I trow,' " quoted Oedipa, " 'Who's once been set his tryst with Trystero.' *Courier's Tragedy*, Act IV, Scene 8."

Bortz blinked at her. "And how," he said, "did you get into the Vatican library?"

Oedipa showed him the paperback with the line in it. Bortz, squinting at the page, groped for another beer. "My God," he announced, "I've been pirated, me and Wharfinger, we've been Bowdlerized in reverse or something." He flipped to the front, to see who'd re-edited his edition of Wharfinger. "Ashamed to sign it. Damn. I'll have to write the publishers. K. da Chingado[39] and Company? You ever heard of them? New York." He looked at the sun through a page or two. "Offset." Brought his nose close to the text. "Misprints. Gah. Corrupt." He dropped the book on the grass and looked at it with loathing. "How did *they* get into the Vatican, then?"

"What's in the Vatican?" asked Oedipa.

"A pornographic *Courier's Tragedy*. I didn't get to see it till '61, or I would've given it a note in my old edition."

"What I saw out at the Tank Theater wasn't pornographic?"

"Randy Driblette's production? No, I thought it was typically virtuous." He looked sadly past her toward a stretch of sky. "He was a peculiarly moral man. He felt hardly any responsibility toward the word, really; but to the invisible field surrounding the play, its spirit, he

---

[39]The publishers' name is an obscenity in Spanish.

was always intensely faithful. If anyone could have called up for you that historical Wharfinger you want, it'd've been Randy. Nobody else I ever knew was so close to the author, to the microcosm of that play as it must have surrounded Wharfinger's living mind."

"But you're using the past tense," Oedipa said, her heart pounding, remembering the old lady on the phone.

"Hadn't you heard?" They all looked at her. Death glided by, shadowless, among the empties on the grass.

"Randy walked into the Pacific two nights ago," the girl told her finally. Her eyes had been red all along. "In his Gennaro suit. He's dead, and this is a wake."

"I tried to call him this morning," was all Oedipa could think of to say.

"It was right after they struck the set of *The Courier's Tragedy*," Bortz said.

Even a month ago, Oedipa's next question would have been, "Why?" But now she kept a silence, waiting, as if to be illuminated.

They are stripping from me, she said subvocally—feeling like a fluttering curtain in a very high window, moving up to then out over the abyss—they are stripping away, one by one, my men. My shrink, pursued by Israelis, has gone mad; my husband, on LSD, gropes like a child further and further into the rooms and endless rooms of the elaborate candy house of himself and away, hopelessly away, from what has passed, I was hoping forever, for love; my one extra-marital fella has eloped with a depraved 15-year-old; my best guide back to the Trystero has taken a Brody.[40] Where am I?

"I'm sorry," Bortz had also said, watching her.

Oedipa stayed with it. "Did he use only that," pointing to the paperback, "for his script?"

"No." Frowning. "He used the hardcover, my edition."

"But the night you saw the play." Too much sunlight shone on the bottles, silent all around them. "How did he end the fourth act? What were his lines, Driblette's, Gennaro's, when they're all standing around at the lake, after the miracle?"

" 'He that we last as Thurn and Taxis knew,' " recited Bortz, " 'Now recks no lord but the stiletto's Thorn,/And Tacit lies the gold once-knotted horn.' "

"Right," agreed the grad students, "yeah."

---

[40]Committed suicide, especially by jumping off a bridge.

"That's all? What about the rest? The other couplet?"

"In the text I go along with personally," said Bortz, "that other couplet has the last line suppressed. The book in the Vatican is only an obscene parody. The ending 'Who once has crossed the lusts of Angelo' was put in by the printer of the 1687 Quarto. The 'Whitechapel' version is corrupt. So Randy did the best thing—left the doubtful part out altogether."

"But the night I was there," said Oedipa, "Driblette did use the Vatican lines, he said the word Trystero."

Bortz's face stayed neutral. "It was up to him. He was both director and actor, right?"

"But would it be just," she gestured in circles with her hands, "just some whim? To use another couple lines like that, without telling anybody?"

"Randy," recalled the third grad student, a stocky kid with hornrims, "what was bugging him inside, usually, somehow or other, would have to come outside, on stage. He might have looked at a lot of versions, to develop a feel for the spirit of the play, not necessarily the words, and that's how he came across your paperback there, with the variation in it."

"Then," Oedipa concluded, "something must have happened in his personal life, something must have changed for him drastically that night, and that's what made him put the lines in."

"Maybe," said Bortz, "maybe not. You think a man's mind is a pool table?"

"I hope not."

"Come in and see some dirty pictures," Bortz invited, rolling off the hammock. They left the students drinking beer. "Illicit microfilms of the illustrations in that Vatican edition. Smuggled out in '61. Grace and I were out there on a grant."

They entered a combination workroom and study. Far away in the house children screamed, a vacuum whined. Bortz drew shades, riffled through a box of slides, selected a handful, switched on a projector and aimed it at a wall.

The illustrations were woodcuts, executed with that crude haste to see the finished product that marks the amateur. True pornography is given us by vastly patient professionals.

"The artist is anonymous," Bortz said, "so is the poetaster who rewrote the play. Here Pasquale, remember, one of the bad guys? actually does marry his mother, and there's a whole scene on their wedding night." He changed slides. "You get the general idea. Notice how often the figure of Death hovers in the background. The moral rage, it's a throwback, it's mediaeval. No Puritan ever got that violent. Except possibly the Scurvhamites. D'Amico thinks this edition was a Scurvhamite project."

"Scurvhamite?"

Robert Scurvham had founded, during the reign of Charles I, a sect of most pure Puritans. Their central hangup had to do with predestination. There were two kinds. Nothing for a Scurvhamite ever happened by accident, Creation was a vast, intricate machine. But one part of it, the Scurvhamite part, ran off the will of God, its prime mover. The rest ran off some opposite Principle, something blind, soulless; a brute automatism that led to eternal death. The idea was to woo converts into the Godly and purposeful sodality of the Scurvhamite. But somehow those few saved Scurvhamites found themselves looking out into the gaudy clockwork of the doomed with a certain sick and fascinated horror, and this was to prove fatal. One by one the glamorous prospect of annihilation coaxed them over, until there was no one left in the sect, not even Robert Scurvham, who, like a ship's master, had been last to go.

"What did Richard Wharfinger have to do with them?" asked Oedipa. "Why should they do a dirty version of his play?"

"As a moral example. They were not fond of the theatre. It was their way of putting the play entirely away from them, into hell. What better way to damn it eternally than to change the actual words. Remember that Puritans were utterly devoted, like literary critics, to the Word."

"But the line about Trystero isn't dirty."

He scratched his head. "It fits, surely? The 'hallowed skein of stars' is God's will. But even that can't ward, or guard, somebody who has an appointment with Trystero. I mean, say you only talked about crossing the lusts of Angelo, hell, there'd be any number of ways to get out of that. Leave the country. Angelo's only a man. But the brute Other, that kept the non-Scurvhamite universe running like clockwork, that was something else again. Evidently they felt Trystero would symbolize the Other quite well."

She had nothing more then to put it off with. Again with the light, vertiginous sense of fluttering out over an abyss, she asked what she'd come there to ask. "What was Trystero?"

"One of several brand new areas," said Bortz, "that opened up after I did that edition in '57. We've since come across some interesting old source material. My updated edition ought to be out, they tell me, next year sometime. Meanwhile." He went looking in a glass case full of ancient books. "Here," producing one with a dark brown, peeling calf cover. "I keep my Wharfingeriana locked in here so the kids can't get at it. Charles could ask no end of questions I'm too young to cope with yet." The book was titled *An Account of the Singular Peregrinations of Dr Diocletian Blobb among the Italians, Illuminated with Exemplary Tales from the True History of That Outlandish And Fantastical Race.*

"Lucky for me," said Bortz, "Wharfinger, like Milton, kept a commonplace book, where he jotted down quotes and things from his reading. That's how we know about Blobb's *Peregrinations.*"

It was full of words ending in e's, s's that looked like f's, capitalized nouns, y's where i's should've been. "I can't read this," Oedipa said.

"Try," said Bortz. "I have to see those kids off. I think it's around Chapter Seven." And disappeared, to leave Oedipa before the tabernacle. As it turned out it was Chapter Eight she wanted, a report of the author's own encounter with the Trystero brigands. Diocletian Blobb had chosen to traverse a stretch of desolate mountain country in a mail coach belonging to the "Torre and Tassis" system, which Oedipa figured must be Italian for Thurn and Taxis. Without warning, by the shores of what Blobb called "the Lake of Piety," they were set upon by a score of black-cloaked riders, who engaged them in a fierce, silent struggle in the icy wind blowing in from the lake. The marauders used cudgels, harquebuses, swords, stilettos, at the end silk kerchiefs to dispatch those still breathing. All except for Dr Blobb and his servant, who had dissociated themselves from the hassle at the very outset, proclaimed in loud voices that they were British subjects, and even from time to time "ventured to sing certain of the more improving of our Church hymns." Their escape surprised Oedipa, in view of what seemed to be Trystero's passion for security.

"Was Trystero trying to set up shop in England?" Bortz suggested, days later.

Oedipa didn't know. "But why spare an insufferable ass like Diocletian Blobb?"

"You can spot a mouth like that a mile off," Bortz said. "Even in the cold, even with your blood-lust up. If I wanted word to get to England, to sort of pave the way, I should think he'd be perfect. Trystero enjoyed counter-revolution in those days. Look at England, the king about to lose his head. A set-up."

The leader of the brigands, after collecting the mail sacks, had pulled Blobb from the coach and addressed him in perfect English: "Messer, you have witnessed the wrath of Trystero. Know that we are not without mercy. Tell your king and Parliament what we have done. Tell them that we prevail. That neither tempest nor strife, nor fierce beasts, nor the loneliness of the desert, not yet the illegitimate usurpers of our rightful estate, can deter our couriers." And leaving them and their purses intact, the highwaymen, in a cracking of cloaks like black sails, vanished back into their twilit mountains.

Blobb inquired around about the Trystero organization, running into zipped mouths nearly every way he turned. But he was able to collect a few fragments. So, in the days following, was Oedipa. From obscure philatelic journals furnished her by Genghis Cohen, an ambiguous footnote in Motley's *Rise of the Dutch Republic*, an 80-year-old pamphlet on the roots of modern anarchism, a book of sermons by Blobb's brother Augustine also among Bortz's Wharfingeriana, along with Blobb's original clues, Oedipa was able to fit together this account of how the organization began:[41]

In 1577, the northern provinces of the Low Countries, led by the Protestant noble William of Orange, had been struggling nine years for independence from Catholic Spain and a Catholic Holy Roman Emperor. In late December, Orange, de facto master of the Low Countries, entered Brussels in triumph, having been invited there by a Committee of Eighteen. This was a junta of Calvinist fanatics who felt that the Estates-General, controlled by the privileged classes, no longer represented the skilled workers, had lost touch entirely with the people. The Committee set up a kind of Brussels Commune. They controlled the police, dictated all decisions of the Estates-General, and threw out many holders of high position in Brussels. Among these was Leonard I, Baron of Taxis, Gentleman of the Emperor's Privy Chamber and Baron of Buysinghen, the hereditary Grand Master of the Post for the Low Countries, and executor of the Thurn and Taxis monopoly. He was replaced by one Jan Hinckart, Lord of Ohain, a loyal adherent of Orange. At this point the founding figure enters the scene: Hernando Joaquín de Tristero y Calavera,[42] perhaps a madman, perhaps an honest rebel, according to some only a con artist. Tristero claimed to be Jan Hinckart's cousin, from the Spanish and legitimate branch of the family, and true lord of Ohain—rightful heir to everything Jan Hinckart then possessed, including his recent appointment as Grand Master.

---

[41]The "history" that follows is a mixture of facts about the Thurn und Taxis postal monopoly and fiction about the Tristero counterforce.

[42]Calavera is the Spanish form of "Calvary," the "place of the skull" where Christ was crucified.

From 1578 until Alexander Farnese took Brussels back again for the Emperor in March, 1585, Tristero kept up what amounted to a guerrilla war against his cousin—if Hinckart was his cousin. Being Spanish, he got little support. Most of the time, from one quarter or another, his life was in danger. Still, he tried four times to assassinate Orange's postmaster, though without success.

Jan Hinckart was dispossessed by Farnese, and Leonard I, the Thurn and Taxis Grand Master, reinstated. But it had been a time of great instability for the Thurn and Taxis monopoly. Leery of strong Protestant leanings in the Bohemian branch of the family, the Emperor, Rudolph II, had for a time withdrawn his patronage. The postal operation plunged deeply into the red.

It may have been some vision of the continentwide power structure Hinckart could have taken over, now momentarily weakened and tottering, that inspired Tristero to set up his own system. He seems to have been highly unstable, apt at any time to appear at a public function and begin a speech. His constant theme, disinheritance. The postal monopoly belonged to Ohain by right of conquest, and Ohain belonged to Tristero by right of blood. He styled himself El Desheredado, The Disinherited, and fashioned a livery of black for his followers, black to symbolize the only thing that truly belonged to them in their exile: the night. Soon he had added to his iconography the muted post horn and a dead badger with its four feet in the air (some said that the name Taxis came from the Italian *tasso*, badger, referring to hats of badger fur the early Bergamascan couriers wore). He began a sub rosa campaign of obstruction, terror and depredation along the Thurn and Taxis mail routes.

Oedipa spent the next several days in and out of libraries and earnest discussions with Emory Bortz and Genghis Cohen. She feared a little for their security in view of what was happening to everyone else she knew. The day after reading Blobb's *Peregrinations* she, with Bortz, Grace, and the graduate students, attended Randolph Driblette's burial, listened to a younger brother's helpless, stricken eulogy, watched the mother, spectral in afternoon smog, cry, and came back at night to sit on the grave and drink Napa Valley muscatel, which Driblette in his time had put away barrels of. There was no moon, smog covered the stars, all black as a Tristero rider. Oedipa sat on the earth, ass getting cold, wondering whether, as Driblette had suggested that night from the shower, some version of herself hadn't vanished with him. Perhaps her mind would go on flexing psychic muscles that no longer existed; would be betrayed and mocked by a phantom self as the amputee is by a phantom limb. Someday she might replace whatever of her had gone away by some prosthetic device, a dress of a certain color, a phrase in a letter, another lover. She tried to reach out, to whatever coded tenacity of protein might improbably have held on six feet below, still resisting decay—any stubborn quiescence perhaps gathering itself for some last burst, some last scramble up through earth, just-glimmering, holding together with its final strength a transient, winged shape, needing to settle at once in the warm host or dissipate forever into the dark. If you come to me, prayed Oedipa, bring your memories of the last night. Or if you have to keep down your payload, the last five minutes—that may be enough. But so I'll know if your walk into the sea had anything to do with Tristero. If they got rid of you for the reason they got rid of Hilarius and Mucho and Metzger—maybe because they thought I no longer needed you. They were wrong. I needed you. Only bring me that memory, and you can live with me for whatever time I've got. She remembered his head floating in the shower, saying, you could fall in love with me. But could she have saved him? She looked over at the girl who'd given her the news of his death. Had they been in love? Did she know why Driblette had put in those two extra lines that night? Had *he* even known why? No one could begin to trace it. A hundred hangups, permuted, combined—sex, money, illness, despair with the history of his time and place, who knew. Changing the script had no clearer motive than his suicide. There was the same whimsy to both. Perhaps—she felt briefly penetrated, as if the bright winged thing had actually made it to the sanctuary of her heart—perhaps, springing from the same slick labyrinth, adding those two lines had even, in a way never to be explained, served him as a rehearsal for his night's walk away into that vast sink of the primal blood the Pacific. She waited for the winged brightness to announce its safe arrival. But there was silence. Driblette, she called. The signal echoing down twisted miles of brain circuitry. Driblette!

But as with Maxwell's Demon, so now. Either she could not communicate, or he did not exist.

Beyond its origins, the libraries told her nothing more about Tristero. For all they knew, it had never survived the struggle for Dutch independence. To find the rest, she had to approach from the Thurn and Taxis side. This had its perils. For Emory Bortz it seemed to turn into a species of cute game. He held, for instance, to a mirror-image theory, by which any period of instability for Thurn and Taxis must have its reflection in Tristero's shadow-state. He applied this to the mystery of why the dread name should have appeared in print only around the middle of the 17th century. How had the author of the pun on "this Trystero *dies irae*" overcome his reluctance? How had half the Vatican couplet, with its suppression of the "Trystero" line, found its way into the Folio? Whence had the daring of even hinting at a Thurn and Taxis rival come? Bortz maintained there must have been some crisis inside Tristero grave enough to keep them from retaliating. Perhaps the same that kept them from taking the life of Dr Blobb.

But should Bortz have exfoliated the mere words so lushly, into such unnatural roses, under which, in whose red, scented dusk, dark history slithered unseen? When Leonard II-Francis, Count of Thurn and Taxis, died in 1628, his wife Alexandrine of Rye succeeded him in name as postmaster, though her tenure was never considered official. She retired in 1645. The actual locus of power in the monopoly remained uncertain until 1650, when the next male heir, Lamoral II-Claude-Francis, took over. Meanwhile, in Brussels and Antwerp signs of decay in the system had appeared. Private local posts had encroached so far on the Imperial licenses that the two cities shut down their Thurn and Taxis offices.

How, Bortz asked, would Tristero have responded? Postulating then some militant faction proclaiming the great moment finally at hand. Advocating a takeover by force, while their enemy was vulnerable. But conservative opinion would care only to continue in opposition, exactly as the Tristero had these seventy years. There might also be, say, a few visionaries: men above the immediacy of their time who could think historically. At least one among them hip enough to foresee the end of the Thirty Years' War, the Peace of Westphalia, the breakup of the Empire, the coming descent into particularism.

"He looks like Kirk Douglas," cried Bortz, "he's wearing this sword, his name is something gutsy like Konrad. They're meeting in the back room of a tavern, all these broads in peasant blouses carrying steins around, everybody juiced and yelling, suddenly Konrad jumps up on a table. The crowd hushes. 'The salvation of Europe,' Konrad says, 'depends on communication, right? We face this anarchy of jealous German princes, hundreds of them scheming, counter-scheming, infighting, dissipating all of the Empire's strength in their useless bickering. But whoever could control the lines of communication, among all these princes, would control them. That network someday could unify the Continent. So I propose that we merge with our old enemy Thurn and Taxis——' Cries of no, never, throw the traitor out, till this barmaid, little starlet, sweet on Konrad, cold-conks with a stein his loudest antagonist. 'Together,' Konrad is saying, 'our two systems could be invincible. We could refuse service on any but an Imperial basis. Nobody could move troops, farm produce, anything, without us. Any prince tries to start his own courier system, we suppress it. We, who have been so long disinherited, could be the heirs of Europe!' Prolonged cheering."

"But they *didn't* keep the Empire from falling apart," Oedipa pointed out.

"So," Bortz backing off, "the militants and the conservatives fight to a standstill, Konrad and his little group of visionaries, being nice guys, try to mediate the hassle, by the time they get all squared away again, everybody's played out, the Empire's had it, Thurn and Taxis wants no deals."

And with the end of the Holy Roman Empire, the fountainhead of Thurn and Taxis legitimacy is lost forever among the other splendid delusions. Possibilities for paranoia become abundant. If Tristero has managed to maintain even partial secrecy, if Thurn and Taxis have no clear idea who their adversary is, or how far its influence extends, then many of them must come to believe in something very like the Scurvhamite's blind, automatic anti-God. Whatever it is, it has the power to murder their riders, send landslides thundering across their roads, by extension bring into being new local competition and presently even state postal monopolies; disintegrate their Empire. It is their time's ghost, out to put the Thurn and Taxis ass in a sling.

But over the next century and a half the paranoia recedes, as they come to discover the secular Tristero. Power, omniscience, implacable malice, attributes of what they'd thought to be a historical principle, a Zeitgeist, are carried over to the now human enemy. So much that, by 1795, it is even suggested that Tristero has staged the entire French Revolution, just for an excuse to issue the Proclamation of 9th Frimaire, An III,[43] ratifying the end of the Thurn and Taxis postal monopoly in France and the Lowlands.

"Suggested by who, though," said Oedipa. "Did you read that someplace?"

"Wouldn't somebody have brought it up?" Bortz said. "Maybe not."

She didn't press the argument. Having begun to feel reluctant about following up anything. She hadn't asked Genghis Cohen, for example,

---

[43]One of the more temporary reforms of the French Revolution was a revamped calendar that began with the year I on September 22, 1792. The date referred to here is November 29, 1794.

if his Expert Committee had ever reported back on the stamps he'd sent them. She knew that if she went back to Vesperhaven House again to talk to old Mr Thoth about his grandfather, she would find that he too had died. She knew she ought to write to K. da Chingado, publisher of the unaccountable paperback *Courier's Tragedy*, but she didn't, and never asked Bortz if he had, either. Worst of all, she found herself going often to absurd lengths to avoid talking about Randolph Driblette. Whenever the girl showed up, the one who'd been at the wakes, Oedipa found excuses to leave the gathering. She felt she was betraying Driblette and herself. But left it alone, anxious that her revelation not expand beyond a certain point. Lest, possibly, it grow larger than she and assume her to itself. When Bortz asked her one evening if he could bring in D'Amico, who was at NYU, Oedipa told him no, too fast, too nervous. He didn't mention it again and neither, of course, did she.

She did go back to The Scope, though, one night, restless, alone, leery of what she might find. She found Mike Fallopian, a couple weeks into raising a beard, wearing button-down olive shirt, creased fatigue pants minus cuffs and belt loops, two-button fatigue jacket, no hat. He was surrounded by broads, drinking champagne cocktails, and bellowing low songs. When he spotted Oedipa he gave her the wide grin and waved her over.

"You look," she said, "wow. Like you're all on the move. Training rebels up in mountains." Hostile looks from the girls twined around what parts of Fallopian were accessible.

"It's a revolutionary secret," he laughed, throwing up his arms and flinging off a couple of camp-followers. "Go on now, all of you. I want to talk to this one." When they were out of earshot he swiveled on her a look sympathetic, annoyed, perhaps also a little erotic. "How's your quest?"

She gave him a quick status report. He kept quiet while she talked, his expression slowly changing to something she couldn't recognize. It bothered her. To jog him a little, she said, "I'm surprised you people aren't using the system too."

"Are we an underground?" he came back, mild enough. "Are we rejects?"

"I didn't mean——"

"Maybe we haven't found them yet," said Fallopian. "Or maybe they haven't approached us. Or maybe we are using W.A.S.T.E., only it's a secret." Then, as electronic music began to percolate into the room, "But there's another angle too." She sensed what he was going to say and began, reflexively, to grind together her back molars. A nervous habit she'd developed in the last few days. "Has it ever occurred to you, Oedipa, that somebody's putting you on? That this is all a hoax, maybe something Inverarity set up before he died?"

It had occurred to her. But like the thought that someday she would have to die, Oedipa had been steadfastly refusing to look at that possibility directly, or in any but the most accidental of lights. "No," she said, "that's ridiculous."

Fallopian watched her, nothing if not compassionate. "You ought," quietly, "really, you ought to think about it. Write down what you can't deny. Your hard intelligence. But then write down what you've only speculated, assumed. See what you've got. At least that."

"Go ahead," she said, cold, "at least that. What else, after that?"

He smiled, perhaps now trying to salvage whatever was going soundlessly smash, its net of invisible cracks propagating leisurely through the air between them. "Please don't be mad."

"Verify my sources, I suppose," Oedipa kept on, pleasantly. "Right?"

He didn't say any more.

She stood up, wondering if her hair was in place, if she looked rejected or hysterical, if they'd been causing a scene. "I knew you'd be different," she said, "Mike, because everybody's been changing on me. But it hadn't gone as far as hating me."

"Hating you." He shook his head and laughed.

"If you need any armbands or more weapons, do try Winthrop Tremaine, over by the freeway. Tremaine's Swastika Shoppe. Mention my name."

"We're already in touch, thanks." She left him, in his modified Cuban ensemble, watching the floor, waiting for his broads to come back.

Well, what about her sources? She was avoiding the question, yes. One day Genghis Cohen called, sounding excited, and asked her to come see something he'd just got in the mail, the U.S. Mail. It turned out to be an old American stamp, bearing the device of the muted post horn, belly-up badger, and the motto: WE AWAIT SILENT TRISTERO'S EMPIRE.

"So that's what it stands for," said Oedipa. "Where did you get this?"

"A friend," Cohen said, leafing through a battered Scott catalogue, "in San Francisco." As usual she did not go on to ask for any name or address. "Odd. He said he couldn't find the stamp listed. But here it is. An addendum, look." In the front of the book a slip of paper had been pasted in. The stamp, designated 163L1, was reproduced, under the title "Tristero Rapid Post, San Francisco, California," and should have been inserted between Local listings 139 (the Third Avenue Post Office, of New York) and 140 (Union Post, also of New York). Oedipa, off on a kind of intuitive high, went immediately to the end-paper in back and found the sticker of Zapf's Used Books.

"Sure," Cohen protested. "I drove out there one day to see Mr Metzger, while you were up north. This is the Scott Specialized, you see, for American stamps, a catalogue I don't generally keep up on. My field being European and colonial. But my curiosity had been aroused, so——"

"Sure," Oedipa said. Anybody could paste in an addendum. She drove back to San Narciso to have another look at the list of Inverarity's assets. Sure enough, the whole shopping center that housed Zapf's Used Books and Tremaine's surplus place had been owned by Pierce. Not only that, but the Tank Theatre, also.

OK, Oedipa told herself, stalking around the room, her viscera hollow, waiting on something truly terrible, OK. It's unavoidable, isn't it? Every access route to the Tristero could be traced also back to the Inverarity estate. Even Emory Bortz, with his copy of Blobb's *Peregrinations* (bought, she had no doubt he'd tell her in the event she asked, also at Zapf's), taught now at San Narciso College, heavily endowed by the dead man.

Meaning what? That Bortz, along with Metzger, Cohen, Driblette, Koteks, the tattooed sailor in San Francisco, the W.A.S.T.E. carriers she'd seen—that all of them were Pierce Inverarity's men? *Bought?* Or loyal, for free, for fun, to some grandiose practical joke he'd cooked up, all for her embarrassment, or terrorizing, or moral improvement?

Change your name to Miles, Dean, Serge, and/or Leonard, baby, she advised her reflection in the half-light of that afternoon's vanity mirror. Either way, they'll call it paranoia. They. Either you have stumbled indeed, without the aid of LSD or other indole alkaloids, onto a secret richness and concealed density of dream; onto a network by which X number of Americans are truly communicating whilst reserving their lies, recitations of routine, arid betrayals of spiritual poverty, for the official government delivery system; maybe even onto a real alternative to the exitlessness, to the absence of surprise to life, that harrows the head of everybody American you know, and you too, sweetie. Or you are hallucinating it. Or a plot has been mounted against you, so expensive and elaborate, involving items like the forging of stamps and ancient books, constant surveillance of your movements, planting of post horn images all over San Francisco, bribing of librarians, hiring of professional actors and Pierce Inverarity only knows what-all besides, all financed out of the estate in a way either too secret or too involved for your non-legal mind to know about even though you are co-executor, so labyrinthine that it must have meaning beyond just a practical joke. Or you are fantasying some such plot, in which case you are a nut, Oedipa, out of your skull.

Those, now that she was looking at them, she saw to be the alternatives. Those symmetrical four. She didn't like any of them, but hoped she was mentally ill; that that's all it was. That night she sat for hours, too numb even to drink, teaching herself to breathe in a vacuum. For this, oh God, was the void. There was nobody who could help her. Nobody in the world. They were all on something, mad, possible enemies, dead.

Old fillings in her teeth began to bother her. She would spend nights staring at a ceiling lit by the pink glow of San Narciso's sky. Other nights she could sleep for eighteen drugged hours and wake, enervated, hardly able to stand. In conferences with the keen, fast-talking old man who was new counsel for the estate, her attention span could often be measured in seconds, and she laughed nervously more than she spoke. Waves of nausea, lasting five to ten minutes, would strike her at random, cause her deep misery, then vanish as if they had never been. There were headaches, nightmares, menstrual pains. One day she drove into L.A., picked a doctor at random from the phone book, went to her, told her she thought she was pregnant. They arranged for tests. Oedipa gave her name as Grace Bortz and didn't show up for her next appointment.

Genghis Cohen, once so shy, now seemed to come up with new goodies every other day—a listing in an outdated Zumstein catalogue, a friend in the Royal Philatelic Society's dim memory of some muted post horn spied in the catalogue of an auction held at Dresden in 1923; one day a typescript, sent him by another friend in New York. It was supposed to be a translation of an article from an 1865 issue of the famous *Bibliothèque des Timbrophiles*[44] of Jean-Baptiste Moens. Reading like another of Bortz's costume dramas, it told of a great schism in the Tristero ranks during the French Revolution. According to the recently discovered and decrypted journals of the Comte Raoul Antoine de Vouziers, Marquis de Tour et Tassis, one element among the Tristero had never accepted the passing of the Holy Roman Empire, and saw the

---

[44] Stamp-Collectors' Library.

Revolution as a temporary madness. Feeling obliged, as fellow aristocrats, to help Thurn and Taxis weather its troubles, they put out probes to see if the house was interested at all in being subsidized. This move split The Tristero wide open. At a convention held in Milan, arguments raged for a week, lifelong enmities were created, families divided, blood spilt. At the end of it a resolution to subsidize Thurn and Taxis failed. Many conservatives, taking this as a Millennial judgement against them, ended their association with The Tristero. *Thus,* the article smugly concluded, *did the organization enter the penumbra of historical eclipse. From the battle of Austerlitz until the difficulties of 1848, the Tristero drifted on, deprived of nearly all the noble patronage that had sustained them; now reduced to handling anarchist correspondence; only peripherally engaged—in Germany with the ill-fated Frankfurt Assembly, in Buda-Pesth at the barricades, perhaps even among the watchmakers of the Jura, preparing them for the coming of M. Bakunin. By far the greatest number, however, fled to America during 1849-1850, where they are no doubt at present rendering their services to those who seek to extinguish the flame of Revolution.*

Less excited than she might have been even a week ago, Oedipa showed the piece to Emory Bortz. "All the Tristero refugees from the 1849 reaction arrive in America," it seemed to him, "full of high hopes. Only what do they find?" Not really asking; it was part of his game. "Trouble." Around 1845 the U.S. government had carried out a great postal reform, cutting their rates, putting most independent mail routes out of business. By the '70's and '80's, any independent carrier that tried to compete with the government was immediately squashed. 1849-1850 was no time for any immigrating Tristero to get ideas about picking up where they'd left off back in Europe.

"So they simply stay on," Bortz said, "in the context of conspiracy. Other immigrants come to America looking for freedom from tyranny, acceptance by the culture, assimilation into it, this melting pot. Civil War comes along, most of them, being liberals, sign up to fight to preserve the Union. But clearly not the Tristero. All they've done is to change oppositions. By 1861 they're well established, not about to be suppressed. While the Pony Express is defying deserts, savages and sidewinders, Tristero's giving its employees crash courses in Siouan and Athapascan dialects. Disguised as Indians their messengers mosey westward. Reach the Coast every time, zero attrition rate, not a scratch on them. Their entire emphasis now toward silence, impersonation, opposition masquerading as allegiance."

"What about that stamp of Cohen's? We Await Silent Tristero's Empire."

"They were more open in their youth. Later, as the Feds cracked down, they went over to stamps that were almost kosher-looking, but not quite."

Oedipa knew them by heart. In the 15¢ dark green from the 1893 Columbian Exposition Issue ("Columbus Announcing His Discovery"), the faces of three courtiers, receiving the news at the right-hand side of the stamp, had been subtly altered to express uncontrollable fright. In the 3¢ Mothers of America Issue, put out on Mother's Day, 1934, the flowers to the lower left of Whistler's Mother had been replaced by Venus's-flytrap, belladonna, poison sumac and a few others Oedipa had never seen. In the 1947 Postage Stamp Centenary Issue, commemorating the great postal reform that had meant the beginning of the end for private carriers, the head of a Pony Express rider at the lower left was set at a disturbing angle unknown among the living. The deep violet 3¢ regular issue of 1954 had a faint, menacing smile on the face of the Statue of Liberty. The Brussels Exhibition Issue of 1958 included in its aerial view of the U.S. pavilion at Brussels, and set slightly off from the other tiny fairgoers, the unmistakable silhouette of a horse and rider. There were also the Pony Express stamp Cohen had showed her on her first visit, the Lincoln 4¢ with "U.S. Potsage," the sinister 8¢ airmail she'd seen on the tattooed sailor's letter in San Francisco.

"Well, it's interesting," she said, "if the article's legitimate."

"That ought to be easy enough to check out." Bortz gazing straight into her eyes. "Why don't you?"

The toothaches got worse, she dreamed of disembodied voices from whose malignance there was no appeal, the soft dusk of mirrors out of which something was about to walk, and empty rooms that waited for her. Your gynecologist has no test for what she was pregnant with.

One day Cohen called her to tell her that the final arrangements had been made to auction off Inverarity's stamp collection. The Tristero "forgeries" were to be sold, as lot 49. "And something rather disturbing, Miz Maas. A new book bidder has appeared on the scene, whom neither I nor any of the firms in the area have heard of before. That hardly ever happens."

"A what?"

Cohen explained how there were floor bidders, who would attend the auction in person, and book bidders, who would send in their bids by mail. These bids would be entered in a special book by the auction firm, hence the name. There would be, as was customary, no public disclosure of persons for whom "the book" would be bidding.

"Then how do you know he's a stranger?"

"Word gets around. He's being super-secretive—working through an agent, C. Morris Schrift, a very reputable, good man. Morris was in touch with the auctioneers yesterday to tell him his client wanted to examine our forgeries, lot 49, in advance. Normally there's no objection if they know who wants to see the lot, and if he's willing to pay all the postage and insurance, and get everything back inside of 24 hours. But Morris got quite mysterious about the whole thing, wouldn't tell his client's name or anything else about him. Except that as far as Morris knew, he was an outsider. So being a conservative house, naturally, they apologized and said no."

"What do you think?" said Oedipa, already knowing pretty much.

"That our mysterious bidder may be from Tristero," Cohen said. "And saw the description of the lot in the auction catalogue. And wants to keep evidence that Tristero exists out of unauthorized hands. I wonder what kind of a price they'll offer."

Oedipa went back to Echo Courts to drink bourbon until the sun went down and it was as dark as it would ever get. Then she went out and drove on the freeway for a while with her lights out, to see what would happen. But angels were watching. Shortly after midnight she found herself in a phone booth, in a desolate, unfamiliar, unlit district of San Narciso. She put in a station call to The Greek Way in San Francisco, gave the musical voice that answered a description of the acned, fuzz-headed Inamorato Anonymous she'd talked to there and waited, inexplicable tears beginning to build up pressure around her eyes. Half a minute of clinking glasses, bursts of laughter, sounds of a juke box. Then he came on.

"This is Arnold Snarb," she said, choking up.

"I was in the little boys' room," he said. "The men's room was full."

She told him, quickly, using up no more than a minute, what she'd learned about The Tristero, what had happened to Hilarius, Mucho, Metzger, Driblette, Fallopian. "So you are," she said, "the only one I have. I don't know your name, don't want to. But I have to know whether they arranged it with you. To run into me by accident, and tell me your story about the post horn. Because it may be a practical joke for you, but it stopped being one for me a few hours ago. I got drunk and went driving on these freeways. Next time I may be more deliberate. For the love of God, human life, whatever you respect, please. Help me."

"Arnold," he said. There was a long stretch of bar noise.

"It's over," she said, "they've saturated me. From here on I'll only close them out. You're free. Released. You can tell me."

"It's too late," he said.

"For me?"

"For me." Before she could ask what he meant, he'd hung up. She had no more coins. By the time she could get somewhere to break a bill, he'd be gone. She stood between the public booth and the rented car, in the night, her isolation complete, and tried to face toward the sea. But she'd lost her bearings. She turned, pivoting on one stacked heel, could find no mountains either. As if there could be no barriers between herself and the rest of the land. San Narciso at that moment lost (the loss pure, instant, spherical, the sound of a stainless orchestral chime held among the stars and struck lightly), gave up its residue of uniqueness for her; became a name again, was assumed back into the American continuity of crust and mantle. Pierce Inverarity was really dead.

She walked down a stretch of railroad track next to the highway. Spurs ran off here and there into factory property. Pierce may have owned these factories too. But did it matter now if he'd owned all of San Narciso? San Narciso was a name; an incident among our climatic records of dreams and what dreams became among our accumulated daylight, a moment's squall-line or tornado's touchdown among the higher, more continental solemnities—storm-systems of group suffering and need, prevailing winds of affluence. There was the true continuity. San Narciso had no boundaries. No one knew yet how to draw them. She had dedicated herself, weeks ago, to making sense of what Inverarity had left behind, never suspecting that the legacy was America.

Might Oedipa Maas yet be his heiress; had that been in the will, in code, perhaps without Pierce really knowing, having been by then too seized by some headlong expansion of himself, some visit, some lucid instruction? Though she could never again call back any image of the dead man to dress up, pose, talk to and make answer, neither would she lose a new compassion for the cul-de-sac he'd tried to find a way out of, for the enigma his efforts had created.

Though he had never talked business with her, she had known it to be a fraction of him that couldn't come out even, would carry forever beyond any decimal place she might name; her love, such as it had been, remaining incommensurate with his need to possess, to alter the land, to bring new skylines, personal antagonisms, growth rates into being. "Keep it bouncing," he'd told her once, "that's all the secret, keep it bouncing." He must have known, writing the will, facing the spectre, how the bouncing would stop. He might have written the testament only to harass a one-time mistress, so cynically sure of being wiped out he could throw away all hope of anything more. Bitterness could have run that deep in him. She just didn't know. He might himself have discovered The Tristero, and encrypted that in the will, buying into just enough to be sure she'd find it. Or he might have even tried to survive death, as a paranoia; as a pure conspiracy against someone he loved. Would that breed of perversity prove at last too keen to be stunned even by death, had a plot finally been devised too elaborate for the dark Angel to hold at once, in his humorless vice-president's head, all the possibilities of? Had something slipped through and Inverarity by that much beaten death?

Yet she knew, head down, stumbling along over the cinderbed and its old sleepers, there was still that other chance. That it was all true. That Inverarity had only died, nothing else. Suppose, God, there really was a Tristero then and that she *had* come on it by accident. If San Narciso and the estate were really no different from any other town, any other estate, then by that continuity she might have found The Tristero anywhere in her Republic, through any of a hundred lightly concealed entranceways, a hundred alienations, if only she'd looked. She stopped a minute between the steel rails, raising her head as if to sniff the air. Becoming conscious of the hard, strung presence she stood on—knowing as if maps had been flashed for her on the sky how these tracks ran on into others, others, knowing they laced, deepened, authenticated the great night around her. If only she'd looked. She remembered now old Pullman cars, left where the money'd run out or the customers vanished, amid green farm flatnesses where clothes hung, smoke lazed out of jointed pipes. Were the squatters there in touch with others, through Tristero; were they helping carry forward that 300 years of the house's disinheritance? Surely they'd forgotten by now what it was the Tristero were to have inherited; as perhaps Oedipa one day might have. What was left to inherit? That America coded in Inverarity's testament, whose was that? She thought of other, immobilized freight cars, where the kids sat on the floor planking and sang back, happy as fat, whatever came over the mother's pocket radio; of other squatters who stretched canvas for lean-tos behind smiling billboards along all the highways, or slept in junkyards in the stripped shells of wrecked Plymouths, or even, daring, spent the night up some pole in a lineman's tent like caterpillars, swung among a web of telephone wires, living in the very copper rigging and secular miracle of communication, untroubled by the dumb voltages flickering their miles, the night long, in the thousands of unheard messages. She remembered drifters she had listened to, Americans speaking their language carefully, scholarly, as if they were in exile from somewhere else invisible yet congruent with the cheered land she lived in; and walkers along the roads at night, zooming in and out of your headlights without looking up, too far from any town to have a real destination. And the voices before and after the dead man's that had phoned at random during the darkest, slowest hours, searching ceaseless among the dial's ten million possibilities for that magical Other who would reveal herself out of the roar of relays, monotone litanies of insult, filth, fantasy, love whose brute repetition must someday call into being the trigger for the unnamable act, the recognition, the Word.

How many shared Tristero's secret, as well as its exile? What would the probate judge have to say about spreading some kind of a legacy among them all, all those nameless, maybe as a first installment? Oboy. He'd be on her ass in a microsecond, revoke her letters testamentary, they'd call her names, proclaim her through all Orange County as a redistributionist and pinko, slip the old man from Warpe, Wistfull, Kubitschek and McMingus in as administrator *de bonis non* and so much baby for code, constellations, shadow-legatees. Who knew? Perhaps she'd be hounded someday as far as joining Tristero itself, if it existed, in its twilight, its aloofness, its waiting. The waiting above all; if not for another set of possibilities to replace those that had conditioned the land to accept any San Narciso among its most tender flesh without a reflex or a cry, then at least, at the very least, waiting for a symmetry of choices to break down, to go skew. She had heard all about excluded middles; they were bad shit, to be avoided; and how had it ever happened here, with the chances once so good for diversity? For it was now like walking among matrices of a great digital computer, the zeroes and ones twinned above, hanging like balanced mobiles right and left, ahead, thick, maybe endless. Behind the hieroglyphic streets there would either be a transcendent meaning, or only the earth. In the songs Miles, Dean, Serge and Leonard sang was either some fraction of the truth's numinous beauty (as Mucho now believed) or only a power spectrum. Tremaine the Swastika Salesman's reprieve from holocaust was either an injustice, or the absence of a wind; the bones of the GI's at the bottom of Lake Inverarity were there either for a reason that mattered to the world, or for skin divers and cigarette smokers. Ones and zeroes. So did the couples arrange themselves. At Vesperhaven House either an accommodation reached, in some kind of dignity, with the Angel of Death, or only death and the daily, tedious preparations for it. Another mode of meaning behind the obvious, or none. Either Oedipa in the orbiting ecstasy of a true paranoia, or a real Tristero. For there either was some Tristero beyond the appearance of the legacy

America, or there was just America and if there was just America then it seemed the only way she could continue, and manage to be at all relevant to it, was as an alien, unfurrowed, assumed full circle into some paranoia.

Next day, with the courage you find you have when there is nothing more to lose, she got in touch with C. Morris Schrift, and inquired after his mysterious client.

"He decided to attend the auction in person," was all Schrift would tell her. "You might run into him there." She might.

The auction was duly held, on a Sunday afternoon, in perhaps the oldest building in San Narciso, dating from before World War II. Oedipa arrived a few minutes early, alone, and in a cold lobby of gleaming redwood floorboards and the smell of wax and paper, she met Genghis Cohen, who looked genuinely embarrassed.

"Please don't call it a conflict of interests," he drawled earnestly. "There were some lovely Mozambique triangles I couldn't quite resist. May I ask if you've come to bid, Miz Maas."

"No," said Oedipa, "I'm only being a busybody."

"We're in luck. Loren Passerine, the finest auctioneer in the West, will be crying today."

"Will be what?"

"We say an auctioneer 'cries' a sale," Cohen said.

"Your fly is open," whispered Oedipa. She was not sure what she'd do when the bidder revealed himself. She had only some vague idea about causing a scene violent enough to bring the cops into it and find out that way who the man really was. She stood in a patch of sun, among brilliant rising and falling points of dust, trying to get a little warm, wondering if she'd go through with it.

"It's time to start," said Genghis Cohen, offering his arm. The men inside the auction room wore black mohair and had pale, cruel faces. They watched her come in, trying each to conceal his thoughts. Loren Passerine, on his podium, hovered like a puppet-master, his eyes bright, his smile practiced and relentless. He stared at her, smiling, as if saying, I'm surprised you actually came. Oedipa sat alone, toward the back of the room, looking at the napes of necks, trying to guess which one was her target, her enemy, perhaps her proof. An assistant closed the heavy door on the lobby windows and the sun. She heard a lock snap shut; the sound echoed a moment. Passerine spread his arms in a gesture that seemed to belong to the priesthood of some remote culture; perhaps to a descending angel. The auctioneer cleared his throat. Oedipa settled back, to await the crying of lot 49.

About the Author

DAVID H. RICHTER received his B.A., M.A., and Ph. D. from the University of Chicago. He is now Associate Professor of English at Queens College, City University of New York, where he has served as Assistant Chairman for Administration. He has also taught at Roosevelt University in Chicago. His specialties are the novel, literary theory, and eighteenth-century literature. Richter is the author of *Fable's End*—a book on form in the didactic novel—and of articles on Jerzy Kosinski, theory of literary genres, and ironic narrative in Defoe, Sterne, Nabokov and Nathanael West. He is at present at work on two books—a collection of formalist criticism and a study of the Gothic novel.

A Note on the Type

The text of this book was set in Palatino, a typeface designed by the noted German typographer Hermann Zapf. Named after Giovanbattista Palatino, a writing master of Renaissance Italy, Palatino was the first of Zapf's type faces to be introduced to America. The first designs for the face were made in 1948, and the fonts for the complete face were issued between 1950 and 1952. Like all Zapf-designed type faces, Palatino is beautifully balanced and exceedingly readable.

Composed by Lehigh-Rocappi from input provided by Random House, Inc., New York, New York.

Printed and bound by R. R. Donnelley & Sons Co., Crawfordsville, Indiana.